OKAN... COLLEGE LIBRARY

62

D0753600

V

J. W. VON GOETHE

SELECTED WORKS

Though one of the towering figures of world literature, Goethe has long been neglected in the English-speaking world. This collection of his four major works, together with a selection of his finest letters and poems, should show that he is not only one of the very greatest European writers: he is also accessible, entertaining and contemporary.

THE SORROWS OF YOUNG WERTHER is a story of self-destructive love which made the twenty-five year old author a celebrity overnight. Its exploration of the conflicts between ideas and feelings, circumstance and desire, continues in ELECTIVE AFFINI-TIES. The cosmic drama of FAUST goes far beyond the realism of the novels in a poetic exploration of good and evil, while the ITALIAN JOURNEY, written in the author's old age, recalls his youth in Italy and the impact of Mediterranean culture on a young Northerner.

EVERYMAN'S   LIBRARY

EVERYMAN,
I WILL GO WITH THEE,
AND BE THY GUIDE,
IN THY MOST NEED
TO GO BY THY SIDE

OKANAGAN UNIVERSITY COLLEGE
LIBRARY
BRITISH COLUMBIA

J. W. von GOETHE

Selected Works

including
The Sorrows of Young Werther
Elective Affinities
Italian Journey, Faust

Introduced by Nicholas Boyle

EVERYMAN'S LIBRARY

Alfred A. Knopf New York Toronto

246

THIS IS A BORZOI BOOK

PUBLISHED BY ALFRED A. KNOPF, INC.

First included in Everyman's Library, 2000

The Sorrows of Young Werther and *Novella*:
Copyright © 1971 by Random House, Inc.
Elective Affinities:
This edition reprinted 1999 by Everyman's Library by arrangement with Oxford
University Press. First published by Oxford University Press in 1994.
© David Constantine, 1994
Italian Journey:
Copyright © 1962 by Pantheon Books
Faust:
© University of Toronto Press, 1970
Reprinted by arrangement.
Selected Letters:
Translations by Dr M. Herzfeld and C. Melvil Sym first published by the
Edinburgh University Press, 1957.
Selected Poetry:
Translations are all from *Johann Wolfgang von Goethe: Selected Poems*, edited by
Christopher Middleton, Goethe Edition: Volume 1. © Suhrkamp/Insel Publishers
Boston, Inc., 1983
Michael Hamburger, 'Prometheus', 'Roman Elegies I, V', 'Nearness of the
Beloved', 'Nature and Art', 'Found', 'On Orginality II', 'Hegira', 'Blessed
Longing', 'The Bridegroom' and Vernon Watkins, 'The Godlike' originally
appeared in *Great Writings of Goethe* by Stephen Spender. Copyright © 1958 by
Stephen Spender.
John Frederick Nims, 'Rosebud in the Heather' and 'To the Moon' first appeared
in *Sappho to Valéry*. Copyright © 1971 by John Frederick Nims. Reprinted by
permission of Princeton University Press.

Introduction, Bibliography, and Chronology © 1999 by David Campbell
Publishers Ltd.
Typography by Peter B. Willberg

All rights reserved under International and Pan-American Copyright
Conventions. Published in the United States by Alfred A. Knopf,
Inc., New York, and simultaneously in Canada by Random House
of Canada Limited, Toronto. Distributed by Random House, Inc.,
New York

ISBN 0-375-41044-9

Book Design by Barbara de Wilde and Carol Devine Carson

Printed and bound in Germany
by Graphischer Grossbetrieb Pössneck GmbH

J . W . von G O E T H E

CONTENTS

INTRODUCTION

Goethe's greatness is singular: it is difficult to think of any parallel to his achievement either in the modern age of which he can claim to be the supreme poetic representative, and which to a great extent he defined, or in any other. His poetic drama *Faust* took a lifetime to write; its rich complexity of tone and structure reflects sixty of the most eventful years in European cultural and political history; it created a modern myth on which writers and composers have drawn for two centuries; and even before its completion contemporaries compared it to Dante's *Divine Comedy*. Yet Goethe was not a man of one work: his plays and his novels, one of which became a European bestseller, had a decisive influence on the course of German literature, and his lyric poetry, which shows his genius at its purest and most condensed, was a source of inspiration to successive generations of Romantic and post-Romantic musicians. In their settings of his songs they have made his words familiar round the world to audiences that know neither his language nor even perhaps his name.

It was certainly part of his achievement that he lived as long and finished as much as he did: there really is nothing in literary history to put beside the last seven years of his life when, from the age of seventy-five onwards, he wrote the Second Part of *Faust* and two concluding volumes of his autobiography, completed the second part of his novel *Wilhelm Meister*, and saw through the press forty volumes of the definitive edition of his *Collected Works*. But what sets him apart from the poetic giants of the Victorian and later eras whom he might otherwise seem to anticipate – from Wordsworth and Hugo, Tennyson and Whitman, or even Pound and Yeats and Borges – is something more remarkable still. At every stage of a long and inwardly turbulent life he rediscovered, or reinvented, himself through his writing, and yet he never significantly repeated himself. For each of the ages of man, which he experienced in his own person, he found a new poetry, not one borrowed or retained, defiantly or mechanically, from an earlier period. He rarely wrote in a genre already established, whether by himself or anyone else, and the unpredictable turns he took left his contemporary readers – and publishers – bewildered; they were expecting more of what had been successful in the past and Goethe declined, or was unable, to provide it. His work was always recognizable but always inimitable: he never adopted a manner, let alone a recipe, and only once, at the beginning of his career, could he be said to have been the leader of a school.

He was of course remarkable in other ways too. For fifty years his literary work was accompanied by precise, methodical and industrious scientific observation and scholarship – and by rather less reliable speculation – particularly in the fields of botany, anatomy, geology and optics. He invented the term and the concept of 'morphology', which in the nineteenth century played a role in preparing the ground for Darwinian evolutionism, and he compiled a history of colour-theory which remained unsurpassed in its comprehensiveness for many years. He was also a statesman in the complex world of the moribund Holy Roman Empire. For over half a century a minister of his small but sovereign duchy, responsible at one point for both its finances and its foreign policy, he was uniquely well-situated and well-connected for a poet of his time. But just as he cannot really be said to have achieved much as a scientist, so his role in contemporary affairs should not be exaggerated: the twentieth century was to see many closer symbioses of poetry and politics. Goethe was more significant as an administrator who deployed the duchy's resources in patronage of art and architecture, the theatre, and especially the local university of Jena: indeed his role as a patron of philosophy, and as a philosopher himself, has been rather undervalued. He was hugely and widely talented, and unusually fortunate. What makes him unique, however, is his literary work – that permanently modulating flow of original, perhaps compulsively original, words in which he gave expression to a varied and deeply pondered life.

*

Johann Wolfgang Goethe (he became 'von Goethe' in 1782, when he was ennobled) was born on 28 August 1749 in what was then the self-governing Imperial Free City of Frankfurt on the Main. His father was a wealthy man, who lived off his capital, his mother was the daughter of the city's principal official. In an age when continental Europe was dominated by rational, and eventually revolutionary, Enlightenment, and by benevolent despotism, he had an urban, bourgeois, upbringing amid flourishing institutions which had changed little since the Renaissance and Reformation and whose roots lay deep in the Middle Ages. He was educated by private tutors with his sister Cornelia (other brothers and sisters died in childhood), and he followed in his father's footsteps by studying law at the universities of Leipzig and Strasbourg. He was already a fluent composer of largely frivolous verse, when, in Strasbourg in 1770–71, something like a literary revolution exploded in him. A serious illness, possibly tuberculosis, had caused him to break off his studies – and a liaison with an innkeeper's daughter – in Leipzig, and during a long and troubled convalescence at home he had first succumbed to religious enthusiasm and then begun to detach himself from it. In Strasbourg, where he quickly gained his legal qualifications, he celebrated his recovery of health and of the world around him. He began an intense but short-lived love-affair with Friederike Brion, the daughter of a pastor in a nearby village, immortalized in the poems 'Welcome and Farewell' and 'May Song' and more indirectly reflected in 'Rosebud in the Heather'*. A group of young intellectuals had gathered in Strasbourg – then still largely German-speaking, but under pressure from French – and when the radical clergyman and literary critic J. G. Herder (1744–1803) spent some time in the town they listened avidly to his theory that literature was born out of national languages and living traditions, not out of dead languages and book-learning, that the true poets were not men of taste and wit, like Pope or Voltaire, but authors of folk-songs or the shadowy epic bards such as Homer and Ossian, and that Shakespeare

---

*For these and other poems mentioned here see the selection of poems towards the end of the present volume. This introduction also provides the context for the selection of letters, in so far as that is not indicated by the footnotes to them.

could provide a better model for the German theatre than the supposedly 'regular' drama of France. Herder seems to have awoken in Goethe a sense that he could give direction to Germany's literary revival, then some thirty years old. Goethe set off to collect folk-songs in the Alsatian countryside, wrote a paean of praise to the Gothic – and so, he thought, German – architecture of Strasbourg cathedral, and back in Frankfurt in the autumn he worked off his depression after the abrupt end to his relationship with Friederike Brion by writing in six weeks a pseudo-Shakespearean chronicle play in unprecedentedly realistic prose, based on the memoirs of a late medieval feuding baron, *Götz von Berlichingen, with the Iron Hand*. When it was published in 1773 *Götz von Berlichingen* (the play which revealed to Walter Scott the potential of the historical novel) made Goethe famous overnight.

Goethe, however, had as yet no public reputation when in 1772 he arrived in the little Hessian town of Wetzlar for a spell of practical legal experience at the Supreme Court of the Holy Roman Empire. He made the acquaintance of J. C. Kestner, another young lawyer, and conceived a sentimental attachment to Kestner's fiancée, Charlotte Buff, who after a summer's awkward dalliance made it clear to Goethe that they could be no more than good friends. The consequences were out of all proportion to this relatively slight affair. In 1773 Goethe, now starting up a legal practice in Frankfurt, had to face the question of what was his true vocation, and to explain to himself his manifest difficulty in achieving a satisfactory relationship with a woman. During that year he seems to have created a series of symbolic figures – Prometheus, Faust, Wilhelm Meister perhaps – which remained for the rest of his changing life the literary instruments for his self-understanding. In the winter he fused together his own experiences with Charlotte Buff and the story of another lawyer in Wetzlar, who had shot himself out of disappointed love shortly after Goethe had left, and gave to the composite figure that resulted the name of Werther. He wrote the novel *The Sorrows of Young Werther* in the first months of 1774; it was published in the autumn and took Germany, and then Europe, by storm. Goethe became a celebrity and the family house became a place of pilgrimage.

INTRODUCTION

Poets and dramatists were springing up all over the German-speaking world, for literature suddenly seemed to offer the younger middle-class generation a meaning and purpose which they had ceased to find in religion and which the despotic constitution of most of the Empire's territories prevented them from finding in public affairs. Herder and others – such as the British thinkers Shaftesbury and Lowth – provided them with a theory of the individual poetic genius as a semi-divine figure, the focus of a nation's culture, who acknowledged no law but that of inspiration. In Goethe, who within a year had published a great play and a great novel, as different from each other as they were original, and was now filling the periodicals with a profusion of lesser dramas, poems and fragments, Germany seemed to have found its genius. For a while Goethe seemed to agree. In the ode 'Prometheus' he cast himself as a modern, autonomous, post-religious man – rather as Nietzsche would define the species over a century later – who seeks assurance of his identity not from the God who made him but from the products of his own 'creative' powers. In 'A Song to Mahomet' he presented the poet-prophet as the inspirational figure who, like a river gathering its tributaries, gathers his contemporaries together into a common cause. But Goethe was too intelligent to imagine that he or any of his fellow-geniuses could live permanently with the demands they were imposing upon themselves, and he was fully aware that 'Storm and Stress' – as the movement of literary revolt came to be known – had a darker side to it. In the first draft of his *Faust* and the related play *Clavigo* he showed intellectual rebels who shoulder all convention aside and then have to face in horror the destructive consequences of their self-assertion.

.Goethe sought personal stability in the frenzied intellectual atmosphere by getting engaged to Elisabeth – 'Lili' – Schönemann, the daughter of a Frankfurt banker, but he was torn apart by the conflict between his desire for her and his fear of what she represented – fixture in Frankfurt and an ever more staid and limited career within the city, perhaps even the suffocation of his literary talent. He broke away suddenly in the summer of 1775 to go on a walking-tour of Switzerland with some well-born poets whom he hardly knew; the poem

'On the Lake' which he jotted into his diary during a picnic on Lake Zurich is outstanding for its combination of a physically and visually realized landscape with the sense of a biographically significant moment, a refusal of nostalgic introspection, and a determination to trust in the natural powers of ripening which will take the poet on to he knows not what future. The engagement to 'Lili' Schönemann did not survive the separation and in the autumn of 1775 Goethe was in a state of bewilderment verging on despair. His father wanted him to embark on the Grand Tour of Italy and France which for him had been the prelude to marriage and a comfortable life of semi-retirement, but there was the promise of an invitation to the ducal court at Weimar, which had a reputation for the patronage of literature and whose young Duke Carl August was, at eighteen, about to marry, come of age, and take over the administration of the duchy from his widowed mother. The invitation, however, seemed to have been forgotten and Goethe threw himself into writing a drama, *Egmont,* about the popular hero of the Dutch wars of liberation and so an onslaught on the despotic powers of princes. Finally his father prevailed on him to leave for Italy but on the way he was overtaken by a personal emissary of Carl August's and persuaded to turn back to Weimar, which became his home for fifty-six years.

Duke Carl August (1757–1828) wanted Goethe as more than a house-guest for a few weeks, or a resident entertainer to adorn his court. Having lost his father so young that he could not remember him, he had in his early years an emotional need for an older man to rely on. Goethe was almost immediately made a member of the three-man Privy Council, under the Duke the ruling body of the duchy. He promptly had Herder summoned to take charge of the local church, and he was the Duke's closest confidant and guide for about ten years. In 1779 he took the Duke on a tour of Frankfurt and the Swiss mountains so that he could see the world incognito and relive some of Goethe's own Storm and Stress experiences. But Goethe's attitude to court society was ambivalent, and as a middle-class parvenu, associated with the immorality and vulgarity of modern German literature, he was unwelcome to the established, French-speaking noble families. As if to mark his distance from them he lived much of his first six years just outside the walls of Weimar in a cottage bought for him by Carl August in the water meadows of the River Ilm (which he was at this time gradually transforming into a landscaped park in the English style). Here he could relax in semi-rural surroundings, as if he were Rousseau or Werther, after days spent in arranging amateur theatricals in town, or, increasingly, in administrative duties, and it was here that he continued to write – the park provides, for example, the scenic background to the poem 'To the Moon'. But Goethe was also attracted to the world of the court: he recognized, probably unconsciously, that the autocratic principalities represented Germany's political future better than the middle-class free city from which he came, or the Empire which was the constitutional framework for its existence; he was anxious, like many a man of the eighteenth-century Enlightenment, to try his hand at social reform on the manageable scale that the duchy offered, and the court was the visible expression of the Duke's political power; and he liked the idea of a society of noble, self-disciplined people devoting themselves to their own culture and the improvement of the world. The reality, naturally, in no way corresponded to that ideal – the Weimar court was petty, backbiting, selfish, snobbish and little interested in culture – but in the wife of the Duke's equerry, Charlotte von Stein, Goethe thought he saw the ideal embodied. He felt destined for her even before he met her and for ten years during which they were lovers in everything except a physical sense he allowed her to exercise over him an extraordinary fascination. In her he saw fulfilled the longing for calm after Storm and Stress which he expressed in his two 'Wanderer's Night Songs', and the ethereal abstractions of 'The Godlike', a hymn to moral rather than hereditary nobility, tell us something of her colourless and firmly inhibited personality. She was perhaps the right patron for an administrative career of exemplary self-denial and devotion to duty. Goethe's responsibilities grew from those of an impresario and tutor: he took on mines, roads, defence and, in 1782 when he acquired his 'von' and with it acceptance into the highest tier of Weimar society, the exchequer. He was then the most powerful man in the duchy and left his cottage for a permanent residence within the walls. But there was a price to be paid: his writing was gradually drying up. In 1779 he completed the first draft of a play, *Iphigenia in Tauris*, in which Iphigenia heals her deranged brother Orestes, rather as Goethe felt he had been healed by the influence of Frau von Stein, and he began one or two more; but he was unable to finish them, or *Egmont*, or the novel *Wilhelm Meister's Theatrical Mission* which had been intended as a realistic account of the enthusiasms of the Storm and Stress era. Behind his disciplined exterior powerful emotions were still at work and if they could not express themselves directly they took on strange forms, as we can see in the ballad 'Erlkönig' or the song of longing for her Italian homeland that, in *Wilhelm Meister*, Goethe puts in the mouth of the hermaphrodite figure Mignon.

*

Goethe still longed to see Italy, and especially Rome, as his father had intended he should, in order to complete his education, grow up at last, and mature sexually. When he resigned from most of his administrative offices in 1785 and still found that his writing was not regenerated, he resolved to try the most powerful medicine he could imagine. He laid plans for a secret trip to Rome, breaking, if only temporarily, all his ties with Weimar, including that with Frau von Stein, and taking with him only the task of completing the eight volumes of the first collected edition of his works, for which he signed a contract just before he left. On 3 September 1786 he slipped away from the Bohemian spa of Carlsbad where he had been spending the summer and raced down through Germany and Austria across the Brenner towards Venice and Rome. Rome lured him on because it was in a sense the capital of the modern world – the German Emperor took his title from it – as well as of the ancient, but when he arrived he found its ruinous state a disappointment. He was looking for the living spirit of pagan antiquity and its art, not for its crumbling monuments. Having originally intended to spend only a few weeks away he was eventually enabled by the generosity of Carl August, who kept prolonging his leave and paying his salary, to live for nearly two years in Italy. But what he came to value most about this time was not the opportunity of seeing ancient works of art and architecture at first hand (he gave as much attention to the better preserved masterpieces of the Renaissance) but rather the opportunity of living as nearly as possible what he thought of as the ancient way of life: experiencing in Naples and Sicily the benign climate and fertile setting in which human beings and Nature were in harmony; pretending in Rome to be one of the expatriate colony of German artists, devoted as it seemed simply to beauty and the development of their craft; and arranging there with a young widow, of whom little is known, his first protracted sexual liaison. The chaste reign of Frau von Stein was over: their relationship never recovered from the hurt of his secret departure and she may have known better than he did that the breach was deliberate.

Altogether, Goethe's Italian journey was a time of discovery not of the ancient past, but of himself. Carl August, who was also away from Weimar, carving out a new career as a general in the Prussian army, crowned his generosity by agreeing a wholly new basis for Goethe's return to the duchy in June 1788: he was to be relieved of virtually all routine administrative tasks and freed to concentrate on what he now knew to be his true identity, that of a poet. Goethe's two years in Italy were not in themselves particularly productive of poetry, however. He put his *Iphigenia* into verse, completed *Egmont* and did one or two other pieces of editorial work for his collected edition, but his inspiration was not renewed until he came back to Weimar, bitterly regretful at his expulsion from 'Paradise' as he called it. He resolved to preserve as much as he could of the Roman atmosphere in Weimar, set about hiring artists he had met in Italy, and at once – before there was time for any second thoughts – he took himself a mistress, Christiane Vulpius (1765–1816), the orphan daughter of the Duke's late archivist. The physical happiness and fulfilment he found with her in the discrete isolation of the cottage by the Ilm he translated into a recreation in verse of his blissful months in Rome, modelled on the forms and manner of the Roman elegists, especially Propertius. (The collection of these *Roman Elegies* was published in 1795 but some were suppressed as too explicit and were not printed until the twentieth century.) At the same time Goethe wrote the greater part of his verse tragedy *Torquato Tasso*, a lament for the Italian world he had lost and the story of a poet driven mad by an uncomprehending court. Frau von Stein was ostentatiously uninterested in his reminiscences of Italy and communication between them finally broke down when the news leaked out that Christiane Vulpius had joined his household.

After the burst of creativity associated with the completion of the collected edition of his works (which included the first publication of much of what we now know as the First Part of *Faust* under the title *Faust. A Fragment*), poetic inspiration seems to have deserted Goethe for some years and he turned to science, particularly botany and the theory of colour. The atmosphere in Weimar was increasingly unfavourable to his attempts to create for himself a private Italian microcosm: he discovered that he had incurred domestic responsibilities when Christiane gave birth to his son August (1789–1830); the Duke asked him to set up and manage a court theatre, which had to cater for the public taste rather than for his personal interests; and the Revolution in France soon came to dominate all thinking, writing and conversation. In 1792 Goethe accompanied the Duke on the joint invasion of France by Prussia, Austria and the Empire which was turned back at Valmy, and he experienced the horrors of a disastrous retreat. This peculiarly ill-judged campaign led to the overthrow and execution of Louis XVI, the establishment of a French republic, and a French counter-attack into Germany. In the summer of 1793 the Allies temporarily recovered Mainz from the French, after a long siege and fierce bombardment, which Goethe also witnessed. He remained completely loyal to his sovereign, Carl August, but he thought the military confrontation with France unnecessary and foolish: France in his view probably needed reform – and only the corruption and intransigence of the ruling classes had led to violence – but conditions in Germany were so different that a Revolution there was neither to be desired nor to be feared. For many years he was alienated from pro-Revolutionary friends, such as Herder or the composer

Reichardt, by the feeling that their attitudes were unrealistic, dangerous and ungrateful to their patrons. Through the pain of their separation while he was on campaign, and the sadness of losing all their children following August after only a few days of life (there may have been a rhesus incompatibility in the parents), Goethe grew closer to Christiane during the Revolutionary period. Though he refused to go through a church ceremony he told his friends that he regarded himself as married.

*

From 1794 Goethe gave nearly all his literary attention to the task of rewriting his old novel as the story of a young man maturing through the search for the personal meaning of his life, and *Wilhelm Meister's Years of Apprenticeship* was published in four volumes in 1795–6. 'Nearness of the Beloved', one of the few rhymed lyrical poems of this period, reflects the religious mood of one of the interpolated narratives in this rambling but profound work, which has been more acclaimed by other novelists than by the reading public. At the same time he collaborated with the poet and dramatist Friedrich Schiller (1759–1805) in editing a literary journal, *The Horae*. Schiller, who had an unestablished chair of history in the University of Jena, had been living in the area for some years but Goethe had kept him at arm's length, out of distaste for *The Robbers* (1781) and the other dramas by which Schiller had made his reputation, and which were among the last and most extreme products of Storm and Stress. Once it became clear that Schiller, like Goethe, had moved on, and that they shared a similar commitment to literature and a similar detached interest in the philosophical upheaval inaugurated in the 1780s by Kant, their relationship developed into a close friendship. Jena in the last decade of the eighteenth century attracted nearly all the best minds in the rising generation of German intellectuals, among them the philosophers Fichte and Schelling, the brothers Wilhelm and Alexander von Humboldt – one a great philologist, the other an outstanding natural scientist – and the founders of Romanticism in literature, Friedrich and August Wilhelm Schlegel. Goethe and Schiller were a main source of the attraction but avoided being identified with any single party. Goethe pretended to be the less philosophically-minded of the pair but probably understood Kant better than Schiller or the post-Kantians, and attributed to Schiller's influence both his sympathy for the new movement and his eventual resumption and completion of *Faust. Part One*, in which the new ideas manifestly play an important role.

He especially admired the brilliance of the young Schelling, who was attempting to unify the new philosophy of the mind with the most recent advances in natural science, particularly in the areas of magnetism and electricity. Goethe, however, believed that the human mind was itself a product of natural processes and should not regard itself as giving laws to Nature, as the Kantians thought it did. In 'The Metamorphosis of Plants' (1798), the last of a number of fine poems written during these years in classical elegiac metres, he summarized the results of his botanical observations so as to show this continuity between the natural and human worlds. But he also learnt from Schelling's emphasis on universal 'polarity'; on the opposition of negative and positive forces throughout Nature, not only in electromagnetic phenomena; and on the process of development through conflict. Some of these ideas are reflected in the sonnet 'Nature and Art' though its immediate occasion was the attempt by August Wilhelm Schlegel to persuade Goethe to take up writing sonnets, one of the numerous strict forms that Schlegel was trying to revive as part of his programme for making all the treasures of world literature available in German. Goethe was willing to show that he could be a virtuoso if he tried (and managed in 'Night Song' a successful imitation of the Persian *ghazel*), but poetry for him was a more spontaneous and mysterious art. After the failure of a last attempt to return to Italy in 1797 he was unable for six years to summon up any sustained literary inspiration, writing only occasional poems and fragments, doing translations, and working on scenes and speeches in *Faust* in short bursts. For Schiller by contrast this was a very creative time: after Goethe had the Weimar theatre refitted in 1798, Schiller produced a series of masterpieces in verse drama which have held the German stage ever since. There has been much argument about which poet derived more from the relationship, and who, if either, was exploiting whom, but it seems better to say that it is one of the most extraordinary examples in literature of cross-fertilization.

*

Goethe suffered a serious illness in the winter of 1800–1 but the burden of his responsibilities for the duchy's cultural affairs continued to increase. He took on the administration of the Weimar and Jena libraries, organized the building of a new summer theatre for the Weimar company in the little Saxon spa of Bad Lauchstädt – where Christiane, whose existence was not officially acknowledged in Weimar, was always welcomed as a celebrity – and in 1803 brought to a successful conclusion a fifteen-year project for rebuilding and refurnishing the ducal palace, which had been destroyed by fire just before Carl August's accession. In the same year, under pressure from Napoleon, the Holy Roman Empire reorganized itself into a collection of virtually sovereign secular states, and Goethe completed and published his first major work since 1797: *The Natural Daughter*, a symbolic drama of extreme abstraction and great poetic beauty, which summed up many years of reflection about the social and aesthetic consequences of the French Revolution, now clearly over. It contains the first full exposition of Goethe's concept of 'renunciation': the resigned acceptance of the historical destiny that condemns us moderns to a life without the human and artistic perfection achieved, for example, in ancient Greece. In early 1805 Goethe and Schiller both fell ill again: Goethe recovered, but Schiller died in May. The sense that an epoch had ended was compounded in 1806 when the Empire was formally dissolved and Weimar, unwisely a party to the Third Coalition against France, was caught up in the disastrous consequences of Napoleon's defeat of Prussia at the battles of Jena and Auerstädt on 14 October. The duchy was occupied and Weimar itself was sacked, though Goethe's house was spared on the express instructions of Napoleon, who was an admirer of *Werther* which he claimed to have reread seven times. Christiane showed great courage in protecting the house against random marauders, and to show his gratitude, and probably in fulfilment of an intention he had formed some time before, Goethe took advantage of the confusion of the moment to go through a ceremony of marriage to her in the vestry of the court chapel. The shock of military defeat probably hastened the death of the Dowager Duchess, Carl August's mother, in 1807 and for a while it seemed possible that her son's domains might be dismembered. But Carl August had married his son to the sister of the Tsar and Napoleon needed Russian co-operation to implement his plan for a blockade of England, so Weimar survived, on condition of giving its support to the new Napoleonic order. After a personal interview with Napoleon in Erfurt in 1808 – 'Voilà un homme,' the Emperor is reputed to have said on setting eyes on Goethe, and he awarded him the Legion of Honour – and especially after Napoleon's remarriage to the daughter of the Emperor of Austria in 1810, Goethe had no difficulty in seeing in Napoleon the legitimate successor to the Holy Roman Emperor as the ruler of Germany. After the landslide of the defeat at Jena and the collapse of Prussia, 'a new life' began for him, he wrote in 1807 in the powerful sonnet 'Immense Astonishment'. It was a reflective life, aware of the unpredictable and potentially destructive forces hidden beneath the surface of daily existence, but aware also of the value of an inherited social order. After the publication, by the Tübingen firm of J. G. Cotta, of a new collected edition of his works, in which the full text of *Faust. Part One* first appeared in 1808, this became the great age of Goethe's prose. He published his novel *Elective Affinities* in 1809, his longest prose work, the treatise *On the Theory of Colour*, in 1810, and at the same time he started work on his autobiography, *Poetry and Truth*, which appeared between 1811 and 1814. In these years also Goethe's correspondence with the Berlin musician and Freemason C. F. Zelter (1758–1832) grew up to take the place of his correspondence with Schiller as the vehicle for his day-to-day reflections on life, personalities, intellectual movements and his own writing. Goethe continued to be benevolent to the younger literary generation, now completely under the spell of Romanticism, and briefly hoped that one of the new dramatists, among them the passionate Heinrich von Kleist, might prove a successor to

Schiller in the theatrical sphere. He could not, however, approve of the unrealistic tendency in the Romantics' often supercilious attitude to their contemporary public or of their increasingly nationalist political stance. Goethe felt at ease in the Napoleonic Empire, he forbade his son August to fight in the so-called Wars of Liberation, and he could not share in the outburst of rejoicing which greeted the Emperor's defeat at the battle of Leipzig in 1813.

In the period of European instability until the battle of Waterloo, Goethe's reaction was, by his own admission, flight. He spent most of the summer in both 1814 and 1815 in the area of Frankfurt and the Rhineland, newly accessible after the end of French occupation, and conceived an escapist affection for Marianne Jung, later Willemer, the young and intelligent fiancée of an elderly Frankfurt banker. The escape was aesthetic and literary too: he allowed himself to be over-whelmed by the wealth of colour in a private collection of medieval art amassed in Heidelberg by two brothers with Romantic leanings; and his reading of a translation of the medieval Persian poet Hafiz struck him with the force of a revelation. He started to write poems in the Persian manner himself, some of them love poems for Marianne Jung, who responded in kind. For two years, before and after her wedding, they played a game of make-believe, impersonating Hafiz and his beloved, using his works as the basis for coded messages, and practising the Arabic script. This semi-adulterous liaison was more intense than earlier sentimental attachments of Goethe to younger women, but probably not different in kind. It did not affect the seriousness with which he regarded his marriage or the protective love he felt for Christiane, best seen in a touching poem ('Found') which he wrote for her in 1813 to mark twenty-five years of their life together. But the game was brought to a brutally abrupt end in June 1816 when Christiane died of a painful gynaecological illness. 'Emptiness and deathly silence within and around me,' Goethe wrote in his diary. He did not return to Frankfurt and virtually ceased writing poems in the Hafiz manner. Put together over the next few years as a collection with explanatory notes, these appeared in 1819 as *The Parliament of West and East* (*West-Oestlicher Divan*), one of his most remarkable achievements. Despite the avowed intention of fleeing from the chaos of European wars ('Hegira'), the poems do not simply present an oriental fantasy-world but insist, like the title Goethe chose , on the coexistence of both eastern and western elements. They are 'single and double' at the same time ('Gingo Biloba'), and not only in a cultural but also in a personal and sexual sense. Goethe's game with Marianne Jung is only one of the love themes: 'Blessed Longing' was written before he met her, 'A Thousand Forms' is as much about God (or Nature) as it is about a woman, and a whole section is devoted to the poet's love for a young boy. Even more than Fitzgerald's *Rubaiyat of Omar Khayyam*, which they anticipate by forty years, the poems of Goethe's *Divan* use orientalism as a pretext for the expression of subversive ideas about divinity and, especially, human identity ('Sublimer and Sublimest'). A sense of polemical distance from a Europe, and a Germany, in the grip of political reaction, artistic and literary Romanticism, and reviving Christianity, also runs through Goethe's main prose work in the years 1814–17: the narrative of his visit to Italy in 1786–7 now known as *Italian Journey*.

*

After the death of his wife, Goethe, at sixty-seven, began methodically to prepare for his own. The Congress of Vienna, from which Weimar emerged as a Grand Duchy and with a considerable accretion of territory, the apparent (rather than real) restoration of the *ancien régime*, and the repressive Carlsbad Decrees of 1819, which turned much of Europe into a police state, all suggested that order had returned after twenty-five years of revolution. Goethe's son married an impoverished member of the Prussian nobility in 1817 and there were soon two grandsons (a grand-daughter followed in 1827), so it was necessary for the poet to put his affairs in order too. He made a new will, resigned from the directorship of the theatre, and gave up at long last his citizenship of Frankfurt. Another collected edition of the works, enlarged by so much recent autobiographical writing, was put in train with Cotta. He began to systematize and publish his papers on scientific subjects, many of them written more than twenty years before and little touched since. A sequel to his earlier novel, *Wilhelm Meister's Years of Wandering, or: The Renunciants*, was quickly put together and published in 1821 – 'renunciation' here appears as a willingness, rather in the spirit of *The Parliament of West and East*, to emigrate to America in order to escape the shortcomings of the Old World. He wrote up for his autobiography his experiences while on campaign in 1792 and 1793 and started a new project, his *Annals*, covering more briefly, sometimes in little more than note form, the years that he could see he would not be able to include in *Poetry and Truth*. Much of this work, he ruefully admitted, was stitching up fragments ('Humility'). Even his poems which, after he stopped writing for *The Parliament of West and East*, were less numerous, became more like summaries of a lifetime's wisdom. Often it was expressed in pungent little rhymed epigrams of almost proverbial directness ('Something like the Sun') or disarming self-irony ('On Originality II', 'The Years'). But longer and more thoroughly composed poems of Goethe's later years can still show great imaginative and symbolic power. 'Primal Words. Orphic' (1817) can stand for several great meditations, at once solemn and playful (one thinks of the later Yeats), on the mysteries of individuality and history, the constrictions of circumstance, and the liberating forces of love and hope for an ideal goal, still to be achieved.

If there was a touch of complacency and illusion about Goethe's assiduous stylization of himself into a Grand Old Man of letters it was painfully shattered in 1823. Having allowed himself, during his recent visits to the Bohemian spa of Marienbad, to be carried away by his infatuation with the nineteen-year-old Ulrike von Levetzow, he proposed marriage to her. The rejection – not by Ulrike, but by her family – was an emotional turning-point and ushered in the last phase of his personal 'renunciation'. In three poems, later put together as 'Trilogy of Passion', he looked back on all he had achieved in a long life, and finding it at first outweighed by the bitterness of parting and death, eventually accepted the transfiguring consolations of music and platonic love. (Goethe played the cello and the piano, and was personally acquainted with Beethoven, Clara Wieck-Schumann, and the young Mendelssohn, whom he greatly admired.) After his return from Marienbad he did not again leave the area of Weimar and devoted himself to the third and last of the Cotta editions of his works, with which he hoped to secure the financial future of his family.

In 1825, a year which saw the fiftieth anniversary of Carl August's accession and of Goethe's arrival in Weimar, he resumed work on *Faust. Part Two*, of which some sketches and drafts went back to the beginning of the century. In 1826 he completed a project first planned in the same period: what had been intended to be a verse epic now became a short story in prose, *Novella*. Other short stories took on their final form as insertions in the second, much enlarged, edition of *Wilhelm Meister's Years of Wandering* which appeared in 1829. Here the sense of 'renunciation' is almost the opposite of what it was in the first edition: it is an acceptance of the need to remain in Europe, for all its constrictions, and to work to meet the challenge of industrialization and social change. Goethe might not move from Weimar, but through his voracious reading of even the most contemporary literature, through the stream of visitors – young unknowns, friends of his son and daughter-in-law, perhaps, as well as royalty and politicians and literary and scientific celebrities – and through his ever more extensive correspondence, he stayed at the heart of 'world literature', a term that he invented. Particularly in these last years – their ripeness and industriousness and the enlivening presence of a sovereign humour, are all perfectly caught in his *Conversations* with his literary assistant J. P. Eckermann – he created for the nineteenth century its picture of what a poet could be, an inspired and secular sage, in the service of an autonomous art. He was, however, doing far more than burnishing up his portrait for posterity. He continued to write reflective verse of great density and authority: 'Lines Written upon Contemplation of Schiller's Skull', for example, reiterates his lifelong belief in the identity of God and Nature and in the interaction of body and spirit. His purely lyrical poems of this period are unparalleled in the intensity with which thought and image are condensed into endlessly resonant symbols and an abrupt, almost inconsequential diction which, however strange, retains a note of personal and colloquial informality ('To the Full

(Prince Albert's duchy of Saxe-Gotha was the immediate neighbour of Saxe-Weimar and Goethe was a frequent visitor at the Gotha court.) For Gwen Raverat's Uncle William, the eldest son of Charles Darwin, 'old Go-eethe' was one of the 'fine fellows' one had to admire along with Homer, Rembrandt and Beethoven. The nineteenth-century sages had no hesitation in claiming him as one of their own: to Carlyle (for whom Goethe wrote a reference when he applied for a professorship at St Andrews in 1828) Goethe demonstrated the possibility of retaining moral seriousness in an age of secular modernity; Emerson selected him as his representative 'man of letters', G. H. Lewes made his reputation with one of the earliest biographies of Goethe in either English or German and was accompanied on his research trip to Weimar by George Eliot; and Bohn's Standard Library brought out cheap multi-volume editions of Goethe in translation. For Matthew Arnold 'no persons' were 'so thoroughly modern, as those who have felt Goethe's influence most deeply', and for them 'Goethe's wide and luminous view' was both a consolation and an ideal.

But in the last decades of the century, economic, then imperial, and finally military rivalry between Britain and Germany clouded the public mind. German culture in general fell into disfavour in England at the very time when Goethe's name and works were being appropriated by the new nation which Bismarck had invented. Under Kaiser Wilhelm II Goethe was made to serve as the centrepiece of a classical literature which was felt to be as much a prerequisite of nationhood as military heroes, colonies and a navy. It also happened that Goethe's archives became publicly accessible only in 1885, on the death without issue of his last grandchild, and as a result the systematic study of his life and works was from the beginning made a part of a half-conscious programme of constructing a national mythology. Reactions in England were understandably and increasingly hostile. The British variant of German Idealism which had dominated university philosophy in the later nineteenth century was on the defensive after 1900 and as war became more likely German literary achievements were more stridently and contemptuously dismissed. (Rupert Brooke in a railway carriage: 'Opposite me two Germans sweat and snore.') In 1915 Ford Madox Hueffer (eventually to change his name to 'Ford', out of hatred for 'Prussianism') published a diatribe against the German culture into which his father had been born, under the title *When Blood is their Argument*. 'There is no such thing as "modern German culture",' he wrote. 'The Goethe legend has done a great deal of harm to the aesthetic standards of the whole world.' Goethe's works in his view will not stand up to critical scrutiny, but their market-price is artificially supported by a conspiracy between the German state and its servile jobbers, the German professors. Those who 'have invested so many foot-poundals of brain-energy in the author of *The Sorrows of Werther* ... dislike seeing what I may call a fall in Goethes'. Hueffer's book was more perceptive, and better-informed, about the political and economic context in which German literature was written and read than many later English studies of the subject, but it was also propaganda and those who win wars do not enjoy the immediate liberation from propaganda which is the fortunate lot of those who lose them. In the decade after 1918, when hundreds of British families of German origin were forcibly repatriated, and those who remained anglicized their names, British intellectual life was ethnically cleansed and the debt of Victorian culture to Germany was erased from memory, or ridiculed. Common sense returned to rule philosophy, Georgian Englishness to rule verse. T. S. Eliot, seeking a new British and post-Victorian identity for himself in the London of the 1920s, adopted Hueffer's estimate of Goethe as a journeyman of letters, a prose moralist: Goethe the poet could be disregarded along with the rest of the Romantic generation. (In these circumstances it was a courageous act by some London academics to refound the English Goethe Society and start the journal *German Life and Letters*, but they did not find the audience outside university circles for which they had hoped.) However, as it became clearer that the age of Empire was drawing to a close and that Britain was culturally no more self-sufficient than she was politically and economically, Germany's experiences became an object of interest again. In the ultra-modern, international and post-imperial world of Berlin in the critical years of the Weimar Republic, W. H. Auden and Christopher

Isherwood found a release into the twentieth century from the complacency of an English middle class which continued in an essentially Edwardian life-style until the demise of domestic service in 1939. Auden's discovery of a world beyond England took him to America and to an environment which had not lost its nineteenth-century affiliations with Germany, and at the end of his life he regarded it as achievement enough to become, he hoped, 'a minor atlantic Goethe' ('The Cave of Making', 1964). Even Eliot, redefining England and history in the purgatorial fires of the Blitz, changed his view of Goethe completely, and kept a drawing of him on his mantelpiece throughout the war. In 1949, the year of Goethe's 200th anniversary, which also saw Louis MacNiece's verse rendering of *Faust*, commissioned by the BBC, Stephen Spender gave a prophetic lecture on 'Goethe and the English mind'. He said that the development of the private and self-scrutinizing tone in English poetry had been made possible by the public air of confidence and success in Britain's imperial epoch, and that 'with the catastrophic breakdown of Britain's position in the world' the basis for that private poetry had been withdrawn. Goethe had thereby become extraordinarily topical: 'Goethe was evidently close to the problem of Joyce, the problem of the disintegration of a very complex modern consciousness within a world whose values do not provide a structure upon which such complexity can realize itself objectively . . . Goethe's search for a realization of objectivity through subjective experience leads straight into the modern movement in poetry, though very few modern poets realize this.' If the British reception of Goethe has made little progress since the anniversary of 1949, it must partly have been because the public and intellectual adaptation to the catastrophe of which Spender spoke has been so slow and the rediscovery of Britain's European and pre-imperial roots has been so reluctant.

Goethe's greatness is inseparable from the factors which have made him difficult of access for an English audience. He fits into none of our established categories. As novelist, dramatist, lyric poet, even essayist, he never does quite what we expect. Essentially, we might say, Goethe is a writer who, with great foresight in his time, understood and presented the problems of the Romantic age in the language and forms of the eighteenth century, and we are not used to looking for the themes of Poe or Baudelaire in the verse of Gray or the prose of Johnson. Landscapes deriving from Claude, or narrative structures deriving from Voltaire or Fielding, do not seem to us the obvious setting in which to treat such issues as the industrialization of society, the breakdown of institutional religion, or the Kantian philosophy of the self and moral freedom. Yet Goethe's work has this hybrid appearance for an English reader not only because it is in the nature of his genius to displace categories even as he seems to be applying them, but for historical reasons too. English literary expectations have been formed by the different or delayed experience, or even by the absence of experience, of events, which have made the modern, and post-modern, world and which influenced Goethe's writing directly and profoundly. The French Revolution was not a period of revolution for England but a time in which the wealthy English middle class refounded its overseas empire and consolidated it in a series of wars against its French rivals. England knew neither the restrictions and formalities of the *ancien régime*, nor the novelties of political Terror and occupation by the conscript armies of the *levée en masse*, nor therefore the shock of the complete historical disjunction in which, on the continent of Europe, the modern form of the state came into being. That upheaval was the central political event in Goethe's life: it destroyed the Holy Roman Empire, which provided the constitutional framework for the society in which he lived his early years, and though the forms he had been familiar with in his youth were preserved in Restoration Germany he knew that they were inhabited by a wholly different spirit. To survive the Revolution into the era of European nation-states was to have an experience of collective detachment from an irretrievable past such as England had not known since the Reformation of the sixteenth century and did not have to face again until the final dissolution of the Empire in the twentieth. The self-conscious and semi-serious formality of Goethe's later writing, its ironical juxtapositions of ancient and modern, of the nineteenth and the eighteenth centuries, which none the less nearly always refuse the temptation to nostalgia, is the expression of a sensibility which has learnt what it is to be the victim of revolutionary historical change. From the 1840s to the 1940s, from Chartism to the Welfare State, that was not a feeling with which the majority of the English public could, or wished to sympathize. But early and mid-Victorian England also had a small proportion of unflinchingly liberal minds who were aware that their country would not for ever remain immune to what had begun on the streets of Paris in 1789, and they saw that Goethe, whatever his public pose, was as modern an intellect as they.

All German literature lay, as far as the nineteenth-century British public was concerned, under the twin suspicions of political Jacobinism and religious impiety. The one was assumed to lead to the other. It is true that the German clergy underwent an Age of Doubt, brought on by biblical criticism and a loss of faith in the scientific evidences for Christianity, in the later eighteenth century, a hundred years before their English counterparts. The result, however, was neither political revolution nor a public outbreak of unbelief but the rapid growth in philosophy and literature of secular reinterpretations of religion and alternatives to it. The rational and aesthetic rewritings of Christianity by Kant and Schiller and the Idealist generation of philosophers and theologians met a warm reception in America, where they helped to generate a major cultural institution, the Transcendentalist movement, but in England they seemed little better than atheism. In the later part of the century, then, the British mood changed; after the publication of Darwin's *Origin of Species* in 1859 doubts became more widespread and more mentionable, and the German substitutes for belief became the object of serious interest. But it was not long before economic and imperial rivalry had its intellectual effect, an Anglican school of biblical criticism was founded to counter the German, and isolationism was restored.

In one sense it was unfair that Goethe's reputation should have suffered through his being associated with the great philosophical and theological movements of his time and being dismissed as just another irreligious German. Goethe never became a disciple of anyone, not even Kant, and he was never tempted by new restatements of doctrines whose old formulations he had already rejected as absurdities. But his religious position was far more radical than that of the Idealists, and the British, had they known it, had far more reason to be suspicious of him than of Schleiermacher or Hegel. Apart from his marriage, Goethe took an active part in no church ceremony after he was twenty-one and consciously and explicitly sought to live as 'a decided non-Christian' a life which was one of the most deeply reflective and emotionally one of the most turbulent of his age. Christianity was for him already a historical phenomenon, only indirectly relevant to what he called the serious task of seeking his own salvation. Nietzsche was right to see in Goethe his predecessor and master, a man who was more at ease than he was with the death of at least Luther's God – something which at the end of the nineteenth century was for many, even in Germany, still unthinkable. The charges of impiety and materialism were those first and most constantly levelled against Goethe in British reviews and the latter charge at least was repeated by Hueffer in 1915. Obscenity and blasphemy were the reasons cited by Coleridge for not translating *Faust* and many nineteenth-century versions of the play excluded the Prologue, since its representation of God was deemed offensive. Even now Goethe's conversations with Eckermann are available in English only in editions purged of his satirical references to the English church and its prelates. But even to raise the question of Goethe's theology is to understate his radicalism. Goethe was no disciple, and he was no apostle either. Though he incorporated many contemporary ideas into his works he never did so with the simply didactic purpose of passing them on. He was interested in what might be called the morality of ideas: what kind of life would you lead if you saw things this way? what kind of person was likely to take up this kind of thinking? He understood those who remained faithful to the old religion (like Gretchen), and those who emancipated themselves from it (like Faust), and those who took up with all kinds of fashions in order to avoid the responsibility of finding the meaning of their life for themselves (like many of the characters in his novels). This sovereign detachment from the ideologies with which his age teemed made him all but incomprehensible in an England where even unbelief, once it had become respectable, was a specially Low form of churchmanship. It even harmed him in Transcendentalist America. Since he was anyway under suspicion for his apparent accommodation with anti-democratic regimes, the charge of unseriousness and moral laxity provided as good an excuse for avoiding the challenge of his writings as in England the charge that he was too metaphysical and obscure.

'My things can never be popular', Goethe confided to Eckermann at the end of his life. A third and crucial aspect of the modernity of his works is their peculiar relation to their audience. For a few years at the start of his literary career he enjoyed an intoxicating intimacy with the public he could reach through print. *Werther* seemed to make all Germany into his friends and correspondents. But the intimacy was based, like the Storm and Stress movement itself, on an illusion. Germany did not consist simply of eager readers and writers of books, held together by a publishing industry which was one of the earliest forms of capitalist mass production. The German middle classes expressed themselves and their values so successfully in literature because more practical and more political forms of self-expression were not available to them. In political terms the lives of the great majority of German readers of *Werther* were determined by their being the subjects of absolute rulers and their bureaucracies, with no say in their own affairs, and by their imprisonment in what was almost a hereditary caste system hostile to the egalitarianism implied by a mass market. Goethe instinctively understood the danger to himself represented by the mismatch between the potentially national middle-class culture of the book and the economic and political realities of German life. He could continue to be popular only at the cost of failing to articulate the full truth about his and any other German existence of his time. Perhaps largely for this reason he gave up his base in republican and bourgeois Frankfurt, and with it his mass public, and moved to princely and authoritarian Weimar. During his first ten years there he published virtually nothing and sought his audience instead in a few select friends in and around the court. But this experiment too was a failure: he needed a genuine public and without it he ceased eventually to be able to write at all. His decision

J. W. VON GOETHE

The age of the empires is over and with it the sense of personal identity which membership of an imperial nation once conferred, or confirmed. That is the solid core of truth within the theorizings of Post-Modernism (if by Post-Modernism we understand intercultural pluralism, the belief in an indefinite deferral of meaning, and the simultaneous dissolution of personality and objectivity into structures of symbolism and interpretation which can never be brought to a final coherence). In that sense Goethe is not so much a modern as a post-modern writer. He had little sympathy with the burgeoning political and cultural nationalism of his time, which for all its artificiality was to have such fateful consequences for the next century and a half, and Spender recognized fifty years ago that in Goethe's works personal identity is fluctuating and unstable (he pointed in particular to the transformations of Mephistopheles in *Faust. Part Two*). In the modern world, as Goethe came to understand far sooner than most of his contemporaries, cultural identity is not unitary and fixed, its sources are multiple, and it is always growing and changing; and personal identity changes with it. That is the explicit theme of *The Parliament of West and East*: the German and Islamic worlds interpenetrate as do the sexualities of the poet and the beloved. Moreover Goethe – the great 'dissolvent' as Arnold called him – learnt at a very early age, and largely through his detachment from Christianity, that poetry and truth cannot be separated. Living, like writing, is a matter of interpretation. Goethe created meanings assiduously in his life and in his art and constantly transferred them from one domain to the other. All poetry for him is personal, but personality is not unified, and perhaps not even our own possession. Goethe – it is especially evident in his novels – was aware that the meanings that make up our lives may come from outside us. *Werther, Wilhelm Meister, Elective Affinities*, all demonstrate how our interpretations of our lives, and even of ourselves, are given to us by others, by fashion, by teachers, by our cultural context. Yet they also show how there is more to us than a chance bundle of interpretations, how there is in us a centre or point of growth always questing for something more than what is given, sometimes transcending it, sometimes tragically betrayed by it, sometimes triumphantly giving it a form like that of a flower, to which duration is irrelevant. That living centre came more and more clearly to be recognized by Goethe as a principle not of self-assertion but of self-forgetfulness: we find ourselves by giving up the search for ourselves and finding instead the world – a world which is there *for us*, presupposing our enjoyment, activity and response, just as the visible world is resplendent with colours that exist only in so far as they are perceived by a human eye. We lose ourselves in order to love, and find ourselves in loving. In Goethe's later works – *Wilhelm Meister's Years of Wandering, Faust. Part Two*, the later instalments of his autobiography – the growing centre is so mysteriously self-effacing that we may seem to be left with only detached and arbitrarily assorted perspectives on things. But the mystery is the condition of the discovery: we cannot know the heart of things, nor of ourselves, but if we refrain from the attempt to penetrate to these inaccessible extremes all experience will be revealed to us, boundless and unpredictable and everywhere alive. Goethe is thus more than a post-modern writer: reaching out to an audience beyond the limits of time and place and culture he first described the post-modern landscape and showed how it is possible to live and grow and find happiness in it, and not fall either into narcissism or despair. The past has not been kind to him, but it is in his nature to belong to the future.

*

The works contained in this selection illustrate some of the different phases and modes of Goethe's writing and show, even through the opaque medium of translation, something of the strength and disconcerting novelty of his imagination. *Werther*, written when he was twenty-four, is remarkable not only for the deftness and compelling *accelerando* of its simple narrative and the overwhelming force of the emotions it contains, but also for the subtlety with which it negotiates a difficulty evident in its literary successors such as *The Catcher in the Rye* and *By Grand Central Station I Sat Down and Wept*. Werther may well at times be guilty of self-pity, but the book which tells his story does not collude with him. Rather more than it is a love-story, *Werther* is the story of a mind being taken over by fashionable obsessions – in that respect it is a true descendant of *Don Quixote* – and it is told with a lucid and dispassionate realism which reaches a climax in the last, shattering pages. As the derangement of the hero grows and his suicide approaches, the necessity for a third-person narrative becomes more apparent, but long before then we have learnt to distinguish between the book and its principal character. The definiteness of the setting, in time and place and social circumstance, and the hints of excess and of a perverse tendency to self-destruction in Werther's make-up encourage us to read the letters selected for us not just as a record of Werther's voice but as evidence for his condition. Above all, our attention is drawn to the role played by books and by topical issues – the heart, the garden, the landscape, the simple life – in the formation of his sensibility. Werther's distance from established religion and his secularizing application of theological terms to profane love is a *leitmotif* throughout, sounded even in the novel's last sentence: its title is itself a play on words and could equally be translated as *The Passion of Young Werther*. Homer and Ossian, heroes of the Herder-influenced intellectual around 1770, are the two geniuses who preside over the two books of the novel and the two phases of Werther's career; there are less explicit allusions to Rousseau and Goldsmith, and the moment when a reminiscence of a poem by Klopstock reveals to Werther and Lotte that they are soulmates must be one of the first occasions in non-comic literature when love is mediated through print. The height of Werther's passion can be communicated by Werther not in his own words but in those of his translation of Macpherson's Ossian. But Werther is no mere specimen and the novel no mere case-study in a forgotten vogue, with only antiquarian appeal. When we emerge into the third-person narrative towards the end of Werther's life we do not find that we have escaped into the comfortable rationality of an eighteenth-century milieu in which we can learn the 'truth' about Werther, or what he looked to like to his friends, or what Lotte or Albert 'really' felt and thought. By an extraordinary stylistic *tour de force* Goethe, in his editorial report to the reader, remains uncompromisingly true to the original insight which gives the novel its power: that experience comes to us only as our own

– that no one else can have it for us – however derivative and sociable the elements of which it is composed. To shift the narrative perspective to that of Lotte or Albert or some other *raisonneur* would only mean reiterating in the context of another life, and so simply postponing, the question which Werther's case posed for Goethe with exemplary clarity and urgency: what is there in the world to match and satisfy the yearnings of a heart that has fully understood the uniqueness of its own destiny?

*

Elective Affinities, published when Goethe was sixty, suggests, behind its inscrutable and at times rebarbative exterior, no diminution in the intensity of that question; indeed there are clearly deliberate formal parallels to *Werther*. Again there are two books; again the conflict comes, at the end of the first book, to a provisional resolution in flight and, at the end of the second, to a definitive conclusion in a death which is virtually a suicide; again the action of the second book repeats motifs from the first in a more intense or complex form (exemplified in the promotion of the Captain to the rank of Major). The plot itself could be seen as a complex recapitulation of the plot of *Werther*: not one unconsummated adultery but two, and with the perspectives of all four parties taken into account. To Werther's revealingly erotic dreams corresponds an extra-ordinary scene of mental adultery during marital intercourse surely without parallel in the non-pornographic literature of the age; and Werther's fantasies of a reunion with Lotte after death are raised to a higher level at the close of *Elective Affinities*, where a similar suggestion about Eduard and Ottilie is put by the (unreliable) narrator, who for the nonce has turned hagiographer. If anything Goethe wrote is unredeemedly tragic it is *Werther*, and of *Elective Affinities* he said that it engendered the fear that Aristotle thought essential to tragedy, 'when we see a moral evil approaching the persons of the action and encompassing them'. The most significant parallel between the two novels lies in the nature of that moral evil. For if *Werther* is the story of one man succumbing to the intellectual and emotional vogues of his time, *Elective Affinities* shows us a similar corruption of a whole society.

It is often assumed, because the title of the novel alludes to the chemical analogy for human behaviour proposed early on by the Captain and by Eduard, that this analogy must be taken as explaining the actions of the characters, who must therefore be seen as the puppets of natural forces unknown to them and to us. But the theory of chemical 'elective affinities' no more explains the relationships between the four characters than the Christological allusion in the title of *Werther* confirms that Werther's story is to be read as a new and secular Passion. In both cases the title refers us not to the source of the malady but to one of its most prominent symptoms. Three of the main characters, and most of the minor ones, seek to explain, and so to tame and obscure, the moral enormity of their conduct, by recourse to convenient interpretative fictions – many of them recognizable features of the German intellectual land-scape in the Romantic era – and by doing so they hasten the potential catastrophe. The Captain, with his tidy mind, invokes scientific theory (probably a bit obsolete, he admits). Charlotte judges everything by the standards of a blinkered common sense. She thinks herself practical, unprejudiced and unsenti-mental, but is a prisoner of convention, painfully unaware of the sensibilities deeper than her own which her crassness offends, and sexually frigid. Eduard, as self-indulgent in his metaphysics as in everything else, interprets events, when con-venient, as the workings of a benevolent destiny, even when they are manifestly random, or the product of some conscious or unconscious intention, or capable of bearing a quite differ-ent significance. Around the characters rises a miasma of further potential interpretative and symbolic schemes provided by such contemporary fads as landscape gardening, medieval-ism in art, or the rational reduction of Christianity to social work and the moral edification of children. These both build up a picture of the furnishings of a Romantic mind, as *Werther* built up a picture of the age of Sentiment, and are the agents of corruption.

The resemblance of *Elective Affinities* to *Mansfield Park* is aston-ishing – though their authors knew next to nothing of each other, the two novels were written at almost the same time, a literary coincidence matched only by that of Voltaire's *Candide* and Johnson's *Rasselas* in 1759. In both books literary and intellectual distractions – in *Mansfield Park* the preparations for acting a play by August Kotzebue, an adversary of Goethe's – are the means of furthering and concealing the spread of 'moral evil'. And just as Fanny Price stands fast, despite her social and economic vulnerability, so Ottilie, also a charity case, is the only character in Goethe's story who, after initially succumbing to the seductive blindness of infatuation, sees through all the self-deceptions to the abyss on the edge of which the entire household is standing. If they carry out the plan for reordering their liaisons that the chemical analogy suggests – Charlotte marrying the Captain/Major, and Eduard marrying Ottilie – they will in effect be retrospectively consenting to the death of a child which has made the divorce of Eduard and Charlotte a practical possibility. Knowing the moral dubiousness of the circumstances which led to the death, Ottilie realizes that to consent to it would be tantamount to murder. Unsustained by any belief in immortality or the reward of virtue, she resists the power both of her own desires and of the chemical analogy and all it stands for – the blandishments of a coarse and self-deluded age to which her refined and unyielding conscience is an obstacle and a reproach, and which soon dispatches her with relief into the safely exceptional status of (dead) sainthood. Goethe's novel, however, is more philosophical and more extreme, and in that sense more religious, than Jane Austen's. Ottilie is totally alone. Indeed, since personality itself seems to be dissolved by the various scientific and symbolic explanations of unconscious motives, and all the characters have virtually the same rather featureless name (the real name of both Eduard and the Captain being Otto), even of Ottilie little is left for certain at the end but a moral assertion in the void. She cannot turn in hope, like Fanny Price, from an episode in chaos to the comfort of a surrounding social order maintained by returning figures of authority. She is not even supported by a sympathetic narrator, for the most obviously post-modern feature of this extraordinary book is a third-person narrative which is at once tendentious and impersonal. A highly sophisticated development of the editorial voice in *Werther*, it has the task of mediating between the perspectives of the four main characters without creating a fifth viewpoint which we might be tempted to take for some socially validated 'truth'. The chosen angle is not identical with that of any character but is sufficiently similar to Charlotte's to be plainly inadequate: Eduard is severely criticized (Goethe himself thought the passionate Eduard, for all his selfishness, 'beyond price because his love is unconditional'); the tedious Captain, though his scientific theories are treated with caution, is presented as far more reliable; lavish praise is heaped on Charlotte's judgement at the most inappropriate moments and her (understandable) jealousy of Ottilie is left uncommented; Ottilie herself is removed to a mysterious distance. Somewhere beyond the reach of narration, like Werther in his last days, she struggles to find her own way through a world that is seemingly oblivious of what she knows to be the one thing necessary.

*

Goethe's autobiographical writings are an easily enjoyable part of his work but they have their own subtlety and certainly cannot be taken as a reliable record, even when, as is the case with *Italian Journey*, they make extensive use of contemporary diaries and letters. They create new patterns in past events and read out of the events a new significance for the time of writing. Goethe's polemical reaction to political change and to the cultural atmosphere in Germany between 1813 and 1817 makes of *Italian Journey* a hybrid work in which present and past interact. Like the *Parliament of West and East* it is a flight from the contemporary world, an extension and multiplication of his personality through a quest for the physical traces, in art and landscape, of ancient culture. After the settled and confident narration of his childhood and youth in *Poetry and Truth*, written when Napoleon seemed secure on the imperial throne, Goethe reverted for *Italian Journey* to the documentary manner of *Werther*, as if the integrity of his identity were again at stake and intensity and immediacy of presentation were again essential. But the story being told could not look less Wertherian: controlled, premeditated, imperturbable, the

Grand Tour unfolds, with landscape and cityscape, art and nature, even botany and geology, all slipping into place in the design, and rounding out the poet's inner image of Rome, and Greece too (for Naples and Sicily, known as Magna Graecia in antiquity, were lands of Greek settlement where some of the best-preserved of all the monuments of Greek architecture had survived, and Goethe even thought it possible that Homer had been a Sicilian). The contrast between matter and manner is deliberate and reinforced by recurrent references to *Werther*, the earlier collection of letters which this is intended to counter: this is the story of the gathering in of the harvest which Werther never lived to see. Werther looked only inward into his own heart and ended in an implosion into nothingness. In Goethe's Italy self and world meet and mingle and sustain each other. The poet's destiny is fulfilled in the lights and colours and forms and solid materials of ancient civilization, and of its Renaissance afterglow, and he joins a happy company of painters and antiquaries disinterestedly devoted to the same tasks as he. It is a journey not towards Arcadia but within it, as Goethe's motto proclaims; with the first sentence we have already entered his Golden Age.

Of course, in 1786–7 it was not really like that at all. Goethe's first venture to Rome and beyond was not intended to be his last, or to be the culmination of his life, and for years afterwards he regarded it as an unsatisfactory foretaste of pleasures still to come. The major recapitulation of his journey which he planned for its tenth anniversary in 1796, during which he hoped to fill the gaps left by his first visit and to return with an educated eye to objects he had been too immature to appreciate before, came to nothing thanks to Napoleon's Italian *blitzkrieg*. The perfect Italian Journey evaded Goethe in life and so, when he came to write his autobiography, he reconstituted it in art: he wrote it up, not as it was, but as it ought to have been. It is possible to see, more or less, how he proceeded since much of his source material has survived for the first sections covering the stretch from Carlsbad to Rome, though he had less at his disposal for Naples and Sicily and most of what he had he subsequently destroyed. It is at any rate clear that Goethe eliminated the agitation of his escape, his anxiety about whether he would get to Rome at all, his uncertainty about the duration of his stay, most of the personal references in his letters, and of course everything to do with his increasingly troubled relationship with Frau von Stein. He suppressed in particular the superstitious aura in which in 1786 he had clothed the sacred places he had made his goals: Rome – he fled not to Italy in general but specifically to the capital of the ancient and modern worlds – and Enna (Castrogiovanni) in Sicily, where Proserpine, about whom he had written a bitterly tragic monodrama, was taken down into the underworld. Enna indeed virtually disappears from his narrative (he probably spent longer there than he admits), though in order to visit it he took an unorthodox route across the island and missed out Syracuse and is hard put to find a convincing explanation for this detour. The sense of an urgent pilgrimage to specific places fades into the background and instead we share in a leisurely, almost timeless, vacation in the warm south, which is given shape by the traveller's growing understanding of ancient art, thanks to his growing experience of its natural setting. Goethe's visit to the Doric temples at Paestum, which shocked him by their archaic simplicity, is transferred from the days after his return from Sicily, when it actually occurred, to the days immediately before he left for Sicily, so that it shall appear to be part of a programme of gradually deepening study of Greek architecture undertaken there. Much attention was given at the drafting stage to reordering the episodes in the conclusion so that Goethe's departure from Naples should be marked by a grand natural spectacle. Human or comic interest was supplied, or gaps in the material were filled out, by the novelistic development of little sub-plots around such themes as the inn in Catania or Kniep's fiancée. The result is not so much a photographic image of the poet's past as a Claude landscape, an ideal picture of what Auden called the Happy Place. The picture, however, is not painted simply in order to gratify the artist but, as the last paragraph reminds us, in order to be shared. The belief that the perfection of human life has proved to be possible at least once in history and that to attain it again is the proper goal of a common endeavour is Goethe's antidote to the hypnotic and predatory solitude at the heart of *Werther* and *Elective Affinities*.

*

The qualities of Goethe's prose writing in his last ten years are peculiarly difficult to render in translation and so personal as to border on the eccentric: he is by turns richly impressionistic, monumentally formal, and disconcertingly off-hand. *Novella* (published 1828) is an outstanding example both of his later style and of the symbolic density to which it can rise. The original intention of the verse epic on this theme, planned in 1797, was to discuss, both directly and metaphorically, the Revolution in France, an outbreak of elemental forces of which both the fire and the exotic beasts which the fire releases seemed at the time an appropriate image. Thirty years later, the Revolution – as we are told at the opening of the story – has done its work and the world has changed, but the image has only become richer in its implications. There are many contexts in which it is possible to show the self-discipline that is needed if natural forces are not to be opposed with equivalent violence, but to be tamed through a harmony of energy and control, of which art gives a model. To the political sphere Goethe's story adds that of personal relations: the most delicate touches hint at Honorio's disordered feelings for the Princess – it is his heroics that put her at risk and lead to the unnecessary death of the tiger – and the open-endedness of his future complements and qualifies the apparently definitive conclusion. But there is an aesthetic and philosophical level to the story too, and beyond that a religious, and here it becomes clear that nothing in this secular parable is definitive. There is at the heart of things, and so in our immediate neighbourhood, an unapproachable mystery. The point where the human and the elemental touch and are brought into harmony cannot be seen, or spoken of, or imagined. Its symbol is the central court of the ruined castle, impenetrably overgrown. Science and art are emissaries that can bring back reports of it, by telescope and notebook, for example, but it remains inaccessible to the narrator and to us. Into this place, where the lion is tamed, only the religious image can go, the little child prophesied by

Isaiah, and we cannot follow. The religion may be secularized – there are overtones of *The Magic Flute* as well as of the Old Testament – and we are dealing with religion as metaphor, no doubt. But it is a metaphor of something which cannot be put into any other words, and perhaps religion has never claimed more than that. 'In old age', Goethe remarked, 'one always professes mysticism'.

*

The whole span of Goethe's development, from the explosive emotions of his youth to the sceptical mysticism of his old age, is encompassed by *Faust*, Europe's greatest long poem since Milton, possibly since Dante. At about the time when he conceived the idea of *Werther* and was still burdened by recollections of Friederike Brion he brought together in his mind the old chap-book and puppet-play theme of Dr Faustus, which had long appealed to him, and the eighteenth-century theme of the woman seduced and abandoned, and created the harrowing tragedy of Faust, Gretchen and Mephistopheles which is the kernel of *Faust. Part One.* Some more philosophical passages were added while he was in Italy, which extended Faust's ambitions into the political and historical spheres; the potential scope of the drama threatened to become unmanageable, and for many years after 1790 it looked as if *Faust. A Fragment* would never be completed. Around the turn of the century, however, Goethe decided to divide the work into two parts. He added the introductory poem, prelude and prologue (an epilogue, postlude and valedictory poem were originally planned too) and composed the passage he had for decades been unable to formulate, Faust's agreement with the devil, and the scenes leading up to it. He was thus able to publish as *Part One* the final version of the play he had first envisaged thirty years before, while postponing – perhaps indefinitely – the writing of a second part to contain the other themes that appealed to him. He had already begun to draft the scenes in which Helen of Troy first makes her appearance but not until the mid-1820s did he take them up again, and *Faust. Part Two* is essentially the work of his last years.

The issues in *Part One* are clearly those of burning and contemporary importance for the younger Goethe – the radical self-assertion of the young intellectual, whether of the Storm and Stress or of the Idealist period, who none the less has to face up to the personal and moral consequences of his revolt against convention. *Part Two* is more retrospective. It is in a sense another autobiographical memoir: an old man's reflection on the great political and cultural events he has experienced, and his transformation of them into symbol. Act I shows us the world of the *ancien régime*, its administrative incompetence and its aesthetic superficiality. Yet that world was also capable at least of conceiving, if not of nurturing, a classical ideal, and however abstract and theoretical that ideal may have been it was an image of human perfection that impassioned Goethe. Faust too falls in love with it but, like Goethe, he can love only flesh and blood and as Goethe had to go to Italy to put flesh on his ideal, so Faust has to go to Greece. Growth and metamorphosis are the unifying themes in the pullulating phantasmagoria of the Classical Walpurgis Night out of which the fully reconstituted Helen of Troy emerges with the suddenness of a crystallization at the end of a successful alchemical operation. In Act III Goethe reflects deeply on the Neo-Classical movement which dominated German taste in his middle years, the years of the French Revolution. Is it not impossible to re-establish contact with the spirit of dead humanity, however perfect it may have been in its own day and however inspiring its memory may be to later generations? Is it not intrinsic to human experience that it belongs to a particular historical time in which it is born and dies, and is not any attempt to resurrect it an absurdity? Such were the questions Mephistopheles might well have put to the German poets and thinkers of the 1790s, who seemed hardly to notice that while they were discussing the incarnation of the ideal, Napoleon was at the gates insisting on a different kind of realism. (In *Faust* it is Menelaus who plays this role.) Act IV transports us into those political realities, though the battle between Emperor and Anti-Emperor which ends, as in 1815, with the restoration of the Emperor, turns out in its own way to be an insubstantial illusion: the Emperor may be back on the throne, but the world has changed. In the new dispensation, as

Act V shows, the old forms count for nothing. 'War, trade, and piracy' are the new gods, as in the burgeoning capitalist and imperialist Europe of the 1820s, and Faust, as always, joins in with a will, anticipating in his own last acts of expropriation and mass enslavement some of the worst crimes of the twentieth century. To put it mildly, he seems no readier for heaven at the end of *Part Two* than at the end of *Part One*. But we should remember that any judgement the play passes on Faust is also being passed on the whole of Goethe's life and times: it is not likely to be unqualified or unsubtle.

Schiller, who knew something of Goethe's plans for what became *Faust. Part Two*, feared that he would not be able to find the 'poetical hoop' to hold together the vast mass of varied material in the play. But Goethe did just that when at last he wrote the lines that constitute his Faust's agreement with the devil: not a pact with a fixed term and conditions, as in the older versions of the story, but a wager between two parties who represent different views of modernity. For Faust is defined by Goethe as a specifically modern man, since he is a man who has explicitly put Christianity behind him. He is trying to live beyond good and evil, as Christianity has hitherto understood them, and he is no more willing to share Mephistopheles' views of what makes for human evil than he is able to share Gretchen's view of what is for human beings the divinely ordained good life. He wagers with Mephistopheles that he can live his secular life to the end without repentance whatever experiences may be put in his way, and the stake he pledges is not his immortal soul, in which he does not believe, but his life. He himself is the only source of value that he recognizes, and his capacity for experience, for moving on to the next thing that life brings, is the only good that he has to lose. This radical individualism, this reliance only on self, Goethe has diagnosed as the characteristic ethical attitude of the modern age, and he makes Faust's assertion of it into the structural principle that holds his drama of modernity together. For Goethe understands Faust's stance but he does not share it: there are other things to life besides the endless appetite of subjectivity for experience, and they are threatened by the triumphant onward march of Fausts, great and little.

INTRODUCTION

Two things in particular are shown by Goethe's play to be
– almost – beyond Faust's grasp, the two things that had been
most important to him personally as a bulwark against the
follies and brutality of his age. There is the moral commitment
to the duties of a limited life represented by Gretchen, whom
Faust cheats of the marriage which would be her proper fulfilment. (Marriage, which Werther abuses, and to which Ottilie
sacrifices herself, was an institution which Goethe always
treated with the greatest seriousness, resenting its appropri-
ation by a church whose authority he did not accept.) And
there is the classical ideal of human perfection, of a harmony
between humanity and nature, which Goethe felt he had
glimpsed in Italy and to which he felt we could remain true if
we kept the ancient models and practices before our minds, as
much in science as in art. Faust, of course, can experience
these, as he can experience anything, thanks to the magical
powers the wager has given him; but he can experience them
only on a condition which empties them of their substance.
He can experience them only for a moment, and it is their
nature to last, to be the commitment and vocation of a lifetime.
The centre and summit of each Part of *Faust* is a moment when
Faust's orbit crosses that of a life wholly different from his own,
a moment when he glimpses what he has lost by his wager
and what, by bringing it into relation with himself, he must
necessarily destroy. In *Part One*, Faust's moment in the summerhouse with Gretchen, their first kiss, reveals to him what
it would be to live permanently in perfectly equal and recip-
rocal love, and he leaves it behind as he has vowed to do and
reduces Gretchen to an object of enjoyment. In *Part Two* the
central scene of the central act is deliberately shaped to recall
that moment in the summerhouse: Faust makes fleeting contact
with the spirit of antiquity and is inspired with a vision of
Arcadian life which was once, and should still be, the true
perfection of humanity. But that too he shakes off to pursue
'power and property' and to establish his own counter-image
of humanity, in the contemplation of which he dies: a wholly
artificial society maintaining itself only by endless collective
effort under the permanent threat of mass extinction. The
wager is therefore the linch-pin in the structure of both parts

SELECT BIBLIOGRAPHY

———

There is now a modern selection from the entire range of Goethe's works (including the scientific writings) in English translation:

Goethe. Collected Works, Suhrkamp Edition in 12 Volumes, edited by V. Lange and others, Suhrkamp Publishers, Inc., New York, 1983–9.

The following usefully complement the selection in the present volume:

Goethe, *Erotic Poems*, translated by David Luke, introduced by H. R. Vaget, Oxford University Press, 1997.

Goethe, *Maxims and Reflections*, translated by Elizabeth Stopp, introduced by Peter Hutchinson, Penguin Classics, London, 1998.

There are many fine translations of *Faust* into modern English verse, notably by Alice Raphael (*Part One* only), David Luke and Martin Greenberg. That of Louis MacNiece is unfortunately severely abridged. Barker Fairley's prose version has the inestimable merit of an accuracy in tone as well as in linguistic detail which is not achievable by the verse translator and it seemed right to make it available again.

Studies of Goethe in English are numerous; in German they are beyond computation. The following should be found both informative and stimulating:

E. A. BLACKALL, *Goethe and the Novel*, Cornell University Press, Ithaca and London, 1976.
N. BOYLE, *Goethe. The Poet and the Age*. Volume One, *The Poetry of Desire (1749–1790)*, Oxford University Press, 1991; Volume Two, *Revolution and Renunciation (1790–1803)*, Oxford University Press, 1999.
N. BOYLE, *Goethe. Faust. Part One*, Cambridge University Press, 1987.
W. H. BRUFORD, *Culture and Society in Classical Weimar 1775–1806*, Cambridge University Press, 1962.
B. FAIRLEY, *A Study of Goethe*, Clarendon Press, Oxford, 1947.
E. HELLER, *The Disinherited Mind. Essays in Modern German Literature and Thought*, Bowes & Bowes, Cambridge, 1952.
T. J. REED, *Goethe*, Oxford University Press, 1984.

T. J. REED, *The Classical Centre. Goethe and Weimar 1775–1832*, Croom Helm, London, New York, 1980.

M. W. SWALES, *Goethe. The Sorrows of Young Werther*, Cambridge University Press, 1987.

J. R. WILLIAMS, *The Life of Goethe*, Blackwell, Oxford, 1998.

J. R. WILLIAMS, *Goethe's 'Faust'*, Allen & Unwin, London, 1987.

CHRONOLOGY

DATE	AUTHOR'S LIFE	LITERARY CONTEXT
1740		Fielding: *Tom Jones*.
1749	Goethe born in Frankfurt am Main, 28 August.	
1751		First volume of the *Encylopédie*.
1756–63		
1759		Lessing: *Faust* scene. Voltaire: *Candide*. Johnson: *Rasselas*.
1765–8	Studies in Leipzig.	
1770–71	Studies in Strasbourg; meets Herder; love-affair with Friederike Brion; poems.	
1771	Shakespearean historical drama, *Götz von Berlichingen* (published 1773); 'Storm and Stress' period begins.	
1773	First work on *Faust*; many small dramas, including *Satryos*.	Herder edits *Of German Character and Art* – 'Storm and Stress' manifesto.
1774	Novel in letters, *The Sorrows of Young Werther*, a European bestseller.	
1775	Engagement to Lili Schönemann broken off; invited to Weimar by Duke Carl August (aged 18); work on *Faust* interrupted.	Sheridan: *The Rivals*.
1776	(to 1786) Growing administrative and theatrical responsibilities in Weimar; friendship with Charlotte von Stein; 'Principal insight that ultimately all things are ethical'.	
1781		Kant: *Critique of Pure Reason*. Schiller: *The Robbers*. G. C. Tobler: essay on Nature (later attributed to Goethe, eg. by T. S. Eliot).
1782	Ennobled, becoming 'von Goethe'.	J. H. Füssli (Fuseli): *The Nightmare*. Rousseau: *Confessions* (and 1789).

HISTORICAL EVENTS

Maria Theresa Empress in Austria. Frederick II (the Great) King in Prussia.

Seven Years' War.

Boston Tea-Party.

Death of Louis XV.

American Declaration of Independence.

DATE	AUTHOR'S LIFE	LITERARY CONTEXT
1786	Rewrites *Werther*; obtains extended leave from Weimar and departs secretly for Italy; completes classicizing drama *Iphigenia in Tauris*.	Mozart: *The Marriage of Figaro*. Tischbein: *Goethe in the Campagna*.
1787	Visits Naples, Sicily, Rome; completes drama, *Egmont*; work on *Faust*.	Blake: *Songs of Innocence*.
1788	Returns to Weimar as poet, rather than administrator; begins living with Christiane Vulpius; *Roman Elegies* begun (to 1790, published 1795).	Schiller: *The Gods of Greece*.
1789	Completes *Tasso*, tragedy of a poet; first, and only surviving, child (August) born.	Lavoisier: *Elementary Treatise on Chemistry*.
1790	*Faust. A Fragment* published; briefly in Venice; turns to optics and botany; reads Kant.	Flaxman: illustrations to Homer.
1791	Director of Weimar Court Theatre.	
1792	On Allied campaign in France; at Valmy.	
1793		David: *Death of Marat*.
1794	Friendship with Schiller begins.	
1795	Novel, *Wilhelm Meister's Years of Apprenticeship*, published (also 1796).	Schiller: *Aesthetic Letters*.
1796	Classical poems: *Alexis and Dora*, *Hermann and Dorothea*.	
1797	Resumes work on *Faust*. Second journey to Italy broken off in Switzerland.	Hölderlin: *Hyperion*. Schlegel's Shakespeare translation begins. Wackenroder: *Lucubrations of a Monastic Art-Lover*.
1798	Starts classicizing journal, *The Propylaea* (to 1800).	Schelling appointed professor in Jena. Schiller: *Wallenstein*. Wordsworth: *Lyrical Ballads*. Schlegels start Romantic journal, *Athenaeum*.
1799	Starts neo-classical Weimar art competition.	Schleiermacher: *On Religion*. Novalis: *Christendom, or Europe*. Fichte leaves Jena (atheism controversy).

CHRONOLOGY

DATE	AUTHOR'S LIFE	LITERARY CONTEXT
1800	Much work on *Faust*, including Helena scenes for *Part Two*.	Fichte: *On the Vocation of Man*.
1801	Serious illness; work on *Faust* interrupted; work on *Theory of Colours* (to 1810).	
1803	Finishes *The Natural Daughter*, play about French Revolution.	Beethoven: *Third Symphony* ('Eroica').
1804		
1805	Ends art competition.	Death of Schiller; Hegel appointed professor in Jena.
1806	*Faust. Part One* finished (13 April); Goethe's house spared during looting of Weimar after battle of Jena; marries Christiane Vulpius.	
1807	Starts novel, *Wilhelm Meister's Years of Wandering*.	Hegel: *Phenomenology of Mind*.
1808	*Faust. Part One* published; meets Napoleon.	Kleist: *Penthesilea*.
1809	*Elective Affinities*, novel.	
1810	*Theory of Colours* published; *Pandora*, drama.	Mme de Staël: *On Germany*. C. D. Friedrich: *Monk beside the Sea*. Goya: *Disasters of War*.
1811	First part of autobiography, *Poetry and Truth*, published (completed 1831).	P. Cornelius: *Faust-Cycle*. Schubert: Goethe settings (to 1826).
1812		
1813		
1814	Poems in Persian style of Hafiz begin; interest in medieval art revives.	Scott: *Waverley*. Jane Austen: *Mansfield Park*. Chamisso: *Peter Schlemihl*.
1815		
1816	Partial production of *Faust* in Berlin; wife, Christiane, dies: 'emptiness and deathly silence in and around me'; *Italian Journey* published (also 1817); schema for *Faust. Part Two* (unpublished).	Coleridge: *Kubla Khan*. Constant: *Adolphe*. F. A. M. Retzsch: illustrations to *Faust*.
1817	Resigns as director of Weimar theatre.	
1818	Reads translation of Marlowe's *Doctor Faustus*.	Keats: *Endymion*. Mary Shelley: *Frankenstein*. Grillparzer: *Sappho*.

HISTORICAL EVENTS

Concordat between France and the papacy signed.

Territorial reorganization of Holy Roman Empire by Napoleon.

Napoleon crowned Emperor.
Napoleon King of Italy. Third Coalition against France. Austrians defeated at Austerlitz.
Confederation of the Rhine constituted; Holy Roman Empire ends. Battles of Jena and Auerstädt; Prussia defeated.

Emancipation of serfs in Prussia.

Peninsular campaign begins.

Napoleon annexes Papal States; enters Vienna.
Regency begins in England. Berlin University opens.

Napoleon's Russian campaign; retreat from Moscow.
War of Liberation; Napoleon defeated at Leipzig.
Allied invasion of France; abdication and exile of Napoleon.

Napoleon's 'Hundred Days'; battle of Waterloo; Congress of Vienna concluded. Holy Alliance between Prussia, Austria and Russia.
First meeting of Diet of new German Confederation.

Nationalist rally of German students at the Wartburg.

Congress of Aix-la-Chapelle; Allied occupation of France ends. Beginning of the Zollverein (German customs union, completed 1844).

DATE	AUTHOR'S LIFE	LITERARY CONTEXT
1819	*The Parliament of West and East*, Persian-style poems, published.	Schopenhauer: *The World as Will and Idea*.
1820		First partial English versions of *Faust*. Shelley: *Prometheus Unbound*.
1821	*Wilhelm Meister's Years of Wandering*, first edition.	Byron dedicates *Sardanapalus* to Goethe. Constable: *The Hay Wain*.
1823	First conversation with J. P. Eckermann; *Marienbad Elegy*.	Gower: translation of *Faust*. Beethoven: *Ninth Symphony*.
1824		Carlyle: translation of *Wilhelm Meister's Years of Apprenticeship*.
1825	Resumes work on *Faust*.	
1826	Work on *Novella* (to 1828).	
1827	*Helena, a classical-romantic phantasmagoria. Interlude for 'Faust'* (i.e. Act III of *Part Two*) published; reads Manzoni's *The Betrothed*; correspondence with Carlyle.	Heine: *Book of Songs*. Hugo: *Preface to 'Cromwell'*. Delacroix: illustrations to Stapfer's French translation of *Faust*.
1828	Part of Act I of *Faust. Part Two* published.	
1829	Numerous productions of *Faust. Part One* to celebrate Goethe's 80th birthday, but he attends none of them. *Second Sojourn in Rome* (continuation of *Italian Journey*). *Wilhelm Meister's Years of Wandering*, second edition.	Balzac: *Les Chouans*. Turner: *Ulysses Deriding Polyphemus*.
1830	Finishes Acts I and II of *Faust. Part Two*; son dies in Rome.	Hugo: *Hernani*. Stendhal: *Scarlet and Black*.
1831	Act V, then Act IV, of *Part Two*, completed (22 July).	Hegel dies. Carlyle: *Sartor Resartus*.
1832	Dies, 22 March. *Faust. Part Two* published.	Scott, Bentham die.

CHRONOLOGY

HISTORICAL EVENTS

Assassination of conservative playwright August Kotzebue; Metternich's repressive Carlsbad Decrees adopted by the Federal Diet. 'Peterloo' Massacre in England; Six Acts.

George IV King of England. Revolutions in Spain, Portugal and Naples. Conference of Troppau.

Greek War of Independence begins. Insurrection in Piedmont. Death of Napoleon.

French invasion of Spain.

Decembrist revolt in Russia. Stockton to Darlington railway.

July Revolution in France.

Polish rebellion suppressed. Mazzini founds 'Young Italy'.

English Reform Bill passed.

THE SORROWS OF
YOUNG WERTHER

*Translated by Elizabeth Mayer
and Louise Bogan*

BOOK ONE

How happy I am to have come away! Dearest friend, how strange is the human heart! To leave you, one so dearly loved, from whom I was inseparable, and yet to be glad! I know you will forgive me. Were not all my other personal relationships definitely chosen by fate to torment a heart like mine? Poor Leonora! And yet I was blameless. Was it my fault that, while the capricious charms of her sister provided me with a pleasant entertainment, her poor heart built up a passion for me? Still – am I altogether blameless? Did I not encourage her emotions? Did I not relish her perfectly genuine and naïve expressions which so often made us laugh, although they were anything but amusing? Did I not – but oh, what is man that he dares so to complain of himself! Dear friend, I promise you I will improve. I will no longer ruminate, as I always used to do, on the petty troubles which Fate puts in my way. I will enjoy the present and let bygones be bygones. You are certainly right, best of friends, that there would be far less suffering in the world if human beings – God knows why they are made like that – did not use their imaginations so busily in recalling the memories of past misfortunes, instead of trying to bear an indifferent present.

Be so kind to tell my mother that I shall attend to her business as well as I can, and that I will give her news about it soon. I have seen my aunt, and found that she is far from being the disagreeable person my family makes her out to be. She is a lively, impetuous woman, but very warm-hearted. I explained to her my mother's complaint concerning that part of the legacy which had been withheld from her. She told me the reasons and motives of her own conduct, and also the terms on which she would be willing to hand over everything, and even more than we asked. In short, I do not like to write more about it just now; tell my mother that all will be well. And again I have found, handling this trifling piece of business, that misunderstandings and neglect create more confusion in this world than trickery and malice. At any rate, the last two are certainly much less frequent.

Otherwise, I am very happy here. The solitude in this heavenly place is sweet balm to my soul, and the youthful time of year warms with its abundance my often shuddering heart. Every tree, every hedge is a nosegay of blossoms; and one would wish to be turned into a cockchafer, to float about in that sea of fragrance and find in it all the nourishment one needs.

The town itself is not pleasant, but all around it Nature expands an inexpressible beauty. This moved the late Count M. to lay out a garden on one of the hills which, intersecting one another in the loveliest natural diversity, form the most charming valleys. The garden is simple, and as soon as one enters, one feels that it was planned not by a scientific gardener but by a sensitive heart wishing to commune with itself alone. I have already shed many a tear to the memory of its former owner, in the crumbling summerhouse which was once his favourite retreat, and now is mine. Soon I shall be the master of the garden; the gardener has taken to me after only a few days, and he will not fare badly.

May 10

A wonderful serenity fills my whole being, like these lovely mornings which I enjoy with all my heart. I am quite alone, and pleased with life in this countryside, which seems to have been created for souls like mine. I am so happy, dear friend, so completely sunk in the sensation of sheer being, that my art suffers. I could not draw anything just now, not a line, and yet I have never been a greater painter than at the present moment. When the mist rises around me from the lovely valley, and the sun at high noon rests on the roof of my impenetrably dark forest, and only single shafts of sunlight steal into the inner sanctuary, and I am lying in the tall grass by the falling brook, discovering the variety of thousands of different grasses closer to the ground; when I feel nearer to my heart the teeming little world among the grass blades, the innumerable, inscrutable shapes of all the tiny worms and insects, and feel the presence of the Almighty who created us in his image, the breath of the All-Loving who sustains us, floating in eternal bliss – my friend, when everything grows dim then before my eyes, and sky and earth rest in my soul like the image of a beloved being – I am often overcome by longing and by the thought: could you only breathe upon paper all that lives so full and warm within you, so that it might become the mirror of your soul, as your soul is the mirror of the infinite God! – My friend – but it is more than I can bear; I succumb to the power and the glory of these visions.

May 12

I do not know if mocking spirits haunt this place, or whether it is the warm heavenly fantasy in my own heart which transforms everything around me into a paradise. Near the entrance to the town is a fountain, a fountain which holds me spellbound like Melusine with her sisters. – Going down a small hill, you find yourself in front of a vault to which some twenty steps lead down, where the clearest water gushes forth from the marble rocks. The enclosing little wall above, the tall trees which give shade all about, the coolness – all this makes the place so attractive and thrilling. Hardly a day passes without my sitting there for an hour. Then the girls will come from the town and fetch water, the most innocent task and the most necessary, in ancient times performed even by the daughters of kings. As I sit there, the patriarchal idea comes to life again for me: I see them, our forefathers, meet at the fountain and do their wooing, and feel how benevolent spirits hover around wells and springs. Anyone who has refreshed himself at a cool fountain after a long walk in summer will understand my feelings.

May 13

You ask me if you should send me my books? – My dear fellow, I implore you, for God's sake, do not bother me with them. No longer do I wish to be guided, excited, stimulated; my own heart storms enough in itself. What I need are cradlesongs, and I have found plenty of these in my Homer. How often do I lull my rebellious blood to rest, for you cannot imagine anything so erratic, so restless as my heart. My friend, need I tell you all this, you, whom I have so often burdened with the sight of my transitions from grief to excessive joy, from sweet melancholy to fatal passion. I treat my poor heart, moreover, as though it were a sick child, and satisfy all its desires. Do not tell this to anyone; there are those who would strongly disapprove.

May 15

The simple folk here already know me and have taken to me, especially the children. When I first joined them, and asked them in a friendly way about this or that, some thought that I wanted to scoff at them, and they sometimes even curtly rebuked me. I did not resent this; I merely felt most vividly what I had observed frequently before: people of a certain rank will always keep a cool distance from common people, as if they were afraid to lose their dignity by too much familiarity. On the other hand, there are superficial fellows and malicious jokers who seem to be condescending and only hurt the feelings of the poor folk all the more by their insolence. I know quite well that we are not and cannot ever be equal; but I am convinced that anyone who thinks it necessary to keep his distance from the so-called mob in order to gain its respect is as much to blame as the coward who hides from his enemy because he fears to be defeated.

A little while ago I came to the fountain and saw a young servant girl who had set her pitcher on the lowest step while she looked about for one of her companions to help her lift it to her head. I went down and looked at her. 'Do you want me to help you?' I asked. She blushed all over. 'Oh, no, sir!' she said. – 'Why not?' – She adjusted the pad on her head, and I helped her. She thanked me and went up the steps.

May 17

I have made all sorts of acquaintances but have not yet found any congenial company. I do not know what there is about me that attracts people; so many like me and become attached to me, and then I am always sorry that we can travel only a short way together. When you ask me what the people here are like, I must answer: Like people everywhere! There is a certain monotony about mankind. Most people toil during the greater part of their lives in order to live, and the slender span of free time that remains worries them so much that they try by every means to get rid of it. O Destiny of Man!

They are a very good sort of people, however. Whenever I forget myself and enjoy in their company the pleasures still granted to human beings, can exchange friendly jokes in all frankness and candour around a well-set table, arrange a drive in a carriage or a ball at the proper time – all this sort of thing has quite a good effect on me; I must only avoid remembering that there are still many other forces dormant in me, all unused and rotting, which I must carefully hide. Ah! it contracts my heart, and yet – it is the fate of a man like myself to be misunderstood.

Alas, that the friend of my youth is gone! Alas, that I ever knew her! I should say to myself: You are a fool to search for something that cannot be found on this earth. But she was mine, I felt her heart, her great soul, in whose presence I seemed to be more than I really was because I was all that I could be. Good God, was there a single force in my soul then unused? Could I not unfold in her presence all the wonderful emotions with which my heart embraces Nature?

Was not our relationship a perpetual interweaving of the most subtle feeling with the keenest wit, whose modifications, however extravagant, all bore the mark of genius? And now? – Alas, the years she had lived in advance of my own brought her to the grave before me. I shall never forget her – neither her unwavering mind nor her divine fortitude.

A few days ago I met a young man by the name of V., an open-hearted youth with pleasant features. He has just left the university and does not consider himself a sage but thinks, nevertheless, that he knows more than other people. He has studied hard, as I can tell from many indications; in short, he has a pretty store of knowledge. As he had heard that I sketch a good deal and know Greek (two unusual phenomena in these parts), he came to see me and displayed all sorts of learning, from Batteux to Wood, from De Piles to Winckelmann, assuring me that he had read the whole first part of Sulzer's 'Theory', and that he possessed a manuscript of Heyne's on the study of antiquity. I let that pass.

I have made the acquaintance of another good man, the Prince's bailiff, an honest, candid character. They say it warms the heart to see him among his children, of whom he has nine. There is much talk about his oldest daughter in particular. He invited me to his house, and I am going to pay him a visit soon. He lives an hour and a half from here in one of the Prince's hunting lodges which he was permitted to occupy after the death of his wife, as he found life here in town, and in his bailiff's quarters, too painful.

I have also come across a couple of odd people whom I consider thoroughly repulsive, and quite intolerable in their demonstrations of friendship.

Farewell! You will approve of this letter, which is entirely historical.

May 22

That the life of man is but a dream is a thought which has occurred to many people, and I myself am constantly haunted by it. When I see the limitations which imprison the active and speculative faculties of man; when I see how all human activity is directed towards procuring satisfaction for needs that have no other purpose than prolonging our miserable existence; when I see, moreover, how any comfort we may derive from certain points of inquiry is merely a dream-like kind of resignation, in which we paint our prison walls with gaily coloured figures and luminous prospects – all this, Wilhelm, leaves me speechless. I withdraw into my inner self and there discover a world – a world, it is true, rather of vague perceptions and dim desires than of creative power and vital force. And then everything swims before my senses, and I go on smiling at the outer world like someone in a dream.

That children do not know the reason of their desires, all the learned teachers and instructors agree. But that grown-ups too stumble like children on this earth, not knowing whence they come or whither they go, acting as little according to true purposes, being ruled like them by cakes and birch rods, no one likes to believe; yet to me it seems quite obvious.

I know your reply to this statement, and I willingly admit that those are the happiest people who, like children, live for the day only, drag around their dolls, putting their clothes on or off, tiptoe around the cupboard where Mummy keeps the sweets locked up, and, after having finally snatched the desired bit, stand with full cheeks and shout: 'More!' – These are indeed happy creatures. Nor are those people unhappy who, giving pompous names to their shabby occupations or even to their passions, pretend that these are gigantic achievements for the happiness and welfare of mankind. Happy the man who can be like this! But whoever realizes in all humility what all this amounts to, who observes with what pleasure every prosperous citizen trims his little garden into a paradise, how patiently even the unfortunate man struggles along his road under the weight of his burden, and how all are eager to see the light of the sun a little longer – well, such a man remains calm and shapes his own world out of himself; and he, too, is happy because he is a human being. And then, however confined he may be, he still holds for ever in his heart the sweet feeling of freedom, and knows that he can leave this prison whenever he likes.

May 26

You know of old my habit of settling down in some pleasant region and living there in a modest way. Here, too, I have discovered again a place which has attracted me.

About an hour from the town is a village called Wahlheim. Its location against a hill is very interesting, and when you leave it by the upper footpath, you can suddenly overlook the whole valley. The good landlady of the inn, pleasant and brisk for her age, provides beer, wine and coffee; and the best feature of all is two linden trees, shading with their spreading branches the little square in front of the church, which is framed on all sides by peasants' cottages, barns and farm-yards. I have seldom found a place so intimate and charming, and often have my little table and a chair brought out from the inn, and there drink my coffee and read my Homer. When I came for the first time, quite by accident, on a fine after-noon, under these linden trees, I found the little square deserted. Everyone was out in the fields. Only one little boy, about four years of age, was sitting on the ground, holding another child of about six months, who sat between his feet close against his breast, so that his arms formed a kind of chair for the little one; and the older boy sat perfectly still in spite of the sprightly way in which he glanced around with his dark eyes. I was amused by the sight and, sitting down on a plough opposite the two, made a drawing of the brotherly pose with great delight. I included the nearest fence, a barn door, and a few broken cartwheels, just as they came into view, and realized, after an hour, that I had made a well-composed and very interesting sketch, without having added the slightest invention of my own. This confirmed me in my resolution to keep close to Nature in the future. Nature alone is illimitably rich, and Nature alone forms the great artist. It is possible to say a good deal in favour of rules, about as much as can be said in praise of bourgeois society. The person who takes his direction from rules alone will never produce anything in bad taste, in the same way as the person who allows himself to be shaped by rules of social convention can never become an intolerable neighbour or a conspicuous villain; on the other hand, any rule is likely to destroy both the true feeling of Nature and its true expression, whatever people may say to the contrary. You will object that this statement is too severe, and that rules only restrain and prune the over-luxuriant vine, etc. My dear friend! Shall I give you an analogy? It is the same with love. A young man's heart is entirely attached to a girl; he spends every hour of the day with her, wastes all his strength, all his fortune, in order to prove to her at every moment that he is wholly devoted to her. Should a philistine then enter the picture, a man of some responsible position, and say to him: 'My dear young man, it is natural to love, but you must love only in a sensible way. Organize your day; some hours for work and some – the hours of relaxation – for your sweetheart. Calculate your means; and it is perfectly permissible to use whatever is left over and beyond your personal needs to buy her a present of some sort, only not too frequently – perhaps for her birthday or a similar occasion.' – Should the young man follow this advice, he will certainly turn into a useful member of society, and I should advise any prince to take him into his Cabinet; but his love is done with, and, if he is an artist, his art as well. O my friends! Why does the stream of genius so seldom break out as a torrent, with roaring high waves, and shake your awed soul? – Dear friends, because there are cool and composed gentlemen living on both banks, whose garden houses, tulip beds and cabbage fields would be devastated if they had not in good time known how to meet the threatening danger by building dams and ditches.

May 27

I am indulging, I see, in rapture, analogies and rhetoric, and I have forgotten to tell you the end of my story about the children. I had been sitting on my plough for almost two hours, completely absorbed in a painter's kind of perception which I described to you very fragmentarily in my letter of yesterday, when, towards evening, a young woman came up to the children, who had sat motionless the whole time. She carried a little basket on her arm and called from a distance: 'Philip, you are a very good boy.' She greeted me; I thanked her and, getting up, asked her if she was the children's mother. She said, yes, she was; and, handing a piece of bread to the older boy, she lifted the younger child on her arm and kissed it with motherly affection. 'I asked Philip to take care of the little one,' she said, 'as I had to go to town with my oldest son to buy white bread, sugar, and an earthen pot.' I noticed all these articles in her basket as the lid had fallen open. 'I wanted to make some soup for Hans (that was the name of the youngest child), but his oldest brother, the rascal, had broken the old pot yesterday while he was quarrelling with Philip for the scrapings.' I asked about the oldest boy, and she had hardly mentioned the fact that he was chasing the geese in the meadow when he came running up with a hazel switch for his younger brother. I continued my talk with the woman and learned that she was the schoolmaster's daughter, and that her husband had gone to Switzerland to collect his inheritance from a cousin. 'They meant to cheat him out of it,' she said, 'and did not answer his letters. That is why he went there himself. If only nothing has happened to him; I have not heard anything from him since he left.' I was quite sorry to have to leave the woman, but I gave a penny to each boy, and another to the mother to buy a roll for the younger one whenever she went to town; and in this way we parted.

I tell you, my dearest friend, when I am completely beside myself, the tumult of my emotions is soothed by the sight of such a woman, who is rounding the narrow circle of her

A young peasant came out of a nearby house and was soon busy mending the plough which I had sketched some days before. As I liked his manner, I spoke to him about his circumstances; we were soon acquainted and, as usually happens to me with such people, were soon quite familiar. He told me that he was in the service of a widow who treated him very well. He told me so much about her and praised her in such a way that I could soon guess that he was heart and soul devoted to her. She was no longer young, he said; her first husband had treated her badly, and she did not want to marry again. It became more than evident from his words how beautiful and how charming she was in his eyes, and how much he wished that she would choose him as a husband so that he might efface the memory of her first husband's faults. I should have to repeat every word of his story in order to give you a true picture of the pure affection, love and devotion of this man. Yes, I should have to possess the gift of the greatest of poets in order to depict to you convincingly the expressiveness of his gestures, the harmony of his voice, the hidden fire of his eyes. No, words fail to convey the tenderness of his whole being; everything I could attempt to say about this would only be clumsy. I was particularly moved by his anxiety that I might receive a wrong impression about his relationship to her or doubt her respectability. The delightful way in which he spoke of her figure, her physical charm, that irresistibly attracted and captivated him in spite of her lack of real youth, I can only repeat to myself in my inmost soul. Never in my life have I seen an urgent and passionate desire combined with such purity of heart; yes, I may well say, never had I myself imagined or dreamed of such purity. Do not scold me if I confess that the memory of this innocence and candour fills my soul with delight, that the picture of this devotion and tenderness follows me everywhere, and that I thirst and languish as if kindled by that flame.

I shall try to see her as soon as possible, or rather, after giving it a second thought, I shall avoid her. It is better that I see her through the eyes of her lover; she might not appear to my own eyes, in reality, as I now see her; and why should I destroy the lovely image I already possess?

June 16

Why do I not write to you? And you, a learned man, ask me this? You should be clever enough to guess that I am in a happy mood because – in a word – I have made an acquaintance who moves my heart in a strange way. I have – I do not know.

It is not easy for me to tell you, in chronological order, just how it happened, how I met such a lovely being. I am contented and happy, and therefore not a good historian.

An angel! – Nonsense! Everyone calls his loved one thus, does he not? And yet I cannot describe to you how perfect she is, or why she is so perfect; enough to say that she has captured me completely.

So much innocence combined with so much intelligence; such kindness with such firmness; such inner serenity in such an active life.

But all this is foolish talk – pure abstract words which fail to describe one single feature of her real person. Another time – no, not another time, right at this moment I will tell you everything. If I don't do it now, it will never be done. Because – between you and me – since I began this letter I have been three times on the point of laying down my pen, having my horse saddled and riding out to her. Although I swore to myself this morning not to do it, I am going every other moment to the window to see how high the sun has climbed.

I could not bear it any longer; I had to see her. Here I am back, Wilhelm; I will now eat my supper and then go on writing to you. What a delight it was to see her among the dear lively children, her eight brothers and sisters!

But if I go on in this way you will know as little at the end as at the beginning. Listen, then, while I force myself to go into details.

The other day I wrote you that I had met the bailiff S., and that he had asked me to visit him in his hermitage, or rather, his little kingdom. I neglected to do so, and probably never would have gone there if I had not by chance discovered the treasure hidden in that quiet part of the district.

The young people here had arranged a ball in the country, and I gladly agreed to go. I asked a good, pretty, but otherwise uninteresting girl to be my partner, and proposed to hire a coach to drive out to the appointed place with her cousin and herself, picking up Charlotte S. on our way. 'You will meet a beautiful girl,' my partner said while we were driving through a broad clearing of the forest towards the hunting lodge. 'Be careful that you do not fall in love with her!' her cousin added. – 'What do you mean?' I said. – 'She is already engaged,' was her answer, 'and to a very worthy man who is not here at present. He left to attend to his affairs after the death of his father, and is also about to apply for an important position.' This information did not particularly impress me.

The sun was still a quarter of an hour from the top of the mountains when we drove up at the lodge gate. The air was very close, and the ladies expressed their concern about a thunderstorm which was evidently gathering around the horizon in small compact whitish-grey clouds. I dispelled their fear by pretending to be a weather expert, although I myself began to feel apprehensive about an interruption of our amusement.

I climbed out of the coach, and the maid who came to the gate asked us to wait a moment – Mamsell Lottchen would soon be down. I crossed the courtyard towards the well-built lodge. When I had gone up the outer staircase and entered the house, I saw the most charming scene I had ever in my life beheld. In the entrance hall six children, between the ages of eleven and two, were swarming around a handsome young girl of medium height, who wore a simple white dress with pink bows on her arms and breast. She was holding a loaf of dark bread and cutting one slice apiece for each of the children around her, in proportion to age and appetite, dealing it out so kindly, and each child cried out 'Thank you!' so artlessly, after having stretched out two tiny hands as high as possible before the slice was cut; after which they all cheerfully jumped away with their supper, or, if of a quieter nature, walked sedately towards the gate to have a look at the strangers and at the coach in which their Lotte would soon drive away. – 'Please, forgive me,' she said, 'that I gave you the trouble to come for me, and that I keep the ladies waiting. While I was dressing and making all sorts of arrangements for the household during my absence, I forgot to give the children their supper, and they won't have their bread sliced by anyone but me.' I paid her an insignificant compliment while my soul was taking in her whole appearance, her voice, the grace of her bearing; and I had just enough time to recover from my surprise when she ran to her room to fetch her gloves and fan. The children meanwhile kept at some distance, casting sidelong glances at me, and I went up to the youngest, an extremely pretty little boy. He drew back just as Lotte returned from her room, saying: 'Louis, shake hands with your uncle.' The boy obeyed her most trustingly, and I could not refrain from kissing him with affection, in spite of his runny little nose. 'Uncle?' I asked, taking her hand. 'Do you consider me worthy of being related to you?' – 'Oh,' she said with a merry smile, 'our circle of relatives is very wide, and I should be sorry if you were to be the worst among them.' – On leaving, she told Sophy, the next oldest to herself, a girl of about eleven, to take good care of the younger children, and to give her love to their father when he returned from his ride. She told the children to obey Sophy as they would herself, and some of them promised to do so; but a pert little blonde of some six years said: 'But she is not you, dear Lotte. We love you much more.' – The two older boys had climbed up behind the coach and, on my pleading for them, were allowed to accompany us to the edge of the wood if they promised not to fight with each other and to hold on fast.

Hardly had we taken our seats and the ladies exchanged their welcomes and their remarks on one another's dresses and particularly on one another's hats, and had gossiped a good deal about the people they expected to meet, when Lotte asked the coachman to stop and ordered her brothers to climb down. They insisted on kissing her hand once more, and the older one did so with all the tenderness which can be characteristic of a boy of fifteen, the younger one in a rough and boisterous way. Once more she sent her love to the younger children, and then we continued our drive.

The cousin asked if Lotte had finished the book she had recently sent her. 'No, I have not,' Lotte said; 'I do not like it; you may have it back. And the one before it was not any better.' I was amazed when, on my asking her what books she meant, she gave me the titles. I was struck by the show of character in everything she said; every word revealed fresh attractions, and her flashes of intelligence showed in her face, which seemed gradually to light up with pleasure when she felt that I understood her.

'When I was younger,' she continued, 'I liked nothing so much as novels. God knows how happy I was if I could sit in a corner on Sundays and share with heart and soul the fortunes and misfortunes of some Miss Jenny. And I won't deny that this sort of book still has some attraction for me; but, as I have so little time now for reading, whatever I read has to be to my taste. And the author whom I like most of all is the one who takes me into my own world, where everything happens as it does around me, and whose story, nevertheless, becomes to me as interesting and as touching as my life at home, which is certainly not a paradise but is, on the whole, a source of inexpressible happiness to me.'

I tried to hide my emotions at these words. I did not, it is true, succeed very well; for when I heard her speak casually, but with much truth, about *The Vicar of Wakefield* and about ——, I lost all my reserve and told her everything I wished to tell, and only noticed, after some time, when Lotte directed the conversation to the other two, that they had been sitting all the while with wide-open eyes, as if they were not there at all. Now and then the cousin puckered up her little nose mockingly, to which, however, I paid no attention.

The conversation turned to the pleasures of dancing. 'If this passion should be a weakness,' Lotte said, 'I readily confess that I don't know anything to surpass dancing. And whenever I have something on my mind, I start strumming some *contredanse* on my clavichord (which is always out of tune), and then all is well.'

How delighted I was to look into her dark eyes while she spoke. How my whole soul was fascinated by her warm lips and her glowing cheeks! I was so deeply lost in the excellence of her conversation that I often did not catch the very words by which she expressed her meaning! – All this you can imagine, as you know me well.

I climbed out of the coach as if in a dream when we stopped in front of the house where the ball would take place, and was so lost in my dreams, with the twilit world all about me, that I hardly noticed the music which rang out to us from the illuminated ballroom above.

Two gentlemen, Herr Audran and another whose name escapes me – who can remember all those names! – who were the partners of Lotte and her cousin, welcomed us at the coach door and took charge of their ladies, and I escorted my partner upstairs.

We went through the steps of a few minuets; I asked one lady after another for a dance, but it seemed that only the most disagreeable ones could not decide to end the dance with a clasp of the hand. Lotte and her partner started an *anglaise*, and you can imagine how delighted I was when she was in the same line with us from the beginning of the first figure. You should see her dance! She concentrates so completely – heart and soul – on the dance itself; her whole body is in harmony, as carefree and as ingenuous as if nothing else mattered, as if she had no other thoughts or feelings; and I am certain that at those moments everything else vanishes from her sight.

I asked her for the second *contredanse*; she promised me the third and assured me with the most charming frankness that she was very fond of dancing in the German way. 'It is a custom here,' she continued, 'that any couple belonging together remain together for the German dance; but my partner is awkward at waltzing and will be grateful if I spare him the effort. Your lady cannot waltz either and does not like to; but I noticed during the *anglaise* that you waltz well; if you, therefore, want to be my partner in the German dance, do go and ask my partner for the favour, and I shall do the same with your lady.' I accepted the promise by taking her hand, and we agreed that her partner should meanwhile entertain mine.

Now the dance began, and we enjoyed ourselves for some time, interlacing our arms in various ways. With what nimble grace she moved! And when at last we changed to waltzing, and all the couples revolved around one another like celestial bodies, there was at first, owing to the inefficiency of most of the dancers, a kind of mix-up. We were wise, and let the others have their fling, but as soon as the clumsiest had left the floor, we stepped out and held the ground firmly with another couple, Audran and his partner. Never have I danced so well! I was no longer a mortal being. To hold that loveliest creature in my arms and to whirl with her like the wind so that the surroundings disappeared – truly, Wilhelm, I swore to myself that a girl whom I loved, on whom I might have claims, should never be allowed to waltz with another man save myself, even if it would spell ruin for me. You will understand!

We took a few turns around the ballroom between dances, to recover our breath. Then she sat down, and the oranges I had secured for her, now the only ones left, had a good effect, except that whenever she shared a little slice in a dutiful way with a greedy lady sitting next to her, I was cut to the heart.

We were the second couple in the third *anglaise*. As we crossed and recrossed the lines of dancers and while I, God knows with what delight, clung to her arm and held her glance, which was reflecting the frankest and purest happiness, we met a lady who had caught my attention before, because of the amiable expression of a face not exactly young.

She looked at Lotte with a smile, lifted a warning finger, and, whirling past, pronounced the name *Albert* twice with much emphasis.

'Who is Albert?' I asked Lotte, 'if I am not too bold to ask.' She was about to answer when we were forced to separate, so as to participate in the Great Figure Eight. I seemed to notice a thoughtful shadow on her brow as we kept passing each other. 'Why should I keep it a secret from you?' she said, offering me her hand for the promenade. 'Albert is a fine man to whom I am as good as engaged.' This was, of course, no news to me (the ladies having spoken to me of the matter in the coach), and yet it was now in some way new to me, as I had never actually thought of it in relation to her, who had become so dear to me in so short a time. At any rate I entangled myself in the dance, became absent-minded and stumbled in between the wrong couple, so that everything was at sixes and sevens, and Lotte's presence of mind as well as much pushing and pulling were necessary quickly to restore order.

The dance was not yet finished when the lightning, for some time seen in flashes on the horizon and which I had always explained away as mere summer lightning, became more powerful, and the thunder drowned out the music. Three ladies ran out of the ranks of dancers, and their partners followed suit. Confusion became general and the music stopped. It is natural, when an accident or something terrifying surprises us in the midst of our pleasures, for us to be more impressed than usual, partly because of the so vividly felt contrast, and partly, even more, because our senses are then susceptible and therefore react much more strongly. To these causes I must attribute the strange grimaces that I noticed on the faces of several ladies. The wisest one sat down in a corner, with her back turned to the window, and covered her ears with her hands. A second one knelt in front of her, hiding her head in the lap of the other. A third pushed herself in between and, bathed in tears, hugged her sisters. Some wanted to drive home; others, even more at a loss, did not have enough presence of mind to check the advances of

some *gourmets* who were busy capturing from the lips of the
pretty ladies in distress their anxious prayers destined for
Heaven. Some of the gentlemen had gone downstairs to
smoke a quiet pipe; and the rest of the company did not
refuse when the hostess had the sensible idea of showing
them into a room protected by shutters and curtains. Hardly
had they got there when Lotte began to arrange the chairs in a
circle, inviting everyone to sit down and join in a parlour game.

I saw more than one fellow purse his lips and stretch
himself in expectation of a delicious forfeit. 'We are going
to play "Counting",' Lotte said. 'Attention now! I'll go round
the circle from right to left, and you all must count in that way
round and round, each of you the number that falls to him;
but it must go like wildfire, and the person who hesitates or
makes a mistake gets his (or her) ears boxed, and so on to a
thousand.' Well, it was great fun to watch her. She went
around the circle with her arm outstretched. 'One' counted
the first; his neighbour 'two'; 'three' the next, and so on. Then
Lotte began to go faster, faster and faster, until someone
made a mistake – bang! a slap on his ear, and while the others
laughed the next also – bang! and faster and faster! I myself
received two slaps and, greatly pleased, thought that they
were harder than those she gave to others. General confusion
and outbursts of laughter brought the game to an end before
the 'thousand' had been counted. Groups of friends disappeared into the background; the thunderstorm was over,
and I followed Lotte into the ballroom. On the way there she
said: 'They forgot the thunderstorm and everything else while
they played the game.' I did not know what to say. 'I was one
of the most frightened,' Lotte continued, 'but by playing the
brave one, in order to cheer up the others, I became courageous myself.'

We stepped to the window. The thunder could still be
heard in the distance, and the blessed rain fell gently on the
ground, from which the most refreshing fragrance rose to us
on the fullness of the warm air. She stood leaning on her
elbow, her eyes searching the landscape; she looked up at the

sky and then at me. I saw her eyes fill with tears; she laid her hand on mine and said: 'Klopstock!' I remembered immediately the magnificent ode which she had in mind, and was overcome by the flood of emotions which she evoked in me with this name. It was more than I could bear. I bowed over her hand and kissed it, moved to the happiest tears. And I again looked into her eyes – noble poet! if you had seen the deep reverence in her eyes! May I never hear again from other lips your so often profaned name!

June 19

I have forgotten where I stopped in my story the other day. I only know that it was two o'clock in the morning when I went to bed, and that if I could have chatted with you instead of writing to you, I should probably have kept you awake until daybreak.

I have not yet told you what happened when we drove home from the ball, and I have not the time to tell you today.

It was a magnificent sunrise. The dripping forest and the refreshed fields lay all about us! Our companions were dozing. Lotte asked me if I would not like to do the same; I should not take any notice of her. 'So long as I see these eyes open,' I said, looking into hers intensely, 'there is no danger of my falling asleep.' And we both kept awake until we arrived at her gate, which was noiselessly opened by the maid, who assured Lotte that her father and the children were well and still asleep. Then I left her, after asking the favour of seeing her again that same day. She granted my request and I went. Since then, sun, moon and stars may continue on their course; for me there is neither day nor night, and the entire universe about me has ceased to exist.

June 21

My days are as blissful as those which God reserves for his saints; and, whatever may happen to me, I shall never be able to say that I have not experienced the purest joys of life. – You know my Wahlheim. I am now completely settled here. It is only half an hour to Lotte's home, where I feel like myself and find all the happiness granted to man.

Had I known, in choosing Wahlheim as the goal of my walks, that it lies so near to Heaven! How often, in my wanderings near and far, have I seen the hunting lodge which now encloses all my desires, sometimes from the mountain, at other times across the river from the plain!

Dear Wilhelm, I have thought over many things concerning man's ambition to extend himself, to make new discoveries, to roam about; and, on the other hand, his inner urge voluntarily to submit to limitation, to jog along in the groove of habit without looking to right or left. It is strange how, when I came here and looked down from the mountain into the lovely valley, everything attracted me. There was the grove! Ah, could I but mingle with its shades! There was the mountaintop! Ah, could I but overlook from there the wide landscape! The interlocked hills and familiar valleys! Ah, could I but lose myself in them! – I hurried here and there and came back, not having found what I hoped to find. Oh, it is the same with the distance as with the future! A vast, twilit whole lies before our soul; our emotions lose themselves in it as do our eyes, and we long to surrender our entire being and let ourselves sink into one great well of blissful feeling. Alas, when we approach, when There has become Here, everything is as it was before, and we are left with our poverty, our narrowness, while our soul thirsts for comfort that slipped away.

So the most restless vagabond yearns in the end for his native land, and finds in his poor hut, in the arms of his wife, in the circle of his children, and in his labour to support them all, the happiness he searched the wide world for in vain.

When I walk in the morning at sunrise to my Wahlheim and pick my own dish of green peas in the garden of the inn, sit down and shell them while I read my Homer, and then choose a pan in the kitchen, cut off some butter and put the peas on the fire, covering the pan and sitting down so that I may shake them from time to time – I feel vividly how the wanton suitors of Penelope slaughtered oxen and swine, cut them up, and roasted them. There is nothing that fills me with more quiet, genuine emotion than those features of patriarchal life which I can, thank God, weave without affectation into my own way of living. How happy I am that my heart is open to the simple, innocent delight of the man who brings a head of cabbage to his table which he himself has grown, enjoying not only the cabbage but all the fine days, the lovely mornings when he planted it, the pleasant evenings when he watered it, so that, after having experienced pleasure in its growth he may, at the end, again enjoy in one single moment all that has gone before.

June 29

The day before yesterday the physician came out here to see the bailiff and found me on the floor among Lotte's children, as some crawled over me, and others teased me, while my tickling them brought on loud cries. The doctor, very dogmatic and stiff as a puppet, who arranges the pleats of his cuffs and pulls out the endless frills of his jabot as he talks, thought all this to be beneath the dignity of an intelligent person, as I saw from the way he turned up his nose. I did not let him discourage me, however; and, while he was discussing very rational matters, I rebuilt the houses of cards that the children had knocked down. He later went all over town complaining that the bailiff's children were naughty enough but that Werther would now spoil them completely.

Yes, dear Wilhelm, children are nearer my heart than anything else on earth. When I watch them and see in these little creatures the seeds of all the virtues, all the forces they will need one day so badly; when I see in their obstinacy the future perseverance and firmness of character, in their mischievousness the happy temper and the facility needed to evade the world's dangers, all so natural and innocent! – always, always

I keep repeating the golden words of the Teacher of mankind: Unless ye become even as one of these! And yet, dearest friend, we treat them, who are our equals, whom we should look upon as our models, as our subjects. We don't want them to have a will of their own! – Do *we* not have one? And in what lies our privilege? Because we are older and wiser! – Good Lord, from your Heaven you look down on nothing but old children and young children; and your Son has already long ago proclaimed in which age you find greater joy. That people believe in Him and yet do not listen to His words – this also is an old story – and model their children upon themselves, and – farewell, Wilhelm! I do not wish to rave any longer.

July 1

What Lotte's presence must mean to a sick person I can feel in my own poor heart, which is worse off than many a one that pines on a sickbed. She is going to spend some days in the town with a good woman who, from what the doctors say, is nearing her end and wishes to have Lotte at her bedside in her last moments. A week ago I accompanied Lotte on her visit to the pastor of St ——, a little village, about an hour away, in the mountains. We arrived there at about four in the afternoon. Lotte had brought her second sister with her. On entering the courtyard of the parsonage, shaded by two tall walnut trees, we found the good old man sitting on a bench in front of the house door; when he saw Lotte, he became very animated, forgot his knotty stick and tried to get up and meet her. She ran towards him, made him sit down again while she seated herself at his side, gave him her father's warmest greetings, and hugged his ugly, dirty youngest boy, the apple of his old father's eye. You should have seen her holding the old man's attention with her talk, raising her voice to reach his almost deaf ears; telling him about the healthy young people who had died unexpectedly, about the excellent effects of Karlsbad, and praising his resolution to go there next summer; and saying how she thought he looked much better and brisker than the last time she had seen him. Meanwhile, I was being polite to the pastor's wife. The old man became very cheerful. And as I could not help but admire the beautiful walnut trees that shaded us so pleasantly, he began to tell us, although with some difficulty, their history. 'We don't know,' he said, 'who planted the older one; some say this pastor, others that one. But the younger tree, behind there, is as old as my wife, fifty next October. Her father planted it the morning of the day she was born. He was my predecessor here, and I cannot tell you how much he loved that tree, and certainly it is no less dear to me. My wife was sitting under it on a log with her knitting when I first entered this courtyard as a poor student twenty-seven years ago.' Lotte inquired after his daughter and was told she had gone out to the labourers in the field with a Herr Schmidt, and the old man took up his story again: how his predecessor had grown fond of him, and his daughter as well; and how he had become first his curate and then his successor. He had hardly finished his story when his daughter came through the garden with Herr Schmidt. She welcomed Lotte with warm affection, and I confess that I found her very pleasing: a lively brunette with a shapely figure, who might have been an entertaining companion during a short stay in the country. Her suitor (for Herr Schmidt was obviously this) was an educated but reserved man who refused to join the conversation, although Lotte kept trying to draw him in. What most distressed me was that I gathered from the expression on his face that it was obstinacy and moodiness rather than limited intelligence that kept him from communication. This fact became gradually only too clear; for when Friederike, later on our walk, changed places with Lotte and, occasionally, with me, the gentleman's face, swarthy by nature, darkened so visibly that soon Lotte tugged my sleeve, giving me to understand that I had been too polite to Friederike. Now, nothing makes me more angry than people who torment one another, particularly if young people in the prime of their lives, when they should be most receptive of all pleasures, mutually spoil their few good days by putting on moody faces, realizing only when it is too late that they have wasted something irrecoverable. It greatly annoyed me; and when we had returned to the parsonage, towards evening, and were seated around the table drinking our milk, and the conversation turned towards the joys and sorrows of this world, I could not help but pick up the thread and fervently attack bad moods. 'We human beings often complain,' I began, 'that there are so few good days and so many bad ones; but I think we are generally wrong. If our hearts were always open to enjoy the good, which God gives us every day, then we should also have enough strength to bear the evil, whenever it comes.' – 'But we cannot command our dispositions,' said the pastor's wife. 'How much depends on the body! If one does not feel well, everything seems wrong.' – I admitted that. 'Then,' I said, 'we'll look at moodiness as a disease and see if there is a remedy for it.' – 'That makes sense,' said Lotte. 'I, for one, believe at least that much depends on ourselves. I speak from my own experience. If something irritates me and is about to make me depressed, I jump up and sing a few dance tunes up and down the garden, and immediately the mood is gone.' – 'That is just what I wanted to say,' I replied. 'Bad humour is exactly like laziness, because it is a kind of laziness. Our nature has a strong inclination towards both, and yet, if we are strong enough to pull ourselves together, our work is quickly and easily done, and we find real pleasure in activity.' Friederike listened very attentively, but her young man made the objection that man is not his own master, least of all master of his emotions. 'Here we are speaking of an unpleasant emotion,' I rejoined, 'and certainly everyone would like to elude it. No one knows the extent of his powers unless he has tested them thoroughly. A sick person will certainly consult all available doctors and will not reject the greatest suffering or the bitterest medicine if he can recover the good health he longs for.' I noticed that the good old pastor was straining his ears to catch the gist of our discussion, and

I raised my voice and turned to him. 'They preach against so many vices,' I said, 'but I never heard anyone attacking bad humour from the pulpit.' 'The pastors in towns should do just that,' he said. 'The peasants are never ill-humoured; but a little preaching might do no harm here sometimes, and it would at least be a lesson for my wife and for the bailiff.' Everyone laughed, and he heartily joined in, until he was seized by a fit of coughing that for a time interrupted our conversation. Then the young man began to speak once more: 'You call bad humour a vice; I think that an exaggeration.' – 'Not at all,' I retorted, 'if that which harms oneself as well as one's neighbour deserves the name. Is it not enough that we cannot make each other happy; should we in addition deprive each other of that pleasure which every heart may sometimes grant itself? And give me the name of the man who is in a bad mood and yet gallant enough to hide it, to bear it alone without blighting other people's happiness! Or is it not perhaps an inner resentment at our own unworthiness, a dissatisfaction with ourselves, which is always bound up with some envy stirred up by foolish vanity? We see people happy whom we have not made happy, and that is unbearable to us.' Lotte gave me a smile, having noticed the emotion with which I spoke, and a tear in the eye of Friederike spurred me on to continue. – 'Woe to them,' I said, 'who abuse their power over the hearts of others and deprive them of any simple joy which there has its source. All the gifts, all the favours in the world cannot for a moment replace the inner happiness which the envious moodiness of our tyrant has spoiled.'

My whole heart was full at this moment; the memory of past events rushed into my mind, and my eyes filled with tears.

'If people would only warn themselves daily,' I exclaimed, 'that one cannot do anything for one's friends but leave them their pleasure and add to their happiness by sharing it with them. Are you able to give them one drop of comfort when their souls are tormented by a violent passion or crushed by grief?

'And when the last fatal sickness assails the beloved whom you have worn out in the days of her youth, and she lies prostrate in pitiable exhaustion, her unseeing eyes fixed on Heaven, the cold sweat of death coming and going on her pale forehead, and you stand at the bedside like a condemned man with the desperate feeling that you can do nothing; and you feel agony cramp your heart so that you wish to sacrifice all in order to inspire the dying person with one invigorating drop, one spark of courage ...'

The memory of a similar scene at which I had been present completely overwhelmed me as I said these words. I raised my handkerchief to my eyes and left the company. Only the voice of Lotte, who called out to me that it was time to leave, brought me to myself. And how she scolded me on our way home for my too warm sympathy with everything, saying it would be my ruin and that I should spare myself! O angel, for your sake I must live!

July 6

She stays with her dying friend and is ever the same active, lovely creature whose presence soothes pain and makes people happy wherever she goes. She went for a walk last evening with Marianne and her youngest sister. I knew of it, and went to meet them, and we walked together. After an hour and a half we returned to the town and stopped at the fountain which is so dear to me, and now will be a thousand times dearer. Lotte sat down on the little wall above, and we stood near her. I looked around and alas! the time when my heart was so lonely returned vividly to my mind. – 'Dear fountain,' I said, 'it is a long time since I rested near your coolness; I have sometimes even passed by in a hurry without giving you a glance.' – I looked down and saw the little girl coming up the steps, carefully carrying a glass of water. I looked at Lotte and felt deeply what she means to me. Meanwhile, the child approached with the glass, and Marianne wanted to take it from her, but 'No!' cried the little one with the sweetest expression. 'No, you must drink first, Lotte!' I was so delighted with the candour, the goodness, with which these words were said, that I could not otherwise express my emotion but lifted the child in my arms and kissed her so fervently that she immediately began to scream and to weep. 'That was not right of you,' said Lotte. – I was puzzled. – 'Come, darling,' she continued, taking the child by the hand and leading her down the steps. 'There, wash your face, quick, quick, in the clear spring water, and everything will be all right again.' – While I stood watching the little girl rub her cheeks with her wet little hands, so trustful that the miraculous spring water would wash away the defilement, and remove the chance of being disgraced by an ugly beard; and when I heard Lotte say: 'Now, that will do!' (but the child went on washing herself eagerly, as though Much would help more than Little) – I tell you, Wilhelm, never did I attend a ceremony of baptism with more reverence; and when Lotte came up the steps again, I would gladly have knelt before her, as before a prophet who has washed away with holy water the crimes of a nation.

That same evening, in the happiness of my heart, I could not help repeating the little incident to a man I thought to have common sense, as he is intelligent; but what was his reaction! He said that Lotte had been very thoughtless; that one should never deceive children; such deceit would give rise to innumerable misconceptions and superstitions from which children should be protected at an early age. – It came to my mind that there had been a christening in the man's family only a week ago; therefore I changed the subject but in my heart remained faithful to the truth: that we should deal with children as God deals with us; and He makes us happiest when He lets us stagger about under a benign delusion.

July 8

What children we are! How we crave for a noticing glance! We had gone to Wahlheim. The ladies were driving out, and

during our walks together I thought I saw in Lotte's eyes –
but I am a fool. Forgive me; you should see those eyes. I must
be brief, for I am so sleepy that I can hardly keep my eyes
open. – Well, the ladies were getting into the carriage and
young W., Selstadt, Audran and I were standing around it.
There was a lively conversation going on through the carriage
door with the other young men, who were lighthearted and
talkative enough. I tried to catch Lotte's glance. Alas, it
wandered from one young man to the other, but it did not
fall on me! Me! Me! Who stood there absorbed in her alone!
My heart bade her a thousand farewells, and she did not
notice me! The carriage drove off, and tears stood in my
eyes. I looked after her, and saw Lotte's headdress lean out of
the carriage window as she turned to look back – ah, at me?
Dear friend, I am torn by this uncertainty. My only consolation is: She may have turned to look back at me! Perhaps!
Good night! Oh, what a child I am!

July 10

You should see what an absurd figure I cut when people talk
about her in company! Even more so if they ask me how I like
her – like! I hate the word like poison. What sort of a person is
he who likes Lotte, whose heart and mind is not completely
possessed by her! Like! The other day someone asked me if
I 'liked' Ossian!

July 11

Frau M. is very ill indeed; I pray for her life because I suffer
with Lotte. I rarely see her at my friend's, but today she told
me a curious incident. Old M. is a hard, close-fisted man who
has tormented and kept a tight rein on his wife all during her
lifetime, but she has always succeeded in managing somehow.
A few days ago, when the doctor had given up hope for
her, she sent for her husband – Lotte was in the room – and
said to him: 'I have to confess something that might cause

confusion and annoyance after my death. Until lately I have managed the household as neatly and as economically as possible; but you will forgive me for having deceived you during the last thirty years. At the beginning of our married life you fixed a very small sum for the purchase of food and for other domestic expenses. When our household became larger and our business grew, you could not be persuaded to raise my weekly allowance in proportion; you very well know that when our expenses were heaviest, you required me to manage on seven florins a week. I accepted this money without protest, but I took the balance needed from the weekly receipts, as nobody suspected that your wife would steal from your till. I have not squandered the money, and I might have met Eternity with hope and confidence, even without confessing all this, if I had not thought of the woman who will have to keep house after me, and who may be at a loss how to make ends meet, as you will always insist then that your first wife managed with so little.'

I spoke to Lotte about the incredible delusion of a man who does not suspect that there must be something wrong when a person manages with seven guilders and expenses are obviously perhaps twice as much. But I have personally known people who would accept the presence of the prophet's 'unfailing cruse of oil' in their home without being surprised.

July 13

No, I do not deceive myself! In her dark eyes I have read a genuine sympathy for me and my destiny. Yes, I feel – and in this I can trust my heart – that she – oh, may I, can I express the Heaven that exists in these words? – that she loves me!

Loves me! – And how precious I become in my own eyes, how I – to you as an understanding person I may say it – how I admire myself since she loves me.

Is this presumption, or a sense of true proportion? I do not know the man whom I once feared as a rival in Lotte's heart.

And yet, when she speaks of her fiancé with such warmth, such affection, I feel like one who has been deprived of all his honours and titles and who has had to yield his sword.

July 16

Oh, how my blood rushes through my veins when my fingers unintentionally brush hers or when our feet touch under the table. I shrink back as though from fire, but a secret force drives me forward again, although everything swims before my eyes. Her innocent, candid soul does not divine how tormenting such small intimacies can be. And when, while we talk, she puts her hand on mine and, animated by what we are saying, moves closer to me, so that the heavenly breath of her mouth reaches my lips, I am close to fainting, as if struck by lightning. And, Wilhelm, if I should ever dare – this heavenly confidence – you understand! No, my heart is not so depraved! Weak! Weak enough! – And is that not depravity?

She is sacred to me. Any desire is silenced in her presence. I never know what I feel when I am with her; it is as if my soul were spinning through every nerve. She plays a melody on her clavichord with the touch of an angel, so simple, so ethereal! It is her favourite tune, and I am cured of all pain, confusion and melancholy the moment she strikes the first note.

Not one word about the magic power of music in antiquity seems to me improbable when I am under the spell of her simple melody. And how well she knows when to play it, at the moment when I feel like blowing out my brains. The confusion and darkness of my soul are then dispersed, and I can breathe more freely again.

July 18

Wilhelm, what would the world mean to our hearts without love! What is a magic lantern without its lamp! As soon as you insert the little lamp, then the most colourful pictures are thrown on your white wall. And even though they are nothing but fleeting phantoms, they make us happy as we stand before them like little boys, delighted at the miraculous visions. I have not been able to see Lotte today; a party which I could not refuse to attend prevented me from going. What should I do? I sent my servant to her, only so that I might have someone near me who had been in her presence today. How impatiently I waited for his return, how happy I was to see him back. I should have liked to take him by his shoulder and kiss him, if I had not been too embarrassed to do so.

It is said that the Bologna stone, when placed in the sun, absorbs the sun's rays and is luminous for a while in the dark. I felt the same with the boy. The consciousness that her eyes had rested on his face, his cheeks, the buttons of his jacket and the collar of his overcoat, made all these sacred and precious to me. At that moment I would not have parted with him for a thousand thaler. I felt so happy in his presence. God forbid that you should laugh at me, Wilhelm. Are these delusions if they make us so happy?

July 19

'I am going to see her,' is my first cry in the morning when I rouse myself and gaze at the glorious sun in a perfectly serene mood. 'I am going to see her!' And thus I have no other wish for the rest of the day. Everything, everything is drowned in this prospect.

July 20

I cannot yet accept your suggestion that I should accompany the envoy to ———. I am not very fond of a subordinate position; and we all know that the man is a disgusting fellow, besides. You write that my mother would like to see me doing some active work; it makes me laugh. Am I not now active? and does it make any real difference whether I count peas or lentils? As everything in the world amounts after all to nothing to speak of, a person who drudges for the sake of others, for money or honours or whatnot, without following his own ambition, his own need, is always a fool.

July 24

Since you are so concerned that I should not neglect my drawing, I would rather skip that subject than confess that I have not done much lately.

Never before have I been happier, never has my sensitiveness to Nature been richer or deeper, even to the smallest stone, the tiniest blade of grass, and yet – I do not know how to express myself, but my powers of perception are so weak that everything floats and fluctuates before my mind, so that I cannot seize any outline; but I imagine I could do better if I had some clay or wax. I shall get some clay if this state lasts much longer, and I shall knead away even if cakes should be the outcome.

Three times I have started Lotte's portrait, and three times I have bungled it, which makes me very cross, the more so because I was at one time quite successful in getting likenesses. Finally I gave up and cut her silhouette, and with that I shall be satisfied.

July 26

Yes, dear Lotte. I shall order and look after everything; please keep on giving me commissions, and frequent ones. But I ask you one favour: no more sand in the notes you write me. I took today's quickly to my lips, and something gritted between my teeth.

July 26

Many times I have made up my mind not to see her so often. If one could only stick to one's resolutions! Every day

I succumb to temptation, and then promise myself most solemnly that I shall stay away tomorrow for once; but when tomorrow comes, I again find some irresistible reason to go, and, before I know it, I am with her. Either she has said the night before, 'You will come tomorrow, won't you?' and who could then stay away? Or she has given me some errand, and I think it is proper to bring her the answer in person; or the day is so very lovely that I walk to Wahlheim, and, when I am there, it is only half an hour to her! – I am so close to her aura – zut! and I am there. My grandmother knew a fairy tale about the Magnetic Mountain. Ships which sailed too close to it were suddenly deprived of all their iron; all the nails flew towards the mountain, and the poor sailors were shipwrecked among the collapsing planks.

July 30

Albert has arrived, and I shall go away. Even if he were the best, the most noble person, one to whom I would be willing to submit myself in every respect – it would still be unbearable to see him before my eyes in possession of so much perfection. Possession! – Enough, Wilhelm, the Bridegroom is here! A worthy, agreeable man whom one cannot help liking. Fortunately, I was not present when he was welcomed back. That would have torn my heart. He has so much sense of decorum that he has not once kissed Lotte in my presence. God bless him! I must love him for the respect with which he treats her. For me he has the kindest feelings, but I suspect that this is Lotte's doing rather than an impulse of his own spirit; for in these matters women have a delicate way, and they are right; if they can keep two devoted admirers on mutual good terms the advantage is always on their side, although it is rarely achieved.

Meanwhile I cannot deny Albert my esteem. His outward composure is in very strong contrast to the restlessness which I cannot conceal of my own character. He feels deeply, and he knows what he possesses in Lotte. He seems seldom to be in a bad mood, a sin which, as you know, I hate more in human beings than any other.

He thinks me a person of sensitive intelligence; and my devotion to Lotte, my warm enthusiasm for everything she does, increases his triumph, and he loves her all the more. I am undecided whether he may not sometimes torment her with petty jealousy; were I in his place, I would not be entirely free from that demon.

Be that as it may! My happiness with Lotte is gone. Shall I call this folly or delusion? What are names! The situation itself is evident. I knew everything I now know before Albert returned; I knew that I could not make any claims upon her, nor did I make any; so far, that is, as it is possible for one not to feel desire in the presence of such sweetness. And yet the idiot now stares with wide eyes because the other man really arrives and carries off the girl.

I firmly set my teeth and mock at my misery: and I would mock twice and thrice at anyone who might suggest that I should resign myself, since nothing can be helped in any case. Don't pester me with those empty-headed people! – I roam about in the woods, and when I arrive at Lotte's house and find Albert sitting with her in the arbour in her garden, and I cannot then leave, I behave in a wild and boisterous way and start all sorts of tomfooleries. 'For Heaven's sake,' said Lotte to me today, 'please don't make a scene, as you did last night! You are dreadful when you show off in that way.' Between ourselves, I wait for the time when Albert is busy; then zut! I am there; and I am always happy when I find her alone.

August 8

Please, dear Wilhelm, do not think that I had you in mind when I called those people intolerable who ask us to resign ourselves to an inevitable fate. I really never thought for a moment that you could hold such an opinion. And, fundamentally, you are right. I have only one objection: in this world we are seldom faced with an Either-Or; all emotions and modes of action show as many varieties of shape and shading as exist between a hooked nose and one that is turned up.

So you won't be angry with me when I grant your whole argument, and yet continue in my attempt to slip in between the Either and the Or.

'Either,' you say, 'you have some reason to hope, so far as Lotte is concerned, or you have none. Very well, in the first case, try to carry the matter through; try to reach the fulfilment of your wishes. Otherwise, pull yourself together and try to get rid of an unfortunate passion that is bound to burn up all your energy.' My dear friend! That is well said, and easily said.

But can you demand it of the unhappy man whose whole life is slowly and irremediably wasting away of a lingering disease; can you demand that he should make a definite end of his misery by the stab of a dagger? And does not the disease, at the very same time that it burns up his strength, also destroy the courage he needs to free himself from it?

In the evening

My diary, which I have neglected for some time, fell into my hands today, and I am amazed how I ran into this situation with full awareness, step by step. How clearly I have seen my condition, yet how childishly I have acted. How clearly I still see it, and yet show no sign of improvement.

August 10

If I were not an idiot, I could lead the best and happiest of lives. One cannot easily imagine the union of pleasanter circumstances for anyone than that in which I am now placed. Oh, how true it is that our heart alone creates its own happiness! To be a member of this charming family, to be loved by the father like a son, by the children like a father, and by Lotte! – And then there is that worthy Albert, who

never disturbs my happiness by peevish bad manners; who
meets me with warm friendship; for whom I am, next to
Lotte, the most cherished being in the world. Wilhelm, it is a
joy to hear us talk about Lotte on our walks together. There is
nothing more ridiculous on this earth than our relationship;
and yet I am often moved to tears when I think of it.

When he tells me of Lotte's kindly mother; how on her
deathbed she entrusted Lotte with the care of her household
and her children, and Lotte herself to Albert's care; how from
that day on Lotte had been animated by an entirely new spirit;
how she had conscientiously taken over the house and
become a real mother to the children; how not one moment
of her time had been spent without tasks and active love, and
yet she kept her former cheerfulness and lightness of heart. –
While he talks I walk along beside him and pick wayside
flowers, arrange them carefully into a nosegay, and – throw
them into the river which flows beside the path, and
watch them float gently downstream. – I do not remember
if I wrote you that Albert is going to remain here; he will
receive a handsome salary from a position with the Court,
where he is in great favour. I have seldom seen his equal in
regard to order and diligence in handling affairs.

August 12

Albert is certainly the best man under the sun. Yesterday a
remarkable scene took place between us. I went to take leave
of him because I was suddenly seized by the desire to ride into
the mountains, where I am now writing to you. As I paced up
and down his room I caught sight of a brace of pistols. 'Will
you lend me your pistols for my trip?' I asked him. 'By all
means,' he replied, 'if you will take the trouble to load them;
I only keep them here *pro forma*.' I took one of them down,
and he continued: 'Since the day that my precaution paid me a
nasty trick, I do not want to have anything more to do with
that sort of thing.' I was curious to hear the story. – 'I was
staying,' he said, 'for about three months with a friend in the

country. I had taken along an unloaded pair of pistols, and I slept unconcerned. One rainy afternoon when I was sitting about, doing nothing, the thought crossed my mind – I do not know why – that we might be attacked and might need the pistols – you know how one sometimes imagines things. I gave them to the servant to clean and load. He was dallying with the maids and wanted to scare them, when, God knows how, the pistol went off. The ramrod was still in the barrel and struck the ball of the right thumb of one of the girls and smashed it. Of course, I had to pay for her tears as well as for the medical treatment; and since that day I have left all my firearms unloaded. But, dear friend, what is the use of caution? One never learns enough about danger! Although –' You already know that I am very fond of the fellow up to the point when he says 'although'. For does it not go without saying that any general statement has its exceptions? But he is so scrupulous that when he thinks he has said anything rash or commonplace or only partly true, he does not stop qualifying, modifying, adding and subtracting until, at last, there is nothing left of the subject. On this occasion he became so deeply entangled in the matter that I finally did not listen to him any longer. I suddenly became dejected, and, with a violent gesture, pressed the mouth of the pistol to my forehead above the right eye. 'Come, come,' Albert exclaimed, taking the pistol from me, 'what are you doing?' – 'It is not loaded,' I said. – 'Even so, what's the idea?' he retorted impatiently. 'I cannot imagine how a person can be so foolish as to shoot himself; the mere thought of it is repulsive.'

'Why must people like you,' I exclaimed, 'when you discuss any action, immediately say: "This is foolish, that is wise; this is good, that is bad!" And what does it all mean? Does it mean that you have really discovered the inner circumstances of an action? Do you know how to explain definitely the reason why it happened, why it had to happen? If you indeed knew, you would be less hasty in your judgements.'

'You will have to admit,' said Albert, 'that certain actions remain vicious, from whatever motives they may have risen.'

I shrugged my shoulders and granted him that. 'But, dear friend,' I continued, 'even in that general case, a few exceptions can exist. It is true that theft is a vice; but does the man who goes out to steal in order to save himself and his family from starvation – does he deserve pity or punishment? Who will be the first to cast a stone at the husband who sacrifices to his just indignation his unfaithful wife and her vile seducer? Or at the young girl who in one blissful hour loses herself in the irresistible joys of love? Even our laws themselves, those cold-blooded pedants, can be moved towards clemency, and refrain from punishing.'

'It is quite a different matter,' Albert replied, 'when a man is carried away by his passions and loses all power of reflection; he can then be considered a drunkard or a madman.'

'O you rational people,' I exclaimed, smiling. 'Passion! Drunkenness! Madness! You stand there so complacently, without any real sympathy, you moralists, condemning the drunkard, detesting the madman, passing by like the Levite, and thanking God that you are not made as one of these. I myself have been drunk more than once; my passions have never been very far removed from madness, and yet I do not feel any remorse. For I have learned in my own way that all unusual people who have accomplished something great or seemingly impossible have always been proclaimed to be drunk or mad.

'But even in everyday life it is unbearable to hear people say of almost anyone who acts in a rather free, noble or unexpected way: "That man is drunk, or he is crazy!" Shame on you sober ones! Shame on you sages!'

'Now, that is another of your whims,' said Albert. 'You exaggerate everything, and you are certainly wrong when you compare suicide, which we discuss here, to great actions, since no one can consider it as anything but a weakness. For it is certainly easier to die than bravely to bear a life of misery.'

I was about to break off, as no kind of argument upsets me more than when someone utters a trivial commonplace while I am speaking from the heart. But I kept my temper, because

I had heard this sort of talk only too often and had been annoyed by it many times before. Therefore I replied rather forcibly: 'You call that weakness? Please, don't be misled by appearances. Would you call a nation weak that groans under the intolerable yoke of a tyrant, when it at last rises and breaks its chains? A man, horrified that his house has caught fire, feels all his strength tighten and carries with ease burdens that he would scarcely be able to move in a calmer mood; or a man in the rage of having been insulted takes on single-handed half a dozen opponents and defeats them – can such people be called weak? If, my friend, exertion means strength, why should overexertion mean the opposite?' – Albert looked at me and said, 'Don't be offended if I say that the examples you give me are irrelevant to our subject.' – 'That may be so,' I replied. 'People have often reproached me for my irrational way of associating things, a way which, they say, often verges on absurdity. Let us see if we have any other way of imagining how a person may feel when he has decided to throw off the ordinarily agreeable burden of life, for only in so far as we can enter into another's emotions have we the right to discuss such matters.

'Human nature,' I continued, 'has its limits; it can bear joy, suffering and pain to a certain degree, but it collapses as soon as that degree is exceeded. The question, therefore, is not whether someone is weak or strong, but what degree of suffering he can actually endure, be it moral or physical; and I find it just as strange to call a man who takes his own life a coward as it would be improper to call a coward a man who is dying of a malignant fever.'

'Paradoxical! Very paradoxical!' Albert exclaimed. – 'Not so much as you may think,' I replied. 'You admit that we call a disease fatal which attacks Nature so violently that her forces are partly consumed or so largely put out of action that they cannot recover and restore the ordinary course of life by some lucky turn.

'Now, my friend, let us apply this same sort of reasoning to the mind. Let us watch man in his limited sphere and see how impressions affect him, how he is obsessed by ideas, until finally a growing passion robs him of any possible calmness of mind and becomes his ruin.

'A composed, sensible person who has a clear view of the condition of the unfortunate man tries in vain to give advice; just as the healthy man, standing at the bedside of the sick, is unable to transfer to the latter the smallest fraction of his own strength.'

Albert thought all this too general in expression. I reminded him of a girl who had been found in the river, drowned some time before, and told him again her history. – She was a good-natured young creature who had grown up within a narrow circle of domestic tasks weekly laid out for her, with no other prospect of possible amusement than Sunday walks about town with her friends, dressed in her Sunday finery which she had gradually acquired; or perhaps once in a long while a dance; or an occasional lively chat with a neighbour interested in the source of a quarrel, or some slander – a girl whose passionate nature sooner or later feels urgent desires, which are fed by the flatteries of men. All her former pleasures little by little become stale; until she finally meets a man to whom she is irresistibly drawn by a strange, unfamiliar feeling, a man on whom she now stakes all her hopes, forgetting the world around her, hearing nothing, seeing nothing, feeling nothing but him alone, longing for him alone. Unspoiled by the shallow pleasures of an inconstant vanity, her desire draws her straight to one goal – she wants to be his, to find in a lasting union all the happiness she has missed, to experience all her yearned-for joy. His repeated promises give certainty to her hope; his bold caresses inflame her desire and hold her whole being in a state of suspense, in anticipation of some supreme delights. She works herself up to the highest pitch of excitement and finally, when she opens her arms to embrace all her wishes – her lover abandons her. Stunned, and almost out of her mind, she finds herself above an abyss; all around her is darkness; no way out, no consolation, no hope! The one person in whom she had found the

centre of her existence has left her. She does not see the wide
world spread out before her or the many others who might
replace her loss; she feels herself alone, abandoned by all –
and blindly hunted into a corner by the terrible agony of her
heart, she throws herself into the depths to drown all her
anguish in the embrace of death. – That, Albert, is the story of
more than one; and now tell me, is not this a case like that of a
disease? Nature is unable to find a way out from the maze of
confused and contradictory forces, and the patient must die.

   'Shame on him who looks on and says: "The foolish girl! If
she had let time do its work, her despair would have lost its
force, and very probably another man would have appeared
willing to comfort her." – This is exactly as if someone should
say: "The fool – to die of fever! If he had waited until he had
recovered his strength, until the sap of life was improved,
until the tumult in his blood had subsided, all would have
been well, and he would still be alive today!"'

   Albert, who had not quite grasped my comparison, had
a few more objections to make, among them that, after all,
I had only spoken of a simple girl. What he could not understand was how a person of intelligence, whose mind was not
narrow, and who was capable of a larger view of things, could
be exculpated. – 'My friend,' I exclaimed, 'man is human, and
the small amount of intelligence one may possess counts little
or nothing against the rage of passion and the limits of human
nature pressing upon him. Moreover – but of that another
time,' I said, and took my hat. Oh, my heart was so full! – And
we parted without having understood each other. How difficult it is to understand one another in this world.

August 15

It is certainly true that nothing in the world makes a person
indispensable but love. I feel that Lotte would not like to lose
me, and the children have no other idea than that I should
appear every morning. I went out there today to tune Lotte's
clavichord but I did not get around to this task, for the

children followed me everywhere, asking to be told a fairy tale, and Lotte herself begged me to do as they wished. I cut the bread for their supper, which they now take from me as eagerly as from Lotte, and told them their favourite story of the princess who was served by ghostly hands. I am learning a good deal from all this, I assure you; and I am amazed what an impression I make. When I sometimes have to invent a small detail which I forget the next time, they at once tell me that the story was different at the previous telling; so now I practise reciting it without alterations from beginning to end, like a chant. This has taught me what harm an author necessarily does to his book in a second revised edition, even though it may gain in poetic merit thereby. The very first impression finds us receptive; and we are so made that we can be convinced of the most incredible things; but these fix themselves immediately in our mind, and woe to him who would erase and eliminate them.

August 18

Must it so be that whatever makes man happy must later become the source of his misery?

That generous and warm feeling for living Nature which flooded my heart with such bliss, so that I saw the world around me as a Paradise, has now become an unbearable torment, a sort of demon that persecutes me wherever I go. When I formerly looked from the rock far across the river and the fertile valleys to the distant hills, and saw everything on all sides sprout and spring forth – the mountains covered with tall, thick trees from base to summit, the valleys winding between pleasant shading woods, the gently flowing river gliding among the whispering reeds and reflecting light clouds which sailed across the sky under the mild evening breeze; when I listened to the birds that bring the forest to life, while millions of midges danced in the red rays of a setting sun whose last flare roused the buzzing beetle from the grass; and all the whirring and weaving around me drew my attention to the ground underfoot where the moss, which wrests its nourishment from my hard rock, and the broom plant, which grows on the slope of the arid sand hill, revealed to me the inner, glowing, sacred life of Nature – how fervently did I take all this into my warm heart, feeling like a god in that overflowing abundance, while the beautiful forms of the infinite universe stirred and inspired my soul. Huge mountains surrounded me, precipices opened before me, and torrents gushed downward; the rivers streamed below, and wood and mountains sang; and I saw them at their mutual work of creation in the depths of the earth, all these unfathomable forces. And above the earth and below the sky swarms the variety of creatures, multifarious and multiform. Everything, everything populated with a thousand shapes; and mankind, huddled together in the security of its little houses, nesting throughout and dominating the wide world in its own way. Poor fool who belittle everything because you are yourself so small! From the inaccessible mountains, across the wasteland untrod by human foot, to the end of the unexplored seas breathes the spirit of the eternal Creator who rejoices in every atom of dust that divines Him and lives. – Oh, the times when I longed to fly on the crane's wings, as it passed overhead, to the shores of the illimitable ocean, in order to drink from the foaming cup of the Infinite an elating sensation of life, and to feel, if only for a moment, in the cramped forces of my being one drop of the bliss of that Being who creates everything in and through Himself.

My friend, only the memory of those hours eases my heart. Even the effort to recall and to express again in words those inexpressible sensations lifts my soul above itself, but also intensifies the anguish of my present state.

It is as if a curtain has been drawn away from my soul, and the scene of unending life is transformed before my eyes into the pit of the forever-open grave. Can you say: 'This is!' when everything passes, everything rolls past with the speed of lightning and so rarely exhausts the whole power of its existence, alas, before it is swept away by the current, drowned and smashed on the rocks? There is not one moment which does not consume you and yours, and not one moment when you yourself are not inevitably destructive; the most harmless walk costs the lives of thousands of poor, minute worms; *one* step of your foot annihilates the painstaking constructions of ants, and stamps a small world into its ignominious grave. Ha! It is not the notable catastrophes of the world, the floods that wash away our villages, the earthquakes that swallow up our town which move me; my heart is instead worn out by the consuming power latent in the whole of Nature which has formed nothing that will not destroy its neighbour and itself. So I stagger with anxiety, Heaven and Earth and their weaving powers around me! I see nothing but an eternally devouring and ruminating monster.

August 21

In vain do I stretch my arms out for her in the morning, when I try to arouse myself from troubled dreams; in vain do I seek her at night in my bed, deluded by some happy and innocent dream in which I am sitting beside her in the meadow, holding her hand and covering it with a thousand kisses. And when, still heavy with sleep, I grope for her and suddenly find myself fully awake, a torrent of tears bursts from my oppressed heart, and I weep bitterly in view of a hopeless future.

August 22

It is disastrous, Wilhelm! All my energies are tuned to another pitch, have changed to a restless inactivity; I cannot be idle and yet at the same time cannot set to work at anything. My power of imagination fails me; I am insensible to Nature, and I am sick of books. If we fail ourselves, everything fails us. I swear that I should sometimes like to be a workman so that I could see, when I wake up in the morning, some prospect for the coming day, some impetus, some hope. I often envy Albert, whom I see buried up to his ears in documents; and I imagine that I should be better off were I in his place. Already more than once the thought of writing to you and to the Minister flashed through my mind, in order to apply for the post at the Legation which, you have assured me, I would not be refused. So I myself believe. The Minister has liked me for a long time, and has frequently urged me to devote myself to some work; and sometimes, for an hour or so, it seems the thing to do. But when I come to consider it a little later, I remember the fable of the horse which, tired of its freedom, let itself be saddled and harnessed and was ridden to death. I don't know what to do. And, my dear fellow, isn't my longing for a change in my situation an innate, uneasy impatience that will pursue me wherever I go?

August 28

One thing is certain; if my disease could be cured, these people would cure it. Today is my birthday, and very early in the morning I received a little parcel from Albert. When I opened it I saw immediately one of the bows of pink ribbon Lotte had been wearing when I first met her and which I had often implored her to give me. The parcel also contained two books in duodecimo: the small Homer printed by Wetstein, which I had often wished to possess, so that I should not have to drag about with me on my walks the large volume edited by Ernesti. You see! that is how they anticipate my wishes, how well they select the small tokens of friendship which are a thousand times more precious than the dazzling presents which humiliate us, betraying the vanity of the giver. I kiss the ribbon over and over again and drink in with every breath the memory of the few blissful moments in those happy and irretrievable days. Wilhelm, so it is, and I do not complain – the blossoms of life are only phantoms. How many fade, leaving no trace behind; how few bear fruit, and how few of these fruits ripen! But still enough are left; but still

– O my brother! should we neglect the ripe fruit, refuse to enjoy it, and let it rot?

Farewell! It is a glorious summer, and I often sit up in the trees of Lotte's orchard and take down with a long pole the pears from the highest branches. She stands below and catches them when I lower the pole.

August 30

Unhappy man! are you not a fool? Do you not deceive yourself? To what use is this endless raging passion? I have no prayers left except prayers to her; my imagination calls up no other image than hers, and I see everything in the world only in relation to her. And thus I spend many happy hours – until I must again tear myself from her. O Wilhelm, what things my heart urges me to do! After I have been with her for two or three hours, delighting in her form, her bearing, in the heavenly expressiveness of what she says, my nerves slowly become tense, my eyes grow dim, my ears no longer take in her words; and it seems as if an assassin had clutched me fast by the throat; if then my wildly beating heart tries to relieve my oppression but only succeeds in increasing my confusion – Wilhelm, in such moments I often do not know if I am indeed in this world. And if melancholy did not sometimes take hold of me, and Lotte grant me the poor comfort of crying my eyes out over her hand, I have to leave; I must get into the open air; I roam about in the fields. To climb a steep mountain is then my joy, working my way through pathless forest, through thickets which bruise me and thorns which tear me. Then I feel some relief. Some! And when I sink to the ground tired and thirsty, or sit on a fallen tree in the lonely forest, in the dead of night, when the full moon hangs over me, to give my wounded feet some relief, and then slip away in a calm sleep of exhaustion in the half-light – O Wilhelm! the solitude of a cell, the hairshirt and the spiked belt would be sweet comfort to my yearning heart. Adieu! I see no end to this misery except in the grave.

September 3

I must go! Thank you, Wilhelm, for having confirmed me in my wavering decision. For two weeks I have been constantly thinking of leaving her. I must go. She is again in the town, staying with a friend. And Albert – and – I must go!

September 10

What a night it has been, Wilhelm! And now I can endure anything. I shall not see her again. Oh, if I could only fall on your neck and describe with a thousand joyous tears all the emotions that are storming in my heart. Here I sit, gasping for breath, trying to calm down, and waiting for the morning to come; horses are ordered for sunrise.

And she sleeps peacefully and does not know that she will never see me again. I have torn myself away and was strong enough not to betray my intention while we talked together for two hours. Good God, what a conversation it was!

Albert had promised me to be in the garden with Lotte immediately after supper. I stood on the terrace under the tall chestnut trees and watched the sun, which was, for me, setting for the last time over the lovely valley and the gentle river. I had so often stood here with her, looking at the beautiful scene, and now – I paced up and down the avenue that was so dear to me. I had often been drawn to this place by a secret impulse before I even knew Lotte; and how delighted we had been when, at the beginning of our acquaintance, we discovered our mutual liking for the place, which is really one of the most romantic I have ever seen planned by art.

First you have the wide view between the chestnut trees – but, I remember having already written you a great deal about it, how one is soon closed in by high screens of beech trees, and how the avenue grows darker and darker, because of the adjoining shrubbery, until at last all ends in a secluded little circle, around which a thrilling solitude hovers. I can still feel the odd sensation which touched me when I first entered it at high noon; I had a faint presentiment of the kind of setting it would make for both happiness and pain.

I had indulged in these sweet and yearning thoughts of parting and reunion for almost half an hour, when I heard them coming up the terrace. I ran to meet them, took Lotte's hand and kissed it with deep emotion. We had just reached the top of the terrace when the moon rose behind the wooded hill; we talked of various things and approached, before we knew it, the sombre recess. Lotte entered and sat down, Albert beside her, as I did too, but my inner restlessness did not allow me to remain seated for long; I stood up, stood in front of them, paced to and fro, and again sat down: it was an agonizing situation. Lotte drew our attention to the beautiful effect of moonlight illuminating the whole length of the terrace before us, which opened where the screening beech trees ended: a lovely sight, the more striking because complete darkness closed us in on all sides. We were silent, until she said, after a time: 'I never take a moonlight walk, never, without thinking of my dear lost ones; without being overawed by the sense of death and of future life. We shall live,' she went on, her voice vibrating with the most beautiful emotion, 'but, Werther, shall we find one another again and know one another? What do you feel? What do you say?'

'Lotte,' I said, giving her my hand as my eyes filled with tears, 'we shall meet again, here and beyond.' My voice failed me. Wilhelm, did she have to ask me that when my heart was in anguish because of our coming separation!

'And I wonder if our dear lost ones know about us,' she continued, 'if they feel that we remember them with warm affection when everything goes well with us? Oh, the image of my mother is always with me when I sit among her children, my children, on a quiet evening, and they gather around me as they used to gather around her, and then I look up to Heaven with longing and tears, and wish that she might for a moment look in on us and see how I have kept my promise given to her in the hour of her death: to be a mother to her children. With what feeling I then cry out: "Forgive me, dearest Mother, if I am not to them what you were. Oh, do I not do everything I can; are they not dressed and fed and, what is more, cared for and loved? Could you only see the harmony among us, dear sainted Mother, you would thank with fervent gratitude the God whom you implored with your last bitter tears to protect your children."'

These were her words! O Wilhelm, who can repeat what she said? How can dead cold written words convey the heavenly flower of her soul? Albert gently interrupted her: 'Dear Lotte, this affects you too much. I know that your soul is immersed in these ideas, but I implore you –' 'O Albert!' she replied, 'I know you have not forgotten those evenings when we sat together at the small round table, when Father was away on a journey, and we had sent the little ones to bed. You often had a good book with you, but you seldom had time to read. Was not the association with her exquisite soul worth more than anything else? The beautiful, gentle, cheerful and always active woman! God alone knows how often, in my bed, I have prayed in tears that He might make me her equal.'

'Lotte,' I cried, kneeling before her and taking her hand, which I covered with tears, 'Lotte, the blessing of God rests upon you, and the spirit of your mother.' – 'If you had only known her,' she said, and pressed my hand. 'She was worthy to be known by you.' I almost fainted. Never had anything more magnificent, more exalting, been said about me. She continued: 'And this woman had to die in the flower of her years, when her youngest son was only six months old. Her illness was not a long one; she was calm and resigned, and she worried only about her children, especially the youngest. When her end drew near, she said to me: "Send them up to me!" and I brought them into her room – the little one, who did not understand, and the older ones, who were very much upset; they stood around her bed and she raised her hands and prayed over them, then kissed one after the other and sent them away, saying to me: "Be their mother!" I gave her my hand and promised. – "You promise a great deal, my daughter," she said, "both the heart of a mother and the eye of a mother. I have often seen from your grateful tears that you feel what that means. Feel this for your sisters and brothers, and for your father the loyalty and obedience of a wife. You will comfort him." She asked to see him, but he had left the house to hide his unbearable grief – he was completely broken.

'Albert, you were in the room with us. She had heard someone walking about, and asked who it was, and called you to her side. How she looked at you and at me, her mind relieved and at rest, knowing that we would be happy, be happy together.' Albert took Lotte in his arms and kissed her, crying: 'We are! We shall be!' The usually imperturbable Albert was shaken, and I was beside myself.

'Werther,' she began, 'and this woman had to die! Dear God! When I sometimes think that the dearest thing in our lives was taken away, and that no one felt it as keenly as the children, who complained for a long time afterwards that the black men had carried away their mother!'

She stood up, and I woke, shaken, from my trance, but remained seated, still holding her hand. 'We must go,' she said, 'it is late.' She tried to withdraw her hand, but I held it all the more firmly. 'We shall meet again,' I exclaimed, 'we shall find one another, and know one another under whatever form. I am going away,' I went on. 'I go voluntarily, but if I should have to say "For ever" I could not bear it. Farewell, Lotte! Farewell, Albert! We shall meet again.' – 'Yes, tomorrow, I suppose,' she replied lightly. How I felt that word 'tomorrow'! Oh, she was unsuspecting, when she drew her hand away. – They walked down the avenue; I stood in the moonlight, looking after them; then I flung myself on the ground and wept until my tears were exhausted, sprang up again and ran out on the terrace, where I still could catch a glimpse of her white dress moving in the shadow of the tall linden trees near the garden gate. I stretched out my arms, and it disappeared.

BOOK TWO

WE arrived here yesterday. The envoy is indisposed and will, therefore, stay at home for a few days. If he were not so disagreeable, all would be well. I feel that Destiny has some hard tests in store for me. But I won't lose courage! A light heart can bear anything! A light heart? I laugh when those words come from my pen. Oh, a little more lightheartedness would make me the happiest being under the sun. What! With others around me of scanty talent and ability, bragging in complacent self-content, should I despair of my abilities and gifts? Good Lord, you who presented me with all these, why did You not keep half, and give me instead self-confidence and contentment!

Patience! Patience! Things will improve. For, my dear friend, I admit that you were right. Since I have been seeing all sorts of people day in and day out, and have observed how they carry on, I am more lenient with myself. It is true that we are so made that we compare everything with ourselves and ourselves with everything. Therefore, our fortune or misfortune depends on the objects and persons to which we compare ourselves; and for that reason nothing is more dangerous than solitude. Our imagination, by its nature inclined to exalt itself, and nourished by the fantastic imagery of poetry, creates a series of beings of which we are the lowest, so that everything else appears more wonderful, everyone else more perfect. And that is completely natural. We so frequently feel that we are lacking in many qualities which another person apparently possesses; and we then furnish such a person with everything we ourselves possess and with a certain idealistic complacency in addition. And in this fashion a Happy Being is finished to perfection – the creature of our imagination.

If, on the other hand, we just continue to do our best in spite of weakness and hard work, we very often find that, with all our delaying and tacking about, we achieve more than others with their sailing and rowing – and – it gives us a true feeling of our worth if we keep pace with others or even overtake them.

November 26

I begin rather to enjoy myself. The best feature is that there is enough work to do, and that the variety of people, the many new characters, form a colourful drama for my spirit. I have made the acquaintance of Count C., a man I am forced to admire more every day; an intelligent, broad-minded man who has not become cold through his quickness of perception, but radiates a great feeling of friendship and affection. He showed an interest in me when I had to deliver a message; from my first words he saw that we understood each other and that he could talk with me as he could not with everyone. I cannot praise sufficiently his candid manner with me. Nothing in this world equals the warm pleasure we take in seeing a great mind opening to us.

December 24

The envoy annoys me greatly, as I knew he would. He is the most meticulous fool that ever lived, proceeding step by step and fussing like an old maid; a man who is never satisfied with his own work, and consequently never satisfied with another's. I do my work quickly and like to leave things written down as they come; but he is capable of returning my memorandum to me, saying: 'It is good, but better look through it once more; one is always able to find a better word, a more precise particle.' It's enough to drive one mad! – No 'and', not the smallest conjunction, must be omitted; and he is a deadly enemy of the inversions that sometimes slip from my pen. If one does not reel off his periods to the traditional tune, he does not understand one word of them. It is a burden to have to work with such a man.

The confidence of Count C. is my only compensation. The other day he told me quite frankly how dissatisfied he is with the slowness and pedantry of the envoy. 'That type of person makes things difficult for himself as well as for others. But,' he added, 'one has to resign oneself like a traveller who has to cross a mountain; of course, if the mountain were not there, the journey would be much shorter and easier; but there it is, and one has to scale it!'

My old gentleman also sensed in a way that the Count prefers me to him and that vexes and annoys him, so that he seizes any opportunity to disparage the Count in my presence. I, of course, contradict him and only make matters worse. Yesterday I even lost my temper, for his words were meant for me, as well, when he said: 'The Count is quite good at worldly affairs, because he works quickly and has a fluent pen, but, like all literary people, he lacks solid erudition.' He then grimaced, as though to say: 'Do you feel the prick?' But it had no effect on me; I felt only contempt for a man capable of so thinking and behaving. I held my ground and parried with considerable heat. I said that the Count was a man one had to respect for both his character and his knowledge. 'I have never met anyone,' I continued, 'whose range of interests is so wide, and who yet expends so much energy on matters of ordinary life.' This was all Greek to him, and I took leave, not wishing to be choked by more gall and having to listen to further nonsense.

And all this I owe to you, who talked me into assuming this yoke, and harped so much on activity. Activity! If it is true that the man who plants potatoes, or rides into town to sell his grain, is not doing more than I, then I shall slave for another ten years on this galley to which I am at present chained.

And the splendid misery, the boredom among the horrid people who are assembled here! Their social ambitions, the way they watch and spy on one another in order to gain another tiny step; their most contemptible passions flaunted without any reticence. One woman, for instance, tells everyone about her nobility and her native country, so that every stranger is forced to think: 'This woman is a fool to pride herself on that little bit of nobility and on her country's fame.' But, to make it worse, the woman is in reality the daughter of a district clerk from this very region. You see, I cannot understand the human race when it has so little judgement and prostitutes itself in such a vulgar way.

In fact, I realize each day more clearly, dear friend, how foolish it is to judge others by oneself. And as I am so preoccupied with myself, and since this heart of mine is so stormy, oh, how gladly would I let others go their way if they would only let me go mine!

What irritates me most of all are the disgraceful social conditions. I know, of course, as well as anyone, how necessary class distinctions are, and how many advantages I myself gain from them; but they should not stand in my way just when I might enjoy some little pleasure, some gleam of joy on this earth. The other day, on a walk, I made the acquaintance of Fräulein von B., a charming creature, who has preserved a great naturalness in the midst of this stiff and conventional life. We were very congenial as we talked, and when we separated I asked permission to visit her. She consented so frankly that I could hardly wait for the proper moment to make my call. She does not come from these parts and lives in the house of an aunt. I thoroughly disliked the old lady's looks, but I showed her much attention and, for the most part, turned the conversation in her direction. In less than half an hour I guessed almost all that the girl later confirmed: namely, that her dear old aunt lacked everything, having neither a decent fortune nor any wits, and no prop but her family tree, and was protected only by her noble rank, behind which she had entrenched herself and enjoyed the last pleasure left her: to look down from her height on the heads of the burghers. They say she was very beautiful in her youth and frittered away her life, at first by tormenting many a poor young man with her whims; but in middle age obediently submissive to the domination of an old officer who, in exchange for this submission and a moderate dowry, spent the Bronze Age with her, and died. She now finds herself alone in the Iron Age; and no one would pay any attention to her if her niece were not so charming.

January 8, 1772

What dreadful people there are, whose minds are completely absorbed in matters of etiquette, whose thoughts and aspirations all year long turn over the single problem how to push oneself one chair higher at table. And it is not as though they had nothing else to do. No, on the contrary, work continues to pile up because trivial annoyances hinder the dispatch of more important matters. Last week a quarrel started during a sleighing party and the whole fun was spoiled.

The fools, who do not understand that actual rank does not matter at all and that he who occupies the top very rarely plays the chief role. How often a king is ruled by a minister; how many ministers by their secretaries! And who is then the first? I believe it is the man who knows his fellow-men at a glance and has sufficient power or shrewdness to harness their forces and passions to the execution of his plans.

January 20

I must write you, dear Lotte, here in the taproom of a poor country inn, where I have taken refuge from a heavy storm. Since the time I have been a stranger wandering around in D., that depressing hole of a town, among strangers to my heart, there has not been one moment, not one, when my heart would have told me to write to you; but now, in this hovel, this solitary narrow place, while snow and hail pelt on my little window, my first thought is of you. The moment I entered, your image, the memory of you, suddenly overwhelmed me, O Lotte, so sacred and so warm! Dear God, it was the first happy moment in a long time.

If you could see me, my dear, in the flood of distractions! How dried up my senses are getting to be; not for one minute does my heart overflow – not one blissful hour! Nothing! Nothing! I seem to be standing before a sort of raree show, watching the little men and little horses jerk before my eyes; and I often ask myself if everything is not an optical illusion. I join in the play or, rather, I am moved about like a marionette, and sometimes, when I grasp the wooden hand of my neighbour, I shrink back with a shudder. Every evening I plan to enjoy the sunrise, and each morning I fail to get up. During the day I look forward to the moonlight, but later I stay in my room. I do not even know why I get up or why I go to bed.

The leaven which set my life in motion is wanting; the charm which kept me awake far into the night and roused me from my sleep in the morning is gone.

I have found only one feminine friend here: a Fräulein von B., who resembles you, dear Lotte, if anyone can possibly resemble you. 'Well, well!' you will say, 'this fellow resorts to pretty compliments!' There is some truth in it, I have lately been very gallant, which is, after all, my nature to be. I have been very witty, and the ladies say that no one can flatter as well as I (or tell lies, you will add, because one cannot flatter without lying, you see). But I wanted to talk about Fräulein von B. She has a great deal of spirit, which shines out from her blue eyes. Her high rank is a burden to her, as it does not satisfy any of the desires of her heart. She longs to escape from the turmoil, and we spend hours with fantasies of country scenes filled with pure happiness; ah, and of you! How often must she do homage to you! She is not compelled to – she does it voluntarily, loves to hear about you, and loves you.

I wish that I could be sitting at your feet in the dear, familiar room, with our little ones dancing about us; and if they became too noisy, I could gather them around me and quiet them with a frightening fairy tale.

The sun is sinking in full glory over the dazzling snow-white countryside; the storm has passed, and I – must return to my cage. Adieu! Is Albert with you? And how – ? God forgive me that question!

February 8

For a week we have had the most horrible weather, but for me it is a blessing. As long as I have been here, there has not been one fine day that has not been spoiled or ruined for me by someone. Now, when it pours, and drizzles, and freezes, and thaws, I think – well, it cannot be worse inside than it is out of doors, or vice versa; and that is good. When the sun rises in the morning and promises a fine day, I can never resist exclaiming, 'Now they again have a heavenly gift which they can spoil for one another.' Nothing exists that these people cannot spoil for one another. Health, reputation, happiness, recreation! And all this largely through silliness, stupidity, and narrow-mindedness. Sometimes I feel like imploring them on my knees not to rage so violently against themselves.

February 17

I fear that my envoy and I will not be together much longer. That man is absolutely unbearable. His way of working and of handling affairs is so ridiculous that I cannot restrain myself from contradicting him; and I often handle some matter at my will and in my own way – a way, of course, which he always disapproves. For this reason he has recently complained of me at Court, and the Minister reproved me, although mildly; but still it was a reproof; and I was about to send in my resignation when I received a personal letter from him – a letter that brought me down on my knees in admiration of its generous, wise and noble feeling. He puts my extreme sensitiveness in the right place, although he credits my exaggerated ideas of efficiency, of influence upon others, of more intelligent management of business, as youthful and praiseworthy courage; and he does not wish to eradicate these ideas but to temper them, and lead them into the right direction where they can be sure of producing a powerful effect. I am now fortified for a week, and have found my balance again. Peace of mind is a wonderful thing, as is pleasure in oneself. Dear friend, if only these treasures were not so fragile as they are precious and beautiful.

February 20

God bless you, dear friends, and give you all the happy days of which I am deprived.

Thank you, Albert, for having kept me in the dark. I was waiting for news about the day of your wedding and had intended on that day solemnly to take down Lotte's silhouette from my wall and bury it among other papers. Now you are a married couple, and her silhouette is still there. Well, it shall stay there! And why not? I know that I am still with you; that I remain in Lotte's heart without doing any harm to you; I have – yes, I have the second place in it, and will and must keep that place. Oh, I should go mad if she were able to forget – Albert, Hell lies in that thought. Albert, farewell! Farewell, angel from Heaven! Farewell, Lotte!

March 15

Something has so humiliated me that I shall be forced to leave this place, and I gnash my teeth! The Devil! The harm is done, and it is *your* fault alone – *you* spurred me on, pushed and tormented me into accepting a position that was not congenial to me. Well, here I am! and you have had your way! And in order to prevent you from telling me that it was my eccentric ideas which ruined everything, I here recount, dear sir, the story, plain and clear, as a chronicler would put it down.

Count C. is very fond of me and singles me out, as is well known, and as I have written you many times. He had invited me for dinner at his house yesterday, on the very day when the whole aristocratic set, ladies and gentlemen, are accustomed to meet there late in the evening. I had completely forgotten this fact; and it also did not occur to me that subordinate officials like myself are not welcome on such occasions. Very well. I dined with the Count, and afterwards we walked up and down the great hall in conversation and were joined later by Colonel B.; so the hour of the party drew near. God knows, I did not suspect anything. Then the more-than-gracious Lady S. entered with her spouse and her nobly hatched little goose of a flat-bosomed and tight-laced daughter. *En passant*, they opened their eyes wide and turned up their noses in the traditional highly aristocratic manner. As that clique is entirely repulsive to me, I had decided to leave, only waiting until the Count could free himself from trivial chatter, when Fräulein von B. entered the room. Since I become always a little more cheerful when I see her, I stayed on, took my place behind her chair, and noticed only after some time had passed that she was not talking to me with her usual frankness but with some embarrassment. This took me by surprise. 'Is she really like the rest of these people?' I asked myself and was piqued. I wanted to leave, but stayed on, because I should have liked to free her from a blame I did not believe, and still hoped for a kind word from her and – whatever you wish. Meanwhile, more and more people were filling the room. Baron F. all got up in a complete outfit dating back to the coronation of Francis I, Hofrat R. (but here *in qualitate* called Herr von N.) with his deaf wife, not to mention the badly-reduced-in-circumstances J., who had patched up the worn places in his old-fashioned clothes with brand-new material – all these people kept arriving in swarms; and I spoke to some of those I knew who were, however, very laconic, I thought – and paid attention only to my Fräulein von B. I did not notice that the dames at the far end of the room were whispering into each other's ears or that this whispering spread to the gentlemen; that Lady S. was talking to the Count (Fräulein von B. recounted all this to me afterwards), until he finally came up to me and drew me into a window recess. 'You know our strange social conventions,' he said, 'and I notice that the company is displeased to see you here, although I should not want you, for anything in the world –' – 'Your Excellency!' I interrupted, 'I apologize exceedingly; I should have thought of this before, and I know you will forgive me my inconsequence. I wanted to leave some time ago, but a malicious spirit held me back,' I added, smiling and bowing to him. The Count pressed my hand with a warmth that expressed everything. I turned my back on the illustrious company, slipped away and took a cabriolet to M., to see the sunset from the hill, while reading in Homer the magnificent passage which describes how Odysseus is entertained by the faithful swineherd. All this was perfect.

In the evening I returned to the inn for supper. There were only a few people in the taproom, playing at dice at the corner of a table, having turned back the tablecloth. The honest Adelin then came in, put down his hat when he saw me, and, coming up closer, said to me in a low voice: 'Did something annoy you?' 'Annoy me?' I said. – 'The Count asked you to leave his party.' – 'The Devil take it!' I said. 'I was glad to get out into the fresh air.' – 'Good that you take it so lightly,' he said. 'The thing that worries me is that everyone is already talking.' Now for the first time the whole thing began to irritate me. I imagined that everyone who came in for supper glanced at me and seemed to know about the incident. My blood was up.

And today when everyone pities me wherever I go and when I hear that my triumphant rivals are saying, 'You see where arrogance leads, when proud people who boast of their little share of brains think they can ignore all conventions' (and whatever else these gossiping dogs may invent), one would like to take a knife and plunge it into one's heart; for, whatever one may say about independence, I should like to see the person who can allow rascals to slander him when they have the upper hand. When it is only empty talk, it is easy to ignore them.

Everything is against me. Today I met Fräulein von B. in the avenue. I could not keep myself from speaking to her; to tell her, as soon as we were at some distance from her companions, how much she had hurt me the other day. 'O Werther,' she said with deep feeling, 'how could you, knowing my heart, interpret my confusion in such a way? How I suffered for you from the moment I entered the room! I foresaw everything, and a warning word was on the tip of my tongue a dozen times. I knew that Lady S. and Lady T. would leave with their husbands rather than remain while you were there; and I knew that the Count cannot risk their displeasure – and now all this scandal!' – 'What do you mean?' I asked, concealing my alarm, because everything that Adelin had told me the previous day made me suddenly feel very uneasy. – 'How much it has already cost me,' said the sweet creature with tears in her eyes. – I was no longer master of myself, and was ready to throw myself at her feet. 'Do tell me the truth,' I cried. The tears ran down her cheeks, and I was almost out of my mind. She dried her tears without trying to conceal them. 'You know my aunt,' she began. 'She was at the party and with her keen eyes kept a close watch on everything. Werther, I had to suffer for it last night, and this morning I was given a lecture on my friendship with you, and was forced to listen to the degrading, discrediting things she said about you, and could not – was not allowed to – defend you half as much as I wished.'

Every word she spoke pierced my heart like a sword. She did not sense how charitable it would have been to keep all this from me; and she went on to say that more gossip would soon begin to run wild, and mentioned the sort of people who would gloat over it. How delighted they all would be about the punishment I had received for my arrogance and haughty contempt towards others, for which they had often blamed me. All this, Wilhelm, I had to hear from her, spoken in a tone of sincerest sympathy. I was completely crushed, and am still furious. I wish that someone would have the courage to blame me openly so that I could thrust my dagger through his body; if I saw blood, I should certainly feel better. Today I have taken up a knife a dozen times, intending to relieve with it my suffocating heart. I have been told that a noble breed of horses, when overheated and hunted almost to death, will by instinct bite open a vein and so recover their breath. I often feel the same. I should like to open one of my veins and gain eternal freedom for myself.

March 24

I have sent in my resignation to the Court, and I hope that it will be accepted. You will forgive me for not asking your permission first. It is absolutely necessary for me to leave; and everything you will say, to persuade me to stay, I myself know. And therefore – sugar the bitter pill for my mother. I cannot help myself, and she must put up with the fact that I cannot help her either. Of course, it is going to hurt her. To see the beginning brilliant career of her son, which might have mounted, perhaps, to the office of privy councillor and envoy, stop so suddenly, and the little horse brought back to its stable! Now think of the matter as you will and try to figure out the possible conditions under which I might and should have stayed. Enough, I am going. But that you may know where I am going, let me tell you that Prince ——, who likes my company extremely, when he heard of my intention, invited me to accompany him to his estates, and to spend the lovely springtime there. He has promised that I will be completely left alone, and as we understand one another very well, up to a certain point, I shall take my chance and go with him.

walk and to enjoy every memory in a new and vivid way to my heart's content. There I now stood under the linden tree which was once the goal and boundary of my walks as a boy. How different from the present moment! In those days, in my happy ignorance, my greatest desire had been to get away, out into the unknown world, where I hoped to find all the joy and all the satisfaction possible for my aspiring and yearning heart. Now I had come back from that wide world – oh, my friend, with so many shattered hopes, so many ruined plans. I saw before me the mountains which had so many times been the goal of my desires. I used to sit here for hours, longing to be beyond, completely absorbed, heart and soul, in those woods, those valleys which appeared to my eyes so pleasant and mysterious. If I knew that I had to return home at a certain hour, how I loathed leaving the beloved spot! – As I approached the town, I greeted all the familiar little garden houses, but heartily disliked the newer ones, as well as all the other changes that had been made. I entered by the town gate; and now I knew my way again at once. Dear friend, I'll not go into any details; for, delightful as they are, such a detailed description might be monotonous. I had planned to take a room overlooking the market place, next to our old house. As I walked in that direction I noticed that the school, wherein a conscientious old dame had penned up our childhood, had been turned into a shop. I vividly remembered the restlessness, the tears, the dullness of mind, the anxiety of heart, that I suffered in that hole. Every single step I took stirred up memories. No pilgrim in the Holy Land could come across so many places of religious memory, or have a soul more filled with pious emotion. – Another example among thousands: I went down along the river to a certain farm, where formerly I had often walked. This was the place where we boys used to compete, skimming flat stones which skipped along the surface of the water. I clearly remembered how often I stood there, following the river with my eyes, with strange presentiments in my heart; how colourfully my imagination painted the countries through which the river flowed, and how soon

I discovered that my imagination had limits. Still I knew that the river ran on and on, and I completely lost myself in the vision of an unseen far country. – You see, dear friend, how limited and how happy were the glorious Ancients! how naïve their emotions and their poetry! When Ulysses speaks of the immeasurable sea and the infinite earth, everything is true, human, deeply felt, intimate, and mysterious. What is the use of my present knowledge, which I share with any school-boy, that the earth is round? Man needs only a few clods of earth whereon to enjoy himself, and even fewer for his last rest.

Here I am in the Prince's hunting lodge. Life with this gentleman goes along very well, for he is simple and sincere. But he is surrounded by a strange crowd of people whom I cannot understand at all. They are evidently not bad fellows, but they do not have the look of honest ones. Sometimes they make an honest impression on me, but I cannot bring myself to trust them. Another thing I regret is that the Prince often talks about matters he has only heard or read, and he then takes a position that some other person may have presented to him.

Besides, he admires my intelligence and my talents more than my heart, which is, after all, my only pride, and the fountainhead of all – all strength, happiness and misery. Anyone can know what I know. My heart alone is my own.

May 25

I had something on my mind which I did not want to tell you until it was carried out; now that nothing has come of it, it does not matter. I wanted to go to the war; that is what I have long had at heart. It was my chief reason for coming here with the Prince, who is a general in the —— service. During one of our walks I told him of my intention; he advised against it, and there would have had to be more passion in me than actually existed in my passing mood to have prevented me from listening to his arguments.

June 11

You can say what you will; I cannot stay here any longer. What is the use? Time hangs heavy on my hands. The Prince treats me very well, yet I do not feel on my own ground. Fundamentally, we have nothing in common. He is an intelligent man, but of the average kind; to talk to him is not too different from reading a well-written book. I shall stay another week and then take up my wandering again. My drawing is the best thing I have done here. The Prince has a feeling for art and might feel still more strongly in that direction if he were not limited by the pseudo-scientific approach and by trite terminology. I often get furious when I talk with him about Nature and Art with warmth and imagination, only to have him attempt to be clever as he stumbles in with some trite term.

June 16

It is true, I am only a wanderer, a pilgrim on this earth! But are you more?

June 18

Where do I want to go? I tell you in confidence that I must stay here another two weeks; and then I pretend to myself that I wish to visit the mines in ———. But, to tell you the truth, there is nothing in that. I only want to be closer to Lotte once more; that is all. And I mock at my heart – and do what it demands.

July 29

No, it is good! Everything is good! I – her husband! O God, who made me, if you had given me that unspeakable happiness, my whole life would be one perpetual prayer. I will not protest – forgive my tears, forgive my hopeless wishes! She –

my wife! If I could have closed in my arms the loveliest creature under the sun – A shudder goes through my whole body, Wilhelm, when I see Albert put his arm around her slender waist.

And may I say it? Why not, Wilhelm? She would have been happier with me than with him. Oh, he is not the man to satisfy all the needs of her heart. A certain lack of sensitiveness, a certain lack of – call it as you will. – His heart does not beat in sympathy with, say, a passage in a favourite book, where my heart and Lotte's beat in the same rhythm; as on a hundred other occasions when our feelings about the action of a third person are in accord. Dear Wilhelm! It is true that he loves her with all his soul; and how much such a love deserves!

A most disagreeable person has interrupted me. My tears are dried. I am distracted. Adieu, dear friend.

August 4

I am not alone in suffering. The hopes of all men are shattered and their expectations betrayed. I went to see the good woman I met under the linden tree. Her older boy ran up to meet me; his joyful shouts brought her near; she looked very downcast. Her first words were, 'Kind sir, my little Hans is dead!' He was the youngest of her sons. I was silent. 'And my husband,' she went on, 'has returned from Switzerland with empty pockets. If some kind people had not helped him, he would have been forced to beg. He caught a fever on the way.' I did not know what to say. I gave something to the little one. She asked me to accept a few apples, which I did, and left this place of melancholy memory.

August 21

As quick as you turn your hand, so quickly everything has changed. Now and then a happier glimpse of life dawns for me, but, alas, only for a moment! – When I become lost in dreams I cannot avoid thinking, 'What if Albert should die? You would! she would –' And then I begin to run after the chimera until it leads me to abysses from which I shrink back in horror.

When I walk out of the town gate, along the road over which I first drove to fetch Lotte to the ball, how changed it all is! Everything, everything is over! No visible trace of the past, not a heartbeat of my former emotion. I feel like a ghost must feel who returns to the burned and destroyed castle which he built in the flower of his youth and filled with splendid objects, and on his deathbed hopefully bequeathed to his beloved son.

September 3

Sometimes I cannot understand how another *can*, how he *dare* love her, since I alone love her completely and devotedly, knowing only her, and having nothing in the world but her!

September 4

Yes, it is so. As Nature declines towards autumn, autumn is in me and around me. My leaves are turning yellow, and already the leaves of the trees nearby have fallen. Did I not once write to you, soon after I arrived here, of a certain peasant lad? I inquired about him again in Wahlheim, and was told that he had been turned out of service; but no one seemed to know his whereabouts. Yesterday I met him by chance on my way to another village; I spoke to him, and he told me his story, which moved me more than I can say, as you will easily understand when I repeat it to you. But why repeat it? Why do I not keep my grief and my anxiety to myself? Why should I worry you? Why do I always give you reason to deplore and to reprove me? Never mind! This may also be part of my destiny!

With subdued sadness, mingled with shyness, the lad answered my questions at first; but soon, as if he suddenly recognized himself and myself once more, he confessed to me with more confidence the mistakes he had made, and mourned over his misfortunes. Dear friend, if I could only lay before your judgement every word of his story! He confessed, in fact he told me with a sort of joyful reminiscence, that his passion for the woman who employed him had daily grown on him, to the degree that he finally had not known what to do; had not known, as he expressed it, which way to turn his head. He had not been able to eat, to drink or to sleep; he had felt as if something was choking him. He did what he was not supposed to do, and forgot what he had been ordered to do; it was as if an evil spirit drove him on, until one day, knowing the woman to be in an upper room, he had followed her, or rather had been drawn after her by some magic power. When she resisted his demands, he was about to use force; he did not know what happened to him, and God was his witness that his intentions towards her had always been honest, that his most ardent wish was that she might marry him and spend the rest of her life with him. – After having talked for a while, he began to falter, like a person who has something more to say but lacks the courage to speak out. At last he confessed rather timidly that she had allowed him a few small familiar-ities and had not grudged him some intimacies. He checked himself two or three times, again and again protesting em-phatically that he did not mention this to defame her, as he put it; he loved and respected her as much as formerly; he had never mentioned the matter before to anyone and now told it to me only to convince me that he was not unnatural and not insane. And now, dear friend, you will again hear my old song, which I am forever repeating: if you could have seen this man as he stood before me, as he still stands before my mind! Could I but describe to you every exact detail so that you could understand what a warm interest I take – must take – in his destiny. But enough of this; as you know my destiny as well, as you know me as well, you will understand only too clearly what attracts me to all unfortunate beings, and parti-cularly to this one.

As I re-read this letter, I see that I have forgotten to finish the story which you can, however, easily imagine for yourself. The woman defended herself, and at this moment her brother came in. This brother had for a long time hated the lad and wished to have him out of the house, being afraid that his children would lose the inheritance of his childless sister if she should marry again (an inheritance they looked forward to with keen expectation). The woman's brother immediately showed him the door and raised such a hue and cry that the woman, even if she had wished to, could not well have taken him back into her service. She had now hired another farm hand; but this man, too, people said, had caused a definite break between the brother and herself; and she was expected almost certainly to marry this new man; but my lad said that he was determined to make an end of himself before that day.

What I recount to you here is not exaggerated or sentimentalized; indeed, I may say that I have told it poorly, very poorly, and vulgarized it, by telling it in our conventional moralizing phrases.

This kind of love, this fidelity, this passion, is, as you see, no poetic invention. It is alive; it exists in its purest form among those people whom we call uneducated and coarse. We educated people – miseducated into nothingness! Read this story with reverence, I beg you. Today I am calm while I write; you see from my handwriting that I do not scribble and scrawl as I usually do. Read, dearest friend, and bear in mind that you are reading the story of your friend as well. Yes, all this has happened to me, and will happen to me, and I am not as good-natured by half, or as determined as the poor wretch with whom I almost haven't the courage to compare myself.

September 5

She had written a little note to her husband, who was in the country attending to some business. It began: 'Best and dearest of men! Come back as soon as you can; I await you with the utmost joy.' – A friend came in and brought a message from Albert saying that he would be delayed because of some circumstance or other. Lotte's note was not sent; and I found it by chance in the evening. I read it and smiled; and she asked me why. 'What a divine gift is imagination!' I exclaimed. 'For a moment I could pretend to myself that this was written to me.' – She did not reply and seemed displeased; and I fell silent.

September 6

I struggled with myself before I decided to discard my plain blue dress coat, which I wore when I first danced with Lotte; but it had become very shabby. I have had a new one made, exactly like the first, down to collar and lapels; and also another yellow waistcoat and a pair of breeches.

But the effect is not quite the same. I don't know – it may be that in time I shall like it better.

September 12

She has been away for a few days to meet Albert and return with him. Today, when I came into her room, she was back and welcomed me; and I kissed her hand with great delight.

A canary flew down from the mirror and perched on her shoulder. 'A new friend,' she said, and called him to her hand. 'It is a present for my little ones. How sweetly he behaves! Look at him! When I give him a crumb of bread, he flutters his wings and pecks so daintily. He also kisses me. Look!'

When she offered her sweet lips to the little bird, he nestled closely to them, as though he could feel the happiness given to him.

'He shall kiss you, too,' she said, handing the bird over to me. The tiny beak made its way from her lips to mine, and the pecking touch was like a breath – a foretaste of the pleasures of love.

'His kiss is not without greed,' I said. 'He looks for food and flies back, not satisfied with an empty caress.'

'He also takes food from my mouth,' she said. She offered some crumbs to the bird with her lips, which smiled with the happiness of innocently sympathizing love.

I turned my eyes away. She should not do this! She should not inflame my imagination with these pictures of heavenly innocence and joy and arouse my heart from the sleep into which the monotony of life often lulls it. But why not? She trusts me so implicitly! She knows how much I love her!

September 15

It is enough to drive one mad, Wilhelm, to see people without any sense or feeling for the few remaining precious things in this world. You know of the walnut trees, where I sat with the good pastor of St —— and Lotte – those noble walnut trees which, God knows, always filled me with a deep sense of joy! How friendly and cool they made the parsonage yard! How beautiful the branches were – and then the recollection of the good clergymen who had planted them so many years ago. The schoolmaster frequently mentioned the name of one of these, heard from his grandfather; he is said to have been such a good man, and his memory was ever sacred to me as I sat under the trees. I tell you, I saw tears in the schoolmaster's eyes when he spoke yesterday of their having been cut down. Cut down! I am furious and could kill the dog who struck the first blow with his axe. I would become utterly despondent if I should see only one such tree, standing in my courtyard, wither with age. Dearest friend, there is at least one redeeming feature in the situation. What a wonderful thing is human sympathy! The whole village grumbles; and I hope that the present pastor's wife will notice, in regard to butter, eggs and other presents, how much she has hurt the feelings of the whole place. For it is *she*, the wife of the new pastor (our old one is dead), a thin and sickly creature who has every reason not to take any interest in the world, as no one takes any interest in her: a foolish woman who pretends to erudition, pokes her nose into an examination of the Canon, works a good deal at the new-fangled critico-moralist reformation of Christianity, and shrugs her shoulders at the excessive enthusiasm of Lavater. Her health is completely shattered, and for this reason she cannot find any pleasure in anything on God's earth. Only that sort of a creature could think of cutting down my walnut trees. You see, I cannot get over the shock! Just imagine, the falling leaves made her yard damp and dirty; the trees deprived her of sunlight; when the nuts were ripe, the boys pelted them with stones, and this made her nervous, this disturbed her profound meditations when she was weighing the merits of the differing arguments of Kennicot, Semler and Michaelis. When I saw how glum the villagers were, especially the old ones, I asked, 'Why did you let it happen?' – 'When the magistrate wants it,' they answered, 'what can you do?' But justice has triumphed. The magistrate, and the pastor (who, after all, wanted to profit from his wife's whims which anyway did not flavour his soup), had thought of sharing the proceeds; but the Board of Revenue still had old claims to the ground where the trees had stood; and the Board sold them to the highest bidder. There they lie! Oh, if I were a prince! I would know what to do – with the pastor's wife, the magistrate, and the Board of Revenue! – Prince! Indeed, if I were a prince, would I really worry about the trees of my country?

October 10

If I only see her dark eyes, I feel happy! But it makes me angry that Albert does not seem as delighted as he – hoped – as I – thought to be, if – I am not fond of dashes, but it is the only way of expressing myself here – and I think I make myself sufficiently clear.

October 12

Ossian has taken the place of Homer in my heart. What a world this sublime poet has opened to me! I wander with him over the heath, where the gale howls on all sides and sweeps along with it the spirits of our ancestors in the flowing mist and in the darkling light of the moon. I hear from the mountains, and in the roar of the torrent the faint groan of spirits in their caverns, and the lament of the maiden who pines for death beside the four moss-covered and grass-grown stones that mark the grave of her fallen hero, her lover. I then come upon the wandering grey bard who searches for the footsteps of his fathers on the vast heath and finds alas! only their tombstones; and then laments as he gazes at the lovely evening star reflected in the rolling waves of the sea. And I see past ages glow into life in the soul of the hero, when the friendly beam shone on the adventures of the brave, and the moonlight illuminated their ships, homeward bound and hung with wreaths of victory. When I read deep sorrow on the bard's brow, and see the last and lonely great one stagger exhausted towards his grave, drinking in ever-fresh, agonizing joys among the helpless shades of his dead companions, and then look down upon the cold earth and the tall waving grass, crying out: 'The traveller will come, will come, who knew me in my beauty, and he will ask: "Where is the bard, Fingal's great son?" His footsteps tread on my grave, and he will seek for me on this earth in vain.' – O friend! I wish I could draw my sword like a noble paladin, and free my lord from the stabbing agony of a slowly ebbing life with one stroke; and then let my soul follow the liberated demigod.

October 19

Oh, this void, this terrifying void I feel in my breast! I often think: if you could once, only once, press her to your heart, this void would be filled.

October 26

Yes, dear friend, I feel more and more certain that the existence of any human being matters little, very little. A

friend had come to visit Lotte, and I went into the next
room and opened a book but could not read; then I took
up a pen to write. I heard them speaking in low voices; they
talked of unimportant matters and exchanged news of the
town: how this girl would marry, how another was very ill.
'She has a dry cough; the bones show in her face, and she
has fainting spells; I wouldn't give a penny for her life,' said
the friend. 'N.N. is also in very poor health,' said Lotte. –
'He is badly swollen,' said the other. And my lively imagination carried me to the bedside of these unfortunates; I saw
them reluctantly turning their backs on life while my little
ladies, Wilhelm, talked as one talks about a stranger who is
dying. And when I look around the room and see on all
sides Lotte's dresses and Albert's papers, and the furniture,
everything so familiar to me, even this inkwell, I think to
myself: 'See what you mean to this house! On the whole
your friends respect you; you often make them happy, and
it seems to your heart that it could not live without them;
and yet – if you should go, if you should leave this circle,
would they – how long would they feel the void which your
loss will create in their destinies? how long?' – Oh, how
transitory is man, that even in the place where he finds real
confirmation of his existence, where he makes the one true
impress of his personality in the memories, in the souls of
those he loves, that even there he must fade and vanish, and
how soon!

October 27

I often feel like tearing open my breast or knocking out my
brains when I think how little human beings can do for one
another. Oh, the love, the joy, the warmth and the delight
which I do not feel myself, no other person will give me;
and, with a heart full of supreme happiness, I still cannot
make another person happy who stands before me cold
and impassive.

October 27, evening

I have so much in me, and the feeling for her absorbs it all; I have so much, and without her it all comes to nothing.

October 30

How many times have I been on the point of embracing her! God knows what a torture it is to see such loveliness moving about, and not to be permitted to stretch out one's hands to it; for this gesture is, after all, one of the most natural of human impulses. Do not children grasp at anything that comes their way? – And I?

November 3

I often lie down to sleep wishing – yes, sometimes hoping not to wake up again; and the next morning I open my eyes, again see the sun, and feel wretched. Oh, if I only could have moods, could shift the blame on the weather, a third person, or on an unsuccessful enterprise, then only half the weight of this unbearable burden of discontent would rest on me. Miserable me! I know only too well that the fault is with me alone – not fault! Enough, the source of all my misery is hidden in myself, as was formerly the source of all my happiness. Am I not the same who not long ago was intoxicated by the abundance of his emotions, and who stepped into a paradise wherever he went, with a heart ready longingly to embrace the whole world? And now this heart is dead, and thrills of delight radiate from it no longer; my eyes are dry, and my feelings, no longer refreshed by the relief of tears, contract my brow into anxious furrows. I suffer terribly because I have lost what was the one delight of my life – the holy, animating power that helped me to create worlds around me – it has gone! When I now look out of my window at the distant hill, and see how the early sun pierces the mist above it and lights up the peaceful meadows, and how the

gentle river between its leafless willows winds towards me –
oh, when this glorious Nature lies before me as immobile as
on a little lacquered painting, and all this beauty cannot pump
one single drop of happiness from my heart to my brain, and
the whole man stands before the face of God like a dried-up
well, like a broken pitcher – I have often thrown myself on
the ground and implored God for tears, as a farmer prays for
rain when the sky is leaden above him, and the ground around
him is parched.

But alas! I feel that God does not send rain or sunshine
because of our impetuous prayers; and those times that so
torment me when I look back – why were they so blessed?
Only because I patiently waited for His spirit, and embraced
the joy that descended on me with an undivided, deeply
grateful heart.

November 8

She has reproached me with my excesses! Oh, with what
sweetness! My excesses: that now and then, when I allow
myself a glass of wine, I drink the whole bottle. 'Don't do it,'
she said. 'Think of Lotte.' – 'Think!' I said, 'do you need to tell
me that? I think or I do not think. You are always before my
soul. Today I sat near the place where you got out of the
carriage the other day –' She began to speak of other matters,
to keep me from pursuing that subject too deeply. Dear
friend, I am lost! She can do with me as she wishes.

November 15

Thank you, Wilhelm, for your warm sympathy and your well-
meaning advice; and, please, do not worry. Let me suffer to
the end; in spite of my listlessness I still have enough strength
to see it through. I have a deep respect for religion, you know
that; I feel that it is a support for many weary souls, a comfort
for many who die of thirst. Only – can it, must it, be that for
everyone? When you look at the great world, you see

thousands for whom it has meant nothing, thousands for whom it will never mean anything, preached or not preached; and must it then mean something to me? Did not even the Son of God say that those would be about Him whom His Father had given Him? What if I should not have been given to Him? Suppose, as my heart tells me, God the Father wanted to keep me for Himself? – Please, do not interpret this wrongly; do not see any sarcasm in these innocent words; it is my whole soul which I lay open to you; otherwise I should prefer to have kept silence; for, as you know, I do not like to waste words concerning matters of which everyone else is as ignorant as myself. Is it not man's destiny to bear his lot patiently and to drain the cup to the dregs? Yet did not the cup become too bitter for the human lips of God's only Son? Why, then, should I brag and pretend that it tastes sweet to me? And why should I be ashamed at the terrible moment when my whole life trembles between being and not-being; when the past flashes like lightning over the gloomy abyss of the future and everything around me collapses, and the world is destroyed with me – is it not then the voice of a creature thrown completely on his own resources, who has failed himself and is resistlessly plunging into the abyss, that grinds out the cry, 'My God! My God! why hast Thou forsaken me?' And should I be ashamed to use those words; should I fear the moment not spared Him who rolls the heavens together like a scroll?

November 21

She does not see, she does not realize, that she is preparing a poison that will be the ruin of us both; and I voluptuously drain the cup she hands me for my destruction. What is the meaning of the friendly glance she often – often? – no, not often but still, at times, gives me, of the pleasure with which she accepts an involuntary expression of my emotion, of the compassion for my suffering which appears on her brow?

Yesterday, when I was leaving, she gave me her hand and said: 'Adieu, dear Werther!' – Dear Werther! It was the first time she had called me 'dear', and the word went to the marrow of my bones. I have repeated it to myself a hundred times; and last night, before I went to bed, I talked all sorts of nonsense. I suddenly said, 'Good night, dear Werther!' and afterwards had to laugh at myself.

November 22

I cannot pray, 'Let her be mine!' And yet how often do I think of her as mine. I cannot pray, 'Give her to me!' because she belongs to another man. I go on joking at my suffering, and if I gave myself up to this game, it would bring on a whole litany of antitheses.

November 24

She feels how I am suffering. Today her glance went straight to my heart. I found her alone; I did not speak and she looked at me. And I no longer saw her lovable beauty, no longer the gentle light of her exquisite spirit; all that disappeared. I saw a far more wonderful look in her eyes: an expression of warmest sympathy, of the sweetest compassion. Why was I not allowed to throw myself at her feet? Why could I not take her in my arms and answer her with a thousand kisses? She took refuge at the clavichord, and her soft voice breathed out a melody to the accompaniment of her playing. Never have I seen her lips so charming; it was as if they opened thirstily, to drink in the sweet tones which welled up from the instrument; as if only a mysterious echo reverberated from her innocent mouth. If I could only describe it to you! I was resigned; I bowed my head and vowed: 'Never shall I dare to kiss those lips, on which heavenly spirits hover.' And yet – I shall – Ha! you see, it stands like a barrier before my soul – this supreme happiness – and then die to atone for my sin – sin?

November 26

Sometimes I say to myself: 'Your destiny is unique; call the others fortunate – no one has been so tormented as you.' Then I read an ancient poet, and it seems to me as though I look into my own heart. I have so much to endure! Oh, were there other men before me as miserable as I?

November 30

I cannot, I cannot regain my balance! Wherever I go I am faced with an apparition which completely upsets me. Today! O Destiny! O Mankind!

I was walking by the river at noon; I had no desire to eat. Everything was bleak; a cold and humid westerly wind blew from the mountains, and the grey rain clouds drifted into the valley. Some distance away I saw a man in a shabby green coat crawling among the rocks and evidently looking for herbs. When I came closer and the noise I made caused him to turn, I saw a very interesting face, whose main feature was a quiet melancholy and which otherwise expressed nothing but a frank good-natured disposition. Part of his long black hair was fastened into two rolls with pins, and the rest, braided into a thick queue, hung down his back. As his clothes indicated a man of the lower classes, I thought he would not resent my interest in what he was doing; so I asked him what he was looking for. 'I am looking for flowers,' he answered with a deep sigh, 'but I do not find any.' – 'This is not the right season of the year,' I said, smiling. – 'There are so many flowers,' he said, coming down towards me. 'In my garden are roses and honeysuckle of two kinds, one of which my father gave me; they grow like weeds; I have already looked for two days for them and cannot find them. There are always flowers out here, too, yellow and blue and red ones; and the thousand-guilder-plant has a lovely little flower. I cannot find any at all.' I noticed something queer about him and therefore asked cautiously, 'What will you do with the flowers?' A strange convulsive smile flashed over his face. 'If you won't betray me,' he said, pressing a finger on his mouth, 'I have promised my sweetheart a nosegay.' – 'That is very nice of you,' I said. – 'Oh,' he said, 'she has a lot of other things; she is rich.' – 'And yet she will like your nosegay,' I said. – 'Oh,' he rambled on, 'she has jewels and a crown.' – 'What is her name?' – 'If the States-General would only pay me,' he replied, 'I would be a different person! Yes, there was a time when I was well off. Now I am done for. Now I am –' A tearful look heavenward expressed everything. 'So you were happy?' I asked. – 'Oh, I wish I were so again!' he answered. 'I felt as fine, as gay, as light as a fish in the water.' – 'Heinrich!' an old woman who came towards us called. 'Heinrich, where are you? We have looked everywhere for you. Come and eat.' – 'Is he your son?' I asked, going up to her. – 'Yes, my poor son!' she replied. 'God has put a heavy cross on my shoulders.' – 'How long has he been like this?' I asked. – 'He has been quiet now for six months,' she said. 'Thank God he has improved; before then he was raving mad for a whole year and lay in chains in the madhouse. Now he wouldn't do harm to anyone, and he talks of nothing but kings and emperors. He was such a good-natured, quiet boy, who helped support me, and wrote a beautiful hand, and all of a sudden he became gloomy, fell into a violent fever, then into stark madness, and he is now as you see him. If I could tell you, sir –' I interrupted the flow of her words with the question, 'What did he mean when he spoke of a time when he was so happy and well off?' – 'The foolish fellow!' she cried, with a compassionate smile, 'by that he means the time when he was out of his mind; he always praises those days; it was when he was at the asylum and did not know himself.' The last expression struck me like a thunderbolt; I pressed some money into her hand and left her in haste.

'When you were happy!' I cried aloud, while I hurried back to the town, 'when you felt as carefree as a fish in the water. God in Heaven! did you make it men's destiny only to be happy before they come to reason and after they have lost it again? Poor fellow! – and yet how I envy you your melancholy mind and the confusion of your senses in which you wander. Full of hope, you set out to pick flowers for your queen – in winter – and you are sad because you do not find any and do not understand why you cannot find any. And I – I set out without hope, without a purpose, and return home just as I came. You imagine what a person you would be if the States-General would pay you. Happy creature, who can blame an earthly impediment for his lack of happiness. You do not feel! You do not know that your misery lies in your ruined heart, in your ruined brain, and that all the kings and emperors of this world cannot help you.'

He should perish without comfort who mocks at a sick man for travelling to the remotest medicinal springs, even though these may only increase his sickness and make his final exit more painful! who feels superior to the oppressed heart that sets forth on a pilgrimage to the Holy Sepulchre to free itself from pangs of conscience and sufferings of the soul. Every footstep on an unbeaten path that bruises the feet is a drop of balm for an anguished spirit, and, at the end of a day's journey thus endured, that heart will lie down to rest, eased of many a sorrow. And can you call all this delusion, you armchair quibblers? Delusion! O God, you see my tears! Did You, who created man so poor, have to give him fellow-creatures who deprive him of his little poverty, of his little confidence in You, You All-loving Father! For what is trust in a healing root, in the tears of the vine – what is it but trust in You, that You have endowed everything that surrounds us with the power of healing and soothing which we need every hour? Father, whom I do not know! Father, who once filled my whole soul and has now turned His face from me! Call me to You! Break Your silence! Your silence will not keep this soul from thirsting. And is it possible that a human father could be angry when his unexpectedly returning son embraces him, crying: 'I am back again, Father. Don't be angry that I interrupted my journey, which you wanted me to continue. The world is everywhere the same – trouble and work, reward and pleasure; but what is that to me? I am only happy where you are, and I want to suffer and to enjoy in your presence.' – And You, dear Heavenly Father, would You turn him away from You?

December 1

Wilhelm! the man I wrote to you about, the happy unfortunate man, was a clerk in Lotte's father's office; and a desperate passion for her, which he fostered, concealed, confessed, and which finally cost him his position, has driven him mad. Try to imagine from these dry words how this story upset me when Albert told it as calmly as you will, perhaps, read it.

December 4

I beg you – you see, I am done for; I cannot bear it any longer. Today I sat near her as she played the clavichord, all sorts of tunes and with so much expression. So much! So much! What could I do? Her little sister sat on my knee and dressed her doll. Tears came into my eyes. I bowed my head and caught sight of her wedding ring. The tears ran down my cheeks – and suddenly Lotte began to play the heavenly old melody. All at once my soul was touched by a feeling of consolation, by a memory of the past, of the other occasions when I had heard the song, of the dark intervals of vexation between, of shattered hopes, and then – I walked up and down the room, my heart almost suffocated by the rush of emotions. 'For God's sake,' I said, in a vehement outburst, 'for God's sake, stop!' She paused and looked at me steadily. 'Werther,' she said with a smile that went deep to my heart, 'Werther, you are very sick. You dislike the things you once liked. Go! I beg you, calm yourself!' I tore myself from her sight, and – God! you see my misery and will put an end to it.

December 6

How her image haunts me! Awake or asleep, she fills my entire being. Here, when I close my eyes, here, in my forehead, at the focus of my inner vision, her dark eyes remain. Here! but I cannot put it into words. When I close my eyes, they are there; like an ocean, like an abyss, they lie before me, in me, taking hold of all my thoughts.

What is man, that celebrated demigod! Does he not lack powers just where he needs them most? And when he soars with joy, or sinks into suffering, is he not in both cases held back and restored to dull, cold consciousness at the very moment when he longs to lose himself in the fullness of the Infinite?

[THE EDITOR TO THE READER]

I should very much prefer that documents written in his own hand concerning the last remarkable days of our friend were at our disposal, and that it were not necessary for me to interrupt the sequence of his posthumous letters by direct narration.

I have taken great pains to collect exact facts by word of mouth from those who were well informed about his history; it is a simple story, and, apart from a few details, all evidence agrees. It is only with regard to the emotional attitude of the actors that opinions differ and judgement is divided.

Nothing remains for us but to relate conscientiously what we were able to gather after repeated efforts, to insert the letters found after our friend's death and to consider the smallest note valuable, for the particular reason that it is so difficult to uncover the true and real motives of even a single action by persons who are not of the usual type.

Depression and apathy had more and more rooted themselves in Werther's mind, had become tangled and gradually had taken hold of his whole being. The harmony of his spirit was totally destroyed; an inner heat and vehemence, unsettling all the forces of his nature, produced the most adverse effects and left him finally in an exhausted condition, out of which he struggled more desperately than when fighting against former troubles. The anguish of his heart consumed his spirit's remaining powers, his vivacity, and his bright intellect. He became a depressing companion, more and more unhappy and more unjust due to this unhappiness. So, at least, say Albert's friends; they maintain that Werther had been unable to judge a simple, quiet man to whom had been given a long-wished-for happiness which he hoped to preserve for the years to come, Werther himself being a person who squandered, as it were, every day all he had, and then suffered and was in need in the evening. Albert, they said, had not changed in so short a time; he was still the same person whom Werther had known, had respected and admired from the beginning of their acquaintance. Albert loved Lotte above everything; he was proud of her and wished that everyone recognize her as a woman above women. Can anyone, therefore, blame him for wishing to avoid even the shadow of suspicion, for not being inclined to share this treasure even in the most harmless way? His friends do not deny that Albert frequently left the room when Werther was with Lotte; but this was neither because of hate nor because of antipathy towards his friend, but only because of his feeling that Werther was depressed by his presence.

Lotte's father felt indisposed and could not leave the house. Therefore, he sent his carriage for her, and she drove out to see him. It was a lovely winter day; the first snow had fallen heavily and covered the whole countryside.

The next morning Werther went out to join her and, if Albert could not come, to accompany her home.

The clear weather had no effect on his gloomy mood; a dull weight pressed on his soul; the sad scenes he had recently witnessed were branded in his memory; and nothing but one painful thought after another crossed his brooding mind. Since he was in constant struggle with himself, the circumstances of others, too, seemed to him precarious and confused. He believed that he had destroyed the harmonious relationship between Albert and his wife, and he reproached himself, at the same time, that he mixed with this reproach a secret indignation against the husband.

His thoughts revolved the same questions while he walked along. 'Yes, yes,' he said to himself, grinding his teeth, 'so that is companionship – intimate, friendly, affectionate, sympathetic – a placid and constant loyalty! It is, as a matter of fact, satiety and indifference! Doesn't he take more interest in any trifling piece of business than in his dear, delightful wife? Does he appreciate his good fortune? Does he know how to respect her as she deserves? He has her – very well – he has her – I know that, as I know some other things too. I thought I had become used to it, but it is going to drive me mad; it is going to kill me. And has his friendship stood the test? Does he not already see in my devotion to Lotte a trespassing on his own rights, and in my attentions to her a mute reproach? I know well. I feel that he does not like my coming to the house; he wishes me away and cannot bear my presence.'

Werther often slowed his brisk pace and often, stopping short, seemed to consider going back; but again and again he directed his steps forward and, engaged in these thoughts and soliloquies, and almost against his will, eventually arrived at the hunting lodge.

He went into the house, asking for Lotte and her father, and found the whole family rather upset. The oldest boy told him that a calamity had occurred in Wahlheim; a peasant had been murdered. This piece of news did not make any special impression on Werther. – He entered the room and found Lotte trying to persuade her father not to go to Wahlheim, as he intended to do, in spite of his illness, in order to hold an inquest on the scene of the deed. The identity of the murderer was still unknown; the murdered man had been found that morning in front of his house. There was some suspicion: the victim had been employed by a widow who formerly had another man in her service, and this former servant had left her house after some altercation.

When Werther heard this, he became very excited. 'Is it possible!' he exclaimed, 'I must go there at once; I could not have a quiet moment otherwise.' He rushed to Wahlheim, living over in his mind all he knew of the matter; he did not for one moment doubt that the murder had been committed by the man with whom he had so often talked and who had become so important to him. As Werther crossed under the linden trees to reach the inn where they had brought the dead man, he shuddered at the sight of this formerly beloved place. The threshold, where the children of the neighbours had so often played, was spattered with blood. Love and loyalty, the most beautiful of human emotions, had turned into violence and murder. The great trees were without foliage and rimmed with hoarfrost; the lovely hedges which arched over the low wall of the churchyard were bare; and the snow-covered gravestones could be seen through the gaps.

When he came nearer to the inn, in front of which the whole village had gathered, shouts were suddenly heard. A group of armed men could be seen in the distance, and everyone cried out that the murderer had been arrested. Werther looked in that direction and was no longer in doubt. Yes! it was the young farm hand who had loved the widow so ardently, and whom he had met not long ago roaming about in a state of suppressed rage and silent despair.

'What have you done, you unfortunate fellow!' exclaimed Werther, going up to the prisoner. The young man looked at him quietly and in silence, but said at last, with great calm: 'No one is going to have her; she will have no one!' They took the prisoner into the inn, and Werther left in haste. The horrible and violent meeting had shaken him through and through. For one short moment he had been torn from his melancholy, his gloom and his apathetic resignation; he was overcome by compassion and moved by an irresistible desire to save this man, whose predicament he felt deeply. He considered him, even as a criminal, to be free of real guilt, and identified himself so completely with him that he was certain to be able also to convince others. He could not wait to plead for him; the most persuasive arguments rose to his lips; he walked quickly back to the hunting lodge and could not keep himself from rehearsing, in an undertone, as he went along, the defence he wanted to present to the bailiff.

When he entered the house, he found that Albert had arrived; this dampened his spirits for a moment but he managed, after a while, to control himself and began to impress his opinions on the bailiff with much warmth. The latter shook his head repeatedly, and although Werther with the greatest brilliance, passion and truth put forward everything a human being could say to exculpate another human being, the bailiff remained unmoved, as one can easily understand. He did not even allow our friend to finish his discourse but eagerly contradicted him and reproached him for defending an assassin. He pointed out to him that in this way every law would be annulled, the whole security of the state endangered; and besides, he added, he himself would not be able to do anything in a case like this without taking upon himself the heaviest responsibility. Everything would have to be done in the legal way, and according to instructions.

Werther did not yet surrender, and implored the bailiff to look the other way if someone tried to help the man escape. This, too, the bailiff refused to do. Albert, who had finally joined in the discussion, sided with the older man. Werther was overruled and left in a terrible state of suffering after the bailiff had said to him several times: 'No, there is no help for him.'

How deeply these words must have struck him we can see from a note found among his papers, undoubtedly written that same day.

'There is no help for you, unfortunate man! I see only too well that there is no help for us!'

Albert's final words in the matter of the prisoner, spoken in the bailiff's presence, had disgusted Werther extremely: he thought he noticed in them a slight irritability towards himself. And though, on further reflection, he could not fail to see that both men were probably right, he still felt that he would sacrifice his integrity if he should confess, if he should admit that it was so. A note related to this conflict, which perhaps expresses his whole relation to Albert, has been found among his papers.

'What is the use of my saying to myself again and again: He is honest and good; but it still breaks my heart; I cannot be just.'

As the evening was mild and the snow had begun to melt, Lotte and Albert walked home. On the way Lotte now and then looked back, as though she missed Werther's company. Albert began to speak of Werther; he criticized him, although he did him full justice. He touched upon his unfortunate passion and expressed the wish that it might be possible to send him away. 'I wish this for your sake, as well,' he said; 'and,' he added, 'I implore you to try and turn his attentions to you in another direction and limit his frequent visits, which have already been generally noticed and have caused a certain amount of talk.' Lotte was silent, and Albert seems to have resented her silence, since from that time on he did not mention Werther again, and, whenever she spoke of him, stopped the conversation or changed the subject.

Werther's unsuccessful attempt to help the unfortunate man was the last flare of a fading light; after this he sank only deeper into his grief and apathy and became almost frantic when he heard that he might be called to testify against the man, who had, by now, taken to denying everything.

All the unpleasantnesses that he had ever faced during his official life, the humiliation at the Count's party, as well as every other situation in which he had failed, now came and went in his mind. Somehow he found in all this a justification for his present inactivity; he felt himself cut off from any prospects, incapable of grasping any of those chances by which one takes hold of the occupations of everyday life; and, completely absorbed in his curious emotional state, his way of thinking and his hopeless passion, in the unchanging monotony of a cheerless relationship with the lovable and beloved creature whose peace he disturbed, straining his powers to the utmost but wearing them out without purpose and prospect – he steadily advanced towards his tragic end.

A few posthumous letters are the most convincing evidence of his confused state of mind, of his passion, of his restless actions and efforts, and of his weariness of life; and we are therefore inserting them here.

'December 12

'Dear Wilhelm, my condition is one which those unfortunate people who were thought to be hunted by evil spirits must have experienced. I am sometimes gripped by something that is neither anxiety nor desire; it is an unfamiliar inner rage which threatens to tear open my breast, which clutches at my throat. Oh, it hurts, it hurts! And then I wander about in the dreadful night scenes of this inhuman time of year.

'Last night something drove me out of the house. A thaw had suddenly set in, and I had heard that the river had over-flowed and all the brooks were swollen, and that my dear valley, in its whole length, from Wahlheim down, was flooded. After eleven at night I hurried out. It was terrifying to see from the rock the churning waters whirling in the moonlight, gushing forth over meadows, fields and hedges; and up and down the broad valley one tempestuous sea under the howling wind! And when the moon came out again and rested on a black cloud, and the flood rolled and roared before me in the terrible, magnificent light, I shuddered with awe and also with longing. Oh, with wide-open arms I faced the abyss and breathed: "Down, down!" and was lost in an ecstatic wish to hurl down all my agonies, all my sufferings! to storm along with the waves! Yet I did not have the strength to lift my feet from the ground and end all my agony. – My hourglass has not yet run out, I feel it! Oh, Wilhelm, how gladly would I have surrendered my mortal existence, to tear the clouds apart with that gale and to embrace the floods. Ha! will not the prisoner some day be granted this bliss? – And when I looked down with nostalgic longing at the spot where I had once rested with Lotte, under a willow, after a long walk in the summer's heat, I saw that it was also flooded; I could hardly make out where the willow stood. Wilhelm! And I thought of her meadows, of the whole countryside around the hunting lodge, of our arbour, now shattered by the raving torrent. And a sun shaft of the past pierced through, as when a prisoner has a vision of flocks and herds, meadows and former dignities. I remained standing there! I do not blame myself, for I have the courage to die. I should have – Now I am sitting here like an old woman who gleans her firewood from the fences and begs her bread from door to door, so as to prolong and to ease her wasting and cheerless existence for another short space of time.'

'December 14

'What is this, what has happened to me, dear friend? I am alarmed at myself. Is not my love for her the most sacred, the purest, the most brotherly love? Have I ever felt any culpable desire in my soul? But I will not protest! – And now – dreams! Oh, how right were the instincts of those peoples who attributed such contradictory effects to unknown powers! Last night – I tremble to confess it – I held her in my arms, close to my breast, and covered her love-murmuring lips with endless kisses; my eyes sank into the intoxication of hers. Dear God! Am I culpable that I even now feel a supreme happiness in again living through those glowing moments of joy in all their intensity? Lotte! Lotte! – And this is the end! My mind is in a daze; for a week I have not been able to concentrate, my eyes are full of tears. I feel nowhere at home, and everywhere at home. I have no wish; I make no demand. It would be better for me to leave.'

It was about this time, and under these circumstances, that Werther gradually became confirmed in his resolution to leave this world. Since his return to Lotte, this resolution had been always his last straw, his last hope; but he had made up his mind that it should result in no headlong or rash act; that he would take this step with full premeditation and with the coolest possible determination.

His doubts, and his inner struggle are evident from a note which was probably the beginning of a letter to Wilhelm and was found, without date, among his papers:

'Her presence, her destiny, and her sympathy with mine press the last tears from my ebbing mind.

'To lift the curtain and step behind it! That is all! And why with fear and trembling? Because no one knows what one may see there? or because one cannot return? Or because it is, after all, a peculiarity of our mind to apprehend that confusion and darkness exist in places of which we know nothing definite?'

Finally the tragic thought became more and more familiar to him, and his plan became firm and irrevocable, as witness the following ambiguous letter written to his friend.

December 20

'I owe it to your love, Wilhelm, that you understood my words as you did. Yes, you are right; it would be better for me to leave. Your suggestion that I return to you all does not quite satisfy me; at least I should like to come by a round-about way, especially as we can expect continued frost and good roads. I am very glad that you intend to come and fetch me; if you will only wait another two weeks until I have written you a second letter with further details. No fruit should be picked before it is ripe. And two weeks more or less make a great difference. Please tell my mother that she should pray for her son, who asks forgiveness for all the trouble he has given her. It was my destiny to hurt those to whom I owed happiness. Farewell, dearest friend! May Heaven bless you. Farewell!'

What happened at this time in Lotte's heart, how she felt about her husband and about her unhappy friend, we hardly dare express in words, though, knowing her character, we can form for ourselves a faint idea; and the sensitive soul of a woman will be able to enter into her thought and feelings.

So much is certain – that she had firmly decided by herself to do everything that would keep Werther at a distance and that her hesitation was based on a warm feeling of pity for her friend, as she knew how difficult, yes, how almost impossible, the separation would be for him. She felt, however, at this time, a still greater pressure in herself to act; her husband had become completely silent about this relationship, and, as she herself had never touched the subject again, she now wished all the more to give actual proof that her feelings towards Albert were worthy of his towards her.

On the same day that Werther wrote the letter to his friend which we have given above – it was the Sunday before Christmas – he came to see Lotte in the evening and found her alone. She was busy arranging some toys she had made for her younger sisters and brothers. Werther spoke of the pleasure the children would have and of the times when the unexpected opening of a door and the sight of a Christmas tree trimmed with wax candles and hung with candies and apples made one speechless with delight. 'You also are going to get Christmas presents,' said Lotte, hiding her embarrassment under a sweet smile, 'if you are very good: a little roll of wax tapers and something more.' – 'And what do you call good?' he cried. 'How shall I be? How can I be, dearest Lotte?' – 'Thursday night is Christmas Eve,' she said, 'when the children will come here with my father, and everyone will receive his presents. Do come, too – but not before.' Werther was taken aback. 'Please,' she continued, 'that's how it is; I implore you, for the sake of my peace of mind. It cannot, cannot go on like this.' He turned away and paced up and down the room, muttering to himself that phrase, 'It cannot go on like this.' Lotte, who sensed the terrible state of mind into which her words had thrown him, tried to divert his thoughts with all sorts of questions, but in vain. 'No, Lotte,' he exclaimed, 'I shall not see you again!' – 'Why not?' she asked. 'Werther! You can, you must see us again; only do be reasonable. Oh, why did you have to be born with this violent temper, this uncontrollable clinging passion for everything you touch! Please,' she said, taking his hand, 'be reasonable! Your intellect, your knowledge, your talents, should offer you such a variety of satisfactions! Be a man! Get rid of this hopeless attachment to one who can do nothing but pity you.' He gritted his teeth and gave her a dark look. She kept his hand in hers. 'Think it over calmly, if only for a moment, Werther!' she said. 'Do you not feel that you deceive yourself, that you deliberately ruin yourself? Why must it be I, Werther? Just I, who belong to another? Why must that be? I am afraid, very much afraid, that it is only the impossibility of possessing me that attracts you so much.' – He withdrew his hand, giving her a fixed and angry look. 'Clever!' he mocked, 'very clever. Did Albert perhaps make that remark? Diplomatic, very diplomatic!' – 'Anyone might make it,' she retorted. 'And should there exist in the wide world no other girl who could satisfy the desires of your heart? Take your courage in both hands and look for her – I swear you will find her. I have been worried for a long time, for you and for us, about your self-banishment to this narrow circle. Make up your mind! Travel will and must distract you! Look around and find an object worthy of your love; then come back and enjoy with us the pure happiness of true friendship.'

'All that should be printed,' he said with a frozen smile, 'and we could recommend it to educators. Dear Lotte, give me a little time and everything will turn out well.' – 'Only one thing more, Werther, do not return before Christmas Eve!' He was about to answer when Albert entered. They exchanged a rather frigid 'Good evening!' and walked up and down the room together in some embarrassment. Werther then began a conversation on unimportant matters, but it soon petered out. Albert did the same and then asked his wife about some errands he had wanted her to do for him. When he heard that they had not been done, he spoke some words to her which sounded to Werther cold and even harsh. Werther wanted to leave, but he did not have the power, and he delayed until eight o'clock. All this time he was becoming more and more irritated and angry; and, when the table was set, he took his hat and stick, although Albert invited him to stay for supper. Werther imagined this to be only a conventional gesture of politeness, thanked him coldly, and left.

He returned to his lodging, took the candle from the hand of his servant, who wanted to light him upstairs, and went alone to his room. There he burst into uncontrolled loud weeping, talked to himself in great agitation, pacing excitedly up and down, and finally flung himself on his bed, without taking off his clothes, where his servant found him when, plucking up courage, he went in about eleven o'clock to ask if his master wanted him to pull off his boots. Werther allowed him to do this but told him not to come into the room in the morning before he called.

On Monday morning, the twenty-first of December, he wrote the following letter to Lotte; it was found sealed on his writing desk after his death and was brought to her. I shall insert parts of it here at intervals, as it appears from later events that it was written in a fragmentary manner.

'It is decided, Lotte, that I shall die, and I am writing you this calmly, without any romantic exaltation, on the morning of the day when I shall see you for the last time. When you read this, my dearest, the cold grave will already cover the stiffened body of the restless, unfortunate man who does not know any sweeter way to pass the last moments of his life than to talk to you. I have had a terrible, but ah, what a wonderful night. It has strengthened and confirmed my resolution: to die! Yesterday, when I tore myself away from you, my whole nature in terrible revolt, everything rushing into my heart, and when my hopeless, cheerless existence so close to you overwhelmed me with a ghastly chill – I was hardly able to reach my room; almost beside myself, I fell on my knees, and, O God, you granted me a last consolation of bitter tears! A thousand plans, a thousand hopes raged in my soul, but finally it was there, firmly, wholly, the one last thought: to die! I lay down, and this morning, in the peace of awakening, it is still firm, still strong in my heart: to die! – It is not despair; it is the certainty that I have suffered enough, and that I am sacrificing myself for you. Yes, Lotte! Why should I hide it from you? One of us three must go, and I am to be that one! O my dearest, my wounded heart has been haunted by a terrible demon – often. To murder your husband! Or you! Or myself! Well, so be it! When you walk to the top of the mountain, on a fine summer evening, remember me; how I often came up there from the valley to meet you; and then look across to the churchyard and to my grave, where the wind gently sways the tall grass in the light of the setting sun. – I was calm when I began to write this letter and now, now I am weeping like a child, when all this comes so vividly to my mind.'

Shortly before ten o'clock Werther called his servant and, while dressing, told him that, since he would leave this place in a few days, he should clean his clothes and prepare everything for packing. He also gave him the order to ask everywhere for any bills to his account, to collect some books which he had loaned, and to pay the poor people to whom he had usually given some money every week, a sum covering two months.

He had his dinner served in his room and afterwards rode out to the bailiff's house but did not find him at home. Lost in thought, he walked up and down in the garden, evidently overwhelmed in his mind with all his sad memories in these last months.

The children did not long leave him in peace but followed him and ran up to him, saying that when tomorrow had come, and again tomorrow, and another day after that, they would go to Lotte's and get their Christmas presents; and they told him about the marvels which their childish imagination promised them. 'Tomorrow,' he cried, 'and again tomorrow and still another day after that!' and kissed them all affectionately and was about to leave when the smallest boy tried to whisper something in his ear. He confided that his big brothers had written beautiful New Year's greetings, *so* big!

one for Papa, one for Albert and Lotte, and one for Herr Werther, too! and that they would themselves deliver them early on New Year's Day. This almost broke Werther's heart. He gave something to each of the children, mounted his horse, sent his greetings to the old man, and rode away with tears in his eyes.

About five o'clock in the afternoon he arrived at his lodging and ordered the housemaid to see that the fire be kept burning until late that night. He told his servant to pack his books and his linen at the bottom of his trunk and to make a bundle of his clothes. It was probably then he wrote the following passage of his last letter to Lotte:

'You do not expect me! You think I shall obey you and not see you again until Christmas Eve. O Lotte! today or never again. On Christmas Eve you will hold this piece of paper in your hand, trembling and covering it with your sweet tears. I will, I must! Oh, how relieved I am now that I have made up my mind.'

Meanwhile, Lotte was in a peculiar frame of mind. After her last talk with Werther she had realized how hard it would be for her to be separated from him, and how he would suffer if he had to leave her.

She had mentioned almost casually in Albert's presence that Werther would not return until Christmas Eve; and Albert had ridden out to see an official in the neighbourhood with whom he had to settle some business, and where he would have to spend the night.

Now she sat at home alone – none of her family was with her – and she gave herself up to her thoughts, which quietly moved over her circumstances. She saw herself united for ever to the husband whose love and loyalty she knew, to whom she was deeply devoted and whose calmness of disposition and whose trustworthiness seemed to be intended by Providence for a good wife to build on it her life's happiness; she keenly realized how much he would always mean to her and to her children. On the other hand, Werther had become very dear to her heart; from the very beginning of their acquaintance the harmony of their minds had showed itself in the most pleasant way, and continued friendly relations with him as well as their many mutual experiences had made a lasting impression on her heart. She had become accustomed to share with him everything of interest she felt or thought; and his departure threatened to create a great gap in her existence which could not be filled again. Oh, if she only had the power to transform him this very moment into a brother, how happy she would be! – had she only been fortunate enough to marry him off to one of her friends, or could she be allowed to hope that his friendship with Albert might be completely restored!

She passed all her friends in review, one after the other, but found a flaw in each and could not think of one girl to whom she would not have begrudged Werther.

As she pondered on all this, she felt for the first time, keenly if subconsciously, that in her heart of hearts she secretly wished to keep him for herself, at the same time saying to herself that she could not, should not, keep him; her innocent, noble nature, usually so light and resourceful, felt the weight of a melancholy that sees all hope for happiness barred. Her heart was oppressed, and a dark mist lay upon her eyes.

It was half past six when she heard Werther coming up the stairs; she immediately recognized his step, and his voice as he asked for her. Her heart beat violently, we may say almost for the first time, at his arrival. She would have preferred to have had him told she was not at home; and when he came into the room, she received him in a kind of frantic confusion with the words, 'You have broken your promise!' – 'I did not promise anything,' was his answer. – 'But you could at least have respected my request,' she said. 'I asked you not to come, for my peace and yours!'

She did not quite know what she did or said as she sent a message to some friends because she did not wish to be alone with Werther. He had brought her some books and asked her about others while she wished, now, that her friends would arrive, now, that they would not. The maid returned, bringing a message that both girls were unable to come.

At first she thought of having her maid sit with her work in the adjoining room, but she then changed her mind. Werther paced up and down the room, and she went to the clavichord and began to play a minuet; but it did not go smoothly. She recovered herself and sat down quietly beside Werther, who had taken his customary place on the sofa.

'Don't you have anything to read to me?' she asked. He had nothing. 'In my drawer over there,' she began, 'is your translation of some of the songs of Ossian. I have not yet read them because I always hoped you would read them to me. But lately there has never been any time or occasion.' He smiled and took out the songs; a shudder ran through him as he took them in his hands, and his eyes filled with tears as he looked at the written pages. He sat down again and read:

'Star of descending night! fair is thy light in the west! Thou liftest thy unshorn head from thy cloud; thy steps are stately on thy hill. What dost thou behold in the plain? The stormy winds are laid. The murmur of the torrent comes from afar. Roaring waves climb the distant rock. The flies of evening are on their feeble wings; the hum of their course is on the field. What dost thou behold, fair light? But thou dost smile and depart. The waves come with joy around thee; they bathe thy lovely hair. Farewell, thou silent beam! Let the light of Ossian's soul arise!

'And it does arise in its strength! I behold my departed friends. Their gathering is on Lora, as in the days of other years. Fingal comes like a watery column of mist; his heroes are around, and, see! the bards of song – grey-haired Ullin! stately Ryno! Alpin, with the tuneful voice! the soft complaint of Minona! How are you changed, my friends, since the days of Selma's feast, when we contended, like gales of spring as they fly along the hill, and bend by turns the feebly whistling grass.

'Minona came forth in her beauty, with downcast look and tearful eye. Her hair flew slowly on the blast that rushed unfrequent from the hill. The souls of the heroes were sad when she raised the tuneful voice. Often had they seen the grave of Salgar, the dark dwelling of white-bosomed Colma. Colma left alone on the hill, with all her voice of song! Salgar promised to come; but the night descended around. Hear the voice of Colma, when she sat alone on the hill!

'COLMA: It is night; I am alone, forlorn on the hill of storms. The wind is heard on the mountain. The torrent is howling down the rock. No hut receives me from the rain; forlorn on the hill of winds!

'Rise, moon, from behind thy clouds! Stars of the night, arise! Lead me, some light, to the place where my love rests from the chase alone! His bow near him unstrung, his dogs panting around him! But here I must sit alone by the rock of the mossy stream. The stream and the wind roar aloud. I hear not the voice of my love! Why delays my Salgar; why the chief of the hill his promise? Here is the rock, and here the tree; here is the roaring stream! Thou didst promise with night to be here. Ah, whither is my Salgar gone? With thee I would fly from my father, with thee from my brother of pride. Our race have long been foes: we are not foes, O Salgar!

'Cease a little while, O wind! stream, be thou silent awhile! Let my voice be heard around; let my wanderer hear me! Salgar! it is Colma who calls. Here is the tree and the rock. Salgar, my love, I am here! Why delayest thou thy coming? Lo! the calm moon comes forth. The flood is bright in the vale; the rocks are grey on the steep. I see him not on the brow. His dogs come not before him with tidings of his near approach. Here I must sit alone!

'Who lie on the heath beside me? Are they my love and my brother? Speak to me, O my friends! To Colma they give no reply. Speak to me: I am alone! My soul is tormented with fears. Ah, they are dead! Their swords are red from the fight. Oh, my brother! my brother! why hast thou slain my Salgar? Why, O Salgar! hast thou slain my brother? Dear were ye both to me! what shall I say in your praise? Thou wert fair on the hill among thousands! he was terrible in fight! Speak to me! hear my voice! hear me, sons of my love! They are silent, silent for ever! Cold, cold are their breasts of clay! Oh, from the rock on the hill, from the top of the windy steep, speak ye ghosts of the dead! Speak, I will not be afraid! Whither are ye gone to rest? In what cave of the hill shall I find the departed? No feeble voice is on the gale: no answer half drowned in the storm!

'I sit in my grief: I wait for morning in my tears! Rear the tomb, ye friends of the dead. Close it not till Colma comes. My life flies away like a dream. Why should I stay behind? Here shall I rest with my friends, by the stream of the sounding rock. When night comes on the hill – when the loud winds arise, my ghost shall stand in the blast, and mourn the death of my friends. The hunter shall hear from his booth; he shall fear, but love my voice! For sweet shall my voice be for my friends: pleasant were her friends to Colma.

'Such was thy song, Minona, softly blushing daughter of Torman. Our tears descended for Colma, and our souls were sad! Ullin came with his harp; he gave the song of Alpin. The voice of Alpin was pleasant; the soul of Ryno was a beam of fire! But they had rested in the narrow house; their voice had ceased in Selma! Ullin had returned one day from the chase before the heroes fell. He heard their strife on the hill; their song was soft, but sad. They mourned the fall of Morar, first of mortal men! His soul was like the soul of Fingal; his sword like the sword of Oscar. But he fell, and his father mourned; his sister's eyes were full of tears, the sister of car-borne Morar. She retired from the song of Ullin, like the moon in the west, when she foresees the shower, and hides her fair head in a cloud. I touched the harp with Ullin; the song of mourning rose!

'RYNO: The wind and the rain are past; calm is the noon of day. The clouds are divided in heaven. Over the green hills flies the inconstant sun. Red through the stony vale comes down the stream of the hill. Sweet are thy murmurs, O stream! but more sweet is the voice I hear. It is the voice of Alpin, the son of song, mourning for the dead! Bent is his head of age; red his tearful eye. Alpin, thou son of song, why alone on the silent hill? why complainest thou, as a blast in the wood, as a wave on the lonely shore?

'ALPIN: My tears, O Ryno! are for the dead – my voice for those that have passed away. Tall thou art on the hill; fair among the sons of the vale. But thou shalt fall like Morar; the mourner shall sit on thy tomb. The hills shall know thee no more; thy bow shall lie in thy hall unstrung!

'Thou wert swift, O Morar! as a roe on the desert; terrible as a meteor of fire. Thy wrath was as the storm; thy sword in battle as lightning in the field. Thy voice was a stream after rain, like thunder on distant hills. Many fell by thy arms: they were consumed in the flames of thy wrath. But when thou didst return from war, how peaceful was thy brow! Thy face was like the sun after rain, like the moon in the silence of night; calm as the breast of the lake when the loud wind is laid.

'Narrow is thy dwelling now! dark the place of thine abode! With three steps I compass thy grave, O thou who was so great before! Four stones, with their heads of moss, are the only memorial of thee. A tree with scarce a leaf, long grass which whistles in the wind, mark to the hunter's eye the grave of the mighty Morar. Morar! thou art low indeed. Thou hast no mother to mourn thee, no maid with her tears of love. Dead is she that brought thee forth. Fallen is the daughter of Morglan.

'Who on his staff is this? Who is this whose head is white with age, whose eyes are red with tears, who quakes at every step? It is thy father, O Morar! the father of no son but thee. He heard of thy fame in war, he heard of foes dispersed. He heard of Morar's renown; why did he not hear of his wound? Weep, thou father of Morar! Weep, but thy son heareth thee not. Deep is the sleep of the dead – low their pillow of dust. No more shall he hear thy voice – no more awake at thy call. When shall it be morn in the grave, to bid the slumberer awake? Farewell, thou bravest of men! thou conqueror in the field! But the field shall see thee no more, nor the dark wood be lightened with the splendour of thy steel. Thou hast left no son. The song shall preserve thy name. Future times shall hear of thee – they shall hear of the fallen Morar!

'The grief of all arose, but most the bursting sigh of Armin. He remembers the death of his son, who fell in the days of his youth. Carmor was near the hero, the chief of the echoing Galmal. Why burst the sigh of Armin? he said. Is there a cause to mourn? The song comes with its music to melt and please the soul. It is like soft mist that, rising from a lake, pours on the silent vale; the green flowers are filled with dew, but the sun returns in his strength, and the mist is gone. Why art thou sad, O Armin, chief of the sea-surrounded Gorma?

'Sad I am, nor small is my cause of woe! Carmor, thou hast lost no son, thou hast lost no daughter of beauty. Colgar the valiant lives, and Annira, fairest maid. The boughs of thy house ascend, O Carmor! But Armin is the last of his race. Dark is thy bed, O Daura! deep they sleep in the tomb! When shalt thou wake with thy songs – with all thy voice of music? Arise, winds of autumn, arise; blow along the heath! Streams of the mountains roar; roar, tempests in the groves of my oaks! Walk through broken clouds, O moon! show thy pale face at intervals; bring to my mind the night when all my children fell – when Arindal the mighty fell, when Daura the lovely failed. Daura, my daughter, thou wert fair – fair as the moon on Fura, white as the driven snow, sweet as the breathing gale. Arindal, thy bow was strong, thy spear was swift on the field, thy lock was like mist on the wave, thy shield a red cloud in a storm! Armar, renowned in war, came and sought Daura's love. He was not long refused: fair was the hope of their friends.

'Erath, son of Odgal, repined: his brother had been slain by Armar. He came disguised like a son of the sea; fair was his skiff on the wave, white his locks of age, calm his serious brow. Fairest of women, he said, lovely daughter of Armin! a rock not distant in the sea bears a tree on its side: red shines the fruit afar. There Armar waits for Daura. I come to carry his love! She went – she called on Armar. Naught answered but the son of the rock. Armar, my love, my love! why tormentest thou me with fear? Hear, son of Arnart, hear! it is Daura who calleth thee. Erath the traitor fled laughing to the land. She lifted up her voice – she called for her brother and her father. Arindal! Armin! none to relieve you, Daura.

'Her voice came over the sea. Arindal, my son, descended from the hill, rough in the spoils of the chase. His arrows rattled by his side; his bow was in his hand, five dark-grey dogs attended his steps. He saw fierce Erath on the shore; he seized and bound him to an oak. Thick wind the thongs of the hide around his limbs; he loads the winds with his groans. Arindal ascends the deep in his boat to bring Daura to land. Armar came in his wrath, and let fly the grey-feathered shaft. It sung, it sunk in thy heart. O Arindal, my son! for Erath the traitor thou diest. The oar is stopped at once: he panted on the rock and expired. What is thy grief, O Daura, when round thy feet is poured thy brother's blood? The boat is broken in twain. Armar plunges into the sea to rescue his Daura, or die. Sudden a blast from a hill came over the waves; he sank, and he rose no more.

'Alone, on the sea-beat rock, my daughter was heard to complain; frequent and loud were her cries. What could her father do? All night I stood on the shore: I saw her by the faint beam of the moon. All night I heard her cries. Loud was the wind; the rain beat hard on the hill. Before morning appeared, her voice was weak; it died away like the evening breeze among the grass of the rocks. Spent with grief, she expired, and left thee, Armin, alone. Gone is my strength in war, fallen my pride among women. When the storms aloft arise, when the north lifts the wave on high, I sit by the sounding shore, and look on the fatal rock. Often, by the setting moon, I see the ghosts of my children; half view-less they walk in mournful conference together.'

A flood of tears which rushed from Lotte's eyes, giving relief to her oppressed heart, interrupted Werther's reading.

He threw down the paper, took her hand, and broke into bitter sobs. Lotte rested her head on her arm and covered her eyes with her handkerchief. Both were in a terrible emotional state. They felt their own misery in the fate of the noble Gaels, felt it together and their tears mingled. Werther's lips and eyes burned on Lotte's arm, and a shudder ran through her body. She wanted to escape, but grief and pity weighed upon her with leaden force. She took a deep breath in order to control herself and, sobbing, asked Werther, in a lovely voice, to continue. Werther trembled; he thought his heart would break, but he took up the paper and read, his voice shaking with emotion:

'Why dost thou awake me, O breath of spring? Thou dost woo me and say: I cover thee with the dew of Heaven! But the time of my fading is near, near is the storm that will scatter my leaves! Tomorrow the wanderer shall come, he that saw me in my beauty shall come. His eyes will search me in the field around, and will not find me.'

The whole power of these words rushed upon the unhappy man. Completely desperate, he threw himself at Lotte's feet, seized her hands, pressed them upon his eyes and against his forehead; and an apprehension of his terrible intention seemed to brush against her soul. A tumult rose in her; she took his hands, pressed them against her breast and, bending towards him with a mournful gesture, their glowing cheeks touched. The world was lost to them. He clasped her in his arms, held her close against him, and covered her trembling lips with a shower of passionate kisses. 'Werther!' she cried with choking voice, turning away, 'Werther!' She pushed him away with a feeble hand. 'Werther!' she cried in a calmer tone, and with admirable dignity. He did not resist, released her from his embrace, and threw himself almost senseless on the floor at her feet. She quickly got up and said in a terrified confusion, torn between love and indignation, 'This was the last time, Werther! You will not see me again.' And with a look full of love for the unhappy man, she rushed into the next room and locked the door behind her.

Werther stretched out his arms towards her but did not have the courage to hold her back. He lay on the floor, his head on the sofa, and remained in his position for more than half an hour, when a noise brought him to himself. It was the maid, who wanted to set the table. He walked up and down the room, and, when he saw that he was again alone, he went to the door of the next room and called gently, 'Lotte! Lotte! only one word more! a farewell!' There was no answer. He waited and implored and again waited; then he rushed away, calling, 'Farewell, Lotte! farewell for ever!'

He came to the town gate. The watchman, who already knew him, opened it for him without a word. It drizzled between rain and snow; and a little before eleven he knocked at the gate again. His servant noticed, when Werther returned to his lodging, that his master had arrived hatless. He did not dare to mention this and helped him to undress; his clothes were wet through. His hat was later found on a steep bluff overlooking the valley, and it is hard to explain how he could have climbed to that height in the dark and wet night without falling to his death.

He went to bed and slept a long time. His servant found him writing when he brought the coffee he ordered the next morning. He was adding the following lines to his letter to Lotte:

'For the last time, then, for the last time I open my eyes to this world. Alas, they shall not see the sun again, for today it is hidden behind a veil of mist. Now, Nature, mourn your son, your friend, your lover who nears his end. Lotte, this is a unique sensation, and yet it resembles a twilight dream, when one says to oneself: "This is the last morning. The last!" Lotte, these words mean nothing to me. Am I not standing here alive, in the possession of all my faculties, and yet tomorrow I shall lie prostrate and motionless on the ground. To die! What does that mean? Look, we are dreaming when we speak of death. I have seen many people die; but so limited is the human mind that it has no clear conception of the beginning and the end of our existence. At this moment I am still mine, yours! yours, my beloved! And the next moment – separated, divorced from you, perhaps for ever? – No, Lotte, no! How can I *not* be? How can you *not* be? We *are* after all. – *Not* be! What does that mean? It is only a word, a mere sound, which stirs nothing in me. – Dead, Lotte! thrown into the cold ground, so narrow, so dark! – I once had a friend who meant everything to me in my awkward youth; she died, and I followed the bier and stood beside her grave when they lowered the coffin, and the ropes that held it whirred as they were loosened and jerked up again; and then the first shovelful of earth fell with a thud, and the fearful chest gave back a hollow sound, more muffled every time, until it was completely covered with earth. I fell to the ground beside the grave – shocked, shaken, frightened, heartbroken; but I did not know what had happened to me – what will happen to me. – Death! The grave! I do not understand these words.

'Oh, forgive me! forgive me! Yesterday! It should have been the last moment of my life. O angel! for the first time, quite without doubt, I had in my heart of hearts the glowing thought: she loves me! she loves me! My lips are still burning with the sacred fire kindled by yours; there is a fresh warm feeling of happiness in my heart. Forgive me! forgive me!

'Oh, I knew that you loved me – knew it from the first warmhearted glance, from the first pressure of your hand; and yet, when I was not with you, when I saw Albert at your side, I was again tormented by feverish doubts.

'Do you remember the flowers you sent me when you had been unable to say one word to me or give me your hand at that hateful party? Oh, I was on my knees before them almost all night; and, for me, they put the seal on your love. But alas! these impressions faded, as the feeling of God's mercy gradually fades from the soul of the believer after it had been showered on him in holy and visible symbols.

'All this is transitory, but no Eternity shall extinguish the warm life that I drank yesterday from your lips and that I still feel within me. She loves me! This arm held her, these lips have trembled on her lips, this mouth has stammered against hers. She is mine! You are mine, Lotte, for ever!

'And what does it mean that Albert is your husband? Husband! That may be for this world – and in this world it is sin that I love you, that I should like to snatch you from his arms into mine. Sin? Very well, and I am punishing myself for it; for this sin, which I have tasted in all its rapture, which gave me life-giving balm and strength. From now on you are mine! mine, Lotte! I go before you. I go to my Father, to your Father. I shall put my sorrow before Him, and He will comfort me until you come; and I shall fly to meet you and clasp you and stay with you before the Infinite Being in an eternal embrace.

'I do not dream; I am not deluded! So near to the grave, I see everything with great clearness. We shall be! we shall see one another again, see your mother. I shall see her, find her and ah! pour out all my heart to her, your mother, your very image.'

Shortly before eleven o'clock Werther asked his servant if he thought Albert had returned. The boy said, 'Yes, I saw his horse led into the stables.' Werther then gave him an unsealed note which contained the words:

'Will you be good enough to lend me your pistols for my intended journey. And goodbye.'

Lotte had slept little that night; everything she had feared had happened, in a manner which she had neither anticipated nor imagined. Her blood, that usually ran so innocently and lightly through her veins, was in a feverish tumult; a thousand emotions tormented her great soul. Was it the passion of Werther's embraces that reverberated in her heart? Was it indignation at his boldness? Was it a dissatisfied comparison of her present condition with those days of completely candid and frank innocence, when she had unclouded confidence in herself? How was she to face her husband? How to confess to him a scene which she might indeed describe without reserve, and yet of which she did not dare to make a clean breast? She and Albert had not talked to each other freely for so long. Should she now be the first to break silence and to give her husband such an unexpected disclosure just at the wrong time? She was afraid that even the mere mention of Werther's visit would make a disagreeable impression; and now this unexpected catastrophe! Was she allowed to hope that her husband would see the whole affair in the right light, would accept it entirely without prejudice? And could she wish him to read her heart? And yet, could she deceive the man in whose eyes she had always been like a crystal-clear glass – open and candid – and from whom she had been incapable of concealing any emotion, nor had wished to conceal any? All these questions worried her and made her uneasy; and all the while her thoughts kept returning to Werther, who was lost to her; whom she could not give up; whom she had, unfortunately, to leave to himself; and to whom, when he lost her, nothing was left.

How heavily the thought of the deadlock between Albert and herself weighed now on her heart, a deadlock which, at this moment, she could not explain. Even such sensible and good-natured people tend to become tongue-tied with each other, because of some latent differences of opinion; each of them thinking himself right and the other wrong; and the situation then becomes so complicated and exasperating that it is impossible to untie the knot at the critical moment on which all depends. If some happy intimacy had brought them together before this; if love and tolerance had mutually revived between them and opened their hearts – perhaps our friend might have been saved.

And yet, another strange circumstance played a part. Werther had never, as we know from his letters, kept his longing to depart from this world a secret. Albert had often argued with him on the subject; and this subject had several times been talked over by Lotte and her husband. The latter had not only felt a strong revulsion against such an act but also more than once said with a kind of irritability, which was otherwise quite incompatible with his character, that he believed he had sufficient reason to doubt the seriousness of any such intention on Werther's part; he had even sometimes allowed himself to ridicule the whole thing and mentioned his sceptical attitude to Lotte. This may have set her mind at rest for a time, whenever her thoughts presented to her the tragic picture – but it also prevented her from communicating to her husband the anxieties that tormented her at this moment.

Albert returned, and Lotte welcomed him with an embarrassed haste. He was not in a cheerful mood, as he had not been successful in settling his business, and the bailiff in the neighbourhood had been a rigid, narrow-minded man. Besides, the roughness of the road had put him in a bad temper.

He asked if anything had happened, and she answered, much too quickly, 'Werther was here last night.' Then Albert asked if any letters had arrived, and was told that one letter and some packets had been put in his room. He went there, and Lotte was alone. The presence of the man whom she loved and respected had made a fresh impression upon her. She remembered his generosity, his love and his kindness, and felt more at ease. A secret impulse urged her to follow him; she took her needlework and went to his room as she often was in the habit of doing. She found him busy opening the packets and reading their contents. A few apparently contained rather unpleasant news. Lotte asked him several questions, which he answered curtly, and he then went to his high desk to write.

In this manner they passed an hour together, and Lotte's spirits were sinking lower and lower. She felt how difficult it would be for her to reveal to her husband, even if he were in the best of moods, all that weighed on her soul; and she lapsed into a sadness which distressed her only the more as she tried to hide it and choke down her tears.

When Werther's young servant appeared, she became very embarrassed. He handed the note to Albert, who calmly turned to his wife and said, 'Give him the pistols!' – 'I wish him a pleasant journey,' he said to the youth. Lotte was thunderstruck; she staggered when she tried to get up, and almost fainted. Trembling, she walked slowly to the wall, took down the pistols, wiped off the dust, hesitated, and would have hesitated still longer if Albert's questioning glance had not urged her on. She gave the fatal weapons to the young man without saying a word; and when he had left the house, she gathered her work together and went to her room in a state of unspeakable anxiety. Her heart prophesied to her the most terrible possibilities. Her first thought was to throw herself at her husband's feet and to tell him the whole truth about last night's events, as well as her own guilt and her forebodings. But again she could not even hope to persuade her husband to go and see Werther. Meanwhile, the table had been set, and a good friend of Lotte's, who had stopped in for a moment to ask her something, said she would go immediately but stayed, making conversation during the meal more bearable. They pulled themselves together; they talked; they told stories, and were even able to forget.

The boy brought the pistols to Werther, who was delighted to hear that Lotte herself had handed them to him. He ordered bread and wine; then sent the boy out for his own supper, sat down and wrote:

'They have passed through your hands; you have wiped the dust from them. I kiss them a thousand times because you have touched them; and you, Heavenly Spirit, approve of my decision! And you, Lotte, offer me the weapon – you, from whose hands I wished to receive death, and ah! not receive it. Oh, how I questioned my servant! You trembled when you gave them to him, but you did not send me any farewell. Alas, alas! no farewell! Should you have closed your heart to me because of the moment that pledged me to you for ever? Lotte, a thousand years cannot efface that memory! And I feel that you cannot hate him who burns with love for you.'

After supper he told the boy to finish packing, tore up many papers, and went out to pay some small remaining debts. He returned and again went out, through the town gate, in spite of the rain, to the Count's garden. He wandered

about the neighbouring countryside, came back at nightfall
and again wrote:

'Wilhelm, I have seen the fields, the woods, and the sky for
the last time. Farewell, you, too! Dear Mother, forgive me!
Comfort her, Wilhelm! God bless you both! My affairs are all
settled. Farewell! We shall meet again and with more joy.'

'Albert, I have repaid your kindness badly, and yet you will
forgive me. I have disturbed the peace of your home; I have
destroyed your confidence in each other. Farewell! I am
about to make an end. Oh, if my death could make you
happy again. Albert! Albert! Make the angel happy, and with
this I implore God's blessing on you!'

In the evening he spent a great deal of time looking
through his papers. He tore some up and threw them into
the fire and sealed some packets addressed to Wilhelm. These
contained short articles and fragmentary ideas, some of
which I have read; and around ten o'clock, when he asked
that the fire be replenished and that he be brought a bottle of
wine, he sent his servant, whose room, like the other bed-
rooms of the house, was at the far end, to bed. The boy lay
down without taking off his clothes so as to be ready at an
early hour, for his master had told him that the post horses
would be in front of the house before six o'clock the
next morning.

'After eleven

'Everything is so quiet around me, and my soul is so calm. I
thank you, God, who gives these last moments such warmth,
such strength! I walk to the window, my dearest, and see –
still see – some stars in the eternal sky, shining through the
stormy, fleeting clouds. No, you will not fall! The Eternal
Father carries you near His heart, and me as well. I see the
stars that make up the shaft of the Dipper, my favourite
constellation. When I used to leave you at night and had
passed your gate, these stars were just opposite me. How
often have I looked up at them with rapture! How often have

I raised my hands to them, regarding them as a symbol, a hallowed token of my happiness. And still now – O Lotte, does not everything remind me of you? Are you not always near me; and have I not, like a child, greedily snatched all sorts of trifles which you, dear saint, had touched!

'Precious silhouette! I return it to you, Lotte, and ask you to take good care of it. I have covered it with many, many kisses; I have greeted it a thousand times whenever I went out or came home.

'I have written your father a note and asked him to take care of my body. In the churchyard are two linden trees, in a far corner, next to the field; there I should like to rest. He can and will do this service to his friend. Do ask him, too. I do not like to hurt the feelings of devout Christians, who might not want to rest beside a poor, unhappy man. Oh, I wished you would bury me by the wayside or in a remote valley, where priest and Levite may pass by the marked stone, thankful that they are not as other men, and the Samaritan may shed a tear.

'Here, Lotte! I do not shudder to grasp the cold and dreadful cup from which I am about to drink the ecstasy of death. Your hand gave it to me, and I do not flinch. All, all the desires and hopes of my life are fulfilled! So cold, so rigid to knock at the iron gate of death.

'Had I been granted the happiness to die for *you!*, Lotte, to sacrifice myself for *you!* I would die bravely, I would die cheerfully, if I could restore to you the peace and happiness of your life. But alas! it is reserved for only a very few noble souls to shed their blood for those who are dear to them, and by their deaths to fan the flame of life of their friends to a new and wonderfully increased splendour.

'I want to be buried in these clothes I wear, Lotte! You have touched them and hallowed them. I have also asked your father to carry out this request. My soul hovers above the coffin. Do not let them look through my pockets. This rose-coloured ribbon which you wore on your breast the first time I saw you, surrounded by your children – oh, give them a thousand kisses, and tell them the fate of their unhappy friend. The darling children! they swarm around me. Ah, how quickly I grew fond of you; I could not keep away from you from the first moment. – Let this ribbon be buried with me; you gave it to me on my birthday. How eagerly I accepted all this! – Ah, I did not think the way would end here! Be calm! Please, be calm!

'They are loaded. – The clock strikes twelve. – So be it! Lotte! Lotte! Farewell! Farewell!'

A neighbour saw the flash of the powder and heard the shot; but, as everything remained quiet, he did not pay further attention to it.

Next morning, around six o'clock, the servant entered the room with a candle. He found his master lying on the floor, the pistol beside him, and blood everywhere. He called, he touched him; no answer came, only a rattling in the throat. He ran for a doctor and for Albert. Lotte heard the bell; a tremor seized all her limbs. She woke her husband; they got up, and the servant, sobbing and stammering, told the news. Lotte fainted and fell to the ground at Albert's feet.

When the doctor arrived, he found the unfortunate young man on the floor, past help; his pulse was still beating; all his limbs were paralysed. He had shot himself through the head above the right eye, and his brain was laid bare. They bled him needlessly; the blood flowed; he was still breathing.

From the blood on the back of the armchair they concluded that he had committed the act while sitting at his writing desk. He had then slid down and rolled around the chair in convulsions. He was lying on his back, facing the window, enfeebled, fully dressed, in his boots, his blue coat and yellow waistcoat.

The house, the neighbourhood, the town, was in a tumult. Albert came in. They had laid Werther on his bed and bandaged his forehead; his face was already the face of a dead man; he did not move. His lungs still gave forth a dreadful rattling sound, now weak, now stronger; they expected the end.

He had drunk only one glass of the wine. Lessing's *Emilia Galotti* lay open on his desk.

I cannot describe Albert's consternation, Lotte's distress.

On hearing the news, the old bailiff rode up to the house at full speed; he kissed his dying friend and wept bitter tears. His older sons arrived soon afterwards on foot; they knelt beside the bed with expressions of uncontrollable grief and kissed Werther's hands and mouth; the oldest, whom Werther had always loved most, clung to him to the bitter end, when they had to tear the boy away by force. Werther died at noon. The presence of the bailiff and the arrangements he made prevented a public disturbance. That night around eleven the bailiff had Werther buried at the place he himself had chosen. The old man and his sons followed the body to the grave; Albert was unable to. Lotte's life was in danger. Workmen carried the coffin. No clergyman attended.

ELECTIVE AFFINITIES

A NOVEL

Translated by David Constantine

PART ONE

CHAPTER ONE

EDUARD – let that be the name we give to a wealthy baron in the best years of his life – Eduard had spent the loveliest hours of an April afternoon in his nursery grafting young trees with shoots newly arrived for him. The job was just finished; he was putting the tools away in their case and contemplating his handiwork with some satisfaction when the Gardener approached and stood smiling at his master's willingness and industry.

'Have you seen my wife?' Eduard asked, making ready to leave.

'Over in the new grounds,' the Gardener replied. 'It is today she finishes the little summer-house she has been building by the rocks facing the Hall. Everything has turned out beautifully. Your Lordship will be sure to like it. The views are excellent: the village down below, the church a little to the right – you look out almost directly over the steeple – the Hall and the gardens opposite.'

'Indeed,' said Eduard, 'a few steps from here and I could see the people working.'

'And to the right', the Gardener continued, 'the valley opens and you can see into the distance over the fields with all their trees. Such a pleasant prospect. The path up the rocks is very prettily done. Her Ladyship knows what she is about. It is a pleasure to work for her.'

'Go now,' said Eduard, 'and ask will she be so kind as to wait for me. Say I look forward to the pleasure of seeing her new creation.'

The Gardener hurried away, and Eduard soon followed.

He descended the terraces, surveying, as he passed, the greenhouses and the forcing-beds; and reaching the water crossed it by a bridge, to where the path into the new grounds forked. One way, which led across the graveyard pretty directly to the rocks, he avoided, and took the other which bore left on a rather longer route through pleasant greenery, climbing gently. Where the two paths came together again he sat down for a moment on a convenient seat; then began the climb itself, and was brought by all manner of steps and terraces along the narrow path, rising more or less steeply, finally to the summer-house.

Charlotte was at the door to welcome her husband. He sat where she placed him so that through windows and door he could oversee at a glance the different views, in which the landscape appeared like a sequence of framed pictures. He was pleased, and expressed the hope that spring would soon bring to everything a yet more abundant life. 'My only criticism', he added, 'would be that one is perhaps a little cramped here.'

'Room enough for the two of us,' Charlotte replied.

'There is indeed,' said Eduard, 'and for a third, no doubt.'

'Why not?' Charlotte replied, 'and even for a fourth. For a larger company we shall make arrangements elsewhere.'

'Since we are here by ourselves,' said Eduard, 'and won't be disturbed and our mood is so cheerful and tranquil, let me admit that for some time now I have had something to say to you and have not been able to, although it is necessary that I should.'

'I rather thought so,' Charlotte replied, 'from your manner lately.'

'And to be frank,' Eduard continued, 'were it not that I am anxious to catch tomorrow morning's post and that we must make up our minds today, I should perhaps have kept silent a while longer.'

'What is it then?' Charlotte asked in a manner that was amicable and encouraging.

'It concerns our friend, the Captain,' Eduard answered. 'You know how unhappily he, like many others, is placed now through no fault of his own. How painful it must be for a man of his knowledge, talents, and abilities to find himself without

proper employment and – I will say at once what I should like
for him: I should like us to have him here for a time.'

'That will need careful consideration,' Charlotte replied. 'It
will need to be looked at from more than one point of view.'

'Let me tell you what *I* think,' said Eduard in reply. 'There
was in his last letter a sense of very deep discontent. Not that
he is in any material need. He is quite capable of living frugally
when he must, and I have myself seen to all the essentials.
Nor does it trouble him to accept things from me. Throughout our lives we have got so much into one another's debt
that it would be impossible now to calculate how our credit
and debit with one another stands. His real misery is that he
has no employment. It was always his pleasure, indeed his
passion in life, to use the many different talents he has
developed in himself daily and hourly for the benefit of
others. And now to be idle, or to engage in further study
and acquire new skills, being unable to use what he already
possesses in such abundance – all in all, my darling, his
situation is an unhappy one and he feels it worse and worse,
being so isolated.'

'But I thought he had had offers from various quarters,'
said Charlotte. 'I myself wrote on his behalf to several very
active men and women among my friends, and not without
good results, as I believed.'

'That is true,' Eduard replied, 'but these various opportunities, these offers themselves, further torment and upset him.
None of the situations is suitable. He is not being asked to
perform any real work, but to sacrifice himself – his time, his
convictions, his whole way of being – and that he cannot do.
The more I think about his predicament, the more I *feel* it, all
the more keenly do I wish to have him here with us.'

'It does you great credit', said Charlotte in reply, 'that you
think of your friend's circumstances with such sympathy, but
you must let me urge you to think also of yourself, and of us.'

'I have,' Eduard replied. 'We can be sure that his presence
here would bring us nothing but advantage and pleasure. We
need not dwell on what he will cost me – certainly, it will be

very little if he moves in with us. And nor will having him here cause us the least inconvenience. He can live in the east wing, and the rest will take care of itself. We should be doing him a great service, and there would be pleasure for us in his company, and profit too. For a long time now I have wanted the property and the district surveying. He will take charge of that, and supervise the work. It was your intention that we should manage the farms ourselves as soon as the present tenancies expire. But what a risky business that may be! He will be able to advise us in so many ways before we begin. I feel the need of a man like him. The local people have the necessary knowledge, but their way of presenting it is confused and not honest. The trained men from the town and the academies are clear and systematic, it is true, but they lack the insight that comes from being on the spot. I can count on our friend for both. And a hundred other opportunities will come of it too, all of them agreeable to contemplate, involving you also, things I am certain we shall be glad of. Enough: I am grateful to you for listening so sympathetically. Now it is your turn to be just as frank and circumstantial. Say whatever you have to say. I promise not to interrupt.'

'Very well then,' Charlotte replied, 'and I will begin by making a general observation. Men attend more to particular things and to the present, and rightly, since they are called upon to act and to influence events. Women, on the other hand, with an equal rightness attend more to the things that hang together in life, since a woman's fate and the fate of her family depend on such things hanging together and it is up to her to see to it that they do. Accordingly, let us look for a moment at our present and our past lives, and you will have to admit that inviting the Captain here does not *wholly* fit in with our intentions, our arrangements, and our plans.

'It always gives me pleasure to think of us as we were in the first years. We were young, we loved one another dearly, but were parted: you from me when your father, in his insatiable greed, bound you to a woman much your senior but rich; I from you when, my prospects being none of the best, I was obliged to say yes to a wealthy man whom I did not love but could respect. We were set free: you first, your good lady leaving you a sizeable fortune; and my turn came just as your travels ended and you were home. So we were reunited. What a pleasure it was then to recall the past! How we cherished our memories! We could enjoy one another's company undisturbed. You were eager for a closer union, I did not consent at once: our ages being roughly the same, I, as a woman, had doubtless grown older than you had as a man. But at length I had no wish to deny you what you seemed to think your only hope of happiness. You wanted to recover, by being with me, from all the unquiet times you had suffered at Court, in the army, and on your travels, to compose yourself and enjoy life; but by being with me alone. I sent my only daughter away to boarding-school, where, admittedly, there has been more variety in her development than would have been possible had she stayed in the country; but not just my daughter – I sent my niece Ottilie there too, though I am fond of her and she might have done better under my guidance here, helping me in the house. All that was done with your consent, solely in order that we should live for ourselves and enjoy undisturbed the happiness we had longed for early on and had now at last achieved. Thus we began our residence here in the country. I was to see to our internal affairs, and you to the external and to whatever concerned our projects as a whole. I have arranged my life so as to accommodate you in everything, so as to live for you alone. Do let us try it for a while at least, and see how well we can manage together as we are.'

'Since, as you say, it is how things hang together that concerns a woman most,' said Eduard in reply, 'any man who listens to your arguments step by step will be bound to acknowledge that you are right. And indeed you *are* right, or have been until today. The grounds on which we have based our lives so far are of a good sort. But shall we build nothing further on them and shall nothing further develop out of them? Is what I am doing in the gardens and you in the park to be only for hermits?'

'All well and good,' said Charlotte. 'But let us not fetch in anything which gets in our way or is foreign to us. Remember that our plans even concerning our recreation to some extent also depended on our being alone together. First you were going to put your travel-diaries in proper shape for me, and sort out the papers that belong with them, and with my help and counting on my interest turn all those notebooks and loose pages, priceless as they are and at present in such disorder, into a whole work that would give pleasure to us and to others. I promised to help you with the writing out, and how nice we thought it would be, so cosy and so very companionable, to travel in recollection through the lands we were not able to see together. And we have already made a start. Then in the evenings you have been getting out your flute again and accompanying me on the piano; and neighbours visit us and we visit them. All this, for me at least, looked like making the summer the happiest I ever thought to have.'

'And still,' said Eduard, rubbing his forehead, 'I cannot help thinking that nothing in what you are so sweetly and sensibly reminding me of would be at all disturbed by the presence of the Captain. On the contrary, it would be moved along more rapidly and with a new life. Some of the journeys he did with me; he made observations of his own, from his own different point of view. Using both sources we really would produce something handsome and complete.'

'Then let me admit quite openly,' said Charlotte, with some impatience, in reply, 'that my feelings are against the idea. I have a presentiment that nothing good will come of it.'

'That would make women quite invincible,' Eduard replied. 'First you are reasonable, so that it is not *possible* to contradict you; then charming, so that giving in to you is a pleasure; then full of feeling, so that a man wishes to avoid causing you any pain; then full of foreboding, which alarms him.'

'I am not superstitious,' Charlotte replied, 'and attach no importance to these vague promptings – if they were only that. But they are most often unconscious memories of fortunate and unfortunate consequences which, in our experience, have resulted from our own or other people's actions. And in any situation nothing is more significant than the intervention of a third party. I have seen friends, brothers and sisters, married couples, and couples in love whose relationships have been wholly altered and their circumstances entirely reshaped by the fortuitous or chosen advent of somebody new.'

'That might happen', said Eduard in reply, 'when people go blindly about their lives, but not if experience has already brought them some enlightenment and they are more conscious of what they are doing.'

'Consciousness, my dear,' said Charlotte to this, 'is an inadequate weapon, and may indeed be a dangerous one for whoever wields it. At the very least what results from our discussion is that we should not be in any hurry. Give me another day or two. Do not decide yet.'

'Things being as they are,' Eduard replied, 'we shall still be acting precipitately even if we leave it for several days. We have advanced the reasons for and against in turn. Now we have to decide, and really the best would be to toss a coin.'

'That or the dice,' said Charlotte in reply. 'I know your way when you cannot make up your mind. But in a matter as serious as this I should think it criminal.'

'But what shall I write to the Captain?' Eduard cried. 'For I must write at once.'

'A calm, sensible, and sympathetic letter,' said Charlotte.

'Then I might as well not write at all,' said Eduard.

'But there are times', said Charlotte, 'when it is necessary and an act of friendship to write nothing rather than not to write.'

CHAPTER TWO

EDUARD was alone in his room. Charlotte's retelling the events of his past life and her calling to mind the circumstances and the projects they now shared had thrown him, excitable as he was, into a pleasant agitation. Whilst still in her company he had felt contented; and had, accordingly, thought out a letter to the Captain which should be friendly and sympathetic but also restrained and non-committal. When he went to his desk, however, and took up the Captain's letter and read it again, all the unhappiness of his excellent friend's situation came back to him; and the feelings by which he had lately been tormented were all renewed and it seemed to him impossible that he should abandon his friend in such a worrying state.

Eduard was not in the habit of denying himself anything. Being the only child of wealthy parents, spoiled by them, induced by them into an odd but highly advantageous marriage with a much older woman and further spoiled by her then in all manner of ways (for she was grateful that he behaved himself and sought to make it up to him with an abundant generosity) and soon becoming his own master when she died, and travelling as he pleased then, making any diversion or alteration as it suited him, wanting nothing excessive but wanting a good deal nevertheless and a good deal of variety; open, charitable, honest, brave when need be – what hindering of his wishes was he ever likely to encounter?

Every outcome had been as he had wished, even Charlotte he had got possession of, by his stubborn, indeed legendary fidelity finally winning her; and now for the first time he felt himself opposed, for the first time thwarted, and just when by having the friend of his youth to join him he might, so to speak, have rounded off his whole existence. He was put out, impatient, several times took up his pen and laid it down again, being unable to satisfy himself as to what he ought to write. He was unwilling to go against his wife's wishes, and unable to act as she had asked him to; feeling so unsettled, how should he write calmly, as he must? The most natural thing was to seek a postponement of the issue. In a few words he asked his friend's pardon that he had not written, and that the present letter would say nothing much, promising something more significant, something reassuring before long.

Next day, on a walk to the same place, Charlotte took the opportunity to resume the conversation, believing perhaps that the best way to blunt a purpose is continually to discuss it.

Eduard welcomed this return to the subject. He spoke after his usual manner, amicably and agreeably; for though, being highly susceptible, he easily took fire and pressed his desires very passionately and could make a person impatient by his persistence, his speech was nevertheless so modified by perfect consideration for whoever he was speaking to that it was impossible to dislike him even though he pestered.

It was thus, on the morning in question, that he first put Charlotte into the best of moods and then, turning the conversation in the nicest way, quite discomposed her, so that at last she exclaimed: 'Clearly you want me to grant my lover what I refused my husband.'

'In any event,' she continued, 'I am not averse to your knowing that your wishes and your lively and considerate way of expressing them have not left me untouched and unmoved. They oblige me to make a confession. I have been concealing something too. I find myself in a situation similar to yours, and have already imposed upon myself just such a discipline as I expect you to impose upon yourself.'

'I am glad to hear it,' said Eduard. 'I see that in marriage it is necessary to quarrel from time to time, for that way we learn something about one another.'

'Let me admit then,' said Charlotte, 'that what you feel about the Captain I feel about Ottilie. It makes me unhappy to think of the poor child in her boarding-school. She is very much oppressed by her circumstances there. Whereas my daughter Luciane, born to be in the world and in that school preparing herself for the world, performs in languages and history and whatever else her teachers put to her with as much facility as she does in her exercises in music; and, naturally lively and blessed with a good memory, can forget everything, as it seems, and instantly remember it when she pleases; and excels all others in freedom of bearing, grace in dancing, ease and civility of conversation and, being by nature inclined to lead, has made herself the queen of her small circle; and whereas the Principal of that establishment views her as a minor divinity who, in her care, is blossoming as she ought, so doing her credit, promoting the school, and bringing it a further influx of young ladies; and whereas the first pages of the Principal's letters and monthly reports are nothing but hymns in praise of the virtues of this wonderful child, which I am well able to translate into my own prose – what she finally has to say about Ottilie is only apology upon apology that a girl becoming otherwise so very attractive will yet not develop, or show any abilities or accomplishments. What little she says besides is likewise perfectly intelligible to me, since I recognize in the child the whole character of her mother, my dearest friend, who grew up beside me and whose daughter, if I could be her teacher or had charge of her, I would bring up to be a quite exceptional person.

'But since it does not fit into our plans and since one should not be forever rearranging one's circumstances and forever fetching in new things, I let it rest, and when my daughter, who knows full well that poor Ottilie is wholly dependent on us, employs her own advantages against her, thereby undoing, to a certain extent, all our kindness, I keep even the distress this causes me under control.

'But who is so well bred that he will never, in a hurtful way, assert his superiority over others? And who stands so high that he will never have to suffer an oppression of that sort? These trials only increase Ottilie's worth; but since fully realizing how painful her situation is I have been doing my best to place her somewhere else. I expect an answer at any time now, and once I have it I shall not delay. That is how things are with me, my dear. So both of us, in the name of true friendship, have been harbouring similar worries. Let us bear them together, since they do not cancel one another out.'

'What strange creatures we are,' said Eduard with a smile. 'As though by removing the thing that worries us out of our sight we could thereby be rid of it. In a general way we are capable of all kinds of sacrifices, but much less so when it comes to something in particular. My mother was like that. So long as I was living at home, as a child and a young man, she was never able to rid herself of the anxieties of the moment. If I was back late from a ride, I was bound to have had an accident; if I ever got soaked, she was sure I should fall ill of a fever. But then I went away, I put some distance between us, and seemed scarcely to belong to her anymore.

'Looking at it more closely,' he went on, 'we are both behaving foolishly and irresponsibly in leaving two exceptionally worthy people, for whom we feel such affection and concern, in unhappy and oppressive circumstances only in order not to expose ourselves to any danger. If this is not selfishness I do not know what is. You take Ottilie, give me the Captain, and in God's name let us make a trial of it.'

'We *might* risk it,' said Charlotte thoughtfully, 'if the danger were only to ourselves. But do you think it advisable to have Ottilie in the same house as the Captain, a man of about your age, of an age, that is – let me say it to your face, although it flatters you – when a man becomes really capable of love at last, and really worthy of it, and have him here with a girl of such qualities as Ottilie's?'

'It puzzles me', said Eduard in reply, 'how you can rate Ottilie so highly. I can only suppose that she has inherited the affection you felt for her mother. It's true, she is pretty, and I do remember that the Captain drew my attention to her when we came back a year ago and met her and you together at your aunt's. She is pretty, her eyes especially are beautiful; but I am not aware that she made the least impression on me.'

'That is to your credit,' said Charlotte, 'for of course I was there too; and although she is a good deal younger than I am you were so taken with the charms of your older friend that you overlooked the beauty coming into being and promising so much. That too is a part of how you are, and it makes me very glad to share my life with you.'

For all her apparent candour, Charlotte was in fact concealing something. When Eduard returned from his travels she had introduced Ottilie to him in the deliberate intention of giving her foster-daughter the chance of an excellent match; for she had ceased to think of herself in relation to Eduard. And the Captain, as an accomplice, was to bring Ottilie further into Eduard's notice; but Eduard had his earlier love for Charlotte obstinately in mind, and looked neither right nor left but was happy in the feeling that the good he had so passionately desired and which a series of events had denied him, as it seemed for ever, might finally now be his.

The couple were about to go down through the new grounds towards the Hall when a servant came climbing in haste to meet them. Laughing, he shouted up to them whilst still some distance below: 'Your Lordship! Your Ladyship! Come quickly! Mr Mittler is here. He arrived all of a sudden. He has been shouting at us to go and look for you and ask if he's wanted. "Am I wanted?" he shouted after us. "Do you hear? But be quick, be quick!"'

'Our comical friend!' Eduard exclaimed. 'He could not have come at a better moment. What do you say, Charlotte? Hurry back,' he said to the servant, 'and tell him he is indeed wanted. He must break his journey. See to his horse. Bring him indoors and give him something to eat. We'll be there directly.'

'Let us go the quickest way,' he said to his wife, and took the path through the churchyard which he usually avoided. But how astonished he was when he saw that Charlotte's considerateness had been at work here too. Whilst taking all possible care of the old monuments she had brought such harmony and order into everything that the place seemed a pleasant one, on which the eyes and the imagination were glad to dwell.

She had treated the tombstones, even the oldest, with a proper respect. In order of age they had been set upright against the wall, or built into it, or in some other way fitted there; the high plinth of the church itself had been adorned and lent variety with them. Eduard was strangely moved and surprised as he came in at the little gate; he pressed Charlotte's hand, and there were tears in his eyes.

But the comical visitor soon chased these tears away. He would not be detained at the Hall but had ridden at a gallop through the village to the churchyard gate, and there he halted and called out to his friends: 'I hope this is not a joke. If I really am wanted I will stay to lunch. But don't hold me up, I still have a great deal to do.'

'Since you have taken the trouble to come this far,' Eduard called out to him, 'ride in. We meet in a solemn place. But see what a pretty appearance sorrow wears, thanks to Charlotte.'

'At this gate', the rider cried, 'I shall enter neither on horseback, nor in a carriage, nor on foot. These here are all at peace, and no concern of mine. When I'm dragged in here feet first, that will be time enough. Come now: are you in earnest?'

'We are indeed,' said Charlotte. 'We newly-weds are for the first time in more difficulty and perplexity than we can extricate ourselves from alone.'

'You don't look it,' he replied, 'but I'll take your word. And if you are fooling, don't turn to me in future. Come quickly now, I expect my horse would be glad of a rest.'

Soon the three of them were in the dining-room together; the meal was served and Mittler told them what he had done that day and what he intended doing. He was a peculiar man. He had previously been a cleric, and in all his restless busyness in office had most distinguished himself by his ability to cool and resolve the quarrels, both domestic and between neighbours, first of particular individuals, then of entire parishes and of several great families. There were no divorces whilst he was in the job, and the local courts were never bothered by disputes and litigation from his district. He soon saw how necessary it was for him to have a knowledge of the law. He devoted himself entirely to legal studies, and before long felt able to hold his own against the cleverest in the profession. His sphere of influence grew astonishingly, and he was about to be called to Court, so that what he had begun from below could be completed from above, when he won a considerable sum of money in a lottery, bought himself a modest estate, let it out, and made it the centre of his activities; and kept firmly to the principle, or rather obeyed his old habit and inclination, never to stay long in any house where nothing wanted resolving and where there was no need of any help. Those with a superstitious conviction that names are meaningful assert that it was his being called Mittler which obliged him to follow this strangest of vocations.

When dessert had been served the visitor earnestly enjoined his hosts not to delay their revelations any longer, since he must leave immediately after coffee. Husband and wife began their confessions then in every detail; but no sooner had he grasped what the matter was than he leapt up from the table in exasperation, rushed to the window, and gave orders to saddle his horse.

'Either you don't know me,' he exclaimed, 'or you don't understand me, or you are making mischief. I see no quarrel. I see no need of help. Do you think I exist to give advice? Giving advice is quite the most foolish job there is. Let everyone advise himself, and do what he can't help doing. If it turns out well, he can congratulate himself on his perspicacity and good luck; if it turns out badly, I'll be there. Any man who wants to be rid of an evil always knows what he wants; and anyone who wants something better than he's got is always as blind as a bat. You may laugh! I tell you, he's playing blindman's buff, he *may* catch it; but what? Do as you like: it's all the same. Have your friends here, or leave them where they are: all one. I've seen the most sensible things come to grief, and the most ridiculous succeed.

Don't torment yourselves, and if one way or the other it ends badly don't torment yourselves then either. Just send for me, and you will have my help. Till then: good day.'

And he bestrode his horse, without waiting for coffee.

'See,' said Charlotte, 'how little help a third person is in the end when two who are close have got a little out of balance. We are more confused now, if that is possible, and less sure of ourselves than we were, wouldn't you say?'

And doubtless they would have wavered a while longer if a letter from the Captain had not arrived, in reply to Eduard's. He had decided to accept one of the positions offered him, even though it was not at all suitable. He was to share in the boredom of certain high and wealthy persons, and be expected to dispel it.

Eduard saw very clearly what the whole arrangement would be like, and put it to Charlotte in very graphic terms. 'Can we bear to think of our friend in such a situation?' he cried. 'You cannot be so cruel, Charlotte.'

'Our strange friend Mittler is right after all,' Charlotte replied. 'All such undertakings are a risk. What might come of it no one can anticipate. Such new circumstances may be productive of happiness and unhappiness without our being able to claim any particular credit or needing to feel ourselves particularly to blame. I do not have the strength to resist you any longer. Let us make a trial of it. All I ask is that it should not be for too long. Let me exert myself even more energetically on his behalf and use my influence and contacts all I can, to get him a place which will suit him and give him some contentment.'

Eduard's gratitude to his wife was very keen, and he thanked her in the nicest way. Light-hearted then, he hurried to convey to his friend some proposals in a letter. Charlotte was required to second him in a postscript in her own hand, and to join her friendly invitation with his. She wrote in a fluent script, agreeably and obligingly, but also in a sort of haste, which was not usual with her; and finished by spoiling the look of the page with a blot, a thing she *never* did and which made her cross, and the more she tried to wipe it away the worse it looked.

Eduard made a joke of it, and since there was still room added another postscript: their friend should see by these signs with what impatience he was awaited, and match the speediness of his journey to the speed with which the letter had been written.

The messenger departed, and Eduard, wishing to show Charlotte his gratitude, sought to do so by insisting again and again that she must fetch Ottilie out of the boarding-school at once.

Charlotte begged for more time, and that evening managed to arouse in Eduard the desire for a musical entertainment. Charlotte was a very good pianist, Eduard not quite so good on the flute; for although from time to time he had worked hard at it he lacked the patience and the staying power necessary for the full development of such a talent. So he performed his part very unevenly – some passages well, though perhaps too quickly; but at others he slowed down, since he was not familiar with them, and it would have been very difficult for anyone else to get to the end of a duet with him. But Charlotte managed; she slowed down where necessary and elsewhere allowed herself to be carried away by him, and accomplished thus the dual responsibility of a good conductor and a shrewd housewife, who manage to keep a measure in the whole, even if the particular passages are not always in time.

CHAPTER THREE

THE Captain came. He preceded his arrival with a letter so full of good sense that Charlotte's mind was entirely set at rest. Such frankness about himself, such clear-sightedness about his own situation and the situation of his friends, augured nothing but good.

Their first hours of talk were, as is usual among friends who have not seen each other for some time, lively, indeed almost exhausting. Towards evening Charlotte suggested a walk to the new grounds. The Captain was delighted by them and took note of all the beauties which the new paths had now made visible and able to be enjoyed. He had a practised eye, but was modest in what he looked for; and although he saw clearly what was desirable he did not, as many do, annoy the people who were showing him around their property by asking for more than the circumstances allowed or, worse still, by mentioning more perfect achievements seen elsewhere.

When they reached the summer-house they found it all decked out; admittedly only with artificial flowers and evergreens, but beautiful sheaves of real corn and other fruits of the field and orchard had been arranged there too, so that the whole made a very gay appearance and did credit to its author's artistic sense. 'I know my husband does not like his birthday or his name-day to be celebrated,' Charlotte said, 'but I am sure that today he will not mind my dedicating these few garlands to a triple occasion.'

'A triple one?' Eduard exclaimed.

'Yes indeed,' Charlotte replied. 'We can surely regard the arrival of our friend as an occasion, and have you both forgotten that today is your name-day? For are you not both called Otto?'

The two friends shook hands across the little table. 'I had forgotten', said Eduard, 'what we did when we were boys, in

139

the name of friendship. We *were* both called Otto, but when we were at school together and it kept causing confusion I voluntarily renounced the name – neat and attractive though it is – in his favour.'

'Which was not so *very* generous of you,' said the Captain. 'For I perfectly well remember that you liked the name Eduard better, and indeed when spoken by pretty lips it does have a most agreeable sound.'

Now they were sitting, the three of them, around the same little table at which Charlotte had spoken so vehemently against the coming of their guest. Eduard, in his contentment, had no wish to remind his wife of that time; but he could not refrain from saying: 'There would be plenty of room for a fourth person besides.'

At that moment the sound of hunting-horns reached them from the direction of the Hall, and seemed to affirm and reinforce the hopes and sympathies of that company of friends. They listened in silence, withdrawing into their separate selves and feeling their happiness doubled by its being so beautifully shared.

It was Eduard who put an end to the interlude. He stood up and went outside the summer-house. He said to Charlotte: 'Let us take our friend to the top at once, or he will suppose this narrow valley to be all our inheritance and abode. Up there you can breathe, and the vision is enlarged.'

'We shall have to go the old way still,' Charlotte replied, 'which is quite an arduous climb. But I hope before long my steps and paths will make the going easier, right to the top.'

Over rocks and through bushes and undergrowth they climbed the last rise. There they were not on level ground but on a continuing and fertile ridge. Behind them the Hall and village had gone out of sight. Down below they could see a line of ponds; and beyond, bordering these, were wooded hills, and finally steep cliffs which vertically and very definitely ended the final reach of the water, their imposing shapes being reflected on its surface. In a cleft there, through which a stream, with some force, fell into the ponds, lay a mill, half hidden, which looked, in that setting, a place it would be delightful to repose in. In the whole arc as it lay under their gaze there was an abundant variation of height and depth, of shrub and woodland whose first green already indicated the richness and fullness that was to come. In one place or another the eye was drawn to particular groups of trees, and first, immediately below the friends as they stood looking, to a group of poplars and plane trees on the bank of the middle pond. These appeared to particular advantage, being in the best years of their growth, fresh, healthy, and striving for height and breadth.

To these trees especially Eduard drew his friend's attention. 'I planted them myself,' he cried, 'when I was young. They were little saplings, my father had them dug up when the big garden was being extended at the Hall, and I rescued them. It was in the summer. I do not doubt that they will be magnificent this year too, and grow a little more, in gratitude.'

In a cheerful contentment they returned to the house. The guest was given spacious and agreeable quarters in the east wing and had very soon arranged his books and papers and set up his instruments so as to continue with his usual activities. But during the first days Eduard would not leave him in peace; he conducted him everywhere, on horse or on foot, and made him acquainted with the district and with the estate; at the same time making known to him the desire he had long felt for a better knowledge and a more profitable use of it all.

'The first thing', said the Captain, 'would be for me to do a survey of the area with the compass. It is an easy job and a pleasant one, and although it will not give us perfect accuracy, still it will be useful and we shall have made an encouraging start. It is also something which can be done without much assistance, and which we can be sure of finishing. If you ever want more accurate measurements no doubt we shall find a way.'

The Captain was an expert at this sort of survey work. He had brought the necessary instruments with him, and began at once. He gave some instruction to Eduard and to a few servants and labourers who were to be his assistants in the business. The days were favourable; the evenings and the early mornings he spent transferring heights and features to the map. Soon everything was washed or shaded or coloured in, and Eduard saw his property coming forth from the paper in all clarity like a new creation. It was as though he were only now becoming acquainted with what he owned, and as though his ownership were only now confirmed.

This was a chance to discuss the estate and the things one might now, having had an overview, do with it more easily than when one's experiments with Nature were isolated, haphazard, and on the basis of only casual impressions.

'We must make that clear to my wife,' said Eduard.

'Do no such thing,' said the Captain, who never liked to put his own opinions in the way of anyone else's, having learned from experience that the views people hold are far too various ever to be collected in a common point, however reasonable the arguments for such agreement might be. 'Do no such thing!' he cried. 'She would surely be upset. Like everyone else who pursues these things in an amateur sort of way, what matters to her is that she is doing something and not whether anything is being done. In their dealings with Nature such people have a hesitant touch; they have a fondness for this little spot or that; they don't dare remove any obstacle, they are not bold enough to make sacrifices; they cannot visualize in advance the desired result, they try things out, which work or don't work, they make alterations, alter what should be left alone perhaps, and leave alone what should be altered, so that in the end it remains a piecemeal sort of job which may prompt and please but which will not satisfy.'

'Admit it,' said Eduard – 'You are not happy with the work she has done.'

'If the idea itself, which is a very good one, had been fully carried out, there would be nothing to object to. She has toiled her way up the rocks and now, as you might say, makes everyone she takes there suffer likewise. Neither side by side nor in single file is it possible to walk with any freedom. One's pace is continually interrupted. And there are all sorts of other things wrong that might be pointed out.'

'Could it easily have been done in any other way?' Eduard asked.

'Very easily,' the Captain replied. 'All she needed to do was break away that one corner, nothing much anyway since the rock there is in small pieces, and she would have gained a fine sweeping curve for the climb and some spare stones besides to build up those places where otherwise the path would have been narrow and unshapely. But let this be in strictest confidence between you and me, or she will be upset and aggrieved. And what is already done we must let stand. If you do want to expend more money and effort there, then various very pleasing things could still be achieved from the summer-house upwards and on to the ridge.'

Thus the two friends found much to occupy them in the present, but they had besides a lively pleasure in remembering the past, and in this Charlotte readily joined them. It was also decided that, as soon as the first work outdoors was completed, a start should be made on the travel-diaries and the past be recalled in that way too.

There was, it must be said, less for Charlotte and Eduard to discuss together alone, especially now that he had on his mind the criticisms – which he thought justified – made of her work in the grounds. For a long time he kept to himself the views that the Captain had confided in him; but at last, when he saw his wife beginning again the labour of her little steps and paths, now from the summer-house towards the ridge, he restrained himself no longer, and after some hesitation came to the point and disclosed his new insights to her.

Charlotte was halted in her tracks. She was intelligent enough to see that the men were right; but what was done, having turned out the way it had, contradicted them; she had thought it right and what was wanted, and even where it had now been criticized she was fond of it, in every part; she fought against being convinced, she defended her little creation, railed against men for immediately thinking on a grand scale, for making a great work out of what had been an amusement and an entertainment, and for not considering the costs which an enlarged plan would be bound to entail. She was upset, hurt, aggrieved; she could not let go of the old, nor quite reject the new; but, decisive as she was, she at once called a halt to the work and gave herself time to think the matter over and come to her own conclusions.

Being now without this activity and amusement, and since the men meanwhile were pursuing their affairs ever more companionably – seeing to the ornamental gardens and the glasshouses with especial eagerness, and in between times keeping up with the usual gentlemanly occupations such as hunting and the buying, swapping, breaking in, and training of horses – Charlotte felt herself daily more alone. Still more of her energies went into letter-writing, also on the Captain's behalf; but there were lonely hours nevertheless. All the more welcome and entertaining, then, were the reports she had from the boarding-school.

To a lengthy letter of the Principal's, expatiating as usual on Luciane's progress, was added a brief postscript, together with an enclosure in the hand of a male assistant in the establishment, both of which are here communicated.

The Principal's Postscript

'On the subject of Ottilie, your Ladyship, I can really only repeat what is contained in my earlier reports. Though I have no reason to chide her, I cannot be content with her either. She is, as she always was, modest and agreeable towards others; but her very self-effacingness and her readiness to be of service are not, in my view, wholly to be approved. Your Ladyship recently sent her some money and various materials. The first she has made no use of; and the latter also are still lying there untouched. It is true she keeps her things very clean and in good order, and seems only for that reason to change her clothes. Nor do I think it meritorious in her that she eats and drinks so little. Our meals are never excessive, but there is nothing I like better than to see children eating their fill of tasty and wholesome food. We give considerable thought to what we set before them, and it should be eaten up. But I can never bring Ottilie to do so. Indeed, if there is ever a pause in a meal because the serving girls are slow, she will invent some task or other, simply in order to pass over one of the dishes or the dessert. In all this it needs, however, to be borne in mind that she does sometimes, as I have only recently found out, suffer from headaches on the left side, which pass, it is true, but which may well be painful and of some significance. So much for Ottilie. She is of course a lovely child and we are very fond of her.'

The Assistant's Enclosure

'Our excellent Principal usually allows me to read the letters in which she communicates her observations on her charges to their parents and guardians. Those which she addresses to your Ladyship I always read with a double attention and a double pleasure; for whilst we must congratulate you on having a daughter who unites in herself all the brilliant qualities through which one rises in the world, I at least must deem you to be no less happy for having, in your foster-daughter, a child born to be a kindness and a content-ment to others and surely also to be happy herself. Ottilie is almost the only child in our care over whom I am unable to be of one mind with our much-esteemed Principal. I do not at all hold it against that always active lady that she should ask to see the fruits of her care both outwardly and clearly; but there are fruits of a hidden kind too, and they are the true and the richest ones and will develop sooner or later into a life of beauty. Such a one is your foster-daughter without a doubt. All the time I have taught her I have seen her going forwards, always at the same pace, slowly forwards, never back. Perhaps children always need to begin at the beginning: she certainly does. If a thing does not derive from what has gone before she cannot grasp it. Confront her with anything, however easily intelligible, and she will appear nonplussed and even recalcitrant if for her it is without connection. But if the connecting links can be discovered and made clear to her she can grasp even the most difficult matters.

'Advancing slowly in this way she falls behind the other girls who, being quite differently gifted, are forever racing ahead and grasp everything, even unconnected things, very easily and easily retain them and put them to use then without trouble. Accordingly, if the pace of instruction is quickened she learns nothing at all and can manage nothing; and that is the case in certain of the courses given by excellent but speedy and impatient teachers. There have been complaints about her handwriting, and about her inability to grasp the rules of grammar. I went into these complaints: it is true, she writes slowly and without fluency if you like, but not timidly and nor does she misshape her letters. What I taught her of the French language, which is admittedly not my subject, she grasped without difficulty since I proceeded step by step. I agree it is very odd: she knows many things and she knows them well; but when she is asked she seems to know nothing.

'If I might finish with a general observation, I should say that she does not learn like one who is being taught but like one who intends to teach; not like a pupil, but like a future teacher. Your Ladyship may think it strange that, being myself a teacher and an educator, I can find no better way of praising a person than to declare her to be one of my own kind. Your Ladyship's finer insight and deeper knowledge of people and of the world will extract the best from my limited but well-meant opinions. You will be persuaded that in this child too there lies the promise of much happiness. I remain your obedient servant and conclude with the hope that I might be permitted to write to you again as soon as I think I have something pleasing and significant to say.'

Charlotte was delighted by this letter. Its contents approximated very closely to her own views of Ottilie; at the same time she could not refrain from smiling, since the teacher's interest seemed to her warmer than simple insight into the virtues of a pupil would usually arouse. In her calm and unprejudiced way she contemplated this relationship, as she had so many others; she valued the sympathy shown to Ottilie by a man of good sense, for her life had sufficiently confirmed her in the view that every true attachment is a very valuable thing in a world where indifference and antipathy are all-too-well established.

CHAPTER FOUR

THE topographical chart, on which the features of the estate and its surroundings were clearly depicted, on quite a large scale, in pen and in different colours, and to which the Captain had given a firm basis by taking trigonometrical measurements, was soon finished; for he was ever active, he needed less sleep than almost anyone, his days were given always to the immediate purpose, and as a consequence by evening something had always been achieved.

'Let us now', he said to his friend, 'move to the rest, to an inventory of the property, for which enough preparatory work has surely already been done. From it our assessments of rents and other matters will follow naturally. And let one thing above all be agreed and instituted: keep everything which is really business separate from life. Business wants seriousness and a strict rule, but life capriciousness; in business we must be thoroughly consequential, but in our lives a certain inconsequentiality is often called for, is indeed delightful and heartening. If you are secure in the first you can move all the more freely in the second; whereas if you mix the two your freedom will carry your security away and end it.'

Eduard felt a gentle reproach in these proposals. Though not by nature untidy he could never manage to order his papers into different categories. Things he had to settle with other people and things which depended upon nobody but himself were not kept separate; and in the same way he did not sufficiently separate business and serious employment from amusement and diversion. Now it was made easy for him by a friend's exertions, by a second self creating the two halves into which the one self is not always willing to divide.

In the wing of the house occupied by the Captain they set up a repository for present matters and an archive for the past; brought together all the documents, papers, and reports from their various containers, closets, cupboards, and chests, and so in no time at all a pleasing tidiness had been imposed upon the chaos and everything was properly classified and sorted under headings. They found what they wanted in a greater completeness than they had hoped. They were much helped in their work by an elderly clerk, who all day long and even into the night never left his desk. He was a man with whom Eduard had always been dissatisfied in the past.

'I scarcely recognize him,' said Eduard to his friend. 'How busy and useful the man is!' The Captain replied: 'That is because we do not give him anything new to do until he has finished the first job in his own good time. In that way, as you see, he accomplishes a great deal. But if we pester him he can do nothing whatsoever.'

The two friends, spending their days together thus, did not fail to pay Charlotte regular visits in the evenings. If no company were present from the neighbouring places and estates, which was often the case, then their conversation and their reading mostly concerned those things by which the well-being, the advantage, and the comfort of civil society are enhanced.

Charlotte, always one to use the present time, seeing her husband contented, felt a fresh motivation in her own life too. Various domestic provisions which she had long wished to make but had not quite known how to were now accomplished through the industry of the Captain. The household medicine chest, which had been poorly stocked, was improved and Charlotte herself made able, through some simple reading and instruction, to put her natural energy and helpfulness to more frequent and more effective use.

Whilst they were giving thought to those emergencies which, though commonplace, all too often come without any warning, they assembled everything which might be necessary for the prevention of drowning, and with good reason, since there were so many ponds, waterways, weirs, and sluices in the vicinity and accidents of that kind did quite often occur. The Captain saw to this item with very great thoroughness, and Eduard let slip the remark that a case of that sort had made a very strange and momentous intervention into his friend's life. But when the Captain said nothing in reply and seemed to be evading some unhappy memory, Eduard likewise went no further, and Charlotte too, being herself in a general way *au courant*, passed over the remark.

'These precautionary measures', said the Captain one evening, 'are all well and good. But we still lack what matters most: a reliable man who knows how to use all the things we have provided. There is a field-surgeon of my acquaintance whom I might suggest as being very suitable and who may be had for a modest remuneration, an excellent man in his job and one by whom, in the treatment of certain violent internal disorders, I have often been better served than by famous doctors; and it is after all immediate assistance that we have most need of in the country.'

He was sent for at once; and husband and wife were delighted to be able to spend on such necessary things sums of money that might otherwise have gone on nothing in particular.

Thus Charlotte made use of the Captain's knowledge and energy in her own fashion and began to be entirely happy at his presence and to feel easy in her mind at whatever might ensue from it. She usually had questions to put to him, and since she was a person who valued life she sought to remove everything harmful and everything lethal. The lead glaze on earthenware and the verdigris on copper vessels had caused her anxiety. She asked for instruction in the matter, which naturally meant going back to basic concepts in physics and chemistry.

Occasional but always welcome stimulus to such conversations was given by Eduard's love of reading aloud. He had a deep and very melodious voice and had once been famous and appreciated for his lively and heartfelt renderings of poetical and rhetorical works. Now other subjects occupied him and he read aloud from other writings, and latterly such as had to do with physics, chemistry, and things of a technical nature.

One of his peculiarities, but one which other people may perhaps share, was that he found it unbearable to have any-body looking over his shoulder as he read. In earlier times, when reading poems, plays, and stories aloud, this was doubt-less due to the intense desire that any reader has, like the poet, actor, or story-teller himself, to surprise, to make pauses, to arouse expectations; which intended effect is of course very much impaired if another person's eyes are hurrying ahead to know what is coming. And for that reason, when he was reading he would always seat himself in such a position as to have nobody behind him. There being only the three of them this precaution was unnecessary; and since it was now not a matter of exciting the feelings or surprising the imagination, Eduard himself paid no especial heed.

But then one evening, having seated himself carelessly, he became aware that Charlotte was reading over his shoulder. His old irritation revived, and he rebuked her in terms that were somewhat ungentle: 'Once and for all I do wish people would refrain from habits that are an annoyance in society. If I am reading aloud to someone is it not as though I were telling him something? What is written or printed stands in place of my own opinions and my own feelings; and would I go to the trouble of speaking if there were a little window in my forehead or in my breast so that the man to whom I was communicating my thoughts one by one and offering him my emotions one by one could always know far in advance what my direction was? Somebody reading over my shoulder always makes me feel I'm being torn in two.'

Charlotte, whose aplomb in larger and smaller gatherings showed especially in her way of neutralizing any unpleasant, vehement, or even merely animated utterance, of interrupting any conversation that was dragging on, and of enlivening any that was faltering, on this occasion too was well served by her gift. 'I am sure you will forgive me,' she said, 'if I confess what happened. I heard you reading about relations between things and at once began thinking about *my* relations, of one or two of my cousins who are rather a worry to me at present. When I began listening again I realized that it was entirely inanimate things you were reading about and I looked over your shoulder to get my bearings.'

'It was an analogy which misled and confused you,' said Eduard. 'All we are concerned with here is earths and minerals, but human beings are very narcissistic, they like to see themselves everywhere and be the foil for the rest of creation.'

'They do indeed!' said the Captain, and he continued: 'That is man's way with everything he encounters outside himself. He credits the minerals and the plants, the elements and the gods with his own wisdom and his own folly and with his will and whims.'

'I wonder,' Charlotte asked, 'though I do not wish to lead you too far from the present topic, whether you would mind telling me in a few words what the nature of these relationships is.'

'I shall be very glad to,' the Captain replied, since it was to him that Charlotte had turned with her question, 'as well as I can, at least, from what I read about it some ten years ago. Whether people in the scientific world still think the same on the subject, whether it accords with the newer doctrines, I could not say.'

'It is a bad business', Eduard cried, 'that we cannot nowadays learn anything that will last a lifetime. Our forefathers stuck to the teaching they were given when they were young, but we have to unlearn everything every five years if we are not to go completely out of fashion.'

'We women', said Charlotte, 'are not quite so particular. And to be honest, all that really concerns me is what the word means. For nothing makes one more ridiculous in society than using a new coinage or a technical term wrongly. I should simply like to know what sense the expression has when it is used with reference to these particular things. The science behind it we can leave to the experts, who in my experience will be unlikely ever to agree.'

'But where shall we begin, so as to get most quickly to the heart of the matter?' said Eduard, after a silence, to the Captain. He, having thought for a moment, replied: 'If I may be permitted to begin, as it might seem, at the very beginning, we shall soon be there.'

'Be assured of my complete attention,' said Charlotte, laying her work aside.

So the Captain began: 'The first thing we notice about all the substances we encounter in Nature is that each is always drawn to itself. It may sound strange to say something so self-evident, but only once we have fully understood the things we are familiar with can we proceed together towards the things with which we are not familiar.'

Eduard interrupted him: 'We might make it easy for her and for ourselves by giving examples. Think of water, oil, or mercury and you will see a unity, a coherence in their composition. From this united state they will never depart, unless by force or some other intervention. Remove that force and they at once restore themselves to wholeness.'

'Quite so,' said Charlotte in agreement. 'Raindrops quickly unite to form streams. And quicksilver amazed us as children when we played with it and split it into little beads and let it run together again.'

'And I may be permitted', the Captain added, 'to mention one significant detail in passing: that what decisively and always characterizes that very pure self-attraction of substances in liquid form is spherical shape. The falling raindrop is round; you yourself have already mentioned the little beads of mercury; and falling drops of molten lead, if they have time to solidify completely, are spherical when they land.'

'Let me run ahead,' said Charlotte, 'and see if I can guess what you are aiming at. Just as everything has an attraction to itself so too there must be a relationship with other things.'

'And that will vary according to the different natures of the things concerned,' said Eduard in haste. 'Sometimes they will meet as friends and old acquaintances and come together quickly and be united without either altering the other at all, as wine for example mixes with water. But others will remain strangers side by side and will never unite even if mechanically ground and mixed. Thus oil and water shaken together will immediately separate again.'

'It would not take much', said Charlotte, 'to see people of one's own acquaintance in these simple forms; and I am particularly reminded of the social circles people move in. But what these inanimate substances most resemble are the large social groups which confront one another in the world: the classes and the different occupations, the nobility and the third estate, the soldier and the civilian.'

'And yet,' Eduard replied, 'just as these may be joined by custom and the law, so in our world of chemistry there are agents which will bind together the things that are holding one another off.'

'Thus,' the Captain interjected, 'we join oil and water by the agency of an alkaline salt.'

'Not so fast with your lecture,' said Charlotte. 'Let me prove I am keeping up. Have we not already come to relationships and affinities?'

'We have indeed,' the Captain replied, 'and let us at once now get to know them in what they are and in what they do. We say of those natures which on meeting speedily connect and inter-react that they have an affinity for one another. This affinity may be very remarkable. Alkalis and acids, although opposed to one another and perhaps precisely because they are so opposed, will in a most decisive way seek out, take hold of, and modify one another and form, in so doing, a new substance together. We have only to think of lime, which manifests towards all acids a strong inclination, a decided wish for union. As soon as our chemistry cabinet arrives we shall show you various experiments which are very entertaining and which will give you a clearer idea than words, names, and technical terms may do.'

'I must confess', said Charlotte, 'that when you speak of these wondrous entities as related they seem to me not so much blood relations as related in spirit and in the soul. In precisely this way true and important friendships may come about between people: opposing qualities make an intenser union possible. I look forward to witnessing what mysterious effects you will produce for me. And now –', she said, turning to Eduard – 'I shan't spoil your reading any more and, being so much better informed, will listen attentively to what you have to say.'

'Since you have asked us for explanations,' Eduard replied, 'we cannot let you off so lightly, for the complicated cases are in fact the most interesting. Only through them do we realize the degree of affinity and how near, strong, remote, or slight the relations are. Affinities are only really interesting when they bring about separations.'

'Does that unhappy word', cried Charlotte, 'which we hear all too often in the world today, occur in the sciences too?'

'Indeed it does,' Eduard replied. 'Significantly, it used to be high praise to say of the chemists that they were skilled in the art of separation.'

'But not any more?' said Charlotte in reply, 'and that is only right and proper. Bringing things together is a harder task, and a worthier one. A man skilled in the art of bringing things together would be welcome in every walk of life. But now since you are launched into your subject do give me a few examples.'

'Then let us return forthwith', said the Captain, 'to things we have already mentioned and discussed. For example, what we call limestone is a more or less pure oxide of calcium tightly combined with a weak acid known to us in gaseous form. If a piece of that rock is placed in dilute sulphuric acid this combines with the calcium to form gypsum; the gaseous weak acid, on the other hand, escapes. A separation and a new combination have come about and one even feels justified in using the term "elective affinity", because it really does seem as though one relationship were preferred to another and a choice made for one over the other.'

'Forgive me,' said Charlotte, 'just as I forgive the scientist, but I would never call that a choice, rather a necessity in

Nature, and scarcely even that since in the end it is perhaps only a matter of opportunity. Opportunity makes thieves, they say, and also relationships; and as for the natural substances you were speaking of, it seems to me that the only choice lies in the hands of the chemist himself, who brings them together. Once they *have* been brought together, heaven help them! In the case in point my sympathy is with the gaseous acid obliged to drift around in space once again.'

'All it need do', the Captain replied, 'is combine with water, to bring refreshment to the sick and the healthy then as a mineral spring.'

'All very well for the gypsum,' said Charlotte. 'He is a finished thing, a body, he is taken care of, whereas that poor creature driven out may have a great deal to put up with before finding a home.'

'Unless I am very much mistaken,' said Eduard with a smile, 'your remarks are not entirely innocent. Admit it! I suppose in your view I am the lime – seized by sulphuric acid in the person of the Captain, torn from your agreeable company and transformed into an unco-operative gypsum.'

'If your conscience', said Charlotte in reply, 'prompts you to such reflections then I need not worry. These comparisons are very entertaining, everyone likes playing with analogies. But a human being is after all superior by several degrees to those natural substances, and having been rather lax in our use of the fine words "choice" and "elective affinity" we might do well to return to our inner selves and ask in all seriousness what the validity of such expressions in this context is. Alas, I know of enough cases in which a close and, as it seemed, indissoluble relationship was annulled by the casual arrival of a third party, and one of the pair, previously joined so beautifully, driven out into empty space.'

'But in that respect', said Eduard, 'chemists are much more gallant. They add a fourth party, so that nobody goes without.'

'Indeed,' said the Captain, 'and those cases are the most significant and the most remarkable in which the attraction and the affinity, the desertion and the uniting, can be seen, so to speak, crosswise: when four substances, united until that moment two by two, are brought into contact, desert their previous union, and unite afresh. In this letting go and seizing hold, this fleeing one thing and seeking another, one is really inclined to discern some higher prescription; one ascribes to such substances a sort of volition and power to choose and the technical term "elective affinities" seems perfectly justified.'

'Describe such a case to me,' said Charlotte.

But the Captain replied: 'One cannot do these things justice in words and one ought not to try. As I said, as soon as I can show you the experiments themselves everything will be clearer and more agreeable. At present you would have to make do with frightful technical terms which would give you no real idea. These entities, which seem lifeless and are yet in themselves always disposed to be active, need to be seen at work. They need an observer who will watch with some engagement of his sympathy how they seek one another out, how they attract and seize, destroy, devour, and consume one another and at once emerge from the closest possible union in a renewed and novel and unexpected form: it is then one credits them with eternal life, indeed with sense and understanding, since our own senses seem scarcely adequate to the task of observing them properly and our reason scarcely competent to grasp them.'

'I do not deny', said Eduard, 'that the strange technical terms will be bound to seem cumbersome and even ridiculous to anyone not reconciled to them by physical observation and by having grasped the concepts they represent. But for the time being we could easily express the relationships we are speaking of here with letters.'

'If you don't think it will seem pedantic,' said the Captain in reply, 'I can doubtless summarize what I was saying by using such symbols. Imagine an A closely bound to a B and by a variety of means and even by force not able to be separated from it; imagine a C in a similar relationship with a D; now bring the two pairs into contact; A will go over to D, C to B, without our being able to say who first left the other, who first with another was united again.'

'Well then,' said Eduard interrupting, 'until we have seen all this with our own eyes we shall think of these formulae as a sort of parable, out of which we can abstract a lesson for our own immediate use. You are the A, Charlotte, and I am your B: for do I not depend on you and come after you as the B does the A? The C is quite obviously the Captain, who for the time being has to some extent taken me away from you. Now it would be right and proper, to prevent you from departing into the void, to provide you with a D, and quite without question that must be the amiable young lady Ottilie, and you must not now make any further objection to her joining us.'

'Very well,' said Charlotte in reply, 'even though the illustration does not seem to me to fit our case exactly. I think it a lucky chance that today we are in complete agreement for once and that these natural and elective affinities have made it easier for me to disclose something to you. Let me then admit that this afternoon I decided to have Ottilie here. My housekeeper, who has served me so faithfully, is leaving to be married. So much for what concerns my side of the matter and my advantage. The reasons which concern Ottilie herself you will read out to us. I shan't look over your shoulder, and of course do not need to, knowing what they are. But read to us.' So saying she took out a letter and handed it to Eduard.

CHAPTER FIVE

The Principal's Letter

'YOUR Ladyship will forgive me if I say very little today. After the public examination, now completed, of our achievements with our pupils in the last year, I must write to all the parents and guardians of the outcome. Besides, I can afford to be brief, since in a very few words I can tell you a great deal. Your daughter has proved herself the first in every sense. The enclosed testimonials and her own letter describing the prizes she has received and expressing the satisfaction she feels at so pleasing a success, will set your mind at rest, and more than that will be a delight to you. My own delight is somewhat tempered since I foresee that we shall not much longer have any cause to hold back among us a young lady who has already advanced so far. I respectfully take my leave and at some date in the near future shall be so bold as to communicate to you what, in my view, her best course would be. My good friend the Assistant will write to you about Ottilie.'

The Assistant's Letter

'Our respected Principal permits me to write about Ottilie in part because, thinking as she does, it would pain her to communicate what has to be communicated, and in part also because she herself has to make an apology and would rather do it through me.

'Since I know only too well how little our dear Ottilie is able to express what she has in her and what her strengths are, I was somewhat anxious about the public examination, and all the more so since absolutely no preparation for it is possible and if it were to take the usual form we should not be able to prepare Ottilie even to make a good appearance. By the outcome my anxieties were all-too-fully justified: she did not receive any prizes and is also among those not given a testimonial. Need I dwell on it? In the handwriting others did not shape their letters quite so well as she did, but had much greater fluency; at reckoning everyone was quicker, and the difficult problems, at which she does better, were not set in this examination. Many outdid her at chattering and holding forth in French; in history she was not ready with her names and dates; in geography she needed to attend more to political classifications. In music she found neither the time nor the necessary calm for the presentation of her few modest pieces. In drawing she would certainly have won the prize: her outlines were clear and the execution both painstaking and intelligent. But unfortunately she had begun something too large, and did not finish.

'When the pupils had been dismissed and the examiners were making up their minds and allowing us, the teachers, to say a word at least, I soon saw that Ottilie was either not being mentioned at all or, if she were, then with indifference if not disapproval. I thought I might win some favour for her by describing frankly what she was like, and this I attempted with a double eagerness, first because I could speak with conviction and secondly because in earlier years I had found myself in the same unhappy predicament. I was listened to attentively; however, when I had finished the principal examiner made the following courteous but very definite reply: "We take it for granted that a person has talents. They must be developed into real abilities. This is the purpose of all education, this is the express and unmistakable intention of parents and guardians and, unspokenly, only half-consciously, of the children themselves. And this is the object of the examination, which judges teachers and pupils together. From what you have told us we may be very hopeful on the child's account, and you are certainly to be praised for your close attention to your pupils' talents. Convert these by this time next year into real abilities and neither you nor your favoured pupil will want for applause."

'I had already resigned myself to what followed, but I had not anticipated a worse thing, which occurred immediately after it. Our excellent Principal who, like a good shepherd, does not like to see even one of her sheep lost or, as was the case here, unadorned, when the gentlemen had taken their leave could not conceal her impatience and said to Ottilie who, whilst the others were enjoying their prizes, stood quite calmly at the window: "But for heaven's sake tell me how it is possible to seem so stupid without being it!" Ottilie replied with perfect composure: "Forgive me, Ma'am, I happen to have my headache again today, and quite badly." "No one would know!" said the Principal, usually such a sympathetic lady, and turned away crossly.

'Now, it is true: no one would know. For Ottilie's features do not alter nor have I ever seen her put her hand to her temple.

'And that was still not everything. Miss Luciane, your Ladyship, always lively and outspoken, was on that day, in her triumph, very boisterous and overweening. She danced round the room with her prizes and testimonials and even waved them in Ottilie's face. "You came off badly, didn't you?" she cried. Ottilie answered her with perfect composure: "There will be other examination days." "But you will always be last," your young lady cried, and danced away.

'Ottilie seemed composed to everyone else, but not to me. If she is combating some inner, unpleasant and powerful emotion this shows itself in the different colouring of her face. Her left cheek becomes red for a moment, whilst the right turns pale. I observed this sign, and my sympathy for her would not be restrained. I took the Principal aside, spoke earnestly with her about the matter. The excellent woman saw her mistake. We conferred, we had a long discussion, and without on that account becoming long-winded let me present to your Ladyship our decision and our request: that you have Ottilie home for a while. You will yourself be the best person to understand our reasons. If you agree to this course, I shall say more about how the dear child might be handled. If your daughter leaves us then, as seems likely, we shall be delighted to have Ottilie back.

'One more thing, which I might perhaps later omit to mention: I have never seen Ottilie demand anything, nor even ask for anything with any urgency. On the other hand there have been occasions, though not many, when she has sought to refuse something which was being asked of her. She does this with a gesture which, for anyone who has understood its meaning, is irresistible. She presses the palms of her raised hands together and brings them towards her breast, bowing very slightly as she does so and giving whoever is making a demand on her such a look that he gladly renounces everything he might be demanding or desiring. If your Ladyship should ever witness this gesture, which is not very likely, treating her as you do, then think of me and be indulgent with Ottilie.'

Eduard had read out these letters, smiling as he did so and shaking his head. Nor was there any lack of comment upon the persons involved and upon the situation.

'Enough!' Eduard cried at last. 'It is decided: let her come! Then you will be taken care of, my dear, and we can now bring forward a proposition of our own. It is becoming very necessary that I join the Captain in the east wing. Evenings and mornings are quite the best times to work together. In exchange you will have the nicest rooms on your side of the house for yourself and Ottilie.'

Charlotte made no objection, and Eduard elaborated upon the lives they would lead henceforth. He said, among other things: 'It is very considerate of our niece to have headaches on the left side; I sometimes have them on the right. If we get them together and are sitting opposite and I am leaning on my right elbow and she on her left, each head on a hand inclined in a different way, we shall make a fine pair of corresponding images.'

The Captain thought this perilous; but Eduard cried: 'Beware of the D, my dear chap. For what would B do if C were taken from him?'

'I should have thought', said Charlotte in reply, 'that that was obvious.'

'Of course it is!' Eduard cried. 'He would go back to his A, to his Alpha and Omega!' And he leapt to his feet and took Charlotte in his arms.

CHAPTER SIX

A CARRIAGE, bringing Ottilie, drew up. Charlotte went to meet her; the child hurried forward, threw herself at her feet, and embraced her knees.

'Why such abasement?' Charlotte asked in some confusion, and sought to raise her.

'I don't really mean it as an abasement,' Ottilie replied, and remained where she was. 'Only I am so happy to remember the time when I was no higher than your knee and was already so sure of your love.'

She stood up, and Charlotte embraced her warmly. She was introduced to the men and at once, as a guest, treated with especial respect. Beauty is everywhere a welcome guest. She seemed to listen closely to the conversation, without herself taking part.

Next morning Eduard said to Charlotte: 'She is an agreeable and entertaining girl.'

'Entertaining?' Charlotte replied with a smile. 'She never opened her mouth.'

'Really?' said Eduard in reply, and seemed to be thinking about it. 'How very strange!'

Charlotte gave the new arrival only a few indications how the house was to be managed. Ottilie had quickly seen – or rather, and better, had quickly *felt* – the whole order of things. She grasped without difficulty what she had to do for everyone and for each person in particular. Everything happened punctually. She could arrange things without seeming to give orders, and if there was any delay she at once did the job herself.

As soon as she saw how many hours she had at her disposal she asked Charlotte to let her make a timetable, which she kept to strictly. She did the work set before her in a manner Charlotte had been informed about by the

Assistant. She was left to do things as she liked. Only occasionally Charlotte sought to prompt her. For example, she would sometimes surreptitiously give her worn quills to use, to induce a greater fluency in her handwriting; but before long they were sharpened again.

The ladies had decided to speak French together whenever they were alone, and Charlotte kept this up all the more keenly seeing that Ottilie was more forthcoming in the foreign language and once practising it had been made into a duty. In French she often seemed to say more than she intended. Charlotte was particularly amused by her occasional, very pointed, and yet affectionate description of everything in her boarding-school. Ottilie became a welcome companion, and Charlotte hoped one day to have in her a reliable friend.

Meanwhile she took out those papers again which had to do with Ottilie, to remind herself what, in the past, the Principal and the Assistant had said about the child, and to compare their judgements with the present person. For Charlotte was of the opinion that it was never too soon to acquaint oneself with the character of the people one had to live with, so as to know what was to be expected of them, what might be improved in them, and what once and for all must be allowed and forgiven them.

Though she found in this examination nothing new, certain things she was already familiar with became more significant and more striking. Ottilie's moderation in eating and drinking, for example, did really cause her concern.

The women next gave their attention to the question of dress. Charlotte asked of Ottilie that she should dress so as to make a finer and more elegant appearance. At once the child, ever willing and assiduous, went to work on the materials she had already had as a present, and with very little help from anyone else soon managed to make clothes of them which were extremely becoming. The new fashions in dress enhanced her appearance; for since that which is attractive in a woman extends also over all she wears, it is as though we see her continually afresh and with new pleasure when she lends her qualities to a new apparel.

She thus became to the men, at once and more and more, what we can properly call a solace to the eye. For if the emerald by its splendid colour is kind to the sight – indeed, may even work healingly on that noble faculty – human beauty works with a far greater power on the outer and the inner senses. Whoever looks on beauty is immune against the advent of any evil; he feels in accord with himself and with the world.

Thus, in many ways their society had gained by Ottilie's arrival. The two men kept more regularly to the hour, indeed to the minute of their appointments. They were always as prompt as should be for meals, or to take tea or a walk. And especially in the evenings they were not in such a hurry to leave the table. Charlotte noticed as much, and observed them both. She wished to establish whether one was more decisive in this than the other; but she could not discern any difference. Both were altogether more sociable. In their conversation they seemed to be mindful of what would be likely to arouse Ottilie's interest, and of what she would be likely to understand or know something about. If they were reading or recounting something, they would break off and wait for her to return. They became gentler and generally more communicative.

In response to this Ottilie's willingness to be of service increased daily. The better she got to know the house, its people, their circumstances, the more eagerly she made her contribution, ever-more quickly understanding every glance, every movement, an unfinished word, a sound. Her quiet attentiveness remained constant, as did also her calm busyness. And so her sitting and standing, coming and going, fetching and carrying, and sitting down again were one eternal change without a hint of agitation, an eternal movement giving pleasure. Furthermore, she trod so softly that they never heard her come or go.

Ottilie's properly obliging ways were a great joy to Charlotte. There was only one thing which seemed to her not quite appropriate, and she let it be known. 'It is a commend-able act of kindness', she said to Ottilie one day, 'to bend down quickly if somebody drops something and to pick it up forthwith. We show ourselves, in a manner of speaking, willing to serve that person. But in society one must consider whom one is showing such submissiveness to. Towards other women I shall not prescribe you any rules. You are young. Towards women who are older than you and who are your superiors in society it is a duty; towards your equals it is an attractive courtesy, and to women younger than you or below you it shows you to be human and good-natured. But it is not quite proper for a woman to show herself submissive and willing to be of service towards men in this way.'

'I shall try to get out of the habit,' said Ottilie in reply. 'Meanwhile you will forgive me this little impropriety if I tell you how I got into it. We were taught history. I have not retained as much as I doubtless ought to have, for I never knew what I should need it for. Only isolated scenes made an impression on me. This one for instance:

'When Charles I of England stood before his so-called judges the gold knob of the little staff he carried fell to the floor. Accustomed, if ever such a thing happened, to having everyone bustling to help he seemed to look around him and to expect that on this occasion too someone would do him this small service. Nobody moved; he bent down himself and picked up the knob. Rightly or wrongly, I thought this such a painful thing – I don't know whether I should have done – that since then I have never been able to see anyone drop anything without bending down for it. But since of course that may not always be a proper thing to do and since –' she continued with a smile – 'I cannot on every occasion tell my story, I shall in future be a little more restrained.'

Meanwhile continuous progress was being made on the schemes the men felt themselves called upon to pursue. Indeed, every day there was something new to be thought about and undertaken.

One day, when they were walking through the village together, they noticed with displeasure how much less clean and tidy it was than those villages whose inhabitants are so for very want of space.

'You will remember', said the Captain, 'that when we were travelling through Switzerland we remarked how pleasingly and effectively one might improve the so-called parkland of a country house by obliging a village situated as this one is to adopt not the Swiss style of building but those very advantageous virtues, Swiss neatness and cleanliness.'

'Here, for example,' said Eduard in reply, 'that would be quite feasible. The hill where the Hall is falls away to a point; the village is built in a fairly regular semicircle facing it; between them runs the stream, and to stop it flooding one man has used stones, another stakes, another old rafters, and his neighbour planks, nobody doing any good to anybody else, but each on the contrary causing himself and everyone else only damage and disadvantage. And the road likewise goes up and down and through the water and over the stones in a very unintelligent way. If the people would only co-operate it would not take much to put up a wall all along here in an arc and raise the road behind it to the level of the houses, create a pleasing open space, encourage some tidiness and, by thinking on a larger scale, be rid of all these trivial annoyances and shortcomings at a stroke.'

'Let us try it,' said the Captain, running his eye over the scene and assessing it rapidly.

'I dislike having to do with peasants and tradespeople,' said Eduard, 'unless I can actually give them orders.'

'I can hardly blame you,' the Captain replied. 'In my own life I have had more than enough trouble from such dealings. How hard people find it to set the sacrifice that must be made against the benefits that would result. Or to want the end and not reject the means. And many even confuse the means and the end, are pleased by the former and lose sight of the latter. They want every evil curing at the point of its appearance, and pay no attention to where it actually has its origins and cause. That is why any consultation is so difficult, especially with the lower classes who in day-to-day matters are perfectly sensible but who seldom see further ahead than tomorrow. And if it happens that in any communal undertaking one party stands to lose and another to gain, then seeking to proceed by agreement will be futile. Anything which is really for the common good will be done by the unrestricted exercise of sovereign power, or not at all.'

Whilst they were standing there in conversation a beggar approached them. His effrontery seemed greater than his need. Eduard, cross at the interruption and unsettled, told him off, having first several times in a more measured fashion but vainly motioned him away; but when the fellow retreated only gradually, muttering and even answering back and defiantly claiming a beggar's rights and that, though he might be refused alms, he should not be insulted since he was as much under the protection of God and the Law as anyone else, Eduard lost all control.

The Captain said then, to soothe him: 'Let us see to it, having had this encounter, that our supervision of local matters extends to cover mendicancy too. Of course, one must give alms, but it is better not to give them oneself, and certainly not on one's home ground. Moderation and consistency in all things, including charity. Too great a generosity will attract beggars, not keep them away; whereas when a man is travelling he might well choose to appear to some pauper by the roadside like Good Luck itself and throw him a gift beyond all expectation as he hurries by. The village and the Hall being situated as they are, we should easily be able to make a suitable arrangement. It is a thing I have already given some thought to.

'At one end of the village is the inn, and an elderly and respectable married couple live at the other. You need to leave a small sum of money in both places. Nothing will be given to a person entering the village, only to a person leaving it, and since both places are also on the roads leading up to the Hall anyone heading that way will be referred to one or other of them instead.'

'Come along,' said Eduard, 'let us arrange it at once. We can always see to the details later.'

They went to the innkeeper and to the elderly couple, and the thing was done.

'I know very well', said Eduard as they climbed the hill back to the Hall together, 'that insight and resolution are what matter in life. You were, for example, entirely right in your judgement of the work my wife was doing in the grounds, and you gave me at the same time an indication as to how it might be improved which, I readily admit, I at once passed on to her.'

'I guessed as much,' said the Captain, 'and wished you hadn't. You made her unsure, she has left everything lying and on this one account is at odds with us, avoids all mention of it and has not invited us to the summer-house again though she does go up there with Ottilie between times.'

'We must not let ourselves be put off by that,' Eduard replied. 'If I am once persuaded that some good thing could and ought to happen I cannot rest until I have seen it done. We have found ways and means in the past, have we not? Let us make it our entertainment one evening that we get out the volumes on English country houses, with the engravings, and then your map of the estate. We treat it first as though it were problematical and not a serious proposition. That we are in earnest will be obvious soon enough.'

It was done as Eduard suggested. When the volumes were opened they saw for each case an outline of the terrain and drawings of the landscape in its first rough and natural state, then on other pages depictions of the changes wrought on it by art in such a way as to utilize and enhance all the good already present there. The transition to their own property, to their own surroundings and to what might be made of them, was an easy one.

Though it was a pleasure now to base their deliberations on the map drawn by the Captain, still they could not entirely get away from that first conception which had been Charlotte's starting point. But they devised an easier ascent to the ridge; and they would put up a sort of pavilion high on the slopes against a pleasant little copse; it would bear on the Hall, it would be visible from the Hall windows, and from it the Hall and the gardens would be overlooked.

The Captain had considered everything carefully and made his calculations; and he returned to the subject of the road through the village, the wall along the stream and the filling in that would be needed there. 'Building an easy way up to the ridge,' he said, 'I shall gain just the quantity of stone I need for that wall. When one thing fits into another like that both can be achieved with less expense and more expeditiously.'

'But now this is my concern,' said Charlotte. 'A definite sum will have to be set aside. If we know how much is needed for a project of this kind then we can divide it up, if not week by week at least month by month. The purse is in my hands, I pay the bills and keep the accounts.'

'You don't seem to trust us very far,' said Eduard.

'No,' Charlotte replied, 'not very far in matters of whim. There we have more control than you do.'

The arrangement was agreed, the work soon begun, the Captain always present and Charlotte now almost daily a witness of his earnest and resolute mind. He for his part learned to know her better and both began to find it easy to work together and get results.

It is in any such undertaking as it is in dancing: two people in step are bound to become dependent on one another, and a mutual goodwill inevitably develops. That Charlotte was indeed well disposed towards the Captain since getting to know him more closely was proved for certain when in all serenity and with no disagreeable feelings whatsoever she allowed him to destroy a very pretty resting place which in her first endeavours she had picked out and beautified particularly but which stood now in the way of his plan.

CHAPTER SEVEN

Since now Charlotte and the Captain were occupied together it followed that Eduard was more in the company of Ottilie. Feelings of a quietly affectionate nature had in any case for some time already inclined him towards her. She was helpful and considerate to everyone, but most of all to him, or so he flattered himself. And without question: she had already noticed exactly what things he liked to eat, how he liked them served, how much sugar he took in his tea – nothing of that sort escaped her. She was most careful to shield him from draughts, since he was inordinately sensitive to them and on that account was sometimes at odds with his wife who liked as much air as possible. She likewise always knew what needed to be done in the orchard and the garden. She sought to further the things he desired and prevent those by which he might be irritated; to such an extent that before long she had become his guardian angel, he could not manage without her, and began to find it painful when she was not there. Added to that, she seemed more talkative and more open when they were alone together.

There was still something childlike about Eduard even as he grew older, and Ottilie, young herself, liked this in him especially. They took pleasure in remembering earlier occasions when they had seen one another; these memories went back into the very first period of Eduard's affection for Charlotte. Ottilie claimed to be able to remember them as the handsomest pair at Court; and when Eduard refused to believe that she could remember anything so early in her childhood, she insisted that one occasion in particular was still perfectly fresh in her mind: how once when he came in she had hidden her face in Charlotte's skirts, and not out of fear but out of a childish astonishment. She might have added: because he had made such a lively impression on her, because she had liked him so much.

Things being thus, a good deal of business which the two men had earlier taken up together now to some extent faltered, so that it became necessary for them to get a clear view again, draft a few memoranda, write letters. Accordingly, they agreed to meet in their office room, where they found their old copyist sitting idle. They set to work, and soon gave him things to do, without noticing that they were putting on to him several matters which formerly they had been accustomed to dealing with themselves. The Captain had difficulties with the very first memorandum, and Eduard with the very first letter. They struggled for a while among rough drafts and rewritings until Eduard, who was making the least headway, asked what the time was.

Then it turned out that the Captain, for the first time in many years, had forgotten to wind his watch; and they began to suspect, if not already actually to feel, that time was becoming unimportant to them.

Whilst the men thus to some extent pursued their affairs less energetically, the industry of the women only increased. In general a family's usual mode of life, engendered by the given persons and by necessary circumstances, will take even an extraordinary new affection, a developing passion, into itself as into a vessel, and quite some time may elapse before this new ingredient causes any noticeable fermentation and rises foaming over the brim.

The affections arising mutually among our friends had the happiest effect. Their souls were opened and a general goodwill came forth out of the particular. Each was contented, and did not begrudge the others a like contentment.

Such a condition elevates the spirit by enlarging the feelings, so that everything one does and projects tends towards boundlessness. The friends no longer kept within the house. Their walks extended, and whilst Eduard and Ottilie hurried ahead to decide the paths and clear a way, the Captain and Charlotte followed behind at a sedater pace, conversing

seriously and taking pleasure in many a newly discovered spot
and in many an unexpected view.

Their walk led them one day from the eastern gate down to
the inn, over the bridge and towards the ponds, which they
kept to then, near the water, as far as it was usual to go, until
the banks became impeded by a bushy hillside and later by
cliffs and ceased to be passable.

But Eduard, who was familiar with the locality from the
days of his going out hunting there, pushed ahead with Ottilie
on an overgrown path, knowing that the old mill, which was
hidden in the gully, could not be far off. The little-used path
soon gave out, however, and they became lost among mossy
rocks in a dense undergrowth. But not for long: they soon
heard the mill-wheels and knew they were close.

Stepping out on to a spur they saw the strange wooden
building, black and ancient, below them in the little ravine,
under the shadow of tall trees and the high rock faces. They
decided without more ado to climb down over the moss and
broken rock, Eduard leading; and when he looked up and
Ottilie, stepping lightly without fear or apprehension, was
following him and keeping her balance beautifully from stone
to stone, he seemed to see a being from heaven hovering
above him. And when at times, coming to a difficult place,
she seized his outstretched hand or even leaned on his
shoulder for support, then there was no denying that it was
a woman, with all her delicacy and lightness, who was touching him. He could almost have wished that she might stumble
and slip so that he could catch her up in his arms and press
her to his heart. But he never would have done this, and for
more than one reason: he was afraid of offending her, and
also of harming her.

Our meaning here will be plain in a moment. For when he
was down and sitting opposite her under the tall trees at the
rustic table, and the miller's friendly wife had been sent for
milk and the miller himself, full of welcome, had been sent to
find Charlotte and the Captain, Eduard after some hesitation
began to speak:

'My dear Ottilie, there is something I want you to do. Forgive me for asking, even if you refuse. You make no secret of the fact – and why should you? – that under your dress, on your bosom, you wear a miniature. It is the portrait of your father, of that excellent man whom you scarcely knew and who in every sense deserves a place near your heart. But forgive me: the picture is unsuitably large, and the metal and the glass alarm me unspeakably whenever you lift up a child or carry something or if the carriage sways or when we are pushing through the undergrowth, or just now coming down the rocks. I am terrified by the possibility that some unforeseen knock or fall or contact might be harmful or even fatal to you. To please me then: remove the picture, not from your thoughts, not from your room – indeed, give it the finest and holiest place in your apartment – but remove from your bosom a thing whose presence seems to me in my perhaps exaggerated nervousness so very dangerous.'

Ottilie said nothing and had looked straight ahead of her as he spoke; then, neither hurrying nor hesitating, looking more towards heaven than at Eduard, she undid the chain, drew out the portrait, pressed it against her forehead, and handed it to her friend with the words: 'Keep it for me until we are home. I have no better way of showing you how much I appreciate your friendly concern.'

Her friend did not dare press the picture to his lips, but he took her hand and pressed it against his eyes. They were perhaps the loveliest hands that had ever been clasped together. It was as if a weight had been lifted from his heart, as if a dividing wall between himself and Ottilie had been removed.

Led by the miller, Charlotte and the Captain came down on an easier path. There was a welcoming, and joyfulness and refreshment. They were unwilling to take the same way home, and Eduard suggested a rocky path on the other side of the stream which brought them, with some exertion on their part, back into a view of the ponds. Now they were traversing a mixed woodland and, looking away, they had sight of frequent villages, little open towns, and dairy farms in green and fertile surroundings; and, nearest, one remote holding that lay very snugly in the woodland high up. The region was revealed most beautifully and in its greatest richness before and behind them once they had climbed the gradual slope, and there they entered a cheerful copse of trees and, emerging from it, found themselves on the rocky eminence facing the Hall.

How delighted they were by their more or less unexpected arrival at that place. They had done the tour of a little world; they were standing where the new building was to be, and looking across again at the windows of their home.

They climbed down to the summer-house and sat there all four together for the first time. It was, very naturally, the unanimous wish that the day's walk, which they had done slowly and not without difficulty, should be so devised and accommodated that it could be done more companionably, at a stroll and in comfort. Everyone made suggestions, and they calculated that the route for which they had needed several hours, if it were well laid out, must lead back to the Hall in an hour. Below the mill, where the stream flowed into the ponds, they were already erecting a bridge which would shorten the way and adorn the landscape when Charlotte reined in their inventive imaginations a little by reminding them of the costs which such an undertaking would entail.

'There too we have a solution,' Eduard replied. 'All we need do is sell the holding in the woods that looks so well situated but brings in so little, and spend the revenue on this project, and in that way, having the pleasure of a priceless walk, we enjoy the profits of a good investment, whereas at present, according to our last accounts at the end of the year, we draw, to our annoyance, only a pitiable income from it.'

Charlotte herself, as a good housekeeper, could make no real objection. The matter had come under discussion before now. The Captain proposed dividing up the parcels of land among the farmers who had their living in the woodlands; but in Eduard's view there was a quicker and easier way of proceeding. The present tenant, who had already made offers, should have it and pay in instalments, and in like instalments their own project would be undertaken stage by stage according to a plan.

So reasonable and measured an arrangement was bound to meet with approval, and the whole company was already imagining the leisurely new paths and along them and near them, waiting to be discovered, the pleasantest places for rest and for a view.

At home that evening, in order to have a picture of everything in greater detail, they at once took out the new map of the estate. They followed the way they had gone and saw how in one or two places it might be improved. All their earlier proposals were discussed again in the light of their most recent thinking; the situation of the new house, opposite the Hall, was given renewed approval, and the whole circular route to it and from it decided on.

Ottilie had not offered any opinion when Eduard finally turned the map, which until then had lain before Charlotte, towards her and invited her to speak her mind and, when she hesitated a moment, urged her in the friendliest way not to be silent, nothing was ruled out, everything was open still.

Ottilie laid her finger on the highest flat surface of the ridge. 'I would build the house here,' she said. 'True, you would not see the Hall, the trees would hide it; but what you would gain would be the feeling of being in a new and different world, since the village and all the dwelling places would be hidden too. The view over the ponds, towards the mill, towards the high ground, the mountains, out into the country, is extraordinarily beautiful, as I noticed when we passed.'

'She is right!' Eduard cried. 'How could it have escaped us? This is what you mean, Ottilie, is it not?' And taking a pencil he drew in a crude and emphatic oblong on the ridge.

The Captain winced; it pained him to see his careful and neatly drawn map disfigured in this way; but, after gently expressing his unhappiness, he controlled himself and considered the proposal: 'Ottilie is right,' he said. 'Would we not after all go quite some distance to drink coffee or eat a fish we should not have enjoyed so much at home? We want novelty, variety. Building the Hall where they did, an older generation showed good sense, for it has shelter from the winds and is near the things we need every day; but a house intended more for social gatherings than for living in will be very well placed up there, and many pleasant hours may be spent in it during the summer months.'

The more they discussed the matter the more persuaded they became; and Eduard could not conceal his delight that it was Ottilie's idea. He was as proud as if he had thought of it himself.

CHAPTER EIGHT

THE very next morning the Captain made an examination of the site, drew first a rough sketch and then, when all four had conferred again at the place itself, did an exact plan along with an estimate of the costs and everything else that might be required. The necessary preparations were begun. The business of selling the farmstead was at once resumed. Again the two men had plenty to do together.

The Captain observed to Eduard that it would be a nice thing, indeed that it was almost their obligation, to celebrate Charlotte's birthday by laying the foundation stone. Eduard's old antipathy towards such occasions was soon overcome, since it quickly occurred to him to celebrate Ottilie's birthday, which fell later, in a similarly ceremonious fashion.

Charlotte, who thought the new projects and what they entailed a significant, serious, even almost a worrying matter, spent her time going over again, for herself, the estimates and the schedule of work and disbursements. They saw less of one another during the day, and were all the more desirous of one another's company in the evening.

Ottilie meanwhile had become entirely the mistress of the household, and how could it be otherwise, given her quiet and steady conduct? Besides, her whole disposition was towards the house and domestic matters, rather than towards the world and a life in the open air. Eduard soon noticed that really she only went with them on their walks to be obliging, and in the evenings stayed longer out of doors only to be sociable, and indeed would sometimes find something that needed doing in the house as an excuse to go indoors again. Very soon, then, he managed to arrange their walks together so as to be home before sunset, and began reading poetry aloud again, which he had not done for a long time, and particularly poems into whose reading he could put the expression of a pure but passionate love.

In the evenings they usually sat around a low table on seats which they fetched to it: Charlotte on the sofa, Ottilie on a chair opposite her, and the men taking the two sides. Ottilie sat on Eduard's right, which was where he pushed the light when he was reading. Thereupon Ottilie moved closer, to see the book itself, for she was another who trusted her own eyes more than somebody else's lips; and Eduard likewise moved nearer, to make it in every way easier for her; indeed, he often made longer pauses than was necessary, so that he would on no account turn the page before she had come to the end of it.

Charlotte and the Captain noticed this, of course, and now and then smiled across at one another; but both were surprised by another occasion when Ottilie's silent affection was made manifest.

Once, when tiresome visitors had deprived the little company of a part of an evening, Eduard proposed that they should remain a while together. He felt in the mood to take up his flute again, which for a long time had not been usual. Charlotte began looking for the sonatas which they were accustomed to perform together, and since they were not to be found Ottilie, after some hesitation, admitted that she had taken them to her room.

'And you could accompany me on the piano?' Eduard cried, his eyes shining with delight. 'And will you?'

'Yes,' said Ottilie. 'We shall manage, I daresay.' She fetched the music and sat down at the piano. Those listening noticed and were amazed how completely Ottilie had learned the piece for herself, but what amazed them even more was how she managed to accommodate it to Eduard's manner of playing. 'Managed to accommodate' is not the right expression; for whereas Charlotte skilfully and of her own free will held back to suit her husband when he hesitated and kept up with him when he raced ahead, it seemed that Ottilie, who had heard them play the sonatas on a number of occasions, had only learned them in the way that belonged to the man she was accompanying. She had made his faults so much her own that in the end something whole and alive came out of them that did not keep proper time, it is true, but was extremely agreeable and pleasing to listen to nevertheless. The composer himself would have been delighted to see his work distorted in such a loving way.·

The Captain and Charlotte watched this strange and unexpected encounter in silence, and with such feelings as one often has when witnessing childish acts which, because of their worrying consequences one cannot entirely approve of but cannot disapprove of either, which one indeed may even be bound to envy. For in fact their own affection was developing no less than that between Eduard and Ottilie, and perhaps even more dangerously since both were more serious, surer of themselves, and more capable of self-restraint.

The Captain was already beginning to feel that a process of irresistible habituation was threatening to bind him to Charlotte. He forced himself to avoid those times when Charlotte usually came out into the grounds; rose very early, saw to everything necessary, and withdrew then to his own wing of the house, to work. For the first few days Charlotte thought it accidental and went looking for him in all the likely places; then she believed she understood his intention, and respected him all the more.

If now the Captain avoided being alone with Charlotte, he was all the more active in furthering and hastening the preparations for the splendid celebration of her approaching birthday; for whilst he was laying the easy path from below, beginning behind the village, he had at the same time, in order to extract stone, as he said, ordered the work to start from the top, and had arranged and calculated everything so that only in the night before the event should the two halves of the path be joined. For the new house up above, the cellar had been not so much dug as hewn out of the rock, and a fine foundation-stone had been sculpted, with little compartments and a coping.

This combination of outward activity, of small, affectionate, and secret purposes, with feelings within which were being more or less repressed, rather dampened the company's enjoyment when they were together; so much so that Eduard, who felt that something was lacking, one evening urged the Captain to get out his violin and accompany Charlotte on the piano. The Captain gave way to the general wish and together they performed one of the hardest pieces with feeling, ease, and freedom, which gave them and their two listeners the greatest satisfaction. They promised one another frequent repeat performances and practices together.

'They do better than we do, Ottilie,' said Eduard. 'Let us admire them, but enjoy our own partnership none the less.'

CHAPTER NINE

THE birthday had arrived and everything was ready. The village street had been raised and bordered by a wall, against the stream. The path which passed the church, continuing for a while on the course laid down for it by Charlotte, now wound its way up among the rocks, having the summerhouse first on the left above it, then, after doubling back entirely, on the left below it, and so gradually reached the top.

There were many guests that day. They went to church where, dressed for a great occasion, the whole parish was assembled. After the service the boys, the young men, and the grown men, as it had been arranged, left first; then came the Hall with all their party and their retinue; girls, young women, and married women brought up the rear.

On the bend a raised-up place had been set into the rock; here, at the Captain's suggestion, Charlotte and the guests paused for breath. They had a view over the whole route, the company of men, already come up, and the women following them, now going past. On a day of splendid weather it was an exceptionally beautiful scene. Charlotte was surprised, moved, and she pressed the Captain's hand affectionately.

They followed the crowd which, at a leisurely pace, had climbed ahead and had by now formed a ring around the site of the new building. The owner himself then and those closest to him, as well as the highest-ranking guests, were invited to descend into the depths where the foundation-stone, supported under one side, was ready to be laid down. A mason, resplendently dressed, trowel in one hand and hammer in the other, gave a fine speech in rhyme which we must do less than justice to and reproduce here in prose.

'Three things', he began, 'are needful in a building: that it is in the right place, that it has good foundations, and that it is perfectly executed. The first is really the business of the man whose house it will be. For just as in town only the prince and the municipality can decide where any building should be allowed, so in the country it is the privilege of the man who owns the land to say: my dwelling place shall be here and nowhere else.'

Eduard and Ottilie did not dare to look at one another when they heard these words, although they were close and face to face.

'In the third, the execution, men of very many trades are involved; indeed, few trades are *not* involved. But the second, the foundation, is the responsibility of the mason and, to speak the truth, it is the most important in the whole undertaking. It is a serious business, and our invitation is a serious one: for this occasion is celebrated in the depths. Here within the confines of this excavated space you do us the honour of appearing as witnesses of our secret proceedings. In a moment this sculpted stone will be laid down and these walls of earth, for the present still decorated with beautiful and dignified living figures, will soon no longer be accessible, they will be underground.

'This foundation-stone, whose corner will mark the right-hand corner of the building, whose squareness will signify its regularity, and whose horizontal and vertical setting will ensure the plumb and level trueness of all the outside and inside walls, might now be laid in place without more ado, for it would surely rest on its own weight. But there shall be lime here too, in a mortar, to bind; for just as people who are naturally inclined to one another hold together better still when cemented by the Law, so likewise stones, suited in shape, are joined even better by these powers that bind; and since it is not proper that you should be idle while others are active, you will, I am sure, be willing to take a part in the work.'

So saying, he gave Charlotte his trowel and with it she threw mortar under the stone. Several others were encouraged to do the same, then the stone was lowered; whereupon Charlotte and the rest were handed the hammer and expressly blessed the union of the stone with the ground, by tapping three times.

The speaker continued: 'The mason's work, now open to the sky, though it is not always performed in concealment will finish in concealment nevertheless. The foundations, properly laid, will be filled in; and even with the walls, which we raise in the daylight, it is rare that we are remembered in the end. The stone-cutter's work and the sculptor's are more visible, and when the decorator extinguishes all trace of our hands and claims our work for his own because he covers it and colours it and smooths it over, that too we must accept.

'Who then more than the mason will be concerned to make what he does right for himself, by doing it right? Who has more reason than he has to nourish his own self-respect? When the house has been built, the floors levelled and tiled, the outside ornamented, he will still see in through all the layers and still discern those regular and careful joints to which the whole owes its existence and its stay.

'But just as anyone who has done something wrong is bound to be afraid that despite all his efforts it will come to light one day, so too a man who has done the right thing in secret must always expect it to surface against his will. For that reason we make this foundation-stone into a memorial stone as well. In the various cavities carved here various things are to be laid, as evidence, for a distant posterity. These sealed metal containers hold written memorials; all manner of curious things have been engraved into these metal plates; the best old wines will be buried in these beautiful glass bottles, with a note of their vintage; and there are besides different coins minted in the present year – all this we have received through the generosity of the man for whom we build. And there is still room, should any guest or spectator feel inclined to make over something to posterity.'

There was a short pause, and the mason looked around him; but as is usually the case on such occasions nobody was prepared, everyone was taken by surprise, until finally a young and cheerful army officer began, and said: 'If I am to contribute something which has not yet been laid down in this treasure house I must cut a couple of buttons off my uniform, for surely they also deserve to be passed on to posterity.' No sooner said than done! Now others had similar ideas. The ladies hurried to put in little combs from their hair; bottles of smelling salts and other fine articles were likewise sacrificed. Only Ottilie hesitated, until Eduard with a friendly word broke in upon her contemplation of all the things which had been contributed and placed in the receptacles. Thereupon she undid from her neck the golden chain on which the picture of her father had hung and laid it down gently over the other jewellery. Eduard then, in some haste, at once had the cover fitted on and sealed.

The young mason, having been the busiest in these proceedings, now resumed his manner of a public speaker, and continued: 'We lay down this stone for ever, to secure the longest enjoyment of the house by its present and future owners. However, whilst here, as it were, burying a treasure we are mindful also, in this most fundamental of all matters, of the fleetingness of human things. We entertain the possibility that the lid here so securely sealed might one day be raised again, which could only happen if all that we have not yet even built were then to be destroyed.

'But precisely in order that it shall be built let us bring our thoughts back from the future and into the present. Let us, as soon as today's festivities are over, at once go on with our work so that none who follow at their own tasks upon our foundations need ever be idle but the building will rise up speedily and be finished and at the windows, which are not yet there, the master of the house with his nearest and dearest and his guests may look around him cheerfully, and their good health and the health of all present we hereby drink to now.'

So saying he emptied, at a draught, a beautifully cut glass and threw it into the air; for we mark the superabundance of our joy by destroying the vessel we made use of when we were joyful. But on this occasion it happened differently: the glass did not fall to the ground again, and not because of a miracle.

In order to get on with the building the ground in the far corner had already been completely dug out and a start made on the walls, and for this purpose scaffolding had been erected to the full height that would be required.

For this occasion, for the benefit of the workers themselves, it had been planked and a crowd of spectators permitted up. The glass rose to their height and was caught by one of them, who thought this a very happy occurrence and omen for himself. He was showing the glass around, without letting it out of his hand, and on it could be seen the letters E and O engraved together in a very decorative intertwining. It was one of the glasses which had been made for Eduard when he was young.

The scaffold was empty again, the most agile among the guests climbed up to look around, and there was no end to their praise of the prospects on all sides; for anyone standing on a high place, and even only one storey higher, discovers all manner of things. Looking out into the open country several new villages became visible; the silver line of the river could be seen clearly; indeed, one viewer claimed to be able to see the towers of the capital. In the other direction, behind the wooded hills, rose the blue peaks of a distant range of mountains; and the immediate vicinity could be seen entire. 'All it needs,' somebody cried, 'is for the three ponds to be made into one lake; then the view would lack nothing grand or desirable.'

'That could be done,' said the Captain. 'They used to be a mountain lake in earlier times.'

'But spare my copse of plane trees and poplars,' said Eduard, 'that stand so handsomely by the middle pond. Look –' he turned to Ottilie, led her a few steps forward and pointed down – 'I planted those trees myself.'

'How long have they been there?' Ottilie asked.

'About as long', Eduard replied, 'as you have been on earth. Yes, I was already planting trees when you were still in your cradle, my dear child.'

The company returned to the Hall. After dinner they were invited to take a walk through the village, to inspect the improvements there too. Instructed by the Captain the villagers had assembled in front of their houses; they were not standing in rows but were grouped naturally in their families, some, as the evening demanded, busy with tasks, others resting on newly provided benches. And they had been given the pleasant duty of repeating this cleanliness and orderliness at least every Sunday and every holiday.

When the true sociability of the heart, such as had arisen among our friends, is interrupted by any larger company, that will always be unwelcome. All four were pleased to find themselves alone again in the spacious drawing-room; but this homely feeling was somewhat spoiled when Eduard was handed a letter announcing the arrival of new guests on the following day.

'As we expected,' Eduard exclaimed to Charlotte, 'the Count will not let us down: he arrives tomorrow.'

'Then the Baroness will not be far away,' Charlotte replied.

'Indeed not!' said Eduard. 'She will make her own way here tomorrow too. They ask to be accommodated overnight and will leave next day together.'

'Then we must prepare things at once, Ottilie,' said Charlotte.

'What orders do you have?' Ottilie asked.

Charlotte gave some general indications, and Ottilie withdrew.

The Captain enquired after the relationship of these two persons, since he knew about it only in the most general way. Some time ago, both already married, they had fallen passionately in love with one another. Two marriages were shaken, and not without scandal; there was talk of divorce. In the case of the Baroness it became possible, but not in the Count's. They were obliged to pretend to separate, but their relationship continued; and though during the winter in the capital they could not be together, they made up for it in summer when they could travel and visit the spas. Both were a little older than Eduard and Charlotte and all four had been close friends since their earliest years at Court together. Good relations had been maintained, without that implying complete mutual approval. But on this occasion Charlotte did feel their arrival to be in a certain sense wholly inopportune, and if she were entirely honest as to the reason, it was on account of Ottilie. The child was too young, too good and innocent, to be exposed to such an example.

'They might have waited a day or two,' said Eduard, just as Ottilie came back into the room, 'until the farm was quite sold. The contract is ready, I have one copy here, we need the second, and our old clerk is not at all well.' The Captain offered his services, Charlotte also; but there were reasons why they should not. 'Give it to me,' said Ottilie, rather in haste.

'You won't manage it,' said Charlotte.

'I should have to have it by the day after tomorrow,' said Eduard, 'first thing. And it is long.'

'It will be ready,' Ottilie cried, and the document was already in her hands.

Next morning when they were looking out from an upper window for their guests, whom they wanted to be sure to go and meet, Eduard said: 'Who is that riding so slowly down the road towards us?' The Captain described the rider's appearance more closely. 'It's him,' said Eduard. 'The details which you see better than I do exactly fit the whole which I see very well. It's Mittler. But why is he riding slowly, and so very slowly at that?'

The figure drew nearer, and it was indeed Mittler. They welcomed him with affection as he came slowly up the steps. 'Why did you not come yesterday?' Eduard shouted.

'I dislike noisy occasions,' he replied. 'But I am here today to celebrate my friend's birthday with you quietly after the event.'

'How can you afford the time?' Eduard asked in jest.

'You owe my visit, which you may or may not be glad of, to a thought which occurred to me yesterday. I had spent half the day very agreeably in a household in which I had acted as a peacemaker, and then I heard that a birthday was being celebrated over here. "Really, one might call it selfishness," I said to myself, "that you are only willing to enjoy yourself with people you have reconciled. Why do you not enjoy yourself for once with friends who are never at odds?" With the result that here I am. I have done as I said I should.'

'Yesterday you would have had a lot of company,' said Charlotte, 'but not much today. There will be the Count and the Baroness, who have given you trouble in the past.'

That strange and welcome man sprang then in lively exasperation out from among the four companions and looked about him at once for his hat and riding-crop. 'Something will always come and spoil it if ever I allow myself a moment's peace and quiet. But why do I not keep to what I am? I should not have come, and now I am driven away. For I will not be under one roof with them; and beware: they bring nothing but ill. They are like leaven, they propagate their own infection.'

They tried to placate him, but in vain. 'Anyone who assaults the estate of matrimony,' he cried, 'anyone who in word and worse in deed undermines that foundation of all moral order has me to deal with; and if I cannot better him I keep out of his way. Marriage is the basis and the pinnacle of culture. It makes the uncultured gentle and in it the most cultured can best demonstrate their gentleness. It must never be dissolved, for it brings so much happiness that in comparison any individual unhappiness is of no significance. And what do people mean when they speak of unhappiness? It is impatience, which comes over them from time to time and then they are pleased to call themselves unhappy. Only let the moment pass and you will think yourselves fortunate that something which has stood so long still stands. There is never a sufficient reason for separation. The human condition is so rich in joy and sorrow that it cannot be calculated what a man and wife owe one another. The debt is infinite, and can only be paid through eternity. It may not always be easy, that I do not doubt, and why should it be? Are we not also married to our consciences, which we should also be glad to be rid of often enough, since they are more difficult than ever a man or woman might be to us?'

Thus he held forth, vehemently, and would doubtless have continued for quite some time if coach-horns had not announced the arrival of the two parties who, as though according to a programme, drove up before the house from their separate directions simultaneously. As the household hurried to meet them Mittler hid himself, had his horse brought down to the inn, and rode away in a bad temper.

CHAPTER TEN

THE guests were welcomed and led inside. They were delighted to be back in the house and in the rooms in which they had once spent many happy days, and which for some considerable time they had not revisited. Our friends were just as glad to see them there. The Count, and the Baroness too, might be numbered among those tall and handsome figures who are almost more pleasing to look at in middle age than in their youth; for though perhaps their first bloom may have passed, now they incline one not only to like them but also to feel towards them a decided confidence. This couple too were very easy to be with. They confronted the circumstances of life in a free and open-minded way, and this and their cheerfulness and their obvious lack of embarrassment were felt at once, and a rare courtesy gave limits to everything yet no one was aware of any constraint.

Their effect upon the company was immediate. The new arrivals, coming straight from society, as was apparent even in their clothes, their belongings, and in everything about them, were something of a contrast to our friends in their rural and secretly passionate state, but this very soon passed as old memories and a present interest mixed and rapid and lively talk quickly drew everyone together.

But before long there was a separation. The women withdrew to their own wing of the house, and in exchanging confidences and at the same time beginning to appraise the newest fashions in morning wear, hats, and suchlike, they found plenty to amuse them, whilst the men gave their attention to the new carriages and had horses brought out and at once began to deal and swap.

Not until dinner did everyone come together again. They had dressed, and in this too the visitors appeared to advantage. Everything they wore was new and as if never seen before and yet through use already accustomed and comfortable.

The conversation was lively and went to and fro, for in such company everything and nothing seems of interest. They conversed in French, to exclude the servants, and ranged with complacent boldness over worldly matters of a high and of a middling importance. On one topic the talk remained longer than perhaps it should have done, when Charlotte asked after an old friend and was dismayed to hear that she was about to be divorced.

'It is very disagreeable,' said Charlotte. 'We imagine our absent friends to be safe and well, we suppose a particular dear person to be quite catered for, and the next we hear her fate is precarious and she has been obliged to set off again on paths that may again be less than safe.'

The Count replied: 'Really, my dear, we have only ourselves to blame if such vicissitudes surprise us. We do so like to think that earthly things will last, and especially marriages, and concerning these we are beguiled by what we see again and again in the theatre into notions which do not accord with the way of the world. In comedy marriage is depicted as the final goal of desires whose fulfilment is postponed and hindered for the duration of several acts, and the instant it is achieved the curtain falls and that moment of satisfaction reverberates in us. In the real world things are different. The play continues behind the curtain, and if the curtain rises again we do not like to watch or listen any further.'

'It cannot be quite so bad,' said Charlotte with a smile, 'since we see people who have already quitted the stage very willing to act a part on it again.'

'There can be no objection to that,' said the Count. 'One might well wish to take on another role, and anyone who knows how the world is must see that in marriage too it is only this settled everlastingness in a world of such mutability which is somewhat out of place. I had a friend whose speciality in humour was suggesting new laws. He used to assert that all marriages should only be contracted for a period of five years. Five, he would say, is a nice, uneven, and holy number and that period is just sufficient to get to know one another, bring a few children into the world, fall out and – the nicest thing of all – make it up again. "How happy the early part would be!" he used to exclaim. Two or three years at least would go by quite pleasantly. Then very likely one of the partners would be anxious to see the relationship last longer, the desire to please would increase the closer they got to the ending of the contract. The indifferent – indeed, even a discontented – partner would be appeased and won over by such behaviour. They would be no more aware of the passage of time than one ever is in pleasant company, and would be very agreeably surprised when at last they noticed that their term had passed and had been tacitly extended.'

Clever and amusing though this was, and although, as Charlotte appreciated, the frivolous suggestion could be given a deep moral sense, talk of that kind was unpalatable to her, and particularly on account of Ottilie. She was well aware that there is nothing more dangerous than a conversation which takes liberties and treats as usual, commonplace, or even praiseworthy a situation which is reprehensible or half reprehensible; and surely it must be deemed dangerous whenever the marriage bond is belittled in that way. She sought, therefore, adroitly as ever, to change the subject; but failing to, she was sorry that Ottilie had managed things so well that there was no cause for her to leave the table. The girl, watchful, never flustered, had a perfect understanding with the major-domo; a glance from her sufficed, and everything ran smoothly, even though two or three of the servants were new and inexpert.

And so the Count, insensitive to Charlotte's efforts to change the subject, continued with it. He was never usually one to be the least tiresome in conversation, but this matter was too close to his heart and his difficulties in getting a divorce from his wife had embittered him against everything that concerned the marriage bond, which he himself none the less passionately desired to enter into with the Baroness.

'That friend of mine', he continued, 'made another legislative proposal. A marriage should only be held to be indissoluble when both partners, or at least one of them, had been married for the third time. For, incontrovertibly, any such person would have demonstrated that marriage for him or her was something he or she could not do without. And it would also have become known how such persons had behaved in their previous relationships, whether they had any peculiarities, which often give more cause for separation than real faults do. It would thus be up to both parties to find out about one another; and attention should be paid to the married and the unmarried alike, since one never knew what the future might bring.'

'That would at least greatly increase society's interest in these matters,' said Eduard. 'For really, as things are, once you marry nobody enquires any further after your virtues or your vices.'

'If that *were* the system,' the Baroness interjected with a smile, 'our good friends here would have already successfully completed two of the stages and could now be preparing themselves for the third.'

'They were lucky,' said the Count. 'In their case Death did willingly what the courts, when it is left to them, do very unwillingly.'

'Let us leave the dead in peace,' Charlotte answered with some seriousness in her look.

'Why should we,' the Count replied, 'if we can remember them with respect? They were not too demanding, they made do with quite a moderate number of years, and when they left they did a great deal of good.'

'If only such situations did not waste the best years of one's life,' said the Baroness, suppressing a sigh.

'Indeed,' said the Count, 'it might drive one to despair, if it were not the case that very few things in the world turn out as one had hoped. Children do not do what they promise; young people very rarely, and if they keep faith the world itself will not keep faith with them.'

Charlotte, glad to see the conversation changing tack, replied in cheerful tones: 'Well, we must in any case accustom ourselves soon enough to only a partial and fragmentary enjoyment of the good things of life.'

'Certainly,' the Count replied, 'you have both enjoyed very happy times. If I think of the years when you and Eduard were the handsomest pair at Court, nothing now approaches the brilliance of those times, nor are there people now as resplendent as you were. When you danced together all eyes were upon you, and how sought after you were whilst having eyes only for one another!'

'Since so much has changed,' said Charlotte, 'we may perhaps, in all modesty, permit ourselves to listen to such flatteries.'

'In my own mind', said the Count, 'I have often blamed Eduard for not being more persistent. His peculiar parents would surely have relented in the end, and an extra ten years, youthful ones at that, are not to be sniffed at.'

'I must put in a word in his defence,' said the Baroness. 'Charlotte was not entirely blameless. She did look elsewhere a little, it must be said. And although she loved Eduard dearly and in secret had decided upon him for her husband, I can vouch for how much she tormented him on occasions, so that he was easily persuaded that he should travel, take himself off, and get used to doing without her, which was a fateful decision.'

Eduard bowed to the Baroness and seemed grateful for her intercession.

'But then', she continued, 'there is one thing I must add to excuse Charlotte. The man who was courting her at that time had long been outstanding in his devotion and was, when one got to know him better, certainly more sympathetic than you are all willing to admit.'

'My dear lady,' the Count replied in somewhat heated tones, 'let us say quite frankly that you were yourself not entirely indifferent to him and that Charlotte had more to fear from you than from anyone else. I think it a very pretty trait in women that they retain their affection for a particular man so long – indeed, that no sort of separation causes them to waver in it or abandon it.'

'This is a quality which men may possess in even higher degree,' the Baroness replied. 'In your own case at least, my dear Count, I have observed that nobody has more sway over you than a woman you were once fond of. I have seen you do more when asked a favour by such a one than you might on behalf of the woman currently in your affections.'

'There may be no answer to a reproach of that kind,' said the Count, 'but as for Charlotte's first husband, I disliked the man for this reason: that he broke up a handsome couple, two people intended by Providence for one another who, once joined, need never have worried about the five-year term nor have looked ahead to any second or third contract.'

'We shall do our best', said Charlotte, 'to catch up on what we have missed.'

'Keep to that,' said the Count. 'For your first marriages', he continued with some vehemence, 'were after all marriages of the detestable kind. But then unfortunately marriage alto-gether has something – forgive me if I put this strongly – rather vulgar about it. It spoils the tenderest relationships, and really all it has to offer is a crass sort of security which perhaps one of the parties at least is pleased enough to have. But it is all a formality, and they seem to have come together only so that both thenceforth may go their separate ways.'

At that moment Charlotte, wishing to get away from this subject once and for all, tried a bold shift of direction and was successful. The talk became more general, husband and wife, and the Captain, were able to take part; even Ottilie was induced to say something, and dessert was taken in the happiest mood, a wealth of fruit piled up in pretty baskets and a bright abundance of flowers beautifully arranged in gorgeous vases doing most to foster it.

There was mention too of what had been done in the grounds, and an inspection took place immediately after dinner. Ottilie withdrew, saying she had things in the house to see to; but in reality she went on with her work of copying. The Count was engaged in conversation by the Captain; Charlotte joined them later. When they had climbed on to the ridge and the Captain had obligingly hurried down again to fetch the map, the Count said to Charlotte: 'I like the man exceedingly. He has both a wide and a coherent knowledge. And what he does seems very serious and consequential too. What he is achieving here would, in a higher sphere, be of great importance.'

To hear the Captain praised like this gave Charlotte intense satisfaction. But she composed herself and reinforced what the Count had said in a clear and level manner. Then how he astonished her when he continued: 'I have made his acquaintance at exactly the right time. I know a position which would suit the man perfectly, and by recommending him, and securing his happiness, I shall oblige a highly placed friend of mine in the best possible way.'

It was as though a thunderbolt had struck Charlotte. The Count noticed nothing; for women, accustomed to controlling themselves at all times, retain even in the most extraordinary situations an apparent composure. But she was no longer listening to what the Count was saying as he went on: 'It is not in my nature to dally once I am convinced of a thing. Mentally I have already written my letter, and now I am in a hurry to set it down. Will you get me a messenger I can dispatch this evening?'

Inwardly Charlotte was distraught. Surprised both by these propositions and by herself, she could not utter a word. Fortunately the Count continued to speak of his plans for the Captain, and it was all-too obvious to Charlotte how advantageous they were. Then, not before time, the Captain appeared and unrolled his map for the Count to see. But what new eyes she saw her friend with now, now that she was to lose him! Bowing hastily she turned away and hurried down to the summer-house. Long before she got there the tears had started from her eyes, and she flung herself into the narrow confines of that little hermitage and gave herself over entirely to a grief, a passion, a despair of whose possibility only a moment since she had had not the slightest apprehension.

Eduard had gone with the Baroness in the other direction, as far as the ponds. She was a shrewd woman, and liked to know everything that was going on. Feeling her way in the conversation, she soon noticed how expansive Eduard was apt to become in praise of Ottilie; and she led him on, always in the most natural way, until it seemed to her certain that here was a passion, and not one at its outset either, but one already established.

Married women, though they may not be fond of one another, are nevertheless in tacit allegiance, especially against young girls. The consequences of such an attachment were immediately obvious to her, knowing the world as she did. Moreover, earlier that morning she had been speaking about Ottilie to Charlotte, had disapproved of the child's residing in the country, especially given the quietness of her temperament, and had proposed taking Ottilie into town, to live with a friend of hers who was much concerned with the education of her only daughter and was, precisely, on the look-out for an agreeable companion who should be instated as a second child and share in all the daughter's advantages. Charlotte had said she would think about it.

Now the insight into Eduard's feelings had confirmed the Baroness in her plan, but the more certain she became the more she feigned still to be indulging Eduard. For no one was more mistress of herself than she, and such self-control in extraordinary situations accustoms us to dissemble even in ordinary ones and inclines us, since we have so much power over ourselves, to extend it over others too and thus to compensate somewhat by an external triumph for an inner loss.

Most often this attitude is accompanied by a sort of secret delight at other people's blindness, at how unwittingly they go into the trap. We take pleasure not only in our own present triumph but also in the thought of the shameful realization awaiting them. Thus the Baroness was malicious enough to invite Eduard and Charlotte for the vintage on her estates and to answer the question whether they might bring Ottilie with them in terms he could interpret after his own desires.

Eduard began at once to speak rhapsodically of the splendid country, the great river, the hills, rocks, vineyards, ancient castles, outings on the water, all the festivities accompanying the picking and the pressing of the grapes, and so forth, and was already, in the innocence of his heart, openly looking forward to the effect such scenes would have on Ottilie's unspoilt mind. At that moment they saw Ottilie approaching, and the Baroness was quick to ask Eduard not to say anything about their autumn journey since things looked forward to so long usually did not happen. Eduard promised, but hurried her forward to meet Ottilie and in the end ran several paces ahead of her, to meet the girl himself. His whole being was expressive of a heartfelt joy. He kissed her hands, and pressed into them a bunch of wild flowers which he had picked along the way. Watching, the Baroness felt something close to bitterness. For though she might not approve of what was perhaps blameworthy in this passion, she could not bear to see what was sweet and delightful in it bestowed on that intruding nobody of a girl.

By the time they sat down to supper an entirely different mood had come over the company. The Count, who had written his letter and dispatched the messenger with it even before supper, was in conversation with the Captain and in a sensible and modest fashion was drawing him out more and more, having seated him at his side for the evening. This meant that the Baroness, to the right of the Count, could have very little talk with him; and she had just as little with Eduard who, thirsty at the start and then excited, did not stint himself with the wine and was conversing very animatedly with Ottilie, whom he had placed by him, whilst Charlotte, sitting on the Captain's left, found it hard, indeed almost impossible, to conceal the trouble she felt.

The Baroness had time enough to observe things. She saw Charlotte's discomfort, and since all she knew of was

Eduard's relationship with Ottilie she soon persuaded herself that Charlotte too was concerned and upset by her husband's behaviour, and she gave more thought to how she might now best achieve her ends.

Even when they rose from table there was a division in the company. The Count, wishing really to fathom the Captain, was obliged to try several approaches before he could find out what he wished to know; for the Captain was a quiet, not at all conceited, and altogether laconic man. They walked up and down along one side of the room, whilst Eduard, excited by the wine and by his hopes, was laughing with Ottilie at the window, Charlotte and the Baroness meanwhile walking together in silence to and fro on the other side of the room. Their silence and their standing idly by at length caused a faltering in the rest of the company. The women withdrew to their wing, the men to theirs, and the day seemed to have been concluded.

CHAPTER ELEVEN

EDUARD accompanied the Count to his room and was easily led by their talk to stay with him for a while. The Count was losing himself in the past, animatedly remembering Charlotte's beauty, expatiating upon it, as an amateur of these things, with a good deal of passion: 'A beautiful foot is one of Nature's greatest gifts. The grace of it never fades. I was watching her today as she walked. One would still like to kiss her shoe and do as the Sarmatians did whose highest tribute to a revered and beautiful woman – barbaric no doubt but heartfelt nevertheless – was to drink a health to her out of her shoe.'

Their praises did not rest there, at the tip of the foot; they were, after all, old friends. They passed from the person herself to old stories and adventures, and recalled the obstacles which at the time had been placed in the way of the two lovers to prevent their meeting, and what trouble they had gone to, what strategies they had devised, simply in order to be able to speak their love.

'Do you remember', the Count continued, 'what a friend in need I was to you and how very unselfish, when their Majesties were visiting an uncle in that immense and labyrinthine house? The day had been spent in ceremonies and formal dress; a part of the night at least was to be for the lovers and their freer discourse.'

'You had taken good note of how to get to where the ladies-in-waiting had their rooms,' said Eduard. 'We made our way successfully to my own beloved lady.'

'Who,' said the Count, 'giving more thought to propriety than to my contentment, had kept a very ill-favoured chaperone by her; so that whilst you, with looks and words, were getting on splendidly, my own lot was most unenviable.'

'Only yesterday,' said Eduard, 'when we knew you were coming, my wife and I were remembering the story, and especially how you and I got back. We missed our way and found ourselves at the guardroom. Since we knew how to proceed from there we saw no reason not to go through, as we had already elsewhere along our route. But what a surprise we had when we opened the doors! The way was blocked with mattresses on which the guards were lying out like giants in several rows asleep. The only man awake looked at us in astonishment. But being full of a youthful courage and impertinence we stepped quite coolly over the stretched-out boots, without even one of those snoring sons of Anak waking up.'

'I was very tempted to stumble and make a noise,' said the Count. 'For what a strange resurrection we should have witnessed then!'

At that moment the great clock struck twelve.

'Midnight,' said the Count with a smile. 'The time has come. My dear Baron, I must ask a favour of you. Guide me tonight as I guided you then. I promised the Baroness I would call on her. We have not had a word alone together all day. It is so long since we saw one another and only natural that we should want a little time in private. Show me how to get there, I shall find my own way back. Certainly I shan't have to stumble over guardsmen's boots.'

'I shall be very glad to do you that favour,' Eduard replied. 'Any host would. But the three ladies are all together in that wing. Who knows whether we might not find them still talking or what else we might do that would look very odd?'

'Have no fear,' said the Count, 'the Baroness is expecting me. She will certainly be in her room by now, and alone.'

'It is a simple matter,' said Eduard, and taking a light he went ahead of the Count down a secret stairway which led to a long corridor. At the end of this he opened a small door. They climbed a spiral staircase; at the top, on a narrow landing, Eduard gave the Count the light and showed him a concealed door on the right which opened at the first touch, admitted the Count, and left Eduard alone in the dark.

Another door on the left led into Charlotte's bedroom. He heard voices and listened. Charlotte was speaking to her maid. 'Is Ottilie already in bed?' 'No,' said the girl, 'she is still downstairs writing.' 'Then light the night-light,' said Charlotte, 'and you can go. It is late. I'll put the candle out and see myself to bed.'

It filled Eduard with joy to hear that Ottilie was still writing. 'She is busy for me!' he said to himself in triumph. Enclosed by the darkness entirely within himself, he could see her sitting there, writing; he seemed to approach her, to see her as she turned to him; he felt an irresistible longing to be near her again. But from where he stood there was no way down to the entresol where she lived. He stood now at the door of his wife's room, a strange confusion took place in his heart; he tried to open the door, he found it locked, he knocked softly, Charlotte did not hear him.

She was walking agitatedly up and down in the larger adjoining room. Again and again she returned to what, since the Count's unexpected proposal, her mind had already wrestled with more than enough. It was as though the Captain were there before her eyes. He filled the house still, the walks were still enlivened by his presence, and he was to go away from her and everything be empty! She said all the things to herself that can be said, indeed she even anticipated, as people do, the poor consolation that even such sorrows will be lessened by the passage of time. She cursed the time it would take to lessen them; she cursed the time when they would have been lessened. How dead that time would be!

Finally, then, having recourse to tears was all the more welcome, since she rarely did. She threw herself down on the sofa and let her sorrow overwhelm her utterly. Eduard, for his part, could not leave the door; he knocked again, and a third time somewhat louder, so that Charlotte heard it quite clearly through the night-time stillness and sprang up in alarm. Her first thought was that it might, that it must be the Captain; her second that that was impossible. She supposed she must have been mistaken; but she had heard it, she

wanted to have heard it, and was afraid she had. She went into
the bedroom and quietly approached the secret door, which
was locked. Now she upbraided herself for being afraid. 'Very
likely the Countess needs something,' she said, and called out
then in a steady and sober voice: 'Is anyone there?' A low
voice answered: 'I am.' 'Who?' Charlotte replied, not being
able to tell. To her it seemed the Captain was at the door.
Then the voice came again, rather louder: 'Eduard!' She
opened, and her husband stood before her. He greeted her
flippantly. She was able to take up the tone. He enveloped his
mysterious visit in mysterious explanations. 'But let me confess my real reason for coming,' he said at last. 'I have vowed
I shall kiss your shoe before the morning.'

'It is a long time since you thought of doing that,'
said Charlotte.

'So much the worse,' Eduard replied, 'and so much
the better.'

She had seated herself in an armchair so that the slightness
of her nightwear would not be so exposed to his eyes. He
went down on his knees before her, and she could not
prevent him from kissing her shoe nor, when the shoe
came off in his hand, from taking hold of her foot and
pressing it tenderly against his breast.

Charlotte was one of those women who, moderate by
nature, in their marriages continue without effort or ulterior
motive to behave as they did during the courtship. She never
sought to arouse her husband, scarcely did she even respond
to his desire; but without coldness or any off-putting severity
she always resembled a loving bride-to-be who in her innermost self still shies away even from what is permissible. And
that night Eduard found her so in a double sense. How
passionately she wished her husband gone; for the phantom
of her friend seemed to be reproaching her. But the things
that should have caused Eduard to leave only attracted him
the more. A certain agitation was apparent in her. She had
been weeping, and if weaker people are mostly less attractive
when they weep, those whom we know to be usually strong

and composed gain by it immeasurably. Eduard was so lovable, so gentle, so pressing; he begged to be allowed to stay with her, he never demanded it, but now in earnest and now amusingly he sought to persuade and never bethought himself that he had rights, and boldly in the end extinguished the candle.

By lamplight then, in a twilight, the heart's desires and the imagination at once asserted their rights over reality. Eduard held Ottilie in his arms; now closer, now receding, the Captain hovered before Charlotte's soul; and thus absent and present in the queerest fashion were intermingled, in excitement and delight.

But the present will not be denied its monstrous due. They spent a part of the night in all manner of talk and pleasantry which was the freer because, alas, the heart had no part in it. But when Eduard woke next morning in the arms of his wife the day seemed to look in upon him ominously, the sun, so it seemed to him, was illuminating a crime; he crept from her side, and she found herself alone, in the strangest way, when she awoke.

CHAPTER TWELVE

WHEN the company reassembled for breakfast an attentive observer would have been able to deduce from each person's bearing how differently they were thinking and feeling. The Count and the Baroness met one another with the cheerfulness and contentment that lovers feel when, having suffered a period of separation, they have again reassured themselves of their mutual affection; whereas Charlotte and Eduard felt something like shame and remorse at the sight of the Captain and Ottilie. For love by its very nature claims all rightness for itself, all other rights vanish in the face of love. Ottilie was like a child in her good humour; she might be said to be open, after her fashion. The Captain looked grave; it had become all too clear to him in his conversations with the Count, who had wakened in him everything that for some time had been lying dormant, that he was not in any real sense doing what he was meant to do, but was only drifting along in a state of semi-idleness. No sooner had the two guests departed than yet more visitors arrived, which suited Charlotte who was anxious to forget herself and be distracted; but did not suit Eduard who felt doubly inclined to concern himself with Ottilie; and they were just as unwelcome to Ottilie herself, since she had not yet finished the copying which had absolutely to be ready early next day. When finally the visitors took their leave she hurried to her room at once.

It was evening. Eduard, Charlotte, and the Captain, who had strolled a little way with the visitors until they got into their carriage, decided to take a further walk as far as the ponds. At considerable expense Eduard had sent away for a rowing-boat, and it had arrived. They wanted to see whether it handled easily.

It was moored on the shore of the middle pond not far from a few ancient oak trees which had already been included in a future project. There was to be a landing-stage here, and under the trees a place to sit and rest, in a structure which would serve as a landmark for anyone coming across the water.

'Where will be the best place to land on the other side?' Eduard asked. 'Near my plane trees, I should think.'

'They are a little too far to the right,' said the Captain. 'Landing lower down, one would be nearer the Hall. But we must think about it.'

The Captain was already standing in the stern of the boat and had taken one of the oars. Charlotte climbed in, then Eduard, who took the other oar; but whilst he was already pushing off he thought of Ottilie, thought that this boating trip would detain him, that he would get back from it who knew when. He made up his mind at once, jumped ashore again, handed the Captain his oar, and, with a hasty excuse, hurried home.

There he learned that Ottilie had shut herself in her room and was writing. Though he was pleased that she was doing something for him it distressed him keenly that he was not able to see her at once. His impatience increased by the minute. He paced up and down in the big drawing-room, tried all manner of things but could concentrate on nothing. What he wanted was to see her, and see her alone, before Charlotte came back with the Captain. It grew dark, the candles were lit.

At last she came in, radiantly lovable. The feeling that she had done something for her friend had enhanced her whole being beyond itself. She laid down the original and the copy on the table in front of Eduard. 'Shall we compare?' she said with a smile. Eduard did not know what to reply. He looked at her, he looked at the copy. The first pages were written with the greatest care, in a delicate female hand; then the writing seemed to change, to become easier and freer; but how great was his astonishment when he ran his eyes over the final pages. 'In heaven's name!' he cried. 'What is this? That is my handwriting.' He looked at Ottilie, and again at the pages.

Especially the ending was exactly as if he had written it himself. Ottilie said nothing, but she was looking into his eyes with the greatest satisfaction. Eduard raised his arms. 'You love me!' he cried. 'Ottilie, you love me!' And they held one another in a tight embrace. It would not have been possible to say who first seized hold of the other.

Thereupon Eduard's world was turned around: he was no longer what he had been, the world no longer what it had been. They stood before one another, he held her hands, they looked into one another's eyes, they were about to embrace again.

Charlotte came in with the Captain. When they apologized for staying out so long Eduard gave a secret smile. 'You are back far too soon,' he said to himself.

They sat down to supper. The day's visitors were discussed. Eduard, excited and full of love, spoke well of everyone, always considerately, often approvingly. Charlotte, not quite of his opinion, noticed this mood and teased him for being so mild and indulgent, since usually when company left his comments on them were very harsh.

Passionately and with heartfelt conviction Eduard cried: 'Only love one person utterly and all the others will seem lovable too.' Ottilie cast down her eyes and Charlotte stared into the distance.

The Captain spoke. 'It is somewhat the same with feelings of respect and reverence,' he said. 'You learn to recognize what is of value in the world only by finding one fit object for such sentiments.'

Charlotte withdrew to her bedroom as soon as she could, and gave herself up to the memory of what had happened that evening between her and the Captain.

When Eduard, springing ashore and pushing off the boat, had thus himself given over his wife and his friend to the unsteady element, Charlotte saw the man on whose account she had already suffered so much in secret now sitting before her in the twilight and with two oars propelling the craft anywhere he liked. She felt a deep melancholy, such as she had rarely felt before. The circuiting boat, the splashing of the oars, a chill breath of wind over the surface, the sighing of the reeds, the last flights of birds, the glimpses and the glimpsed reflections of the first stars: there was something ghostly about it all in the general stillness. It seemed to her that her friend was taking her far away, to expose her, to leave her alone. In her heart she was strangely agitated, and she could not weep.

The Captain meanwhile was explaining to her what form the new projects ought to take, in his view. He was full of praise for the boat, which could be rowed and steered easily by one person with the two oars. She would learn herself, it was a pleasure sometimes to be moving on the water all alone and to be one's own ferryman and helmsman.

At these words his friend was afflicted by the thought of their coming separation. 'Is he saying that on purpose?' she asked herself. 'Does he know? Does he suspect? Or did he mean nothing by it and was he foretelling my fate unawares?' She was seized by a great sadness, an impatience; she asked him to land just as soon as he could and go back to the Hall with her.

It was the first time the Captain had rowed over the ponds, and although he had made a general survey of the depths there were still particular places he was not familiar with. Darkness was coming on, he directed his course towards where he supposed there might be an easy place to disembark and where he knew it was not far to the path which led to the Hall. But from this course he was somewhat distracted when Charlotte, in a sort of fearfulness, again expressed the wish to be ashore. He redoubled his exertions and was approaching the bank, but unfortunately found himself halted whilst still at a little distance from it; he had run aground, and his efforts to get free again were in vain. What was to be done? He had no choice but to climb into the water, which was shallow enough, and carry his friend to the shore. Glad of his burden he crossed safely, being strong enough not to stagger or give her any cause for alarm, but still she had wound her arms fearfully round his neck. He held her tight and pressed her against him. Not until they had reached a grassy slope did he put her down, and not without agitation and confusion. She still hung on his neck; he took her into his arms again and kissed her, with intensity, on the mouth – but lay a second later at her feet, pressed her hands to his lips, and cried: 'Charlotte, will you forgive me?'

The kiss which her friend had dared to give her and which she had almost given him in return brought Charlotte to her senses. She pressed his hand but did not raise him. Bending down to him and laying a hand on his shoulder she cried: 'We cannot prevent this moment from marking an epoch in our lives; but whether it be one worthy of us, that we can still decide. You must leave, my dear friend, and you will leave. The Count is making arrangements to advance you, which is a cause of joy to me and also of grief. I wanted to say nothing about it, until it was certain; but now the moment obliges me to reveal my secret. I can forgive you and forgive myself only if we have the courage to alter our situation, since it is not within our power to alter our feelings.' She raised him up, took his arm to support herself, and they returned to the Hall in silence.

But now she stood in her bedroom where she was bound to feel and think of herself as Eduard's wife. Help in this contradictory state came to her from her character which, already much tested, was sound. Accustomed always to being self-aware and to having control over herself, now too she did not find it difficult, by force of earnest consideration, to approach the desired equilibrium; indeed, she could not help smiling at herself when she thought of the strange visit Eduard had paid her in the night. But at once she was seized by a curious apprehension, a joyous and anxious trembling, which resolved itself into a woman's most sacred hopes and longings. She was moved to kneel and repeat the vows she had made to Eduard at the altar. Friendship, affection, and renunciation passed before her in serene images. She felt herself inwardly restored. Soon a sweet tiredness came over her, and peacefully she slept.

CHAPTER THIRTEEN

EDUARD, for his part, was in a quite different mood. He was so little disposed to sleep that it did not even occur to him to undress. A thousand times he kissed the copy of the document, the beginning in Ottilie's childish and diffident hand; he hardly dared kiss the ending since the writing looked so much like his own. 'If only it were a different document!' he said to himself; but even so it was the loveliest assurance that what he most desired was fulfilled. And would it not remain in his hands and for ever and ever be pressed to his heart, even after a stranger's signature had defaced it?

The waning moon came up over the woods. The warm air drew him out of doors; he went here and there, he was the most restless and the happiest of mortal men. He walked through the gardens, they were too confining; he ran into the fields, there the space was too great. He was drawn back to the Hall; he found himself under Ottilie's windows. He sat down on the terrace, on a flight of steps. 'Now walls and locks and bolts keep us apart,' he said to himself, 'but our hearts are not kept apart. If she were here she would fall into my arms and I into hers, and what do I need beyond that certainty?' There was quietness all about him, not a breath of wind; so quiet he could hear the burrowing of busy creatures under the earth where night and day are alike. He gave himself up entirely to his dreams of happiness, fell asleep at last, and when he woke the sun was already rising with a splendid aspect and getting the better of the early mists.

He found he was the first awake on his property. His workers seemed to him late arriving. When they came they seemed to him too few and the work planned for the day was too little for his wishes. He wanted more workers, they were promised and taken on in the course of the day. But even then he thought the numbers insufficient to get his intentions carried out quickly. The work gave him no pleasure any more; he wanted everything finished, and for whom? He wanted the paths laid so that Ottilie could walk on them in comfort, and seats already in place so that Ottilie could sit and rest. And at the new house too he did what he could to hasten things along: he wanted the roof on by Ottilie's birthday. Neither in his feelings nor in his actions was there any measure. Knowing that he loved and was loved drove Eduard into boundlessness. How changed in their appearance were all the rooms and all his surroundings! He no longer knew where he was in his own home. Ottilie's presence consumed everything; he was entirely absorbed in her, no other consideration occurred to him, his conscience uttered not a word; everything in his nature which had been restrained broke loose, his whole being streamed towards Ottilie.

The Captain observed this passionate activity and wished he might prevent its unhappy consequences. The works being thus one-sidedly and excessively hastened along were based, as he had intended them, on a model of tranquil and amicable co-existence. He had effected the sale of the farmstead, the first payment had been received, Charlotte, as agreed, had added it to her funds. But in the very first week she was obliged to practise and encourage sobriety, patience, and orderliness even more than usual; for in all the haste the money set aside would not go far.

Much had been begun and much remained to be done. How could he leave Charlotte in that situation? They conferred, and agreed they would rather speed up the schedule of work themselves, borrow money for that purpose, and pay it back as the instalments still due on the sale of the farm came in. By ceding the franchise this could be done almost without loss; their hands would be untied, and since everything was now under way and there were enough workmen, they would get more done at one time and so bring matters to a successful conclusion quickly. Eduard was happy with the arrangement since it accorded with his own intentions.

In her innermost heart, meanwhile, Charlotte was abiding by what she had thought and decided for herself, and her friend, in a manly fashion, gave her his support, being of one mind with her. But this only increased their intimacy. They exchanged their views on the subject of Eduard's passion; they exchanged advice. Charlotte drew Ottilie closer, kept a stricter watch over her, and the more she got to know her own heart the deeper she was able to see into the girl's. It seemed to her there was no help but to send the child away.

She now thought it a happy chance that Luciane had received such outstandingly good reports at school; for her great aunt, having been informed, now wished her to move into her house once and for all, to have her company and to take her into society. Ottilie could go back to the boarding-school; the Captain would leave, his future assured; and everything would be as it was a few months previously – indeed, even better than it was. Charlotte hoped she would quickly restore her own relationship with Eduard, and in her thinking she arrived at such a rational settlement of everything that she became more and more confirmed in the illusion that a return to an earlier and more restricted condition would be possible, that a thing now violently released could be brought back into confinement.

Eduard meanwhile was acutely aware of the obstacles being placed in his way. He soon noticed that he and Ottilie were being kept apart, that it was being made difficult for him to speak to her alone or even to be near her except in company; and feeling exasperated by this he began to feel the same about other things too. When he did manage to snatch a word with her it was not only to assure her of his love but also to complain about his wife and about the Captain. He had no sense that by his haste in the business he was himself on the way to exhausting their funds; he was bitterly critical of Charlotte and the Captain, saying they were acting against the original agreement; but he had himself accepted the second agreement and had indeed occasioned it and made it necessary.

Hatred is partisan, but love even more so. Ottilie too began to be somewhat estranged from Charlotte and the Captain. When on one occasion Eduard was complaining about the latter, saying that as a friend, and their circumstances being what they were, he was not acting entirely honestly, Ottilie made a thoughtless reply: 'He has displeased me before now by not being entirely honest with you. I once heard him say to Charlotte: "I do wish Eduard would not subject us to his flute-playing. He will never get any better at it, and it is tiresome to have to listen to it." You can imagine how much that hurt me, since I love accompanying you.'

She had no sooner said this than her spirit whispered to her that she ought to have kept silent; but too late. Eduard's expression changed. He had never been so angered; he was assailed in his dearest ambitions; without in the least overestimating himself he did have an innocent desire to do well. And what amused him and gave him pleasure should surely be treated considerately by his friends. He did not think how frightful it is for others to have their ears tormented by a mediocre talent. He was insulted, furious, beyond ever forgiving. He felt himself absolved from all responsibilities.

The need to be with Ottilie, to see her, to whisper something to her, to confide in her, grew daily. He decided to write to her and to ask her to begin a secret correspondence with him. The scrap of paper on which, not wasting any words, he had done this was lying on his desk and blew off in a draught as his valet entered to curl his hair. To test the heat of the tongs the man was used to picking up scraps of paper from the floor; on this occasion he picked up the note, twisted it swiftly, and it was scorched. Seeing what had happened Eduard snatched the paper out of his hand. Soon afterwards he sat down to write it again; the words did not come quite so easily the second time. He had doubts, anxieties, which he overcame, however. He pressed the note into Ottilie's hand when next he was able to approach her.

Ottilie's reply came without delay. Eduard put the note, unread, into his waistcoat which, fashionably short, did not retain it very well. It slipped out and fell to the floor without his noticing. Charlotte saw it and picked it up, glanced at it, and handed it to him. 'Here is something you have written,' she said, 'which you would perhaps be sorry to lose.'

He was shaken. 'Is she acting?' he wondered. 'Does she know what is in the note or is she misled by the similarity of the handwriting?' He hoped and believed it was the latter. He was warned, doubly warned, but these strange accidental signs by means of which a higher power seems to be speaking to us were unintelligible to his passion; indeed, as his passion led him on it irked him more and more to be held, as he thought deliberately, under constraint. Their companionableness was vanishing. His heart had closed, and when he was obliged to be together with his friend or with his wife he could not discover and reanimate the old affection for them in his bosom. In silence reproaching himself for this, as he was bound to, only made him uncomfortable, and he had recourse to a sort of gaiety which, being without love, was also without any of his usual grace.

Her own deep feeling helped Charlotte through these trials. She harboured the earnest intention to renounce her affections, beautiful and noble though they were.

It was her heartfelt wish to be able to help Eduard and Ottilie too. She saw very well that separation alone would not be sufficient to cure such an ill. She resolved to discuss the matter openly with the child; but could not, the memory of her own moment of weakness stood in her way. She tried to express herself generally on the subject; but generalities fitted her own state too, which she was shy of uttering. Every hint she might give Ottilie pointed back into her own heart. She wanted to warn, and felt that she herself might still be in need of warning.

So she continued to keep the lovers apart and to say nothing, but by that the situation was not improved. Gentle insinuations, which escaped her occasionally, had no effect on Ottilie since Eduard had persuaded her of Charlotte's affection for the Captain and that Charlotte herself desired a divorce which he was now intending to bring about, in a decent fashion.

Ottilie, borne along by the feeling of her own innocence, heading towards the happiness she most desired, lived only for Eduard. Strengthened in everything good by her love for him, more joyful, on his account, in everything she did, more open to others, she found herself in a heaven on earth.

So all in their different fashions pursued their daily lives, thoughtfully or not; everything seemed to be following its usual course, as is the way in monstrously strange circumstances when everything is at stake: we go on with our lives as though nothing were the matter.

CHAPTER FOURTEEN

IN the meantime a letter had arrived for the Captain from the Count. Two letters really: one to make public, which opened up very fine prospects but for some time in the future; and another which contained a definite offer for the present, an important position at Court and as an administrator, the rank of major, a handsome salary, and other advantages, but which because of various contingent circumstances was to be kept secret still. Accordingly, the Captain told his friends about his future prospects and concealed from them what was so imminent.

He went on with his present business very actively, and in secret made arrangements so that everything should proceed unhindered once he was gone. It suited him too, now that a date should be fixed for things to be finished, that Ottilie's birthday was hastening things along. Without there being any express understanding between them the two friends were once again glad to be working together. Eduard was delighted that by raising money in advance their resources had been strengthened; the whole undertaking was advancing rapidly.

In the Captain's view they ought not now to have gone ahead with making the three ponds into a lake. The lowest dam would need fortifying, the two middle ones removing; it was a considerable and somewhat dubious undertaking, in more ways than one. But both tasks, which could of course be connected, had already been begun, and in them they were glad of a certain young architect, a former pupil of the Captain's, who, by hiring competent artisans and by whenever possible allocating the different jobs himself, was making good progress in a work that looked solid and likely to last; which secretly delighted the Captain, for his own withdrawal would thus not be felt. On principle he would never quit any business he had taken on and had not finished until he was sure he had been adequately replaced. Indeed, he despised men who make their own departures felt by first creating confusion where they are employed and who, in their gross self-importance, seek to undo whatever they themselves will no longer be engaged in.

Thus there was constant hard work towards the celebration of Ottilie's birthday, without anyone saying so, or even to themselves fully admitting it. As Charlotte saw things – which was not with any jealousy – the celebration should not be of too emphatic a kind. Given her youth, her fortune, her relationship to the family, it would not be right for Ottilie to seem too much the queen of the day. And Eduard would not have it discussed, since everything was to arise as if of itself, and give surprise and be delightful in a natural way.

Tacitly then, they all came to agree upon a pretext: the day should be for the roofing of the new house, without mention of anything else, and for that occasion it could be announced to friends and to the local people that there would be a celebration.

But Eduard's affections were boundless. Desiring to possess Ottilie, he was just as immoderate in the giving of himself and of presents and promises. For some of the gifts with which he wanted to honour Ottilie on the day Charlotte made proposals that were far too poor. He spoke with his valet who saw to his wardrobe and was constantly in dealings with tradespeople and people from the fashion houses. The valet, knowledgeable not only about the nicest things to give but also about how best to give them, at once placed an order in town for an extremely attractive box: covered in red morocco, studded with steel nails, and filled with presents that were worthy of such a vessel.

And he suggested something else to Eduard. There were a few fireworks, which no one had ever bothered to let off. These could be added to and improved. Eduard seized on the idea, and the valet undertook to see it carried out. It was to remain a secret.

The Captain, meanwhile, as the day approached, had made his arrangements for proper order, arrangements which he deemed very necessary when large numbers of people were invited or attracted to one location. And he had gone to some trouble to prevent begging and other things which are a nuisance and detract from the charm of a festive occasion.

But Eduard, together with his accomplice in the matter, busied himself principally with the fireworks. They were to be let off at the middle pond, in front of the great oak trees; on the opposite bank, under the plane trees, the spectators would foregather and at a proper distance, in comfort and safety, would see the show reflected in the water and floating and burning on the surface itself.

Accordingly, under another pretext, Eduard had the undergrowth, grass, and moss removed from the space beneath the plane trees, and when this was done and the ground was clear it became apparent just how splendidly the trees had grown, how tall they were and how broad. Eduard was overjoyed. 'It was about this time of year when I planted them,' he said to himself. 'How long ago would that be?' As soon as he got home he looked through the old diaries which his father, especially when in the country, had kept very conscientiously. There could be no mention of Eduard's having planted the trees, but another important domestic event on the same day which he still remembered was bound to have been noted. He leafed through a few volumes, found the particular circumstance, then to his amazement, to his delight, he noticed a most marvellous coincidence. The day and the year when the trees were planted was also the day and the year when Ottilie was born.

CHAPTER FIFTEEN

At last the day Eduard had longed for dawned, and guests began to arrive, a great number, for invitations had been sent out far and wide and some who had not been at the laying of the foundation-stone and had heard so many delightful things about it were all the more eager not to miss this second occasion.

Before lunch the carpenters appeared in the courtyard, making music and bearing numerous hoops of greenery and flowers all piled unsteadily in one abundant crown. They recited a greeting and requested, as was the custom, silk scarves and ribbons from the ladies, for decoration. Whilst lunch was in progress they went on their way in a jovial procession, and having halted in the village for a while, there too relieving the women and girls of a good number of ribbons, they came at last, accompanied and expected by a large crowd, on to the ridge where the new house stood, roofed.

After lunch Charlotte held the company back somewhat. She did not want there to be any ceremonious and formal procession, and so people made their way to the site in a leisurely fashion, in their different groups, without attention to rank and order. Charlotte lingered with Ottilie, which rather made matters worse; for since Ottilie was actually the last to arrive it seemed as if the fanfare and the drums had only waited for her, as if the commencement of the celebrations were signalled by her arrival.

To soften the appearance of the house it had been decorated, according to the Captain's tasteful directions, with greenery and flowers; but unknown to him Eduard had got the Architect to inscribe the date, in flowers, on the cornice. To that there could perhaps be no objection; but the Captain arrived just in time to prevent Ottilie's name appearing in floral splendour on the space below. He found a tactful way of putting a stop to this and of removing from view those letters which had already been made up.

The pole of flowers had been set in place and was visible for miles around. Its scarves and ribbons fluttered gaily, and a short speech went away with the wind, largely unheard. The ceremony was at an end, and now the dancing was to begin on the space before the house which had been levelled and set around with greenery. A smart young carpenter came forward with a girl to be Eduard's partner, and himself invited Ottilie, who was at Eduard's side. The two pairs at once had others following them, and before long Eduard swapped his nimble peasant girl for Ottilie and danced the round with her. The younger among Eduard's and Charlotte's guests joined cheerfully with the local people in the dancing whilst the older ones watched.

Then, before the company dispersed along different walks, it was agreed they would reassemble at sunset under the plane trees. Eduard was there first, made all the arrangements, and conferred with his valet who, across the water, together with the firework-maker, was to have charge of the spectacle.

When the Captain saw what provision had been made he was not best pleased; he wished to speak with Eduard about the crush of spectators that must be expected, but Eduard begged him, somewhat abruptly, to leave this part of the festivities in his sole care.

The people had already pressed forward on to the dams whose upper surfaces, which had been scoured clean of their grass, were uneven and unsafe. The sun went down, it was twilight, and whilst they were waiting for it to be darker the guests under the plane trees were served with refreshments. They thought the place incomparably fine and took pleasure in imagining the view from there across a wide lake with such variety around it.

A quiet evening, not a breath of wind, for the nocturnal festivity conditions promised to be ideal; but suddenly there was a terrible uproar. Large clods of earth had come loose from the dam, several people were seen falling into the water. The ground had given way under the pressing and stamping of an ever-increasing crowd. Everyone wanted the best place, and now nobody could advance or retreat.

The company leapt up and ran to the spot, but more to see what was happening than to do anything about it. And what *could* they do when no one could get through? Together with a few others equally determined, the Captain hurried over and at once drove the crowd down off the dam on to the banks so that the rescuers hauling the people out of the water should not be hindered. Soon all, by their own or others' exertions, were on dry land again, all but one, a boy whose panic-stricken efforts, instead of bringing him nearer the dam, had carried him further away. He seemed at the end of his strength, only now and then a hand or a foot lifted above the surface. Unhappily, the rowing boat was on the far side, laden with fireworks, it could only be unloaded slowly, help was a long time coming. Then the Captain made up his mind, he threw off his outer garments, all eyes were upon him, and his solid and powerful form filled everyone with confidence; but a cry of amazement rose out of the crowd when he dived into the water. He was watched all the way, and soon, being a strong swimmer, he had reached the boy and brought him, but dead as it seemed, to the dam.

Meanwhile the boat had been rowed across, the Captain climbed in and enquired very closely among all those present whether indeed everyone was saved. The Surgeon arrived and took charge of the boy believed dead; Charlotte approached, she begged the Captain to look after himself, to go back to the Hall and change his clothes. But he lingered, until people whose judgement could be trusted, who had been close witnesses of events and had themselves been among the rescuers, gave him the most solemn assurances that everyone was safe.

Charlotte watched him set off for the Hall; it occurred to her that the wine and the tea and whatever else might be needed were locked away, and that in such situations people often do not manage things properly; she hurried through the guests who, after the distraction, were still under the plane trees. Eduard was busy persuading them all to stay; he was about to give the signal, the fireworks would begin. Charlotte approached and begged him to postpone an entertainment that was no longer appropriate, that in the present moment could not be enjoyed. They must consider the child, she said, and the man who rescued him. 'The Surgeon will do his duty,' Eduard replied. 'He has everything he needs, if we press around him we shall only be in his way.'

Charlotte insisted, and motioned to Ottilie who at once made ready to leave. Eduard seized her hand and cried: 'We will not end our day in a hospital. She is wasted as a nurse. The seeming dead will revive without our help and the living will dry off.'

Charlotte said nothing, and left. Some followed her, others followed Eduard and Ottilie; in the end nobody wanted to be last and they all followed Charlotte. Eduard and Ottilie found themselves alone under the plane trees. He insisted on staying, though she begged him urgently and fearfully to return to the Hall with her. 'No, Ottilie,' he cried. 'Extraordinary things do not come to pass in smooth and usual ways. This evening's extraordinary event brings us together sooner. You are mine. I have said it and sworn it so often already, and that is enough of saying it and swearing it. Now let it happen.'

The boat had come over from the other side. It was the valet, who asked in some embarrassment what was to happen now about the fireworks. 'Let them off,' Eduard shouted across to him. 'You were the one they were intended for, Ottilie, you alone, and now you will be the only one to watch them. Let me sit at your side and enjoy them with you.' He was gentle, diffident, and sat down by her without touching her.

Rockets lifted off in a rush, crackers banged, Roman candles ascended, fiery serpents twisted and burst, sprays of sparks came off the Catherine wheels, and all were single first, then paired, then all together and ever more violently coming after and together. Eduard, inflamed, watched the fiery spectacle in a lively contentment. But to Ottilie's gentle and agitated spirit this constant creation and disappearance in noise and flashing light was more alarming than pleasant. She leaned timidly against Eduard, and this greater closeness, this trust, filled him with the feeling that now she was completely his.

Darkness had scarcely resumed its proper sovereignty when the moon rose and lit up the paths for the pair as they returned. A figure, hat in hand, barred their way and begged them for alms, since on that festive day he had not had his due. The moon shone into his face, and Eduard recognized the beggar who had importuned him previously. But in his great happiness now he could not be indignant, and he forgot that on that day more than ever begging was especially frowned upon. He did not search his pockets long, and gave a gold coin. He would have liked to make everyone happy, his own happiness seemed so boundless.

At the Hall meanwhile everything had ended well. The Surgeon's ministrations, the fact that all they needed was to hand, Charlotte's assistance, everything worked together and the boy was returned to life. The guests dispersed, either to see something of the fireworks from a distance, or, after such mixed events, to return to the peace and quiet of their own homes.

The Captain too, quickly changing his clothes, had taken an active part in all the work of welfare; now there was peace of mind and he found himself alone with Charlotte. Gently he let her know that he would soon be leaving. She had experienced so much in the course of the evening that this revelation had little effect upon her; she had seen how her friend had offered the sacrifice of himself, how he had saved a life, and that his own life was safe. These wondrous events seemed to her to presage a significant future, but not an unhappy one.

Eduard, entering with Ottilie, was likewise informed of the Captain's imminent departure. He suspected that Charlotte

must have known for some time, but was far too preoccupied with himself and his own plans to have any sense of
grievance.

On the contrary, he listened attentively and contentedly to
the account of the advantageous and prestigious position
which the Captain would occupy. His own secret wishes
hurried, without restraint, ahead of events. Already he
saw Charlotte united with the Captain and himself with
Ottilie. On that festive day he could not have been given a
better present.

But Ottilie's astonishment was great when she went to her
room and found the marvellous box on the table. She opened
it at once. The things inside were all so beautifully packed and
arranged that she shrank from taking any out, and scarcely
lifted them. Muslins, cambrics, silks, shawls, and lace-work
outdid one another in their delicacy, prettiness, and costli-
ness. And there was jewellery too. She understood the
thought behind it all: to dress her from head to foot, and
more than once; but everything was so costly and exotic that
she could not bring herself to think of it as hers.

CHAPTER SIXTEEN

NEXT morning the Captain was gone. He left behind him a heartfelt and grateful letter to his friends. He and Charlotte had said their poor, tongue-tied farewells the night before. She felt the separation to be final, and accepted it; for in the Count's second letter, which finally the Captain had shown her, there was mention of the prospect of an advantageous marriage as well; and although he himself paid no attention to this point, she thought it a certainty and renounced him utterly.

But now she felt justified in demanding of others what she had demanded of herself. Since she had not found it impossible others ought to find it possible too. In this belief she broached the subject with her husband, and did so openly and confidently, feeling that the matter must now be settled once and for all.

'Our friend has left us,' she said, 'you and I are as we were, and might return now completely to our former condition, if we wished.'

Eduard, who heard nothing except what favoured his passion, thought Charlotte must be referring to the time before their marriage and, in a rather indirect manner, be raising hopes of a divorce. Therefore he answered, with a smile: 'Why not? All it needs is that we come to an agreement.'

He was then grievously disappointed when Charlotte replied: 'And it also rests with us to change Ottilie's circumstances. We have a double opportunity of providing for her in a way which will be desirable. She can go back to the boarding-school, since my daughter has now moved to her great aunt's; or she can have a place in a very respectable household and share with an only daughter there all the advantages of an appropriate upbringing.'

'But by now', Eduard replied with some composure, 'Ottilie has been so spoilt among friends here that any other company will hardly be welcome to her.'

'We have all been spoilt,' said Charlotte, 'and you not least. But now the time has come for us to be sensible and to give serious thought to what will be best for all the members of our little circle, and not to refuse to make sacrifices.'

'I certainly do not think it right', said Eduard, 'that Ottilie should be sacrificed, which would be the case if at the present moment we thrust her down among strangers. The Captain was visited by good fortune whilst he was here; we can say goodbye to him with quiet minds and even with some satisfaction. But who knows what lies in store for Ottilie? Why the hurry?'

'What lies in store for us is obvious,' Charlotte replied in some agitation, and since she was determined to speak her mind once and for all she continued: 'You love Ottilie, you are growing accustomed to her. Affection and passion have been engendered and are thriving on her side too. Why not say outright what every hour of the day admits and confesses to us? Shall we not at least have the foresight to ask ourselves how it will end?'

'Though one cannot make any immediate reply to that,' said Eduard, taking a hold on himself, 'this much can be said: that we should first of all decide to wait and see what the future will teach us if we cannot at the moment already tell how a thing may turn out.'

'But in our case', Charlotte replied, 'no great prescience is needed to see how things will turn out, and this much, at the very least, can be said here and now: that we are both too old to go wandering blindly where we either do not want to or ought not to go. We are our own responsibility, nobody else's; we must ourselves be friends and mentors to ourselves. Nobody is asking us to ruin our lives, nor to expose ourselves to censure and, very likely, ridicule.'

'But can you blame me,' said Eduard, unable to match the clear, pure language of his wife, 'can you reproach me for having Ottilie's happiness at heart? And I do not mean some future happiness – that can never be counted on – but her happiness now. Imagine it honestly and allow yourself no illusions: Ottilie wrenched from our company and answerable to strangers – to ask her to suffer such an alteration would take more cruelty than I, at least, feel myself capable of.'

Charlotte could see very well that behind his pretence her husband was resolute. Only now did she feel how far he had moved away from her. In some agitation she exclaimed: 'Can Ottilie be happy if she causes our separation? If she robs me of a husband and his children of their father?'

'I should have thought our children were provided for,' said Eduard smiling coldly; but he added then in rather friendlier tones: 'Besides, it is surely premature to think of going to such extremes.'

'Passion goes to extremes immediately,' Charlotte remarked. 'Do not refuse the good advice and the help I am offering us both. Soon it will be too late. In a dark time the one who sees clearest must be the one to act and help. I am that one on this occasion. My dear, my dearest Eduard, do as I ask. Surely you cannot expect me to give up my hard-won happiness, the rights I treasure most, and you – and all without demur?'

'Who said any such thing?' Eduard replied in some embarrassment.

'You did,' said Charlotte. 'By wanting to keep Ottilie with us are you not agreeing to everything that will surely come of it? I have no wish to insist, but if you are not able to overcome your inclinations at least you will have to stop deceiving yourself.'

Eduard felt the truth of what she said. Words uttered are a terrible thing when they suddenly express what the heart has already long since permitted itself; and only in order to gain a moment's respite Eduard replied: 'I am still not quite clear what it is you intend.'

'My intention was', said Charlotte, 'to discuss the two proposals with you. There is much good in each. The school would suit Ottilie best, if I consider how the child is at present. But the larger and wider situation promises more if I consider what she must become.' Thereupon she gave her husband a detailed account of the two situations, and concluded with the words: 'I would myself prefer the lady's house to the boarding-school, and for several reasons, but especially because I do not wish to increase the affection, indeed the passion, of the young man whose heart Ottilie won when she was there.'

Eduard let it seem that he agreed with her, but only to buy time. Charlotte, determined to do something that would be decisive, at once seized the opportunity, since Eduard made no immediate objection, to settle it that Ottilie's departure, for which in secret she had already made all the preparations, should take place in a day or so.

Eduard shuddered, he thought himself betrayed and his wife's affectionate language calculated, contrived, and shaped to separate him from his happiness for ever. It seemed he was leaving the matter all to her; but inwardly his own decision had already been taken. To win at least a breathing-space, to prevent the imminent and incalculable disaster of Ottilie's removal, he decided to leave home himself, and not without Charlotte's knowledge either; but in the way he put it to her she was led to think that he did not wish to be present at Ottilie's departure, indeed that thenceforth he did not wish to see her again. Charlotte, believing herself victorious, did everything to help. He ordered the horses, gave his valet the necessary instructions, what he should pack and how he should follow on, and then, at the very last moment, he sat down and wrote.

Eduard to Charlotte

'The misfortune which has befallen us, my dear, may be able to be remedied or not, but I know this much: that if I am not here and now to succumb to despair I must find a respite for me and for us all. Since I am sacrificing myself I can make demands. I am leaving my house and will only come back when the prospects are more favourable and more peaceable. Be the owner of it meanwhile, but with Ottilie. I want to live in the knowledge that she is with you and not among strangers. Look after her, treat her as you used to, as you always have, and more lovingly still, be kinder and gentler. I promise I shall not seek to have any secret dealings with Ottilie. Let me be rather for a while in complete ignorance of your lives; I shall think the best. Think of me likewise, you and she. There is only one thing: I beg and beseech you not to make any attempt to send Ottilie to live anywhere else or to change her situation. Outside the sphere of your house and grounds, in the care of strangers, she belongs to me and I will have possession of her. But if you honour my affections, my wishes, my grief, if you flatter my illusions and my hopes, I will not resist the remedy should it be offered me.'

These last phrases came from his pen, not from his heart. Indeed, seeing the words on the page he began to weep bitterly. Was he then in some way to give up the happiness, or misery, of loving Ottilie? Now he began to realize what he was doing. He was going away, without knowing what would result. For the time being at least he was not to see her; could he feel at all certain of ever seeing her again? But the letter was written, the horses were waiting; at any moment he risked catching sight of Ottilie and having his resolution instantly destroyed. He took hold of himself, thought that after all he could come back whenever he liked and that from a distance he might actually approach more closely to the satisfaction of his wishes. And he contemplated the alternative: that if he stayed Ottilie would be driven from the house. He sealed the letter, ran down the steps, and mounted his horse.

Riding by the inn he saw the beggar to whom he had given so generously the night before. The man was sitting in the garden, at ease, eating a midday meal. He got to his feet and bowed respectfully, indeed reverentially to Eduard. This figure had stood in Eduard's way when he was walking with Ottilie on his arm only the night before, and grieved him now

CHAPTER SEVENTEEN

OTTILIE went to the window, having heard somebody ride away, and caught a last glimpse of Eduard. She thought it strange that he should leave the house without seeing her and without wishing her good-day. She grew anxious and ever-more puzzled when Charlotte took her for a long walk and spoke of many things but never – and it seemed deliberate – mentioned her husband. She was doubly surprised then on their return to find the table only set for two.

Things we are used to, small in themselves perhaps, are never easy to do without, but we suffer real pain at their absence only when the occasion itself is significant. Eduard and the Captain were missing, for the first time in months Charlotte had arranged the table herself, and it seemed to Ottilie that she had been deposed. The two women sat opposite one another; Charlotte spoke quite openly of the Captain's new appointment and of the small hope they had of seeing him again in the near future. Ottilie's only comfort in her situation was to be able to suppose that Eduard had ridden after his friend to go with him a part of the way.

But when they rose from table they saw Eduard's travelling carriage under the window, and when Charlotte asked rather crossly who had ordered it there she was told it was the valet who still had things to collect. It took all of Ottilie's self-control to conceal her astonishment and her pain.

The valet entered with further requests. He wanted his master's tankard, a few silver spoons, and some other items, which seemed to Ottilie to indicate a long journey and a lengthy absence. Charlotte rebuked him for asking: she did not understand what he meant, surely all his master's things were in his, the valet's, keeping. The valet, whose sole interest was of course to speak with Ottilie and for that reason under whatever pretext to lure her from the room, excused himself adroitly and repeated his requests, which Ottilie wished to grant him; but Charlotte refused, he was obliged to withdraw, and the carriage rattled away.

It was a terrible moment for Ottilie. She did not understand or comprehend, but that Eduard had been taken away from her for a lengthy period, that much she could feel. Charlotte sensed what her condition was, and left her alone. We dare not describe her pain, her tears. She suffered boundlessly. All she asked was that God would help her through the day; she survived that day and the night, and when she found herself again it seemed to her a meeting with a different person.

She was neither composed nor resigned, but after so great a loss she still had her being, and now there were other things to be afraid of. Her first anxiety, as soon as she began to think again, was that she might be sent away herself, now that the men were gone. She never guessed that Eduard by his threats had seen to it that she would remain at Charlotte's side; but Charlotte's own behaviour reassured her somewhat. She kept the child busy and only rarely and unwillingly let her out of sight; and although she was well aware that words can do very little against a determined passion, still she knew the power of calm reflection and so made a point of discussing things with Ottilie.

Thus it was a great comfort for Ottilie when one day Charlotte, very conscious of the import of her words, made the following judicious observation: 'People whose passions have got them into difficulties will always be grateful if we, by our calmness, can help them free again. Let us engage ourselves joyfully and cheerfully in the things the men have left unfinished; that way we can best look forward to their return, by preserving and furthering through our moderation those things which their tempestuous and impatient natures threatened to destroy.'

'Since you are speaking of moderation, my dear aunt,' said Ottilie in reply, 'I will admit that what at once occurs to me is how immoderate men are, and especially in relation to wine. It has often saddened and distressed me to watch good sense, intelligence, consideration for others, charming and amiable manners being lost for hours at a time, and instead of all the good that a talented man can do or permit, to see catastrophe and confusion threatening. And how often it results in rash decisions!'

Charlotte agreed with her, but did not continue the conversation since she was well aware that once again Ottilie was only thinking of Eduard, who if not habitually at least more often than might be wished would raise the degree of his pleasure, his talkativeness, and his practical energies by drinking wine.

When Charlotte made her remarks the men, and especially Eduard, were able to approach again in Ottilie's thoughts, and so it was all the more remarkable to her when Charlotte spoke of a marriage the Captain was about to enter into as of something well known and definite, for this made everything look very different from how she had envisaged it on the basis of Eduard's earlier assurances. These things caused Ottilie to pay ever-more attention to Charlotte's every utterance, every hint, every act, every step. Ottilie had grown astute, sharp, suspicious, without knowing it.

Charlotte meanwhile, having looked hard at all the details of her circumstances, addressed herself to them in her usual decisive and orderly manner, and insisted on Ottilie's constant participation too. Though she did not stint, she drew her household tightly in again; and now, all things considered, she viewed the passionate events as a sort of happy chance. For as things were going they might easily have got beyond all limits; and their agreeably fortunate and comfortable situation, had they not come to their senses in time, might, by living life at too rapid a rate, have been if not destroyed at least severely shaken.

She did not interrupt the work already begun in the grounds. On the contrary, she pushed ahead with whatever had to be ready as a basis for future development, but that was all. Her husband, when he came home, must find enough that would keep him pleasantly occupied.

In these works and projects the Architect's way of proceeding seemed to her beyond praise. Soon the lake stretched out before her eyes and the newly created shores were grassed over or beautified by all manner of planting. All the rough work on the new house was finished off and everything necessary for its preservation seen to; then she made a halt at a point where it would be a pleasure to begin again. In so doing she was cheerful and tranquil. Ottilie only seemed it, for she saw in all things only signs as to whether Eduard was expected soon or not. In all things nothing interested her except this consideration.

Thus she welcomed an arrangement by which the local boys were enrolled to keep the gardens tidy, for these had become extensive. It was an idea Eduard himself had entertained. The boys were fitted out with a sort of cheerful livery which they put on in the evenings after a thorough cleansing of their persons. This wardrobe was kept at the Hall; the most sensible and meticulous boy had been given charge of it; the whole exercise was directed by the Architect, and very soon all the boys had acquired a certain dexterity. Their training showed off well, they performed their duties in something of a military manner. Certainly, when they arrived with their scrapers, billhooks, rakes, little spades, mattocks, and fan-shaped brooms, others coming after with baskets to carry away the weeds and stones, or dragging the enormous iron roller, they made a pretty and heart-warming procession in which the Architect noted a charming sequence of poses and activities for the frieze of a summer-house, whereas Ottilie saw only a sort of parade in it which would soon be welcoming home the returning lord.

This gave her the heart and the desire to welcome him with something similar. Efforts had been made already to encourage the village girls in sewing, knitting, spinning, and other female tasks. These virtues too had increased with the promotion of cleanliness and a pretty appearance in the village. Ottilie was always involved, but in a rather casual fashion, as the occasion arose and as her mood dictated. Now she resolved to pursue it more thoroughly and consequentially. But girls cannot be marshalled into a company as boys can. She followed her instincts, and without being quite explicit about it she sought to do nothing more than inculcate upon every girl an attachment to home, to parents and brothers and sisters.

She was successful with many. But about one lively little girl there were constant complaints that she lacked all address and would do nothing whatsoever in the house. Ottilie could not be unsympathetic to the child since she was especially friendly towards Ottilie herself. She came up and walked with her and ran alongside whenever Ottilie allowed it. On those occasions she was busy, cheerful, and tireless. The child seemed to need to be attached to a beautiful mistress. At first Ottilie tolerated her company; then grew fond of her; finally they became inseparable, and Nanni went with her mistress everywhere.

Often Ottilie made her way to the garden; it gladdened her heart to see everything coming on so beautifully. The soft fruits and the cherries were finishing, though on the last of them Nanni feasted with particular relish. As he looked to the fruit that would be ready in such abundance in the autumn the Gardener was constantly put in mind of his master, and never without wishing him home. Ottilie loved listening to the old man. He was perfect in his job, and never ceased speaking of Eduard when she was there.

When Ottilie said how pleased she was that the grafting done in the spring had taken so well, the Gardener expressed some concern: 'I sincerely hope that his Lordship will not be disappointed. If he were here this autumn he would see what delicious kinds there are still in the old garden from his father's day. Fruit-growers nowadays are not so reliable as the Carthusians used to be. The names in the catalogues sound honest enough, of course. But you graft and bring them on, and finally when they fruit it is not worth having such trees in the garden.'

But again and again, almost as often as he saw her, the faithful old servant asked Ottilie about his master's return and when it would be. And when Ottilie could not tell him, though he said nothing Ottilie could see it distressed him and that he believed she would not confide in him, and it pained her to have her ignorance thus forcibly brought home. But still she could not keep away from these beds and borders. Seeds they had in part and plants they had entirely put in the ground together were now in full bloom and scarcely needed any more tending except by Nanni, always ready with her watering-can. How feelingly Ottilie contemplated the later flowers now just showing! Their brightness and abundance were to have been the glory of Eduard's birthday and the expression of her affection and her gratitude; and though sometimes she still promised herself that she would see the day celebrated, her hope was not always equally vigorous. Doubts and anxieties were forever whispering around the poor girl's soul.

Nor was it likely that any real and frank understanding would again be established with Charlotte. For of course the situations of the two women were very different. If everything remained as it had been, if they returned again into the way of lawful life, then Charlotte's present happiness increased and the prospect of a happy future opened before her; Ottilie, on the other hand, lost everything. And it is right to say everything: for it was in Eduard that she had first found life and joy, and in her present condition she felt an infinite emptiness such as she had scarcely had any inkling of before. For a heart that is searching will of course feel a lack; but a heart that has suffered a loss feels deprived. Longing is transformed into discontent and impatience, and a woman's spirit, used to waiting upon an outcome, inclines her now to step outside her normal sphere, to be active and enterprising and to do something for her happiness herself.

Ottilie had not given Eduard up. And how could she, even though Charlotte, shrewdly enough, despite her own conviction to the contrary, pretended she had and that it was understood and had been decided that between her husband and Ottilie a friendly and tranquil relationship was possible. But how often at nights, having locked herself in, Ottilie knelt before the open box and looked at her birthday presents, not one of which she had used or cut or made up. And how often the poor girl hurried at sunrise from the house in which previously she had found all her happiness into the open air, into places she had used not to like. She was not even content remaining on dry land. She jumped into the boat and rowed herself out into the middle of the lake, then took up a travel book, let the waves of the agitated surface rock her, read, dreamed herself into foreign lands, and always found her friend there. All along she had remained close to his heart, and he to hers.

CHAPTER EIGHTEEN

WE have already made the acquaintance of Mittler. It was only to be expected that he, always so curiously busy, hearing of the misfortune which had befallen his friends (though none of them had as yet sent to him for help), should be disposed to prove and practise his friendship and his skill in their case too. But it seemed to him advisable that first he should wait a while; for he knew only too well that in confusions of a moral kind educated people are harder to assist than uneducated. Accordingly, he left them to themselves for a time; but in the end could not bear it any longer, and hastened to visit Eduard, having already discovered his whereabouts.

The way led him to a pleasant valley over whose sweet green floor, through meadows and many trees, the abundant waters of an ever-lively stream meandered or rushed. Fertile fields and plentiful orchards stretched away over the gentle slopes. There was space between the villages, the whole scene had a peaceful character, and the particular parts, if not especially suitable for painting, seemed so for life itself.

His eyes lit finally on a well-kept farmstead with a clean and simple dwelling-house surrounded by gardens. He supposed this to be Eduard's present home, and he was not mistaken.

We can say this much about our solitary friend: that in his privacy he had abandoned himself wholly to his passion and was making many plans and nourishing many hopes. He could not deny that he wished to see Ottilie here, that he wished to bring her, to lure her here, and there were other things besides, permissible and impermissible, that he let his thoughts entertain. Then his imagination reeled among the possibilities. If he was not to possess her here, rightfully possess her, then he would make over to her the possession of the property. Here she should live quietly for herself and be independent; she should be happy and, whenever he let his imagination torment him further, then perhaps be happy with another man.

So his days passed in a perpetual veering between hope and pain, between tears and cheerfulness, between plans, preparations, and despair. He was not surprised to see Mittler. He had been expecting his arrival for quite some time, and was thus even half glad of it. Against him, if he came as Charlotte's emissary, he had already devised a variety of prevarications, excuses, and, to follow them, some more-decisive proposals; but if he brought news of Ottilie Mittler was as welcome as a messenger from heaven.

He was cross, therefore, and aggrieved when he learned that Mittler had not come from home but of his own accord. Eduard's heart closed against him and the conversation could not get under way. But Mittler knew very well that a mind preoccupied with love has an urgent need to speak and be disburdened before a friend of what is happening within, and he was for that reason willing, after a few exchanges, to relinquish his usual role on this occasion and play the confidant instead of the go-between.

Having then censured Eduard, in a friendly fashion, for the solitariness of his life, he was given this reply: 'Oh, I do not know how I might spend my time more agreeably! I am always preoccupied with her, always close to her. I have the inestimable advantage of being able to imagine where Ottilie is, where she walks, where she stands, where she takes her rest. I see her before me doing what she usually does, always busying herself and always, it is true, with things that please me best. But I go further than this, for how can I be happy away from her? I fall to imagining how Ottilie might come to me. I write tender loving letters in her name to myself; I answer her, and keep the pages in one place together. I have promised not to make a move in her direction, and I will keep my promise. But what binds her, that she should not turn to me? Has Charlotte perhaps been so cruel as to require her to promise and swear that she will not write to me and will not give me any news of herself? That would be natural and likely, yet I find it outrageous and unbearable. If she loves me, as I believe she does, as I know she does, why will she not resolve, why does she not dare to flee and throw herself into my arms? She ought to, I sometimes think, she could do. When there is some movement in the hall I look towards the door. I think and hope it might be her about to enter. Oh, and since what is possible is impossible I imagine the impossible must be possible. At night when I wake and the lamp casts an unsteady light over the room I think her shape, her ghost, a sense of her must come flitting by and approach and take hold of me if only for a moment, so that I should have a sort of assurance that she is thinking of me and is mine.

'One joy remains. When I was near her I never dreamed of her; but now at a distance we are together in dreams, and, strangely enough, since I have made the acquaintance of other attractive women in the neighbourhood it is now that her image appears to me in dreams, as if to say: "Look where you like. You will not find anyone more beautiful or fitter to be loved than I am." And thus her image enters all my dreams. Everything that happens to me with her gets confused and transposed. We might be signing a contract: her hand is there and so is mine, her name and mine, they erase one another, they intertwine. Nor are these blissful tricks of the imagination without pain. Sometimes she does something which offends against the pure idea I have of her; and then indeed I feel how much I love her for I become distressed beyond all expression. Sometimes she teases me quite against her nature and torments me; but then at once her image changes, her beautiful, round, heavenly little face is elongated – she is someone else. But still I am tormented, unsatisfied, and broken into pieces.

'Don't smile, my dear Mittler. Or smile if you like. Oh, I am not ashamed of this devotion, or call it a foolish and raging passion if you will. No, I have never been in love, only now am I discovering what it means. Everything in my life to date has been only a prelude, a postponement, only passing the time, wasting time, until I got to know her, until I loved her and wholly and really loved her. It has been said against me – if not to my face then certainly behind my back – that I am an amateur, that I have no particular talent for anything. That may be so, but only because I had not found the thing I can excel at. Now show me the man whose talent for loving exceeds mine.

'Admittedly, it is a talent full of misery, and rich in pain and tears; but I find it so natural to me, so peculiarly mine, that I am not likely ever to give it up.'

Doubtless this vivid and heartfelt utterance had afforded Eduard some relief; but now also and all at once every single detail of his strange situation had become clear to him, the painful contradictions overwhelmed him, and he began to weep and did so unrestrainedly, for he had been made weak by his confidences.

Mittler, not able to go against his own hasty temperament and implacable good sense and less than ever likely to since he saw himself deflected from the purpose of his journey by Eduard's painful and passionate outpourings, now frankly and emphatically expressed his disapproval. Eduard, he said, should pull himself together, should consider what his standing as a man required of him, should bear in mind that what does most honour to a human being is that he keep a grip on himself in misfortune and suffer pain with equanimity and decorum, so as to be highly esteemed, honoured, and set up as a model.

Upset as he was and riven by feelings of the most painful kind, these words were bound to seem hollow and worthless to Eduard. 'Easy for a comfortable and contented man to talk like that,' he cried, 'but he would be ashamed if he knew how he grates on a man who is suffering. We are supposed to be infinite in our patience, but people set in their comfortable ways will not acknowledge that there might be such a thing as infinite torment too. There are cases, indeed there are, in which solace is despicable and the only honourable course is to despair. The noble poets of Greece, who knew how to depict heroes, did not at all mind letting them weep when they were in the grip of pain. "Tears are a sign of goodness in a man," they used to say. I will not live with people whose hearts are stony and whose eyes are dry! I curse those who are happy and who want the unhappy man for a spectacle or not at all. To have their approval he must conduct himself nobly even in the cruellest physical and mental tribulation; and for their applause at his death he must die before their eyes with a proper decency, like a gladiator. My dear Mittler, I am grateful for your visit; but you would do me a great favour now if you would take a stroll in the garden and round about. Come back later. Meanwhile I shall seek to compose myself and to be more like you.'

But Mittler softened, preferring not to break off a conversation which it might be hard to start up again. Nor was Eduard averse to going on, since their talk was in any case heading towards its natural end.

'All this thinking about it and discussing it will do no good,' said Eduard, 'but at least in speaking I have for the first time realized and for the first time definitely felt what I ought to do and what I am now determined to do. I see my present and my future life before me. My only options are misery or delight. Bring about a divorce, my dear fellow. That is what is needed, and it has already happened. Get me Charlotte's consent. I shan't go into why I believe it to be obtainable. Go and see her, there's a good fellow, ease all our minds, make us happy.'

Mittler was taken aback. Eduard continued: 'My fate cannot be separated from Ottilie's, and we are not destined to perish. See this glass. Our initials are cut in it. A man full of joy in an act of celebration flung it into the air so that no one else should ever drink out of it. It was to have shattered on the stony ground, but it was caught before it fell. Now I have bought it back at a high price and I drink from it daily and daily confirm myself in the belief that relationships fate has decided are indestructible.'

'Woe is me!' cried Mittler. 'What a deal of patience one has to have with one's friends! Now of all things I am up against superstition – which I have always detested as the most pernicious interferer in human affairs. We play around with prophecies, presentiments, and dreams, to lend some significance to our everyday lives. But when life itself becomes significant and when everything about us is in commotion those phantoms only make the tempests all the more terrible.'

'But in the uncertainty of life,' Eduard cried, 'leave a heart struggling between hope and fear at least some sort of guiding star that it can look to, even if not steer by.'

'I should be glad to,' Mittler replied, 'if there were any hope of consistency in it; but I have always found that nobody takes any notice of warning signs; only the flattering and promising ones receive attention, and only in them do people have any faith.'

Since Mittler saw himself being led now even into the regions of darkness, where he felt more and more uncomfortable the longer he stayed, he agreed with a rather greater readiness to do as Eduard was urging him to do, and visit Charlotte. For what further arguments could he bring against Eduard at present? What he could still do, as he saw it, was gain time and find out how things stood with the women.

He hurried to Charlotte, and found her, as ever, composed and cheerful. She gladly informed him of all that had happened, for Eduard's words had only enabled him to grasp the effects. He advanced from his own side cautiously, but could not bring himself to utter the word 'divorce' even in passing. How great then were his surprise, astonishment, and – in accordance with his views – delight when Charlotte, after so much that was disagreeable, went on to say: 'I cannot but believe, cannot but hope that all will be well, that Eduard will come back again. How can it be otherwise, since I am expecting a child?'

'Do I hear aright?' Mittler exclaimed.

'Indeed you do,' Charlotte replied.

'A thousand blessings on this piece of news!' he cried, clapping his hands. 'I know the power of this argument on a man's mind. How many marriages have I not seen it hasten, strengthen, restore! Hope such as you now have is worth any number of words. Truly, it is the best hope in the world. But,' he went on, 'for my own part I should have every reason to feel aggrieved. I see very well that this particular case does nothing for my self-esteem. My efforts will not earn me any thanks from you. I am rather like that doctor, a friend of mine, who was always successful in curing the poor, for wages in heaven, but rarely cured a rich man who would have paid him well. It is fortunate that this present matter will resolve itself, for my exertions and my speeches would have done no good.'

Charlotte now asked him to convey the news to Eduard, take a letter from her, and see what was to be done and set in train. But Mittler declined. 'There is nothing more to do!' he cried. 'Write your letter. Any messenger will serve as well as I. For I must be off now to where I am needed more. I shan't come again, except to congratulate you. I shall come to the christening.'

On this occasion, as often before, Charlotte was displeased with Mittler. Being quick, he did some good, but his hastiness caused some failures too. Nobody was more dependent on opinions arrived at very rapidly in advance.

Charlotte's messenger came to Eduard, and was received by him half in fright. The decision in the letter could just as well be no as yes. For a long time he did not dare open it. He was dumbfounded when he read it. By the following passage, with which the letter ended, he was as if turned to stone:

'Think of that night when you came like an adventurous lover to visit your wife and drew her irresistibly and took her as a mistress, as a bride, into your arms. Let us honour in this strange chance a disposition of Heaven by which there will be a new bond in our relationship just as our life's happiness threatens to come asunder and disappear.'

It would be hard to describe what happened in Eduard's soul after that moment. In such a press of feelings old habits and old inclinations finally come to the fore again, to kill time and to fill life up with something. Hunting and war are one such recourse a nobleman always has at his disposal. Eduard longed for some external danger to balance the inner one. He longed to go under, for his existence was threatening to become unbearable; indeed, he found solace in the thought that he would no longer exist and might thereby make his friends and loved ones happy. Nobody put any obstacle in the way of his desire, since he kept his decision secret. In all proper form he drew up his will. It was a sweet feeling being able to leave his present dwelling-place to Ottilie. Charlotte, the unborn child, the Captain, the servants, were all provided for. His plans were helped by a renewal of the war. His youthful soldiering, being of a trivial kind, had irritated him greatly, and he had left the service for that reason. Now it was a splendid feeling to follow a general of whom he could say to himself: under his leadership death is probable and victory certain.

Ottilie, once Charlotte's secret was known to her too, being shocked as Eduard had been, and even more so, withdrew into herself. She had nothing more to say. She could not hope, nor was wishing allowed her. But her diary gives us an insight into her inner life, and we have in mind to disclose some items from it.

PART TWO

CHAPTER ONE

IT often happens in ordinary life as in an epic poem (where we admire it as poetic artifice) that when the principal characters withdraw, remove themselves from view, become inactive, at once some second or third and until then scarcely noticed person takes their place and, by the entire engagement of himself, like them seems worthy of our attention, sympathetic interest, and even our approval and our praise.

Thus day by day after the departure of the Captain and of Eduard, the Architect became more important. So many matters depended on him entirely for their organization and execution. He was exact, sensible, and energetic in carrying out his duties; assisted the ladies in a variety of ways and kept them entertained when their quiet lives grew tedious. His very appearance was of a kind to inspire trust and kindle affection. He was a youth in the full sense of the word, a fine figure, slim, if anything a little too tall, modest without being timid, eager to confide but never importunate. He would gladly take on any responsibility and go to any trouble, and having a very good head for figures he had soon understood all the management of the household and his helpful influence extended everywhere. It was usually left to him to receive visitors, and if they arrived unexpectedly he either succeeded in putting them off or, at the very least, so prepared the women that no inconvenience resulted.

Among those giving him a good deal of trouble was a young lawyer sent one day by a gentleman of the neighbourhood to discuss a matter which, though of no very great significance, nevertheless touched Charlotte closely. We are obliged to consider this incident because it gave an impetus to various things which might otherwise have lain dormant for a long time.

The reader will remember the changes Charlotte had made in the churchyard. All the memorial stones had been removed from their places and set along the wall and along the plinth of the church. The space thus vacated had been levelled. Apart from one broad path which led to the church and past it to a little gate on the far side, everywhere else had been sown with different kinds of clover, now beautifully verdant and flowering. New graves were to be dug in a certain order starting from the far corner, but the site afterwards was always to be levelled and sown in the same manner. Nobody could deny that by this arrangement churchgoers on Sundays and holy days were afforded a prospect that was both cheerful and in keeping. Even the parson, though advanced in years and attached to the old ways and at first not especially happy with what had been done, was now delighted to sit like Philemon with his Baucis under the old lime trees at his back door and see before him not the bumpy graves but a fine colourful carpet, which moreover would be of benefit to his household since Charlotte had granted the parsonage sole use of the piece of land.

But notwithstanding all this several parishioners had earlier expressed their disapproval of the fact that the place where their ancestors lay buried was now no longer marked and that the memory of them was thereby, as it were, extinguished; for though the well-preserved headstones showed who was buried they did not show where, and where was what really mattered in the view of many.

Precisely that view was taken by a local family who, several years before, had reserved a portion of this general resting-place for their own members and had made a small endowment to the church in exchange. Now the young lawyer had been sent to cancel the endowment and to announce that the payments would be discontinued because the conditions under which they had so far been made had been unilaterally set aside and all representations and objections ignored. Charlotte, the author of the change, wished to speak to the young man herself. Forcefully, yet without undue vehemence, he set out his own and his client's arguments, and in doing so gave those present much to think about.

'We see', he said after a short preamble in which he explained to their satisfaction why he had intruded upon them, 'we see the meanest and the highest much concerned to mark the place where their dear ones lie. The poorest farm labourer, burying his child, finds some kind of comfort in setting a frail wooden cross on the grave and adorning it with a wreath to keep the memory alive at least as long as his sorrow lasts, even though such a mark, like grief itself, is annulled by time. The better-off turn such crosses into iron ones, strengthen and protect them in a variety of ways, and several years might be the length of their survival. But since these too sink down in time and become unnoticeable the landed families think it supremely important to raise a stone that may be counted on to last for several generations and can be renewed and refurbished by their descendants. But it is not the stone itself we are drawn to, but what is contained beneath it, what nearby has been committed to the earth. It is not just a matter of remembrance, but of the person too, and not of memory so much as of presence. I can more easily and intimately approach a departed loved one in a grave than in a memorial stone, for the stone itself is of little importance. But around it, as around a milestone, husbands and wives, relatives and friends should still foregather, even after death, and the living must have the right to turn away strangers and ill-wishers and keep them at a distance from their own loved ones who are at rest.

'Thus I think it entirely just that my client should revoke the endowment; and it is moreover a very moderate response, for his family has been offended in a way for which no compensation is imaginable. They must forego the bitter-sweet satisfaction of paying their respects to their beloved dead and also the hope and comfort of one day resting with them side by side.'

'The matter is not so important', Charlotte replied, 'that we need upset ourselves by going to law over it. I so little regret what I have done that I will gladly compensate the church for its losses. But I must tell you frankly that your arguments have not convinced me. The pure sense of a final and general equality, at least after death, seems to me of more solace than this selfish and stubborn continuation of our personalities, allegiances, and material circumstances. And what is your view?' she asked, turning to the Architect.

'In such a dispute', he replied, 'I should prefer neither to take part nor to have the casting vote. But let me in all modesty say what touches me most, in my way of seeing things, as an artist. Since we are no longer so fortunate as to be able to hold in our arms the remains of our loved ones in a funerary vase; since we are neither rich enough nor serene enough to preserve them unspoilt in large and ornate sarco-phagi; since even in the churches there is no longer room for us and our kith and kin, but we are turned out of doors – we all have reason to approve of the procedure your Ladyship has introduced. If the members of a parish lie side by side in rows then they are indeed lying next to and among their own; and if the earth is one day to receive us all I can think of nothing more natural and cleanly than that the mounds accidentally created and gradually subsiding should be levelled at once so that the coverlet, borne by all, shall be made to rest lightly on all.'

'And must it all pass without any sign of remembrance?' Ottilie asked. 'With nothing that will aid our memory?'

'By no means!' the Architect continued. 'We are not being asked to give up remembrance, only the particular place. It is the dearest wish of every architect and sculptor that people should turn to him, to his art, to work of his hands, for some perpetuation of their lives; which is why I should like to see well-thought-out and well-executed monuments, and not strewn around singly and casually but set up in one place where they can expect to last. Since nowadays even the saintly and the mighty no longer insist on lying in person in the churches, let us at least, either there or in beautiful buildings near the places of burial, set up monuments and memorial inscriptions. There are a thousand forms they might be given and a thousand ways of ornamenting them.'

'If artists are as well off as you say,' Charlotte replied, 'why is it all we ever get from them are urns and petty obelisks and broken columns? Instead of the thousand good ideas you were boasting of I have only ever seen a thousand repetitions.'

'That may be so in these parts,' the Architect answered, 'but not everywhere. And then good ideas and their proper application are altogether a difficult matter. Especially in this case it is hard to counter the seriousness of the subject, and in treating what is distressing to avoid merely causing distress. As far as sketches for all kinds of monument are concerned, I have a large collection and will show you them when you like; but the finest memorial is always the person's own image. Better than anything else this gives an idea of what he was; it provides the best text to his life's greater or lesser quantity of music; but it needs to be done when he is at his best, and normally it isn't. Nobody thinks of preserving living forms, or when they do it happens in an unsatisfactory way. They take a quick cast of the dead man's face, set the resulting mask on a block of stone, and call it a bust of him. Only very rarely is the artist able to bring such a thing wholly back to life again.'

'Perhaps without knowing it or intending it', said Charlotte, 'you have turned this conversation entirely to my advantage. The likeness of a person is surely an independent thing; wherever it stands, it stands for itself and we shall not require it to designate the actual place of burial. But, to be honest, I have a strange sort of antipathy even towards such images, for they seem always to be silently reproaching me; they point towards something distant and departed, and remind me how difficult it is properly to honour the present. If we think how many people we have seen and known, and admit how little we have been to them and how little they to us, what a strange feeling that is! We meet a witty man and have no conversation with him, a learned man and learn nothing from him, a well-travelled man and find nothing out, and one full of love and do nothing that would have pleased him.

'And this happens, unfortunately, not just with those who are passing through. Societies and families behave in this way towards their dearest members, cities towards their worthiest citizens, peoples towards their finest princes, nations towards their most outstanding men and women.

'I have heard it asked why we speak so unreservedly well of the dead but of the living always with a certain caution. And the answer was: because from the dead we have nothing to fear, whereas the living may still cross us. Of such impurity is our concern for the memory of others; it is mostly only selfish and unserious. But nothing is more serious than that we keep our dealings with the living always active and alive.'

CHAPTER TWO

STIRRED by this encounter and by the ensuing conversations, they went next day to the burial-ground and the Architect made several happy suggestions as to how it might be beautified and rendered more cheerful. Thereafter his concern extended to the church itself, a building which from the start had attracted his attention.

The church had stood for several centuries; it was a thoroughly German work, well proportioned and pleasingly ornamented. There was good reason to believe that the man who had built a nearby monastery had proved his worth here too, with insight and affection, on this smaller building. Its effect was earnest and agreeable still, even though the conversion of the interior to suit the Protestant form of worship had deprived it of some of its quiet and majesty.

The Architect easily begged a little money from Charlotte, to restore both the outside and the interior of the church in the early style and bring the whole into harmony with the field of resurrection in which it stood. He was very skilled himself, and some of the workers still building the new house could of course be kept on until this pious work too was completed.

They were now exploring the building itself with all its surroundings and outbuildings when, to the great astonishment and delight of the Architect, they came upon a small and hitherto almost unnoticed side chapel whose proportions were even more subtle, even lighter, and whose ornamentation was even more pleasing and conscientious. It also contained several carved and painted remnants of the older form of worship, when the different festivals had been marked by different images and implements and celebrated each in its special way.

The Architect could not resist at once including the chapel in his plans. This small space should be restored particularly as a memorial of earlier times and of their taste. He saw how he would like the empty surfaces decorated, and looked forward to using his talents as a painter; but for the time being he kept this a secret from the others.

First of all he did as he had promised and showed the women the various copies and sketches he had made of ancient funerary monuments, urns, and related things, and when the conversation turned to the simpler burial mounds of the northern peoples he produced his collection of weapons and implements which had been found in them. He had everything together very neatly and portably in drawers and compartments on trays fitted into these and lined with cloth, so that the ancient and solemn objects seemed in his handling of them almost modish, it was a pleasure to look at them, like looking into little trinket boxes at a milliner's. And once he had got into the way of showing things, since their solitude required some entertainment, he appeared before them every evening with a part of his treasures. They were mostly of German origin: tiny one-sided and weightier coins, seals, and other things of that kind. These all directed the imagination to earlier times, and when he illustrated his discourses with the beginnings of printing, with woodcuts and the first engravings, and since one might say that the church too, day by day, in the same spirit, in its colours and other decoration, was growing towards the past, they almost began to wonder whether they were living in the modern age at all, and whether their dwelling now among quite different customs, habits, modes of life, and convictions were not merely a dream.

After such preparation, a larger portfolio which he produced last had the best effect of all. True, it contained for the most part only line drawings of figures which, however, having been traced from the pictures themselves, had retained their ancient character entirely, and how this charmed the company when they saw! A perfect purity of existence gazed out from all the figures; there was an undeniable goodness, if not nobility, in them all. Joyous composure, willing acknowledgement of something above us worthy of reverence, a quiet giving of the self in love and expectation were expressed in every face and every gesture. The old man with the bald crown, the curly-headed boy, the cheerful youth, the earnest adult, the transfigured saint, the hovering angel, all seem blessed in a state of innocent sufficiency, in a pious waiting. The most commonplace occurrence had in it a trace of heavenly life, and every character there seemed meant for an act of worship.

Most no doubt gaze at such a region as at a vanished golden age, a lost paradise. Perhaps only Ottilie could feel herself to be among her own kind there.

Who then could have refused the Architect when he offered to decorate the panels of the chapel ceiling after the prompting of these archetypal images, and in so doing to make a definite memorial of himself in a place where he had been so happy? He expounded on this with some wistfulness. He could see that as things stood he would not be able to stay for ever in such perfect company; indeed, that he might have to depart before very long.

These days, though not rich in events, did offer many occasions for serious conversation. We shall therefore take this opportunity to communicate something of what Ottilie noted down from them, and can think of no better transition than a comparison forcefully suggested to us by a reading of her charming pages.

We have heard of a peculiar custom in the English navy. All the ropes, however strong or weak, on all of His Majesty's ships, are woven in such a way that a red thread goes through the whole length and cannot be extracted from it without undoing it all, and by this thread even the smallest pieces are recognizable as belonging to the Crown.

In the same way there runs through Ottilie's diary a thread of love and devotion which unites everything and characterizes the whole. Thus the remarks, observations, the quoted maxims and whatever else may appear all become quite peculiarly the writer's own and significant for her. Every single item here selected and communicated constitutes a most decided proof of that.

From Ottilie's Diary

'To be at rest one day with those we love is the sweetest thing we can imagine if ever we let our thoughts go beyond this life. "To be gathered to one's people" is such a warm expression.

'By various kinds of reminder and memorial our distant and departed ones may be brought a little nearer. None is so important as a portrait. There is something oddly pleasurable in talking with a beloved portrait, even if it is not a good likeness, just as there is sometimes in quarrelling with a friend. In an enjoyable way we feel our separateness and yet we cannot part.

'We sometimes converse with a person who is present as though with a portrait. He does not need to speak, or look at us, or concern himself with us; we see him, we feel our relationship with him, indeed our relations with him may even develop, without his doing anything about it, without his feeling anything of it, but relating to us merely as a portrait would.

'We are never content with portraits of people we know. For that reason I have always felt sorry for portrait painters. We rarely ask the impossible of anyone, but of them we do. They are required to get everybody's relationship with the subject, everybody's affection or dislike, into the picture; and not merely represent their own view of a person but what everybody else's might be too. I do not wonder if such artists gradually close up and become indifferent and wilful. This would be of no consequence except that it costs us the like-nesses of many well-loved people.

'It must be agreed that the Architect's collection of weapons and ancient utensils, which were buried along with the body under great mounds of earth and slabs of stone, is proof of how futile is the provision human beings make for the preservation of their personalities after death. And how paradoxical we are! The Architect admits that he has himself opened such ancestral tombs and continues nevertheless to concern himself with memorials for posterity.

'But why take it so strictly? Is everything we do done for eternity? Do we not dress in the morning only to undress in the evening? Do we not leave on journeys only to return? And why should we not wish to be beside our loved ones even if only for a century?

'When we see the many gravestones sinking down or being worn away by the feet of churchgoers, and even churches themselves fallen in on their memorial stones, still life after death may seem a sort of second life into which we enter as a picture with its caption and dwell there longer than in our real and living lives. But then that picture too, that second existence, fades sooner or later. As over people, so over their monuments, Time maintains its rights.'

CHAPTER THREE

I T is such an agreeable feeling to be busy with something one is only half-competent to do that nobody should criticize the dilettante for taking up an art he will never learn, or blame the artist who leaves the territory of his own art for the pleasure of trying himself in a neighbouring one.

This seems an appropriate way of viewing how the Architect proceeded to paint the chapel. The colours were ready, measurements taken, cartoons done; he had given up any claim to originality; he stuck to his tracings; his sole endeavour was to dispose the seated and the hovering figures in the best manner and tastefully decorate the space with them.

The scaffolding was in place, the work advanced, and once something the eyes could appreciate had already been achieved he was content that Charlotte should visit him with Ottilie. The living faces of the angels, the lively drapery on the background of a blue heaven delighted the eye, their tranquil and pious natures called on the soul to collect itself, and a very tender effect was brought about.

The women had climbed up to join him on the scaffolding, and no sooner had Ottilie seen how measuredly and easily the work was going forward than all she had earlier received through teaching at once seemed to grow in her and she took a brush and paint and, being directed what to do, put in the numerous folds of a robe with as much neatness as skill.

Charlotte, who was always glad to see Ottilie in any way occupied and distracted, left the pair to it, and went off to follow her own thoughts and work through for herself all the reflections and concerns which she could not communicate to anyone else.

When ordinary people are agitated and made anxious by everyday inconveniences they may extract a smile of

sympathy from us; but we look with reverence at a personality in which the seed of a large fate has been sown and which
must wait upon the future growth of this conception and is
not permitted and is not able to hasten the good or the ill, the
happiness or the unhappiness, destined to come forth from it.

Through Charlotte's messenger, sent to him in his solitude, Eduard had replied in a friendly and sympathetic manner, but with more composure and seriousness than intimacy
and love. Shortly afterwards he had vanished, and his wife
could get no news of him until at last she came across his
name in the newspapers, where he was mentioned with
honour among those who had distinguished themselves in
an important military engagement. Now she knew which way
he had taken, she learned he had escaped from grave dangers;
but she realized at once that he would seek out even graver
ones, and it was all too clear to her that, in every sense, he
would be hard to hold back from a final extreme. In her
solitary thinking she dwelled constantly upon these cares, and
might turn them any way she liked but no perspective gave
her any comfort.

Ottilie, suspecting nothing of all this, had meanwhile taken
a very great liking to her new work and easily obtained
Charlotte's permission to continue with it regularly. Now
they made rapid progress and the azure heavens were soon
populated with fit inhabitants. Through sustained practice
Ottilie and the Architect attained to a greater freedom in the
last pictures; they grew markedly better. The faces too, which
were left to the Architect to paint, gradually began to manifest
a quite peculiar quality: they all began to look like Ottilie. The
presence of the beautiful child must doubtless have made
such a lively impression upon the soul of the young man, who
had no preconceptions as to faces, either from art or life, that
gradually in passing from the eye to the hand nothing was
lost, indeed by the finish both worked wholly in harmony.
Enough, one of the last faces succeeded perfectly so that it
seemed as if Ottilie herself were looking down out of the
heavenly regions.

The ceiling was finished; it had been intended simply to leave the walls and only go over them with a lighter brownish colour and pick out the delicate columns and the ornamental carvings in something darker. But, as always happens, one thing led to another and it was decided to have festoons of fruit and flowers as well which would, so to speak, join heaven and earth together. Here Ottilie was wholly in her element. The gardens provided her with the loveliest patterns, and although the garlands were very richly done, the work was completed earlier than expected.

Still everything looked untidy and unfinished. The scaffolding lay in confusion, the planks thrown down anyhow, and the uneven floor was further disfigured by splashes of paint. The Architect begged a week's grace, during which time the ladies were not to enter the chapel. At length then, on a beautiful evening, he asked them both to make their way there; but wished to be excused from accompanying them, and at once took his leave.

'Whatever surprise he may have prepared for us,' said Charlotte when he had gone, 'I am really not in the mood for it at present. Go by yourself, will you, and tell me about it. He is certain to have done something we shall be pleased with. I shall enjoy it first in your account, then gladly in reality afterwards.'

Ottilie, who knew that in many respects Charlotte was protecting herself, avoiding any emotional excitement and above all any surprises, at once set off alone, and could not help looking out for the Architect, who was, however, nowhere to be seen and had perhaps concealed himself. She went into the church, which she found open. The work here had been finished some time before, and the place cleaned and opened for services again. She approached the door of the chapel. It was heavy, set with bronze, but it opened easily on a sight which, being unexpected in a familiar place, astonished her.

Through the single high window a solemn radiance entered, a beautiful fusion of different colours of glass. This lent the whole an unfamiliar air and produced a quite peculiar mood. The beauty of the vaulted ceiling and the walls was enhanced by an attractive floor of specially shaped tiles laid in a pleasing pattern on a screed of plaster. The Architect had ordered these in secret, as well as the little panes of coloured glass, and was able to put everything together very quickly. Places to sit had been provided too. Several beautifully carved choir-stalls had been found among the antiquities of the church and set around the walls in a tasteful manner.

Ottilie was delighted by the familiar parts now appearing before her as an unfamiliar whole. She stood, walked to and fro, looked and looked again; finally she sat down in one of the stalls, and it seemed to her, as she looked up and around, as though she existed and did not exist, as though she had feelings and had none, as though everything might vanish before her eyes or she herself might vanish even as she looked; and only when the sun went from the window, which until then it had illuminated very brilliantly, did Ottilie wake and come back to herself, and hurry away to the Hall.

She felt how strangely this event had fallen. It was the evening before Eduard's birthday. Needless to say, she had hoped to celebrate the day in quite another fashion. Was not everything to have been decorated for the occasion? But the whole abundance of autumn flowers was still unplucked. There were the sunflowers still, turning towards heaven, and the asters looking ahead with quiet and modest faces; and what had at all been made into garlands had served as patterns to decorate a place which, if it were not to remain an artist's whim, if it were ever to have a proper use, only seemed fit to be their common burial place.

Then she could not help thinking of the noise and bustle with which Eduard had celebrated her birthday, and of the newly roofed house and the great amity they had looked forward to in it. And she seemed to see with her very eyes, hear with her very ears, the fireworks going off again, and imagined them more and more the lonelier she became; but only felt herself to be yet more alone. She could no longer take his arm and had no hope of ever finding support in him again.

From Ottilie's Diary

'I must note down something the young artist said: "Artists and artisans both demonstrate with perfect clarity that a person is least able to appropriate for himself those things which are most peculiarly his. His works leave him as birds do the nest in which they were hatched."

'In this respect an architect's fate is the strangest of all. How often he employs his whole intellect and warmth of feeling in the creation of rooms from which he must exclude himself. Royal halls owe their splendour to him, and he may not share in the enjoyment of their finest effects. In temples he draws a line between himself and the holy of holies; the steps he built to ceremonies that lift up the heart, he may no longer climb; just as the goldsmith worships only from afar the monstrance he wrought in the fire and set with jewels. With the keys of the palace the architect hands over all its comforts to the wealthy man, and has not the least part in them. Surely in this way art must little by little grow away from the artist, if the work, like a child provided for, no longer reaches back to touch its father. And how much better off art was in the days when it had to do almost only with what was public, with what belonged to everyone and thus to the artist too.

'One idea the ancient peoples had is very solemn and may seem terrifying. They imagined their ancestors sitting on thrones, in a circle, in a vast cave, conversing without words. For a new arrival, if he merited it, they rose, and welcomed him with a bow. Yesterday when I was sitting in the chapel, and opposite my carved seat there were several others set around, that idea seemed to me very sympathetic and pleasing. "Why can you not remain seated," I said to myself, "seated in silence in an inward contemplation, for a long long time, until the friends arrived for whom you would rise and show them to their places with a friendly bow?" The stained-glass window turns the daylight to a solemn twilight, and someone ought to donate a sanctuary lamp so that the night would not be entirely dark either.

'Whatever we do, we always conceive of ourselves as seeing. I think we only dream so as not to cease seeing. It might well be that one day the inner light will break forth from us so that we shall no longer have need of any other.

'The year is dying away. The wind passes over the stubble and there is nothing for it to seize and shake; only the red berries on those slender trees seem to wish to remind us of something more cheerful, just as the beat of the thresher wakes in us the thought that in the corn that has fallen to the sickle much life and nourishment lies hidden.'

CHAPTER FOUR

AFTER such events, after such a bringing-home to her of the transience and rapid passing of things, how strangely must Ottilie have been affected by the news, which could no longer be kept from her, that Eduard had put his life under the fickle sway of war. She thought then, alas, all the things that in her situation she had reason to think. Fortunately a human being can comprehend only a certain degree of unhappiness; anything beyond it destroys him or leaves him cold. There are situations in which fear and hope become one and the same, cancel one another out, and lose themselves in a dark insensateness. How else could we know the people we love best to be in continual danger and yet go on with our daily lives as usual?

Thus it looked like an intervention of Ottilie's guardian angel when suddenly into the quiet in which, being lonely and unoccupied, she seemed about to founder, a tumultuous host was fetched, which by engaging her outwardly as much as could be and by bringing her out of herself, at the same time awoke in her a feeling of her own strength.

Charlotte's daughter Luciane had scarcely left her school and made her entry into society and surrounded herself in her aunt's house with a numerous company, than her wish to please was gratified and a very wealthy young man soon felt a passionate desire to possess her. His considerable fortune gave him a right to call the best of everything his own and he seemed to want nothing but a perfect wife whom the world could envy him as they envied him everything else.

This family matter had already caused Charlotte a good deal of work, all her thoughts and her correspondence were given over to it, except when they were directed towards seeking more news of Eduard; with the result that latterly Ottilie had been left more to herself than usual. She was aware that Luciane was expected and had accordingly made what domestic provision was most necessary; but the visit was not thought to be so very imminent. They were still thinking they would write, make arrangements, be more particular, when suddenly the storm broke over the Hall and over Ottilie.

Servants and ladies' maids arrived, and horse-litters bearing trunks and boxes; it was already like a double or triple contingent of visitors; but only then did the guests themselves appear; the great aunt with Luciane and some lady friends, the intended himself, likewise not unaccompanied. The vestibule was full of valises, portmanteaus, and other leather containers. The numerous little boxes and cases were only with difficulty sorted out. The baggage and the carrying of it were endless. Between times it rained in torrents, which caused much discomfort. In the face of this frenzy Ottilie remained efficient and unperturbed; indeed, her cheerful competence was shown at its very best, for she had soon found a proper place for everyone and everything. Every guest was accommodated, all were made comfortable in the ways that suited them, and all felt well looked after because they were not prevented from looking after themselves.

After their very arduous journey they would all have been glad of a little peace and quiet; the young man would have liked to get to know his future mother-in-law and assure her of his love and goodwill; but Luciane could not rest. She had been allowed to take up riding, and now it was her joy. Her husband-to-be owned some fine horses, and forthwith the company was obliged to mount. The wind and the weather made no difference; it was as though the whole purpose of life was to get wet and dry off again. If it occurred to her to go out on foot she never considered what clothes she was wearing or how she was shod. She had to see the park she had heard so much about. What could not be done on horseback was hurried through on foot. She had soon seen everything and given her opinion on everything. Being so quick in her manner she was hard to contradict. The company had to put up with a good deal, her maids especially, who never got to the end of washing and ironing, undoing and sewing things on.

No sooner had she exhausted the house and the grounds than she felt herself called upon to pay visits in the neighbourhood. Since they rode and drove at a pace, this neighbourhood extended pretty far. The Hall was swamped with return visits and before long, so as not to miss one another, particular days were set.

Whilst Charlotte was settling the details of the business with the aunt and the young man's agent, and Ottilie, and those under her, were mobilizing huntsmen and gardeners, fishermen and tradespeople so that with such a crowd in the house there should not be any shortages, Luciane appeared still like a fiery comet towing a long train behind. She soon found the usual entertainments quite insipid. It was as much as she would do to leave the most elderly visitors in peace at the card table; whoever was at all mobile – and she might charm or bully almost anybody into mobility – was commandeered, if not for dancing then for animated guessing games and forfeits. And although all this, including the paying of the forfeits, centred on herself, it was also true that nobody, and especially none of the men, whatever he might be like, went quite without some recompense; indeed, a few elderly persons of consequence were won over entirely when she found out that it happened to be their birthdays or name-days and celebrated them specially. She was helped by her very characteristic talent for making everyone feel favoured but each privately the most favoured of all, the man most conspicuously guilty of this weakness being in fact the oldest present.

Though she seemed bent on winning over men who counted for something – who had rank, consequence, reputation, or some other important quality in their favour – on being the ruination of wisdom and good sense, and on gaining approval for her wild and fantastical nature even among the sober-minded, she nevertheless did not neglect the young; each had his part, his day, an hour when she chose to charm and captivate him. She had quickly set her sights on the Architect who, however, looked forth so untroubledly from among his long dark locks, stood at a distance with such upright serenity, answered all questions briefly and sensibly, but seemed so disinclined to enter further into anything, that finally she decided, half crossly and half schemingly, to make him the star of the day and win him for her court with all the rest.

It was not for nothing that she had brought so much luggage with her, and more had followed. She had made provision for endless changes of clothes. Three or four times in the course of the day she would change for the fun of it into and out of the clothes that society is used to seeing, but now and again would appear in thorough fancy dress, as a peasant girl or a fisher-wife, a fairy, a flower-girl. She would even dress up as an old woman, all the better to show off her fresh young face from under the cap; and really she so confused the actual and the imaginary it was as if there were a sort of nixie in the family.

But what these costumes chiefly served for were *poses plastiques* and mime dances, in which she was adept at representing different characters. One cavalier in her entourage had made himself capable of accompanying her gestures at the piano with what little music was necessary; conferring briefly beforehand, they were at once in accord.

One day, when they had paused for a while during a very lively ball, being urged as it seemed on the spur of the moment (though in fact at her own secret instigation) to give one of her performances, she appeared confused and surprised, and contrary to her usual habit had to be asked several times. She seemed undecided, would not choose, asked for a subject as the *improvisatori* do, until at last her piano-playing assistant, very likely by prior arrangement, sat himself down, began to play a funeral march, and said she should give them her Artemisia, a role she had learned to excel in. She yielded, and appeared after a brief absence, to the tender and melancholy notes of the funeral march, as the royal widow, with measured steps, bearing an urn. Behind her a large blackboard was carried in, and a golden drawing-pen into which was fitted a sharp piece of chalk.

One of her admirers and adjutants, to whom she whispered something, at once went and invited, obliged, and more or less dragged forth the Architect, to do a drawing of the tomb of Mausolus, and play alongside her in the performance, not as an extra, but importantly, in his professional capacity. Though outwardly appearing most embarrassed – for in his modern, tight-fitting, entirely black plain clothing he contrasted very strangely with the gauzes, crapes, fringes, spangles, tassels, and crowns – inwardly he at once took hold of himself; but that only increased the strangeness of the spectacle. With the greatest seriousness he stepped up to the large blackboard, which was held by a couple of page-boys, and carefully and exactly drew a mausoleum, which it is true would have been more appropriate for a Lombard king than for a Carian, but so beautifully proportioned, so solemn in its parts, so inventive in its ornamentation, that the audience watched with pleasure whilst it was being created and admired it finished.

Throughout he had scarcely turned to the queen, but had given all his attention to what he was doing. Finally, when he bowed to her and indicated that he believed her orders had been carried out, she held out the urn to him and showed that she wished to see it depicted on the summit of the monument. He obliged, though unwillingly, for the urn was not in character with the rest of the sketch. As for Luciane, she was now at long last delivered from her state of impatience, for it had not been at all her wish to have a scrupulous drawing from him. Had he sketched in very roughly something looking vaguely like a monument and spent the rest of the time attending to her, that would have been more in accordance with her real purpose and her wishes. As it was, his behaviour put her into the greatest embarrassment. Grieving, giving instructions, making suggestions, expressing approval at what was gradually being created, she did her best to ring the changes, and once or twice she almost forcibly turned him round so as to be in some sort of relationship with him, but his manner was far too stiff and all too often she had to have recourse to the urn, pressing it against her heart, gazing at heaven, and in the end, since such situations must always intensify, she looked more like a widow of Ephesus than a queen of Caria. Thus the performance went on and on; the pianist, patient enough on other occasions, was at a loss to know where his playing should go next. He sent up a prayer of thanks when he saw the urn in place on the pyramid, and involuntarily, as the queen was about to express her gratitude, he struck up a jolly tune, which was quite out of keeping with the character of the performance but entirely restored the good spirits of the audience, who hurried then in two halves to offer to the lady, for her expressiveness, and to the Architect, for his skilful and attractive drawing, their warm congratulations.

Chief among those who talked to the Architect was Luciane's fiancé. 'I am sorry', he said, 'that the drawing is so impermanent. You must at least allow me to have it brought up to my room, and to discuss it with you.' 'If you would like me to,' said the Architect, 'I can show you careful drawings of such buildings and monuments. This one is only a casual and rapid sketch.'

Ottilie was near, she approached the two men. 'Be sure', she said to the Architect, 'that you find an occasion to show the Baron your collection. He is a friend of the arts and of antiquity. I should be glad if you got to know one another better.'

Luciane came by and asked what they were speaking about.

'About a collection of works of art,' the Baron replied, 'which this gentleman owns and which he would be willing to show us on some occasion.'

'But he must fetch them at once,' Luciane cried. 'Will you not bring them at once?' she added caressingly, and took his hands in hers with affection.

'This might not be the right moment,' the Architect replied.

'What!' Luciane cried in an imperious voice. 'Will you disobey your queen's command?' Then she began to beg him, teasingly.

'Don't be stubborn,' said Ottilie, half under her breath.

The Architect withdrew with a bow that was neither acquiescence nor refusal.

He had no sooner gone than Luciane began rushing around the room with a pet greyhound. 'Oh dear,' she cried, happening to bump into her mother, 'how very unhappy I am! I didn't bring my monkey with me. I was advised against it, but it was only the servants not wanting to be bothered. And now I have to do without him. But I shall have him sent for, somebody must go and fetch him for me. If I could only see a picture of him, that would make me happy. I shall certainly have him painted and he shan't leave my side ever again.'

'Perhaps I can console you,' said Charlotte in reply. 'We have a whole volume of pictures of monkeys in the library, the strangest things. Shall I have it fetched?' Luciane screamed with delight, and the folio was brought. The sight of these abominable creatures, already human enough in their appearance and made still more so by the artist, filled Luciane with the greatest delight. But what pleased her best was to find in every one of the animals some resemblance to people she knew. There she was merciless.

One looked like an uncle of hers, another like M. who dealt in women's trinkets, another like the Reverend S., and another was the spitting image of a certain somebody else whose name escaped her. 'Oh, monkeys are wonderful!' she cried. 'Really, they quite outdo the *Incroyables*, and I cannot think why they are barred from polite society.'

She said this in polite society, but nobody took it amiss. First charming enough to get away with many things, in the end she was ill-behaved enough to get away with anything.

Ottilie meanwhile was in conversation with Luciane's fiancé. She was hoping the Architect would return, and with his more serious and more tasteful exhibits liberate the company from the world of monkeys. It was in this expectation that she had been speaking with the Baron and had mentioned certain items to him particularly. But the Architect failed to appear, and when at last he did return he mingled with the company, bringing nothing with him and giving no indication that anything had been asked of him. Ottilie was for a moment — how shall we describe it? — aggrieved, indignant, taken aback. She had spoken kindly to him, she wanted the Baron to have some enjoyment more in his own style since, though he loved Luciane infinitely, her behaviour did seem to be paining him.

The monkeys had to make way for some refreshments. Then party games, and even dancing again, and finally a joyless sitting around, joyless but feverish efforts to revive an already defunct pleasure, lasted on this occasion, as on others, well beyond midnight. For Luciane was already accustomed to not being able to get out of her bed in the morning nor into it at night.

Fewer events are recorded in Ottilie's diary around this time, but maxims and aphorisms having to do with life and abstracted from life are more abundant. But since most of them cannot have come from her own thinking it is likely that somebody must have given her a book from which she copied out what was congenial. Some things of her own and of a more intimate relevance will no doubt be recognizable by the red thread.

From Ottilie's Diary

'We like looking into the future because we should like, by wishing, to draw what is still fluid and shapeless in it towards us here to our advantage.

'It is difficult to be at any large gathering without thinking that chance which has brought so many together ought to have brought our friends there too.

'However retiringly you live, before you know it you become a borrower or a lender.

'If we ever meet anyone who owes us thanks we think of it at once. How often do we meet someone we owe thanks to and do not think of it?

'To speak of ourselves to others comes naturally; to take in what others say about themselves, in the spirit in which they say it, is a matter of culture.

'No one would speak much in company if he were aware how often he misunderstands other people.

'The reason we garble things when we pass them on is doubtless that we did not understand them in the first place.

'A person who holds forth without ever flattering his listeners, excites disgust.

'Every word spoken excites its contradiction.

'Contradiction and flattery both make for poor conversation.

'The pleasantest society is one in which a genial respect is observed among all its members.

'Nothing so characterizes a man as what he finds ridiculous.

'We laugh when the elements of a moral discrepancy are brought home to our senses in a harmless way.

'A sensual man often laughs when there is nothing to laugh at. Whatever provokes him, he expresses his inner well-being.

'A commonsensical man finds almost everything ridiculous, a wise man almost nothing.

'An elderly man was reproved for still bothering with young women. He replied: "It is the only way to rejuvenate oneself, and everyone wants that."

'We do not mind having our faults pointed out to us, we do not mind being punished for them, patiently we suffer a good deal on their account; but we become impatient should we have to cure ourselves of them.

'Certain failings are necessary for an individual's existence. We should be sorry if old friends were ever cured of certain of their peculiarities.

'We say "He is not long for this world" if a man does something out of character.

'What sort of failings may we keep and even cultivate in ourselves? Those which are more congenial than harmful to other people.

'Passions are failings or virtues, only intensified.

'Passions are real phoenixes. As the old one burns out the new one rises immediately out of the ashes.

'Great passions are a hopeless sickness. What might cure them is what really makes them dangerous.

'Passion is both intensified and moderated by being confessed. Perhaps nowhere else is a middle course more desirable than in what we say and what we do not say to those we love.'

CHAPTER FIVE

THUS Luciane made them drunk on life and drove them on and on through a social whirl. Her court increased daily, in part because her doings excited and attracted people, in part because others were attached to her by courtesies and acts of kindness. She was in the highest degree generous; for since, through the goodwill of her aunt and her fiancé, so much that was beautiful and expensive had suddenly come to her she seemed to possess nothing that was really her own, nor to know the value of the things heaped upon her. So without a moment's hesitation she might take off an expensive shawl and put it around the shoulders of a young woman who seemed to her, in comparison with others, to be poorly dressed, and she did this in such an adroit and teasing manner that nobody could refuse the gift. One of her entourage always carried a purse and was commanded wherever they went to find out the oldest and the sickest and relieve them, at least for the moment. In this way she acquired an excellent reputation throughout the neighbourhood, which became inconvenient at times since it attracted too many people in need, who importuned her.

But what most enhanced her reputation was her conspicuous, kind, and persistent behaviour towards an unfortunate young man who would not come into society because he had lost his right hand, even though this had happened honourably in battle and he was good-looking and well-proportioned otherwise. His injury caused him such unhappiness, it was so distasteful to him always, on being introduced, to have to tell the story of his misfortune, that he preferred to hide himself away, give himself up to reading and other studies, and once and for all have nothing to do with society.

This young man's existence became known to her. He was made to appear, first in a small party, then in a larger, then in

275

the largest. She behaved more charmingly towards him than towards anyone else; indeed, by her very pressing willingness to be of service, by her acts of compensation, she succeeded in making him value his loss. He had to sit by her at table, she cut up his food so that he only needed to use his fork. If persons of greater age or higher rank replaced him next to her she extended her attentiveness right across the table and sent the servants hurrying to supply what her being at a distance threatened to deprive him of. Finally she encouraged him to write with his left hand; all his attempts had to be sent to her, so that near and far she was always in a relationship with him. The young man scarcely recognized himself, and really from that time on he began a new life.

It might be supposed that behaviour of this sort would be displeasing to the man she was to marry; but quite the opposite was the case. He thought it a great virtue in her that she went to such trouble, and was all the more unperturbed by it for knowing her almost exaggerated tendency to rebuff anything in the least little bit compromising. She would come at anyone just as she pleased, everyone was in danger of being pushed, jostled, or in some other way tormented by her; but nobody was permitted to do the same in return, nobody might take hold of her if he felt like it, nobody respond in kind, not even remotely, to the liberties she took herself; and thus she held other people within the strictest bounds of decency towards herself, whilst seeming at every moment to transgress those bounds in her dealings with them.

Altogether it was as though she had decided as a matter of principle to expose herself equally to praise and blame, affection and dislike. For whilst in many ways seeking to make people fond of her, she most often undid it again by speaking maliciously of everyone. So always after visiting in the neighbourhood, when she and her company had been welcomed in apartments and great houses, returning home she would demonstrate in the most unrestrained fashion how inclined she was to view all human relations only from their ridiculous side. Here were three brothers overtaken by old age whilst still courteously disputing who should marry first; here a young woman small in stature married to a very large old man; elsewhere, contrariwise, a cheerful little man and a clumsy giant of a wife. In one house children were forever getting in the way; in another a most numerous party seemed to her lacking because no children were present. Childless old couples should be off to their graves as quickly as possible, so that there might be some laughter in the house again at long last. Young couples should travel, keeping house was not the thing for them. And as she was with people so she was also with their possessions, with their houses, their furnishings, their tableware. She was especially inclined to make jokes about what people put on their walls. From the oldest high-warp tapestries to the most modern papers, from the most dignified family portraits to the most frivolous modern engravings, they all suffered, they were all so to speak annihilated by her mocking remarks, so that it was a wonder anything was left alive for fifteen miles around.

There was perhaps no real malice in this perpetual negation; it was mostly a sort of self-centred mischievousness; but a real bitterness had developed in her relationship with Ottilie. She looked down contemptuously on the sweet child's tranquil and ceaseless activity, which everyone noticed and commended; and when Ottilie's care of the gardens and greenhouses was mentioned she not only made fun of it by appearing to wonder – though they were in the depths of winter – that neither flowers nor fruit were to be seen, but thenceforth ordered in so much greenery, so many sprays of anything with buds on, to waste every day on decorating the room and the table, that it grieved Ottilie and the Gardener who saw their hopes for the coming year and perhaps for some time longer thus destroyed.

Nor would she leave Ottilie in peace in the domestic routine where she was content to be. Ottilie must come with them on their drives and sleigh-rides; to the balls given in the neighbourhood; and why should she fear the snow and the cold and the violent storms at night-time since numerous other people were able to survive them? The delicate child suffered a good deal from all this, and Luciane gained nothing; for although Ottilie dressed very simply she was always the most beautiful, or seemed it at least to the men. Her gentle attractiveness drew all the men around her, whether her place in the great rooms was first or last; indeed, Luciane's fiancé himself often conversed with her, and all the more so because he wanted her advice and collaboration in a matter that was concerning him.

He had got to know the Architect better, had spoken at some length with him about historical matters whilst looking at his collection of works of art, and on other occasions too, especially when viewing the chapel, had begun to appreciate his talents. The Baron was young, rich; he was a collector, he had in mind to build; his passion was lively, his knowledge slight; it seemed to him that in the Architect he had found a man who would serve his purposes in more ways than one. He had spoken to his future wife of this intention; she commended him on it and was delighted with the proposal, but perhaps more in order to take the young man away from Ottilie, for whom she suspected him of having a fondness, than because she supposed she might make any use of his talents herself. For although he had been very active in her impromptu performances and for this or that occasion had often come forward with the necessary materials, she still always thought that she knew best; and since her ideas were mostly commonplace, a nimble servant was as competent to carry them out as the finest artist. When she thought of staging a celebration for a person's birthday or for some other day of honour in his life she never rose beyond an altar, to sacrifice at, or the placing of a wreath upon a head that might be a living one or might be a plaster cast.

When the Baron asked about the Architect's position in the house Ottilie was able to answer him precisely. She knew that Charlotte had already made efforts to get him a new situation; for if Luciane's party had not arrived the young man would have departed as soon as the chapel was completed, since all building work was to be suspended throughout the winter, necessarily; and thus it would be a very good thing if this skilful artist could be employed again and advanced by a new patron.

Ottilie's personal relationship with the Architect was entirely pure and straightforward. His agreeable and energetic presence had entertained and delighted her as would that of an older brother. Her feelings for him remained on the placid, passionless surface of a blood relationship; for there was no more room in her heart; it was packed full with her love for Eduard, and only God, who permeates all things, could share in its possession.

Meanwhile, as winter deepened, as the weather grew wilder, the roads more impassable, it seemed all the more attractive to spend the diminishing days in such good company. There were brief ebbs, but again and again a flood-tide of visitors came over the house. Officers arrived from distant garrisons, the cultured ones bringing great benefit, the coarser ones annoyance to the company; there were civilians too, in any number, and one day, quite unexpectedly, the Count and the Baroness drove up together.

Now truly by their presence a real court seemed to be constituted. The men of rank and good reputation surrounded the Count, and the women gave the Baroness her due. They were not long wondering why the pair were together and so cheerful; for they learned that the Count's wife had died and that a new union would be concluded just as soon as was decent. Ottilie remembered their first visit and every word that had been spoken on the subject of marriage and divorce, union and separation, hope, expectation, loss, and renunciation. Both parties, then quite without prospects, now stood before her so close to the happiness they had hoped for, and she could not help sighing.

As soon as Luciane heard that the Count was a lover of music she organized a concert; she wanted them to hear her sing and play the guitar. The concert took place. She did not play badly, her voice was agreeable; but as for the words, they were as unintelligible as they always are whenever a beautiful German girl sings and accompanies herself on the guitar. But everyone assured her that her singing had been most expressive, and the applause was as loud as she could have wished. One strange upset occurred, however. There was a poet in the party whom she particularly wished to attach to herself in the hope that he would address some of his poems to her, and for that reason she had sung during the evening almost only things by him. He was, as everyone was, altogether polite to her, but she had expected more. She several times prompted him; but he said nothing further until at last, at the end of her patience, she sent one of her courtiers to him, to ascertain whether he had not been charmed to hear his superb poems so superbly rendered. 'My poems?' he replied in astonishment. 'Forgive me, my dear sir,' he went on, 'I heard nothing but vowel sounds, and not all of those. But it is certainly my duty to show myself grateful for so charming an intention.' The courtier was silent, and kept what he had heard to himself. The poet tried to extricate himself from the affair with a few mellifluous compliments. She let it be understood that it was her wish to have something written especially for her. He would not have been so uncivil, of course, but really he might as well have handed her the alphabet to make up whatever eulogy she liked out of it for whatever melody she happened to have available. In the end her pride *was* hurt, as things turned out. Soon afterwards she discovered that on the very same evening he had taken one of Ottilie's favourite melodies and set some exceptionally lovely and more-than-obliging verses to it.

Luciane, who like all her sort was forever mixing up things that were right for her and things that were not, decided now to try her hand at recitations. She had a good memory but, if we are to be honest, her delivery was unintelligent, and vehement without being passionate. She recited ballads, stories, and other things usually thought suitable for such performance. But she had acquired the unfortunate habit of

accompanying the words with gestures, which in a disagreeable fashion confuses rather than connects what is really epic
and lyrical with the dramatic.

The Count, a man of some insight who had soon
appraised the party, their likings, passions, and forms of
amusement, happily or unhappily directed Luciane towards
a new form of presentation which suited her personality very
well indeed. 'I see around me', he said, 'several fine-looking
people who ought certainly to be able to imitate the movements and poses one sees in pictures. Have you never tried
representing actual well-known paintings? Reproductions of
that sort, though they require a good deal of preparation, are
unbelievably charming in their effects.'

It was soon clear to Luciane that she would be quite in her
element here. Her height, her full figure, her regular but
interesting face, her light-brown plaited hair, her slim neck,
everything seemed intended for a painting; and had she
realized that she looked more beautiful when she stood still
than when she moved (for then she did not always manage
to be graceful, which spoiled things) she would have
given herself up with even more eagerness to this art of
living pictures.

Now followed a search for engravings of famous paintings. The first choice was *Belisarius* by van Dyck. An elderly
man, tall and well-built, was to represent the blind general,
seated, and the Architect the grieving warrior who stands
before him, which character he indeed rather resembled.
Luciane, half in modesty, had chosen for herself the young
girl in the background who is counting money from a purse
into the palm of her hand, whilst an old woman seems to be
trying to dissuade her from giving so much. Another female
figure, actually offering him alms, was represented too.

With this and other paintings they occupied themselves
most earnestly. The Count gave the Architect some indications as to what would be necessary, and he at once set up a
theatre for it and took charge of the lighting. They were
already deep in the preparations before realizing that an

enterprise of this sort involves considerable expense, and that in the country in the middle of winter they were lacking many things they needed. Accordingly, so that the proceedings should not be halted, Luciane had almost her entire wardrobe cut up to supply the various costumes as the painters, whimsically enough, had decided them.

The evening came, the tableaux were presented before a large audience to general applause. There was music first, of a kind to raise expectations. They opened with *Belisarius*. The figures were so matching, the colours distributed so felicitously, the lighting so well contrived that the audience did indeed think themselves in another world; except that the presence of the real instead of the illusory produced a sort of unease.

The curtain fell, and on request was raised again more than once. The company was then diverted by a musical interlude, prior to being astonished by a picture of a loftier kind. It was Poussin's well-known depiction of Ahasuerus and Esther. This time Luciane had bethought herself better. In the figure of the queen fallen down in a faint she had scope for the display of all her charms, and for the girls surrounding and supporting her she had cleverly selected only such as were pretty and shapely, among them, however, none being in the least able to compare with her. Ottilie was excluded from this tableau, as from all the others. To be seated on the golden throne, to represent the Zeus-like king, they had chosen the strongest and handsomest man of the party, so that in this tableau a truly incomparable perfection was achieved.

For the third they had chosen the so-called *Paternal Admonition* by Ter Borch. Our own Wille's splendid engraving of it must surely be known to all. A noble and chivalrous-looking father, seated, one leg thrown over the other, is addressing his daughter, who is standing before him, with what seems to be the utmost seriousness. She herself, a splendid figure in a wonderfully pleated white satin gown, is only seen from behind, but her whole being seems to indicate that she is taking his words to heart. At the same time it is obvious from the father's bearing and gestures that the admonition is neither vehement nor humiliating. As for the mother, she seems to be hiding a slight embarrassment by gazing into a wine glass which she is about to empty.

On this occasion Luciane was to appear in her full glory. Her plaits, the shape of her head, neck, and nape were beautiful beyond belief, and her waist, which is a part scarcely able to be seen in the classical dresses women wear nowadays, was shown off to its best advantage, in all its neatness and grace, by the older costume; and the Architect had been at pains to arrange the abundant folds of white satin with the utmost naturalness, so that unquestionably this living repro-duction by far exceeded the original and threw the whole audience into raptures. There was no end to the encores, and the quite natural desire that so beautiful a creature, having been seen sufficiently from the back, should also be looked at face to face grew so pressing that one impatient and comical fellow shouted out the words sometimes written at the foot of a page: 'Tournez s'il vous plaît', and his cry was taken up. But the actors were too well aware of their own advantage and had understood the sense of these productions far too well to give in to the general clamour. The contrite-looking daughter stood as she was without letting the audience see the expression on her face; the father remained seated in the pose of admonition, and the mother never lifted her nose and eyes from the transparent glass in which, though she seemed to be drinking, the wine was never less. – We need do no more than mention the little pieces that came after. They were Dutch tavern and fairground scenes.

The Count and the Baroness departed, promising to return in the first happy weeks of their imminent union; and Charlotte hoped that after two strenuous months she might now be rid of the rest of the company too. She was sure of her daughter's happiness, once the first tumult of her youthful and bridal days was done, for her husband-to-be thought himself the luckiest man in the world. Abundantly wealthy and moderate in his temperament he seemed curiously flattered by the privilege of possessing a woman all the world was bound to admire. He had got so much into the way of relating everything to her, and to himself only through her, that it made him uncomfortable if a newcomer did not immediately and wholly address himself to her but instead sought a closer connection with him, paying her no particular attention, which often happened, especially with older people, because of his own good qualities. It was soon settled that the Architect should join them in the New Year and spend Shrovetide in town with them, where, in further performances of the magnificent tableaux and in a hundred other things, Luciane counted on being blissfully happy, the more so since her aunt and her fiancé seemed to think any expense insignificant if it were necessary for her pleasure.

It was time to leave, but they were incapable of doing so in a normal way. They were saying in jest, but loud enough to be heard, that Charlotte's winter supplies would soon be exhausted when the gentleman who had stood as Belisarius and who was certainly not without funds, being carried away by Luciane's qualities, which for a long time now he had been an admirer of, grew reckless and cried: 'Then let us do as the Poles do! Come to me next and exhaust my supplies, and so on, each in turn.' What he offered was at once accepted. Luciane gave him her hand on it. Next day they had packed, and the swarm fell upon another property. There they had room enough, but less comfort and convenience. Much ensued that was not quite right, which delighted Luciane at least. Their lives became wilder and ever-more riotous. There were shooting parties in the deep snow, and other such discomforts. The women were not excused any more than the men, and so they proceeded, hunting, horse-riding, sleigh-riding and making a noise, from one estate to the next, until they approached the capital. There news and tales of pleasure at Court and in town turned their imaginations in another direction, and drew Luciane and all her company, her aunt having gone on ahead, irresistibly into other circles of life.

From Ottilie's Diary

'The world will always take a man as he presents himself; but it is up to him to present himself as something. Difficult people are more bearable than insignificant ones.

'There is nothing that cannot be imposed upon society, except what matters.

'We do not get to know people when they come to us; we have to go to them to find out what they are like.

'I almost find it natural that we object to things in visitors and that as soon as they have gone our comments on them are not of the kindest; for in a sense we have a right to judge them by our own standards. Even sensible and fair-minded people are inclined to be harsh on such occasions.

'On the other hand when we have been visiting and have seen others in their own surroundings, in their familiar ways, in their necessary and unavoidable circumstances, and how they busy themselves and how they have adapted, it shows only ignorance and ill will if we find ridiculous things which in more than one sense ought to seem to us worthy of respect.

'We should achieve through what we call politeness and good manners the things which may otherwise only be achieved by force or not even by force.

'The natural element of good manners is the company of women.

'How may a person be well-mannered and yet preserve his character and his peculiarity?

'It would be nice if what is peculiar about him were brought out precisely by his manners. Everyone appreciates exceptional qualities, so long as they give no trouble.

'The greatest advantages in life, as in society, are enjoyed by the soldier who is also a man of culture.

'Coarse military men at least do not betray their characters, and since underneath their brute strength there is most often affability it is possible to get on with them too, should that be necessary.

'Nobody is more tiresome than an awkward civilian. We have a right to expect some polish in his case since he never has to concern himself with anything coarse.

'If we live with people who have a keen sense of what is proper we become anxious on their account whenever anything improper occurs. Thus I always feel for and with Charlotte if anyone rocks in his chair, because that pains her unbearably.

'Nobody would intrude upon us with his spectacles on his nose if he knew that we women at once lose all desire to look at him or speak to him.

'Being intimate where one should be respectful is always ridiculous. Nobody would lay aside his hat having scarcely said good-day if he knew how comical it looks.

'There is no outward sign of politeness that does not have a basis deep in morality. A proper education would convey both the sign and that basis together.

'Good manners are a mirror in which everyone is reflected.

'There is a politeness of the heart, akin to love. From it derives the easiest politeness of outward behaviour.

'Voluntary dependence is the finest condition, and how would that be possible without love?

'We are never further from our wishes than when we imagine ourselves in possession of what we wished for.

'No one is more enslaved than the man who believes himself to be free and is not.

'So soon as a man declares himself to be free he at once feels bound by circumstances. If he dares to declare himself bound, he feels himself free.

'Against the great advantages of another person there is no remedy but love.

'It is a frightful thing to see stupid people proud of an outstanding man.

'A servant is said not to have any heroes. But that is only because it takes a hero to recognize a hero. The servant will doubtless know how to value people of his own kind.

'There is no greater comfort for mediocrity than that genius is not immortal.

'Even the greatest men are connected to the times they live in by some weakness.

'We usually think people more dangerous than they are.

'Fools and the wise are equally harmless. But half-fools and the half-wise, these are the most dangerous.

'There is no surer way of evading the world than art, and no surer way of attaching oneself to it.

'Even in moments of the greatest happiness and the greatest tribulation we need the artist.

'Art concerns itself with that which is weighty and good.

'To see what is difficult handled with ease gives us a sight of the impossible.

'Difficulties increase the nearer we get to our goal.

'To sow is not so onerous as to reap.'

CHAPTER SIX

A COMPENSATION for the upheaval caused to Charlotte by the visit was that she came to understand her daughter perfectly. She was much helped in this by her own experience of the world. It was not the first time she had encountered such a strange character, though never before one so extreme. And yet she knew from experience that people of that kind, when life and different events and parental circumstances have worked on them, may mature to become very congenial and lovable, as their selfishness moderates and their wild enthusiasms and energies take some definite course. Charlotte, as Luciane's mother, was understandably more tolerant of what was perhaps for other people a disagreeable spectacle; for strangers will ask that a child be agreeable or at least not tiresome now, but a parent may rightly and properly look to the future.

In an odd and unexpected way, however, Charlotte was to be affected by her daughter after she had gone. For Luciane had left a bad name behind her, and not just because of things she had done that were blameworthy but also because of other things too that might have been thought commendable. Luciane seemed to have made it a rule not only to rejoice with them that rejoiced but also to weep with them that wept and, fully to indulge her spirit of contradiction, on occasion to turn rejoicing into glumness and tears to laughter. Wherever she visited she asked after those too sick and weak to appear. She went to them in their rooms, played the doctor, and out of a medical chest which she always had with her in her carriage forced some drastic remedy on each; such treatment then, as might be expected, succeeded or failed as chance decided.

She was quite pitiless in these good works and would brook no opposition, being entirely convinced of the merit of what she was doing. But she was unsuccessful also in an attempt on the moral front, and it was this that made work for Charlotte, since it had repercussions that were being talked about. She only got to hear of it after Luciane had gone. Ottilie, who had been present at that very party, was required to give her a detailed account.

One of the daughters of a well-respected house had had the misfortune to cause the death of a younger sibling and could not get over it or be herself again. She kept to her room, in a silent preoccupation, and could only bear the sight even of her own family if they came to her singly; for if there were several people together she at once suspected they were talking about her and her condition among themselves. With any person alone her conversation was perfectly rational and she would talk then for hours.

Luciane had got to hear of her and had at once secretly determined, when she visited the house, to work a sort of miracle and restore the young woman to society. She behaved more circumspectly than usual, got herself admitted alone into the troubled girl's presence, and won her trust, apparently through music. Only at the end she spoiled things. Since what she wanted was to make a stir she brought the beautiful pale child, whom she thought sufficiently prepared, one evening suddenly into a lively and brilliant company; and perhaps even that might have come off but the people themselves were clumsy, out of curiosity and apprehension, first crowding around the invalid, then avoiding her, and by their whispering and their furtive stares making her confused and agitated. It was more than the girl's delicate sensibility could bear. With fearful screams of horror at the approach of something monstrous, as it seemed, she fled. The party dispersed in all directions, and Ottilie was one of those who brought the girl, by now completely unconscious, back to her room.

Luciane meanwhile, in a manner characteristic of her, had given the remaining members of the party a severe dressing down, without in the least considering that all the blame was hers, and without allowing this or any other failure to deter her from continuing to busy herself.

The girl's condition had worsened since then; indeed, the malady in her soul had so intensified that the parents could no longer keep the poor child at home but had been obliged to put her into the care of a public institution. There was nothing Charlotte could do except seek, by being especially kind towards the family, to alleviate in some measure at least the suffering caused by her daughter. The affair had made a deep impression on Ottilie; she pitied the poor girl all the more since she was convinced, and told Charlotte as much, that the illness would have been curable had it been treated in a consequential manner.

And since we usually speak more about past chagrins than about past pleasures, Ottilie brought up the little misunderstanding she had had with the Architect that evening when he had been unwilling to show the company his collection, despite her having asked him to in the friendliest manner. His unco-operative behaviour, perplexing at the time, had continued to trouble her, she did not know why. Her feelings were entirely right; for what a girl like Ottilie might ask, a young man like the Architect ought not to refuse. But when at last she gently reproached him with it his excuses had some validity.

'If you knew', he said, 'how roughly even cultured people handle the most precious works of art, you would forgive me for not wishing to have mine passed around. They seem not to know that a medal should be held along the edge. Instead they touch the face, however beautifully and cleanly stamped it is, they rub the loveliest pieces between finger and thumb as if that were the way to appreciate artistic forms! They never think that you need both hands for a large sheet of paper and they reach for a priceless engraving, an irreplaceable drawing, with one, just as an insolent politician seizes hold of a newspaper and shows you in advance what he thinks about world events by crumpling its pages. It never occurs to them that if twenty people in succession treat a work of art like that there will be very little left for the twenty-first to see.'

'Have I not sometimes upset you in that way?' Ottilie asked. 'Have I not perhaps occasionally damaged your treasures without suspecting it?'

'Never!' the Architect replied. 'Never! How could you? You were born with a sense of what is right and proper.'

'Be that as it may,' Ottilie replied, 'it would be no bad thing if in future a very full chapter were included in the books of good manners, after the chapters on how to behave at table, on how to behave in museums and with collections of works of art.'

'Certainly,' said the Architect, 'curators and private collectors would then be much more willing to show people their rarities.'

Ottilie had long since forgiven him; but when he seemed to take her reproach very much to heart and again and again assured her that he liked people to see his collection, that he would gladly put himself out for friends, then she felt that his delicate feelings had been hurt by her and that she must make it up to him. She was thus not well placed to refuse absolutely a request he made to her in the aftermath of this conversation, even though, quickly consulting her heart, she did not see how she could do as he wished.

The matter was as follows. It had pained him greatly that Luciane's jealousy had kept Ottilie out of the tableaux; and he had also noticed, with regret, that Charlotte, not feeling well, had been present only intermittently at this brilliant item in their entertainments. Now before he left he wished to give further proof of his gratitude by staging, for the honour of the former and the amusement of the latter, a far more beautiful production than all the others had been. And there was perhaps another secret motive, one he was not aware of himself: that he was finding it so hard to leave this house, this family, indeed it seemed to him impossible that he should go away from the sight of Ottilie's eyes, whose calm and friendly looks had lately been almost the whole sustenance of his life.

It was approaching Christmas, and he suddenly realized that the representation of paintings through figures in the round must have derived from the cribs, from the pious presentations dedicated at this holy time to the Mother of God and the child, when in their apparent lowliness they are worshipped by shepherds and soon after by kings.

He had a perfect conception of the possibility of such a tableau. A beautiful baby boy had been found; nor would there be any shortage of shepherds and shepherdesses; but they could not carry it through without Ottilie. In his thinking the young man had made her the Virgin Mary, and if she refused there was no question for him but the whole enterprise must founder. Ottilie, half embarrassed by his plea, directed him to Charlotte. She gladly gave him permission and also, in a friendly fashion, overcame Ottilie's reluctance to presume to impersonate that holy figure. The Architect worked day and night so that nothing should be wanting on Christmas Eve.

And indeed literally day and night. He had in any case few needs, and Ottilie's presence seemed to serve him for all refreshment. Working for her sake it was as if he needed no sleep, and being occupied with her, no food. Thus for that evening, for that solemn and festive hour, everything was finished and ready. He had managed to put together a small ensemble of wind instruments whose melodious playing served as introduction and produced an appropriate mood. When the curtain rose Charlotte was in truth astonished. The picture offered her had been seen so many times before that one could scarcely expect it to have any novel effect. But on this occasion reality itself, making up the tableau, enjoyed some particular advantages. The whole scene was more night than twilight, but in its component details nothing was unclear. By a clever arrangement of the lighting, which was concealed by the figures in the foreground, themselves in shadow and lit only glancingly, the artist had succeeded in giving expression to the incomparable idea that all light emanates from the child. Joyful girls and boys stood round, their fresh faces sharply lit from below. There were angels too, whose own radiance seemed dimmed by that of the divinity and whose ethereal bodies seemed, in the presence of the divinely human, somehow more solid and in need of light.

Fortunately the child had fallen asleep, and as prettily as could be wished, so there was no distraction when the eyes rested on the figure of his mother who, with infinite grace, had lifted back a veil to reveal the hidden treasure. In that instant the picture seemed held and frozen. Dazzled in the body, astounded in the soul, the ring of common people seemed to have moved a moment since to avert their smitten eyes and then to stare again in curiosity and delight and with more wonder and joy than admiration and reverence; though these were not lacking either but were expressed in one or two of the older faces.

But Ottilie's pose, bearing, expression, and looks excelled anything a painter has ever depicted. Any sensitive connoisseur, seeing this sight, would have been fearful lest anything move; would have been alarmed by the thought that perhaps nothing would ever please him so much again. Unhappily there was no one present quite able to appreciate the effects in their entirety. Only the Architect, who in the person of a tall, slim shepherd was looking in from the side over the heads of those kneeling, though his perspective was not the very best, nevertheless his enjoyment exceeded everybody else's. And indeed how shall anyone describe Ottilie's appearance as the newly created Queen of Heaven? Purest humility, the sweetest modesty in the receipt of a great and undeserved honour and of an inconceivably immeasurable happiness, were pictured in her face, such being her own feelings as well as her conception of what she was acting.

Charlotte was delighted by the beautiful tableau, but what most affected her was the child. The tears streamed down her face, and with great intensity she dwelled on her hopes of soon having such a sweet infant in her lap.

The curtain had been lowered, in part to give the performers some relief and in part to change the subject of the tableau. The artist had had the idea of transforming the first image, one of night and lowliness, into one of daylight and glory, and to that end had assembled on all sides the means of a vast illumination and in the interval put them into service.

Ottilie's chief solace in her half-theatrical state had been that, apart from Charlotte and a very few members of the household, nobody had been watching this pious and sophisticated dumb show. She was then somewhat perturbed to hear during the interval that a stranger had arrived in the room and had been warmly welcomed by Charlotte. Who it was nobody could tell her. She submitted, not wishing to spoil the performance. Candles and lamps were burning and a truly infinite brightness was all about her. The curtain rose, the spectators were amazed by what they saw: the whole tableau was all light, and in the place of the shadows, now entirely abolished, only the colours remained and they, being skilfully selected, produced a sweet, mellow effect. Looking up from under her long lashes Ottilie noticed a male figure seated next to Charlotte. She could not make out who it was, but thought she recognized the voice of the Assistant from her school. A strange sensation took hold of her. How much had happened since she last heard the voice of that loyal teacher! As in a thunderflash the succession of her joys and sorrows passed rapidly before her soul, and she asked herself how much of it all she would dare admit to him. 'Then how little right I have', she thought, 'to appear before him in this sacred guise and how strange he must find it to see me, whom he has only ever seen as nature made me, now behind a mask.' There followed at once a hurried to-ing and fro-ing in her thoughts and feelings. Her heart was constrained, her eyes filled with tears, as she forced herself to continue in the appearance of a frozen image; and how glad she was when the child began to stir and the artist was obliged to signal for the curtain to fall again.

Added to Ottilie's other feelings in the last moments had been the painful sense that she could not hasten to greet an estimable friend, but now she was in a still greater trouble. Should she go to him in this strange costume and finery? Should she change? There was no question: she did the latter and sought in the meantime to take hold of herself, calm herself, and had just regained her balance and composure when finally she met the new arrival and greeted him in her accustomed clothes.

CHAPTER SEVEN

In so far as the Architect wished the best for the ladies to whom he owed so much he was glad, when he finally had to depart, to know that a man as admirable as the Assistant would be keeping them company; but when he thought of himself as the object of their favour it did pain him somewhat to see himself replaced so swiftly and, as it seemed to him in his modesty, so well, indeed so completely. He had been putting off the moment, but now he was in haste to leave; for he wished to spare himself at least the present sight of things he would have to accept once he was gone.

His half-unhappy mood was brightened considerably at the moment of departure when the ladies presented him with a waistcoat which for a long time he had watched them both working at and envied in silence whoever it was intended for. A gift of that sort is the most pleasing a man full of love and reverence can receive; for thinking of the tireless play of a woman's fingers over it he will be bound to flatter himself that from a work of such duration the heart itself will not have been entirely absent.

The women now had another man to look after, whom they were well disposed towards and wished to make welcome. The female sex has its own inner immutable interest which nothing in the world will cause it to desert; but in outward, social relations they gladly and easily let themselves be determined by the man currently engaging their attention; and thus refusing and accepting, resisting and yielding, in fact they rule, and no man in the civilized world dares disobey.

The Architect had used and demonstrated his talents for the amusement and benefit of his friends pretty much as his own inclinations moved him, and it was in that spirit and with such intentions that their activities and entertainments had been organized; but now through the presence of the Assistant a new mode of life soon established itself. His great gift was speaking well and discussing human relations, especially in the context of the education of young people. And thus arose a quite palpable contrast with their previous way of life, and all the more so since the Assistant did not entirely approve of what had latterly been their exclusive occupation.

He said nothing at all about the *tableau vivant* that had greeted him on his arrival. But when they showed him, with some satisfaction, the church, the chapel, and related things, he could not refrain from expressing his opinion and his sentiments. 'For myself,' he said, 'I do not at all like this *rapprochement* and mingling of the sacred and the sensuous; and that certain special rooms should be set aside and consecrated and decorated, and that only in them should feelings of piety be preserved and nourished, is not to my liking either. No surroundings, not even the meanest, should disturb the sense of the divine in us, for that sense can accompany us everywhere and make any place a temple. I like to see family prayers conducted in the room where people eat, come together, and enjoy themselves playing games and dancing. The highest and the best in man is formless, and one ought to be wary of giving it form except in noble acts.'

Charlotte, in a general way already acquainted with his sentiments and soon getting to know them in more detail, was quick to engage him in his professional capacity, and had her young gardeners, whom the Architect had mustered just before leaving, march into the great hall and be presented. Their clean, bright, cheerful uniforms, orderly movements, and lively and natural ways made a very good impression. The Assistant examined them after his particular method, and by means of a variety of questions and strategies had very soon brought out their personalities and abilities and, without seeming to, in the space of less than an hour, had quite significantly instructed and advanced them.

'How ever do you do it?' Charlotte asked as the boys withdrew. 'I listened very carefully, the things that came up were not in the least extraordinary, but to utter them in such good order in so short a time when the talk was going backwards and forwards all the while, would be quite beyond my power.'

'One ought perhaps to make a mystery of one's professional successes,' the Assistant replied. 'But I will give you a simple rule for achieving what you have just seen and much more besides. Seize hold of your subject, your material, your idea, or whatever, and keep tight hold of it. Make sure you have understood it with perfect clarity in all its parts. Then when you talk to a group of children you will easily discover what of your subject has already been developed in them, what needs further encouragement, and what there is still to impart. Their answers to your questions may be as inappropriate as can be, may lead entirely away from the point, but so long as your next question reintroduces sense and meaning, so long as you do not allow yourself to be moved from your own position, in the end the children will be obliged to think, understand, and be persuaded of the truth of only those things the teacher wishes, and only as he wishes it. His greatest mistake is to let himself be carried away by his pupils, if he fails to hold them fast to the one point he is presently dealing with. Try it yourself when you can, you will be greatly entertained.'

'How nice!' said Charlotte. 'Good practice in teaching is entirely the opposite of good manners. In company one should never dwell on anything, whereas it seems that in the classroom the first commandment is to combat any changing of the subject.'

'Variety without distraction would be the best motto, in education as in life, if such commendable equilibrium were that easy to achieve,' said the Assistant, and was about to continue when Charlotte called out to him to look at the boys again, who were at that moment moving in a cheerful procession across the courtyard. He said how pleased he was to see that the children were required to wear uniforms. 'Men', he said, 'ought to wear uniforms from childhood onwards since they must accustom themselves to acting in concert, losing themselves among others of their kind, obeying as a mass, and working for the whole. Then every sort of uniform encourages a military sense and a brisker, smarter bearing, and all boys are in any case born soldiers – look at their games of battle and combat and how they are forever storming this and climbing that.'

'But you will not chide me', said Ottilie, 'for not making my little girls all wear the same. I hope that when I present them it will give you pleasure to see such a colourful mixture.'

'Quite right,' he replied. 'Altogether, women should dress with great variety, each in her own manner and style, so that each may learn to feel what suits her best and is appropriate for her. And a further reason, and a more important one, is this: that women are fated to stand alone all their lives and to act alone.'

'That seems to me very paradoxical,' said Charlotte in reply. 'Surely we almost never act for ourselves?'

'Indeed you do,' the Assistant replied, 'and most certainly in your relations with other women. Consider a woman when she is in love, or engaged to be married, or as a wife, house-wife, and mother, she is always isolated, always alone, and wishes to be alone. Vain women are just the same. Every woman excludes all other women, by her very nature, since it is incumbent upon every woman to do everything that the whole sex is required to do. With men it is different. Men need men. A man would create another man if none existed, a woman might live an eternity without it ever occurring to her to bring forth another of her kind.'

'Only let the truth appear strange,' said Charlotte, 'and before long what is strange will appear true. We shall put the best complexion we can upon your remarks and hold together as women despite them, and work together too, or we give men too great an advantage over us. And you must not mind us feeling a certain satisfaction, which will be all the keener in future, when we see the gentlemen too falling out among themselves.'

With close attention then, in his sensible fashion, the Assistant examined how Ottilie was managing the children in her charge, and expressed decided approval. 'You do very well,' he said, 'having this authority over them, to aim only at making them immediately useful. Cleanliness makes children feel pleased with themselves, and once they are prompted to do things cheerfully and with some self-esteem, then the battle is won.'

He was besides especially pleased to see that nothing was being done for outward appearance only, but for what lies within and for the children's real needs. 'Why,' he cried, 'the whole business of education might be summed up in a very few words, if anyone had ears to hear.'

'Will you try whether I have?' said Ottilie with a smile.

'Gladly,' he replied. 'But you must keep it a secret. Educate the boys for service and the girls for motherhood, and all will be well.'

'For motherhood,' said Ottilie, 'women might let that stand, since whether they become mothers or not they must always expect to have to look after somebody. But as for being servants, our young men would consider themselves far too good for that. You can see it in every one of them that he thinks he should be the one to give the orders.'

'Precisely why we keep it a secret from them,' said the Assistant. 'We flatter ourselves about our chances in life, and life soon undeceives us. But how many people will concede willingly what they will be forced to concede in the end? Now enough of these thoughts. They do not concern us here.

'I think you fortunate that you are able to proceed correctly with your charges. If your littlest girls run around with their dolls and fasten a few bits of rag together for them, if older sisters look after the younger children and the household looks after itself through its own members and helps itself along, then to start in life after that is not a very big step, and such a girl will find in her husband's house what she left behind at her parents'.

'But in the educated classes the task is very complicated. We have to take higher, finer, and subtler relations – and especially social relations – into account. There as teachers we must shape our pupils for an outward life. It is necessary, it is indispensable, and may well be a good thing, always providing we do not go too far. For as we endeavour to shape a child for the wider world it is easy to push him to where there are no boundaries at all and to lose sight of what his inner self actually requires. That is the task, and the educators succeed or fail at it in varying degrees.

'I am alarmed by a good deal of what we provide our girls with in the boarding-school, because experience tells me that it will be of very little use to them in future. How much a young woman discards and consigns to oblivion as soon as she becomes a mother and the mistress of a household!

'Nevertheless, having dedicated myself to this profession, I still cherish hopes that one day, with a loyal companion at my side, I shall fully develop in my pupils the qualities they will need when they enter into their independence and the sphere of their own endeavours; that I should then be able to say to myself: in this sense their education is complete. Admittedly, education of another kind will continually ensue, in almost every year of our lives, if not by our own doing then through circumstances.'

Ottilie felt the truth of this last remark. How much had been brought on in her by an unforeseen passion in the past year! And what trials she saw approaching if she looked only a very little way ahead!

It was not unintentionally that the young man had mentioned a helpmeet, a wife; for, however diffident he might be, he could not help giving some remote hint of his intentions. Indeed, several factors and occurrences had prompted him to try to get a little closer to his goal in the course of this visit.

The Principal of the school was already elderly, for some time she had been casting about among her male and female colleagues for one who would in practice enter into partnership with her, and had at length put to the Assistant, in whom she had good cause to have every confidence, the proposition that he should continue the running of the establishment in tandem with her, co-operate in it as in a thing of his own, and come into it as heir and sole owner after her death. The chief consideration in all this seemed to be that he must find himself a wife of the same mind. Though he said nothing, Ottilie was before his eyes and in his heart. Doubts arose, but were then countered by certain favourable events. Luciane had left the school; it would be easier for Ottilie to return; there were rumours about her relationship with Eduard, it is true, but like other cases of its kind the matter was not taken very seriously, and it might indeed help bring Ottilie back. No decision would have been taken, however, and nothing would have been done, if here too an unexpected visit had not given added impetus. But the arrival of people of importance in a particular circle will never be without some effect.

The Count and the Baroness, who were often asked about the relative merits of different boarding-schools, since almost everyone finds the education of his children a problem, had decided to acquaint themselves particularly with this one, which was so well spoken of, and in their new circumstances could now undertake such an enquiry together. But the Baroness had a further purpose. When she was last at Charlotte's they had gone over the whole matter of Eduard and Ottilie in every detail. She insisted again and again that Ottilie must be sent away. She sought to give Charlotte, still fearful of Eduard's threats, the courage to act. Various expedients were discussed, and when the school was mentioned the Assistant's fondness for Ottilie was mentioned also, and the Baroness became all the more determined to pay the intended visit.

She arrived, met the Assistant, they were shown the school, and they spoke of Ottilie. The Count himself was glad to talk about her, having got to know her better during their recent stay. She had drawn nearer to him, indeed she was attracted by him, because in his conversation, which was so rich in matter, she seemed to see and recognize things which previously had been quite unknown to her. And whereas in her dealings with Eduard she forgot the world, through the Count's presence the world seemed to her for the first time truly desirable. Every attraction is mutual. The Count felt a fondness for Ottilie, such that he liked to think of her as his daughter. Here too, and more than on the first occasion, she was an irritation to the Baroness. Who knows what she might have engineered against Ottilie in more violently passionate times! Now she contented herself with seeking to render her less harmful to married women by marrying her off.

Cleverly then, but also discreetly, she prompted the Assistant to take a trip to the Hall and there move nearer the accomplishment of his plans and wishes, which he had not kept secret from her, without further delay.

And so, with the Principal's full support, he set off on his journey and his hopes were high. He knew that Ottilie was not ill-disposed towards him, and though a little mismatched socially, modern ways of thinking would help them over that. Besides, the Baroness had more than hinted that Ottilie would always be poor. Being related to a wealthy family was no advantage, she said; for however large the fortune they will never feel they ought to deprive their closer relatives, who have more obvious claims, of any large part of it. And indeed it is curious how very rarely we use the great privilege of being able to dispose of our goods even after death to the advantage of those we love best, and that we, out of respect for tradition as it seems, only benefit those who would inherit from us whether we had any say in the matter or not.

In his feelings, as he travelled towards her, the Assistant became Ottilie's complete equal. A warm welcome raised his hopes. It is true, Ottilie did not seem quite so open with him as she had been; but she was more adult, more formed and, it might be said, in a general way more communicative than he had known her. He was made privy to things which concerned him particularly in his capacity as Ottilie's teacher; but whenever he wished to get nearer to his purpose a certain inner shyness held him back.

But then on one occasion Charlotte gave him the opportunity when, though Ottilie was with them, she said: 'Well, now you have been the examiner of most things that are growing up around me, how do you find Ottilie? I am sure you can tell me in her presence.'

The Assistant's reply was calmly delivered and full of insight. He found her, he said, much changed for the better, her manner less constrained, more at ease in her conversation, and with a more developed view of the world that expressed itself in her actions at least as much as in her words; but still he believed she might benefit very greatly by returning to the school for a while, so as to assimilate in proper order thoroughly and for ever the things which the world imparts only brokenly and more confusingly than satisfyingly, and often, indeed, too late. But he need not labour the subject; Ottilie herself would know what interconnected studies she had been torn from.

Ottilie was bound to agree; but she could not admit what she felt at his words, since she could hardly make sense of it herself. When she thought of the man she loved nothing in the world seemed unconnected any longer, and without him she could not see how things would ever connect again.

Charlotte's response to the Assistant's suggestion was kindly and also shrewd. She said that both she and Ottilie had for some time thought a return to the school desirable; but latterly she would not have been able to manage without her dear friend and helper; in the future, however, she would not object if it remained Ottilie's wish to return for as long as was necessary to complete what had been begun and to assimilate entirely what had been interrupted.

This proposal delighted the Assistant; Ottilie was in no position to say anything against it, though she shuddered at the thought. What Charlotte wanted was to gain time. First let the fact of a happy fatherhood return Eduard to his senses and bring him home; after that, so she believed, everything would fall into place again and Ottilie too would be taken care of in one way or another.

After a serious conversation, when all parties have been given food for thought, it usually happens that a sort of standstill is reached, which rather resembles a general embarrassment. They walked up and down in the room, the Assistant glanced at a book or two and eventually lit upon the folio that was still lying about from the time of Luciane's visit. When he saw that there was nothing in it but monkeys he shut it again at once. This incident may, however, have given rise to a conversation of which traces are to be found in Ottilie's diary.

From Ottilie's Diary

'How can anyone bring himself to do such careful pictures of those horrible monkeys? We debase ourselves even by looking at them as animals; but there is a greater evil still in giving in to the temptation to look for people we know behind those masks.

'Altogether it requires a certain perversity to enjoy looking at caricatures and grotesques. I can thank our excellent Assistant that I was spared the torment of studying natural history. I never could get on with worms and beetles.

'On this occasion he admitted that he felt the same. "We should know nothing about the natural world," he said, "except what we have as our immediate living surroundings. With the trees that blossom, leaf, and bear fruit around us, with every plant along our way, every blade of grass we walk on, we have a real relationship, they are our true compatriots. The birds hopping to and fro on our branches and singing in our greenery belong to us, speak to us, have done so since we were children, and we have learned their language. Is it not the case that every foreign creature, torn from its own environment, fills us with a sort of uneasiness which only familiarity will relieve? We should have to live very tumultuous and colourful lives to bear the company of monkeys, parrots, and blackamoors."

'Whenever a curiosity and longing for exotic things came over me I used to envy the traveller who sees such wonders in a living and daily connection with other wonders. But even he becomes another person. Nobody lives among palm trees unpunished, and it is certain one's sentiments alter in a country where elephants and tigers are at home.

'A naturalist only deserves respect if he can depict and present the most strange and foreign things in their locality, with all their neighbouring circumstances, always in their own peculiar element. How I should love to hear Humboldt talk.

'A natural-history cabinet can seem like an Egyptian tomb with the different animal and plant gods standing around embalmed. No doubt it would be right for a mysterious priesthood to busy itself with such things in semi-darkness; but they should not be let into our general education, particularly since they can easily keep out something closer to home and worthier of respect.

'A teacher who can arouse our feelings over a single deed or a single poem does more than one who gives us the whole series of inferior forms of life with all their names and structures; for the end-result is what we may know already: that the best and nearest likeness of divinity is worn by man.

'Let each retain the freedom to occupy himself with what he finds attractive, what gives him pleasure, what seems to him useful; but the proper study of mankind is man.'

CHAPTER EIGHT

Few people are capable of concerning themselves with the most recent past. Either the present holds us violently captive, or we lose ourselves in the distant past and strive with might and main to recall and restore what is irrevocably lost. Even in the great and wealthy families who owe their ancestors so much it is very often the case that the grandfathers are remembered more than the fathers.

Thoughts such as these were prompted in our friend the Assistant when, on one of those beautiful days that raise false hopes of the end of winter and the beginning of spring, he had walked through the extensive old grounds of the Hall and admired the tall avenues of lime trees and the formal gardens that went back to Eduard's father's time. They had come on superbly, just as the man who planted them had intended, and now, when by rights they should have been saluted and enjoyed, nobody ever mentioned them; they were scarcely visited; instead, money and enthusiasm went elsewhere, towards a greater liberty and spaciousness.

He made this observation to Charlotte on his return, and she did not disagree. 'As life hurries us along,' she replied, 'we suppose ourselves to be the authors of our actions, and that what we undertake and how we amuse ourselves are matters of our own choosing; but looked at closely, of course, they are only the plans and tendencies of the times, in whose execution we are obliged to co-operate.'

'Indeed,' said the Assistant, 'and who can resist the trend of his surroundings? Time hurries on, and with it our own sentiments and opinions, our prejudices and our hobbies. If the son grows up in a time of change you can be sure he will have nothing in common with his father. If in the father's time the mood was for acquiring things, securing their possession, reining in, delimiting, and affirming one's own pleasure by cutting oneself off from the world, the son will seek to spread himself, give out, expand, and open up what was enclosed.'

'Whole epochs', said Charlotte in reply, 'resemble the father and son you are describing. We can nowadays scarcely imagine the times when every little town had to have its walls and ditches, every manor was set in a marsh, and every tiny chateau had to be entered over a drawbridge. Now even the larger towns are doing away with their walls, even the royal palaces are filling in their moats, the towns are wide open, and when you travel and see these things you would think a general peace were here for good and the Golden Age very near. No one feels comfortable in a garden unless it looks like the open country; there must be nothing that makes us think of art or rules; we want room to breathe, and no constraints at all. Do you think it possible we might ever quit this state for another one, for the old one perhaps?'

'Why not?' said the Assistant in reply. 'There are difficulties in every condition, in restraint and in unrestraint. The latter presupposes superfluity, and leads to waste. Let us keep to your example, which is striking enough. As soon as there is a shortage self-restraint is reimposed. People obliged to put their land to use wall in their gardens again so they can be sure of keeping what they produce. That gradually gives rise to a new view of things. Usefulness gets the upper hand again, and even the man who owns a great deal in the end, like everyone else, feels bound to make use of it all. Take my word for it, your son may want nothing to do with the new park, and may well withdraw behind the solemn walls and beneath the tall lime trees of his grandfather instead.'

Charlotte was secretly delighted to have a son foretold, and so pardoned the Assistant his rather pessimistic view as to what might happen one day to her beautiful and beloved park. She answered him therefore in perfectly friendly terms: 'Neither of us is old enough to have experienced such reversals more than once; but if we think back into childhood and remember what we used to hear older people complaining about, and if we consider different regions and cities too, then there is probably no denying the truth of your observation. But should we do nothing to counter such a process of nature? Should it not be possible to establish some agreement between fathers and sons, parents and children? You were kind enough to prophesy a son for me. Must he then necessarily contradict his father and destroy what his parents have built, instead of completing it and raising it higher, as he might if he continued in their spirit?'

'There is indeed a sensible rule for ensuring precisely that,' said the Assistant in reply, 'but people seldom follow it. The father should promote his son into co-ownership, they should build and plant together, he should allow him, as he does himself, a harmless freedom of action. One activity may be woven into another, but not simply tacked on to it. A young shoot will graft very easily and gladly on to an old stem, but a grown branch never will.'

The Assistant was glad that, just as he was obliged to leave, he had happened to say something Charlotte was pleased to hear, for thus he kept her well-disposed towards him. He had been away too long already, but could not bring himself to leave until he was entirely convinced that he must wait out the period of Charlotte's confinement, now imminent, before he could hope for any decision concerning Ottilie. Then he bowed to the circumstances, and with those prospects and hopes returned to the Principal.

Charlotte's confinement approached. She kept more to her rooms. The women who had gathered around her were more and more the only company she kept. Ottilie looked after the house, and scarcely dared think what she was doing. True, her acceptance was total; she wished that in future too she might serve Charlotte, the child, and Eduard in every helpful way; but she did not see how that would be possible. She was saved from complete confusion only by carrying out her duties day after day.

A son came safely into the world, and all the women agreed that he was the living image of his father. Only Ottilie, though she said nothing, could not see the likeness when she went to offer her congratulations to the mother and her first heartfelt greetings to the child. Charlotte had been grieved by the absence of her husband during the preparations for her daughter's wedding; and now the father was not present at the birth of his son either, and would not decide what name he should be called by in the future.

The very first friend to come with congratulations was Mittler, who had sent out his spies so as to have word of the event at once. He arrived, and was all complacency. Barely concealing his triumph from Ottilie he expressed it loudly to Charlotte and set about dispelling all anxieties and removing every present difficulty. They must hurry ahead with the christening. The old parson, one foot in the grave, would unite past and future with his blessing; the child must be called Otto; he could have no other name but the name of the father and the friend.

It took all Mittler's determined bullying to overcome the thousand-and-one doubts, objections, hesitations, falterings, better ideas, other ideas, and the dithering, and the thinking one thing, then another, then the first again; since on such occasions whenever a worry is removed more and more spring up, and wishing to spare everybody's susceptibilities we always wound a few.

Mittler saw to all the notices and letters to godparents; he wanted them done without delay, for it was to him a matter of the utmost importance that a happiness in his view so significant for the family should be made known to the wide world too where not everyone was kind in what they thought and said. And the recent passionate events had of course been noticed by a public in any case convinced that whatever happens happens in order that they shall have something to talk about.

The christening ceremony was to be dignified, but limited and brief. They assembled; Ottilie and Mittler were to act as sponsors. The old parson approached, his steps were slow, he was supported by the verger. Prayers had been said, the child laid in Ottilie's arms, and looking down fondly at him she was more than a little startled by his open eyes, for she seemed to be looking into her own. Anyone would have been astonished by such likeness. Mittler, taking the child next, was similarly shocked, for he saw in its features a resemblance, but to the Captain, that was more striking than anything he had ever seen of the kind before.

The old clergyman's frailty had prevented him from accompanying the baptism with more than the usual liturgy. Mittler meanwhile, full of the occasion, remembered the times he had himself officiated. It was altogether his way in every situation to imagine what he would say and how he would phrase things, and on this occasion he was even less able to restrain himself because the gathering was only a small one and only of friends. Accordingly, towards the end of the proceedings, he usurped the parson's place and began with cheerful self-satisfaction to list the hopes and duties that were his as a sponsor, and dwelled on them at length, reading an encouragement to do so in Charlotte's contented looks.

Forging ahead, the speechmaker failed to notice that the poor cleric would have liked to sit down, and still less did he realize that he was about to be the cause of something much worse. For having, with considerable emphasis, described the relationship of everyone present to the child, thereby putting Ottilie's composure severely to the test, he turned last to the old man himself, with these words: 'And you, the respected patriarch among us, can say with Simeon, "Lord, now lettest thou thy servant depart in peace, for mine eyes have seen the salvation of this house."'

He was rising now to a glorious peroration, but soon saw that the old man, to whom he was holding out the child, though he first seemed to bend towards it, then at once fell back. Scarcely kept from sinking to the floor he was got to a chair, and notwithstanding every effort at first aid, was there pronounced dead.

To see birth and death, coffin and cradle, so immediately side by side, to envisage them thus, to connect these colossal opposites not just in the imagination but with their very eyes was a hard task for those assembled, it was put to them so abruptly. Only Ottilie gazed at the parson, now gone to his rest and still amiable and kindly in his appearance, with a sort of envy. The life of her soul had been killed, why should her body be preserved?

But if in this way unpleasant events of the day quite often turned her thoughts towards transience, parting, and loss, she had wondrous night-time apparitions for comfort, and by them she was reassured of the existence of the man she loved and her own existence was affirmed and enlivened. When she lay down at night and was floating in the sweet sensation between sleep and waking, she seemed to have a view into a room that was at once perfectly bright and yet lit gently. In this room she saw Eduard quite distinctly, clothed not as she was used to seeing him but for war, each time in a different posture which was, however, always entirely natural and had nothing fantastic about it: standing, walking, lying, or riding. The figure, depicted in every detail, moved willingly before her without her having to do the least thing herself, without her volition, without her having to strain her imagination. Sometimes she also saw him surrounded, especially by something in motion which was darker than the light background; but the most she could distinguish was shadows, which might appear to her variously as people, horses, trees, or mountains. Usually she fell asleep while the apparition lasted, and waking next morning after a peaceful night she was refreshed, comforted, she felt convinced: Eduard was still alive, she stood with him still in the closest possible relationship.

CHAPTER NINE

Spring had arrived, later but also more suddenly and more joyfully than usual. In the garden now Ottilie was rewarded for her foresight. Everything budded, leafed, and blossomed at its proper time; things brought on carefully under glass and in the beds now lifted quickly to meet Nature herself working in the open air again at last; and everything that needed doing and seeing to was no longer, as it had been, a hopeful labour but became a cheerful pleasure.

She had to console the Gardener however for the gaps that Luciane's wildness had caused among the pot-plants and the damage done to the shapes of some of the trees. Ottilie urged him to take heart, it would right itself again before very long; but he had too deep a sense and too pure a conception of his work to be much comforted by her arguments. Just as the gardener himself must not be distracted by other hobbies and passions, so there must be no interruption of the tranquil process by which a plant attains a lasting or a transient perfection. Plants are like obstinate individuals – entirely amenable if you treat them their way. The gardener, more than anyone else perhaps, needs a steady eye and a quiet steadiness of purpose to do exactly what is appropriate in every season and in every hour.

These were qualities he possessed in a high degree, which was why Ottilie enjoyed working with him; but for some time now he had not had the contentment of doing what he was really best at. For although he was perfectly competent in everything concerning fruit-growing and the kitchen garden and could manage an old-style ornamental garden too (and it is generally the case that different people do well at different things), and although what he did in the orangery and with bulbs, carnations, and auriculas was a challenge to Nature herself, he had never entirely got to like the new ornamental

313

trees and fashionable flowers, and the limitless world of botany then opening up and all the foreign names buzzing around in it filled him with a sort of timidity, which made him cross. What the lord and lady had begun sending away for in the previous year he regarded as useless expense and down-right waste, particularly since quite a few of the plants that cost so much then came to nothing, and his dealings with the suppliers, whom he thought less than honest, were not of the happiest.

After several attempts he had devised a sort of plan to answer these circumstances, and Ottilie supported him in it, the more so since its real premiss was the return of Eduard, whose absence in this as in so many matters was daily more grievously felt.

As the plants rooted deeper and sent forth more and more shoots Ottilie likewise felt the tightening of her attachment to that place. Exactly a year before she had arrived as a stranger and person of no consequence; how much she had acquired since then! And since then lost again, alas! She had never been so rich, and never so poor. Feelings of each alternated in her by the minute, indeed were very deeply intermixed, so that her only recourse, again and again, was to put her sympathies, her passions, into whatever things were nearest.

Naturally she was most attentive to all the things Eduard loved best. For why should she not hope he would soon return and notice with a present gratitude how carefully she had served him in his absence?

But in a quite different way besides she had cause to be active on his behalf. The baby was now principally in her care, and that care was all the more immediate because it had been decided not to give him to a wet nurse but to bring him up on milk and water. In that lovely season he was to enjoy the fresh air; and she much preferred to take him out herself and carried him sleeping and oblivious among the flowers and the blossom that would in time smile kindly on his childhood, and among the shrubs and plants which seemed intended, being in their infancy, to accompany his growing with their own. When she looked around her she saw how ample was the condition the child had been born to enjoy; for almost everything as far as the eye could see would be his one day. Given so much then, how desirable it was that he should grow up under the eyes of his father and mother and be the confirmation of their renewed and joyful union.

Ottilie felt all this in such purity that she thought of it as a decided reality and felt nothing on her own account. Under those clear skies, in that bright sunshine, it was suddenly clear to her that her love, to be perfected, must become wholly unselfish; indeed, there were moments when she believed she had already attained those heights. All she wanted was her friend's well-being; she believed herself capable of giving him up, even of never seeing him again, if she could be sure he was happy. But for herself she was quite decided never to belong to anyone else.

Care had been taken that the autumn should be as magnificent as the spring. All the summer annuals, everything that will not give up flowering in autumn but pushes on bravely into the coming cold, asters especially, had been sown in abundance and great variety and, transplanted now into all four corners, would make, when the time came, a starry sky over the earth.

From Ottilie's Diary

'If in a book we come across a good idea or hear something striking in conversation we very likely copy it into our diaries. But if we also took the trouble to excerpt characteristic remarks, original opinions, fleeting witticisms from the letters of our friends, we should be very rich. We keep letters, but never read them again; then finally one day we burn them, to be discreet; and thus the loveliest and most immediate breath of life disappears irrevocably for us and for others. I have resolved to make good this omission.

'So the fairy tale of the seasons begins again at the beginning. Here we are once more now, thankfully, in the prettiest chapter. Violets and lilies of the valley are like captions or vignettes in it. We are always pleased when we open the book of life at their page again.

'We scold the poor, and especially the youngsters among them, when they loiter at the roadside and beg. We seem not to have noticed that they are busy again just as soon as there is something for them to do. Scarcely has smiling Nature displayed her gifts again than the children are after them, to begin a trade; then no child begs, every one offers you a bouquet; it was plucked before you woke, and the supplicant looks at you as smilingly as the gift itself. No one looks wretched who feels he has some right to ask.

'Why is the year sometimes so short and sometimes so long, and why does it seem so short, and yet so long when we look back on it? That is how I feel about the year which has passed, and nowhere more acutely than in the garden where fleeting things and lasting things go hand in hand. And yet nothing is so fleeting that it leaves no trace and no continuation of its kind.

'We can enjoy the winter too. We seem to extend ourselves more freely when the trees stand before us so ghostly and transparent. They are nothing, but they hide nothing either. But once the buds and the blossom come then we are impatient for all the foliage to be there and for the landscape to become substantial again and the trees to press towards us each in its own shape.

'Everything which is perfect in its kind must exceed its kind and become something else, something incomparable. In some of its sounds the nightingale is still a bird; then it goes beyond its class, as though to show every feathered thing what singing is really like.

'A life without love, without the presence of the beloved, is only a *comédie à tiroir*, a thing all in little episodes. You pull out one after the other and push them back in again and hurry to the next. What there is in it of any value and meaning scarcely hangs together. Everywhere you have to begin again, and everywhere you feel like ending it.'

CHAPTER TEN

CHARLOTTE for her part was cheerful and well. Her thriving boy was a delight to her, she dwelled on him, so full of promise, constantly with her eyes and in her thoughts. He had given her a new relationship with the world and with the estate. Her old energy revived; wherever she looked she saw the many things that had been done in the previous year, and was pleased by them. On a strange impulse she climbed up to the summer-house with Ottilie and the child, and laying him on the little table, as on a household altar, and seeing two places empty, she remembered times past and was filled with a new hope for herself and for Ottilie.

A girl herself may cast a modest look at the young men around her perhaps, and secretly consider whether she would like this one or that for a husband; but whoever has to make provision for a daughter or a female ward looks further afield. Charlotte was doing so at that moment, and a union of the Captain and Ottilie, who had sat side by side in that very place, now seemed to her not impossible. She had learned that the Captain's prospects of an advantageous marriage had come to nothing.

Charlotte climbed higher, Ottilie carrying the child. She gave herself up to a host of reflections. There are shipwrecks on dry land too; the proper and laudable thing is to recover and recuperate from them as quickly as possible. Life is a matter of profit and loss after all. How often we make provision and are thwarted! How often we set off only to be diverted! How often we are distracted from a goal clearly sighted, in order to achieve a higher one! A traveller, to his vast annoyance, breaks a wheel, and through this disagreeable accident he makes acquaintances and relationships of a most delightful kind which have an influence on the rest of his life. Fate grants us our wishes, but in its own way, so as to be able to give us something beyond our wishes.

Thinking these and similar thoughts Charlotte made her way to the new house on the ridge, and there they were entirely confirmed. For the surroundings were far more beautiful than one could have imagined. On all sides everything trivial and distracting had been removed; all the good in the landscape, all that Nature and time had done to it, appeared cleanly and was evident; and where new planting had been done, to fill out a few gaps and pleasantly connect the separated parts again, there was already some greenness.

The house itself was almost habitable; the views, especially from the upper rooms, were extraordinarily various. The longer one looked, the more beauties were discovered. What effects the different times of day and sun and moonlight would bring forth! It was a place one longed to live in, and how quickly the desire to build and be busy awoke in Charlotte when she saw that all the rough work was complete. A joiner, an upholsterer, a painter who could manage stencils and do a little gilding – they were all that was needed, and in no time the building was ready. Cellar and kitchen were rapidly fitted out, for at that distance from the Hall all the necessities of life had to be on hand. So now the women lived up there with the child and from this dwelling-place, as from a new mid-point, unexpected walks were opened up for them. There in a higher region they savoured the fresh open air in beautiful weather.

Ottilie's favourite walk, sometimes alone, sometimes with the baby, was down to the plane trees on an easy path which then led further to where one of the boats was moored that were used for crossing over. She enjoyed going on the water sometimes; but without the child, since at that Charlotte showed some anxiety. But Ottilie was sure to go to the Hall every day, to visit the Gardener and take a friendly interest with him in the numerous young plants now all enjoying the fresh air.

In this beautiful season Charlotte had a very welcome visitor. It was an Englishman who had got to know Eduard whilst travelling, had met him on a few occasions, and was now curious to see the grounds whose attractions he had so often heard praised. He brought with him a letter of introduction from the Count, and himself introduced a quiet but very agreeable gentleman as his travelling companion. Then as he explored the estate – sometimes with Charlotte and Ottilie, or with the garden staff, the gamekeepers; often with his companion, but sometimes alone – it was obvious from his remarks that he was a lover and connoisseur of such parkland and gardens and had doubtless laid out more than one himself. Although getting on in years he took part cheerfully in all the things by which the beauty and significance of life may be enhanced.

It was in his company that the women first fully appreciated their surroundings. His practised eye took in every effect with a complete freshness, and his pleasure in what had come into being was all the greater since he had not known the landscape beforehand and could scarcely distinguish the things that had been done to it from those that Nature had supplied herself.

It could indeed be said that through his observations the park grew and was enriched. He saw in advance what a place newly planted and only now coming on would one day be like. Wherever some beautiful feature could be accentuated or a new one added, he spotted it. Here he drew their attention to a spring which, if it were cleaned out, might be the ornament of a whole area of shrubbery; and here a cave which, if it were cleared and extended, would make a very desirable place to sit, since from it, after the removal of only a few trees, they would have magnificent rock formations towering in their sight. He congratulated the proprietors on having so much still to do, and urged them not to be in a hurry but to store up some of the pleasant work of creation and design for future years.

Nor did he ever mind being left to himself, since for most of the day he was busy taking picturesque views of the park in a portable camera obscura and sketching them so that he, and others, should have something beautiful and profitable from his travels. He had been doing this for several years now wherever the surroundings merited it, and had put together a most agreeable and interesting collection as a result. He showed the ladies the large portfolio he carried with him and entertained them with the pictures and also with his commentary. They were delighted to be able to travel the world so comfortably and to see shores and harbours, mountains, lakes and rivers, cities and fortresses, and many places famous in history pass before them in their solitude.

Each of the women had her own particular interest: Charlotte's the more general, wherever there was something historically remarkable; whilst Ottilie dwelled especially on the regions Eduard had been most used to speak about, places he liked being in and to which he often returned. Every man has particular localities, near home and far away, which attract him and are, after his character, peculiarly dear and exciting to him, for the first impression they make, for certain circumstances attaching to them, and for their accustomedness.

Ottilie asked the English lord where he liked being best and where he would make his home now if he had to choose. He mentioned several beautiful regions, and with obvious pleasure, in his peculiarly accented French, he spoke of the experiences in those places which had made them so precious to him.

When asked, however, where he usually resided and where he was happiest to return to he replied quite straightforwardly but, for the women, surprisingly:

'I have accustomed myself to being at home everywhere and have come to feel it the best possible arrangement that others should build, plant, and exert themselves domestically on my behalf. I have no longing to return to my own estates, partly for political reasons but principally because my son, for whom, in the end, all the work I did was done, to whom I hoped to bequeath it all, with whom I hoped for a time still to enjoy it, takes no part in any of it but has gone to India like many another to lead a more useful life there or, for all I know, to waste himself completely.

'It is certain that we spend far too much time and money merely preparing to live. Instead of settling down at once in a moderate condition of life we go on and on expanding, to our greater and greater discomfort. Who has any pleasure in my buildings now, and in my park and gardens? Not I, nor even my own kith and kin: only visiting strangers, sightseers, restless travellers.

'Even the very wealthy are only half at home, especially in the country where things we are used to in town are missing. The book we desire to read above all others is not to hand, and what we need most we have left behind. We are forever settling in only to depart again, and if we do not do it to suit our own whims and wishes then circumstances, passions, accidents, necessity, and whatever else will force it anyway.'

The Englishman had no idea how deeply the two friends were affected by his observations. And indeed how often any one of us may run that risk by making a general observation even when we mainly know the circumstances of the company we are in. Being accidentally hurt thus, even by people who were sympathetic and meant well, was nothing new to Charlotte; and the world in any case lay in such clarity before her that she felt no particular pain when somebody thoughtlessly and carelessly obliged her to gaze upon this or that unpleasant place. Ottilie on the other hand, who in her half-conscious youthfulness sensed more things than she saw, and might, indeed had to, avert her eyes from what she did not wish to and was not supposed to see, Ottilie was thrown by these confidences into the cruellest state: the agreeable veil before her eyes was torn asunder and it seemed to her as if everything done till then for the house, the garden, the park, and the whole environment was in fact for nothing, because the man to whom it all belonged had no joy of it since he, like their present visitor, was wandering the world, and in the most dangerous fashion, having been driven to do so by those who were closest in his love. She had grown used to listening in silence, but her situation now was painful in the extreme, and was made worse rather than better by what their guest, with peculiar gravity and serenity, then went on to say.

'It seems to me,' he said, 'that I do best to think of myself as a perpetual traveller, giving up a great deal in order to enjoy a great deal. I am used to change, indeed I find it necessary, just as at the opera we are always waiting for a scene-change precisely because there have already been so many. I know what I can expect of the best inn and the worst. It can be as good or as bad as it likes, I am never in one place long enough to grow accustomed, and what does it matter in the end whether our lives are determined entirely by fixed habits or entirely by the most casual accidents? At least I no longer have the irritation of misplacing or losing things, or of not being able to use my living-room because it has to be deco- rated, or of somebody breaking my favourite cup and nothing tasting right out of any other for an age. I am free of all that, and if the place goes up in flames the servants will calmly pack my bags and load my carriage and I leave town. And with all these advantages, when I reckon it up I have not spent more by the end of the year than it would have cost me at home.'

In this description Ottilie saw no one but Eduard, saw him too now deprived and suffering hardships, travelling the unmade roads, lying under the stars in want and in danger, and amid so much precariousness and risk accustoming himself to being homeless and friendless and to throwing away everything so as to have nothing to lose. Fortunately then the company broke up for a while. Ottilie found space to weep in solitude. None of her dull griefs had been so hard on her as this clarity which she now strove to make even clearer, as people will indeed torment themselves once they have begun to be tormented.

Eduard's condition seemed to her so poor, so pitiable, that she decided, cost what it might, to do everything in her power to bring about his reunion with Charlotte, then in some quiet place to hide her grief and love and cheat them with some sort of work.

In the meantime the English lord's companion, a sensible, tranquil, and observant man, had noticed the *faux pas* in the conversation and had pointed out to his friend the similarity of his and Eduard's lives. He for his part knew nothing about the family circumstances; but the companion, whom, as he travelled, nothing interested more than the strange things which are caused to occur by natural and artificial circumstances, by the conflict of law and unrestraint, pragmatism and reason, passion and prejudice, had in advance, but then especially when arriving in the house, made himself acquainted with all that had happened and was still happening.

His Lordship was sorry, but not seriously embarrassed. To avoid such errors it would be necessary to say nothing whatsoever in society; for not only serious observations but even the most trivial remarks may happen to chime badly with the interests of those present. 'We shall put things right this evening,' he said, 'and avoid all conversation of a general kind. I suggest you give them one or two of the curious anecdotes and stories with which you have so enriched your portfolio and your memory on our travels.'

But despite the best of intentions the visitors still did not manage to cause the women no distress with the entertainment. For when the companion, through a series of strange, instructive, cheerful, moving, and terrible stories, had excited their attention and roused their interest to the highest degree, he thought to close with an admittedly odd but none the less gentler happening, and did not guess how near it was to his listeners.

STRANGE NEIGHBOURS
A NOVELLE

'Two children of wealthy neighbouring families, a boy and a girl, similar in age, were brought up together in the pleasant expectation that they would one day be man and wife, and their parents looked forward joyfully to this eventual union.

But before long it began to be apparent that what they had planned would be unlikely to come about, for a strange antipathy arose between the characters, both excellent, of the two children. Perhaps they were too alike. Both self-absorbed, clear in their wishes, firm in their intentions; both loved and respected by their play-fellows; always opponents when they came together; each separately creative, but mutually destructive when they met; not competing after a distant goal, but forever fighting for some immediate purpose; entirely good-natured and lovable, and only full of hatred, indeed wicked, in their dealings with one another.

'This strange relationship was already manifest in their childish games, and thereafter as they grew older. And as boys play at war and divide into sides and fight battles, so the proud and spirited girl once set herself at the head of one of the armies and fought with such fierceness and force that the other would have been shamefully routed if her sole real opponent had not stood his ground and in the end disarmed her and taken her prisoner. But even then she defended herself with such ferocity that he, to save his eyes and so as not to harm his enemy, had to tear off the silk kerchief he wore around his neck and use it to tie her hands behind her back.

'She never forgave him this, indeed she went to such secret lengths to harm him that the parents, who had for some time been keeping a watchful eye on these bizarre passions, conferred together and agreed to separate the hostile pair and to abandon the hopes they had been cherishing.

'The boy soon excelled in his new circumstances. He took in everything he was taught. His patrons as well as his own inclinations directed him towards the army. Wherever he might be he was loved and respected. His good qualities seemed to promote only well-being and contentment in others; and in himself, without fully realizing it, he was glad to have lost the one opponent Nature had given him.

'The girl on the other hand now suddenly entered into a changed condition. Her years, her increasing culture, and more, a certain inner sense, drew her away from the rough games she had been used to playing in the boys' company. Altogether, she seemed to be lacking something. There was nothing around her fit to excite her hatred, and no one had come her way yet who was worthy of being loved.

'A young man, older than her former neighbour and enemy, a man of rank, wealth, and consequence, well liked in society, sought after by women, bestowed upon her his entire affection. It was the first time that a man had approached her as friend, lover, and devoted servant. She was greatly flattered to be thus preferred by him over many others older, more cultured, more brilliant, more sophisticated than herself. His sustained attentions, that were never importunate, his faithful support in various contretemps, the candid yet – since she was still very young – temperate and no more than hopeful expression of his sentiments to her parents, all this inclined her towards him, and the accustomedness of the situation, its outward form becoming known and accepted in the world, this also played a part. She had been spoken of so often as a bride-to-be that in the end she thought of herself as one, and neither she nor anybody else thought any further trial necessary when she exchanged rings with the man so long thought of as her future husband.

'The placid course which the whole business had taken was not accelerated by the engagement either. Both sides simply let things carry on. They took pleasure in one another's company and wished to enjoy the pleasant time of year really as a springtime before the more serious life that was to come.

'The younger man meanwhile, away from home, had developed as well as anyone could have wished. He had achieved a deserved advancement in his career, and was given leave to visit his family. In a quite natural and yet strange fashion he stood again now face to face with his beautiful neighbour. Latterly all her feelings had been kindly ones, having to do with her family and with matrimony, she was at one with everything that surrounded her; she thought herself happy, and was so in a certain sense. But now for the first time in years something again confronted her – and not something fit to be hated, she had become incapable of hatred; rather that childish hatred, really only an obscure acknowledgement of inner merit, expressed itself now in a joyful astonishment, a glad contemplation, a pleased admission, and in a half-willing, half-involuntary, and yet inevitable drawing near; and all that was mutual. Their long separation gave rise to long conversations. Even their childish unreasonableness was now, as they remembered it in their more enlightened state, a source of amusement, and it was as if they must make up for that teasing hatred at least by friendly and attentive dealings now, as if that violent mistaking must now be countered by explicit recognition.

'On his side everything kept a sensible and desirable measure. His rank, his circumstances, his wish to advance, preoccupied him abundantly, so that to have the friendliness of this beautiful bride-to-be was a grateful extra which he was well pleased to receive, without then viewing her in any connection with himself or begrudging her fiancé, with whom moreover he was on excellent terms, the possession of her.

'But for her things looked very different. It seemed to her that she had woken from a dream. The battle against her young neighbour had been her first passion and that violent fighting, under the guise of resistance, was only, after all, a violent and, as it were, inborn affection. And now as she remembered things she had no other sense than that she had always loved him. She smiled at those hostile searchings with a weapon in her hand; she seemed to remember the pleasantest possible sensation when he disarmed her; she imagined she must have felt the intensest bliss when he tied her hands, and everything she had ever undertaken to harm and annoy him seemed to her now only innocent means by which she might attract his attention. She cursed their separation, she rued the sleep she had fallen into, she damned the slow and dreamy process of habit which had betrothed her to such an insignificant man; she was changed, doubly changed, for-wards and backwards, according to how one views it.

'If anyone had been able to untangle and share her feelings (which, however, she kept to herself), he would not have blamed her; for it had to be admitted that in any comparison of the two men her husband-to-be came off much the worse. Though he could be said to inspire a certain confidence, his rival called forth the completest trust; though he was good company, the latter was a man you might want for a lifelong companion; and in exceptional circumstances, were there ever a need for a higher understanding and sympathy, you might have had doubts about the one but felt an entire certainty about the other. Women have a particularly fine feeling, inborn in them, for these distinctions, and have reason, as well as opportunity, to develop it.

'The more the lovely bride-to-be nourished such senti-ments secretly in her heart, the less she liked hearing, from anyone at all, what her fiancé had in his favour, what circum-stances and duty seemed to recommend and dictate, indeed what an unalterable necessity seemed irrevocably to require, all the more did her feelings favour their own beautiful one-sidedness; and being on the one hand indissolubly bound by the world and family, by her fiancé and her own consent, and since on the other the youth, going his ambitious way, made no secret of his sentiments, plans, and prospects and behaved towards her only like a faithful and not even very loving brother, and when there was even talk of his imminent departure, then it seemed as if her early childish spirit awoke again with all its ploys and violence and now on a higher level of life armed itself in dudgeon, to act with more consequence and with more dire effect. She decided to die, to punish the man she had hated and now so passionately loved for his indifference, and, since she could not have him, at least to marry herself for ever to his imagination and his remorse. She wanted him never to be able to rid himself of her dead image, never cease reproaching himself that he had not recognized, explored, and valued her feelings.

'This strange madness went with her everywhere. She hid it under all manner of outward appearances; and though people thought her odd no one was attentive or shrewd enough to discover the true inner cause.

'Meanwhile friends, relatives, and acquaintances had been exhausting themselves in the staging of numerous festivities. Scarcely a day went by without something novel and unexpected being put on. There was hardly a beauty spot around that had not been decorated and made ready for the reception of crowds of happy guests. And our young homecomer too wished to play his part before leaving again and invited the bridal couple and a few close family for an outing on the river. They boarded a large, beautiful, well-fitted ship, one of those yachts that offer rooms and a small suite and aim to transpose on to the water all the comforts of the land.

'They sailed, with music, down the great river; the company had gone below out of the heat and were amusing themselves with quizzes and games of chance. The young host, never able to remain inactive, had seated himself at the helm to relieve the elderly captain, who had fallen asleep at his side; and thus, left as the one awake, he needed precisely then to use all possible care since he was approaching a place where two islands narrowed the bed of the river and their flat pebble shores, extending now from the one side and now from the other, made a dangerous rapids. Steering cautiously, staring intently ahead, he was almost tempted to wake the skipper, but trusted his own ability and headed for the narrows. At that moment his beautiful enemy appeared on deck wearing a wreath of flowers in her hair. Removing the wreath she flung it at the helmsman. "Take this to remember me by," she cried. "Get out of my way!" he cried, catching the wreath. "I need all my strength and concentration." "I shall," she cried. "You will never see me again." Those were her words, then she hurried to the bows and jumped into the water. "Oh, save her, save her!" voices cried. "She is drowning!" He was in the most frightful dilemma. The noise woke the old captain, who made to take over the helm and the younger man to give it him; but there was no time to change command: the ship stranded, and at that moment, throwing off the more encumbering of his clothes, he dived into the water and swam after his beautiful enemy.

'Water is a friendly element for whoever knows it well and is able to manage it. It bore him up, and being a good swimmer he mastered it. He had soon reached the girl carried away ahead of him; he seized her, raised, and bore her; both were then carried away by the violent force of the water until the islands and the shoals were far behind them and the river again began to flow with breadth and ease. Now at last he took heart and revived from the first pressing danger in which he had acted without thought and only mechanically. Keeping up his head he looked around him and steered then with all his strength towards a flat and bushy place which ran out prettily and conveniently into the water. There he brought his beautiful catch ashore; but could discern no breath of life in her. He was in despair, when his eyes lit upon a well-trodden path through the bushes. Again he took up his precious burden, soon saw an isolated dwelling, and reached it. There he found good people, a young married couple. The misadventure, the grave danger were soon uttered. What, after a moment's reflection, he asked, was done. A bright fire burned; woollen blankets were laid upon a bed; furs and fleeces and whatever else they had in the house that was warming, were quickly fetched. Now the intense desire to save overrode every other consideration. Nothing was left undone that might bring the beautiful, stiffening, naked body back to life. It worked. She opened her eyes, she saw her friend, she fastened her wonderfully beautiful arms around his neck. So she remained for a long while; tears flowed from her eyes, which completed her recovery. "Will you leave me now?" she cried – "Now that I have found you again like this?" "Never!" he cried – "Never!" and knew neither what he said nor what he did. "But now be still," he added, "be still. Think of yourself, for your sake and for mine."

'She did think of herself, and only now became aware of the condition she was in. Before her rescuer, before the man she loved, she could not feel any shame; but she was content to let him go so that he could see to himself, for what he had on was still dripping wet.

'The young married couple conferred: he offered the youth and she the girl their wedding clothes which still hung ready to dress two people through from head to toe. Before long the two adventurers were not only dressed but they stood in finery. They looked delightful, gazed at one another in astonishment when they met, and with immoderate passion and yet half laughing at their disguises violently embraced. Youthful strength and the quickness of love very soon restored them entirely, and had there been music they would have danced.

'To have come from the water to dry land, from death to life, from the circle of the family into a wilderness, from despair to ecstatic happiness, from indifference to affection, to passion, all in the space of a moment – the mind would not be adequate to comprehend it, the mind would burst or lapse into confusion. Then the heart must do most if such a wondrous reversal is to be borne.

'Being entirely lost in one another it was some time before they could give any thought to the anxiety and the fears of those they had left behind; and they were themselves almost not able to think without fears and anxiety of how they should ever confront them again. "Shall we flee? Shall we hide?" the young man asked. "We will stay together," she said, her arms around his neck.

'The countryman, having heard from them the story of the stranded ship, hurried without further questions to the riverbank. The vessel was coming safely by; with a great deal of effort it had been got off again. They had sailed on in all uncertainty, in the hope of finding the lost pair. When therefore the countryman attracted the attention of those on board by shouting and waving, and ran to a place where it was safe to land, and kept on with his shouting and waving, the ship bore in towards the bank, and what a spectacle that was when they came ashore! The parents of the betrothed couple hurried off first; the husband-to-be was almost distracted with grief. Scarcely had they learned that the two beloved children were safe when the couple themselves came out of the bushes in their strange costumes. Nobody knew them until they came up close. "Who are you?" the mothers cried. "What are you?" cried the fathers. The two now safe threw themselves down at their feet. "Your children," they cried. "Two joined as one." "Forgive us," the girl cried. "Give us your blessing," cried the boy. "Give us your blessing," they cried together, when for astonishment nobody spoke. "Your blessing," it came again for the third time, and who could have refused it?'

CHAPTER ELEVEN

THE story-teller paused, or rather had already finished before he noticed that Charlotte was greatly agitated; indeed, she rose and with a gesture of apology left the room. She knew the story. Those things had happened in reality to the Captain and the daughter of a neighbouring family, not entirely as the Englishman had described them, it is true, but in the chief features there was no distortion, only in the details it had been developed and embellished, as is usually the case when stories of that kind pass from mouth to mouth and finally through the imagination of an intelligent and sensitive story-teller. In the end scarcely anything and almost everything is as it was.

Ottilie followed Charlotte, being urged to do so by the two visitors. And now it was the nobleman's turn to remark that perhaps once again a *faux pas* had been committed and a story told that was known to the household or even intimately associated with it. 'We must beware', he continued, 'of doing yet more harm. We seem to have given these ladies very little pleasure in return for all the kindness and enjoyment we have had here. We must look for a tactful way of taking our leave.'

'I have to confess', his companion replied, 'that there is something else holding me here, and without an explanation and closer knowledge of it I should be very loath to leave. Yesterday, my lord, when we were in the park with the camera obscura, you were busy choosing the very best perspective and did not notice what was going on besides. You left the main path to get to a place by the lake, one not much visited, with a charming view across. Ottilie, who was with us, seemed reluctant to follow and asked if she might make her way there in the boat. I got in too. Her beauty and her skill with the oars were a great delight. I assured her that not since Switzerland (for there too the most charming girls do the ferryman's job) had I had such an agreeable ride across the water, but could not resist asking why she had not wanted to take that little path. For really there was a kind of anxious embarrassment in her avoiding it. "If you promise not to make fun of me," she answered with a smile, "I can give you a sort of explanation, though even for me it is something of a mystery. I have never gone that way without feeling a quite peculiar cold shudder such as I never feel anywhere else and which I cannot explain. I prefer not to expose myself to such a sensation, especially since I at once then get a headache on the left side, which is something I do suffer from occasionally." We landed, Ottilie talked to you, and I went and examined the place which she had pointed out to me quite distinctly in the distance. How great was my amazement when I found very clear traces of coal there, so that I am certain that with some digging a rich seam might be discovered in the depths.

'Forgive me, my lord – I see you smiling and am well aware that you indulge my passionate interest in these things, to which you yourself do not give any credence, only as a wise man and a friend – but I cannot possibly leave here without having that beautiful child try the oscillations too.'

Invariably when this matter was discussed the English lord repeated the reasons for his scepticism, the companion listened to them with all patience and deference, but in the end abided by his own opinion and his wishes. He also reiterated the consideration that one ought not to give up the business merely because such experiments did not succeed with everybody, indeed one ought rather to pursue it all the more seriously and thoroughly, since many more relationships and affinities of inorganic entities among themselves, of organic entities with them and also among themselves, at present unknown to us, would surely be revealed.

He had already set out his apparatus – the golden rings, marcasites, and other metallic substances which he always carried with him in a handsome box – and now laid out certain metals and lowered others over them, on threads, to make a trial, saying as he did so: 'I see it amuses you, my lord, that nothing will move for me nor in me either, and I do not begrudge you your amusement. My procedures however are only a subterfuge. When the ladies return I intend them to be curious to know what strange things we are up to.'

The women came back. Charlotte knew immediately what was going on. 'I have heard a good deal about such things,' she said, 'but never seen it done. Since you have everything so nicely ready here, let me try if it will work with me.'

She took the thread in her hand, and being serious in her desire she held it steadily and without emotion; but not the slightest oscillation was to be observed. Then Ottilie was bidden to try. She held the pendulum even more calmly and with even less inhibition and conscious intention over the metals. But at once the dangling metal was seized, really as if in a whirlpool, and veered to one side or the other, according to what new substances were placed below, now in a circle, now in an ellipse, or swinging in straight lines, just as the gentleman's companion might have hoped, indeed in a way exceeding all his hopes.

The gentleman himself was somewhat taken aback, but his friend's delight and avidity were such that he would not cease and begged again and again for the experiments to be repeated and varied. Ottilie was accommodating enough to do as he wished, until at last, in the nicest way, she asked him to let her desist, since her headache was coming on again. Amazed, indeed delighted, he assured her with great enthusiasm that he would entirely cure her of this malady if she would entrust herself to his treatment. There was a moment's hesitation; but Charlotte, who soon realized what he had in mind, declined the well-intentioned offer, being unwilling to permit in her presence something she had always felt gravely apprehensive about.

The visitors had departed, and although their impact had been a strange one still, when they left, a desire to meet them again somewhere remained behind. Charlotte now took advantage of the fine weather to repay visits in the neighbourhood, but could scarcely get to the end of them since everyone for miles around, some out of real kindness, others only as a matter of custom, had been diligently solicitous of her welfare. At home she was enlivened by the sight of the child; and certainly he deserved every love and care. They thought him a wonderful child, indeed a wonder, in his size and shapeliness, his strength and good health, a delight to behold, and even more astounding was that double likeness which developed more and more. In his features and in the whole shape of his body the child more and more resembled the Captain, and his eyes were less and less distinguishable from Ottilie's.

Led by this strange relatedness and perhaps even more by the beautiful inclination a woman feels to lavish affection on the child of a man she loves though it is not her own, Ottilie became as good as a mother to the growing boy, or rather she became another sort of mother. When Charlotte went away Ottilie was left alone with the child and his nurse. Nanni had left her some time ago, in pique, and had gone home to her parents, being jealous of the boy on whom all her mistress's affection now seemed to be bestowed. Ottilie continued taking the child into the fresh air, and got used to longer and longer walks. She had the feeding bottle with her, to give the child his milk whenever necessary. Almost always she had a book with her too and made thus, the child in her arms, reading and taking her walks, a very charming *penserosa*.

CHAPTER TWELVE

THE main aim of the campaign had been achieved and Eduard, decorated for his services, had been honourably discharged. He returned at once to his little estate and there was given precise news of those at home whom, without their noticing or knowing it, he had kept under close surveillance. His quiet dwelling-place was a joy to enter again; for there had been many alterations and improvements and much progress in the meantime according to his instructions, so that now the gardens and the grounds made up in intimacy and in the immediacy of their amenities for what they lacked in extensiveness.

Eduard, accustomed by the quicker pace of his recent life to acting more decisively, now resolved to do what he had had time enough to think about doing. And first he summoned the Major. Their joy at seeing one another again was great. Youthful friendships, like blood relationships, have the considerable advantage that aberrations and misunderstandings of whatever kind never fundamentally harm them and after a while the old dealings are restored.

Thus warmly welcoming the Major Eduard asked about his present circumstances, and learned how completely in accordance with his wishes fortune had treated him. Half-teasingly then, but in the tones of intimacy, Eduard enquired whether any romantic engagement were not also under way. 'None,' said his friend with meaningful seriousness.

'I cannot be devious,' Eduard continued. 'It would be wrong. I must at once reveal to you my feelings and intentions. You know my passion for Ottilie, and have long since understood that it was she who drove me into these wars. I do not deny that I had wished to be rid of a life that without her was no longer any use to me; but I must also at once admit to you that I could not bring myself to despair completely.

Happiness with her was so beautiful, so desirable that I remained unable to renounce it fully. There were many consoling hints and many cheering signs which strengthened me in the belief, in the delusion, that Ottilie could be mine. A glass marked with our initials thrown into the air when the foundation stone was laid, instead of smashing to pieces it was caught and is in my hands again. "Well then," I cried to myself, having spent many uncertain hours in this solitude, "I will make myself into a sign in the place of that glass, to see whether our union shall be possible or not. I will go and seek my death, and not as a madman but as one who hopes to live. Ottilie shall be the prize I am fighting for, and she will be what I hope to win and to conquer behind the enemy lines on every battlefield and behind every fortification and in every siege. I will perform miracles, in the wish to be spared and in the intention to win Ottilie and not to lose her." These feelings guided me, they stood by me in all the dangers; but now I feel like a man arrived at his goal, all obstacles overcome and nothing now in my way. Ottilie is mine, and what still lies between that thought and its execution is not, as I see it, of any significance.'

'With a few strokes,' the Major replied, 'you cancel out everything that might and ought to be said on the other side; but said it must be nevertheless. It is not for me to remind you of your relationship with your wife and of what that is worth; but you owe it to her and to yourself not to be in any doubts. And I cannot bring to mind that a son has been given you without at the same time telling you that you belong to one another eternally, that you owe it to the child to live united so that unitedly you may see to his upbringing and his future good.'

'It is only the parents' conceit,' Eduard replied, 'if they imagine their children to have any such need of them. All living things find nourishment and succour, and if the father dies young and the son's early years are not so favoured and not so comfortable as a consequence, that itself might equip him all the more quickly for the world by making him realize betimes that he has to fit in with others; a thing we all have to learn sooner or later. But that is not the issue here: we are rich enough to look after several children, and it is certainly neither a duty nor a kindness to heap so many goods upon one head.'

When the Major began to say something about Charlotte's worth and about Eduard's long-lived attachment to her, Eduard broke in abruptly: 'We were foolish,' he said, 'as I now see only too well. Anyone in middle age who seeks to realize the hopes and wishes of his youthful past is always a dupe, for every decade in a person's life has its own happiness and its own hopes and prospects. Woe betide the man whom circumstances or his own delusions cause to reach forwards or back! We made a foolish mistake: must it be for the rest of our lives? Shall we, because of doubts of whatever kind, deny ourselves something that the morals of our times do not forbid? People so often go back on their intentions and their deeds: why should not we whose case is the whole, not an individual part, and not one particular requirement of life but life in its entirety?'

The Major did of course set out before Eduard, in a way that was as tactful as it was emphatic, all the different considerations relating to his wife, the families, society, and the estates; but Eduard was quite unmoved.

'All this, my dear friend,' he said in reply, 'passed before my soul in the chaos of battle when the earth was shaken by a constant thunder, when musket balls whined and whistled, to right and left my comrades fell, my horse was hit, my hat shot through; it hovered before me at nights by the quiet fire under the starry vault of heaven. Then all my attachments presented themselves to my soul; and in my thinking and in my feelings I went through them all; I made them truly mine, I was reconciled, again and again, and now for ever.

'At such times, why should I hide it from you, you too were present, you too belonged in my circle; and have we not for many years belonged to one another? If I have got into your debt at all I am now in a position to pay you back with interest; and if you are in my debt in any way you are enabled now to make it up to me. I know you love Charlotte, and she deserves your love; I know she has feelings for you in return, and why should she not recognize your worth? Take her as a gift from me, bring me Ottilie, and we are the happiest people on earth.'

'Precisely because you are bribing me with such precious gifts,' the Major replied, 'I must be all the more cautious and all the more severe. Your proposal, which in my heart I honour and respect, instead of easing the matter renders it more difficult. For now what concerns you also concerns me, and it is not just a matter of the destiny but also of the reputation, of the honour of two men who have come thus far uncensured, but who now through this strange drama, not wishing to call it by any other name, run the risk of appearing before the world in a most peculiar light.'

'The very fact that we are uncensured', said Eduard in reply, 'gives us the right to be for once. If a man is sound all his life that lends soundness to things he does which would appear equivocal if done by others. For my part I feel justified by the ordeals to which I have lately submitted myself and by the difficult and dangerous things I have done for others in doing something for myself as well. For yourself and Charlotte, let the future decide; but neither you nor anyone else will hold me back from doing what I have resolved to do. Offer me your hand and I will again be entirely amenable; but if I am left to myself, or worse if I am opposed, then certainly, whatever the outcome, it will be extreme.'

The Major thought it his duty to resist Eduard's intention for as long as possible, and now he employed a skilful tactic against his friend by seeming to give in and by turning to the formalities, the official procedures which would be necessary to bring about this separation and these unions. Then so much surfaced that was unpleasant, onerous, and distasteful that Eduard's humour was made worse and worse.

'It is clear to me', he cried at last, 'that a man must take what he wants by storm from friends as well as foes. What

I want, what I cannot do without, never leaves my sight. I shall seize hold of it, and that before long, you may be sure. I know very well that relationships of this kind are neither annulled nor formed unless things fall that are at present standing and unless things shift that only desire to stay. Such matters will never be settled by reflection, all rights are equal when the reason views them and on the rising scale you can always lay a counter-weight. Therefore, my friend, decide to act on my behalf and on your own, decide for my side and for yours to unravel, dissolve, and fasten anew these relations. Do not let any considerations hold you back. We have in any case already made ourselves talked about, we shall be talked about again and then, like everything when it loses its novelty, we shall be forgotten and left to get on with our lives as best we can and nobody will mind us.'

The Major's arguments were at an end. Eduard, beyond any possibility of a change of view, was treating the matter as a decided fact, and had moved on to discuss in detail how it might all be arranged, and in the cheerfulest manner, even jestingly, was expatiating upon the future.

Then becoming serious and thoughtful he said: 'Were we to trust to the hope or the expectation that everything will work itself out and that chance will guide and favour us, we should be criminally deluding ourselves. We cannot possibly save ourselves that way, nor restore a communal peace of mind; and how will I ever console myself, having innocently caused it all? I pestered Charlotte into inviting you to live with us, and Ottilie only came as a consequence of that change. We cannot undo what ensued, but we can render it harmless and direct our circumstances for our own happiness. If you will not contemplate the smiling prospects I have opened up for us, if you impose on me, impose on us all, a sad renunciation, in so far as you think that possible and in so far as it might really be possible, surely in that case also, if we resolve to return to our former conditions, much unpleasantness, inconvenience, and bitterness will return there with us, and still nothing good or cheerful ever come of it. Would your present happy situation give you any pleasure if you were prevented from visiting me and living in my house? And after what has happened it would be bound to be always painful. Charlotte and I, with all our wealth, would be in a poor state. And if like other men of the world you are inclined to think that absence and the passage of the years will dull such feelings and expunge such deeply graven marks, then, precisely, it is those years we are speaking of, and we wish to spend them not in pain and doing without but in well-being and joy. And lastly let me put to you the most important consideration of all. Though we, our inner lives and our material lives being what they are, might at a pinch be able to bear these things, what will become of Ottilie who would have to leave our house and in society do without our loving care and make shift pitiably in the cold and wicked world? Describe to me any circumstances in which Ottilie might be happy without me, without us, and then you will have uttered a stronger argument than any other and one which, even if I cannot concede it, cannot bow to it, I will nevertheless very gladly add to the debate.'

This was no easy task, at least no sufficient answer occurred to Eduard's friend, and all he could do was insist again and again how serious, worrying, and in many senses dangerous the whole enterprise was, and that at the very least they must consider with all possible earnestness how best to manage it. Eduard agreed, but on condition that his friend would not leave him until they were entirely of one mind in the matter and had taken the first steps.

CHAPTER THIRTEEN

EVEN people who are entirely strange and indifferent to one another will exchange confidences if they live together for a while, and a certain intimacy is bound to develop. All the more then is it to be expected that our two friends, being side by side, daily and hourly in each other's company, kept nothing back. They revived the memory of their earlier circumstances, and the Major revealed that Charlotte had intended Ottilie for Eduard when he came back from his travels, that it had been her intention to marry the beautiful child to him when the time was right. Eduard, beside himself with delight at this disclosure, spoke without any restraint now about the mutual affection of Charlotte and the Major, depicting it, since it suited and favoured him, in the liveliest colours.

The Major could neither entirely deny nor entirely concede it; but Eduard only grew firmer and more definite. Everything seemed to him not merely possible but already achieved. All parties only needed to agree to do what they in fact wished to do; a divorce could certainly be got; soon after there would be a marriage, and Eduard would leave with Ottilie.

None among all the mind's sweet fantasies are sweeter than those of lovers and persons newly married when they look forward to the enjoyment of their fresh new relationship in a fresh new world and to the testing and confirmation of a lasting union in circumstances that are forever changing. The Major and Charlotte, meanwhile, were to have complete authority over everything concerning property, wealth, and all other things desirable and needful in the world, and make such arrangements and fairly and properly initiate such courses of action as would leave all the parties satisfied. But the thing Eduard seemed to take more than any other as his

342

basis and from which he seemed to be promising himself the greatest advantage was this: since a child ought to remain with its mother, the Major would be able to bring the boy up, guide him according to his lights, and develop his gifts. Not for nothing then had he been christened with the name they shared: Otto.

This had all become so decided in Eduard's mind that he was reluctant to linger even one more day before beginning to make it a reality. On their way towards the estate they arrived in a small town where Eduard owned a house, and there he would stay and wait for the Major to return. But he could not bring himself to halt, and accompanied his friend further, through the town. They were both on horseback and, being involved in serious conversation, they rode on together, further still.

Suddenly in the distance they saw the new house on the ridge, saw for the first time its red tiles catch the light. Eduard was seized by a longing he could not withstand; it must all be settled the same evening. He would remain in hiding in a village very close by; the Major would put the matter to Charlotte with every degree of urgency, overwhelm her cautiousness, and force her by the unexpected proposition into the frank revelation of her sentiments. For Eduard, transferring his own desires on to her, fully believed that he was answering her own decided wishes, and hoped to have her agreement so rapidly because he was incapable of wishing for anything else.

A happy outcome shone before his eyes, and so that it should be speedily announced to him lurking there, a few cannon shots were to be fired off and, if it were already dark, a few rockets sent up.

The Major rode towards the Hall. He did not find Charlotte; on the contrary, he learned that at present she was living in the new house on the ridge, but was just then visiting in the neighbourhood and might be some time yet before returning home. He went back to the inn where he had left his horse.

Eduard meanwhile, driven by an impatience he could not master, crept from his hiding-place, on remote paths known only to fishermen and hunters, in the direction of the park and towards evening had arrived among the bushes near the lake whose surface he saw now for the first time pure and entire.

That afternoon Ottilie had walked out to the lake. She was carrying the child and reading as she walked in her usual way. She reached the oaks at the crossing-point. The boy had fallen asleep; she sat down, laid him beside her, and went on reading. The book was one of those that draws a tender-hearted reader in and will not let go. She forgot time and the hour and that over land she would have a long way back to the new house; but she sat lost in her book, in herself, such a sweet sight that the trees and the bushes around her ought to have been given life and eyes to admire her and take delight in her. And at that moment a warm light from the setting sun shone in behind her and gilded her shoulder and her cheek.

Eduard, having made his way so far unseen, finding his park empty and the whole vicinity deserted, was emboldened to advance even further. Finally he emerged from among the bushes near the oak trees; he saw Ottilie and she him; he ran to her and lay at her feet. After a long silence, in which both struggled to compose themselves, he explained to her briefly why and how he had come. He had sent the Major to Charlotte, the course of all their lives was perhaps being decided at that very moment. He had never doubted her love and she, he was sure, had never doubted his. He begged her to consent. She hesitated, he besought her; he was ready to assert his former rights and enfold her in his arms; she pointed to the child.

Eduard looked, and was amazed. 'Dear God,' he cried, 'if I had any reason to be suspicious of my wife and my friend this living shape would tell against them terribly. Is he not the image of the Major? I never saw such a likeness.'

'No, no,' said Ottilie in reply, 'everyone says he is like me.'

'Can that be possible?' said Eduard, and at that moment the child opened its eyes, two large, black penetrating eyes, profound and affectionate. The boy already viewed the world so understandingly; he seemed to know them both standing there before him. Eduard threw himself down by the child, then again he knelt before Ottilie. 'It is you!' he cried. 'Those are your eyes. But yours, your own, are the only ones I want to look into. Let me cast a veil over the ill-fated hour that gave this creature life. Shall I frighten your pure soul with the unhappy thought that a man and wife, estranged, in their embraces may defile a legal union by their real living desires? Or since we have come so far, since my relationship with Charlotte must be brought to an end, since you will be mine, why should I not say it? And I will, though it is harsh: this child was begotten and conceived in a double adultery! It severs me from my wife and my wife from me when it ought to have united us. May it be a witness against me, and may those beautiful eyes tell yours that in the arms of another woman I belonged to you, and may you feel, Ottilie, truly feel, that only in your arms can I expiate that error, that crime.

'Hark!' he cried, and sprang up, believing he had heard a shot, the sign the Major had agreed to give. It was a hunter, shooting, on the hills nearby. Nothing followed; Eduard was impatient.

Only now did Ottilie notice that the sun had sunk behind the mountains. Its light still shone a moment off the windows of the house on the ridge. 'Go now, Eduard,' Ottilie cried. 'We have done without one another so long and have been patient so long. Think what we owe Charlotte, both of us. She must decide, do not let us pre-empt her. I am yours if she allows it; if not I must give you up. Since you think the decision will be very soon, let us wait. Go back to the village where the Major thinks you are. There may be any number of things that need to be explained. Is it likely he will fire off a gun? That would be a very crude way of announcing the success of his negotiations. He may be looking for you at this very moment. I do know that he has not seen Charlotte.

He may have gone to meet her, they knew where she went to. But how many things might have happened! Leave me now! She must be back any minute. She will be expecting me up there with the child.'

Ottilie spoke in haste. She was imagining all the possibilities. She was happy there with Eduard and felt that now she must make him go away. 'I beg you, my love, I beseech you!' she cried. 'Go back and wait for the Major.' 'I shall do as you ask,' Eduard cried, first gazing at her full of love and clasping her tightly in his arms. She enfolded him in hers and pressed him lovingly against her heart. Hope, like a star falling from heaven, soared above their heads and away. It seemed to them they belonged to one another, they believed it; for the first time ever they gave and received kisses that were sure and free, and when they parted it was like an act of violence and they suffered pain.

The sun had gone down, it was getting dark, there were damp scents around the lake. Ottilie stood confused and agitated; she looked across to the house on the hill and thought she saw Charlotte's white dress on the balcony. The detour round the lake was a long one; she knew how impatiently Charlotte would be waiting for the child. She could see the plane trees opposite, only a stretch of water was between her and the path which climbed directly to the house. In her thoughts she was already over, as she was with her eyes. The risk of going on the water with the child vanished in her urgency. She hurried to the boat, was unaware that her heart was pounding, her feet unsteady, her senses threatening to desert her.

She sprang into the boat, seized an oar, and pushed off. It was hard, she had to push again with some force, and the boat rocked and glided a little way out on to the lake. She had the child on her left arm, the book in her left hand, the oar in her right and she unbalanced herself, with the rocking, and fell into the boat. She lost the oar on one side and, as she sought to steady herself, the child and the book on the other, all overboard. She managed to seize hold of the child's clothing;

but her awkward position prevented her from getting up. Her free right hand was insufficient to help her turn and rise; when at last she succeeded and dragged the child out of the water its eyes were closed and it had ceased to breathe.

At that moment all her good sense returned to her, but her anguish, correspondingly, was all the greater. The boat was drifting near the middle of the lake, the oar was far away, she could see no one on the land and how would it have helped her had she seen anyone? Cut off from everything, she drifted on the faithless element as its prisoner.

She sought her own help. So often she had heard of the resuscitation of the drowned. She had witnessed it on the evening of her birthday. She undressed the child and dried him with her own muslin skirt. She tore open her bodice and for the first time showed her breasts uncovered under the open sky; for the first time ever she pressed something living against her pure and naked bosom, alas! – not living at all. The cold limbs of the unfortunate creature chilled her bosom through into her innermost heart. Tears welled without end from her eyes and cast over the stiffened form a semblance of warmth and life. She would not let up, she wrapped him in her shawl, and thought by caressing him and pressing him close and breathing on him and by her kisses and her tears to compensate for all the remedies denied her where she was, cut off.

All in vain! The child lay motionless in her arms, and the boat motionless on the surface of the water; but even then her sweet spirit did not give her up to helplessness. She looked for help above. She fell on her knees in the boat and with both hands lifted up the stiffened child above her innocent bosom which in its whiteness and also, alas, in its coldness was like marble. Tearfully she looked up and cried for help from where a feeling heart will always hope to find abundance when the lack of it is all around.

And nor was it in vain that she appealed to the stars which one by one were now beginning to shine. A breeze arose and drove the boat towards the plane trees.

CHAPTER FOURTEEN

SHE hurried to the new house, called for the Surgeon, handed him the child. Never unprepared, he treated the infant corpse step by step according to his accustomed method. Ottilie aided him in everything; fetched, carried, saw to whatever was needed, existing in another world, it is true, for the greatest unhappiness, like the greatest happiness, changes the appearance of all things; and only when the Surgeon, at the end of his efforts and his science, shook his head and answered her hopeful questions first with silence then with a gentle 'No', only then did she leave Charlotte's bedroom where all this had taken place, and scarcely had she entered the living-room than, unable to reach the sofa, she fell exhausted headlong, face-down on the carpet.

They heard Charlotte draw up. The Surgeon begged those present to keep back, he would meet her, prepare her; but she had already entered the room. She found Ottilie on the floor, and a maid rushed towards her screaming and in tears. The Surgeon entered and she learned everything at once. But how should she give up every hope at once? Experienced, skilled, and wise, he begged her not to look at the child; he withdrew, pretending there was more he might try. She sat on the sofa, Ottilie still lay on the floor, but raised now to her friend's knees, her beautiful head resting there. The Surgeon came and went, seemed to be seeing to the child, but was seeing to the women. So it came to midnight, and the stillness of death grew deeper and deeper. Charlotte no longer pretended that the child would come back to life; she asked to see him. He had been laid in clean, warm, woollen wraps, in a cradle, which they set next to her on the sofa, only the little face uncovered; he lay there at peace, beautiful.

The accident had soon excited the village and word of it at once reached the inn. The Major had taken the familiar path up the hill; he went round the house and, catching a servant who was running to fetch something from the annex, he informed himself more fully, and asked that the Surgeon be sent out to him. The Surgeon came, and was astonished to see his old protector there; he told him how things stood, and undertook to prepare Charlotte for his appearance. He went back in, began to speak of things that would lead her thoughts away, and led her thus from one subject to another and at last brought her friend to mind, and to her spirit and to her feelings made his certain sympathy, his presence, palpable, and so from there soon passed to the reality. In short, she learned that her friend was at the door, knew everything, and desired to be admitted.

The Major entered; Charlotte greeted him with a painful smile. He stood before her. She lifted the green silk coverlet which concealed the corpse, and in the dark light of a candle he saw, with a thrill of horror which he managed to conceal, his frozen image. Charlotte pointed to a chair and so they sat, in silence, facing one another, all night through. Ottilie still lay quietly, her head in Charlotte's lap; she was breathing gently; she slept, or seemed to sleep.

It began to get light, the candle went out, the two friends seemed to wake from a heavy dream. Charlotte looked at the Major and said composedly: 'Explain to me, my dear friend, what fate brings you here to share in this spectacle of grief?'

'This is no time,' the Major replied, as softly as he had been asked, as though they were afraid of waking Ottilie, 'this is neither the time nor the place to hold back or lead in gently. The situation I find you in is so monstrous that my reasons for coming here, important though they are, lose their value by comparison.'

Thereupon he disclosed to her, very calmly and simply, what the purpose of his mission was, in so far as Eduard had sent him; and what the purpose of his coming was, in so far as his own free will and his own interest were concerned. He presented both very gently, but honestly; Charlotte listened, kept her composure, and seemed neither surprised nor angered.

When the Major had finished Charlotte replied, so softly that he was obliged to move his chair nearer. 'I have never been in such a situation before,' she said, 'but in situations at all resembling this I have always asked myself: "How will it be tomorrow?" I feel very keenly that I hold the fates of a number of people in my hands, and there is no doubt in my mind as to what I should do. It is soon said. I agree to a divorce. I ought to have agreed to it sooner; by hesitating, by resisting, I have killed the child. There are certain things which Fate determines on very obstinately. Reason and virtue, duty and everything holy stand in its way in vain. Something is set to happen as Fate sees fit but which to us does not seem fit; and at length it will accomplish its own end however we behave.

'But what am I saying? Really, all Fate is doing is to set my own wishes and my own intentions on course again, when I was foolish enough to work against them. Did I not myself think Eduard and Ottilie the best possible couple and join them in my thoughts? Did I not seek to bring them together? And were you not yourself, my dear friend, my accessory in this plan? And why could I not distinguish mere insistency from true love? Why did I accept his hand in marriage when as his friend I should have made him and another wife happy? And only look at this unhappy sleeper here. I tremble to think of the moment when she will wake out of this sleep which is almost a death and be conscious again. How shall she live, how shall she be comforted, if she may not hope through her love to give back to Eduard what she, as the instrument of the strangest chance, has robbed him of? And she can give him back everything, seeing how devotedly and passionately she loves him. Love can bear anything, but it can do much more than that: make good everything. There must be no thought of my own position at this time.

'Go now while it is quiet, my dear Major. Tell Eduard I agree to a divorce and that I leave it to him, you, Mittler, to initiate it; that I am easy in my mind as regards my future situation, and in every sense have reason to be. I will sign any paper you bring me; but please do not ask me to play any active part or give any thought to it or offer an opinion.'

The Major rose. She gave him her hand across the sleeping Ottilie. He pressed it to his lips. 'And for myself,' he whispered, 'what am I permitted to hope?'

'Do not oblige me to give you an answer now,' said Charlotte in reply. 'We have not done anything to deserve unhappiness, but nor have we deserved to be happy together either.'

The Major left. Though he felt the deepest sympathy for Charlotte he could not grieve over the poor departed child. Such a sacrifice seemed to him necessary for the happiness of them all. He thought of Ottilie with her own child in her arms as the best possible compensation for what she had caused Eduard to lose; he thought of a son in his own lap who would be the image of himself with more right than the one who had died.

Such flattering hopes and images were passing through his soul when on his way back to the inn he met Eduard, who had spent the whole night out of doors waiting for the Major, with never any sign of fire or noise of thunder announcing the success. He had heard of the unhappy accident and he too, instead of grieving over the poor creature, saw this event, though he would not quite admit it to himself, as an act of providence by which everything in the way of his happiness was instantly removed. Thus he was easily persuaded by the Major, who lost no time in telling him of his wife's decision, to return to the village and from there to the little town where they would consider and initiate what needed doing next.

When the Major had gone Charlotte sat only a few moments longer sunk in her own thoughts, for then Ottilie sat up, looking at her friend with wide eyes. First she raised herself from Charlotte's lap, then from the floor, and stood before her.

'It has happened again' – so the extraordinary child began with an irresistible seriousness and grace – 'the same thing has happened to me again. You said to me once that similar things often happen to people in their lives in a similar way, and always at important moments. Now I see that what you said is true, and I feel impelled to confess something. Shortly after my mother's death, when I was a little child, I had pushed my stool up close against you. You were sitting on the sofa as you are now; my head was on your knees, I was not asleep, I was not awake, I was between the two. I could hear everything that was going on around me, and especially everything that was being said, very clearly; and yet I could not stir, or speak, or indicate, even if I had wanted to, that I felt conscious of myself. You were talking with a friend about me at the time; you were pitying me, being left a poor orphan in the world; you were describing my condition of dependence, and how doubtful my prospects were unless some particular lucky star came and shone over me. I comprehended everything you seemed to be wishing for me and everything you seemed to be asking of me, I comprehended it all perfectly and exactly, only perhaps too strictly. And on the basis of my limited insights I made rules for myself concerning all those things; for a long time now I have lived in accordance with those rules, have done things or not done things as they dictated, in the days when you loved me and cared for me and when you took me into your house and for some time after that.

'But I went off course, I broke my rules, I have even lost my sense of them, and after a terrible occurrence again you have enlightened me about my situation, which is more wretched than the first one was. Lying in your lap, half-stricken, again, as out of another world, I heard you speaking softly above my ear. I heard what my situation appears to be, I shuddered at my own self; but as on the previous occasion so too on this, in my sleep that was half like death I have set out my new course for myself.

'I have decided, as I did then, and what I have decided I must tell you at once. I will never be Eduard's. In a terrible fashion God has opened my eyes to the crime in which I am caught up. I will atone for it; and do not anybody seek to dissuade me from my intention. Dearest friend, take what steps you must in the light of that. Have the Major come back; write to him that nothing must happen. What anguish I felt that I could not move or stir when he was leaving. I wanted to jump up and cry out that you must not let him go with such criminal hopes.'

Charlotte saw Ottilie's condition, and felt it; but she hoped that in time and by argument she would be able to sway her. But when she said one or two words that suggested a future, a lessening of grief, some hope – 'No,' cried Ottilie in exalted tones. 'Let none of you try to move me or cheat me. The moment I hear you have agreed to a divorce, in that selfsame lake I will atone for my offence and crime.'

CHAPTER FIFTEEN

When people are living peacefully and happily together more time is spent than is necessary or proper in discussing things that have happened or ought to happen; relations, friends, others in the house are forever swapping plans and the details of their projects and occupations, and without exactly ever taking advice from one another they do nevertheless go through the motions of seeking it on every occasion. At times of crisis, on the other hand, when it might be thought that a person would be most in need of assistance and support, the individuals all withdraw into themselves, everyone tries to act for himself, everyone in his own way, and the particular means all being thus concealed, only the outcome, the ends, the thing achieved, become common property again.

After so many wondrous and unhappy events a certain quiet seriousness had come over the two friends, expressing itself as a sweet regard for one another's feelings. With all secrecy Charlotte had removed the child to the chapel. It rested there as the first victim of the fate still lowering over them.

Charlotte, so far as she was able to, turned her attention to living again, and found Ottilie the first in need of her support. She paid her very particular attention, without letting it appear so. She knew how much the heavenly girl loved Eduard; little by little, partly from Ottilie herself and partly from the Major in letters, she had learned every detail of what had happened before the calamity.

Ottilie for her part did much to lighten Charlotte's immediate life. She was open, even talkative, but there was never any mention of the present nor of the recent past. She had always been attentive, always observant, she was knowledgeable; all that became apparent now. She entertained and

354

diverted Charlotte, who still secretly hoped to see the union of two people so dear to her.

But Ottilie had a different sense of things. She had disclosed to her friend the secret of how she lived; she was released from her earlier constraints and subservience. By her remorse, by her decision, she also felt freed from the weight of her misfortune and offence. She needed no further law over herself; in the depths of her heart she had forgiven herself, but on one condition, which was complete renunciation; and there could be no release from that condition, ever.

So a little time passed, and Charlotte felt how much the house and the park, the lakes, the rocks and trees daily renewed in both of them only sadness. It was clear they must leave the place, but how was not so easy to decide.

Should the two women remain together? Eduard's earlier wishes seemed to demand it, his declaration, his threat, to make it necessary; but there could be no disguising the fact that the two women, for all their goodwill, their reasonableness, and their efforts, were in a painful situation being together. Their conversations were evasive. Sometimes they were content to only half-understand a thing, but often an expression might be misinterpreted nevertheless, if not by the mind then by the feelings. They were fearful of hurting one another, and precisely in that fear they were most likely to be hurt, and also to hurt.

If they were to move from there and also, for a time at least, lead separate lives, the old question arose: where should Ottilie go? That great and wealthy house already mentioned had tried in vain to find girls to live in with the promising young heiress, to entertain her and compete with her. When the Baroness had last visited, and recently again in letters, Charlotte had been urged to send Ottilie there; now Charlotte mentioned it herself. But Ottilie refused categorically to go where she would encounter what we call society.

'My dear aunt,' she said, 'so that I shall not seem narrow-minded and obstinate, let me say something which in other circumstances it would be one's duty to keep quiet about and conceal. Any peculiarly unhappy person, even if he is blameless, is marked in a terrible way. His presence excites a sort of horror wherever he is seen and noticed. Everyone searches his appearance for traces of the monstrous fate which has been laid upon him; everyone is curious and at the same time fearful. In the same way a house or a town in which something monstrous has happened remains frightful to anyone entering it. Daylight is not so bright there and the stars seem to lose their radiance.

'How great, and yet perhaps excusable, are the indiscretion, the silly intrusiveness, and clumsy goodwill shown towards unhappy persons of that kind. Forgive me for speaking like this; but I suffered unbelievably with that poor girl when Luciane fetched her out of her secluded rooms, took a friendly interest in her, and with the best intentions tried to make her join in the dancing and the games. When the poor child grew more and more anxious and in the end fled and fainted, when I held her in my arms and people were alarmed, excited, and everyone more than ever was curious to look at the unfortunate girl, I never thought a fate like that awaited me. The pity I felt then, which was true and intense, is still alive. Now I can apply that pity to myself and see to it that I am never the occasion of such a scene.'

'But my dear child,' said Charlotte in reply, 'where could you go and not be seen by people? We have no nunneries nowadays where feelings such as yours used to be able to find sanctuary.'

'It is not solitude which gives sanctuary, my dear aunt,' said Ottilie in reply. 'Sanctuary of the most valuable kind is to be found in places where we can be busy. Penance and deprivation, in whatever amount, are not at all the best way to escape a fate we feel is determined to hunt us down. Only if I have to be idle and be on show to people are they antipathetic and frightening to me. But if I can be cheerfully busy and tirelessly doing my duty then I do not mind what human eyes are looking at me, because then I can face the eyes of heaven too.'

'Unless I am very much mistaken,' said Charlotte in reply, 'you are inclined to go back to the school.'

'Yes,' Ottilie replied, 'I do not deny it. I think it would be a very happy calling to educate others along the usual ways when my own education has been along the strangest. And has it not happened in history that people who, on account of grievous moral accidents, have gone into the wilderness were by no means hidden and shielded there as they had hoped? They were called back into the world to lead the lost on to the proper paths again, which they could do better than anybody else, being themselves already initiated into the errors of life. They were called to help the unfortunate, and could do so supremely well, having themselves already met with every earthly misfortune.'

'That is a strange choice of vocation,' Charlotte replied, 'but I shall not oppose you. So be it, if only, as I hope, for a short time.'

'I am very grateful to you,' said Ottilie, 'for allowing me this trial, this experience. I may be deluding myself, but I do think it will work. In that place I shall remember the ordeals I went through, and how small, how negligible they were compared with those I have had to go through since. I shall contemplate the youngsters' difficulties quite serenely, smile over their childish griefs, and lead them with a gentle hand out of all their little confusions. Happiness is no qualification for a person in charge of happy people. Whoever has received a great deal will ask a great deal of himself and of others. That is human nature. Only an unhappy person, who is recovering, knows how to nourish for himself and for others the sense that even a moderate good should be enjoyed with intense delight.'

'Let me say one more thing against your plan,' said Charlotte at last, after some thought, 'and it seems to me the most important thing of all. I am not thinking of you but of another person. The Assistant, who is a good, sensible, and pious man, has feelings which are known to you. Proceeding as you intend to, you will become more precious and indispensable to him every day. Since already, his feelings being what they are, he is unhappy living without you, he will in future, having grown used to your working at his side, no longer be able to do his job without you. Being first a source of strength to him in his work, you will finish by making him hate it.'

'Fate has not dealt kindly with me,' said Ottilie in reply, 'and perhaps whoever loves me cannot expect much better. But since our friend is so good and sensible he will, I hope, in his feelings develop a pure relationship with me. He will see in me somebody consecrated, who has a hope of countering a monstrous evil for herself and others only if she dedicates herself to that holy power which, invisibly all around us, can alone protect us against the monstrous forces that are pressing in.'

All this, uttered by the sweet child with such conviction, Charlotte took in, to reflect upon it quietly later. In various ways, but always very gently, she had tried to ascertain whether any rapprochement of Ottilie and Eduard were thinkable; but even the gentlest mention, the faintest expression of a hope, the smallest suspicion seemed to agitate Ottilie to the depths; indeed, on one occasion, when she could not avoid doing so, she spoke her mind on the subject quite unequivocally.

'If your decision to give up Eduard is so firm and unalterable,' Charlotte said to her, 'then only beware of ever seeing him again. Away from the person we love, the intenser our feelings are the more we seem to gain mastery over ourselves, because we turn inwards the whole violence of the passion, which formerly extended outwards from ourselves; but how soon, how rapidly we are undeceived when the person we thought ourselves able to do without suddenly stands before us again, and doing without him is impossible. Do what you think most suitable to your situation. Be sure. Indeed, it would be better to change your mind, but of your own accord, of your own free volition and inclination. Do not let yourself be dragged back into the earlier state of affairs by accident or by surprise, for then there really will be a division in your soul, and one that will not be bearable. As I have said, before you take this step, before you go away from me and begin a new life which will lead you who knows where, ask yourself once again whether you can really give up Eduard for ever and ever. But if you say you can then let it be agreed between us that you will have nothing to do with him, will not even speak with him if he should come looking for you and force his way into your presence.' With not a moment's further thought Ottilie gave Charlotte the promise she had already given herself.

But now Charlotte was mindful of the threat Eduard had made that he could only be without Ottilie so long as she stayed with Charlotte. Admittedly their circumstances had changed since then, so much had happened that those words forced from him by the moment were to be thought of as annulled by subsequent events; nevertheless she did not care to risk doing anything that might conceivably offend him, and so Mittler was asked to ascertain what Eduard's feelings would be.

Since the death of the child Mittler had often visited Charlotte, if only briefly. The accident, which made the reunion of man and wife seem to him extremely improbable, had troubled him greatly; but it was in his nature to be always hopeful, always striving for the best, and privately now he was delighted by Ottilie's decision. He trusted to the soothing passage of time, still thought he might hold husband and wife together, and saw these passionate agitations only as trials of marital love and fidelity.

At the outset Charlotte had informed the Major by letter of Ottilie's first declaration, and implored him to persuade Eduard to take no further steps; rather they should keep calm and wait and see whether the beautiful child's spirits might recover. And she had also told him all he needed to know about events and feelings since then, and now Mittler had been given the difficult job of preparing Eduard for a change in the situation. But Mittler, knowing that it is easier to get acceptance of an accomplished fact than the agreement to accomplish it, persuaded Charlotte that it would be best to send Ottilie to the school at once.

Accordingly, as soon as he had gone, they made preparations for the journey. Ottilie packed her things, but Charlotte noticed that she intended taking neither the beautiful box nor anything out of it. She said nothing, and let the girl, who also said nothing, do as she wished. The day of her departure arrived; Charlotte's carriage was to convey Ottilie on the first day as far as a place they knew where she would spend the night, and on the second as far as the school; Nanni was to accompany her, and remain as her maid. The passionate little girl had made her way back to Ottilie immediately after the death of the child, and by nature and affection was as attached to her now as ever; indeed, she seemed in her entertaining garrulousness to be seeking to make up for what she had missed and to devote herself to her beloved mistress utterly. She was quite beside herself with joy at going on the journey and seeing new places, since she had never left home before, and ran from the Hall to the village, to her parents, her relatives, announcing her happiness and saying goodbye. Unfortunately in so doing she went into rooms where children were sick with the measles and was at once infected. They did not wish to postpone the journey; Ottilie herself insisted on going, she had done it before, knew the people who kept the inn where she would stay, the coachman from the Hall was driving her; there was nothing to worry about.

Charlotte made no objection; in her thoughts she was herself already hurrying away from the surroundings of her home; only she first wanted to put the rooms Ottilie had lived in back as they were before the arrival of the Captain, for Eduard. Hopes of restoring a former happiness will rise in a person again and again, and once more now Charlotte had a right to such hopes, indeed a need for them.

CHAPTER SIXTEEN

WHEN Mittler arrived to discuss the matter with Eduard he found him alone, leaning on the table and pressing his right hand against his head. He seemed to be in great pain. 'Is your headache troubling you again?' Mittler asked.

'It is troubling me,' Eduard replied, 'but I cannot hate it for doing so, since it reminds me of Ottilie. Perhaps she is in pain herself at this very moment, leaning on her left arm, and doubtless more in pain than I am. And why should I not bear it as she does? The pain is good for me, I can almost say I am glad of it, it brings the image of her patience, accompanied by all her other virtues, ever-more intensely, clearly, vividly into my soul. Only in suffering do we feel with perfect complete-ness all the great qualities necessary to bear it.'

Finding his friend so resigned Mittler did not hold back with what he had come to say, but he delivered it stage by stage, as a narrative: how the thought had occurred to the women, how gradually then it had ripened into an intention. Eduard made almost no objection. What little he said seemed to imply that he would leave it all to them; the pain he was in seemed to have made him indifferent to everything.

But as soon as he was alone he stood up and paced the room. He no longer felt his pain, he was entirely preoccupied outside himself. Even during Mittler's narrative his imagina-tion, the imagination of a man in love, had been intensely at work. He saw Ottilie, alone or as good as, on a route he knew well, in a familiar inn whose rooms he had so often entered; he thought, he pondered, or rather he did neither; all he did was desire and want. He had to see her, speak to her. To what end, why, what could come of it? No matter. He did not resist, he had to.

His valet was taken into his confidence, and had soon found out the day and the hour of Ottilie's journey. The morning dawned; without delay Eduard set off alone on horseback to where Ottilie would spend the night. He arrived far too early; the astonished landlady greeted him joyfully; she owed him thanks for a great good fortune in her family. He had got her son decorated for bravery in the field by making a particular mention of his deed, which he alone had been present at, and by vigorously bringing it to the attention of the commander-in-chief and overcoming the objections of a few ill-wishers. She hardly knew where to begin in her efforts to please him. Quickly she tidied up as well as possible in her best parlour, which was also, it must be admitted, her cloak-room and pantry; but he announced that a young lady would be arriving, and got her to prepare a room for him, in a rough-and-ready way, on the corridor at the back of the house. The landlady thought it mysterious, and was delighted to do something for her benefactor, who clearly had an interest in the matter and was very busy about it. He himself, in what emotion he spent the long long time till evening! He looked about the room in which he would see her; in all its domestic strangeness it seemed to him a heavenly abode. He thought and thought: whether he should surprise Ottilie or prepare her first. In the end the latter view prevailed; he sat down and wrote. She was to receive this letter.

Eduard to Ottilie

'Dearest, when you read this letter I shall be near to you. Do not be frightened, do not be horrified, you have nothing to fear from me. I shall not force myself upon you. You will not see me until you allow it.

'First think of your position and of mine. How grateful I am to you that you are not intending to take any conclusive step; but what you have in mind to do is serious enough. Don't do it. Here, at a sort of crossroads, think again: Can you be mine, will you be mine? Oh, you would do us all a great good, and me an immeasurable one.

'Let me see you again, see you again joyfully. Let me put my beautiful question to you with the words of my mouth

and you answer it with the beauty of your person. Come into
my arms, Ottilie, where I have held you once or twice and
where you belong always.'

As he wrote he was seized by the feeling that now what he
longed for more than anything was approaching, would at
any moment be there, present. 'She will come in at this door,'
he said to himself, 'she will read this letter, she will be really
here, as she used to be, after all my longing for her to appear.
Will she still be the same? Will she look the same? Have her
feelings changed?' He was holding the pen in his hand and
was about to set down what he was thinking; but the carriage
rolled into the yard. In haste he added: 'I hear you arriving.
Farewell, but only for a moment.'

   He folded the letter and wrote her name on it; there was no
time to seal it. He hurried into the bedroom from where he
knew a way on to the corridor, and at once it occurred to him
that he had left his watch and seal on the table. He did not
wish her to see these things first; he hurried back, and
retrieved them. In the hall he could hear the landlady, she
was already approaching the room, to show the guest in. He
ran to the door of the bedroom, but it had closed. He had
caused the key to fall out as he ran through, it lay on the other
side, the lock had sprung shut, he stood as if in a trance. With
some violence then he pressed against the door; it would not
give. How he wished he were a ghost and could slip through
the crack! All in vain. He hid his face against the doorpost.
Ottilie came in, the landlady, seeing him, withdrew. Not for
one moment could he remain hidden from Ottilie either. He
turned to her, and so the lovers faced one another again, in
the strangest fashion. She looked at him calmly and earnestly,
neither advancing nor retreating, and when he made a move
to approach her she stepped back a few paces as far as the
table. He too then stepped back. 'Ottilie,' he cried, 'let me
break this terrible silence. Are we only shades that we face
one another thus? But listen at least. It is an accident that you
have come upon me here immediately. There you have a

letter which was to have prepared you. Read it, I beg you, read it. And then decide what you can.'

She looked down at the letter, thought for a while, then took it up, opened it, read it. Her expression did not change as she was reading, and likewise she laid it gently aside; then, raising her hands and pressing the palms together, she brought them to her breast, inclining herself very slightly, and looked with such a look at the impassioned and demanding man that he was obliged to desist from demanding or desiring anything. That gesture rent his heart. He could not bear how Ottilie looked nor the posture of her body. It seemed certain that she would fall to her knees if he persisted. He ran from the room in despair and sent the landlady in to the solitary girl.

He paced up and down in the hall. It had grown dark, there was silence in the room. At last the landlady appeared and took the key out of the lock. The woman was moved, embarrassed, she did not know what she should do. In the end, as she was leaving, she offered the key to Eduard, who refused it. She left the light burning and went away.

Eduard in deepest grief threw himself down on the threshold of Ottilie's room, and wept. Perhaps lovers in such proximity have never spent a sadder night.

Dawn broke; the coachman hustled, the landlady unlocked the room and went in. She found Ottilie asleep fully clothed. She went back and signalled to Eduard with a smile of sympathy. Both then approached the sleeping girl; but this sight too was more than Eduard could bear. The landlady did not have the heart to wake the child from her rest, she sat down opposite. At last Ottilie opened her beautiful eyes and stood up. She refused any breakfast, and then Eduard came in to her. He begged her to speak, to explain what she wanted. He swore he wanted only what she wanted; but she remained silent. Again, full of love and urgently, he asked would she be his. In the sweetest way, her eyes cast down, she shook her head in a gentle refusal. He asked did she want to go on to the school. She signified no, with indifference. But when he asked whether he might conduct her back to Charlotte, then with relief, inclining her head, she agreed. He hurried to the window to give the coachman orders; but behind him like lightning she had left the room, and was down the stairs and in the carriage. The coachman set off for home, Eduard following on horseback at a little distance.

CHAPTER SEVENTEEN

CHARLOTTE was greatly surprised to see Ottilie draw up in the courtyard and Eduard dash in on horseback immediately after her. She hurried to the door. Ottilie got out and approached with Eduard. With a violent eagerness she took hold of the hands of the man and wife and pressed them together, then ran to her room. Eduard flung himself into Charlotte's arms, and wept; there was no explanation he could give, he begged her to be patient with him, look after Ottilie, help her. Charlotte hurried to Ottilie's room, and went cold as she entered: it had already been entirely cleared, there were only the bare walls. It looked as vast as it did cheerless. Everything had been taken away, only the box was left, since nobody knew where to put it, left standing in the middle of the room. Ottilie lay on the floor embracing the box, her head on it. Charlotte knelt down by her, asked what had happened, and received no answer.

She left her maid, bringing refreshments, with Ottilie, and hurried to Eduard. She found him in the drawing-room; but he would tell her nothing either. He fell on his knees before her, bathed her hands in tears, fled to his rooms, and when she sought to follow him she was met by the valet who gave her what explanation he could. The rest she pieced together herself, then at once determinedly put her mind to what needed doing forthwith. Ottilie's room was restored with all speed. Eduard had found his own as he left them, down to the last scrap of paper.

The three seemed to resume their relations with one another, but Ottilie still would not speak and Eduard could do nothing but beg his wife to be patient, whilst seeming himself incapable of patience. Charlotte sent messengers to Mittler and to the Major. The first could not be found; the Major came. To him Eduard poured out his heart, confessed

every least detail, and so Charlotte learned what had happened, what had altered the situation so strangely and caused
such a turmoil of the emotions.

In the gentlest way she spoke about it with her husband.
Her one request was that for the present the girl should not
be subjected to any more persuasion. Eduard felt his wife's
worth, her love, her reasonableness; but his passion possessed him exclusively. Charlotte urged him not to lose
hope, she promised to agree to a divorce. He did not believe
it; he was in such a sickness that hope and faith were deserting
him in turn. He demanded that Charlotte should promise to
marry the Major; he was in the grip of an insane discontent.
Charlotte, to soothe him, to keep him from collapse, did as he
asked. She promised to marry the Major in the event of
Ottilie's agreeing to a union with Eduard, but only under
the express condition that for the time being the two men
would go away together. The Major had some business to
conduct in another part of the country for the court he was at,
and Eduard promised to go with him. They made their
preparations, and grew a little calmer since at least something
was being done.

Meanwhile it was noticeable that Ottilie was scarcely eating or drinking as she continued in her refusal to speak. They
sought to persuade her, she became distressed; they let her
be. And is it not a weakness in most of us that we shy away
from tormenting a person even for his own good? Charlotte
cast around for a remedy and at last hit upon the idea
of sending for the Assistant from the school since he had a
good deal of influence over Ottilie and had made friendly
enquiries after her failure to arrive – without, however,
receiving a reply.

They spoke of this intention when she was present, so that
she should not be surprised. She seemed not to agree to it; she
thought for a while; finally she appeared to have reached
some decision, she hurried to her room, and before it was
evening sent the following note to the others who were
still together.

Ottilie to her Friends

'Dear ones, why must I say outright what is self-evident? I have left my proper course and am not to be allowed to resume it. Even if I were at one with myself again, still in the world outside a malevolent spirit has me in its power and seems to be thwarting me.

'My intention to give up Eduard and go away from him was quite unqualified. I hoped I would not meet him again. It happened otherwise; he appeared before me even against his own will. Perhaps I took and interpreted my promise too literally that I would never have any conversation with him. But as my feeling and my conscience at that moment prompted me I fell silent, I became dumb before my friend, and now I have nothing more to say. The vows I have taken are very strict, and perhaps they would worry a person who had thought about them first; but I submitted to them on the spur of the moment, forced by my feelings. Let me persist in them as long as my heart commands. Do not call in anyone to negotiate with me. Do not press me to speak or to take more food and drink than I absolutely need. Help me over this time by your indulgence and your patience. I am young, young people recover quite unexpectedly. Let me be in your company, give me the joy of your love and the benefit of your conversation; but leave my inner self to me.'

The men's departure, long prepared for, was put off, because of delays in the business on which the Major was to be sent. This pleased Eduard. Ottilie's note had roused him again, her words, which gave both comfort and some hope, had encouraged him, he felt he had reason to go on steadfastly waiting, and suddenly declared that he would not leave. 'How foolish', he cried, 'to throw away deliberately and prematurely what we can least do without, what we need most, when, though its loss does threaten, we might still be able to preserve it. And why do such a thing? Really only so that a man may seem to have a will of his own and to be free to choose. In that ridiculous conceit I have often torn myself away from friends hours and even days too early, only so as not to be under the duress of the last, implacable moment. But this time I will stay. Why should I go away? Has she not already gone away from me? There is no likelihood that I will take her hand or hug her to my heart; I must not even think of it, I go cold at the thought. She has not gone away from me, she has risen above me.'

And so he stayed, as he wanted to and had to. But nothing could equal his well-being when he was in her company. And in her too the same feeling had remained; she was no more able than he was to escape that blessed necessity. Now as before they exerted an indescribable, almost magical power of attraction over one another. They were living under one roof; but even without exactly thinking of one another, busy with other things, pulled this way and that by the company they were in, still they drew near to one another. If they were in a room together before long they were standing or sitting side by side. Only complete nearness could make them tranquil, but then utterly tranquil, and this nearness was enough; neither a look, nor a word, nor a gesture, nor any contact was necessary, only a pure being together. Then they were not two people but only one in an unthinking and complete well-being, content with themselves and with the world. Had one of them been held fast at the far end of the house the other, little by little, involuntarily would have been impelled thither. Life was a mystery to them, and they found its solution only in each other's company.

Ottilie was altogether serene and calm, so that their minds could be entirely at rest on her account. She rarely left them, except that she had got their permission to eat alone. Only Nanni served her.

There is more repetition in a person's life than we suppose. His own nature is the immediate cause of it. Character, individuality, disposition, bent, locality, surroundings, and habits make up an entirety in which each person lives, as in an element, an atmosphere, and only in that element does he feel himself contented and at ease. And so we find human beings, about whose changeability there is so much complaint, after many years, to our amazement, not changed at all, and after an infinite number of inner and outward stimuli in fact unchangeable.

Thus now in our friends' daily lives together almost everything had resumed its former course. Still Ottilie, never speaking, expressed her helpful nature in many an act of kindness; and everyone likewise, after his or her own fashion. In this way their domestic round was the illusory image of their former lives, and it was forgivable that they should delude themselves into thinking things were still the same.

The autumn days, equal in length to those of spring, brought the company back indoors at exactly the same hour. The seasonal beauty of fruits and flowers was such that they could think this the autumn of that first spring; the time in between had fallen into oblivion. For now the kinds of flowers in bloom were those they had sown in those first days also; now fruits were ripening on the trees which then they had seen in blossom.

The Major came and went; Mittler too appeared from time to time. Their evening sessions mostly had the same pattern. Usually Eduard read aloud, and with a greater liveliness, with more feeling, better, indeed, as one might say, more cheerfully than before. It was as if he were seeking through gaiety as well as through passion to reanimate Ottilie out of her stone-coldness and to melt her silence. He sat as he had done formerly in such a way that she could read over his shoulder, indeed he was uneasy, distracted, if she were not doing so, if he were not certain that she was following the words with her eyes.

The disagreeable and uncomfortable feelings of their middle period had been entirely extinguished. No one had any grudge against anyone else; no bitterness of any kind remained. Charlotte played the piano, the Major accompanied her on the violin, and Ottilie's particular management of the keys came into unison, as formerly, with Eduard's flute. So they drew near to Eduard's birthday, whose celebration they had missed the previous year. This time it was to be celebrated quietly, by friends at ease, without festivities. That was the understanding they had arrived at, half tacitly, half expressly. But as the day approached so the solemnity of Ottilie's being, more felt than noticed till then, grew ever greater. In the garden it was often as though she were making an assessment of the flowers. She had directed the Gardener to spare all of the late summer blooms, and spent most time among the asters, which that year more than any other were flowering in extreme abundance.

CHAPTER EIGHTEEN

BUT most significantly, as the friends continued their silent observation of Ottilie, they saw that for the first time she had unpacked the chest, taken different things out of it, and cut them up to make an outfit of clothes, only one, but that full and complete. When with Nanni's help she tried then to pack the rest back in again she could hardly manage it. The space was overfilled even though a part had been taken out. The young girl gazed and gazed. She was desperate to have something for herself, especially when she saw that all the smaller items of an outfit were provided too. Shoes and stockings, embroidered garters, gloves, and numerous other things remained. She begged Ottilie to give her something from these. Ottilie refused, but at once opened a drawer in her dressing-table and let the child take what she liked. She did so, hastily and clumsily, and ran off with her booty to announce her good fortune to everyone else in the house and show them what she had got.

At last Ottilie managed to put everything back, in careful layers; then she opened a secret compartment let into the lid. There she had hidden Eduard's little notes and letters, a few dried flowers as reminders of earlier walks, a lock of her beloved's hair, and other things besides. Now she added one more thing – it was the portrait of her father – and locked the whole box, hanging the tiny key on its golden chain around her neck again, in her bosom.

All sorts of hopes meanwhile had been awakened in her friends. Charlotte was convinced that on the day itself she would begin to speak again; for there had been an air of secret busyness about her and of serene self-contentment, and she wore a smile such as shows on the face of a person harbouring something good and joyful for the ones he loves. Nobody knew that Ottilie was spending many hours in a condition of great weakness, and only by strength of spirit lifted herself out of it for the times when she appeared in company.

During this period Mittler had quite often called, and had stayed longer than formerly. Never one to give up, he knew he must not miss his chance if it presented itself. Ottilie's silence and refusal seemed to him auspicious. So far no steps had been taken towards a divorce; he hoped he might determine the poor girl's fate in some other and more favourable way. He listened, he made concessions, or he let it be thought that he had, and in his own fashion he acted sensibly enough.

But again and again it got the better of him if ever he had occasion to deliver an opinion on subjects he held to be very important. He lived a good deal in himself and when he was with other people his dealings with them mostly took the form of actions. If words burst forth from him in the company of friends then, as we have seen more than once already, they rolled on heedlessly, they hurt or healed, brought benefit or harm, just as it happened.

On the evening before Eduard's birthday Charlotte and the Major were sitting together waiting for Eduard who had ridden out. Mittler was walking up and down the room; Ottilie had remained in hers laying out her clothes for the next day and giving various directions to her maid, who understood her perfectly and did her silent bidding in a trice.

Mittler had just got on to one of his favourite topics. He was given to asserting that in the education of children, as in the government of peoples, nothing is more out of place and more barbaric than prohibitions, than laws and regulations which forbid. 'Human beings are born doers,' he said, 'and for anyone who knows how to manage them they will set to work at once and busy themselves and get things done. For my part I would rather put up with mistakes and failings around me until such time as I have the opposing virtues at my command, than get rid of the failings and have nothing proper to put in their place. People are very glad to do what is right and useful if they only can; they do it in order to have something to do, and think no more about it than about the stupidities they commit out of idleness and boredom.

'I have never liked listening to children being made to repeat the Ten Commandments. The fifth is fine and sensible, being a commandment to do something: "Honour thy father and thy mother." If the children really take that to heart they can spend all day practising it. But the sixth! I ask you: "Thou shalt do no murder." As though anyone had the slightest desire to murder anyone else. You might hate someone, grow angry, grow hasty, and as a consequence of one thing and another it might indeed happen that on occasion you strike somebody dead. But is it not a barbarous practice to forbid a child to commit an act of murder? Now if it said: Take care of your neighbour's life, put out of his way whatever might be harmful to him, save his life even at the risk of your own, if you harm him consider that you are harming yourself – those are commandments such as obtain among cultured and rational peoples, and all we have of them in our catechism is the poor addendum: "What dost thou learn by this?"

'And then the seventh! Really quite abominable! All it does is cause the wondering minds of children to lust after dangerous secrets, it excites their imaginations with such peculiar images and ideas that the very thing we are seeking to remove is brought forcibly into view. Far better to have things of that sort punished arbitrarily by secret courts than to have them gossiped about in front of the whole congregation.'

At that moment Ottilie came in. ' "Thou shalt not commit adultery," ' Mittler continued. 'How coarse, how very indecent! Now would it not sound quite different if it said: Show reverence for the marriage bond. Seeing a loving man and wife, be glad, take pleasure in it as you do in the happiness of a sunny day. Should any cloud come over their union, seek to dispel it, strive to appease and soothe them, make clear to them what advantages they have in one another, and with a beautiful selflessness further the good of others by making them sensible of the happiness that derives from every duty done and especially from this which binds a man and a woman together indissolubly.'

Charlotte sat in torment, all the worse since she felt sure that Mittler did not realize what he was saying and where he was saying it, and before she could interrupt him she saw Ottilie, altered in appearance, leave the room.

'You will spare us the eighth commandment,' said Charlotte with a forced smile. 'And all the others too,' said Mittler in reply, 'so long as I save the one on which all those others rest.'

There was a terrible scream. Nanni rushed in, crying: 'She is dying! Miss is dying! Oh, come quick!'

When Ottilie, staggering on her feet, had returned to her room, her fine clothes for the next morning lay all spread out across several chairs and the little girl, passing from one piece to the next in a wondering contemplation, exclaimed triumphantly: 'Oh, Miss, do look. It's a wedding outfit, and just right for you!'

Ottilie heard these words and sank down on the sofa. Nanni saw her mistress turn pale and stiffen. She ran to Charlotte, they came. Their friend the Surgeon was soon on the scene; he thought it only exhaustion. He had them fetch some beef tea; Ottilie refused it with disgust, indeed she almost fell into convulsions when the cup was brought to her lips. He asked then gravely and quickly, as the circumstances prompted him to, what Ottilie had eaten that day. The little girl hesitated; he repeated his question, the girl confessed that Ottilie had eaten nothing.

There was something suspicious in the degree of Nanni's distress. He hurried her next door, Charlotte followed, the girl fell on her knees, confessed that Ottilie had been eating almost nothing for some considerable time. Urged to by Ottilie, Nanni had eaten the meals herself; she had kept quiet about it because, with gestures, her mistress had pleaded and threatened, and also, she added innocently, because it tasted so good.

The Major and Mittler came in, they found Charlotte busy in the company of the Surgeon. The pale, ethereal girl sat, self-possessed as it seemed, in the corner of the sofa. They begged her to lie down; she refused, but indicated that they should bring her box. She placed her feet on it and, half-recumbent then, was comfortable. She seemed to want to say goodbye, her gestures expressed the tenderest affection for those around her, love, gratitude, a plea for forgiveness and the most heartfelt farewell.

Eduard, dismounting, learned of her condition, rushed into the room, threw himself down beside her, seized her hand and, never speaking, wetted it with his tears. So he remained a long while. At last he cried: 'Am I not to hear your voice again? Will you not come back into life with a single word for me? Well then, I shall follow you over. There we will speak with other tongues.'

She pressed his hand, hard, looked at him full of life and full of love, and after a deep breath, after a heavenly, silent moving of the lips: 'Promise me you will live!' she cried out, sweetly and tenderly expending her strength, and at once fell back.

'I promise,' he answered, but he was already calling after her. She had departed.

After a night of weeping it fell to Charlotte to see to the burial of the beloved remains. The Major and Mittler supported her. Eduard's condition was pitiable. Once he was able to lift himself at all out of despair and compose his mind somewhat he insisted that Ottilie should not be removed from the Hall, she must be tended, cared for, treated like a living woman, for she was not dead, she could not be dead. They did as he wished, at least in the sense that they forbore to do what he had forbidden. He did not ask to see her.

There was a further shock, a further worry for the friends. Nanni, severely scolded by the Surgeon, brought to confess by threats and then reproached, abundantly, after her confession, had fled. After much searching she was discovered; she seemed beside herself. Her parents took her back. The kindest treatment seemed without effect, she had to be locked up since she threatened to run away again.

Step by step they managed to retrieve Eduard from the most violent level of despair, but only into unhappiness, for it was clear to him, it was a certainty, that he had lost his life's happiness for ever. They plucked up the courage to suggest to him that if Ottilie were buried in the chapel she would still be among the living and would still have a friendly and quiet dwelling as her own. It was hard to get his agreement, and only on condition that she would be carried out in an open coffin and in the chapel itself should have at most a glass lid over her, and that a lamp be donated to be kept always alight, did he at last give his consent and seemed then to have acquiesced in everything.

They dressed the precious body in the fine clothes she had prepared for herself; they wreathed her head with asters that shone like stars, sadly and full of portent. To decorate the bier, the church, the chapel, all the gardens were stripped of what had decorated them. They lay like a waste, as though winter had already erased the joy from all the beds. Very early in the morning she was carried out of the Hall in an open coffin, and the rising sun gave the flush of life again to her ethereal face. Those accompanying her crowded around the bearers, nobody wanted to go ahead or follow behind, everyone wanted to be around her and enjoy her presence for the last time. Among the boys, the men, the women, no one was unmoved. The girls were inconsolable, feeling the loss of her the most immediately.

Nanni was absent. They had kept her away, or rather they had kept the day and the hour of the funeral a secret from her. She was locked up at her parents' house in a little room overlooking the garden. But when she heard the bells she knew at once what was happening and when the woman in charge of her, being curious to see the procession, left her alone she escaped through a window on to a passageway, and from there, since she found the doors all locked, on to the roof.

At that very moment the cortège was swaying through the village down the clean street strewn with leaves. Nanni saw her mistress clearly below her, more clearly, more perfectly, in a greater beauty than any who were following in the procession. She seemed no longer earthly, but to be borne along on clouds or waves, and seemed to be beckoning to her maid and she, in confusion, swaying, tottering, fell.

With a terrible scream the crowd dispersed in all directions. In the press and tumult the bearers were obliged to set down the bier. The child lay near it; all her limbs seemed shattered. They lifted her up; and by chance or by some intervention of fate they rested her across the corpse, indeed with the life that remained to her she seemed herself to be trying to reach her beloved mistress. But no sooner had her shaking limbs touched Ottilie's dress and her nerveless fingers Ottilie's folded hands than the girl sprang up, first raised her arms and her eyes to heaven, then fell on her knees by the coffin and in ecstatic reverence gazed up at her mistress.

At last she leapt to her feet as if inspired, and with a religious joy cried out: 'Yes, she has forgiven me. What no human being could forgive me, what I could not forgive myself, God has forgiven me through her look, her gesture, and her mouth. Now she is lying down again so quiet and gentle, but you saw how she sat up and opened her hands and blessed me and how she looked at me and smiled. You all heard it, you are my witnesses that she said to me: "You are forgiven." Now I am not the murderess among you any more, she has forgiven me, God has forgiven me, and nobody can have anything against me any more.'

The crowd was pressing round; they were astonished, they listened, looked this way and that, and scarcely knew what to do next. 'Carry her to her rest now,' said the girl. 'She has done and suffered all her share and can no longer dwell among us.' The bier moved on, Nanni immediately behind it, and they reached the church and the chapel.

Thus Ottilie's coffin lay now, at her head the coffin of the child, at her feet the little chest, and around all a stout enclosure of oak. They had arranged that for a period there should be a woman who would watch over the body lying so sweetly under the glass cover. But Nanni would not let any-one have this office but herself; she wished to be there alone, without any companion, and diligently look after the lamp now for the first time lit. She requested this so eagerly and so insistently that they let her, in order to prevent any worsening of her state of mind, which there was reason to fear.

But she was not alone for long. Just as night fell and the hanging lamp, coming into its own, cast a brighter light, the door opened and the Architect entered the chapel whose piously decorated walls, now in so mild a radiance, pressed forward to meet him more full of the past and heavier with futurity than he would ever have believed.

Nanni was sitting on one side of the coffin. She recognized him at once; but without a word she pointed to her dead mistress. And so he stood on the other side, in youthful strength and grace, thrown back upon himself, stiff, inward looking, his arms hung down, his hands clasped, wrung in pity, bowing his head, lowering his gaze upon the lifeless girl.

Once before he had stood like that in front of Belisarius. Involuntarily now he assumed the same posture; and how natural it was on this occasion too. Here too something inestimably valuable had fallen from its height; and if in the former case courage, intelligence, power, rank, and wealth were lost irrevocably and lamented in the person of one man, if qualities necessary at critical times to the nation and its prince had there been disregarded, indeed rejected and repu-diated, here a like number of other, quiet virtues, brought forth by Nature out of her abundant depths only a short time since, had now been quickly erased again by her indifferent hand; rare, beautiful, and lovable virtues whose peaceable influence the needy world at all times welcomes with delighted satisfaction and laments the loss of with longing and grief.

The young man said nothing, nor the girl for a while; but when she saw the tears start frequently from his eyes, when he seemed to be utterly dissolved in grief, then she spoke to him, and with so much truth and power, with so much kindness and certainty, that he, astonished at her eloquence, was able to compose himself, and his beautiful friend hovered before him living and working in a higher region. His tears ceased, his grief was less; kneeling he said goodbye to Ottilie, and to Nanni, warmly pressing her hands, and that same night rode away, having seen no one besides.

The Surgeon, unbeknown to the girl, had spent the night in the church, and visiting her next morning he found her cheerful and comforted. He was prepared for all sorts of delusions; he expected her to tell him of conversations with Ottilie during the night and of other such phenomena; but she was normal, calm, and entirely self-possessed. She remembered earlier times and circumstances all perfectly well and with great exactness, and nothing in her talk left the usual course of what is true and real except the happening at the funeral, and that she often recounted with delight: how Ottilie had sat up, blessed her, forgiven her, and in so doing set her mind at rest for ever.

The continuing beauty of Ottilie's state, more like sleep than death, attracted numbers of people. Those who lived there or nearby wanted to see her while they could and everyone was eager to hear Nanni's incredible story from her own lips; some then made fun of it, most were sceptical, and there were a few whose attitude towards it was one of belief.

Every need denied its real satisfaction perforce engenders faith. Nanni, all broken by her fall in full view of everyone, was made whole again by touching the virtuous corpse. Why should not a similar benefit be vouchsafed others from it? Loving mothers brought their children, at first in secret, if they were afflicted with any ill, and believed they discerned a sudden improvement. Belief in this grew, and in the end even the oldest and the weakest came looking for some refreshment and relief. The numbers grew, and it became necessary to close the chapel; indeed, except for services, to close the church itself.

Eduard never had the heart to visit the departed girl. He lived by rote, seemed to have no more tears, to be incapable of any more grief. His participation in the talk, his appetite for food and drink, lessened daily. He imbibed some comfort still, a little, so it seemed, only out of the glass, for all it had been a false prophet to him. He still took pleasure in contemplating the entwined initials, and his look then, solemn and serene together, seemed to suggest that even now he was still hoping for reunion. And just as a happy man seems favoured by every trivial circumstance and raised up high by every chance, so the littlest occurrences will easily combine to distress and bring to perdition the unhappy man. For one day, as Eduard was raising the beloved glass to his lips, he set it down again in horror; it was the same and not the same, he missed one small identifying mark. They confronted the valet, who admitted that the real glass had been broken recently and a similar one, also from Eduard's boyhood, had been put in its place. Eduard could not be angry, his fate was spoken by the deed – why should the symbol move him? And yet it pressed him down. Thenceforth he seemed to find it repugnant to drink; he seemed to be purposely abstaining from food and from conversation.

But from time to time he became restless. He called for something to eat again, began speaking again. 'Alas,' he said on one occasion to the Major, who rarely left his side, 'it is my deep misfortune that all my striving remains an imitation and a false exertion. What was blessedness for her is a torment to me; and yet for the sake of that blessedness I am obliged to take on that torment. I must go after her, and along this way. But my own nature holds me back, and my promise. It is a terrible task to imitate the inimitable. Now I understand that genius is necessary for everything, even martyrdom.'

In this hopeless condition why dwell on the efforts in which, as wife, as friend, as doctor, Eduard's loved ones for a while exhausted themselves? At last he was found dead. It was Mittler who made the sad discovery. He called the Surgeon and took note, in his customary fashion, of the exact circumstances in which the deceased was found. Charlotte rushed to the scene; she suspected suicide; she was ready to blame herself and the others for an unforgivable negligence. But the Surgeon, with reasons in nature, and Mittler, with reasons in morality, were soon able to convince her she was wrong. It was quite obvious that Eduard had been surprised by his end. At a quiet moment he had taken out of a little box, and out of his pocket-book, all the things left him by Ottilie, things he had previously been careful to conceal, and had laid them all out before him: a lock of her hair, flowers plucked in an hour of happiness, all the notes she had written him, from that first one which his wife had so casually and with such consequence, handed over to him. He would not intentionally have exposed all that to chance discovery. And so he too, whose heart until a moment since had suffered a ceaseless agitation, lay now in peace, unassailably; and since he had gone to his rest in thinking of that saintly girl, surely he could be called blessed. Charlotte gave him his place next to Ottilie and ordered that no one else should be buried under that roof. On that condition she made sizeable bequests for the benefit of the church, the school, the clergyman, and the schoolteacher.

So the lovers are side by side, at rest. Peace hovers over their dwelling-place, cheerful images of angels, their kith and kin, look down at them from the vaulted ceiling, and what a sweet moment it will be for their eyes when on some future day they wake together.

ITALIAN JOURNEY

(1786–1787)

*Translated by W. H. Auden
and Elizabeth Mayer*

CONTENTS

ITALIAN JOURNEY

Et in Arcadia ego

PART ONE

FROM CARLSBAD TO THE BRENNER

I SLIPPED out of Carlsbad at three in the morning; otherwise, I would not have been allowed to leave. Perhaps my friends, who had so kindly celebrated my birthday on 28 August, had thereby acquired the right to detain me, but I could wait no longer. I packed a single portmanteau and a valise, jumped into the mailcoach, and arrived in Zwota at 7.30. The morning was misty, calm and beautiful, and this seemed a good omen. The upper clouds were like streaked wool, the lower heavy. After such a wretched summer, I looked forward to enjoying a fine autumn. At noon I arrived in Eger. The sun was hot, and it occurred to me that this place lay on the same latitude as my native town. I felt very happy to be taking my midday meal under a cloudless sky on the fiftieth parallel.

On entering Bavaria, the first thing one sees is the monastery of Waldsassen. The clerics who own this valuable property have been wiser than most people. It lies in a saucer- or basin-like hollow amid beautiful meadows and surrounded on all sides by fertile, gently rolling hills. The monastery owns property all over the countryside. The soil is a decomposed clayey slate. The quartz which is found in this type of rock formation does not decompose or erode, and it makes the soil loose and fertile. The land rises steadily all the way to Tirschenreuth, and the streams flow towards the Eger and the Elbe. After Tirschenreuth, the land falls to the south and the streams run towards the Danube. I find I can quickly get a topographical idea of a region by looking at even the smallest stream and noting in which direction it flows and which drainage basin it belongs to. Even in a region which one cannot overlook as a whole, one can obtain in this way a mental picture of the relation between the mountains and the valleys.

Before reaching Tirschenreuth, we struck a first-class high road of granitic sand. This decomposed granite is a mixture of feldspar and argillaceous earth which provide both a firm foundation and a solid binding, so that the road is as smooth as a threshing floor, all the more desirable because the region through which it runs is flat and marshy. The gradient was now downhill and we made rapid progress, a pleasant contrast after the snail's pace of travel in Bohemia (I enclose a list of the places at which we stopped). By ten o'clock next morning we reached Regensburg, having covered a hundred and four miles in thirty-one hours. Dawn found us between Schwandorf and Regenstauf, and I noticed that the soil had already changed for the better. It was no longer debris washed down from the mountains, but mixed alluvial earth. In primeval times tides from the Danube area must have passed up the Regen and invaded all the valleys which now discharge their waters into that basin. This invasion formed the polders upon which agriculture depends. This holds good for all river valleys, large or small, and by noting their presence or absence, any observer can discover at a glance whether the soil is fit for cultivation.

Regensburg has a beautiful situation. The lie of the land was bound to invite the founding of a town, and its spiritual lords have shown good judgement. They own all the fields around, and in the town itself church stands by church and convent by convent. The Danube reminds me of the Main. The river and the bridges at Frankfurt are a finer sight, but the Stadt-am-Hof on the far bank of the Danube looks very impressive.

The first thing I did was to visit the Jesuit College, where the students were performing their annual play. I saw the end of an opera and the beginning of a tragedy. The acting was no worse than that of any other group of inexperienced amateurs, and their costumes were beautiful indeed, almost too magnificent. Their performance reminded me once again of the worldly wisdom of the Jesuits. They rejected nothing which might produce an effect, and they knew how to use it with love and care. Their wisdom was no coldly impersonal calculation; they did everything with a gusto, a sympathy and personal pleasure in the doing, such as living itself gives. This great order had organ-builders, wood-carvers and gilders among its members, so it must also have included some who, by temperament and talent, devoted themselves to the theatre. Just as they knew how to build churches of imposing splendour, these wise men made use of the world of the senses to create a respectable drama.

I am writing this on the forty-ninth parallel. The morning was cool, and though, here too, people complain of the cold, damp summer, a glorious day unfolded. Thanks to the presence of the great river, the air is extraordinarily mild. The fruit, however, is not particularly good. I ate some nice pears, but I am longing for grapes and figs.

I keep thinking about the character and the activities of the Jesuits. The grandeur and perfect design of their churches and other buildings command universal awe and admiration. For ornament, they used gold, silver and jewels in profusion to dazzle beggars of all ranks, with, now and then, a touch of vulgarity to attract the masses. Roman Catholicism has always shown this genius, but I have never seen it done with such intelligence, skill and consistency as by the Jesuits. Unlike the other religious orders, they broke away from the old conventions of worship and, in compliance with the spirit of the times, refreshed it with pomp and splendour.

A peculiar mineral is found here, which is worked up into specimens for collectors. It looks like a sort of puddingstone, but it must be older, primary or even porphyritic. It is greenish in colour, porous, mixed with quartz, and embedded in it are large pieces of solid jasper in which again small round specks of breccia may be seen. I saw one very tempting specimen, but it was too heavy, and I have vowed not to burden myself with stones on this journey.

I left Regensburg at 12.30 p.m. From Abach, where the Danube dashes against the cliffs, to Saale the countryside is beautiful. The limestone is of the same kind as that round Osterode in the Harz Mountains – compact but porous.

I arrived here at six in the morning. After looking around for twelve hours, I have little to remark. In the picture gallery I felt rather lost; my eyes have not yet reaccustomed themselves to looking at paintings. But I saw some excellent things. The sketches by Rubens from the Luxembourg Gallery, for instance, delighted me. There was one precious and curious object, a miniature model of the Trajan column – the ground was lapis lazuli, the figures were gilt. A fine piece of craftsmanship and pleasant to look at.

In the Hall of Classical Antiquities I became acutely aware that my eyes have not been trained to appreciate such things. For this reason I felt I should be wasting my time if I stayed there long. There was little that appealed to me, though I cannot say why. A Drusus attracted my attention, there were two Antonines and a few other pieces which I liked. On the whole, the arrangement is none too happy. The intention behind it was obviously good, but the Hall, or rather the large vaulted room, would have looked better if it had been kept cleaner and in better repair. In the Museum of Natural History I found beautiful minerals from the Tirol. I was already familiar with these and even own some specimens myself.

I met an old woman selling figs, the first I have ever tasted. They were delicious. But although Munich lies on the forty-eighth parallel, on the whole the fruit here is not particularly good. Everyone is complaining about the cold, wet weather. Before reaching Munich, I ran into a fog which was almost rain, and all day long a cold wind has been blowing from the mountains of the Tirol. When I looked towards them from the tower, they were hidden in clouds and the whole sky was overcast. Forgive me for talking so much about wind and weather: the land traveller is almost as dependent upon them as the mariner. It would be a shame if my autumn in foreign lands should turn out to be as unpropitious as my summer at home has been.

I am on my way to Innsbruck. How much I fail to notice to right and left because of the goal by which I have been so long obsessed that it has almost gone stale in my mind!

Mittenwald, 7 September. Evening

My guardian angel, it seems, says Amen to my Credo, and I am grateful to him for having guided me to this place on such a perfect day. My last postilion exclaimed with joy that it was the first of the whole summer. I cherish a secret superstition that the fine weather will continue.

My friends must forgive me for talking again about temperature and clouds. By the time I left Munich at five, the sky had cleared. The clouds were still massed over the mountains of the Tirol and their lower layers were motionless. The road keeps to the high ground over hills of alluvial gravel from which one can see the Isar flowing below. The tidal action of the primeval ocean is easy to grasp. In many a pile of granite rubble I found cousins of the specimens in my collection which Knebel gave me. The mist which rose from the river and the meadows persisted for a time but finally dispersed. Between the gravel hills, which you must picture as stretching far and wide, hour after hour, the soil is fertile and similar to that of the Regen valley. We came back again to the Isar at a point where the hills end in a bluff some one hundred and fifty feet high. When I got to Wolfrathshausen, I had reached the forty-eighth parallel. The sun was blazing fiercely. No one believes the fine weather will last; they all grumble because the weather of the declining year has been so bad and lament that the Good God does nothing about it.

As the mountains slowly drew nearer, a new world opened before me. The situation of Benediktbeuren is surprising and enchanting. The abbey, a long, sprawling white building, stands on a fertile plain beyond which rises a high, rocky ridge. The road climbs to the Kochelsee and then still higher into the mountains until it reaches the Walchensee. There I saw my first snow-capped peaks, and when I expressed my surprise at being already so close to the snow line, I was told that only yesterday there had been a thunderstorm followed by snow. People here interpret these meteorological events as a promise of better weather, and from the early snows they anticipate a change in temperature. All the surrounding cliffs are of limestone – the oldest formation which contains no fossils. These limestone mountains stretch in an immense, unbroken chain from Dalmatia to Mount St Gotthard and beyond. Hacquet has travelled over much of it. It leans against the primal mountain range which is rich in quartz and clay.

I reached Walchensee at half past four, having met with a pleasant adventure an hour or so before. A harp player who had been walking ahead of us with his eleven-year-old daughter begged me to let her ride with me in the coach. He himself walked on, carrying his instrument. I let her sit by my side, and she placed a large new bandbox carefully at her feet. She was a pretty young creature who had already seen a good deal of the world. With her mother, she had made a pilgrimage on foot to Maria-Einsiedeln, and both of them had been planning a longer pilgrimage to S. Jago de Compostela. But her mother had been carried away by death before she could fulfil her vow. One could never, she told me, do too much in veneration of the Mother of God. After a great fire in which a whole house had been burned to the ground, she had seen with her own eyes that the picture of Our Lady in the niche over the door had remained undamaged and the glass as well. This was certainly a true miracle. She always travelled on foot, and on her last journey she had played in Munich before the Elector. All in all, she had performed before twenty-one royal personages. She had large brown eyes, an obstinate forehead, which she sometimes screwed up, and I found her quite good company. When she talked, she was natural and agreeable, especially when she laughed out loud like a child, but when she was silent, wishing, evidently, to look important, she pouted her upper lip, which gave her face an unpleasant expression. I talked with her on many topics; she was familiar with them all and observant of everything about her. Once, for instance, she asked me the name of a tree. It was a beautiful tall maple, the first I had seen on my journey. She had noticed it immediately and was delighted when more and more of them appeared and she was able to recognize them. She told me she was on her way to the fair in Bolzano and assumed I was going there too. Should we meet there, I must buy her a fairing. This I promised to do. She was also going to wear her new bonnet which she had had made to order in Munich and paid for out of her earnings. She would show it to me in advance. At which she opened her bandbox and I had to share her admiration for the richly embroidered, gaily beribboned headdress.

We shared another cheerful prospect as well: she assured me we would have fair weather, because she carried a barometer with her – her harp. When the treble string went sharp it was a sign of good weather, and this had happened today. I accepted the good omen and we parted gaily, hoping to meet again soon.

On the Brenner Pass, 8 September. Evening

Led, or rather driven, I reached at last as quiet a resting place as I could have hoped for. It has been one of those days which I shall remember with joy for many years. I left Mittenwald at six. A bitter wind had cleared the sky completely. It was as cold as one only expects it to be in February, but, in the radiance of the rising sun, the dark pine-grown foothills, the grey limestone cliffs between them and the snow-capped peaks in the background against a deep-blue sky were a rare and ever-changing vision.

Near Scharnitz one enters the Tirol. At the frontier the valley is closed in by a rock wall which joins the mountains on both sides. On one side the cliff is fortified, on the other it rises perpendicularly. It is a fine sight. After Seefeld the road becomes more and more interesting. From Benediktbeuren on, it had been climbing steadily from one height to another and all the streams ran towards the basin of the Isar, but now I looked down from a ridge into the valley of the Inn and saw Inzing lying below me. The sun was high in the heavens and shone so hotly that I had to take off some of my outer garments. Because of the ever-varying temperature, I have to make several changes of clothing during the course of the day.

Near Zirl we began to descend into the Inn valley. The landscape is of an indescribable beauty, which was enhanced by a sunny haze. The postilion hurried faster than I wished; he had not yet heard Mass and was devoutly eager to hear it in Innsbruck because it was the Feast of the Virgin's Nativity, so we rattled downhill beside the Inn and past St Martin's Wall, a huge, sheer limestone crag. I would have trusted myself to reach the spot where the Emperor Maximilian is said to have lost his way and to have come down safely without the help of an angel, though I must admit it would have been a reckless thing to do.

Innsbruck is superbly situated in a wide fertile valley between high cliffs and mountain ranges. My first thought was to make a stop there, but I felt too restless. I amused myself for a little by talking to the innkeeper's son, who was 'Söller'* in person. It is curious how I keep meeting my characters one after the other.

Everything has been made clean and tidy for the Feast of the Virgin's Nativity. Healthy, prosperous-looking people are making a pilgrimage to Wilten, a shrine an hour's walk from the town in the direction of the mountains. At two o'clock when my coach rolled through the gay and colourful crowd, the procession was in full swing.

After Innsbruck the landscape becomes increasingly beautiful. On the smoothest of roads we ascended a gorge which

---

* Söller. Character in Goethe's comedy *The Accomplices* (*Die Mitschuldigen*), 1768.

discharges its waters into the Inn and offers the eye a great variety of scenery. The road skirts the steepest rock and in places is even hewn out of it. On the other side one could see gentle cultivated slopes. Villages, large and small houses, chalets, all of them whitewashed, lay scattered among fields and hedges over a high, wide slope. Soon the whole scene changed: the arable land became pasture and then the pasture, too, fell away into a precipitous chasm.

I have gained some ideas for my cosmological theories, but none of them is entirely new or surprising. I have also kept dreaming of the model I have talked about for so long, with which I should like to demonstrate all the things which are running through my head but which I cannot make others see in nature.

It grew darker and darker; individual objects faded out and the masses became ever larger and more majestic. Finally everything moved before my eyes like some mysterious dream picture and all of a sudden I saw the lofty snow peaks again, lit up by the moon. Now I am waiting for dawn to light up this cleft in which I am wedged on the dividing line between north and south.

Let me add some more remarks about the weather, which is treating me so kindly, perhaps because I pay it so much attention. On the plains, one accepts good or bad weather as an already established fact, but in the mountains one is present at its creation. I have often witnessed this as I travelled, walked, hunted or spent days or nights among cliffs in the mountain forests, and a fanciful idea has taken hold of my mind which is as difficult to shake off as all such fancies are. I seem to see its truth confirmed everywhere, so I am going to talk about it. It is my habit, as you know, to keep trying the patience of my friends.

When we look at mountains, whether from far or near, and see their summits, now glittering in sunshine, now shrouded in mists or wreathed in storm-tossed clouds, now lashed by rain or covered with snow, we attribute all these phenomena to the atmosphere, because all its movements and changes are visible to the eye. To the eye, on the other hand, shapes of the mountains always remain immobile; and because they seem rigid, inactive and at rest, we believe them to be dead. But for a long time I have felt convinced that most manifest atmospheric changes are really due to their imperceptible and secret influence. I believe, that is to say, that, by and large, the gravitational force exerted by the earth's mass, especially by its projections, is not constant and equal but, whether from internal necessity or external accident, is like a pulse, now increasing, now decreasing. Our means for measuring this oscillation may be too limited and crude, but sensitive reactions of the atmosphere to it are enough to give us sure information about these imperceptible forces. When the gravitational pull of the mountains decreases even slightly, this is immediately indicated by the diminished weight and elasticity of the air. The atmosphere can no longer retain the moisture mechanically or chemically diffused through it; the clouds descend, rain falls heavily, and shower clouds move down into the plain. But when their gravitational pull increases, the elasticity of the air is restored and two significant phenomena follow. First the mountains gather round their summits enormous cloud masses, holding them firmly and immovably above themselves like second summits. Then, through an inner struggle of electrical forces, these clouds descend as thunderstorms, fog or rain. The elastic air is now able to absorb more moisture and dissolve the remaining clouds. I saw quite distinctly the absorption of one such cloud. It clung to the steepest summit, tinted by the afterglow of the setting sun. Slowly, slowly, its edges detached themselves, some fleecy bits were drawn off, lifted high up, and then vanished. Little by little the whole mass disappeared before my eyes, as if it were being spun off from a distaff by an invisible hand.

If my friends smile at the peripatetic meteorologist and his strange theories, I shall probably make them laugh out loud with a few further reflections. Having taken this journey in order to escape the inclemencies I had suffered on the fifty-first parallel, I had hoped, I must confess, to enter a true

Goshen on the forty-eighth. I found myself disappointed, as I should have known beforehand, because latitude by itself does not make a climate but mountain ranges do, especially those which cross countries from east to west. From the great atmospheric changes which are continually going on there, the northern countries suffer most. Thus it seems that the weather last summer in all the northern lands was determined by this great Alpine chain from which I am now writing. Here it has rained without stopping for the last months, and winds from the south-west and south-east have blown the rain northward. The weather in Italy is reported to have been fine and, indeed, almost too dry.

Now a few words about the plant life, which is also greatly influenced by climate, altitude and moisture. So far I have seen no marked change, but a certain improvement is observable. In the valley, before reaching Innsbruck, I frequently saw apples and pears on the trees. Peaches and grapes are brought here from Italy or, rather, South Tirol. Around Innsbruck much maize is grown as well as buckwheat. On the way up the Brenner Pass I saw the first larch trees and near Schönberg the first pine. I wonder if the harper's daughter would have asked me their names too.

As for the plants, I am very conscious of how much I have still to learn. Until I reached Munich I was only aware of seeing familiar ones. But then my hasty travelling day and night did not lend itself to careful observations, even though I carried my Linnaeus with me and had his terminology firmly stamped on my mind. (When shall I find the time and the peace for analysis which, if I know anything about myself, will, in any case, never become my forte?) I keep a sharp lookout for general characteristics; when I saw my first gentian by the Walchensee, it struck me that it has always been in the vicinity of water that I have found new plants.

My attention was drawn to the obvious influence of high altitude. I not only saw new plants but also familiar ones with a different kind of growth. In the low-lying regions, branches and stems were strong and fleshy and leaves broad, but up here in the mountains, branches and stems became more delicate, buds were spaced at wider intervals and the leaves were lanceolate in shape. I observed this in a willow and in a gentian, which convinced me that it was not a question of different species. Near the Walchensee, the rushes I saw were also taller and thinner than those of the plain.

The limestone Alps through which I have been travelling so far have a grey colour and beautiful irregular shapes, even though the rock is divided into level strata and ridges. But since bent strata also occur and the rock does not weather equally everywhere, the cliffs and peaks assume bizarre shapes. This formation continues up the Brenner to a considerable altitude. In the neighbourhood of the Upper Lake, I came across a modification of it. Against a dark-green and dark-grey mica schist, strongly veined with quartz, there leaned a white solid limestone which towered glimmering above its screes, a huge, deeply fissured mass. Further up, I found mica schist again, though it seemed of a softer texture than that lower down. Higher still, appeared a special type of gneiss or, rather, a kind of granite approximating to gneiss, such as one finds in the district of Elbogen. Up here, opposite the Inn, the cliff is mica schist. The streams which flow from these mountains deposit nothing except this rock and grey limestone.

The granite massif upon which all this leans cannot be far away. My map shows that we are on the slope of the Great Brenner proper where all the streams of the surrounding region have their sources.

My impression of the outward appearance of the people is as follows: they look brave, straightforward and, in their physique, very much alike. They have large, dark eyes; the eyebrows of the women are dark and finely traced, whereas those of the men are fair and bushy. The green hats worn by the men add a gay note to the grey rocks; these are decorated with ribbons or wide fringed taffeta sashes pinned on with great elegance. Everyone wears a flower or a feather in his hat as well. The women, on the other hand, disfigure themselves by wearing very large caps of shaggy white cotton which look like monstrous men's nightcaps. They look all the odder because everywhere except in this region the women wear the same becoming hats as the men.

I frequently had occasion to observe that the people here attach great value to peacock feathers and, indeed, to any brightly coloured feather. A person who intends to travel in these mountains should carry some with him, for such a feather, given at the right moment, will serve as the most welcome gratuity.

As I collect, sort and sew these pages together in order to give my friends a brief review of my adventures up to the present moment and at the same time relieve my mind of all I have experienced and thought, I look with alarm at some of the packages of manuscript which I have brought with me. Still, are they not, I say to myself, my travelling companions, and may they not have a great influence on my future?

I took all my writings with me to Carlsbad in order to prepare the definitive edition which Göschen is going to publish. Of those which had never been printed, I already possessed copies beautifully written by the practised hand of my secretary Vogel, who also came to Carlsbad with me. Thanks to his help and Herder's loyal co-operation, I had been able to send the first four volumes to the publisher and was intending to send the last four. Some of their contents were only outlines of works and even fragments, because, to tell the truth, my naughty habit of beginning works, then losing interest and laying them aside, had grown worse with the years and all the other things I had to do.

Since I had these with me, I gladly yielded to the request of the intellectual circle in Carlsbad, and read aloud to them everything they had not yet seen. Whenever I did, there were bitter complaints about the unfinished pieces which they wished were longer.

Most of my birthday presents were poems about my projected but unfinished works in which their authors complained of my habits of composition. One bore the distinguished title of 'The Birds'. A deputation of these gay creatures sent to the 'True Friend'* besought him earnestly to found and furnish forthwith the kingdom he had promised them for so long. The allusions to my other fragmentary pieces were no less intelligent and amiable, so that they suddenly came to life again for me, and I told my friends about other projects I had, and outlined them in detail. This gave rise to more insistent requests and played into Herder's hand, who tried to persuade me to take all my manuscripts with me and, above all, to reconsider *Iphigenie* with the attention it deserved. In its present form it is rather a sketch than a finished play. It is written in a poetic prose which occasionally falls into iambics and even other syllabic metres. I realize that, unless it is read with great skill, so that the blemishes are artfully concealed, this is detrimental to the effect of the play.

Herder urged all this very seriously. I had concealed from him my plans to extend my journey. He believed it was to be merely another mountain excursion, and as he has always ridiculed my passion for mineralogy and geology, he suggested that it would be much better if, instead of tapping dead rocks with a hammer, I were to use my tools for literary work. I promised to try, but so far it has been impossible. Now, however, I have extracted *Iphigenie* from a bundle of manuscripts and shall carry her with me as my travelling companion in a warm and beautiful country. The days are long, nothing distracts my thoughts and the glories of the scenery do not stifle my poetic imagination: on the contrary, favoured by motion and the open air, they excite it.

---

* Truefriend (*Treufreund*). Character in Goethe's comedy *The Birds* (*Die Vögel*), modelled on Aristophanes, 1780.

FROM THE BRENNER TO VERONA

AFTER fifty crowded lively hours I arrived here at eight o'clock last night, went early to bed and am now once more in a condition to continue with my narrative. On the evening of the ninth, after finishing the first instalment of my diary, I thought I would try to make a drawing of the inn, a post-house on the Brenner, but I was unsuccessful. I failed to catch the character of the place and returned indoors in somewhat of an ill-humour. The innkeeper asked me if I would not like to start on my way at once because the moon would soon be rising and the road was excellent. I knew that he wanted the horses back early next morning to bring in the second hay crop, so that this advice was not disinterested, but, since it corresponded with my heart's desire, I accepted it with alacrity. The sun came out again, the air was balmy: I packed and at seven o'clock I set off. The clouds had dispersed and the evening became very beautiful.

The postilion fell asleep and the horses trotted downhill at great speed along a road they knew. Whenever they came to a level stretch they slowed down. Then the driver would wake up and goad them on again. Very soon we came to the Adige, rushing along between high cliffs. The moon rose and lit up the gigantic masses of the mountains. Some watermills, standing above the foaming river among age-old pines, looked exactly like a painting by Everdingen.

When I reached Vipiteno at nine o'clock, it soon became obvious that they wanted me to leave at once. We reached Mezzaselva on the stroke of midnight. Everyone except the new postilion was fast asleep. On we went to Bressanone, where again I was, so to speak, abducted, so that I arrived in Colma as dawn was breaking. The postilions tore along the road so fast that it took my breath away, but in spite of my regret at travelling in such haste and by night through this lovely country, deep down inside I was happy that a propitious wind was behind me, hurrying me on towards my goal. At dawn I saw the first hillside vineyards. We met a woman selling pears and peaches.

On we drove. I reached Trinità at seven and was immediately carried off again. For a while we travelled north and at last I saw Bolzano, bathed in sunshine and surrounded by steep mountains which are cultivated up to a considerable height.

The valley is open to the south and sheltered on the north by the mountains of the Tirol. A balmy air pervaded the whole region. Here the Adige turns south again. The foothills are covered with vineyards. The vines are trained on long, low trellises and the purple grapes hang gracefully from the roof and ripen in the warmth of the soil so close beneath them. Even on the valley bottom, which is mostly meadowland, vines are grown on similar trellises, which are placed closely together in rows, between which maize is planted. This thrusts out higher and higher stalks: many I saw were ten feet high. The fibrous male flowers had not yet been cut off, for this is not done until some time after fertilization has taken place.

The sun was shining brightly when I arrived in Bolzano. I was glad to see the faces of so many merchants at once. They had an air about them of purpose and well-being. Women sat in the square, displaying their fruit in round, flat-bottomed baskets more than four feet in diameter. The peaches and pears were placed side by side to avoid bruising. I suddenly remembered a quatrain I had seen inscribed on the window of the inn at Regensburg:

> *Comme les pêches et les melons*
> *Sont pour la bouche d'un baron,*
> *Ainsi les verges et les bâtons*
> *Sont pour les fous, dit Salomon.*

Evidently this was written by a northern baron, but one can be equally sure that, if he had visited these parts, he would have changed his mind.

In the Bolzano market there is a lively traffic in silk; traders also bring cloth there and all the leather they can procure in the mountain districts. Many merchants, however, come mainly to collect money, take orders and give new credits. I should much have liked to inspect all the various products offered for sale, but my heart's desire will not let me rest, and I am as impatient as ever to leave at once.

I console myself with the thought that, in our statistically minded times, all this has probably already been printed in books which one can consult if need arise. At present I am preoccupied with sense-impressions to which no book or picture can do justice. The truth is that, in putting my powers of observation to the test, I have found a new interest in life. How far will my scientific and general knowledge take me? Can I learn to look at things with clear, fresh eyes? How much can I take in at a single glance? Can the grooves of old mental habits be effaced? This is what I am trying to discover. The fact that I have to look after myself keeps me mentally alert all the time and I find that I am developing a new elasticity of mind. I had become accustomed to only having to think, will, give orders and dictate, but now I have to occupy myself with the rate of exchange, changing money, paying bills, taking notes and writing with my own hand.

From Bolzano to Trento one travels for nine miles through a country which grows ever more fertile. Everything which, higher up in the mountains, must struggle to grow, flourishes here in vigour and health, the sun is bright and hot, and one can believe again in a God.

A poor woman hailed me and asked me to let her child ride in my coach because the hot ground was burning its feet. I performed this deed of charity as an act of homage to the powerful Light of Heaven. The child was dressed up in a peculiar and showy fashion, but I could not get a word out of it in any language.

The Adige now flows more gently and in many places forms broad islands of pebbles. Along the river banks and on the hills everything is planted so thickly that you would imagine each crop must choke the other – maize, mulberries, apples, pears, quinces and nuts.

Walls are covered with a luxuriant growth of dwarf-elder, and thick-stemmed ivy clambers and spreads itself over rocks; lizards dart in and out of crevices, and everything that wanders about reminds me of my favourite pictures. The women with their braided hair, the bare-chested men in light jackets, the magnificent oxen being driven home from the market, the little heavily laden donkeys – all this animated scene makes one think of some painting by Heinrich Roos.

As evening draws near, and in the still air a few clouds can be seen resting on the mountains, standing on the sky rather than drifting across it, or when, immediately after sunset, the loud shrill of crickets is heard, I feel at home in the world, neither a stranger nor an exile. I enjoy everything as if I had been born and bred here and had just returned from a whaling expedition to Greenland.

I even welcome the dust which now sometimes whirls about my coach, as it used to in my native land, and which I had not seen for so long. The bell-like tinkling noise the crickets make is delightful – penetrating but not harsh – and it sounds most amusing when some impish boys try to outwhistle a field of such singers: they seem to stimulate each other. Every evening is as perfectly calm as the day has been.

If someone who lives in the south or was born there were to overhear my enthusiasm at all this, he would think me very childish. But I already knew all about it when I was suffering, alas, under an unfriendly sky, and now I have the pleasure of feeling as an exception this happiness which by rights we ought to be able to enjoy as a rule of our nature.

Trento, 11 September. Evening

I wandered about the town, which is very old though there are a few well-built modern houses. In the church hangs a painting of the assembled Council listening to a sermon by the Vicar-General of the Jesuits. I should much like to know what he put over on them. The church of these Fathers is immediately recognizable by the pilasters of red marble on its façade. The door is covered by a heavy curtain to keep out the dust. I lifted it and stepped into a small antechapel. The church proper is closed off by a wrought-iron grille through which, however, one can view the whole without difficulty. It was quiet and empty, for it is no longer used for divine service. The door was open only because all churches must be open at the hour of vespers.

As I was standing there looking at the architecture, which seemed to me like that of all churches built by this order, an old man entered and immediately took off his black biretta.

His worn and dingy black habit showed that he was an impoverished priest. He knelt down before the grille, said a short prayer and got up. As he turned round he muttered to himself: 'Well, they have expelled the Jesuits but they ought at least to have paid them what the church cost them to build.* I know very well how many thousands they spent on it and on the Seminary.' With that he left and the curtain fell back behind him. I lifted it again and waited quietly. He was still standing at the top of the steps and talking to himself: 'The Emperor didn't do it. The Pope did it.' Unaware of my presence, he turned his face towards the street and continued: 'First the Spaniards, then we, then the French. The blood of Abel cries out against his brother Cain.' Then he descended the steps and walked down the street, still muttering continuously. Probably he was some poor old man who had been supported by the Jesuits, lost his wits after the tremendous fall of that order, and now comes every day to look in this

* The Jesuit Order had been suppressed by Clement XIV in 1773.

empty shell for its former inhabitants, pray for them a little and then curse their enemies.

A young man from whom I had inquired about the points of interest in this town showed me a house which is called the Devil's House because the Devil, though usually bent on destruction, is said to have got the stones together and built it in a single night. The good fellow failed to notice what was really remarkable about it. It is the only house in good taste which I have seen in Trento and was probably built at an earlier period by some good Italian.

I left at five in the evening. Last night's performance was repeated, for immediately after sunset, the crickets began their shrill chorus. For nearly a mile the road ran between walls, over the tops of which I could see vineyards. Other walls which were not high enough had been built up with stones, brambles and so forth to prevent passers-by from picking the grapes. Many vineyard owners spray the vines nearest to the road with lime. This makes the grapes unpalatable but does not spoil the wine, since it is all eliminated during fermentation.

11 September. Evening

Here I am in Rovereto, where the language changes abruptly. North of this point it had wavered between German and Italian. Now, for the first time, I had a pure-bred Italian as a postilion. The innkeeper speaks no German and I must put my linguistic talents to the test. How happy I am that, from now on, a language I have always loved will be the living common speech.

Torbole, 12 September. Afternoon

How I wish my friends could be with me for a moment to enjoy the view which lies before me.

I could have been in Verona tonight, but I did not want to miss seeing Lake Garda and the magnificent natural scenery along its shores, and I have been amply rewarded for making this detour. After five, I started off from Rovereto up a side valley which discharges its waters into the Adige. At its head lies an enormous rocky ridge which one must cross before descending to the lake. I saw some limestone crags which would make fine subjects for pictorial studies. At the end of the descent one comes to a little village with a small harbour, or rather, landing place at the northern end of the lake. Its name is Torbole. On my way up the ridge I had frequently seen fig trees beside the road, and when I descended into the rocky amphitheatre I saw my first olive trees, which were laden with olives. I also saw, growing freely, the small white figs which Countess Lanthieri promised me.

From the room where I am sitting, a door opens on to the courtyard below. I placed my table in front of it and made a quick sketch of the view. Except for one corner to my left, I can see almost the entire length of the lake. Both shores, hemmed in by hills and mountains, glimmer with innumerable small villages.

After midnight the wind starts blowing from north to south. Anyone who wishes to travel down the lake must do so at this hour, for some hours before sunrise the air current veers round into the opposite direction. Now it is afternoon and the wind is blowing strongly in my face, which is cooling and refreshing. Volkmann* informs me that the lake was formerly called Benacus and quotes a line from Virgil where it is mentioned:

Fluctibus et fremitu assurgens Benace marino.†

This is the first line of Latin verse the subject of which I have seen with my own eyes. Today when the wind is increasing in force and higher and higher waves are dashed against the landing place, the verse is as true as it was many

---

* J. J. Volkmann, author of *Historical and Critical News from Italy*, Goethe's guidebook.

† *The Georgics* of Virgil, II, v, 159–60.

centuries ago. So much has changed, but the wind still churns up the lake which a line of Virgil's has ennobled to this day.

Written on a latitude of 45° 50'

In the cool of the evening I took a walk. Here I am really in a new country, a totally unfamiliar environment. The people lead the careless life of a fool's paradise. To begin with, the doors have no locks, though the innkeeper assures me that I would not have to worry if all my belongings were made of diamonds. Then the windows are closed with oil paper instead of glass. Finally, a highly necessary convenience is lacking, so that one is almost reduced to a state of nature. When I asked the servant for a certain place, he pointed down into the courtyard. '*Qui abasso può servirsi!*' '*Dove?*' I asked. '*Da per tutto, dove vuol!*' was his friendly answer. Everywhere one encounters the utmost unconcern, though there is noise and lively bustle enough. The women of the neighbourhood chatter and shout all day long, but at the same time they all have something to do or attend to. I have yet to see one idle woman.

The innkeeper announced with a true Italian flourish that he would have the happiness of serving me the most exquisite trout. These are caught near Torbole where a brook comes down from the mountains and the fish look for a way upstream. The Emperor receives ten thousand gulden for the fishing rights. They are a large fish – some of them weigh over fifty pounds – speckled all over from head to tail. They are not the real trout, but their taste is delicate and excellent – something between that of trout and salmon.

What I enjoy most of all is the fruit. The figs and pears are delicious, and no wonder, since they ripen in a region where lemon trees are growing.

13 September. Evening

At three o'clock this morning I set off with two rowers. At first the wind was favourable and they could use the sails.

At dawn the wind dropped and the morning, though cloudy, was glorious. We passed Limone, whose terraced hillside gardens were planted with lemon trees, which made them look at once neat and lush. Each garden consists of rows of square white pillars, set some distance apart and mounting the hill in steps. Stout poles are laid across these pillars to give protection during the winter to the trees which have been planted between them.

Our slow progress favoured contemplation and observation of such pleasing details. We had already passed Malcesine when the wind suddenly veered right round and blew northwards, as it usually does during the day. Against its superior force, rowing was of no avail and we were compelled to land at the harbour of Malcesine, the first Venetian town on the eastern shore of the lake. When one has water to deal with, it is no good saying: 'Today I shall be in this place or that.' I shall make as good use of this stop as possible, in particular, by drawing the castle, which is a beautiful building near the shore. I made a preliminary sketch of it while we were passing this morning.

14 September

The contrary wind which drove me yesterday into Malcesine harbour involved me in a dangerous adventure from which, thanks to keeping my temper, I emerged victorious and which highly amuses me in retrospect.

As I had planned, early in the morning I walked to the old castle, which, since it is without gates, locks or sentries, is accessible to anyone. I sat down in the courtyard facing the old tower, which is built upon and into the rock. I had found an ideal spot for drawing, at the top of three or four steps that led to a locked door. In the frame of this door stood a little carved stone seat of the kind one can still come across in old buildings in our country.

I had not been sitting there long before several persons entered the courtyard, looked me over and walked up and

down. Quite a crowd gathered. Then they came to a stop and
I found myself surrounded. I realized that my drawing had
created a sensation, but I did not let this disturb me and went
calmly on with my work. At last a somewhat unpreposses-
sing-looking man pushed himself forward, came up close to
me and asked what I was doing there. I replied that I was
drawing the old tower so as to have a memento of Malcesine.
This was not allowed, he said, and I must stop at once. Since
he spoke in Venetian dialect which I hardly understand,
I retorted that I didn't know what he was saying. At this,
with typical Italian nonchalance he tore the page up, though
he left it on the pad. When this happened I noticed that some
of the bystanders showed signs of indignation, especially one
old woman who said this wasn't right. They should call the
podestà, who was the proper judge of such matters. I stood on
the step with my back against the door and took in the faces
of the crowd, which still kept growing. The eager stares, the
good-natured expression on most of them and all the other
characteristics of a crowd of strange people afforded me
much amusement. I fancied I saw before me the chorus of
'Birds', whom, as the 'True Friend', I had so often made fun
of on the stage of the Ettersburg theatre. By the time the
podestà arrived on the scene with his actuary, I was in the
highest spirits and greeted him without reserve. When he
asked me why I had made a drawing of their fortress, I said
modestly that I had not realized that these ruins were a
fortress. I pointed to the ruinous state of the tower and the
walls, the lack of gates, in short, to the general defenceless
condition of the whole place, and assured him it had never
crossed my mind that I was drawing anything but a ruin. He
answered: If it were only a ruin, why was it worth noticing?
Wishing to gain time and his good will, I went into a detailed
exposition; they probably knew, I said, that a great many
travellers came to Italy only to see ruins, that Rome, the
capital of the world, had been devastated by the Barbarians
and was now full of ruins which people had drawn hundreds
of times, that not everything from antiquity had been as well

preserved as the amphitheatre in Verona, which I hoped to see soon.

The *podestà* stood facing me, but on a lower step. He was a tall, though hardly a lanky, man of about thirty. The dull features of his stupid face were in perfect accord with the slow and obtuse way in which he put his questions. The actuary, though smaller and smarter, also did not seem to know how to handle such a novel and unusual case. I kept on talking about this and that. The people seemed to enjoy listening, and when I directed my words at some kindly-looking women, I thought I could read assent and approval in their faces.

But when I mentioned the amphitheatre in Verona, which is known here by the name 'arena', the actuary, who had been collecting his wits in the meantime, broke in: that might be all very well, he said, in the case of a world-famous Roman monument, but there was nothing noteworthy about these towers except that they marked the frontier between Venetia and the Austrian Empire, for which reason they were not to be spied upon. I parried this by explaining at some length that the buildings of the Middle Ages were just as worthy of attention as those of Greek and Roman times, though they could not be expected to recognize, as I did, the picturesque beauty of buildings which had been familiar to them since childhood. By good luck, the morning sun at this point flooded the tower, rocks and walls with a lovely light and I began describing the beauty of the scene with great enthusiasm. Since my audience was standing with their backs to it and did not want to withdraw their attention from me completely, they kept screwing their heads round, like wrynecks, in order to see with their eyes what I was praising to their ears. Even the *podestà* turned round, though with greater dignity; they looked so absurd that I became quite hilarious and spared them nothing, least of all the ivy which had luxuriantly covered the rocks and walls for so many centuries.

The actuary returned to his argument: this was all very well, but the Emperor Joseph was a troublesome *signore* who certainly had evil designs on the republic of Venice. I might well be a subject of his, sent to spy on the frontier.

'Far from being a subject of the Emperor,' I exclaimed, 'I can boast of being, like yourselves, the citizen of a republic which, though it cannot compare in power and greatness with the illustrious state of Venice, nevertheless also governs itself and, in its commercial activity, its wealth and the wisdom of its councillors, is inferior to no city in Germany. I am, that is to say, a native of Frankfurt-am-Main, a city of whose name and renown you must certainly have heard.'

'From Frankfurt-am-Main!' cried a pretty young woman. 'Now you will be able to find out at once, Signor Podestà, the kind of man this stranger is. I am certain he is honest. Send for Gregorio – he was in service there for a long time – he is the best person to clear up the whole matter.'

The number of kindly-disposed faces around me had increased, the original troublemaker had disappeared, and when Gregorio arrived, the tide turned definitely in my favour. Gregorio was a man in his fifties with one of those familiar olive-skinned Italian faces. He spoke and behaved like someone to whom anything strange is not strange at all. He at once told me that he had been in service with Bolongaro and would be happy to hear news from me about this family and about the city which he remembered with great pleasure. Fortunately, he had resided there when I was a young man, so that I had the double advantage of being able to tell him exactly what had happened in his day and what changes had taken place later. I had been acquainted with all the Italian families, so I gave him news of them all and he was delighted to hear many facts: that Signor Alessina, for instance, had celebrated his golden wedding in 1774, and that a medal, struck on that occasion, was in my possession. He remembered that the maiden name of this wealthy merchant's wife had been Brentano. I was also able to tell him many things about the children and grandchildren – how they had grown up, been provided for, married and had children in their turn.

While I gave him the most accurate information I could about everything, his features grew jovial and solemn by turns. He was moved and happy. The bystanders got more and more excited and hung on every word of our conversation, though he had to translate some of it into their dialect.

At the end he said: 'Signor Podestà, I am convinced that this man is an honest and educated gentleman who is travelling to enlarge his knowledge. We should treat him as a friend and set him at liberty, so that he may speak well of us to his countrymen and encourage them to visit Malcesine, the beautiful situation of which so well deserves the admiration of foreigners.'

I gave added force to these friendly words by praising the countryside, the town and its inhabitants, nor did I forget to mention the prudence and wisdom of its authorities.

All this was well received and I was given permission to look at anything in the neighbourhood I liked, in the company of Master Gregorio. The keeper of the inn where I had engaged a room now joined us and was delighted at the prospect of foreigners flocking to his inn, once the attractions of Malcesine were properly known. He examined my various articles of clothing with lively curiosity and was especially envious of my small pistols, which can be conveniently slipped into one's pockets. He thought people fortunate indeed who were allowed to carry such beautiful firearms, which were prohibited to them under the severest penalties. From time to time, I interrupted his friendly importunity to express my gratitude to my liberator.

'Do not thank me,' replied the honest fellow, 'you do not owe me anything. If the *podestà* knew his business and if the actuary thought about anything except his self-interest, you would not have got off so easily. The one was more embarrassed than you were and the other had not a penny to gain by your arrest, the report he would have to make, or sending you to Verona. He realized this very soon and you were already at liberty before our conversation ended.'

Towards evening this good man came to take me to see his vineyard, which was pleasantly situated on the shore of the lake. His fifteen-year-old son accompanied us and was told to climb the trees and pick me the finest fruit, while his father selected the ripest grapes.

Alone with these two simple, kindhearted persons, in the immense solitude of this corner of the world, it struck me, as I meditated on my adventure of the morning, that man is indeed a strange creature, who, in order to enjoy something which he could perfectly well have enjoyed in peace and comfort and pleasant company, gets himself into trouble and danger because of an absurd desire to appropriate the world and everything it contains in a manner peculiar to himself.

Shortly before midnight the innkeeper accompanied me to the boat, carrying a little basket of fruit which Gregorio had given me as a present. And so, with a propitious wind, I left that shore which had threatened to become for me the coast of the Laestrygones.

Now about my trip down the lake. This ended happily, after the beauty of the mirror-like water and the adjacent shore of Brescia had refreshed my whole being. Along the western shore, where the mountains were no longer precipitous and the land sloped more gently down to the lake, Gargnano, Bogliaco, Cecina, Toscolano, Maderno, Gardone and Salò stretched in one long row for about an hour and a half. No words can describe the charm of this densely populated countryside. At ten in the morning I landed in Bardolino, loaded my baggage on to one mule and myself on to another. The road crossed a ridge which separates the lake basin from the Adige valley. The primeval waters from both sides probably met each other here, causing powerful currents which raised this gigantic dam of gravel. In quieter epochs fertile soil was then desposited on it, but the ploughmen are constantly bothered by the boulders which keep cropping up. They try to get rid of as many of them as possible by piling them on top of each other in rows, so that the road is lined by very thick and compact walls. Owing to the lack of moisture at this altitude, the mulberry trees are a sorry sight. There are no springs at all. Occasionally one comes across puddles of accumulated rain water, at which the mules and even the drivers quench their thirst. Below, along the river, water-wheels have been erected to irrigate the low-lying fields when necessary.

The magnificence of the new landscape which comes into view as one descends is indescribable. For miles in every direction there stretches a level, well-ordered garden surrounded by high mountains and precipices. Shortly before one o'clock on 14 September I arrived in Verona, where I am writing this to complete the second instalment of my journal. Now I must sew the sheets together. I am greatly looking forward to seeing the amphitheatre tonight.

As to the weather during this period, I have the following to report. The night of the ninth and tenth was clear and cloudy by turns and there was a constant halo around the moon. At about 5 a.m. the whole sky became overcast with grey but not heavy clouds, which disappeared during the day. The lower I descended, the finer the weather became, and by the time we had reached Bolzano and left the great massif behind us, the whole character of the atmosphere had changed. Various shades of blue distinguished one part of the background landscape from another, and against this I could see that the atmosphere was charged with water vapour, evenly distributed, which it was able to hold in suspension, so that this moisture neither fell as dew or rain nor gathered into clouds. When I came down still further, I observed clearly how the water vapour rising from the Bolzano valley and the stratus clouds rising from the mountains to the south were moving towards the higher regions in the north, which they did not hide but veiled in a haze. Above the mountains in the far distance I could see a so-called water gall. South of Bolzano, the weather had been beautiful all summer with only occasionally a little 'water' (they say *acqua* when speaking of a light shower), followed immediately by sunshine. Yesterday a few drops fell now and then, but the sun shone all the time. They have not had such a good year for ages; all the crops have done well; the bad weather they have sent to us.

I shall only briefly mention the mountain rocks and minerals, since *Journey to Italy* by Ferber and Hacquet's *Across the Alps* have already dealt adequately with them.

At dawn, a quarter of an hour after crossing the Brenner Pass, I came, near Colma, to a marble quarry. Almost certainly this marble rests upon the same kind of schist as I saw on the other side of the pass. Further down, I saw indications of porphyry. The cliffs were so splendid and the heaps of stones along the high road of such a convenient size that, if I weren't so greedy and were willing to limit myself to small specimens, I could easily have made myself a little mineralogical museum like that of Voigt's. Soon after leaving Colma, I found a kind of porphyry which splits into regular horizontal plates, and between Bronzolo and Egna another kind which splits vertically. Ferber took them to be volcanic in origin, but that was fourteen years ago, when eruptions were all the rage.* Even Hacquet ridiculed this hypothesis.

Of the inhabitants, I have little to say and that unfavourable. After crossing the Brenner, I noticed as soon as it was daylight a definite change in their physical appearance. I thought the sallow complexion of the women particularly disagreeable. Their features spoke of misery and their children looked just as pitiful. The men looked little better. Their physical build, however, is well-proportioned and sound. I believe that their unhealthy condition is due to their constant diet of maize and buckwheat, or, as they call them, yellow polenta and black polenta.

These are ground fine, the flour is boiled in water to a thick mush and then eaten. In the German Tirol they separate the

---

* An allusion to the controversy over the building of the earth's crust between the Vulcanists who held volcanic action to be the prime factor, and the Neptunists who held rock formations to be oceanic deposits. Goethe was a Neptunist.

dough into small pieces and fry them in butter, but in the Italian Tirol the polenta is eaten just as it is or sometimes with a sprinkling of grated cheese. Meat they never see from one year's end to the other. Such a diet makes the bowels costive, especially in children and women, and their cachectic complexion is evidence of the damage they do themselves. They also eat fruit, and green beans which they boil in water and dress with garlic and olive oil. I asked if there were no well-to-do peasants. 'Of course.' 'Don't they ever treat themselves to something better?' 'No, that is all they're used to.' 'But what do they do with their money? What do they spend it on?' 'Oh, they have their masters all right, who relieve them of it again.' This was the sum of a conversation I had in Bolzano with the daughter of my innkeeper.

From her, too, I heard about the winegrowers. Though apparently the best off, their position is the worst of all. They are completely at the mercy of the merchants, who, in bad years, lend them money to keep them going and then, in good years, buy their wine for a mere song. But life is like that everywhere.

My theory about their diet is confirmed by the fact that the women in the towns all look healthier. I saw pretty plump faces with bodies that were a little too short for their weight and their big heads. Now and then I encountered some who looked really friendly and good-natured. The men we know from itinerant Tiroleans. In their own land they look less healthy than the women, probably because the women do more physical labour and take more exercise, while the men lead a sedentary life as shopkeepers or craftsmen. The people I met around Lake Garda were very dark-skinned without the least touch of red in their cheeks, but they looked cheerful and not at all unhealthy. Their complexion is probably due to their constant exposure to the rays of the sun, which beats so fiercely at the feet of their mountains.

FROM VERONA TO VENICE

THE amphitheatre is the first great monument of the ancient world I have seen, and how well preserved it is! When I entered it, and even more when I wandered about on its highest rim, I had the peculiar feeling that, grand as it was, I was looking at nothing. It ought not to be seen empty but packed with human beings, as it was recently in honour of Joseph I and Pius VI. The Emperor, who was certainly accustomed to crowds, is said to have been amazed. But only in ancient times, when a people were more of a people than today, can it have made its full effect. Such an amphitheatre, in fact, is properly designed to impress the people with itself, to make them feel at their best.

When something worth seeing is taking place on level ground and everybody crowds forward to look, those in the rear find various ways of raising themselves to see over the heads of those in front: some stand on benches, some roll up barrels, some bring carts on which they lay planks crosswise, some occupy a neighbouring hill. In this way in no time they form a crater. Should the spectacle be often repeated on the same spot, makeshift stands are put up for those who can pay, and the rest manage as best they can. To satisfy this universal need is the architect's task. By his art he creates as plain a crater as possible and the public itself supplies its decoration. Crowded together, its members are astonished at themselves. They are accustomed at other times to seeing each other running hither and thither in confusion, bustling about without order or discipline. Now this many-headed, many-minded, fickle, blundering monster suddenly sees itself united as one noble assembly, welded into one mass, a single body animated by a single spirit. The simplicity of the oval is felt by everyone to be the most pleasing shape to the eye, and each head serves as a measure for the tremendous scale of the whole. But when the building is empty, there is no standard by which to judge if it is great or small.

The Veronese are to be commended for the way in which they preserved this monument. The reddish marble of which it is built is liable to weather, so they keep restoring the steps as they erode, and almost all of them look brand-new. An inscription commemorates a certain Hieronymus Maurigenus and the incredible industry he devoted to this monument. Only a fragment of the outer wall is left standing and I doubt if it was ever even completed. The lower vaults which adjoin a large square called *il Bra* are rented to some artisans, and it is a cheerful sight to see these caverns again full of life.

The most beautiful of the city gates is called *Porta stupa* or *del Palio*, but it has always been bricked up. From a distance it does not look well designed as a gate, and it is only when one gets close to it that one can recognize its beauty. All sorts of explanations are given for its being bricked up. Personally, I suspect that the artist intended it as a gateway to a new alignment of the Corso, for its relation to the present street is all wrong. To its left there are nothing but some barracks, and a line drawn at right angles to the gate through its centre leads to a nuns' convent, which it would certainly have been necessary to demolish. That was probably realized; also, the nobility and the men of wealth may have disliked the idea of building their houses in such a remote quarter of the town. Then, perhaps, the artist died, the gate was bricked up and the project abandoned for good.

16 September

The portico of the Teatro Filarmonico looks very impressive with its six tall Ionic columns. By comparison, the life-size bust of the Marchese Maffei in an enormous wig, situated in a painted niche over the door, supported by two Corinthian columns, looks all the more puny. The place is honourable enough, but to be worthy of the grandeur of the columns, the bust should have been colossal. As it is, it stands ineffectually upon a little stone corbel and is out of harmony with the whole.

The gallery which runs around the vestibule is also too small, and the fluted Doric dwarfs look mean beside the smooth Ionic giants. But this must be forgiven for the sake of the fine museum which has been established under this colonnade. Here antique relics, most of them dug up in or around Verona, are arranged on exhibit. Some, even, are said to have been found in the amphitheatre. There are Etruscan, Greek and Roman works from the oldest times and some of more recent date. The bas-reliefs are set into the walls and bear the numbers Maffei gave them when he described them in his *Verona illustrata*. There are altars, fragments of columns and similar relics, also a beautiful tripod of white marble on which genii busy themselves with attributes of the gods. Raphael has copied and transfigured similar figures in the lunettes of the Farnesina.

The wind that blows from the tombs of the ancients is charged with fragrance as if it had passed over a hill of roses. The sepulchral monuments are intimate and moving and always represent scenes from everyday life. Here a husband and wife look out from a niche as from a window. Here a father and mother and son look at each other with an indescribable tenderness. Here a married couple join hands, here a father reclines on a couch and appears to be chatting with his family. To me, the immediacy of these sculptures was extremely moving. They date from a late period in art, but all are very simple, natural and expressive. There is no knight in armour kneeling in anticipation of a joyful resurrection. With varying degrees of skill, the artist has represented only the simple realities of human beings, perpetuating their existence and giving them everlasting life. No one folds his hands or looks up to heaven. Here they are still the people they were on earth, standing together, taking an interest in each other, loving each other. All this, despite a certain lack of craftsmanship, is charmingly expressed in these works. A richly ornamented marble pillar also gave me something to think about.

Admirable though this museum may be, it is clear that the noble desire to preserve which inspired its founders is no longer alive. The precious tripod will soon be ruined, for it stands in the open and is exposed on the western side to the inclemencies of the weather. This treasure could easily be preserved by providing it with a wooden cover.

Had the Palazzo del Provveditore ever been finished, it might have made a fine piece of architecture. The nobility still build a good deal, but, unfortunately, everyone builds on the site of his old residence – often, therefore, in small, narrow lanes. At the moment, for instance, they are putting a magnificent façade on a seminary which is situated on an alley in one of the remotest suburbs.

As I was passing the huge, sombre gateway of a strange-looking building in the company of a chance acquaintance, he good-naturedly asked me if I would like to enter the inner courtyard for a moment. The building was the Palazzo della Ragione, and on account of its height, the courtyard seemed nothing more than an enormous well. 'Here,' he told me, 'all criminals and suspects are held in custody.' Looking about me, I saw that on every floor there was an open corridor railed off by iron bars, which ran past numerous doors. Whenever a prisoner steps out of his cell to be brought for interrogation, he gets a breath of fresh air but he is also exposed to the eyes of the public; since, moreover, there must be a number of rooms for interrogation, chains kept rattling in the corridors, now on this floor, now on that. It was a horrid experience and I must confess that the good humour with which I shook off the 'Birds' would here have been put to a severer test.

At sunset I wandered along the rim of the crater-like amphitheatre, enjoying the view over the town and surrounding countryside. I was completely alone. Below me crowds of people were strolling about on the large flagstones of *il Bra* – men of all ranks and women of the middle class. From my bird's-eye view the women in their black outer garments looked like mummies.

The *zendale* and the *vesta* which constitute the whole *garde-robe* of women of this class is a costume clearly suited to a people that does not care too much about cleanliness, but likes to move about in public all the time, now in church and now on the promenade. The *vesta* is a skirt of black taffeta worn over other skirts. If the woman has a clean white petti-coat underneath, she knows how to lift the black one grace-fully to one side. This is held in place by a belt which narrows the waistline and covers the lappets of the bodice, which may be of any colour. The *zendale* is a hooded shawl with long fringes; the hood is raised above the head on a wire frame and the fringes tied around the body like a scarf, so that their ends hang down at the back.

16 September

Today, about a thousand paces from the arena, I came upon a modern public spectacle. Four noblemen from Verona were playing a kind of ball game with four men from Vicenza. The Veronese play this game among themselves all year round for an hour or two before nightfall. On this occasion, because the match was with a foreign team, a vast crowd, at least four or five thousand, had gathered to watch. I could not see one woman of any rank in life.

When I spoke earlier of the needs of the crowd on such occasions, I described the kind of amphitheatre it makes accidentally, as those in the rear try to look over the heads of those in front. And this was what I now saw being created. Even at a distance I could hear the vigorous clapping which greeted every successful stroke. The game is played as fol-lows: two slightly sloping planks are placed at an appropriate distance from each other. The striker stands at the top end of his plank, wielding in his right hand a large wooden ring set with spikes. When one of his own team throws the ball towards him, he runs down to meet it so as to increase the force of the stroke with which he hits it. The opposing team try to return the ball, and in this way it keeps flying back and forth until someone misses it and it falls to the ground. The postures the players assume during the game are often very beautiful and deserve to be imitated in marble, especially that assumed by the striker as he runs down the plank and raises his arm to hit the ball. I was reminded of the gladiator in the Villa Borghese. Almost all the players were well-developed muscular young men in short, tight-fitting white clothes. The teams were distinguished by badges of different colours. It seems odd that they should play this game near an old city wall where there is no proper provision for spectators. Why don't they play in the amphitheatre, where there is ample room?

17 September

I shall comment only briefly on all the pictures I have seen. My purpose in making this wonderful journey is not to delude myself but to discover myself in the objects I see. I must admit quite honestly that I understand very little about art or the craft of the artist, and must confine my observations to the subjects of the paintings and their general pictorial treatment.

The Church of San Giorgio is like an art gallery. All the pictures are altarpieces which vary in merit but all are well worth seeing. But what subjects these poor artists had to paint! And for what patrons! A rain of manna, thirty feet long and twenty feet high, and, as a companion picture, the miracle of the five loaves! What is there worth painting about that? Hungry persons pounce upon some small crumbs, bread is handed out to countless others. The painters have racked their brains to give these trivialities some significance. Still, genius, stimulated by these demands, has created many beautiful works. One painter, faced with the problem of representing St Ursula with her eleven thousand virgins, solved it very cleverly. The saint stands in the foreground, looking as though she has conquered the country. She has the noble, but quite unattractive, appearance of a virgin Amazon. In diminished perspective her little troop is seen stepping ashore from the ship and approaching in procession. Titian's *Assumption of the Virgin in the Cathedral* has become very black. One is grateful to this painter for letting the Goddess-to-be look down at her friends below, instead of gazing up to Heaven.

In the Gherardini Gallery I found some beautiful things by Orbetto. This was the first time I had heard of him. When one lives far away, one hears only of the major artists in the galaxy and is often satisfied with merely knowing their names; but when one draws closer, the twinkle of stars of the second and third magnitude becomes visible until, finally, one sees the whole constellation – the world is wider and art richer than one had hitherto supposed. One picture I must especially praise. It contains only two half-length human figures. Samson has just fallen asleep in the lap of Delilah, who is reaching furtively across his body for a pair of scissors which lies on a table by a lamp. The execution is very fine. I was also struck by a *Danaë* in the Palazzo Canossa.

The Palazzo Bevilacqua houses many treasures. A so-called *Paradise* by Tintoretto – actually it is the Coronation of Mary in the presence of all the patriarchs, prophets, apostles, saints, angels, etc. – gave that happy genius the opportunity to display all his riches. To appreciate his vision, the facility of his brush and the variety of his expressive means, one would have to own this composition and have it before one's eyes for a whole lifetime. The technique is flawless. Even the heads of the most distant angels, vanishing into the clouds of glory, have individual features. The tallest figures are about a foot high; Mary and Christ, who is placing the crown on her head, measure about four inches. The loveliest creature in the picture, without any doubt, is Eve – still, as of old, a bit voluptuous.

A few portraits by Paul Veronese have increased my respect for this artist. The collection of antiques is magnificent, especially a son of Niobe prostrate in death. Most of the portrait busts, which include an Augustus wearing the civic crown and a Caligula, are interesting in spite of their restored noses. My natural disposition is to reverence the good and the beautiful, so to be able to cultivate it day after day and hour after hour in the presence of such noble objects makes me feel very happy.

In a country where everyone enjoys the day but the evening even more, sunset is an important moment. All work stops; those who were strolling about return to their homes; the father wants to see the daughter back in the house – day has ended. We Cimmerians hardly know the real meaning of day. With our perpetual fogs and cloudy skies we do not care if it is day or night, since we are given so little time to take walks and enjoy ourselves out of doors. But here, when night falls, the day consisting of evening and morning is definitely over, twenty-four hours have been spent, and time begins afresh. The bells ring, the rosary is said, the maid enters the room with a lighted lamp and says: '*Felicissima notte!*' This period of time varies in length according to the season, and the people who live here are so full of vitality that this does not confuse them, because the pleasures of their existence are related, not to the precise hour, but to the time of day. If one were to force a German clock hand on them, they would be at a loss, for their own method of time measurement is closely bound up with their nature. An hour or an hour and a half before sunset, the nobility set out in their carriages; first they drive to the Bra, then down the long broad street to the Porta Nuova, through the gate and round the city walls. As soon as the hour of night rings, they all return; some drive to churches to recite the Ave Maria della Sera, others stop in the Bra, when the cavaliers approach the carriages and engage the ladies in conversation. This goes on for quite a while. I have never stayed to the end, but pedestrians remain in the streets until far into the night. Today it rained just enough to lay the dust. It was a gay and lively sight.

In order to adapt myself to one of the important customs of this country, I have invented a method which makes it easier for me to learn their system of counting the hours. The enclosed diagram will give you an idea of it. The inner circle shows our twenty-four hours from midnight to midnight, divided into two periods of twelve hours, as we count them and our clocks mark them. The middle circle shows how the bells are rung here at this time of year; they also ring up to twelve twice within twenty-four hours, but when our clocks would strike eight, they strike one, and so on till the twelve-hour cycle is completed. The outer circle shows how they reckon up to twenty-four. At night, for instance, if I hear seven strokes and I know that midnight is at five, I subtract five from seven and get the answer two in the morning. If, during the day, I hear seven rings and know that noon is at five, I do the same subtraction and the answer is two in the afternoon. But if I wish to refer to those hours according to local usage, I have to remember that noon is called seventeen hours; then I add this seventeen to the two and say nineteen hours. When you learn about this for the first time and start to figure it out, it seems extremely complicated and difficult to put into practice. But one soon gets used to it, and even finds the calculation as entertaining as the local inhabitants, who delight in this constant counting and recounting, like children who enjoy difficulties which are easy to master. They always have their fingers in the air, anyway, do all their counting in their heads and are fascinated by numbers.

Besides, the whole business is much easier for them because they do not pay the slightest attention to noon and midnight or compare, as we do, the two hands of a clock. They simply count the evening hours as they ring, and, during the day, add this number to the variable noon number with which they are familiar. The rest is explained by the table accompanying the diagram (see p. 430).

People here are always busily on the move, and certain streets where the shops and stalls of the artisans are crowded close together look especially merry. These shops have no front doors, but are open to the street, so that one can look straight into their interiors and watch everything that is going

on – the tailors sewing, the cobblers stretching and hammer-
ing, all of them half out in the street. At night, when the lights
are burning, it is a lively scene.

On market days the squares are piled high with garlic and
onions and every sort of vegetable and fruit. The people
shout, throw things, scuffle, laugh and sing all day long.
The mild climate and cheap food make life easy for them.
At night the singing and the music get even louder. The ballad
of Marlborough* can be heard in every street, and here and
there a dulcimer or a violin as well. They whistle and imitate
all kinds of birdcalls; one hears the most peculiar sounds. In
the exuberance of their life this shadow of a nation still seems
worthy of respect.

The squalor and lack of comfort in their houses, which
shock us so much, spring from the same source; they are
always out of doors and too carefree to think about anything.
The lower classes take everything as it comes, even the
middle classes live in a happy-go-lucky fashion, and the rich
and the nobility shut themselves up in their houses, which are
by no means as comfortable as a house in the north. They
entertain company in public buildings. The porticos and
courtyards are filthy with ordure and this is taken completely
for granted. The people always feel that they come first. The
rich may be rich and build their palaces, the nobility may
govern, but as soon as one of them builds a courtyard or a
portico, the people use it for their needs, and their most
urgent need is to relieve themselves as soon as possible of
what they have partaken of as often as possible. Any man
who objects to this must not play the gentleman, which
means, he must not behave as though part of his residence
was public property; he shuts his door and that is accepted. In
public buildings the people would never dream of giving up
their rights and that is what, throughout Italy, foreigners
complain of.

* *Malbrouk* [Marlborough] *s'en va-t-en guerre*. Popular satirical ballad on the
English General dating from the War of the Spanish Succession (1701–14).

Comparative circle giving the Italian and German time measurements and the Italian hours for the latter half of September

Midday

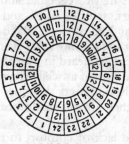

Midnight

From August to November the night increases in length by half an hour every half-month			From February to May the day increases in length by half an hour every half-month		
Month	Sunset by our clocks	Midnight by Italian time [hours]	Month	Sunset by our clocks	Midnight in Italy [hours]
Aug. 1	8.30 p.m.	3½	Feb. 1	5.30 p.m.	6½
Aug. 15	8.00 p.m.	4	Feb. 15	6.00 p.m.	6
Sept. 1	7.30 p.m.	4½	Mar. 1	6.30 p.m.	5½
Sept. 15	7.00 p.m.	5	Mar. 15	7.00 p.m.	5
Oct. 1	6.30 p.m.	5½	Apr. 1	7.30 p.m.	4½
Oct. 15	6.00 p.m.	6	Apr. 15	8.00 p.m.	4
Nov. 1	5.30 p.m.	6½	May 1	8.30 p.m.	3½
Nov. 15	5.00 p.m.	7	May 15	9.00 p.m.	3
In December and January the time does not change			In June and July the time does not change		

Month	Sunset by our clocks	Midnight in Italy [hours]	Month	Sunset by our clocks	Midnight in Italy [hours]
Dec. Jan.	5.00 p.m.	7	July June	9.00 p.m.	3

Today I strolled about the city studying costumes and manners, especially those of the middle classes, who are the most numerous and the most active. They swing their arms as they walk. Persons of higher rank, who wear swords on occasion, only swing the right arm, since they are accustomed to keeping their left arm at their side.

Though the people go about their business with such unconcern, they have a sharp eye for anything unusual. When I first arrived, everybody looked at my high boots, which, even in winter, are not worn here because they are too expensive. Now that I am wearing shoes and stockings, nobody any longer pays me attention. But early this morning, when they were all running this way and that with flowers, vegetables, garlic and other market products, to my great surprise they could not take their eyes off some cypress branches I had in my hands. These branches had green cones hanging from them, and I was also carrying some sprigs of blossom from a caper bush. Everybody, young and old, kept staring at my fingers, and strange thoughts seemed to be passing through their heads.*

I had picked them in the Giardino Giusti, where huge cypresses soar into the air like awls. The yew trees, which, in our northern gardens, are clipped to a point, are probably imitations of this magnificent product of nature. A tree whose every branch, from the lowest to the highest, aspires to heaven and which may live three hundred years deserves to be venerated. Judging from the date when the garden was planted, these cypresses must already have reached such a great age.

Vicenza, 19 September

The road from Verona to Vicenza runs in a north-westerly direction parallel to the mountains. To the left one sees a continuous range of foothills, composed of sandstone,

* Cypress branches were usually carried by mourners.

limestone, clay and marl, dotted with villages, castles and isolated houses. A vast plain stretches to the right, across which we drove on a wide, straight and well-kept road through fertile fields. There trees are planted in long rows upon which the vines are trained to their tops. Their gently swaying tendrils hung down under the weight of the grapes, which ripen early here. This is what a festoon ought to look like.

The road is much used and by every sort of person. I was delighted to see carts with low wheels shaped like plates and drawn by four oxen carrying large tubs in which the grapes are brought from the vineyards to the wine presses. When the tubs are empty, the drivers stand in them. It reminded me very much of a triumphal Bacchanalian procession. The soil between the vine rows is used for the cultivation of all kinds of grain, especially maize and millet.

Near Vicenza a new range of hills rises, running north and south – they are said to be volcanic – which closes off the plain. At their feet, or rather in their semicircular recess, lies the city.

19 September

I arrived some hours ago and have already seen the Teatro Olimpico and other buildings by Palladio. An excellent little book with copperplates and a text has been published for the benefit of foreigners by someone with an expert knowledge of art. You have to see these buildings with your own eyes to realize how good they are. No reproductions of Palladio's designs give an adequate idea of the harmony of their dimensions; they must be seen in their actual perspective.

Palladio was a great man, both in his conceptions and in his power of execution. His major problem was that which confronts all modern architects, namely, how to make proper use of columns in domestic architecture, since a combination of columns and walls must always be a contradiction. How hard he worked at that, how the tangible presence of his creations makes us forget that we are being hypnotized!

There is something divine about his talent, something comparable to the power of a great poet who, out of the worlds of truth and falsehood, creates a third whose borrowed existence enchants us.

The Teatro Olimpico is a re-creation of a Classical theatre on a smaller scale and indescribably beautiful. Yet, compared to our own modern theatres, it looks like an aristocratic, rich and well-educated child as against a clever man of the world who, though not as rich, distinguished or educated, knows better what it is within his means to do.

Looking at the noble buildings created by Palladio in this city, and noting how badly they have been defaced already by the filthy habits of men, how most of his projects were far beyond the means of his patrons, how little these precious monuments, designed by a superior mind, are in accord with the life of the average man, one realizes that it is just the same with everything else. One gets small thanks from people when one tries to improve their moral values, to give them a higher conception of themselves and a sense of the truly noble. But if one flatters the 'Birds' with lies, tells them fairy tales, caters daily to their weaknesses, then one is their man. That is why there is so much bad taste in our age. I do not say this to disparage my friends; I only say – that is what they are like, and one must not be surprised if things are as they are.

Beside the Basilica stands an old building resembling a citadel and studded with windows of unequal sizes. It is impossible to describe how wrong this looks. Undoubtedly the architect's original plan called for it to be demolished together with its tower. But I must control my feelings because here, as elsewhere, I so often come upon what I seek and what I shun side by side.

20 September

Yesterday I went to the opera, which lasted until long after midnight, and I was dying to get some sleep. Scraps of melodies from *The Three Sultanas* and *The Abduction from the*

Seraglio had been not very skilfully pieced together. The music was easy to listen to, but probably the work of an amateur; there was not an idea in it which struck me as new. The two leading dancers performed an *allemande* with the utmost grace.

The theatre is new, of a modest elegance, and uniform in its decoration as befits a provincial town. From every box hangs a carpet of the same colour; only the box of the *Capitan grande* is distinguished by a slightly longer carpet.

The prima donna is very popular and received a tremendous ovation every time she came on stage, and the 'Birds' went wild with joy when she sang anything well, which she often did. She had a natural manner, a good figure, agreeable features, a beautiful voice, and behaved very modestly; only her arm gestures were a little lacking in grace. But I do not think I shall go again. As a 'Bird' I feel I am a failure.

21 September

Today I paid a visit to Dr Turra, who for five years devoted himself passionately to the study of botany, compiled a herbarium of Italian flora and laid out a botanical garden for the late Bishop. Now all this is over. His medical practice has crowded out the study of natural history, worms have eaten the herbarium, the Bishop is dead, and the botanical garden has been planted with useful cabbages and garlic.

Dr Turra is a civilized and learned man. He told me his history frankly and modestly and with unfailing courtesy, but he showed no inclination to show me his collections, which may not have been in a presentable state. So our conversation soon came to a standstill.

Evening

I called upon Scamozzi, an old architect who has brought out a book on Palladio and is himself a competent and dedicated artist. He showed great pleasure at my interest and gave me some information. The building of Palladio's for which I have a special predilection is said to be the house in which he himself lived. Seen at close range, there is far more to it than one would imagine from a picture. I should like to see a drawing of it in colour which would reproduce the tints that the stone and the passage of time gave it. But you must not think that the architect built himself a palace. It is the most unpretentious house in the world and has only two windows, separated by a wide expanse of wall which would easily have admitted of a third. One might make an amusing picture, showing how this house is wedged between its neighbours. Canaletto would have been the man to do this.

Today I went to see a magnificent house called the Rotonda. It stands on a gentle elevation half an hour out of town. It is a square block, enclosing a round hall lit from above. On each of the four sides a broad flight of steps leads up to a portico of six Corinthian columns. Architecture has never, perhaps, achieved a greater degree of luxury. Far more space has been lavished on the stairs and porticos than on the house itself, in order to give each side the impressive appearance of a temple. The house itself is a habitation rather than a home. The hall and the rooms are beautifully proportioned, but, as a summer residence, they would hardly satisfy the needs of a noble family. But from whatever direction one approaches it, the Rotonda is a fine sight. If one walks round it, the variety of visual effect created by the square block and the projecting columns is quite extraordinary. The owner's ambition, to leave his heirs an enormous *fideicommissum* and a tangible memorial to his wealth, is perfectly realized. Just as the house can be seen in all its splendour from every point of the surrounding countryside, so the views of the countryside from the house are equally delightful. You see the Bacchiglione gliding along as they steer their barges downstream from Verona to the Brenta, and you overlook the immense estates of the Marchese Capra, who desired that his family preserve them undivided. The inscriptions on the four gables, which together form a whole sentence, deserve to be recorded.

MARCUS CAPRA GABRIELIS FILIUS
QUI AEDES HAS
ARCTISSIMO PRIMOGENITURAE GRADUI SUBJECIT
UNA CUM OMNIBUS
CENSIBUS AGRIS VALLIBUS ET COLLIBUS
CITRA VIAM MAGNAM
MEMORIAE PERPETUAE MANDANS HAEC
DUM SUSTINET AC ABSTINET.

The last line is very odd; a man who had so much wealth at his disposal and could do what he liked with it still feels that he ought to sustain and abstain. That lesson, surely, could have been learned at less expense.

22 September

Tonight I attended a meeting at the Academy of the Olympians. It is hardly a serious affair but still a desirable one, for it adds some spice to the lives of these people. They had gathered in a large well-lit hall next door to the Teatro Olimpico. The Capitan and several representatives of the nobility were present. All told, there was an audience of about five hundred, all of them educated people.

The motion proposed by the President was: Which has been of greater benefit to the Arts – Invention or Imitation? Not a bad idea, for if one treats the alternatives as exclusive, one can go on debating it for centuries.

The Academicians took full advantage of the occasion and produced all sorts of arguments in prose and in verse, some of them very good ones. Moreover, they had an enthusiastic audience who shouted bravos, clapped and laughed. If only it were possible to stand up in front of one's own countrymen like this and entertain them in person, instead of having to confine one's best thoughts to the printed page of some book at which a solitary reader, hunched up in a corner, then nibbles as best he can.

Naturally, Palladio's name kept cropping up whenever the speakers were in favour of Imitation. At the end of the debate, when jokes are always expected, one of them wittily remarked that Palladio had already been taken care of by others, so he intended to praise Franceschini, the great silk manufacturer. Then he started to show how greatly his imitation of the fabrics of Lyon and Florence had profited this resourceful man and, through him, the town of Vicenza as well; therefore, Imitation was far superior to Invention. He said all this with such humour that the audience never stopped laughing. By and large, the advocates of Imitation received the greater applause because they voiced what the common herd thinks, so far as it is able to think.

At one point, for instance, the audience clapped enthusiastically at a very crude sophism because they had not felt the force of the many excellent arguments which had been offered in favour of Invention.

I am glad to have had this experience, and it was gratifying to see that, even after such a long time, Palladio is still revered by his fellow citizens as a lodestar and an example.

22 September

Early this morning I was in Thiene, which lies northward in the direction of the mountains. There they are putting up a new building on the ground-plan of the old, a laudable practice, showing a proper respect for the good heritage of the past. The castle is superbly situated on a wide plain against a background of limestone mountains without any intervening foothills. The traveller who comes by the road that runs in a dead-straight line towards the castle is greeted by lively streams on either hand, gushing down to water the vast rice fields he has just crossed.

So far I have seen only two Italian cities and only spoken to a few persons, but already I know my Italians well. They are like courtiers and consider themselves the finest people in the world, an opinion which, thanks to certain excellent qualities which they undeniably possess, they can hold with impunity. In my opinion, they are a very good people; to realize this, one has only to observe the children and the common folk as I do constantly, for I am in their company all the time and always enjoy it. And what beautiful faces and figures they have! I must particularly praise the people of Vicenza, for, in their town, one enjoys all the advantages of a great city. They do not stare at you, regardless of what you are doing; yet, when you speak to them, they are polite and ready to talk. I found the women especially agreeable. I do not wish to find fault with the women of Verona: they have well-developed figures and clear-cut features, but most of them are pale and the *zendale* is to their disadvantage, for, naturally, beneath such a charming costume one expects to see something especially fetching. Here, however, I have seen some very pretty creatures. Those with black curly hair were singularly attractive. There were blondes as well, but they are not really to my taste.

Padua, 26 September. Evening

I arrived here today, bag and baggage, after a three-and-a-half-hour drive from Vicenza in a single-seated little chaise called a *sediola*. The journey could have been made in half the time, but, as I wanted very much to enjoy a delightful day in the open air, I was not sorry that my *vetturino* failed to fulfil his obligation. We drove south-east across a fertile plain between hedges and trees without seeing anything special. At last, on the right, there rose a beautiful range of mountains stretching north and south. The profusion of flowers and fruits, hanging down from the trees and over the hedges and walls, was extraordinary. Roofs were laden with pumpkins, and the strangest-looking cucumbers hung from poles and trellises.

From the Observatory, I got a glorious view of the surrounding countryside. To the north lay the Tirolean Alps, snow-capped and almost hidden in clouds, and joined in the north-west by the hills of Vicenza. In the west and nearer, I could make out distinctly the folded shapes of the hills of Este. To the south-east an unbroken plain stretched away like a green sea, tree after tree, bush after bush, plantation after plantation, and, peeping out of this green, innumerable white houses, villas and churches. The Campanile of San Marco and other lesser towers of Venice were clearly visible on the horizon.

27 September

At last I have acquired the works of Palladio, not the original edition with woodcuts, but a facsimile with copperplate engravings, published by Smith, an excellent man who was formerly English consul in Venice. One must give the English credit for having so long appreciated what is good and for their munificence and remarkable skill in publicizing it.

On the occasion of this purchase, I had entered a bookshop, which, in Italy, is a peculiar place. The books are all in stitched covers and at any time of day you can find good company in the shop. Everyone who is in any way connected with literature – secular clergy, nobility, artists – drops in. You ask for a book, browse in it or take part in a conversation as the occasion arises. There were about half a dozen people there when I entered, and when I asked for the works of Palladio, they all focused their attention on me. While the proprietor was looking for the book they spoke highly of it and gave me all kinds of information about the original edition and the reprint. They were well acquainted both with the work and with the merits of the author. Taking me for an architect, they complimented me on my desire to study this master who had more useful and practical suggestions to offer than even Vitruvius, since he had made a thorough study of classical antiquity and tried to adapt his knowledge to the needs of our times. I had a long conversation with these friendly men and learned much about the sights of interest in the town.

Since so many churches have been built in honour of the saints, it is good that a place should be found in them to erect memorials to the intelligent. The portrait bust of Cardinal Bembo stands between two Ionic columns. He has a beautiful face, withdrawn upon itself by force of will, and an enormous beard. The inscription runs as follows:

Petri Bembi Card. imaginem Hier. Guerinus Ismeni f. in publico ponendam curavit ut cujus ingenii monumenta aeterna sint ejus corporis quoque memoria ne a posteritate desideretur.

As a building, in spite of all its fame, the university shocked me. I am glad I did not have to study there. Such a cramped school is unimaginable even to a German student, who often suffered agonies on the hard benches of the auditorium. The anatomical theatre, in particular, is an example of how to squeeze as many students together as possible. The listeners sit in tiers one above the other in a kind of high funnel. They look down from their precipice on to the narrow platform where the dissecting table stands. This gets no daylight, so that the professor has to demonstrate by the light of a lamp.

The Botanical Garden is much more cheerful. Many plants can stay in the ground all through the winter if they are planted near the walls. But towards the end of October the place is roofed over and kept heated during the short winter months. To wander about among a vegetation which is new to one is pleasant and instructive. It is the same with familiar plants as with other familiar objects: in the end we cease to think about them at all. But what is seeing without thinking? Here, where I am confronted with a great variety of plants, my hypothesis that it might be possible to derive all plant forms from one original plant becomes clearer to me and more exciting. Only when we have accepted this idea will it be possible to determine genera and species exactly. So far this has, I believe, been done in a very arbitrary way. At this stage in my botanical philosophy, I have reached an impasse, and I do not yet see how to get out of it. The whole subject seems to me to be profound and of far-reaching consequence.

The square called Prato della Valle, where the principal fair takes place in June, is of vast extent. The wooden stalls in the centre are not an attractive sight, but the Paduans assure me that they will soon have a *fiera* of stone like the one in Verona.

Even now the surroundings of the square look impressive and promise well for this plan.

All around the edge of its enormous oval stand statues of famous men who either taught or studied here. Any native or foreigner is permitted to put up a statue of a certain size to any relative or fellow countryman, as soon as his merits and his connexion with the university have been proved.

The oval is surrounded by a canal. On the four bridges which span it stand colossal statues of Popes and Doges, together with smaller ones erected by guilds, private individuals and foreigners. The King of Sweden has donated a statue of Gustavus Adolphus, who, supposedly, once attended a lecture in Padua. The Archduke Leopold has revived the memory of Petrarch and Galileo. The statues are in a good modern style, very few over-mannered, some quite lifelike, and all in the costume of their period and their official rank. There is nothing undignified or in bad taste about the inscriptions, either.

At any university this would have been a felicitous idea, but nowhere so much as in Padua, for here one sees the evocation of a past which is now closed.

In the place of assembly belonging to a religious brotherhood dedicated to St Anthony, there are some ancient paintings, reminiscent of the old German school, among them some by Titian, which show a progress in the art which no painter on the other side of the Alps has so far made. I also saw some more modern paintings. Though no longer able to reach the sublime dignity of their predecessors, these artists have been extremely successful in the lighter genre. The beheading of St John the Baptist by Piazzetta is, after allowing for the mannerisms of this master, a very good painting.

St John is kneeling, with his right knee against a rock and with folding hands, looking up to heaven. Behind him, holding him bound, a soldier bends forward to look into his face as if he were surprised at the saint's composure. In the upper part of the picture, another soldier is standing who is supposed to deal the fatal blow; but he has no sword and is only making a gesture with his hands as if he were practising the stroke beforehand. Below him is a third soldier, drawing a sword out of a scabbard. The idea, though not great, is felicitous, and the composition unusual and effective.

In the Church of the Eremitani I saw some astonishing paintings by Mantegna, one of the older masters. What a sharp, assured actuality they have! It was from this actuality, which does not merely appeal to the imagination, but is solid, lucid, scrupulously exact and has something austere, even laborious about it, that the later painters drew their strength, as I observed in Titian's pictures. It was thanks to this that their genius and energy were able to rise above the earth and create heavenly forms which are still real. It was thus that art developed after the Dark Ages.

The audience chamber of the Palazzo Comunale, justly designated by the augumentative title *salone*, is such a vast closed-in shell that, even when one has just come from seeing it, one can hardly retain its image in one's mind. It is three hundred feet long, one hundred feet wide and, from floor to vaulted ceiling, one hundred feet high. People here are so used to living out of doors that the architects were faced with the problem of vaulting over a market square, so to speak. Such a huge vaulted space gives one a strange feeling. It is a closed-in infinity more analogous to human nature than the starry sky is. The sky draws us out of ourselves, but this gently draws us back into ourselves.

For the same reason, I like to rest for a while in the Church of St Giustina, which is four hundred and eighty-five feet long, and proportionately high and wide. Tonight I sat there meditating in a corner. I felt very alone, since no one in the world, even had he thought of me at that moment, would have looked for me in such a place.

I have now packed my bags once more. Tomorrow morning I am going to travel on the Brenta by boat. It rained today but it is now clear again, and I hope to see the lagoons in brilliant sunshine and send greetings to my friends from the embrace of the Queen Bride of the sea.

VENICE

It was written, then, on my page in the Book of Fate that at five in the afternoon of the twenty-eighth day of September in the year 1786, I should see Venice for the first time as I entered this beautiful island-city, this beaver-republic. So now, thank God, Venice is no longer a mere word to me, an empty name, a state of mind which has so often alarmed me who am the mortal enemy of mere words.

When the first gondola came alongside our boat – this they do to bring passengers who are in a hurry to Venice more quickly – I remembered from early childhood a toy to which I had not given a thought for perhaps twenty years. My father had brought back from his journey to Italy a beautiful model of a gondola; he was very fond of it and, as a special treat, he sometimes allowed me to play with it. When the gondolas appeared their shining steel-sheeted prows and black cages greeted me like old friends.

I have found comfortable lodgings in the Queen of England, not far from the Piazza San Marco. My windows look out on to a narrow canal between high houses; immediately below them is a single-span bridge, and opposite, a narrow, crowded passage. This is where I shall live until my parcel for Germany is ready and I have had my fill of sightseeing, which may be some time. At last I can really enjoy the solitude I have been longing for, because nowhere can one be more alone than in a large crowd through which one pushes one's way, a complete stranger. In all Venice there is probably only one person who knows me, and it is most unlikely that I shall meet him at once.

Venice, 28 September 1786

A few words about my adventures since leaving Padua. The passage down the Brenta in a public boat and in well-behaved company, since the Italians observe good

443

manners among one another, was tolerably pleasant. The banks are studded with gardens and summer houses, small properties stretch down to the edge of the river and now and then the busy high road runs beside it. Since we descended the river by a chain of locks, there was a short delay every now and then when we could step ashore and enjoy the fruit which was offered us. Then we would board the boat again and continue gliding through a fresh and animated world.

To so many varied images was added a new apparition – two pilgrims who, though they came from Germany, seemed to have found their proper place here. They were the first I ever saw so close. They have right to free transportation on this public conveyance, but, since the other passengers avoided them, they did not sit in the covered space but astern with the steersman. Such pilgrims are rare in these days. They were stared at by everybody and treated with scant respect, for, in earlier times, many rascals roamed the countryside in this disguise. When I heard that they were Germans and could not speak any other language, I went aft to talk to them and learned that they came from the region of Paderborn. Both men were nearing fifty and had dark, good-natured faces. Their main goal had been the Shrine of the Three Magi in Cologne; then they had wandered across Germany and were now on their way to Rome. After that they planned to return to northern Italy; then one would wander back home to Westphalia, while the other made a further pilgrimage to S. Jago de Compostela.

Their habit was the conventional one but, with their tucked-up skirts, looked much better than the trailing taffeta habits we usually wear when we appear as pilgrims at our fancy-dress balls. The wide cape, the round hat, the scallop shell, that most primitive of drinking vessels, everything had its meaning and immediate use. Their passports were in a tin box. The most curious of their belongings were the small portfolios of red morocco in which they carried the small articles they needed for daily necessities. They had taken them out because they had found something in their clothes that needed mending.

Our steersman was happy to have found an interpreter and asked me to put various questions to them. In this way I learned much about their opinions and their journey. They complained bitterly of their fellow believers, even of secular priests and monks. Piety, they said, seemed to be very rare, for no one was inclined to believe in theirs, and in Catholic districts, almost without exception, they were treated as vagabonds, even though they immediately produced their itinerary, drawn up by their superior, and their passports, issued by their bishop. On the other hand, they told me with great feeling how well they had been received by Protestants, particularly by a country pastor in Swabia and even more so by his wife, who had persuaded her somewhat reluctant husband to allow her to give them a much needed meal. When they left, she even presented them with a *thaler*, which had been a godsend to them as soon as they were back again in a Catholic district. After telling me all this, one of them said with the utmost seriousness: 'Of course, we remember this woman every day in our prayers, praying that God may open her eyes in the same way that He opened her heart to us, and that, even this late, He may receive her into the bosom of the One True Church. And so we hope and believe that we shall meet her hereafter in Paradise.'

I sat on the small flight of stairs which led to the main deck and interpreted what was relevant in this conversation to the steersman and a few others who had left the cabin and crowded into this narrow space. Meanwhile the pilgrims were given some food, though not much, for Italians are not fond of giving. The pilgrims then produced small consecrated slips of paper on which were pictures of the Three Magi and appropriate devotional prayers in Latin, and asked me to distribute them among the small group of bystanders and explain their great value. I was quite successful at this, too. When they seemed worried as to how, in a great city like Venice, they would find the monastery which puts up pilgrims, the sympathetic steersman promised that, when they landed, he would give three *centavi* to a boy who would guide them to that faraway place. He added, in an undertone, that they would find small comfort there. The institution which had been founded on a grand scale to house God knows how many pilgrims was now rather reduced and its revenues had been turned over to other purposes. As we talked, we sailed down the lovely Brenta, leaving behind us many wonderful gardens and magnificent palaces, and catching fleeting glimpses of prosperous coastal towns. At last we entered the lagoons and, immediately, gondolas swarmed around our boat. A passenger from Lombardy, a man well known in Venice, invited me to join him in one so that we might arrive in the city more quickly and avoid the ordeal of the Dogana. Some people wanted to detain us, but, with the help of a modest tip, we succeeded in shaking them off and, in the peaceful sunset, went gliding quickly towards our goal.

29 September. Michaelmas Eve

So much has been said and written about Venice already that I do not want to describe it too minutely. I shall only give my immediate impression. What strikes me most is again the people in their sheer mass and instinctive existence.

This race did not seek refuge in these islands for fun, nor were those who joined later moved by chance; necessity taught them to find safety in the most unfavourable location. Later, however, this turned out to their greatest advantage and made them wise at a time when the whole northern world still lay in darkness; their increasing population and wealth were a logical consequence. Houses were crowded closer and closer together, sand and swamp transformed into solid pavement. The houses grew upward like closely planted trees and were forced to make up in height for what they were denied in width. Avid for every inch of ground and cramped into a narrow space from the very beginning, they kept the alleys separating two rows of houses narrow, just wide enough to let people pass each other. The place of street and square and promenade was taken by water. In consequence, the Venetian was bound to develop into a new kind of creature, and that is why, too, Venice can only be compared to itself. The Canal Grande, winding snakelike through the town, is unlike any other street in the world, and no square can compete with the vast expanse of water in front of the Piazza San Marco, enclosed on one side by the semicircle of Venice itself. Across it to the left is the island of San Giorgio Maggiore, to the right the Giudecca with its canal, and still further to the right the Dogana with the entrance to the Canal Grande, where stand some great gleaming marble temples. These, in brief, are the chief objects which strike the eye when one leaves the Piazza San Marco between the two columns.

After dinner I hurried out without a guide and, after noting the four points of the compass, plunged into the labyrinth of this city, which is intersected everywhere by canals but joined together by bridges. The compactness of it all is unimaginable unless one has seen it. As a rule, one can measure the width of an alley with one's outstretched arms; in the narrowest, one even scrapes one's elbows if one holds them akimbo; occasionally there is a wider lane and even a little square every so often, but everything is relatively narrow.

I easily found the Canal Grande and its principal bridge, the Ponte Rialto, which is a single arch of white marble. Looking down, I saw the Canal teeming with gondolas and the barges which bring all necessities from the mainland and land at this point to unload. As today is the Feast of St Michael, the scene was especially full of life.

The Canal Grande, which separates the two main islands of Venice, is only spanned by a single bridge, the Rialto, but it can be crossed in open boats at various points. Today I watched with delight as many well-dressed women in black veils were ferried across on their way to the Church of the Solemnized Archangel. I left the bridge and walked to one of the landing points to get a closer look at them as they left the ferry. There were some beautiful faces and figures among them.

When I felt tired, I left the narrow alleys and took my seat in a gondola. Wishing to enjoy the view from the opposite side, I passed the northern end of the Canal Grande, round the island of Santa Chiara, into the lagoons, then into the Giudecca Canal and continued as far as the Piazza San Marco. Reclining in my gondola, I suddenly felt myself, as every Venetian does, a lord of the Adriatic. I thought with piety of my father, for nothing gave him greater pleasure than to talk of these things. It will be the same with me, I know. Everything around me is a worthy, stupendous monument, not to one ruler, but to a whole people. Their lagoons may be gradually silting up and unhealthy miasmas hovering over their marshes, their trade may be declining, their political power dwindling, but this republic will never become a whit less venerable in the eyes of one observer. Venice, like everything else which has a phenomenal existence, is subject to Time.

30 September

Towards evening I explored – again without a guide – the remoter quarters of the city. All the bridges are provided with stairs, so that gondolas and even larger boats can pass under their arches without difficulty. I tried to find my way in and out of the labyrinth by myself, asking nobody the way and taking my directions only from the points of the compass. It is possible to do this and I find my method of personal experience the best. I have been to the furthest edges of the inhabited area and studied the way of life, the morals and manners of the inhabitants. They are different in every district. Good heavens! what a poor good creature man is after all.

Many little houses rise directly from the canals, but here and there are well-paved footpaths on which one can stroll very pleasantly between water, churches and palaces. One agreeable walk is along the stone quay on the northern side. From it one can see the smaller islands, among them Murano, a Venice in miniature. The intervening lagoons are alive with innumerable gondolas.

Evening

Today I bought a map of the city. After studying it carefully, I climbed the Campanile of San Marco. It was nearly noon and the sun shone so brightly that I could recognize both close and distant places without a telescope. The lagoons are covered at high tide, and when I turned my eyes in the direction of the Lido, a narow strip of land which shuts in the lagoons, I saw the sea for the first time. Some sails were visible on it, and in the lagoons themselves galleys and frigates were lying at anchor. These were to have joined Admiral Emo, who is fighting the Algerians, but unfavourable winds have detained them here. North and west, the hills of Padua and Vicenza and the Tirolean Alps made a beautiful frame to the whole picture.

1 October

Today was Sunday, and as I walked about I was struck by the uncleanliness of the streets. This set me thinking. There appears to be some kind of police regulation on this matter, for people sweep the rubbish into corners and I saw large barges stopping at certain points and carrying the rubbish away. They came from the surrounding islands where people are in need of manure. But there is no logic or discipline in these arrangements. The dirt is all the more inexcusable because the city is as designed for cleanliness as any Dutch town. All the street are paved with flagstones; even in the remotest quarter, bricks are at least placed on the kerb and, wherever it is necessary, the streets are raised in the middle and have gutters at their sides to catch the water and carry it off into covered drains. These and other technical devices are clearly the work of efficient architects who planned to make Venice the cleanest of cities as well as the most unusual. As I walked, I found myself devising sanitary regulations and drawing up a preliminary plan for an imaginary police inspector who was seriously interested in the problem. It shows how eager man always is to sweep his neighbour's doorstep.

2 October

I hurried off first thing to the Carità. I had discovered in the writings of Palladio a reference to a monastery in which he had intended to reproduce a typical private home of a rich and hospitable man in classical times.

His plan, both in general design and in detail, had delighted me and I expected to see a miracle of beauty. Alas, scarcely a tenth of it has been built, but even this little is worthy of his divine genius. I am convinced I am right when I say that I never saw anything more sublime, more perfect, in my life. One ought to spend years contemplating such a work.

The church is older. Leaving it, one enters an atrium of Corinthian columns which immediately makes one forget all ecclesiastical hocus-pocus. On one side is the sacristy, on the other the chapter house, and the most beautiful winding staircase in the world. This has a broad open newel and the stone steps are built into the wall and so tiered that each supports the one above it. How beautifully it is constructed can be gathered from the fact that Palladio himself was satisfied with it. From the atrium, one steps into a large inner courtyard. Unfortunately, of the building which was planned to surround it, only the left-hand side was finished – three superimposed orders of columns. The ground floor has porches, the first floor an arcade with cells opening into it; the top floor is a wall with windows.

Now a word about the construction. Only the capitals and bases of the columns and the keystones of the arches are carved in marble. All the rest is made, I cannot say of bricks, but of burnt clay. I never saw this kind of tile before. The friezes, the cornices and the sides of the arches are all made of it. The material was partly fired and the whole building held together with very little mortar. Even as it stands, it seems all of one piece, so what a wonderful sight it would have been if it had been finished and properly polished and coloured. But the scheme, as with so many buildings today, was on too large a scale. The artist had assumed, not only that the existing convent would be torn down, but also that some adjoining houses would be bought up. Probably the money ran out and he lost interest. O kindly Fates, who favour and perpetuate so many stupidities, why did You not allow this work to be completed!

3 October

The Church of Il Redentore, another noble work by Palladio, has an even more admirable façade than that of San Giorgio. Palladio was strongly imbued with the spirit of the Ancients, and felt acutely the petty narrow-mindedness of his times, like a great man who does not wish to conform to the world but to transform it in accordance with his own high ideals. From a casual remark in the book, I infer that he was dissatisfied with the custom of building Christian churches in the form of old basilicas, and tried to make his sacred buildings approximate to the form of the Classical temple. This attempt led to certain incongruities, which seem to me to have been happily avoided in Il Redentore, but are very conspicuous in San Giorgio. Volkmann says something about this but he fails to hit the nail on the head.

The interior of Il Redentore is as admirable as the exterior. Everything, including the altars, is by Palladio. Unfortunately, the niches, which were meant to be filled with statues, are occupied by mediocre figures, carved in wood and painted all over.

The Capuchin friars had sumptuously decorated one of the side altars in honour of St Francis. The only marble left visible was the Corinthian capitals; all the rest was covered with what looked like a magnificent arabesque embroidery. I was particularly impressed by the tendrils and leaves embroidered with gold thread, and when I looked closer, I discovered an ingenious trick. Everything I had taken for gold was actually straw, pressed flat and pasted on paper in beautiful designs. The ground was painted in vivid colours and everything was executed in excellent taste. If, instead of having been made in the convent for nothing, the material of this piece of fun had been genuine gold, it would probably have cost several thousand *thalers*. On occasions one might very well follow their example.

On a quay overlooking the water I have several times noticed a low fellow telling stories in Venetian dialect, of which, unfortunately, I cannot understand a word. His audience consisted for the most part of people of the humblest class. No one laughed; there was rarely even a smile. There was nothing obtrusive or ridiculous about his manner, which was even rather sober; at the same time the variety and precision of his gestures showed both art and intelligence.

Map in hand, I tried to find my way through the labyrinth to the Church of the Mendicants. Here is the Conservatorio, which at the present time enjoys the highest reputation. The women were singing an oratorio behind the choir screen; the church was filled with listeners, the music beautiful and the voices superb. An alto sang the part of King Saul, the protagonist in the work. I have never heard such a voice. Some passages in the music were of infinite beauty and the text was perfectly singable – a kind of Italian Latin which made one smile at times but which gave the music wide scope.

The performance would have been even more enjoyable if the damned conductor had not beaten time against the screen with a rolled sheet of music as insolently as if he were teaching schoolboys. The girls had so often rehearsed the piece that his vehement slapping was as unnecessary as if, in order to make us appreciate a beautiful statue, someone were to stick little patches of red cloth on the joints.

This man was a musician, yet he did not, apparently, hear the discordant sound he was making which ruined the harmony of the whole. Maybe he wanted to attract our attention to himself by this extraordinary behaviour; he would have convinced us better of his merits by giving a perfect performance. I know this thumping out the beat is customary with the French; but I had not expected it from the Italians. The public, though, seemed to be used to it. It was not the only occasion on which I have seen the public under the delusion that something which spoils the enjoyment is part of it.

Last night I went to the opera in San Mosè (here the theatres are named after the nearest church) and did not enjoy it much. The libretto, the music and the singers all lacked that essential energy which such performances need to reach perfection. One could not say that everything was bad, but only the two women took the trouble both to act well and to please. That, at least, was something to be thankful for. Both had beautiful figures and good voices and were lively, agreeable little creatures. The men, on the other hand, sang without any gusto and their voices lacked all brilliance.

The ballet was deficient in ideas and was booed most of the time. But one or two of the dancers, male and female, were wildly applauded. The girls considered it their duty to acquaint the audience with every beautiful part of their bodies.

Today I saw a very different kind of comedy which I enjoyed much more. In the Palazzo Ducale I witnessed an important trial, which, luckily for me, had come on during the vacation. One of the advocates was everything an exaggerated buffo should be: short and fat but agile, a very prominent profile, a booming voice and an impassioned eloquence, as though everything he said came from the bottom of his heart.

I call it a comedy because everything has probably already been settled before the public performance takes place; the judges know what they have to say, and the contending parties what they have to expect. Nevertheless, I much prefer this kind of proceeding to our fussy and complicated bureaucratic system. Let me try to give some idea of the amusing, informal and natural way in which such things are conducted here.

In a large hall of the palazzo, the judges sit on one side in a semicircle. Opposite them, on a platform large enough to seat several persons side by side, sit the advocates of both parties. On a bench facing them sit the plaintiff and the defendant. When I entered, the advocate for the plaintiff had left the platform, since today's session was not to be a legal duel. All the documents, pro and con, were to be read aloud, although they had already been printed. A scraggy clerk in a dingy black coat with a bulging file in his hands was preparing to perform his duties as a reader. The hall was packed and it was obvious that the legal issue was as important to the Venetian public as it was to the parties involved.

Fideicommissums enjoy a high legal status in the Republic. Once an estate is stamped with this character, it keeps it permanently, even though, for some special reason or other, it may have been sold several centuries ago and passed through many hands. If the question of ownership is ever raised, the descendants of the original family can claim their rights and the estate must be restored to them.

On this occasion the litigation was of particular importance because the complaint was against the Doge himself, or rather against his spouse, who was sitting there, on the little bench, wrapped in her *zendale*, with only a small space between her and the plaintiff. She was a lady of a certain age with a noble stature, regular features and a serious, even sour expression. The Venetians were very proud to see the princess appear before the court, in public and in her own palace.

The clerk started reading, and only then did I realize the significance of a little man sitting on a low stool behind a little table, not far from the advocates' platform, and of the hourglass he had in front of him. So long as the clerk is reading, the time is not counted, but if the advocate wishes to interrupt the reading, he is granted only a limited time. While the clerk reads, the hourglass lies on its side with the little man's hand touching it. As soon as the advocate opens his mouth, the hourglass is raised; as soon as he stops talking, it is laid down again.

Therefore, when the advocate wishes to attract the attention of the public or to challenge the evidence, it requires great skill on his part to do this effectively with brief comments. When he does, the little Saturn is completely nonplussed; he has to keep switching the hourglass from a horizontal to a vertical position and back every minute and finds himself in a similar situation to that of the evil spirits in the puppet play when the mischievous harlequin cries 'Berlicke! Berlocke!'* in such rapid succession that they never know whether they should come or go.

Only someone who has heard the collating of documents in a law court can have any idea of this method of reading – rapid monotonous, but quite articulate. A skilful advocate knows how to relieve the general boredom with facetious remarks, and the public responds to them with roars of laughter. I remember one joke, the most amusing of those I could understand.

The clerk was reciting a document in which the owner, whose right was in doubt, disposed of the property in question. The advocate asked him to read slower, and when the clerk came to the words 'I bestow, I bequeath' flew out at him, shouting: 'And what do *you* want to bestow? What do *you* want to bequeath? You poor starved devil, without a penny to your name! However,' he continued, apparently pulling himself together, 'the same could be said of our illustrious

* *Berlicke, Berlocke.* Magic spell from the old puppet play *Dr Faustus.*

proprietor. He also wanted to bestow and to bequeath what belonged to him as little as it belongs to you.' A burst of laughter ensued which went on for a long time, but the hourglass was immediately returned to its horizontal position, and the clerk went on droning and pulling faces at the advocate. All this clowning, however, is arranged in advance.

4 October

At the Teatro San Luca yesterday I saw an improvised comedy, played in masks with great bravura. The actors were, of course, unequal. Pantalone, very good; one woman, without being an outstanding actress, had an excellent delivery and stage presence. The subject was a fantastic one, similar to that which is played in our country under the title *Der Verschlag*.

We were entertained for more than three hours with one incredible situation after the other. But once again, the basis of everything is the common people; the spectators join in the play and the crowd becomes part of the theatre. During the daytime, squares, canals, gondolas and palazzi are full of life as the buyer and the seller, the beggar and the boatman, the housewife and the lawyer offer something for sale, sing and gamble, shout and swear. In the evening these same people go to the theatre to behold their actual life, presented with greater economy as make-believe interwoven with fairy stories and removed from reality by masks, yet, in its characters and manners, the life they know. They are delighted, like children, shouting, clapping and generally making a din. From sunset to sunset, from midnight to midnight, they are just the same. Indeed, I never saw more natural acting than that of these masked players, an art which can only be achieved by an extraordinarily happy nature and long practice.

As I write this, a regular bedlam has broken loose under my window, although it is past midnight. Whether for good or ill, they are always up to something together. Now I have

heard three fellows telling stories on a square and a quay, also
two lawyers, two preachers and a troupe of comic actors. All
of them had something in common, not only because they are
all natives of a country where people live in public all the time,
and are all passionate talkers, but also because they imitate
each other, and share a common language of gesture which
accompanies what they say and feel.

Today is the feast of St Francis, and I went to the Church
alle Vigne, which is dedicated to him. The loud voice of a
Capuchin friar was accompanied like an antiphon by the
shouts of the vendors in front of the church. I stood in the
doorway between them and it sounded rather curious.

5 October

This morning I visited the Arsenal, which I found most
interesting because I am ignorant of naval matters and managed to learn a few elementary facts there. It was like visiting
some old family which, though past its prime, still shows
signs of life. I always enjoy watching men at work and I saw
many noteworthy things. I climbed up on to a ship of eighty-
four cannon, the finished hull of which was standing there.
Six months ago, in the Riva degli Schiavoni, a similar ship
burned down to the waterline. The powder magazine was not
very full, so not much harm was done when it exploded; all
that happened was that the houses in the neighbourhood lost
their windows.

Watching the men working with the finest Istrian oak
provoked some mental reflections on the growth of this
valuable tree. I cannot repeat often enough how much my
hard-won knowledge of those natural things, which man
takes as his raw material and transforms to suit his needs,
helps me to get a clearer idea of the craftsman's technique.
Just as my knowledge of mountains and the minerals
extracted from them is of great advantage to me in my
study of architecture.

*

To describe the *Bucentaur* in one word, I shall call it a show-galley. The old *Bucentaur*, of which pictures still exist, justifies the epithet still more than the present one which, by its splendour, makes one forget the original. I always return to my old contention that any artist can create something genuine if he is given a genuine task. In this case, he was commissioned to construct a galley worthy of carrying the heads of the Republic on their most solemn day to the sacrament of their traditional sea power, and this task was admirably performed. One should not say that it is overladen with ornaments, for the whole ship is one single ornament. All the wood carving is gilded and serves no purpose except to be a true monstrance showing the people their masters in a splendid pageant. As we know, people who like to decorate their own hats like to see their superiors elegantly dressed as well. This state barge is a real family heirloom, which reminds us of what the Venetians once believed themselves to be, and were.

At night

I have just got back from the Tragedy and am still laughing, so let me commit this farce to paper at once. The piece was not bad; the author had jumbled together all the tragic matadors, and the actors had good roles. Most of the situations were stale, but a few were fresh and quite felicitous. Two fathers who hated each other, the sons and daughters of these divided families passionately in love crosswise, one couple even secretly married. Violent, cruel things went on and in the end nothing remained to make the young people happy but that their fathers should stab one another, whereupon the curtain fell to thundering applause. The audience did not stop shouting '*fuora*' until the two leading couples condescended to creep round from behind one side of the curtain, make their bows and go off on the other.

The audience was still not satisfied but continued clapping and shouting '*I morti!*' until the two dead men also appeared and bowed, whereupon a few voices cried: '*Bravi i morti*'; and it was some time before they were allowed to make their exit. To get the full flavour of this absurdity, one must see and hear it for oneself. My ears are ringing with the *bravo! bravi!* which Italians are forever shouting, and now I have even heard the dead acclaimed with this compliment. *Good night!* We northerners say this at any time after sundown when we take leave of each other; the Italian says '*Felicissima notte!*' only once, to wit, when the lamp is brought into the room at the moment that separates day from night, so that the phrase has quite a different meaning. The idioms of every language are untranslatable, for any word, from the noblest to the coarsest, is related to the unique character, beliefs and way of life of the people who speak it.

6 October

I learned many things from yesterday's tragedy. To begin with, I heard how the Italians declaim their iambic hendecasyllabics. Then I now see with what skill Gozzi combined the use of masks with tragic characters. This is the proper spectacle for a people who want to be moved in the crudest way. They take no sentimental interest in misfortune and enjoy themselves only if the hero declaims well. They set great store by rhetoric and, at the same time, they want to laugh at some nonsense.

Their interest in a play is limited to what they feel is real. When the tyrant handed his son a sword and ordered him to kill his own wife, who was standing before him, the public expressed its displeasure at such an unreasonable demand, and so noisily that they almost stopped the play. They yelled at the old man to take his sword back, an action which would, of course, have wrecked the subsequent situations in the play. In the end, the harassed son came down to the footlights and humbly implored the audience to be patient for a little because the business would certainly conclude exactly as they hoped. But, artistically speaking, the situation of which

the public complained was absurd and unnatural, and I heartily approved of their feelings.

I now understood better the long speeches and the many
passages of dialectic in Greek tragedy. The Athenians were
even fonder of talking than the Italians, besides being better
at it. Their dramatists must certainly have learned something
at the tribunals, where they spent whole days.

Looking at the buildings which Palladio completed, in
particular at his churches, I have found much to criticize
side by side with great excellence. While I was asking myself
how far I was right or wrong about this extraordinary man,
he seemed to be standing beside me, saying: 'This or that
I did against my will, nevertheless I did it because it was
the closest approximation to my ideal possible under the
circumstances.'

The more I think about him, the more strongly I feel that,
when he looked at the height and width of an old church or
house for which he had to make a new façade, he must have
said to himself: 'How can you give this building the noblest
form possible? Because of contradictory demands, you are
bound to bungle things here and there, and it may well
happen that there will be some incongruities. But the building
as a whole will be in a noble style, and you will enjoy doing the
work.' It was in this way that he executed the great conception he had in mind, even when it was not quite suitable and
he had to mangle it in the details.

The wing of the Carità, therefore, must be doubly precious
to us because here the artist was given a free hand and could
obey his genius unconditionally. Had the convent been finished, there would probably be no more perfect work of
architecture in the whole world today.

The more I read his writings and note as I do his treatment
of classical antiquity, the more clearly I understand how he
thought and worked. He was a man of few words, but every
one of them carries weight. As a study of Classical temples,
his fourth volume is an excellent introduction for the intelligent reader.

Last night, at the Teatro San Crisostomo, I saw Crébillon's *Electra* – in translation, of course. I cannot express how tasteless I found it and how terribly bored I was.

As a matter of fact, the actors were quite good and knew how to put over certain passages on the public. In one scene alone Orestes has no less than three separate narrations, all poetically embroidered. Electra, a pretty, vivacious little woman, spoke the verse beautifully, but her acting was as extravagant as her role, alas, demanded. However, I again learned something. The Italian iambic hendecasyllabic is ill-suited to declamation because the last syllable is always short and this causes an involuntary raising of the voice at the end of every line.

This morning I attended High Mass at the Church of Santa Giustina, where, on this day of the year, the Doge has always to be present to commemorate an old victory over the Turks. The gilded barges, carrying the Prince and some of the nobility, land at the little square; oddly liveried boatmen ply their red-painted oars; on shore the clergy and religious orders, holding lighted candles on poles and silver candelabra, jostle each other and stand around waiting; gangways covered with carpets are laid across from the vessels to the shore: first come the *Savii* in their long violet robes, then the Senators in their red ones, and, last, the old Doge, in his long golden gown and ermine cape and wearing his golden Phrygian cap, leaves the barge while three servants bear the train of his robe.

To watch all this happening in a little square before the doors of a church on which Turkish standards were displayed was like seeing an old tapestry of beautiful colour and design, and to me, as a fugitive from the north, it gave keen pleasure. At home, where short coats are *de rigueur* for all festive occasions and the finest ceremony we can imagine is a parade of shouldered muskets, an affair like this might look out of place, but here these trailing robes and unmilitary ceremonies are perfectly in keeping.

The Doge is a good-looking, imposing man. Although, apparently, in ill health, he holds himself, for the sake of dignity, erect under his heavy gown. He looks like the grand-papa of the whole race and his manner is gracious and courteous. His garments were very becoming and the little transparent bonnet he wore under his cap did not offend the eye, for it rested upon the most lovely snow-white hair.

He was accompanied by about fifty noblemen, most of them very good-looking. I did not see a single ugly one. Some were tall and had big heads, framed in blond curly wigs. As for their faces, the features were prominent and the flesh, though soft and white, had nothing repellently flabby about it. They looked rather intelligent, self-assured, unaffected and cheerful.

When they had all taken their places in the church and High Mass had begun, the religious orders entered in pairs by the west door, were blessed with holy water, bowed to the high altar, to the Doge and to the nobility, and then left by a side door to the right.

For this evening I had made arrangements to hear the famous singing of the boatmen, who chant verses by Tasso and Ariosto to their own melodies. This performance has to be ordered in advance, for it is now rarely done and belongs, rather, to the half-forgotten legends of the past. The moon had risen when I took my seat in a gondola and the two singers, one in the prow, the other in the stern, began chant-ing verse after verse in turns. The melody, which we know from Rousseau,* is something between chorale and recita-tive. It always moves at the same tempo without any definite beat. The modulation is of the same character; the singers change pitch according to the content of the verse in a kind of declamation.

I shall not go into the question of how the melody evolved. It is enough to say that it is ideal for someone idly singing

* J. J. Rousseau, *Recueil d'Airs, Romances et Duos*, Paris, 1750.

to himself and adapting the tune to poems he knows by heart.

The singer sits on the shore of an island, on the bank of a canal or in a gondola, and sings at the top of his voice – the people here appreciate volume more than anything else. His aim is to make his voice carry as far as possible over the still mirror of water. Far away another singer hears it. He knows the melody and the words and answers with the next verse. The first singer answers again, and so on. Each is the echo of the other. They keep this up night after night without ever getting tired. If the listener has chosen the right spot, which is halfway between them, the further apart they are, the more enchanting the singing will sound.

To demonstrate this, my boatmen tied up the gondola on the shore of the Giudecca and walked along the canal in opposite directions. I walked back and forth, leaving the one, who was just about to sing, and walking towards the other, who had just stopped.

For the first time I felt the full effect of this singing. The sound of their voices far away was extraordinary, a lament without sadness, and I was moved to tears. I put this down to my mood at the moment, but my old manservant said: '*è singolare, come quel canto intenerisce, e molto più, quando è più ben cantato.*' He wanted me to hear the women on the Lido, especially those from Malamocco and Pellestrina. They too, he told me, sing verses by Tasso to the same or a similar melody, and added: 'It is their custom to sit on the seashore while their husbands are out sea-fishing, and sing these songs in penetrating tones until, from far out over the sea, their men reply, and in this way they converse with each other.' Is this not a beautiful custom? I dare say that, to someone standing close by, the sound of such voices, competing with the thunder of the waves, might not be very agreeable. But the motive behind such singing is so human and genuine that it makes the mere notes of the melody, over which scholars have racked their brains in vain, come to life. It is the cry of some lonely human being sent out into the wide world till it reaches the ears of another lonely human being who is moved to answer it.

8 October

I visited the Palazzo Pisani Moretta to look at a painting by Paolo Veronese. The female members of the family of Darius are kneeling at the feet of Alexander and Hephaestus. The mother mistakes Hephaestus for the King, but he declines the honour and points to the right person. There is a legend connected with this picture according to which Veronese was for a long time an honoured guest in this palace and, to show his gratitude, painted it in secret, rolled it up and left it under his bed as a gift. It is certainly worthy of such an unusual history. His ability to create a harmony through a skilful distribution of light and shade and local colours without any single dominant tone is conspicuous in this painting, which is in a remarkable state of preservation and looks as fresh as if it had been painted yesterday. When a canvas of this kind has suffered any damage, our pleasure in it is spoiled without our knowing the reason.

Once it is understood that Veronese wanted to paint an episode of the sixteenth century, no one is going to criticize him for the costumes. The graded placing of the group, the mother in front, behind her the wife, and then the daughters in order, is natural and happy. The youngest princess, who kneels behind all the rest, is a pretty little mouse with a defiant expression. She looks as if she were not at all pleased at coming last.

My tendency to look at the world through the eyes of the painter whose pictures I have seen last has given me an odd idea. Since our eyes are educated from childhood on by the objects we see around us, a Venetian painter is bound to see the world as a brighter and gayer place than most people see it. We northerners who spend our lives in a drab and, because of the dirt and the dust, an uglier country where even reflected light is subdued, and who have, most of us, to live in cramped rooms – we cannot instinctively develop an eye which looks with such delight at the world.

As I glided over the lagoons in the brilliant sunshine and saw the gondoliers in their colourful costume, gracefully posed against the blue sky as they rowed with easy strokes across the light-green surface of the water, I felt I was looking at the latest and best painting of the Venetian school. The sunshine raised the local colours to a dazzling glare and even the parts in shadow were so light that they could have served pretty well as sources of light. The same could be said of the reflections in the water. Everything was painted clearly on a clear background. It only needed the sparkle of a white-crested wave to put the dot on the *i*.

Both Titian and Veronese possessed this clarity to the highest degree, and when we do not find it in their works, this means that the picture has suffered damage or been retouched.

The cupolas, vaults and lateral wall-faces of the Basilica of San Marco are completely covered with mosaics of various colours on a common gold ground. Some are good, some are poor, depending upon the master who made the original cartoon. Everything depends on that, for it is possible to imitate with square little pieces of glass, though not very exactly, either the Good or the Bad.

The art of mosaic, which gave the Ancients their paved floors and the Christians the vaulted Heaven of their churches, has now been degraded to snuff boxes and brace-lets. Our times are worse than we think.

The Casa Farsetti houses a collection of casts taken from the finest pieces of antique sculpture, a few of which I had already seen in Mannheim and elsewhere. A colossal Cleo-patra with the asp coiled around her arm, sleeping the sleep of death – a Niobe shielding her youngest daughter from the arrows of Apollo with her cloak – a few gladiators – a winged genius resting – sitting or standing philosophers.

Many striking portrait busts evoked the glorious days of antiquity. I feel myself, alas, far behind in my knowledge of this period, but at least I know the way. Palladio has opened it to me, and the way to all art and life as well. This may sound a little strange, but it is not quite so paradoxical as the case of Jacob Boehme, to whom Jove's thunderbolt revealed the secret of the universe while he was looking at a pewter bowl. The collection contains also a fragment of entablature from the temple of Antoninus and Faustina in Rome which, in its striking modernity, reminded me of the capital from the Parthenon which stands in Mannheim. How different all this is from our saints, squatting on their stone brackets and piled one above the other in the Gothic style of decoration, or our pillars which look like tobacco pipes, our spiky little towers and our cast-iron flowers. Thank God, I am done with all that junk for good and all.

Before the gate of the Arsenal, there are two enormous lions of white marble; one is sitting erect, planted firmly on his forepaws, the other is lying stretched out. They are so huge that they make everything around them look small, and one would feel crushed oneself if sublime works of art did not always elevate the spirit. They are said to belong to the best period of Greek art and to have been brought here from the Piraeus during the glorious days of the Republic.

Some bas-reliefs let into the wall of the Church of Santa Giustina, the vanquisher of the Turks, probably come from Athens as well, but they are difficult to see properly because of the high choir stalls. They show genii dragging about attributes of the gods. The sacristan drew my attention to them because, so the story goes, Titian took them as models for the angels in his painting: the *Murder of St Peter Martyr*. They certainly are indescribably beautiful.

In the courtyard of a palazzo, I saw a colossal nude statue of Marcus Agrippa; the wriggling dolphin at his side indicates that he was a naval hero. How true it is that a heroic representation of the human being simply as he is makes him godlike.

I took a close look at the horses on the Basilica of San Marco. From below one can see that in some places they have a beautiful yellow metallic sheen but in others show a copper-green tarnish. We are told that once they were gilded, and at close quarters one sees that they are scored all over, because the barbarians could not be bothered to file away the gold but hacked it off with chisels. Still, it might have been worse; at least their forms have been preserved.

Early this morning a gondola took me and my old factotum to the Lido. We went ashore and walked across the spit of land. I heard a loud noise: it was the sea, which presently came into view. The surf was breaking on the beach in high waves, although the water was receding, for it was noon, the hour of low tide. Now, at last, I have seen the sea with my own eyes and walked upon the beautiful threshing floor of the sand which it leaves behind when it ebbs. How I wished the children could have been with me! They would so have loved the shells. Like a child, I picked up a good many because I have a special use for them. There are plenty of cuttlefish about, and I need the shells to dry the inky fluid they eject.

Not far from the beach lies the Cemetery for the English and, a little further on, that for the Jews, neither of whom are allowed to rest in consecrated ground. I found the graves of the good consul Smith and his first wife. To him I owe my copy of Palladio, and I offered up a grateful prayer at his unconsecrated grave, which was half buried in the sand.

You must think of the Lido as a dune. The wind stirs up the sand, blows it in all directions and piles it up on all sides in drifts. Soon no one will be able to find this grave, though it is raised fairly high above the ground level.

What a magnificent sight the sea is! I shall try to go out in a boat with the fishermen; the gondolas dare not risk putting out to open sea.

Along the shore I found various plants whose common characteristics gave me a better understanding of their individual natures. All are plump and firm, juicy and tough, and it is clear that the salt content of the sand and, even more, the salt in the air is responsible. They are bursting with sap like aquatic plants, yet hardly like mountain flora. The tips of their leaves have a tendency to become prickly like thistles, and when this happens, the spikes grow very long and tough. I found a cluster of such leaves which I took to be our harmless coltsfoot, but it was armed with sharp weapons, and the leaves, the seed capsules and the stalks were as tough as leather. Actually, it was sea holly (*Eryngium maritimum*). I shall bring seeds and pressed leaves with me.

The fish market offers countless varieties of sea food. It is delightful to wander through it inspecting the luckless denizens of the sea which the nets have caught.

9 October

A precious day from beginning to end! I visited Pellestrina, opposite Chioggia, where the Republic is constructing huge defences against the sea called *i murazzi*. These are built of uncemented stone blocks and are intended to protect the Lido in times of storm. The lagoons are a creation of nature. The interaction of tides and earth, followed by the gradual fall in level of the primeval ocean, formed an extensive tract of swampland at the extreme end of the Adriatic, which was covered at high tide but partly exposed at low.

Human skill took over the highest portions of ground and thus Venice came into being as a cluster of hundreds of islands surrounded by hundreds of other islands. At great cost and with incredible energy, deep channels were dredged to enable warships to reach the vital points even at low tide.

All that intelligence and hard work created in times past, intelligence and hard work have now to preserve. There are only two gaps in the Lido through which the sea can enter the lagoons – one near the Castello and one near Chioggia. Normally the tide flows in and out twice a day, and the current always follows the same course. The high tide covers the marshy patches but leaves the higher ground still visible, if not dry.

But it would be a very different matter if the sea should attack the spit of land and make new breaches so that it could flow in and out at will. Not only would the little towns on the Lido, Pellestrina, S. Pietro and others, be submerged, but also the system of communicating channels would be silted up. The Lido would be transformed into islands and the islands behind it into tongues of land. To prevent this, the Venetians must make every effort to protect the Lido, so that the angry element cannot destroy or alter that which man has already conquered and to which he has given shape and direction for his own purposes.

In times of abnormally high tides it is especially fortunate that the sea can only enter at two points and is shut out elsewhere. The fury of its entry is curbed and in a few hours it has to submit again to the law of reflux.

Actually, the Venetians have little to worry about: the slowness with which the sea is receding guarantees them security for millennia, and, by intelligently improving their system of dredged channels, they will do their best to keep their possessions intact.

If only they would keep their city cleaner! It may be forbidden, under severe penalties, to empty garbage into the canals, but that does not prevent a sudden downpour from sweeping into them all the rubbish that has accumulated at the street corners, or, what is worse, from washing it into the drains, which are only meant to carry off water, and choking them, so that the main squares are in constant danger of being flooded. I have even seen the drains in the little square of San Marco, which are as sensibly distributed as those on the big one, choked to overflowing.

On rainy days a disgusting sludge collects underfoot; the coats and *tabarros*, which are worn all year round, are bespattered whenever you cross a bridge, and, since everybody goes about in shoes and stockings – nobody wears boots – these get soiled, not with plain mud, but with a vile-smelling muck.

Everybody curses and swears, but as soon as the weather clears up, nobody notices the dirt any more. It has been truly said that the public is forever complaining that it is badly served but won't take the first step to see that it is served better. All this could be put right at once if the city authorities cared.

This evening I again climbed to the top of the Campanile. Last time I saw the lagoons in their glory at the hour of high tide; this time I wanted to see them in their humiliation at low tide, so as to have a complete mental picture. It was very strange to see dry land all around where previously I had seen only a mirror of water. The islands were islands no longer but patches of higher ground rising from a large greenish-grey morass intersected by channels. The swampland is over-grown with aquatic plants and should, for that reason, be gradually rising, in spite of the pluck of the tides which never leave the vegetation alone.

To get back to the sea. Today I watched the amusing behaviour of the mussels, limpets and crabs. What an amazing thing a living organism is! How adaptable! How there, and how itself! How useful my knowledge of natural history, scrappy though it is, has been to me, and how I look forward to increasing it! But, when there is so much to share with them, I must not excite my friends with exclamations alone.

The sea walls of which I spoke are constructed as follows. First come some steep steps, then a gently inclined surface, then another step, then another incline and finally a vertical wall with a coping on top. The rising sea climbs the steps and slopes and only when exceptionally violent does it break against the wall and its coping.

In the wake of the tide come small mussels, univalved limpets and any other small creature that is capable of motion, crabs in particular. But they have hardly secured a hold on the sea wall before the tide begins to recede. At first the crawling swarm does not know what has happened to it, and expects the briny flood to return. But it does not return. The stone quickly dries in the blazing sun, and, at that, they

begin to beat a hasty retreat. This gives the crabs their chance
to go hunting. Nothing is more entertaining to watch than the
movements of these creatures. All one can see is a round
body and two long pincer claws; their spindly legs are
invisible. They strut along as if on stilts, and as soon as a
limpet starts moving, they rush forward and try to insert their
claws into the narrow span between the limpet's shell and the
ground so as to turn it upside down and devour the now
defenceless mollusc. But as soon as the limpet senses the
presence of its enemy, it attaches itself to the stone by suc-
tion. Now the crab puts on a bizarre and graceful performance. It capers around the shell like a monkey, but lacks the
strength to overpower the powerful muscle of the soft little
creature. Presently it abandons its quarry and hurries off to
stalk another wanderer, while the first limpet continues
slowly on its way. I did not see a single crab succeed, although
I watched for hours.

10 October

At last I have seen a real comedy! At the Teatro San Luca
today they played *Le Baruffe Chiozzotte*, one of the few plays by
Goldoni which is still performed. The title might be roughly
translated as *The Scuffles and Brawls in Chioggia*. The characters
are all natives of that town, fishermen and their wives, sisters
and daughters. The habitual to-do made by these people,
their quarrels, their outbursts of temper, their good nature,
superficiality, wit, humour and natural behaviour – all these
were excellently imitated. I was in Chioggia only yesterday, so
their faces were still vivid in my mind's eye and their voices
still ringing in my ears. I enjoyed the play immensely, and
could follow it fairly well, even though I did not understand
all the local allusions. The plot is as follows: The women of
Chioggia are sitting as usual in front of their houses along the
water front, spinning, knitting, sewing or making lace. A
young man passes by and greets one of them with greater
warmth than the others. This sets off a gibing match.

Tongues grow sharper and more sarcastic, one insult outdoes another, accusations are hurled back and forth until one virago blurts out the truth. At this, all hell breaks loose and the authorities are forced to intervene.

The second act takes place in a courtroom. It is not allowed to represent the nobility on the stage, so the place of the *podestà* is taken by the actuary. He orders the women to appear before him one by one. This arouses suspicion because he is in love with the leading lady and is only too glad of an opportunity to speak with her in private. Instead of interrogating her, he declares his love.

Another woman, who is in love with him and madly jealous, bursts into the room, followed by the enraged lover of the first lady and then by all the others. Fresh accusations are hurled, and hell breaks loose again in the courtroom as it had previously on the quayside.

In the third act the fun reaches its climax and the play ends with a hasty forced solution.

One character is a very happy dramatic invention. Among all these scandal-loving, loquacious people, there is one old fisherman whose physical faculties are impeded as the result of a hard life since childhood. Speech, in particular, costs him immense effort. He has to move his lips and wave his hands violently in the air before he at last manages to stutter out what he is thinking. Since he can only express himself in short sentences, he has developed a laconic and solemn manner of speech, which gives all his remarks the character of a proverb or an aphorism. This provides a perfect counterbalance to the uninhibited passionate behaviour of the other characters.

I have never in my life witnessed such an ecstasy of joy as that shown by the audience when they saw themselves and their families so realistically portrayed on the stage. They shouted with laughter and approval from beginning to end. The actors did an excellent job. Between them they represented all the types of character one finds among the common people. The leading lady was particularly charming – much better than she was the other day as a tragic heroine. By and large, all the actresses, but especially this one, imitated the voices, gestures and temperaments of the people with uncanny skill, but the highest praise is due to the playwright for creating such a delightful entertainment out of thin air. Only someone in intimate contact with this pleasure-loving people could have done it. It is written with an expert hand.

Of Sacchi's company, for which Gozzi wrote and which is now scattered, I have only seen Smeraldina, who is short and plump but full of vivacity, and Brighella, a lean, well-built man whose facial play and gestures are particularly expressive.

Masks, which in our country have as little life and meaning for us as mummies, here seem sympathetic and characteristic expressions of the country: every age, character type and profession is embodied in some extraordinary costume, and since people run around in fancy dress for the greater part of the year, nothing seems more natural than to see faces in dominoes on the stage as well.

11 October

Since solitude amid a large crowd does not, in the long run, seem possible, I have struck up an acquaintance with an old Frenchman. He does not know one word of Italian and, in spite of all his letters of introduction, feels completely at sea. He is a man of some standing and has perfect manners, but he cannot come out of his shell. He must be in his late fifties. He has left a seven-year-old son at home and is waiting anxiously for news of him. He is travelling through Italy in great comfort but at great speed. All he wants is to have at least seen the country and learned as much as possible in passing. I have managed to do him a few good turns and give him some useful information. As I was talking to him about Venice, he asked how long I had been there. When I told him: 'Two weeks and for the first time,' he remarked: '*Il paraît que vous n'avez pas perdu votre temps.*' This is the first testimonial to my good conduct that I can present. He had been here a

week and is leaving tomorrow. To have met in a foreign
country such an incarnation of Versailles is an experience
I shall treasure. 'Now, here's another kind of traveller for
you,' I said to myself. It was amazing to me that a man who, in
this way, was well educated, brave and decent could travel
without noticing anything in the world outside himself.

12 October

Yesterday, at San Luca, they played a new piece, *L'Inglicismo in
Italia*. Since there are a great many Englishmen living in Italy,
it is only natural that notice should be taken of their behaviour, and I hoped to hear what the Italians think about their
wealthy and welcome guests. But the play amounted to
nothing. There were a few of the usual farcical scenes, but
the rest was heavy and pedantic. Moreover, there was not a
trace of the English character; just the usual Italian moral
platitudes about the most commonplace matters.

It was not a success and came near to being booed. The
actors did not feel in their element as they had on the square
of Chioggia. This was the last play I saw here, and it at least
did one thing for me. By contrast, it heightened my enthusiasm for the representation of real Italian life as I saw it the
other night.

Having gone over my journal for the last time and inserted
a few observations from my notes, I shall now arrange everything in the proper order, roll it up and send it off, to be
submitted to the judgement of my friends.

There is much in this record, I know, which I could have
described more accurately, amplified and improved, but
I shall leave everything as it stands because first impressions,
even if they are not always correct, are valuable and precious
to us. Oh, if only I could send my distant friends a breath of
the more carefree existence here! It is true that the Italian has
only the shadowiest idea of the ultramontane countries, but
Beyond the Alps now seems dim to me too, though friendly
faces beckon to me all the time out of the mists. The climate

alone would lead me to prefer these regions to all others, if birth and habit were not powerful bonds. I should not like to live here permanently or anywhere else where I had no occupation. For the present the novelty of everything keeps me constantly busy. Architecture rises out of its grave like a ghost from the past, and exhorts me to study its precepts, not in order to practise them or enjoy them as a living truth, but, like the rules of a dead language, in order to revere in silence the noble existence of past epochs which have perished for ever.

Since Palladio keeps referring to Vitruvius, I have bought Galliani's edition, but this tome weighs as heavy in my luggage as it weighs on my brain when I study it. I find Palladio, by his own way of thinking and creating, a much better interpreter of Vitruvius than his Italian translator. Vitruvius is not easy reading: the book is written in an obscure style and needs to be studied critically. I skim through the pages or, to be more exact, I read it like a breviary, more from devotion than for instruction. Already the sun sets earlier and I have more time for reading and writing.

Everything that was important to me in early childhood is again, thank God, becoming dear to me, and, to my joy, I find that I can once again dare to approach the classics. Now, at last, I can confess a secret malady, or mania, of mine. For many years I did not dare look into a Latin author or at anything which evoked an image of Italy. If this happened by chance, I suffered agonies. Herder often used to say mockingly that I had learned all my Latin from Spinoza, for that was the only Latin book he had ever seen me reading. He did not realize how carefully I had to guard myself against the classics, and that it was sheer anxiety which drove me to take refuge in the abstractions of Spinoza. Even quite recently, Wieland's translation of Horace's *Satires* made me very unhappy; after reading only a couple, I felt beside myself.

My passionate desire to see these objects with my own eyes had grown to such a point that, if I had not taken the decision I am now acting upon, I should have gone completely to pieces. More historical knowledge was no help. The things were in arm's reach, yet I felt separated from them by an impenetrable barrier. Now I feel, not that I am seeing them for the first time, but that I am seeing them again.

14 October. Two hours after sunset

Written during my last moments here. The packet boat for Ferrara is about to leave at any minute. I am not sorry to leave, because if I were to stay longer with any pleasure and profit, I should have to alter my original plan. Besides, everybody is leaving Venice now for their gardens and estates on the mainland. I have only been here a short time, but I have absorbed the atmosphere of this city sufficiently, and I know that I shall carry a picture away with me which, though it may be incomplete, is clear and accurate so far as it goes.

FROM FERRARA TO ROME

16 October. On the boat. Early morning

MY fellow travellers are still asleep in the cabin, but I have passed the last two nights on deck, wrapped in my cloak. It only cooled off in the early hours of the morning. I have now crossed the forty-fifth parallel and must return to my old song: I would gladly let the inhabitants of this country keep everything if only, like Dido, I could enclose in strips of bull's hide enough of their climate to surround our houses with it. Climate, truly, makes all the difference to one's life. The weather during the voyage was glorious, and the ever-shifting landscape idyllic. The Po runs gently between vast plains. One can see no distant views, only the bushy and wooded banks. I saw some of the same sort of childish levees I had seen on the Adige. They are just as inefficient as those along the Saale.

Ferrara, 16 October. Night

I arrived here at seven in the morning, German time, and expect to leave again tomorrow. For the first time on my trip, I am in low spirits and feel utterly indifferent to this beautiful, depopulated city in the middle of a flat plain. Once upon a time these same streets were animated by a brilliant court. Here Ariosto lived disappointed and Tasso unhappy, and we persuade ourselves that we are edified by visiting their shrines. The mausoleum of Ariosto contains a great deal of badly distributed marble. Instead of Tasso's prison we are shown a woodshed or coal cellar in which he was certainly not confined. At first nobody in the house knows what one wants to see. After a while they remember, but not before they have been tipped. I was reminded of Dr Luther's famous ink stain which is touched up from time to time by the custodian of the castle. There must be something of an itinerant journeyman about most travellers to make them want to look for such signs. I got more and more depressed and was only moderately attracted by a beautiful academic institute which a native-born cardinal had founded and endowed. But some monuments of antiquity restored me to life.

I was further cheered up by a painting of John the Baptist confronting Herod and Herodias. The prophet, in his conventional desert costume, is pointing at the lady with a vehement gesture. She looks impassively at the king sitting beside her, while he looks calmly but shrewdly at the enthusiast. At the feet of the king stands a white dog of medium size, while a small Bolognese dog peeps out from under Herodias' skirt. Both dogs are barking at the prophet. What a jolly idea!

Cento, 17 October. Evening

I am writing from Guercino's home town and in a better mood than I was in yesterday. Cento is a small, clean and friendly town of about five thousand inhabitants. As usual, the first thing I did was to climb the tower. I saw a sea of poplars among which were small farms, each surrounded by its own field. It was an autumn evening such as our summer rarely grants us. The sky, which had been overcast all day, was clearing as the cloud masses moved northward and southward in the direction of the mountains. I expect a fine day tomorrow.

I also got my first glimpse of the Apennines, which I am approaching. Here the winter is confined to December and January; April is the rainy month, and for the rest of the year they have fair, seasonable weather. It never rains for long. This year September was better and warmer than August. I welcomed the sight of the Apennines in the south, for I have had quite enough of flat country. Tomorrow I shall write from their feet.

Guercino loved his native town as most Italians do, for they make a cult of local patriotism. This admirable sentiment has been responsible for many excellent institutions and, incidentally, for the large number of local saints. Under the master's direction, an academy of painting was founded here, and he left the town several pictures which are appreciated by the citizens to this day, and rightly so.

I liked very much one painting of his which represents the risen Christ appearing to His mother. She is kneeling at His feet, looking up at Him with indescribable tenderness. Her left hand is touching His side just below the wound, which is horrible and spoils the whole picture. He has His arm around her neck and is bending backward slightly so as to see her better. The picture is, I will not say unnatural, but a little strange. In spite of it, the figure remains immensely sympathetic. He looks at her with a quiet, sad expression as if the memory of His suffering and hers had not yet been healed by His resurrection, but was still present in His noble soul. Strange has made an engraving of this picture and I should be happy if my friends could at least see that. I was also attracted by an exquisite picture of the Madonna. The Child is reaching for her breast, which she modestly hesitates to bare. In another, the Child is in the foreground facing us, while the Madonna behind Him is lifting His arm so that He may bless us with His raised fingers. A happy idea, and very much in the spirit of Catholic mythology.

As a painter, Guercino is healthy and masculine without being crude. His work has great moral beauty and charm, and a personal manner which makes it immediately recognizable, once one's eye has been trained to look for it. His brush work is amazing. For the garments of his figures he employs particularly beautiful shades of reddish-brown which harmonize very well with the blue he is so fond of using. The subjects of his other paintings are not so happy. This fine artist tortured himself to paint what was a waste of his imagination and his skill. I am very glad to have seen the work of this important school of painting, though such a hasty look is insufficient for proper enjoyment.

Bologna, 18 October. Night

I left Cento early this morning and arrived here soon after. As soon as he heard that I had no intention of staying long, an alert, well-informed guide raced me through the streets and so many churches and palaces that I scarcely had time to mark in my Volkmann the places I visited, and who knows, if I look at the marks in the future, how many of them I shall remember? But now for a few highlights.

First of all, the Cecilia by Raphael. My eyes confirmed what I have always known: this man accomplished what others could only dream of. What can one really say about this picture except that Raphael painted it! Five saints in a row – their names don't matter – so perfectly realized that one would be content to die so long as this picture could endure for ever. But, in order to understand and appreciate Raphael properly, one must not merely glorify him as a god who appeared suddenly on earth without a father or a mother, like Melchizedek; one must consider his ancestors, his masters. These were rooted in the firm ground of truth; it was their labour and scrupulous care which laid the broad foundation; it was they who vied with each other in raising, step by step, the pyramid, on the summit of which the divine genius of Raphael was to place the last stone and reach a height which no one else will surpass or equal.

My historical interest has been greatly stimulated by looking at paintings by some of the older masters, such as Francesco Francia, a very fine painter, or Pietro di Perugia, such a good man that one feels like calling him an honest German soul. If only Dürer had had the good fortune to go further south in Italy. Poor Dürer! To think how such a genius – I saw some incredibly great works by him in Munich – miscalculated in Venice and made a deal with a priestly gang which lost him months of his time, and how, when he was travelling in the Netherlands, he bartered the supreme works of art with which he had hoped to make his fortune for parrots, and made portraits of the servants, who had brought him a plate of fruit, to save himself tips! The thought of such a poor fool of an artist is especially moving to me because, at bottom, my fate is the same as his; the only difference is that I know better how to look after myself.

This is a venerable, learned city, thronged with people. They wander about under the arcades which line most of the streets and shelter them from sun and rain as they buy and sell, do business, or stand and gape. Towards evening I escaped from these crowds and climbed the tower to enjoy the fresh air and the view. To the north I could see the hills of Padua, and beyond them the Swiss, Tirolean and Friulian Alps, the whole northern chain, in fact, which at the time was wrapped in mist; in the west, a limitless horizon, broken only by the towers of Modena; to the east, a dead level plain stretching to the Adriatic and, to the south, the foothills of the Apennines, cultivated right up to their summits and dotted with churches and country houses like the hills of Vicenza.

There was not a cloud in the sky, but on the horizon hung a haze which the watchman of the tower told me had not disappeared for the last six years. The hills of Vicenza with their houses and little churches used to be clearly visible through a telescope, but nowadays this is rare, even on the clearest days. This fog clings by preference to the northern mountain chain and it is this that makes our dear fatherland such a Cimmerian country. The watchman also pointed out that, thanks to the healthy air, all the roofs of the town looked brand-new; not a tile had been affected by damp or over-grown by moss. This was true, but probably the quality of the tiles has something to do with it. In former times, at least, the tiles baked in this region were of excellent quality.

The leaning tower is frightful to look at, but it was prob-ably built that way on purpose. My theory is that, during the times of civic feuds, every great building became a fortress and every powerful family built its own tower. After a bit, this became both a hobby and a point of honour; everybody wished to boast of having a tower. In due time perpendicular towers became too commonplace, so someone built a leaning one. If so, one must admit that architect and owner achieved their aim, for people are no longer interested in all the straight towers but only in the crooked one. I went up it later. The layers of bricks run horizontally. Given a good mortar and iron bars, it is possible to build the craziest things.

19 October. Evening

I have spent the day well just looking and looking. It is the same in art as in life. The deeper one penetrates, the broader grows the view. In the sky of art countless new stars keep appearing, the Carracci, Guido, Domenichino, and they puzzle me. To enjoy these children of a later, happier period properly would require a knowledge and a competence of judgement which I lack and which can only be acquired gradually. The main obstacle to understanding these painters is their absurd subjects, which drive me mad, though I would like to admire and love them.

It is as if the sons of gods had married the daughters of men and begotten of them a variety of monsters. It is always the same, even with a genius like Guido. You find yourself in the dissecting room, at the foot of the gallows, on the edge of the corpse pit. His heroes always suffer and never act. Never an interest in everyday life, always the expectation of something fantastic about to appear from outside. The figures are either of criminals or lunatics except when, as a last resource, the painter introduces a nude boy or a pretty girl into the crowd of spectators or treats the saintly heroes as if they were mannequins, draping them in cloaks arranged in beautiful folds. That is no way to convey an idea of human beings. Out of ten subjects, only one should have been painted and even that one the artist was not allowed to paint from the proper angle.

The large picture by Guido in the Church of the Mendicanti is, technically, everything a painting should be, but the subject is the ultimate in absurdities which can be forced upon an artist. It is a votive picture. The Senate, I gather, unanimously praised it, and thought it up as well. Two angels, worthy of comforting a Psyche in distress, are obliged to mourn over a dead body.

St Proculo is a fine figure, but the others! – all these idiotic bishops and priests! Below them cherubs are playing with attributes; the painter, with the knife at his throat, did what he could for himself and tried his utmost to indicate that it was not he who was the barbarian.

Two nudes by Guido: a St John the Baptist in the desert and a Sebastian, exquisitely painted, but what do they *say*? One gapes, the other writhes.

When I look at history in this black mood, I feel inclined to say: First faith ennobled the arts, then superstition took over and ruined them.

After supper, feeling a little gentler and less arrogant than I did this morning, I jotted down the following notes:

In the Palazzo Tanari there hangs a famous picture by Guido of Mary suckling her child. She is larger than life and her head might have been painted by a god. Her expression, as she looks down on the child at her breast, is one of speechless and utter submission, as if it were not a child of love and joy to which she is giving her breast, but a heavenly changeling; she cannot do otherwise and, in her deep humility, cannot understand why this should have happened to her. The remaining space is filled by a voluminous garment which is highly admired by connoisseurs, but I did not know quite what to make of it. For one thing, the colours have darkened, the room is badly lit and it was a cloudy day.

In spite of my state of confusion, I already feel that using my eyes, experience and curiosity are beginning to help me through these mazes. I was, for instance, much impressed by a *Circumcision* of Guercino's, because, by now, I know his work fairly well and love it. I forgave him his indelicate subject and enjoyed his execution. He has left nothing to the imagination, but everything is painted in a decent manner and as perfectly as if it were done in enamel.

And so it is with me as it was with Balaam, the confused prophet who blessed when he had come to curse; and this would happen more often if I were to stay longer.

But as soon as I see a picture by Raphael again, or one which can probably be attributed to him, I am immediately and completely restored to health and happiness. I found a St Agatha, an exquisite picture, though not too well preserved. The painter has given her a healthy, self-confident virgin quality, yet devoid of either coldness or crudity. I have this figure firmly printed on my mind. To her, in the spirit, I shall read my *Iphigenie*, and I shall not allow my heroine to say anything this saint would not like to say.

Thinking again of this 'sweet burden', which I am carrying with me on my pilgrimage, compels me to confess that, along with all the great objects of art and nature I have to cope with, a train of new and rather disturbing poetic images keeps running through my mind. After I left Cento, I meant to start working again on *Iphigenie*, but what happened? My imagination conjured up a plot about Iphigenia in Delphi and I had to develop it. Here it is, in briefest outline.

Electra, confident that Orestes will bring the image of Diana from Tauris to Delphi, appears in the temple of Apollo carrying the cruel axe which had wrought such disaster in the House of Pelops and dedicates it to the god as a final expiatory offering. By ill luck, a Greek enters and tells her that he accompanied Orestes and Pylades to Tauris and saw the two friends being led to death, while he fortunately escaped. The passionate Electra is beside herself and does not know whether to vent her fury on the gods or on men.

In the meantime Iphigenia, Orestes and Pylades have also arrived in Delphi. When the two sisters meet without recognizing one another, Iphigenia's divine composure makes a strong contrast to the human passion of Electra. The Greek who had escaped sees Iphigenia and recognizes her as the priestess who, he believes, had sacrificed the friends, and discloses her identity to Electra. Electra snatches back the axe from the altar and is about to kill Iphigenia when a fortunate turn of events averts this horrible crime. If this scene were written properly, it could be as great as anything ever put on the stage, but, even if the spirit were willing, how should I find the time to write it?

Since this rush of so many good and desirable things rather alarms me, I must tell my friends of a dream I had about a year ago which I felt to be significant. I dreamed that I landed from a fairly large boat on the shore of a fertile island with a luxuriant vegetation, where I had been told one could get the most beautiful pheasants. I immediately started bargaining for these birds with the natives, who killed them and brought them to me in great numbers. I knew they were pheasants, although, since dreams usually transform things, they had long tails covered with iridescent eyelike spots similar to those of peacocks or rare birds of paradise. The natives brought them on board and neatly arranged them so that the heads were inside the boat and their long gaily-coloured feather tails hung outside. In the brilliant sunshine they made the most splendid pile imaginable, and there were so many of them that there was hardly room for the steersman and the rowers. Then we glided over calm waters and I was already making a mental list of the names of friends with whom I meant to share these treasures. At last we reached a great port. I lost my way among huge masted ships, and climbed from one deck to another, looking for some place where I could safely moor my little boat.

Such fantastic images give us great delight, and, since they are created by us, they undoubtedly have a symbolic relation to our lives and destinies.

I have visited the famous scientific academy called The Institute or The Studies. This large building, especially its inner courtyard, looks austere enough, although the architecture is not of the best. On the stairs and in the corridors, though there is no lack of stucco ornament and decorative frescoes, everything is correct and dignified and I was astounded, I must admit, by the wealth of beautiful and interesting things which have been collected here. But, as a German, accustomed to a more liberal system of education, I do not feel quite at ease.

An earlier observation came back to my mind: though Time changes everything, men cling to the form of a thing as they first knew it, even when its nature and function have changed. The Christian Churches still cling to the basilica form, though that of a temple would be better suited, perhaps, to their ritual. Scientific institutions still look like monasteries because it was in such pious precincts that study found its first quiet refuge. The law courts in Italy are as lofty and spacious as the wealth of the community permits – one might be in a market square out of doors, where in ancient times justice was administered. And do we not go on building our largest theatres with all their appurtenances under one roof, as though it were the first fair booth to be temporarily hammered together with a few boards and nails? At the time of the Reformation the great influx of people thirsty for knowledge compelled students to board in private houses, but how long it took us before we laicized our orphanages and gave poor children the secular education which is so necessary for them!

20 October. Evening

I spent the whole of this beautiful day in the open air. The moment I get near mountains, I become interested again in rocks and minerals. I seem to be an Antaeus who always feels new strength whenever he is brought into contact with his mother earth.

I rode on horseback to Paderno, where the so-called Bolognese heavy spar is found. This they make into little cakes which, after they have been calcined, glow in the dark if they have been previously exposed to the light. Here they simply call them *fosfori*.

On the way there, after leaving behind some sandstone hills, I came upon whole boulders of muscovite mica, sticking up out of the ground. The hill where the spar is found is not far from a brick kiln and a stream formed by the conjunction of a number of brooks. At first I thought it was alluvial clay which had probably been washed down from the mountains by rain, but, on closer inspection, I found that its solid rock was a finely laminated schist, alternating with bands of gypsum. The schist is so mixed with iron pyrites that, in contact with air and moisture, it undergoes a complete change. It swells, the lamina disappear and a kind of clayey slate is formed, conchoidal and crumbly, with surfaces that glitter like bituminous coal. Only after examining large specimens and breaking several in pieces so that I could clearly see both surfaces, could I convince myself of the transformation. The conchoidal surfaces are spotted with white particles and sometimes with yellow. Gradually the whole surface of the hill decomposes until it looks like a large mass of weathered iron pyrites. Among the solid layers, there are some green and red ones which are hardened. I also saw frequent traces of sulphur ore.

I then climbed up a boulder-strewn gulley washed out of the mountains by the rains, and was delighted to see many specimens of the spar I was looking for, sticking out of its weathered sides. Some were quite clean, others still encased in clay. One can see at once that they are not alluvial detritus, but to determine whether their formation was simultaneous with that of the schist, or a result of the tumefaction or decomposition of the latter, would require a more careful examination. The specimens I found, large and small, are roughly egg-shaped and the smallest look vaguely like crystals. The heaviest piece weighs eight ounces and a half. In the same clay I also found perfect loose crystals of gypsum. Experts will be able to draw more precise conclusions from the specimens I shall bring with me. So here I am again burdened with stones! I have packed up more than twelve pounds of the heavy spar.

20 October. At night

How much I could write if I were to tell you of all the ideas which ran through my head today. But I feel irresistibly drawn onward and can only concentrate with an effort on the present moment. Heaven, it seems, has been listening to my prayers, for I have just heard that a *vetturino* is leaving for Rome, and I shall go with him the day after tomorrow. Tonight and tomorrow, therefore, I must make my preparations, settle many things and do some work.

Lojano, in the Apennines.
21 October. Evening

I don't know whether I drove out of Bologna today or was driven out. In other words, I was given an opportunity of leaving even earlier and I jumped at it. So now, here I am in a miserable inn, in the company of a papal officer who is going to his home town of Perugia. To start a conversation when I joined him in the two-wheeled carriage, I paid him a compliment. As a German, I said, accustomed to associating with soldiers, I was very happy to be travelling in the company of a papal officer. 'I can easily understand', he replied, 'that you have a sympathy for the military profession, since I have been told that, in Germany, everybody is a soldier, but please don't be offended if I say that, though our duties are light and I can live perfectly comfortably in my garrison at Bologna, I, personally, would rather be rid of this uniform and look after my father's small estate. But I am the younger son and must take things as they come.'

22 October. Evening

Giredo is a dismal little hole in the Apennines, but I am very happy, knowing that the road is leading me ever nearer to my heart's desire. Today we were joined by a couple, an Englishman and his so-called sister. They have beautiful horses and are travelling without servants, and the gentleman evidently acts as groom and valet combined. They grumble incessantly about everything and might come straight out of the pages of Archenholz.*

The Apennines are a curious part of the world. At the edge of the vast plain of the Po, a mountain range rises from the lowlands and extends to the southern tip of Italy with a sea on each side. If this range had not been so precipitous, lofty and intricate that tidal action in remote epochs could have little influence, it would be only slightly higher than the rest of the country, one of its most beautiful regions, and the climate would be superb. Instead, it is a strange network of criss-crossing mountain ridges; often one cannot even find out where the streams are running to. If the valleys were filled up and the level areas smoother and better watered, the country might be compared to Bohemia, except that the mountains look totally different. But you must not picture it as a desert. Though mountainous, it is well cultivated, the chestnuts thrive, the wheat is excellent and the crops are green already. The road is bordered with evergreen oaks, and around the churches and chapels stand slender cypresses.

Last night the sky was cloudy, but today it is again fair and clear.

Perugia, 25 October. Evening

For two evenings I have written nothing. The inns were so bad that I could not find room even to spread out a sheet of paper. Moreover, since leaving Venice, my travelling spool does not reel off as pleasantly and smoothly as it did before, and everything is beginning to get in a muddle.

At ten o'clock our time, on the twenty-third, we emerged from the Apennines and saw Florence lying in a broad valley which was amazingly densely cultivated and scattered with villas and houses as far as the eye could see.

---

*J. W. Archenholz (1743–1812), author of *England and Italy*.

I took a quick walk through the city to see the Duomo and the Battistero. Once more, a completely new world opened up before me, but I did not wish to stay long. The location of the Boboli Gardens is marvellous. I hurried out of the city as quickly as I entered it.

One look is sufficient to show one that the people who built it were prosperous and enjoyed a lucky succession of good governments. The most striking thing about Tuscany is that all the public works, the roads and the bridges, look beautiful and imposing. They are at one and the same time efficient and neat, combining usefulness with grace, and everywhere one observes the care with which things are looked after, a refreshing contrast to the Papal States, which seem to keep alive only because the earth refuses to swallow them.

All that I recently said the Apennines might have been, Tuscany is, for it lies so much lower, the ancient sea has done its duty and piled up a deep loamy soil. This is light yellow in colour and easy to work. The peasants plough deep furrows but still in the old-fashioned manner. Their plough has no wheels and the share is not movable. Hunched behind his oxen, the peasant pushes his plough into the earth to break it up. They plough up to five times a year and use only a little light manure which they scatter with their hands. At sowing time they heap up small, narrow ridges with deep furrows between them in which the rain water can run off. The wheat grows on the top of the ridges, so that they can walk up and down the furrows when they weed. In a region where there is a danger of too much rain, this method would be very sensible, but why they do it in this wonderful climate, I cannot understand. I saw them doing this near Arezzo. It would be difficult to find cleaner fields anywhere; one cannot see the smallest clod of earth; the soil is as clean as if it had been sifted. Wheat seems to find here all the conditions most favourable to its growth, and does very well. Every second year, they grow beans for the horses, which are not fed on oats. The lupines are already green and will be ripe in March.

The flax is coming up. It is left out all winter and the frost only makes it all the more hardy.

Olives are strange trees; they look almost like willows, for they lose their heartwood and their bark splits open, but they look sturdier. The wood grows slowly and is very fine-grained. The leaf is similar to a willow leaf, but there are fewer to a branch. Around Florence, all the hill slopes are planted with olives and vines, and the soil between them is used for grain. Near Arezzo and further on, the fields are less cluttered. In my opinion, they do not check the ivy enough; it does great damage to the olives and other trees, and it would be easy to destroy. There are no meadows anywhere. I was told that maize had exhausted the soil. Since it was introduced, agriculture has declined in other ways. I believe this comes from using so little manure.

Tonight I took leave of my papal captain after promising to visit him in Bologna on my way back. He is a perfect type of the average Italian. Here are a few anecdotes to illustrate his character.

Having often seen me lost in silent thought, he once said: '*Che pensa! Non deve mai pensar l'uomo, pensando s'invecchia,*' or, in translation, 'Why do you think so much! A man should never think. Thinking only makes him grow old.' Then, after we had talked a bit: '*Non deve fermarsi l'uomo in una sola cosa, perchè allora divien matto: bisogna aver mille cose, una confusione nella testa*' – 'A man should never think about one thing only, because then he will go crazy: one should have a thousand things whirling about in one's head.' The mentality of such an Italian is even better revealed by the following conversation. He had obviously noticed that I was a Protestant, so, after some beating about the bush, he asked if I would mind answering a few questions, because he had heard so many odd things about Protestants and would like to obtain some first-hand information at last. 'Are you really allowed', he said, 'to have an affair with a pretty girl without being married to her? Do your priests permit you that?' I replied: 'Our priests are sensible men who do not bother themselves about such minor matters; of course, if we asked their permission, they would not give it.' 'And you really don't have to ask them?' he cried. 'Oh, you lucky people! And, since you don't go to confession, they won't hear about it.' Whereupon he began abusing his priests and praising our blessed freedom. 'But confession,' he went on, 'what about that? We are told that all people, even those who are not Christians, must confess their sins. Since they are impenitent and cannot do it in the proper way, they make confession to an old tree, which is certainly silly and wicked, but still a proof that they recognize the necessity for confession.' I explained our views about confession and its practice. He thought it all very convenient but pretty much the same as confessing to a tree. He hesitated for a moment and then asked me in all earnestness to tell him the honest truth about another point. One of his priests, an absolutely truthful man, had told him personally that we were allowed to marry our sisters. This, after all, would be going rather far. When I denied this and tried to give him a few sane ideas about our beliefs, he seemed to think them too commonplace and paid no attention. Then he turned to another question. 'We have been told as a fact that Frederick the Great, who has won so many victories, even over true believers, and fills the world with his fame, is really a Catholic though everybody imagines he is a heretic. He has special dispensation from the Pope to keep his faith a secret. As you know, he never enters one of our churches, but worships in a subterranean chapel and is deeply contrite that he cannot publicly profess the sacred religion because, if he did, his Prussians, a brutish nation of fanatical heretics, would kill him immediately, and then he could be of no more help to the cause. That is why the Holy Father has given him this dispensation, and, in return, Frederick quietly favours and propagates the one true faith.' I let all this pass without argument and merely said that, as it was such a deep secret, no one could verify it. The rest of our conversation ran on the same lines. I was surprised at the shrewdness of the priests who deny or misrepresent anything which might infringe upon the mysterious circle of their traditional doctrine or cast doubts upon it.

Foligno, 26 October. Evening

I left Perugia on a glorious morning and felt the bliss of being once more alone. The situation of the town is beautiful and the view of the lake charming. I shall remember them both. At first the road went downhill, then it ran along a lovely valley, flanked on either side by distant hills, until, finally, Assisi came into view.

From reading Palladio and Volkmann, I knew there was a Temple of Minerva here, built during the reign of Augustus and still perfectly preserved. When we got near Madonna degli Angeli, I left my *vetturino* and let him go on to Foligno. I was longing to take a walk by myself in this silent world, and climbed the road to Assisi on foot with a high wind blowing against me. I turned away in distaste from the enormous substructure of the two churches on my left, which are built one on top of the other like a Babylonian tower, and are the resting place of St Francis. I was afraid that the people who gathered there would be of the same stamp as my captain. I asked a handsome boy the way to the Maria della Minerva, and he accompanied me up into the town, which is built on the side of a hill. At last we arrived in the Old Town and – lo and behold! – there it stood, the first complete classical monument I have seen. A modest temple, just right for such a small town, yet so perfect in design that it would be an ornament anywhere.

Since I have read in Vitruvius and Palladio how cities should be laid out and how temples and public build-ings should be situated, I have learned to treat these matters with great respect. In this, as in so much else, the ancients were great by instinct. The temple is situated halfway up the mountain at a point where two hills meet and on a piece of level ground which today is called the *piazza*. The square itself slopes slightly and four roads meet there, two from above and two from below, forming an irregular St Andrew's Cross. In ancient times the houses which face the temple and obstruct the view probably did not exist. If they were removed, one could look down on the fertile countryside to the south and the sanctuary of Minerva would be visible from every side. The layout of the roads may be of early date, since they follow the contours of the mountain. The temple does not stand in the centre of the square but is so placed that it can be seen in foreshortened perspective by anyone approaching it from the direction of Rome. Besides drawing the building, one ought to draw its well-chosen site.

One could never tire of looking at the façade and admiring the logical procedure of the architect. The order is Corinthian and the space between the columns about two modules. The bases of the columns and the plinths below them appear to be standing on pedestals, but this is only an illusion, for the stylobate has been cut through in five places, and through each gap five steps lead up between the columns. By these one reaches the platform on which the columns actually stand, and enters the temple. The bold idea of cutting through the stylobate was a very sensible one, given the site. Since the temple stands on a hill, the stairs up to it would otherwise have jutted out too far into the square and made it too cramped. How many steps there were originally is now impossible to determine, because, except for a few, they lie buried under the earth and paved over. I tore myself away reluctantly and firmly resolved to call the attention of all architects to this building so that an accurate plan may be made available to us. I realized once more how little accepted tradition is to be trusted. Palladio, on whom I had relied implicitly, made a sketch of this temple, but he cannot have seen it personally, for he puts real pedestals on the ground, which gives the columns a disproportionate height and makes the whole a Palmyra-like monstrosity instead of the great loveliness of the real thing. I cannot describe the sensations which this work aroused in me, but I know they are going to bear fruit for ever.

The evening was beautiful and I was walking down the Roman Road in a state of blissful content when suddenly behind me I heard loud, rough voices in lively argument. I thought they must be *shirri*, for I had previously noticed some in the town. Without turning round, but straining my ears to catch what they were saying, I walked calmly on. Soon I realized that I was the subject of their quarrel. Four men, two of them armed with guns, passed me, muttering something. After a few steps they turned, surrounded me, and asked what I was doing here. I replied that I was a stranger and had walked to Assisi while my *vetturino* drove on to Foligno. This they found hard to believe – that someone should pay for a carriage and then walk. They asked if I had been to the Gran Convento. I said no, but assured them I had known the building for many years. This time, since I was an architect, I had gone to look at the Maria della Minerva, which, as they knew, was an architectural masterpiece. This they did not deny, but they were offended because I had not paid my respects to the saint and did not conceal their suspicion that I might be a dealer in contraband goods. I pointed out how ridiculous it was to take someone for a smuggler who was walking by himself without a knapsack and with empty pockets. I offered to return to the town with them and go to the *podestà*. I would show him my documents and he would acknowledge me as a respectable foreigner. After muttering among themselves again, they said this would be unnecessary. I behaved all the time with dignity and, at last, they went away towards the town. I followed them with my eye. There, in the foreground, walked those rude fellows while, behind them, Minerva looked down on me kindly, as if she wanted to console me. I turned to look at the dreary Duomo of St Francis on my left and was just about to continue my way when one of the unarmed members of the band left it and approached me in a friendly manner. 'Dear Mr Foreigner,' he said, 'you ought, at least, to give me a tip, for, I assure you, I knew at once that you were an honest man and frankly told my companions so. But they are hot-headed, quick-tempered fellows who do not know the ways of the world. You must also have noticed that I was the first to applaud your words and back you up.' I complimented him on this and urged him to protect in future any distinguished foreigner who might come to Assisi for the sake of religion and art, especially any architect who might come to measure and sketch the Temple of Minerva, which had never yet been drawn or engraved. Such people would bring glory to the town, and if he gave them a helping hand, they would certainly show their gratitude – and with these words I pressed a few silver coins into his hand, which made him very happy, as they were more than he had expected. He begged me to come back to Assisi soon; I must on no account miss the feast of the saint, when I could certainly expect both edification and amusement. Indeed, if a good-looking man like me should wish to meet a handsome female, he could assure me that, on his recommendation, the most beautiful and respectable woman in Assisi would gladly receive me. He then took his leave, after solemnly promising that he would remember me that very evening in his devotions at the tomb of the saint and pray for the success of my journey. So we parted, and I felt much relieved at being alone again with Nature and myself. The road to Foligno along the side of the mountain overlooking the valley is beautiful, and my walk, which took fully four hours, was one of the most enchanting I have ever taken.

Travelling with *vetturini* is an exhausting affair; the only thing to be said for it is that one can always get out and walk. All the way from Ferrara I have submitted to being dragged along in this fashion. This Italy, so greatly favoured by Nature, has lagged far behind all other countries in mechanical and technical matters, which are, after all, the basis of a comfortable, agreeable life. The carriage of the *vetturino* is called *una sedia*, 'a seat', and is undoubtedly derived from the ancient litters in which women and elderly or prominent persons were carried by mules. The mule that was harnessed between the shafts of the rear has been replaced by two wheels, and that is all the improvement they have made. One is still joggled along as one was centuries ago. It is the same with their houses and everything else. The idyllic dream of the first men living out of doors and retiring to caves only in an emergency is a reality here, and to see it, one has only to enter their dwellings, especially in rural districts, which still preserve the character of caves.

They are utterly carefree because they are afraid that thinking might make them age quicker. With an unheard-of negligence they fail to make provision for the longer winter nights and, consequently, suffer like dogs for a considerable part of the year. The inn here in Foligno is exactly like a Homeric household. Everyone is gathered in a large vault around an open fireplace, shouting and talking. They all eat together at one long table, as in a painting of the Wedding Feast at Cana. To my great surprise, someone has brought me an inkwell, so I am taking the opportunity to write, though these pages will bear witness to the cold and the inconvenience of my writing table.

I have only just realized how bold I was to travel unprepared and alone through this country. The different currencies, the *vetturini*, the prices, the wretched inns are a daily nuisance, and anyone who travels alone for the first time, hoping for uninterrupted pleasures, is bound to be often disappointed and have much to put up with. But, after all, my one wish has been to see this country at any cost and, were I to be dragged to Rome on Ixion's wheel, I should not utter a single word of complaint.

Terni, 27 October. Evening

Once again I am sitting in a cave which was damaged in an earthquake last year. Terni lies between limestone hills on the edge of a plain and, like Bologna on the other side, at the foot of a mountain range.

Now that the papal officer has left me, I have a priest as a travelling companion. He has of course recognized me as a heretic, but is willing to answer all my questions about ritual and similar matters. Through meeting new people all the time, I am acquiring what I came for; it is only by listening to the people talking among themselves that one can get a true picture of the country. They are all bitter rivals; they indulge in the oddest provincialism and local patriotism, and cannot stand each other. There are eternal feuds between the different classes, conducted with such lively passion that one seems to be taking part day and night in a comedy, in which everyone exposes himself. Yet they can quickly control themselves too, and they immediately notice when a foreigner disapproves of their behaviour.

I walked up to Spoleto and stood on the aqueduct, which also serves as a bridge from one hill to the other. The ten brickwork arches which span the valley have been quietly standing there through all the centuries, and the water still gushes in all quarters of Spoleto. This is the third work of antiquity which I have seen, and it embodies the same noble spirit. A sense of the civic good, which is the basis of their architecture, was second nature to the ancients. Hence the amphitheatre, the temple, the aqueduct. For the first time I understand why I always detested arbitrary constructions, the Winterkasten* on the Weissenstein, for example, which is a pointless nothing, a monstrous piece of confectionery – and I have felt the same about a thousand other buildings. Such things are still-born, for anything that does not have a true *raison d'être* is lifeless and cannot be great or ever become so. For how many pleasures and insights must I thank these last eight weeks! But they have also cost me a great deal of effort. I try to keep my eyes open all the time, remember as much as I can and not judge more than I can help.

The strange wayside chapel of San Crocefisso is not, in my opinion, the remnant of a temple which once stood there. Evidently, columns, pillars and entablatures have been found and patched together. The result, though not unskilful, is

---

* Winterkasten. A huge octagonal castle on the Wilhelmshöhe near Kassel.

absurd. It is impossible to describe, but there certainly exists an engraving of it somewhere. The curious difficulty about trying to form an idea of antiquity is that we only have ruins to go by, so that our reconstructions must be inadequate.

The so-called classic soil is another matter. If we do not approach it fancifully but consider this soil in its reality as it presents itself to our senses, it still appears as the stage upon which the greatest events were enacted and decided. I have always looked at landscape with the eye of a geologist and a topographer, and suppressed my imagination and emotions in order to preserve my faculty for clear and unbiased observation. If one does this first, then history follows naturally and logically in all its astonishing wonder. One of the things I now most want to do is to read Tacitus in Rome.

I must not forget my observations of the weather. When I drove through the Apennines after leaving Bologna, the clouds were still drifting north, but later they changed their direction and moved towards Lake Trasimeno. There they were arrested and only a few moved on further south. This proves that, in summer, the great plain of the Po does not send all its clouds towards the Tirolean Alps, but sends some of them to the Apennines, which probably is the explanation of their rainy season. People are beginning to harvest the olives. Here they pick them by hand; in other places they knock them down with sticks. If winter comes early, the remaining fruit are left on the trees until the spring. I saw some very big and very old olive trees in a patch of very stony ground.

The Muses, like the daemons, do not always visit us at the right moment. Today they drove me to develop a most untimely idea. As I approached the centre of Catholicism, surrounded by Catholics, boxed up in a *sedia* with a priest and trying to feel and understand the truth of Nature and the nobility of Art, the thought rose unbidden in my mind that all traces of early Christianity have been obliterated. Indeed, when I visualized it in its purity, as recorded in the Acts of the Apostles, I shuddered at the thought of the distorted baroque paganism which has imposed itself upon those simple and innocent beginnings. Once again the legend of the Wandering Jew came to mind, who witnessed all these strange developments and lived to take part in that extra-ordinary scene when Christ returns to look for the fruits of His teaching and is in danger of being crucified a second time. The words *Venio iterum crucifigi* must serve me as an epigraph for this catastrophe.

Other dreams like it hover before me. In my impatience to get on, I sleep in my clothes and can think of nothing more agreeable than to be roused before dawn, quickly take my seat in the carriage and travel dayward half asleep, letting dream images do what they like with me.

Città Castellana, 28 October

My last day must not go unrecorded. It is not yet eight o'clock, but everybody is in bed and I am free to think of the past and look forward to the near future. The morning was very cold, the day clear and warm, the evening somewhat windy but beautiful. We left Terni very early and reached Narni before daybreak, so I could not see the bridge. All around were limestone hills without a trace of any other rock formation.

Otricoli lies on an alluvial mound, formed in an early epoch, and is built of lava taken from the other side of the river. As soon as one crosses the bridge, one is on volcanic terrain, either lava or an earlier metamorphic rock. We climbed a hill which I am inclined to define as grey lava. It contains many white crystals with the shape of garnets. The high road to Città Castellana is built of it and worn wonder-fully smooth by the carriages. This town is built upon a volcanic tufa in which I thought I could recognize ashes, pumice stone and lava fragments. The view from the castle is magnificent. Soracte stands out by itself in picturesque soli-tude. Probably this mountain is made of limestone and belongs to the Apennines. The volcanic areas lie much lower, and it is only the water tearing across them which has carved them into extremely picturesque shapes, overhanging cliffs and other accidental features.

Well then, tomorrow evening Rome! Even now I can hardly believe it. When this wish has been fulfilled, what shall I wish for next? I can think of nothing better than safely landing at home in my pheasant-boat, to find my friends in good health, cheerful and happy to see me again.

ROME

AT last I can break my silence and send my friends a joyful greeting. I hope they will forgive me for my secretiveness and my almost subterranean journey to this country. Even to myself, I hardly dared admit where I was going and all the way I was still afraid I might be dreaming; it was not till I had passed through the Porta del Popolo that I was certain it was true, that I really was in Rome.

Let me say this: here in Rome, in the presence of all those objects which I never expected to see by myself, you are constantly in my thoughts. It was only when I realized that everyone at home was chained, body and soul, to the north, and all desire to visit these parts had vanished, that, drawn by an irresistible need, I made up my mind to undertake this long, solitary journey to the hub of the world.

Now that this need has been satisfied, my friends and my native land have once again become very dear to my heart, and my desire to return very keen, all the keener because I am convinced that the many treasures I shall bring home with me will serve both myself and others as a guide and an education for a lifetime.

1 November

Now, at last, I have arrived in the First City of the world! Had I seen it fifteen years ago with an intelligent man to guide me, I should have called myself lucky, but, since I was destined to visit it alone and trust to my own eyes, I am happy, at least, to have been granted this joy so late in life.

Across the mountains of the Tirol I fled rather than travelled. Vicenza, Padua and Venice I saw thoroughly, Ferrara, Cento, Bologna casually, and Florence hardly at all. My desire to reach Rome quickly was growing stronger every minute until nothing could have induced me to make more stops, so that I spent only three hours there. Now I have arrived, I have calmed down and feel as if I had found a peace that will last for my whole life. Because, if I may say so, as soon as one sees with one's own eyes the whole which one had hitherto only known in fragments and chaotically, a new life begins.

All the dreams of my youth have come to life; the first engravings I remember – my father hung views of Rome in the hall – I now see in reality, and everything I have known for so long through paintings, drawings, etchings, woodcuts, plaster casts and cork models is now assembled before me. Wherever I walk, I come upon familiar objects in an unfamiliar world; everything is just as I imagined it, yet everything is new. It is the same with my observations and ideas. I have not had a single idea which was entirely new or surprising, but my old ideas have become so much more firm, vital and coherent that they could be called new.

When Pygmalion's Galatea, whom he had fashioned exactly after his dreams, endowing her with as much reality and existence as an artist can, finally came up to him and said: 'Here I am,' how different was the living woman from the sculptured stone.

Besides, for me it is morally salutary to be living in the midst of a sensual people about whom so much has been said and written, and whom every foreigner judges by the standard he brings with him. I can excuse those who criticize and disapprove of them because their life is so far removed from ours that it is difficult and expensive for a foreigner to have dealings with them.

3 November

One of the main reasons I had given myself as an excuse for hurrying to Rome, namely, that All Saints' Day was on 1 November, turned out to be a delusion. If, I had said to myself, they pay such high honours to a single saint, what a spectacle it must be when they honour them all at once. How utterly mistaken I was. A conspicuous general feast has never become popular in the Church; originally, perhaps, each religious order celebrated the memory of its patron saint privately, for now the feast on his name day, the day appointed for his veneration, is the one on which each appears in all his glory.

Yesterday, however, which was the Feast of All Souls, I had better luck. The Pope* celebrated their memory in his private chapel on the Quirinal. Admission was free to all. I hurried with Tischbein to the Monte Cavallo. The square in front of the palazzo, though irregular in shape, is both grand and graceful. There I set eyes on the two Colossi. To grasp them is beyond the power of the eye or the mind. We hurried with the crowd across the spacious courtyard and up an enormous flight of stairs, and into the vestibules opposite the chapel. To think that I was under the same roof as the Vicar of Christ gave me a strange feeling. The office had begun and the Pope and cardinals were already in the church – the Holy Father, a beautiful and venerable figure of a man, the cardinals of various ages and statures.

I was suddenly seized by the curious wish that the Head of the Church would open his golden mouth and, in speaking of the transports of joy felt by the souls of the blessed, transport us with joy as well. When I saw him merely moving from one side of the altar to the other and muttering just like any ordinary priest, the original sin of the Protestant stirred in me and I felt no pleasure whatsoever in the sacrifice of the Mass as it is traditionally offered here. Did not Christ, even as a child, interpret the Scriptures in a loud voice? As a young man, He certainly did not teach or work miracles in silence, for, as we know from the Gospels, He liked to speak and He spoke well. What would He say, I thought, if He were to see His representative on earth droning and tottering about? The

* Pius VI (1775–99).

words *Venio iterum crucifigi* came to mind and I nudged my companion to come out with me into the free atmosphere of the vaulted and frescoed rooms. There we found a lot of people who were looking at the paintings, for the Feast of All Souls is also the feast of all artists in Rome. On this day not only the chapel but also all the rooms in the palazzo are open to the public for many hours. Entrance is free and one is not molested by the custodian.

I looked at the frescoes and found some excellent ones by artists whose names I hardly knew – Carlo Maratti, for example, whom I soon came to love and admire. But it was the masterpieces of the artists whose style I had already studied which gave me the keenest pleasure. I saw a St Petronilla by Guercino. This canvas was formerly in St Peter's, where it has now been replaced by a copy in mosaic. The body of the dead saint is lifted out of the tomb, restored to life and received into Heaven by a divine youth. Whatever objections there may be to this twofold action, the painting is beyond price.

I was even more surprised by a Titian which outshines all of his pictures which I have seen so far. Whether it is only that my visual sense is now more trained, or whether it really is his most stupendous picture, I cannot judge. It shows the imposing figure of a bishop, enveloped in a gorgeous chasuble stiff with gold embroideries and figures. Holding a massive crozier in his left hand, he gazes up to Heaven, rapt in ecstasy. In his right hand he holds an open book, from which he seems to have just received divine inspiration. Behind him, a beautiful virgin, carrying a palm, looks with tender interest into the book. On his right, a grave old man is standing quite close to the book but does not seem to be paying it any attention. Perhaps the keys in his hand assure him that he can elucidate its secrets by himself. Facing this group, a nude, well-shaped young man, bound and pierced with arrows, looks out with humble resignation. In the space between them two monks, bearing a cross and a lily, turn their devout gazes heavenward, where, above the semicircular ruin which encloses all the human figures, a mother in her highest glory looks down in compassion while the radiant child on her lap holds out a wreath with a gay gesture as if eager to throw it down. Above them and the triple aureole, like a keystone, hovers the Holy Dove.

Behind this composition there must lie some ancient tradition which made it possible to combine all these various and seemingly incongruous figures into a significant whole. We do not ask how or why; we take it as it is and marvel at its inestimable art.

Less enigmatic but still mysterious is a fresco by Guido. A childlike Virgin sits quietly sewing, flanked by two angels who are ready at the slightest gesture to minister to her wishes. What this charming picture says is that youthful innocence and diligence are protected and honoured by the Heavenly Powers. No legend or interpretation is necessary.

But now for an amusing anecdote to lighten these somewhat ponderous reflections on art. For some time I had been aware that some German artists, evidently acquaintances of Tischbein's, would give me a stare, go out and come back for another look. Presently Tischbein, who had left me alone for a few minutes, returned and said: 'This is going to be great fun. The rumour that you are in Rome has already spread and aroused the curiosity of the artists about the only foreigner whom nobody knows. One of our circle has always boasted of having met you and even lived with you on terms of intimacy, a story we found hard to believe. So we asked him to take a look at you and resolve our doubts. He promptly declared that it was not you but a stranger without the slightest resemblance to you. So your incognito is safe, at least for the moment, and later we shall have something to laugh about.'

Since then, I have moved more freely among these artists and asked them to tell me the authors of various paintings, the style of which is still unfamiliar to me. I was especially attracted by a painting of St George, the slayer of the dragon and the liberator of virgins. Nobody could tell me the name of the master until a short, modest man, who had not opened his mouth before, stepped forward and said it was by the Venetian painter Pordenone, and one of his finest paintings. I realized then why I had been drawn to it; being already familiar with the Venetian school, I could better appreciate the virtues of its members. The artist who gave me this information is Heinrich Meyer, a Swiss, who has been studying here for several years in the company of a friend named Cölla. He makes remarkable drawings in sepia of antique busts and is well versed in the history of art.

5 November

I have been here now for seven days and am gradually beginning to get a general idea of the city. We walk about a good deal, I study the layout of Ancient Rome and Modern Rome, look at ruins and buildings and visit this villa or that. The most important monuments I take very slowly; I do nothing except look, go away, and come back and look again. Only in Rome can one educate oneself for Rome.

I find it a difficult and melancholy business, I must confess, separating the old Rome from the new, but it has to be done and I can only hope that, in the end, my efforts will prove well worthwhile. One comes upon traces both of magnificence and of devastation, which stagger the imagination. What the barbarians left, the builders of Modern Rome have destroyed.

Here is an entity which has suffered so many drastic changes in the course of two thousand years, yet is still the same soil, the same hill, often even the same column or the same wall, and in its people one still finds traces of their ancient character. Contemplating this, the observer becomes, as it were, a contemporary of the great decrees of destiny, and this makes it difficult for him to follow the evolution of the city, to grasp not only how Modern Rome follows on Ancient, but also how, within both, one epoch follows upon another. I shall first of all try to grope my way along this half-hidden track by myself, for only after I have done that shall I be able to benefit from the excellent preliminary studies to which, from the fifteenth century till today, eminent scholars and artists have devoted their lives.

As I rush about Rome looking at the major monuments, the immensity of the place has a quietening effect. In other places one has to search for the important points of interest; here they crowd in on one in profusion. Wherever you turn your eyes, every kind of vista, near and distant, confronts you – palaces, ruins, gardens, wildernesses, small houses, stables, triumphal arches, columns – all of them often so close together that they could be sketched on a single sheet of paper. One would need a thousand styluses to write with. What can one do here with a single pen? And then, in the evening, one feels exhausted after so much looking and admiring.

7 November

My friends must excuse me if, in future, I become rather laconic. When one is travelling, one grabs what one can, every day brings something new, and one hastens to think about it and make a judgement. But this city is such a great school and each day here has so much to say that one does not dare say anything about it oneself. Even if one could stay here for years, it would still be better to observe a Pythagorean silence.

7 November

I am feeling in fine shape. The wind is *brutto*, as the Romans say. There is a wind at noon, the sirocco, which brings some rain daily, but I do not find this sort of weather disagreeable because it is warm all the time, which it never is on rainy days in our country.

I am coming to appreciate Tischbein more and more, his talents, his ideas on art and his aims as a painter. He showed me his drawings and sketches. Many are very promising. His stay with Bodmer has turned his thoughts towards the earliest ages of man when he found himself on earth and was expected to solve the problem of becoming the lord of creation.

As an introduction to a series of pictures, he has tried to represent this great age symbolically – mountains covered with majestic forests, ravines carved out by torrents, moribund volcanoes emitting only a thin column of smoke, and, in the foreground, the massive stump of an ancient oak with its roots uncovered on which a stag is testing the strength of its antlers – all well conceived and charmingly executed.

He has made one very curious drawing showing man as the tamer of horses, superior not in strength but in cunning to all the beasts of the field, the air and the waters. This composition is of extraordinary beauty and should look most effective when done in oils. We must certainly acquire a drawing of it for Weimar. He also plans to paint an assembly of wise old men, which will give him an opportunity of doing some real figures. At the moment he is enthusiastically making sketches for a battle scene in which two bands of horsemen are attacking each other with equal fury. They are separated by a tremendous ravine over which a horse can vault only by a tremendous effort. Defence is out of the question. Bold attack, reckless decision, victory or a plunge into the abyss. This picture will give him a chance to reveal his knowledge of the anatomy and movements of the horse.

He would like to see this planned series of scenes linked together by a poem which would explain their meaning and itself gain in substance from the figures in them. The idea is an excellent one, but, to bring it to fruition, we should have to spend years together.

The loggias of Raphael, the huge paintings of the School of Athens, etc., I have seen only once. This was much like studying Homer from a faded and damaged manuscript. A first impression is inadequate; to enjoy them fully, one would have to look at them again and again. The best preserved are those on the ceiling with Biblical stories for their subjects; these look as fresh as if they had been painted yesterday. Even though only a few of them are by Raphael himself, they were all done from his designs and under his personal supervision.

When I was a young man, I sometimes indulged in a day-dream of being accompanied to Italy by an educated Englishman, well versed in general history and the history of art. This has now come to pass in a still happier way than I dreamed of. Tischbein has long been devoted to me, and has always wanted to show me Rome, where he has lived for so long. We were old friends by correspondence and now we are new friends in the flesh. Where could I have found a better guide? Thanks to him, I shall be able to learn and enjoy as much as possible in the limited time I have. As I see things at present, when I leave here, I shall wish I was arriving instead.

8 November

My peculiar and perhaps capricious semi-incognito has some unforeseen advantages. Since everyone feels it his duty to ignore my identity, no one can talk to me about me; so all they can do is talk about themselves and the topics which interest them. In consequence I get to know all about what everyone is doing and about everything worthwhile that is going on. Even Hofrat Reiffenstein* respects my whim, but since for some reason of his own he dislikes the name I adopted, he soon made me a Baron and now I am known as The-Baron-who-lives-opposite-the-Rondanini. This title is sufficient because Italians always call people by their first names or their nicknames. This is the way I wanted it, and I escape the endless annoyance of having to give an account of myself and my writings.

---

* Hofrat Reiffenstein (1719–93). Diplomat, formerly in the service of Gotha and Russia, archaeologist and art connoisseur.

9 November

Sometimes I stand still for a moment and survey, as it were, the high peaks of my experiences so far. I look back with special joy to Venice, that great being who sprang from the sea like Pallas from the head of Jupiter. In Rome the Pantheon, so great within and without, has overwhelmed me with admiration. St Peter's has made me realize that Art, like Nature, can abolish all standards of measurement. The Apollo Belvedere has also swept me off my feet. Just as the most accurate drawings fail to give an adequate idea of these buildings, so plaster casts, good as some I have seen are, can be no substitute for their marble originals.

10 November

I am now in a state of clarity and calm such as I had not known for a long time. My habit of looking at and accepting things as they are without pretension is standing me in good stead and makes me secretly very happy. Each day brings me some new remarkable object, some new great picture, and a whole city which the imagination will never encompass, however long one thinks and dreams.

Today I went to the pyramid of Cestius and in the evening climbed to the top of the Palatine, where the ruins of the imperial palaces stand like rocks. It is impossible to convey a proper idea of such things. Nothing here is mediocre, and if, here and there, something is in poor taste, it, too, shares in the general grandeur.

When I indulge in self-reflection, as I like to do occasionally, I discover in myself a feeling which gives me great joy. Let me put it like this. In this place, whoever looks seriously about him and has eyes to see is bound to become a stronger character: he acquires a sense of strength hitherto unknown to him.

His soul receives the seal of a soundness, a seriousness without pedantry, and a joyous composure. At least, I can say that I have never been so sensitive to the things of this world as I am here. The blessed consequences will, I believe, affect my whole future life.

So let me seize things one by one as they come; they will sort themselves out later. I am not here simply to have a good time, but to devote myself to the noble objects about me, to educate myself before I reach forty.

11 November

Today I visited the Nymph Egeria, the Circus of Caracalla, the ruined tombs along the Via Appia and the tomb of Metella, which made me realize for the first time what solid masonry means. These people built for eternity; they omitted nothing from their calculations except the insane fury of the destroyers to whom nothing was sacred.

I also saw the ruins of the great aqueduct. What a noble ambition it showed, to raise such a tremendous construction for the sake of supplying water to a people. We came to the Colosseum at twilight. Once one has seen it, everything else seems small. It is so huge that the mind cannot retain its image; one remembers it as smaller than it is, so that every time one returns to it, one is astounded by its size.

Frascati, 15 November

The rest of our company are already in bed, and I am writing in the sepia I use for drawing. We have had a few rainless days of genial sunshine, so that we don't long for the summer. This town lies on the slope of a mountain, and at every turn the artist comes upon the most lovely things. The view is unlimited; you can see Rome in the distance and the sea beyond it, the hills of Tivoli to the right, and so on. In this pleasant region the villas have certainly been built for pleasure. About a century ago, wealthy and high-spirited Romans began building villas on the same beautiful spots where the ancient Romans built theirs. For two days we have roamed the countryside, always finding some new attraction.

Yet I find it hard to decide which are the more entertaining, our days or our evenings. As soon as our imposing landlady has placed the three-branched brass lamp on the table with the words *'Felicissima notte!'* we sit down in a circle and each brings out the drawings and sketches he has made during the day. A discussion follows: shouldn't the subject have been approached from a better angle? Has the character of the scene been hit off? We discuss, in fact, all those elements in art which can be judged from a first draft.

Thanks to his competence and authority, Hofrat Reiffenstein is the natural person to organize and preside at these sessions, but it was Philipp Hackert who originated this laudable custom. An admirable landscape painter, he always insisted on everyone, artists and dilettantes, men and women, young and old, whatever their talents, trying their hand at drawing, and he himself set them a good example. Since his departure this custom of gathering together an interested circle has been faithfully kept up by Hofrat Reiffenstein; and one can see how worthwhile it is to stimulate in everyone an active interest.

The individual characters of the members of our circle are charmingly revealed. Tischbein, for example, being a painter of historical scenes, looks at landscape in a completely different way from a landscape painter. He sees important groupings and significant objects where another would see nothing and then manages to catch many traits of simple humanity, in children, country folk, beggars and other similar unsophisticated people, even in animals, which he can render most successfully with a few characteristic strokes, providing us with new topics for discussion.

When we run out of conversation, some pages are read aloud from Sulzer's *Theory*, another custom introduced by Hackert. Though, judged by the strictest standards, this work is not altogether satisfactory, I have observed with pleasure its good influence on people of a middling level of culture.

Rome, 17 November

Here we are back again! Tonight there was a tremendous downpour with thunder and lightning. It still goes on raining, but remains warm. Today I saw the frescoes by Domenichino in Sant' Andrea della Valle and the Carracci in the Farnese Gallery. Too much for months, let alone for a single day.

18 November

The weather has been fine and clear. In the Farnesina I saw the story of Psyche, colour reproductions of which have for so long brightened my rooms. Later I saw Raphael's *Transfiguration* in San Pietro in Montorio. These paintings are like friends with whom one has long been acquainted through correspondence and now sees face to face for the first time. The difference when one lives with them is that one's sympathies and antipathies are soon revealed.

In every corner there are magnificent things which are almost never mentioned and have not been disseminated over the world in etchings and reproductions. I shall bring some with me, done by excellent young artists.

18 November

Tischbein is well versed in the various types of stone used both by the ancient and the modern builders. He has studied them thoroughly and his artist's eye and his pleasure in the physical texture of things have greatly helped him. Some time ago he sent off to Weimar a choice collection of specimens which will welcome me on my return. Meanwhile, an important addition to them has turned up. A priest who is now living in France planned to write a book on Stones in Antiquity and, by special favour of the Propaganda, received some sizeable pieces of marble from the island of Paros. They range in grain from the finest to the coarsest and are of perfect purity except for a few which contain some mica.

These were used for building, whereas the pure marble was used for sculpture. In judging the works of artists, an exact knowledge of the material they used is obviously a great help.

There are plenty of opportunities here for assembling such a collection. Today we walked in the ruins of Nero's palace over fields of banked-up artichokes and could not resist the temptation to fill our pockets with tablets of granite, porphyry and marble which lay around in thousands, still bearing witness to the splendour of the walls which they once covered.

I must now speak of a curious, problematic painting which is one of the most extraordinary things I have ever seen.

There was a Frenchman living here some years ago who was well known as a collector and lover of the arts. He came into possession, nobody knows how, of an antique chalk drawing, had it restored by Mengs and added it to his collection as an item of great value. Winckelmann mentions it somewhere with enthusiasm. It shows Ganymede offering Jupiter a cup of wine and receiving a kiss in return. The Frenchman died and, in his will, left the picture to his landlady, stating it to be an antique. Then Mengs died and on his deathbed declared that it was not an antique but had been done by him. This started an endless feud between all parties. One person swore that Mengs had dashed it off as a joke, another that Mengs could never have done anything like it, that it was almost too beautiful for a Raphael. Yesterday I saw it for myself and I must confess that I do not know of anything more beautiful than the figure of Ganymede, especially the head and the back – all the rest has been much touched up. However, the picture is discredited and no one wants to relieve the poor woman of her treasure.

20 November

Experience has taught us often enough that there is a demand for drawings and etchings to go with every kind of poem, and that even a painter himself will dedicate his most descriptive pictures to some passage of poetry, so Tischbein's idea, that in order to achieve a proper unity poets and painters should collaborate from the start, is a very praiseworthy one. The difficulty would obviously be greatly lessened if the poems were short enough to be composed at a sitting and read at a glance. Tischbein, it so happens, has pleasing idyllic subjects in mind and, to my surprise, they are of a character which neither poetry nor painting by itself could treat adequately. On our walks he has told me all about them and urged me to fall in with his plan. He has already designed a frontispiece for our joint effort. If I were not afraid to embark on something new, I might perhaps be tempted.

22 November
On the Feast of St Cecilia

I must write a few lines to keep alive the memory of this happy day or, at least, make a historical report of what I have been enjoying. The day was cloudless and warm. I went with Tischbein to the square in front of St Peter's. We walked up and down until we felt too hot, when we sat in the shadow of the great obelisk – it was just wide enough for two – and ate some grapes we had bought nearby. Then we went into the Sistine Chapel, where the light on the frescoes was at its best. Looking at these marvellous works of Michelangelo's, our admiration was divided between the Last Judgement and the various paintings on the ceiling. The self-assurance, the virility, the grandeur of conception of this master defy expression. After we had looked at everything over and over again, we left the chapel and entered St Peter's. Thanks to the brilliant sunshine outside, every part of the church was visible. Since we were determined to enjoy its magnitude and splendour, we did not, this time, allow our overfastidious taste to put us off and abstained from carping criticism. We enjoyed everything that was enjoyable.

Then we climbed up on to the roof, where one finds a miniature copy of a well-built town with houses, shops, fountains, churches (at least they looked like churches from the outside) and a large temple – everything in the open air with beautiful walks between. We went into the Cupola and looked out at the Apennines, Mount Soracte, the volcanic hills behind Tivoli, Frascati, Castel Gandolfo, the plain and the sea beyond it. Below us lay the city of Rome in all its length and breadth with its hill-perched palaces, domes, etc. Not a breath of air was stirring, and it was as hot as a greenhouse inside the copper ball. After taking in everything, we descended again and asked to have the doors opened which lead to the cornices of the dome, the tambour and the nave. One can walk all the way round and look down from the height on the whole church. As we were standing on the cornice of the tambour, far below us we could see the Pope walking to make his afternoon devotions. St Peter's had not failed us. Then we climbed all the way down, went out into the square and had a frugal but cheerful meal at an inn nearby, after which we went on to the church of St Cecilia.

It would take pages to describe the decorations of this church, which was packed with people. One could not see a stone of the structure. The columns were covered with red velvet wound around with ribbons of gold lace, the capitals with embroidered velvet conforming more or less to their shape – so, too, with the cornices and pillars. All the intervening wall space was clothed in brightly coloured hangings, so that the whole church seemed to be one enormous mosaic. More than two hundred candles were burning behind and at the sides of the high altar, so that one whole wall was lined with candles, and the nave was fully illuminated. Facing the high altar, two stands, also covered with velvet, had been erected under the organ loft. The singers stood on one; the orchestra, which never stopped playing, on the other.

Just as there are concertos for violins or other instruments, here they perform concertos for voices: one voice – the soprano, for instance – predominates and sings a solo while, from time to time, the choir joins in and accompanies it, always supported, of course, by the full orchestra. The effect is wonderful.

All good days must come to an end and so must these notes. In the evening we got to the opera house, where *I litiganti** was being given, but we were so sated with good things that we passed it by.

23 November

Useful as I find my incognito, I must not forget the fate of the ostrich who believed that he could not be seen when he buried his head in the sand. While sticking to it on principle, there are occasions when I must relax my role. I was not unwilling to meet Prince Liechtenstein, the brother of Countess Harrach, since I have the greatest regard for her, and I have dined several times at his house. I soon realized, however, that my surrender to his invitations would have further consequences, and so it did. I had heard in advance about the Abbate Monti and his tragedy *Aristodemo*, which was soon to be performed, and I had been told that the author had expressed a wish to read it to me and get my opinion. Without actually refusing, I did nothing about it, but at last I met the poet and one of his friends at the Prince's house, where the play was read aloud.

The hero, as you know, is a king of Sparta who, to satisfy various conscientious scruples, commits suicide. It was tactfully insinuated that the author of *Werther* would certainly not resent finding that some passages from his admirable book had been used in the play. So, even within the walls of Sparta, I was not to be allowed to escape the angry manes of that unfortunate young man.

The work reveals a remarkable talent. It moves simply and quietly, and both the sentiments and the language, strong but delicate, are in accord with the theme. In my own fashion, if not in the Italian one, I pointed out the virtues of the play,

* *Tra i due litiganti il terzo gode*. Operetta by Giambattista Lorenzi.

and everybody was fairly satisfied, though, with southern impatience, they had expected something more. In particular, they wanted to hear from my lips some prophetic words about the impression it would make on the public.

I evaded this by saying that I was unfamiliar with this country, its preconceptions and its taste. But I was sincere enough to add that Roman audiences were spoiled, being accustomed to a three-act comedy with a complete two-act opera as an interlude or to a grand opera with utterly irrelevant ballets as intermezzi, so that I could not see them enjoying the noble calm progression of a tragedy without interruptions. Moreover, I said, it seemed to me that, to Italians, suicide was something utterly outside the range of their comprehension. One killed other people. Yes. That one heard of almost every day. But to take one's own precious life, or even contemplate doing so, that I had never heard of in Rome. I would be glad, however, to hear any evidence and arguments which would prove that my doubts were mistaken, for nothing would please me better than to see the play performed and to applaud it sincerely and loudly with a chorus of friends.

This statement was very warmly received and I had every reason this time to be glad I had unbent. Prince Liechtenstein is kindness itself, and, more than once, he has given me the opportunity to see in his company treasures of art which can only be seen by special permission of the owners, and to get that, one must be influential in high circles.

But it was asking too much of my good humour when the daughter of the Young Pretender also expressed her wish to see the 'rare marmoset'. I refused and have very firmly gone underground again.

Yet there is something unsatisfactory about this. I am more convinced than ever of a conclusion I came to earlier in my life: a man of good will should be just as active and energetic in social life as the egotistic, the narrow-minded and the evil. It is easy to see the truth of this, but difficult to put it into practice.

All I can say about the Italians is this: they are children of Nature, who, for all the pomp and circumstance of their religion and art, are not a whit different from what they would be if they were still living in forests and caves. What strikes any foreigner are the murders which happen almost every day. In our quarter alone there have been four in the last three weeks. Today again the whole city is talking of one, but it only *talks*. An honest artist called Schwendimann, a Swiss medallist and the last pupil of Hedlinger, was assaulted exactly like Winckelmann. His assailant, with whom he had got into a scuffle, stabbed him twenty times, and when the guards arrived, the villain stabbed himself. This is not the fashion here. Usually, the murderer takes sanctuary in a church, and that is the end of that.

Truth demands that I put some shadows into my rosy picture by reporting crimes, disasters, earthquakes and floods. Most of the foreigners are wildly excited over the present eruption of Vesuvius, and it takes a strong character not to be swept away oneself.

This natural phenomenon has something of the irresistible fascination of a rattlesnake. At the moment it seems as if all the art treasures of Rome were of no account; all the foreigners have interrupted their sightseeing tour and are hurrying off to Naples. But I shall resist the temptation and stay here, trusting that the mountain will keep something in reserve for me.

1 December

Moritz is here, who first attracted my attention by his biography, *Anton Reiser*, and his travel book, *Wanderings in England*. He is a really first-rate man and we greatly enjoy his company.

In Rome, where there are so many foreigners who have not come to study its art but for quite other kinds of amusement, one must be prepared for anything.

ceiling can be seen at closer range. The gallery is rather narrow and we squeezed into it along the iron railing with some difficulty and some feeling of danger – people who suffer from vertigo would be advised to stay below – but this was more than made up for by the masterpiece which met our eyes. At present I am so enthusiastic about Michelangelo that I have lost all my taste for Nature, since I cannot see her with the eye of genius as he did. If only there were some means of fixing such images firmly in one's memory! At any rate, I shall bring home as many engravings and drawings made after his work as I can get hold of. From the chapel we went to the loggias of Raphael, and, though I hardly dare admit it, I could not look at them any longer. After being dilated and spoiled by Michelangelo's great forms, my eye took no pleasure in the ingenious frivolities of Raphael's arabesques, and his Biblical stories, beautiful as they are, do not stand up against Michelangelo's. What a joy it would give me if I could see the works of both more frequently and compare them at leisure without prejudice, for one's initial reactions are bound to be one-sided.

The sun was almost too warm as we dragged ourselves to the Villa Pamfili and stayed in its lovely gardens until evening. A large meadow, bordered with evergreen oaks and tall stone-pines, was dotted with daisies which all had their little heads turned to the sun. This set me off again on botanical speculations, which I resumed the next day during a walk to Monte Mario, Villa Mellini and Villa Madama. It is fascinating to observe how a vegetation behaves when its lively growth is never interrupted by severe cold. One sees no buds here and realizes for the first time what a bud is. The arbutus is again in bloom while its last fruits are still ripening. The orange trees also show blossoms, as well as half- and fully-ripe fruits, but these, unless they stand between buildings, are covered at this time of year. There is room for speculation about the cypress, which, when it is very old and full-grown, is the most digni-fied of all trees. Soon I shall pay a visit to the Botanical Garden, where I hope to learn a good deal. Nothing, above all, is comparable to the new life that a reflective person experiences when he observes a new country. Though I am still always myself, I believe I have been changed to the very marrow of my bones.

3 December

Till now the weather has followed a six-day cycle – two cloudless days, one overcast day, two or three wet days and then again fine weather. I try to make the best use I can of each one of them.

The noble objects with which I am surrounded never lose their freshness for me. I did not grow up with them. I have not wrung from each its peculiar secret. Some attract me so powerfully that, for a while, I become indifferent, even unjust, to others. For example, the Pantheon, the Apollo Belvedere, one or two colossal heads and, recently, the Sistine Chapel have so obsessed me that I see almost nothing else. But how can we, petty as we are and accustomed to pettiness, ever become equal to such noble perfection? Even when one has adjusted oneself to some degree, a tremendous mass of new things crowd in on one, facing one at every step, each demanding the tribute of one's attention. How is one to find one's way through? Only by patiently allowing it all to grow slowly inside one, and by industriously studying what others have written for one's benefit.

I immediately bought the new edition of Winckelmann's *History of the Art of Antiquity*, translated by Fea. Read on the spot where it was written and with an able and learned company to consult, I find it a great help.

Roman antiquity is beginning to give me about as much pleasure as Greek. History, inscriptions, coins, in which hitherto I took no interest, are forcing themselves on my attention. My experience with natural history is repeating itself here, for the entire history of the world is linked up with this city, and I reckon my second life, a very rebirth, from the day when I entered Rome.

5 December

In the few weeks I have been here, I have already seen a number of foreigners come and go, and have been amazed at the lack of respect so many of them show for all these objects which are so worth seeing. In the future, thank God, none of these birds of passage will ever be able to impress me again. If, when I get back to the north again, one of them should start telling me about Rome, he will never again make me sick with envy. I have seen her for myself and I already know more or less where I stand.

8 December

Now and again we get a really beautiful day. The rain that falls from time to time is making the grass grow and the gardens green. The presence of evergreens here and there prevents one from noticing the fallen leaves of the others. The orange trees in the gardens, growing uncovered straight out of the ground, are heavy with fruit.

I meant to give a full account of a carriage drive we took to the sea and of the fishing catch we saw there, but our good friend Moritz returned in the evening on horseback and broke his arm when his horse took a fall on the slippery Roman pavement. This has put a stop to our merrymaking and brought domestic calamity into our little circle.

13 December

I am so happy that you have taken my disappearance as well as I hoped you would. Please make my peace with any heart that may have been offended at it. I did not mean to upset anyone and I cannot yet say anything to justify myself. God forbid that the motives which led to my decision should ever hurt the feelings of a friend.

I am slowly recovering from my '*salto mortale*', and I study more than I amuse myself. Rome is a world, and it would take years to become a true citizen of it. How lucky those travellers are who take one look and leave.

This morning I came by chance on the letters which Winckelmann wrote from Italy, and you can imagine with what emotion I have started to read them. Thirty-one years ago, at the same time of year, he arrived here, an even greater fool than I was. But, with true German seriousness, he set himself to make a thorough and accurate study of antiquity and its arts. How bravely he worked his way through! And, in this city, what it means to me to remember him!

Aside from the objects of Nature, who in all her realms is true and consistent, nothing speaks so loudly as the impression left by a good and intelligent man, or by authentic works of art which are just as unerring as Nature. One feels this particularly strongly in Rome, where so many caprices have been given free rein and so many absurdities perpetuated by wealth and power.

I was especially delighted by one passage in a letter of Winckelmann's to Francke. 'In Rome you must seek out everything with a certain phlegm, otherwise you are taken for a Frenchman. I believe that Rome is the school for the whole world and I, too, have been purged and tested here.'

What he says exactly describes my methods of investigation. No one who has not been here can have any conception of what an education Rome is. One is, so to speak, reborn and one's former ideas seem like a child's swaddling clothes. Here the most ordinary person becomes somebody, for his mind is enormously enlarged even if his character remains unchanged.

This letter will reach you in time for the New Year. May its beginning bring you much happiness and may we all meet again before its end! What a joy that will be! The past year has been the most important in my life; whether I die tomorrow or live yet awhile, it has been good to me. Now a few words for the children, which you may read to them or tell them in your own words.

Here you do not notice the winter. The only snow you can see is on the mountains far away to the north. The lemon trees are planted along the garden walls. By and by they will be covered with rush mats, but the orange trees are left in the open. Hundreds and hundreds of the loveliest fruits hang on these trees. They are never trimmed or planted in a bucket as in our country, but stand free and easy in the earth, in a row with their brothers. You can imagine nothing jollier than the sight of such a tree. For a few pennies you can eat as many oranges as you like. They taste very good now, but in March they will taste even better.

The other day we went to the seashore and saw fishermen hauling in their nets. The oddest creatures came up – fish, crabs and weird freaks of nature. Among them was the fish which gives anyone who touches it an electric shock.

20 December

But all this is more effort and trouble than it is pleasure. The rebirth which is transforming me from within continues.

Though I expected really to learn something here, I never thought I should have to start at the bottom of the school and have to unlearn or completely relearn so much. But now I have realized this and accepted it, I find that the more I give up my old habits of thought, the happier I am. I am like an architect who wanted to erect a tower and began by laying a bad foundation. Before it is too late, he realizes this and deliberately tears down all that he has built so far above ground. He tries to enlarge and improve his design, to make his foundations more secure, and looks forward happily to building something that will last. May Heaven grant that, on my return, the moral effect of having lived in a larger world will be noticeable, for I am convinced that my moral sense is undergoing as great a transformation as my aesthetic.

Dr Münter is here, having returned from Sicily. He is an energetic, impetuous man. I don't know his plans, but he is going to visit you in May and will have much to tell you. He has been travelling in Italy for two years, but is very disappointed with the Italians because they have paid too little respect to the important letters of recommendation he carried, which were supposed to give him access to certain archives and private libraries. As a result, he has failed to do as much as he hoped. He has collected some beautiful coins and is, so he tells me, in possession of a manuscript which classifies coins historically by certain specific characteristics, on similar lines to Linnaeus's classification of plants. Herder will probably be able to get more information about this. Perhaps permission will be given to have a copy made. Something of this kind can and must be done, and, sooner or later, we too will have to concern ourselves more seriously with this field.

25 December

I am now starting to look at the best things for the second time. As my initial amazement changes to a feeling of familiarity, I acquire a clearer sense of their value. For a profound understanding of what man has created, the soul must first have won its complete freedom.

Marble is an extraordinary material. Because of it, the Apollo Belvedere gives such unbounded pleasure. The bloom of eternal youth which the original statue possesses is lost in even the best plaster cast.

In the Palazzo Rondanini opposite, there is an over-life-size mask of a Medusa in which the fearful rigidity of death is admirably portrayed. I own a good cast of it, but nothing is left of the magic of the original. The yellowish stone, which is almost the colour of flesh, has a noble, translucent quality. By comparison, plaster always looks chalky and dead. And yet, what a joy it is to enter a caster's workshop and watch the exquisite limbs of the statues coming out of the moulds one after the other. It gives one a completely fresh view of the figures. All the statues which are scattered over Rome can here be seen set side by side. This is invaluable for purposes of comparison. I could not resist buying the cast of a colossal head of Jupiter. It now stands in a good light facing my bed, so that I can say prayers to him the first thing in the morning. However, for all his majesty and dignity, he has been the cause of a comic incident.

When our old landlady comes in to make our beds, she is usually accompanied by her favourite cat. I was sitting outside in the hall and heard her busying herself in my room. Suddenly she flung the door open – to hurry is not like her – and called to me to come quickly and witness a miracle. When I asked her what had happened, she replied that her cat was worshipping God the Father.

She had noticed for some time that the creature had the intelligence of a Christian, but, even so, this was a miracle. I ran into the room to see for myself, and it really was miraculous. The bust stands on a high pedestal, and the body is cut off far below the chest, so that the head is near the ceiling. The cat had jumped up on to the pedestal, placed its paws on the chest of the God and stretched itself up until its muzzle could just reach the sacred beard, which it was now gracefully licking, oblivious of the exclamations of the landlady or my entrance.

I did not spoil the enthusiasm of the good woman by telling her my own explanation for this strange feline devotion. Cats have a keen sense of smell and probably it had scented the grease from the mould, some of which still remained sunk in the grooves of the beard.

29 December

I must tell you more about Tischbein and his admirable qualities: how, for instance, true German that he is, he has educated himself. I must also say with gratitude what a true friend he has been to me during his second stay in Rome. He has looked after me constantly and had a whole series of copies from the best masters made for me, some in black crayon, others in sepia and water colour. These will be invaluable to me in Germany when I am far away from the originals.

Tischbein at first set out to become a portrait painter, and in the course of his career has come into contact with eminent men, especially in Zurich, who improved his taste and enlarged his vision.

I brought along with me *Scattered Leaves*, which are doubly welcome here. As a reward, Herder ought to be told in full detail what a good impression this little book makes at repeated readings. Tischbein could hardly believe that its author could have written it without ever having been in Italy.

In this artistic colony one lives, as it were, in a room full of mirrors where, whether you like it or not, you keep seeing yourself and others over and over again.

I had often noticed Tischbein giving me a close scrutiny and now the reason has come out; he is thinking of painting my portrait. The sketch is finished, and he has already stretched the canvas. The portrait is to be life-size. He wants to paint me as a traveller, wrapped in a white cloak, sitting on a fallen obelisk and looking towards the ruins of the Campagna di Roma in the background. It is going to be a fine painting, but it will be too large for our northern houses. I shall, I hope, again find some corner for myself, but there will be no room for my portrait.

In spite of all the attempts that are made to draw me out of my obscurity, in spite of all the poets who read me their productions in person or get others to do so, and though I would only have to say the word to cut quite a figure here, I stick to my resolution. I am only amused at discovering what they are after. Each little circle, though they all sit at the feet of the Queen of the world, now and then displays the spirit of a small provincial town. In fact, they are no different here than they are anywhere else. I am already bored at the thought of what they would like to do with me and through me. It would mean joining a clique, championing its passions and intrigues, praising its artists and dilettantes, belittling their rivals, and putting up with everything that pleases the Great and the Rich. Why should I add my prayer to this collective litany which makes me wish I were on another planet, and what good would it do?

No, I refuse to become any more deeply involved, and for my part, I mean to keep away, and when I get home, to discourage in myself and others the desire to gad about the wide, wide world.

What I want to see is the Everlasting Rome, not the Rome which is replaced by another every decade. If I had more time, I would use it better. It is history, above all, that one reads quite differently here from anywhere else in the world. Everywhere else one starts from the outside and works inward; here it seems to be the other way around. All history is encamped about us and all history sets forth again from us. This does not apply only to Roman history, but to the history of the whole world. From here I can accompany the conquerors to the Weser and the Euphrates, or, if I prefer to stand and gape, I can wait in the Via Sacra for their triumphant return. In the meantime I have lived on doles of grain and money, and have my comfortable share in all this splendour.

2 January 1787

One may say what one likes in praise of the written or the spoken word, but there are very few occasions when it suffices. It certainly cannot communicate the unique character of any experience, not even in matters of the mind. But when one has first taken a good look for oneself at an object, then it is a pleasure to read or hear about it, for now the word is related to the living image, and thought and judgement become possible.

You often used to make fun of my passion for observing stones, plants and animals from certain definite points of view, and tried to make me give it up. Now my attention is fixed on the architect, the sculptor and the painter and in them, too, I shall learn to find myself.

6 January

I have just come back from seeing Moritz, whose arm is now out of a cast. Things are going well. What I learned during these two weeks I spent with my suffering friend as nurse, confessor, confidant, finance minister and private secretary may bear good fruit in the future. During all this time the acutest suffering and the rarest pleasure went hand in hand.

Yesterday, for my eye's delight, I set up in the hall outside my room a new cast, a colossal head of Juno, the original of which is in the Villa Ludovisi. She was my first Roman love and now I own her. No words can give any idea of this work. It is like a canto by Homer. But I really deserve such good company because I can now announce that *Iphigenie* is finished at last, that is to say, it lies on the table before me in two almost identical copies, one of which will soon be on its way to you. Please receive it kindly. Though you will not, of course, find in its pages what I should have written, you will at least be able to guess what I would like to have written.

You have complained several times about obscure passages in my letters which hinted at some conflict under which I was suffering, even in the midst of the noblest sights. My Greek travelling companion was in no small part responsible by urging me to work when I ought to have been looking about me.

It reminds me of an excellent friend who had made all the preparations for a journey which might well have been called a journey of exploration. For years he studied and saved up his money and then, thinking to kill two birds with one stone, he suddenly eloped with the daughter of a distinguished family.

In a similar reckless mood I decided to take *Iphigenie* with me to Carlsbad. Let me now tell you briefly of the places where I was most occupied with my heroine.

After leaving the Brenner behind me, I took her out of the largest parcel and took her to my heart. On the shores of Lake Garda, where the strong noonday wind was dashing the

waves against the shore and I felt at least as lonely as my
heroine on the shores of Tauris, I drafted the first lines of a
new version. I continued this in Verona, Vicenza, Padua, and
with especial ardour in Venice. After that I came to an
impasse and even felt tempted to write a new play, *Iphigenie
in Delphi*. This I would have done at once if distractions and
my sense of obligation towards the older play had not
deterred me.

But once in Rome I began working again steadily. In the
evening, before going to bed, I prepared myself for the next
morning's allotted stint, which I attacked the moment I woke.
My method was very simple. I wrote a rough draft straight
off, then I read this aloud to myself, line by line, period by
period, until it sounded right. The result is for you to judge. In
writing it, I have learned more than I have achieved. I shall
enclose some comments with the play itself.

6 January

Again I have some more ecclesiastical matters to tell you
about. We spent a roaming Christmas Eve visiting the
churches where services were being held. One of the most
popular is equipped with a special organ and other musical
devices, so that not a pastoral sound is lacking, from the
shepherd's pipes to the chirping of birds and the bleating
of sheep.

On Christmas Day I saw the Pope with the assembled
clergy in St Peter's, where he celebrated High Mass. At times
he sat on his throne, at others he stood in front of it. It is a
spectacle unique in its kind, magnificent and dignified. But
I am so old a protestant Diogenes that the effect on me of this
splendour was more negative than positive. Like my pious
predecessor, I should like to say to these spiritual conquerors
of the world: Do not come between me and the sun of
sublime art and simple humanity.

Today is the Feast of the Epiphany, and I have heard Mass
said according to the Greek rite. These ceremonies seemed

to me more impressive, austere and thoughtful than the Latin ones.

As I watched, I again felt that I am too old for anything but truth. Rites, operas, processions, ballets, they all run off me like water off a duck's back. But an operation of Nature, like the sunset seen from the Villa Madama, or a work of art, like my revered Juno, leaves a deep and lasting impression.

I am already beginning to shudder at the thought of the forthcoming theatre season. Next week seven theatres will open. Anfossi himself is here and will perform *Alexander in India. Cyrus* will also be given and a ballet, *The Conquest of Troy.* This would be something for the children.

10 January

Here, then, is my 'child of sorrows'. *Iphigenie* deserves the epithet in more senses than one. When I read it to our circle I marked several lines. Some of them I think I have improved; others I have left as they stood, hoping Herder will put them right with a stroke or two with his pen. I have worked myself into a stupor over it.

The main reason why, for several years, I have preferred to write prose is that our prosody is in a state of great uncertainty. My intelligent and scholarly colleagues left the decision on such matters to instinct and taste. What has been lacking is any prosodic principle. I would never have dared rewrite *Iphigenie* in iambics if I had not found my guiding star in Moritz's *Prosody*. My association with the author, especially while he was laid up, has enlightened me still further on the subject, and I ask my friends to give his theory sympathetic consideration.

It is a striking fact about our language that we have very few syllables which are definitely long or short; with most of them, it is a matter of taste and option. Moritz has now worked out that there exists a certain syllabic hierarchy. The syllable which is more important to the meaning of a word is long and makes the less important syllable next to it short. On the other hand, the same syllable is short if it comes before or after a syllable which carries a greater weight of meaning. Here is certainly something to hold on to, and, even if not everything has been solved, we have at least a thread by which we can grope our way along. I have often obeyed the advice of this maxim and found it conform to my own feelings about language.

I mentioned earlier my reading of the play. Let me now tell you briefly how it turned out. Accustomed to my earlier impassioned and explosive work, these young men were expecting something in the manner of *Berlichingen** and at first could not reconcile themselves to the calm flow of the lines, though some elevated and simple passages did not fail to make their effect. Tischbein, who also has little taste for such emotional restraint, expressed this in a charming allegory or symbol. He compared my work to a burnt offering, the smoke from which is prevented from rising by a gentle air current and creeps along the ground, while its flame struggles to rise upward. His drawing, which I enclose, has both charm and point, I think.

And so this work which I had expected to finish much sooner has entertained, detained, occupied and tortured me for three whole months. It is not the first time I have treated what was most important as if it were a side issue; but we won't wrangle or philosophize any more over this.

I enclose a pretty carved stone – a little lion with a gadfly buzzing in front of its nose. This was a favourite subject of the Ancients, who treated it time and time again. I should like you to seal your letters with it in future so that the little thing may serve as a kind of artistic echo travelling back and forth between you and me.

13 January

Every day I have so much to tell and every day activities and distractions prevent me from putting one sensible word

* *Götz von Berlichingen*, early drama by Goethe, 1773.

down on paper. Furthermore, the days are getting chilly and
one is better off anywhere than indoors when the rooms have
neither stoves nor fireplaces and are only good for sleeping or
feeling uncomfortable in. Still, there are some incidents of the
past week which must not go unrecorded.

In the Palazzo Giustiniani there stands a statue of Minerva
which I admire very highly. Winckelmann scarcely mentions
it, and when he does, in the wrong context. And I do not
feel myself competent to say anything about it. We had
been standing for a long time looking at the statue when
the wife of the custodian told us that it had once been a sacred
image. The *inglesi*, she said, who belong to the same religious
cult, still come to worship it and kiss one of its hands. (One
hand, indeed, is white, while all the rest of the statue is a
brownish colour.) She went on to say that a lady of this
religious persuasion had been here recently, thrown herself
on her knees and worshipped it. She herself, being a Christian, had found this behaviour so funny that she had run out
lest she should burst out laughing. Seeing that I could not tear
myself away from the statue either, she asked me if I had a
sweetheart whom it resembled. Worship and love were the
only things the good woman understood; disinterested
admiration for a noble work of art, brotherly reverence
for another human spirit were utterly beyond her ken. We
were delighted with the story of the English lady and left with
the desire to return soon. If my friends want to hear more
about the High Style of the Greeks, they should read what
Winckelmann has to say about it. He does not mention
this Minerva in his discussion, but, if I am not mistaken,
the work is a late example of the high, austere style at the
point of its transition to the style of beauty: the bud is about
to open. A transitional style is appropriate to her character
as Minerva.

Now for a spectacle of another sort! On the Feast of
Epiphany, which celebrates the bringing of the Glad Tidings
to the Heathen, we went to the Propaganda. There, in the
presence of three cardinals and a numerous auditory, we first

heard an address on the theme: In what place did Mary receive the three Magi? In a stable? If not, where else? Then some Latin poems on similar themes were read, and after that about thirty seminarists appeared and read, one after another, little poems, each in his native tongue: Malabarian, Epirotian, Turkish, Moldavian, Hellenic, Persian, Colchic, Hebrew, Arabic, Syrian, Coptic, Saracenic, Armenian, Iberian, Madagassic, Icelandic, Egyptian, Greek, Isaurian, Ethiopian, etc., and several others which I could not understand. Most of the poems seemed to be written in their national metres and were recited in their national styles of declamation, for some barbaric rhythms and sounds came out. The Greek sounded as if a star had risen in the night. The audience roared with laughter at all the foreign voices, and so this performance, too, ended in farce.

Here is another little story to show how lightly the sacred is taken in holy Rome. The late Cardinal Albani was once present at just such a festive gathering as I have described. One of the seminarists turned towards the Cardinal and began in his foreign tongue with the words *'gnaja! gnaja!'* which sounded more or less like the Italian *'canaglia! canaglia!'* The Cardinal turned to his colleagues and said: 'This fellow certainly knows us!'

13 January

In spite of all he did, Winckelmann left much undone and his work leaves much to be desired. With the materials he had assembled, he built quickly so as to get a roof on his house. If he were still alive and in good health, he would be the first to revise what he wrote. How much more he would have added to his observations, what good use he would have made of all that others, following in his footsteps, have done and of all the results of recent excavations. And then Cardinal Albani, for whom he wrote so much and for whose sake, perhaps, he left many things unsaid, would be dead.

15 January

Well, *Aristodemo* has been performed at last and with great success. Since Abbate Monti is related to the Pope's nephew and is very popular in high society, one could take it for granted that nothing but good would be heard from that quarter, and, sure enough, the boxes were generous with their applause. From the start the parterre was captivated by the poet's beautiful diction and the excellent delivery of the actors, and let no occasion pass to voice its satisfaction. The German artists in the back rows were no less vociferous, appropriately for once, since they are apt to be noisy on all occasions.

The author was so nervous about the reception of his play that he stayed at home, but after each act he received favourable reports, which by degrees transformed his anxiety into joy. There will be no lack of repeated performances and everything looks fine. The success of the play proves that a strong dramatic contrast, provided each element has any obvious real merit on its own, can win the approval of both the connoisseur and the general public.

It was a praiseworthy performance, and the acting and delivery of the chief actor, who is on stage nearly all the time, were excellent; it was like seeing one of the kings of antiquity in person. The costumes which impress us so much when we see them on statues had been most successfully imitated in the actor's costume and it was obvious that he had studied the antique period well.

16 January

Rome is threatened with a great loss. The King* of Naples is going to transport the Farnese Hercules to his palace. All the artists are in mourning. However, as a result, we are going to see something our predecessors never saw. The upper part of

* Ferdinand IV (1751–1825).

the statue, from the head to the knees, and the feet with the pedestal on which they stand were discovered on the estates of the Farnese. The legs from the knees to the ankles were missing, and Guglielmo della Porta had made substitutes for them, upon which Hercules had been standing up till now. But recently the original legs were discovered on the Borghese estates and have been on exhibit in the Villa Borghese.

Prince Borghese has now decided to present these precious fragments to the King of Naples. The legs which Porta made have been removed and replaced by the authentic ones. Though everyone up till now has been perfectly satisfied with the statue as it was, there is a hope that we may be going to have the pleasure of seeing something quite new and more harmonious.

18 January

Yesterday, the Feast of St Anthony, we had a wonderful time. Though there had been frost in the night, the day turned out beautifully warm and clear.

It is a matter of historical observation that all religions, as their ritual or their theological speculation expands, must sooner or later reach the point of allowing the animals to share to some extent in their spiritual patronage. St Anthony, abbot or bishop, is the patron saint of all four-footed creatures and his feast is a saturnalia for these otherwise oppressed animals and for their keepers and drivers as well. The gentry must either walk or stay at home, and the people love to tell fearful stories of unbelieving masters who forced their coachmen to drive on this day and were punished by serious accidents.

The church stands on a square which is so large that, normally, it looks empty, but today it is full of life. Horses and mules, their manes and tails gorgeously braided with ribbons, are led up to a small chapel, detached from the church proper, and a priest, armed with an enormous brush, sprinkles them with holy water from tubs and buckets

in front of him. He does this generously, vigorously and even
facetiously so as to excite them. Devout coachmen offer
candles of various sizes, their masters send alms and gifts,
so that their valuable, useful beasts may be protected against
every kind of accident during the coming year. Donkeys and
horned cattle also get their modest share of blessing.

Later we took a long diverting walk under the blesssed
Italian sky. We were surrounded by objects of interest, but
this time we ignored them and abandoned ourselves to fun
and frolics.

19 January

We took another holiday today and looked at a part of the
Capitol which I had hitherto neglected. Then we crossed the
Tiber and drank Spanish wine aboard a ship which had just
landed. Romulus and Remus are said to have been found in
this neighbourhood. For us it was a triple Pentecost as we got
drunk on the holy spirit of art, the memories of the ancient
past and the sweet wine simultaneously.

20 January

The enjoyment which a beginner derives from his first superficial look depresses him later when he realizes that, without
solid knowledge, such pleasure is an illusion.

I am fairly well up in anatomy and have acquired some
knowledge of the human body, though not without much
effort. Now, thanks to my constant observation of statues,
I find myself becoming more and more interested in the
subject and at a more serious level. In surgical anatomy,
knowledge of the part is the only thing which matters, and
for that, one wretched little muscle is quite sufficient. But in
Rome the parts are of no account except in so far as they
contribute to a shape which is noble and beautiful.

In the large military hospital of Santo Spirito they have
made a model of the muscular system for artists to study,

which is universally admired. It looks just like a Marsyas or a saint who has been flayed alive.

I am also educating myself by following the customs of the Ancients and studying the skeleton, not as an artificially assembled mass of bones, but with the natural ligaments to which it owes life and motion.

If I now tell you that I am also studying perspective in the evenings, it will show, I hope, that I have not been idle. For all that, I am always hoping to do more than I actually manage to do.

22 January

As for the artistic tastes of the German colony here, I can only say: the bells ring loudly enough, but not in unison.

When I think what wonderful things there are all around us and how little advantage I have taken of them, I could despair. But now I look forward eagerly to returning and hope that, next time, I shall see clearly these masterpieces, after which I was, until now, groping like a blind man.

Even in Rome, too little provision is made for the person who seriously wants to study the city as a whole. He is compelled endlessly to piece it together from fragments, though these are certainly superabundant. The truth is, few visitors are really serious about seeing and learning anything that matters. They are governed by their caprices and their vanity, as all who have dealings with them are well aware. Every guide has his designs on one, everybody wants to recommend some tradesman or other, or promote the career of his favourite artist. And why shouldn't he? Don't these ignoramuses reject the best when it is offered them?

It would be of the greatest advantage to the serious student if the government, which must give its permission before an antique work of art is exported, would insist in such cases that a cast be made first. These casts might be collected in a special museum. But even if a Pope were to have such an idea, he would have all the traders against him because, in a few years, there would be an outcry at the loss of so many valuable and important works, for which, in some cases, the permission to export has been obtained by secret and devious ways.

For some time, but particularly since the performances of *Aristodemo*, the patriotic feelings of the German colony have been aroused. They never stopped singing the praises of my *Iphigenie*. Again and again I was asked to read excerpts and in the end I was forced to repeat my reading of the whole work. When I did this, I found several more lines which sounded better when read than they looked on paper, which proves that poetry is not written for the eye.

Rumours of this reading at last reached the ears of Reiffenstein and Angelica,* and I was urged to give another at their house. I asked for some days' grace, but gave them a lengthy outline of the story and the plot development. This presentation was more favourably received by the aforesaid than I had dared hope; even Signor Zucchi, from whom I expected it least, showed a sincere and sympathetic interest. This, however, is easy to explain, for in its formal structure my play conforms more or less to the traditional form of Greek, Italian and French drama. And this still has the greatest appeal for those who have not yet grown accustomed to the English audacities.

25 January

I find it becoming more and more difficult to give a proper account of my stay in Rome. The more I see of this city, the more I feel myself getting into deep waters.

It is impossible to understand the present without knowing the past, and, to compare them with each other, I should need more time and fewer distractions. The very site of the city takes one back to the time of its foundation. We soon see

* Angelica Kauffmann, Swiss painter, married to the Italian painter Antonio Zucchi.

that it was no great, wisely led people who settled here and prudently established it as the centre of an empire. No powerful ruler chose it as a suitable spot for the seat of a colony. No, it began as a refuge for shepherds and riffraff. A couple of vigorous young men laid the foundations for the palaces of the masters of the world on the very same hill at the foot of which a despotic usurper had once had them exposed among reeds and swamps. In relation to the land behind them, the seven hills are not hills at all; it is only in relation to the ancient river bed of the Tiber, which later became the Campus Martius, that they appear to be heights. If the spring allows me to make further excursions possible, I shall be able to describe the disadvantages of the site more fully. Even now, with pity in my heart, I can hear the anguished lamentations of the women of Alba as they see their city destroyed and are driven from that beautiful location which some intelligent leader had chosen. I can picture them, huddled on the miserable Coelian hill and exposed to the mists of the Tiber, looking back at their lost paradise. I still know little of the surrounding country, but I am convinced that no inhabited site among the peoples of old was as badly placed as Rome. In the end, when they had swallowed up everything, in order to live and enjoy life, the Romans had to move out again and build their country villas on the sites of the cities they had destroyed.

25 January

It is comforting to observe how many people here live quietly, each pursuing his own interests. In the house of a priest who, though without original talent, has devoted his life to art, we saw some interesting copies of great paintings which he had reproduced in miniature. The best of all was of the Last Supper by Leonardo da Vinci. Christ is sitting at the table with His intimate disciples, and the painter has chosen the moment when He prophesies and says: 'Verily, one of you shall betray me.'

I am trying to make arrangements to have an etching made, either after this copy or another. It would be the greatest blessing if a faithful reproduction could become available to a wide public.

Some days ago I visited a Franciscan called Father Jacquier who lives on the Trinità dei Monti. He is a Frenchman by birth and well known for his books on mathematics. He is very old, but very nice and sympathetic. He has known many eminent men in his time and even spent some months with Voltaire, who grew very fond of him.

I have made the acquaintance of many other good and sound people among the clergy. There are plenty of them about but, because of some priestly mistrust, they avoid each other.

The bookshops here are not centres for the exchange of ideas and the literary novelties seldom have much in them. The proper thing, therefore, for a solitary man to do is to seek out the hermits.

After the success of *Aristodemo* which I really did a good deal to promote, I was again led into temptation. But it soon became only too obvious that they were not interested in me personally. They wanted to use me as a tool to strengthen their party and, if I had been prepared to come out and take sides, I too could have played a brief shadowy role. But now that they have seen I am not to be made use of, they leave me alone, and I go my own way in peace.

Yes, my life has acquired a ballast which gives it the proper balance; I am no longer afraid of the ghosts who so often used to make me their sport. Be of good cheer yourselves; that will give me added strength to stand on my own feet and will draw me back to you.

28 January

Everything I see around me suggests two lines of inquiry which I shall not fail to pursue when I see my way more clearly. The first is this:

At the sight of the immense wealth of this city, even though it consists of scattered fragments, one is inevitably led to ask about the age when it came into being. It was Winckelmann who first urged on us the need of distinguishing between various epochs and tracing the history of styles in their gradual growth and decadence. Any true art lover will recognize the justice and importance of this demand.

But how are we to obtain this insight? Little spade-work has been done; the general principle has been clearly laid down, but the details remain uncertain and obscure. A special training of the eye over many years would be required, and we must first learn what questions to ask. But hesitating and temporizing are no help. Once his attention has been drawn to the question and its importance realized, any serious student will understand that, in this field as in others, judgement is impossible without a knowledge of historical development.

The second line of inquiry is concerned exclusively with the art of the Greeks: What was the process by which these incomparable artists evolved from the human body the circle of their god-like shapes, a perfect circle from which not one essential, incidental or transitional feature was lacking? My instinct tells me that they followed the same laws as Nature, and I believe I am on the track of these. But there is something else involved as well which I would not know how to express.

2 February

Nobody who has not taken one can imagine the beauty of a walk through Rome by full moon. All details are swallowed up by the huge masses of light and shadow, and only the biggest and most general outlines are visible. We have just enjoyed three clear and glorious nights. The Colosseum looked especially beautiful. It is closed at night. A hermit lives in a small chapel and some beggars have made themselves at home in the crumbling vaults. These had built a fire on the level ground and a gentle breeze had driven the smoke into the arena, so that the lower parts of the ruins were veiled and only the huge masses above loomed out of the darkness. We stood at the railing and watched, while over our heads the moon stood high and serene. By degrees the smoke escaped through holes and crannies and in the moonlight it looked like fog. It was a marvellous sight. This is the kind of illumination by which to see the Pantheon, the Capitol, the square in front of St Peter's, and many other large squares and streets.

Like the human spirit, the sun and the moon have a quite different task to perform here than they have in other places, for here their glance is returned by gigantic, solid masses.

13 February

I must mention a stroke of luck. It was a small one, but, great or small, luck is luck and always welcome. On the Trinità dei Monti they are digging the foundation for a new obelisk. The top of the hill is covered with mounds of earth taken from the ruins of the Gardens of Lucullus, which were later inherited by the Caesars. My wig-maker was passing by one morning and found in the rubble a flat piece of terracotta with some figures on it. He washed it and showed it to us, and I promptly bought it. It is almost as big as my hand and seems to be part of a large bowl. The figures on it are two griffins flanking a sacrificial altar; they are beautifully done and give me extraordinary pleasure. If they had been carved in stone, they would have made a lovely seal.

15 February

Before leaving for Naples, I could not escape giving another reading of *Iphigenie*. The audience consisted of Signora Angelica, Hofrat Reiffenstein and even Signor Zucchi, who insisted on coming because his wife wished him to. At the time he was working on a large architectural drawing done in decorative style, at which he is a master. He used to be closely associated with Clerisseau and they were in Dalmatia together. He drew the figures for the buildings and ruins which Clerisseau later published. In doing so, he learned so much about perspective and effects that now, in his old age, he can amuse himself with a sheet of paper in a worthwhile way.

Angelica, tender soul that she is, responded to my play with a sympathetic understanding that astounded me. She has promised to make a drawing based on one passage and give it to me as a souvenir. And so, just as I am on the point of leaving Rome, I have become tenderly attached to these kindhearted people. It is both a pleasure and a pain for me to know that someone will be sorry to see me go.

16 February

The safe arrival of *Iphigenie* was announced to me in a surprising and pleasant way. Just as I was leaving for the opera, a letter in a familiar hand was brought to me – doubly welcome because it had been sealed with the little lion, so that I knew that my package must have arrived safely. I pushed my way into the opera house and looked for a seat under the large chandelier. There, in the middle of a crowd of strangers, I suddenly felt so close to my distant friends that I wished I could jump up and embrace them. I thank you heartily for the bare notice of its arrival. I hope your next letter will be accompanied by some kind word of approval.

Here follows a list, telling you how the copies which are due to me from Göschen are to be distributed among my friends. I don't care in the least how the general public responds to my piece, but I do wish to give my friends some pleasure with it.

I am always inclined to undertake too much. If I think of my next four volumes as a whole, my head swims; when I think of them separately, I feel a little better. Perhaps it would have been wiser to have done as I originally intended, and sent these things out into the world in fragments. Then

I could have embarked with fresh courage and strength on new subjects in which I felt a fresher interest.

Would I not have done better to write *Iphigenie in Delphi* instead of grappling with the moods of Tasso? But I have already put much too much of myself into the play, fruitlessly to abandon it now.

I am sitting in the hall by the fireplace, and the heat of a fire that is, for once, well fed gives me the courage to start a new page. How wonderful it is that one can reach out so far into the distance with one's latest thoughts and transport thither one's immediate surroundings.

The weather is beautiful, the days are becoming visibly longer, the laurel and boxwood are in flower and so are the almond trees. This morning I came upon an unusual sight. In the distance I saw what looked like some tall poles which were the most beautiful purple all over. On closer inspection, they turned out to be what in our hothouses is called the Judas tree and, by botanists, *Cercis siliquastrum*. Its violet, butterfly-shaped flowers blossom directly out of the trunk. They had been lopped during the winter, which accounted for the poles I had seen, and flowers had burst forth from the bark by the thousands. Daisies are pushing up out of the ground in swarms like ants. The crocus and the adonis appear less often but look all the more decorative and graceful when they do.

What new joys and profitable experiences the southern regions of this country must have in store for me! It is the same with the works of Nature as with works of art: so much has been written about them and yet anyone who sees them can arrange them in fresh patterns.

When I think of Naples or, even more, of Sicily as I know them from stories and pictures, it strikes me that these earthly paradises are precisely the places where volcanoes burst forth in hellish fury and have for centuries terrified and driven to despair the people who live there and enjoy these regions.

But, important though I hope they will be to me, I must banish these things from my thoughts so that I may make the most of my last few days in the ancient capital of the world.

For two weeks now I have been on the go from morning to night, seeing the things I had not seen before and giving the best a second or third look. Everything is beginning to make a pattern; the major works fall into their proper places and there is room between them for many minor ones. My preferences are becoming clearer and my emotional response to what is greatest and most authentic is now freer and more relaxed.

At this stage one naturally envies the artist, who, through reproducing and imitating these great visions, comes closer to them in every way than the person who merely looks and thinks. Still, after all, each can do only what lies in his power, and so I spread all the sails of my spirit that I may circumnavigate these coasts.

Today the grate has been stacked up with the finest coal, something which rarely happens, since it is hard to find someone with the time or the inclination to devote an hour or two to looking after the fire. I shall take advantage of the agreeable temperature to rescue some of my notes before they become completely illegible.

On February the second we went to the Sistine Chapel for the ceremony of the blessing of the candles. This upset me very much and I soon left with my friends. I thought to myself: These are the very candles which for three centuries have blackened the frescoes, and this is the very incense which, with sacred insolence, not only wraps the sun of art in clouds, but also makes it grow dimmer every year and in the end will totally eclipse it.

We went outside and, after a long walk, came to Sant'Onofrio, where Tasso lies buried in a corner. His bust stands in the convent library. The face is of wax, and I can well believe that it is a death mask. It is a little blurred and damaged in places, but it still reveals better than any of his other portraits a gifted, delicate, noble and withdrawn personality.

So much for today. Now I must tackle the honest Volk-mann's second volume on Rome and copy out excerpts concerning the things I have not yet seen. Before I go to Naples, the harvest should at least be reaped. The good day will certainly come when I can gather it into sheaves.

17 February

Except for four rainy days, all through February the sky has been cloudless, and in the middle of the day it is almost too warm. Everyone prefers to be out of doors. Hitherto we gave ourselves up to gods and heroes, but now the landscape comes into its rights, and the beauty of these days draws us into the countryside. I sometimes remember how in the north artists tried to make something of thatched roofs and ruined castles, to capture a picturesque effect from brooks, bushes and dilapidated rocks, and then I wonder at the change in myself, all the more so because these things still cling to me from habit. In the last two weeks, however, I have plucked up courage and have been going out, equipped with small pieces of drawing paper, to the hills and valleys where the villas are. Without too much deliberation I make sketches of typical southern or Roman subjects, chosen at random, and, trusting to luck, try to give them some light and shade. I can see clearly what is good and what is even better, but as soon as I try to get it down, it somehow slips through my fingers and I capture, not the truth, but what I am in the habit of capturing. Progress would require the discipline of steady practice, but where shall I find the time for such concentration? Still, I feel I have improved in many ways during these two weeks of passionate endeavour.

The artists like giving me lessons because I am quick to understand. But understanding is not the same as doing. Quickness of understanding is a mental faculty, but right doing requires the practice of a lifetime. However, feeble as his efforts may be, the amateur should not despair. The few lines I draw on the paper, often too hasty and seldom exact, help me to a better comprehension of physical objects. The more closely and precisely one observes particulars, the sooner one arrives at a perception of the whole.

One must not, however, compare oneself with the artist, but proceed in one's own manner. Nature has provided for all her children: even the least of them is not hindered in his existence by the existence of the greatest. 'A little man is still a man.'* Let us leave it at that.

I have seen the sea twice, first the Adriatic, then the Mediterranean, but both, as it were, only in passing. In Naples we shall get better acquainted. Everything in me is suddenly beginning to merge clearly. Why not earlier? Why at such a cost? I have so many thousands of things, some new, some from an earlier time, which I would like to tell you.

In the evening, when the Carnival madness has abated

I am not happy about leaving Moritz alone when I go away. He has made good progress, but the moment he is left to look after himself, he immediately withdraws into his favourite hiding holes. With my encouragement he has written a letter to Herder, which I enclose, and I hope that the answer will contain some useful advice. Moritz is an unusually good person; he would have made better progress if, now and then, he had met sympathetic people capable of explaining his condition to him. At the moment, if Herder would allow him to write a letter once in a while, it would do him more good than anything. He is engaged on an archaeological work which really deserves to be encouraged. Our friend Herder could not easily have lent his kind offices to a better cause, nor sown his teachings in a more fertile field.

The large portrait of me, which Tischbein has started on, is already beginning to grow out of the canvas. He has ordered a small clay model from a skilful sculptor and draped it

---

* *A little man.* A quotation from Goethe's satirical puppet play *Das Jahrmarktsfest zu Plundersweilern*, 1773.

elegantly in a cloak. From this model he is now hard at work painting, for the picture ought, of course, to be brought to a certain stage before we leave for Naples, and merely to cover such a large canvas with paint takes plenty of time.

19 February

To my annoyance, I wasted the whole day among the fools. When night fell, I went for a walk in the Villa Medici to recover. The new moon is just past. Next to its tenuous sickle, I could almost make out the dark portion of the disc with the naked eye, and through a telescope it was clearly visible. During the day a haze hovers over the earth like that I know from the drawings and paintings of Claude Lorrain, but this phenomenon cannot easily be seen in Nature more beauti- fully than here. The almond trees, blossoming among the dark-green oaks, are a new vision of grace. The sky is like a light-blue piece of taffeta, lit up by the sun. But how much more beautiful it will be in Naples! All this confirms my botanical fancies, and I am on the way to establishing impor- tant new relations and discovering the manner in which Nature, with incomparable power, develops the greatest complexity from the simple.

Vesuvius is throwing up stones and ashes, and at night people can see the summit glowing. I hope that ever-active Nature will make me the present of a flow of lava. I can hardly wait to make these mighty objects my own.

21 February. Ash Wednesday

At last the folly is over. Yesterday evening the innumerable little candles created another scene of Bedlam. One has to see the Roman Carnival to lose all wish ever to see it again!

It is not worth writing about, though it might make an amusing topic of conversation. What I find unpleasant about it is the lack of genuine gaiety in the people, who have not enough money to gratify the few desires which they may still have. The great are stingy about spending, the middle class is impecunious and the populace without a penny. On the last day the noise was incredible, but there was no genuine merriment. The pure and lovely sky looked down in innocence on all these buffooneries.

Since, however, one cannot entirely refrain from describing such scenes and to amuse the children, I am sending you some coloured drawings of carnival masks and characteristic Roman costumes. The dear little ones may use them to replace some missing chapter in their Orbus Pictus.

I am using the moments between packing to write down a few things I forgot to mention. Tomorrow we leave for Naples. I am looking forward to finding a new freedom in that paradise of Nature, and a fresh impulse to resume my study of art when I return to the solemnities of Rome.

Packing is no trouble. I do it with a lighter heart than I did six months ago when I severed my ties with all that was dear to me. Yes, that was six months ago already, and of the four I have spent in Rome, not a moment has been wasted. That is saying a good deal, but it is no exaggeration.

I know that *Iphigenie* arrived; by the time I reach the foot of Vesuvius, I hope I shall hear that she has been kindly received.

To be travelling in Tischbein's company, who has such a remarkable eye for nature and art, is a great privilege for me. Like true Germans, we cannot refrain from making plans to work. We have bought the finest drawing paper, though the number and splendour of the objects we shall encounter will probably set limits to our good intentions.

I have made up my mind about one thing: the only one of my poetic works which I shall take with me is *Tasso*. I set great hopes on him. If I only knew your opinion of *Iphigenie*, this might serve me as a guide, for *Tasso* is a similar work. The subject, which is even more strictly circumscribed than the former play, needs still further elaboration in detail. All I have written so far must be thrown away; it has been lying around too long and neither the characters, the plot nor the tone have the slightest affinity with my present views.

As I was putting my things in order I came across your reproach that I contradict myself in my letters. I was not aware of this, but, since I always send them off the moment I have written them, it is highly probable. I feel myself being tossed about by tremendous powers, and it is only to be expected that I do not always know where I stand.

There is a tale about a fisherman who was caught at night by a storm and was trying to steer his boat homeward. His little son clung to him and asked: 'Father, what is that funny little light I see, now above us, now below?' His father promised to give him the answer the next day. It turned out to have been the beacon of the lighthouse, which to the child's eyes, as the boat rocked up and down on the wild waves, had appeared now below him, now above.

I too am steering my boat towards port over a wild sea and am keeping a steady eye on the lighthouse beam, even though to me too it seems to be constantly shifting its position, so that at last I may come safe and sound to shore.

At any departure, one inevitably thinks of earlier journeys and of that final future one. The thought is borne in on me, more forcibly than ever, that we make far too many provisions for life. Tischbein and I, for example, are about to turn our backs on so many wonderful things, including our well-stocked private museum. We now have three Junos standing side by side for comparison, but we are leaving them behind as though we had none.

PART TWO

NAPLES

WE made good time getting here. Two days ago the sky grew overcast, but there were some signs in the atmosphere which promised the return of good weather, and so it was. The clouds gradually dispersed, patches of blue sky appeared from time to time and, finally, the sun shone upon our course. We passed through Albano, and, before reaching Genzano, made a stop at the gates of a park which the owner, Prince Chigi, might be said to retain but not to maintain. Perhaps that is why he does not want anyone to look at it. It has turned into a complete wilderness – trees, shrubs, weeds, creepers grow as they like, wither, tumble down and rot. The valley of the park is enclosed by a high wall, but there is a little lattice gate through which one can peer into it, and see the hill slope beyond and the castle on its crown. It would make a fine subject for a good painter.

Enough of description. Let me merely add that, from this high ground, we could see the mountains of Sezze, the Pontine Marshes, the sea and the islands. A heavy shower was moving seaward over the marshes, and ever-changing patterns of light and shade played over the level waste. Some columns of smoke rising from scattered and barely visible huts gave an added beautiful effect as the sunlight struck them.

Velletri stands on a volcanic hill which is joined to other hills only on its northern side and commands a wide view in the other three directions.

We paid a visit to the museum of the Cavaliere Borgia, who, thanks to his connexions with the Cardinal and the Propaganda, has been able to collect some remarkable antiques – Egyptian idols, carved in the hardest kind of stone, metal figurines from earlier and later periods, and terracotta bas-reliefs which were dug up in this region. These last lead one to conclude that the ancient Volsci had a style of their own.

Among the many other rare objects in this museum, I particularly noticed two small paint-boxes of Chinese origin. On one the whole process of raising silkworms was portrayed, on the other the cultivation of rice, both very naïvely imagined and elaborately executed.

It is disgraceful, I know, that one does not come more often to look at these treasures, seeing how near to Rome they are. One's only excuse is the discomfort of any excursion into these parts and the binding spell of the Roman magic circle. As we were walking towards our inn, we passed some women sitting in front of their houses who called out to us and asked if we would like to buy some antiques. When we showed an eager interest, they brought out old kettles, fire-tongs and other worthless household utensils, and split their sides with laughter at having made fools of us. At first we were furious, but our guide set matters right when he assured us that this trick was an old custom here and every foreign visitor must submit to it with good grace.

I am writing this in a miserable inn and am too tired and uncomfortable to write any more. So – a very, very good night!

Fondi, 23 February

As early as three in the morning we were again on our way. Day break found us in the Pontine Marshes, which do not actually look as dreary as people in Rome usually describe them.

From one cross-journey, one cannot, of course, really judge such a vast and ambitious project as the drainage operations which have been undertaken at the Pope's orders, but it looks to me as though they are going to be largely successful.

Imagine a wide valley running from north to south with hardly any fall, but dipping towards the mountains in the east and rising towards the sea in the west. Down its whole length runs the straight line of the restored Via Appia, flanked on its right by the main canal which drains all the land on the seaward side, so that this has now been reclaimed for agriculture. Except for a few patches which lie too low, it is in cultivation as far as the eye can see, or would be if the farmers could be found to lease it.

The land on the mountain side of the road presents a more difficult problem. Cross-channels emptying into the main canal have been dug through the embankment of the road, but these cannot drain off the water. I am told there is a plan for digging a second drainage canal along the base of the mountains. Over large areas, especially around Terracina, willows and poplars have been accidentally sown by the wind.

Each posting station is merely a long shed with a thatched roof. Tischbein drew one and was rewarded by a sight such as only he can fully enjoy. A white horse had broken loose on the drained land and was rejoicing in its freedom, galloping over the brown earth like a flash of light. It looked superb, and Tischbein's rapture gave it added significance.

On the site of the former village of Mesa, at the very centre of the area, the Pope has erected a beautiful great building to inspire hope and confidence in the whole undertaking. So on we rolled in animated conversation but remembering the warning not to fall asleep on this road. If we had forgotten, the blue exhalation which, even at this time of year, hangs above the ground at a certain height would have reminded us of the dangerous miasma. It made the rocky perch of Terracina all the more desirable, and presently we saw the sea before us. The other side of that rock city offered us a view of a vegetation which was entirely unfamiliar. Indian figs forced their large, fleshy leaves between humble grey-green myrtles, yellow-green pomegranates and pale-green olive branches. Beside the road grew flowers we had never seen before. The meadows were full of narcissus and adonis. We had the sea on our right for a time, but the limestone hills close on our left remained unbroken. They are a continuation of the Apennines and run down from Tivoli till they reach the sea from which they have been separated, first by the Campagna di Roma, then by the extinct volcanoes of Frascati, Albano and Velletri, and finally by the Pontine Marshes. Monte Circello, the promontory which faces Terracina and marks the end of the Pontine Marshes, is probably limestone as well.

We now turned away from the sea and soon reached the plain of Fondi. This small area of fertile soil enclosed by not too rugged mountains welcomes every traveller with a smile. Most of the oranges are still hanging on the trees, the young crops – chiefly wheat – are showing green in the fields and there, below us, lay the little town. A solitary palm tree stood out, and we gave it a greeting. So much for tonight. Forgive my hasty pen. The objects of interest are too many and our quarters too miserable. But I could not resist my desire to get something down on paper. We arrived here at sunset and now it is time for bed.

Sant'Agata, 24 February

The room is cold, but I must give you some account of a perfect day. Dawn had just broken when we drove out of Fondi, and we were immediately greeted by oranges hanging over the walls on either side of the road. The trees are so loaded with fruit, I could hardly believe my eyes. On top, the young foliage is yellowish, but below, a very lush green. Mignon* was quite right to yearn for this country.

Then we came to well-tilled wheat fields planted with properly spaced olive trees. When the wind stirred, they turned the silvery undersides of their leaves to the light while the branches swayed gracefully. It was a grey morning, but a strong north wind promised to disperse the clouds.

---

* See the poem *Mignon*, below, p. 1086.

Presently the road ran along a valley between fields which were full of stones but well cultivated, their young crops of the freshest green. In several places we saw large, circular, paved threshing floors enclosed in low walls. They do not bring the corn home in sheaves, but thresh it on the spot. The valley narrowed, the road climbed steadily, sheer limestone crags rose on either side, the storm blew violently at our backs, and sleet fell which melted very slowly.

Our curiosity was aroused by the walls of some old buildings which were laid out in a network pattern. The high ground was rocky but planted with olive trees wherever there was the smallest patch of soil for them to grow in. Next we crossed a plain covered with olive groves and came to a small town. There we noticed, built into garden walls, ancient tombstones and all sorts of fragments, and the well-constructed floors of ancient villas, now filled up with earth and overgrown with thickets of olives. And then ... then, there was Vesuvius, capped with a cloud of smoke.

When we reached Mola di Gaeta, we were again greeted by orange trees in profusion. We stayed there a few hours. The bay in front of the little town commands a beautiful vista of sea and shore. The coast is the shape of a crescent moon. The tip of the right horn, the rock on which stands the fortress of Gaeta, is not far away, but its left horn extends much further. Following it with the eye, one sees first a chain of mountains and then Vesuvius and the islands beyond. Facing the crescent and almost at its centre lies the island of Ischia.

On the beach I found my first starfish and sea urchins, which had been washed ashore. I also picked up a lovely green leaf, as thin as the finest vellum, and some curious pebbles. Limestone pebbles were the most common, but serpentine, jasper, quartz, granite, porphyry, various kinds of marble and green-blue glass were also to be seen. These last can hardly come from this region and are most probably fragments from ancient buildings. Thus one can watch the waves playing before one's eyes with the splendour of an earlier world. We tarried with pleasure and were much amused by the nature of the people, whose behaviour was rather like that of some primitive tribe. After leaving Mola behind us, we had beautiful views all the way, even after the sea left us. The last we saw of it was a lovely cove, which we sketched. A good fruit country followed, fenced in by hedges of aloes. We also saw an aqueduct which ran from the mountains towards some unrecognizable jumble of ruins.

After crossing the river Garigliano, the road ran in the direction of a mountain range through a fairly fertile but uninteresting region. At last, the first hill of volcanic ash. From then on we entered a vast system of hills and valleys with snow-capped mountains rising in the background. A straggling town on a nearby hill caught my eye. In the valley lay Sant'Agata, where a respectable inn welcomed us with a cheerful fire burning in a fireplace built like a cabinet. Our room, however, is icy cold and has no windows, only shutters – so I must hurry to finish this.

Naples, 25 February

We have arrived safely at last and the omens are favourable. I haven't much to report about the last day of our journey. We left Sant'Agata at sunrise. All day a north-east wind blew fiercely at our backs without slackening, but it was afternoon before it succeeded in dispersing the clouds, and we suffered acutely from the cold.

Our road led us again between and over volcanic hills, among which, so far as I could tell, limestone formations occurred much less frequently. At last we came to the plain of Capua and soon afterwards to the town itself, where we made our midday halt. In the afternoon a beautiful, flat expanse lay before us. The broad high road ran between fields of green wheat; this is already a span high and spread out before our eyes like a carpet. Rows of poplars are planted in the fields and vines trained between their widespreading branches. It was like this all the way to Naples. The soil is loose, free from stones and well cultivated. The stems of the vines are unusually strong and tall and the tendrils sway like nets from one poplar to another.

Vesuvius was on our left all the time, emitting copious clouds of smoke, and my heart rejoiced at seeing this remarkable phenomenon with my own eyes at last. The sky grew steadily clearer and, finally, the sun beat down on our cramped and jogging quarters. By the time we reached the outskirts of Naples the sky was completely cloudless, and now we are really in another country. The houses with their flat roofs indicate another climate, though I dare say they are not so comfortable inside. Everybody is out in the streets and sitting in the sun as long as it is willing to shine. The Neapolitan firmly believes that he lives in Paradise and takes a very dismal view of northern countries. *Sempre neve, case di legno, gran ignoranza, ma denari assai* – that is how he pictures our lives. For the edification of all northerners, this means: 'Snow all the year round, wooden houses, great ignorance, but lots of money.'

Naples proclaims herself from the first as gay, free and alive. A numberless host is running hither and thither in all directions, the King is away hunting, the Queen is pregnant and all is right with the world.

26 February

Alla Locanda de Sgr Moriconi al Largo del Castello – at this jolly, high-sounding address, letters from all four quarters of the globe can reach us from now on.

In the vicinity of the great citadel by the sea there is a vast space which, though it is surrounded on all sides by houses, is not called *piazza* but *largo* – the Broad Place, a name which probably dates from a time long ago when it was still open country. At one corner stands a large house in which we have taken a spacious corner room so that we can enjoy an uninterrupted view of the ever-lively square. An iron balcony runs along the outside past many windows and even round the corner. One would never leave it if the nipping wind did not chill one to the bones. Our room is gaily decorated, especially the elaborately coffered ceiling, where hundreds of arabesques announce that we are not far from Pompeii and Herculaneum. All this would be very fine, but there is neither fireplace nor stove, and, since February exercises its rights even here, I was longing for some means of keeping warm.

They brought me a tripod, high enough to hold one's hands over without stooping. To this is fastened a shallow pan filled with very fine live charcoal which is covered by an even layer of ashes. As we learned in Rome, it has to be used very economically. From time to time the overlying ashes must be carefully pushed aside with the head of a key, in order to let a little air reach the coals. If one gets impatient and stirs up the glowing embers, one may feel warmer for the moment, but very soon they burn themselves out, and then one must pay something to get the brazier refilled.

I was not feeling very well, so, naturally, I wanted more comfort. A rush mat protected me against the worst consequences of the cold stone floor. Since furs are unknown here, I decided to put on a pea-jacket which we had brought with us as a joke. This served me in good stead, especially after I fastened it round my waist with a cord from my valise. I must have looked a comic sight, something between a sailor and a Capuchin friar. When Tischbein returned from visiting some friends, he could not stop laughing.

27 February

Yesterday I spent indoors reading, waiting for my slight indisposition to pass. We spent today in ecstasies over the most astonishing sights. One may write or paint as much as one likes, but this place, the shore, the gulf, Vesuvius, the citadels, the villas, everything, defies description. In the evening we went to the Grotta di Posillipo and reached it just at the moment when the rays of the setting sun were shining directly into the entrance. Now I can forgive anyone for going off his head about Naples, and think with great affection of my father, who received such lasting impressions from the very same objects as I saw today. They say that someone who has once seen a ghost will never be happy again; vice versa, one might say of my father that he could never be really unhappy because his thoughts could always return to Naples. In my own way, I can now keep perfectly calm and it is only occasionally, when everything becomes too overwhelming, that my eyes pop out of my head.

28 February

Today we paid a visit to Philipp Hackert, the famous land-scape painter, who enjoys the special confidence and favour of the King and Queen. One wing of the Palazzo Francavilla has been reserved for his use. He has furnished this with the taste of an artist and lives very contentedly. He is a man of great determination and intelligence who, though an invet-erate hard worker, knows how to enjoy life.

Afterwards we went to the seashore and saw all kinds of fish and the weirdest-shaped creatures being hauled in out of the waves. The day was lovely, the tramontana bearable.

1 March

In Rome I had already been obliged, more often than I liked, to abandon my obstinate hermit existence and take some part in social life. It does seem rather odd, I must admit, to go into the world with the intention of remaining alone. I was unable, for instance, to resist Prince Waldeck's kind invitations, and, thanks to his rank and influence, I was able to see many good things in his company.

For some time now, he has been staying in Naples, and we had hardly arrived before he sent us an invitation to take a drive with him out to Pozzuoli and the neighbouring country-side. I had been thinking of a trip to Vesuvius today, but Tischbein persuaded me to accept, saying that, in this perfect weather and the company of such a cultured prince, the other excursion promised to be as profitable as it certainly would be pleasant. While in Rome we made the acquaintance of a beautiful lady and her husband who are both inseparable friends of the Prince's. She is to be one of the party, so we are counting on having a delightful time.

I was already well known in this high circle from an earlier occasion. At our first meeting, the Prince had asked me what I was working on, and I was so preoccupied with my *Iphigenie* that one evening I told them the whole story in considerable detail. There was some discussion afterwards, but I got the impression they had been expecting something livelier and more violent.

1 March. Evening

Who has not had the experience of being swept off his feet and perhaps decisively influenced for life by a cursory reading of a book which, when he read it again and thought about it, had hardly anything more to say to him? (This happened once to me with *Sakuntala.**) And does not much the same thing happen to us in our encounters with eminent persons?

How shall I describe a day like today? – a boat trip; some short drives in a carriage; walks on foot through the most astonishing landscape in the world; treacherous ground under a pure sky; ruins of unimaginable luxury, abominable and sad; seething waters; caves exhaling sulphur fumes; slag hills forbidding all living growth; barren and repulsive areas; but then, luxuriant vegetation, taking root wherever it can, soars up out of all the dead matter, encircles lakes and brooks, and extends its conquest even to the walls of an old crater by establishing there a forest of noble oaks.

Thus one is tossed about between the acts of nature and the acts of men. One would like to think, but feels too

---

* *Sakuntala*, dramatic poem by the sixth-century Indian poet Kalidasa.

incompetent. Meanwhile the living merrily go on living. We, of course, did not fail to do the same, but people of culture, who belong to the world and know its ways, and are also warned by grave events, are inclined to reflections. As I was lost in contemplation of an unlimited view over earth, sea and sky, I was called back to myself by the presence of an amiable young lady who is accustomed to receive attentions and is not indifferent to them.

But even in my transports, I did not forget to take some notes. For a future redaction, the map I made on the spot for our use and a quick sketch of Tischbein's will be of great help. Today I am incapable of adding another word.

2 March

Today I climbed Vesuvius, although the sky was overcast and the summit hidden in clouds. I took a carriage to Resina, where I mounted a mule and rode up the mountain through vineyards. Then I walked across the lava flow of 1771 which was already covered with a fine but tenacious moss, and then upward along its edge. High up on my left I could see the hermit's hut. Climbing the ash cone, which was two-thirds hidden in clouds, was not easy. At last I reached the old crater, now blocked, and came to the fresh lava flows, one two months, one two weeks, and one only five days old. This last had been feeble and had already cooled. I crossed it and climbed a hill of ashes which had been recently thrown up and was emitting fumes everywhere. As the smoke was drifting away from me, I decided to try and reach the crater. I had only taken fifty steps when the smoke became so dense that I could hardly see my shoes. The handkerchief I pressed over my mouth was no help. In addition, my guide had disappeared and my steps on the little lava chunks which the eruption had discharged became more and more unsteady. I thought it better, therefore, to turn back and wait for a day with less cloud and less smoke. At least I now know how difficult it is to breathe in such an atmosphere.

Otherwise the mountain was perfectly calm, with none of the flames, rumbling or showers of stone there had been during the weeks before we arrived. Well, I have now made a reconnoitre, so that I can make my regular attack as soon as the weather clears.

Most of the types of lava I found were already known to me, but I discovered one phenomenon which struck me as unusual and which I intend to investigate more closely after I have consulted experts and collectors. This was the lining of a volcanic chimney which had once been plugged up, but then burst open and now juts out from the old filled-up crater. This hard, greyish, stalactitic mass seems to me to have been produced simply by the condensation of the finest volcanic vapours, unassisted by moisture or chemical action. This gives matter for further thought.

3 March

Today the sky is overcast and a sirocco is blowing – just the weather for writing letters.

Besides, I have seen quite enough people (and a mixed bag they are), beautiful horses and extraordinary fish.

I won't say another word about the beauties of the city and its situation, which have been described and praised so often. As they say here, '*Vedi Napoli e poi muori!* – See Naples and die!' One can't blame the Neapolitan for never wanting to leave his city, nor its poets for singing the praises of its situation in lofty hyperboles: it would still be wonderful even if a few more Vesuviuses were to rise in the neighbourhood.

I don't want even to think about Rome. By comparison with Naples's free and open situation, the capital of the world on the Tiber flats is like an old wretchedly placed monastery.

The sea and shipping make one aware of new possibilities. Yesterday the frigate for Palermo sailed before a strong tramontana, and her passage cannot have taken more than thirty-six hours.

With longing, I watched her spread sails as she passed between Capri and Cape Minerva and finally disappeared. If I were to watch a person I loved sail away in this fashion, I should pine away and die. Today a sirocco is blowing; if the wind increases, the waves near the harbour wall should be a merry sight. It being a Friday, the great coach drive of the nobility took place, when they show off their carriages and even more their horses. Nothing could be more graceful than these creatures. For the first time in my life, my heart went out to them.

3 March

I am sending you some pages, summarizing my first days in this new world, and enclose with them the envelope of your last letter, scorched in one corner, as evidence that it has been with me on Vesuvius.

You mustn't, either in your dreams or your waking hours, think of me as surrounded by dangers; where I go, I can assure you, I am in no greater peril than I would be on the high road to Belvedere.* I can aptly quote the Psalmist: 'The earth is the Lord's and all that is in it.' I don't seek adventure out of idle curiosity or eccentricity, but, since I have a clear mind which quickly grasps the essential nature of an object, I can do more and risk more than others. The voyage to Sicily is perfectly safe, and Sicily itself is by no means as dangerous as people who have never come within miles of it like to make out.

No earthquakes have been felt in southern Italy recently; only Rimini and neighbouring places in the north have suffered any damage. Earthquakes have moods of their own; here people talk of them as they talk of the weather or as, in Thuringia, they talk of forest fires.

I am glad you have now taken kindly to the new version of *Iphigenie*; I should be still happier if you were more aware of

* The summer residence of the Dukes of Weimar.

how much it differs from the first. I know what I have done to it and am entitled, therefore, to talk about it. I could have gone much further. If what is good gives one joy, what is better gives one even more, and, in art, only the best is good enough.

5 March

We have spent the second Sunday in Lent wandering from one church to another. What is treated in Rome with the utmost solemnity is treated here with a lighthearted gaiety. The Neapolitan school of painting, too, can only be properly understood in Naples.

We were amazed to see the whole west front of a church painted from top to bottom. Over the portal, Christ was driving the money-changers out of the temple; on both sides, the latter were falling gracefully down a flight of stairs with a startled look on their faces.

In the interior of another church the span above the entrance is copiously decorated with a fresco depicting the expulsion of Heliodorus. No wonder Luca Giordano had to be quick, having such vast spans to fill. Even the pulpit is not always, as it is elsewhere, a cathedra, a chair for a single preacher. One I saw was a gallery up and down which walked a Capuchin, scolding the congregation for their sins, now from one end, now from the other.

I can't begin to tell you of the glory of a night by full moon when we strolled through the streets and squares to the endless promenade of the Chiaia, and then walked up and down the seashore. I was quite overwhelmed by a feeling of infinite space. To be able to dream like this is certainly worth the trouble it took to get here.

During the last few days I have made the acquaintance of a remarkable man, the Cavaliere Filangieri, who is well known for his work *Science of Legislation*. He is one of those noble-hearted young men to whom the happiness and freedom of mankind is a goal they never lose sight of. His manners are those of a gentleman and a man of the world, but they are tempered by a delicate moral sense which pervades his whole personality and radiates charmingly from his speech and behaviour. He is devoted to his King and the present monarchy, even though he does not approve of everything that is going on. He is also oppressed by his fears of Joseph II. The thought of a despot, even as a phantom possibility, is horrible to noble minds. He told me quite frankly what Naples might expect from this man. He likes to talk about Montesquieu, Beccaria and his own writings – all in the same spirit of good will and of a sincere youthful desire to do good. He must still be in his thirties.

Soon after we met, he introduced me to the work of an older writer, whose profound wisdom is so refreshing and edifying to all Italians of this generation who are friends of justice. His name is Giambattista Vico, and they rank him above Montesquieu. From a cursory reading of the book, which was presented to me as if it were sacred writ, it seems to me to contain sibylline visions of the Good and the Just which will or should come true in the future, prophecies based on a profound study of life and tradition. It is wonderful for a people to have such a spiritual patriarch: one day *Hamann* will be a similar bible for the Germans.

6 March

Reluctantly, but out of loyal comradeship, Tischbein accompanied me today on my ascent of Vesuvius. To a cultured artist like him, who occupies himself only with the most beautiful human and animal forms and even humanizes the formless – rocks and landscapes – with feeling and taste, such a formidable, shapeless heap as Vesuvius, which again and again destroys itself and declares war on any sense of beauty, must appear loathsome.

We took two cabriolets, since we didn't trust ourselves to find our own way through the turmoil of the city. The driver shouted incessantly, 'Make way! Make way!' as a warning to donkeys, burdened with wood or refuse, carriages going in the opposite direction, people walking bent down under their loads or just strolling, children and aged persons, to move aside so that he could keep up a sharp trot.

The outer suburbs and gardens already gave sign that we had entered the realm of Pluto. Since it had not rained for a long time, the leaves of the evergreens were coated with a thick layer of ash-grey dust; roofs, fascias and every flat surface were equally grey; only the beautiful blue sky and the powerful sun overhead gave witness that we were still among the living.

At the foot of the steep slope we were met by two guides, one elderly, one youngish, but both competent men. The first took me in charge, the second Tischbein, and they hauled us up the mountain. I say 'hauled', because each guide wears a stout leather thong around his waist; the traveller grabs on to this and is hauled up, at the same time guiding his own feet with the help of a stick.

In this manner we reached the flat base from which the cone rises. Facing us in the north was the debris of the Somma. One glance westward over the landscape was like a refreshing bath, and the physical pains and fatigue of our climb were forgotten. We then walked round the cone, which was still smoking and ejecting stones and ashes. So long as there was space enough to remain at a safe distance, it was a grand, uplifting spectacle. After a tremendous, thundering roar which came out of the depth of the cauldron, thousands of stones, large and small, and enveloped in clouds of dust, were hurled into the air. Most of them fell back into the abyss, but the others made an extraordinary noise as they hit the outer wall of the cone. First came the heavier ones, struck with a dull thud and hopped down the slope, then the lighter rattled down after them and, last, a rain of ash descended. This all took place at regular intervals, which we could calculate exactly by counting slowly.

However, the space between the cone and the Somma gradually narrowed till we were surrounded by fallen stones which made walking uncomfortable. Tischbein grew more depressed than ever when he saw that the monster, not content with being ugly, was now threatening to become dangerous as well.

But there is something about an imminent danger which challenges Man's spirit of contradiction to defy it, so I thought to myself that it might be possible to climb the cone, reach the mouth of the crater and return, all in the interval between two eruptions. While we rested safely under the shelter of a projecting rock and refreshed ourselves with the provisions we had brought with us, I consulted our guides. The younger one felt confident that we could risk it; we lined our hats with linen and silk handkerchiefs, I grabbed his belt, and, sticks in hand, we set off.

The smaller stones were still clattering, the ashes still falling about us as the vigorous youth hauled me up the glowing screes. There we stood on the lip of the enormous mouth; a light breeze blew the smoke away from us but also veiled the interior of the crater; steam rose all around us from thousands of fissures; now and then we could glimpse the cracked rock walls. The sight was neither instructive nor pleasing, but this was only because we could not see anything, so we delayed in the hope of seeing more. We had forgotten to keep our slow count and were standing on a sharp edge of the monstrous abyss when, all of a sudden, thunder shook the mountain and a terrific charge flew past us. We ducked instinctively, as if that would save us when the shower of stones began. The smaller stones had already finished clattering down when, having forgotten that another interval had begun and happy to have survived, we reached the foot of the cone under a rain of ashes which thickly coated our hats and shoulders.

After an affectionate scolding from Tischbein and some refreshment, I was able to make a careful examination of both the older and the fresher lavas. The older guide could pick them out and give the exact year of each. The more ancient were already covered with ash and quite smooth; the more recent, especially those which had flowed more sluggishly, looked very peculiar.

When lava flows sluggishly, the surface cools into solid masses. From time to time some obstruction brings these to a standstill. The masses behind are borne forward on the molten stream beneath and forced over the stationary ones. This process is repeated again and again until finally the whole flow petrifies in jagged shapes. Something similar happens with ice floes on a river, but it looks odder in lava. Among the formless melted products there were some large chunks which, on fracture, showed a resemblance to a type of more primitive rock. The guides maintained that they were old lavas from the lowest depths of the volcano which it expels from time to time.

On our way back to Naples I noticed some one-storey little houses constructed in a curious way without windows; the only light the rooms receive comes through the door opening on to the street. From early morning until late into the night, the occupants sit outside until it is time to retire into their caves.

This city, which, even in the evening, is in an uproar too, though one of a somewhat different kind, makes me wish I could stay here longer to make such sketches as I can of its animated scenes. But nothing so nice, I fear, is likely to happen.

7 March

This week Tischbein has conscientiously taken me to see most of the art treasures in Naples and explained them to me. As a connoisseur and excellent painter of animals, he had already aroused my interest in the bronze head of a horse in the Palazzo Colubrano, and today we went to see it. This amazing fragment stands in a niche above the courtyard fountain, directly facing the front gates. What an effect it must have produced when it was seen in relation to the limbs and body as a whole.

The horse, as it was originally, must have been much larger than the horses on the Basilica of San Marco, and, even from the head alone, when examined closely and in detail, one gets an overwhelming impression of character and power. The magnificent frontal bone, the snorting nostrils, the pricked ears, the bristling mane! What a passionate, powerful creature!

When we turned round, we noticed a female statue standing in a niche over the gates. Winckelmann held that it represents a dancer, for he believed that it was the lively and ever-changing motions of such performers which the sculptors immortalized for us in the frozen marble forms of nymphs and goddesses. This one is very graceful and lovely; at some time or other her head must have come off, but it has been skilfully replaced; the rest is perfectly intact, and she really deserves a better place.

9 March

Today I received your dear letters of 16 February. Please go on writing. I have given precise orders about my mail while I am away and shall go on doing so if I should travel further. At such a distance, it seems strange to me to read that my friends do not come together more often, but of course, when people live so near each other, it is quite natural if they seldom meet.

The weather has become gloomier – a sign of change. Spring is near and we are going to have rain. The summit of Vesuvius has not been visible since I was up there. During the last few nights we sometimes saw flames, but now everything is quiet again. A more violent eruption is expected.

The storms of the last days have presented us with the picture of a magnificent sea and allowed me to study the motions and the forms of the waves. Nature is, indeed, the only book whose every page is filled with important content.

The theatre, on the other hand, no longer gives me any pleasure. Here, during Lent, they perform sacred operas. The only difference between them and profane operas is that they have no ballets between the acts; otherwise, they are as gay as possible. At the Teatro San Carlo they are giving *The Destruction of Jerusalem by Nebuchadnezzar*. To me the theatre is merely a peepshow on a larger scale. I seem to have lost my taste for such things.

Today we paid a visit to the Prince of Waldeck in the Palazzo Capodimonte, which houses a large collection of paintings, coins, etc., not too well displayed, but including some precious things. What I saw clarified and confirmed many traditional concepts for me.

In our northern countries we know such things, coins, carved gems, vases, even lemon treees, only from single specimens; seen here, where they belong, and in profusion, they look quite different. For where works of art are rare, rarity itself is a value; it is only where they are common, as they are here, that one can learn their intrinsic worth.

Large sums are currently being paid for Etruscan vases and, to be sure, you can find some beautiful and exceptional pieces among them. Every foreigner wants to possess one. You grow less cautious with your money here than you would be at home. I am afraid that I myself will be tempted.

One agreeable aspect of travel is that even ordinary incidents, because they are novel and unexpected, have a touch of adventure about them. After returning from Capodimonte, I made still another visit in the evening to the Filangieri's. There, on the sofa with the lady of the house, sat a young person whose outward appearance did not seem to me to be quite in keeping with her free-and-easy behaviour. Dressed in a light little frock of striped silk, with her hair arranged in a capricious fashion, the pretty little creature looked like one of those modistes who spend so much time dressing other women that they can't be bothered to pay attention to their own appearance. Since they are accustomed to getting paid for their work, they cannot see why they should look after themselves for nothing. My entrance did not disturb her in the least, and on she chattered, telling a number of droll little stories about things which had happened to her during the last few days, or rather, things which her harum-scarum behaviour had caused to happen.

The lady of the house tried to help me to get a word in edgewise by talking about Capodimonte and its magnificent situation and art treasures, but all in vain. The lively little lady jumped up – when standing, she looked even prettier – took her leave, ran to the door and, as she passed me, said: 'The Filangieri are coming to dine with me one of these days. I hope to see you too.' And off she went before I could open my mouth to accept. I was then told that she was the Princess —,* and closely related to the family. The Filangieri are not rich and live in modest but decent style. I fancied that the little Princess must be in the same position, especially since I know that such high-sounding titles are not rare in Naples. I wrote down her name, the day and the hour, to be certain of turning up at the right place and the right time.

11 March

Since my stay in Naples is not going to be a long one, I visit the more distant points of interest first; those nearby offer themselves of their own accord. As Tischbein and I drove to Pompeii, we saw on every hand many views which we knew well from drawings, but now they were all fitted together into one splendid landscape.

Pompeii surprises everyone by its compactness and its smallness of scale. The streets are narrow, though straight and provided with pavements, the houses small and window-less – their only light comes from their entrances and open arcades – and even the public buildings, the bench tomb at the town gate, the temple and a villa nearby look more like architectural models or dolls' houses than real buildings. But their rooms, passages and arcades are gaily painted. The walls have plain surfaces with richly detailed frescoes painted on them, most of which have now deteriorated. These frescoes

* Filangieri's sister, Teresa, Princess Ravaschieri di Satriano.

are surrounded by amusing arabesques in admirable taste: from one, enchanting figures of children and nymphs evolve, in another, wild and tame animals emerge out of luxuriant floral wreaths. Though the city, first buried under a rain of ashes and stones and then looted by the excavators, is now completely destroyed, it still bears witness to an artistic instinct and a love of art shared by a whole people, which even the most ardent art lover today can neither feel nor understand and desire.

Considering the distance between Pompeii and Vesuvius, the volcanic debris which buried the city cannot have been driven here, either by the explosive force of the eruption or by a strong wind: my own conjecture is that the stones and ashes must have remained suspended in the air for some time, like clouds, before they descended upon the unfortunate city.

To picture more clearly what must have happened historically one should think of a mountain village buried in snow. The spaces between the buildings, and even the buildings themselves, crushed under the weight of the fallen material, were buried and invisible, with perhaps a wall sticking up here and there; sooner or later, people took this mound over and planted vineyards and gardens on it. It was probably peasants digging on their allotments who made the first important treasure hauls.

The mummified city left us with a curious, rather disagreeable impression, but our spirits began to recover as we sat in the pergola of a modest inn looking out over the sea, and ate a frugal meal. The blue sky and the glittering sea enchanted us, and we left hoping that, on some future day, when this little arbour was covered with vine leaves, we would meet there again and enjoy ourselves.

As we approached Naples, the little houses struck me as being perfect copies of the houses in Pompeii. We asked permission to enter one and found it very clean and neatly furnished – nicely woven cane chairs and a chest which had been gilded all over and painted with brightly coloured flowers and then varnished. Despite the lapse of so many centuries and such countless changes, this region still imposes on its inhabitants the same habits, tastes, amusements and style of living.

12 March

Today I rambled through the city in my usual fashion, noting many points which I hope to describe more fully later, for now, unfortunately, I have not the time.

Everything one sees and hears gives evidence that this is a happy country which amply satisfies all the basic needs and breeds a people who are happy by nature, people who can wait without concern for tomorrow to bring them what they had today and for that reason lead a happy-go-lucky existence, content with momentary satisfaction and moderate pleasures, and taking pain and sorrow as they come with cheerful resignation. Here is an amazing illustration of this.

The morning was cold and damp, for it had been raining a little. I came to a square where the large paving stones seemed to me to have been swept unusually clean, and was surprised to see a number of ragamuffins squatting in a circle with their hands pressed to the flat stones as if they were warming them. At first I thought they were playing a game, but the serious expression on their faces suggested some more practical purpose for their behaviour. I racked my brains trying to guess what they were up to, but found no satisfactory explanation, so I had to ask someone why these little monkeys formed this circle and took up such a peculiar posture.

I was told that a blacksmith in the neighbourhood had been putting a tyre on a cartwheel. This is done as follows: the iron band is laid on the ground, shavings are piled on it in a circle and set alight to make the iron sufficiently malleable. When the shavings have burnt themselves out, the tyre is fitted on to the wheel, and the ashes are carefully swept up. The little street arabs take advantage of the fact that the paving stones are still hot and stay there till they have absorbed the last bit of warmth from them.

I could give you countless other examples of this capacity to get the most out of the least and make careful use of what would otherwise be wasted. This people displays the most ingenious resource, not in getting rich, but in living free from care.

Evening

In order to get to the whimsical little Princess on time, and not to miss the right house, I hired a servant, who conducted me to the gates of a large palazzo. Since I did not credit her with living in such a magnificent residence, I spelled out her name once more, letter by letter, but he assured me that this was the right place. I entered a spacious empty courtyard, enclosed by the main building and several annexes – all in the gay Neapolitan style of architecture – and faced an enormous portal and a wide though not very long staircase, on either side of which servants in splendid livery were lined up, who bowed deeply as I passed. I felt like the sultan in Wieland's Fairy Tale and, following his example, took my courage in both hands. At the head of the staircase, I was received by the upper servants, and, in due course, the grandest of them opened a door and I was confronted by a magnificent but perfectly empty salon. As I paced up and down I caught a glimpse of a side gallery where a table was laid for about forty persons on the same scale of splendour as everything else. A secular priest entered: without asking who I was or where I came from, he took my presence for granted and made polite conversation.

Double doors were thrown open to admit an elderly man, and immediately closed behind him. The priest advanced to meet him, so I did the same. We greeted him with a few polite words to which he replied with some barking and stammering noises. For all that I could make of them, he might have been speaking Hottentot. When he had taken up a position by the fireplace, the priest stepped back and I followed his example. Now an imposing Benedictine entered, accompanied by a younger brother. He, too, greeted our host and, after being barked at, withdrew and joined us by the window. The members of religious orders, especially the more elegantly dressed ones, are at great advantage in society; their habit, though it indicates humility and renunciation, at the same time lends them a decided dignity. They can appear submissive without abasing themselves, and when they draw themselves up to their full height, they are invested with a certain self-complacency which would be intolerable in any other profession but becomes them rather well. The Benedictine was this kind of man. I asked him about Monte Cassino; he invited me to come there and promised me the warmest reception. In the meantime, officers, courtiers, secular priests, even some Capuchins had arrived, and the salon was full of people.

I looked in vain for a lady. At last, the double doors opened and closed again and a lady entered who looked even older than the master of the house. The presence of the lady of the house – for that is what I took her to be – convinced me that I was in the wrong palazzo and a total stranger to its owners.

Dinner was now announced and I stuck close to the ecclesiastics, hoping to sneak in with them into the paradise of the dining room. At this moment Filangieri and his wife entered hurriedly, apologizing for being late; and a moment later the little Princess came running into the salon, curtsying, bowing, and nodding to all the guests as she passed, and made straight for me. 'How nice of you to keep your promise!' she cried. 'Sit next to me at table, and you shall have all the titbits. But wait a moment! First I have to find my place. Then you must immediately take the chair next to me.' Thus bidden, I followed her various gyrations and at last we reached our places. The Benedictines were seated opposite me and Filangieri on my right. 'The food is excellent,' said the Princess, 'everything Lenten fare but choice. I will tell you which dishes are the best. But first I must take our precious clerical friends down a peg. I can't abide them. They're all knaves. Every time they come to the house they make off with some food. What we have, we should eat with our friends.'

The soup had been served, and the Benedictine was eating it with decorum. 'Don't be shy, your Reverence!' she cried gaily. 'Is your spoon too small? Let me send for a bigger one! You gentlemen must be used to large mouthfuls.' The Father replied that, in this princely home, everything was so well ordered that even guests who were accustomed to far greater comforts than he would be perfectly satisfied.

When little tarts were offered, he took only one. Why, she cried, didn't he take half a dozen? Surely he must know that puff-paste is easy on the bowels. The sensible man took another one and thanked her for her kind attentions, as if he hadn't heard her indelicate joke.

A more substantial piece of pastry gave her a further opportunity for venting her malice. 'Take a third one, Father! You seem determined to lay a good foundation.' 'When such excellent materials are provided,' replied the priest, 'the builder has an easy time.' And so she went on and on, only pausing now and then to help me select the most delicious morsels. Meanwhile I talked with my neighbour on serious topics. As a matter of fact, I have never heard Filangieri say anything commonplace. In this respect, as in so many others, he resembles my friend Georg Schlosser,* except that, being a Neapolitan and a man of the world, he has a softer nature and is more approachable.

Throughout the meal, the mischievous lady on my left did not leave the clergy in peace for a moment. During Lent the fish is served in forms which make it look like meat, and this gave her inexhaustible opportunities for making irreverent and unseemly comments. She made great play with the expressions 'a liking for flesh' and 'a fleshly liking', saying that one ought at least to enjoy the form, even though the substance was forbidden. I heard her make more jokes of the same kind, but have not the courage to repeat them. Certain

*J. G. Schlosser, advocate and Goethe's brother-in-law.

things may sound tolerable when spoken, especially on beautiful lips, but set down in black and white, they lose all charm for me. An impudent remark is peculiar in that it amuses at the moment because one is taken aback, but if repeated later, it sounds merely offensive.

Dessert was served, and I was afraid she would continue her banter, but, unexpectedly, she turned to me and said with good humour: 'The dear clergy shall swallow their Syracusan wine in peace. I have never yet succeeded in teasing one of them to death or even in spoiling his appetite. But now, let's talk sense. What were you and Filangieri talking about so seriously? That good man worries too much. As I keep telling him: if you make new laws, we shall have all the bother of devising ways and means to break them; we already know what to do about the old ones. Just think what a nice city Naples is, and how long people have lived here carefree and contented. From time to time, of course, someone gets hanged, but life goes on swimmingly for the rest.'

She then suggested that I go and stay on her large estate in Sorrento; her agent would serve me the finest fish and delicious *mungana*, the meat of suckling calves. The mountain air and heavenly view would soon cure me of all philosophy; later, she would come herself and then all my wrinkles – at my age I had no business to have any – would vanish without trace, and we would lead a very jolly life together.

13 March

Today I shall write a few more words and let one letter chase after another. I am well, but I see less than I should. This place encourages languor and an easygoing life. In spite of this, I am rounding out my picture of the city bit by bit.

On Sunday we went to Pompeii again. There have been many disasters in this world, but few which have given so much delight to posterity, and I have seldom seen anything so interesting. The city gate and the avenue of tombs are unusual. There is one tomb of a priestess, shaped like a semicircular bench and with an inscription carved in large letters on its stone back. As I looked over it, I saw the sun setting into the sea.

We met a company of lively Neapolitans, who were as natural and lighthearted as could be, and we all ate at the Torre dell'Annunziata. Our table was set close to the shore with a delightful view of Castellammare and Sorrento, which seemed very near. One of the Neapolitans declared that, without a view of the sea, life would not be worth living. Personally, it is enough for me that I now carry this picture in my memory and I shall quite happily return to the mountains, when the time comes.

We are lucky to have a very accurate landscape painter here, who captures the atmosphere of these rich and open surroundings in his drawings. He has already done some work for me.

I have now carefully studied my Vesuvian specimens; things look quite different when seen in relation to each other. If, as perhaps I should, I were to devote the rest of my life to observation, I might discover some things which would enlarge human knowledge.

Please tell Herder that my botanical insights are taking me further and further. My basic hypothesis remains the same, but to work everything out would take a lifetime. One day, perhaps, I shall be capable of giving a general outline.

I am now looking forward to seeing the Portici museum. For most people it is the place they visit first; for us it will be the last. I still don't know where I am going next; they all want me to be back in Rome for Easter. I shall wait and see.

Angelica is engaged in painting a scene from my *Iphigenie*. Her idea is a very happy one and she will carry it out admirably. She has chosen the turning point in the play, the moment when Orestes comes out of his swoon and finds himself in the presence of his sister and his friend. She has transformed the lines which the three characters speak one after another into simultaneous gestures. This shows both her delicate sensibility and her capacity to translate life into terms of her own medium.

Farewell and keep on loving me! Everyone here treats me kindly, even though they do not know what to make of me. They find Tischbein more congenial. This evening, immediately after supper, he painted some life-size heads, and they reacted like Maoris at the sight of their first man-of-war. Tischbein has a great gift for sketching in pen and ink the figures of gods and heroes, large as life or larger. He dashes them off with a few strokes and then puts in the shadows with a broad brush, so that the head stands out in relief. The company were amazed at the ease with which he did this and expressed their enthusiastic delight. Then their fingers began itching to try it themselves. They picked up the brushes and started daubing beards on each other's faces.

This happened in a cultured circle and in the house of a man who is himself a sound painter and draughtsman. Is not such behaviour an expression of some primitive trait in the human race?

Caserta, 14 March

Saw Hackert at his apartment in the old castle where he lives very comfortably and has room enough to entertain his guests. The new castle is a palace worthy of a king, a huge quadrilateral building like the Escorial with a number of inner courtyards. Its location is extraordinarily beautiful – upon one of the most fertile plains in the world with a park extending to the feet of the mountains. From the latter an aqueduct carries a whole river to supply the castle and surrounding countryside with water. This can be released to hurl itself over some artificially arranged rocks in a stupendous cascade. The gardens are beautifully laid out and in perfect harmony with a region that is itself a garden.

The castle, though truly regal, seemed to lack life, and people like myself cannot feel at ease in its immense empty rooms. The King probably feels the same, for he has been provided with a lodge in the mountains, the scale of which is less out of proportion to a human being and better suited to hunting and other pleasures of this life.

15 March

Though Hackert is always busy drawing and painting, he remains sociable and has a gift for attracting people and making them become his pupils. He has completely won me over as well, since he is patient with my weaknesses and stresses to me the supreme importance of accuracy in drawing and of a confident and clearheaded approach. When he paints, he always has three shades of colour ready. Using them one after the other, he starts with the background and paints the foreground last, so that a picture appears, one doesn't know from where. If only it were as easy to do as it looks! With his usual frankness he said to me: 'You have talent but you don't know how to use it. Stay with me for eighteen months and then you will produce something which will give pleasure to yourself and others.' Is this not a text on which one should never stop preaching to all dilettantes? What fruit it is going to bear in me remains to be seen.

The fact that he is not only giving drawing lessons to the Princesses but is also called upon in the evening to give lectures on art and other related subjects is evidence of the special trust with which the Queen honours him. For his talks he uses Sulzer's dictionary as a textbook, selecting some passage or other which he likes or believes in.

I could not but approve, but, at the same time, I could not help smiling at myself. What a difference there is between a person who wishes to build his life from within and one who wishes to influence the world and instruct others for domestic uses. I have always hated Sulzer's theory because its basic principles are false, but I realize now that his book contains much which people need to know. The many pieces of information which it offers and the way of thinking which satisfied the worthy Sulzer make it good enough, surely, for society people.

We spent many interesting hours with Andres, the restorer of old paintings, who has been summoned from Rome and is also living in the old castle. The King takes a great interest in his work. I shall not try to describe his unique craftsmanship because I would have to begin by enlarging upon the difficulty of the task and the immense labour required to arrive at a successful solution.

16 March

Your welcome letter of 19 February reached me today and shall be answered at once. I am always happy to be brought to my senses again by thinking of my friends.

Naples is a paradise; everyone lives in a state of intoxicated self-forgetfulness, myself included. I seem to be a completely different person whom I hardly recognize. Yesterday I thought to myself: Either you were mad before, or you are mad now.

From here I went to see the remains of the ancient town of Capua and its environs. Only in these regions can one understand what vegetation really is and what led man to invent the art of cultivation. The flax is already in bloom and the wheat a span and a half high. The country round Caserta is completely flat and the fields are worked on till they are as smooth and tidy as garden beds. All of them are planted with poplars on which vines are trained, yet in spite of the shadow they cast, the soil beneath them produces the most perfect crops. How will they look later, when spring is come in all its power? Till now, though we have had lovely sunshine, the wind has been cold and there is snow on the mountains.

During the next two weeks I must make up my mind whether to go to Sicily or not. I have never before been so torn by conflicting feelings as I am now when I contemplate this decision. One day something happens which makes me in favour of the trip, the next some circumstance turns me against it. Two spirits are fighting over me.

And now, for my friends of the gentler sex, in strict confidence – don't breathe a word to the men! I am quite aware that my *Iphigenie* has met with a strange reception. Everyone was used to the original version and, through hearing and reading it so often, knew some passages almost by heart. Now it all seems different, and I realize well enough that, at bottom, nobody appreciates the endless pains I have taken over the play. A work of this kind is never really finished; one only calls it finished because one has done all that is possible in the time and the circumstances.

But this is not going to discourage me from trying to perform a similar operation on *Tasso*. Sometimes I feel like throwing it into the fire, but I shall stick to my resolution, and I intend, if things go as they should, to make it an unusual work. So I am rather glad that the printing of my writings is proceeding so slowly. On the other hand, it is always good for me to feel the distant threat of the compositor. Strangely enough, even the things I undertake purely for love benefit from some kind of external pressure.

In Rome I was glad to study: here I want only to live, forgetting myself and the world, and it is a strange experience for me to be in a society where everyone does nothing but enjoy himself. Sir William Hamilton, who is still living here as English ambassador, has now, after many years of devotion to the arts and the study of nature, found the acme of these delights in the person of an English girl of twenty with a beautiful face and a perfect figure. He has had a Greek costume made for her which becomes her extremely. Dressed in this, she lets down her hair and, with a few shawls, gives so much variety to her poses, gestures, expressions, etc., that the spectator can hardly believe his eyes. He sees what thousands of artists would have liked to express realized before him in movements and surprising transformations – standing, kneeling, sitting, reclining, serious, sad, playful, ecstatic, contrite, alluring, threatening, anxious, one pose follows another without a break. She knows how to arrange the folds of her veil to match each mood, and has a hundred ways of turning it into a headdress. The old knight idolizes her and is enthusiastic about everything she does. In her, he has found all the antiquities, all the profiles of Sicilian coins, even the Apollo Belvedere. This much is certain: as a performance it's like nothing you ever saw before in your life. We have already enjoyed it on two evenings. This morning Tischbein is painting her portrait.

Everything I have been told (or learned for myself by putting two and two together) about the personages and conditions at the Court must now be sorted out and checked. Today the King has gone wolf-hunting; they expect to kill at least five.

Naples, 17 March

Every time I wish to write words, visual images come up, images of the fruitful countryside, the open sea, the islands veiled in a haze, the smoking mountain, etc., and I lack the mental organ which could describe them.

Here the soil produces everything, and one can expect from three to five harvests a year. In a really good year, I am told, they can grow maize three times in the same fields.

I have seen much and thought even more. The world is opening itself to me more and more, and all that I have long known intellectually is now becoming part of me. What an early-to-know, late-to-practise creature man is!

It is only a pity that, at the moment, I have nobody with whom I can share my thoughts. Tischbein is with me, to be sure, but, both as a man and an artist, his mind is the shuttle-cock of a thousand ideas, and hundreds of people have a claim on his time. His is a curious case: a man who cannot take an unforced interest in the existence of anyone else because he feels so frustrated in his own efforts.

Certainly the world is only a simple wheel and every point on its circumference is equidistant from its centre. It only looks so strange to us because we ourselves are revolving with it.

What I have always said has been confirmed: there are certain natural phenomena and certain confused ideas which can be understood and straightened out only in this country.

As for my voyage to Sicily – the gods still hold the scales in their hands. The little needle still oscillates back and forth.

Who can the friend be whose coming has been so mysteriously announced to me? I hope I shan't miss him because of my erratic excursions and my proposed trip to the island.

The frigate has returned from Palermo. In a week from today she will sail back. I still don't know whether I shall sail with her or return to Rome in time for Holy Week. Never in my life have I felt so undecided. A single moment, a trifle, may turn the scales.

I am beginning to get along better with other people. The important thing to remember is always to weigh them by the shopkeeper's scales and never by the goldsmith's, as friends, in hypochondriac or exacting moods, are only too apt to do with each other, alas.

Here people know nothing whatever about each other. Each runs hither and thither and hardly notices his neighbours. All day long they race back and forth in their paradise, without looking about them much, and when the mouth of hell nearby begins to roar, they have recourse to the blood of St

Januarius. Well, in the rest of the world, too, in their fight with death and devil, people resort to blood, or would if they could.

To thread one's way through an immense and ever-moving crowd is a peculiar and salutary experience. All merge into one great stream, yet each manages to find his way to his own goal. In the midst of so many people and all their commotion, I feel peaceful and alone for the first time. The louder the uproar of the streets, the quieter I become.

I sometimes think of Rousseau and his hypochondriac out-pourings of misery. I can quite understand how a mind as delicately organized as his could become deranged. If I didn't take such an interest in the things of nature, or see that there are ways of sorting out and comparing hundreds of observa-tions despite their apparent confusion – as a surveyor checks many separate measurements with a single straight line – I should often think I was mad myself.

18 March

We could not put off any longer going to see Herculaneum and the Portici museum of objects excavated there. Hercula-neum lay at the foot of Vesuvius and was completely buried under lava, to which subsequent eruptions added fresh layers, so that the ancient city is now sixty feet below ground level. It was discovered when, in the course of digging a well, some workmen came upon floors of paved marble. It is a thousand pities that the site was not excavated methodically by German miners, instead of being casually ransacked as if by brigands, for many noble works of antiquity must have been thereby lost or ruined.

   We descended a flight of sixty steps to a vault, where we admired by torchlight the former open-air theatre, while the guard told us about the things which were found there and brought to the light of day.

We had good letters of recommendation to the museum and were well received, but we were not allowed to make any drawings. Perhaps this made us pay attention all the more closely to what we saw, so that we were all the more vividly transported into the past, when all these objects were part and parcel of their owners' daily life. They quite changed my picture of Pompeii. In my mind's eye its homes now looked both more cramped and more spacious – more cramped because I now saw them crowded with objects, and more spacious because these objects were not made merely for use but were decorated with such art and grace that they enlarged and refreshed the mind in a way that the physical space of even the largest room cannot do.

There was one beautiful jar, for example, with an exquisitely wrought rim which, on closer inspection, turned out to be two hinged semicircular handles, by which the vessel could be lifted and carried with ease. The lamps are decorated with as many masks and scrolls of foliage as they have wicks, so that each flame illuminates a different work of art. There were high, slender bronze pedestals, evidently intended as lamp stands. The lamps which were suspended from the ceiling were hung with all sorts of cunningly wrought figures which surprise and delight the eye as they swing and dangle.

We followed the custodians from room to room, trying to enjoy and learn as much as possible in the little time we had. We hope to come back.

19 March

In the last few days I have entered into a new and intimate relationship. For four weeks Tischbein has been a loyal and useful partner in all my excursions into the realm of nature and art. When we were at Portici yesterday we had a talk and both of us came to the conclusion that his artistic career, his duties at court and in the city, which may lead to a permanent post in Naples, were incompatible with my plans and particular interests. Helpful as ever, he suggested as a possible companion a young man whom I have seen a lot of ever since we arrived, and not without interest and sympathy.

His name is Kniep. He lived for some time in Rome, then came to Naples, the ideal place for a landscape painter. In Rome I had already often heard that his draughtsmanship was admirable, though the same could not be said for his willingness to work. Now that I have got to know him pretty well, I think that this fault for which he is blamed is really a lack of self-confidence which can certainly be overcome if we spend some time together. In confirmation of this, he has made a good start already, and, if things go as I wish, we are going to be good travelling companions for quite some time.

19 March

One has only to walk the streets and keep one's eyes open to see the most inimitable pictures.

Yesterday, at the Molo, which is the noisiest corner of the city, I came across a wooden stage on which a Pulcinella was having a quarrel with a monkey. On a balcony overhead a pretty girl exposed her charms to all. Beside the stage with the monkey stood a quack offering his nostrums against all ailments to a credulous crowd. Painted by Gerard Dow, such a scene would delight our contemporaries and posterity.

Today is the Feast of St Joseph, the patron saint of all *frittaruoli*, or pastry cooks, using the word 'pastry' in its crudest sense. Since, under the black, boiling oil they use for frying, there is a constant flare of flame, all fiery torments are assigned to their mystery. Last night they decorated their house fronts with appropriate paintings: Souls in Purgatory and Last Judgements were blazing on all sides. In front of their doors large frying pans stood on hastily erected stoves. One apprentice kneaded the dough, while a second shaped it into crullers and threw them into the boiling oil. A third stood beside the pan with a small skewer, picked out the crullers when they were cooked and put them on another skewer, held by a fourth apprentice, who then offered them to the bystanders. The third and fourth apprentices were young boys wearing blond, elaborately curled wigs, which are regarded as the attribute of angels. To complete the group, there were some persons who handed wine to the cooks, drank themselves and cried their wares. Angels, cooks, everybody shouted at the top of their voices. They drew a great crowd because, on this night, all pastry goods are sold at greatly reduced prices and even a portion of the profits is given to the poor.

One could go on for ever describing similar scenes, each crazier than the last, not to mention the infinite variety of costumes or the hordes of people you can see on the Toledo alone.

You can find many other original entertainments if you live among these people, who are so natural that one might even become natural oneself. As an example, take Pulcinella, the mask native to this country, as Harlequin is to Bergamo or Hanswurst to the Tirol. Pulcinella is the imperturbable servant, somewhat careless, almost lazy, but humorous. You can find waiters or house servants of this type everywhere. I got enormous fun today out of ours, though it was over nothing more than sending him to buy me paper and pens. Partial misunderstanding, procrastination, good will and a touch of roguery combined created a charming scene which would be successful on any stage.

20 March

The news that another emission of lava had just occurred, invisible to Naples since it was flowing towards Ottaiano, tempted me to make a third visit to Vesuvius. On reaching the foot of the mountain, I had hardly jumped down from my two-wheeled, one-horse vehicle before the two guides who had accompanied us the last time appeared on the scene and I hired them both.

When we reached the cone, the elder one stayed with our coats and provisions while the younger followed me. We bravely made our way towards the enormous cloud of steam which was issuing from a point halfway below the mouth of the cone. Having reached it, we descended carefully along its edge. The sky was clear and at last, through the turbulent clouds of steam, we saw the lava stream.

It was only about ten feet wide, but the manner in which it flowed down the very gentle slope was most surprising. The lava on both sides of the stream cools as it moves, forming a channel. The lava on its bottom also cools, so that this channel is constantly being raised. The stream keeps steadily throwing off to right and left the scoria floating on its surface. Gradually, two levels of considerable height are formed, between which the fiery stream continues to flow quietly like a mill brook. We walked along the foot of this embankment while the scoria kept steadily rolling down its sides. Occasionally there were gaps through which we could see the glowing mass from below. Further down, we were also able to observe it from above.

Because of the bright sunshine, the glow of the lava was dulled. Only a little smoke rose into the pure air. I felt a great desire to get near the place where the lava was issuing from the mountain. My guide assured me that this was safe, because the moment it comes forth, a flow forms a vaulted roof of cooled lava over itself, which he had often stood on. To have this experience, we again climbed up the mountain in order to approach the spot from the rear. Luckily, a gust of wind had cleared the air, though not entirely, for all around us puffs of hot vapour were emerging from thousands of fissures. By now we were actually standing on the lava crust, which lay twisted in coils like a soft mush, but it projected so far out that we could not see the lava gushing forth.

We tried to go half a dozen steps further, but the ground under our feet became hotter and hotter and a whirl of dense fumes darkened the sun and almost suffocated us. The guide who was walking in front turned back, grabbed me, and we stole away from the hellish cauldron.

After refreshing our eyes with the view and our throats with wine, we wandered about observing other features of this peak of hell which towers up in the middle of paradise. I inspected some more volcanic flues and saw that they were lined up to the rim with pendent, tapering formations of some stalactitic matter. Thanks to the irregular shape of the flues, some of these deposits were in easy reach, and with the help of our sticks and some hooked appliances we managed to break off some pieces. At the lava dealer's I had already seen similar ones, listed as true lavas, so I felt happy at having made a discovery. They were a volcanic soot, precipitated from the hot vapours; the condensed minerals they contained were clearly visible.

A magnificent sunset and evening lent their delight to the return journey. However, I could feel how confusing such a tremendous contrast must be. The Terrible beside the Beautiful, the Beautiful beside the Terrible, cancel one another out and produce a feeling of indifference. The Neapolitan would certainly be a different creature if he did not feel himself wedged between God and the Devil.

22 March

If my German temperament and my determination to study and practise rather than amuse myself did not drive me on, perhaps I might tarry a little longer in this school for easy, happy living and try to profit more from it. It is possible to live very comfortably in this city on only a small income. The situation and the climate are beyond praise; but they are all the resources the foreigner has. Of course, someone with leisure, money and talent could settle down here and live most handsomely. This is what Sir William Hamilton has done in the evening of his days. The rooms in his villa, which he has furnished in the English taste, are charming and the view from the corner room may well be unique. The sea below, Capri opposite, Mount Posillipo to the right, near by the promenade of the Villa Reale, to the left an old building of the Jesuits, in the distance the coast line from Sorrento to Cape Minerva – probably nothing comparable could be found in the whole of Europe and certainly not in the middle of a great city.

But now the Sirens from beyond the sea are luring me away from this delight and a hundred others, and, if the wind is favourable, I shall be leaving at the same time as this letter – it will go north as I go south.

Man is headstrong in spirit, and at this moment I am in particular need of unconfined spaces. It is not perseverance I have to learn so much as quickness of perception. Once I can get hold of a matter by its fingertip, listening and thinking will enable me to grasp the whole hand.

Strangely enough, a friend recently spoke of *Wilhelm Meister* and begged me to go on with it. Under these skies, I doubt if it would be possible, but perhaps in the last books I shall manage to capture something of this heavenly air. I pray that my existence may develop further, the stem grow taller, the flowers blossom forth in greater abundance and beauty. If I cannot come back reborn, it would be much better not to come back at all.

Today I saw a painting by Correggio which is up for sale. Though not in perfect condition, it still retains an indelible charm. It depicts a Madonna and Child at the moment when the latter is hesitating between her breast and some pears offered Him by a cherub – in other words, The Weaning of Christ. It immediately reminded me of the Betrothal of St Catherine, and is also, I am convinced, from the hand of Correggio.

23 March

My relationship with Kniep has been put to a practical test and promises to give great satisfaction to us both. We made an excursion to Paestum together, and he proved himself a most hard-working draughtsman. The fruits of our journey are some superb sketches, and he is very happy because he finds that this exacting busy life stimulates his talent, which he had come to doubt. Drawing calls for resolution and it is just in this that his precise and tidy proficiency becomes evident. He never forgets to draw a square round the paper on which he is going to make a drawing, and sharpening and resharpening his excellent English pencils gives him almost as much pleasure as drawing. In consequence, his outlines leave nothing to be desired.

We have made the following bargain: from now on we shall live and travel together and all he will be expected to do is draw. All his drawings will become my property, but, in order that they may serve as a basis for further activity on our return, he is going to execute a number of subjects, selected by me, which I shall buy till I have spent a certain sum, after which, thanks to his skill and the importance of the views he has drawn, he will be able to sell the rest. I am very happy about this arrangement.

Now let me give a brief account of our excursion. Our carriage was a light two-wheeled affair, and our groom a rustic but good-natured boy. He stood behind us as, taking the reins in turn, we rolled through an enchanting countryside which Kniep greeted with a painter's eye. Soon we came to a mountain defile through which we sped on the smoothest of roads past picturesque groups of trees and rocks. Near La Cava we halted because Kniep could not resist making a drawing of a splendid mountain which stood out sharply against the sky. His neat and characteristic sketch took in the whole mountain from its summit to its base. The pleasure it gave us both seemed a good beginning to our friendship.

That same evening he made another drawing from the window of our inn in Salerno, which will make any description of this lovely region superfluous. Who would not have felt inclined to study in this place when the university was in its heyday?

Very early next morning, we drove by rough and often muddy roads towards some beautifully shaped mountains.

We crossed brooks and flooded places where we looked into the blood-red savage eyes of buffaloes. They looked like hippopotamuses.

The country grew more and more flat and desolate, the houses rarer, the cultivation sparser. In the distance appeared some huge quadrilateral masses, and when we finally reached them, we were at first uncertain whether we were driving through rocks or ruins. Then we recognized what they were, the remains of temples, monuments to a once glorious city. Kniep quickly chose a favourable spot from which to draw this very unpicturesque landscape, while I found a country-man to conduct me round the temples. At first sight they excited nothing but stupefaction. I found myself in a world which was completely strange to me. In their evolution from austerity to charm, the centuries have simultaneously shaped and even created a different man. Our eyes and, through them, our whole sensibility have become so conditioned to a more slender style of architecture that these crowded masses of stumpy conical columns appear offensive and even terrifying. But I pulled myself together, remembered the history of art, thought of the age with which this archi-tecture was in harmony, called up images in my mind of the austere style of sculpture – and in less than an hour I found myself reconciled to them and even thanking my guardian angel for having allowed me to see these well-preserved remains with my own eyes. Reproductions give a false impression; architectural designs make them look more ele-gant and drawings in perspective more ponderous than they really are. It is only by walking through them and round them that one can attune one's life to theirs and experience the emotional effect which the architect intended. I spent the whole day doing this, while Kniep was busy making sketches. I felt happy to know that I had nothing to worry about on that score, but could be certain of obtaining faithful records to assist my memory. Unfortunately, there was no place nearby where we could stay the night, so we returned to Salerno and drove back to Naples early the next morning. This time we

saw Vesuvius from its other side. The country was fertile and
the main road was lined with poplars, as colossal as pyramids.
We made a brief halt to make this pleasing picture our own.
Then we came to the top of a ridge and a grand panorama
unfolded before us: Naples in all its glory, rows of houses for
miles along the flat coast line of the Gulf, promontories,
headlands, cliffs, then the islands and, beyond them, the
sea. A breathtaking sight!

A horrible noise, more a screaming and howling for joy
than a song, startled me out of my wits. It came from the boy
who was standing behind me. I turned on him furiously. He
was a good-natured lad, and this was the first time he had
heard a harsh word from either of us.

For a while he neither moved nor spoke; then he tapped
me on the shoulder, thrust his right arm between Kniep and
myself, pointed with his forefinger and said: '*Signor, perdonate!
Questa è la mia patria!*' which means: 'Sir, forgive me. This is
my native land!' And so I was startled for the second time.
Poor northerner that I am – something like tears came into
my eyes.

25 March. Lady Day

Although I felt Kniep was very glad to be accompanying me
to Sicily, I could not help noticing that there was something
he hated to leave. Thanks to his sincerity, it did not take me
long to discover that this something was a sweetheart to
whom he is deeply attached. His story of how they became
acquainted was touching. The girl's conduct so far spoke
highly in her favour: now he wanted me to see how pretty
she was. A meeting place was arranged where I could, incidentally, enjoy one of the most beautiful views over Naples.
He led me on to the flat roof of a house, directly overlooking
the lower part of the city and facing towards the harbour
mole, the Gulf and the coast of Sorrento. Everything that lies
to the right takes on a peculiar perspective which cannot
easily be seen from any other point.

While we were admiring this view, all of a sudden the pretty little head we had been expecting popped up out of the floor, for the only access to this kind of terrace is through a square opening which can be closed by a trap door. When the little angel had emerged completely, it suddenly occurred to me that some old masters depict the Angel of the Annunciation as coming up a staircase. Our angel had a lovely figure, a charming little face and natural good manners. I was glad to see my new friend so happy under this wonderful sky and in view of the loveliest landscape in the world.

After the girl left us, he confessed to me that the reason why he had so far endured voluntary poverty was because it had enabled him to enjoy her love and learn to prize her simple and modest way of life. Now, however, he welcomed the prospect of improving his circumstances, mainly because this would enable him to make her life more comfortable as well as his own.

After this agreeable encounter, I took a walk along the seashore. I was feeling calm and happy. Suddenly I had a flash of insight concerning my botanical ideas. Please tell Herder I am very near discovering the secret of the Primal Plant. I am only afraid that no one will recognize in it the rest of the plant world. My famous theory about the cotyledons has now been so elaborated that it would be difficult to take it any further.

26 March

I shall send this letter off tomorrow. On Thursday the twenty-ninth I am due to sail for Palermo at last on the corvette which, in my ignorance of things nautical, I promoted in an earlier letter to the rank of a frigate.

During my stay here, my state of indecision – should I go or not? – made me restless and irritable at times; now I have made up my mind, I feel much better. Given my temperament, this trip is salutary and even necessary. To me Sicily implies Asia and Africa, and it will mean more than a little to me to stand at that miraculous centre upon which so many radii of world history converge.

In Naples I have lived like a Neapolitan. I have been anything but studious, and when I get back I must make up for a few of my omissions – but only a few, I'm afraid, since I have to be in Rome by 29 June. Having missed Holy Week, I want at least to celebrate the Feast of St Peter. I must not let my Sicilian trip make me deviate too far from my original plan.

The day before yesterday there was a violent thunderstorm and torrents of rain; now it is clear again and a tramontana is blowing from the north. If it keeps up, we shall have a very swift passage.

Yesterday Kniep and I visited the corvette to take a look at our cabin. A sea voyage is something I still have to experience. This short crossing and perhaps a cruise along the coast will stimulate my imagination and enlarge my vision of the world. The captain is a likeable young man; the ship, built in America, is neat, elegant and sails well.

Here everything is beginning to turn green; in Sicily it will be even greener. By the time you get this letter, I shall already have left Trinacria* behind me and be on my return voyage. There's man for you! Forever jumping backwards and forwards in his thoughts. I have not yet been there but already I am with you again. It is not my fault if this letter is confused. I am interrupted all the time, but I should at least like to finish this page.

I have just had a visit from the Marchese Berio, a young man who appears well informed. He wished to make the acquaintance of the author of *Werther*. By and large, the Neapolitans have a great desire for culture and a thirst for knowledge, but they are too happy-go-lucky to set about it in the right way. If I had more time, I would gladly give them more. Four weeks – what are they to set against the immensity of life?

* Trinacria, the Three-Pointed, i.e., Sicily.

And now, farewell! On this journey I shall certainly learn how to travel; whether I shall learn how to live, I don't know. The people I meet who possess this art are so different from me in their nature and habits that I doubt whether I have the talent.

Farewell, and think of me with the same love that I cherish for you in my heart.

28 March

What with packing, saying goodbye, shopping, paying bills, catching up with this and preparing that, these last days have been completely wasted.

My peace of mind has been disturbed at the last minute by the Prince of Waldeck. When I went to say good-bye to him, he would talk of nothing else but the arrangements I was to make after my return to accompany him to Greece and Dalmatia. Once one has stepped into the great world and accepted its ways, one has to be careful not to get trapped or even spirited away. I am too exhausted to write another word.

29 March

For some days the weather has been uncertain, but on this day of our departure, it is as beautiful as could be. A favourable tramontana, a sunny sky, just the day for wishing to go round the world. Once more, I sincerely bid farewell to all my friends in Weimar and Gotha. May your love accompany me; I shall certainly always need it. Last night I dreamed I was at home and again at my usual occupations. I know this much: I could never unload my boat of pheasants anywhere but on your shores. Let us hope that by then it will be laden with precious cargo.

SICILY

On her last voyage the packet set sail with a favourable north-east wind behind her. Not so this time. The wind had veered to the south-west and we were forced to learn how dependent the navigator is upon the moods of the weather. We spent an impatient morning between the shore and the café. At noon we went on board at last. The corvette was anchored not far from the Molo. Bright sunshine and a slight haze made the shadows of the cliffs of Sorrento look intensely blue; Naples was full of life and a blaze of colour. It was sundown before the boat began to move and very slowly at that. The head wind drove us towards Posillipo and its promontory. Throughout the night the ship made its quiet progress. The cabins below deck are pleasant and furnished with single berths. Our fellow passengers, opera singers and dancers with engagements in Palermo, are gay and well behaved.

Daybreak found us between Ischia and Capri and about a mile from the latter, as the sun rose magnificently behind the crags of Capri and Cape Minerva. Kniep kept himself busy drawing the shifting outlines of the coast and islands as we sailed along, and the slowness of our progress was to his advantage. The wind remained slack. By about four in the afternoon we lost sight of Vesuvius, but Cape Minerva and Ischia were still visible. As evening drew near, they too disappeared. The sun sank into the sea accompanied by clouds and a streak of purple light a mile long. Kniep made a drawing of this phenomenon as well. Now there was no more land to be seen, the horizon was a circle of water and the night sky was lit up by the moon.

But I was not to enjoy this gorgeous sight for long before I was overcome by seasickness. I retired to my cabin, assumed a horizontal position, took nothing but some bread and red wine, and soon felt very snug. Isolated from the outside world, I let my thoughts run freely on the inner one, and, since I anticipated a slow passage, I set myself forthwith a serious task which would keep me fully occupied. The only manuscripts I had taken with me on this voyage were the first two acts of *Tasso*. These, though roughly similar in plot and action to the ones I have now done, were written ten years ago in a poetic prose. I found them too weak and nebulous, but these defects vanished when, in accordance with my present ideas, I introduced a metre and let the form dominate.

31 March

The sun rose out of the sea into a clear sky. At seven we caught up with a French boat which sailed two days before we did. Although we had sailed much faster, the end of our voyage was still not in sight. The appearance of the island of Ustica gave us some encouragement, but, alas, it lay on our left when we should have left it, like Capri, on our right. By now the wind was completely adverse and we could not move an inch. The waves were running high and almost everybody on board was sick.

I remained in my horizontal position, revolving and reviving my play in my mind. The hours passed by and I would not have known what time of day it was if Kniep had not periodically brought me bread and wine. The rough sea had not affected his appetite in the least, and he took a malicious glee in telling me what an excellent dinner they had had, and how sorry our nice young captain was that I couldn't be with them to eat my share. The various ways in which the passengers behaved, as good cheer and pleasure gave way to discomfort and sickness, also provided him with rich material for mischievous description.

At four in the afternoon the captain changed course. The mainsails were hoisted again and we steered in a straight line towards Ustica, beyond which, to our great delight, we could see the mountains of Sicily. We now had the wind with us and the speed of the ship increased as we headed for Sicily. We passed several other islands. The setting sun was veiled in an evening haze. The wind remained fairly propitious. About midnight the sea began to get very rough.

1 April

By three in the morning, it was blowing a gale. Half awake, half asleep, I kept thinking about my drama. On deck there was a great commotion as the sails were taken in. The sea was high and the boat tossed and rolled. Towards dawn the sky cleared and the storm subsided. Ustica was now definitely on our left. The sailors pointed out a large turtle swimming in the distance, and through our telescopes we could follow its living dot quite clearly. By noon we could make out the promontories and bays of the Sicilian coast, but the ship had fallen considerably to leeward. Now and then we tacked. In the afternoon we came closer to the shore, where the west coast, from Cape Lilibeo to Cape Gallo, lay in bright sunshine. A school of dolphins accompanied our ship on both sides of the prow, always darting ahead. It was delightful to watch them swimming through the transparent waves and often leaping clean out of the water, so that their fins and the spines along their backs made an iridescent play of green and gold.

Since we were still too far to leeward, the captain set a straight course for a bay beyond Cape Gallo. Kniep did not lose this good opportunity to make detailed sketches of the various vistas. At sunset the captain again turned out to sea and headed north-eastward in order to reach the latitude of Palermo. Once in a while I ventured on deck but kept my poetic project always in mind – by now I had almost mastered the whole play.

The sky was slightly overcast, but the moon was bright and its reflection in the sea incredibly beautiful. For the sake of the effect, many painters would have us believe that the reflection of the celestial lights in the water is at its widest where it is strongest, that is to say, at the point nearest the observer. But now I saw for myself that the reflection was widest on the horizon and tapered, as it approached the ship, till it ended, like a glittering pyramid, in a point. During the night the captain repeated his manoeuvre several times.

2 April

By eight in the morning we stood directly opposite Palermo. I was in high spirits. During these last days in the belly of the whale, I have made considerable progress in planning my play. I felt so well that I was able to stand on the foredeck and devote my attention to the coast of Sicily. Kniep kept sketching all the time. Thanks to his skill and accuracy, several sheets of paper have become valuable records of our belated arrival.

Palermo, 2 April

After a great deal of trouble and effort, we finally reached port at three in the afternoon. I had completely recovered and was able to enjoy everything thoroughly. The city faces north with high mountains rising behind it. The rays of the afternoon sun were shining across it, so that all the buildings facing us were in shadow but lit by reflected light. The delicate contours of Monte Pellegrino to the right were in full sunshine, and a shore with bays, headlands and promontories stretched far away to the left.

In front of the dark buildings, graceful trees of a tender green, their tops illuminated from behind, swayed like vegetal glow-worms. A faint haze tinted all the shadows blue.

Instead of hurrying impatiently ashore, we remained on deck until we were driven off. It might be long before we could again enjoy such a treat for the eyes from such a vantage point.

We entered the city through a wonderful gate, consisting of two huge pillars but no crosspiece, so that the towering chariot of Santa Rosalia can pass through on her famous feast day, and were taken to a large inn. The landlord was a jovial old man who had long been accustomed to receiving strangers of all nationalities. He led us to a spacious room with a balcony overlooking the harbour and the mountain of Santa Rosalia. We were so delighted with the location of our room that at first we didn't notice a raised alcove, whose curtains concealed an enormous sprawling bed surmounted by a silk canopy. This was quite in keeping with the rest of the old-fashioned, stately furniture. A little embarrassed by such pomp and splendour, we were prepared, as is customary, to haggle about terms, but the old man said he would leave it to us to name them; he only hoped we would like it here. We might also, he added, use the *sala* adjoining our room, which, thanks to its wide balcony, was light, airy and cheerful.

For an artist, there was an inexhaustible wealth of vistas to be seen, and we studied them one by one with an eye to painting them all.

The same evening the bright moonlight tempted us to take a walk down to the harbour and back. Before going to bed, we stood for a long time on our balcony. The light was unusual and all was stillness and charm.

3 April

We went out first thing to take a closer look at the city, which is easy to grasp in its overall plan, but difficult to get to know in detail. A street a mile long runs from the lower to the upper gate; this is bisected by another street, so that everything which lies along these axes is easy to find. But the inner part of the city is a confusing labyrinth, where a stranger can find his way about only with the help of a guide.

Towards evening we watched with great interest the famous carriage parade of the nobility, who at that hour drive out of the town towards the harbour in order to take the air, chat with each other and, above all, flirt with the ladies. Two hours before sunset, a full moon rose, bathing the evening in an inexpressible glory. Owing to the mountains behind Palermo to the south, sunlight and moonlight are never seen reflected in the water at these hours. Even on this brightest of days, the sea was dark blue, sombre and, so to speak, intrusive, whereas in Naples, from noon on, it always becomes increasingly serene, brilliant and, so to speak, extensive.

Kniep went off to make a drawing of Monte Pellegrino and left me to take walks and make observations by myself.

Here are a few more notes, hastily thrown together:

We left Naples at sundown on Thursday, 29 March, and did not reach Palermo till three in the afternoon four days later. I have never set out on a journey as calmly as I did on this one and have never had a quieter time, though our voyage was much prolonged by continuously adverse wind, and for the first days I was violently seasick and confined to my cabin. If anything was ever a decisive event for me, it is this trip.

No one who has never seen himself surrounded on all sides by nothing but the sea can have a true conception of the world and of his own relation to it. The simple, noble line of the marine horizon has given me, as a landscape painter, quite new ideas.

My artist-companion is a merry, loyal and warmhearted young man who makes very accurate drawings, which you will enjoy when I bring them back with me. To shorten the long hours of the voyage, he had written down a description of the technique of water-colour painting, showing me how to use certain colours to produce certain tones. If one were not told, one could mix away for ever trying to discover the secret. I had already heard something about it in Rome, but only scrappily. In no country has this art been brought to such perfection as in Italy.

I cannot begin to describe the way in which this Queen of the Islands has received us – with mulberry trees in their freshest green, evergreen oleanders, hedges of lemon trees, etc. In a public garden I saw great beds of ranunculi and anemones. The air is mild, warm and fragrant. Furthermore, the full moon rose over a promontory and was reflected in the sea, and all this after being tossed by the waves for four days and nights! Forgive my scribbling with a blunt pen dipped in the sepia which my friend uses when he retraces his drawings. It will come to you like a whisper while I am preparing another memorial to these happy hours. I shan't tell you what it is, and I can't tell you when you will receive it.

3 April

The enclosed sheet, dear friends, is meant to let you share a little in our joys and give you some idea of the vast expanse of water which this incomparable bay encloses. Starting in the east, where a low promontory extends far out into the sea, and moving west, the eye passes from wooded crags to the suburbs where the fishermen live, then to the city itself, where all the houses, which like ours line the waterfront, face the sea, then to the gate through which we entered, then to the landing-place for smaller boats, then to the port proper, the Molo and the anchorage for large ships. Beyond that rises graceful Monte Pellegrino, which shelters all vessels from the winds, and finally, stretching down to the sea on the other side of the mountain, a lovely, fertile valley. Kniep made a drawing and I made a rough sketch. We both had great fun doing this and came home in high spirits. We have not yet felt strong and brave enough to work over it and finish it properly, so our sketches must stay as they are for the time being. This sheet is merely a proof of our incapacity to cope with such subjects, or rather of our presumption in trying to master them in such a short time.

4 April

This afternoon we visited the pleasant valley in the mountains to the south of Palermo, along which meanders the river Oreto. To make a good picture of this valley calls for a skilful hand and an unerring eye for colour. Kniep succeeded in finding an excellent viewpoint for one. In the foreground water cascades over a dilapidated weir, which lies in the shadow of a cheerful-looking clump of trees; in the background an unobstructed vista of the valley with a few farm buildings.

The fair spring weather and the luxuriant vegetation lent an air of grace and peace to the whole valley, which our stupid guide proceeded to ruin with his erudition, for he started telling us in great detail how, long ago, Hannibal* had given battle here and what stupendous feats of valour had taken place on this very spot. I angrily rebuked him for such an odious evocation of defunct ghosts. It was bad enough, I said, that from time to time crops have to be trampled down, if not always by elephants, still by horses and men, but at least one need not shock the imagination out of its peaceful dreams by recalling scenes of savage violence from the past.

He was very astonished that I, on such a spot, should not want to hear anything about classical times, and, of course, I could not make him understand my objections to this mixing-up of the past and the present.

He must have thought me still more of an eccentric when he saw me searching for pebbles in the shoals which the river had left high and dry, especially when I pocketed several specimens. Again, I could not explain to him that the quickest way to get an idea of any mountainous region is to examine the types of rock fragments washed down by its streams, or that there was any point in studying rubble to get the idea of these eternal classical heights of the prehistoric earth.

---

* It was not Hannibal but Hasdrubal who was defeated near Panormus by Caecilius Metellus in 251 B.C.

My haul from the river turned out to be a rich one. I collected nearly forty specimens, though I must admit they could possibly all be classified under a few rubrics. The majority are probably some kind of jasper or chert or schist. Some were round and smooth, some shapeless rubble, some rhomboid in form and of many colours. There was no lack, either, of pebbles of shell-limestone.

Shell-limestone underlies the plain on which Palermo stands, the region outside the city, called Ai Colli, and part of the Bagheria. The city has been built of it, hence the large quarries in the neighbourhood. Near Monte Pellegrino there is one quarry more than fifty feet deep. The lower strata are whiter than the upper and contain many fossil corals and shellfish, scallop shells in particular. The uppermost stratum is mixed with red clay and contains few fossils, if any. Above this there is only a very thin layer of red clay.

The limestone of Monte Pellegrino itself is an older formation and full of holes and fissures; these are irregularly distributed, but, when examined carefully, they seem to follow the lines of demarcation between the strata. The rock is compact and resonant when struck with a hammer.

There are no meadows, so there is no hay. In spring the horses are fed on barley fresh from the ear, '*per rinfrescar* – to refresh them' as they say; at other seasons on chaff and bran. There is some pasture in the mountains and some in the fields, for a third of them lie fallow. There are some sheep of a breed introduced from Barbary, but very few, and more mules than horses, because the dry food agrees better with the former.

5 April

We explored the city thoroughly. The architecture is similar to that of Naples, but the public monuments – the fountains, for instance – are even further removed from the canons of good taste. There is no instinctive feeling for art here, as there is in Rome, to set a standard. The monuments owe their existence and their form to accidental circumstances. One fountain, much admired by all the islanders, would not exist had Sicily not happened to have deposits of beautiful marble of every colour at a time when a sculptor who was an expert in making animal figures happened to be in high favour. This fountain is hard to describe.

In a square of moderate size stands a circular stone construction a little less than one storey high, the socle, wall and cornice of which are coloured marble. Let into it all the way round are niches from which all sorts of animal heads, carved in white marble, look out, craning their necks – horses, lions, camels, elephants in succession. Within this circular menagerie, one is rather surprised to see a fountain. Four flights of marble steps lead up it from openings cut in the enclosing wall, allowing people to draw the copiously flowing water.

It is the same with the churches, which surpass even those of the Jesuits in splendour, but accidentally, not deliberately. It's as if an artisan, a carver of figures or foliage, a gilder, a varnisher or a worker in marble, without taste and without guidance, had wished to show what he could do in a given spot.

On the other hand, one finds plenty of talent for the realistic imitation of Nature; for example, the animal heads I mentioned are very well done. This, of course, is just what the masses admire, for the only artistic pleasure they know lies in finding that the copy is like the original.

Towards evening I made an amusing acquaintance when I entered a modest shop on the main street to buy various odds and ends. While I was standing outside looking at the goods, a gust of wind whirled down the street, stirring up a cloud of dust which blew into the shops and covered the windows. 'By all the saints,' I cried when I went in, 'why is your city so filthy? Can nothing be done about it? In its length and beauty this street would stand comparison with the Corso in Rome; it has pavements which every shopkeeper and owner of a workshop keeps clean by continually sweeping everything into the middle of the street. At the slightest breeze all the rubbish which has accumulated there is blown back again and everything is dirtier than it was before. In Naples the refuse is carried away daily to the gardens and fields on the backs of donkeys. Couldn't some similar measure be devised for your city?' 'That is the way things have always been,' he replied. 'What we throw out of our homes immediately starts to rot on our doorsteps. As you can see, there are piles of straw, weeds, kitchen garbage, and rubbish of every kind. It all dries and is blown back with the dust. We fight it all day and what happens? Our busy pretty little brooms wear out and go to increase the rubbish.'

The joke was that this was quite true. They have pretty little brooms, made from dwarf palms, which with hardly any alteration would make fine fans, but these are soon worn out, and when this happens, they are left lying in the streets in thousands. When I asked him once again if they could not adopt some other method, he answered: 'People say that the very persons who are responsible for keeping the city clean have too great political influence to be forced to spend the public funds as they are in duty bound; they are further afraid that, if all the muck were removed, the disgraceful condition of the paving would clearly reveal the embezzlement of the public money. But all this', he added with a waggish look, 'is what malicious people say. Personally, I share the view of those who maintain that the nobility keep the streets this way because they like a soft, elastic surface for their carriages over which they can take their usual evening drive in comfort.' Having got into his stride, he went on to poke fun at various examples of police corruption, giving me a reassuring proof that man still retains enough sense of humour to mock at what he cannot mend.

6 April

Santa Rosalia, the patron saint of Palermo, has become so universally famous through Brydone's description of her feast day that my friends will certainly be pleased to read something about the spot where she is especially venerated.

Monte Pellegrino is a huge mass of rock, broader than it is high, which stands at the north-west end of the Gulf of Palermo. There is an inaccurate picture of it in *Voyage pittoresque de la Sicile*. It is composed of a grey limestone from an early epoch. Its cliffs are completely barren without so much as a tree or a shrub, and even its level patches are only scantily covered with a little turf and moss.

At the beginning of the last century, the bones of the saint were discovered in one of its caves and brought down to Palermo. Her presence delivered the city from the plague and, from that moment on, Rosalia became its patron saint, chapels were built in her honour and magnificent ceremonies observed. Her devotees made frequent pilgrimages up the mountain, and, at great cost, a road was constructed, supported on piers and arches like an aqueduct, which zigzags upward between two crags.

The shrine itself is more appropriate to the humility of the saint who took refuge there than the pomp of the festival which is celebrated in honour of her renunciation of the world. In all Christendom, which for eighteen hundred years has founded its wealth, its splendours, its solemn festivities upon the poverty of its first founders and most fervent confessors, there may well be no other sacred spot as naïvely decorated and touchingly venerated as this.

On reaching the top of the mountain, one turns a corner and faces a steep cliff to which the church and convent appear to be joined. There is nothing particularly attractive or interesting about the façade of the church, and one opens the door expecting little, but, once inside, one gets an extraordinary surprise. One finds oneself in a great hall which runs the whole breadth of the church and opens into the nave. There are the usual holy-water stoups and a few confession boxes. The nave is an open courtyard bounded on its right by rugged rocks and on the left by a continuation of the hall. It is paved with stone slabs set at a slight angle to drain off the rain water, and at its centre stands a small fountain. The cave itself has been transformed into a chancel without robbing it of its natural, rugged character.

After climbing a few steps which lead up to it, one is confronted by a high lectern with choir stalls on either side. The only daylight comes from the courtyard and from the nave. In the centre, right at the back of the dark cave, stands the high altar.

As I said, the cavern has not been altered, but since there is a constant trickle of water from the rocks, some means had to be devised to keep the place dry. Leaden pipes, interconnected in various ways, have been attached to the face of the rock. These are wide at the top and narrow at the bottom and painted a drab green, so that the interior of the cave seems to be overgrown with some large species of cactus. The pipes catch the water as it drips from the sides and back of the cave and conduct it into a clear cistern from which the faithful scoop it to use it as a protection against every kind of ill.

As I was looking at all this, a priest approached and asked me if I were a Genoese and would like to have some masses said. I told him that I was visiting Palermo with a Genoese who would come up for the feast day tomorrow. Since one of us always has to stay at home, I had come up today to look around. He said I was quite free to look at everything I liked and make my devotions. He drew my attention to a side altar on the left which was especially sacred and went away.

Through a large trellis of wrought brass I could see lamps gleaming under the altar. I knelt down and peered through. Inside there was another screen of very fine brass wire, so that the object behind it appeared as if through gauze.

By the quiet light of the lamps I saw a beautiful woman who seemed to be reclining in a kind of ecstasy; her eyes were half closed and her head rested on her right hand, which was heavily adorned with rings. Her garment of gilded tinfoil was a perfect imitation of a cloth richly woven with gold thread. Her head and hands, made of white marble, were perhaps not in the best style, but had been carved so naturally that one expected her to start breathing and moving at any moment. At her side a cherub seemed to be fanning her with a lily. I could not take my eyes off this picture, which seemed to me to possess a quite extraordinary charm.

In the meantime, the priests had entered the cave, taken their seats in the stalls and were saying vespers. I sat down on a bench facing the altar and listened for a while, then I returned to the altar, knelt down and gazed once more at the beautiful image of the saint, surrendering myself completely to the magic of the figure and the place.

The chanting died away; the water trickled down into the cistern. The church had again become an empty desert, as it were, a savage cave, where a great silence, a great purity now reigned. The tinsel trappings of Catholic worship, especially in Sicily, were displayed here in all their artlessness. The illusion created by the figure of the fair sleeper appealed even to a discriminating eye. It was only with difficulty that I tore myself away, and I got back to Palermo very late at night.

7 April

I spent some happy, peaceful hours alone in the Public Gardens close to the harbour. It is the most wonderful spot on earth. Though laid out formally and not very old, it seems enchanted and transports one back into the antique world. Green borders surround exotic plants, espaliers of lemon trees form gracefully arched walks, high hedges of oleander, covered with thousands of red blossoms which resemble carnations, fascinate the eye. Strange trees, probably from warmer climes, for they are still without leaves, spread out their peculiar ramifications. At one end there is a bank with a bench on it from which one can overlook the garden and intricate vegetation; at the other are some large ponds in which goldfish swim about gracefully, now hiding under moss-grown pipes, now swarming together in great numbers, attracted by a piece of bread.

The green of the plants is of a different shade, either more yellow or more blue, than the green we are used to. What gives this scenery its greatest charm, however, is the haze uniformly diffused over everything, which has a peculiar effect. Even when one object is only a few steps further away than another, the difference in depth is clearly distinguished by a different tint of light blue. If one looks at them for long, their own colour is lost and they appear, at least to the eyes, to be blue all over.

The enchanting look which distant objects like ships and promontories take on in this haze is most instructive for a painter who has to learn to distinguish distances and even measure them exactly, as I discovered when I walked to the top of a hill. I no longer saw Nature, but pictures; it was as if some very skilful painter had applied glaze to secure a proper gradation of tone.

The enchanted garden, the inky waves on the northern horizon, breaking on the curved beaches of the bays, and the peculiar tang of the sea air, all conjured up images of the island of the blessed Phaeacians.

I hurried off to buy myself a Homer so that I could read the canto in which he speaks of them. When I got back, I found Kniep enjoying a well-earned rest after a hard day's work, and I recited to him a hastily improvised translation as we sat over our glasses of good red wine.

8 April. Easter Sunday

The noisy rejoicing in the Resurrection of the Lord began at dawn: rockets, firecrackers, squibs and the like exploded in great numbers in front of the churches, while crowds of the faithful fought their way in through the open doors. Bells rang, organs pealed, processions sang in unison, priestly choirs chanted antiphonally – to ears unaccustomed to such a rowdy worship of God, the noise was quite deafening.

The first Mass had hardly ended before two runners, in the elegant livery of the Viceroy, arrived at our inn on a double errand: first, to bring greetings to all foreigners on this feast day and receive tips in return; second, to invite me to dinner, a message which obliged me to increase my donation.

After spending the morning visiting churches and studying the faces and behaviour of the people, I drove to the Viceroy's palace, which is situated at the upper end of the city. I arrived a little early, and the reception rooms were empty except for one cheerful little man whom I recognized at once as a Knight of Malta.

When he heard that I was a German, he asked if I could give him any news of Erfurt, where he had once spent a pleasant time. He mentioned the Dacheröden family and the Coadjutor von Dalberg, and I was able to give him news which pleased him very much. Then he inquired about the rest of Thuringia and, with special interest, about Weimar. 'Whatever happened to the man – in my day he was young and high-spirited – who at that time set the tone in Weimar? What was his name? You know – the author of *Werther*.' I paused for a moment, as if I was trying to remember, and then said: 'As a matter of fact, the person you ask about so kindly is myself.' He was visibly taken aback and exclaimed: 'Then how things must have changed!' 'Yes, indeed,' I replied, 'between Weimar and Palermo I have changed in many ways.'

At this moment the Viceroy entered with his suite. He behaved with the dignified ease which befits a gentleman of his rank, but he could not help smiling when the Knight of Malta went on and on expressing his amazement at seeing me here. At dinner I was seated next to the Viceroy, who discussed my journey with me and promised that he would send out orders that I be allowed to see everything in Palermo and given every assistance on my way across Sicily.

9 April

Our entire day has been taken up with the madness of the Prince of Pallagonia. His follies turned out to be quite different from anything I had imagined after hearing and reading about them.

When a person is expected to describe some absurdity, he is always at a loss, because however great his love for the truth, merely by describing it, he makes it something, whereas, in fact, it is nothing that wants to be taken for something. So let me preface my remarks with another general reflection: neither tasteless vulgarity nor assured excellence is the creation of one single man or one single epoch; on the contrary, with a little thought, one can trace the genealogy of both.

The fountain I mentioned earlier can be counted as one of the ancestors of the Pallagonian mania, the only difference being that the latter has its own territory where it has complete liberty to display itself on a grand scale. I shall now try to trace its history.

In these regions country houses are built in the middle of the estate, so that, to reach the house itself, one has to drive through cultivated fields, vegetable gardens and other agriculturally useful premises. But people are more economical here than they are in northern countries, where a large acreage of valuable soil is often sacrificed to the layout of a park so that the eye may be flattered by unprofitable shrubs. These southerners, on the contrary, erect two walls between which one reaches the big house without being aware of what is happening on either side. The drive usually begins with a huge gateway – sometimes there is a vaulted hall as well – and ends in the courtyard of the house.

To give the eye something to look at, a moulding runs along the top of the walls, decorated with scrolls and brackets on which vases are sometimes placed. The wall surfaces are divided into whitewashed panels. The circular courtyard of the big house is surrounded by one-storey dwellings where the servants and farm labourers live, and high above all this rises the rectangular block of the house itself.

This is the traditional layout, and probably existed long before the Prince's father built the house. His taste, if not the best, was still tolerable, but his son, the present owner, without departing from the general design, has given free rein to his passion for deformed and revolting shapes, and it would be paying him too great a compliment to credit him with the faintest spark of imagination.

On entering the great hall on the boundary of the estate, we found ourselves in an octagon, very high in proportion to its width. Four colossal giants in modern gaiters support the cornice over which, facing the gate, hovers the Holy Trinity. The drive to the house is unusually broad, and each wall has been transformed into an uninterrupted socle on which excellent pedestals sustain strange groups interspersed with vases. The repulsive appearance of these deformities, botched by inferior stonecutters, is reinforced by the crumbly shell-tufa of which they are made, but a better material would, no doubt, have made the worthlessness of the form still more conspicuous. I called them groups, but the word is inappropriate, for they are not the products of calculation or even of caprice; they are merely accidental jumbles.

Each square pedestal carries three groups, the bases of which are so arranged that, together, their various postures fill the whole space. The predominant group usually consists of two figures and its base takes up a great part of the front of the pedestal. These figures are mostly animal and human monsters. Two more pieces are needed to fill up the space at the rear. There is one of medium size which usually represents a shepherd or a shepherdess, a cavalier or a lady, a dancing monkey or a dog. The last gap is most often filled by a dwarf, since this unfortunate race is a great subject for boorish jokes.

The following list may give you a better idea of what Prince Pallagonia has perpetrated in his madness.

Human beings. Beggars of both sexes, men and women of Spain, Moors, Turks, hunchbacks, deformed persons of every kind, dwarfs, musicians, Pulcinellas, soldiers in antique uniforms, gods and goddesses, persons dressed in French fashions of long ago, soldiers with ammunition pouches and leggings, mythological figures with grotesque accessories; for instance: Achilles and Chiron with Pulcinella.

Animals.   Only parts of them; a horse with human hands, the head of a horse on a human body, deformed monkeys, many dragons and snakes, every kind of paw attached to every kind of body, double heads and exchanged heads.

Vases.   Every kind of monster and scroll, emerging from their bellies or their bases.

Now imagine similar figures multiplied *ad infinitum*, designed without rhyme or reason, combined without discrimination or point, pedestals and monstrosities in one unending row, and the painful feelings they must inspire, and you will sympathize with anyone who has to run the gauntlet of this lunacy.

When we reached the big house, we were received into the arms of a semicircular courtyard and faced a gateway and a wall constructed like a fortress. Here we found an Egyptian figure built into the wall, a fountain without water, a monument and, scattered about everywhere, overturned vases and statues deliberately laid on their noses.

The inner courtyard is the traditional circular shape, but, just so that there should be no lack of variety, the low buildings which surround it have been built in small semi-circles. The paving was overgrown with grass, and the court-yard looked like a dilapidated graveyard. Oddly scrolled marble urns, inherited from the owner's father, and dwarfs and freaks of a later date, lay higgledy-piggledy, waiting to be found their right place. In addition there was an arbour, crammed with antique vases and stone scrolls of various shapes.

But the bad taste and folly of an eccentric mind reaches its climax in the cornices of the low buildings which slant this way and that, so that our sense of hydrostatic balance and the perpendicular, which is what primarily makes us human beings and is the fundamental principle of all eurhythmics, is upset and tortured. Even these roofs are also decorated with hydras and small busts, an orchestra of monkeys and similar absurdities; dragons alternate with gods, and an Atlas carries a wine cask instead of the celestial globe.

If one hopes to escape all this by entering the house, which, since his father built it, looks relatively sane from the outside, just inside the door one is confronted by the laurel-wreathed head of a Roman emperor on the body of a dwarf who sits on a dolphin.

In the house the fever of the Prince rises to a delirium. The legs of the chairs have been unequally sawn off, so that no one can sit on them, and we were warned by the castellan himself not to use the normal chairs, for they have spikes hidden under their velvet-cushioned seats. In corners stood candelabra of Chinese porcelain, which turned out, on closer inspection, to be made up of single bowls, cups and saucers, all glued together. Some whimsical object stares out at you from every corner.

Even the unrivalled view of the sea beyond the foothills is spoiled because the panes of coloured glass in the windows either make warm tones look cold or cold tones blazing. I must not forget a cabinet. Its panels are made from antique gilt frames which have been sawn in pieces and then put together again. The hundred different styles of carving, ancient and modern, crammed into these panels, from which the gilt was peeling when it wasn't smothered in dust, made it look like a mangled piece of junk.

A description of the chapel alone would fill a book. Here lies the clue to the whole madness. Only in the brain of a religious fanatic could it have grown to such rampant proportions. I must leave you to imagine how many caricatures of a perverted piety have been assembled here, and only mention the most conspicuous one.

A carved crucifix of considerable size, painted in realistic colours and varnished and gilded in places, is fixed flat to the ceiling. Into the navel of the Crucified a hook has been screwed from which hangs a chain. The end of this chain is made fast to the head of a man, kneeling in prayer and painted and varnished like everything else. He hangs suspended in the air as a symbol of the ceaseless devotions of the present owner.

The house is only partly built; a large hall, designed and elaborately decorated, though not at all in atrocious taste, remains unfinished. There are some limits, it seems, to what even the Prince can do to indulge his mania.

It was the first time I had seen Kniep lose patience. His feelings as an artist were outraged by this madhouse, and when I tried to study the details of these misbegotten horrors, he hustled me away. But, good-natured fellow that he is, he finally drew one of the groups, the only one that at least made some sort of picture. A woman with a horse's head is seated in a chair playing cards with her vis-à-vis, a cavalier in old-fashioned clothes. He has a griffin's head, dressed in a full-bottomed wig with a crown perched on top of it. Which reminds me: the coat-of-arms of the House of Pallagonia is a satyr holding up a mirror to a woman with a horse's head. Even after having seen the other absurdities, this seems to me the most peculiar of all.

10 April

Today we drove up the hill to Monreale on an excellent road built by an abbot of the monastery at the time of its enormous wealth. The road was broad, its gradient easy, with trees here and there and, more conspicuously, both high-spouting and running fountains, decorated with scroll ornaments of an almost Pallagonian eccentricity, but refreshing, nevertheless, to beasts and men.

The monastery of San Martino is a venerable institution. One confirmed old bachelor by himself has rarely produced anything sensible – witness the case of Prince Pallagonia –

but a celibate group can create the greatest of works, as many churches and cloisters testify. But the real reason why religious communities have achieved so much is probably that, unlike the other kind of family father, they can count upon an unlimited number of descendants.

The monks showed us their museum. They own many beautiful things, both objects of antiquity and products of Nature. We were especially taken by a coin bearing the figure of a young goddess. The good fathers would have gladly given us a replica but they hadn't anything handy which might have served as a mould.

After showing us everything, not without some melancholy comparisons between the past and the present day, they took us to a pleasant little room with a lovely view from its balcony. Here a table had been laid for the two of us, and nothing was lacking to make an excellent meal. After the dessert had been served, the abbot came in, accompanied by his oldest monks, sat down with us and stayed for almost half an hour, during which time we had to answer many questions. They bade us a very cordial farewell; the younger monks took us back to the museum and then walked us to our carriage.

We returned home in a very different frame of mind from that of yesterday. It seemed deplorable that such a great institution should be in decline at the very time when an enterprise as vulgar as the one we had seen the day before should be vigorously flourishing.

The road to San Martino climbs limestone hills of an early formation. The stone is quarried, crushed and burned to a very white lime. For fuel they use a long, strong kind of grass which is dried in bundles. In this way they obtain what they call *calcara*. The topsoil right up to the steepest heights is a red alluvial clay. The greater the height, the redder it becomes, as it is less darkened by vegetation. In the distance I saw a quarry with walls almost the colour of cinnabar.

The hills among which the monastery stands are well cultivated and rich in springs.

Having seen the two principal places of interest outside the city, we now visited the Palazzo Reale, where the Viceroy's obliging runner showed us around. To our dismay, the hall where the antiques usually stand was in a state of the greatest disorder, because the walls were being redecorated.

The statues had been moved, covered with sheets, and hidden from view by scaffolding, so that, despite the good will of our guide and occasional help from the workmen, we couldn't see them properly. I was mainly interested in two bronze rams, which, even in these unpropitious circumstances, delighted me. They are represented in a reclining position with one hoof stretched out and their two heads turned in opposite directions, so that they complement each other. Their fleeces are not short and curly but flow in long waves. Two powerful figures from the mythological family, worthy of carrying Phrixus and Helle; a work of great veracity from the best Greek period. They are said to have stood in the port of Syracuse.

The runner then took us to see the catacombs outside the city. These must have been designed by someone with a feeling for architecture; they do not look in the least like quarries which happen to have been used as a burial place. The sides are perpendicular and made of a compact tufa. Vaulted openings were dug into them, and in these the stone coffins were placed, one on top of the other. Those above are smaller than those below, and in the space over the pilasters there are niches for the coffins of children. Everything is of tufa without any masonry to support it.

12 April

Today we were shown Prince Torremuzza's collection of coins. I went there almost reluctantly. I understand too little about this field, and a merely inquisitive tourist is the bane of the true connoisseur. But after all, one has to begin somewhere, so I relented and derived great pleasure and some profit from our visit.

The ancient world was dotted with cities and even the smallest of them has left us, in its precious coins, a record, if not of the whole course of art history, at least of some epochs of it. An eternal spring of art's immortal fruits and flowers smiled up at us out of these drawers, telling of a craftsmanship perfected and practised over a lifetime, and of much else besides.

Alas, we others possessed in our youth nothing but family medals which say nothing and coins bearing the portraits of emperors in which the same profile is repeated *ad nauseam*, of overlords who cannot be regarded as paragons of humanity. It makes me sad to think that in my youth my historical knowledge was limited to Palestine, which had no images at all, and Rome, which had far too many. Sicily and Magna Graecia have given me hope of a new life.

The fact that I indulge in general reflections on these objects is proof that I still know precious little about them; but I hope I shall gradually improve in this, as in everything else.

This evening another of my wishes was fulfilled and in a surprising fashion. I was standing in the main street, joking with my old shopkeeper friend, when I was suddenly accosted by a tall, well-dressed runner who thrust a silver salver at me, on which lay several copper coins and a few pieces of silver. Since I had no idea what he wanted, I shrugged my shoulders and ducked my head, the usual gesture for showing that one has not understood or does not wish to. He left as quickly as he had come, and then I saw another runner on the opposite side of the street, occupied in the same fashion.

I asked the shopkeeper what all this was about, and he pointed with a meaningful, almost furtive glance to a tall, thin gentlemen, dressed in the height of fashion, who was walking down the middle of the street through all the dung and dirt with an air of imperturbable dignity. In a freshly curled and powdered wig, carrying his hat under his arm and wearing a silk coat, a sword and neat shoes with jewelled buckles, the elderly gentleman walked solemnly on, ignoring all the eyes that were turned in his direction.

'That is Prince Pallagonia,' said the shopkeeper. 'From time to time he walks through the city collecting ransom money for the slaves who have been captured by Barbary pirates. The collection never amounts to much, but people are reminded of their plight, and those who never contribute during their lifetime often leave a considerable legacy to this cause. The Prince has been president of this charity for many years now, and has done a great deal of good.'

'If,' I said, 'instead of spending vast sums on follies for his villa, he had used them for this cause, no prince in the world would have accomplished more.' My shopkeeper disagreed: 'Aren't we all like that? We pay gladly for our follies but we expect others to pay for our virtues.'

13 April

Anyone with an interest in mineralogy who goes to Sicily must feel highly indebted to Count Borch, who was the first to make a thorough study of its minerals. To honour the memory of a predecessor is at once a pleasure and a duty. After all, what am I, both in my life and my travels, but a precursor of those who shall come after me?

The Count's industry seems to me to have been superior to his learning; his approach is somewhat self-complacent, lacking in the modesty and seriousness with which important issues should be treated. On the other hand, his quarto volume devoted to the minerals of Sicily is extremely useful, and with its help I prepared myself for a visit to the stone polishers. Though they are not as busy as they used to be, when churches and altars had to be faced with marble and agate, they still carry on their craft. I ordered specimens of soft stones and hard stones – these are their terms for marble and agate, the only difference in their eyes being a difference in price. They are also showing great skill in handling another material which is a by-product from their lime kilns. Among the calcined lime they find lumps of a sort of glass paste, varying in colour from a very light to a very dark or almost black blue. These, like other minerals, are cut into thin sheets and priced according to their purity and brilliance of colour. They can be used as successful substitutes for lapis lazuli in the veneering of altars, tombs and other church ornaments.

I have ordered a complete collection, but it is not yet ready and will have to be sent to Naples. The agates are of a rare beauty, especially those in which irregular specks of yellow or red jasper alternated with a white and, as it were, frozen quartz. An exact imitation of these, produced by coating the back side of thin glass panes with lacquer dyes, was the only sensible thing I saw in the Pallagonian madhouse. They have a more decorative effect than windows made with true agate, because, instead of having to piece together many small stones, the architect can make the panes any size he likes. This artistic trick deserves to be more widely used.

13 April

To have seen Italy without having seen Sicily is not to have seen Italy at all, for Sicily is the clue to everything.

We are now in the rainy season – today we had a thunderstorm – but this is continually interrupted by fine days, and how powerfully everything waxes green! Some of the flax has already formed nodules, some is still in flower, and the blue-green fields of flax at the bottom of the valleys look like little ponds. My companion is a true 'Hopewell'* to whom I shall continue to play the 'True Friend'. He has already made many sketches and will continue to do so. The thought of one day coming home with all my treasures fills me with joy.

So far I have said nothing about the food – an important subject, after all. The vegetables are delicious, especially the

---

* *Hopewell* (*Hoffegut*). Like *Truefriend*, a character in *The Birds*.

lettuce, which is very tender and tastes like milk; one can understand why the Ancients called it *lactuca*. The oil and the wine are also good, but would be even better if prepared with greater care. The fish – excellent and of a most delicate flavour. We have always had good beef, too, though most people here do not recommend it.

But let's leave the table now and go to the window to look down into the street. As always happens at this season, a criminal has been reprieved in honour of Holy Week, and is being accompanied by a religious brotherhood to a mock gallows. There he says his prayers, kisses the ladder and is led away again. He is a good-looking, well-kempt man of the middle class, dressed completely in white, white tail coat, white hat. He carries his hat in his hand. Pin some coloured ribbons on him here and there, and he could attend any fancy-dress ball as a shepherd.

13 and 14 April

I must now set down the details of a singular adventure which befell me just before I left Palermo.

During my stay I have often heard people at our public eating place discussing Cagliostro, where he came from and what has happened to him. The people of Palermo are all agreed on one point: that a certain Giuseppe Balsamo was born in their city, became notorious for his many hoaxes and was exiled. But opinions are divided as to whether this man and Count Cagliostro are one and the same person. Some who once knew Balsamo insist that they can recognize his features in the well-known engraving which has also reached Palermo. During these discussions one guest mentioned the efforts which a Palermo lawyer has made to clear up the whole question. He has been commissioned by the French authorities to investigate the early history of the man who, in the course of an important and dangerous trial,* had

---

* The famous 'Diamond Necklace Affair', 1783–4.

the insolence to insult the intelligence of France and, indeed, the whole world with the most ridiculous cock-and-bull stories.

This lawyer, someone told me, has drawn up Giuseppe Balsamo's family tree, and sent it, along with an explanatory memoir and certified appendices, to France, where it will probably be published.

Everybody spoke highly of this lawyer, and when I expressed a wish to make his acquaintance, my informant offered to take me to his house and introduce me.

A few days later we went there together and found him in consultation with some clients. When he had finished with them, he produced a manuscript containing Cagliostro's family tree, the necessary confirmatory documents and the draft of his memoir.

He gave me this family tree to look at while he explained it. I shall quote enough of what he said to make it intelligible.

Giuseppe Balsamo's great-grandfather on his mother's side was Matteo Martello. The maiden name of his great-grandmother is unknown. There were two daughters of this marriage: Maria, who married Giuseppe Bracconeri and became the grandmother of Giuseppe Balsamo; and Vincenza, who married Giuseppe Cagliostro, a native of La Noara, a village eight miles from Messina. (Incidentally, two bell-founders named Cagliostro are still living in Messina.) This Vincenza Cagliostro subsequently stood godmother to her grand-nephew, who received at baptism the Christian name of her husband, Giuseppe. When, later, this Giuseppe Balsamo went to live abroad, he also adopted his great-uncle's surname, Cagliostro. Giuseppe and Maria Bracconeri had three children: Felicitas, Matteo and Antonino.

Felicitas married Pietro, the son of Antonino Balsamo, a Palermo haberdasher who seems to have been of Jewish extraction. Pietro Balsamo, the father of the notorious Giuseppe, went bankrupt and died at the age of forty-five. His widow, who is still alive, bore him one other child, a daughter, Giovanna Giuseppe-Maria. This daughter married Giovanni

Batista Capitummino, who died, leaving her with three children.

The memoir which the author obligingly read to me and, at my request, lent me for a few days is based on baptism certificates, marriage contracts and other legal instruments which he has collected with great care.* It describes the good use Giuseppe made of his gift for imitating any hand. He forged, or rather manufactured, an old document, on the strength of which the ownership of certain estates was contested in court. He fell under suspicion, was examined and imprisoned, but succeeded in escaping and was cited edictally. He travelled through Calabria to Rome, where he married Lorenza, the daughter of a brassworker. From Rome he went to Naples under the name of Marchese Pellegrini. He took the risk of returning to Palermo, was recognized and imprisoned, but managed to get himself set free. The story of how this happened deserves telling.

A prominent Sicilian prince, a great landowner who held several high offices at the court of Naples, had a son who combined a violent temper and powerful physique with all the arrogance to which, when they lack culture, the rich and the great imagine themselves to be entitled.

Donna Lorenza Cagliostro, alias Pellegrini, succeeded in ingratiating herself with the son, and the bogus Marchese pinned his hopes on this. The young Prince made no secret of being the protector of the newly arrived couple. But the party who had been injured by the fraud lodged an appeal, and Giuseppe Balsamo was again thrown into prison. The Prince, naturally, was furious. He tried by various means to have him

* *Added by Goethe some years later*: It contained, as I see from an extract I made at the time, more or less the same particulars as those given in the minutes of the Roman trial, namely, that Giuseppe Balsamo was born in Palermo at the beginning of June 1743, that, in his youth, he took the habit of the Brothers of Mercy, an order dedicated to the care of the sick, that he showed early promise of an unusual intelligence and talent for medicine but was expelled from the order for bad conduct, and that afterwards he posed in Palermo as a magician and treasure seeker.

set free and, when these failed, he made a scene in the very
antechamber of the President, when he threatened to give the
plaintiff's attorney a thrashing if he did not immediately
revoke Balsamo's arrest. The attorney refused, whereupon
the Prince grabbed him, threw him on the floor, trampled on
him and would have assaulted him still further had not the
President, hearing the fracas, hurried out in person and put a
stop to it. But, being a weak and servile man, he did not dare
punish the offender; the plaintiff and his attorney lost heart
and Balsamo was released. There is no record in the official
files of who ordered this or of the circumstances in which it
came about.

Balsamo left Palermo soon afterwards, and the author of
the memoir has only incomplete reports to give of his subsequent travels. It ended with a closely reasoned proof that
Cagliostro and Balsamo are one and the same person.*

When I saw from the genealogical tree that several members of the family, Cagliostro's mother and sister in particular,
were still living, I told the author of the memoir that I would

---

* *Added by Goethe some years later*: At that time this thesis was more difficult to
sustain than it is today when all the facts are known and we can see how the
story hangs together. If I had not had reason to suppose that this document
was to be made public in France, so that, on my return, I should probably find
it in print, I would have made a copy and my friends and the public would have
learned many interesting facts much earlier. Since then we have learned most
of its contents from a source which has usually been a source of errors only.
Who would have thought that Rome, of all places, would contribute so much
to the enlightenment of the world and the unmasking of an impostor by
publishing a précis of the court minutes! Though this précis could be and
should have been more interesting than it is, every sensible reader will be
grateful for it. For years we had to look on in dismay while the deceived, the
half-deceived and the deceivers worshipped this man and his conjuring tricks,
prided themselves upon their association with him, and from the height of
their credulous conceit pitied those who had common sense enough not to be
impressed.

Who did not prefer to keep silent during those times? Only now, when the
whole affair is closed and beyond discussion, can I bring myself to complement the official document by telling what I know.

like to see them and make the acquaintance of the relatives of such an extraordinary personality. He replied that this would be difficult, since they were poor but respectable people who lived a very retired life and were not used to meeting strangers. Furthermore, Sicilians are very suspicious by nature, and my visit might be misinterpreted in various ways. He promised, however, to send me his clerk, who had access to the family and had procured all the information and documents for him.

Next day the clerk appeared but expressed some scruples about the business. 'So far', he told me, 'I have always avoided letting these people see my face again because, in order to get my hands on their marriage contracts, baptismal certificates, etc., and make legal copies of them, I had to resort to a deception. I mentioned casually one day that there was a family stipendium vacant somewhere for which the young Capitummino was probably qualified, but to see if this were so, the first thing which would have to be done would be to draw up a family tree. After that, of course, everything would depend upon negotiations. I would take care of these, if they would promise me a compensation.

'The good people agreed with alacrity. I received the necessary document, the copies were made and the family tree drawn up, but since then I have been careful to keep out of their way. Only a few weeks ago I ran into Mother Capitummino, and the only excuse I could make was the slowness with which all such negotiations are transacted here.'

That is what the clerk said, but when he saw that I did not want to give up my idea, we agreed after some deliberations that I should introduce myself as an Englishman, delegated to bring his family news of Cagliostro, who had been released from the Bastille and had just arrived in London.

At the appointed hour – it must have been about three in the afternoon – we set off together. The house stood at the end of an alley not far from Il Cassaro, the main street. We climbed some dilapidated stairs which led directly into the kitchen. A woman of medium height, broad and sturdy without being stout, was busy washing dishes. Her dress was clean, and when we entered, she turned up one corner of her apron to hide the part which was dirty. She seemed glad to see the clerk and said: 'Signor Giovanni, have you good news for us? Have you straightened things out?' He replied: 'I still haven't settled our business yet, but here is a foreigner who brings you greetings from your brother and can tell you how he is.'

The greetings I was supposed to bring were something I hadn't bargained for, but at least I had been introduced. 'You know my brother?' she asked. 'The whole of Europe knows him,' I replied, 'and I think you will be happy to hear that he is well and safe, for you have probably been worried about his fate.' 'Go in,' she said, 'I won't be long.' So the clerk and I entered the next room.

It was what we would call a parlour, spacious and lofty, but it also seemed to be almost the entire living space for the family. There was only one window. The walls, which had once been painted, were covered with the blackened pictures of saints in gold frames. Two large beds without curtains stood against one wall, a small cupboard, shaped like a secretaire, against another. Old chairs, with rush bottoms and backs which had once been gilt, stood around, and the tiles of the floor were worn out in places, but everything was very clean. We now approached the family, who were assembled at the other end of the room near the window. While the clerk was explaining the reason for my visit to old Mother Balsamo – the old woman was very deaf – I had time to take a good look at the others. By the window stood a girl of about sixteen, with a good figure but a face scarred from smallpox, and beside her a young man whose face was also pockmarked and who looked disagreeable. In an armchair facing the window sat, or rather slumped, a very ugly person who seemed to be afflicted with some kind of lethargy.

When the clerk had finished, they invited us to sit down. The old woman asked me several questions in Sicilian dialect, which had to be translated for me, since I could not understand every word. She was pleasant to look at; the regular lines of her face expressed a serenity which one often notices on the faces of deaf people, and her voice sounded gentle and agreeable.

I answered her questions, and my answers had to be translated as well. The slowness of our conversation gave me the chance to weigh my words carefully. I told her that her son had been acquitted in France and was now in England, where he had been well received. The happiness she voiced on hearing this news was accompanied by expressions of deep piety. Now that she spoke louder and slower, I could understand her better.

Meanwhile her daughter had come in and sat down next to the clerk, who repeated to her all I had said. She had put on a fresh apron and arranged her hair neatly under a net. She must have been a woman of about forty. The more I looked at her and compared her with the mother, the more I was struck by the difference between them. The daughter's whole bearing expressed determination and a lively, healthy sensuality. She looked about her with intelligent gay blue eyes in which I could not detect the slightest shade of suspicion. She sat leaning forward on her chair with her hands resting on her knees, and looked better in this position than she had standing up. Her unpronounced features reminded me of her brother's as we know him from an engraving of his portrait. She asked me several questions about my journey and my reasons for visiting Sicily, and was convinced that I would return to celebrate with them the feast of Santa Rosalia.

The grandmother again had some questions to ask me, and while I was answering them, her daughter spoke with the clerk in an undertone. When I got the chance, I asked what they were talking about. The clerk said that Signora Capitummino had told him her brother still owed her fourteen ounces. When he had to leave Palermo in a hurry, she had redeemed some of his belongings from the pawnshop. She had never heard from him since, and although she had heard that now he was very rich and lived like a lord, he had never repaid her or given her any financial help. Would I, she asked, when I returned to England, please take it upon me to remind him in a friendly way of this debt and obtain some support for her? Would I also take a letter with me and, if possible, deliver it personally? I said I would, whereupon she asked where I was staying so that she could send me this letter. As I did not want her to know my address, I offered to come the next evening to fetch it. She then began to tell me about her precarious situation. She was a widow with three children. One of them, a girl, was being educated in a convent; the other two, a girl and a boy, were living at home – the latter had just left for school. Besides them, she had her mother to support and, out of Christian charity, she had taken in the poor sick person I had seen, which made her burden still heavier. All her industry was hardly sufficient to procure the bare necessities for herself and her family. She knew, of course, that God would not let her good works go unrewarded, but nevertheless, she groaned under the burden which she had borne for such a long time.

The young people now joined in the conversation, which became more lively. While I was talking with them, I heard the old woman ask her daughter if she thought I was a devotee of her sacred religion. The daughter cleverly evaded the question by telling her mother, so far as I could understand, that the foreigner seemed to have their welfare at heart and it would not be proper to question anyone about this matter on the first meeting.

When they heard that I intended to leave Palermo soon, they again urged me to be sure to return and praised the paradisiacal days of the Feast of Santa Rosalia. Nothing like it, they said, was to be seen and enjoyed in the whole world. My companion, who had wanted to leave long before and had repeatedly made signs to me that we should go, at last brought the conversation to an end, and I repeated my promise to come next day in the late afternoon to fetch the letter. The clerk was glad that our visit had gone off so well, and we parted from each other with expressions of mutual satisfaction.

You can imagine the impression this poor, pious, friendly family made on me. My curiosity had been satisfied, but their unaffected good manners had aroused an interest which increased the more I thought about them. At the same time I was worried about the next day. It would be only natural if, after I left, my surprise visit had set them thinking. From their family trees I knew that several other members of the family were still living, and they would, of course, call them and their friends together to discuss the amazing news they had heard from me. I had achieved my purpose and the only thing left for me to do was to bring this adventure to an end as tactfully as possible. Accordingly, the next day, soon after my midday meal, I went to the house by myself. They were astonished to see me so early. The letter, they said, was not ready yet. Furthermore, several relatives were coming in that evening who also wished to make my acquaintance. I told them I had to leave early the next morning and still had to pay some other visits and do my packing, so I had decided to come early rather than not come at all.

Meanwhile the grandson, who had not been there the day before, came in carrying the letter I was to take. This had been written, as is customary here, by one of the public scribes who sit in the squares. In height and build, the young man resembled the sister I had already seen, and his manner was quiet, melancholy and modest.

He asked me about his uncle's wealth and expensive style of living, remarking sadly: 'Why has he so completely forgotten about his family? How fortunate it would be for us if he would only return to Palermo. But how', he continued, 'did he come to tell you that he still has relatives in Palermo? They say he passes himself off as a man of noble birth and denies any connexion with us.' I answered this question, for which the clerk's imprudence had been inadvertently responsible, as plausibly as I could by saying that his uncle might have reasons for concealing his humble birth from the general public, but that he made no secret of it to his friends.

His sister, encouraged by the presence of her brother and also, perhaps, by the absence of her friend of yesterday, now joined in our conversation and began to talk in a very well-mannered and lively way. Both of them implored me to remember them to their uncle, if I should write to him. They also insisted that, after travelling across the kingdom, I was to come back and celebrate the Feast of Santa Rosalia with them. Their mother supported them in this. 'Signor,' she said, 'although it is not proper for me, really, with a grown-up daughter in the house, to invite foreigners to call, since one has to be wary not only of danger but also of gossip, you will always be welcome here whenever you come back to this city!'

'Yes, yes,' said her children. 'We shall show him round and sit with him on the stands from which you get the best view of the festivities. How he will admire the great car of the Saint and the magnificent illuminations!'

Meanwhile their grandmother had read through the letter several times. When she heard I was about to leave, she rose from her chair and handed me the folded sheet of paper. 'Tell my son how happy the news you have brought has made me! Tell him also that I take him to my heart – like this.' With these words she opened her arms wide and pressed them again to her breast. 'Tell him that I recommend him every day in my prayers to God and the Blessed Virgin, that I send him and his wife my blessing, and that my only wish is to see him again before I die, with these eyes which have shed so many tears for him.'

The graceful music which only the Italian language possesses enhanced the choice and noble arrangement of her words, which were further accompanied by those lively gestures with which the southern peoples give such extraordinary fascination to their speech. Deeply moved, I bade them farewell. All shook hands with me. The young people saw me to the door, and when I descended the stairs, they ran to the kitchen balcony overlooking the street and, as they waved goodbye, called out repeatedly that I was on no account to forget to come back. They were still standing on the balcony when I turned the corner.

I need hardly say that the interest I took in this family made me keenly anxious to do something practical to relieve their need. They had been twice deceived: first by the lawyer's clerk, now by an inquisitive North European, and it looked as if their hopes of help out of the blue were going to be dashed for the second time.

My first idea was to send them, before I left, the fourteen ounces which the fugitive owed them, under the pretext that I could count on Cagliostro reimbursing me. But when I had paid my bill at the inn and made a rough estimate of what I had left in cash and letters of credit, I realized that, in a country where lack of communications makes all distances infinite, so to speak, I would find myself in difficulties if I presumed, out of kindness of heart, to remedy the injustice of a scoundrel.

That same evening I went to see my friend, the shopkeeper, and asked him how the feast tomorrow would pass off. A great procession, headed by the Viceroy, was to move through the city, accompanying the Host on foot, and it was inevitable that the slightest wind would wrap God and man in a dense cloud of dust. The cheerful little fellow said that the people of Palermo are content to rely on a miracle. On several similar occasions a heavy downpour had washed down the sloping street and made a fairly clean road for the procession. The same thing was expected this time, and not without reason, for clouds were beginning to gather in the sky, promising rain during the night.

15 April

And so it happened! Last night a torrent of rain came down from heaven. First thing next morning, I hurried down into the street to witness the miracle. It was indeed extraordinary.

The flood, channelled between the pavements, had dragged the lighter rubbish down the street, pushing some of it into the sea and some into the drains, at least into those which were not choked. It had shifted the coarser litter from one place to another, so that curious meanders had been formed on the paving stones. Hundreds and hundreds of people with shovels, brooms and pitchforks were now busy enlarging these clean patches and joining them together by piling the remaining refuse on one side or the other. In consequence, when the procession started, it could proceed down a clean road, serpentining between the mud, and the clergy in their long skirts and the Viceroy and nobility in their elegant footwear could pass without being incommoded and bespattered. In my imagination I saw the Children of Israel, for whom the angel prepared a dry path through the midst of swamp and slough, and tried to ennoble with this simile the shocking spectacle of so many devout and proper people praying and parading their way down an avenue of wet piles of muck.

Where the streets have pavements, it is always possible to walk without getting dirty, but today, when we visited the inner city in order to see various things we had neglected so far, despite all the sweeping and heaping that had gone on, we found it almost impossible to get through.

Today's ceremonies gave us occasion to visit the cathedral and see its remarkable monuments. As we were stretching our legs in any case, we thought we would visit some more buildings. Among them a well-preserved Moorish house delighted us. It was not a big house, but its rooms were spacious and well proportioned; in a northern country it would not really be habitable, but in a southern it would make a most desirable residence. Expert architects should make a ground plan and a perspective view of it.

In a dismal quarter we saw several fragments of antique marble statues, but we hadn't the patience to try and identify them.

16 April

Since we have now to reckon with our imminent departure from this paradise, I hoped today to find a few more hours of perfect peace in the Public Gardens, and then to take a walk in the valley at the foot of the mountain of Santa Rosalia, so that I could do my daily stint of the Odyssey and consider the dramatic possibilities of Nausicaa. All this came to pass, and if I did not have perfect luck, I had much to be satisfied with. I made a draft of the whole, and could not resist roughing out and even composing several passages which particularly tempted me.

17 April

It is really and truly a misfortune to be haunted and tempted by so many spirits. Early this morning I went alone to the Public Gardens with the firm intention of meditating further upon my poetic dreams, but, before I knew it, another spirit seized me, one that had already been haunting me during the last few days.

Here where, instead of being grown in pots or under glass as they are with us, plants are allowed to grow freely in the open fresh air and fulfil their natural destiny, they become more intelligible. Seeing such a variety of new and renewed forms, my old fancy suddenly came back to mind: Among this multitude might I not discover the Primal Plant? There certainly must be one. Otherwise, how could I recognize that this or that form was a plant if all were not built upon the same basic model?

I tried to discover how all these divergent forms differed from one another, and I always found that they were more alike than unlike. But when I applied my botanical nomen-clature, I got along all right to begin with, but then I stuck, which annoyed me without stimulating me. Gone were my fine poetic resolutions – the garden of Alcinous had vanished and a garden of the natural world had appeared in its stead.

Why are we moderns so distracted, why do we let ourselves be challenged by problems which we can neither face nor solve!

Alcamo, 18 April

Very early in the morning we left Palermo on horseback. Kniep and the *vetturino* had proved themselves most efficient at packing and loading. We rode slowly up the excellent road we had travelled on before when we visited San Martino, and once more admired the magnificent fountains along it. Then an incident occurred which taught us something about the temperate habits of this country. Our groom was carrying a small barrel of wine slung over his shoulder like one of our *vivandières*. This looked big enough to hold sufficient wine to last us a few days. So we were surprised when he rode up to one of the water spouts, took out the spigot of the barrel and let water run in. Being Germans, we were flabbergasted and asked what he was doing. Wasn't the barrel full of wine? He replied, with the utmost nonchalance, that he had left a third of it empty because nobody ever drank unmixed wine. It was better to add the water while the wine was still in the barrel because then they would mix better. Besides, one couldn't always be certain of finding water. By this time, the barrel was full and there was nothing to be done but accept what used to be the custom at Oriental wedding feasts in days of old.

After passing Monreale and reaching the top of the ridge, we saw a beautiful landscape which spoke more of history than of agriculture. On our right stretched the level horizon of the sea, interrupted by picturesque foothills and wooded or treeless shores, its absolute calm in perfect contrast to the rugged limestone cliffs. Kniep quickly made some thumbnail sketches.

We are now in Alcamo, a quiet, clean little town with a well-appointed inn and within convenient distance of the Temple of Segesta, which we can see standing in solitary grandeur not so far off.

Our lodgings are so attractive that we have decided to spend the whole day here.

First, let me say something about our experiences yesterday.

After Monreale, we left the good road and entered a region of rocky mountains. High up on the ridge, I came across stones which, judging by their weight and sparkle, I took to be iron pyrites. All the flat land is cultivated and fairly fertile. The outcrops of limestone are red in colour like the weathered soil. This red, calcareous clay covers a wide area and makes a heavy soil with no sand in it, but nevertheless yields excellent wheat. We saw some lopped olive trees, old and very sturdy.

Under the shelter of an airy pergola attached to a miserable inn, we took a light midday meal. Dogs greedily gobbled up the discarded skins of our sausages; a beggar boy chased them away and hungrily consumed our apple parings until he, in his turn, was chased away by an old beggar. Professional jealousy is to be found everywhere. The old beggar ran up and down in his tattered toga, acting as both boots and waiter. I had observed on earlier occasions that if you order anything from an innkeeper which he hasn't got in the house at the moment, he calls a beggar to fetch it from the grocer's.

As a rule we are spared such slovenly service, thanks to our excellent *vetturino*, who is groom, guide, watch, buyer and cook in one.

On the higher slopes of the mountains we still found olive, carob and mountain ash. Here cultivation follows a three-year cycle – beans, corn and rest. Manure, the peasants say, works greater miracles than the saints. The vines are trained very low.

Alcamo stands on a hill at some distance from the Gulf. The landscape is impressive in its majesty – high crags, deep valleys, vastness and variety. Beyond Monreale one enters a beautiful double valley, divided down the middle by a mountain ridge. The cultivated fields lie green and still, the broad

road is lined with wild bushes and tangled shrubs lavishly decked with brilliant blossoms: the lentisk, so covered with yellow, papilionaceous flowers that not a green leaf is visible, bush after bush of hawthorn, aloes, already tall and showing signs of bloom, rich carpets of amaranthine clover, insect-orchids, small alpine roses, hyacinths with closed bells, borage, alliums, asphodels.

The stream which comes down from Segesta carries with it not only calcareous debris but also many particles of hornstone which are very compact and in every shade of dark blue, yellow and brown. Before one reaches Alcamo, one finds complete hills of such deposits. In the limestone cliffs I also saw veins of hornstone and silica with a *salband* of lime.

Segesta, 20 April

The Temple of Segesta was never completed. They never levelled the area around it, only the periphery on which the columns were to be set up. One can tell this from the fact that in some places the steps are sunk nine or ten feet into the ground, though there is no hill nearby from which the stones and earth could have been washed down. Moreover, the stones are still lying in their natural places and there are no broken fragments among them.

All the columns are standing, the two which had fallen having recently been raised again. It is difficult to decide whether or not they were meant to have socles, and it is difficult for me to explain why this is so, without a drawing. In some places it looks as though the columns must have stood on the fourth step, in which case one would have had to descend a further step to enter the temple. In other places the top step has been cut through and it looks as though the columns had bases. But then one comes to places where there is no cut and one is back at the first hypothesis. Some architect ought to settle this point definitely. The two long sides have twelve columns each, not counting the corner columns; the façade and the rear side have six each, including the corner ones. One sign that the temple was never completed is the condition of the temple steps. The peglike projections to which ropes were attached when the blocks were transported from the quarry to the site have not been hewn off. But the strongest evidence is the floor. Here and there slabs indicate where its edges must have been, but the centre is natural rock which rises higher than the sides, so that the floor can never have been paved. In addition, there is no trace of an inner hall, and the temple was never coated with stucco, though one can presume that this was intended, because, on the abaci of the capitals, there are projections where stucco could possibly be applied. The whole temple is built of a travertine type of limestone, which is now very badly weathered. The restoration of 1781 has done a lot of good. The new stonework is simple but beautiful. I could not find the particular great blocks Riedesel speaks of: perhaps they were used up when the columns were restored.

The site of the temple is remarkable. Standing on an isolated hill at the head of a long, wide valley and surrounded by cliffs, it towers over a vast landscape, but, extensive as the view is, only a small corner of the sea is visible. The countryside broods in a melancholy fertility; it is cultivated but with scarcely a sign of human habitation. The tops of the flowering thistles were alive with butterflies; wild fennel, its last year's growth now withered, stood eight or nine feet high and in such profusion and apparent order that one might have taken it for a nursery garden. The wind howled around the columns as though they were a forest, and birds of prey wheeled, screaming, above the empty shell.

The fatigue of clambering about among the unimpressive ruins of a theatre discouraged us from visiting the ruins of the city. At the foot of the temple, I found large pieces of hornstone, and on our way back to Alcamo, I saw that the road bed was largely composed of this rock, to which the soil owes the silica content that makes it friable. Examining a young fennel, I noticed a difference between the upper and the lower leaves; the organism is always one and the same, but it evolves from simplicity to multiplicity. The peasants are now busy weeding, walking up and down their fields like men on a *battue*. There are some insects about. (In Palermo I saw only glow-worms.) The leeches, lizards and snails here are no more beautiful in colour than ours; indeed, all those I saw were grey.

Castelvetrano, 21 April

From Alcamo up to Castelvetrano one approaches the limestone mountains over gravel hills. Between the steep barren mountains lie broad upland valleys – the ground is all cultivated, but there are scarcely any trees. The extensive alluvial deposits which form the gravel hills indicate by their alignment the course of the currents in the primeval ocean. The soil is well mixed and, owing to its sand content, more friable. Salemi lay to our right, an hour's ride away. We crossed hills where the limestone was overlaid with beds of gypsum, and the composition of the soil improved still further. The foreground was all hills; far away to the west we could see the sea. We came upon fig trees in bud and, to our delight, great masses of flowers, which had formed colonies on the broad road and kept repeating themselves, one large multicoloured patch following closely on the last. Beautiful bindweeds, hibisci, rose-mallows and a great variety of clovers predominated by turns, interspersed with allium and bushes of goat's rue. We wound our way on horseback, crossing and recrossing narrow paths. Russet-coated cattle grazed here and there, small but well built and with small, graceful horns.

In the north-east the mountains stood in row after row with the peak of Il Cuniglione soaring up in their midst. Among the gravel hills there were no signs of a spring or a stream, and evidently there is little rainfall here, since we saw neither ravines nor debris from flash floods.

During the night I had a strange experience. We were dead tired and had thrown ourselves on our beds in an inn which was anything but elegant. At midnight I woke up and saw over my head a star so beautiful that I thought I had never seen one like it. Its enchanting light seemed a prophecy of good things to come and my spirit felt utterly refreshed, but soon it disappeared, leaving me alone in the dark. It was not till daybreak that I discovered what had caused this miracle. There was a crack in the roof and I had woken up just at the very moment when one of the most beautiful stars in the firmament was crossing my private meridian. The travellers, of course, unhesitatingly interpreted this natural phenomenon as an omen in their favour.

Sciacca, 22 April

The road from Castelvetrano ran all the time over gravel hills and was devoid of mineralogical interest. When it reached the seashore, we could see a few limestone cliffs. The whole plain is immensely fertile; the oats and barley were in excellent condition, *salsola kali* had been planted, the fruit stalks of the aloes were higher than those we saw during the past two days, and the various clovers never left us. We came to a copse – mostly bushes, but with a tree rising here and there. And then, at last, cork-trees.

Girgenti, 23 April. Evening

From Sciacca to this place is a good day's ride. Shortly after Sciacca we halted to look at the thermal baths. A hot spring, with a pungent odour of sulphur, gushes out of a rock. The water tastes salty but not foul. Can it be that the sulphur fumes are not produced till it issues into the open air? A little higher up, there is a spring of cool, odourless water, and on top of the hill stands the cloister where the steam baths are: a dense cloud of vapour was rising from them into the pure air.

The beach here is made up of limestone fragments only; quartz and hornstone have abruptly disappeared. I inspected the small rivers: Caltabellotta, Macaluba and Platani. The first two carried limestone debris only, but in the bed of the Platani I found yellow marble and iron pyrites, the eternal companions of that more noble rock. Some small pieces of lava caught my eye, for I did not expect to find any volcanic material in these parts. I even believe they must have been transported here from far away to serve human purpose; probably they were fragments of old millstones. In the neighbourhood of Monteallegro thick beds of solid gypsum overlie and interlie the beds of limestone. The little town of Caltabellotta looks so odd, perched up on its crag.

24 April

I swear that I have never in my whole life enjoyed such a vision of spring as I did at sunrise this morning. The new Girgenti stands on the site of the ancient citadel, which covers an area large enough to house a city. From our windows we look down over a wide, gentle slope, now entirely covered with gardens and vineyards, so that one would never guess this was once a densely populated urban quarter. All one can see rising out of this green and flowering area is the Temple of Concord near its southern edge and the scanty ruins of the Temple of Juno to the east. All the other sacred ruins, which lie along a straight line between these two points, are invisible from this height. At the foot of the slope, looking south, lies the shore plain, which extends for about two miles till it reaches the sea. We had to forego an immediate descent through branches and creepers into that marvellous zone of green foliage with its flowers and promise of fruit, because our guide, a good-natured little secular priest, begged us to devote our first day to seeing the city.

First he showed us its well-built streets, then he led us to some higher ground to enjoy an even more extensive view and finally, to satisfy our artistic appetite, brought us to the cathedral. This contains an ancient sarcophagus which, since it was converted into an altar, has been well preserved.

It depicts Hippolytus with his hunting companions and horses. Phaedra's nurse has bidden them halt and is about to hand Hippolytus a small tablet. The artist's main concern was to portray beautiful young men. In order that the eye should concentrate its attention on them, he has made the old nurse very small, almost a dwarf. I have never seen a bas-relief as wonderful or as well preserved. If I am not mistaken, it is an example of Greek art from its most graceful period.

A priceless vase of considerable size carried me back to some still more remote epoch, and, in the structure of the church itself, there were places where the pieces of antique buildings seemed to have been incorporated.

Since there are no inns in Girgenti, a family kindly made room for us in their own house and gave us a raised alcove in a large chamber. A green curtain separated us and our baggage from the members of the household, who were manufacturing macaroni of the finest, whitest and smallest kind, which fetches the highest price. The dough is first moulded into the shape of a pencil as long as a finger; the girls then twist this once with their finger tips into a spiral shape like a snail's. We sat down beside the pretty children and got them to explain the whole process to us. The flour is made from the best and hardest wheat, known as *grano forte*. The work calls for much greater manual dexterity than macaroni made by machinery or in forms. The macaroni they served us was excellent, but they apologized for it, saying that there was a much superior kind, but they hadn't enough in the house for even a single dish. This kind, they told us, was only made in Girgenti and, what is more, only by their family. No other macaroni, in their opinion, can compare with it in whiteness and softness.

In the evening our guide again managed to appease our impatient longing to walk down the hill by leading us to other points along the heights from which, as we gazed at the noble view, he gave us a general survey of the position of all the remarkable things we were to see on the morrow.

At sunrise we were at last permitted to walk down the hill, and at every step the scenery became more picturesque. Convinced that he was only serving our best interests, the little man led us through the lush vegetation without stopping once, though we passed thousands of singular views, any one of which would have made a subject for an idyllic picture. The ground beneath our feet was undulated like waves over the hidden ruins. The shell-tufa of which these were built ensures the fertility of the soil which now covers them. In due course we came to the eastern limit of the city where, year after year, the ruins of the Temple of Juno fall into ever greater decay because their porous stone is eroded by wind and weather. We only meant to make a cursory examination today, but Kniep has already chosen the points from which he will sketch tomorrow.

This temple stands on a foundation of weathered rock. From this point the city wall ran due east along the edge of a limestone hill which falls in precipices to the shore plain. The sea which once washed the base of these cliffs must have receded to its present shoreline in a fairly remote age. The city walls were partly built of quarried stone and partly hewn out of the solid rock. Behind the walls rose the temple. It is easy to imagine what a stupendous sight the rising tiers of Girgenti must have looked from the sea.

The slender architecture of the Temple of Concord, which has withstood so many centuries, already conforms more nearly to our standard of beauty and harmony than the style which preceded it – compared to Paestum, it is like the image of a god as opposed to the image of a giant.

Since the intention was so laudable, one ought not to complain, I suppose, but what has recently been done to preserve these monuments is in very poor taste. The cracks have been repaired with a dazzling white gesso which quite spoils the look of the whole temple. It would have been so easy to give the gesso the colour of the weathered stone. On the other hand, when one sees of what friable shell-limestone the walls and columns are built, one must admit that it is surprising the temple has survived at all. It is clear, though, that the builders themselves, in the hope of a grateful posterity, took steps for its preservation; on the columns one can still see traces of a thin coat of plaster which they applied both to flatter the eye and to ensure durability.

Next we stopped before the ruins of the Temple of Jupiter, which lie scattered far and wide like the disjointed bones of a gigantic skeleton, amid and beneath several small-holdings, which are divided by fences and overgrown with plants of every size. The only recognizable shapes in all this heap of rubble are a triglyph and half of a column, both of gigantic proportions. I tried to measure the triglyph with my outstretched arms and found I could not span it. As for the column, this will give you some idea of its size. When I stood in one of the flutings as in a niche, my shoulders barely touched both edges. It would take twenty-two men, placed shoulder to shoulder, to form a circle approximating in size to the circumference of such a column. We left with a feeling of disappointment because there seemed nothing here for a draughtsman to do.

The Temple of Hercules, on the other hand, still reveals traces of the classic symmetry. The two rows of columns on its front and rear side all lie pointing north and south, one row uphill, the other down, as if they had all fallen together at the same moment. The hill itself may have been formed from the ruins of its *cella*. The columns which were probably held together by the entablature may have been blown down in a raging storm. The separate blocks of which they were composed are still lying in their proper order. Kniep has already mentally sharpened his pencils in anticipation of depicting this unusual occurrence.

The Temple of Aesculapius, standing in the shade of a lovely carob tree and almost walled in by some kind of small farm buildings, makes a pleasant picture.

Last we climbed down to the Tomb of Theron and felt happy to be standing in the presence of a monument we had seen in so many reproductions. It provides the foreground to an extraordinary vista. The eye travels faster from west to east along the rocky cliff with its crumbling walls, through which and above which it sees the remains of the temples. This view has been painted by Hackert with a skilful hand, and Kniep will certainly sketch it too.

26 April

By the time I woke up, Kniep was all ready to set off on his artistic excursion with a boy he had hired to carry his cardboard sheets. I stood by the window and shared the glory of the morning with my secret, quiet, but by no means speechless friend. A certain shy reverence has hitherto kept me from pronouncing the name of this mentor to whom I turn and listen from time to time. It is von Riedesel,* that excellent man whose little book I carry near my heart like a breviary or a talisman.

I have always enjoyed seeing myself in the mirror of natures who possess what I lack, and he is one of them. Calm resolution, sureness of aim, apt and precise method, good grounding and scholarship, intimate association with a masterly teacher, in his case, Winckelmann – I lack them all, and everything which comes from having them. So I cannot blame myself for trying to gain, by stealth, storm and cunning, what my life has so far not permitted me to acquire in the ordinary way. Would that this good man, amid the tumult of this world, could be aware that, at this very moment, a grateful disciple is doing homage to his merits, lonely in a lonely place which had so much attraction for him that he wished to spend his lifetime here, far from family and friends, forgetting and forgotten.

* J. H. von Riedesel (1740–85), Prussian ambassador to the Court of Vienna, author of *Journey across Sicily and Magna Graecia*.

So, consulting my assiduous friend from time to time, I walked the roads of yesterday with my clerical guide, looking at the same objects from many different angles.

He drew my attention to a beautiful custom of this powerful, ancient city. Set in the rocks and masses of masonry which once served Girgenti as ramparts are tombs which were probably reserved for the Brave and the Good. What fairer resting-place could they have found as a memorial to their glory and an immortal example to the living?

In this wide plain between the cliffs and the sea are the remains of a small temple which has been converted into a Christian chapel. The harmonious combination of the half-columns and the square blocks of the walls was a joy to the eye. I felt I was witnessing the exact moment when the Doric order reached its highest measure of perfection. We took a brief look at some insignificant monuments of antiquity and a longer one at the large subterranean vaults in which wheat is stored at the present day. My good old guide gave me much information about the conditions here, both civil and ecclesiastical. Nothing he told me sounded very encouraging, and our conversation seemed in keeping with our surroundings, where everything is steadily crumbling away. I learned from him, incidentally, that there is still much hatred of the French for having made peace with the Barbaresques. They are accused of betraying Christendom to the infidels.

Looking at the cliffs, one observes that all the strata dip towards the sea. The lower layers have eroded, so that the upper overhang like suspended fringes.

Halfway up the road from the shore plain there is an ancient gate hewn out of the rock. The walls which still stand are built on rock foundations in tiers.

Our *cicerone* is called Don Michele Vella, the-antiquary-who-lives-near-Santa-Maria-in-the-house-of-Mastro-Gerio.

The broad beans are planted thus: they dig holes in the soil at suitable intervals, put in a handful of manure, wait for rain

and then sow the beans. The bean-straw is burned and the
ashes used for washing their linen. They never use soap.
Instead of soda, they use the burned outer shells of almonds.
They wash their laundry first with water and then with this
kind of lye.

The rotation of crops is as follows: broad beans, wheat,
tumenia; during the fourth year, the field lies fallow and
serves as pasture. Tumenia – the name is said to be derived
from either *bimenia* or *trimenia* – is a precious gift from Ceres.
It is a kind of a summer corn and takes three months to ripen.
They keep sowing it from January till June, so that, at any
given moment, some of it is ripe. It needs little rain but much
heat. At first it has a very tender leaf, but it grows as fast as
wheat and when ripe is very strong. Wheat is sown in October
and November and is ripe in June, barley in November. Here
the latter is ripe by the first of June, but earlier along the coast
and later in the mountains.

The flax is ripe already. The acanthus has unfolded its
magnificent leaves. *Salsola fruiticosa* grows luxuriantly, and
sainfoin is abundant on the uncultivated slopes. Some of
these crops are leased to people who carry them to the city
in sheaves. The oats which they weed out of the wheat are
also sold in sheaves.

When they plant cabbages, they dig neat trenches with
little borders of soil to catch the rain. The fig trees are
showing all their leaves; the figs have begun to form and
will be ripe by St John's Day. Later in the year, however, the
trees will bear a second crop. The almond trees are laden with
fruit. I saw a lopped carob tree bearing innumerable pods.
The vines which yield eating grapes are trained over pergolas,
supported on high poles. Melons are planted in March and
ripe in June. I saw them cheerfully growing among the ruins
of the Temple of Jupiter, though there was no moisture for
them at all.

Our *vetturino* eats raw artichokes and kohlrabi with the
greatest gusto; it must be said, though, that these are much

tenderer and more succulent here than they are in our climate. The same is true of other vegetables. When one passes through the fields, the peasants let one eat, for example, as many young broad beans as one likes, pods and all.

When I showed interest in some black stones that resembled lava, the antiquary told me that they came from Mount Etna, and that more specimens could be found near the harbour, or rather, the anchorage.

Except for quails, there are few birds in this region. The other migrants are swallows, *rinnine* and *ridene*. *Rinnine* are small black birds which come from the Levant, breed and nest in Sicily and then either fly back or further on. *Ridene*, or wild duck, arrive from Africa in December and January, descend on Acragas in great numbers and then move off into the mountains.

A word about the vase in the cathedral. It shows a hero in full armour, a stranger apparently, who has just arrived and is standing in the presence of a seated old man whose wreath and sceptre show him to be a king. Behind the King stands a woman with lowered head, supporting her chin with her left hand in a watchful and pensive pose. Behind the hero facing them, another old man, also wearing a wreath, is talking to a man who carries a spear and is possibly a member of the King's bodyguard. He appears to have introduced the hero and to be saying to the guard: 'Just let him speak to the King, he is a good man.' The ground colour of this vase seems to have been red and the figures to have been painted over it in black; the woman's garment is the only place where red seems to have been laid on black.

27 April

If Kniep really means to carry out all his plans, he will have to draw without stopping, while I roam about with my little old guide. Today we walked as far as the seashore, from which, the ancients assure us, Girgenti was a wonderful sight.

As we gazed out at the vast watery expanse, my guide pointed to a long bank of cloud like a mountain ridge on the southern horizon; this, he said, indicated the coast of Africa. I was struck by another strange phenomenon: a slender arc of light clouds, with one foot resting on Sicily and the other on the sea somewhere in the south, vaulted into the blue sky, which was otherwise cloudless. Almost motionless and richly dyed by the rays of the setting sun, it was a strange and a beautiful spectacle. My guide told me that its other foot probably rested on Malta, which lay exactly in the direction to which the arc pointed, and that this phenomenon was not rare. It would really be very odd if the mutual attraction between the two islands should manifest itself atmospherically in this way.

Our conversation revived an idea I had once had and dismissed as being too difficult and dangerous: Why not take a trip to Malta? But the same objections remained and I decided to keep our *vetturino* till we reached Messina.

In taking this decision, I was influenced by another of my stubborn fancies. So far, on my excursions through Sicily I had only seen a few regions which were rich in wheat; the horizon had always been limited by mountains, so that my impression was of an island entirely lacking in plains, and I could not understand why Ceres was said to have shown it such especial favour. When I asked about this, I was told that, instead of going along the coast by way of Syracuse, I should cut straight across the interior; then I would see wheat fields in plenty. Though it meant leaving out Syracuse, Kniep and I readily yielded to this tempting suggestion because we had heard that little now remained of that once glorious city but its name. Besides, it would be easy to visit it from Catania.

Caltanissetta, 28 April

At last we can say we have seen with our own eyes the reason why Sicily earned the title of 'The Granary of Italy'. Soon after Girgenti, the fertility began. There are no great level areas, but the gently rolling uplands were completely covered with wheat and barley in one great unbroken mass. Wherever the soil is suitable to their growth, it is so well tended and exploited that not a tree is to be seen. Even the small hamlets and other dwellings are confined to the ridges, where the limestone rocks make the ground untillable. The women live in these hamlets all the year round, spinning and weaving, but during the season of field labour, the men spend only Saturdays and Sundays with them; the rest of the week they spend in the valleys and sleep at night in reed huts. Our desire had certainly been granted; indeed, we soon came to long for the winged chariot of Triptolemus to bear us away out of this monotony.

After riding through this deserted fertility for hours under a scorching sun, we were glad to arrive in the well-situated and well-built town of Caltanissetta. However, we looked in vain for a tolerable inn. The mules are housed in superbly vaulted stables, the farm hands sleep on the heaps of clover which is used for fodder, but the foreigner has to start his housekeeping from nothing. Even when he has found a room which might possibly do, this has first to be cleaned. Chairs, benches, even tables do not exist; one sits on low blocks of solid wood.

If one wants to convert these blocks into the legs of a bed, one goes to the carpenter and rents as many boards as are needed. The large leather bag which Hackert lent us was temporarily filled with chaff and proved a godsend. But first we had to do something about our meals. On our way we had bought a chicken, and our *vetturino* went off at once to buy rice, salt and spices. But since he had never been near this place before, it was some time before we could solve the question of where we could do our cooking, as there were no facilities for this at the inn. At last an elderly citizen offered, in return for a small sum, to provide firewood, to lend us a stove, kitchen utensils and table requisites, and, while the meal was being prepared, to conduct us round the town.

This he did and brought us finally to the market square, where, in accordance with immemorial custom, the town notables were sitting around, talking among themselves and expecting us to entertain them as well.

We had to tell them stories about Frederick the Second, and the interest they showed in that great king was so lively that we kept his death a secret for fear we might become objects of hatred to our hosts as bearers of ill tidings.

A few more geological observations. As one descends from Girgenti, the soil turns whitish: the older type of lime-stone appears to be followed immediately by gypsum. Then comes a new type of limestone, more friable, slightly decom-posed and, as one can see from the tilled fields, varying in colour from a light yellow to a darker, almost violet tint. Halfway between Girgenti and Caltanissetta, gypsum reappears. This favours the growth of a beautiful purple, almost rose-red sedum, while the limestone harbours a bright yellow moss.

Near Caltanissetta the decomposed limestone frequently outcrops again. Its strata contain few fossilized shells, and the outcrops have a reddish, slightly violet colour, almost like red lead. I had observed similar ones on the hills near San Martino.

Quartz I only saw once, halfway down a little valley, enclosed on three sides and opening in the east towards the sea. In the distance on our left the high mountain which rises above Camerata came into view and another shaped like a truncated cone. The immense wheatfields looked incredibly clean – no weeds at all. At first we saw nothing but green fields, then ploughed ones, and here and there, where the ground was moister, a patch of pasture. Trees are very rare; we came upon a few apple and pear trees soon after leaving Girgenti, and fig trees on the summits of ridges and in the neighbourhood of the occasional villages.

The valleys are beautiful in shape. Even though their bottoms are not completely level, there is no sign of heavy rain, for it immediately runs off into the sea; only a few little brooks, which one hardly notices, trickle along.

The dwarf palms and all the flowers and shrubs of the south-western zone had disappeared and I did not see much red clover. Thistles are allowed to take possession only of the roads, but all the rest is Ceres' domain. As a matter of fact, the whole region looks very like certain hilly, fertile regions in Germany, that between Erfurt and Gotha, for example, especially when one looks in the direction of the Gleichen.* It took a combination of many factors to make Sicily one of the most fertile countries in the world. They plough with oxen and it is forbidden to slaughter cows or calves. We have met many goats, donkeys and mules on our trip, but few horses. Most of these were dapple greys with black feet and black manes. They have magnificent stables with built-in stone mangers.

Manure is used only in growing beans and lentils; the other crops are grown after they have been harvested. Red clover and sheaves of barley, in the ear but still green, are offered for sale to passing riders.

On the mountain above Caltanissetta we saw a hard fossiliferous limestone: the large shells lay below, the small on top. In the paving stones of the little town we found pectinites.

After Caltanissetta the hills descend steeply into a number of valleys which discharge their waters into the river Salso. The soil is reddish and very clayey. Much of the land lies fallow, and, where it is cultivated, the crops, though tolerably good, are far behind those of the regions we had traversed earlier.

Castrogiovanni, 29 April

Today we saw an even more fertile and even more uninhabited region. It rained steadily, which made travelling very

---

* Gleichen. Three mountains near Gotha.

unpleasant, since we had to cross several rivers which were in flood. When we came to the bank of the Salso and looked in vain for a bridge, a surprising adventure awaited us. Some sturdy men grabbed the mules by the girth in pairs and led them, with their riders and baggage, across a deep arm of the stream to a gravel bank, alternately checking and pushing the beasts to keep them on the right course and prevent them from being swept off their feet by the current. After the whole cavalcade had assembled on the bank, they transported us across the second arm of the river in the same fashion.

Brushwood grew along the banks but soon disappeared after we reached dry land. The Salso carries down particles of granite, a metamorphosed gneiss, and marble, both speckled and plain.

Presently we saw ahead of us the isolated crest on which Castrogiovanni is perched. It gives the whole landscape a curiously sombre character.

As we ascended the flank of this hill by a long, winding road, we saw that it was made of shell-limestone. We picked up some specimens containing large calcified shells. Castrogiovanni itself is not visible until one reaches the summit, since it is built on the northern slope. The little town, the tower and the village of Calascibetta a little way off to the left confront each other very solemnly. The beans were blossoming in the plains below, but who could enjoy the view! The roads were horrible, the more so because they had once been paved, and the rain beat down without stopping. The ancient Enna gave us a most unfriendly welcome – a room with a plastered stone floor and shutters but no windows, so that either we had to sit in the dark or put up with the drizzling rain, from which we had just escaped. We consumed some of our remaining provisions, spent the night in misery and took a solemn vow never to let ourselves be tempted again on our travels by a mythological name.

We left Castrogiovanni by a path so steep and rugged that we had to lead the mules. For most of the descent, everything at eye level was wrapped in clouds, but at a great height we were astonished to see a grey-and-white-striped something which seemed to be a solid body. How could there be a solid body in the sky? Our guide explained that it was one flank of Etna, seen through rents in the clouds; the stripes were snow and the bare rock of the ridge; even so, the ridge we could see was not the summit.

Leaving the steep rock of the ancient Enna behind us, we rode through long, long, lonely valleys, uncultivated, uninhabited, abandoned to pasturing cattle which were as graceful and lively as deer. These good creatures had pasture acreage enough, but they were hemmed in by enormous masses of encroaching thistles which were steadily reducing their grazing ground. Here these plants find the ideal conditions for increasing and multiplying their kind. The area they have usurped would provide sufficient pasture for several large estates. Since they are not perennials, they could easily be exterminated at this season by mowing them down before they have flowered.

As we were solemnly making strategic plans for our war on the thistles, we were put to shame by the discovery that they were not quite as useless as we thought. At a lonely inn where we had halted to fodder our mules, two Sicilian noblemen had just arrived. They were on their way across country to Palermo to settle a lawsuit. To our amazement, we saw these two dignified gentlemen standing in front of a clump of thistles and cutting off the tops with their sharp pocket knives. Carefully holding their prickly acquisitions by the finger tips, they pared the stalk and consumed the inner portion with great gusto, an operation which took them some time. Meanwhile we refreshed ourselves with some wine, undiluted for once, and some good bread. Our *vetturino* prepared some of this thistle pith for us, insisting that it was both healthy and refreshing, but to us it seemed as tasteless as the raw kohlrabi of Segesta.

On the way, 30 April

In the pleasant valley down which the S. Paolo river zigzags its course, the soil, a dark-red decomposed limestone, is twenty feet deep in places. The aloes had grown tall, the harvest looked good, though here and there spoiled by weeds and far behind the crops in the south of the island. Much fallow land, wide fields, an occasional small house and, except just below Castrogiovanni, no trees. Along the river banks, extensive pasture land crowded with enormous clumps of thistles. In the detritus of the river, more quartz, some plain, some like breccia.

Molimenti is a modern hamlet, with a good location on the bank of the S. Paolo and beautiful fields all round it. In this neighbourhood the wheat is ready for harvesting by the twentieth of May. The district shows as yet no trace of a volcanic character; even the river carries no volcanic detritus. The soil is a good mixture, rather heavy, and usually of a coffee-brown purplish colour. The mountains along the left bank of the river are limestone and sandstone. I was unable to examine the order of the strata, but undoubtedly the decomposition of these two rocks has contributed to the great and constant fertility of the valley. Shortly after leaving Molimenti, we saw peasants harvesting the flax.

1 May

Down this so diversely cultivated valley, destined by Nature to universal fertility, we rode in rather a gloomy mood because, in spite of all our hardships, we had not seen anything which was paintable. Kniep made one sketch of an interesting distant view, but the middle and foreground were so awful that he introduced into the latter an elegant group in the style of Poussin which cost him little trouble and transformed the drawing into a delightful little picture. I wonder how many 'Travels of a Painter' contain such half-truths.

In an effort to put us in a better temper, our muleteer had promised us good lodgings for this evening and actually brought us to a real inn which was built only a few years ago. As it is situated at just a day's journey from Catania, it must be welcome to any traveller. The accommodation was tolerable, and, after our twelve days' journey, we were able to make ourselves fairly comfortable at last. But, to our surprise, we found an inscription pencilled on the wall in a beautiful English script, which read:

Traveller, bound for Catania, whoever you may be, beware of staying at the Golden Lion; it is worse than falling into the clutches of the Cyclops, the Sirens and Scylla.

Though we fancied that the benevolent warning was probably a mythological exaggeration, we nevertheless made up our minds to give a wide berth to this fierce beast of a Golden Lion, so, when our muleteer asked us where we wanted to put up in Catania, we said: 'Anywhere, except at the Lion.' At this, he suggested that we might be satisfied with the place where he stabled his mules, though we would have to provide our own food, as we have done hitherto. So great was our wish to escape the jaws of the lion, that we readily agreed.

Near Hybla Maior, pieces of lava begin to appear which the stream has brought down from the north, and, on the far side of the ferry, limestone, mixed with particles of hornstone and lava, and hardened volcanic ash coated with a tufa of lime. The alluvial hills continue all the way to Catania; beside them and over them lie lava flows from Mount Etna. On our left we passed what was probably a crater. Here Nature shows her predilection for high colours and amuses herself by arraying the black-blue-grey lava in vivid yellow moss, red sedum, and a variety of purple flowers. Cacti and vines give evidence of meticulous cultivation. Lava everywhere, one enormous flow after another. Motta is a beautiful and imposing crag. The beans grow in tall bushes. The fields vary in quality; in some the soil is of good composition, in others very flinty.

Our *vetturino*, who had probably not seen this spring vegetation of the south-east coast for a long time, broke out into loud exclamations of joy at the beauty of the crops and asked us with complacent patriotism if we knew anything like it in our country. A girl with a pretty face and lovely figure – an old acquaintance of his – ran along beside his mule, chattering and spinning her thread at the same time. Now yellow flowers began to predominate. As we neared Misterbianco, cacti reappeared in the hedges, but entire hedges of these bizarre-shaped plants, each more beautiful than the last, appeared more frequently as we reached the outskirts of Catania.

Catania, 2 May

It is no good denying that, as regards lodging, we found ourselves very badly off. Such fare as our muleteer could manage was not of the best. A chicken boiled with rice is certainly not to be despised, but an immoderate use of saffron made it as yellow as it was inedible. Our sleeping-quarters were so uncomfortable that we seriously thought of having recourse again to Hackert's leather bag. Early next morning, therefore, we had a talk with our friendly host, who expressed his regrets at being unable to provide us with better accommodation. 'But over there,' he said, pointing to a large corner house across the street, 'you will be well looked after and have every reason to be satisfied.' From the look of the place, it promised well and we hurried over immediately. The proprietor was not at home, but an alert-looking man, who introduced himself as a waiter, assigned us a pleasant room next to a large sitting room and assured us that the terms would be reasonable. We asked him, as we always do, for precise details about the price of lodging, meals, wine, breakfast, etc. Everything did sound very cheap, so we moved our few belongings across the street and stowed them in the drawers of the spacious gilded commodes. For the first time Kniep had a chance to sort out his cardboard sheets and put his drawings in order, while I did the same with my notes.

Feeling very happy about the rooms, we stepped out on to the balcony to enjoy the view. When we had admired it long enough, we were just turning to go back to our work when – lo and behold! – there above our heads, like a threat, was a big golden lion. Our eyes met, and our smiles turned to laughter. From now on we would be on constant watch lest one of the Homeric bogies should suddenly appear out of some corner. But nothing of the sort happened; all we found in the sitting room was a pretty young woman playing with a two-year-old child. Our semi-landlord told her in harsh tones to clear out at once. She had no business there. 'Don't be so cruel,' she said, 'don't drive me away. I cannot manage the child at home when you are not there. Surely these gentlemen won't mind my soothing it in your presence.' The husband would not leave it at that, but tried to drive her away. The child stood in the doorway howling, so that, in the end, we were obliged to beg that she be allowed to stay where she was.

After the Englishman's warning, it didn't take a genius to see through the comedy: we played the innocent greenhorns and he played the loving father to perfection. Strangely enough, the child seemed to like him better than the pre- tended mother; probably, she had given it a pinch on the sly. When the man left to take a letter of recommendation for us to the house chaplain of Prince Biscari, she remained and, with the most innocent air in the world, went on playing with the child till he returned to report that the Abbé would come in person to show us round.

3 May

Early this morning, the Abbé, who had already come yester- day to pay his respects, arrived and took us to the palace, a one-storey building on a high foundation. We first visited the museum with its collection of marble and bronze statues, vases and many other such-like antiquities.

We were fascinated by a torso of Jupiter, which I knew already from a cast in Tischbein's studio, but which has greater merits than one would guess from the cast. A member of the household gave us the most essential historical information, and then we moved on into a large, high-ceilinged room. The many chairs along the walls indicated that it was sometimes used for large social gatherings. We sat down, expecting a gracious reception. Two ladies entered the salon and walked up and down its whole length, engaged in lively conversation. When they noticed us, the Abbé rose, we did the same, and we all bowed. I asked who they were and was told that the younger one was the Princess, the older a noblewoman from Catania. We sat down again, and the ladies continued to walk up and down like people in a public square.

Next we were taken to the Prince, who showed us his collection of coins. This was a special mark of confidence, since, both in his father's day and in his own, several objects were missing after they had been shown to visitors, and he was now chary of showing them. I had learned a good deal from looking at Prince Torremuzza's collection, and added to my knowledge by reading Winckelmann, whose book provides a reliable thread to guide us through the various epochs of art, so this time I was able to do much better. When he saw that, though amateurs not connoisseurs, we were observant, the Prince, who is an expert in these matters, willingly explained to us everything we wanted to know. After spending quite some time, though not enough, over these objects, we were about to take our leave when he took us to his mother's suite to see the rest of his smaller works of art.

There we were introduced to a distinguished-looking lady, with an air of instinctive breeding, who received us with the words: 'Look around, gentlemen; you will find everything just as my dear husband arranged it. This I owe to the filial devotion of my son, who not only allows me to live in his best rooms, but also will not allow a single object in his father's collection to be removed or displaced. In consequence I enjoy the double advantage of living in the fashion

I have been accustomed to for so long, and of making the acquaintance of eminent foreigners who, as in former times, come here from far-off countries to look at our treasures.'

With that she opened the glass cabinet in which the amber collection was kept. What distinguishes Sicilian amber from the northern kind is that it passes from the colour of transparent or opaque wax or honey through all possible shades of yellow to a most beautiful hyacinthine red. We were shown urns, cups and other things which had been carved from it, and it was clear that remarkably large pieces must have been needed. These, some incised shells from Trapani and some exquisite ivories were the lady's special pride and joy, and she had some amusing stories to tell about them. The Prince pointed out the more important things, and in this manner we spent some entertaining and instructive hours.

When the Dowager Princess realized we were Germans, she asked us for news of von Riedesel, Bartels and Münter, all of whom she knew, and spoke of their characters and activities with great discrimination and affection. We were sorry to have to leave her, and she appeared sorry to see us go. There is something lonely about the life of these islanders which needs to be refreshed and nourished by chance meetings with sympathetic persons.

We then went with the Abbé to the Benedictine monastery. We entered a cell and he introduced us to a middle-aged monk whose melancholy and reserved features did not promise a very cheerful conversation. He was, however, a gifted musician, the only monk who could master the enormous organ in their chapel. When he divined our wishes – one can't say he heard them – without a word he led us into the vast chapel and began to play the admirable instrument, filling the remotest corners with sounds that ranged from the gentlest whisper to the most powerful trumpet blasts.

If one had not already seen this man, one would have thought that such power could only be exercised by a giant; now, knowing his personality, we could only wonder that he had not, long ago, succumbed in such a struggle.

Soon after dinner, the Abbé came with a carriage to show us the remoter quarters of the city. Just as I was getting into the carriage, a curious *contretemps* occurred. I had climbed in first, meaning to sit on his left, but when he got in, he positively ordered me to move and let him sit on my left. I begged him not to stand on ceremony. 'Excuse me', he said, 'for insisting that we sit this way. If I sit on your right, people will think I am driving with *you*, but when I sit on your left, it is understood that you are driving with *me*, that is to say, that, in the name of the Prince, I am showing you the city.' I had no answer to that, so I let the matter rest.

We drove up the streets, where the lava which destroyed most of the city in 1669 has remained visible to this day. The solidified stream of fire had been used like any other stone; streets had been marked out on it and some even built. Remembering what passions had been aroused before I left Germany by the dispute over the volcanic nature of basalt, I chipped off a piece; it is magma without any doubt. I did this in several other places so as to obtain a variety of specimens.

If the native inhabitants did not love their part of the country and take the trouble, from scientific interest or in hope of gain, to collect everything of note in their local neighbourhoods, the foreigner would long rack his brains to no purpose. The lava dealer in Naples had been of great help to me and now I found a much superior guide in the person of the Cavaliere Gioeni. In his extensive and elegantly displayed collection, I found the lavas of Etna, the basalt from its foot and various metamorphosed rocks, some of which I could recognize. I was received most kindly and shown everything. What I liked best were the zeolites from the stacks which rise out of the sea off the coast near Jaci.

When we asked the Cavaliere how we should go about climbing Etna, he refused even to discuss an enterprise which was so hazardous, especially at this time of year. He

apologized for this and said: 'Most foreign visitors are too apt
to consider the ascent a trifling affair. But we, who are near
neighbours of the mountain, are content if we have reached
the summit twice or thrice in a lifetime, for we never attempt
it except under ideal conditions. Brydone, whose description
first inspired people with a longing for the fiery summit,
never reached it himself. Count Borch leaves the reader in
doubt, but he too only reached a certain altitude, and the
same can be said of many others. At the present moment the
snow stretches too far down and presents insurmountable
obstacles. If you will follow my advice, ride early tomorrow
morning to the foot of Monte Rosso: you will enjoy the most
magnificent view and at the same time see the place where the
lava of 1669 poured down on our unfortunate city. If you are
wise, you will let others tell you about the rest.'

5 May

We took the Cavaliere's good advice and set off early this
morning on mules, turning our heads every so often to look at
the view behind us. After some time we reached the lava
zone. Unsoftened by time, jagged clumps and slabs stared us
in the face, and the mules could only pick their way at
random. On the first high ridge we halted and Kniep made
a sketch of what lay ahead of us – masses of lava in the
foreground, the twin summits of Monte Rosso on the left,
and directly above us the forests of Nicolosi, out of which the
snow-covered and faintly fuming peak emerges. We retraced
our steps a little in order to approach Monte Rosso, which
I climbed. It is nothing but a heap of red volcanic cinders,
ashes and stones. It would have been easy to walk all round
the rim of the crater if a blustering morning wind had not
made every step unsafe; to advance at all, I tried taking off my
overcoat, but then my hat was in danger of being blown into
the crater at any moment and myself after it. I sat down to
pull myself together and survey the landscape, but this did not
help much, as the gale was blowing directly from the east. A

magnificent panorama was spread out far and wide below me.
The whole coast from Messina to Syracuse with its curves
and bays lay open to my view or only slightly hidden by
coastal hills. I descended, half dazed, to find Kniep sitting
in a sheltered place where he had made good use of his time.
With delicate strokes he had fixed on paper what the fury of
the wind had hardly allowed me to see, let alone imprint on
my memory.

On re-entering the jaws of the Golden Lion, we found the
waiter. We had had great difficulty in preventing him from
accompanying us. He now commended our decision to
abandon the ascent of the peak, but kept pressing us to hire
a boat the next day and visit the stacks of Jaci. No more
delightful an excursion could be made from Catania. We
would take food and drink and cooking utensils with us.
His wife would be only too glad to take care of everything.
He recalled the happy occasion when some English people
hired a second boat to accompany them and play music. They
had a hilarious time.

To me, the stacks of Jaci were a great temptation, for I was
dying to chip off for myself some of those beautiful zeolites
I had seen in Gioeni's collection. After all, we could decline
his wife's offer and still make a brief visit. But the Englishman's ghostly warning triumphed; I gave up the zeolites and
felt inordinately proud of my self-control.

6 May

Our clerical guide did not fail us, but took us to see some
ancient architectural remains, water tanks, a *naumachia* and
other ruins of a similar sort.

These, to be honest, demand of the spectator a considerable talent for imaginative reconstruction. Owing to the
frequent destruction of the city by lava, earthquake and war,
they are sunk in the ground or completely buried, so that only
a professional expert can derive any pleasure or instruction
from them.

The Abbé dissuaded us from paying the Prince a second visit, and we parted with cordial expressions of mutual gratitude and good will.

Taormina, 7 May

Thank goodness, everything we saw today has been sufficiently described already. Furthermore, Kniep has decided to spend the whole day up here sketching.

After climbing the steep cliffs near the sea, one reaches two summits connected by a half-circle. Whatever shape it may have had originally, Art has assisted Nature to build this semicircle which held the amphitheatre audience. Walls and other structures of brick were added to provide the necessary passages and halls. The proscenium was built in a diagonal at the foot of the tiered half-circle, stretching from cliff to cliff to complete a stupendous work of Art and Nature.

If one sits down where the topmost spectators sat, one has to admit that no audience in any other theatre ever beheld such a view. Citadels stand perched on higher cliffs to the right; down below lies the town. Though these buildings are of a much later date, similar ones probably stood in the same places in older days. Straight ahead one sees the long ridge of Etna, to the left the coast line as far as Catania or even Syracuse, and the whole panorama is capped by the huge, fuming, fiery mountain, the look of which, tempered by distance and atmosphere, is, however, more friendly than forbidding.

If one turns round, beyond the passages which ran behind the spectators' backs one sees the two cliffs and, between them, the road winding its way to Messina, the sea dotted with rocks and reefs, and in the far distance the coast of Calabria. I had to strain my eyes to distinguish it from a bank of gently rising clouds.

We descended into the theatre and stayed for a while among the ruins, which a talented architect should attempt to restore, at least on paper.

When we tried to beat a downhill path for ourselves through the gardens into the town, we discovered what an impenetrable barrier a hedge of closely planted cacti can be. You look through gaps in the tangle of leaves and think you can make your way through them, but the prickly spikes on their edges are a painful obstacle; you step on a colossal leaf, expecting it to support you, but it collapses and you fall into the arms of the next plant. But we extricated ourselves from this labyrinth at last and had a quick meal in the town. We could not tear ourselves away until after sunset. To watch this landscape, so remarkable in every aspect, slowly sinking into the darkness, was an incredibly beautiful sight.

On the seashore below Taormina, 8 May

I cannot praise Kniep enough or the good fortune which sent him to me. He has relieved me of a burden which would have been intolerable and set me free to follow my natural bent. He has just left to sketch all that we saw yesterday. He will have to sharpen his pencils again and again, and I cannot imagine how he is going to finish the job. I might have seen it all again too, and at first I was tempted to go with him, but in the end decided to stay where I was. Like a bird that wants to build its nest, I searched for a cranny and perched myself on the branches of an orange tree in a mean, abandoned peasant's garden. It may sound a bit strange to speak of sitting on the branch of an orange tree, but it is quite natural if you know that, when an orange tree is left to itself, it starts putting out branches above its roots which in time become real boughs.

There I was soon lost in fancy, thinking about a plot for my *Nausicaa*,* a dramatic condensation of the *Odyssey*. I think this can be done, provided one never loses sight of the difference between a drama and an epic.

Kniep has come back in high spirits with two enormous drawings which he is going to elaborate for me in everlasting memory of this wonderful day.

* One act and some fragments of *Nausicaa* were published in 1827.

I must not forget to mention that we are looking down from a small terrace, looking over this beautiful seashore, seeing roses and hearing nightingales, which, we are told, sing for six months without stopping.

IN RETROSPECT

Thanks to the companionship and activity of a talented artist and to my own humble and sporadic efforts, I knew that, after this trip was over, I would possess permanent records of it in the form of sketches and finished drawings of all the most interesting landscapes. Consequently, I was all the more ready to yield to a desire of mine which had been growing ever stronger: namely, to take the magnificent scenery which surrounded me, the sea, the islands, the harbours, and bring it to life in noble poetic images, to compose in their presence and out of them a more homogenous and harmonious work than any I had written before.

The purity of the sky, the tang of the sea air, the haze which, as it were, dissolved mountains, sky and sea into one element – all these were food for my thoughts. As I wandered about in the beautiful Public Gardens of Palermo, between hedges and oleander, through orange trees and lemon trees heavy with fruit, and other trees and bushes unknown to me, I took this blessed strangeness to my heart. There could be no better commentary on the *Odyssey*, I felt, than just this setting. I bought a copy and read it with passionate interest. It fired me with the desire to produce a work of my own, and very soon I could think of nothing else: in other words, I became obsessed with the idea of treating the story of Nausicaa as a tragedy.

I cannot say now what I would have made of it, but I quickly had the plot clearly worked out in my mind. Its essence was this: to present Nausicaa as an admirable young woman with many suitors, but no inclination towards any one of them, so that she has refused them all. This indifference is overcome by a mysterious stranger whom she meets, and she compromises herself by a premature declaration of her love, a tragic situation in the highest sense.

A wealth of secondary motives was to have added interest to this simple fable, and there was to have been a sea-island quality about the imagery and atmosphere to give a pervading tone to the whole play.

The action, as I planned it, was to have gone as follows:

Act I. Nausicaa is playing with a ball with her maids. The unexpected encounter takes place. Her hesitation about accompanying the stranger personally into the city is the first sign that she feels drawn towards him.

Act II. The palace of Alcinous. The characters of the suitors are revealed. The act ends with the entrance of Ulysses.

Act III. The importance of the adventurer is brought out. I planned to produce an interesting artistic effect with a narration in dialogue of his adventures. Each listener responds to this with a different emotion. As the narration proceeds, passions run higher, and the strong attraction which Nausicaa feels for the stranger is at last revealed in action and counter-action.

Act IV. Off stage, Ulysses gives proof of his prowess, while on stage, the women give free expression to their sympathies, hopes and tender sentiments. Nausicaa cannot control her feelings and compromises herself irrevocably before her own people. Ulysses, the half guilty, half innocent cause of this, is finally forced to announce his determination to depart.

Act V. Nothing is left for the good girl but to kill herself.

There was nothing in this composition which I could not have drawn from life. I too was a wanderer; I too was in danger of arousing sympathies which, though not perhaps of the kind which end in tragedy, could still be painful and destructive; I too was far from my native land, in circumstances where one entertains an audience with glowing descriptions of distant objects, adventures while travelling, incidents in one's life; where one is considered a demigod by the young and a braggart by the sedate; where one experiences many an undeserved favour, many an unexpected obstacle. It was facts like these which gave the plot its particular fascination for me. I spent all my days in Palermo and most of the time I was travelling through Sicily dreaming about it. On this classic soil I felt in such a poetic mood that I hardly suffered from all the discomforts, but could take in all I saw and experienced and enshrine it in my heart for ever.

As is my good or bad habit, I wrote down little or nothing but worked out most of it in detail in my head. Later a hundred distractions prevented me from going on with it, until, today, I can only recall it as a fleeting memory.

8 May. On the way to Messina

On our left we have high limestone cliffs. As we go on, they become more colourful and form beautiful coves. A type of rock appears which one might call a schist or a conglomerate. In the brooks we begin to find particles of granite. The river Nisi and the brooks further on carry mica. The yellow apples of solanum and the red blossoms of the oleander strike a cheerful note in the landscape.

9 May

Struggling against a strong east wind, we rode between the surging sea on our right and the cliffs from which we looked down yesterday on our left. All day we battled with water. We crossed numerous brooks, the largest of which, the Nisi, bears the honorary title of river; but all these were easier to deal with than the raging sea, which in many places swept across the road, dashed against the cliffs and doused us as it receded. But the magnificence of the spectacle made up for the discomfort.

There was no lack of geological interest. Weathering causes enormous rockfalls from the limestone cliffs. The softer parts of these are ground away by the action of the waves and only the more solid conglomerates are left on the beach, which is covered with colourful pebbles of iron pyrites. We picked up several specimens.

Messina, 10 May

We arrived in Messina and, since we did not know of any other place to stay, we agreed to pass the first night in the quarters of our *vetturino*, with the understanding that we would look for better accommodation in the morning. The immediate result of this decision was that we got a terrifying picture of a devastated city.* For a good quarter of an hour we rode on our mules through ruin after ruin till we came to our inn. This was the only house which had been rebuilt, and from its upper floor we looked out over a wasteland of jagged ruins. Outside the premises of this sort of farmstead, there was no sign of man or beast. The silence during the night was uncanny. The doors could neither be locked nor barred, and there was as little provision for human guests as in any other stable.

In spite of this, we slept peacefully on the innkeeper's mattress, which our *vetturino*, efficient as ever, had wheedled him into surrendering.

11 May

Today we bade farewell to our valiant *vetturino* and rewarded him for his conscientious services with a liberal gratuity. We parted in friendship, after he had found us a local factotum who was to take us at once to the best inn and show us the sights of Messina. Our host of last night was eager to get rid of us as quickly as possible and lent a helping hand with the transport of our baggage to a pleasant lodging nearer the living part of the city, that is to say, outside it. After the enormous disaster in which twelve thousand people were

---

* Messina had been destroyed by an earthquake in 1783.

killed, there were no houses left in Messina for the remaining thirty thousand. Most of the buildings had collapsed and the cracked walls of the rest made them unsafe. So a barrack town was hastily erected in a large meadow north of the city. To get a picture of this, imagine yourself walking across the *Römerberg* in Frankfurt or the market square in Leipzig during the Fair. All the booths and workshops are open to the street. Only a few of the larger buildings have entrances which can be closed, and even these rarely are, because those who live in them spend most of their time out of doors. They have been living under these conditions for three years now, and this life in shacks, huts and tents, even, has had a definite influence on their characters. The horror of that tremendous event, the fear of its repetition, drive them to take their delight in the pleasures of the moment. The dread of a new catastrophe was revived about three weeks ago, on April the twenty-first, when a noticeable tremor shook the grounds. We were shown a little church which was crowded with people at the time. A number of them, it is said, have not yet recovered from the shock.

A kindly consul volunteered to take care of us and acted as our guide; and, in a world of ruins, this was something to be grateful for. When he heard that we wished to sail soon, he introduced us to the captain of a French merchant vessel, who was about to sail for Naples – an opportunity which was doubly desirable, because the white flag would be a protection against pirates.

We had just been telling our guide that we would like to see the interior of one of the larger single-storey barracks, and get a picture of the furnishings and improvised way of life, when we were joined by a friendly man who introduced himself as a teacher of French. After we had finished our walk, the consul told him of our wish and asked him to show us his house and introduce us to his family.

We entered the hut, which was built and roofed with planks. It looked exactly like one of those booths at a fair, where wild animals and other curiosities are exhibited for money. The timberwork was visible and a green curtain separated off the front part, which had no flooring but seemed to have been beaten flat like a threshing floor. A few chairs and tables were the only furniture, and the only light came through chance chinks in the boards. We talked for a while and I was looking at the green curtain and the rafters above it when, all of a sudden, the heads of two pretty girls with black curls and inquisitive black eyes appeared from behind the curtain. When they saw they had been observed, they vanished in a flash, but, at the consul's request, they reappeared as soon as they had had time to get properly dressed. With their graceful figures and colourful dresses, they looked very elegant against the green curtain. From their questions it was easy to guess that they took us for legendary beings from another world, and our answers only confirmed them in their endearing delusion. The consul painted an amusing picture of our fabulous appearance in Messina. The conversation was very pleasant and we found it hard to leave. It wasn't till we had closed the door behind us that we realized we had never seen the inner rooms, for our interest in the construction of the hut had been driven out of our minds by the charm of its inhabitants.

12 May

The consul told me, among other things, that it would be expedient, if not absolutely necessary, for me to pay my respects to the Governor, because he was an odd old man who was capable of doing others a lot of good or a lot of harm, depending upon his mood or his prejudice. The consul would get into his good graces by introducing an eminent foreign visitor, and the visitor could never know when he might not need the support of such a personage in some way or other. So, to oblige my friend, I went.

When we came into the antechamber, we heard a tremendous racket going on in the room beyond. A runner, gesticulating like a Pulcinella, whispered in the consul's ear:

'An evil day! A dangerous moment!' Nevertheless, we entered and found the aged Governor sitting at a table near the window with his back to us. Before him was a pile of old letters and documents, from which he was cutting off the blank sheets with great deliberation, demonstrating thereby his love of economy. While engaged in this peaceful occupation he was bawling horrible insults and curses at a respectable-looking man who, to judge from his clothes, might have some connexion with the Knights of Malta. He defended himself quietly but firmly, though he was given little opportunity to speak.

The Governor apparently regarded him as a suspicious person, because he had entered and left the country several times without the necessary permit. In refutation of this, he produced his passports and spoke of his well-known position in Naples, but it did no good. The Governor went on cutting up his old letters, carefully putting the blank sheets on one side, and stormed away without stopping for breath. Besides the two of us, there were some twelve persons there, standing in a wide circle and witnessing this combat of beasts. They probably envied us our advantageous position near the door, for it looked as if at any moment, the irascible old man might raise his crooked stick and strike out. The consul's face fell; but I was comforted by the droll runner beside me, who, every time I looked round, pulled all kinds of faces to reassure me that matters were not very serious.

And indeed, the violent argument was finally settled quite mildly, with the Governor declaring that, though there was nothing to prevent him from arresting the accused and letting him cool his heels in prison, he had decided to let him go this time. He might stay in Messina for a certain number of days, but he was never to return. Without moving a muscle of his face, the accused took his leave, and bowed to all those present, and especially to us, who had to make way for him as he went out by the door. The Governor turned and was about to shout some more abuse after him, when he became aware of our presence. He controlled himself immediately, made a sign to the consul, and we both approached.

We saw a man of advanced years, who kept his head bent, but looked out with penetrating dark eyes from under his grey and bushy eyebrows. He now looked a very different person from what he had the moment before. He invited me to sit down beside him and, without interrupting his occupation, asked me a number of questions, which I did my best to answer. Finally he said that, as long as I stayed in Messina, I was invited to be a guest at his table. The consul was even more pleased than I was, since he knew better what danger we had escaped. He flew down the stairs, and I had lost all desire to venture a second time into this lion's den.

13 May

We woke on a clear sunny morning and in much pleasanter lodgings, but we still found ourselves in this accursed city.

There can be no more dreary sight in the world than the so-called Palazzata, a crescent of palazzi which encloses about a mile of the harbour waterfront. Originally they were all four-storey stone buildings. Several façades are still intact up to the coping; in other cases one, two or three floors have collapsed, so that this string of once splendid palazzi now looks revoltingly gap-toothed and pierced with holes, for the blue sky looks through nearly all the windows. The rooms inside are all in ruins.

There is a reason for this. The grandiose project was begun by the rich. The less well-to-do wished their houses to look as impressive from the street, so they concealed their old houses, which were built of rubble cemented with lime, behind new façades of quarried stone blocks. Such structures were unsafe in any case, and when there was an earthquake, they were bound to collapse. There are many stories of miraculous escapes which illustrate this. An inhabitant of one such building, for example, at the very moment of the catastrophe had just stepped into the deep enclosure of a window. The whole house collapsed behind him, but he was left safe and sound up there, waiting to be liberated from his airy prison.

That it was shoddy building, due to the lack of decent stone in the neighbourhood, which was the main reason for the almost total destruction of the city, is confirmed by the fact that the few buildings which were solidly constructed survived. The Jesuit college and church, which were built of quarried stone, are still intact. Be that as it may, Messina is a very disagreeable sight and reminded me of that primitive age when Sicels and Siculians quitted this unquiet soil to settle on the west coast of the island.

We spent the whole morning looking round, then went to our inn and ate a frugal meal. We were still sitting there together, feeling very content, when the consul's servant rushed in and breathlessly informed me that the Governor had sent people to hunt for me all over the city because he had invited me to dinner and I had failed to come. The consul, he said, implored me to go immediately, regardless of whether I had dined or not, or forgotten the hour or ignored it on purpose. Now I realized how incredibly reckless of me it had been, in my joy at escaping the first time, to dismiss from my mind the Cyclops' invitation.

The servant would brook no delay and his argument was urgent and convincing: the despot would take his fury out on the consul and any of his fellow countrymen who might be staying in Messina. I made myself tidy, plucked up my courage and followed my guide, secretly invoking Odysseus, my patron, and asking him to intercede for me with Pallas Athene. When I arrived at the lion's den, the comical runner I had seen the first time took me into a large banquet hall where about forty people were sitting at an oval table in absolute silence. He led me to an empty chair on the Governor's right. After bowing to my host and his guests, I gave as my excuse for failing to arrive on time the vast size of the city and the local method of counting the hours to which I was not yet accustomed and had been several times misled by.

The Governor glared at me and said that in a foreign country one should learn its local customs and behave accordingly. I parried this by saying that I always tried to learn them, but it had been my experience that in a new place and unfamiliar circumstances one was apt, with the best will in the world, to make mistakes, for which one could only plead in excuse the fatigue of travelling, the distraction of seeing so many new things, and the preoccupation with finding decent lodging or making preparations for the next stage of one's journey. He asked me how long I intended to stay in Messina. 'I should like', I replied, 'to stay a very long time, so that I might show my gratitude for your kindness by an exact observance of all your orders and regulations.' After a pause, he asked what I had actually seen in Messina. I gave him a brief account of this morning and added that what I had admired most of all was the tidiness and cleanliness of the streets. This was true. The rubble had been piled up within the areas enclosed by the ruined walls and a row of stone blocks set up against the houses to keep the middle of the streets free and open to traffic. Nor was it a lie when I flattered the worthy man by telling him that all the inhabitants of Messina gratefully admitted that they owed this benefit to him. 'Do they admit it?' he growled. 'They have yelled long enough about the severity of the measures we were forced to take for their own good.' Then I talked about the wise forethought of the government, of those higher purposes which are only recognized and appreciated later, and so forth. He asked if I had seen the Jesuit church and, when I said no, proposed to let me see it and everything it contained.

During our conversation, which went on with hardly a pause, I observed that the rest of the company were sitting in utter silence and without moving except to put food into their mouths. And so they remained. When dinner was over and coffee served, they stood along the walls like wax dolls. I went up to the chaplain who was to show me the church, and tried to thank him in advance for his kind offices; but he was evasive and said that he was only carrying out His

Excellency's orders. Then I addressed a young foreigner standing next to him. Although he was a Frenchman, he too seemed ill at ease and was as petrified and speechless as all the others, among whom I recognized several who had anxiously looked on at yesterday's scene with the Maltese Knight.

The Governor left, and soon after the chaplain said it was time for us to go. I followed him while the others sneaked silently away. He brought me to the west door of the Jesuit church, which, in the familiar architectural style adopted by these fathers, soars into the air with impressive pomp. We were received by the verger, who invited us to enter, but the chaplain stopped me, saying we must wait for the Governor. Presently the latter arrived in his coach, which drew up in a neighbouring square. He beckoned to us and the three of us joined him at the door of the coach. He ordered the verger, not only to show me every part of the church, but also to give me a detailed history of the altars and other donations; further, he was to unlock the sacristies and show me everything of interest which they contained. I was a man, he said, whom he wished to honour, so that I might have good reason, when I got home, to speak of Messina in the highest terms. Then, turning to me with a smile – in so far as those features were capable of one – he said: 'Be sure to appear at dinner at the proper hour, and you will be welcome so long as you are here.' I hardly had time to thank him with proper respect before his coach rolled away.

From now on the chaplain became more cheerful and we entered the church. The castellan, as one may be permitted to call him in this deconsecrated, enchanted palace, had just begun to carry out the orders he had been so peremptorily given, when Kniep and the consul rushed into the empty shrine and embraced me with loud exclamations of joy at seeing me again, for they thought I must have been arrested. They had been waiting in mortal anxiety when the nimble runner, amply rewarded no doubt by the consul, came to tell them of the happy ending to my adventure. The antics and gestures with which he told the story had cheered them up immensely. After hearing of the Governor's courtesy with regard to the church, they had set off at once to look for me.

By this time we were standing in front of the high altar, while the ancient treasures were explained to us. Columns of lapis lazuli, fluted, as it were, with gilded bronze bars; pilasters and panels, inlaid after the Florentine manner; superb Sicilian agates in profusion – everything combined again and again with bronze and gilt.

Now a strange contrapuntal fugue began, with Kniep and the consul reciting the complications caused by my adventure on the one side, and the verger reciting the history of the treasures on the other, each party engrossed in its subject and ignoring its rival. For my part, I had the twofold pleasure of feeling how lucky my escape had been, and of seeing the minerals of Sicily, which I had so often examined in the mountains they came from, employed for an architectural purpose.

My knowledge of the various substances out of which this splendour was composed helped me to discover that the so-called lapis lazuli of the columns was actually only calcara, but of a beautiful colour I had never seen before, and assembled with superb skill. A great quantity of this material must have been needed in order to select pieces of uniform colour, not to mention the highly important labour of cutting, grinding and polishing. But to the Jesuits, was anything impossible?

The consul continued to enlighten me about the danger with which I had been threatened: the Governor was annoyed with himself because, at my first visit, I had witnessed his violent behaviour towards the quasi-Maltese. He had therefore made up his mind to show me special honour, but, by failing to appear at dinnertime, I had upset his plan at the very outset. After waiting quite a time, the despot had sat down at his table without concealing his impatience and displeasure, so that his guests were in terror of having to assist at another scene, either when I appeared or after dinner.

Meanwhile the verger was trying to get a word in edgewise. He opened the secret repositories, which were well proportioned and tastefully, even ornately, decorated, where several portable sacred vessels were kept, shapely and polished like everything else. I could see no precious metal or any works of art from ancient or modern times that were authentic.

Our Italian–German fugue – the chaplain and verger psalmodizing in the first tongue, Kniep and the consul in the second – was drawing to a close, when we were joined by a member of the Governor's suite whom I had seen at the dinner table. This looked like more trouble, especially when he offered to accompany me to the port and show me some points of interest which were normally inaccessible to strangers.

My friends exchanged glances, but I was not going to let myself be deterred from going off alone with him. After some trivial conversation, I began to speak more confidentially. When I was sitting at the Governor's table, I told him, I had not failed to notice that several members of the silent guests were trying, with friendly signs, to assure me that I was not a stranger among strangers, but among friends, even perhaps among brothers,* and had nothing to worry about. 'I consider it my duty', I said, 'to thank you and I beg you to convey my gratitude to the others.' He replied: 'We tried to reassure you because, knowing the temperament of our master, we were fairly certain you had nothing to fear. An explosion like that with the Maltese is very rare. After one, the old man usually blames himself, watches his temper and is content to perform the duties of his office calmly and coolly, until some unexpected incident takes him by surprise, and he explodes again.'

My honest companion added that nothing would please him and his friends better than to make my closer acquaintance. I would therefore oblige them if I would reveal my identity, and this evening would be an excellent opportunity. I politely evaded this request by asking him to forgive what must seem to him a caprice, but, on my travels, I wished to be

---

* Brothers, i.e. Freemasons. Goethe was one.

treated simply as a human being; if, as such, I could inspire confidence and gain sympathy, it would make me very happy, but many reasons forbade me from entering into other relations.

I did not try very hard to convince him, for I did not dare tell him my real reason. I was interested to learn, though, how under a despotic government men of innocence and good will had banded together for the protection of foreigners and themselves. I did not hide from him the fact that I knew much about their relations with other German travellers, and I spoke at length about the laudable goals at which they aimed. He grew more and more puzzled at this mixture of confidence and reserve and tried in every possible way to make me lift my incognito. He did not succeed, partly because, having escaped one danger, I had no intention of needlessly exposing myself to another, and partly because I knew very well that the ideas of these honest islanders were so different from mine that a closer acquaintance would afford them neither pleasure nor consolation.

This evening we spent several hours with the sympathetic consul who has helped me so much. He explained how the scene with the Maltese had come about. Though not actually an adventurer, this man was a rolling stone. The Governor came from a great family, and his ability and achievements were highly respected and appreciated; on the other hand, he had a reputation for unlimited caprice, violent temper and an adamant obstinacy. A despot by nature, and full of suspicions, as old men often are, he hated the sort of person who keeps moving from place to place, and believed they were all simply spies. The 'redcoat' had crossed his path just at a time when, after a considerable period of calm, he felt the need to lose his temper in order to relieve his liver.

Messina, and at sea, 13 May

We both woke with the same feeling: we were cross with ourselves for having let our first disagreeable impression of

Messina make us so impatient to depart that we were now committed to the captain of the French merchant vessel. After the lucky outcome of my adventure with the Governor, my meeting with the upright man to whom I would only have had to make myself known, and a visit to my banker, who was living in the country in very pleasant surroundings, I had every reason to believe I would have enjoyed myself if I had arranged to stay longer. As for Kniep, he had made the acquaintance of some pretty girls, and was praying that the unfavourable wind, normally so odious, would go on blowing as long as possible.

Meanwhile we sat in discomfort; we could not unpack anything because we had to be ready to leave at any moment. Before noon the summons came and we hurried on board. Among the crowd gathered on the shore, we found our good consul and said goodbye to him with grateful hearts. The yellow-coated runner also pressed forward to get his *douceur*. I gave it him and instructed him to inform his master of our departure and apologize for my absence from his table. 'He who sails away is excused,' he cried, turned a somersault and disappeared.

As we moved slowly away from the shore, we were entranced by the wonderful view – the crescent-shaped Palazzata, the citadel, the mountains rising behind the city. On the other side of the straits we could see the shore of Calabria. While we were enjoying the unlimited vistas, we noticed a commotion on the water at some distance to our left and, somewhat nearer on our right, a rock rising out of the sea; one was Charybdis, the other Scylla. Because of the considerable distance in nature between these two objects which the poet has placed so close to one another, people have accused poets of fibbing. What they fail to take into account is that the human imagination always pictures the objects it considers significant as taller and narrower than they really are, for this gives them more character, importance and dignity. A thousand times I have heard people complain that some object they had known only from a description was disappointing when seen in reality, and the reason was always the same. Imagination is to reality what poetry is to prose: the former will always think of objects as massive and vertical, the latter will always try to extend them horizontally. The landscape painters of the sixteenth century, when contrasted with those of our own times, offer the most striking example of this. A drawing by Jodokus Momper set beside a sketch by Kniep would illustrate the difference perfectly. We spent the time talking about such matters, since, even for Kniep, the coastlines were not attractive enough to draw, though he had come prepared to do so.

Our boat was very different from the Neapolitan corvette. I was beginning to feel seasick and my condition was not relieved by a comfortable privacy as it had been on our previous passage. However, the common cabin was at least large enough to hold several people and there were plenty of good mattresses. As before, I assumed a horizontal position, while Kniep looked after me and fed me with red wine and good bread. In the condition I was in, our whole Sicilian trip did not present itself to me in a very rosy light. After all, what had we seen but the hopeless struggle of men with the violence of Nature, the malice and treachery of their times, and the rancours of their own rival factions. The Carthaginians, the Greeks, the Romans, and countless peoples after them built and destroyed. Selinunt was systematically laid waste. Two thousand years have not succeeded in demolishing the temples of Girgenti; Catania and Messina were destroyed in a few hours, if not a few minutes.

But I did not allow myself to become too much obsessed with these seasick reflections of a person tossed about by the waves of life.

At sea, 13 May

My hopes that the voyage would be quicker this time and that I would recover from my seasickness sooner did not materialize. At Kniep's suggestion, I tried several times to go on deck, but any enjoyment of the beautiful scenes was denied; only an occasional incident made me forget my dizziness. The sky was overcast with a haze of white clouds. Though we could not see the face of the sun, its light filtered through the haze and lit up the sea, which was an unimaginable blue. We were accompanied all the time by a school of dolphins, swimming and leaping. To them, evidently, from below and from a distance, our floating house appeared as a black point, which they took for prey or some other welcome food. The crew, at any rate, treated them as enemies, not escorts; they harpooned one, but did not haul it on board.

The wind remained unfavourable and our boat had constantly to change its course. The passengers were growing impatient, and some of the more knowledgeable declared that neither the captain nor the helmsman knew his job, that the former might do well as a merchant and the latter as a simple sailor, but neither was qualified to guarantee the safety of so many valuable lives and goods.

I begged these people, who no doubt meant well, to keep their misgivings a secret. The number of passengers was considerable and among them were women and children of various ages. Everybody had crowded aboard the French vessel with only one thought in their minds – the white flag would protect them against pirates. I warned the grumblers that their mistrust and alarm, if known, would cause great distress to those who had so far put their trust in a colourless piece of cloth without any insignia.

As a specific talisman, this white pennon between sky and sea is very curious. On occasions of departure, those who are leaving and those who are left behind wave to each other with white handkerchiefs, evoking by this sign mutual feelings of friendship and affection which are seldom felt so deeply as at the moment of separation. Here, in this simple flag, the basic idea behind this symbol is hallowed. It is as if someone should fix his handkerchief to the mast to proclaim to the whole world that a friend is coming across the sea.

From time to time I refreshed myself with bread and wine – to the annoyance of the captain, who demanded that I should eat what I had paid for. I was able at last to sit on deck and occasionally take part in the conversation. Kniep succeeded in cheering me up, not, as on the corvette, by boasting of the excellent meals, but by telling me how lucky I was to have lost my appetite.

14 May

The afternoon passed without our having entered the Gulf of Naples. On the contrary, we were steadily drawn in a westerly direction; the boat moved further and further away from Cape Minerva and nearer and nearer to Capri.

Everybody was glum and impatient, except Kniep and myself. Looking at the world with the eyes of painters, we were perfectly content to enjoy the sunset, which was the most magnificent spectacle we had seen during the whole voyage. Cape Minerva and its adjoining ranges lay before us in a display of brilliant colours. The cliffs stretching to the south had already taken on a bluish tint. From the Cape to Sorrento the whole coast was lit up. Above Vesuvius towered an enormous smoke cloud, from which a long streak trailed away to the east, suggesting that a violent eruption was in progress. Capri rose abruptly on our left and, through the haze, we could see the outlines of its precipices.

The wind had dropped completely, and the glittering sea, showing scarcely a ripple, lay before us like a limpid pond under the cloudless sky. Kniep said what a pity it was that no skill with colours, however great, could reproduce this harmony and that not even the finest English pencils, wielded by the most practised hand, could draw these contours. I was convinced, on the contrary, that even a much poorer memento than this able artist would produce would be very valuable in the future, and urged him to make an attempt at it. He followed my advice and produced a most accurate drawing which he later coloured, which shows that pictorial representation can achieve the impossible.

With equally rapt attention we watched the transition from evening to night. Ahead of us Capri was now in total darkness. The cloud above Vesuvius and its trail began to glow, and the longer we looked the brighter it grew, till a considerable part of the sky was lit up as if by summer lightning.

We had been so absorbed in enjoying these sights that we had not noticed that we were threatened with a serious disaster; but the commotion among the passengers did not leave us long in doubt. Those who had more experience of happenings at sea than we bitterly blamed the captain and his helmsman, saying that, thanks to their incompetence, they had not only missed the entrance to the straits but were now endangering the lives of the passengers, the cargo and everything else confided to their care. We asked why they were so anxious, for we did not see why there could be any cause to be afraid when the sea was so calm. But it was precisely the calm which worried them: they saw we had already entered the current which encircles Capri and by the peculiar wash of the waves draws everything slowly and irresistibly towards the sheer rock face, where there is no ledge to offer the slightest foothold and no bay to promise safety.

The news appalled us. Though the darkness prevented us from seeing the approaching danger, we could see that the boat, rolling and pitching, was moving nearer to the rocks, which loomed ever darker ahead. A faint afterglow was still spread over the sea. Not the least breath of wind was stirring. Everyone held up handkerchiefs and ribbons, but there was no sign of the longed-for breeze. The tumult among the passengers grew louder and louder. The women and children knelt on the deck or lay huddled together, not in order to pray, but because the deck space was too cramped to let them move about. The men, with their thoughts ever on help and rescue, raved, and stormed against the captain. They now attacked him for everything they had silently criticized during the whole voyage – the miserable accommodation, the outrageous charges, the wretched food and his behaviour. Actually, he had not been unkind, but very reserved; he had never explained his actions to anyone and even last night he had maintained a stubborn silence about his manoeuvres. Now they called him and his helmsman mercenary adventurers who knew nothing about navigation, but had got hold of a boat out of sheer greed, and were now by their incompetent bungling about to bring to grief the lives of all those in their care. The captain remained silent and still seemed to be preoccupied with saving the boat. But I, who all my life have hated anarchy worse than death, could keep silent no longer. I stepped forward and addressed the crowd, with almost the same equanimity I had shown in facing the 'Birds' of Malcesine. I pointed out to them that, at such a moment, their shouting would only confuse the ears and minds of those upon whom our safety depended, and make it impossible for them to think or communicate with one another. 'As for you,' I exclaimed, 'examine your hearts and then say your prayers to the Mother of God, for she alone can decide whether she will intercede with her Son, that He may do for you what He once did for His apostles on the storm-swept sea of Tiberias. Our Lord was sleeping, the waves were already breaking into the boat, but when the desperate and helpless men woke Him, He immediately commanded the wind to rest, and now, if it should be His will, He can command the wind to stir.'

These words had an excellent effect. One woman, with whom I had had some conversation about moral and spiritual matters, exclaimed: '*Ah, il Barlamè. Benedetto il Barlamè,*'* and as they were all on their knees anyway, they actually began to say their litanies with more than usual fervour. They could do this with greater peace of mind, because the crew were now trying another expedient, which could at least be seen and understood by all. They lowered the pinnace, which could hold from six to eight men, fastened it to the ship by a long rope, and tried, by rowing hard, to tow the ship after them.

* Il Barlamè. Probably St Barlaam, a figure in a Byzantine legend.

But their very efforts seemed to increase the counter-pull of the current. For some reason or other, the pinnace was suddenly dragged backwards towards the ship and the long towing rope described a bow like a whiplash when the driver cracks it. So this hope vanished.

Prayers alternated with lamentations and the situation grew more desperate, when some goatherds on the rocks above us whose fires we had seen for some time shouted with hollow voices that there was a ship below about to founder. Much that they cried was unintelligible, but some passengers, familiar with their dialect, took these cries to mean that they were gleefully looking forward to the booty they would fish out of the sea the next morning. Any consoling doubt as to whether our ship was really dangerously near the rocks was soon banished when we saw the sailors taking up long poles with which, if the worst came to the worst, they could keep fending the ship off the rocks. Of course, if the poles broke, all would be lost. The violence of the surf seemed to be increasing, the ship tossed and rolled more than ever; as a result, my seasickness returned and I had to retire to the cabin below. I lay down half dazed but with a certain feeling of contentment, due, perhaps, to the sea of Tiberias; for, in my mind's eye, I saw clearly before me the etching from the Merian Bible.* It gave me proof that all impressions of a sensory-moral nature are strongest when a man is thrown completely on his own resources.

How long I had been lying in this kind of half-sleep I could not tell, but I was roused out of it by a tremendous noise over my head. My ears told me that it came from dragging heavy ropes about the deck, and this gave me some hope that the sails were being hoisted. Shortly afterwards Kniep came down in a hurry to tell me we were safe. A very gentle breeze had sprung up; they had just been struggling to hoist the sails, and he himself had not neglected to lend a hand. We had, he

* A folio Bible after Luther, illustrated by the Swiss engraver Matthaeus Merian (1627).

said, visibly moved away from the cliff, and, though we were not yet completely out of the current, there was hope now of escaping from it. On deck everything was quiet again. Presently, several other passengers came to tell me about the lucky turn of events and to lie down themselves.

When I woke on the fourth day of our voyage, I felt refreshed and well, just as I had after the same period during the passage from Naples; so that even on a longer voyage I would probably have paid my tribute with an indisposition lasting three days.

From the upper deck I was pleased to see that the dangerous island was a considerable distance away, and that the course of our ship promised us an entrance into the Gulf, and this soon happened. After such a trying night, we could now admire the same objects in the morning light which had previously delighted us at sunset. Capri had been left behind and the right coast of the Gulf was close ahead of us. We could see the citadels, the town, with Posillipo to the left and the headlands which thrust out into the sea between Procida and Ischia. All the passengers had come on deck. In the foreground there stood a Greek priest, who must have been biased in favour of his native Orient, for when the Neapolitans, who had enthusiastically greeted their glorious homeland, asked him what he thought of Naples compared with Constantinople, he replied in a sad, homesick tone: '*Anche questa è una città!* – This is a city, too.'

In due time we arrived in the harbour, which was buzzing with people as it was the liveliest time of the day. Our trunks and gear had just been unloaded and were standing on the shore, when two porters grabbed them. We had scarcely told them we would be staying at Moriconi's before they ran off with the load as if it were loot, and we had some difficulty keeping track of them through the crowded streets and across the square. Kniep carried his portfolio under his arm so that the drawings at least would be saved if the porters robbed us of all which the surging waves had spared.

NAPLES

TO HERDER

HERE I am again, dear friends, safe and sound. My journey across Sicily was quick and easy, and when I get home, you shall judge for yourselves how well I have used my eyes. My old habit of sticking to the objective and concrete has given me an ability to read things at sight, so to speak, and I am happy to think that I now carry in my soul a picture of Sicily, that unique and beautiful island, which is clear, authentic and complete. There is nothing else I want to see in the south, especially since yesterday, when I revisited Paestum, the last vision I shall take with me on my way north, and perhaps the greatest. The central temple is, in my opinion, better than anything Sicily has left to show.

The sea and the islands gave me both joy and pain. I am satisfied with the results of my journey, but I must save the details for my return. Even in Naples, I find it impossible to collect my thoughts, though I hope I shall be able now to give you a better description of this city than I did in my earlier letters. On the first of June, unless a higher power prevents me, I shall go to Rome, and at the beginning of July, I plan to leave again. I must see you as soon as possible and am counting the days till we meet. I have accumulated a good deal of material and need the leisure to sort it out and work on it.

I am infinitely grateful to you for all your affection and kindness and all you have done for my writings. We may not see eye to eye on everything, but in all important matters our ways of thinking are as alike as it is possible for two people's to be. If you have made great self-discoveries during the past months, I too have acquired much, and look forward to a happy exchange of ideas.

The more I see of the world, the less hope I have that humanity as a whole will ever become wise and happy. Among the millions of worlds which exist, there may, perhaps, be one which can boast of such a state of affairs, but given the constitution of our world, I see as little hope for us as for the Sicilian in his.

A word about Homer. The scales have fallen from my eyes. His descriptions, his similes, etc., which to us seem merely poetic, are in fact utterly natural though drawn, of course, with an inner comprehension which takes one's breath away. Even when the events he narrates are fabulous and fictitious, they have a naturalness about them which I have never felt so strongly as in the presence of the settings he describes. Let me say briefly what I think about the ancient writers and us moderns. *They* represented things and persons as they are in themselves, *we* usually represent only their subjective effect; *they* depicted the horror, *we* depict horribly; *they* depicted the pleasing, *we* pleasantly, and so on. Hence all the exaggeration, the mannerisms, the false elegance and the bombast of our age. Since, if one aims at producing effects and only effects, one thinks that one cannot make them violent enough. If what I say is not new, I have had vivid occasion to feel its truth.

Now that my mind is stored with images of all these coasts and promontories, gulfs and bays, islands and headlands, rocky cliffs and sandy beaches, wooded hills and gentle pastures, fertile fields, flower gardens, tended trees, festooned vines, mountains wreathed in clouds, eternally serene plains and the all-encircling sea with its ever-changing colours and moods, for the first time the *Odyssey* has become a living truth to me.

I must also tell you confidentially that I am very close to the secret of the reproduction and organization of plants, and that it is the simplest thing imaginable. This climate offers the best possible conditions for making observations. To the main question – where the germ is hidden – I am quite certain I have found the answer; to the others I already see a general solution, and only a few points have still to be formulated more precisely. The Primal Plant is going to be the strangest creature in the world, which Nature herself shall envy me. With this model and the key to it, it will be possible to go on for ever inventing plants and know that their existence is logical; that is to say, if they do not actually exist, they could, for they are not the shadowy phantoms of a vain imagination, but possess an inner necessity and truth. The same law will be applicable to all other living organisms.

18 May

Tischbein has returned to Rome, but I find that he has been doing everything he can to ensure that I shall not feel his absence. He has evidently persuaded his friends that I am a person to be trusted, for they all prove to be friendly, kind and helpful. In my present situation this is especially welcome, because not a day passes without my having to turn to someone for some courtesy or assistance. I am just about to draw up a summary list of all the things I still would like to see; then the little time I have left will decide and dictate how much can really be retrieved.

22 May

Today I had a delightful adventure which set me thinking and deserves to be told.

A lady who had done me several favours during my first stay here invited me to come to her house on the stroke of five: an Englishman wished to meet me because he had something to say to me about my *Werther*.

Six months ago I would certainly have refused, even if I was twice as interested in her as I am: the fact that I accepted told me that the Sicilian journey had had a good influence: in short, I promised to be there.

Unfortunately, the city is so big and there are so many things to see that I was a quarter of an hour late when

I climbed her stairs. I was just about to ring her bell when the door opened and out came a good-looking middle-aged man whom I immediately recognized as an Englishman. He had hardly spotted me before he said: 'You are the author of *Werther.*' I admitted this and apologized for being late. 'I couldn't wait another minute,' said the Englishman. 'What I have to say to you is very short and can just as well be said here, on this rush mat. I don't intend to repeat what you must have heard a thousand times. Indeed, your work has not made as violent an impression on me as it has on others. But every time I think what it must have taken to write it, I am amazed.'

I was about to say a few words of thanks when he cut me short by saying: 'I can't wait a moment longer. I wanted to tell you this personally. I have. Goodbye and good luck!' – and with that he rushed down the stairs. I stood there for a few moments reflecting on the honour of being so lectured, and then rang the bell. The lady was very pleased to hear of our encounter and told me many things about this extraordinary man which were greatly to his credit.

25 May

I am unlikely to see my frivolous little princess again. She has really gone to Sorrento, and, before she left, so her friends told me, she paid me the compliment of abusing me for having preferred the stony desert of Sicily to her company. They also told me more about this odd little person. Born of a noble but impecunious family and bred in a convent, she made up her mind to marry a wealthy old prince. She needed all the less persuasion because, though she was kind-hearted, she was by nature perfectly incapable of love. Finding herself, in spite of her wealth, imprisoned in a life entirely governed by family considerations, her intelligence became her only resource; being restricted in her company and her actions, she could give full rein, at least, to her loose tongue.

I was assured that her actual conduct was irreproachable, but that she seemed to have firmly made up her mind to fly in the face of all convention with her freedom of speech. It was said, jokingly, that no censorship could possibly pass her discourses if they were written down, for everything she uttered was an offence against religion, morals or the state. Many strange and amusing stories are told of her, one of which I shall tell here, though it is slightly improper.

Shortly before the earthquake devastated Calabria, she had retired to an estate there, owned by her husband. Not far from the big house there was a barrack, that is to say, a one-storey wooden house with no foundation, but otherwise papered, furnished and properly equipped.

At the first signs of the earthquake, she took refuge there. She was sitting on the sofa with a small sewing-table in front of her, tatting, and opposite her sat their old house chaplain. Suddenly the ground shook and the whole building tilted towards her, so that the sewing-table and the Abbé rose in the air. 'Fie!' she cried, leaning her head against the sinking wall. 'Is this proper for such a venerable old man? Why, you're behaving as if you wished to fall on top of me. This is against all morality and decorum.' In the meantime the house had resettled itself, but she could not stop laughing at the ridiculous and lustful figure which she said the good old man had made of himself. She showed no concern for the calamities and loss of life and property which had affected her family and thousands of others, as if this joke had made her forget everything else. Only an extraordinarily happy disposition could have enjoyed a joke at the very moment when the earth seemed about to swallow her up.

26 May

There is a good deal to be said for having many saints, for then each believer can choose his own and put his trust in the one who most appeals to him. Today was the feast day of my favourite saint, and, following his example and teaching, I celebrated it with devotion and joy.

Filippo Neri is held in high honour and at the same time remembered with gladness. One is edified and delighted when one hears about his reverent fear of God, and at the same time is told many stories about his good humour. From his earliest youth he was conscious of a fervent religious impulse and in the course of his life he developed the highest gifts for mystical experience – the gift of spontaneous prayer, of profound, wordless adoration, of tears, ecstasy, and even, as a crowning grace, the gift of levitation – all were his.

With these mysterious spiritual graces, he combined the clearest common sense, an absolute valuation or rather de-valuation of earthly things, and an active charity, devoted to the bodily and spiritual needs of his fellow men. He was strict in observing all the duties which are demanded of a faithful member of the Church, attendance at worship, prayers, fast-ing, and in the same spirit he occupied himself with the education of the young, instructing them in the study of music and rhetoric and arranging other discussions and debates for the improvement of their minds as well as their souls.

In all this, moreover, he acted of his own accord without any direction from authority, and lived for many years with-out joining any religious order or even becoming ordained.

But the most interesting fact of all is that right in the middle of Rome and at the very same time as Luther, a gifted, God-fearing and energetic man should, like the Reformer, have thought of combining the spiritual, even the sacred, with the secular and relating the supernatural order to the natural, for this is the only key which can unlock the prison of papalism and restore to the free world its God.

In a short motto, Neri formulated his basic teaching 'Spernere mundum, spernere te ipsum, spernere te sperni.' This expresses everything. A hypochondriac may sometimes imagine he can fulfil the first two of these demands, but, to submit to the third, a man must be far on the way to saintliness.

27 May

Yesterday, through the kindness of Count Fries, all your dear letters from the end of last month arrived from Rome. It gave me such joy to read and reread them. The little box I had waited for so anxiously also arrived, and I thank you a thousand times for everything.

It is high time for me to escape from here. What with revisiting various spots in Naples and its surroundings, in order to refresh my memory, and winding up some of my affairs, the days have been running away like water. Moreover, there were several very nice people, both old and new acquaintances, whom I couldn't possibly refuse to see. One of them was an amiable lady with whom I passed some very agreeable days in Carlsbad last summer. We spent many hours talking about one dear good friend after the other, above all about our beloved, good-humoured Duke. She had kept the poem with which the girls of Engelhaus surprised him as he was riding away. The words brought back the occasion, the merry scene, their witty teasings and mystifications, their ingenious attempts to exercise the right of mutual retaliation. In no time we felt we were on German soil and in the best German society, surrounded on all sides by cliffs, united by the strangeness of the spot, but even more by respect and friendship. But then, as soon as we went to the window, the Neapolitan crowd went rushing by like a river and carried our peaceful memories away with it.

It was also impossible for me to get out of making the acquaintance of the Duke and Duchess von Ursel – an excellent couple with a genuine feeling for Nature and people, a real love of art and benevolent to everyone they meet. We had many long and fascinating conversations.

Sir William Hamilton and his Fair One continue to be very friendly. I dined at their house, and in the evening, Miss Hart gave a demonstration of her musical and melic talents.

At the suggestion of Hackert, who is kinder to me than ever and doesn't want me to miss anything worth seeing, Sir

William showed us his secret treasure vault, which was crammed with works of art and junk, all in the greatest confusion. Oddments from every period, busts, torsos, vases, bronzes, decorative implements of all kinds made of Sicilian agate, carvings, paintings and chance bargains of every sort, lay about all higgledy-piggledy; there was even a small chapel. Out of curiosity I lifted the lid of a long case which lay on the floor and in it were two magnificent candelabra. I nudged Hackert and asked him in a whisper if they were not very like the candelabra in the Portici museum. He silenced me with a look. No doubt they somehow strayed here from the cellars of Pompeii. Perhaps these and other such lucky acquisitions are the reason why Sir William shows his hidden treasures only to his most intimate friends.

I was greatly intrigued by a chest which was standing upright. Its front had been taken off, the interior painted black and the whole set inside a splendid gilt frame. It was large enough to hold a standing human figure, and that, we were told, was exactly what it was meant for. Not content with seeing his image of beauty as a moving statue, this friend of art and girlhood wished also to enjoy her as an inimitable painting, and so, standing against this black background in dresses of various colours, she had sometimes imitated the antique paintings of Pompeii or even more recent masterpieces. This phase, it seems, is now over, because it was difficult to transport the apparatus and light it properly, and so we were not to share in this spectacle.

This reminds me that I have forgotten to tell you about another characteristic of the Neapolitans, their love of crèches, or *presepe*, which, at Christmas, can be seen in all their churches. These consist of groups of large, sumptuous figures representing the adoration of the shepherds, the angels and the three Magi. In this gay Naples the representation has climbed up on to the flat roof tops. A light framework, like a hut, is decorated with trees and evergreen shrubs. In it, the Mother of God, the Infant and all the others stand or float, dressed up most gorgeously in a wardrobe on which the family spends a large sum. The background – Vesuvius and all the surrounding countryside – gives the whole thing an incomparable majesty.

In depicting this sacred scene, it is possible that living figures were sometimes substituted for the dolls, and that in time this gave rise to one of the great diversions of noble and wealthy families, who pass many evenings in their palaces representing profane scenes from history or poetry.

If I may be permitted a comment, which a guest who has been so well treated ought really not to make, I must confess that our fair entertainer seems to me, frankly, a dull creature. Perhaps her figure makes up for it, but her voice is inexpressive and her speech without charm. Even her singing is neither full-throated nor agreeable. Perhaps, after all, this is the case with all soulless beauties. People with beautiful figures can be found everywhere, but sensitive ones with agreeable vocal organs are much rarer, and a combination of both is very rare indeed.

I am eagerly looking forward to reading the third part of Herder's book. Please keep it for me until I can tell you where to send it. I'm sure he will have set forth very well the beautiful dream-wish of mankind that things will be better some day. Speaking for myself, I too believe that humanity will win in the long run; I am only afraid that at the same time the world will have turned into one huge hospital where everyone is everybody else's humane nurse.

28 May

Once in a while the good and ever-useful Volkmann forces me to dissent from his opinion. He asserts, for instance, that there are thirty to forty thousand lazy ne'er-do-wells in Naples, and who does not repeat his words? Now that I am better acquainted with the conditions in the south, I suspect that this was the biased view of a person from the north, where anyone who is not feverishly at work all day is regarded as a loafer. When I first arrived, I watched the common people both in motion and at rest, and though I saw a great many who were poorly dressed, I never saw one who was unoccupied. I asked friends where I could meet all these innumerable idlers, but they couldn't show me any either.

So, seeing that such an investigation would coincide with my sightseeing, I set off to hunt for them myself. I always began my observations very early in the morning, and though, now and then, I came upon people who were resting or standing around, they were always those whose occupation permitted it at that moment.

In order to get a just picture of this vast throng, I began by classifying by appearance, clothes, behaviour and occupation. This is much easier to do in Naples than anywhere else, because here the individual is left alone much more, so that his external appearance is a much better indication of his social status. Let me give some illustrations to back up my statements.

Porters. Each has his privileged standing place in some square or other, where he waits till someone needs his services.

Carriage Drivers. These with their ostlers and boys stand beside their one-horse chaises in the larger squares, grooming their horses, and at the beck and call of everyone who wants to take a drive.

Sailors and Fishermen. These are smoking pipes on the Molo or lying in the sun because a contrary wind does not permit them to leave port. In this area I saw several people wandering about, but almost all of them carried something which indicated they were busy.

Beggars. The only ones I saw were very old men, no longer capable of work, and cripples. The longer and closer I looked, the fewer real idlers I could observe, either of the lower classes or the middle, either young or old, men or women, either in the morning or during most of the rest of the day.

Small Children.   These are occupied in many different ways. A great number carry fish from Santa Lucia to sell in the city. Little boys, ranging from five- or six-year-olds down to infants who can only crawl on all fours, are frequently to be seen near the Arsenal or any other place where carpenters work, collecting shavings, or on the shore, gathering the sticks and small pieces of wood which have been washed up and putting them into little baskets. When these are full, they go to the centre of the city and sit down, holding a market, so to speak, of their small stocks of wood. Working men and people of modest means buy them to use as kindling, as wood for their simple kitchen stoves, or as potential charcoal for the braziers with which they warm themselves.

Other children go round selling water from the sulphur springs, which is drunk in large quantities, especially in the springtime. Others again try to make a few pennies by buying fruit, spun honey, sweets and pastries, which they offer for sale to other children – possibly, only so as to get their share for nothing. It is amusing to watch such a youngster, whose entire equipment consists of one wooden board and one knife, carrying round a watermelon or half a pumpkin. The children flock round him; he puts down his board and starts cutting the fruit up into small portions. The buyers are intensely in earnest and on tenterhooks, wondering if they will get enough for their small copper coins, and the little merchant takes the whole transaction just as seriously and cautiously as his greedy customers, who are determined not to be cheated out of the smallest piece. I'm certain that if I could stay here longer, I would be able to collect many other examples of such child industry.

Garbage Collectors.   A very large number of people, some middle-aged men, some boys, all very poorly dressed, are occupied in carrying the refuse out of the city on donkeys.

The immediate area around Naples is simply one huge kitchen garden, and it is a delight to see, first, what incredible quantities of vegetables are brought into the city every market day, and, second, how human industry immediately returns the useless parts which the cooks reject to the fields so as to speed up the crop cycle. Indeed, the Neapolitans consume so many vegetables that the leaves of cauliflowers, broccoli, artichokes, cabbages, lettuce and garlic make up the greater part of the city's refuse. Two large, flexible panniers are slung over the back of a donkey: these are not only filled to the brim, but above them towers a huge mound of refuse, piled with peculiar cunning. No garden could exist without a donkey. A boy or a farm hand, sometimes even the farmer himself, hurry as often as possible during the day into the city, which for them is a real gold mine. You can imagine how intent these collectors are on the droppings of mules and horses. They are reluctant to leave the streets at nightfall, and the rich folk who leave the opera after midnight are probably unaware of the existence of the industrious men who, before daybreak, will have been carefully searching for the trail of their horses.

I have been assured that, not infrequently, such people have gone into partnership, leased a small piece of land, and, by working untiringly in this blessed climate, where the vegetation never stops growing, have been so successful that they were able to add considerably to their profits.

Pedlars, etc. Some go about with little barrels of ice water, lemon and glasses, so that, on request, they can immediately provide a drink of lemonade, a beverage which even the poorest cannot do without. Others carry trays, on which bottles of various liqueurs and tapering glasses are held safely in place by wooden rings. Others again carry baskets containing pastries of various kinds, lemons and other fruit. All of them, it seems, want nothing better than to contribute to the daily festival of joy.

There are other small traders who wander about with merchandise displayed on a plain board, or the lid of a box, or arranged in a square on the bare ground. They do not deal, like a shop, in any single line of goods, but they sell junk, in the proper sense of the word. There is no tiny scrap of iron, leather, cloth, linen, felt, etc., which does not turn up in this market for secondhand goods and cannot be bought from this vendor or that.

Finally, many persons of the lower class are employed by tradesmen and artisans as errand boys or general drudges.

True, one cannot take many steps before coming on some poorly clad, even ragged, individual, but it does not follow that he is a loafer or a good-for-nothing. On the contrary, I would say, though this may seem like a paradox, that in Naples it is the poorest class which works hardest.

What is meant here by working is not, of course, to be compared with what working means in the north, for there Nature compels people to make provision, not merely for the next day or the next hour, but for the distant future, to prepare in fair weather for foul, in summer for winter. With us the housewife has to smoke and cure the meat so that the kitchen will have supplies for the whole year; her husband must see to it that there are sufficient stores of wood, grain and cattle feed, etc. As a result, the finest days and best hours cannot be given over to play, because they are dedicated to work. For several months of the year we do not go out of doors unless we must, but take shelter in our houses from rain, snow and cold. The seasons follow each other in an inexorable round, and everyone must practise household management or come to grief. It is senseless to ask, Does he like it? He has to like it. He has no option, for he is compelled by Nature to work hard and show foresight. No doubt their national environment, which has remained unchanged for millennia, has conditioned the character of the northern nations, so admirable in many respects. But we must not judge the nations of the south, which Heaven has treated so benevolently, by our standards. What Cornelius von Pauw had the temerity to say, when speaking of the Cynic philosophers in his book, *Recherches philosophiques sur les Grecs*, fits in perfectly with my argument. It is false, he says, to think of these people as miserable; their principle of going without was favoured by a climate which gave them all the necessities of life. Here a poor man, whom, in our country, we think of as wretched, can satisfy his essential needs and at the same time enjoy the world to the full, and a so-called Neapolitan beggar might well refuse to become Viceroy of Norway or decline the honour of being nominated Governor of Siberia by the Empress of all the Russias.

A Cynic philosopher would, I am certain, consider life in our country intolerable; on the other hand, Nature invited him, so to speak, to live in the south. Here the ragged man is not naked, nor poor he who has no provision for the morrow.

He may have neither home nor lodging, spend summer nights under the projecting roof of a house, in the doorway of a palazzo, church or public building, and when the weather is bad, find a shelter where, for a trifling sum, he may sleep, but this does not make him a wretched outcast. When one considers the abundance of fish and sea food which the ocean provides (their prescribed diet on the fast days of every week), the abundance and variety of fruits and vegetables at every season of the year, when one remembers that the region around Naples is deservedly called '*Terra di Lavoro*' (which does not mean the land of *work* but the land of *cultivation*) and that the whole province has been honoured for centuries with the title '*Campagna Felice*' – the happy land – then one gets an idea of how easy life is in these parts.

Someone should try to write a really detailed description of Naples, though this would take years of observation and no small talent. Then we might realize two things: first, that the so-called *lazzarone* is not a whit less busy than any other class and, second, that all of them work not merely to *live* but to *enjoy* themselves: they wish even their work to be a recreation. This explains a good many things: it explains, for instance, why, in most kinds of skilled labour, their artisans are technically far behind those of the northern countries, why factories do not succeed, why, with the exception of lawyers and doctors, there is little learning or culture considering the size of the population, why no painter of the Neapolitan school has ever been profound or become great, why the clergy are happiest when they are doing nothing, and why most of the great prefer to spend their money on luxury, dissipation and sensual pleasures. I know, of course, that these generalizations are too glib and that the typical features of each class could only be established precisely after a much closer scrutiny and longer acquaintance, but I believe that, on the whole, they would still hold good.

To return to the common people again. They are like children who, when one gives them a job to do, treat it as a job but at the same time as an opportunity for having some fun. They are lively, open and sharply observant. I am told their speech is full of imagery and their wit trenchant. It was in the region around Naples that the ancient *Atellanae fabulae* were performed, and their beloved Pulcinella is a descendant from these farces.

Pliny, in Book III, Chapter V, of his *Historia naturalis*, considers Campania worth an extensive description.

In what terms to describe the coast of Campania taken by itself, with its blissful and heavenly loveliness, so as to manifest that there is one region, where Nature has been at work in her joyous mood! And then again all that invigorating healthfulness all the year round, the climate so temperate, the plains so fertile, the hills so sunny, the glades so secure, the groves so shady! Such wealth of various forests, the breezes from so many mountains, the great fertility of its corn and vines and olives, the glorious fleeces of its sheep, the sturdy necks of its bulls, the many lakes, the rich supply of rivers and springs, flowing over all its surface, its many seas and harbours, and the bosom of its lands offering on all sides a welcome to commerce, the country itself eagerly running out into the seas, as it were, to aid mankind. I do not speak of the character and customs of its people, its men, the nations that its language and its might have conquered.

The Greeks themselves, a people most prone to gushing self-praise, have pronounced sentence on the land by conferring on but a very small part of it the name of Magna Graecia.*

29 May

One of the greatest delights of Naples is the universal gaiety. The many-coloured flowers and fruits in which Nature adorns herself seem to invite the people to decorate themselves and their belongings with as vivid colours as possible. All who can in any way afford it wear silk scarves, ribbons and flowers in their hats. In the poorest homes the chairs and chests are painted with bright flowers on a gilt ground; even the one-horse carriages are painted a bright red, their carved woodwork gilded; and the horses decorated with artificial flowers, crimson tassels and tinsel. Some horses wear plumes on their heads, others little pennons which revolve as they trot.

We usually think of a passion for gaudy colours as barbaric or in bad taste, and often with reason, but under this blue sky nothing can be too colourful, for nothing can outshine the brightness of the sun and its reflection in the sea. The most brilliant colour is softened by the strong light, and the green of trees and plants, the yellow, brown and red of the soil are dominant enough to absorb the more highly coloured flowers and dresses into the general harmony. The scarlet skirts and bodices, trimmed with gold and silver braids, which the women of Nettuno wear, the painted boats, etc., everything seems to be competing for visual attention against the splendour of sea and sky.

As they live, so they bury their dead; no slow-moving black cortège disturbs the harmony of this merry world. I saw them carrying a child to its grave. The bier was hidden under an ample pall of red velvet embroidered with gold, and the little coffin was ornamented and gilded and covered with

* Transl. Loeb Classical Library. Book III, v, 40–42.

rose-coloured ribbons. At each of its four corners stood an angel, about two feet high, holding a large sheaf of flowers over the sleeping child, who lay dressed in white. Since these angels were only fastened in place with wires, they shook with every movement of the bier and wafted the fragrance of the flowers in all directions. One reason why they tottered so was that the procession was hurrying down the street at such a pace that the priest and candle-bearers at its head were running, rather than walking.

There is no season when one is not surrounded on all sides by victuals. The Neapolitan not only enjoys his food, but insists that it be attractively displayed for sale. In Santa Lucia the fish are placed on a layer of green leaves, and each category – rock lobsters, oysters, clams and small mussels – has a clean, pretty basket to itself. But nothing is more carefully planned than the display of meat, which, since their appetite is stimulated by a periodic fast day, is particularly coveted by the common people.

In the butchers' stalls, quarters of beef, veal or mutton are never hung up without having the unfatty parts of the flanks and legs heavily gilded.

Several days in the year and especially the Christmas holidays are famous for their orgies of gluttony. At such times a general *cocagna* is celebrated, in which five hundred thousand people vow to outdo each other. The Toledo and other streets and squares are decorated most appetizingly; vegetables, raisins, melons and figs are piled high in their stalls; huge paternosters of gilded sausages, tied with red ribbons, and capons with little red flags stuck in their rumps are suspended in festoons across the streets overhead. I was assured that, not counting those which people had fattened in their own homes, thirty thousand of them had been sold. Crowds of donkeys laden with vegetables, capons and young lambs are driven to market, and never in my life have I seen so many eggs in one pile as I have seen here in several places.

Not only is all this eaten, but every year a policeman, accompanied by a trumpeter, rides through the city and announces in every square and at every crossroad how many thousand oxen, calves, lambs, pigs, etc., the Neapolitans have consumed. The crowd show tremendous joy at the high figures, and each of them recalls with pleasure his share in this consumption.

So far as flour-and-milk dishes are concerned, which our cooks prepare so excellently and in so many different ways, though people here lack our well-equipped kitchens and like to make short work of their cooking, they are catered for in two ways. The macaroni, the dough of which is made from a very fine flour, kneaded into various shapes and then boiled, can be bought everywhere and in all the shops for very little money. As a rule, it is simply cooked in water and seasoned with grated cheese. Then, at almost every corner of the main streets, there are pastrycooks with their frying pans of sizzling oil, busy, especially on fast days, preparing pastry and fish on the spot for anyone who wants it. Their sales are fabulous, for thousands and thousands of people carry their lunch and supper home, wrapped in a little piece of paper.

30 May

Seen tonight from the Molo. The moon lighting up the edges of the clouds, its reflection in the gently heaving sea, at its brightest and most lively on the crest of the nearest waves, stars, the lamps of the lighthouse, the fire of Vesuvius, its reflection in the water, many isolated lights dotted among the boats. A scene with such multiple aspects would be difficult to paint. I should like to see van der Neer tackle it.

31 May

I am so firmly set on seeing the Feast of Corpus Christi in Rome, and the tapestries woven after Raphael's designs, that no natural beauty, however magnificent, can lure me away from my preparations for departure.

I ordered my passport. The custom here is the exact opposite of ours; a *vetturino* gave me the earnest money as a guarantee of my safety.

Kniep has been very busy moving into new lodgings which are much better than his old ones. While the moving was going on, he hinted more than once that it is considered strange, even improper, to move into a house without bringing any furniture with you. Even a bedstead would be enough to make the landlord respect him. Today, as I was crossing the Largo del Castello, I noticed, among countless second-hand household goods, a couple of iron bed-frames painted a bronze colour. I bargained for these and gave them to my friend as a future foundation for a quiet and solid resting-place. One of the porters who are always hanging about carried them, together with the requisite boards, to the new lodgings. Kniep was so pleased with them that he decided to leave me immediately and establish himself there, after quickly buying large drawing-boards, paper and other necessaries. According to our contract, I gave him a certain number of the sketches he had made in the Two Sicilies.

1 June

The Marchese Lucchesini* has arrived, and on his account I have postponed my departure for a few days. It was a real pleasure to make his acquaintance. He impressed me as being one of those people who have a sound moral digestion which allows them to enjoy themselves at the great world banquet, whereas a person like myself sometimes overeats like a ruminant, and then must chew and chew for a long time before he can take another bite. I also liked his wife very much; she is a good German soul.

I shall be glad to leave Naples; indeed, I must leave. During these last days I have done nothing but pay courtesy

* Marchese Lucchesini, Prussian Secretary of State, on a diplomatic mission in Italy.

calls. Most of the people I met were interesting and I do not regret the hours I spent with them, but another two weeks and all my plans would be upset. Furthermore, the longer one stays here, the idler one gets. Apart from the treasures of Portici, I have seen very little since my return from Paestum. There is still a lot I ought to see, but I don't feel in the mood to stir a foot. The Portici museum is the alpha and omega of all collections of antiquities. It makes one realize how far superior to us the ancient world was in artistic instinct, even though it was far behind us in solid craftsmanship.

The servant I hired to bring me my passport said he was sorry to see me go, and told me that the great lava stream which has just issued from Vesuvius is moving towards the sea; it has already reached a point far down the steeper slopes and may well reach the shore in a few days. This news has put me in a dilemma. I have spent the whole day paying farewell visits which I owed to people; there have been many of them who have been kind and helpful to me, and I can guess what tomorrow will be like. When travelling, it is impossible to avoid social life altogether, but the truth is, I can do nothing for these people, and they get in the way of the things which really matter to me. I am in a black mood.

1 June. Evening

My round of thank-you visits was not without pleasure and profit; I was shown several things which I had neglected. Cavaliere Venuti even let me see some hidden treasures. I took another reverent look at his priceless, though mutilated, Ulysses, and together we paid a farewell visit to the porcelain works, where I lingered over the Hercules and the beautiful Campanian vases.

He was most affectionate when we parted, and said that he only wished I did not have to leave him so soon. My banker, too, at whose house I arrived just at dinner-time, would not let me go. This would have been all very well if my thoughts had not been running on lava all the time. I was still settling bills, packing and doing this and that when night began to fall, and I hurried to the Molo to watch the lights and their trembling reflections in the agitated sea, the full moon in all its glory, the flying sparks of the volcano and, above all, the lava, which had not been there two nights ago, moving on its fiery, relentless way.

I thought of driving out to see it, but this would have been complicated to arrange and it would have been morning before I got there. Besides, I did not want impatience to spoil my present enjoyment, so I stayed where I was, sitting on the Molo, oblivious of the passing crowds, their explanations, stories, comparisons and senseless arguments about the direction the lava would take, until I could no longer keep my eyes open.

2 June

Another beautiful day, spent usefully and pleasantly, no doubt, with admirable people, but against my will and with a heavy heart. All the time I looked longingly at the cloud of smoke as it slowly moved towards the sea, indicating hour by hour the advance of the lava. Even my evening was not to be free. I had promised to visit the Duchess of Giovene, who is living in the royal palace. I climbed stairs and wandered along many corridors, the uppermost of which was obstructed by chests, closets and all the impedimenta of a court wardrobe, and was shown into a room which was large and lofty but not particularly spectacular. There I found an attractive young lady whose conversation revealed her to be a person of delicacy and refinement. Born in Germany, she is familiar with the development of our literature towards a more liberal and clear-sighted humanism. She especially admires everything Herder is doing and the lucid intellect of Garve. She has tried to keep up with the women writers of Germany, and it was obvious from what she said that she would like to become a famous writer herself and influence young ladies of noble birth – such a conversation is without beginning or end. No candles had been brought in, though it was already twilight and the window shutters were closed. We were walking up and down the room, when, all of a sudden, she flung open a shutter. If she meant to give me a surprise, she certainly succeeded, for the sight was such as one sees only once in a lifetime. The window at which we were standing was on the top floor, directly facing Vesuvius. The sun had set some time before, and the glow of the lava, which lit up its accompanying cloud of smoke, was clearly visible. The mountain roared, and at each eruption the enormous pillar of smoke above it was rent asunder as if by lightning, and in the glare, the separate clouds of vapour stood out in sculptured relief. From the summit to the sea ran a streak of molten lava and glowing vapour, but everywhere else sea, earth, rock and vegetation lay peaceful in the enchanting stillness of a fine evening, while the full moon rose from behind the mountain ridge. It was an overwhelming sight.

From the point where we were standing, though it was impossible to discern every detail of the picture, the whole could be taken in at a glance. For a time we watched in silence, and when we resumed our conversation, it took a more intimate turn. We had before our eyes a text to comment on, for which millennia would be too short. As the night advanced, every detail of the landscape stood out ever more clearly; the moon shone like a second sun; with the aid of a moderately strong lens, I even thought I could see the fragments of glowing rock as they were ejected from the abyss of the cone. My hostess, as I shall call her, since I have seldom eaten a more exquisite supper, had ordered the candles to be placed on the side of the room away from the window. Sitting in the foreground of this incredible picture with the moonlight falling on her face, she looked more beautiful than ever, and her loveliness was enhanced for me by the charming German idiom in which she spoke. I forgot completely how late it was till, at last, she had to ask me to leave because in a short while the doors would be locked as they are in a convent. And so to beauty, both near and distant, I bade a reluctant farewell, but blessing the Fates who, at its close, had so wonderfully rewarded me for a day unwillingly spent in being polite.

When I got outside, I thought to myself that, after all, a closer view of this great lava stream would only have been a repetition of the small one I did see, and that the evening I had spent was the only possible conclusion to my stay in Naples. Instead of going home at once, I started walking towards the Molo with the intention of seing the great spectacle with a different foreground. I don't know how it was – perhaps it was weariness after such a full day, perhaps a feeling that I ought not to spoil the beautiful picture I had just seen by any more looking – but I changed my mind and went back to Morconi's. There I found Kniep, who had come over from his new lodgings to pay me an evening visit, and we discussed our future relations over a bottle of wine. I promised him that as soon as I was able to exhibit some of his work in Germany, I would recommend him to the Duke of Gotha, who would probably give him commissions, and so, as close friends who look forward to a fruitful co-operation in the future, we said goodbye to each other.

3 June. Trinity Sunday

I drove away through the teeming crowds of this incomparable city which I shall probably never see again – half dazed but glad that I am leaving neither pain nor remorse behind me. I thought of my good friend Kniep and made a vow to do all I can for him when I am far away.

At the last police station on the outskirts of the suburbs, I was startled for a moment by a waiter who smiled in my face and then ran away. The customs inspectors had not yet finished with my *vetturino* when the door of the coffee house opened and out came Kniep, carrying on a tray a huge china cup of black coffee. He walked slowly to the door of my coach with a serious expression on his face, which, as his emotion was heartfelt, became him very well. I was surprised and moved: one does not often encounter such a visible sign of gratitude. He said to me: 'You have been so kind and good to me that I shall remember you all my life, and I want to offer you this as a symbol of my gratitude.'

I never know what to say on such occasions, so I only said very laconically that the work he had done had already made me his debtor, and that the use of our common treasure would put me under still greater obligation to him.

We parted as two persons seldom do whom chance has thrown together for a short time. Perhaps we should find more satisfaction and gratitude in our lives if we always said quite frankly what we expect from one another. If we did, both parties would be satisfied, and we should find sympathy, which is the beginning and end of everything, into the bargain.

On the road, 4, 5, 6 June

As I am travelling alone this time, I have leisure to think over all I have seen and done during the past months, and I do so with great pleasure. At the same time, I become aware of gaps in my observations. When a journey is over, the traveller himself remembers it as an unbroken sequence of events, inseparable from each other. But when he tries to describe this journey to someone else, he finds it impossible to communicate this, for he can only present the events one by one as separate facts.

This is why nothing has cheered me more than the assurances in your last letters that you have been busy reading travel books about Italy and Sicily and looking at engravings, and it is a great comfort to learn that your studies have made my letters clearer, as I knew they would.

Had you done this earlier, or told me so, I would have been even more zealous in my efforts than I was. The knowledge that men like Bartels, Münter and architects of various nationalities preceded me – men who, no doubt, pursued their investigations more carefully and objectively than I, who had only the inner significance of things in view – has often eased my mind when I was forced to recognize the inadequacy of my efforts.

If every human individual is to be considered only as a supplement to all the others, if he is never so useful or so lovable as when he is content to play this part, this must be particularly true for travellers and writers of travel books. Personality, purpose, the times, the chances of fortune and misfortune, are different in every case. If I know a traveller's predecessors, I find profit in reading him too, and shall welcome his successor with pleasure, even if, in the meantime, I have been so fortunate as to visit the same country myself.

NOVELLA

Translated by Elizabeth Mayer and Louise Bogan
Poems translated by W. H. Auden

At daybreak a thick autumn mist still flooded the spacious inner court of the Prince's castle; but when the veil gradually lifted, the hustle and bustle of the hunting party, on horseback and on foot, became more or less visible. The hurried preparations of those nearest at hand could be recognized: stirrups were lengthened or shortened, rifles and cartridge pouches passed around, knapsacks of badger skin adjusted, while the impatient hounds almost pulled their keepers along by their leashes. Here and there a horse pranced nervously, pricked by its own fiery temper or by the spur of its rider who, even in the dim light of the early morning, could not suppress a certain vanity to show off. All, however, were waiting for the Prince, whose farewells to his young wife had already caused too much delay.

Although those two had been married for only a short time, they already felt deeply the happiness of harmonious minds; both had active and lively dispositions and each enjoyed sharing the other's tastes and pursuits. The Prince's father had lived long enough to see, and to put to good use, the day when it became clear that all the members of a state should spend their lives in the same industrious way; that everyone should work and produce according to his faculties, should first earn and then enjoy his living.

How successful this policy had been became evident during these days when the great market was held, which might well be called a trade fair. The day before, the Prince had escorted his wife on horseback through the maze of piled-up merchandise and had drawn her attention to the favourable exchange of products here between the mountainous regions and the plain; he was able to demonstrate to her, at this very centre, the industry of his own domain.

Although the Prince's conversation with his entourage had turned, during these days, almost exclusively upon these pressing topics, and although he was constantly conferring, in particular, with his Minister of Finance, yet the Master of the Hounds also carried his point when he made the tempting suggestion, impossible to resist, that he arrange a hunt – already once postponed – during these favourable autumn days, to give friends and the many guests, lately arrived, a special and rare treat.

The Princess was not very happy to be left behind; but the plan was to penetrate far into the mountains in order to harass the peaceful inhabitants of those forests by an unexpected invasion.

The Prince, at the moment of departure, did not forget to suggest that she should take a leisurely ride in the company of Prince Friedrich, his uncle. 'And then,' he added, 'I also leave with you our Honorio as equerry and personal attendant. He will take care of everything.' After saying these words he gave, on his way downstairs, the necessary instructions to a handsome young man; and then rode off with his guests and his attendants.

The Princess, after having waved her handkerchief to her husband in the courtyard below, went to the rooms on the other side of the castle, from which she had a clear view of the mountains – a view all the more beautiful since the rather elevated position of the castle above the river offered a variety of remarkable prospects on either side. She found the excellent telescope still in the position in which it had been left the evening before, when they had talked about the lofty ruins of the old family castle which could be seen over bush, mountain and wooded summit, and which had stood out unusually clear in the evening glow, the great masses of light and shade throwing into sharp relief this mighty monument of times long past. Now, in the early-morning light, the autumn colours of the various kinds of trees which had soared up unchecked and undisturbed through the masonry for so many years were startlingly distinct through the strong lenses which brought everything closer to the eye. The lovely lady, however, lowered the telescope slightly towards a barren stony tract where the hunting party would pass; she waited patiently for that moment and was not disappointed: because of the clarity and magnifying power of the instrument, her bright eyes clearly recognized the Prince and the Grand Master of the Horse. She could not resist waving her handkerchief again when she more imagined than saw that they briefly halted and looked back.

At this moment Friedrich, the Prince's uncle, was announced. He entered the room with his draughtsman who carried under his arm a large portfolio. 'My dear niece,' said the still-vigorous old gentleman, 'we want to show you the drawings of the old castle, which have been made to demonstrate from various angles how remarkably well the powerful structure, built for shelter and defence, has resisted all seasons and all weathers from time immemorial, and how its masonry, nevertheless, has had to give way, here and there collapsing into desolate ruins. We have already taken steps to make this wilderness more accessible, for it is all that is needed to surprise and delight any wanderer or visitor.'

After having explained to her in detail each single drawing, the old Prince continued: 'Here, as we ascend through the hollow path in the outer ring of walls, we come to the castle itself, where a rock rises before us – one of the most massive rocks in the whole mountain range. Upon it a watchtower was built; but nobody would be able to say where nature ends and art and workmanship begin. Walls are annexed on both sides, and outworks slope downward in terraces. But this is not quite accurate, for it is actually a forest which girds this age-old summit. For the last hundred and fifty years no stroke of an axe has rung out here, and everywhere gigantic trees have grown to a great height. When you push your way along the walls, the smooth maple, the sturdy oak and the slender fir tree obstruct your progress with their trunks and roots, and you have to wind your way around them and choose your footing with caution. Look, how admirably has our masterly artist shown, in his drawing, these characteristic features; how clearly you can recognize the various kinds of trunk and root interwoven with the masonry, and the strong branches interlaced through the gaps in the walls. This wilderness has no parallel; it is a unique place, where ancient traces of long-vanished human strength can be seen in a deadly struggle with the everlasting and ever-acting forces of nature.'

Taking up another drawing, he went on: 'And what do you think of this courtyard, which became inaccessible after the collapse of the old gate tower and has never been entered by any human being for countless years! We tried to force an entrance from one side; we broke through walls, blasted vaults, and in this way made a convenient but secret passage. We did not have to clear up the inner court which is paved by a flat-topped rock made smooth by nature; but, even so, here and there huge trees have succeeded in anchoring their roots; they have grown up slowly but resolutely and are now thrusting their branches right up into the galleries where, once upon a time, knights paced up and down; they have become the true Lords and Masters, and Lords and Masters they may remain. After removing deep layers of dead leaves we discovered the most extraordinary level place, the like of which will probably not be found again in the whole world.

'We should, therefore, be grateful to our fine artist, whose various drawings have so convincingly reproduced the scene that we can imagine ourselves present. He has spent the best hours of the day and of the season on his work, and has studied these objects for weeks on end. On this corner we have arranged a small and pleasant lodging for him and the caretaker whom we have assigned to him. You cannot imagine, my dear, what a beautiful outlook and view into the open country and also towards the courtyard and ruins he can enjoy from there. But now, after sketching everything so neatly and faithfully, he will carry out his work down here at his convenience. We plan to decorate our garden room with these pictures, and no one will let his eyes wander over our symmetrically designed flowerbeds, our arbours and shady walks, without wishing to meditate in the castle itself, seeing both old things and new, that which is solid, inflexible and indestructible, and that which is vigorous, flexible and unresisting.'

When Honorio entered and announced that the horses were ready, the Princess turned to her uncle and said: 'Let us ride up there so that I can actually see everything you have shown me in these drawings. I have heard about that project ever since I came here; and now I feel a great desire to see with my own eyes what seemed to me impossible when described to me, and still unbelievable even after seeing the drawings.'

'Not yet, my dear,' replied the old Prince. 'What you have just seen is what it can and will be. At present some of the work has come to a standstill. Art must first complete its task, if it is not to be put to shame by nature.'

'Then we'll at least ride in that direction, even if only to the foot of the crag. Today I am very much in the mood for having a look around far and wide.'

'Just as you wish,' answered the old Prince.

'But I should love to ride through the town,' added the Princess, 'across the great market place where all those booths give the illusion of a small town or a tented encampment. It is as though the needs and occupations of all the families round about were gathered at this central point and laid out to be seen in broad daylight; for the watchful observer can see here everything man produces and needs, and one can imagine for a moment that money is unnecessary, that any business can be transacted here by barter, which is also fundamentally true. After the Prince gave me an opportunity for this observation yesterday, I am pleased at the thought that in this place, where mountains border the plains, the people of both regions so clearly express what they need and want. Because the mountain dweller knows how to shape the wood of his forests into a hundred forms, and how to convert iron to any purpose, the plainsman comes here to meet him with goods of such great variety that one can often hardly recognize their material, nor guess the purpose they may serve.'

'I know that my nephew takes a great interest in these matters,' said the old Prince, 'and just at this time of year it is most important to receive more than to spend; to accomplish this purpose is, ultimately, the sum of our whole state economy as well as of the smallest household budget. But forgive me, my dear, I never like to ride across a market place when a fair is going on; at every step obstacles block your way and stop you, and on such an occasion my imagination becomes kindled once more by the memory of that dreadful disaster which is branded, as it were, upon my eyes, when I saw similar piles of goods and merchandise go up in flames. I had scarcely –'

'Let us not waste these lovely morning hours,' the Princess interrupted him, for the old gentleman had several times before frightened her by describing that catastrophe in detail, telling her how once, on a long journey, he had stopped at the best inn on a market place which was on that day packed with the commotion of a fair; how he had, in the evening, gone to bed, extremely tired, and had been roused during the night in a ghastly manner by screams and by flames that were rolling against his lodging.

The Princess hurried downstairs and mounted her favourite horse, but, instead of leaving through the back gate and riding uphill, she led her reluctantly willing companion through the front gate and downhill; for who would not be delighted to ride by her side, who would not have willingly followed her? Even Honorio, who had been looking forward to joining the hunters, had willingly stayed behind to devote himself entirely to her service.

As was to be expected, they could ride only step by step in the market place; but the lovely, gracious Princess cheered her companions with intelligent remarks whenever they were delayed. 'I repeat my lesson of yesterday, for it is necessity that wishes to test our patience.' And this was true, for the whole crowd pressed the riders so closely that they could move on only very slowly. The people were happy to catch a glimpse of the young lady, and many smiling faces showed definite pleasure in discovering that the first lady in the land was also the most beautiful and the most charming. There were mountain people, having come down from their quiet homes among rocks, firs and pines, and mixing with the plains people, who lived among hills, field and meadows; also tradespeople from small towns, and others who had assembled here. After having quietly surveyed the crowd, the Princess remarked to her companion how all these people, wherever they came from, used for their clothing more material than was necessary, more cloth and linen, more ribbon for trimming. 'It seems to me that the women cannot pad themselves enough, nor the men puff themselves out enough to their satisfaction.'

'And we won't begrudge them that pleasure,' said the old gentleman. 'People are happy, happiest indeed, when they can spend their surplus money on dressing themselves up and decking themselves out.' The lovely lady nodded in agreement.

They had gradually advanced in this manner towards an open square near the outskirts of the town, where they saw at the far end of a row of small booths and stalls a much larger wooden structure. Hardly had they sighted it when a deafening roar struck their ears. The feeding time for the wild animals on display there had evidently come; the lion raised his powerful forest-and-desert voice; the horses trembled; and one could hardly fail to realize the terrifying manner in which the King of the Desert announced his presence in the midst of the peaceful existence and pursuits of the civilized world. As they approached the building they could not help but see the huge, garish posters which represented in strong colours and striking images those strange animals and were meant to fill the peaceable citizen with an irresistible desire to see the show. A fierce, formidable tiger was seen attacking a blackamoor, about to tear him to pieces; a gravely majestic lion did not seem to see any prey worthy of his dignity; beside these mighty beasts, other strange and colourful creatures deserved less attention.

'On our way back,' said the Princess, 'let's dismount and have a closer look at these unusual guests.'

'It is quite remarkable that human beings always want to be excited by something horrifying,' said the old Prince. 'In there, the tiger lies quietly in his cage, while out here he must make a furious leap on the blackamoor to make you believe that you will see him do the same within. As if there were not enough murder and bloodshed, fire and destruction in the world! The ballad singers have to repeat all this at every street corner. The good people want to be intimidated, so that they can afterwards feel, all the more intensely, how pleasant and relaxing it is to breathe freely.'

Whatever uneasy feelings those alarming pictures may have given them, these were at once blotted out when they passed through the town gate into a perfectly serene country-side. They rode at first along the river, which was here still a rivulet, fit only for the traffic of small craft, but which farther on gradually widened to become one of the largest streams, retaining its name and bringing prosperity to distant coun-tries. The gently rising road then led them through well-tended fruit and pleasure gardens, until a densely populated region gradually opened before them where, after having passed first a thicket and then a grove, charming villages limited but refreshed their view. A green valley, leading uphill, was a welcome change for the riders, as the grass had been lately mown for the second time, making the turf look like velvet; it was watered by a lively spring which came gushing down from some higher place. They now rode on to a higher and more open viewpoint which they reached, coming out of a wood, after a brisk ascent. It was then that they saw, though still at a considerable distance and over other groups of trees, the object of their pilgrimage – the old castle, rising aloft like the peak of some wooded crag. But when they turned around – and nobody arrived at this point without looking back – they saw to the left, through occasional gaps in the tall trees, the Prince's new castle, illuminated by the morning sun, the well-built upper part of the town, slightly obscured by light clouds of smoke, and farther to the right the lower town, the river with some of its windings, its meadowlands and gristmills, while straight before them extended a wide, fertile region.

After they had feasted their eyes on the beautiful panorama, or rather, as usually happens when we look about us from such a height, were feeling a strong desire for an even wider and unbounded view, they rode uphill on a broad and stony tract, with the mighty ruin facing them like a green-crested pinnacle with only a few old trees deep down at its foot. Riding through these trees, they found themselves confronted with the steepest, most inaccessible flank where enormous, age-old rocks, untouched by change, massive and firm, towered above. Between them huge stone slabs and fragments, tumbled down in the course of time, were lying across each other in confusion and seemed to forbid even the boldest climber to advance. But anything precipitous and abrupt seems to appeal to youth. To dare, to attack, to conquer is a delight for young limbs. The Princess indicated that she would like to make the attempt; Honorio was at hand, and the old gentleman, though not so enterprising, did not protest, being reluctant to confess to lesser energy. They decided to leave the horses below under the trees and to try and reach a certain point where an enormous projecting rock presented a level space from which they would have a view, almost a bird's-eye view, of scenery still picturesque, though slowly receding into the distance.

The sun, almost at its highest point, shed a brilliant light on everything: the new castle with its various parts, the main buildings, the wings, cupolas and towers looked very impressive. The upper part of the town could be seen in its full extent; they could even easily look into the lower town and, through the telescope, recognize the different stalls in the market place. It was Honorio's habit to carry this useful instrument with him, strapped over his shoulder. They looked up and down the river, where the land on this side was broken by mountainous terraces; on the other side was an undulating, fertile plain, alternating with moderate hills and innumerable villages – it was an old custom to argue how many could be counted from this spot.

Over this vast expanse reigned a serene stillness, as is usual at noon when Pan is sleeping, as the ancients said, and all nature is holding its breath for fear of wakening him.

'It is not for the first time,' said the Princess, 'that, standing on such a high place with a view in all directions, I have thought how pure and peaceful nature looks on a clear day, giving the impression that there could be nothing unpleasant in the world; but when we return into the habitations of human beings, be they high or low, large or small – there is always something to fight over, to dispute, to straighten out and set right.'

Honorio, who had meanwhile been looking across at the town through the telescope, suddenly exclaimed: 'Look! Look! A fire has started in the market place!' The others also looked and noticed some smoke, but the sunlight subdued the flames. 'The fire is spreading!' all cried, looking by turns through the lenses; the good eyes of the Princess could now recognize the disaster even without the help of the instrument. Now and then they could perceive red tongues of flames; smoke rose up, and the old Prince suggested: 'Let's ride back, this is bad; I have always been afraid that I might have this unfortunate experience a second time.' When they had climbed down and had reached their horses, the Princess turned to her uncle. 'Please, ride back quickly, and take your groom with you. Leave Honorio with me; we'll follow at once.' Her uncle, feeling that her suggestion was as reasonable as it was necessary, rode down the rough, stony slope as quickly as the condition of the ground allowed.

When the Princess had mounted her horse, Honorio said: 'I implore Your Highness to ride slowly! Both in the town and at the castle everything for fighting fires is in the best order and nobody will lose his head in such an unusual and unexpected emergency. But the road here is bad, small stones and short grass, to ride fast is unsafe; in any case, the fire will certainly have been put out by the time we arrive.' The Princess did not believe this. She saw the smoke spreading; she thought she saw a blazing flame and heard an explosion; and now all the terrifying scenes of the fire at the fair, witnessed by her uncle and described to her repeatedly, were evoked in her imagination on which they were unfortunately impressed all too deeply.

That former incident had been terrible, unexpected and shocking enough to leave behind a lifelong impression as well as an anxious apprehension of a possible recurrence of that kind of disaster. In the dead of night a sudden blaze had seized stall after stall on the great crowded market place, even before the people who were sleeping in or near those flimsy booths had been shaken from their dreams. The old Prince, a stranger, tired after a long journey, had retired early but, wakened from his first sleep, he had rushed to the window to see the ghastly illumination, flame upon flame, darting on every side and licking fiery tongues towards him. The houses on the market place, tinted red by the reflection, seemed to glow, threatening to catch fire at any moment and to burst into flames; below, the irresistible element kept raging, the boards crashed to the ground, laths cracked, pieces of tent canvas flew up, and the tatters, blackened and with jagged and flaming edges, reeled in the air, as if evil spirits, shaped and reshaped by their element, would consume themselves in a playful round dance, trying to emerge now and then out of the flames. Meanwhile, with piercing screams, people were saving whatever they could take hold of; servants and hired men helped their masters to drag to safety bales of goods already on fire, to snatch at least something from the racks and stuff it into the crates, although they were forced in the end to abandon everything to the destruction of the swiftly advancing flames. How many, wishing that the roaring fire would stop for a moment, had looked around for a possible breathing space and been seized by the flames with all their

possessions. Everything that smouldered or was burning on
the one side lay on the other still in deep darkness. Determined characters, men with a strong will, fiercely fought their
fiery adversary and saved a few things, though they lost
their hair and their eyebrows. It was unfortunate that the
wild confusion of that past event was now evoked again in the
pure mind of the Princess. The serene horizon of the morning seemed suddenly clouded, her eyes dimmed, and even
wood and meadow took on a strangely ominous look.

Riding into the peaceful valley, but oblivious to its refreshing coolness, they had hardly passed the lively source of the
stream, flowing nearby, when the Princess caught sight of
something unusual far below in the bushes of the meadowland, which she at once recognized as the tiger; leaping, it
came up towards them, just as she had seen it on the poster a
short time ago, and its sudden appearance, adding to the
terrifying scenes which occupied her mind at this moment,
affected her very strongly. 'Flee, Madam!' shouted Honorio,
'flee at once!' She turned her horse and rode up the steep hill
from which they had just descended. But the young man rode
towards the beast, drew his pistol and, when he thought he
was within range, fired; but, unfortunately, he missed his
mark. The tiger jumped aside, Honorio's horse shied, and
the enraged animal continued on its way upward, closely
following the Princess. She raced her horse as fast as it
would go up the steep and stony slope, forgetting for the
moment that the gentle creature, unaccustomed to such
efforts, might not stand the strain. Urged on by its hard-
pressed rider, the horse overtaxed itself, stumbled now and
then over the loose stones of the slope and, after one last
violent effort, fell exhausted to the ground. The lovely lady,
resolute and expert, managed to get quickly to her feet; the
horse, too, scrambled up, but the tiger was coming nearer,
although at a slower pace; the rough ground and the sharp
stones seemed to check its progress, and only the fact that
Honorio was in close pursuit appeared to irritate and goad it
on again. Racing towards the place where the Princess was

standing beside her horse, both runners arrived at the same time. The chivalrous young man leaned from his horse, fired his second pistol, and shot the beast through the head. The tiger fell at once and, stretched out at full length, showed more clearly than ever its tremendous power, the physical frame of which was now all that was left. Honorio had jumped from his horse and knelt on the animal, stifling any last sign of life, his drawn hunting knife ready in his right hand. He was a handsome youth whom the Princess had often before seen galloping his horse, as he had just now, at the tournaments. In the same way, while riding in the manège at a full gallop, his bullet had hit the Turk's head (mounted on a pole) right under the turban; and again, approaching at an easy gallop, he had speared the Moor's head from the ground with the point of his drawn sword. In all such arts he was skilled and lucky, and both skill and luck had now stood him in good stead.

'Give it the finishing stroke!' cried the Princess. 'I'm afraid the beast may still hurt you with its claws.'

'Excuse me, but it is already dead,' the young man answered, 'and I do not want to spoil its pelt which shall adorn your sledge next winter.'

'Don't be frivolous at a moment like this, which calls forth all feelings of reverence in the depth of our hearts,' said the Princess.

'I too have never in my life felt more reverence than at this moment,' exclaimed Honorio, 'but just for that reason I think of something cheerful and can look at this pelt only in the light of your future pleasure.'

'It would always remind me of this dreadful moment,' she replied.

'But isn't it a much more innocent trophy than the weapons of defeated enemies which used to be carried in the triumphal procession before a conqueror?' asked the young man with glowing cheeks.

'I shall always remember your courage and skill when I look at it; and I need not add that you can count on my gratitude and the Prince's favour as long as you live. But do stand up now! There is no longer any life in the beast, and we must think of what to do next. First of all, stand up!'

'Since I am already on my knees before you, in an attitude which would be forbidden to me in any other circumstances, I beg of you to give me at once a proof of the kindness and good will which you just promised me,' said the young man. 'I have asked your husband, the Prince, several times before to give me leave and the permission to go abroad. Any person who has the good fortune to sit at your table and have the privilege of your company should have seen the world. Persons who have travelled widely come here from all parts, and as soon as the conversation turns to a certain town or any place of importance in some part of the world, we are asked if we have been there. No one who has not seen all these things is considered an educated person; it seems as if we should inform ourselves only for the benefit of others.'

'Stand up!' the Princess said once more. 'I do not like to ask my husband for anything that runs contrary to his opinions; but if I am not mistaken, the reason why he has kept you here until now will soon be removed. His intention was to see you matured into an independent nobleman who would do credit both to himself and to his Prince when abroad as he did here; and I should think that your action today would be the best letter of recommendation a young man could carry with him into the world.'

The Princess did not have time to notice that a shadow of sadness rather than youthful delight passed over Honorio's face; nor did he himself have time to give way to his feelings, for a woman, holding a boy by the hand, came running in great haste up to where they were standing; and hardly had Honorio collected himself and got up, when she flung herself, weeping and crying, on the lifeless body of the tiger. Her behaviour as well as her picturesque and odd, though clean and decent, dress showed that she was the owner and keeper of the creature stretched on the ground. The dark-eyed boy with curly dark hair, holding a flute in his hand, knelt down beside his mother and also wept with deep feeling, although less violently.

This unhappy woman's wild outburst of passion was followed by a stream of words which, though incoherent and fitful, flowed like a brook gushing from one rocky ledge to another. This natural language, short and abrupt, was most impressive and touching. As it would be impossible to try and translate her words into our idiom, we can give only an approximate meaning.

'They have murdered you, poor creature! murdered you needlessly! You were tame and would have loved to lie down quietly and wait for us, for your pads hurt you and your claws had no strength left. You missed the hot sun, which would have made them grow strong. You were the most beautiful of your kind; no man ever saw a royal tiger, so splendidly stretched out in sleep, as you lie now, dead, never to rise again! When, in the morning, you woke at daybreak, opened your jaws wide and put out your red tongue, you seemed to smile at us; and even though you roared, you still took your food playfully from the hands of a woman, from the fingers of a child! How long we travelled with you on your journeys; how long was your company important and rewarding to us! To us, yes, to us it came true: "Out of the eater came forth meat, and out of the strong came forth sweetness." All this is now over! Alas, alas!'

Her lament was not yet finished when riders came down the slope from the castle, galloping at full speed. They were soon recognized as the hunting party, headed by the Prince himself. While hunting in the mountains beyond, they had seen the smoke clouds rising from the fire and had taken a direct path towards these ominous signs, racing through valleys and gorges as if in eager pursuit of game. Galloping over the stony ground, they now stopped short and stared at the unexpected group, which stood out with remarkable distinctiveness on the level clearing. After the first recognition nobody spoke a word, and when everyone had somewhat recovered from the surprise, a few words were sufficient to explain what had not been obvious at a first glance. As he heard about the extraordinary and unheard-of occurrence, the Prince stood among his attendants on horseback and the men who had hurried after him on foot. There was no doubt about what to do; the Prince gave his orders and instructions, when suddenly a tall man forced his way into the circle. He was dressed in the same strange and colourful fashion as his wife and child. And now the whole family was united in mutual surprise and grief. The man, however, collected himself and, standing at a respectful distance from the Prince, said to him: 'This is not a moment for lament. Oh, my lord and mighty hunter, the lion too is at large and has come to these hills, but spare him, have pity and let him not be killed like this good animal here.'

'The lion?' said the Prince. 'Have you found his tracks?'

'Yes, my lord! A peasant in the valley who needlessly took refuge in a tree directed me to go up this hill to the left; but when I saw the crowd of men and horses I hurried here, being curious and in need of help.'

'Then the hunt must start in that direction,' the Prince ordered. 'Load your guns; go cautiously to work. It will do no harm if you drive the animal into the woods below; but in the end, my good man, we won't be able to spare your favourite creature. Why have you been so careless as to let both animals escape?'

'The fire broke out,' the man replied. 'We kept quiet and waited to see what would happen. It spread very fast but was far away. We had enough water to protect ourselves, but some gunpowder exploded, and burning fragments were blown over to us and beyond. We left in haste and confusion and are now very unhappy people.'

The Prince was still busy giving instructions, but for a moment everything seemed to come to a standstill, for a man was seen running down from the old castle – a man they soon recognized to be the castellan who was in charge of the painter's workroom where he lived, being also the supervisor of the workmen. He arrived out of breath, but quickly told his story in a few words: behind the upper rampart the lion had peacefully settled down in the sunshine, at the foot of a hundred-year-old beech tree. But the castellan angrily concluded: 'Why did I take my gun to town yesterday to have it cleaned! If I had had it handy, the lion would not have stood up again; the skin would be mine, and I would have bragged about it all my life, and justly so!'

The Prince, whose military experience was now of value to him, for he had found himself before in situations where inevitable trouble had threatened from several sides, turned to the first man, saying: 'What guarantees can you give me that your lion, should we spare him, will do no harm to my people in this region?'

'My wife and my child offer to tame him, and to keep him quiet until I have managed to bring up here the iron-barred cage in which we'll take him back again, harmless and unharmed,' answered the father hastily.

The boy evidently wished to try out his flute, an instrument of the kind formerly called 'flauto dolce', which had a short mouthpiece like a pipe. Those who know how to play it can produce the most pleasant sounds. Meanwhile, the Prince had asked the castellan how the lion had managed to enter the castle grounds. The man answered: 'By the narrow passage which is walled in on both sides and has, for ages, been the only approach and is meant to remain so. Two footpaths, formerly leading up, have been so completely obstructed that, except by this narrow approach, no one can enter the magic castle which the mind and taste of Prince Friedrich intended it to become.'

After some moments of reflection, watching the child who all the time had been playing softly his flute as if preluding, the Prince turned to Honorio, saying: 'You have accomplished much today, finish now what you began. Take some men with you and hold the narrow passage, have your guns ready but do not shoot unless you cannot drive back the beast in any other manner. If necessary, build a fire to scare it if it should try to come down. This man and his wife may take responsibility for the rest.' Honorio at once set about carrying out these orders.

The child went on playing his tune, which was actually only a sequence of notes without any precise order and perhaps for this very reason was so deeply moving. Those standing around seemed to be under the spell of the melodious rhythm, when the father of the boy began to speak with appropriate enthusiasm:

'God has given the Prince wisdom and also the knowledge that all the works of God are wise, each in its own way. Look at that rock, how firm it stands; it does not move and braves the storms and the sunshine. Ancient trees surround its summit, and proudly it looks around far and wide. If one of its parts should crumble, it does not want to remain where it was but falls down, shattered to pieces, and covers the side of the slope. But even there the pieces will not stay; playfully they leap into the depth below; the brook receives them and carries them to the river. Neither resisting nor obstinate and angular, but smooth and rounded, they move along with increasing speed and pass from river to river, till they finally reach the ocean, where a host of giants are marching and the deep is swarming with dwarfs.

'But who sings the glory of the Lord, whom the stars praise for ever and ever? And why do you look in distant places? Look at the bees! Late in the fall they are still harvesting and build themselves a house, true and level, at once masters and workmen. Watch the ants: they know their way and never lose it; they build themselves a home of grass, crumbs of earth and pine needles; they build it up and cover it with a vaulted roof; but they have worked in vain, for the horse paws the ground and destroys everything. Look! it crushes their rafters and scatters their planks; it snorts impatiently and is restless; for the Lord has made the horse a brother to the wind and a companion of the storms, to carry man wherever he wishes, and woman wherever she desires to go. But in the palm grove the lion appeared. At a dignified pace he crossed the desert, where he reigns over all the other animals and nothing withstands him. Yet man knows how to tame him, and the cruellest of creatures has respect for him, the image of God, in which the angels too are made who serve the Lord and His servants. For in the lion's den Daniel was not afraid; he stood firm and was confident, and the wild roaring did not interrupt his hymn of praise.'

This speech, delivered with an expression of natural enthusiasm, the child accompanied with occasional melodious sounds on his flute; but when his father had finished, the boy began to sing in a clear, ringing voice, with skilful modulations, whereupon the father took the flute and accompanied the child, who sang:

> From the deep and from the darkness
> Rises now the prophet's song;
> God and Angels hover round him –
>   Why should he fear wrong?
> Lion and lioness together
> Rub against his knees and purr,
> For that melting holy music
>   Stills their savage stir.

The father continued to accompany each strophe on the flute, while the mother joined in, from time to time, as a second voice. But it was particularly moving when the child began to change the order of the lines of the verse; and even though he did not give a new meaning to the whole, he intensified his own feeling and the feelings of the listeners.

> Round the child those Angels hover
> Guarding him with sacred song;
> In the deep and in the darkness
>   Why should he fear wrong?
> In the presence of that music
> Never may misfortune dwell;
> Round my path the Angels hover:
>   All things shall be well.

All three then sang together with force and exaltation:

For the Eternal rules the waters,
Rules the earth, the air, the fire;
Like a lamb the lion shall gambol
　　And the flood retire.
Lo! the naked sword of anger
Hangs arrested in midair:
Strong the Love and great its wonders
　　That abides in prayer.

All were silent; all heard and listened; and only when the sounds had died away could one notice and observe the general impression. Everyone seemed to have calmed down; everyone was touched in a different manner. The Prince, as if he only now realized the disaster which had threatened him a short time ago, looked down at his wife, who was leaning against him and was not ashamed to take her small embroidered handkerchief and press it to her eyes. It did her good to feel her youthful heart relieved of the oppression that had weighed on it during the last hour. Complete silence reigned in the crowd; all seemed to have forgotten the dangers around them: the fire in the town below and, from above, the possible appearance of a suspiciously quiet lion.

The Prince was the first to get the crowd moving again when he gave the order to lead the horses nearer. Then he turned to the woman and said: 'Do you really believe that you can attract and tame the escaped lion, wherever you find him, by your singing and the sounds of your child's flute, and that you can take him back under lock and key without harm to others and to the beast itself?' They assured him that they could certainly do this, whereupon the castellan was appointed to be their guide. The Prince now left hurriedly with a few of his men, while the Princess followed more slowly with the others; but the mother and her son, accompanied by the castellan, who had meanwhile armed himself with a gun, climbed up the steep slope.

At the entrance to the narrow passage, the only approach to the old castle, they found the huntsmen busily piling up dry brushwood to build, if necessary, a large fire.

'It will not be necessary,' said the woman. 'Everything will be done in a friendly manner.'

Farther on they saw Honorio sitting on a spur of the wall, his double-barrelled gun across his knees, like a sentry prepared for anything that might happen. But he hardly seemed to notice them as they approached. He sat there as if sunk deep in thoughts and looked around in an absent-minded way. The woman spoke to him, imploring him not to let his men light the fire, but he seemed to give little attention to what she said; she went on to speak with great animation and exclaimed: 'Handsome young man, you killed my tiger – I do not curse you. Spare my lion, good young man, and I shall bless you.'

But Honorio looked straight ahead at the sun, which was slowly going down.

'You look westward,' the woman cried, 'and that is well, for there is much to be done there. But hurry, do not delay! You will conquer. But first conquer yourself!' At this, Honorio seemed to smile; the woman continued on her way but could not refrain from looking back once more at the young man; the red glow of the sun flushed his face, and she thought she had never seen a more handsome youth.

'If your child,' said the castellan, 'can really charm and quiet the lion with his song and his flute, as you are convinced he can, we shall quite easily subdue the powerful beast, for it has settled down quite close to the vaults through which we have broken an entrance into the courtyard, since the main gate has been blocked up by ruins. If the child can lure the lion in there, I can close the opening without any difficulty, and the boy can, if he wants, escape from the animal over one of the narrow winding stairs which he can see in the corners. We two are going to hide; but I shall take up a position from where my bullet can come to the child's aid at any moment.'

'All these preparations are unnecessary. God and our own skill, faith and good fortune are our best aides.'

'That may be so,' said the castellan, 'but I know my duty. First I shall lead you by a difficult ascent up to the battlements just opposite the entrance I mentioned before. Your child may descend then, as it were, into the arena of a theatre and lure the trusting beast into it.'

And so it happened: from their hiding place above, the castellan and the mother saw the child walking down the winding stairs into the bright courtyard, and then disappearing into the dark opening opposite; but they could immediately hear the sounds of his flute which gradually died away and finally stopped. The silence was ominous enough; the old hunter, though familiar with danger, felt ill at ease in this strange case concerning a human being. He thought to himself that he would prefer to face the dangerous animal himself; the mother, however, with a cheerful face, leaned far over the parapet and listened, not showing the slightest sign of uneasiness.

At last they heard the flute again; with eyes radiant with joy the child came out of the dark vault, the lion following him slowly and apparently walking with some difficulty. Now and then the animal seemed inclined to lie down, but the boy led it around in a half circle among the trees, which still showed some of their bright autumn foliage. Finally he sat down, almost transfigured by the last rays of the sun shining through a gap in the ruins, and began once more his soothing song, which we cannot refrain from repeating:

> From the deep and from the darkness
> Rises now the prophet's song;
> God and Angels hover round him –
>   Why should he fear wrong?
> Lion and lioness together
> Rub against his knees and purr,
> For that melting holy music
>   Stills their savage stir.

The lion had meanwhile nestled close to him, placing his heavy right forepaw in the lap of the boy, who, continuing to sing, stroked it gently but soon noticed that a sharp thorn was stuck between the pads. Carefully removing the painful point, the boy took off his bright-coloured scarf with a smile and bandaged the fearful paw, so that his mother, leaning back, flung up her arms in delight and would probably have applauded – clapping her hands in the usual manner – had not a firm grip of the castellan's fist reminded her that the danger was not yet over.

After playing a few notes on the flute as a prelude, the child sang triumphantly:

> For the Eternal rules the waters,
> Rules the earth, the air, the fire;
> Like a lamb the lion shall gambol
>   And the flood retire.
> Lo! the naked sword of anger
> Hangs arrested in midair:
> Strong the Love and great its wonders
>   That abides in prayer.

If it is possible to believe that an expression of friendliness, of grateful satisfaction, can be perceived on the features of such a fierce creature, the tyrant of the forests, the despot of the animal kingdom, then here it was seen; for the child, in his transfiguration, seemed really like a powerful and victorious conqueror, and the lion, though not looking like a defeated being, for his strength was only for a time concealed, did yet seem a tamed being, having surrendered to his own peaceable will. The child went on playing the flute and singing, transposing the verses and adding new ones in his own way:

> So good children find the Angels
> Near them in their hour of need,
> To prevent designing evil
> And promote the shining deed.
> So the dear child walks in safety,
> For the notes, bewitching sweet,
> Bring the tyrant of the forest
> Gentle to his gentle feet.

FAUST

Translated by Barker Fairley

CONTENTS

FAUST

A TRAGEDY

PART ONE

DEDICATION

You shifting figures, I remember seeing you dimly long ago, and now I find you coming back again. I wonder should I try to hold on to you this time. Have I the inclination, have I the heart for it? You draw closer out of the mist. Very well then, have your way. The magic breeze that floats along with you fills me with youthful excitement.

You bring back joyful days and joyful scenes and you recall many folk who were dear to me. Early love, early friends rise from the past like an old tale half-forgotten. The pain comes back and with it the lament that life should be so wayward, so confused, and I go over the names of those good people who left this life before me, cut off by some ill chance from further happiness.

Those that I wrote for then will not see what follows now. The friendly throng is dispersed; the early responses have died away. I write now for the unknown crowd whose very approval I dread. If there are any now alive who were pleased with my verses, they are scattered far and wide.

And a great desire seizes me – a desire I have not felt for years – to return to this solemn realm of the spirit. My song resumes hesitantly, insecurely, like an Aeolian harp. I am shaken through and through. The tears come freely and my heart is softened. All my world now seems far away, and what was lost has become real and immediate.

PRELUDE ON THE STAGE
The director, the poet, the clown

DIRECTOR

Tell me, you two, you've stood by me so many times when
things were bad. What luck do you think we shall have on this
tour of ours through the country? The crowd is so easy-going
I'd like to please them. The posts are up and the stage is ready.
And there they are, all sitting with their eyes wide open,
looking forward to a treat and perhaps a real surprise.
I usually know how to satisfy them, but I've never been so
much at a loss as now. Of course, they're not used to seeing
the best, but they've read an awful lot. We want something
lively, something novel, and it has to be pleasant too, and not
meaningless. For I must say I like the sight of people streaming in crowds to the tent, thrusting in bursts like birthpangs
through the narrow gate, and fighting their way to the box
office all in broad daylight at four in the afternoon or earlier.
Yes, breaking their necks almost to get a ticket, like starving
men in a famine at a baker's door. No one but a poet can work
this miracle on such a mixed public. My friend, do it today.

POET

Don't talk to me about the vulgar mob, the seething vortex
that sucks you in against your will. The very sight of it para-
lyses me. Lead me rather to the quiet nook that is my heaven,
the only place where a poet can be happy and can cultivate his
precious gift among those who love and cherish him.

   The verses, good or bad, that spring to his lips from deep
within him are crowded out in the rough-and-tumble of the
day. You have to wait for years to see them in their true light.
Showy things are just meant for the moment, but whatever is
really good comes through to posterity.

CLOWN

Posterity, I hate the word. What if I were to talk about
posterity? Who would amuse people now? They want their

fun and they're going to get it. Having a lad like me on hand is worth something, isn't it? If you know how to reach your audience, you'll never quarrel with it, and the bigger it is, the easier they are to work on. So be a good boy and do your best. Give us something with all sorts of imagination in it, give us wisdom, good sense, feeling, passion, if you like, but don't forget there has to be some clowning too.

DIRECTOR
Plenty of action, that's the first thing that's needed. People want to use their eyes, they want to see. If you keep the scene moving all the time, if you keep them staring and gaping, it's more than half the battle. They'll love you. Give them lots of stuff and you'll appeal to lots of people. Everyone will be free to make his choice. If you offer plenty there'll be this or that for so many of them and they'll all go home contented. Whatever piece you do, do it in pieces. With a mixed grill you can't miss. It's easy to think up, easy to stage. If you present them with an artistic whole, what's the use? They'll only take it in snatches anyway.

POET
You don't know what a cheap trade that is, unworthy of a true artist. Botchwork, the lowest of the low, that's what you've come down to.

DIRECTOR
Talk like that doesn't bother me. If a man wants to be effective, he must use the right tools. Just remember what sort of people you're addressing. It's not hardwood you have to split, it's soft. One of them comes because he's bored and another comes from gorging at the dinner table. And, what is worse, quite a lot of them have just been reading the newspaper. They come with their minds on something else, the way you go to a carnival. It's curiosity at most that brings them along. The ladies come in their finery and this helps too without costing us anything. What are you poets dreaming of in your ivory towers? Don't give yourself illusions about a full house. Take a closer look at our patrons, coarse cold-hearted people, one hoping for a game of cards after the play, and

another for a wild night in bed with a girl. You silly fools, there's no sense in tormenting the nine muses here. I tell you, give us plenty, pile it on, and you can't go wrong. Just get them all mixed up, they're hard to please. What's got you now? Are you in pain, or is it ecstasy?

POET

Off you go, and get someone else to do your dirty work. Do you expect a poet wantonly to trifle away his greatest gift, nature's gift to his humanity, merely to oblige you? By what power is it that a poet masters the elements and moves the hearts of all men? Is it not the sense of harmony extending from him to embrace the world? Without him nature is like an endless thread, indifferently, discordantly turning on the spindle, no harmony in it. Who is it that breaks up the monotony, enlivens it, gives it rhythm? Who is it that can take a single thing and make it part of the great chorus extolling the universe? Who is it that blends storms and tempests with the human emotions or mingles the glow of sunset in our thoughtful moods? Who scatters all the spring flowers in the paths where lovers walk? Who makes the meagre laurel into a crown of honour for all who deserve it? Who assures us there are gods in council on Olympus? It is the power of man as revealed in the poet.

CLOWN

All right. Get to work with it, this pretty gift of yours. Try it on a love-story. You know how it goes. You meet someone, you feel something, you stick around, and bit by bit you get involved. You're all happiness and then trouble comes. First the rapture and then the misery, and before you know where you are you have a whole romance. Write us a play on these lines. But scoop it up out of real life, life at the full. Everybody lives it, few know it. And it's interesting, no matter where you scratch it. Variety, colour, confusion, error, and a grain of truth. That's the right brew, it suits everyone. The handsome young folk will turn up, tense with expectation. The sentimental ones will get their fill of melancholy. You'll touch life at many points and so each of them will learn about himself.

They're young, they're ready to laugh, ready to cry. They're still growing, they still have their ideals, their illusions. You can appeal to that. Adults are so set in their ways you can never please them. But the young will always be grateful for what you offer.

POET

Then give me back the days when I was like that, the days when a fountain of song welled out of me, one song after another, and never stopped. The world was veiled in mist; the budding branch was a miracle of promise; the valleys were clothed with flowers, thousands of flowers, for me to pluck. I had nothing, yet I had enough – the urge towards truth and the joy of illusion. Oh, give me back those driving passions – the deep happiness that hurts, the force of hate, the power of love. Oh, make me young again.

CLOWN

Youth, my friend, is what you may need in the stress of battle, or in love when pretty girls hang on your neck and won't be repressed, or if you're running a race and see the winning-post so near and yet so far, or on riotous nights, first whirling in the dance and then feasting and drinking till daybreak. But when it comes to playing the old familiar tune and doing it boldly, yet gracefully, and setting yourself a task and working it out in a happy, casual way, that, old gentlemen, is your job and we respect you for it. They say old age makes us childish, but it isn't so. Old age brings out the true child in all of us.

DIRECTOR

We've had arguments enough, what we want now is action. You're wasting your time over these compliments when we might be doing something useful. What's the good of talking about being in the mood or not in the mood. The mood never comes to those who hesitate. If you pretend to be poets make your poetry do what you tell it to do. You know what we want. We want strong drink, so on with the work. We've no time to lose. What you don't do today, you won't find done tomorrow. Tackle something within your reach and go at it with a will. Once started, you won't want to let go and you'll work on because you're committed.

You know that in the German theatre each of us is free to experiment. Today you can be lavish with scenery and all the furnishings. You have sun and moon at your disposal and stars in plenty. Water, fire, rocks, beasts, birds – we're not short of any. So on this little stage of ours you can run through the whole of creation and with fair speed make your way from heaven through the world to hell.

PROLOGUE IN HEAVEN

The Lord. The heavenly host. Then Mephistopheles. The three arch-angels step forward

RAPHAEL

The sun resounds among the singing spheres with its ancient music and, thundering loud, completes its course. The angels cannot fathom it, but the mere sight gives them strength. The great, the incomparably great, works of creation are splendid as on the first day of the world.

GABRIEL

And with speed incredible the earth revolves in its glory, the radiance of paradise alternating with deep and dreadful night. Sea-floods storm at the base of the rocks, and sea and rocks alike are whirled in the swift motion of the spheres.

MICHAEL

And tempest on tempest rages from sea to land, from land to sea, forming a chain of mightiest energy. Dread light-nings flash before the thunderclap. But your messengers, O Lord, revere the gentler processes.

ALL THREE

The angels cannot fathom it, but the mere sight gives them strength. And all your mighty works are splendid as on the first day.

MEPHISTOPHELES

Since you, O Lord, are receiving once more and wish to know how we're getting on, here I am again among those present. You've never made me feel unwelcome in the past. Only you must forgive me, I can't talk big. If I tried, you'd laugh at my rhetoric. But I forget, you haven't laughed for a long time. On the sun and the planets etcetera I've nothing to report. I only see the life of man – how wretched it is. These little lords of creation haven't changed in the least. They're just as queer as they were on the first day. It would be better for them if you hadn't given them the light of heaven. They call it their reason and all they use it for is to make themselves more bestial than the beasts. With your Grace's permission, they seem to me like those long-legged grasshoppers that make their little flying jumps and then settle in the grass and sing the same old song. If only they would stay in the grass. But they bury their noses in all the dirt they find.

THE LORD

Is this all you have to say to me? Must you always come complaining? Is there never anything on earth that you approve of?

MEPHISTOPHELES

No, sir, I find it pretty bad there, as I always have. Men's lives are so miserable I'm sorry for them. Poor things, I haven't the heart to plague them myself.

THE LORD

Do you know Faust?

MEPHISTOPHELES

What? The professor?

THE LORD

He is my servant.

MEPHISTOPHELES

Well, I must say, he has his own way of serving you. The common food and drink is not for him. There's an unrest in him that drives him off the map. He half knows how crazy he is. He claims that heaven ought to yield him the pick of the stars and earth its uttermost delights. And nothing, near or remote, can ever satisfy him.

THE LORD

I admit he's not yet rid of his confusion, but I shall soon lead him into the light. The gardener knows when he sees the tree in leaf that flower and fruit will follow in due season.

MEPHISTOPHELES

What will you wager? I'll take him from you yet, if you give me permission to lead him gently my way.

THE LORD

You're free to do that for the rest of his days. Striving and straying, you can't have the one without the other.

MEPHISTOPHELES

Much obliged. I've never enjoyed having to do with the dead. Rosy cheeks are what I like. I've no use for corpses. I'm like a cat with a mouse.

THE LORD

Very well, I leave it to you. Draw his mind away from its true source and, if you can get a grip on him, set him on your downward path. And confess in the end to your shame: man in his dark impulse always knows the right road from the wrong.

MEPHISTOPHELES

Good enough. But I shan't be long over it. I'm not afraid of losing my bet. If I succeed, you must allow me to celebrate my triumph. I'll make him eat the dust and enjoy it, like my old friend, the serpent.

THE LORD

I give you complete freedom, as I always have. I've never hated your sort. Of all the negative spirits your roguish kind gives me the least concern. It's so easy for men to slump and before long they want to do nothing at all. So I don't object to their having your company. You act as a stimulant and so serve a positive purpose in spite of yourself.

But you, the true sons of heaven, I bid you rejoice in the living beauty of the world, its growth, its love. Seek in your minds for what is permanent in its change.

The heavens close, the archangels withdraw

MEPHISTOPHELES *alone*

I like to see the old man now and then, and I take good care to keep in with him. It's nice of so great a personage to talk to the devil himself in this human way.

NIGHT
A high, narrow, vaulted Gothic chamber

FAUST *sitting at his desk, restless*

Look at me. I've worked right through philosophy, right through medicine and jurisprudence, as they call it, and that wretched theology too. Toiled and slaved at it and know no more than when I began. I have my master's degree and my doctor's and it must be ten years now that I've led my students by the nose this way and that, upstairs and down-stairs, and all the time I see plainly that we don't and can't know anything. It eats me up. Of course I'm ahead of these silly scholars, these doctors and clerics and what not. I have no doubts or scruples to bother me, and I snap my fingers at hell and the devil. But I pay the price. I've lost all joy in life. I don't delude myself. I shall never know anything worth knowing, never have a word to say that might be useful to my fellow men. I own nothing, no money, no property, I have no standing in the world. It's a dog's life and worse. And this is why I've gone over to magic, to see if I can get secrets out of the spirit world and not have to go on sweating and saying things I don't know, discover, it may be, what it is that holds the world together, behold with my own eyes its innermost workings, and stop all this fooling with words.

Oh if this were the last time the full moon found me here in my agony. How often have I sat at this desk among my books watching for you in the deep of night till at last, my melancholy friend, you came. Oh to be out on the hilltops in your lovely light, floating among spirits at some cavern's mouth or merging into your meadows in the dimness. Oh to be clear, once and for all, of this pedantry, this stench, and to wash myself in your dew and be well again.

But where am I? Still a prisoner in this stifling hole, these walls, where even the sunlight that filters in is dimmed and discoloured by the painted panes, surrounded from floor to ceiling by dusty, worm-eaten bookshelves with this sooty paper stuck over them, these instruments everywhere, these beakers, these retorts, and then, on top of that, my family goods and chattels. Call that a world?

Is it any wonder that your heart should quail and tremble and that this ache, this inertia, should thwart your every impulse? When God created man he put him in the midst of nature's growth and here you have nothing round you but bones and skeletons and mould and grime.

Up then. Out into the open country. And what better guide could I have than this strange book that Nostradamus wrote. With its help I shall follow the movement of the stars. Nature may teach me how spirits talk to spirits. It is futile to brood drily here over the magic signs. You spirits, hovering about me, hear me and answer. *He opens the book and sees the sign of the macrocosm*

What a vision is this, flooding all my senses with delight, racing through my nerves and veins with the fire and the freshness of youth. Was it a god who set down these signs that hush my inner fever, fill my poor heart with happiness, and with mysterious power make visible the forces of nature about me. Am I myself a god? Such light is given to me. In these pure lines I see the working of nature laid bare. Now I know what the philosopher meant: 'The spirit-world is not closed. It is your mind that is shut, your heart that is inert. Up, my pupil, be confident, bathe your breast in the dawn.' *He contemplates the sign*

Oh what a unity it is, one thing moving through another, the heavenly powers ascending and descending, passing the golden vessels up and down, flying from heaven to earth on fragrant wings, making harmonious music in the universe. What a spectacle. But ah, only a spectacle. Infinite nature, how shall I lay hold of you? How shall I feed at these breasts, these nurturing springs, for which I yearn, on which all life depends? When these are offered, must I thirst in vain? *He turns the pages angrily and sees the sign of the Earth-spirit*

How differently this sign affects me. You, Earth-spirit, are closer to me, warming me like wine and filling me with new energy. I'm ready now to adventure into life, endure the world's joy and the world's pain, wrestle with its storms, and not lose courage in the grinding shipwreck. See, the room is clouded, the moon is hid, the lamp goes out, vapours rise, redness flashes, terror comes down on me from the vaulted roof. You spirit that I have sought, I feel your nearness. Reveal yourself. My whole being gropes and struggles towards sensations I never knew. My heart goes out to you. Reveal yourself. You must, though it costs me my life. *He seizes the book and spells out the mysterious sign, a red flame flashes, and the spirit appears in the flame*

SPIRIT

Who calls?

FAUST *with face averted*

Appalling.

SPIRIT

You sought me mightily, you sucked and pulled long at my sphere. And now?

FAUST

Ah! I cannot face you.

SPIRIT

You begged breathlessly to see me, to see my face, hear my voice. I yield to your implorations. Here I am. And now, you would-be superman, what abjectness is this? Where now is your spirit's call? Where is the heart that swelled to world-size, created its own world, and cherished it rapturously, thinking itself the equal of us spirits? Where are you, Faust, whose voice came to me with such pressure, such urgency? Is this Faust, shattered when my breath reaches him, a worm wriggling away in terror?

FAUST

Must I give in to you, you flame-shape? Yes, here I am. This is Faust, your equal.

SPIRIT

In floods of life, in storms of action, I range up and down.

I flow this way and that. I am birth and the grave, an eternal ocean, a changeful weaving, a glowing life. And thus I work at the humming loom of time, and fashion the earth, God's living garment.

FAUST

You busy spirit, roaming the wide world, how close I feel to you.

SPIRIT

You are not close. You are not equal. You are only equal to what you think I am. *disappears*

FAUST *collapsing*

Not equal to you. Me created in God's image. And not even equal to you. (*A knock*) Oh, death. That's my famulus knocking. Oh that at the supreme moment this dull creeping fellow should spoil my wealth of visions.

Wagner in his nightcap with a lamp in his hand. Faust turns in annoyance

WAGNER

Forgive me. I heard you declaiming. From a Greek tragedy, I've no doubt. This is an art. I wish I was better at it. It's worth a lot nowadays. They do say an actor could teach a parson.

FAUST

Yes, if the parson's an actor, as may sometimes be the case.

WAGNER

Oh, dear me. When a man is stuck in his study all the time and only sees the world on holidays, from far away, through a telescope, you might say, hardly that, how is he to persuade them of anything?

FAUST

You'll never do this, if you don't feel it. If it doesn't come from deep down and win the hearts of your hearers with energy unforced. Oh yes, stay put in your chairs, paste your clippings together, concoct a stew from other men's tables, blow the petty little flames from your ashheaps to entertain the simple-minded, if that's what suits you. But you'll never move and unite the hearts of men, unless your own heart is behind it.

WAGNER

But the delivery, the technique, is what makes a good orator. I realize how much I have to learn.

FAUST

Make your living honestly. Don't be a bell-tinkling fool. Intelligence and good sense can be left to speak for themselves. If you really have something to say, do you have to hunt for words and phrases to say it? These smart speeches of yours, packed with titbits from everywhere, are as unrefreshing as the wind in autumn rustling the dry leaves.

WAGNER

But art is long, God knows, and this life of ours is short. I often lose heart in my studies, and lose confidence too. There's so much to master before you can get back to the sources. And, poor fellows, we snuff out before we're halfway through.

FAUST

Manuscripts. Is that the sacred spring to quench your thirst for ever? You'll never find true refreshment unless it comes from within you.

WAGNER

You must pardon me, though. It's a great satisfaction to enter into the spirit of the times, to see what a wise man once said and then to consider what wonderful progress we've made since.

FAUST

Oh yes, wonderful indeed. Past ages, my friend, are a book with seven seals. What you all call the spirit of the times is just your own spirit with the times reflected in it. A sorry sight it often is, I must say. One glance is enough to make you run. A garbage can and a lumber-room. Or, at best, a blood-and-thunder play with excellent moral saws and sayings, good enough perhaps for a puppet-show.

WAGNER

But the world around us, the human heart and mind. Everyone wants to know about it.

FAUST

Know about it. What sort of knowing? Who'll tell you the

honest truth? The few men who really knew and didn't keep
what they knew to themselves but told the world what
they felt and saw have been burned and crucified from the
beginning of time. But excuse me, friend, it's very late, we
must stop now.

WAGNER

I could have stayed up all night, conferring with you so
intellectually. But tomorrow is Easter Sunday and you must
allow me to come and ask you one or two more questions.
I've kept my nose to the grindstone and I know a lot, but
I want to know everything. *off*

FAUST *alone*

Strange they don't lose hope altogether, always busy with
things that don't matter, digging greedily for treasure and
happy when they come across an earthworm.

   To think that this prosaic voice sounded here in my
room when the air was thronged with spirits. But for once,
you miserable wretch, I'm grateful to you. You saved me
from despair that was not far from destroying me. This
apparition was so tremendous, it made a dwarf of me,
a nothing.

   Shaped in God's image, was I? Conceitedly indulging in
the clear light of heaven, thinking I was soon to look into the
mirror of eternal truth after leaving mortality far behind me.
What presumption. Imagining I was greater than the angels,
able to move of my own accord in nature's veins and create
like one of the gods. Oh, the punishment. One thundering
word has brought me low.

   Equality with you I cannot claim. I had the strength to
summon you, but not the strength to hold. In that supreme
moment I felt at once so great and so small. And then
ruthlessly you thrust me back into uncertainty, the common
lot of men. Who will tell me what next to do, or what not
to do? Shall I abandon my quest or not? The things
we do cramp us not less surely than the things that are
done to us.

   Our noblest thoughts soon lose their purity in the dross

that invades them. Then mere comforts suffice and ideals are despised. The lofty sentiments that were the breath of life to us are smothered in the earthly rubble.

Time was when your imagination with bold and hopeful flight would reach out into infinity, but when, in the whirligig, misfortunes come, then little room is all the room it needs. Care at once lodges deep in the heart, clothing itself in endless disguises and bringing disquietude and those mysterious pains. Whatever crosses our mind, nothing is free from it — fire, water, dagger, poison, family, property. You quake at the thought of what doesn't happen and you weep for the loss of what you never lose.

I'm not like the gods. I know it now. I'm like the worm, wriggling in the dust, the worm that feeds on the dust and is crushed to nothing by the passing foot.

What is it but dust, this high wall shutting me in with its hundred compartments? And all this rubbish, these countless moth-eaten trivialities that beset me? Can I be expected to find what I want here? Am I to read in a thousand books that men have always been harassed and that one of them was happy here or there? You empty grinning skull, what have you to say to me? All you can say is that your poor brain like mine once groped for the light and the truth only to go grievously astray at the close. As for these instruments, they mock me, these wheels and cogs and rollers. I stood at the gate, they were the keys. Complicated enough, but they didn't lift the latch. You can't pluck nature's veil, she stays a mystery in full daylight. What she doesn't choose to reveal you can't force out of her with screws and levers. These old things are only here because they were my father's, I never used them. This parchment has been gathering soot from my smoky lamp for years. Better by far, it would have been, to squander the little I had than to go on sweating here under the weight of it. What you inherit from your forebears isn't yours unless you do something with it. Things unused are a sore burden. Only your creativeness moment by moment can turn them to account.

But now this flask here? Can it be magnetic? Why does it suddenly rivet my attention, easing and clearing my mind, like moonlight flooding the dark forest?

Come down, you rare, you sacred draught, you tribute to man's cunning, you blend of subtle poisons, quintessence of opiates.

Show your master what you can do for him. I look at you, my pain is less. I take hold of you, my stress relaxes. The flood-tide of my spirit ebbs and ebbs, and the high sea beckons. The great waters sparkle at my feet. A new day invites me to new shores.

A fiery chariot comes swinging down for me. I'm ready to follow a new course, ready for a new activity in a purer sphere. What exaltation, what divine joy. And what a reversal, deserved or not. A worm and now this. Yes, turn your back on the sweet sunlight. Tear open the gates that others shrink from approaching. The time has come to show by your deeds that man in moral courage is equal to the gods, bold enough to face that dark horrific cavern and force his way to the narrow passage, girt with flames of hell, and do it serenely, even at the risk of lapsing into nothingness.

And now I take this long-forgotten crystal loving-cup down from its old case. I remember how it figured at family parties and how the guests were amused when the pledger did his duty, invented a rhyme to interpret the decorations, and emptied the cup at a draught. There is no friend of my youth to pass it on to this time, nor any need for rhyming. This is a drink that soon intoxicates, the drink that I prepared, the chosen drink darkening the brimming cup. I pledge it with all my heart to the new day. *He puts the cup to his lips. Church bells and choir*

CHOIR OF ANGELS

Christ is risen. Joy to the mortal no longer swathed in fleshly ills, inherited, insidious, ruinous.

FAUST

What heavy bourdon, what high note is this, that pulls the glass from my lips with such force. Do these deep bells announce the Easter festival? Is this the choir singing the comforting words, first sung by angels at the darksome grave, giving assurance of a new faith, a new covenant?

CHOIR OF WOMEN

We, his faithful ones, anointed and laid him in shrouds, and now he is no longer here.

CHOIR OF ANGELS

Christ is risen. Happy the lover of mankind, his sad and saving ordeal passed.

FAUST

Why do you seek me in the dust, you heavenly notes, strong and gentle at once? Ring out elsewhere for weaker men. I hear your message well enough, but I lack the faith, the faith that fathers your miracle. I don't aspire to those regions whence your message comes. And yet, these sounds, known to me from early years, call me back to life. I remember sabbaths when in the stillness the kiss of heavenly love was granted me. In those days the pealing bells were full of promise and to utter a prayer was a rapture of delight. A strange, sweet yearning would draw me out into the fields and woods where floods of tears gave birth, it seemed, to an inner world. This is the song that ushered in the merry games of childhood and the festive springtime, so free, so happy. Memory, piety, holds me from this last step of all. Ring out, sweet bells. My tears come. Earth has won me back again.

CHOIR OF DISCIPLES

He that was sublime in life has gone up from the sepulchre and is beginning now to share the joy of creation. Master, we who languish here on earth bemoan your fortune.

CHOIR OF ANGELS

Christ is risen out of corruption. Rejoice and free yourselves. Go forth and praise him in good works, promising blessedness. Then the master will be near, he will be among you.

OUTSIDE THE TOWN-GATE
People of all sorts out for the day

SOME JOURNEYMEN
Why go that way?

OTHERS
We're going to the Huntsman.

THE FIRST ONES
But we want to go to the Old Mill.

ONE
I say, go to Riverview.

SECOND
The road there's so dull.

THE SECOND ONES
What'll you do?

THIRD
I'll go with the rest.

FOURTH
Come on up to the village. That's where you're sure to find
the prettiest girls and the best beer. And a good scrap too.

FIFTH
You never have enough. Is your hide itching for the third
time? I don't want to go there. I hate the place.

SERVANT GIRL
No, I'm going back home.

ANOTHER
We're sure to find him beside those poplars.

FIRST
That's no fun. It's you he'll walk with. You're the only one he
dances with. What's that to me?

THE OTHER
He won't be by himself today for sure. He told us Curly was
coming with him.

STUDENT
The way those wenches step out. They're hefty. Come on,

let's join them. That's what I like – a maid in her Sunday best, a good strong beer, and a nippy tobacco.

GIRL

Just look at those nice boys. It's a shame. They could have anyone they wanted and they go running after those servant girls.

SECOND STUDENT *to the first*

Not so fast. There's two others coming. Nicely dressed. One of them lives next door. I've taken a real fancy to her. They're just strolling along. They'll let us pick them up.

FIRST STUDENT

No, I don't want to be put on my best behaviour. Come on quick or we'll lose the others. The hand that wields a broom on Saturdays will fondle you best on Sundays.

TOWNSMAN

No, I don't approve of our new mayor. Now he's appointed, he's getting bolder every day. And what is he doing for the town? Aren't things getting worse all the time? We have to toe the line more than ever and pay bigger taxes too.

BEGGAR *singing*

Good sirs, fair ladies, so gay, so shining, pray look on me and ease my lot. Let me not grind my organ here for nothing. If you don't give, you won't be happy. This is a holiday, make it a good day for me.

ANOTHER TOWNSMAN

I know nothing better on Sundays and holidays than talking about war and rumours of war when the nations are at one another's throats far off in Turkey and places. You stand at the window and empty your glass and watch the boats gliding downstream, then go home in the evening in good spirits, thankful for peace and peaceful times.

THIRD TOWNSMAN

Yes, neighbour. I'm with you there. Let them split one another's heads and all go topsy-turvy, so long as things stay just the same at home.

OLD WOMAN *to the girls*

Oh, how smart you are, you pretty creatures. You could turn anybody's head. But go easy. Don't put on such airs. I know how to get you what you want.

GIRL

Come on, Agatha. I take good care not to be seen with those old witches. But on St Andrew's night she did show me my future lover.

THE OTHER

She showed me mine in a crystal, like a soldier, in riotous company. I keep a look-out for him, but I've had no luck.

SOLDIERS *singing*

High-walled castles and haughty girls, these we assail. A bold endeavour, a great reward. Death or delight, we follow the trumpet. Girls or castles, surrender they must. A bold endeavour, a great reward. And the soldiers march away.

Faust and Wagner

FAUST

The ice is gone in the brooks and rivers under the sweet spring's quickening glance. And the valleys are green with hope. Old winter, the dodderer, has shrunk into the hills, streaking the sprouting meadows with impotent hail. But the sun will have no whiteness, where all is thrust and growth. She wants colour everywhere. Being short of flowers, she makes the gay crowd serve. Turn round here on the rise and look back at the town. See the motley throng pouring out through the dark gate into the sunlight. They all love it. They're celebrating the resurrection, because they're resurrected themselves, out of cramped houses, stuffy rooms, out of the toils of trade, the weight of roofs and gables, the narrow streets, the church darkness. Back into the daylight. See how soon they scatter among the fields and plots. See these boats all dancing in the river, wherever you look. And here this last boat setting out loaded to the gunwale. You can make out the colour of the dresses sprinkled right up the hillside. And now I can hear the noise of the village. This is the people's heaven, young and old contentedly saying: Here I can be free, here I am human.

WAGNER

It's an honour to go for a walk with you, professor, and profitable too. But I would never come here alone, because I can't bear any coarseness. I hate this fiddling and shrieking, and this skittle-alley. They make an infernal noise and call it enjoyment, call it singing.

Peasants under the linden tree

Dance and Song

The shepherd put on his best for the dance. And smart he looked in his gay jacket. They were dancing like mad round the linden tree. There was no room there. Hooray, hooray, on went the fiddles.

He pushed his way in and bumped a girl with his elbow. She whipped round and yelled 'Stupid.' Hooray, hooray. Don't be so rough.

Round and round they went, this way and that way. Skirts were flying. They got hot and rested arm in arm. Hooray, hooray. And hip to elbow.

And don't make so free. Lots of girls have been had. But he got her off to one side all the same. They could just hear the noise of the dance. Hooray, hooray, on went the fiddles.

OLD PEASANT

It's nice of you, doctor, to come among us common folk today and not feel above it, you being so learned a scholar. So take this drink in our best cup with our compliments. We don't want it just to quench your thirst. We hope that for every drop that is in it a day will be added to your life.

FAUST

I accept this refreshment with thanks and drink to the health of all of you.

The people gather round

OLD PEASANT

Indeed it was right of you to come on this happy day.
I remember what you did for us once in evil days. There's
many a one here now whom your father saved from the fever
when he stopped that epidemic. You were a young man
then. You went into all the houses. Many never came out
alive, but you did. You stood a lot. You helped us and God
helped you.

ALL

Your health, sir, we wish you a long life to go on helping us.

FAUST

Bow down to him from whom help comes. *He passes on
with Wagner*

WAGNER

What satisfaction it must give you to be revered by all these
people. Lucky is he who can derive such advantages from his
talents. They all come running and enquiring. Fathers show
you to their little boys. The fiddling stops, the dancers stop.
They line up when you move on. Caps fly in the air. It
wouldn't take much and they'd go down on their knees as if
the sacred host was coming.

FAUST

It's only a few steps further to that rock where we'll rest a
while. I often used to sit here alone with my thoughts,
tormenting myself with prayer and fasting. I was firm in my
faith then and full of hope. And with sighs and tears and
wringing of hands I believed I could force the Lord in heaven
to end the plague. The approval I get from these people is a
mockery to me now. If only you could read in my heart how
little my father and I deserved the approval. My father was a
quiet gentleman who studied nature in his own queer way, but
honestly enough. He joined a society of alchemists who went
in for the black kitchen, laboriously mixing opposites in
search of remedies. A red lion was wedded in a warm liquid
to the lily, then the two were distilled again and again over an

open flame till finally the young queen appeared in many
colours. This was our remedy. The patients died. No one
asked any questions. With our hellish drugs we did more
harm in this part of the country than the plague. I administered the poison myself to thousands, they pined away, while
I have lived to see the time when they praise their murderers.

WAGNER

You shouldn't let it bother you. If you carefully and conscientiously practise the arts that have been handed on to you,
it's all that can be expected. A man who respects his father
will be glad to learn from him and if he in his turn can add to
science his son will profit.

FAUST

What a sea of confusion and error we live in, finding no use
for the knowledge we have and lacking the very knowledge
we need. There is solace in the mere thought of escape. But
why spoil this happy hour with such lamenting? See how the
evening rays pick out the little houses in their green setting.
The day is over and the sun is almost gone, speeding away on
its life-giving journey. And now I long for wings to lift me off
the ground and let me follow it. Then I should have the quiet
earth ever below me in an eternal sunset, with all the heights
aflame and the valleys at rest and the silvery streams turning
to gold. Not the grim mountain with all its chasms would
check my marvellous flight. And next the great ocean
would come in sight with the day's warmth lying in its bays.
If the sun seems near to sinking, a burst of new energy carries
me after it, to drink its eternal light, the day always before me
and the night behind, the heavens above me and the waves
beneath. A lovely dream, but not for long. The body has not
wings to match the spirit's wings. Yet it is natural for our
feelings to soar upward and onward, when we see the lark
trilling its song, a speck lost in the blue, or the eagle in hilly
country floating above the pines, or the heron over flats and
lakes winging its way to roost.

WAGNER

I've had some queer thoughts myself, but I never wanted to

do that. You get your fill of woods and fields so quickly. And
I've no desire to fly like a bird. What I like is the pleasures of
the mind that carry you from page to page and from book to
book and make winter evenings a delight. You're snug and
warm in every limb and, with an old parchment spread before
you, it's heavenly.

FAUST

This is the force that drives you. You don't know the other
force, and I hope you never will. As for myself, there are two
of me, unreconciled. The one clings to the earth with its
whole body sensually, while the other soars with all its
might to the abodes of the blest. If there are spirits about,
ranging and ruling in the atmosphere, come down to me out
of this golden light, and transport me where life is rich and
new. If I only had a magic carpet to take me abroad I wouldn't
part with it for anything, not for the costliest of gowns, not
even for a king's mantle.

WAGNER

Don't summon those spirits that throng the air and threaten
us with danger on every hand. We know them too well. In the
sharp North wind they attack us with their arrowy tongues or
they eat out our lungs in the withering East. In the South they
come out of the desert to blaze down on our poor heads and
the West wind only refreshes in order to flood our fields and
drown us out. They're all ears, because they're full of mischief. They do what we ask, because they like to fool us. They
pretend to come from heaven and they lie with the tongues of
angels. But let us push on. The colour has all faded from the
scenery, it's chilly now and damp. Home's the place after
dark. But what are you standing and staring at so? There's
nothing to see here in the twilight.

FAUST

Do you notice the black dog running there in the stubble?

WAGNER

Oh yes. I saw it a while back. It's just a dog.

FAUST

Look again. What do you think it really is?

WAGNER

A poodle, following us the way dogs do.

FAUST

Don't you see that he's circling us and getting nearer and nearer? If I'm not mistaken, there's a streak of fire trailing behind him.

WAGNER

All I see is a black poodle. Your eyes must be deceiving you.

FAUST

I believe he's drawing magic snares round our feet and wants to come to terms with us.

WAGNER

He's just confused, because he finds we're strangers and not his master.

FAUST

The circle is narrowing, he's not far away.

WAGNER

There you see. He's no ghost. He's just a dog like any other dog, whining and lying down and wagging his tail.

FAUST

Come here. Stay with us.

WAGNER

A silly creature. You stop, he's at your service. You speak to him, he jumps up at you. Throw something away, he'll fetch it. He'll fetch your stick out of the water.

FAUST

You must be right. It's just his tricks, no trace of a spirit.

WAGNER

Even a philosopher might enjoy having a well-behaved dog. Some student has trained him well, he'll do you no discredit.

They enter the town-gate

FAUST'S STUDY (i)

FAUST *entering with the poodle*

It's dark now in the fields and everywhere. Night has come, bringing its strange intimations and premonitions. Our better self is awakened, our unruliness, our dangerous impulses abated. Thoughts of love begin to stir in me, love of mankind, love of god.

Be quiet, poodle. Don't run about so. What are you sniffing at in the doorway? Lie down behind the stove, I'll give you my best cushion. You entertained us nicely with your antics when we came down the hill. Now let me make you comfortable as my guest. You're welcome to stay if you don't make a noise.

This is the time when a man feels clear in his own mind, sitting in his den with the friendly lamp burning. Reason raises its voice again and hope revives. You long to reach the springs of life, you long for the source.

Poodle, stop your whining and growling. There's no place for these animal noises beside the lofty music that I hear within me. We know that if people don't understand a thing they ridicule it, they complain about the good and the beautiful because it embarrasses them. Is the dog going to follow suit?

But ah, in spite of myself my inner contentment is beginning to fail. Why must the flow so soon give out and leave us thirsting? I've seen it many times. But there's another way, if we put our trust in the supernatural and yearn for revelation. And where does the light of revelation burn better and brighter than in the New Testament? I must look at the original without delay and see if I can render it honestly in my beloved German. *He opens a volume and begins*

The text reads: In the beginning was the word. But stop. What about this? I can't rate the word nearly as high as that. I'll have to translate it some other way. Unless I'm mistaken, the true reading is: In the beginning was the mind. But let's not be in a hurry with the first line. Can it be the mind that creates the world? Surely we ought to read: In the beginning was the energy. But no sooner do I write this than something tells me not to stop there. And now I see the light and set down confidently: In the beginning was the act.

Poodle, if you and I are to share the room, you'll have to

stop your yelping. I can't do with so bothersome a companion. One of us will have to go. I'm sorry. You can't be my guest any longer. The door's open. Off with you. But what do I see? Can it be natural? Can it be real? This poodle is swelling so. It can't be a poodle. It's more like a hippopotamus. Eyes of fire and dreadful jaws. What a spectre I brought home with me. But I'll get you. The key of Solomon is the thing for the likes of you.

SPIRITS *on the landing*

> There's someone trapped in there. Don't go in. Stay out. The old devil's caught like a fox in a trap. But watch. Float about for a minute and you'll see he'll get loose. Help him if you can. He's done us many a good turn.

FAUST

First I'll go at him with the spell of the four elements.

> Let the salamander glow, let the undine writhe, let the sylph disappear, let the cobold toil.

No man could be master of the spirits, if he didn't know the elements, their strength and their properties.

> Salamander, disappear in flame; Undine, rustle and collapse; Sylph, shine like a meteor; Cobold, bring help, come out and make an end of it.

None of the four is in the beast. There he lies grinning at me. I haven't hurt him yet. But I'll make you sit up with a stronger one.

> Fellow, are you a fugitive from hell? Then look at this sign, before which the black angels bow down.

He's swelling up with bristling prickles.

> You base creature, can you read his story here, the never begotten, the ineffable one, filling the heavens, wantonly transfixed.

Caught behind the stove, he's swelling like an elephant, filling the whole room, turning into cloud. Don't go through the ceiling. Lie down at your master's feet. You see I'm as good as my word. I'll roast you with holy fire. Don't wait till I give you the threefold light. Don't wait till I turn on the strongest of my arts.

MEPHISTOPHELES *the cloud fades, he comes out from behind the stove, dressed like a wandering scholar*

What's the noise about? What can I do for you, sir?

FAUST

So you were the poodle, were you? A wandering scholar. Very amusing.

MEPHISTOPHELES

I salute the learned gentleman. You certainly made me sweat.

FAUST

What's your name?

MEPHISTOPHELES

I call that a silly question, coming from a man who holds words in such contempt and cares only for depth and nothing for appearance.

FAUST

With birds like you one can usually tell the nature by the name, and tell it only too clearly, if your name happens to be lord of the flies, or liar, or destroyer. Well, who are you?

MEPHISTOPHELES

A part of the force that always tries to do evil and always does good.

FAUST

You're speaking in riddles. Explain.

MEPHISTOPHELES

I am the spirit that always negates, and rightly so, since everything that comes into existence is only fit to go out of existence and it would be better if nothing ever got started. Accordingly, what you call sin, destruction, evil in short, is my proper element.

FAUST

You call yourself a part and yet you look like a whole.

MEPHISTOPHELES

I'm just speaking the modest truth. I know that man in his silly little world thinks he's a whole, or usually does. But I am part of the part that was everything in the beginning. Part of the darkness that gave birth to light. Light that in its arrogance challenges Mother Night and claims the possession of space.

But, try as it may, it will never succeed, because it can't free itself from objects. It flows from objects, it beautifies objects, it is intercepted by them. And so, when we get rid of objects, we shall get rid of light as well. I hope it won't be long.

FAUST

Now I see what you're up to. You can't destroy on a big scale, so you're working on a small.

MEPHISTOPHELES

Yes, and not achieving much either. This thing, this clumsy world, confronting nothingness, I haven't been able to get at it yet. After all the pounding waves, the storms, the fires, the earthquakes, land and sea stay just as they were. And as for that cursed brood of men and animals, I can do nothing with them. To think how many of them I've buried already and yet there's always some new blood circulating. Always. It's enough to drive you mad. Germs spring up by the thousand in earth, air, or water, dry or wet, warm or cold. If I hadn't reserved fire for myself, there'd be nothing I could call my own.

FAUST

So you are pitting that cold malignant devil's fist of yours against the power of creation, against the life-force that never halts. A futile endeavour. Better try something else, you crazy son of Chaos.

MEPHISTOPHELES

We must certainly look into this. I'll have more to say about it another time. Do you mind if I go now?

FAUST

I can't see why you ask. We're now acquainted. Come and see me when you like. Here's the window. There's the door. And there's always the chimney.

MEPHISTOPHELES

Unfortunately there's a little thing that stops me going out. The mandrake's foot in the doorway.

FAUST

What? The pentagram? Does that bother you? Tell me then. If this blocks you, how did you get in? Can devils be fooled?

MEPHISTOPHELES

Take a look. It isn't well drawn. You see, the corner pointing out has a break in it.

FAUST

A lucky accident. So, by pure chance, you're my prisoner.

MEPHISTOPHELES

The poodle never noticed when it came running in. Now it's different. The devil can't get out.

FAUST

Why don't you go through the window?

MEPHISTOPHELES

It's a rule among ghosts and devils. They have to go out the way they came in. Going in, we can choose. Going out, we're tied.

FAUST

So even hell has its laws? I like that. We might come to terms with one another.

MEPHISTOPHELES

What we promise we keep, to the full. No haggling. But it isn't simple. We'll talk about this some day soon. For the present, I beg you please to let me go.

FAUST

Oh, stay another minute and chat with me.

MEPHISTOPHELES

Let me go now and I'll soon be back. Then you can ask all the questions you like.

FAUST

I didn't try to trap you. You walked into the trap yourself. A man doesn't catch the devil every day. Better hang on to him when he has him.

MEPHISTOPHELES

If you wish, I'm prepared to stay and keep you company, provided you allow me to entertain you in my own way.

FAUST

Excellent. Do what you choose, only let it be pleasant.

MEPHISTOPHELES

You'll get more sensuous pleasure from my entertainment

than in all the dull round of the year. What these gentle spirits sing, the lovely scenes they show, is not just empty magic. Nose and palate will get their share. You'll be delighted. No preparation is needed. We're all assembled. Begin.

SPIRITS

Let the vaulted ceiling lift, the dark clouds scatter, and the friendly blue sky appear, with milder suns and sparkling stars. Hosts of angels pass by in the air, awakening our desire. Their robes and ribbons fill the landscape, cover the arbours where lovers unite. Vines sprout, grapes pour into the presses, rivers of foaming wine trickle through the clean rocks, leave the heights, spread into lakes, with green shores sloping, birds drink delight, fly towards the sun and the happy isles rocking in the waves, with jubilant choirs singing, dancing in the meadows. Some climb the hills, others swim, others float in the air, all finding life and divine happiness.

MEPHISTOPHELES

He's off. Well done, you airy youngsters. You've performed your duty and sung him to sleep. Thank you for the concert. You, Faust, are not the man to keep the devil in your grasp. Play on him now with sweet dreams, plunge him into depths of illusion. But to burst this threshold's spell I need a rat's tooth. And I shan't have to wait long. There's a rat rustling here, he'll hear me at once.

The lord of rats and mice, of flies, frogs, bugs, and lice commands you to come out of hiding and nibble this threshold where I'm putting a drop of oil. There you are. And now to work. The corner that blocks me is the forward one here. Another bite and it's done.

Now, Faust, dream away till we meet again.

FAUST *waking*

Have I been duped a second time? Is this all I have from my rendezvous with spirits? Did I just see the devil in a dream and lose a poodle?

FAUST'S STUDY (ii)
Faust. Mephistopheles

FAUST

A knock. Come in. Who's pestering me now?

MEPHISTOPHELES

It's me.

FAUST

Come in.

MEPHISTOPHELES

You have to say it three times.

FAUST

Oh well then, come in.

MEPHISTOPHELES

That's the way. I trust we shall hit it off together. You see, I want to cheer you up and so I've put on the costume of a nobleman, red with gold braid, a cape of stiff silk, a cock's feather in my hat, and a long rapier. And I want you to wear the same, so that you may feel completely on the loose, free and ready to find out what life is like.

FAUST

No matter what I wear, I shall feel the misery of our petty, earthly existence just the same. I'm too old to take it lightly, too young to back down altogether. What has the world to offer me? Renunciation. You can't do this, you can't do that. This is the eternal refrain that rings and jangles in our ears hour by hour all our life long. When I wake in the morning, I wake with horror. I could shed bitter tears to think of the day beginning that will not grant me one thing I wish for, no not one, the day that with senseless carping will nip all pleasure in the bud and thwart every generous impulse with its ugliness and its mockery. When I lie down on my bed at night I am full of fears. There will be no repose, wild dreams will come to terrify me. The divinity that resides in me, master of my powers, can shake me to the depths, but that is all. It effects nothing outwardly. And so life to me is a burden, and death what I desire.

MEPHISTOPHELES

And yet death when it comes is never wholly welcome, never.

FAUST

Oh happy the man whom death reaches at the moment of victory to twine the bloody laurels about his brow, or it finds him after the mad whirl of the dance lying in a girl's embrace. Oh would that I had collapsed and died in ecstasy under the earth-spirit's impact.

MEPHISTOPHELES

Someone I know didn't drain his draught on that particular night.

FAUST

Spying round is your game, it seems.

MEPHISTOPHELES

I don't know everything, but I know a lot.

FAUST

I was fooled. Sweet, familiar music, thoughts of happy days, awoke what was left of the child in me and lifted me out of my horrible confusion. But not again. Now I put my curse on everything, the decoys, the enticements, that confront us on every side, all the trumpery and flattery that detains us in this vale of misery. I curse the high and mighty notion the mind has of itself; I curse the dazzle of the outer world that assails our senses; I curse the dreams we dream, the hypocrisy of them; I curse the illusion that our names can last and make us famous. I curse property in every form, be it wife and child or man and plough. I curse Mammon, whether he incites us to action with promise of rewards or smooths the pillow for us in our lazy moments. I curse the winecup and its comforts. I curse love and its heights. I curse hope. I curse faith. And, most of all, patience I curse.

SPIRIT CHORUS *invisible*

Alas, alas for the lovely world destroyed. A demi-god has shattered it with a mighty blow. See, it is falling, crumbling.

We carry the remnants over into limbo and lament the beauty lost. Man in your strength build it again. Build it better. Build it in your heart. Begin a new life with clear mind and let new songs be sung.

MEPHISTOPHELES

These are my lesser minions. Note how shrewdly they urge you to be active and cheerful. They want to draw you out of your stagnant solitude into the wide world.

Stop playing with this misery that gnaws at your life like a vulture. Any company, the meanest, will make you feel that you're a man among men. Not that I propose to thrust you among riff-raff. I'm not one of the great, but if you care to join forces with me for life, I shall be happy to oblige you on the spot. I'll be your companion and, if I suit, I'll be your servant, your slave.

FAUST

And what have I to do in return?

MEPHISTOPHELES

There's plenty of time for that.

FAUST

Not a bit of it. The devil's an egoist and not disposed to help others free gratis. State your terms. You're not the safest of servants.

MEPHISTOPHELES

I pledge myself to your service here and will always be at your beck and call. If we meet over there, you can do the same for me.

FAUST

Over there is no concern of mine. If you can shatter this world to pieces, let the other come. My joys and sorrows belong to this earth and this sunlight. When I part with them, the rest can follow, whatever it is. There may be top and bottom in that other place; people there may go on loving and hating. I simply don't care.

MEPHISTOPHELES

I see no difficulty in that. Come, agree. My tricks will delight you. I'll show you things no one has ever seen before.

FAUST

You poor devil, what can you have to show me? Did the likes of you ever comprehend the mind of man and all its great endeavour. But come on. Perhaps you have food that never fills you; red gold that trickles through your fingers like quicksilver; a game at which you can't win; a girl who while lying in the arms of one lover with the wink of an eye picks up someone else; honours that lift you to the seventh heaven and then go out like shooting stars. Come along with your fruit that rots in the hand when you try to pick it, and your trees that grow new leaves and shed them every day.

MEPHISTOPHELES

There's nothing there that I don't feel equal to. Entertainments like those are just in my line. But, my friend, the day will come when we shall want to relax and savour a good thing quietly.

FAUST

If ever I lie down in idleness and contentment, let that be the end of me, let that be final. If you can delude me into feeling pleased with myself, if your good things ever get the better of me, then may that day be my last day. This is my wager.

MEPHISTOPHELES

Agreed.

FAUST

And shake again. If ever the passing moment is such that I wish it not to pass and I say to it 'You are beautiful, stay a while,' then let that be the finish. The clock can stop. You can put me in chains and ring the death-bell. I shall welcome it and you will be quit of your service.

MEPHISTOPHELES

Consider what you're saying. We shan't forget.

FAUST

Quite right. I haven't committed myself wildly. If I come to a stop, if I stagnate, I'm a slave. Whether yours or another's, what does it matter?

MEPHISTOPHELES

There's the doctoral dinner this very day. I shall be there as your servant. But, to meet all emergencies, could I have a word in writing?

FAUST

So you want it in writing, do you, you pedant? Don't you know the worth of a man, the worth of a man's word? Isn't it enough that my given word is to rule my life for the rest of my days? I know that, when you see the world raging along like so many torrents, you may well ask why a mere promise should bind me. But this is the way we are. We cherish the illusion and cling to it, it keeps us clear, and clean-spirited, and responsible. But a parchment all filled out and stamped is a spectre that everyone dreads. The written word dies, leather and sealing-wax take over. What do you want, you devil? Bronze, marble, parchment, paper? Shall I write with a style or a chisel or a pen? Take your choice.

MEPHISTOPHELES

Why do you get so heated and exaggerate so when you start speechifying? Any scrap of paper will do. Only you must sign with a drop of blood.

FAUST

If this really satisfies you, we'll go through with the tom-foolery.

MEPHISTOPHELES

Blood. Blood is special.

FAUST

Don't be afraid of me breaking the contract. My full effort and energy is what I promise. I aimed too high. I'm only fit to be in your class. The great Earth-spirit has rejected me. Nature is closed to me. I can't think. I'm sick of learning, have been for ages. Let us spend our passions, hot in sensual deeps. Let us have miracles galore, all the miracles, round us in magic veils. Let us plunge into the rush of time, the race of events, hit or miss, pain or pleasure, just as it comes, always on the move, always doing something. It's the only way.

MEPHISTOPHELES

We don't make any restrictions. If you like to flit about, here a nibble, there a nibble, or just sample things on the high run, well and good. I hope you'll like it. Only help yourself and don't be bashful.

FAUST

Am I not telling you that it's not a question of enjoyment? A whirl of dissipation is what I seek, this and nothing else, pleasures that hurt, torments that enliven, hate that is instinct with love. Having got the desire for knowledge out of my system, I mean to expose myself to all the pain and suffering in the world. Nay more. All that is given to humanity, total humanity, to experience I desire to experience in my own person, the heights and the depths of it, the weal and the woe, to enlarge myself in this way to humanity's size, and to smash up with the rest of humanity in the end.

MEPHISTOPHELES

Mark my words. I've been chewing at this old leaven for thousands of years. In the short space of a lifetime no man will ever digest it. This totality, this whole, is God's affair and no one else's. I can assure you of that. You see, he dwells in eternal light, us devils he thrusts into darkness, and all you are fit for is day and night, half and half.

FAUST

But my mind is made up.

MEPHISTOPHELES

Good enough. There's only one thing I'm afraid of. Time is short and art is long. Take my advice. Engage a poet. Let him turn on his imagination and load you with all the virtues and distinctions – the courage of the lion, the speed of the stag, the hot blood of Italy, the endurance of the North. Let him solve the problem of combining generosity with cunning, and plan a young man's impulsive love-affair for you. I'd like to know the gentleman. I'd call him Mr Microcosm.

FAUST

What am I then, if it isn't possible to reach the peak of humanity, as I so vehemently desire?

MEPHISTOPHELES

You are what you are. Put on as many wigs as you like, and boots a yard high, you'll never be bigger than you are.

FAUST

So it was all to no purpose – I feel it now – that I took on me the whole treasury of the human mind. No new strength has been awakened in me. I'm no larger than I was, no nearer to the infinite.

MEPHISTOPHELES

My dear sir, you're looking at things in a conventional way. We must do better than that, or the joys of life will escape us. Hang it. You have your hands and feet, you have a headpiece and a codpiece. And anything else you can enjoy is yours, isn't it? If I can afford a coach and six, isn't their energy mine? I can ride around as proudly as if I had twenty-four legs. So come, no more ruminating. Let us set off together. I tell you, when you talk this theoretical stuff, you put me in mind of a donkey on a barren heath, led round and round by an evil spirit, while all the time there's nice green grass near by.

FAUST

How do we begin?

MEPHISTOPHELES

We just get out of here. Out of this torture chamber. What sort of a life is this, boring yourself and these young men? Leave that to your portly neighbour. Why go on threshing straw? After all, you daren't tell them the best of what you know. I can hear one of them outside on the landing.

FAUST

I can't possibly see him.

MEPHISTOPHELES

The poor boy's been waiting a long time. He deserves a friendly word. Lend me your cap and gown. I shall look well in them.

He puts them on Now leave it to me. I only need a quarter of an hour. Meanwhile make yourself ready for our tour.

Faust off

MEPHISTOPHELES *in Faust's gown*

Keep it up. Go on despising reason and learning, man's greatest asset. Let me entangle you in my deceits and magic

shows and I'll get you for sure. This man was born with
a spirit that drives him on incessantly and will not be curbed.
All at such a pace that he overleaps the common pleasures.
I'll drag him through a round of riotous living, where everything is shallow and meaningless, till I have him at my mercy
like a fly on a fly-paper. I'll dangle food and drink before
his greedy mouth. He'll beg in vain for refreshment. He'd be
sure to go under anyway, even if he hadn't given himself to
the devil.

A student enters

STUDENT
Excuse me, sir, I'm a newcomer, wishing to introduce himself
to a man respected and revered by everyone.

MEPHISTOPHELES
I appreciate your courtesy. As you see, I'm a man no different
from others. Have you called on anyone else?

STUDENT
Please be kind to me, advise me. I'm young and eager. I have
a little money, enough. Mother would hardly let me leave
home. I want to study something worthwhile, now I've come
so far.

MEPHISTOPHELES
Well, you're in the right place.

STUDENT
Honestly, I feel like pulling out again. I'm not happy in these
big buildings, these walls. It's so shut in. You don't see a tree,
not a blade of grass. And sitting in the lecture room my head
goes round, I nearly pass out.

MEPHISTOPHELES
It's all a matter of habit. A child doesn't immediately take to
the breast, but before long it feeds lustily. At the breasts of
wisdom you'll find your appetite growing every day.

STUDENT
I'll cling to her neck with delight. But how do I get there?

MEPHISTOPHELES
First you must tell me what faculty you choose.

STUDENT

I want to be a really learned man. I want to master nature and science and earth and heaven, all of it.

MEPHISTOPHELES

You're on the right track there, but you'll have to apply yourself.

STUDENT

I'm heart and soul in it, but I'd like a little relaxation on summer holidays.

MEPHISTOPHELES

Time flies so fast you mustn't waste it. But with a little method you can save time. And therefore, my friend, I advise you to begin with a course in logic. There they'll put you through your paces, lace your mind up tight in a pair of murderous jackboots and set it crawling ponderously along the straight road, not flitting about all over the place like a will-o'-the-wisp. And they'll tell you and tell you again that things you used to do in one, like eating and drinking, have to be done now in a one-two-three. Our thinking apparatus, you know, works like a weaver's loom, where a single tread starts a thousand connections, the shuttles go back and forth and the threads flow invisibly. And then a philosopher comes and proves that it had to be so. The first statement was thus and so, and the second was thus and so, and that's why the third and the fourth are thus and so. If the first and the second weren't there, there'd never be a third and fourth at all. This impresses his hearers, but it doesn't make weavers of them. If they want to discuss a living thing they begin by driving out the spirit, and this leaves them with the parts in their hands, lifeless and disconnected. The chemists call it manipulating nature, but they're fooling themselves.

STUDENT

I don't quite follow you.

MEPHISTOPHELES

You'll soon find it easier, once you learn to simplify and classify.

STUDENT

It all makes me feel as stupid as if I had a mill-wheel going round in my head.

MEPHISTOPHELES

Next, and above everything else, you must have a go at metaphysics and make sure you profoundly comprehend the things that don't fit into the human brain. Whether a thing fits or doesn't fit, there's always an excellent word for it. Attend regularly, for your first term, five lectures every day, be there on the dot, do your homework and your preparation carefully so as to be sure afterwards that the professor said nothing that wasn't in the book. But mind you write everything down, as if it was the Holy Ghost himself dictating to you.

STUDENT

You don't need to tell me twice. I know the value of that. If you get a thing down in black and white you can take it home with you and not worry.

MEPHISTOPHELES

But what about a faculty?

STUDENT

Well, I know I don't want to study law.

MEPHISTOPHELES

I'm with you there. I know what that stuff's worth. Laws and statutes, inherited like a disease, dragging on endlessly from generation to generation and from place to place, sense turning into nonsense, benefaction into bane and boredom. A pity you have to be someone's grandson. About the rights and privileges you're born with they never have a word to say.

STUDENT

You make me hate the stuff more than ever. How lucky I am to get your advice. Now theology attracts me.

MEPHISTOPHELES

I don't want to lead you astray. But this is a subject where it's not easy to keep on the right track. There's so much poison concealed in it and you can hardly tell the poison from the cure. The best way here again is to keep to one man and take his word. Swear by what he says. But stick to words anyway. Then you'll find your questions answered and your doubts removed. You'll join the church of the know-it-alls.

STUDENT

But a word has to mean something. It must have a concept behind it.

MEPHISTOPHELES

I grant you that. But you mustn't be fussy about it. Because when you run out of concepts a word can come in very handy. You can argue with words, believe in words, you can do nearly anything with words, make them into a whole system, and you can't rob them of an iota.

STUDENT

I'm afraid I'm taking up a lot of your time. But there's one thing more. Could you give me a lead on medicine? Three years is so short a time and the field is so vast. A hint or two is a great help.

MEPHISTOPHELES *aside*

I'm sick of this sobriety. I'll have to play the devil again.
Aloud

Medicine is easy to grasp. When you've finished studying the universe, you'll find you just have to let it go its own sweet way as before. Your science won't help you much. You learn what you can. But see that you make the most of your opportunities. That's the thing. You're well set up, you're not backward. If you trust yourself, others will trust you. Above all else learn to manage women. There's one treatment that will cure all their manifold troubles. And if you make some show of honesty, you'll have them where you want them. It's useful to be an M.D., it wins their confidence and makes them think you're an expert. You'll be able to feel around for little things right away that others have to wait years to lay their hands on. You'll know how to give her the right look, ardent but cunning, and squeeze her pulse and take her round the hips to see how tightly she's laced.

STUDENT
This sounds better. At least you know what you're at.

MEPHISTOPHELES
My friend, all theory is grey, the tree of life is golden-green.

STUDENT
I assure you, it's all like a dream. Might I trouble you again some day and hear more of your wisdom?

MEPHISTOPHELES
I'll gladly do what I can.

STUDENT
I can't leave without asking you to sign my autograph book. Please.

MEPHISTOPHELES
Very good. *He signs and returns the book*

STUDENT *reads*
'Eritis sicut Deus, scientes bonum et malum.' *He closes the book reverently and leaves*

MEPHISTOPHELES
Just follow my motto and my old crony, the serpent, and you'll land yourself in trouble sooner or later, whether you're made in God's image or not.

Faust enters

FAUST
Where do we go now?

MEPHISTOPHELES
Wherever you like. We'll see the little world and then the great. Just think, you're going to get the whole course without paying a penny. It'll be fun and profitable too.

FAUST
But how am I to lead a gay life with this long beard? It'll all be a failure. I've never been at home in the world. In company I feel so small. I shall always be ill at ease.

MEPHISTOPHELES
My friend, you'll get over that. Just have more confidence in yourself and you'll be all right.

FAUST

How do we start? I don't see your carriage and horses anywhere.

MEPHISTOPHELES

We'll spread my cloak, it'll carry us through the air. But you mustn't bring a heavy pack on this bold venture. A little hydrogen, supplied by me, will send us up. Quickly and easily if we travel light. Congratulations on your new career.

AUERBACH'S TAVERN IN LEIPZIG
A merry company, drinking

FROSCH

What! Nobody drinking? Nobody laughing? And all these long faces? This won't do. You're fire and flame mostly. Today you're like a heap of wet straw.

BRANDER

It's your fault. You're so flat yourself. Can't you give us some fooling, some filth?

FROSCH *pours a glass of wine over his head*

There you have both.

BRANDER

You dirty swine.

FROSCH

Well, you asked for it and you got it.

SIEBEL

Out you go, if you start quarrelling. Come on, let's sing a hearty song, all together. Oho, oho.

ALTMAYER

Ouch. I can't stand it. He's splitting my ears. Hey, cottonwool.

SIEBEL

That's the true bass, when it echoes from the vault.

FROSCH

Right. Out with them that can't take a joke. Oho, oho.

ALTMAYER

Doh. Ray. Me. Fah.

FROSCH

We're all tuned up. *sings*

> The Holy Roman Empire. Oh, poor thing. How does it
> hold together?

BRANDER

That's a miserable song, a nasty song, a political song. Woof.
You can think yourselves lucky when you wake up in the
morning that you don't have to worry over the Holy Roman
Empire. Me, I thank my stars I'm not an emperor or his
chancellor. But we need a head man here. Let's elect a pope.
You know what a man has to have to be a pope, don't you?

FROSCH *sings*

> Dame nightingale, fly. Fly to my sweetheart. Give her
> my love.

SIEBEL

None of that. You and your sweetheart.

FROSCH

Yes, give her my love, and kisses too. You can't stop me.
He sings

> Unbar the door in the quiet night when my lover is waiting.
> Bar it again in the morning early.

SIEBEL

Okay. Sing all you want about that girl of yours. I'll have the
laugh yet. She made a fool of me. She'll do it to you. I'd give
her a goblin for a lover to flirt with at the cross-roads. Let
an old billy-goat on his way home from the Brocken bleat at
her as he trots past. A decent man of flesh and blood's too
good for her. I'd smash her windows in. That's all I have to
say to her.

BRANDER *rapping the table*

Listen to me, fellows. You all know I have the savvy. We have
lovers sitting here. I ought to treat them to something special,
just for them. Part of a good night's fun. Now listen to this.
One of the latest songs. Mind you come in on the refrain.
He sings

> There was a rat lived in the cellar, feeding on lard and
> butter. Gave itself a tidy paunch and looked like Dr

Luther. The cook put poison down for it. The poison griped and twisted it, like love-pangs in the belly.

CHORUS *shouting*

Like love-pangs in the belly.

BRANDER

It rushed around, rushed up and down, and drank at every puddle, gnawed the whole house and scratched at it, it didn't help it any. It got the jitters, jumped about, the pain was more than it could stand, like love-pangs in the belly.

CHORUS

Like love-pangs in the belly.

BRANDER

In broad daylight its throes were such it ran into the kitchen, dropped by the stove and twitched and lay, in torture, hardly breathing. The naughty cook just laughed and said: The creature's had its medicine now, like love-pangs in the belly.

CHORUS

Like love-pangs in the belly.

SIEBEL

The fun those louts are having. A real art, I call it, to scatter poison for the poor rats.

BRANDER

You seem to favour them.

ALTMAYER

Look at the fat one with a bald head. He thinks the bloated rat is him exactly. His troubles make him as quiet as a lamb.

Faust and Mephistopheles

MEPHISTOPHELES

What I must do now, first and foremost, is find some good company for you to let you see how smooth and easy life can be. Here they make every day a holiday. They're not brainy, but they like their comforts and each of them dances in his little round like a kitten chasing its tail. They're as happy as larks, provided they don't have a headache and the landlord isn't pressing for cash.

BRANDER

You can see they're travellers. They look so queer. I'll bet they've just arrived.

FROSCH

By golly, you're right. Good for Leipzig. It's a regular little Paris, civilized and civilizing too.

SIEBEL

What do you think they are?

FROSCH

Just leave it to me. Drinks round once and I'll pump them dry like drawing a child's teeth. They must be well-born, they look so proud and dissatisfied.

BRANDER

Quacks, I'll bet they are.

ALTMAYER

Maybe.

FROSCH

Watch me. I'll give 'em the works.

MEPHISTOPHELES *to Faust*

These people never can spot the devil even when he has them by the collar.

FAUST

Good day, gentlemen.

SIEBEL

Good day to you.

Sotto voce, looking sideways at Mephistopheles

What is it makes him lame in one foot?

MEPHISTOPHELES

May we join you? The company will be good, though we can't expect the same of the drink.

ALTMAYER

You must be very hard to please.

FROSCH

I suppose you were late leaving Rippach. Did you have supper with Jack Ass?

MEPHISTOPHELES

We didn't stop this time. But we had a word with him last

time. He had a lot to say about his cousins and sends you his best. *He bows to Frosch*

ALTMAYER *sotto voce*

There you see. He's no fool.

SIEBEL

A sly dog.

FROSCH

Just wait. I'll get him yet.

MEPHISTOPHELES

If I'm not mistaken, we heard you singing excellently in chorus. Singing must sound well in this vault.

FROSCH

Are you by any chance a pro?

MEPHISTOPHELES

No, I haven't the voice, but I have the liking.

ALTMAYER

Will you sing us a song?

MEPHISTOPHELES

As many as you wish.

SIEBEL

But no old stuff. Something new.

MEPHISTOPHELES

We're just back from Spain, the land of wine and song. *He sings*

   There once was a king and he had a great big flea.

FROSCH

Jesus, do you hear that? A flea. Do you get it? A flea. I'll say that's something.

MEPHISTOPHELES *sings*

   There once was a king and he had a great big flea.
   It might have been his very son, he doted on it so.
   And he sent for his tailor and gave him his orders:
   Measure this junker and dress him in full.

BRANDER

Yes, and you tell the tailor to watch his step, if he values his head, and not give him crinkles in his pants.

MEPHISTOPHELES

   So now there he was, arrayed in silks and satins.

Ribbons on his coat and a cross on it too.
He was made a royal minister and wore a great star.
And his brothers and his sisters, they were big folk at court.
And all the lords and ladies were eaten alive,
the queen and her lady's maid bitten up and chewed.
They didn't dare nip them, they didn't dare touch them.
Let them come biting us, and we nip them and we squash
    them,
we squash them as we please.

CHORUS *with a shout*
Let them come biting us, and we nip them and we squash
    them,
we squash them as we please.

FROSCH
Bravo. That was swell.

SIEBEL
May all the fleas be squashed.

BRANDER
Like this. Finger and thumb. And then quick.

ALTMAYER
Here's to freedom. Here's to wine.

MEPHISTOPHELES
I'd be happy to drink to freedom, if only your wines were
a little better.

SIEBEL
Don't say that to me again.

MEPHISTOPHELES
I'm afraid the landlord will object. But if not, I'd like to give
you gentlemen something out of our own cellar.

SIEBEL
Go right ahead. I'll vouch for it.

FROSCH
If you have something good, we'll give you credit for it.
But don't let it be a mere sip. If I'm to judge, I need a
real mouthful.

ALTMAYER *sotto voce*
Looks like they're from the Rhine.

MEPHISTOPHELES
Let me have a gimlet.

BRANDER
What do you want a gimlet for? You don't mean to say you've
brought the barrels with you?

ALTMAYER
There's a basket of tools behind there.

MEPHISTOPHELES *taking the gimlet. To Frosch*
Now tell me what you'd like.

FROSCH
How come? Are you offering us a choice?

MEPHISTOPHELES
You can have whatever you wish.

ALTMAYER *to Frosch*
Ha. Ha. You're licking your lips already.

FROSCH
Good. If I can choose, I'll have a Rhine wine. I'll stick to the
fatherland every time.

MEPHISTOPHELES *boring a hole in the table where Frosch is sitting*
Give me some wax to cork with quickly.

ALTMAYER
It's just a conjuring trick.

MEPHISTOPHELES *to Brander*
Now it's your turn.

BRANDER
I want champagne, and sparkling.

*Mephistopheles bores, one of them has made the corks and is sticking
them in*

BRANDER
You can't find all you want at home. Often a good thing
comes from abroad. If you're a true German you can't
stand the French, but you like to drink their wines all the
same.

SIEBEL *as Mephistopheles approaches him*
I must confess I don't care about your dry wines. Give me
a real sweet one.

MEPHISTOPHELES *boring*
I'll give you Tokay.
ALTMAYER
Look here, good sirs, you're fooling us.
MEPHISTOPHELES
Come now. That would be a bit risky with gentlemen like you.
Quick. Tell me. What wine shall I give you?
ALTMAYER
Any you like. Don't ask me.

After the holes are all bored and corked

MEPHISTOPHELES *with strange gestures*
> The goat grows horns, the vine grows grapes. The grapes
> are juicy, the vine is woody. The wood table can yield wine
> too. A natural miracle, believe it you.
ALL *drawing the corks. The wine chosen fills the cups*
Oh, what a well-spring, all for us.
MEPHISTOPHELES
Take care not to spill any of it.

They drink repeatedly

ALL *singing*
> We're happy as cannibals, happy as swine, hundreds of
swine.
MEPHISTOPHELES
See how free these people are, see what a good time they
have.
FAUST
I wish we could pull out now.
MEPHISTOPHELES
Wait a minute. You'll see their swinishness come to a head
beautifully.
SIEBEL *drinking carelessly, spills some wine on the floor and it bursts
into flame*
Help. Fire. Help. All hell's blazing.
MEPHISTOPHELES *exorcizing the flame*
Gently my elemental friend.

To Siebel
This was only a touch of purgatorial fire.

SIEBEL
What's all this? Just wait. I'll make you pay for this. You don't seem to know who you're dealing with.

FROSCH
No more of this. I tell you once is enough.

ALTMAYER
We'd better get rid of these chaps quietly.

SIEBEL
Mister, do you think you can play your monkey-tricks here?

MEPHISTOPHELES
Be quiet, you old tub.

SIEBEL
Broomstick, yourself. Are you going to insult us now?

BRANDER
Let's beat them up.

ALTMAYER *draws a cork out of the table and flames come out*
I'm on fire. I'm on fire.
It's witchcraft. At him. He's fair game.

They draw their knives and close in on Mephistopheles

MEPHISTOPHELES *solemnly*
  False words, false forms, new meanings, new places. Be
  here and there.

They stand in astonishment and stare at one another

ALTMAYER
Where am I? What a lovely land.

FROSCH
Vineyards, can it be?

SIEBEL
And grapes under my nose.

BRANDER
Here in this green arbour, what vines, what grapes.

He seizes Siebel by the nose. The others do likewise and raise their knives

MEPHISTOPHELES *as above*
Illusion, free their eyes. Mark how the devil plays his pranks.

He disappears with Faust, the men spring apart

SIEBEL
What's happened?

ALTMAYER
What?

FROSCH
Was that your nose?

BRANDER *to Siebel*
And I'm still holding yours.

ALTMAYER
There was a shock went right through me. Bring me a chair.
I'm all in.

FROSCH
Tell me, whatever was it?

SIEBEL
Where's that fellow? If I get hold of him I'll finish him.

ALTMAYER
I saw him sailing out of the cellar-hatch astride of a tub. I've
such a drag in my legs. (*turning to the table*) My. Do you think
that wine's still running?

SIEBEL
It was all a trick, an illusion.

FROSCH
I really thought I was drinking wine.

BRANDER
And what was that with the grapes?

ALTMAYER
And they say there's no such thing as miracles.

WITCH'S KITCHEN

A low hearth with a cauldron on the fire. Various figures are seen in the
steam rising from it. A she-ape sits by the cauldron, skimming it and
seeing that it doesn't boil over. Her mate is sitting beside her with the

little ones. Walls and ceiling are covered with the strangest appurtenances
of a witch's household. Faust. Mephistopheles

FAUST

This insane witchcraft disgusts me, I find it revolting. Are you
telling me that I shall get rejuvenated in this idiotic collection
of junk? Am I to take an old hag's remedy? Is this foul brew
going to lift thirty years off my back? It's a poor look-out for
me if you can't think of something better. It's hopeless, I give
up. But isn't there a natural way? Isn't there some healing
balm that man has discovered?

MEPHISTOPHELES

Now you're talking sense. There is a natural way. But that's
another story, and a curious one.

FAUST

I want to know.

MEPHISTOPHELES

Well, I'll tell you a way. It'll cost you nothing, no witches,
no doctors. Go right off into the country and start digging
and hoeing. Keep yourself, and keep your thoughts, strictly
confined in a small circle. Eat the simplest food. Live
with your cattle as cattle. Don't be above manuring the
field you plough with your own dung. If you want to stay
young till you're eighty, believe me, this is the best way
to do it.

FAUST

I'm not used to that sort of thing. I can't come down to
handling a spade. And that narrow existence doesn't suit me.

MEPHISTOPHELES

Then it has to be the witch.

FAUST

Why her? Can't you concoct the potion yourself?

MEPHISTOPHELES

A nice waste of time that would be. I could be doing a host of
things, I could build a thousand bridges, meanwhile. This is
a job that calls for patience as well as science. A strange and
complicated process. The draught takes years before it's

potent. The devil taught her how to make it, but the devil can't make it himself.

Seeing the apes

Look, what dainty creatures. This is the girl and this is the boy. (*to the apes*) Your mistress seems to be away.

THE APES

Left by the chimney, to feast with company.

MEPHISTOPHELES

How long is she usually out on the spree?

THE APES

Just as long as we sit here warming our paws.

MEPHISTOPHELES *to Faust*

How do you find them?

FAUST

As gross as anything I ever saw.

MEPHISTOPHELES

Now for me, a chat like this is just what I enjoy. (*to the apes*) Tell me, you monkeys, what are you stirring the pot for?

THE APES

We're making thin soup for beggars.

MEPHISTOPHELES

Then you have a large public.

THE APE *comes towards Mephistopheles obsequiously*

   Quick, throw the dice, and let me win, and make me rich.
   I'm badly off. If I had cash, I'd have sense too.

MEPHISTOPHELES

How happy the ape would be, if he could buy lottery tickets.

In the meantime the young apes have been playing with a big ball which they roll forward

THE APE

   This is the world. It rises and falls, and never stops rolling.
   It rings like glass, so easy to break. It's hollow inside. It's
   shiny here. And shinier there. I'm quick on my pins. Take
   care, my son, and keep away. You might get killed. The
   thing's of clay. The clay can break.

MEPHISTOPHELES

What's the sieve for?

THE APE *lifting it down*

If you were a thief, I'd spot you at once.

He runs to the she-ape and lets her look through it

Look through the sieve. Do you recognize him and daren't name him?

MEPHISTOPHELES *moving towards the fire*

And what's the pot for?

THE TWO APES

The silly sot. Doesn't know the pot. Doesn't know the kettle.

MEPHISTOPHELES

Don't be so rude.

THE APE

Here, take the whisk and sit you down. *seats Mephistopheles in the armchair*

FAUST *who has been standing in front of a mirror, going close to it and then stepping back*

What can this be? A magic mirror? And what a marvel of a woman. O Love, lend me your swiftest wings and take me where she is. Oh, I can't get close to her. If I try, she fades away. How beautiful she is, how unbelievably beautiful, reclining there. The quintessence of all that is heavenly. To think the earth has this to show.

MEPHISTOPHELES

Naturally, if God works his head off for six whole days and then claps his hands at the finish, there must be something mighty good there. Go on gazing at her as long as you wish. I can find you a sweetheart like that. The man that gets her for keeps can count himself lucky.

Faust goes on staring at the mirror. Mephistopheles stretches out in the armchair and plays with the whisk

Sitting here, I feel like a king on his throne. I have the sceptre in my hand. All I need is a crown.

THE APES *after executing all sorts of intricate dance-movements, they bring a crown to Mephistopheles with shouts*

Oh, be so good and glue the crown, with blood and sweat.
Clumsily they break the crown into two pieces and jump about with them
Now we've done it. We talk and watch, and listen and rhyme.

FAUST *looking into the mirror*
I'm beside myself.

MEPHISTOPHELES *pointing to the apes*
My head's beginning to go round too.

THE APES
And if we're lucky, and if it sorts, our rhymes are thoughts.

FAUST *as above*
I'm going out of my mind. Let's get out of here.

MEPHISTOPHELES *still in the armchair*
At least you must admit these poets are honest.

The cauldron, which the she-ape has been neglecting, begins to boil over. This produces a big flame which reaches up the chimney. The witch comes riding down through the flame with a great shriek

THE WITCH
Ouch, ouch, you ape, you swine, curses on you, forgetting the pot and singeing me.
Catching sight of Faust and Mephistopheles
What's this? Who are you? What do you want? Hell-fire take you.

She dips the spoon in the cauldron and throws flame on Faust, Mephistopheles, and the apes. The apes whine

MEPHISTOPHELES *turning round with the whisk in his hand and striking glasses and bottles with it*
Smash, smash. Broken glass. A pretty mess. It's all a joke. Just beating time, to your stinking tune.
The witch starts back in a rage
Don't you know me, you bag of bones? Don't you know your lord and master? I could just light into you and your monkeys and make mincemeat of you all. Have you no respect for my red doublet? Can't you see my cock's feather? Did I try to hide? Must I tell you who I am?

THE WITCH

O sir, forgive my rudeness. But you're not letting anyone see your hoofed foot. And where are your two ravens?

MEPHISTOPHELES

I'll let you off this time. I know we haven't seen one another lately. And culture has put its finger on the devil as on everyone else. You won't see the northern spectre any more. No more horns and tail and claws. As for this horse's hoof of mine, it would tell against me. That's why for years I've padded my calves. Lots of young men do it.

THE WITCH

Fancy Satan, my lord Satan, come to see me again. It makes me all dithery.

MEPHISTOPHELES

Woman, don't call me by that name.

THE WITCH

Why not? What's the matter with it?

MEPHISTOPHELES

Relegated to the book of fable long ago. But it hasn't helped mankind in the least. They've got rid of the evil one, but the many evil ones are still with us. Just call me Baron and it'll be all right. I'm a man of the world, like others. If you doubt my noble birth, here's my escutcheon. *He makes an indecent gesture*

THE WITCH *laughing immoderately*

Ha, ha. That's just like you. You were always a rogue, you rogue you.

MEPHISTOPHELES *to Faust*

Take note of this, partner. This is the way to handle witches.

THE WITCH

Well, gentlemen, what will you have?

MEPHISTOPHELES

A good-sized glass of you know what. But let it be your oldest. The older it is, the better.

THE WITCH

Gladly. There's a bottle of it here that I sometimes take a nip of myself. It's turned quite mellow. I'm pleased to oblige.

Quietly But if your companion drinks it unprepared, it might be the death of him, as you know.

MEPHISTOPHELES
He's a good friend of mine. I want him to get the benefit. Make it the best you have. Draw your circle, do your incantations, and then give him a glassful.

The witch with strange gestures draws a circle and puts fantastic things inside it. The glasses begin to hum and the cauldron rings, making music. Finally she fetches a big book and brings the apes into the circle, using them as a desk. They also hold the torches. She beckons to Faust to join her

FAUST *to Mephistopheles*
This is going too far. These silly contraptions, these lunatic gestures, this crassness, this falsity. I've seen it all and I despise it.

MEPHISTOPHELES
Come, come. Take it lightly. Don't be so critical. She has to perform some hocus-pocus, if the stuff is to work. *He pushes Faust inside the circle*

THE WITCH *declaiming from the book with great emphasis*
Know this, know this. Make one a ten. And let two go. Make an even three. Your fortune is made. Then lose your four. Turn five and six into seven and eight. So says the witch. That's all there is. And nine is one and ten is nothing. This is the witch's two-times-two.

FAUST
The old woman seems to be off her head.

MEPHISTOPHELES
There's plenty more to come. The whole book's like this. I know it well. Lost a lot of time over it. You see, a complete contradiction is a mystery to wise and foolish alike. It's an old trick, spreading lies with three-in-one and one-in-three. You're safe with that, and can talk and teach undisturbed. Who wants to argue with fools? Usually people think when they hear words there must be some meaning in them.

THE WITCH *continuing*

The power of science, hidden from the world. If you don't think, you get it given, no trouble at all.

FAUST

What rubbish is she talking now? I can't endure it any longer, it's like a pack of fools, talking all at once.

MEPHISTOPHELES

Enough, enough, most excellent sibyl. Come, give us your potion and brim the cup. It won't hurt this fellow. He's a man of many promotions. He's had good drinks before.

THE WITCH *with much ceremony pours the potion into a cup*
When Faust puts it to his lips, there is a slight flame

MEPHISTOPHELES

Down with it. You'll be glad of it. A man that's pals with the devil doesn't need to fear a little fire.

The witch breaks the circle and Faust steps out

MEPHISTOPHELES

Come on out with me now. You mustn't rest.

THE WITCH

I hope it'll agree with you, sir.

MEPHISTOPHELES *to the witch*

If I can do you any little service, remind me at the Walpurgis.

THE WITCH

Here's a song. If you sing it now and then, it'll help.

MEPHISTOPHELES *to Faust*

Come away with me now. You have to perspire freely, so that the drink works both ways, inwards and outwards. I'll show you then how a gentleman can enjoy his leisure. We'll set Cupid hopping about and you'll soon be delighted.

FAUST

Just let me have another look in the mirror. That woman was so very lovely.

MEPHISTOPHELES

No, no. You'll soon have the fairest of the fair right in front of you. (*aside*) Any woman will be a Helen to him with this drink under his belt.

STREET
Faust. Gretchen passing by

FAUST
May I? May I walk with you, O fairest lady?

GRETCHEN
I'm not a lady, I'm not fair. I can go home by myself. *She disengages herself and goes off*

FAUST
By God, there's a beauty for you. I never set eyes on the likes. Such a good girl, so pure, but she knows how to cut you too. Those bright red lips and shining cheeks, as long as I live I'll never forget them. The way she dropped her eyes would break a man's heart. And that quick temper, well, that was priceless.

Enter Mephistopheles

FAUST
Listen here. You must get me that girl.

MEPHISTOPHELES
Which girl?

FAUST
She just went past.

MEPHISTOPHELES
What? Her? She's just been to confession. The priest couldn't find a thing. I slipped close by and overheard them. An innocent creature, no need to confess at all. I can't do anything with her.

FAUST
She's over fourteen, isn't she?

MEPHISTOPHELES
You talk like a regular John Thomas, flattering yourself that any favour, any flower you fancy is yours to pluck. But it can't be done, not always.

FAUST
Stop your preaching, Mr Sermonizer. I tell you this. If that

813

sweet young thing doesn't sleep in my arms tonight, we part company. I'll give you till the stroke of twelve.

MEPHISTOPHELES

Please be reasonable. I need at least a couple of weeks just to reconnoitre.

FAUST

Let me have a couple of hours and I could seduce one like her and not need the devil to help me.

MEPHISTOPHELES

You talk just like a Frenchman. But don't take it hard. What's the good of having your pleasure point-blank? The fun isn't nearly as great as when you've worked on her in all sorts of ways and got her going. You can read about it in those Italian tales.

FAUST

I don't need them to get me going.

MEPHISTOPHELES

Now, to put it bluntly, this pretty girl of yours isn't to be had in a hurry. You can't take her by storm. We have to use our wits.

FAUST

Get me something of hers. Take me to her bedroom. Get me a scarf she wears or, closer to my desire, get me one of her garters.

MEPHISTOPHELES

To let you see that I'll do what I can, we'll not lose a minute. I'll take you to her bedroom this very day.

FAUST

Shall I see her? Shall I have her?

MEPHISTOPHELES

No, she'll be at a neighbour's. But you'll be able to feast your senses there and think of the delights that await you.

FAUST

Can we go at once?

MEPHISTOPHELES

It's too early yet.

FAUST

Find some present for me to give her. *off*

MEPHISTOPHELES
Presents? Already? That'll do the trick. I know some good spots with hidden treasure in them. I'll have to scout around a bit.

EVENING
A tidy, little room

GRETCHEN *plaiting and binding up her hair*
I'd give something to know who the gentleman was today. He certainly seemed all right, and he must be well-born. You could tell that from the look of him. And he wouldn't have acted so free, if he wasn't. *off*

Mephistopheles. Faust

MEPHISTOPHELES
Come in, come in, quietly now.
FAUST *after an interval*
Please leave me here by myself.
MEPHISTOPHELES *poking around*
Not all the girls are as clean and tidy as this one. *off*
FAUST *looking round*
Welcome, sweet twilight, flooding this holy place. Now let the pangs of love that live and languish on the dew of hope lay hold of me. Here where everything breathes quietude, order, contentment. So rich is this poverty, so blissful this confinement.
He sits down in the leather armchair by the bed
Let me sit here where so many have sat in joy or in sorrow in days gone by, where children time and time again have gathered round their old grandfather. Perhaps my sweetheart, yet a child, once kissed his aged hand in piety and in gratitude for her Christmas gift. O girl, I feel your spirit of order and of comfort whispering in the air about me, the spirit that lovingly teaches you day by day to spread the clean cloth and sprinkle the sand on the floor with that dear hand

of yours, making this lowly dwelling a heaven indeed.
And here.

He lifts a bed-curtain

This makes me tremble with delight. I could linger here for
hours. Here is where she has slept her tender sleep, dreaming
nature's dreams and slowly growing into the angel she was
born to be.

But me? What brings me here? What do I want here? Why
am I so oppressed, so moved? Poor Faust, I hardly know you.

Is there some spell at work? I was out to gratify my lust and
I find myself lost in a love-dream. Are we a prey to every
breeze that blows?

And if she came in this minute, I should pay dearly for my
offence. How small I should feel, prostrate at her feet.

MEPHISTOPHELES *entering*

Quick. I see her coming down below.

FAUST

Away. I'll never come here again.

MEPHISTOPHELES

Here's a jewel-box I got somewhere. Stick it in her cupboard.
It'll turn her head, you'll see. It's fairly heavy. I put a few
things in that were meant for someone else. But, after all, one
girl's as good as another, and it's all in the game.

FAUST

I don't know whether I ought.

MEPHISTOPHELES

A silly question. Perhaps you want to keep the box for
yourself. Are you a miser by any chance? If you are, waste
no more time and save me further trouble. Here I am,
scratching my head and rubbing my hands –

He puts the box in the cupboard and closes it

Now quick, we must be off. – Trying to bring the little girl
round to where you want her. And you stand there looking as
if you were going to give a lecture, with the grey ghosts of
physics and metaphysics staring at you. Come on. *off*

GRETCHEN *with a lamp*

It's so close here, so stuffy. *She opens the window*

And yet it's fresh enough outside. I feel so queer. I wish mother was home. I'm all of a tremble. What a foolish, frightened girl I am. *She sings while undressing*

> There was a King in Thule once, he was faithful to the very end. His lover on her death-bed gave him a gold cup.
>
> He prized it above everything, he emptied it at every feast. And when he put it to his lips, the tears always came into his eyes.
>
> When his turn came to die, he went over his possessions and left them all to his heir. But not the gold cup.
>
> He sat at the royal banquet with his retainers round him in the high ancestral hall of his castle by the sea.
>
> Then the old fellow rose, drained the cup for the last time, and threw it into the water.
>
> He saw it fall and fill and sink deep into the sea. His eyes closed. He never drank again.

She opens the cupboard to put her clothes away and sees the box

How did this lovely box get in here? I know I locked the cupboard. It's strange. I wonder what's inside. Perhaps someone left it in pawn with mother. And there's the key on a ribbon. I've a good mind to open it. What's this? I never saw anything like it. Jewels. Jewels that a great lady could wear on special holidays. I wonder how I should look in the necklace. Who can all these splendours belong to?

She puts it on and stands before the mirror

I wish the earrings were mine. You look so different with them at once. Ah poor me, a pretty face doesn't help. It's all very well, but no one heeds. Or they praise me and pity me. It's money they're after, money does everything. And we're just the poor.

ON A WALK
Faust in thought pacing up and down. Mephistopheles joins him

MEPHISTOPHELES

By unrequited love. By all the fires of hell. I wish there was something worse that I could swear by.

FAUST

What's got you? What's eating you? I never saw such a face in all my life.

MEPHISTOPHELES

If I wasn't the devil myself, I'd say devil take me.

FAUST

Have you got a tile loose? It's funny to see you behaving like a lunatic.

MEPHISTOPHELES

Just think. The jewels I got for Gretchen, the priest has swiped them. Her mother saw them and got cold feet right away. She has a sensitive nose. She's always sniffling in her prayer-book and knows by the smell whether a thing is sacred or profane. She knew at once there was something wrong with the jewels. Child, she said, unlawful property snares the soul and dries the blood. We'll give them to the Virgin and she'll reward us with manna from heaven. Gretchen pulled a long face and said to herself they needn't have looked her gift-horse so in the mouth, and surely it can't have been a wicked man that gave her it. Her mother sent for the priest and told him what had happened and he liked what he saw. You did right, he said, to resist temptation, it always pays. The church has a good stomach, it has gobbled up whole countries and never overeaten. The church alone, good women, can digest unlawful property.

FAUST

This is the way it goes, they all do it.

MEPHISTOPHELES

Whereupon he pocketed the lot – bracelets, rings, chains like so many trifles, a mere bagatelle, and barely thanked them. Told them they'd get their reward in heaven and left them all uplifted.

FAUST

And Gretchen?

MEPHISTOPHELES

She's restless, doesn't know what to do, doesn't know what

she wants. Thinks about the jewels day and night and thinks still more about who gave her them.

FAUST
This distresses me. Get her some more jewels. There wasn't much to the first batch.

MEPHISTOPHELES
Oh yes, sir, all child's play to you.

FAUST
Hurry up and do as I wish. Get hold of her neighbour. Don't be such a pudding-head. And don't forget the new jewels.

MEPHISTOPHELES
Yes, sir, yes. Happy to oblige.

Faust off

These foolish lovers would blow up the whole works – sun, moon, and stars – to please their women.

A NEIGHBOUR'S HOUSE

MARTHE *alone*
God forgive that husband of mine. He didn't treat me right. Went off, disappeared, and left me in the lurch. I never gave him any trouble. God knows I was fond of him. (*She weeps*) Perhaps he's dead. Oh dear. If only I had a death certificate.

Enter Gretchen

GRETCHEN
Frau Marthe!

MARTHE
O Gretchen, what is it?

GRETCHEN
My knees are shaking. I've just found another of those boxes in my cupboard, an ebony one, lovely things in it, much better than the first.

MARTHE
Don't let your mother know. She'd take it to the priest again.

GRETCHEN
Oh look. Just look.

MARTHE *adorning her*
You lucky, lucky thing.

GRETCHEN
But I can't be seen in the street with them, nor in church either.

MARTHE
Come to see me whenever you like, and put them on, just for you and me. Walk about in them for an hour or so in front of the mirror. And some day, some holiday, there'll be a chance to let people see you in them, bit by bit. A necklace to begin with, and then an earring. Your mother won't notice and if she does we'll bluff her.

GRETCHEN
Whoever could have brought these jewel-boxes? There's something wrong about it. (*a knock*) Heavens. Can that be mother?

MARTHE *looking through the curtain*
It's a strange man. Come in.

Enter Mephistopheles

MEPHISTOPHELES
Forgive me, ladies, for butting in like this. *to Gretchen, very respectfully*
I'm looking for Frau Marthe Schwerdtlein.

MARTHE
That's me. What is it, sir?

MEPHISTOPHELES *whispering to her*
No more for the present, now I know you. You have a lady visiting you. Forgive me for disturbing you. I'll come back this afternoon.

MARTHE *aloud*
Think of it, lass, he takes you for a lady.

GRETCHEN
The gentleman is very kind. But I'm just a poor girl. The jewels aren't mine.

MEPHISTOPHELES

It isn't only the jewels, it's herself, her eyes so clear. How nice that I don't have to leave immediately.

MARTHE

What brings you here? I'm curious to know.

MEPHISTOPHELES

I wish I had better news. Please don't blame me for it. Your husband's dead. He sends you his best.

MARTHE

Dead. The good man dead. Oh, I can't bear it.

GRETCHEN

Please don't take it too hard.

MEPHISTOPHELES

Let me tell you the sad story.

GRETCHEN

I don't want ever to love anyone. Losing him would be so cruel.

MEPHISTOPHELES

Joy needs sorrow, sorrow needs joy.

MARTHE

Tell me how he died.

MEPHISTOPHELES

He's buried in Padua, near to St Anthony, sleeping peacefully in consecrated ground.

MARTHE

Is that all?

MEPHISTOPHELES

I bring a request from him. He wants you to have three hundred masses sung for him. For the rest, I haven't a penny in my pocket.

MARTHE

What! Not a keepsake? Not a piece of jewellery? Not what every journeyman carries at the bottom of his wallet as a souvenir. And would sooner go hungry, sooner beg, than lose it.

MEPHISTOPHELES

Madam, I'm very sorry. He didn't squander his money. He regretted his weaknesses and he lamented his misfortune.

GRETCHEN

Why must there be so much unhappiness? I'll say plenty of
requiems for him.

MEPHISTOPHELES

You're a nice girl, just right for marrying.

GRETCHEN

It's early for that.

MEPHISTOPHELES

Well, if not a husband, why not a lover meanwhile? What can
compare with having a girl like you in your arms?

GRETCHEN

It isn't the custom in these parts.

MEPHISTOPHELES

Custom or not. It's done.

MARTHE

Tell me.

MEPHISTOPHELES

I was with him when he died. On a foul bed of straw. But he
died as a Christian and knew he deserved worse. Oh how
I hate myself, he said, running away like that from my trade and
my wife. Dreadful to think of. If only she would forgive me.

MARTHE *weeping*

The dear man. I forgave him long ago.

MEPHISTOPHELES

But, God knows, she was more to blame than me.

MARTHE

It's a lie! What! Lie like that on the brink of the grave!

MEPHISTOPHELES

True, he was wandering in his mind at the last, if I know
anything. I never had any fun, he said, what with children and
then feeding them all, feeding them in more ways than one.
I hardly had a chance to eat in peace myself.

MARTHE

How could he forget how I toiled for him day and night and
loved him and was true?

MEPHISTOPHELES

You're wrong there. He didn't forget. Far from it. He said:

When we set out from Malta I prayed for my wife and children fervently. Then we ran into luck and captured a Turkish vessel laden with treasure of the Sultan's. Courage had its reward and I got my full share.

MARTHE

Oh dear. Oh dear. Do you think he buried it?

MEPHISTOPHELES

Who knows where in the world it's gone. A pretty lady took up with him, when he was going about in Naples all alone. She was kind to him, so very kind, that he felt it to the end of his days.

MARTHE

The wretch. Robbing his own children. And going on living that wicked life for all his troubles.

MEPHISTOPHELES

Well. He's dead now. That's the other side of the story. If I were you, I'd put in a decent year's mourning and then look about for someone else.

MARTHE

Oh dear. It won't be easy for me to find another as good as my first. He was such fun he was hard to beat. Only he was too restless, always after women, and wine, and gambling.

MEPHISTOPHELES

Come now, that wasn't so bad, provided he was as indulgent with you. On those terms I wouldn't mind taking you on myself.

MARTHE

Oh sir, what a joker you are.

MEPHISTOPHELES *aside*

Now I must get away. She'd take even the devil at his word. *To Gretchen* What about your love-affairs?

GRETCHEN

What do you mean?

MEPHISTOPHELES *aside*

You poor little innocent.
Aloud Goodbye.

GRETCHEN
Goodbye.

MARTHE
Tell me quick. Can I get a certificate to say where and when and how my man died and where he's buried? I like things done the right way and I want to see his death printed in the paper.

MEPHISTOPHELES
Yes, my good woman. The truth calls for two witnesses. I have a friend, a gentleman. I'll get him to swear before the notary and I'll bring him to see you.

MARTHE
Oh, please do that.

MEPHISTOPHELES
And will your young friend be here? He's a nice man, travelled a lot, very courteous to ladies.

GRETCHEN
He'd put me to shame.

MEPHISTOPHELES
No king on earth has the right to do that.

MARTHE
Well, we'll expect you both tonight in my garden at the back.

STREET
Faust. Mephistopheles

FAUST
What about it? Are things moving? Will it be long?

MEPHISTOPHELES
Bravo. I see you're all primed. Well, Gretchen will soon be yours. You'll see her tonight in Marthe's garden. There's a woman simply cut out for pandering and such.

FAUST
Excellent.

MEPHISTOPHELES
But we have to do something on our part.

FAUST

One good turn deserves another.

MEPHISTOPHELES

We have to testify that her husband's bones are resting in Padua in consecrated ground.

FAUST

That's a bright idea. We'll have to make the trip.

MEPHISTOPHELES

You silly fellow. We don't have to. Just testify out of the blue.

FAUST

If this is the best you can do, our scheme's a failure.

MEPHISTOPHELES

That's just like you, you goody-goody. Is it the first time in your life you've borne false witness? Haven't you held forth mightily, impudently, impiously about God and the world and all that moves in the world, and about man, the heart of man and the head? And, when you come down to brass tacks, you have to confess you knew no more than you do about Schwerdtlein's death.

FAUST

You're a liar and a sophist, and you always were.

MEPHISTOPHELES

You're telling me! Aren't you going to turn poor Gretchen's head tomorrow and swear you love her, and feel virtuous about it?

FAUST

Yes, and with all my heart.

MEPHISTOPHELES

Wonderful. And the talk will be all about faithful unto death and desire irresistible. Will that come from the heart too?

FAUST

Stop. It will. When I feel deeply and find no name for the throng of my emotions and ransack the universe for words to express it and I call the fire that consumes me infinite, eternal, is that only a pack of devil's lies?

MEPHISTOPHELES

But I know.

FAUST

Mark this, please, and spare my breath. Have it your own way, if that's the way you want it. But come now. I'm sick of arguing. I have no choice. I give in.

GARDEN

Gretchen arm in arm with Faust. Marthe with Mephistopheles. They stroll up and down

GRETCHEN

I can tell you're just being nice to me, sir, because I'm not in your class. When you're on a journey you make the best of things, good-naturedly. I'm sure there's not much a poor girl like me can say to a man that's seen all you have.

FAUST

A look from you, a word from you, is more to me than all the wisdom in the world. *He kisses her hand*

GRETCHEN

Don't put yourself out. How can you kiss it? It's so horrid, so rough. After all the work I've had to do. And mother's so particular. *They pass*

MARTHE

And you, sir, travel a lot, don't you?

MEPHISTOPHELES

In my business I have to. It's not easy. It hurts to leave places you like. And you just have to push on.

MARTHE

It's all very well to travel up and down the world when you're young and equal to it. But you can't keep it up for ever and, when the end comes in sight, who wants to be a bachelor?

MEPHISTOPHELES

I shiver at the thought of what's ahead.

MARTHE

Then, sir, don't wait too long. *They pass*

GRETCHEN

Yes, out of sight, out of mind. You know how to flatter

a girl. But you must have lots of friends, much cleverer than me.

FAUST

What you call clever, my dear, is mostly vanity, all on the surface.

GRETCHEN

How do you mean?

FAUST

Oh to think that the innocent never appreciate themselves at their true worth. Modesty, lowliness, the best of nature's gifts ...

GRETCHEN

You may spare a moment to think of me. I shall have plenty of time to think of you.

FAUST

Are you often alone?

GRETCHEN

Yes, there's not much housekeeping, but it has to be done. We have no help. I have to cook and sweep and knit and sew and run errands early and late and mother is so close about everything. Not that she hasn't enough. We could spread ourselves better than many. Father left a nice little bit of money and a cottage and garden outside. But I'm living quietly these days. My brother's a soldier, my little sister's dead. I had a lot of trouble with her, but I loved her so, I'd do it all again and gladly.

FAUST

A lovely child, if she was like you.

GRETCHEN

I looked after her and she was fond of me. She was born after father died. We gave mother up for lost; she was so low and she only got better very, very slowly. So she couldn't think of nursing the little one. I brought her up myself on milk and water. She was my baby. It was in my arms, on my lap, she kicked and smiled and grew.

FAUST

It must have made you very happy.

GRETCHEN

Yes, but it was often hard on me too. Her cradle stood by my bed at night. I was wide awake, if she so much as stirred. I either had to feed her or take her in bed with me and, if she wouldn't be quiet, dance up and down the room with her and be at the washtub early next morning, then do the shopping and the cooking, and so on one day after another. You don't always feel light-hearted, but you like your food and your sleep. *They pass*

MARTHE

It's hard on us poor women. Bachelors are so hard to get.

MEPHISTOPHELES

If women were all like you, it might be easy.

MARTHE

But honest, sir, are you still free? Haven't you lost your heart to anyone?

MEPHISTOPHELES

The proverb says: A place of your own and a good wife are beyond price.

MARTHE

I mean, have you never been tempted?

MEPHISTOPHELES

People have always been polite to me, very polite.

MARTHE

What I mean is did you never feel drawn?

MEPHISTOPHELES

You can't ever take women lightly.

MARTHE

Oh, you don't understand.

MEPHISTOPHELES

Sorry. You're very kind, I do understand that. *They pass*

FAUST

So you knew me again the moment I came into the garden.

GRETCHEN

Didn't you see? I dropped my eyes.

FAUST

And you forgive me for being so free, so bold, when you came out of church?

GRETCHEN

I was taken aback, no one had ever done that to me. No one could say anything bad about me. I wondered did I do something vulgar, something not nice. It seemed to come all over him as if he could do business right away. But I confess, something drew me to you. Whatever it was, I was cross with myself for not being crosser with you. But I couldn't help it.

FAUST

Oh, you dear thing.

GRETCHEN

Don't. *She plucks a daisy and pulls at the petals one by one*

FAUST

What's this? A posy?

GRETCHEN

No, it's just play.

FAUST

How do you mean, play?

GRETCHEN

Don't look. You'll laugh at me. *pulls the petals and mutters to herself*

FAUST

What are you saying?

GRETCHEN *inaudibly*

He loves me – loves me not.

FAUST

You angel.

GRETCHEN *continuing*

Loves me – loves me not – loves me – loves me not –
Plucks the last petal, jubilantly
He loves me.

FAUST

Yes, dear. Let the flower's word be final. He loves you. Do you know what it means? He loves you. *He takes her hands*

GRETCHEN

I'm trembling.

FAUST

Don't be afraid. Let my face, let my hands tell you what words

can't say. This surrender, this delight must be for ever. Or
I despair. No, it must be for ever.

*Gretchen presses his hands, frees herself, and runs away. He pauses
a moment in thought, then follows her*

MARTHE *coming up*
It's getting dark.

MEPHISTOPHELES
Yes, and we have to be going.

MARTHE
I'd ask you to stay longer. But people here aren't nice. You'd
think they had nothing to do but watch their neighbours'
every move. They gossip about you, whatever you do. And
what about the other two?

MEPHISTOPHELES
They ran up the path there.

MARTHE
He seems to like her.

MEPHISTOPHELES
And she him. That's the way of the world.

A SUMMER HOUSE

*Gretchen runs in, hides behind the door, puts her finger to her lips, and
peeps through the crack*

GRETCHEN
He's coming.

FAUST *entering*
Oh, you tease. Have I got you now? *kisses her*

GRETCHEN *returning the kiss*
Oh, I love you.

Mephistopheles knocks

FAUST *stamping his foot*
Who's there?

MEPHISTOPHELES
A friend.
FAUST
A beast.
MEPHISTOPHELES
It's time we were off.
MARTHE
Yes, sir, it's late.
FAUST
May I accompany you?
GRETCHEN
Mother would ... Goodbye.
FAUST
Must we part? Goodbye.
MARTHE
Bye, bye.
GRETCHEN
See you again soon.

Faust and Mephistopheles leave

GRETCHEN
What thoughts a man like that must have. It puts me to shame. I say yes to everything. I'm a poor ignorant girl. I don't know what he sees in me.

FOREST CAVERN

FAUST *alone*
You sublime spirit, you gave me all I asked for, gave me everything. It was not for nothing that you showed your face to me, blazing with fire. You gave me nature for my kingdom, nature in its splendour, and gave me the power to feel and enjoy it, not just coldly at a distance, but like a friend who takes me to his heart. You pass the whole range of living things before my eyes and teach me to know my brothers, my kindred, in the quiet woods, in the air and in the water. And

when the storm-wind rages and crashes through the forest, bringing down the giant pine that in its fall ruins the neighbouring trees and makes the hillside boom back with hollow noise, then you guide me to the sheltering cave, you reveal me to myself, and the mysteries that reside in me unfold. And, when as now I see the pure and gentle moon go up the sky, the silvery forms and figures of the early world come hovering out of the rock-steeps and the dripping bushes and temper the austere joy of contemplation.

Oh but now I realize that nothing perfect ever comes. Along with this rapture, bringing me closer and closer to the gods, I am given a companion, who with his cold and withering words humiliates me continually and turns your gifts to nothingness with a whisper. Yet I cannot do without him. He fans in me a burning passion for that fair woman's form, making me go blindly from desire to the fulfilment of desire and in the fulfilment making me yearn again for the desire.

Enter Mephistopheles

MEPHISTOPHELES
Haven't you had enough of it yet, carrying on this way? There can't be much fun in it in the long run. It's all right to try a thing once, but then you want a change.

FAUST
I wish you had something more to do than torment me when I'm feeling better.

MEPHISTOPHELES
Well, I'll let you alone. Only you mustn't say these things to me. I don't get much out of having you for a companion. You're so harsh, so crazy, I have my hands full from morning to night. Impossible to guess what you want and what you don't want.

FAUST
That's the right note to strike. You'd like me to thank you for boring me.

MEPHISTOPHELES
How would you, you poor mortal, ever have managed your

life without me? Haven't I cured you finally of your fantastic muddled way of thinking? If it wasn't for me, you'd have shuffled off this mortal coil already. Why do you want to go hiding in cracks and crevices like a screech-owl? Feeding like a toad on these wet rocks and clumps of moss. A nice way to spend your time. You haven't got the professor out of your system yet.

FAUST

Have you any idea what renewed energy I get from this sojourn in the wilds? If you have, you're devil enough to begrudge me my good fortune.

MEPHISTOPHELES

A queer sort of pleasure, almost unearthly. Lying about among the hills in the dark and in the wet, rapturously embracing earth and heaven, puffing yourself up until you think you're a god, permeating the marrow of the earth with your vague anticipations, experiencing the six days of creation in your own heart, extracting I don't know what satisfaction from feeling so high and mighty, merging amorously into the universe and forgetting your mortality altogether, and then – (*with a gesture*) terminating your deep insight I won't say how.

FAUST

Shame on you.

MEPHISTOPHELES

This doesn't suit you, it seems. But what right have you to throw your superior 'Shame on you' at me? Chaste ears can't bear to hear what chaste hearts can't do without. In short, I don't mind if you delude yourself a little now and then. But you won't be able to keep it up. You're worn out again already and before long you'll be dead with fright or go clean off your head. Enough. Your sweetheart's sitting at home, all shut in and sad. She can't get you out of her mind. She's desperately in love with you. Your passion swept her off her feet like a river that overflows its banks when the snow melts. You've won her heart, and now the flood has receded. It seems to me that instead of presiding in the forest as if you were somebody you ought to reward the silly young thing for her affection. Time is dragging terribly for her. She stands at the window and watches the clouds passing over the old town-wall. Oh for the wings of a dove. That's the song she sings all day long and half the night. Sometimes she's up, mostly she's down. She cries her heart out and then she's quiet. And she's love-sick all the time.

FAUST

You serpent.

MEPHISTOPHELES *aside*

I'll get you yet.

FAUST

Monster. Away with you. Don't speak of her to me. Don't revive in me the desire for her sweet and lovely body. I'm half insane with it already.

MEPHISTOPHELES

What else are we to do? She thinks you've run away and you nearly have.

FAUST

I'm close to her, no matter how far from her I go. I can never forget her. I even envy the sacred host when her lips touch it.

MEPHISTOPHELES

Right you are, my friend. I've often envied you the twins that feed among the lilies.

FAUST

Get out of my sight. You pander.

MEPHISTOPHELES

Wonderful. This abuse from you makes me smile. The god who created boys and girls at once saw the virtue of oppor-tunity-making. Off with you. It's a disgrace. It isn't death that awaits you, it's your girl's bedroom.

FAUST

Suppose I do delight in her embrace and warm myself in her bosom. Do I not feel her plight just the same? Do I not remain the homeless fugitive, an inhuman creature lacking any peace or purpose, roaring down from rock to rock like a cataract in my greed and fury? There she was in her childlike half-awakened state, living in her sequestered little alpine cottage, knowing nothing of life beyond the little round. And I, the accursed of God, was not satisfied with shattering the rocks to ruins. I had to destroy her peace of mind. This is the sacrifice that hell demanded. Help me, you devil, to speed these anxious days. Let what must happen, happen now. Let her fate come down on me and let us both perish together.

MEPHISTOPHELES

There you are again, all froth and fire. You fathead, go in and comfort her. Where your sort can't see the way out, you think the end has come. Long live the bold of heart. Aren't you bedevilled enough already? I can't think of anything more ridiculous than a devil in despair.

GRETCHEN'S ROOM

GRETCHEN *alone, at the spinning-wheel*

My heart is heavy, my peace is gone. I shall never find my peace again.

When he's not there, it's like the grave. The whole world, all of it, is soured.

My poor head is quite unhinged, my thoughts are broken pieces.

My heart is heavy, my peace is gone. I shall never find my peace again.

If I go to the window, I'm looking for him. I'm looking for him, when I leave the house.

His tall figure, his walk, his smile, his piercing gaze.

His magic words, the feel of his hands. And, oh, when he kisses me.

My heart is heavy, my peace is gone. I shall never find my peace again.

My body, yes, my body wants him. Oh just to take him and just to hold him.

And kiss and kiss him the way I'd like, though I die of the kissing.

MARTHE'S GARDEN
Gretchen. Faust

GRETCHEN

Tell me truly.

FAUST

If I can.

GRETCHEN

Tell me. What about your religion? You're a good, kind man. But I don't believe religion matters to you.

FAUST

Let it go. You know I like you. I'd die for those I love. I let people feel and worship as they choose.

GRETCHEN

That's not enough. You have to believe.

FAUST

Do you have to?

GRETCHEN

Oh. How I wish you cared about what I think. You don't respect the sacraments.

FAUST

I do respect them.

GRETCHEN

But you don't want them. You haven't gone to mass, you haven't confessed for a long time. Don't you believe in God?

FAUST

Sweetheart, who can say I believe in him? Ask the priests and the philosophers and the answer they give sounds like mockery.

GRETCHEN

So you don't believe in him?

FAUST

Don't misunderstand me, darling. Who can name him and say: I believe in him? Who with honesty can make bold to say: I don't believe in him? He who sustains and embraces all

836

things, does he not sustain and embrace you and me and himself? Isn't the earth firm beneath our feet? Doesn't the sky arch above us? Don't the friendly stars rise aloft? Don't you and I behold one another face to face? Isn't there something filling your heart and mind, something eternally mysterious working visibly, invisibly in the world about you? Fill your heart with it as full as it will hold and when you're filled with it, serenely filled with it, call it what you like: happiness, heart, love, God. I have no words for it. Feeling is everything. Words are just sound and smoke, bedimming the light of heaven.

GRETCHEN

This sounds all right. It's almost what the parson says, but not quite the same way.

FAUST

It's what all men say under the sun, each in his own language. Why shouldn't I say it in mine?

GRETCHEN

When you hear it said, it may seem good enough. But it isn't right. Because you aren't a Christian.

FAUST

Oh, my dear child.

GRETCHEN

It's been distressing me for a long time to see you with that man.

FAUST

How do you mean?

GRETCHEN

That man that's always with you, he revolts me. Nothing ever gave me such a start as the sight of his horrible face.

FAUST

Little girl, don't worry about him.

GRETCHEN

My blood mounts when I'm where he is. Mostly I like people. But while I long to see you, I have a secret horror of him. And I don't trust him either. God forgive me, if I'm unfair to him.

FAUST
There are people like him, so what?

GRETCHEN
I wouldn't care to live with any of them. When he puts his head round the door, he always has that sneering, half infuriated look. You can see he has no feeling for anything. It's written all over his face that he couldn't possibly love anyone. I'm so happy with you, so easy, so relaxed, so snug. But when he comes, it gripes me.

FAUST
You with your fears, you little angel.

GRETCHEN
It overcomes me so, when he joins us, I almost stop loving you. I couldn't say a prayer with him there. I nearly die. Aren't you the same?

FAUST
It's just your prejudice.

GRETCHEN
I have to go now.

FAUST
Shall I never have a quiet hour with you, the two of us, heart to heart?

GRETCHEN
Oh if only I slept by myself, I'd draw the bolt for you tonight. But mother's a light sleeper and if she caught us, it'd be the death of me.

FAUST
Don't worry about that, dear. Here's a bottle. Put three drops in what she drinks and she'll sleep deep and happy.

GRETCHEN
What wouldn't I do for your sake? I hope it isn't dangerous.

FAUST
Would I give you it, if it was?

GRETCHEN
When I look you in the face, I have to agree somehow. I've done so much for you already, there's hardly anything left for me to do. *off*

Enter Mephistopheles

MEPHISTOPHELES
Has she gone, the little minx?

FAUST
Spying again, were you?

MEPHISTOPHELES
I heard everything, professor. She put you through your
catechism. I hope it does you good. The girls always want
to find out whether a man keeps the old faith or not. They say
to themselves, if he does what he's told there, he'll do what
we tell him.

FAUST
You dreadful creature, you don't comprehend how this dear
soul, so full of her faith, is tormented by the thought that her
lover is damned.

MEPHISTOPHELES
What a queer lover you are, down to earth and up in the sky.
This slip of a girl is leading you by the nose.

FAUST
You abortion of filth and hell-fire.

MEPHISTOPHELES
And she has physiognomy down cold. When she sees me, it
comes all over her. This phiz of mine has a deep meaning. She
knows that. She's sure I'm a man of genius, she wonders
whether I'm the devil himself. And now, tonight...?

FAUST
What business is it of yours?

MEPHISTOPHELES
I get my fun out of it too.

AT THE WELL
Gretchen and Lieschen with jugs

LIESCHEN
Have you heard about Barbara?

GRETCHEN

Not a word. I'm not going out much.

LIESCHEN

There's no doubt about it. Sybil told me today. She's landed herself now. This is what comes of putting on airs.

GRETCHEN

How do you mean?

LIESCHEN

You can smell it a mile off. At mealtimes now she's feeding two.

GRETCHEN

Oh.

LIESCHEN

It serves her right. She's been running after that fellow for so long. Taking her out walking, taking her out to the village and dancing with her. She had to be first wherever she went. Making up to her with cakes and wine. So conceited she was about her beauty. She had the cheek to accept presents from him. Fondling and licking one another. And now she's got it.

GRETCHEN

Poor girl.

LIESCHEN

You don't mean to say you're sorry for her. When you and me had to work at the spinning-wheel and mother wouldn't let us out at night, there she was, standing outside with her boy in the dark passage or sitting on the bench, she didn't mind how long. Now she has to take her medicine, do penance at church in the smock.

GRETCHEN

Surely he'll marry her.

LIESCHEN

A fool he'd be. A smart lad like him. He can have fun with others. Besides, he's gone away.

GRETCHEN

That was bad of him.

LIESCHEN

Even if she gets him, she won't like it. The boys'll spoil her wreath of flowers for her and we'll scatter chaff in the doorway. *off*

GRETCHEN
Going home
I used to rail so myself like the best of them when a poor girl went wrong. Couldn't find words enough for other people's sins. Black as they were, I made them blacker, and never made them black enough to suit me. Prided myself and paraded it and now it's me that's the sinner. Yet, everything that drove me to it was sweet and dear, God only knows.

BY THE TOWN WALL

Set in the wall is an image of the Mater Dolorosa. Flower pots in front of it

GRETCHEN *putting fresh flowers in the pots*
> You who have suffered so, mistress of suffering, turn your face to me in my trouble and be kind.
> With the sword in your heart and pains beyond number you gaze at your son dying.
> You look at the father and your sighs go up for his ordeal and yours.
> But who is there to feel with me the pangs that thrill me and the dread in my heart? Only you know its trembling, its desire, only you.
> Wherever I go, this anguish goes with me. No sooner am I alone, than I weep and weep. My heart is breaking.
> This morning I plucked these flowers for you in the pots at my window. I watered them with my tears.
> The sun came early into my room, to find me already upright in my bed in utter misery.
> Help me, save me from shame, save me from death. You who have suffered so, mistress of suffering, turn your face to me in my trouble and be kind.

NIGHT. STREET AT GRETCHEN'S DOOR

VALENTIN *a soldier, brother of Gretchen*

It used to be that I could sit at a banquet, with everyone blowing his horn and the boys singing the praises of the girls they liked and emptying their glasses to them, and all I had to do was to sit quietly with my elbows on the table and, when they'd finished their boasting, smile and stroke my beard and raise my glass and say: Every man to his taste, but is there a girl in the country to touch my Gretchen, is there any girl that can hold a candle to her? Round went the toasts, clink, clank, and some of them would yell: He's right, she's the pick of the lot, the pick of womanhood, and the others hadn't a word to say. But now it's enough to make you pull your hair out in tufts or climb up the wall. Now any Tom, Dick, or Harry can turn up his nose at me and make his snide remarks and I have to sit there, like a culprit, breaking into a sweat at any chance word. I'm fit to smash their heads, all of them, but I can't call them liars.

But who's this slinking along? I believe there's two of them. If it's him, I'll collar him, he won't leave here alive.

Faust. Mephistopheles

FAUST

See how the light from the ever-burning lamp in the little chapel shines up through the window and spreads, getting weaker and weaker till the surrounding darkness quenches it. I feel just like that inside, dark, nocturnal.

MEPHISTOPHELES

And I'm all aching for something, like an alley cat creeping past the fire-escapes and then hugging the wall. I don't feel exactly wicked about it, just a little bit thievish, a little bit lecherous. It's the Walpurgis Night getting into my system. It's due the day after tomorrow. Wonderful. That's when you know what it is to be alive.

FAUST

Is it the light from a hidden treasure that I see flickering over there?

MEPHISTOPHELES

Yes, you'll soon have the pleasure of lifting it yourself. I peeped at it the other day, saw some lovely coins in it.

FAUST

Wasn't there a ring or a piece of jewellery for my girl to wear?

MEPHISTOPHELES

I did see something of the sort. Maybe a string of pearls.

FAUST

Good. It hurts me to go to see her without any presents.

MEPHISTOPHELES

I don't see why you should mind having your pleasure for nothing occasionally. And now, with the sky full of stars, I'll let you hear a song, a real work of art. It's a moral song, just the sort that'll fool her. *He sings to the zither*

> What are you after, here at your lover's door, at daybreak, Cathy?
>
> Don't do it. He'll let you in as a virgin. You won't be one when you come out.
>
> Take care, once it's done, then good night, you poor things. If you care for one another, give nothing away for love, unless with the ring on your finger.

VALENTIN *steps forward*

Who are you enticing here, you cursed ratcatcher? To hell first with your instrument. And then to hell with the singer.

MEPHISTOPHELES

You've split the zither. It's no good now.

VALENTIN

Now we'll split heads.

MEPHISTOPHELES *to Faust*

Hold your ground, professor. Quick now. I'll lead. Stick close to me. Out with your sword. At him. I'll parry.

VALENTIN

Parry this one.

MEPHISTOPHELES
Why not?

VALENTIN
And this.

MEPHISTOPHELES
Certainly.

VALENTIN
I believe the devil's fighting me. What's this? My hand's gone lame.

MEPHISTOPHELES *to Faust*
Let him have it.

VALENTIN *falls*
Oh.

MEPHISTOPHELES
That's settled him, the lout. But now we must be off, we must disappear. There'll be a hue-and-cry in no time. I'm on good terms with the police, but when it comes to murder, there's not much I can do.

MARTHE *at the window*
Help. Help.

GRETCHEN *at the window*
Bring a light.

MARTHE *as above*
They're scrapping, shouting, yelling, and fighting.

CROWD
One of them's killed.

MARTHE *coming out*
Have the murderers got away?

GRETCHEN *coming out*
Who lies here?

CROWD
The son of your mother.

GRETCHEN
Almighty God. This is fearful.

VALENTIN
I'm dying. It's soon said, and sooner done. What are you

women standing around for, weeping and wailing? Come
here and listen to me.

They all come closer

Gretchen, you're young still, young and foolish. You've made
a mess of things. I'll tell you. Between you and me, you're just
a plain whore. So be a real one.

GRETCHEN

My brother. O God. What will you say next?

VALENTIN

You leave God out of it. What's done can't be undone. So on
you go. You started off with one, secretly. There'll be others
soon. When a round dozen have had you, the whole town'll
have you.

   When shamefulness is born, it's born in secret. You pull
the veil of night over its head. You're ready to strangle it.
But if it grows, if it gets bigger, it goes about by day, though it
isn't any better to look at. The uglier it is, the more it seeks
the light.

   I see the time coming when decent folk will keep away
from you, shun you, you wanton, as if you were a putrid
corpse. When they look you in the face, your heart will quail.
No more gold necklaces then. No more standing at the
altar. No more fun at the dance in a lace collar. You'll have
to hide in dark corners with beggars and cripples. God may
forgive you, but on earth you'll be accurst.

MARTHE

Commend your soul to God. Do you want to die a blas-
phemer?

VALENTIN

If I could only get at your scraggy body, you foul go-between,
I might hope to find forgiveness – yes, and to spare – for all
my sins.

GRETCHEN

Oh my brother. Oh what agony.

VALENTIN

I tell you, stop your blubbering. When you disgraced yourself, you dealt me the worst blow. I was a soldier, a good soldier, and now I must sleep the sleep of death and find my God. *He dies*

CATHEDRAL

Service, organ, singing. Gretchen in a crowded congregation. The evil spirit behind her

EVIL SPIRIT

How different it used to be, Gretchen, when in your childhood innocence you came to the altar and lisped your prayers from the worn little prayer-book, God mingled in your thoughts with the games you played. How is it now? With what sin in your heart? Are you praying for your mother's soul who passed in sleep to endless torment? Through you? At your door whose blood is it? And inside you can't you feel it yet, the something stirring, threatening you both, always with you?

GRETCHEN

Oh, oh, oh, to be rid of these thoughts that shuttle to and fro, reproaching me.

CHOIR

> Dies irae, dies illa
> Solvet saeclum in favilla.

Organ

EVIL SPIRIT

The wrath of heaven seizes you. The trumpets sound. The graves are quaking. And your heart, roused from its ashes to suffer the flames, leaps in agony.

GRETCHEN

Oh to be out of here. These organ tones suffocate me. The chanting breaks me utterly.

CHOIR

> Judex ergo cum sedebit,
> Quidquid latet ad parebit,
> Nil inultum remanebit.

GRETCHEN

I can't move. The pillars imprison me. The great vault crushes me. I'm stifling.

EVIL SPIRIT

Hide yourself, would you? Sin and shame cannot be hidden. You want air? You want light? No.

CHOIR

Quid sum miser tunc dicturus?
Quem patronum rogaturus,
Cum vix justus sit securus?

EVIL SPIRIT

Angels turn their faces from you. The pure shudder at the thought of touching you.

CHOIR

Quid sum miser tunc dicturus?

GRETCHEN

Neighbour. Your smelling-bottle. *She swoons*

WALPURGIS NIGHT

Harz mountains. Neighbourhood of Schierke and Elend Faust. Mephistopheles

MEPHISTOPHELES

Don't you wish you had a broomstick to ride on? The thing for me would be a tough old billy-goat. We've a good way to go yet by this route.

FAUST

As long as my legs hold out, this cudgel of a walking-stick will do for me. What's the point of shortening our route? Having to find our way through a tangle of valleys and then climb these rocks with the everlasting waterfalls splashing down is just what spices a trip of this sort. Spring's already got into the birch trees and even the pines are beginning to feel it. Why shouldn't we feel it too?

MEPHISTOPHELES

Myself, I don't notice it. I'm all wintry. I wish the snow was here. Look at this melancholy red moon rising so late, what there is of it, and not giving enough light to keep us from bumping into the trees or stumbling over a rock. Excuse me if I engage a will-o'-the-wisp. I see one there, shining merrily. Hello, my friend, will you join us? No use wasting your light. Give us the benefit of it like a good fellow. Here's where we're going up.

WILL-O'-THE-WISP

Perhaps my respect for you will enable me to control my frivolous nature. I usually go in a zigzag.

MEPHISTOPHELES

Listen to this. He's trying to imitate mankind. Go straight, damn it all, or I'll blow you and your flimsy light out altogether.

WILL-O'-THE-WISP

I see, sir, that you're the boss and I'll do my best to oblige. But please don't forget that the mountain tonight is bewitched and, if a will-o'-the-wisp is to guide you, you mustn't be too particular.

FAUST, MEPHISTOPHELES, WILL-O'-THE-WISP *singing in turn*

It seems we have entered the realm of dreams and magic. Now do your best and lead us forward in the big barren spaces.

Look at the trees, trees behind trees, whizzing past and the cliffs reaching out over us and the long-nosed rocks blowing and snoring.

And little streams, tiny streams, speeding through the rocks, through the grass. I hear a rustling. Is it song? Is it love's sweet lament, voices from those heavenly days, voices of love, of hope? And there comes the echo like a tale of days gone by.

And hark at the screech-owl, the night-owl, the plover, the jay, coming nearer and nearer. Have they all stayed awake? Is it lizards in the shrubs, long legs, fat bellies? And see the gnarled roots, twisting snake-like out of the rocks, out of the sand, to frighten us, to catch us, stretching their fibrous tentacles at the passer-by. And the mice, hordes of mice, of every colour, running through the moss, the heather, and glow-worms flying in swarms, leading us off the trail.

And tell me, are we standing still or moving? Everything's spinning round, the rocks and the trees pulling faces at us. And will-o'-the-wisps, more and more of them, puffing themselves out.

MEPHISTOPHELES

Take a good hold of my coat-tails. This is one of the middle-sized peaks, where you can see something that will surprise you – the whole mountain made luminous by Mammon, the lord of wealth.

FAUST

What a curious dim light there is in the lower regions, like the red sky at dawn. And feeling its way into the very deepest chasms. Mist rising here, stretches of it there, the glow shining through, creeping along in threads, breaking out like a cascade, reaching down the valley in countless veins, and a patch of it in a nook there all by itself. Look at those sparks flying close by like golden sand scattered in the air. And see, the whole rocky cliff's lit up from top to bottom.

MEPHISTOPHELES

Yes, doesn't Mammon do a good job of illuminating his palace for the festival? You're lucky to have seen it. And now I can hear the unruly guests arriving.

FAUST

My, what a raging gale. Hitting me, slamming me, in the back of the neck.

MEPHISTOPHELES

You must hang on to these ribs of rock, or down you'll go into the depths. The mist makes it darker than ever. Do you hear the cracking in the trees, flinging up the startled owls? Do you hear the columns of the ancient green palaces splintering, the branches creaking and snapping, the roots grinding, gaping, the tree trunks thundering down, falling on one another in dreadful confusion, with the wind howling in the chasms they cover? Can you hear voices in the air, some near, some far off? Yes, the mad, magic singing is streaming across the hillside.

CHORUS OF WITCHES

The witches are heading for the Brocken. The stubble is yellow, the crop is green. That's where they all gather, with Urian presiding. So on we go over stump and stone. The billy-goat stinks, the witch takes it.

VOICE

Mother Baubo's coming by herself, riding on a sow.

CHORUS

Let Mother Baubo take the lead, the place of honour is hers. With those two in front the rest of the witches will follow.

VOICE

Which way did you come?

VOICE

I came by Ilsenstein. I peeped into an owl's nest. Oh, how it stared.

VOICE

To hell with you, why ride so fast?

VOICE

She's scraped me, look at my wounds.

CHORUS OF WITCHES

The road is broad, the road is long. What a mad throng this is. The hayfork pricks, the broom scratches, the child chokes, the mother bursts.

HALF-CHORUS OF WITCHMASTERS

We're crawling like snails. The women are all in the lead. When it's a visit to the devil, the women are a thousand paces ahead.

THE OTHER HALF

We don't worry about that. The woman does it in a thousand paces. But, however fast she goes, the man does it in one big jump.

VOICE *from above*

Come with us, come up from the rocky lake.

VOICE *from below*

We'd like to come up. We're all washed and clean, but we shall never bear.

BOTH CHORUSES

The wind has dropped, the stars are gone. The moon likes to hide too. The magic chorus, roaring along, is scattering thousands of sparks.

VOICE *from below*

Stop. Stop.

VOICE *from above*

Who's calling out of the cleft?

VOICE *from below*

Take me with you. Take me with you. I've been climbing for three hundred years and I can't reach the summit, where I belong.

BOTH CHORUSES

You can ride a broom, ride a stick, ride a hayfork, ride a goat. If you can't get a move on today, you're lost.

HALF-WITCH *from below*

I've been trotting behind for ages. The others are so far ahead. I have no peace at home and can't find any here.

CHORUS OF WITCHES

The salve makes witches bold. A rag will do for a sail. Any tub will do for a boat. Fly in the air today or you never will.

BOTH CHORUSES

And when we reach the summit spread out and cover the whole ground with witches.

They settle

MEPHISTOPHELES

They crowd and push and rush and rattle. They hiss and twirl and tug and babble. They shine and crackle, and stink and burn. There's witches for you. Now stick close to me or we'll lose one another in a minute. Where are you?

FAUST *at a distance*

Here.

MEPHISTOPHELES

Have they carried you that far? I'll have to use my authority. Make way, Voland, the devil, is coming. Make way, good people, make way. Here, professor, grab hold of me and, in one dash, we'll get out of the crowd. It's too much even for me. There's a queer light shining yonder. I feel drawn to those bushes. Come on, we'll slip over there.

FAUST

You spirit of contradiction. But anyway, lead on. I begin to think you managed it well. We came to the Brocken on Walpurgis Night and then, having arrived, we go off into a corner.

MEPHISTOPHELES

See there, what a nice bonfire. It's a merry club-meeting. We shall feel more at home in a small circle.

FAUST

But I'd rather be up on top. I can see the lights and the smoke whirling. The crowd is streaming up to the evil one. We'd be solving some riddles there.

MEPHISTOPHELES

Yes, and setting up some new ones. You just let the great world wag. We'll have a quiet time here. We'll make a little world inside the big one. It's often done. I see some young witches there, all naked, and some old ones who know what to cover up. Be nice to them for my sake. No effort and lots of fun. I can hear music playing. A cursed noise. You have to get used to it. Come along, you can't back out now. I'll lead the way and introduce you, find you some new friends. What do you say? It isn't so small a place. Look. You can hardly see the end. There's a hundred bonfires burning in a row, people dancing, chatting, cooking, drinking, making love. Tell me now where you'd find anything better.

FAUST

Are you going to play the devil here or the magician?

MEPHISTOPHELES

I usually travel incognito. I'm very careful about it, as you know. But on gala days you can be seen wearing your orders.

I can't boast of a garter, but the horse hoof commands respect. Do you see the snail there, crawling towards me, feeling its way with its face? It's smelt me out already. No use trying to conceal myself here. Come along. We'll go from fire to fire. I'll be the wooer and you'll be the lover.

To a few, sitting by a dying fire

Well, old gentlemen, what are you doing here? I'd think better of you if I found you in the midst of things, in all the youthful revels. We're alone enough when we're at home.

GENERAL

You can't trust nations. However much you do for them, the young are always first. It's the same with nations as with women.

MINISTER

We've strayed too far off the right track. Give me the good people we once had. When we were on top, that was the golden age.

PARVENU

We weren't such fools, yet we often did what we shouldn't. But now everything's gone topsy-turvy and just when we wanted to hang on to it.

AUTHOR

Who today wants to read a book of even moderate intelligence? As for the younger generation, they're cheekier than ever.

MEPHISTOPHELES *who suddenly appears very old*

On this my last ascent of the witches' mountain I feel that the people are ready for the Judgment Day. My sands are running out and so the world is on the way out too.

HUCKSTER-WITCH

Gentlemen, don't hurry past, don't miss this opportunity. Look at my wares. I have all sorts of things in my store, but nothing that hasn't done serious harm. Not a dagger but has drawn blood, not a cup but has poured burning poison into a healthy body, not a jewel but has seduced a good woman, not a sword but has played false, maybe run its opponent through the back.

MEPHISTOPHELES

My old friend, you're behind the times. What's done is done with. Go in for novelties, novelties is what we want now.

FAUST

What a riot it all is. I almost lose my identity.

MEPHISTOPHELES

They're all streaming up to the summit. You think you're pushing and you're being pushed.

FAUST

Who's that?

MEPHISTOPHELES

Take a close look at her. It's Lilith.

FAUST

Who?

MEPHISTOPHELES

Adam's first wife. Beware of her lovely locks, unique in their beauty. When she catches a young man with them, she doesn't soon let go.

FAUST

There's two there, an old witch and a young one. They've hopped about plenty already.

MEPHISTOPHELES

There's no rest for anyone today. Here's another dance starting. Come on, we'll help ourselves.

FAUST *dancing with the young one*

Once I had a lovely dream. I saw an apple tree with two shining apples on it. I climbed up after them.

THE PRETTY ONE

You've always liked apples, ever since paradise. It pleases me to think that my garden bears them.

MEPHISTOPHELES *with the old one*

Once I had a lurid dream. I saw a cleft tree. It had a hole in it. Big as it was, I liked it.

THE OLD WITCH

My compliments to the knight of the hoof. Hold ready you know what, unless you funk it.

PROKTOPHANTASMIST

You cursed people. What presumption. Haven't we proved it to you long ago that a spirit has no feet to stand on, and here you are, dancing like ordinary mortals.

THE PRETTY ONE *dancing*

What's he doing at our ball?

FAUST *dancing*

Oh, he goes everywhere. Others dance and he judges them. If he can't discuss every step, it's as if it was never taken. What annoys him most is when we progress. If you would just go round in a circle, as he does in that old mill of his, he might approve, especially if you praised him for it.

PROKTOPHANTASMIST

Are you still there? This is an outrage. Off you go. Haven't we had the age of reason? These devil folk, they won't obey the rules. We're so bright now and yet there still are ghosts in Tegel. I've worked so long against superstition, yet we never get rid of it. It's an outrage.

THE PRETTY ONE

Will you just stop making yourself a nuisance.

PROKTOPHANTASMIST

I tell you spirits to your face, I won't have this tyranny of the spirits. I have no spirit for it.

They go on dancing

Today I see is one of my bad days, but I don't mind taking a journey and I trust before I finish I shall exorcize both devils and poets.

MEPHISTOPHELES

He'll go now and sit in a puddle. That's his way of relieving himself. If leeches settle on his arse, he'll be cured of spirit and spirits too.

To Faust who has withdrawn from the dance

Why did you let the pretty girl go? She sang so beautifully when she was dancing.

FAUST

While she was singing, a red mouse jumped out of her mouth.

MEPHISTOPHELES

That's all right. You mustn't be too fussy. At least the mouse wasn't grey. Who cares anyway in a flirtation?

FAUST

Then I saw...

MEPHISTOPHELES

What?

FAUST

Mephisto, look there. A lovely girl, so pale, standing off by herself. She's sliding slowly away, as if her feet were bound together. I confess she looks to me like my dear Gretchen.

MEPHISTOPHELES

Keep away from her. She's no good to anyone. She's a phantom, an image, not living. She's not safe. That fixed stare of hers congeals your blood and nearly turns you into stone. You've heard of the Medusa, haven't you?

FAUST

Yes, I see, it's the eyes of the dead, not closed by a loving hand. This is the breast that Gretchen offered me, the sweet body that I enjoyed.

MEPHISTOPHELES

All magic, you simpleton. She looks like his sweetheart to every man.

FAUST

What joy, what suffering. I can't take my eyes off her. Strange how the red line round her lovely neck suits her. Not wider than the back of a knife.

MEPHISTOPHELES

You're right, I can see it too. She can carry her head under her arm as well. Perseus cut it off. Can't you get over this love of illusions? Come along up this little hill. It's as merry here as in the Prater. And, unless I'm mistaken, there's a theatre there. What are they doing?

SERVIBILIS

They're just beginning again. A new piece, the last of seven. It's usual here to do seven. A dilettante wrote it and dilettantes act it. Excuse me, sirs, if I leave you. I have a dilettante impulse to draw up the curtain.

MEPHISTOPHELES
It's right and proper that I should find you on the Brocken. This is where you belong.

WALPURGIS NIGHT'S DREAM OR OBERON AND TITANIA'S GOLDEN WEDDING INTERMEZZO

PROPERTY MASTER
We stagehands have an easy day today. This old mountain and the misty valley are all the scenery needed.

HERALD
It takes fifty years to make a golden wedding. But if the quarrel is over, that's the golden wedding for me.

OBERON
Any spirits that are near, show yourselves now. The king and queen are one again.

PUCK
Here comes Puck and does a spin and trails his foot. Hundreds follow him in the merry dance.

ARIEL
Ariel leads the song in tones divinely pure. Many crude natures are attracted, but the refined are drawn to it too.

OBERON
Wives and husbands, learn from us how to get along. Go apart and love will bring you together again.

TITANIA
Yes, if he sulks and she mopes, take him off to the far north and take her to the south.

ORCHESTRA *fortissimo*
A fly's snout and a midge's nose, and all their relatives. Frog in the leaves and cricket in the grass. These are the musicians.

SOLO

Here comes the bagpipes. He's only a soap-bubble. Can you hear him go clickety-clack with his pug-nose?

MIND IN THE MAKING

Give him a spider's foot, a toad's belly, and give him wings. He won't come alive unless in verse.

A COUPLE

A tiny step and then a jump in the honeysweet air. You trip along nicely, but we don't take off.

INQUISITIVE TRAVELLER

This must be a carnival joke. I can hardly trust my eyes. Oberon, the handsome god, on view here even at this late day.

ORTHODOX

He may have neither claws nor tail, but there's no doubt. He's just as much a devil as the gods of Greece.

NORTHERN ARTIST

Anything I undertake today is just sketchy. But I am preparing betimes for my Italian journey.

A PURIST

Oh, it's my bad luck that brought me here where all is snares and temptation. And out of all this crowd of witches only two are powdered.

YOUNG WITCH

Let those that are old and grey powder themselves and wear a skirt. Me, I sit naked on my billy-goat and show my husky body.

MATRON

We're too polite to quarrel with you here, you young and tender things. All we say is: 'May you rot in your tracks.'

CONDUCTOR

Fly's snout and midge's nose, don't buzz around this naked beauty. Frog in the leaves and cricket in the grass, see that you keep time.

WEATHERCOCK *pointing one way*

You couldn't wish for better company. Would you believe it, nothing but brides and bachelors, all brimming with hope.

WEATHERCOCK *pointing the other way*
If the earth doesn't gape to swallow them, I'll go straight to hell on the high run.

EPIGRAMS
Here we come as insects with sharp little claws to honour Papa Satan as he deserves.

EDITOR
Look at the crowd of them there, naïvely chatting and joking. Next thing, they'll claim to be kind-hearted.

LEADER OF THE MUSES
I love to lose myself among all these witches. I'd find them easier to lead than the Muses.

QUONDAM JOURNAL
It pays to get among the right people. Hang on to my coat-tails. The Brocken is like the German Parnassus – there's plenty of room at the top.

INQUISITIVE TRAVELLER
Who's that striding along so stiff and haughty? He's sniffing and sniffing for all he's worth. 'He's hunting for Jesuits.'

CRANE
I like to fish in clear waters, I like to fish in muddy. This is why you find me, pious as I am, consorting with devils.

PAGAN
Believe me, these men of piety can function anywhere. They often hold their conventions on the Brocken.

DANCER
That must be a new gang arriving. I can hear their distant drums. Don't worry. It's the bitterns *unisono* in the reeds.

DANCING-MASTER
See how each of them picks his way, as best he can. The crooked ones jump, the heavy ones hop. They don't care how they look.

FIDDLER
These low people hate one another, murderously. The bag-pipes unite them, as Orpheus with his lyre tamed the beasts.

DOGMATIST
You can't shake me with your noisy doubts and objections.

The devil must be somebody, else why should there be devils at all?

IDEALIST

Imagination in my sense has gone too far this time. Truly, if I'm a part of all that, I'm off my nut.

REALIST

These goings-on are a torment, they're more than I can take. For the first time I don't know where I stand.

SUPERNATURALIST

I'm happy to be here and enjoy this company. I can reason from devils to good spirits.

SCEPTIC

They're tracking out the little flames and think they're near the treasure. Doubt goes with devil, d with d. This suits me entirely.

CONDUCTOR

Frog in the leaves and cricket in the grass. You cursed dilettantes. Fly's snout and midge's nose, what musicians!

OPPORTUNISTS

This host of merry creatures is called sans-souci. We can't walk any longer on our feet, so we walk on our heads.

THE NE´ER-DO-WELLS

We've scrounged many a meal so far, but now God help us. We've danced right through our shoes and we're down to our bare feet.

WILL-O´-THE-WISPS

We come from the swamp where we were born. But here we rate at once as shining gallants.

SHOOTING STAR

I came from high up in the starry light. Now I lie sprawling in the grass. Who'll help me on to my feet?

THE CRUDE ONES

Make way, make way. We tread down the grass. Spirits can be heavy-footed too.

PUCK

Don't stamp so, like baby elephants. Let Puck be the heaviest of us.

ARIEL

If nature or the spirit gave you wings, follow my light tracks to the rosy hill-top.

ORCHESTRA *pianissimo*

Clouds and mist are lit from above. A breeze in the trees and wind in the reeds, and everything vanishes.

DULL DAY. A FIELD
Faust. Mephistopheles

FAUST

An outcast, driven to despair. Wretchedly wandering the wide earth and now at long last a prisoner, a condemned criminal, locked in a dungeon, exposed to the cruellest torture, the dear girl and so ill-fated. Had it to come to this? And you kept it from me, you vile, you treacherous spirit. Yes, you can stand there and roll your devil's eyes in fury. Stand and defy me with your intolerable presence. A prisoner. In hopeless misery. At the mercy of evil spirits and the unsparing censure of mankind. And meanwhile you distract me with your vulgar entertainments, keep her desperate plight from me, and leave her to meet her end alone.

MEPHISTOPHELES

She's not the first.

FAUST

You beast. You foul monster. O infinite spirit, turn this reptile back into its canine form, the dog, that used to run ahead of me on my evening walks, roll at the feet of unsuspecting strangers and jump on their shoulders when they tripped over him. Turn him back into the shape that suited him so that he may crawl again in the sand at my feet and let me spurn him, him the lowest of the low. Not the first! Oh the shame of it, beyond human power to comprehend, that more than one of us mortals reached this depth of misery, that the death-agony of the first was not enough to clear all the others in the eyes of the great forgiver. The suffering of this single one racks me, marrow and bones. But you pass over the fate of thousands with a grin, unmoved.

MEPHISTOPHELES

Here we are again at the far edge of our intelligence. A step more and you people go stark mad. Why do you have dealings with us if you can't go through with it? You want to fly and you're afraid your head'll swim. Did we force ourselves on you or you on us?

FAUST

Don't gnash your savage teeth at me that way. It revolts me. You mighty spirit who deigned to appear before me, you know me heart and soul. Why did you tie me to this abominable creature who feeds on mischief and destruction and rejoices in it?

MEPHISTOPHELES

Have you finished now?

FAUST

Save her, or it'll be worse for you. It'll be curse on you, the direst curse, for centuries to come.

MEPHISTOPHELES

I'm powerless to loose the avenger's chains or to draw his bolts. You say 'Save her.' Who was it that brought her to ruin? Was it me or was it you?

Faust looks about him wildly

MEPHISTOPHELES

You're looking for a thunderbolt. It's good that thunderbolts weren't given to wretches like you. This is the way of tyrants, when they're in a jam, to free themselves by shattering their innocent opponents.

FAUST

Take me there. She must be free.

MEPHISTOPHELES

Think of the risks you're running. Remember there's blood on the town, blood that you shed. Avenging spirits are hovering over the place where the victim fell and waiting for the murderer to return.

FAUST

Must I hear this from you? May a whole world of death and destruction come down on you, you monster. Take me there, I tell you, and set her free.

MEPHISTOPHELES

I'll take you there and now I'll tell you what I can do. Do you think I have unlimited power in earth and heaven? I'll cloud the mind of the jailer. You grab the keys and lead her out by a mortal hand. I'll keep watch. The magic horses are ready. I'll abduct you. This I can do.

FAUST

Up and away.

NIGHT. OPEN FIELD
Faust, Mephistopheles, galloping past on black horses

FAUST

What's going on there at the raven-stone?

MEPHISTOPHELES

I can't say what they're brewing and doing.

FAUST

They go up and then down. They're bending and bowing.

MEPHISTOPHELES

A meeting of witches.

FAUST

They're scattering something, blessing something.

MEPHISTOPHELES

Come on, come on.

PRISON

FAUST *with a bunch of keys and a lamp, at an iron door*

I shudder so. I thought I had forgotten how. The whole misery of mankind comes over me. Here she is behind these dripping walls. And her sole offence came of a harmless wish. You hesitate to go to her? You dread seeing her again? Folly. If I delay I only bring death nearer. *He takes hold of the lock*

Singing within
> My mother, the whore,
> She murdered me.
> My father, the rascal,
> He ate me up.
> My little sister
> Gathered my bones
> In a cool place;
> I turned into a song-bird.
> Fly away, fly away.

FAUST *opening the door*

She doesn't dream her lover's listening and can hear the chains rattling, the straw rustling. *He goes in*

GRETCHEN *trying to hide on her pallet*

Oh, oh, they're coming. Oh death, oh bitter death.

FAUST *quietly*

Quiet now. Quiet. I've come to rescue you.

GRETCHEN *writhing at his feet*

Are you human? Then share my suffering.

FAUST

You'll wake the guards. *He takes hold of the chains to unlock them*

GRETCHEN *on her knees*

Headsman, who gave you this power over me? You've come for me at midnight. Wouldn't tomorrow morning do? Have pity on me. Let me live a little longer.

Standing up

I'm so young, so young. Too young to die. I was pretty too, and that was my ruin. My lover was close, now he's far away. My wreath of flowers torn and scattered. Don't take hold of me so roughly. Spare me. I never hurt you. I never saw you before. Are all my pleas in vain?

FAUST

This is fearful. This is too much.

GRETCHEN

I'm in your hands. I'm at your mercy. Let me nurse my baby first. I cuddled it all night. They took it from me, just to be unkind. And now they say I killed it. I shall never be happy again. They sing songs about me. It's horrid of them. An old tale ends this way. Why tell it of me?

FAUST *throwing himself down*

This is your lover, your lover at your feet, ready to take you out of this miserable bondage.

GRETCHEN *throwing herself down beside him*

Oh let us kneel down together and pray to the saints. See, under these steps, under this door, hell is blazing, the evil one raging, shouting in his fury.

FAUST *louder*

Gretchen. Gretchen.

GRETCHEN *paying heed*

That was my sweetheart's voice.

She jumps up, the chains fall off her

Where is he? I heard him call. I'm free. No one can stop me. I'll cling to his neck. I'll lie in his arms. He called Gretchen. He was standing at the door. I heard his voice, that dear, dear voice of his, right through the howling and the chattering, and the cruel mockery of hell.

FAUST

Yes, it's me, me.

GRETCHEN

It's you. Oh say it again.

Taking hold of him

It's him. It's him. Where is all the agony now? Where is the prison, the chains, the fear and torment of it all? It's you. You've come to save me. I'm saved. Now I can see the street where I first saw you, and the happy garden and me and Marthe waiting for you.

FAUST *trying to pull her away*

Come along. Come along.

GRETCHEN

Oh stay. I so like to be around where you are. *fondling him*

FAUST

Hurry, hurry. If you don't hurry, we'll pay for it in the worst way.

GRETCHEN

What, can't you kiss me any more? Oh my love, you've been away so short a time and you've forgotten how to kiss. I have your arms round me and I'm so frightened. It used to be like heaven when you looked at me and said things and kissed me fit to choke me to death. Kiss me now or I'll kiss you.

She embraces him

Oh, oh, your lips are cold. You don't say a word. You don't love me. Where's your love gone? Who took it away? *She turns from him*

FAUST

Come. Follow me. Sweetheart, be brave. I'll hug you with my heart on fire. Only follow me. Just follow me. That's all.

GRETCHEN *turning to him*

Is it really you? Are you sure?

FAUST

Yes, it's me. Come now.

GRETCHEN

You've taken the chains off. You've taken me on your lap. How come you aren't afraid of me? Do you know who it is you're setting free?

FAUST

Come, come. It'll soon be daylight.

GRETCHEN

I killed my mother. I drowned my baby. Wasn't it my baby and yours? Yours too? It's you. I can hardly believe it. Give me your hand. Yes, it's not a dream. It's your hand, your dear, dear hand. But it's wet. I think there's blood on it. Wipe it. Oh God, what have you done? Put up your sword. Please, please.

FAUST

Forget the past. You're killing me.

GRETCHEN

No. You must live. I'll tell you about the graves. You must see to them tomorrow. Give mother the best place and put my brother beside her, and me a little distance away, not far. And put the baby to my right breast. Else I shall lie there alone. It was lovely, lovely to snuggle up to you. But I can't do it any more. It seems I have to force myself on you and you're pushing me away. And yet it's you. And you look so good and kind.

FAUST

Come on then, if you're sure it's me.

GRETCHEN

What, out there?

FAUST

Yes, out into the open.

GRETCHEN

If the grave's out there and death waiting, come with me. From here to my last rest and not a step further. Are you going? Oh, I wish I could go too.

FAUST

You can. If you want. The door's open.

GRETCHEN

I can't go. There's no hope for me. What's the good of running away? They'll watch out for me. It's wretched to have to beg, and with a bad conscience too. It's wretched to roam about in strange places. And they'll get me anyway.

FAUST

I'll stick with you.

GRETCHEN

Quick, quick, save your poor child. Off you go. Up the path by the brook. Over the little bridge. Into the wood where the board fence is. In the pond. Get hold of it. It's trying to rise. It's struggling. Save it. Save it.

FAUST

Think. Only think. One step and you're free.

GRETCHEN

If only we were past the hill. Mother's sitting there on a rock, wagging her head. It gives me the shivers. She doesn't nod, she doesn't wave. Her head's heavy. She's slept so long she'll never wake. She slept so we could have fun. Those were happy days.

FAUST

It's no use talking any more. I'll have to carry you off.

GRETCHEN

Leave me alone. I won't have violence. Loose your grasp. I always did what you wanted before.

FAUST

Day's coming. Darling. Darling.

GRETCHEN

Yes, day. The last day. It was to have been my wedding day. Don't tell anyone you were at Gretchen's. Oh my flowers. Well, it's done. We'll meet again, but not at the dance. The crowd's gathering. You can't hear them. The streets, the square won't hold them. The bell calls. The staff is broken. They're seizing hold of me, binding me, dragging me to the block. Everyone feels at his neck the axe blade that's meant for me. The world is silent as the grave.

FAUST

I wish I'd never been born.

MEPHISTOPHELES *appearing outside*

Up. Or you're lost. This delay, this chattering's useless. My horses are shivering. It'll soon be light.

GRETCHEN

Who is that rising out of the ground? Send him away. What's he doing here in this holy place? He's after me.

FAUST

I want you to live.

GRETCHEN

God's judgment. I submit to it.

MEPHISTOPHELES *to Faust*

Come, or I'll leave the two of you.

GRETCHEN

Heavenly father, I'm yours. Save me. Angelic hosts, surround me, preserve me. Faust, I shudder at you.

MEPHISTOPHELES

She is doomed.

VOICE *from above*
She is saved.
MEPHISTOPHELES *to Faust*
Come here. *He disappears with Faust*
VOICE *dying away*
Faust, Faust.

PART TWO

ACT I

A PLEASANT LANDSCAPE.
Faust couched on flowery grass, tired, restless, trying to sleep

DAWN

Chorus of Spirits, pleasant little creatures, hovering in the air

ARIEL *singing, accompanied by Aeolian harps*
Now when the spring blossoms are floating down on the world and everywhere green crops catch the eye with their promise, we little elf-spirits eagerly give what help we can. We grieve for a man in misfortune, no matter who he is, a saint or a sinner.

You elves, circling above him, behave as good elves should. Ease the dire conflict in the man's heart, pluck out the bitter, burning arrows of reproach, purge his soul of horror. Take charge of the four watches of the night and make them cheerful. Lay his head down on a cool pillow, then bathe him in Lethe's dew. As he sleeps and gathers strength to meet the new day, his limbs will relax. Perform the fairest of elfin services. Return him to the sacred light.

CHORUS *singly, in pairs, or full chorus, in turn*
With gentler breezes fanning this woodland plot, twilight lets fall its veil of mist and its sweet scents, whispering peace, lulling the heart like a child's, closing the day's door for these weary eyes.

Night has fallen. The holy stars come one by one. Great lights and little lights, shining afar, glittering near, glittering in the lake, shining aloft in the clear night. The full moon, presiding in its splendour, sets its seal on rest, rest perfect and profound.

The hours are spent. Pain and joy have vanished. You will be strong and well again. Let yourself feel it coming. Trust the new daylight. See, the valleys are turning green, the little hills are swelling, showing their trees and shade, and in waves of swaying silver the season's crop advances.

To get your wish, your every wish, turn your eyes to the light. Your bonds are fragile. Sleep is a husk, throw it off. Lose no time, be bold, let others doubt and linger. A real man can achieve anything if he takes hold intelligently and doesn't delay.

A tremendous noise announces the approach of the sun

ARIEL
Listen. Listen to the tempest of the hours. The new day is being born, the spirit's ears can hear it. Rock-portals grind and rumble. Phoebus's wheels are rattling along. What noise comes with the coming of the light. A drumming, a trumpeting. Dazzling the eyes, and staggering the ears with more than they can hear. Slip away into the flower-cups, into the leaves, into the rocks, deeper, deeper, out of hearing, or you'll never hear again.

FAUST
Life's pulse in me is beating strong again, ready to hail and welcome this ethereal dawn. And you too, earth at my feet, have been constant through the night and are breathing now with new vigour, surrounding me with delights and rousing my ambition to strive and strive to reach the summit of existence. The world lies revealed in the half-light. The forest has come alive and rings with a thousand voices. Valleys up and down are streaked with mist, but the clear light of heaven reaches the depths. And twigs and branches there revive and spring out of the dimness they were sleeping in. Colour too upon colour comes out clear against the ground where leaf and flower are trembling with dew-drops. Whichever way I turn, I see a paradise.

Look up. The mighty mountain peaks are announcing the solemn hour. Already they're enjoying the eternal sunlight, which later creeps down to us. Meanwhile the upper meadows stand out clear and brilliant in their greenness. And now step by step it approaches. There. The sun has risen. But ah, it dazzles me, hurts me, and I have to turn aside.

This is what happens, when you hope and yearn for

something and work your way towards realizing it and believe
you are near. You find the great gates of fulfilment flung wide
open to receive you. But now, from the eternal sources
beyond, a flame bursts on you, an excess of flame, a conflagration. We are taken aback. We wanted to light life's torch,
and we find ourselves instead engulfed in a fiery ocean. Oh
what fire! Is it love? Is it hate? that wraps its flames about us,
pain alternating stupendously with joy, so that we are driven
back to earth again and try to hide ourselves in earth's most
youthful veils.

Very well, let me turn my face from the sun and have it at
my back. This waterfall, noising down the crags – the more
I look at it, the more I delight in seeing it plunge thousandfold
from level to level, throwing its spray high, so high, in the air,
scattering cool showers round about. And then, rising gloriously out of the commotion, comes the arch of the changing-
unchanging rainbow, now sharply drawn, now blurred and
lost. This is the mirror of our human endeavour. Ponder it
and you will see: The many-coloured life we know is life
reflected too.

IMPERIAL PALACE

*Throne Room. State Council awaiting the emperor. Trumpets. Courtiers
of every kind, richly dressed, step forward. The emperor ascends the
throne, the astrologer at his right hand*

EMPEROR
I greet you all, you faithful ones, assembled from near and far.
I have the philosopher at my side, but whatever has happened
to the fool?
NOBLEMAN
He collapsed on the stairway right behind you. They carried
him off in his fat. Dead or drunk, they don't know yet.
SECOND NOBLEMAN
But immediately, instantaneously, another offered himself.
Amusingly dressed, but weird-looking. The watch is holding

him at the door with crossed spears. There he is, the brazen fool.

MEPHISTOPHELES
Kneeling before the throne
What is accursed and always welcome? What is desired and then dismissed? What is forever being protected? What is first censured, then accused? Whom mustn't you summon? Whose name does everyone like to hear? Who is approaching your throne? Who has banished himself?

EMPEROR
Spare your words. This is no place for riddles. I leave it to these gentlemen. Here you, you answer. I'd be curious to hear what you'd say. I'm afraid my old fool has gone for good. Take his place and come beside me.

Mephistopheles mounts the steps and stands on the left

VOICES IN THE CROWD
A new fool – New trouble – Where does he come from? How did he get in? – The old fool collapsed – He's done – First it was a barrel – Now it's a shaving.

EMPEROR
And so, my faithful ones, welcome from near and far. You have come together at a favourable moment. Good fortune is promised us from above. But tell me why in these days when we were intending to forget our troubles, put on our masks for the carnival, and altogether have a good time, tell me why we should torment ourselves with a council meeting. However, you said it had to be, and we've called one, so let us proceed.

CHANCELLOR
Justice, the highest of the virtues, rests on the emperor's head like a halo. He alone can execute it. What all men love, demand, desire, and sorely need – it is for him to grant it to them, as his people. But what use are intelligence, kindness, readiness to head, heart, and hand when the body politic is in a raging fever and a single evil breeds a host of evils? If you cast your eye over the vast empire from this high chamber, it's

like a nightmare, where one rank disorder operates through another, lawlessness becomes law and has its way, and a whole world of wrong is the result.

One man helps himself to a herd of livestock, another to somebody's wife, and a third steals cup, cross, and candlestick from the altar and they boast about what they've done for years after and get away with it without so much as a scratch. The courthouse is thronged with plaintiffs and there sits the judge in all his upholstery; meanwhile the angry mob outside is swelling and seething in waves of revolt. It's easy to parade your crimes and your sins when you can count on accomplices who have a worse record than you. Where innocence is its own defence, you'll hear a verdict of guilty every time. And so, you see, the whole world is breaking up, destroying all decency and propriety. How in such case is the state of mind to develop that alone can give us direction? Things have gone so far that a worthy man has to compromise with the unworthy, with flatterers and corrupters. A judge who has lost his judge's power joins forces with the criminal. I've drawn a black picture. I only wish I could make it blacker.

A pause

Decisions will have to be made. When everyone suffers and everyone is harmful, the throne itself is threatened.

MINISTER OF WAR

What madness is abroad in these disordered days. There isn't anyone that isn't either killing or being killed. And the word of command falls on deaf ears. The townsman behind his town walls, the knight perched in his rockbound castle have put their heads together and decided to hold their resources and stick it out. Our mercenaries are getting impatient and shouting for their pay. They'd take off altogether if we didn't owe them money. Let them all want a thing and it's like putting your head in a wasp's nest to forbid it. They're supposed to guard the empire, and the empire's been pillaged and devastated from end to end, violently. We do nothing to stop it. Half the world's wrecked already. And our neighbouring kingdoms think it's no concern of theirs.

LORD TREASURER

You can't count on allies. The subsidies they promise us are like tapwater that doesn't run. Besides, in your vast empire, sir, who owns the property? Wherever you go, you find a newcomer settled in, and he wants his independence. All you can do is to look on. We've surrendered so many privileges, we haven't one left. And as for parties, as they're called, you can't trust them either nowadays. Whether they like us or don't like us, praise us or blame us, it makes no difference. Both the Guelphs and the Ghibellines have gone into hiding and are taking a rest. Who in these times wants to help his neighbour? Every man has to look after himself. There's no gold to be had, the gates are barred. Everyone is scratching and scraping and hoarding. And the treasury's empty.

COURT STEWARD

And what misfortunes beset me too. We try day by day to save and day by day we need more. And every day brings new troubles. The cooks have nothing to complain about. Boars, venison, hares, turkeys, chickens, geese, ducks – all these come in pretty regularly as payments in kind. But we're short of wine. We used to have barrel on barrel in the cellar, the best vineyards, the best years. But the endless boozing of these noble gentlemen has consumed our last drop. The city hall has had to tap its supplies. They come with bowls and basins, and next thing they're all under the table. Now I have to pay wages, foot bills, and take out loans that set me years back. We can't wait to fatten the pigs. Everything's on borrowed money, the beds we sleep in and the bread we eat.

EMPEROR *to Mephistopheles after some reflection*

Tell me, fool, haven't you any complaints?

MEPHISTOPHELES

Not me. When I see you and your retainers in all this splendour. How could confidence be lacking, when your majesty is obeyed unqestioningly; the army is ready to scatter its enemies; goodwill, shrewd practical goodwill, is at your service, and activity of every kind? Under these circumstances how could evil forces gather against you? When such stars as these are shining, how could there be darkness?

VOICES

He's a scamp – He knows the game – Bluffs his way in – For as long as it lasts – I can tell you now – I know what's behind it – What is it then? – Some new proposal.

MEPHISTOPHELES

Wherever you go in this world there's always a shortage of something. It might be this, it might be that. Here it's money we're short of. Now you can't just pick up money from the floor. But there's nothing sunk so deep we can't get hold of it, if we use our wits. There's gold, coined or uncoined, under old walls or in the belly of the hills. And if you ask me who is to unearth it: An intelligent man using the brains that nature gave him.

CHANCELLOR

Nature! Brains! You can't talk this way to Christians. We burn atheists for that, because such talk is most dangerous. Nature is sinful, brains are of the devil. Between them they breed doubt. A misshapen bastard. Don't talk that way to us. In our ancient domains two powers have arisen to support the throne, the clergy and the nobility. They beat off all attacks and they take church and state as their reward. If a rebellion breaks out in the confused mind of the mob, who's behind it? The heretics and witchmasters. They're the ruin of the country, and this fool's one of them. He's trying now with his smart talk to smuggle them into this high company. Don't trust them, they're treacherous.

MEPHISTOPHELES

Just like you learned gentlemen. If you can't touch a thing, it doesn't exist. If you can't grasp it, it's miles away. If you can't put it into figures, it's not true. If you can't weigh it, it has no weight. If you can't coin it, you say it's false.

EMPEROR

This won't solve our problems. What's the good of your lenten sermon? I'm sick of all this arguing. We're short of money, get us some.

MEPHISTOPHELES

I'll get you what you want and get you more. It's easy enough, but easy isn't easy. The stuff's there, but the trick is how to get it. Who knows? But just consider. In those terrible times when human floods swamped the land and the people how many a one in his fear and dread hid away what was dearest to him in some place or other. They did it in the days of the Romans, they did it yesterday, they're doing it now. It's all lying buried in the ground. The ground belongs to the emperor. Let him have it.

LORD TREASURER

For a fool he isn't doing badly. What he claims is the law.

LORD CHANCELLOR

There's something wrong about this. Satan's laying his golden snares.

COURT STEWARD

I don't mind being a bit in the wrong, if he gives the court something it likes.

MINISTER OF WAR

The fool is wise, he promises benefits to all. A military man doesn't ask where they come from.

MEPHISTOPHELES

And if you don't trust me, there's a man here, the astrologer, ask him. He knows his way about in the heavens, circle upon circle. Tell us how it looks there.

VOICES

A pair of rogues – They're in cahoots – A fool and a dreamer – So near the throne – An old, old song – We're tired of it – The fool prompts – The sage speaks.

ASTROLOGER *speaks*

Mephistopheles prompts

The sun is all gold. Mercury is running errands for pay. Venus is putting it over all of you, eyeing you sweetly, early and late. The moon is chaste and moody. Mars is either striking or threatening. Jupiter is the handsome one. Saturn is large, but looks small so far away. Not greatly valued as metal, but heavy. Yes, when sun and moon accord, gold with silver, then all is well in the world. Everything else can be had, palaces, gardens, women's breasts, red cheeks. We can't do it ourselves, but this learned man can procure them for you.

EMPEROR

Everything he says I hear double, but still it doesn't convince me.

VOICES

What does this mean? – A worn out joke – An old wives' tale – A phony science – I've often heard it – Been fooled before – Just let him come – He's a swindler.

MEPHISTOPHELES

There they are, standing around and gaping. They don't believe in the great find. One of them's babbling about mandrakes. Another's seen the black dog. It won't help them, this talking clever, this charge of witchcraft, when suddenly the soles of their feet begin to prickle and they find themselves stumbling about.

You can all feel the secret working of nature. The living trace finds its way up from the lowest regions. When you're plagued in every limb and the place seems creepy, don't lose a minute, start digging for all you're worth. That's the lucky spot.

VOICES

My foot's like lead – Can it be the gout? – My big toe's tickling – I've cramps in my arm – My back aches all the way down – To go by these indications – This must be a wonderful place for treasure.

EMPEROR

Be quick then. You can't slip away now. Give us the proof of your vapourings, and show us these noble regions at once. I'll put sword and sceptre aside, dig with my own imperial hands, and finish the job, if you are to be trusted. If not, I'll consign you to hell.

MEPHISTOPHELES

Well, I could find the way there all right. – But I can't overstate it about the wealth that's lying around everywhere, waiting to be picked up. The farmer, ploughing his furrow, turns up a gold jug. He tries to scratch saltpetre from some clay pot and with trembling joy finds his poor hand filled with gold. What vaults there are to open, what clefts, what passages the treasure-hunter must enter to join the company of the underworld. In old cellars he'll find rows and rows of plate, ruby goblets, and, if he's so minded, there's casks of old wine to hand. But – would you believe it – the wooden staves have rotted away and the inner crust holds. Wines seek the night not less than gold and jewels. A wise man searches undismayed. It's easy to work in daylight, but mysteries belong to the dark.

EMPEROR

I leave mysteries to you. What good is gloom? If a thing's worth having, it should be brought into the daylight. You can't tell a thief in the dark, when all the cows are black and all the cats are grey. These gold-filled pots of yours, plough them up, let us see them.

MEPHISTOPHELES

Take pick and spade and dig yourself. This peasant labour will make you strong. And a herd of golden calves will rise up from the soil. Then delight is yours. You can adorn yourself and your lady in shining jewels, enhancing beauty and majesty both.

EMPEROR

Only be quick. How long must I wait?

ASTROLOGER *as above*

Sire, curb your eagerness. Let us wait till the carnival is over. When people are distracted, they're useless. We must first compose ourselves penitently. Earn the lesser things by way of the higher. Only a good man can do good. If you want joy, calm yourself. If you want wine, press ripe grapes. If you want miracles, strengthen your faith.

EMPEROR

Very well, let us pass the time in merriment. And then Ash Wednesday, when it comes, will be welcome. Meanwhile we must celebrate the carnival as riotously as we can.

Trumpets. Exeunt

MEPHISTOPHELES
The fools don't realize the connection between reward and merit. Even if they had the philosopher's stone, it would be no use to them.

A SPACIOUS HALL WITH SIDEROOMS DECORATED FOR THE CARNIVAL

HERALD
Remember, this is not Germany with its dances of death, devils, and fools. A bright and happy festival is awaiting you. Our sovereign on his visits to Rome has made the journey serve our pleasure as well as his advantage, and he's brought back a merry world with him from beyond the Alps. First at the pope's feet he was given the authority to rule and next he picked up the fool's cap along with the crown. Now we are all as if born again. Any man who knows the world will cheerfully pull the cap over his head and ears, making himself look like a crazy fool, and then use his discretion inside it. I can see them assembling, sorting themselves out and pairing off, one group forcing itself on another, in and out, quite unperturbed. After all, the world with its countless absurdities remains the great big fool that it always was.

FLOWER GIRLS *singing, accompanied by mandolins*
We girls have come from Florence, following the German court. We've dressed up for tonight in the hope of pleasing you.

You see our dusky locks all decked with flowers. Threads and wisps of silk are what we used.

We thought you would approve. Our artificial flowers stay in bloom the whole year round.

We trimmed all sorts of coloured cuttings. You may disapprove of this and that, but the whole is attractive.

We're nice to look at, we flower girls, and stylish too. Artifice sits well on a woman.

HERALD

Show us the lovely baskets that you have on your heads or bulging in your arms. Everyone is free to choose what he likes. Quick, let us turn the walks and alcoves into a garden. These girls are worth looking at, not less than what they offer.

FLOWER GIRLS

Buy away, but on this happy occasion there must be no haggling. Let a few neat words tell each of you what he's getting.

OLIVE BRANCH WITH FRUITS

I don't feel envious of flowers. I avoid all conflict, it's against my nature. I'm the marrow of the earth, a sure token of peace everywhere. Today I hope to be so lucky as to adorn a fair and worthy head.

WREATH OF GOLDEN-RIPE CORN

Ceres' gifts, man's need of needs, are beautiful too. They'll look well on you.

A MIXED WREATH

A surprise. All these flowers that look like mallows, growing out of moss. It isn't quite natural, but fashion can do it.

A MIXED NOSEGAY

Even Theophrastus wouldn't venture to name me. Yet I hope to find favour with some at least, one perhaps who would bind me in her hair or wear me on her heart.

ROSEBUDS *hidden, challenging*

Let these caprices pass as things of fashion, oddly put together, foreign to nature, green stems, golden bells, peeping out of rich hair, but we ...

ROSEBUDS *showing themselves*

We hide away. Lucky those who can find us. When summer comes and roses break into bud, who would not care to see? This promise, this fulfilment in Flora's realm captures the eye, the mind, and the heart.

The flower girls display their wares along the arboured walks

GARDENERS *singing, accompanied by lutes*

See how the flowers decorate and adorn. The fruits we offer are honest. You must taste them to enjoy them.

Cherries, peaches, plums, all sun-browned. Buy them. Tongue and palate will tell you more than the eye.

Come, feast on our ripe fruits. You can write verse about roses, but apples you have to eat.

Allow us to join your young folk and dispose our ripe offerings among theirs.

In these festoons, in bays and bowers, you'll find everything at once – bud, leaf, flower, and fruit.

Singing in alternate choirs, with guitars and lutes, they continue to bargain and decorate

Mother and Daughter

MOTHER
Daughter, when you were a baby, I put a little hood on you. You were so sweet, so delicate. I saw you at once betrothed, married, and well off. I saw you as a woman.

But now so many years have passed and nothing has happened. The wooers, so gay, so many, quickly flitted by, though you danced with one and nudged another with your elbow.

Whatever parties we planned, they led to nothing. Forfeits and such-like games never worked. The silly men are all on the loose today. Sweetheart, try uncrossing your legs. You might catch one that way.

Other young girls join the party, and there is intimate chatter among them. Fishermen and bird-catchers with nets, fishing-rods, limed sticks, etc. enter and mix with the girls. Attempts on both sides to capture or evade lead to pleasant dialogue

WOODCUTTERS *entering, boisterous and clumsy*
Make way, make way. Give us lots of room. We cut down trees. They fall with a crash. And when we carry them, we're rough and ready. Don't take this wrong. Just say to yourselves: If there were no crude ones like us in the country, how could refined ones be there at all, no matter how clever? Remember this: We have to sweat, to keep you from freezing.

CLOWNS *awkward, almost silly*

Fools you are. Born with your backs bent. We, the clever ones, never carried a load. The things we wear, caps, rags, and jackets, sit light on us. We're always easy, always idle, lightly shod, ready to run through the crowded market, or stay and gape or, hearing a catcall, glide through the throng, slippery as eels, or dance or shout, all of us together. You're free to blame us, you're free to praise us, we don't mind at all.

PARASITES *fawning*

You woodcutters and your fellows, the charcoal-burners, are the men for us. For all our bowing and all our scraping, our yes-yes nodding, and flowery phrases, and blowing cold or blowing hot, to suit the moment, what good would it be? Even fire from heaven would be no use, unless there were logs, and loads of charcoal, to fill the hearth and make a fire, for food to fry on and cook and sizzle. The real gourmand that licks his plate will smell the roast and smell the fish and outdo himself at his patron's table.

DRUNKARD *blind drunk*

Today must go without a hitch. I never felt so grand. Let's have some fun and sing some songs, if I sing the songs myself. So here goes again. We'll drink together. You behind there, come here, come here. When our glasses clink, then all is well.

My wife got mad, she yelled at me, when she saw me strutting in these gay colours. She called me a dummy, a tailor's dummy. But me, I drink with the other dummies. When our glasses clink, then we're all right.

Don't tell me I'm lost. I'm where I want to be. I'm where I'm happy. The landlord chalks it up. If not, his wife'll do it. At a pinch the barmaid will. I just drink, drink with everyone, clink, clink. There you are, that's the way.

I don't mind how I have my fun. I don't mind where I have it. It's all the same to me. Leave me lying where I lie. I'm sick of standing.

CHORUS

Drink, brothers, drink. Clink, brothers, clink. Stay glued to your seats. He's under the table. He's finished.

The herald introduces various poets, poets of nature, court poets, love poets, sweet or passionate. In the pressure of competition none lets the other speak. But one of them gets a word in

SATIRICAL POET

Do you know what would really delight me as a poet? To write and recite what no one wants to hear.

The night and graveyard poets beg to be excused, because they are having a most interesting conversation with a newly arrived vampire, which might lead to a new form of poetry. The herald has no choice but to agree and he fills the gap by calling on Greek mythology which, while in modern costume, remains true to character and retains its appeal

The Graces

AGLAIA

We bring grace into life. Put grace into your giving.

HEGEMONE

Put grace into your getting. It is lovely to get your wish.

EUPHROSYNE

And in the quietness of your days make saying thank you gracious too.

The Fates

ATROPOS

Today they've given me the spinning to do, me the old one. There's much to think about, much to ponder, when you have life's delicate thread before you.

To make the thread supple and soft I had to sort out the finest flax. My skilful fingers will make it smooth and even.

If you're tempted to go too far in your sport and your dancing, remember the thread's limits. Take care, the thread can break.

CLOTHO

Please note that the shears have lately been entrusted to me. They weren't pleased with the way the old one handled them.

Interminably dragging out lives most futile; cutting off

others full of hope and promise, and consigning them to the grave.

But I too, young as I am, have made many mistakes, so tonight, to keep myself in check, I've put the shears away.

I'm happy to do this and I look on with a friendly eye. Make the most of the opportunity and have your fun.

LACHESIS

They left the winding to me, the only sensible one. My distaff never stops, never hurries.

Threads come, I wind the threads and guide each one, never letting any slip, always keeping them in place.

If ever I forgot myself, I should fear for the world. Hours add up, years add up, and the weaver takes the skein.

HERALD

You won't recognize the next batch, no matter how learned you are. To look at them, you'd never dream what mischief they've done. You'd say they were welcome guests.

You'd never believe that these were the Furies. They're so pretty, such good figures, friendly, and not old at all. But you just have dealings with them and you'll soon see what serpents they are, for all their harmless look.

They're malicious, sure enough. But today, when every fool boasts of his failings, they don't want to pose as angels either. They confess they're the plague of town and country.

The Furies

ALECTO

He's warned you, but you'll trust us just the same, we're so young, so pretty, and such flatterers. If one of you has a sweetheart, we'll scratch him behind the ears.

And tell him face to face that she's going after one or two others, and she's stupid anyway and doesn't stand straight and has a limp and, if he's thinking of marrying her, she's a poor choice.

And we'll get after the girl too and say to her that not long ago he was running her down to that other girl. Some of this'll stick, even if they make it up again.

MEGAERA

That's nothing. Let them once get joined together and I take over. I know how to sour their happiness for them and never miss. There's always a weak point or a weak moment, if you watch out.

And no one ever attains his heart's desire and clasps it to him, but he tires of it after a while and foolishly starts longing for something else. He runs away from the sun and tries to warm an iceberg.

I know how to manage all this, and at the right time I introduce my faithful Asmodeus and let him scatter the seeds of calamity. In this way, couple by couple, I bring mankind to ruin.

TISIPHONE

No whispering and slandering for me. I mix poison for all traitors, I sharpen daggers. If you go after other girls you'll come to grief sooner or later, I promise you.

Your sweetest ecstasy will turn to gall. You won't get a hearing. You'll pay the price in full for what you did.

Don't babble to me about forgiveness. I make my charge to the rocky cliff and the echo says revenge. The unfaithful lover must perish.

HERALD

Would you please draw to one side. Something is coming now that is different. Look, there's a whole mountain approaching, its loins proudly draped with gay carpets. It has a tusked head, and a squirming trunk – very mysterious, but I'll give you the key. Seated on its neck and driving neatly with a slender staff you see a dainty slip of a woman. And standing behind her another most imposing, most exalted, with a dazzling light playing round her. On either side two noblewomen chained, the one fearing for her freedom, the other happily assured of it. Let each of the two tell us who she is.

FEAR

Smoky torches, lamps, and lights half-illuminate the festive throng. And here I am with no escape, chained, among these phantoms.

Off with you, you and your grinning and giggling. Who would trust you? All my enemies must be after me tonight.

There, a friend's become a foe. I can see through his disguise. Another here would murder me. I've found him out and now he's slinking off.

What would I give to run away no matter where in the world. But everywhere destruction threatens me. I'm caught among these misty horrors.

HOPE

Greetings, dear sisters. You may have revelled in your disguises for these two days, but I know for certain that you will leave them off tomorrow. And if you weren't altogether at ease in this torchlight, we shall soon walk happily again at our own sweet will, alone or not alone, in the lovely open country, and rest when we choose, or busy ourselves, in a life free from care, never going short of anything or failing in our endeavour, knowing too that whatever house we enter we shall be welcome. Surely, the best of life is waiting for us somewhere.

PRUDENCE

I'm protecting this company from two of mankind's greatest enemies, Fear and Hope, whom you see here in chains. Make way and let them pass. You're safe.

I'm in charge of this living colossus with its towered back. It makes its way unperturbed, step by step, on steep paths.

But up there on top you can see a goddess with quivering wings outstretched, ready to move, for gain, in any direction.

The glitter, the splendour, that encircles her can be seen shining on every side from far away. Her name is Victoria and she is the activity goddess.

ZOILO-THERSITES

Ha, ha. I've come just at the right moment, to tell you all you're no good. But Victoria up there's my real target. With those white wings of hers she must think she's an eagle, thinks everything is hers wherever she goes. But when anything worthy or praiseworthy happens, that's when I get angry. Make low high and high low, crooked straight and straight crooked. That's the only way for me. It's the way I want things everywhere.

HERALD

Then let my good staff work its trick on you, you dirty dog. Now you may twist and turn. See how the creature, doubly dwarfed, rolls up into a horrid lump. But what a thing. The horrid lump has turned into an egg. And see, the egg has swelled up and burst and given birth to twins, an adder and a bat. The one's crawling off in the dust and the other's flying to the ceiling. They mean to meet outside. I wouldn't care to join them.

VOICES

Quick, they're dancing over there – Oh, I wish I was out of here – Can't you feel these weird creatures all round us? – I can feel something in my hair – I've got it in the foot – None of us are hurt – But we all got a fright – The fun's over – That's what they wanted, the vermin.

HERALD

Being your appointed herald on such occasions, I'm keeping watch carefully at the door and I never leave it lest anything should intrude that would mar our merriment. But I'm sorry to say that some ghostly creatures are coming in through the window and I can do nothing with ghosts or with magic. I was dubious about that dwarf. But now there's something more powerful thrusting in from the back. I would explain these intruders if I could, but you can't explain what you don't understand. You must help me. Do you see it coming? It's a gorgeous carriage and four, passing through the crowd, but not dividing it. There's no disturbance anywhere. I can see coloured lights away off and stars floating round. It's like a magic lantern. Now the thing comes snorting up. Give it room. It's frightening.

BOY CHARIOTEER

Whoa. Horses, check your flight. Answer the rein as usual. Slow down at my command. Put on speed when I incite you. But let us do honour to these halls. See the revellers gathering round us, more and more of them, in admiration. But come, herald, do your job before we leave. Name us, describe us. It shouldn't be hard. You can see we're allegorical.

HERALD

I can't name you. I might be able to describe you.

BOY CHARIOTEER

Come on then.

HERALD

Well, to begin with, I must admit you're young and handsome. You're only a boy half-grown, but one that the other sex will want to see when you're bigger. A budding ladies' man; in fact, a born seducer.

BOY CHARIOTEER

Good. Go on. Solve the riddle.

HERALD

Dark, flashing eyes, thick dark hair, a jewelled headband, a pretty robe hanging down to your feet with purple hem and tinsel. Nearly like a girl, but, for better or for worse, one that the girls would already appreciate. They'd teach you your letters.

BOY CHARIOTEER

But what do you say to this one, throned so splendidly in my chariot?

HERALD

He looks like a king most rich and kind. Happy the man who enjoys his favour. He has nothing to seek for himself. He's quick to see where there's a need. The sheer joy of giving means more to him than possessions or good fortune.

BOY CHARIOTEER

You can't stop there. You must describe him.

HERALD

Dignity can't be described. But I see a healthy face, round as the full moon, a generous mouth, fresh cheeks, a handsome turban, flowing robes that sit easy. What can I say of his noble bearing? As a ruler of men I believe I know him.

BOY CHARIOTEER

He is Plutus, whom they call the god of wealth, travelling in

splendour on his way to the Emperor who urgently wishes
to see him.

HERALD

But now you. Tell me who you are.

BOY CHARIOTEER

I am poetry, the spendthrift, the poet who fulfils himself by
throwing away what is intimately his. I too am wealthy, as
infinitely wealthy as Plutus, whose festivities I enrich and
enliven, supplying the things he lacks.

HERALD

Your boasting sits well on you. But show us your tricks.

BOY CHARIOTEER

See here. I just snap my fingers and at once there's a shine and
a glitter all round the chariot. There comes a string of pearls.
He goes on snapping his fingers here, there, and everywhere
Here's golden clasps for neck or ear, brooches, crowns,
jewelled rings. Sometimes I scatter flames too and watch
them set things on fire.

HERALD

See the dear folk grabbing and snatching, crowding him,
almost jolting him. They're snatching away all over the hall.
And he's snapping out his treasures as if in a dream. But now
comes a new trick. For all their efforts they get little in return.
The gifts fly away. The pearl necklace has turned into so many
beetles in a man's hand. He's thrown them away, poor fellow,
and now they're buzzing round his head. Others, expecting
something solid, are finding they've only captured silly butterflies. What a rogue he is, promising so much and only
giving what glitters but isn't gold.

BOY CHARIOTEER

I see you know how to interpret costumes, but it isn't your
official business as herald to go to the heart of the matter.
This calls for a sharper vision. But I won't quarrel with you.
I'll turn to you, my master, and ask you (*turning to Plutus*). Did
you not entrust your whirlwind chariot to me? Haven't
I driven it well and taken you where you said? Didn't I with
bold flight win the palm of victory for you? When I fought for

you, did I ever fail? If laurels deck your brow, wasn't it me that thoughtfully twined them?

PLUTUS

If I have to give you a testimonial, I am happy to say you are spirit of my spirit. You always act in my sense. You're richer than I am. I value the green branch I reward you with above all the crowns I wear. I can declare frankly to everyone: My beloved son, in thee I am well pleased.

BOY CHARIOTEER *to the crowd*

I've scattered my finest gifts among you. There's a head here and there with a little fire burning in it that I started. It jumps from one to another, it stays with this one and leaves that. Sometimes, but not often, it flares up in a quick blaze, but in many cases it goes out altogether, unnoticed.

WOMEN CHATTERING

That's a charlatan for sure, up on top of the chariot. And crouching behind him the clown, all starved and shrunken. We've never seen him like that before. You might pinch him now, he'd never feel it.

THE SCRAGGY ONE

Keep away from me, you disgusting women. I know I'm not wanted. In the days when women ran the house, my name was Lady Avarice, and all went well. A lot came in and not much went out. I kept a jealous eye on chests and cupboards. It gave me a bad name. But now that women have stopped being economical and are bad with money and care more for desires than dollars, the menfolk have a great deal to put up with, debts confronting them, whichever way they turn. What cash the women can scrape together they spend on their finery or on their lovers. They eat better and drink more in their wretched company. All this makes me greedy for gold. I'm male, not female any more. Call me the miser.

LEADER OF THE WOMEN

Let the old dragon stick to his dragons. The whole thing's a hoax. He's come to stir up the men and they're trouble enough already.

CROWD OF WOMEN

A man of straw. Give him a punch. He's thin as a lath, can't frighten us. Paper dragons too. Let's have a go at them.

HERALD

See my staff. Calm yourselves. But I'm not needed. These fierce monsters have got excited. They've quickly cleared a space. They're spreading their double pairs of wings and spitting fire angrily from their scaly jaws. The crowd has scattered. The place is clear.

Plutus dismounts

HERALD

He's stepping off. How like a king. He raises his hand. The dragons at once lift down the treasure chest with the miser sitting on it and set it in front of him. It's a miracle.

PLUTUS *to the charioteer*

Now I release you from your irksome duties. Off you go lightly to where you belong. This is no place for you, beset as we are all round by things garish, confused, ugly, turbulent. You need to be where you can look with a clear eye into the clear, be master of yourself and confident, in a world that cares for the good and the beautiful. Seek an abode in solitude and create your world there.

BOY CHARIOTEER

I shall value myself as your envoy and love you as my nearest of kin. Wherever you go, there is plenty, there is abundance. Where I go, everyone feels himself gloriously the gainer. Men often hesitate in this contrary life: Should they go with you or go with me? If they go with you, they can idle their time away. With me there's always something to be done. I never act in secret. I only have to breathe and I give myself away. Good-bye then. I know you wish me well. But say the word, whisper it, and I'll be back.

PLUTUS

The time has come to release our treasures. I touch the locks with the herald's staff and the chest springs open. And see, red gold rising molten in these bronze vessels, threatening to engulf the treasures – crowns, chains, rings.

SHOUTS FROM THE CROWD

Oh, look, just look, it's welling up in the chest. It's over-flowing. – Gold vessels melting away, turning into rolls of coins. – Ducats brand-new bobbing up and down, what a temptation. – See my heart's desire bouncing on the floor. – Don't miss the opportunity, bend your backs and get rich. – Let's grab the whole chest in a flash.

HERALD

You fools, what are you up to? It's only a joke. You'll forget it all by tonight. Do you think the money's real? Counters would be too good for you. Stupidly taking a pretty effect for the truth. The truth would be wasted on you, you snatch-ers at illusion and obscurity. – Plutus, hero of the masquer-ade, scatter these people, clear the floor.

PLUTUS

Your staff is handy. Lend me it for a moment. I'll dip it in the brew. Now, you masqueraders, look out. See the flashes, the sparks flying. The staff's catching fire already. If you come near, you'll get singed and no mistake. Now I'll go the round.

SHOUTS FROM THE CROWD

Oh, we're done for. – Escape, if you can. – Get back, you behind there, it's spraying right into my face. – My, that staff's heavy as well as hot. – It's the end for all of us. – Get back, you mummers, back, you idiots. – If I'd wings, I'd fly.

PLUTUS

The crowd has scattered. – They're all pushed back and no one hurt. But I'll draw an invisible line for safety.

HERALD

Splendid work. I'm grateful to you.

PLUTUS

Be patient, good friend. There's plenty of disorder yet to come.

AVARICE

Now, we can take a friendly look at these people, all ranged round in a circle. And why shouldn't we? The women are always to the fore, when there's anything to nibble or to stare at. I'm not so shrivelled up yet that I don't find a pretty woman pretty. And today, seeing that it costs nothing, I'll try my luck among them. But it isn't easy to make yourself heard in all this crowd, so I'll see what I can get across to them with a little pantomime. There are things you can't say with your hands and feet. I'll have to fall back on one of my pranks. I'll treat this lump of gold as wet clay. After all, you can do anything with gold.

HERALD

What's the skinny fool doing? You wouldn't think he had a sense of humour. He's working the gold in his hands like dough, squeezing it, rounding it, but it's still shapeless. And now he's turned to the women and they're all shrieking and shrinking back in disgust. He's a mischief. I'm afraid he's being indecent and liking it. I can't let this pass. Give me my staff and I'll drive him out.

PLUTUS

He has no notion what is about to descend on us. Leave him to his fooling. He'll soon be pushed aside by forces stronger than himself.

RIOTOUS CROWD *singing*

Here we come, from hill and dale, the riotous army of Pan's worshippers, forcing our way into the empty circle. We know something. You don't know what.

PLUTUS

But I know you and your great god Pan. You've taken a bold step. And I know what you know. It is my duty to let you in and I hope your bold adventure will not turn out badly. There's no telling what can happen. They aren't prepared. They don't know what they're in for.

RIOTERS´ SONG

Look out, you tinselled, titivated people, we're coming on the run, coming in great jumps. We're a rough crowd.

FAUNS

We fauns are dancing a merry dance, with oakleaves in our curly hair and pointed ears peeping out, a broad face and a blunt little nose. This doesn't hurt with women. When a faun offers his paw, no woman, even the fairest, would care to say no.

SATYR

The satyr comes hopping with his goat's foot and his scraggy, sinewy legs, the kind of legs he needs. He loves to survey the world like the chamois from a mountain-top and, thus refreshed, mock the human kin, young and old, down in the stuffy valleys, so smug and contented, when all the time he's the only one who really lives, in the freedom of the heights.

GNOMES

We little gnomes don't like to stay in pairs, we flit about all over the place in mossy jackets with our little lamps, thronging like ants, always busy, each by himself.

We belong to the good-fellow family, well-known as rock-surgeons. We cup the veins of the high mountains and pour the metals down with the miners' cheery hail. We mean it well. We are the friends of man. But the gold we turn out only furthers theft and lechery. The iron is wanted by those who in their pride invented wholesale murder. If you ignore these three commandments, you won't respect the others. This isn't our fault. We are patient. You must be patient too.

GIANTS

We are the so-called wild men, well-known in the Harz mountains, giants in our naked strength, with pine trunks in our right hands and thick, rough girdles of leaves and branches slung round our loins. The pope himself has no such body-guard.

CHORUS OF NYMPHS *encircling Pan*

Here he comes, the great god Pan, the god of the universe. You happy ones, enclose him in a lively dance. He's grave, but kindly too, he wants us to be merry. He's stayed awake all the time under his blue roof, but the brooks murmur to him and the breezes soothe him and when he sleeps at noon not a leaf stirs, the balmy scent of plants fills the air, all is silent and still. The nymph daren't stay awake, she falls asleep where she stands. But if suddenly his mighty voice is heard like a peal of thunder or the sea roaring, then everyone is in a panic, armies scatter in the field, heroes tremble in their midst. So, do homage where it is due, hail him who has brought us here.

DEPUTATION OF GNOMES *addressing Pan*

When the shining precious metal streaks through chasms so hidden that only the divining-rod can trace its windings, there in the gloom we delve our dwelling, all for you to apportion the treasures we bring in the clear daylight. But now we have discovered close by a source of treasure exceeding our expectation, and easy to reach. From here on you, sir, please take charge. We shall all get the benefit of any treasure that is in your hands.

PLUTUS *to the herald*

We must now most solemnly compose ourselves and let what happens happen. You've always shown yourself a man of courage. Now something most horrible is about to come. People will deny it, stubbornly. But you must set it down faithfully in your minute-book.

HERALD *taking hold of the staff which Plutus keeps in his hand*

The dwarfs are conducting great Pan to the fire. It boils up from deep down and then falls back, leaving the dark mouth gaping. Then it foams up hot again. Pan is standing undisturbed, enjoying the strangeness, while pearly drops are scattered right and left. Why is he so unsuspecting? He bends over to look down inside and his beard has fallen in. Whose can that smooth chin be? He's put his hand over it and we can't see. And now comes a catastrophe. His beard has caught fire and flown back on, setting his wreath and his head and his breast alight. Our pleasure has turned into pain. The crowd has run up to put the blaze out, but none of them escape it themselves, and the more they beat about them the more the flames grow. A whole group of masqueraders are involved in them and consumed.

But what are they announcing now, passing the word from mouth to mouth, ear to ear. O unhappy night, ever unhappy, what suffering you have brought on us. Tomorrow the unwelcome news will be heard on every hand: It is the emperor who was burned. Oh that this should be the truth.

The emperor is burned and those with him. Cursed be the company that led him astray, dressing up in resinous twigs and coming here yelling their heads off and bringing everyone to grief. O young people, when will you learn to keep your merry-making within bounds? O majesty, when will you learn to combine power with reason?

The whole wood has gone up in flames, with sharp tongues that are licking the timbered roof and threatening to burn the palace down. What grief. It is too much. Who can save us? All this imperial splendour reduced to ashes in a single night.

PLUTUS

We have had shocks enough. Now relief is needed. You sacred staff, strike the floor till it shakes and rings again. And you, circumambient air, fill with freshness. Come, you mists and pregnant lines of cloud, spread out and cover this raging fire. Rustle, roll, sprinkle, moisten, quench. Turn the silly flames into summer lightning. When spirits threaten us, magic must step in.

PARK

A sunny morning. The Emperor, Courtiers. Faust and Mephistopheles in conventional dress, not conspicuous, both kneeling

FAUST

Has your majesty forgiven us for putting on that magic fire-show?

EMPEROR *beckoning to them to stand up*

I could do with many such entertainments. I saw myself suddenly transported into a glowing region, almost as if I was Pluto. It was a rocky valley, dark and smouldering, with deep pits in it and here and there flames whirling out of them, arching and closing overhead in a flickering vault that came and went incessantly. Through twisted columns of fire I saw far off ranks of people approaching in a wide sweep and doing homage to me as usual. I recognized a courtier or two among them. I felt as if I was lord of countless salamanders.

MEPHISTOPHELES

And so you are, sir, because each of the elements recognizes your majesty as supreme. You've tested the fiery element and found it obedient. Now throw yourself into the sea where it is roughest and you'll at once find you're treading a pearly floor, beautifully enclosed in shifting light-green waves edged with purple, a lovely place to dwell in, and yourself at the centre of it. When you move, step by step the palaces move with you. The walls themselves are alive with things thronging, darting swiftly this way and that. Sea monsters crowd towards the strange, soft light, they come with a rush, but they can't enter where you are. You'll see richly coloured dragons with gold scales, sharks with open jaws; you can look right down their throats. You may be delighted with all your court round you, but you never saw such a throng as this. And you won't lack what is sweetest. Nereids will come, all curious to see this new dwelling-place in the watery world, the young ones like fishes timid and lustful, those behind them more experienced. Thetis will hear the news and offer her hand and her lips to a second Peleus. And now for your seat on Olympus . . .

EMPEROR

You can keep Olympus and the airy spaces. That's a throne we shall mount only too soon.

MEPHISTOPHELES

And, as your majesty knows, you already own the earth.

EMPEROR

What a stroke of luck it was that brought you here straight out of the Arabian Nights. If you are as inexhaustible as Scheherazade you may be assured of my highest favour. Stand ready to oblige when the daily world disgusts me, as it often does.

MARSHAL *in a hurry*

Your highness, I never dreamed in all my life that I should have such a piece of good fortune to announce. I'm delighted and doubly so in your presence. We've paid off all our debts and got out of the usurer's clutches. Those hellish worries are over. I couldn't be happier if I was in heaven.

MINISTER OF WAR *also in a hurry*

We've issued an instalment of pay and the whole army's loyal again. The men are in good spirits. The pubs are full and the girls are busy.

EMPEROR

To think how you ran to tell me. And you're breathing freely again and your faces are all smoothed out and smiling.

LORD TREASURER *entering*

Enquire of these two. They did the job.

FAUST

It is for the chancellor to explain.

CHANCELLOR *approaching slowly*

Feeling great happiness in my old age on account of all this. – Hear me then and look at this momentous piece of paper, which has turned all our woe to weal. *He reads* 'To whom it may concern, this paper here is worth a thousand crowns, its collateral lying safely in the wealth of buried treasure within our borders. Steps have been taken for this treasure to be raised without delay so as to redeem the pledge.'

EMPEROR

This, I suspect, is criminal, a gigantic fraud. Who forged the emperor's signature? Has this offence gone unpunished?

LORD TREASURER

Don't you remember? You signed yourself only last night. The chancellor came up and said to you in our presence: Allow yourself the high pleasure on this festive occasion of ensuring your people's welfare with a few strokes of the pen. You signed, and our conjurors, the printers, quickly ran off a thousand copies. We stamped them at once to let everyone share the benefit without delay. Tens, thirties, fifties, and hundreds are all ready. You can't imagine how happy the people are. Look at your city. It was rotting and half dead, and now it's alive again with pleasure-seekers. Your name has always spelt happiness, but never before has it looked so benign. We don't need the rest of the alphabet now. Your signature's enough to make them all as happy as lords.

EMPEROR

Do you mean to say they take it for good money? The army's satisfied with it, the court? It looks queer to me, but I must let it pass.

COURT STEWARD

It was impossible to hold them back. They scattered in the twinkling of an eye. The money-changers have their doors wide open, cashing all the bills in gold and silver – at a discount, of course. And from there, people go to the butchers and bakers or to the pubs. Half the world has no thought of anything but eating, the other half's strutting about in new clothes. The drapers are cutting out, the tailors are busy sewing. In the wine-cellars they're toasting the emperor in torrents. The frying-pans are sizzling, the plates are clattering.

MEPHISTOPHELES

If you stroll along the terraces by yourself, you'll soon spot a pretty lady, gorgeously decked out, smirking at you and peeping with one eye from behind her peacock fan to see if you'll produce one of these bills, and quicker than by any smart talk or rhetoric it will procure you the best that love can offer. You don't have to bother with a purse or a satchel. You can carry a bill easily in your bosom alongside of a love-letter. The priest can carry it piously in his prayer-book, and the soldier can take the weight off his legs and move more freely. Your majesty must pardon me if I seem to be making light of this great achievement by going into these details.

FAUST

The unlimited treasures lying buried in your territory are not being used. A wealth exceeding the farthest range of thought. Let your imagination strain to the limit, it will still fall short. But deep-seeing minds have infinite confidence in the infinite.

MEPHISTOPHELES

Compared with gold and pearls a paper like this is so convenient, and you know what you've got, no bargaining over it, no exchange needed, nothing to stop you taking your fill of love and wine. If you want cash for it, you can have it.

Otherwise you do a little digging. You can auction your valuables, your cups or chains, and the bills you get can be redeemed at once, thus putting all the doubters and mockers to shame. You become quite used to this and don't want it otherwise. There'll always be treasure, gold, and paper enough anywhere in the empire.

EMPEROR

The emperor has to thank you both for this great benefit. I propose to make the reward as nearly as possible equal to the service. I put our underground territory in your charge and I appoint you custodians of its treasures. You're well informed about them. All digging must be under your control. Join your forces, you masters of our treasures, and enjoy the dignity of your office, in which the underworld and the upper world will work harmoniously together.

LORD TREASURER

I welcome the magician as my colleague. There will be no friction between us whatsoever. *off, with Faust*

EMPEROR

I am now going to give each one of you a present, but you must tell me what you will do with it.

PAGE *receiving*

I shall be merry, light-hearted, content.

ANOTHER *likewise*

I shall buy rings and chains for my sweetheart.

CHAMBERLAIN

From now on I shall treat myself to choicer wines.

ANOTHER

The dice are already itching in my pocket.

BANNERET *deliberately*

I shall clear the encumbrances on my property.

ANOTHER

It's valuable; I'll put it away with the rest of my valuables.

EMPEROR

I hoped to hear talk of new activities, but anyone who knows you can soon see through you. With all your wealth, you'll just remain what you were.

FOOL *entering*
You're giving presents. Give me one.
EMPEROR
You'll only spend it on drink.
FOOL
These magic pieces of paper. I can't figure it out.
EMPEROR
I can believe that. You make such poor use of them.
FOOL
There's more of them falling on the floor. What shall I do?
EMPEROR
Pick them up. They're meant for you. *off*
FOOL
Five thousand crowns. Can these be mine?
MEPHISTOPHELES
You guzzler, have you come back to life again?
FOOL
I've done it many times, but this is the best yet.
MEPHISTOPHELES
You're so delighted you're all in a sweat.
FOOL
Look here, is this worth real money?
MEPHISTOPHELES
Yes, you can eat and drink your fill with it.
FOOL
Can I buy land with it, a house and livestock?
MEPHISTOPHELES
Of course. Bid and you'll get it.
FOOL
And a castle, a forest to hunt in, a trout stream?
MEPHISTOPHELES
I must say I'd like to see you as lord of the manor.
FOOL
I'll be a landowner this very night. *off*
MEPHISTOPHELES *alone*
Who'll say now that our fool's a fool?

A DARK GALLERY
Faust and Mephistopheles

MEPHISTOPHELES

What are you dragging me off into these dark passage-ways for? Isn't there fun enough in there, all the opportunities you want for your tricks and pranks, among that mixed crowd of courtiers?

FAUST

Don't say that to me. You've talked that way too many times before. This running about now is just to avoid speaking with me. But I'm in a fix and don't know what to do. Both the marshal and the steward are after me. The emperor wants to see Helen and Paris right away. It has to be a clear picture of them. The ideal man and the ideal woman. So get to work at once. I've given my word and I must keep it.

MEPHISTOPHELES

Silly of you to promise so casually.

FAUST

You didn't consider where your arts would lead us. We've made him wealthy. Now he expects us to amuse him.

MEPHISTOPHELES

It can't be done in a minute. Don't fool yourself. This is unfamiliar ground, most unfamiliar. It's a stiffer climb altogether. You'll end by getting wickedly involved again. You think it's as easy to call up Helen as to call up those ghosts of paper money. Now if it was witches you wanted, dwarf deformities, or spooky spectres, I could supply them. But the devil's girls, though not to be despised, can't pose as classical heroines.

FAUST

There you are again, grinding out the same old tune. With you I never know where I am. You make difficulties at every turn, new demands all the time. You only need to mutter a few

words and it's done. I know that. They'd be here before you
could say Jack Robinson.

MEPHISTOPHELES

Those pagans are no concern of mine. They have a hell of
their own. But there is a means.

FAUST

Out with it then and don't prevaricate.

MEPHISTOPHELES

I dislike letting out one of the higher secrets. There are
goddesses throned in solitude, outside of place, outside of
time. It makes me uneasy even to talk about them. They are
the Mothers.

FAUST *startled*

The Mothers.

MEPHISTOPHELES

Does it give you the shivers?

FAUST

The Mothers. The Mothers. It sounds so queer.

MEPHISTOPHELES

Queer it is. Goddesses unknown to mortal men, hardly to be
named by them. You'll need to dig deep to reach them. It's
your fault if we have to do it.

FAUST

Show me the way.

MEPHISTOPHELES

There is no way. You'll enter the untrodden, the untreadable,
the unpermitted, the impermissible. Are you ready? There'll
be no locks or bolts. You'll be pushed about from one
emptiness to another. Have you any notion what emptiness
is? Barrenness?

FAUST

I should have thought you'd spare me this jargon. It all
smacks of the witch's kitchen to me and the long, long ago
when I had to mix with others, learn meaningless things and
teach them too. If I talked good sense as I saw it, I was
contradicted more than ever. There were disagreeable incidents. I had to run off into the wilds and be alone. And finally,

lacking all other company, I was driven to joining up with the devil.

MEPHISTOPHELES

And even if you'd swum across the ocean and seen its infinitude and feared you were done for, you'd at least have seen something. You'd have seen waves following waves and when the sea was quiet you'd have seen dolphins gliding through the green water. You'd have seen sun, moon, and stars, and clouds passing. But here you'll see nothing in all the empty distances. You won't hear the tread of your own feet. You'll find nowhere to rest your head.

FAUST

You talk like the biggest mystagogue that ever fooled his simple pupils. Only you're in reverse. You're sending me into nothingness, where I'm supposed to improve myself in my art. You're making me pull the chestnuts out of the fire for you like the cat in the fable. Well, here goes. We'll see what's at the bottom of it all. In this nothing of yours I hope to find the everything.

MEPHISTOPHELES

I see you understand the devil and I'll give you a word of approval before you go. Here, take this key.

FAUST

That little thing.

MEPHISTOPHELES

Take hold of it and don't underrate it.

FAUST

It's growing in my hand. It's shining, flashing.

MEPHISTOPHELES

Now you're beginning to see what it's worth. This key will nose out the way for you. Follow its lead. It'll conduct you to the Mothers.

FAUST *shuddering*

The Mothers. It hits me every time. What is this word that I can't bear to hear?

MEPHISTOPHELES

Why let a new word disturb you? Are you as narrow-minded

as that? Do you only want to hear what you've heard before? Don't let anything bother you, whatever comes. You're well used now to the strangest happenings.

FAUST

To slacken and come to a stop will never suit me. The thrill of awe, of wonderment, is the best we have. The world may make us pay heavily for our feelings, but when the tremendous thing comes we know how to respond.

MEPHISTOPHELES

Down you go, then. I might equally say: Up you go. It's all the same. Escape the created world and enter the world of forms. Take your pleasure in what has long ceased to exist. You'll see it all as drifting clouds. Swing your key and keep it from you.

FAUST *enthusiastically*

Good. I feel a new access of strength as soon as I grip it firmly. My chest expands. On to the great task.

MEPHISTOPHELES

When you come to a glowing tripod you'll know you're as far down as you can go. By the light it throws you'll see the Mothers. Some sitting, some standing or walking about. It just depends. Formation, transformation, the eternal mind eternally communing with itself, surrounded by the forms of all creation. They won't see you. They only see ghosts. You'll be in great danger and you'll need a stout heart. Go straight up to the tripod and touch it with your key.

Faust strikes a commanding attitude with the key

MEPHISTOPHELES *looking at him*

That's the way. It'll connect and follow you as your servant. Now you'll calmly ascend. Your good fortune will hoist you. And before they notice, you'll be here with it. And once you have it here you can call up hero and heroine from the shades. You'll be the first to pull it off. It'll be done and you'll have done it. The clouds of incense will turn into gods as part of the magic process and so remain.

FAUST

And what do I do now?

MEPHISTOPHELES

Let your nature will your descent. Stamp your foot and you'll go down. Stamp again and you'll come up.

Faust stamps his foot and disappears

MEPHISTOPHELES

I hope that key works. I'll be curious to know if he ever gets back.

HALLS BRIGHTLY LIT
Emperor and princes. Courtiers moving about

COURT STEWARD *to Mephistopheles*

You haven't yet put on the ghost scene you promised. Get to work. The emperor's impatient.

MARSHAL

His majesty has just been enquiring. Make haste. You mustn't let him down.

MEPHISTOPHELES

It's this very business that's taken my partner away. He knows what to do and he's working quietly. It requires a very special effort. When you're evoking that precious thing called the beautiful, you need the highest of the arts, you need the philosopher's magic.

MARSHAL

It's all the same to me what arts you need. The emperor wants results.

BLONDE

A word with you, sir. You can see that I have a clear complexion. But in summer, I'm sorry to say, I get freckles by the hundred all over my white skin. Give me a remedy.

MEPHISTOPHELES

Too bad. To think of a handsome girl like you all spotted in maytime like a leopard. Take some frogs' eggs and mix them with toads' tongues. Distil carefully in the full moonlight and apply to your skin when the moon is waning.

When spring comes, you'll find your freckles have disappeared.

BRUNETTE

People are beginning to crowd round you. Please tell me what to do. I have a game leg. It makes me limp when I walk or try to dance or even make a bow.

MEPHISTOPHELES

May I put my foot on yours?

BRUNETTE

Well, that's what lovers do.

MEPHISTOPHELES

The touch of my foot means more than that. Like to like is the thing for all ailments. Foot cures foot. It's the same with the other parts. Come here and watch out. Don't respond.

BRUNETTE *shrieking*

Ouch. It burns. That was a hard tread you gave me. It felt like a horse's hoof.

MEPHISTOPHELES

But it's cured you. You can dance all you want now. Touch feet under the table with your sweetheart.

LADY *pressing forward*

Let me through. I'm in great trouble. It makes me boil with rage. I was his dream until yesterday. And now he's dropped me and gone after her.

MEPHISTOPHELES

Difficult. But listen to me. Take this piece of charcoal, sidle up to him, and mark him with it as best you can on his sleeve, shoulder, and cloak. He'll feel a pang of remorse. But you must eat the charcoal at once and touch neither wine nor water. He'll be sighing at your door before the day's over.

LADY *pressing forward*

I trust it's not poisonous.

MEPHISTOPHELES *enraged*

Madam, do you wish to insult me? This is no ordinary piece of charcoal. It comes from far away, from a funeral pyre that we used to work harder.

PAGE

I'm in love, but they don't believe I'm old enough.

MEPHISTOPHELES *aside*

I don't know which way to turn. (*to the page*) Don't set your heart on the youngest of them. The older ones will appreciate you better.

Others press him

More coming. What a tussle I'm having. I'll have to start telling the truth. That's the poorest way out. But what can you do in a crisis like this. O you Mothers, do let go of Faust.

Looking around

The lights in the hall are burning low. The courtiers are all moving off, passing quietly down long corridors, distant galleries, and assembling in the old baronial hall, big but hardly big enough to hold them. Tapestries hanging on the walls. Armour in every nook and corner. No magic words needed here, I should think. The ghosts will come of themselves.

BARONIAL HALL

Dimly illuminated. Emperor and Courtiers already assembled

HERALD

It is my longstanding duty to announce the play, but there are supernatural forces at work which make it difficult. It's impossible to find any rational explanation of the confusion that prevails. The seating arrangements have been completed, the emperor facing the wall where he can enjoy the tapestries recording the great battles. Here they are then, emperor and courtiers, all ranged round with the crowded benches behind them where lovers can sit close together in the uncanny twilight. And so, since all are now seated, we are ready, the spirits may come.

Trumpets

ASTROLOGER

Let the play begin. The emperor so commands. Open up, you

walls. It's plain sailing now, with magic at our disposal. See, the carpets are disappearing as if curled up in fire. The wall divides and reverses. To all appearance we now have a deep stage before us, and there's a mysterious light coming from somewhere. I'll go up on the proscenium.

MEPHISTOPHELES *sticking his head out of the prompter's box*
I hope you'll all approve of me in my present capacity. Prompting is the devil's rhetoric.
To the astrologer You know the rhythm of the stars. You'll understand my whisperings perfectly.

ASTROLOGER
Here, revealed by the power of magic, is an ancient temple, massive as you see. The row of pillars makes us think of the giant Atlas who once held up the sky. They're certainly equal to the weight of stone they have to bear. Any two of them would suffice for a big building.

ARCHITECT
You call that classical? I don't like it. I call it crass and over-loaded. If a thing's crude, they say it's noble. Clumsy, they say it's great. What I love is slender columns, soaring up into the infinite, pointed arches that uplift the spirit. There's the style that truly edifies.

ASTROLOGER
Accept this heaven-sent occasion with reverence due. Let magic words suspend your rational thinking and, instead, let fantasy, the rich and free, come from far away and rule us. Look now on the scene you so boldly demanded. It's quite impossible and for that very reason worthy of belief.

Faust mounts the proscenium from the other side

ASTROLOGER
See the wonder-worker in priestly robes with a wreath on his head, fulfilling the task he so confidently undertook. A tripod has risen with him from below and he is about to consummate his achievement. If I'm not mistaken, I can smell the incense from the bowl. Things can't go wrong now.

FAUST *impressively*

In your name, O Mothers, enthroned in the illimitable, always alone, yet not unsociable. The forms of life revolve around you, mobile, but lifeless. All that once was in all its splendour is in motion there, seeking to be made eternal. You supreme powers part them in two, assigning some to the tent of day, to be drawn into life's sweet course, others to the vault of night where the magician seeks them out. Whatever wonders are desired, he has in full measure the power to reveal them.

ASTROLOGER

No sooner does the red-hot key touch the bowl than a mist gradually fills the scene, rolling in clouds that spread or shrink or cross or part or join. And now comes a masterpiece of magic. The clouds, as they drift, make music, airy notes like nothing that ever was. Everything, even the columns, the triglyph, is turning into melody. I verily believe the whole temple is singing. Now the mist is dropping and through the thin veil a handsome youth comes forward with measured step. And here I must pause. I don't need to name him. Who could fail to see that this is Paris.

Paris steps forward

LADY

Oh what a picture of youth in its bloom and its strength.

SECOND LADY

Fresh and juicy as a peach.

THIRD LADY

And those lips, so delicately drawn, and yet so sweet and full.

FOURTH LADY

A sip from that cup is what you'd like.

FIFTH LADY

He's very pretty, but not exactly refined.

SIXTH LADY

I do wish he was a little less awkward.

KNIGHT

He still bears the marks of a shepherd boy, I feel. Nothing princely about him, no courtly manners.

SECOND KNIGHT

No doubt he's good-looking when he's half naked. But how would he be in a coat of mail?

LADY

He's seating himself in an attractively feminine way.

KNIGHT

I daresay you wouldn't mind sitting on his lap.

ANOTHER LADY

He's putting his arm behind his head so gracefully.

COURT STEWARD

How vulgar. It shouldn't be allowed.

LADY

You gentlemen find fault with everything.

COURT STEWARD

Stretching out like that in front of the emperor.

LADY

He's only acting. He thinks he's alone.

COURT STEWARD

In this place the play itself ought to be polite.

LADY

The charmer has dropped asleep.

COURT STEWARD

And he's immediately beginning to snore. It's so natural. It's perfect.

YOUNG LADY *delighted*

What is that scent that mingles with the incense and so gladdens my heart?

OLDER LADY

You're right. There's a breath of something that moves me deeply. It comes from him.

STILL OLDER LADY

It's ambrosia, the scent of youth flowering, filling the air about us.

Helen appears

MEPHISTOPHELES

So there she is. She wouldn't bother me. Pretty, no doubt, but not my sort.

ASTROLOGER

To be honest, I must confess I'm helpless here. When beauty comes, tongues of fire are not enough. The praises of beauty have been sung and sung again from the beginning. Those who behold it are swept beyond themselves. Those who ever enjoyed it were rewarded beyond their deserts.

FAUST

Do I see with my eyes? Or is it deep in my inner mind that the source of beauty is thus poured out before me? My fearful journey has brought a marvellous reward. How futile the world was, before it was opened to me. What is it now after my term of priesthood? Desirable, deep-founded, permanent as never before. May the breath of life leave me if ever I go back on you. The fair form that once delighted me, swept me away, in the magic mirror was mere froth beside this. To you I owe the springs of every action and the quintessence of passion. I devote myself to you in affection, love, worship, yes in madness.

MEPHISTOPHELES *from the prompter's box*

Pull yourself together and remember your part.

OLD LADY

Tall, well-built, but the head rather too small.

YOUNG LADY

Look at her feet. Could they be clumsier?

DIPLOMATIST

I've seen great ladies just like her. It seems to me she's beautiful from top to toe.

COURTIER

She's slowly, cunningly approaching the sleeper.

LADY

How ugly she looks beside his youthful purity.

POET
The light of her beauty is shining on him.

LADY
Just like the painting of Endymion and Luna.

POET
You're right. The goddess seems to be coming down from above. Now she's bending over him to drink his breath. A kiss. The lucky man. It's the limit.

DUENNA
In front of everybody. It's too much.

FAUST
What a terrific favour to this lad.

MEPHISTOPHELES
Be quiet. Let the ghost do what it wants.

COURTIER
She's tripping away stealthily. He's waking up.

LADY
She's looking back. I thought she would.

COURTIER
He's astonished. He thinks it's a miracle.

LADY
What she sees is no miracle to her.

COURTIER
She's turned round and coming back, with great decorum.

LADY
I can see she's taking him in hand. In this situation all men are simpletons. He probably thinks he's the first.

KNIGHT
I won't have a word said against her. She's majestic and most refined.

LADY
The jade. I call that vulgar.

PAGE
I wish I was where he is.

COURTIER
What man wouldn't get entangled with her?

LADY

She's a jewel that's passed through many hands. The gilt's a bit worn.

ANOTHER LADY

She's been no good since she was ten years old.

KNIGHT

Everyone on occasion takes the best. This lovely leftover would do for me.

PEDANT

I can see her all right, but I must confess I doubt if she's the right one. Face to face with her you lose your judgement. For myself I stick to the books and the books say she delighted all the old men of Troy. It seems to me that this holds good now. I'm not young, but I like the look of her.

ASTROLOGER

He's a boy no longer. He's heroic and daring. He's seized hold of her. She's practically defenceless. He's hoisted her up on his mighty arm. Is he going to run off with her?

FAUST

The reckless fool. To be so bold. Can't you hear? Stop. This is too much.

MEPHISTOPHELES

Aren't you the man that's putting it on, this crazy ghost-play?

ASTROLOGER

One word more. To go by what we've seen, I'd call it *The Rape of Helen*.

FAUST

Rape indeed. Do I count for nothing here? Have I not this key in my hand? The key that led me through horrid seas of solitude to a firm landing where I could set down my two feet. These are realities. Standing here, my spirit can hold its own with spirits and master the two realms. She was so far off and now she could hardly be nearer. If I rescue her, she'll be doubly mine. I'll take the risk. O Mothers, grant me this. When you've once set eyes on her, you can't give her up.

ASTROLOGER

Faust, Faust, what are you up to? He's grabbed hold of her.

She's beginning to blur. He's turned his key towards the boy and touched him with it. Oh dreadful, dreadful.

Explosion. Faust collapses. The spirits disappear in smoke

MEPHISTOPHELES *throwing Faust over his shoulder*
Now we've got it. Taking up with fools, even the devil's the loser in the long run.

Darkness, confusion

ACT II

A HIGH, NARROW, VAULTED GOTHIC CHAMBER
Formerly Faust's, unchanged

MEPHISTOPHELES *coming from behind a curtain. He raises the curtain and looks back at Faust lying prostrate on an old-fashioned bed*
Lie there, you luckless man, caught in bonds of love not easy to break. When Helen's knocked you out, you don't get your wits back in a hurry. *looking about him*
If I look round me here, I find everything just as it was, nothing moved, nothing damaged. The stained glass seems a bit darker. More cobwebs. The ink's dried, the paper's yellowed. But everything's in its place. There's even the pen here that Faust signed himself to the devil with. And deep down in the reed a drop of the blood that I coaxed out of him on that occasion. A curiosity, unique, one that any collector might be proud of. And look, there's the old gown on the old hook. Reminds me of the crazy notions I once put into that boy's head. He's probably drawing on them still, now he's a little older. I really feel tempted, with this warm gown on, to play the professor again, very pompous, very sure of himself. Learned men know how to carry it off, but the devil's right out of practice. *He shakes the furry gown and crickets, moths, and beetles fly out of it*

CHORUS OF INSECTS

Welcome, boss, welcome, dad. Here we are again, flying and buzzing. We know you all right – you quietly planted us one at a time, and now we come in hundreds and thousands. The devil may like to hide his thoughts, but we little things soon slip out of the fur.

MEPHISTOPHELES

How this young brood delights me. You just sow the seed and some day you'll reap the harvest. I'll give the old sheep-skin another shake. Here's one or two more fluttering out. Off you go now, my dears, and hide in holes and corners. Plenty of them over there among those old boxes, faded parchments, dusty flowerpots, or even in those skulls' eye-sockets. In a place as messy and mouldy as this there'll always be some queer notions and things stirring. *He slips into the gown*

Come, drape me again. I'm the head of the firm once more. But what's the use calling myself that? Who recognizes me as such? *He pulls the bell which rings with a piercing, shrieking tone, making the halls rock and the doors fly open*

FAMULUS *tottering down the long, dark corridor*

Oh what a frightening, shattering noise. The stairs and walls and windows all quaking. And lightning flashing through the stained glass. The floor's giving way under me and there's mortar and rubble coming down from overhead. By some magic or other the door's burst its bolts. And standing there – how dreadful – a giant wearing Faust's old gown, staring at me and waving his hand. My knees are nearly giving way under me. Shall I run or shall I stay? Oh what will happen next?

MEPHISTOPHELES *with a gesture*

Come here, my friend. Your name is Nicodemus.

FAMULUS

Yes, your honour, it is – Oremus.

MEPHISTOPHELES

You can leave that out.

FAMULUS

I'm so glad you know me.

MEPHISTOPHELES

I know you well enough. Older now and still at college, an old-timer in fact. Even a man of learning goes on studying because he can't stop. Building his little house of cards. But the best among you never finishes. Your professor, though, is smart, that Dr Wagner whom we all know and respect. The leading figure in the world of knowledge, the one man that holds it together, and adds a little every day to the world's wisdom. He's a shining light in the lecture room. People crowd after him to hear him and learn from him. He handles the keys like St Peter, both to the higher world and the lower. He's so brilliant no one can stand up against him. Even Faust's name is overshadowed. Wagner gets the credit for everything.

FAMULUS

Forgive me, venerable sir, if I make bold to contradict you. It isn't the way you say. He's modest through and through and he can't reconcile himself to Faust's unaccountable disappearance. He prays that the great man may return happily and put his mind at rest. Faust's room here is waiting for him; it's never been touched since he went away. I hardly dared to come in. What can be happening now, at this great moment? The very walls seem terror-struck. The door-posts rocked. The bolts sprang. Otherwise you'd never have got in yourself.

MEPHISTOPHELES

Where's Wagner gone? Take me to him or bring him here.

FAMULUS

I don't see how I can. He's strictly forbidden it. He's been working for months in the utmost seclusion on his great project. He's the gentlest of his kind and he looks like a charcoal-burner, with his face black all over, his eyes red with puffing the flames. He hangs with bated breath on every moment. The mere sound of the tongs is music in his ears.

MEPHISTOPHELES

Is he going to refuse me, when I'm the very man to speed the good work?

Famulus goes out. Mephistopheles solemnly seats himself

No sooner have I got myself in place than I see something moving. Yes, it's a visitor I recognize. But this time he's one of the *avant-garde*. He's sure to go the limit.

BACCALAUREUS *striding down the corridor*

> The place is wide open today. It makes you wonder whether this fusty death-in-life mightn't come to an end and life be liveable here at last.
>
> The walls are collapsing. If I don't get out quick, I'll be buried underneath them. I'm not a coward by any means, but this is as far as I'm prepared to go.
>
> But what a thing. Isn't this the spot where years ago I came as a freshman, quaking in my shoes, trusting those old greybeards and feeding on their prattle.
>
> From those ancient books of theirs they dished out the lies they had ready. Had them ready but didn't believe them, and made life miserable for them and me. But what's this? Someone's sitting back there in the study, half in the dark. And how surprising. When I get nearer, it's him, still sitting there in that fur-lined gown, just as I left him. I thought he was clever then, when I hadn't got his number. It won't work today. So here goes.

Well, old chap, I see your head is bald and bowed, but if Lethe's waters haven't wetted it yet, you may recognize me, your former pupil. I've outgrown the academic drill now and can claim your approval. You look as if you hadn't changed a bit, but me, I've changed a lot.

MEPHISTOPHELES

I'm glad my bell brought you along. I never thought badly of you. The grub, the chrysalis always gives a hint of the bright butterfly that is to come. I remember your childish pleasure in curly hair and a lace collar. I'm sure you never wore a pigtail. Today you have your hair cut short. You look quite sturdy, quite resolute. All very well. But you mustn't be absolute.

BACCALAUREUS

Old man, here we are in the old place. But consider how times have changed and stop this talking two ways at once. We aren't as stupid as we used to be. You made fun of me without much effort when I was young and innocent, but that's all over now.

MEPHISTOPHELES

If you tell young people the honest truth, which they never like to hear, and then years after they arrive at it by their own bitter experience, they flatter themselves it came from them and they haven't a good word for their teachers.

BACCALAUREUS

He's a sly one. Did you ever hear before of a teacher who told you the straight truth face to face? They all know how to ring the changes, soft pedal or loud, grave or gay, according to need.

MEPHISTOPHELES

There's a time for learning, but, as I see, you're ready to start teaching. You've no doubt collected a lot of experience over the months and years.

BACCALAUREUS

Experience – empty stuff. Not comparable with the mind of man. Come now, confess, nothing we've ever known was worth knowing.

MEPHISTOPHELES *after a pause*

I've often wondered. I was a fool. I feel now how superficial, how silly I am.

BACCALAUREUS

Pleased to hear you say so. You're talking sense. The first old buffer to do it that I've met.

MEPHISTOPHELES

I was searching for hidden gold and came back with dust and ashes.

BACCALAUREUS

Tell me, is that bald pate, that skull, of yours any better than those hollow ones?

MEPHISTOPHELES *cheerfully*

You've no idea, my friend, how rude you are.

BACCALAUREUS

In German, if you're polite, you're not being honest.

MEPHISTOPHELES *who has been approaching the front in his wheelchair, addresses the audience*
Up here I can hardly breathe or see. Have you any room for me down there?

BACCALAUREUS
I find it presumptuous, when the game is up, for you to go on pretending to be something when you're nothing at all. Life is in the blood, and where is the blood so active as in a young man, where it's fresh and vigorous and creative too? Never inert, never wasted, rejecting the weak, favouring the strong. And while we've been conquering half the world, what have you done? Nodded, meditated, dreamed, pondered, plan upon plan. There's no doubt about it, old age is an ague, a cold fever, all whims and worries. A man over thirty's as good as finished. Best thing would be to bump you off.

MEPHISTOPHELES
From the devil at this point no comment.

BACCALAUREUS
The devil only exists with my approval.

MEPHISTOPHELES *aside*
The devil will get you yet, you'll see before long.

BACCALAUREUS
This is the glorious mission of the young. There was no world at all till I created it, fetched the sun up out of the sea and set the moon on its changing course. For me, in all my paths, the earth grew green and blossomed and was beautiful. A sign from me on that first night of all and the stars came out in their splendour. Who was it but me that rescued your minds from the clutches of philistinism? For my own part I'm happy and free to follow the promptings of my spirit and my inner light. And so, in raptest joy of self, I speed along my way, the dark behind me and all bright and clear ahead. *off*

MEPHISTOPHELES
On you go in your glory. This lad is priceless. How it would hurt his feelings to know there's nothing wise and nothing foolish that hasn't been thought of long, long ago. But he won't do any harm. A few years from now and he'll be

different. The new wine may play its pranks, but it mellows with time. *To the younger members of the audience who have refrained from applauding*

You don't approve of what I say. You're young and I forgive you. Remember, the devil is old. When you're old, you'll understand him better.

LABORATORY
Medieval; clumsy, sprawling apparatus, for fantastic ends

WAGNER *at the furnace*

That dreadful bell's ringing, making these sooty walls shake and tremble. It can't be long now before this extreme tension is relieved, and the result known. The dark is lessening, in the innermost bottle there's a glow like live coal, almost like a lovely carbuncle, sending its rays out into the gloom. And now there comes a clear white light. Oh, I hope it won't go wrong this time. But there, what's that rattling the door?

MEPHISTOPHELES *entering*

Greetings, a friend.

WAGNER *nervously*

Greetings to you, at this great moment. (*quietly*) But don't say a word, don't breathe. A grand piece of work is being completed.

MEPHISTOPHELES *more quietly*

Tell me.

WAGNER *still more quietly*

We're making a man.

MEPHISTOPHELES

A man. Did you lock a pair of lovers up the chimney?

WAGNER

God forbid. That old way of doing it is quite out of fashion now. We call it nonsensical. The tender point of life beginning, the sweet energy forcing its way out from within, taking and giving, imposing its pattern, appropriating what is near, then what is less near – all this is discredited. Animals may still take their pleasure in it, but man with his great gifts must have a higher origin, a purer one, henceforth. (*turning to the furnace*) See the light there. Now we can really hope that after duly mixing these hundreds of substances – it's all a matter of mixing – to make the human substance, and then sealing it up and thoroughly redistilling it, the work'll prove to be a quiet success in the end. (*turning again to the furnace*) It's coming now. The mass is clearing. I feel surer and surer. What we used to acclaim as nature's mystery we now boldly try to perform with our intelligence. Where nature used to grow things, we crystallize them out.

MEPHISTOPHELES

A man learns a lot if he lives long enough. Nothing new can happen anywhere for him. I've run into this crystallized sort of people before, on my travels.

WAGNER *who has kept his eye on the bottle*

It's rising, flashing, mounting. In a jiffy it'll be done. A great project seems crazy at the beginning, but the day will come when we'll laugh at our luck. Sooner or later a thinking man will be able to make a thinking brain. (*looking delightedly at the bottle*) The glass is ringing with amorous force. It fogs and then clears. It must be coming. I can see a neat little mannikin gesturing. What do you want? What more would you have? The secret's out now. Just listen to the sound. It's turning into a voice, it's speaking.

HOMUNCULUS *addressing Wagner from the bottle*

Well, father, how are you? That was no joke. Come, give me a hug, but gently, gently, or you'll break the glass. This is the way of things. The whole world's hardly big enough for natural life. But artificial life has to be contained. (*to Mephistopheles*) You here, brother, you rogue. Thank you for coming, and at the right moment too. Very fortunate. While there's life in me, I must be up and doing and I want to get to work right away. You're just the man to help me.

WAGNER

But one word more. I've always been embarrassed. People old and young come at me with problems. For instance, no

one can understand how body and soul go so well together,
cling as if they would never go apart, and yet are forever
quarrelling. Then ...

MEPHISTOPHELES

Stop. I'd rather enquire why man and wife don't hit it off
better. My friend, you'll never get to the bottom of it. But
there's a job of work here, the little fellow wants it.

HOMUNCULUS

Direct me.

MEPHISTOPHELES *pointing to a side-door*

Show your talents here.

WAGNER *still staring into the bottle*

You surely are a darling boy.

The side-door opens, showing Faust stretched out on the bed

HOMUNCULUS *astonished*

Important, this. (*The bottle slips out of Wagner's hands, hovers over
Faust, and shines a light on him*) A beautiful setting. A clear pool
shut in among trees. Women undressing. Delightful women.
It's getting better all the time. But one there is outshines the
rest in splendour, a woman sprung from a line of heroes, if
not from the gods. She dips her foot in the transparent flood,
cools her lovely body's flame in the yielding, glittering water.
But what a din of swiftly flapping wings. A plunging and
splashing that shatters the smooth mirror. The girls run off in
fright, but she, the queen, calmly looks on and, with a
woman's pride and pleasure, watches the prince of swans
nestle at her knees and, gently insistent, stay. He seems to like
it there. But suddenly a mist rises and quite blots out this most
charming of scenes.

MEPHISTOPHELES

The things you have to tell. You're a little fellow, but my, what
an imagination you have. I can't see anything.

HOMUNCULUS

I don't wonder. You that came from the north and grew up in
the dark ages, in all that jumble of popery and chivalry. How
could you expect to see with a clear eye? You're only at home

in the gloom. (*looking round him*) Look at this stonework, brown with age, mouldy, horrid. And pointed arches, twirligigs, so confining. If he wakes up on us, there'll be more trouble. He'll drop dead on the spot. Woodland springs, swans, naked beauties. That was his wishful dream. How could he get used to this? I, the most adaptable of men, can hardly bear it. Away with him.

MEPHISTOPHELES

I'd like to know what you propose.

HOMUNCULUS

Send the soldier into battle, take the girl to the dance, and all will be well. But it suddenly comes into my mind that the Classical Walpurgis Night is on. He'll be in his element there. We couldn't do better than take him to it.

MEPHISTOPHELES

I never heard of anything like that.

HOMUNCULUS

How should you? Romantic ghosts is all you know about. Ghosts, to be genuine, have to be classical too.

MEPHISTOPHELES

Well, which way do we go? Classical colleagues, I hate the thought.

HOMUNCULUS

Your stamping-ground, Satan, is north-west, but we fly south-east, to a great plain with the river Peneios ambling through it, fringed with trees and bushes, widening into loops and bays. The plain stretches back to rugged hills and on the slope lies Pharsalus, the old town and the new.

MEPHISTOPHELES

Oh, take it away, forget those wars of tyranny and slavery. They bore me. No sooner is the fighting done than they start all over again. And neither side notices that it's just Asmodeus who's at the back of it all, teasing them. They're supposed to be fighting for freedom, but, when you come to look at it, it's slaves against slaves.

HOMUNCULUS

Don't bother about the contrariness of mankind. Everyone

has to stick up for himself from the time he's a boy. In the end it makes a man of him. But our problem is with Faust and how to get him well again. If you have anything to propose, let's try it. If not, leave it to me.

MEPHISTOPHELES
We might try some of the Brocken's tricks. But the heathen gates are bolted against me. Those Greeks were never much good, dazzling you with their free play of the senses, enticing you into happy sinfulness. Our sins, you'll find, are always gloomy. So what now?

HOMUNCULUS
You're not backward as a rule. And if I drop a word about the witches in Thessaly, I presume it registers with you.

MEPHISTOPHELES
Witches in Thessaly. Those are people I've been enquiring about for a long time. I don't know that I care about night after night with them. But I'll try anything once.

HOMUNCULUS
Bring the mantle and put it round him. It'll carry you both as before, and I'll go in front and shine my light.

WAGNER *anxiously*
And what about me?

HOMUNCULUS
Well, you'll have to stay at home and do important work. Unroll your old parchments, collect the elements according to rule and mix them carefully. Consider the what and, still more, consider the how. Meanwhile I'll see a piece of the world and possibly discover the dot on the 'i'. Then my great purpose will be served. The reward is worth the effort. Wealth, honour, fame, health, and long life. And knowledge and virtue as well – who knows? Goodbye.

WAGNER *distressed*
Goodbye. This makes me very sad. I'm afraid I'll never see you again.

MEPHISTOPHELES
Quick now. Off to the Peneios. Our cousin is not to be despised.

To the audience After all, we're bound to be dependent on our own creatures.

CLASSICAL WALPURGIS NIGHT
Battlefield of Pharsalia. Darkness

ERICHTHO

The festival of ghosts met here tonight has seen me many times, and now I come again, Erichtho, the dismal one. Dismal, but not as repulsive as those wretched poets make me out to be with their endless gibing. Praising or blaming, they never know when to stop...The valley in all its length is paled and whitened with army tents spread like a sea. An after-vision of that most harrowing, that cruellest of nights. How often it has repeated, how often will it repeat, year after year after year, for the rest of time. Neither one yields the empire to the other. Not willingly, least of all when the other, having taken it with force, rules it with force. Men who cannot master their inner selves are all too ready in their arrogance to dominate their neighbours. But here, on this spot, a great issue was fought out. It's the old story of strength pitted against greater strength, the many-flowered wreath of freedom torn to shreds and the stiff laurel twisted about the conqueror's brow. This is where Pompey dreamed his dream of early triumphs come again, while Caesar there tensely watched the tongue of the balance waver. The fight is on. We know, the world knows now, which was the winner.

Bonfires are blazing red. The soil exhales the shadow of blood once spilt. And, drawn by the rare beauty of this shining night, mythical figures of the Greek world are here in multitude. Fabulous forms of ancient days can be half seen flitting about the fires, or they sit beside them at their ease...The moon is up, not yet at the full, but radiant, shedding its friendly light on everything. The spectral tents have disappeared. The fires are burning blue.

But now, over my head, a meteor shining. How unexpected. And lighting up a ball of something. I catch the scent of human life and must not let it near me, being harmful to it. It would hurt my name and serve no purpose. Now the meteor's dropping. Discretion bids me keep away. *withdraws*

The Aeronauts aloft

HOMUNCULUS
I'll take another turn over these spooky bonfires. The whole valley bottom has the weirdest look.

MEPHISTOPHELES
I can make out some appalling ghosts here. It's like looking through the old window at the horrors of the north.

HOMUNCULUS
Look. There's a lanky one striding past.

MEPHISTOPHELES
It almost looks as if she's had a fright, saw us coming through the air.

HOMUNCULUS
Let her go. Set our gallant friend down and life will immediately come back to him. Here in the world of fable is where he's looking for it.

FAUST *touching the ground*
Where is she?

HOMUNCULUS
Can't quite say. But this is where you'll probably find out. You might, between now and daylight, quickly scout around among the bonfires. A man who's been to the Mothers needn't be afraid of anything.

MEPHISTOPHELES
I have my reasons for being here too. But what better could we do than let each of us go his own way among the fires and have his own fun? Then, when we have to join up again, the little chap can light his glass and make it buzz.

HOMUNCULUS
This is how I'll flash it and ring it. (*The glass lights up and buzzes strongly*) Now off we go in search of more surprises.

FAUST *alone*

Where is she? No need to ask now. If it isn't the soil she trod
and the seashore she knew, it's the air that spoke her speech.
Here, by a miracle, here I am, in Greece. I felt the ground
under me at once, warming me with new life after my sleep,
making me like some Antaeus of the spirit. And, finding all
manner of strange things assembled here in this labyrinth of
fire, I'll make a thorough search of it.

THE UPPER PENEIOS

MEPHISTOPHELES *nosing around*

When I start roaming around among these bonfires, I find
myself quite put off. Almost all of them stark naked, and only
one here and there with a shift on. The sphinxes utterly
indecent, and the griffins brazen too. And then all the rest,
winged and hairy, catching your eye from in front or from
behind. I don't mean we aren't thoroughly indecent too, but
this antique stuff's too vivid altogether. It needs modernizing
and plastering over with the newest fashions ... Offensive
people. But I shouldn't let this deter me. As a newcomer I
must be polite. Greetings to you, fair ladies. And to you too,
the knowing greyfins.

GRIFFINS *snarling*

Not greyfins, griffins. Who wants to be called grey? The
sound of a word tells you where it comes from: Grey,
grave, grating, gruesome. They're all alike, but we don't
like them.

MEPHISTOPHELES

But, to stick to the subject, you don't mind being called
griffins with a 'grrr'.

GRIFFINS *as above*

Of course not. Griffin goes with grip and grab. It's been
proved and proved. Often condemned, but mostly commended. Try grabbing at girls and gold and greatness. Fortune usually favours the grabber.

ANTS *giant variety*

Gold, you say gold. We collected a lot of it and rammed it into caves and holes. Now those arimasps have tracked it down. We don't know where they've taken it. There they are, laughing at us.

GRIFFINS

We'll make them tell.

ARIMASPS

But not tonight. It's a holiday. And by tomorrow we'll have gone through it all. So this time we think we'll score.

MEPHISTOPHELES *who has sat down among the sphinxes*

I find myself so readily at home here. I can understand every one of you.

SPHINX

We utter our ghostly sounds and you folk embody them. And now, for a start, tell us your name.

MEPHISTOPHELES

People have many names for me. Are there any Englishmen here? They generally travel, inspecting battlefields, waterfalls, ruins, dreary classical spots. This would be just the place for them. They identified me as Old Iniquity in one of their early plays.

SPHINX

How did they hit on that?

MEPHISTOPHELES

I can't tell you.

SPHINX

Well now. Do you know how to read the stars? What can you say about the present moment?

MEPHISTOPHELES *looking up*

One shooting star after another. A clipped moon, shining bright. I feel snug here, warming myself against your lion skin. A pity to waste time on the upper regions. Give us some riddles, some charades.

SPHINX

Express yourself and it'll be riddle enough. Try self-analysis. Thus: 'The pious man needs you as much as the wicked. The first needs you as a fencing-jacket for ascetic sword-play. The other as a partner in wild undertakings. And all of it just to amuse the gods.'

FIRST GRIFFIN *snarling*
I don't like him.

SECOND GRIFFIN *snarling louder*
What does he want here?

BOTH TOGETHER
He's nasty. He doesn't belong here.

MEPHISTOPHELES *savagely*
Perhaps you don't think my nails are as sharp as your claws. Try, and we'll see.

SPHINX *gently*
You may stay. You'll soon want to go of your own accord. You may think you're somebody at home, but, if I'm not mistaken, you're not at ease with us.

MEPHISTOPHELES
Your upper half is quite nice. But down below you're beastly, horrible.

SPHINX
You'll pay for this yet, you scamp, because our claws are sound. You with your shrunken hoof don't feel happy in our company.

Sirens practising overhead

MEPHISTOPHELES
What birds are those rocking in the poplars by the river?

SPHINX
Look out for yourself. Their singing has been too much for some of the best.

SIRENS
Why dally with this fabled ugliness? Listen to us. We come in flocks and sing most sweetly, as sirens should.

SPHINXES *mocking them to the same tune*
Make them come down. They're hiding their savage claws in the branches. They'll kill you if you listen to them.

SIRENS

Away with this hate and this envy. We offer the purest delights under heaven, the happiest welcome on land or sea.

MEPHISTOPHELES

There's the new-style playing and singing for you, one note twining around another. Their warbling's wasted on me. It tickles your ear, but it doesn't reach your heart.

SPHINXES

Your heart, indeed. Don't flatter yourself. Your heart's only a shrunken, leather pouch, to go by the look of you.

FAUST *approaching*

How wonderful. The seeing is enough and more than enough. Forbidding, but their features are great and vigorous. All will be well, they seem to say. Where does this solemn sight take me?

Referring to the sphinxes Before these Oedipus once stood.

Referring to the sirens Ulysses writhed before these in hempen bonds.

Referring to the ants These gathered the great treasure.

Referring to the griffins These faithfully guarded it. This freshness of spirit thrills me through and through. The forms are grand. Grand are the memories.

MEPHISTOPHELES

You don't usually tolerate this sort of thing, but today you do. When you're searching for your loved one, even monsters can help.

FAUST *to the sphinxes*

You that are woman-shaped must answer me. Have any of you seen Helen?

SPHINXES

She came after our time. Hercules slew the last of us. But Chiron will be able to tell you. He's galloping about on this ghost-night. If he stops for you, you'll be lucky.

SIRENS

You could find out from us. Ulysses didn't scorn us and hurry past. He stayed with us and he told us many things. We'd pass it all on to you, if you'd come down to where we live by the sea.

SPHINX

Don't be deceived, good man. Ulysses made them bind him. Let the advice we gave you be binding on you. If you can find Chiron, he'll tell you.

Faust off

MEPHISTOPHELES *vexatiously*

What's that flying past and croaking? So fast, one after another, you can hardly bear to look. Very trying for a hunter.

SPHINX

These are the stymphalids. They have webbed feet and a vulture's beak and they fly like the storm-wind in winter, almost too swiftly for the arrows of Hercules. Their croaking is friendly. They'd like to join our company, as relatives.

MEPHISTOPHELES *as if in fright*

There's something else hissing here.

SPHINX

You needn't be afraid of them. They're the heads of the Lernean dragon, severed from the rump and pleased with themselves. But tell me, what's the matter with you? You're flinging yourself about so. Off you go, where you want. I see that bevy over there has made you crane your neck. Pretty faces. Introduce yourself. They're lamiae, smiling, bold, seductive, favoured by the satyrs. A goat's-foot can let himself go with them.

MEPHISTOPHELES

You'll be staying here, won't you? In case I come back.

SPHINXES

Yes, join the merry crowd. We've been used to sitting enthroned for a thousand years ever since our Egyptian days. Pay us due respect. We sit in front of the pyramids, regulating the months and years and the fate of nations, impassively witnessing floods and war and peace.

THE LOWER PENEIOS
Stretches of water, nymphs everywhere

PENEIOS

Bestir yourselves, you reeds and rushes, you slender stems of willow, you trembling poplars, breathe ever so lightly, whisper to me in my broken dreams. A strangely disquieting vibration everywhere has shaken me out of my sleepy flow.

FAUST *coming to the river bank*

Can it be human voices I hear coming from these hidden arbours? It almost seems so. The ripples in the water seem to chatter. The little breezes joke and play.

NYMPHS

Lie down here, rest your weary limbs in this cool place, taste the repose you so seldom find. That would be best. And we'll sing to you in a running whisper, a rustling sound.

FAUST

Now I'm awake. Oh, let them have their way with me, the incomparable forms that my eye recovers here. So marvellously am I affected. Is it dreams? Is it memories? Once before I had this joy. Cool water sliding slowly through dense and faintly swaying bushes, sliding so slowly hardly a ripple can be heard. Springs innumerable flowing together from every side to form this clear, clean, evenly shallowed bathing-pool. And healthy young women in it, the liquid mirror making the eye's delight twofold. The women playing gaily together, or boldly swimming or wading timidly, or shrieking and splashing one another. This should be enough for me to feast on, but my thought presses further. And I turn my gaze to where behind that rich green foliage the queen is concealed.

Wonderful. Swans are entering the pool from the outer bays, majestic, poised, tender, but proudly independent in the movement of head and beak. One of them seems to stand out in pride and boldness, sailing through the rest with spreading feathers, like a wave riding on waves, on its way to the queen... The others move quietly to and fro and then dart at the timid girls to divert them from their duty with concern for their own safety.

NYMPHS

Sisters, put your ears to the ground on the grassy brink. Unless I'm mistaken, I can hear a horse galloping. Who can be bringing news tonight?

FAUST

The ground seems to ring under a horse's tread. Can my good fortune be here, by a miracle? Now I see a man on horseback, a white horse, dazzling white ... and the rider looks like a man of mind and courage. But I know him. It's the famous son of Philyra. Chiron, stop. I've something to say to you...

CHIRON

What is it?

FAUST

Slow down a bit.

CHIRON

I never stop.

FAUST

Then, please, take me with you.

CHIRON

Jump up. Then I can take my time asking. Where are you going? Here you are on the river bank. I'm willing to take you across.

FAUST *mounting*

Wherever you like. I'm eternally indebted to you ... the great man, the noble tutor, who to his glory brought up a race of heroes, the Argonauts, and others who enlarged the world of song.

CHIRON

Forget it. Even Pallas Athene did herself little honour in that role. In the end they carry on just as if they'd never been taught at all.

FAUST

You're the physician who knew his botany well and salved the wounds and cured the sick. I embrace you here in body and in spirit.

CHIRON

If by my side a hero was hurt, I knew what to do. But I finally left all that to the old women and the priests.

FAUST

You're the truly great man who can't bear to be praised. You modestly put it aside and pretend there are others as good as you.

CHIRON

You seem to be one of those clever hypocrites who manage to flatter both the ruler and the ruled.

FAUST

At least you must admit you knew the great ones of your day, you strove to be like the noblest in what you did, and you lived a life worthy of a demi-god. But which of all the heroes did you think the best?

CHIRON

Each of the Argonauts was good in his way and, according to his gifts, could step in where the others were at a loss. The Dioscuri always led in point of youth and beauty. The Boreads, when quick, resolute saving action was needed. As a leader, Jason was strong, thoughtful, accommodating, pleasing to the fair sex. Then there was Orpheus, sensitive, withdrawn, supreme master of the lyre, and keen-eyed Lynceus, who safely piloted their ship through the rocks by day and night. Courage can only be tested in comradeship, when one shows it and the others approve.

FAUST

Have you nothing to say about Hercules?

CHIRON

Oh, don't break my heart . . . I'd never seen Phoebus, Ares, Hermes, and the rest. And then I saw a heavenly sight. He was a king among men, marvellously handsome in his youth, subject to his elder brother and to pretty women too. Earth will not see his like again, nor Hebe lead him into heaven. Poets in vain labour their verses. Sculptors only torture the stone.

FAUST

Yes, they may be proud of their works, but they never truly captured him. You've told me about the most beautiful of men. Now tell me about the most beautiful of women.

CHIRON

Beauty in women, there's nothing to it. It's often so rigid, so self-contained. The woman for me must be brimming with life and happiness. And graceful with it. Like Helen when she rode on my back.

FAUST

She rode on your back?

CHIRON

She did.

FAUST

I'm dazed enough already. And now this.

CHIRON

She held my mane, just as you do.

FAUST

Oh, now I'm beside myself. She's my heart's desire. Tell me about it. Where was it? Where did you take her?

CHIRON

I can soon tell you. Her brothers, the Dioscuri, had rescued her from brigands who didn't take a beating lightly. They gave chase. The brothers waded through and I swam. Once across, she dismounted, stroked my dripping mane and thanked me and said nice things. She was so sweet, so assured. And so young and charming too. An old man's joy.

FAUST

And only ten years old.

CHIRON

I see the philologists have fooled you as well as themselves. It's queer about women in mythology. A poet does what he likes with them. They never grow up, they're never old, they're always enticing, they're carried off in youth, courted in old age. Chronology means nothing to a poet.

FAUST

Then let chronology mean nothing to her. Didn't Achilles

find her on the island of Pherae, quite outside of time. What a consummation. Love achieved in defiance of fate. And why shouldn't I, with this fierce yearning in me, bring her back to life, this figure the like of which never was? This creature at once so sweet and so sublime and, like the gods, undying. You saw her once. I saw her today. She was as lovely as I imagined her. Now I'm a man possessed. Life without her is impossible.

CHIRON

You strange fellow. Humanly speaking, you're enraptured. But to us spirits you seem nothing short of crazy. However, you're in luck today. Once a year I call on Manto for a few minutes, Aesculapius's daughter. She's praying to her father to enlighten the medical profession at last and make them stop killing people ... Of all the sibyls I like her best. She's not uncouth and restless, she's kind and full of good works. If you stay with her for a while, she'll probably be able to cure you completely with her herbs.

FAUST

I don't want to be cured. That would be despicable. My mind is firm.

CHIRON

Don't fail to drink at the healing well. And now jump down. We're there.

FAUST

Where have you brought me through pebbly streams on this weird night?

CHIRON

This is where Greece and Rome fought, Peneios on the right, Olympus on the left. The great empire lost in the sand. The king fled, the citizens won. Look up. There's the eternal temple facing you in the moonlight.

MANTO *dreaming within*

A horse's hoof sounds at my door. Demi-gods arriving.

CHIRON

You're right. Open your eyes.

MANTO *awaking*

Welcome. So you didn't fail me.

CHIRON

Your temple's standing too.

MANTO

Are you always on the move? Do you never tire?

CHIRON

You stay quietly in your sanctuary, while I like to go the round.

MANTO

I wait, and time goes round me. And who's this?

CHIRON

The swirl of this uncanny night has dropped him here. He's mad. He wants Helen and doesn't know where to start. If anyone needs Aesculapian treatment, he does.

MANTO

I like a man who desires the impossible.

Chiron is already far away

MANTO

Come in, adventurer, and rejoice. This dark passage leads to Persephone in the hollow foot of Olympus where she watches for forbidden guests. I once smuggled Orpheus down. Be bold. Make better use of your opportunity. *They go down*

THE UPPER PENEIOS
As before

SIRENS

Come, plunge into the Peneios, sport and swim there, and start our songs for the benefit of these unfortunates. There can be no good life away from the water. If the whole crowd of us went down to the Aegean, every pleasure would be ours.

Earthquake

SIRENS

The water came foaming back, but not in its old bed. The ground quaked, the flood piled up, the shore cracked and smoked. Let's away from here, all of us. This miracle's no good to anyone.

Away to the sea-festival, all you guests, where the glinting, trembling waves lightly lap the shore, and the moon shines double and wets us with its sacred dew. Life there is unconfined, and here – this fearful earthquake. The place is dreadful. No prudent man would stay.

SEISMOS *making noises under the earth*

Another good shove. Another good heave with my shoulders. Then I'll be out and they'll all have to scatter.

SPHINXES

What a horrid vibration. What fearful tension in the air. Such a swaying and tottering and rocking this way and that. It's intolerable, it's monstrous. But we won't move, though hell itself breaks loose.

The ground's lifting like a vaulted roof, marvellous. It's the same old man, the same old greybeard, who made the island of Delos, pushed it up out of the sea to oblige a woman in travail. Now straining and squeezing away untiringly with all his might, his arms tensed and his back bent like the giant Atlas, he's lifting the grass, the soil, the sand, and everything in the peaceful river-bed, and cutting a gap right across the quiet valley. He's like a colossal caryatid, still buried below the waist and holding up a huge mass of rock. But this is where he stops, because we're here.

SEISMOS

I managed this all by myself. You'll have to admit it. And if I hadn't done so much shoving and shaking, how would it have been with this lovely world? You'd never have had your mountains towering aloft against the blue sky in its purity and splendour if I hadn't thrust them up for your pleasure, showing off in front of our great ancestors, Chaos and Old Night, and in company with the titans tossing Pelion and Ossa about like playthings. We carried on this way in youthful exuberance till we got tired of it and wickedly clapped the two mountains on top of Parnassus as a double night-cap... Apollo sojourns happily there with his muses. And who was it but me that planted the throne on high for Jupiter and his thunderbolts? Now once more I've forced my way with an immense effort out of the bowels of the earth and call for happy settlers to begin a new life here.

SPHINXES

You'd say this pile was ancient, if we hadn't just seen it forced up from under the ground. There's a forest spreading across it and more rocks arriving. A sphinx pays no heed. Our seat is sacred. We refuse to be disturbed.

GRIFFIN

I see gold in the cracks, gold in leaf, gold in sparkles. This is a treasure you mustn't miss. Off with you, you ants, and pick it out.

CHORUS OF ANTS

Now that the giants have raised it, up the mountain you go as fast as you can, you wrigglers. Go in and out of the crannies. Every grain is worth having, even the smallest. Search every corner, no slackening, no loafing. In with the gold, you throngs upon throngs. Let the rest go.

GRIFFINS

Gold in heaps. In with it. We put our claws on it. No bolts are stronger. The greatest treasure would be safe with us.

PYGMIES

We've really moved in. We don't know how it happened. Don't ask us where we came from. We're just here. Every land lends itself to cheerful living. And if there are cracks in the rocks, the dwarfs soon turn up, not in ones, but in twos, man and wife. They lose no time in getting to work. They're models of their kind. Perhaps it was like this in paradise. But we're glad to be here and we thank our stars. East or west, mother earth is fruitful everywhere.

DACTYLS

If she produced these little ones in a single night, she'll produce the littlest too, and they'll find one another.

PIGMY ELDERS

Quick, occupy this good place. Get to work. We're still at peace. Build the forges to make munitions.

You ants, so nimble, get us the metals. You dactyls, so tiny, so many, fetch us the wood. Make hidden fires for charcoal-burning.

GENERAL

Set out now with your bows and arrows to that pond and shoot the herons nesting there so haughtily and in such numbers. Shoot them all in one go. Then we can wear their feathers in our helmets.

ANTS AND DACTYLS

Oh, who will save us? We smelted the iron. They're forging chains. It's too early to revolt. We'll have to lie low.

CRANES OF IBYCUS

Shrieks and moans of murdering and dying. Wings flapping wildly in alarm. What sounds of anguish and agony reach us as we fly. They've all been slaughtered. The lake is red with blood. Foul greed has despoiled them. See their feathers in the helmets of those fat-bellied, bandy-legged dwarfs. You coastal birds, our allies, we call on you in a common cause. Let us swear undying hostility to this brood and take vengeance on them, putting all we have into the attack. *They scatter in the air, shrieking*

MEPHISTOPHELES *in the plain*

Northern witches I've always known how to handle, but these foreign ones bother me. After all, the Brocken's easygoing. You can fit in wherever you happen to be. Frau Ilse's always on the look-out at Ilsenstein. And Heinrich likewise at his place. Elend and the Schnarchers don't hit it off, but, at least, everything stays put for ages. Here you don't know where you are. You don't know whether the ground's going to gape under your feet... I come strolling down a smooth valley, and suddenly a mountain goes up at my back, well hardly a mountain, but big enough to cut me off from my sphinxes. There's more fires further down, lighting up the scene. That gay crowd's still hovering and tripping in front of me with their tricks, drawing me on, then pulling back. I'd better be careful. I'm so used to nibbling. I can't forgo an opportunity.

LAMIAE *drawing Mephistopheles after them*

Quick, quick, keep moving, keep chatting and then slowing down. It's amusing to make the old sinner come chasing after us and then get punished. He's hobbling and stumbling along with his club-foot, dragging his leg. Trying to catch us. But we won't let him.

MEPHISTOPHELES *coming to a halt*

What cursed luck. Poor Jack gets fooled. Fooled every time, beginning with Adam. We all grow old, but who's the wiser? And to think of the times it's happened before.

    We know this breed is utterly worthless, with their bodies laced and their faces painted. They've nothing sound to offer a man. Rotten in limb, the wretches, wherever you touch them. We know it, we see it plain as day. Yet theirs is the tune we always dance to.

LAMIAE *stopping*

He's hesitating, stopping. Go towards him. Don't let him escape.

MEPHISTOPHELES *advancing*

On with it. Don't get into a tangle of doubts. That's silly. If there were no witches, who the devil would want to be a devil?

LAMIAE *at their most charming*

Let's encircle him. He's sure to take one of us.

MEPHISTOPHELES

In this flickering light I must admit you look pretty. I can't complain about you.

EMPUSA

Nor about me, I hope. So let me join you.

LAMIAE

We don't want her. She always spoils things.

EMPUSA *to Mephistopheles*

Greetings from little Empusa, the lass with the donkey's foot. You only have a horse's. And yet I wish you good-day.

MEPHISTOPHELES

I thought they'd all be strangers. And here I am, landed among relatives. It's an old, old story: from Harz to Hellas cousins all the way.

EMPUSA

I can transform myself in many ways and do it promptly. But today in your honour I've put on my donkey's head.

MEPHISTOPHELES

I see these people set great store by relationship. But, no matter what, this donkey's head is more than I can take.

LAMIAE

Don't bother with that horrid woman. She drives away any thought of charm and beauty. Where she is, charm and beauty don't exist.

MEPHISTOPHELES

These others that look so slender and so tender, I suspect all of them. Their rosy cheeks may hide another metamorphosis.

LAMIAE

Come, try. There's lots of us. Help yourself. With luck you'll catch the best. What's the good of this harping on desire. A nice suitor you are, strutting along and giving yourself airs. – Now he's coming in among us. Drop your masks bit by bit and show what's behind them.

MEPHISTOPHELES

I've picked the prettiest. *embracing her*
Oh what a broomstick, dry as a bone.
Seizing another
And this one?... What a face.

LAMIAE

Do you think you deserve better? Don't kid yourself.

MEPHISTOPHELES

I'll try the little one... and a lizard slips through my fingers. Her plaited hair's like a snake. And when I take hold of the tall one... she's a bacchic wand with a pine-cone on top. Where will it end?... Here's a fat one that might be fun. I'll make a last attempt. Here goes. She's all flabby and wobbly. Orientals pay high prices for this sort. But ugh, she's burst, a fungus.

LAMIAE

Scatter, flit about like lightning. Flutter round the son of a witch in wavering shuddering circles, black-winged and noiseless like bats. He's getting off too cheap.

MEPHISTOPHELES *shaking himself*

I never seem to learn. It's as ridiculous here as it is in the north. Ghosts just as unpleasant. Poets and people just as crass. A masquerade's a sensual frolic everywhere. I go after a charmer and what I get my hands on gives me the shivers. I wouldn't mind being duped, if it only lasted longer.

Going astray among the rocks

Where am I going? I was on a path and now there's no path. The road was smooth before, and now I'm faced with rubble. I climb helplessly up and down. How shall I ever get back to my sphinxes? I never dreamed such things would happen. A mountain that size in a single night. There's a witches' ride for you. They bring their Brocken with them.

OREAD *in the older rock*

Come up here. My mountain is old, unchanged from the start, with these rocky steeps, the last spurs of Pindus. It was imperturbably the same when Pompey crossed it in his flight. Those illusions, by contrast, vanish at cock-crow. I've often seen them come and go – go quite suddenly.

MEPHISTOPHELES

All honour to you and veneration, with your mighty forest of oak trees, where even the brightest moon never enters. – But there's a modest light moving in the bushes here. How fortunate. It's Homunculus of all people. Where have you been, little fellow?

HOMUNCULUS

I sort of float about from place to place, wanting to get born the best way and eager to shatter my glass. I haven't seen anything yet that I'd trust myself to. But, just between you and me, I'm on the track of two philosophers. I listened to them and they kept saying 'Nature, nature.' I mean to stick to them. They surely understand the living world and I'll find out from them where it would be wisest to go.

MEPHISTOPHELES

Act on your own. Where there's ghosts about, the philo-sopher is welcomed. He at once creates a dozen new ones, in order to show them his favours. You have to make mistakes or you'll never learn. If you want to get born, do it yourself.

HOMUNCULUS
Good advice is not to be despised.

MEPHISTOPHELES
So off you go. We'll see what happens.

They separate

ANAXAGORAS *to Thales*
Will that rigid mind of yours never relent? What more is needed to convince you?

THALES
Water yields to any wind, but it keeps away from the sharp rock.

ANAXAGORAS
This rock was made by explosion, by fire.

THALES
Life began in the wet.

HOMUNCULUS *between the two*
Let me go with you. I also want to begin.

ANAXAGORAS
Tell me, Thales, did you ever, in one night, make a mountain out of mud?

THALES
Nature, the flow of nature, never depended on hours and days. She lets every form grow under her control. Even on a big scale there's no violence.

ANAXAGORAS
But there was violence here. Cruel, plutonic fire, the tremendous bursting of aeolian vapours, broke through the old flat crust, so that at once a mountain had to arise.

THALES
What does it help? What does it lead to? The mountain's there. So far, so good. This sort of argument's a waste of time. It only leads people by the nose, if they let it.

ANAXAGORAS

The mountain's already alive with myrmidons, occupying the cracks. Ants and pygmies and other little busy-bodies.

To Homunculus

You've never aimed high. You've always lived a hermit's life, shut in. If you can adapt yourself to rulership, I'll have you crowned king here.

HOMUNCULUS

What does good Thales say?

THALES

I say don't. Among little people you do little things. Great people make a little man great. Look at that black cloud of cranes. They're threatening the pygmy nation – see how disturbed they are – and they'd threaten the king. They're attacking with beak and claw. Destruction is near. It was criminal to destroy the herons gathered at their quiet pond. But that murderous assault is being savagely avenged. It's aroused the thirst of their kin for the blood of the pygmies. What use to them are shield and spear and helmet now? What use are the herons' plumes? Look at the ants and dactyls trying to hide. Their army's breaking, running. It's collapsed.

ANAXAGORAS *solemnly after a pause*

Till now I've always looked to the powers under the earth, but in this case I turn upwards ... You above, ageless and eternal, triple in form, triple in name, I call on you in my nation's crisis, Diana, Luna, Hecate. You, the heart-inspirer, the philosopher, you so calm-seeming, so passionate, reveal your ancient spell, but without magic. Put on your dread eclipse.

Pause

Has my prayer been granted too soon? Has my appeal to those above upset the order of nature?

See, the goddess's circular throne coming closer and closer, monstrous, fearful to behold. Its blaze is reddening. Come no nearer, you giant disc. You'll destroy the world.

So it's true, is it, that Thessalian witches once, with impious magic, sang you down out of your course and wrung ruinous concessions from you? . . . The luminous disc has darkened. Suddenly it's tearing apart and flashing. What a hissing, rattling noise, with wind and thunder crossing it. I cast myself down at the steps of the throne. Forgive me. I evoked all this. *throws himself down on his face*

THALES

The things this man hears and sees. I don't quite know what happened, but I can't go along with him. Let's agree, these are queer times. And there's the moon rocking comfortably in the same place as before.

HOMUNCULUS

Look at where the pygmies settled. The mountain was rounded. Now it's a peak. I felt a tremendous crash. A piece of rock fell out of the moon. It squashed and killed people right and left and asked no questions. But I can't help admiring the skill that created this mountain in a single night, working from above and from below.

THALES

Calm yourself. It wasn't real. Let that horrid brood go their ways. It's just as well you didn't become their king. And now off we go to the happy sea-festival. They expect strange visitors there and honour them. *They withdraw*

MEPHISTOPHELES *climbing on the other side*

Here I am, struggling up the rocks and stumbling over the roots of these old oaks. In my Harz mountains there's a resinous atmosphere with something of pitch in it. A smell I like, next after sulphur . . . Here among these Greeks there's no trace of anything of the sort. But I'd be curious to know what they stoke their hell-fires with.

DRYAD

You may have your native wisdom for domestic purposes, but abroad you aren't adaptable enough. You shouldn't be thinking of home at all. You should be paying homage to these sacred oak trees.

MEPHISTOPHELES

You can't help remembering what you've lost. The life you were used to is always like a paradise. But tell me. What is it, crouching in that cavern? The light's bad. There's three of them.

DRYAD

The Phorkyads. Go in and speak to them, if you have the pluck.

MEPHISTOPHELES

Why not? I'm amazed at what I see. I thought I'd seen everything, but I have to climb down and admit I never saw the like of this. They're worse than mandrakes. When you've once set eyes on this three-fold monster, no sin will ever look ugly to you again. No hell of ours, not the cruellest, would let them near its door. And here it is, rooted in beauty's land, the land proudly called antique. They're stirring, they seem to be aware of me, they're whistling, twittering, like vampire bats.

PHORKYAD

Sisters, lend me the eye so that I may see who's coming to our temple.

MEPHISTOPHELES

Revered ones, permit me to approach and receive your threefold blessing. I present myself to you, a stranger, yet, if I'm not mistaken, a remote relative. I've seen ancient gods before, prostrated myself before Ops and Rhea. Even the fates, your sisters, daughters of Chaos, I saw them yesterday, or was it the day before. But I never saw anything like you. I'm delighted and have no more to say.

PHORKYADS

This one seems to have a head on his shoulders.

MEPHISTOPHELES

What surprises me is that no poet has sung your praises. Tell me, how did this come about? I've never seen statues of you. Yet you are what the sculptor should attempt. Not Juno, Pallas, Venus, and the rest.

PHORKYADS

Sunk, as we are, in deepest darkness and solitude, we never thought of it.

MEPHISTOPHELES

The question never arose. No one ever sees you. You ought

to be living in places where art and splendour are enthroned side by side, and every day another new marble statue comes running up at the double-quick. Places where...

PHORKYADS

Be silent. Don't awaken our desires. What good would it do us to know more? We are born in the night, close to the night, unknown to the world, almost unknown to ourselves.

MEPHISTOPHELES

There's no problem there. All you have to do is to transfer yourselves to someone else. You have one eye and one tooth among you. It might be mythologically possible to compress yourselves from three into two and lend me the third one's figure for a short time.

ONE

What do you think? Could it be done?

THE OTHERS

Let's try – but without the eye and the tooth.

MEPHISTOPHELES

There you're leaving out the best part. The figure'll never look right.

ONE

Close one eye. It's easy. Then show one of your buck-teeth and you'll have our profile exactly like one of the family.

MEPHISTOPHELES

Good. You honour me.

PHORKYADS

Good.

MEPHISTOPHELES *a phorkyad in profile*

There I am. The favourite son of Chaos.

PHORKYADS

And we're certainly his daughters.

MEPHISTOPHELES

But oh the shame of it. They'll say I'm a hermaphrodite.

PHORKYADS

A new trio of sisters. How lovely we are. We have two eyes and two teeth.

MEPHISTOPHELES

Now I'll have to hide myself and then go and terrify all the devils in hell.

ROCKY INLETS IN THE AEGEAN SEA
The moon, stationary at the zenith

SIRENS *reclining on the rocks, fluting and singing*

There was a night of terror when witches in Thessaly wantonly drew you down to earth. But tonight is different. Shine peacefully tonight from the circling sky on these trembling, glittering waves. Illuminate the throngs now rising to the surface. O lovely moon, be gracious. We are your servants.

NEREIDS AND TRITONS *as sea-wonders*

Pipe a shriller note, one that will sound across the sea and call up the nations of the deep. We took refuge from engulfing storms in this quiet retreat, drawn by the sweet singing.

See with what delight we put on these gold chains and match crown and jewels with buckle and girdle. All this we owe to you, the demons of our bay. Your singing lured and wrecked the ships laden with these treasures.

SIRENS

We know that fishes like the sea-life so fresh and flitting, so painless, but today, you festive crowds, we'd like to be assured that you are more than fishes.

NEREIDS AND TRITONS

We thought of this before we came. Sisters and brothers, be quick. The shortest of journeys will serve to assure you completely. *They go off*

SIRENS

Off they go in a flash, heading straight for Samothrace. The wind is with them. They're out of sight. What do they expect from their visit to the Kabiri, those curious divinities, self-creating, self-ignorant?

Stay where you are, O gracious moon, lest the night pass and the daylight dispel us.

THALES *on the shore, to Homunculus*
I'd like to take you to Nereus. We're quite close to his cavern.
But he's a sour old thing, hard as nails. The whole of the
human race can do nothing to please him. But he sees into the
future and people respect him for that and honour him.
Besides, he's been helpful to many.

HOMUNCULUS
Let's risk it and call on him. It won't cost me my bottle.

NEREUS
Is it human voices I hear? They infuriate me. Always striving
to be like the gods and always doomed to stay the same as
before. I could have had a fine time for years if I hadn't felt
impelled to advise the best of them. When I came to look at
what they did, it was exactly as if I'd never spoken.

THALES
And yet, old man of the sea, we trust you. Don't drive us
away. See this flame, human-looking I admit, but ready to
follow your advice unquestioningly.

NEREUS
Advice. What man ever listened to advice? Wise words always
fall on deaf ears. Men may do things that afterwards they
bitterly condemn, yet they stay just as obstinate as ever.
Wasn't I like a father to Paris and warned him, before he
went after that woman and ensnared her. There he stood on
the shore and I told him what my inner vision showed me: the
air full of smoke, red flames, burning beams, death and
murder underneath. Troy's fearful judgment day, known to
the centuries in enduring verse. An old man's words – they
meant nothing to him. He went his lustful way and Ilium fell,
a giant corpse rigid after long torment, a welcome feast for
Pindus's eagles. Ulysses too. Didn't I foretell him the wiles of
Circe, the horrors of the Cyclops? His dilly-dallying, the
frivolity of his companions. And all the rest. Did it help?
No. Till finally, after all his tossing at sea, the waves dropped
him on a friendly shore.

THALES
Behaviour of that sort distresses a man of wisdom. But if he's

a good man too, he gives it another try. A grain of thanks outweighs a ton of ingratitude and delights the heart. It's no small thing we're asking of you. This boy here wants to get born and needs advice.

NEREUS

Don't put me out of humour on this very happy day. I have quite other things in prospect. I've invited all my daughters, the Dorids, the Graces of the sea. For beauty and daintiness you won't find their equal, not on earth, not on Olympus. You should see how gracefully they spring from their sea-dragons to Neptune's horses. So closely allied are they to the watery element that the very spray seems to lift them. Galatea, the fairest of them all, will come riding in Venus's irised scallop-shell, because Venus deserted us long ago and she inherited her temple-city and chariot-throne and is wor-shipped in Paphos as a goddess.

Away. In this hour of paternal bliss there must be neither rancour in the heart nor abuse on the lips. Off you go to Proteus, the wonder-man. Ask him to tell you how to get born or get transformed. *He goes off towards the sea*

THALES

We're not a bit better off. Even if we run into Proteus, he'll just dissolve and disappear. Or if he doesn't, he'll only say things that'll startle and confuse us. However, you need the advice, so let's go along and try. *off*

SIRENS *on the higher rocks*

What is this we see far off, coming across the water? It's like white sails, running before the wind. Now it's clear. They're mermaids transfigured. Let's go down. Can you hear their voices?

NEREIDS AND TRITONS

What we're bringing will please you all. Austere forms, riding in Chelone's giant tortoise-shell. They are gods. Sing songs of praise.

SIRENS

Ancient divinities, small but powerful. Savers of the shipwrecked.

NEREIDS AND TRITONS
We're bringing the Kabiri to a peaceful festival. Where they prevail, Neptune will be kind.

SIRENS
We yield to you. When a ship is wrecked, you protect the crew. Your power is irresistible.

NEREIDS AND TRITONS
We've brought three. The fourth wouldn't come. He said he was the right one, who did the thinking for all of them.

SIRENS
One god makes a fool of the other. Honour all the gods. Fear all harm.

NEREIDS AND TRITONS
Strictly there are seven of them.

SIRENS
Where are the other three?

NEREIDS AND TRITONS
We can't tell you. You could find out on Olympus. That's where the eighth is, whom no one has ever thought of. They're well disposed, but not ready yet. They always press on, hungry for the unattainable. They're unique.

SIRENS
We worship all the gods, no matter where. It pays.

NEREIDS AND TRITONS
It's our greatest glory to lead this festival.

SIRENS
The heroes of antiquity will suffer in reputation, if they only bring the golden fleece, while you bring the Kabiri.

Repeated in chorus
If they only bring the golden fleece, while we/you bring the Kabiri.

Nereids and Tritons off

HOMUNCULUS
They're ungainly. Like so many old clay pots. Philosophers bump into them and crack their skulls.

THALES
That's what's wanted. The value of the coin is in the rust.

PROTEUS *unseen*

This is just the thing for an old fabler like me. The odder it is, the more acceptable.

THALES

Proteus, where are you?

PROTEUS *ventriloquizing, now near, now far off*

Here, and here.

THALES

Have your old joke, I forgive you. But don't deceive a friend. I know you're speaking from the wrong place.

PROTEUS *as if far off*

Goodbye.

THALES *whispering to Homunculus*

He's quite near. Turn up your light. He's as inquisitive as a fish. And where-ever he may be and whatever shape he's in, a flame attracts him.

HOMUNCULUS

Here's my light, plenty of it. But I must be careful not to break the glass.

PROTEUS *in the form of a giant turtle*

What can it be that gives this lovely light?

THALES *concealing Homunculus*

Good. If you want, you can have a better look. Let us see you on your human pair of legs. You can easily do it. Remember, it's for us to say whether or not you can look at what I'm hiding here.

PROTEUS *in human form*

You still know all the cunning tricks.

THALES

And you still like to change your shape. *He uncovers Homunculus*

PROTEUS *astonished*

An incandescent little dwarf. I never saw one before.

THALES

He wants advice about how to get born. The way I have it from him, he came into the world only half-born. It's strange. He has plenty of mental attributes, but he's very short on body. So far the bottle is all the weight he has. He longs to be embodied properly.

PROTEUS

A real virgin birth. You're there before you ought to be.

THALES

And there's another difficulty. If I'm not mistaken, he's a hermaphrodite.

PROTEUS

Then all the better. Wherever he lands, he'll fit in. But there's no need to deliberate. You must make your start in the open sea. Begin on a small scale and enjoy swallowing what is smaller. You must grow bit by bit and rise to higher forms.

HOMUNCULUS

The air's so soft here. I love this odour, just like green things growing.

PROTEUS

I believe you, boy. And farther out on this narrow tongue of land the atmosphere is more enjoyable still. You wouldn't believe it. There's the procession coming. It's not far away now. Let's go to meet it.

THALES

I'll come too.

HOMUNCULUS

Three strange spirits marching in a row.

Telchines of Rhodes on hippocamps and sea-dragons, wielding Neptune's trident

CHORUS

We forged the trident for Neptune that rules the wildest waves. If the thunder god unleashes his swollen clouds, Neptune retaliates. However fiercely the forked lightning flashes down, wave on wave is thrown up from below. Those who are caught between the two are tossed about and finally swallowed by the deep. This is why he's given us his sceptre for the day. Now we can feel easy and enjoy ourselves.

SIRENS

On the occasion of this moon festival we greet you sun-worshippers, devotees of the happy daylight.

TELCHINES

Dearest goddess, shining aloft, you are happy to hear your brother praised. So lend an ear to Rhodes, where a never-ending paean is sung to him. Whether at the start of his daily course or at the end he looks at us with fiery gaze. Our mountains, cities, shores, waters are lovely and bright. We have no mists. If a mist creeps in – a flash of sun and a little breeze and the island is clear again. The sun god sees himself here in a hundred statues as youth, giant, great, gentle. We were the first to present the gods in human form.

PROTEUS

Let them sing, let them boast, all they want. Dead works of this sort mean nothing to the sun's life-giving rays. They go on persistently with their smelting and moulding and when they have it cast in bronze they think it is really something. What does it come to in the end with these proud images of the gods? An earthquake destroyed them. They were all melted up again.

This earth-life, even at its best, is just a weariness of the flesh. The sea suits life better. Proteus, the dolphin, will carry you out into the eternal waters.

He transforms himself

There, I've done it. Here's the ideal place for you. I'll take you on my back and wed you to the ocean.

THALES

The desire to begin creation at the beginning is most excellent. Surrender to it and be ready for quick action. You'll move in accordance with eternal laws through thousands and thousands of forms. It'll be a long, long time before you're a man.

Homunculus mounts Proteus, the dolphin

PROTEUS

Come with me, what there is of you, into this wet expanse.

There you can start living across and along and move about as you choose. Only don't try to climb the scale. When once you come to man's estate, it'll be all up with you.

THALES

It depends. There's something to be said for being a worthy man in your day.

PROTEUS *to Thales*

Yes, if it's one of your sort. They last for a while. I've seen you for centuries among the pallid ghosts.

SIRENS *on the rocks*

See that splendid ring of clouds round the moon. They're doves aflame with love. Wings as white as the light. Paphos sent them. They are hers. Our festival is now complete, our joy unblemished.

NEREUS

A wanderer in the night might call this an atmospheric phenomenon, but we spirits think differently and we're right. It's doves, accompanying my daughter's ride. A marvellous feat of flying, learned by them in early days.

THALES

I too think it best to trust simple humanity, cherishing a sacred belief in warmth and quietude.

PSYLLI AND MARSI *riding on sea-cows, sea-calves, and sea-rams*

In Cyprus's deep caverns, not swamped by the sea god, not shattered by earthquake, fanned by eternal breezes, we guard Venus's chariot with quiet contentment, as in the earliest days. And in the whispering night-time we bring out our lovely mistress, daughter of Nereus, and ride her here through the woven waves, invisible to the younger generation of men. We busy ourselves quietly, fearing neither eagle nor winged lion, neither cross nor moon, that rule the upper earth, always restlessly changing, banishing, murdering, ruining crops and cities. Meanwhile we bring our dear mistress along.

SIRENS

Come, you sturdy Nereids, primitive and pleasing both. We see you lightly, easily circling the chariot, ring within ring, sometimes snakelike intertwined. And you, tender Dorids, bring your mother Galatea, who is grave like the gods and worthy of immortality, but also graceful and enticing like earthly women.

DORIDS *passing by Nereus in chorus, all on dolphins*

Luna, lend us your light and shade, to show this galaxy of youth, these dear husbands of ours, to our father, with a request. *to Nereus*

We rescued these boys from the raging surf and brought them back to life and warmth on beds of moss. And now with ardent kisses they're faithfully repaying us. Look on them favourably.

NEREUS

A double reward, not to be despised. You're being charitable and you're having fun.

DORIDS

If you approve, father, of what we've done and don't begrudge us our well-earned pleasure, let us keep them and hold them close and stay young for ever.

NEREUS

Enjoy your lovely prizes, and bring them from youth to manhood. But I can't grant you what Zeus alone can grant. The sea that rolls and rocks you will not let love last. When your dalliance is over, put them quietly back on land.

DORIDS

You charming boys, we know your worth, but we must part in sadness. We wanted fidelity for ever, but the gods won't have it so.

THE YOUTHS

If you can go on being so kind to us sailor-boys, we ask no better, we never had it better.

Galatea approaches in her shell

NEREUS

There you are, my darling.

GALATEA

O father, what joy. Stay, my dolphins. The sight of him holds me.

NEREUS

They're gone, gone past, in their sweeping motion. What do they care for my feelings. Oh, if only they would take me with them. But a single glimpse is good for a whole year.

THALES

Hail, hail, once again. How I exult, possessed as I am with the true and the beautiful . . . Everything came out of the water. Everything is sustained by the water. Ocean, may you hold your sway for ever. If you didn't send your clouds, and brooks in abundance, and streams twisting this way and that, and the great rivers, where would our mountains and plains be, where the world? It is you who keep life at its freshest.

ECHO *all in chorus*

It is you who keep life at its freshest.

NEREUS

They're coming back in wavering course, but not coming back to me. They're all moving, vast in numbers, in extended chains and circles, as part of the festival. But I can see Galatea's scallop again and again, shining through the host like a star, my dear one. Clear and bright, far yet always new and true.

HOMUNCULUS

In all this lovely wetness, wherever I shine my light, every-thing charms me with its beauty.

PROTEUS

In all this vital wetness, your light shines and rings more splendidly than ever.

NEREUS

What new secret is being revealed to us in the heart of the throng. What is it flames about the scallop, at Galatea's feet, pulsing alternately strong and gentle, as if with pulsations of love.

THALES

It's Homunculus with Proteus in charge. What you see is the symptoms of his imperious desire. Do I not also hear him gasping and droning in anguish? He's going to smash himself against the shining scallop-throne. There, a flame and a flash, and he's spilt himself.

SIRENS

What a luminous miracle transfigures the waves, breaking against one another in fiery sparkles. Everything is lit up, flickering, brightening. All the figures are aglow in the night. Fire is playing over the whole scene. So let Eros prevail. Eros who started everything. Hail to the sea, hail to the waves with the sacred fire over them. Hail to the fire. Hail to the water. Hail to this rare happening.

ALL

Hail to the soft breezes. Hail to the mysterious caves. Hail above all to the four elements.

ACT III

IN FRONT OF THE PALACE OF MENELAUS AT SPARTA

Enter Helen and a chorus of captive Trojan women, with Panthalis as leader of the chorus

HELEN

Helen, the much admired, the much maligned, I am that Helen, come now from the beach where our ship landed, still dizzy with the restless rocking of the waves that with Poseidon's favour and the east wind helping brought us on their stiff high backs from the plains of Phrygia into home waters. Down on the shore Menelaus and the pick of his warriors are rejoicing to be back again. But I address myself to this great house and bid it welcome me, the house that after his return Tyndareus, my father, built not far from the slope of Pallas's hill, and fitted out more splendidly than any house in Sparta. So I remember it from childhood when I played here happily with my sister Clytemnestra and with Castor and Pollux too. I greet you now, you brazen double entrance-doors that stood wide open once invitingly on a festive day and Menelaus, my shining bridegroom chosen among many, came in to meet me. Open again for me, that I may deliver an urgent message from the king, as befits the wife. Let me in and let everything stay behind that has raged around me so disastrously till now. From the day I crossed this threshold with a light heart to visit the temple on Cythera, as a sacred duty bade, and that Phrygian brigand seized me, much has happened that people far and wide love to relate, but she of whom the story and the legend grew has little joy to hear.

CHORUS

Do not make light, O noble lady, of the honour, the great good fortune, the supreme gift that is yours. Yours and yours alone. It is beauty, beauty that transcends everything. A hero's name precedes his coming. Hence his pride. But before all-compelling beauty the stubbornest of heroes humbles his mind.

HELEN

Enough. I came here on shipboard with my husband and now am sent to his city ahead of him. But what he intends to do I cannot guess. Coming here, am I his wife? Am I his queen? Or am I to be a sacrifice to his royal grief and the long endured misfortunes of the Greeks? I am a captive. Whether a prisoner or not I cannot say. Truly the immortals gave me a dubious name and a dubious fate as companions of my beauty that even here on this threshold stand, dark and threatening, at my side. In the hollow ship Menelaus seldom glanced at me and never said a heartening word, but sat facing me as if he was planning evil. Then when we were in the mouth of the Eurotas and our front ships' prows had hardly touched the beach he commanded as if god-inspired: Let my men disembark in due order. I will muster them in their ranks along the shore. But you must proceed up the luxuriant banks of the Eurotas, guiding your horses through the lush meadows, until you come to the plain, once rich in crops and beautiful still, where Lacedaemon stands, ringed by solemn mountains. Go into the high-towered palace and inspect the servants I left there and the shrewd old housekeeper. Let her show you the treasures your father handed on, a rich array that I have added to continually in war and peace. You'll find everything in order. It is the ruler's privilege to come back and find the house exactly as he left it, seeing that the servant has no authority to alter anything.

CHORUS

Refresh your eyes and your heart with the sight of these ever-increasing treasures. You'll find them there, beautiful chains and ornate crowns in their pride and their conceit. Go in and challenge them. They'll quickly gather their forces. But I should love to see beauty contesting with gold and pearls.

HELEN

Then there came a further command from our lord and master. When you've gone over everything in proper order, take as many tripods as you think necessary and take such other vessels of one sort or another as are needed in fulfilling the sacred ritual. Kettles, bowls, and shallow basins. Bring tall jugs of the purest water from the sacred spring. Also have ready dry kindling wood that quickly ignites and finally a knife well-sharpened. All the rest I leave to your care. This is what he said, as he hurried me off. But he said nothing of the living thing he means to sacrifice in honour of the Olympians. This has an ominous look, but I pay no heed and leave it on the the lap of the high gods who do what seems good to them, whether men approve of it or disapprove. We mortals, we endure it. Many a time a man has raised his heavy axe over the consecrated beast's neck bowed to earth and could not bring it down, because an enemy came upon him or some god intervened and prevented him.

CHORUS

What is to happen, thinking will never tell you. Proceed, queen, with an easy mind. Good and ill comes to us unexpectedly. Even when foretold, we don't believe it. Didn't Troy burn, were we not faced with death, shameful death? And yet here we are, with you, your joyful servants, seeing the dazzling sun in the sky and you, the fairest thing on earth, our gracious mistress, making us happy.

HELEN

Be that as it may. Whatever awaits us, it is for me now to go up without delay into the palace that I have not seen for years and longed for so much and nearly trifled away. There it is again before my eyes, almost unbelievably. My feet won't carry me up the high steps as confidently as when I skipped up them as a child. *off*

CHORUS

Come sisters, unfortunate captives that you are, throw grief aside and share your mistress's happiness, share Helen's happiness at coming back again to her father's house, more assured in her return, because so long delayed.

Praise the gods who restore such happiness and grant such home-comings. He who is liberated rises as with wings over what is harshest, while the captive yearns and exhausts himself with arms outstretched above his prison's battlements.

But a god took hold of her when she was far away and brought her back from ruined Troy to the old home now newly restored, where after endless joy and pain she can revive her memories of early years.

PANTHALIS *as leader of the chorus*

Sisters, stop your joyful singing now and turn your eyes to the great door. What do I see? Is that not the queen hurrying back in alarm? What is it, queen, what can it be, that has shaken you so in your own precincts where you expect a welcome? You cannot hide it. I see it written on your brow – anger, righteous anger, struggling with surprise.

HELEN *who has left the double door open. She is disturbed*

The common fears of men are not for Zeus's daughter. And terror's fleeting finger never touches her. But the horror that has risen out of primal darkness since the beginning of the world and still comes in many shapes like fiery clouds rolling up from a volcano can daunt the heart even of a hero. And thus the infernal gods have cruelly marked my entry into the house today so that I could gladly turn my back on this longed-for threshold and leave it like a parting guest. But no. I've come out into the daylight. Farther you shall not drive me, you powers, whoever you are. The house must now be purified. Then fire can burn in the hearth and welcome the husband and the wife.

CHORUS

Tell us, lady, what has happened. We're your faithful servants who honour you. Tell us.

HELEN

You shall see with your own eyes what I have seen, unless Old Night has already swallowed its creation back into its dark womb. But to let you know, I'll put it into words: When I went into the palace, thinking dutifully in that grave interior of what was next to do, I was surprised to find the place completely silent. Not a sign or sound of people bustling about doing this and that. No servants, no housekeeper to say the usual word of welcome to a stranger. But when I approached the hearth I saw a tall woman with her head covered, sitting by the dying ashes more in a thinking posture than a sleeping. I ordered her to go back to work, assuming she was the housekeeper my husband had left in charge during his absence. But there she sat, covered and motionless as before. Then when I rebuked her, she raised her right arm as if to dismiss me from the house, whereupon I turned from her in anger and hastened towards the steps leading to the bedchamber and the treasure room beside it. But she sprang quickly to her feet and blocked my way, and now I could see how tall and gaunt she was, with hollow bloodshot eyes and curious build disturbing to behold. I'm talking to the wind. Words always fail to bring a figure back to life. But there she is. She's come out into the light. And here we are the masters, till the king comes. Phoebus, the lover of beauty, drives these fearsome births of darkness back to their caverns or at least holds them in check.

CHORUS

I've been through much, although these tresses of mine are a young woman's. I've seen terrible things, the misery of warfare and Ilium the night it was taken.

Through the cloud, the dust, and the din of the fighters I heard the fearful voice of the gods calling. I heard the brazen noise of conflict ringing across the battlefield, coming towards the walls.

Ilium's walls were still standing, but the blaze leaped from house to house, spreading with its own storm-wind over the city at night.

As I was escaping, I could see the gods approaching through the smoke and the heat and the leaping flames, in dreadful anger, marvellous giant figures, crossing the fiery gloom.

Did I see all this confusion or did I imagine it in my terror? I shall never know. But I know for sure that I'm seeing this horror before my eyes. I could touch it with my hands but that for sheer dread I dare not. Which of Phorkys's daughters are you? You make me think of them. Are you perhaps one of the Graiae, sharing a single eye and a single tooth?

Do you dare, you horror, to expose yourself to the expert eye of Phoebus side by side with beauty? But come out. After all, Phoebus doesn't see ugliness, any more than he ever sees a shadow.

But it is the sad fate of us mortals to endure the torture all lovers of beauty feel at sight of the despicable and the eternally damned.

Listen then. If you defy us, you shall hear curses, threats and curses unlimited, from the lips of those happy ones whom the gods have shaped.

PHORKYAS

It's an old saying, old but as true as ever, that modesty and beauty never join hands and walk the green world together. There's an old hostility between them so deep-seated that if they ever meet, no matter where, they turn their backs on one another and hurry away, modesty distressed, but beauty always bold and impudent till the day when Hades' darkness closes over her at last, unless old age has tamed her first. You hussies, come from abroad in all your arrogance, you make me think of a strung-out flock of cranes passing overhead with shrieking calls that make a quiet traveller look up at them. But they go their way, he goes his. So it will be with us.

Who are you anyway, to come noising around the king's high palace like raving maenads or like so many drunk women? Who are you, howling at the housekeeper like dogs that bay the moon? Do you think I don't know your kind? You war-begotten, battle-bred young things, you wantons, first seduced and then seducers in your turn, sapping the strength of soldiers and civilians both. When I look at the lot of you, you're like a plague of locusts settling on the green crops. Consumers of others' labour, nibbling destroyers of good life growing, that's what you are. Spoils of war, bartered goods, or sold on the market-place.

HELEN

Whoever scolds the servants in the presence of the mistress is interfering seriously with her domestic rights. It is for her and for no one else to bestow praise where praise is due and to punish what is reprehensible. Moreover I am well pleased with the service they have rendered me thus far, first at mighty Ilium during the siege and after, and then not less in the vicissitudes of our devious journey where each is apt to think only of himself. I expect the same of them here. The master doesn't ask who his servant is, but only how he serves. Therefore stop grinning at them and hold your tongue. If you've looked after the king's house properly in my absence, it is to your credit. But I am here now. You must step back and not incur reproof after earning our thanks.

PHORKYAS

It is the lady's privilege to be severe with members of the household, and abundantly your privilege, the noble wife of a fortunate leader after so many years of prudent management. Since you, whom I now recognize, are reassuming your old position as queen and mistress, by all means pick up the reins that have long hung slack and rule, take charge of the treasure and take charge of us. But, above all, protect me, who am older, from this gang, who beside the swan of your beauty are nothing more than clumsy geese gaggling.

PANTHALIS
How ugly ugliness is beside the beautiful.
PHORKYAS
How stupid stupidity beside intelligence.

From here on members of the chorus step forward singly and speak

CHORUS 1
Tell us of father Erebus, tell us of Mother Night.
PHORKYAS
Then you must talk about Scylla, your flesh-and-blood cousin.
CHORUS 2
Your family tree has plenty of monsters climbing it.
PHORKYAS
Away you go to Hades to find your ancestors.
CHORUS 3
Those that are living there are all too young for you.
PHORKYAS
Go and make love to old Tiresias.
CHORUS 4
Orion's nurse was your great-great-grand-daughter.
PHORKYAS
You must have been fed by harpies in filth and foulness.
CHORUS 5
How do you nourish that studied skinniness?
PHORKYAS
Not with the blood that you're so greedy for.
CHORUS 6
You're after corpses, revolting corpse yourself.
PHORKYAS
Now I see vampire teeth gleaming in that insolent mouth.
PANTHALIS
It'll close yours if I say who you are.
PHORKYAS
Name yourself first, the riddle will be solved.
HELEN
I have to come between you, not in anger but in sorrow, and

put a stop to this brawling. The master of the house has nothing more troublesome to deal with than a secret feud festering among his faithful servants. At such a time his orders are not echoed back harmoniously in prompt obedience. No, the echo blunders about noisily, confusing him and making him complain to no purpose. And there is something else. In your unbridled rage you have evoked unhappy visions that beset me on every side and fill me with terror, as if, in spite of having my feet on home ground, I was being dragged down to Hades. Can it be memory? Or is it some illusion that has taken hold of me? Was I all that? Am I that now? Shall I be that in future? The dream image and the dread image of those destroyers of cities. The girls are alarmed, but you, the old one, are unmoved. Say a sensible word to me.

PHORKYAS

Whoever can look back on long years of varied happiness will think the highest favour of the gods a dream. You more than any, you favoured beyond all measure – your life has been a succession of men desiring you passionately, one after another, all of them ready and eager for any foolhardy adventure. Theseus in his excitement seized you early, a man as strong as Hercules and beautifully built.

HELEN

Carried me off, a slender fawn, a ten-year-old, and kept me in Aphidnus's castle in Attica.

PHORKYAS

And when, before long, Castor and Pollux rescued you, you were sought by many heroes, sought by the best of them.

HELEN

But I admit I quietly favoured Patroclus most of all. He was the image of Achilles.

PHORKYAS

But your father insisted on Menelaus, the bold seafarer and man of property too.

HELEN

Yes, he gave away his daughter, gave the kingdom as well. Hermione was born of the marriage.

PHORKYAS

But when he was far away in Crete, securing an inheritance, and you were alone, there came to you too handsome a visitor.

HELEN

But why recall the time I spent half-widowed and all the cruel misfortune that came of it?

PHORKYAS

And that journey of his brought me into captivity and into slavery, long slavery, me a free-born Cretan woman.

HELEN

He sent you here at once as housekeeper, entrusting a great deal to you, the palace and the treasures so boldly acquired.

PHORKYAS

The palace you deserted for the towers of Ilium and the never exhausted joys of love.

HELEN

Speak not of the joys. Upon my head was poured an infinitude of bitter, bitter suffering.

PHORKYAS

But they say you were seen twofold, in Ilium and in Egypt.

HELEN

Don't add confusion to a mind distraught. Even now I don't know which I am.

PHORKYAS

And they say Achilles came up from the underworld and was with you passionately after loving you earlier contrary to fate's decree.

HELEN

I joined him, phantom with phantom. It was a dream, as the words say. I'm losing myself and becoming a phantom again.
She falls into the arms of the half-chorus

CHORUS

Silence, silence, you ill-favoured, ill-spoken creature. What sounds are these, coming up from that foul gullet, past those loathsome lips and the one tooth.

   Malevolence in friendly guise, a wolf in sheep's clothing, is far more to be feared than the jaws of the three-headed hound. Apprehensively we stand and watch and ask: When and where will it strike, this lurking monster of malice.

And now, instead of proffering the few gentle Lethe-giving words of comfort, you stir up all that was worst in the past and little that was good, darkening the bright light of today and the glimmer of hope for the future.

Silence, silence. Let the queen's spirit, now ready to take flight, not lose its hold on the fairest form under the sun. (*Helen has recovered and stands again in the centre*)

PHORKYAS

Come, come clear of fleeting clouds, you sun that lights our day. Lovely enough you were when veiled, but now your brilliance dazzles. How the world unfolds before you you yourself can see. Ugly they say I am, but beauty, beauty I quickly recognize.

HELEN

Coming round from the swoon that seized me, my steps are so shaky, all my bones so utterly weary, rest would be welcome. Suddenly faced with dangers, however, we have to be ready. All men must, but a queen, a queen more than others.

PHORKYAS

Standing there before us now in all your grandeur, your beauty, your look is commanding. Tell us then, speak, what is your command?

HELEN

After this impudent altercation amends must be made. Quick then, prepare a sacrifice, as the king ordered.

PHORKYAS

Everything's there in the house, bowl, tripod, and axe, all that is needed for sprinkling and purifying. Name only the victim.

HELEN

The king never said.

PHORKYAS

Never said. Oh the pity of it.

HELEN

Why the pity? Why do you care?

PHORKYAS
Queen, he means you.

HELEN
Me?

PHORKYAS
And these here.

CHORUS
Oh misery, misery.

PHORKYAS
The axe is for you.

HELEN
Dreadful for me, but I feared as much.

PHORKYAS
Inevitable, it seems to me.

CHORUS
And what about us?

PHORKYAS
She will die a noble death. But you will twitch and dangle one after another from the roof-tree, like throstles in a snare.

Helen and Chorus astonished and terrified, in significant grouping

PHORKYAS
You ghosts. There you stand like dummies, dreading to leave the daylight that isn't yours. Men and ghosts alike are as loath as you to see the last of the sun in its splendour. But the time comes and there's no stopping it. They all know it, few of them like it. Enough. You are done for. So now to the work in hand.

She claps her hands, whereupon mummied dwarfs appear at the door and quickly carry out their orders

Come along, you dingy, podgy creatures. There's mischief here to do, as much as you could wish. Put the gold-horned altar in its place, lay the shining axe on its silver edge. Fill the water jugs. There'll be black and filthy blood enough to wash away. Lay the rich carpet here in the sand for the royal victim to kneel on and then be wrapped in and buried with dignity, headless though she be.

PANTHALIS

The queen is standing apart and aloof, thinking her thoughts. But the girls are wilting like mown grass in a meadow. Being the oldest of them, I think it my sacred duty to have a word with you, you the ancient one, who are wise and experienced and seemingly well-disposed, notwithstanding the mistaken and brainless way these women received you. Tell me then of any means of escape you know.

PHORKYAS

The answer is easy. It depends on the queen and her alone, whether her life should be saved and your lives too, thrown in as extras. But resolution is called for now and the speediest possible.

CHORUS

Most venerable of the fates, wisest of sibyls, stay your golden shears and save our lives. Already we feel our limbs hanging, swinging wretchedly, when we'd sooner be dancing with them and then resting in our lovers' arms.

HELEN

Leave them to their panic. I feel no fear at all, I feel only the pain. But if you offer a way of escape, you have our gratitude. I know the wise and circumspect can often make the impossible possible. Come, tell us what it is.

CHORUS

Yes, tell us, tell us quickly, how we ever shall elude these nasty snares that threaten us like necklaces that tighten. We can feel it coming now, that breathless, choking feeling only Rhea, the mother-goddess, can protect us from in mercy.

PHORKYAS

Have you the patience to hear my story quietly? There's much to tell. It can't be told in a minute.

CHORUS

Patience, of course, we have. So long as we listen, we live.

PHORKYAS

A man who stays at home and guards his treasures, keeps his

palace walls in good repair and roofs it thoroughly against the rain can look forward to prosperity and a long life. But if he carelessly, irresponsibly, takes himself off, he won't find the old place the same when he returns. He may even find it destroyed.

HELEN

What is the point of these sententious sayings now? Stirring unhappy thoughts. Say what you have to say.

PHORKYAS

No reproach is intended. I'm speaking of what has happened. Menelaus roamed the sea from bay to bay as a pirate, raiding island or mainland as he chose, and bringing the booty home that is piled up here indoors. Ten long years he spent at Ilium. How many years on his way home I cannot say. But how is it now with this great house and estate of Tyndareus? How is it up and down his kingdom?

HELEN

Are you so inveterate a fault-finder that you can't open your mouth without showing it?

PHORKYAS

North of Sparta there is hill country that has lain neglected for a long, long time. The Taygetos range stands behind it, where our Eurotas has its source, a merry brook at first and now this broad stream flowing down the valley with its reed-beds and these swans of yours. Back there in the hills a bold race of invaders from the Cimmerian north have quietly settled in and built a stronghold unassailable, and from there they harry the country round about just as they choose.

HELEN

You mean they did all this? It seems impossible.

PHORKYAS

Well, they had time enough. It must be twenty years.

HELEN

Have they a leader? Are they united? Or just robbers?

PHORKYAS

Not robbers. They have a leader. He came down on us once, but I have no quarrel with him. He might have taken all we had, but he was content with little, a few presents. He didn't say they were tribute.

HELEN

What does he look like?

PHORKYAS

Not bad at all. I quite liked him. He's free and easy, a good figure. He has more sense than most of your Greeks. You call them barbarians, but I doubt if any of them are as savage as your men often were at Ilium. I think he's generous. I'd be prepared to trust him. And then the castle he's built. Oh, you should see his castle! A different thing from what your ancestors threw together, rudely piling blocks of stone one on another like cyclops. There everything is vertical and horizontal, and planned. Seen from outside, it soars to heaven, straight, poised, smooth as steel. The thought of scaling it unthinkable. And inside, spacious courtyards, enclosed with buildings of all kinds, for all purposes, pillars and arches big and little, balconies, galleries, interesting inside and out. And coats-of-arms.

CHORUS

What are coats-of-arms?

PHORKYAS

Ajax had a coiled snake on his shield. You all have seen it. The seven against Thebes also had figures on their shields, rich and significant ones. Moon and stars in the night-sky, goddesses and heroes, ladders, swords, torches, and whatever else threatens and assails a beleaguered city. Our heroes have always had the same, dating from long ago, very colourful, lions, eagles, beak and claws, buffalo horns, wings, roses, peacocks' tails, and strips of colour gold and black and silver, blue and red. They have them hanging in their halls, row upon row, halls of endless size, wonderful for you to dance in.

CHORUS

Are there dancers there?

PHORKYAS

The very best, blond and gay, and scented with youth as Paris was scented for Helen.

HELEN

You forget your role completely. Finish what you have to say.

PHORKYAS

It is for you to finish and say a resolute yes. At once I'll take you, transport you, to that castle.

CHORUS

Oh, say the word, the little word, and save us all.

HELEN

What? Have I reason to fear that Menelaus would go the length of treating me cruelly, brutally?

PHORKYAS

Have you forgotten what he did to Deiphobus who after his brother Paris was slain took you himself, risking the consequences, and you were happy together. He cut off his nose and ears and went on mutilating him, stopping at nothing. It was a horror to witness.

HELEN

If he did that, it was on my account he did it.

PHORKYAS

Yes, and it'll be on his account that he'll do it to you. Beauty is indivisible. Whoever has wholly possessed it would sooner destroy it with a curse than share it.

Trumpets are heard. The chorus is startled

Note how the blare of the trumpets tears your ears and tears your very insides. This is how jealousy tears the heart of a man who cannot forget what once was his and now is lost to him.

CHORUS

Can't you hear the horns blowing? Can't you see the flashing arms?

PHORKYAS

Welcome, lord and master, I am ready to give account.

CHORUS

But what about us?

PHORKYAS

You know already. First you'll see her death. Then yours will follow inside. There is no help for it.

Pause

HELEN

My mind is made up now what next I have to do. Something tells me you are not a friendly spirit. I fear that any help from you will prove our loss. No matter, I have decided to go to this castle with you. The rest is my affair. None shall know what the queen is thinking privately, deep in her secret heart. Now lead the way.

CHORUS

Oh how happy we are to go, with tripping foot, leaving death behind us, and coming a second time to a towering impenetrable fortress. Guard it as well as Troy was guarded, which only the basest cunning finally conquered.

Clouds spread, veiling the background and nearer objects too

But, sisters, what is this? Look about you. Wasn't the weather bright? And now mists are streaking up from sacred Eurotas. The beautiful rushy shore is blotted out and the swans too that were swimming together so freely, gently, proudly.

But I can hear them calling. It must be that. Calling a harsh distant call foretelling death, they say. Oh what if instead of the promised rescue it says we shall perish, we with our lovely long white swan-necks and our swan-begotten mistress too.

The mist has covered everything. We can't see one another. Whatever is happening? Are we walking or are we floating, barely touching the ground? Can you see anything? Can that be Hermes hovering in front with his golden staff, bidding us return to Hades, that grey cheerless place filled and overfilled with intangible forms, and eternally empty?

Yes, the mist is suddenly lifting on a gloomy scene, walls dark grey, dark brown, starkly confronting us, blocking the view. Is it a courtyard? Is it a deep pit? Dreadful in any case. Sisters, we are captives again, as captive as ever.

COURTYARD OF A CASTLE
Surrounded by rich and fantastic medieval buildings

PANTHALIS

Just like women, this snatching at conclusions foolishly. A prey to the passing moment or any shift of weather. Good luck or bad luck, you can't take either with calmness. One of you always contradicting another, then others contradicting her. Whether in joy or pain you laugh and lament on the selfsame note. But now be quiet and wait to hear the decision our noble mistress comes to for herself and for us.

HELEN

Where are you, Pythoness, or whatever your name is? Come out from behind these gloomy castle vaults. If you went in to tell your wonderful hero of my arrival and ensure me a welcome, thank you. Take me to him without delay. I am weary of wandering. Rest is what I want.

PANTHALIS

There's no one to be seen, lady, not anywhere. That ugly thing has disappeared. She may be still in the mist we came out of so suddenly, somehow, without even taking a step. Or she may be astray in this labyrinth of a castle – it seems like several turned into one – seeking her master to ask him about receiving you. But look, all at once there's a lively commotion of servants flitting about up there in the galleries, at the windows and doorways. It points to a formal reception, welcoming you.

CHORUS

My heart leaps up. Oh look, a procession of young people coming down the stairs, so charming, so decorous, so measured. Who can have ordered it? And assembled it so quickly? What shall I most admire in these handsome boys? Their graceful walk, their locks of hair, their shining brows, their cheeks as red as peaches, and as downy? I'd love to bite them, but dare not when I think in a similar case – oh horror –

981

of the mouth that was filled with ashes. But here they come, the beauties. What can they be carrying? Steps to a throne, carpet and chair, a canopy embroidered, drawn slowly like wreaths of cloud over the queen who, on invitation, has mounted the throne. Move forward and range yourselves in rows on the steps. Blessed, thrice blessed, be this stately ceremony.

What the chorus says here has been enacted step by step. When the long procession of squires and pages are all down, Faust appears at the top of the stairs, dressed like a medieval courtier, and slowly descends

PANTHALIS *observing him closely*

Unless these are passing gifts, lent by the gods for a brief space only, as is their way, this man's admirable figure, his lofty bearing, and agreeable presence will ensure him success in everything he undertakes, whether in serious battle or in the lighter warfare with fair women. I must say I prefer him to many I have seen that were thought most highly of. Now I see the prince reverently advancing with slow and solemn step. O queen, turn your head.

FAUST *approaching, with a man in chains*

Instead of the solemn words of welcome appropriate to the occasion I bring you this man in chains, who by failing in his duty made me fail in mine. Kneel down here and confess your fault to this greatest of women. Here is a man with a rare gift of seeing, appointed to keep close watch from the tower on sky and land for anything that happens either here or in the valley or the hills beyond, the movement of flocks and herds, it may be, or the approach of an enemy. We protect the one and confront the other. But today, what a lapse! You came and he never reported it. We were unable to receive so great a guest with honour due. His life is forfeited. He would have already died the death he deserves save that it is for you, and only you, to punish or pardon at your discretion.

HELEN

This is a great dignity you confer on me, making me both judge and ruler. Perhaps tentatively, but I accept it and exercise the judge's duty to hear the accused. Let him speak.

LYNCEUS, THE WATCHMAN

Let me kneel and let me look, whether death or life awaits me. I am devoted utterly to this woman whom the gods have sent. Watching for the morning light with my eyes fixed on the east, suddenly by a miracle the sun came up in the south. It drew me away from everything else, the heights, the depths, the expanse of earth and sky. I looked only for her. I have eyes as keen as a lynx in a tree-top, but now I found myself fighting my way out of a deep, dark dream. Could I see a thing? No. Not the battlements, the tower, the gate. Such a goddess had come in sight. She dazzled me. I stood there and drank it in, forgetting my watchman's duty, forgetting to blow my horn. If this has aroused her scorn, I still see only her beauty.

HELEN

I cannot punish an offence when I was the cause of it. Oh what a relentless fate pursues me, making me turn men's hearts and heads so that they spare neither themselves nor anything else worth sparing. Abducting, seducing, fighting, shifting from place to place. Gods and demi-gods, heroes, yes, and phantoms dragged me about confusedly hither and thither. When there was only one of me, I caused trouble in the world. More trouble when there were two. Now that I am threefold, fourfold, it's one calamity after another. Set this good man free and let him depart. If a divinity turned his head, it's no disgrace.

FAUST

It amazes me, O queen, to see the sure marksman and the mark attained. I see the bow that sped the arrow and I see the man it pierced. And now comes arrow after arrow piercing me. I feel and hear the feathered missiles whirring everywhere around. What am I now? In an instant you make my staunchest followers rebellious, you make my very walls unsafe. I fear the army will now go over to you, the conquering, unconquered heroine. What can I do but give you myself and all that I vainly thought was mine. I lay myself at your feet and accept you unreservedly as the ruler who, the moment she appeared, assumed the throne.

LYNCEUS

Carrying a chest, followed by men also carrying chests

O queen, here I come again, a rich man begging, begging for a look. When I set eyes on you, I feel both poverty-stricken and fabulously rich. What was I before? What am I now? What can I now desire or do? What use is my keen sight when you on your throne defeat it? Out of the east we came. It was all up with the west. We were a multitude too vast to know how vast it was. If a man went down, another stepped in. A third was ready, lance in hand. There was always a hundred to replace one. Thousands might fall. It went unnoticed. We drove and smashed our way forward, conquering place after place. Where one day my word was law, the next day it was another's turn, robbing, plundering, spying in haste, carrying off the prettiest of the women and the best of the cattle and never leaving a horse behind. But I was on the look-out for rarities. What satisfied others was worthless to me. I was always after treasure, trusting my sharp vision, seeing into pockets, seeing through caskets. I acquired gold in heaps and wonderful jewels. Emeralds alone are fit for you to wear over your heart. Let oval pearls from the sea-floor hang from your ears. Your red cheeks would outshine rubies. So here I set these riches at your feet, the spoils of many a bloody fight. I've brought all these chests, but I have many more, hooped with iron. Let me be your follower and I'll fill your treasure vaults, because no sooner did you mount the throne than everything submitted to you – reason, wealth, power. All this that I clung to as mine now leaves me and is yours. I thought it valuable. Now it is no more to me than withered grass. But one happy glance from you will give it all its value back.

FAUST

Take away this load of yours, so boldly acquired. Be quick about it. No reward. No reprimand. Everything the castle contains is already hers. Any particular gift is superfluous. Go and assemble these treasures never seen before. Put their magnificence on display. Make our vaulted halls as bright as the sky, a paradise of living lifelessness. Roll flowered carpets everywhere as a soft flooring for her to tread. Let her eyes, which only the gods can meet, dwell on a scene of utmost brilliance.

LYNCEUS

Your orders, sir, are simply fun. They're little sooner said than done. Her beauty is of such command, it makes her mistress of the land. The army is abashed before her. Their hands are limp, their swords are blunted. The sun itself is cold and dull, compared with her. Beside the wonders of her face, all the rest is empty space. *off*

HELEN *to Faust*

I want to speak with you. But come up here. Take the ruler's seat beside me and make mine secure.

FAUST

First, O lady, allow me to do you homage on my knees, then kiss the hand that lifts me up. Confirm me as co-regent of your boundless realm and make me your worshipper, your servant, and your guardian all in one.

HELEN

I keep seeing and hearing things that surprise me, astonish me. And I have many questions to ask. But tell me first why the man's words felt so strange, so strange and at the same time so friendly. One sound seems to fit another. When a word has lodged in the ear, a second word follows and caresses it.

FAUST

If you like the way our people talk, you'll be delighted with their song. It will satisfy your ear and satisfy your mind. But the thing to do is to practise together at once. Conversing will encourage it, draw it out.

HELEN

Well, tell me then how I can speak that way.

FAUST

It's easy. Trust your heart. Your heart will say. And when it is so full you cannot bear it, you cast about and wonder –

HELEN

Who will share it.

FAUST

And now we neither look back nor before. The present is
our joy.

HELEN

What need we more?

FAUST

It is our all, our treasure, our domain. And as a pledge –

HELEN

I give my hand again.

CHORUS

Who would hold it against our mistress if she favours the lord
of the castle? You mustn't forget we're all captives, as we have
been again and again, what with the collapse of Troy and the
twists and trials of our endless journey.

Women, used to having men, may be experts, but they
can't be choosers. They take what comes and give the freedom of their luxurious bodies alike to a fair-haired shepherd
boy or a black and bristly faun.

They're getting closer and closer, leaning on one another,
shoulder to shoulder, knee to knee, hand in hand, rocking to
and fro on the great cushioned throne, not afraid of displaying their majesty's intimacy before the eyes of the people.

HELEN

I seem so far away, and yet so near. But here I am and happy
to say it.

FAUST

I tremble, I can hardly breathe, hardly speak. It's all a dream,
not of this world.

HELEN

I feel both done with and newly made, involved in you, true
to the unknown.

FAUST

Don't pry into our unique fate. Our duty is to life now, if only
for the moment.

PHORKYAS

Entering in haste

Spelling out your love-story, trifling with it, idling, dawdling, brooding over it. There's no time for that now. Can't you hear a thundering, a trumpeting? Your destruction is near. Menelaus is approaching with his hordes. Prepare for a bitter struggle. If they get hold of you, they'll mutilate you like Deiphobus. You'll pay for your escort. These light girls will tread the air, and the axe newly sharpened is waiting for her at the altar.

FAUST

Outrageous, this intrusion, jarring on my nerves. Even in time of danger I hate precipitancy. The handsomest of messengers looks ugly if his news is bad. You, the ugliest of all, take pleasure in bad news only. But it won't work this time. Go on shaking the air with your empty breath. There is no danger here. If there were, it would be no more than an idle threat.

Signals, explosions in the towers,
trumpets and clarions, martial music.
A powerful army marches past

FAUST

No, indeed. I'll show you at once my heroic generals assembled and united. A man who can't protect his lady to the utmost doesn't deserve her favour. (*to the generals, who detach themselves from their columns and step forward*) You young blossoms from the north, you the strength and flower of the south, meet the enemy with the suppressed fury that will ensure your victory. The army, clad in glittering steel, has shattered empire after empire. It makes the earth shake under its tread. Thunder echoes in its wake. We landed at Pylos. Old Nestor's days were past. The roving army broke up the little kingdoms. Push Menelaus back to the sea at once. There let him roam and lie in wait and plunder, following his destiny and his inclination, as before. The queen of Sparta bids me appoint you dukes. Lay your territories at her feet and reap the benefit from them. You Germans must defend the bays of Corinth. You Goths, Achaia with its hundred gullies. The Frankish army will move to Elis, the Saxons to Messenia, and the Normans will clean up the seas and make Argolis great. Then each of you can settle down, while keeping up a sharp defence. But Sparta, the queen's ancient seat, will preside over you all. She will see you severally enjoying life in a land where nothing lacks. You will look confidently to her for approval and for justice.

Faust comes down. The dukes form a circle round him, awaiting further instructions

CHORUS

Whoever desires to possess the fairest of women, let him be practical above all and see to his armoury. Flattery may have won him earth's topmost prize, but he won't hold it easily. Cunning men will entice her away from him. Brigands will boldly carry her off. Let him give thought to this.

Accordingly I commend our ruler. I rate him higher than others, when I see him boldly making shrewd alliances, getting strong men on his side, ready to obey his orders instantly, each of them acting in his own interest, earning his overlord's thanks, and bringing glory to both.

Who can snatch her away from him now? She is his and he is strong. Let him keep her, as we have good reason to say, seeing that he is protecting us along with her behind his strong walls and with his mighty army in the field.

FAUST

The gifts I have bestowed on these men are great – a rich country for each of them. But let them go now. We hold the central position. They will vie with one another in protecting this all-but-island, linked to Europe's furthest mountains by only a slight chain of hills, and circled by the running waves. The land of lands – may it give happiness to all the tribes – belongs now to my queen, whom it has known from the moment she broke, shining, through her shell among the Eurotas's whispering reeds and dazzled her great mother and her brothers and sisters. This land looks only to you. It offers you its flowering wealth. The whole earth is yours, but surely you put your home country first. And though the jagged summits of the mountain range are barren in the chilly sunlight, the rock is greening in patches and goats there are nibbling scanty nourishment. Springs begin and join with others as they come cascading down. Already the ravines, the slopes, the meadows are green and in the endlessly broken plain flocks of woolly sheep are grazing. Scattered cattle come cautiously to the precipice edge, but there is shelter for all in many rocky caves, where the god Pan protects them. Nature nymphs live in cool moist places in the bushy clefts, and trees crowd trees with their branch-work reaching up aspiringly to higher regions. This is the ancient forest. The mighty oaks stand stiffly, zigzagging in their contours, while the gentle maples, rich in sweet sap, rise clear and carry their weight lightly. In the quiet shade the mother-ewes' warm milk is always there for the lambs and the children. Fruit is not far to seek. Crops ripen in the fields and honey can be found dripping from a hollow trunk. This is where well-being is hereditary, cheeks and lips ever fresh and happy. Each one is immortal in his place. They are healthy. They are contented. And so in perfect days the child grows to manhood. We are amazed. We ask and ask again, whether these are men or gods. When Apollo lived among shepherds he was so like them you couldn't distinguish. Where nature rules unchallenged, all the worlds are interlocked.

Sitting down beside her

This is what we two have achieved. Let us put the past behind us. Remember you are sprung from the greatest of the gods and in a special sense belong to the early world. No fortress must enclose you. This Arcadia lies not far from Sparta in all its eternal youth and vigour for us to dwell in with delight. If you agreed to live on such a heavenly soil you would reach the happiest consummation. Our thrones would turn into arbours. Let us accept this Arcadian joy and freedom.

[ARCADIA]

The scene is transformed. A row of rocky caves with closed arbours in front of them. A shady grove of trees extending to the foot of the cliff. Faust and Helen are not on the scene. The chorus are lying around, sleeping

PHORKYAS

How long the girls have been asleep I cannot say. Nor can I say whether they have seen in dreams what I have seen before my eyes. And so I'll wake them and give these young folk a surprise. And you too, you greybeards, sitting down there, waiting to see what comes of all these miracles. Up with you, up. Shake off your sleepiness. Don't blink so. Open your eyes, and listen to me.

CHORUS

Go on then, tell us, tell us what fantastic things have happened. Most of all we'd like to hear what surpasses all believing. Bored to death we are with nothing else but all these rocks to stare at.

PHORKYAS

Bored to death already, are you, when your eyes are hardly opened? Listen then, our lord and lady have withdrawn into these arbours, finding there and in the caves and grottoes a secure retreat, a lovers' idyll.

CHORUS

What, in there?

PHORKYAS

Cut off from the world, making me their sole attendant. No small honour, but I acted as became me, looked away, searched about for roots and mosses, being versed in nature's lore, and left them to themselves.

CHORUS

You talk as if there was a world in there, a world of woods and meadows, brooks and lakes. What rigmarole is this?

PHORKYAS

Certainly there is, you novices. Depths unexplored, halls

upon halls, courts upon courts, as I cunningly discovered. But suddenly a burst of laughter echoed through the spacious caverns, and behold, there was a boy there, jumping to and fro between the father and the mother. Such a cooing and caressing, shouts and shrieks of fun and folly. Deafening. I could hardly stand it.

He was naked; like a genius, but wingless; like a faun, but nowise brutish. When he jumped, the ground, reacting, flung him high into the air. He touched the vaulted roof the third time.

His mother, growing anxious, shouted: Jump, jump as often and as freely as you want to, but no flying. Flying is forbidden. And his father warned him likewise, saying: In the earth lies the force that throws you upwards. Touch the earth even with your toe, you'll be strengthened like the son of earth, Antaeus. The boy hopped up the rock, sprang from one brink to another like a ball bouncing freely. Suddenly, then, he disappeared in a crevice, and it seemed as if we'd lost him. His mother grieved, his father soothed her, anxiously I shrugged my shoulders. But soon he was back again. And what a surprise! Were there treasures hidden down there? He was now finely dressed in robes striped and flowered, tassels hanging from his arms and ribbons on his breast. In his hand a golden lyre, just like a little Phoebus. He came, all serene, to the rock-edge overhanging us. Wonderful. His parents embraced in their excitement. Round his head there was a halo. Where it came from, hard to say. Was it gold he was wearing? Was it mental energy flaming? Announcing, as he stood there in his boyhood, he was master-to-be of the beautiful, one through whose limbs the eternal melodies sounded. This is how you'll see him, this is how you'll hear him, to your uttermost amazement.

CHORUS

You call this a miracle, you Cretan woman? Have you never heeded the lesson of the poets, never listened to Ionia's, or Hellas's, wealth of ancient legends of gods and heroes?

Nothing happens nowadays but is a sorry echo of the glorious ancestral past. Your story doesn't compare with the lovely fable – a fable more credible than truth – of the son of Maia.

No sooner born, this neat and healthy child, than his gossipy nurses, little suspecting, swaddled him in spotless napkins, wound him in precious purple, but the rogue in his infant strength and skill slily extricated his supple limbs, leaving the tight swathings where they lay, like the butterfly slipping out of its stiff chrysalis and spreading its wings to fly at will in the sunny atmosphere.

This is he who, nimblest of the nimble, quickly showed by his artful devices that he was the spirit-patron of thieves and rogues and all self-seekers. He lost no time in stealing the sea-god's trident, Ares's sword out of the sheath, Phoebus's bow and arrow, Hephaestus's tongs. Even Father Zeus's lightning he would have taken, but for fear of the fire. He tripped and beat Eros in a wrestling match and filched Venus's girdle while she was fondling him.

Charming melodious stringed music is heard in the cavern. They all give heed to it and are moved by it. The music continues in full till the pause indicated below

PHORKYAS

Listen to these sweet sounds. Rid yourselves of fable and let the old gods go. They have no meaning for us. We demand something better now. What moves the heart must come from the heart. *She withdraws to the rocks*

CHORUS

If you, monster that you are, respond to these accents, we are moved to tears by them and revived. When our inner light shines, we can dispense with the sun, finding in our hearts all that the outer world withholds.

Helen, Faust, Euphorion in the above-described costume

EUPHORION

If you hear children singing, you share the singing with them.

If you see me dance in measure, you are my parents and your hearts dance too.

HELEN

When love brings the right pair together, there is human happiness. Make it three and the rapture is divine.

FAUST

Nothing is lacking then, I am yours and you are mine. We stand united. Might it always be so.

CHORUS

Many years of happiness with this shining boy are promised them. Oh how touching!

EUPHORION

Let me hop and jump. I long to fly up into the sky. I can't wait.

FAUST

Careful, careful. Don't be rash, lest you meet with disaster and ruin us all.

EUPHORION

I won't stay on the ground. Let go of my hands and hair and dress. They're mine, aren't they?

HELEN

Oh think whose you are, think how it would hurt us to lose what the three of us have won.

CHORUS

Won, yes, but not for long, I fear.

HELEN AND FAUST

For the love of your parents keep this violence in check. Stay here in this rural spot. You adorn it.

EUPHORION

I'll do it for your sake. (*moving about among the chorus and inducing them to dance*) I float lightly in this gay company. Is the time right? And the step?

HELEN

Yes, excellent. Lead these beauties in a formal round.

FAUST

I wish it was over. These antics make me uneasy.

Euphorion and the chorus, singing and dancing, move in involved patterns

CHORUS

When you move your arms in that lovely way and shake your bright locks and trail your foot so lightly and twine your limbs, you win all our hearts. You've reached the goal.

Pause

EUPHORION

You are fleet-footed deer, suddenly appearing, close at hand, inviting play. I am the huntsman, you are the game.

CHORUS

If you want to catch us, you needn't exert yourself. After all, our only wish is to embrace you, you fair creature.

EUPHORION

Off you go through the trees, over rough ground. If a thing comes easy, it repels me. I can only enjoy what I take by force.

HELEN AND FAUST

What exuberance! What rashness! No hope for moderation. Do I hear horns blowing across the woods and valleys? And this shrieking. It shouldn't be.

CHORUS *running in, one by one*

He ran past us, he despised us. He just seized the wildest one and is dragging her here.

EUPHORION *carrying a young girl*

Here I come dragging this sturdy girl along to enjoy her with violence. She resists me, but I kiss her mouth and press her to my breast and show her who is master.

GIRL

Let go of me. There's strength of mind in me too and a will as strong as yours. You won't soon overcome it. If you think I'm beaten, you're being over-confident. Hang on, you fool, and I'll burn you just for fun.

She bursts into flame and soars up

Follow me into airy spaces. Follow me into close caverns. Catch me if you can.

EUPHORION *shaking off the last of the flames*

I feel shut in among these rocks and bushes. This is no place for youth and vigour like mine. I hear winds and waves, but far, far away. I want to be near them. *He runs farther and farther up the rock*

HELEN, FAUST, AND CHORUS

Do you want to rival the chamois? You might fall. We shudder at the thought.

EUPHORION

I must go on mounting and enlarging the view. Now I know where I am. In the middle of the island, Pelops's island, close to continent and ocean.

CHORUS

Can't you stay peaceably in these wooded hills? We can search for vines, rows of vines on the slopes, figs and golden apples too. Oh stay, and be good, in this sweet country.

EUPHORION

Are you dreaming of peace? Dream if you like. The password is war and victory, sounding on and on.

CHORUS

Whoever in peace-time wants war back again must have abandoned all hope.

EUPHORION

May it inspire all the fighters this land has produced, men free and utterly fearless in danger after danger, careless of their lives, filled with unquenchable fervour.

CHORUS

Look up. See how high he's climbed. And yet he doesn't seem small. He looks harnessed for victory in bronze and steel.

EUPHORION

No walls, no ramparts. Let each be sure of himself. A man's stronghold is a stout heart. If you want to live in freedom, go into the battlefield lightly armed. Women will become Amazons, children heroes.

CHORUS

Sacred poesy, let it mount to heaven. Let it shine, the fairest of stars, receding and receding, yet still reaching us and still delighting us.

EUPHORION
No, I'm not a child. I'm a young man armed. In company
with the strong, the free, the brave I've shown my worth.
Now off we go to tread the road to glory.

HELEN AND FAUST
Barely ushered into life, new to the joyful light of day, you
climb dizzy stairs, seeking space and its dangers. Are we
nothing to you? Was our lovely union a dream?

EUPHORION
Do you hear the thundering out at sea, re-echoing in the
valleys, army against army, by sea and land, onset upon onset,
pain and torment? Once and for all, death is imperative.

HELEN, FAUST, AND CHORUS
Oh, horror! Must it be?

EUPHORION
Should I look on from afar? No, I must share the suffering.

HELEN, FAUST, AND CHORUS
High spirits and jeopardy. A tragic fate.

EUPHORION
Nothing shall stop me. And now, see, a pair of wings unfolding. I must go. Don't rob me of this.

*He throws himself aloft. His garments sustain him for a moment. His
head is illuminated, trailing a beam of light*

CHORUS
Icarus, Icarus. Oh the pity of it.

*A handsome youth collapses at his parents' feet. In his death he resembles
a known personage, but his mortal part disappears immediately. The
aureole mounts comet-like. Dress, cloak, and lyre are left lying*

HELEN AND FAUST
Cruel torment follows swiftly after joy.

EUPHORION *voice from below*
Mother, don't desert me in the dark kingdom. *pause*

CHORUS *elegy*
Desert you, no, wherever you may be. We believe we recognize you. When you take leave of life, all our hearts go with

you; not so much lamenting as envying your fate. In good days as in bad your song and your courage were supreme.

Born into happiness, with high lineage and health and strength, you soon lost control, your early bloom scattered. Yours was a keen eye to view the world, a fellow-feeling for any warmth of heart, a passion for fair women, and a poetic voice all your own.

But nothing could stop you. Of your own accord you rushed into the fatal net, alienating law and order. At the last your noble ambition showed your integrity. You aimed high, but you failed.

Failed, but who succeeds? A vain question. Fate gives no answer to it on the day of doom when all are suffering and silent. Nevertheless raise your bowed heads and sing new songs. Earth has always begotten them and will beget them again.

Complete pause. The music ceases

HELEN *to Faust*

An old saw says that beauty and happiness cannot stay united. Sooner or later they part. And to my sorrow this is now borne out in me. The bonds of life are broken, and so in grief and pain I say goodbye, throwing myself in your arms for the last time. Persephone, receive my boy and me. *She embraces Faust. Her bodily part disappears, leaving the dress and veil in his arms*

PHORKYAS *to Faust*

Cling to what is left. The dress, keep hold of it. Demons already are plucking at it, eager to drag it down to the underworld. Don't let them. It may not be the divinity you lost, but it is divine. Make the most of this inestimable favour. Rise aloft. It will sweep you through the ether, above all that is commonplace, for the rest of your days. We shall meet again, far, very far, from here.

Helen's garments dissolve into cloud, surround Faust, raise him aloft, and pass with him

PHORKYAS *picks up Euphorion's clothing and his lyre, steps forward,
lifts them high, and speaks*
A lucky find, no matter what. The fire and flame is gone,
I know. But I'm not sorry for the world. There's plenty of
room for poets still, and poets' guilds and poets' grudges.
I can't supply the talent, but at least I can lend the costume.
She sits down at the front of the stage, beside a pillar

PANTHALIS
Be quick now, girls, are we not rid of the incubus, the spell
this old Thessalian hag threw over us all. Rid too of the
tinkling music that was so jumbled, confusing the ear and,
worse, confusing the mind. Down now to Hades where the
queen with solemn step has gone already. Her faithful servants must follow her without delay. We shall find her at the
throne of the inscrutable one.

CHORUS
Queens to be sure, are all right anywhere. Even in Hades
they're up at the top associating proudly with equals, intimate
with Persephone herself. But we background figures, deep in
fields of asphodel, among barren willows and rows of poplar,
how are we to pass the time? Squeaking and twittering like
bats, a dismal, ghostly sound?

PANTHALIS
Whoever neither makes his name nor strives for higher things
belongs to the elements. So away with you. For myself I crave
to be with my mistress, the queen, again. Not merit only,
faithful allegiance can preserve our person. *off*

ALL
We are returned to the light of day. Persons no longer, we feel
it and know it. But back to Hades, never. Living nature claims
us. We spirits have our claim on her.

PART OF THE CHORUS
In these thousands of branches that sway and tremble, rustle
and whisper in the air, we gently, playfully, coax the springs of
life up from the roots into the wavering twigs. We deck them
lavishly with leaves, and then with blossoms, to grow and
thrive unchecked. When the ripe fruits fall to the ground,

people and cattle come at once in busy crowds to gather or nibble them, and everyone in sight is bowed to earth just as men bowed to the earliest gods.

SECOND PART

We stay close to these rocky cliffs and the smooth reflecting water. We move caressingly in gentle vibrations over the surface. And here we listen for every sound, bird-song, or fluting in the reeds, even Pan's dreadful shout. We always have an echo ready. A rustling sound. We rustle back. Thunder, then our thunder rolls and mightily repeats twice, three times, up to ten times.

A THIRD PART

Sisters, we, more mobile-minded, hasten away with the running brooks, drawn by the rich-looking lines of distant hills. Down and down we go meandering, watering first the meadows, then the pastures, then the gardens round the houses. Those pointed cypresses our waymark, towering above the landscape and the shoreline and the mirror of the sea.

A FOURTH PART

You others may go where you like. But we whisperingly haunt this hillside given wholly to vineyards. Here at any time we can see the vinedresser labouring devotedly for a dubious result. With hoe or with spade, heaping, trimming, binding, he makes his prayer to the gods, but first and most usefully to the sungod. Bacchus, the weakling, cares little about his faithful servants. He just rests or lolls in caves and arbours, trifling with a young faun, and eternally finding what he needs to sustain him in his tipsy reveries in skins and jugs and suchlike to right and left of him in the cool grottoes. But when the gods, and Helios above all, have done the airing and the wetting, the warming and the baking, and filled the cornucopia with all the grapes it will hold, then suddenly, where before there was only the solitary labourer, a great stirring of life begins, a rustling in every vine and a going from one to the next. A creaking of baskets, a clattering of pails, a groaning under the loads all on their way to the great vat and the dance of the winepressers. And so the sacred wealth of grapes is rudely trampled to a horrid, foaming, splashing mess. Now the brazen clash of cymbals assails the ear, announcing the mysterious arrival of Dionysus with his following of goat-footed satyrs swinging their women, goat-footed too. Silenus's long-eared beast comes in with its outrageous braying. No respecting here of persons. The cloven hoof treads down all decency. Your senses are in a whirl, your ears are deafened. Drunkards feel their way to the cup, their heads and bellies filled to bursting. Apprehensions here and there only aggravate the tumult. The old skins must be emptied to make way for the new wine.

Curtain. Phorkyas rises to giant proportions, then steps down from her buskins, removes mask and veil, and reveals herself as Mephistopheles, ready, if need be, to supply an epilogue

ACT IV

HIGH MOUNTAINS, ROCKY PEAKS

A cloud comes up, attaches itself, settles on a ledge of rock, and divides

FAUST *emerging*
Here at this outermost mountain-brink where, stepping cautiously, I can look sheer down into deepest depths of solitude, I relinquish the cloud-chariot that conveyed me gently over land and sea through the serene atmosphere and now, slowly disengaging itself, not scattering, begins to move eastward in a single mass. My eye follows it closely with astonishment, to see it dividing, shifting, changing with a wave-like motion. But surely now it is taking shape. Yes, there is no doubt of it. A wonderful giant form, a woman's form, reclining on a sunlit couch. Divine-looking. Like Juno, or like Leda, or it might be Helen. Majestic and how lovely too, but quivering to the sight. Already it has broken up and

comes to rest across the eastern sky, a formless pile, like distant dazzling ice peaks, mirroring for me the deep meaning of those fleeting days.

But what is this delicate, shining wisp of cloud that comes and woos me, cool to the brow, refreshing, and now lightly, hesitantly, rises higher and higher and gathers into one? Am I deluded or do I see a rapturous image of what I prized and cherished most in youth and lost so long ago? A wave of my earliest emotions sweeps through me. Dawn-love it is. That buoyancy and zest. The first look, so quickly felt, so little understood, which, if one could only keep it, would outshine everything in worth. Beauty of soul, the essence of it, the gracious image shows me now. And it holds. It mounts into the higher air and takes the best of me along with it.

A seven-league boot clumps down. A second boot follows. Mephistopheles dismounts. The boots stride off

MEPHISTOPHELES
That was some walking, if you ask me. But what's your idea? Dismounting in the midst of these horrors, these ghastly, grinning rocks? I know them well enough, though not just here, because, strictly speaking, this used to be the floor of hell.

FAUST
You're never at a loss for crazy mythology. Now you're at it again.

MEPHISTOPHELES *solemnly*
When the Lord God – and I know why – threw us out of the air into the lowest depths of hell where a central fire was blazing eternally, we had plenty of illumination, but we were in a very crowded and awkward spot. The devils all began to puff from above and below to put the fire out. There was an awful acid stink of sulphur everywhere and a pressure of gas so stupendous, that it burst through the flat crust of earth, thick as it was, with a great bang. And now it's a different story. What was once the bottom is now the top. They base on this the very theories they need to stand things on their heads. Anyway we escaped that hot imprisonment under the earth

and gained the freedom and dominion of the air. An open secret, well-preserved, and not revealed to the world till later.

FAUST

Those mountains, noble as they are, have nothing to say to me. I ask neither why nor whence. When nature established herself, she neatly rounded off the earthly sphere, assembling the rocks and the hills, taking her pleasure in peaks and chasms, and leading down by easy stages to the foothills and the lowlands, where all is greenery and growth. Nature can rejoice in this without needing your wild upheavals.

MEPHISTOPHELES

That's what you say. You think it's all clear. But those who were there know better. I was there myself and saw the abyss boiling and flaming, and Moloch with his hammer shattering the rocks and hurling mountain-fragments all over the place. The land is still littered with these erratic blocks. Who can explain the force that hurled them? The philosophers can do nothing with it. The rock is there and there we let it lie after cudgelling our brains to no purpose. But the common people in their decency have always understood and are not to be shaken in their belief. They know it's a miracle, and Satan gets the credit. This is the crutch of faith that brings the traveller hobbling to the Devil's Rock and the Devil's Bridge.

FAUST

Well, it's useful to have a glimpse of nature from the devil's point of view.

MEPHISTOPHELES

Let nature be as it may, what do I care? This is a point of honour: the devil was in on it. We are the ones to achieve greatness — tumult, violence, madness. Behold the sign. But, nonsense apart, is there nothing that satisfies you on this earth of ours? You're so hard to please. You've surveyed the kingdoms of the world and the glory of them in all their vastness. Is there anything at all you'd like to do?

FAUST

There is indeed. A great thing has taken hold of me. Guess what it is.

MEPHISTOPHELES

That's easy. Me, I'd seek out one of those big cities, with people scrabbling for food in the heart of it, twisted narrow streets, pointed roofs, a smallish market-place all cabbages and carrots and onions, butchers' stalls infested with flies, feasting on the fat joints. Plenty of bustle, plenty of stinks, all the day long. Then I'd have open squares and broad streets for my upper-class pretensions, and finally endless suburbs, unchecked by city walls, and there I'd ride around in a carriage, up and down, in all the noisy throng of human ant-heaps. And wherever I went, driving or on horseback, I'd be the centre of attraction, honoured by thousands, hundreds of thousands.

FAUST

That wouldn't do for me. One likes to see the people prospering and living well in their fashion, and even studying and getting educated. But in the end it only makes rebels of them.

MEPHISTOPHELES

Then I'd proudly build myself a fancy castle on some pleasant site with lovely gardens, woods, fields, hills, and lawns all round it, rows of trees and velvety turf, straight walks and shady seats well-planned, waterfalls tumbling over rocks, fountains of every kind, impressive here, petty and piddling in many another place. Then I'd build some intimate little cottages to house my pretty ladies and I'd spend endless time there in sweet seclusion. I said ladies, because I always think of them in the plural.

FAUST

Vulgar and up-to-date. Like Sardanapalus.

MEPHISTOPHELES

How is anyone to guess what you want? No doubt something vast and bold. You've just been travelling through the upper air, so I daresay you want the moon.

FAUST

Far from it. This earth is roomy enough for great deeds. I mean to astonish the world. And I have the energy for it.

MEPHISTOPHELES

So it's fame you want. This comes from the heroic company you've kept.

FAUST

Not fame. Fame is nothing. I want action. I want property, power.

MEPHISTOPHELES

There'll be plenty of poets to sing your achievement to posterity and perpetuate your folly.

FAUST

What should you know of man's desire? You simply haven't it in you. With a nature like yours, all hatred and bitterness, how should you grasp the human need?

MEPHISTOPHELES

Have your way then. Let me hear the extent of your latest craze.

FAUST

The open sea arrested my attention. I watched it and saw how it mounted and mounted and then relaxed and spilt its storm-waves along the level shore. And this annoyed me. A man of free mind, who respects the rights of others, is always uneasy when he sees arrogance asserting itself immoderately, violently. And it was like this here. I thought it might be an accident and I looked again more closely. The waves halted, rolled back, and withdrew from their proud conquest. The hour will come and they'll do it all over again.

MEPHISTOPHELES *to the audience*

Nothing new in that for me. I've seen it for hundreds and thousands of years.

FAUST *excitedly*

The water comes creeping up, barren in itself, to spread its barrenness wherever it goes, in every hole and corner. Now it has flooded that desolate stretch of land and there waves upon waves run riot. Then they recede and nothing has been gained. It nearly drives me mad to see the elements so uncontrolled, wasting their energy so blindly. And here my spirit goes all out and boldly resolves to make this its battle-ground and prove itself the master.

And it is possible. With its fluid nature water can slip past any hillock. However much it rages, a slight rise can divert it, a slight drop can pull it down. Seeing this, I quickly made my plans: Get permission to exclude the imperious ocean from the shore, set limits to its watery expanse and force it back on itself. What satisfaction that would be! Step by step I thought it out. This is my wish. Help me to achieve it.

Distant drums and martial music from behind the audience, on the right

MEPHISTOPHELES
I see no difficulty there. Do you hear those drums in the distance?

FAUST
Yes, war again. No man in his senses would welcome it.

MEPHISTOPHELES
War or peace, it's sensible to try and get what you can out of it. We all watch for opportunities that favour us. Well, Faust, the opportunity's here. Seize it.

FAUST
Spare me this enigmatic jargon. Come to the point. What do you mean? Out with it.

MEPHISTOPHELES
I couldn't help observing *en route* that our worthy emperor is in great straits. You know what he's like. When we were entertaining him and put that paper money in his hands he thought the whole world was his. He'd been given his crown early in life and he drew the false conclusion, very comfort-able for himself, that it was both easy and desirable to rule the empire and have his fun at the same time.

FAUST
A gross mistake. A ruler must find his reward in rulership. His heart is filled with a strong will and purpose, but no man must be able to fathom it. Only his intimates may share the secret. Then when the work is done, the whole world will be amazed,

and he will retain his supreme authority and prestige. Self-indulgence debases.

MEPHISTOPHELES

He's not like that. He indulged himself, and how! Meanwhile the empire lapsed into anarchy. Great and small at one another's throats on every side. Brothers banishing and murdering brothers. Castles warring with castles, cities with cities, guilds with nobles, bishops with chapters and people. Merely exchange glances with a man and you were enemies. Your life wasn't safe in a church. It was all up with a merchant or journeyman, if he ventured beyond the city gates. People got bolder and bolder. You had to stand up for yourself, or you were a goner. Well, things dragged on that way.

FAUST

Dragged on, hobbled, fell down, got up, tumbled again, and rolled to a stop.

MEPHISTOPHELES

And you couldn't complain about it either. Everyone had his rights and was able to assert them. Any juvenile could play the adult. But in the end, the best people, the sound people, got fed up. They roused themselves in a body and said: Whoever can bring the country to order can rule it. The emperor can't and won't. Let us elect a new emperor who'll revive the empire, give us security, and wed peace with justice in a newly created world.

FAUST

That sounds like the priesthood talking.

MEPHISTOPHELES

Priests it was. Seeing to their own fat bellies. They had more to lose than any. The revolt spread and became respectable. And our emperor, whom we made happy, has withdrawn to this spot, perhaps to fight his last fight.

FAUST

I'm sorry for him. He was so kind and open.

MEPHISTOPHELES

Come. While there's life, there's hope. We'll have a look. Suppose we rescue him from this narrow pass. Once out of it, he'll be safe henceforth. Who knows which way the dice will fall. And if he has the luck, he'll soon have a following.

They cross the lower hills and inspect the disposition of the army in the valley. Drums and martial music are heard below

MEPHISTOPHELES

I see the position is well chosen. We'll join them and the victory's won.

FAUST

What's the good of it? Trickery, illusion, nothing else.

MEPHISTOPHELES

No, military cunning to win battles. Remember your purpose and keep your mind on big issues. If we can restore throne and country to the emperor, all you will have to do will be to kneel down and be presented with an endless shoreline in fief.

FAUST

You've done so much, so why not go in and win a battle?

MEPHISTOPHELES

Not me. You'll win it. You're the commander-in-chief this time.

FAUST

That would be the limit. Issuing orders where I don't know a thing.

MEPHISTOPHELES

Leave it to the general staff, and the field marshal has nothing to fear. I know what a mess war is and I've appointed my council in good time from among the old giants. If you can assemble them, you're lucky.

FAUST

What's that over there? An armed force. Have you roused all the mountain folk?

MEPHISTOPHELES

No, just the cream of the lot, like Shakespeare's Quince.

Enter the three giants

MEPHISTOPHELES

Why here the boys come! You see they're not all the same age.

Not dressed the same way. Nor armed the same way. They'll serve you well. (*to the audience*) Nowadays everyone loves to see a knight in armour. And if these wretches are allegorical, so much the better.

RAUFEBOLD *young, lightly armed, gaily dressed*

Whoever faces up to me, gets my fist in his teeth right away. Cowards that run – I grab them by the hair.

HABEBALD *in his best years, well armed, richly dressed*

Empty scrapping. Not worth a thing. A waste of time. Get hold of what you can and let the rest wait.

HALTEFEST *old, well-armed, not in mail*

That won't get you far either. You can soon run through a great fortune. Getting hold is good, but keeping's better. Just you leave it to the old man and you'll lose nothing.

They all go downhill

IN THE FOOTHILLS

Drums and martial music from below. The emperor's tent is thrown open. Emperor. Commander-in-chief. Retinue

COMMANDER-IN-CHIEF

It still seems to me that our strategy was well conceived when we withdrew the whole army into this valley. I have great hopes of success.

EMPEROR

We'll see how it goes. But I don't like this pulling back and this semblance of flight.

COMMANDER-IN-CHIEF

Look at our right flank, your majesty. The terrain is just what we could wish, the hills not steep, but steep enough to favour us and entangle the enemy. With our forces half-hidden in rolling country their cavalry won't venture in.

EMPEROR

I can only give my approval. It will be a test of strength, hand to hand.

COMMANDER-IN-CHIEF

Here in these flat meadows in the centre you can see our phalanx in good battle-spirit, their pikes flashing in the sunny morning mist. The rest a dark heaving square, power-ful, thousands of them, eager for the fight. You can see how strong they are. I trust them to break their opponents' ranks.

EMPEROR

This is the first good view of them I've had. They look splendid. An army like that is worth double the number.

COMMANDER-IN-CHIEF

Our left flank speaks for itself. I have stout forces in the rocky cliffs covering the important pass into the valley. You can see their arms glittering. This is where I expect the enemy to be taken unawares and collapse in savage fighting.

EMPEROR

And there they come, those treacherous relatives that used to call me uncle, cousin, brother, and took one liberty after another till they undermined my royal power and authority. Then, with their quarrelling among themselves, they deva-stated the empire and now they've ended by joining forces against me. The populace wavered this way and that and finally drifted with the stronger current.

COMMANDER-IN-CHIEF

I see one of my trusty spies hurrying back down the cliff. I hope he has something useful to report.

FIRST SPY

We managed to work our way in among them, not without the usual risks, but our news is not very favourable. There are many who swear allegiance, as others have before them, but they plead inner disorder and danger to the nation and say their hands are tied.

EMPEROR

Self-interest always tells people to look after number one and forget about gratitude, duty, honour, and such. But don't you realize that when your neighbour's house is on fire your own house is bound to go too?

COMMANDER-IN-CHIEF
There's a second one coming down the hill, but slowly. He's
worn out and trembling in every limb.

SECOND SPY
It was amusing at first to see confusion everywhere, but then,
suddenly, a new emperor came on the scene and now the
whole crowd is on its way under direction, following those
spurious flags like so many sheep.

EMPEROR
A counter-emperor is all to the good. It makes me feel at last
that I am the true one. I only dressed in armour as a uniform,
but now it's converted to a higher purpose. At all our festivals, even at their most brilliant, I felt the lack of one thing –
danger. You always favoured tilting at a ring, but my heart
beat high and I was for jousting proper. If you hadn't been
opposed to war I should be a shining hero by now. I felt
powerfully fortified when I saw myself mirrored in the fire.
The flaming element pressed me close and it seemed real and
dangerous enough, though it was illusory. I've always
dreamed vaguely of victory and fame. I mean now to make
up for having failed so grievously before.

*The heralds are sent off to challenge the counter-emperor. Faust in
armour, the visor half-raised. The giants armed and costumed as before*

FAUST
Here we come and trust we're not unwelcome. Caution can
be useful even when not needed. You know the mountain
people are deep in the lore of nature and the rocks. The spirits
left the flat land long ago and are more attracted by the hills,
and there, in cavernous labyrinths, they're steadily at work on
the gases and the metals, testing, separating, combining, with
the sole purpose of making discoveries. And with subtle
power of mind they construct transparent forms and read
in silent crystals what is happening in the upper world.

EMPEROR
So I have heard and I believe you. But tell me, my good man,
what concern it is of ours.

FAUST

May I remind you of the time in Rome when a dreadful fate awaited that Sabine necromancer from Norcia, who remains your devout and deserving servant. The twigs were crackling, the flames were leaping, the dry logs were all in place, mingled with pitch and sticks of sulphur. There was no hope for him, it seemed, from man or god or devil. But your majesty burst those chains of fire and saved him. He's eternally indebted to you and he thinks only of your welfare, forgetting himself from that day forward and consulting the stars and the depths on your behalf alone. He has enjoined upon us urgently to give you our support. Nature's resources are unlimited in that region and unimpeded, though the church in its stupidity calls it sorcery.

EMPEROR

On feast days when we're receiving and the merry guests arrive expecting to have a good time, jostling one another and crowding the halls, we welcome them all. This worthy man will be doubly welcome if he comes bringing strong support tomorrow morning when our fate hangs in the balance. Nevertheless you must hold back at this crucial moment when thousands are met to battle for me and against me. A man must be self-reliant and, if he claims the throne, prove in person that he's worthy of it. This ghost of a man who has risen against us, calling himself emperor, ruler, commander-in-chief, and feudal lord – let this fist of mine despatch him to the hell where he belongs.

FAUST

It can't be wise for you to risk your head in this way, no matter what. Isn't your helmet crested and plumed, protecting the head that fires our courage? Without the head, what use are the limbs? If the head weakens, they all weaken. If it is wounded, they're all wounded. They revive at once when it revives. The arm is quick to shield the skull, the sword parries and returns the stroke, the foot plants itself gaily on the slain man's neck.

EMPEROR

That's just what I burn to do. To set my foot on his proud head and make it my footstool.

HERALDS *returning*

They received us with disrespect, brushed us aside, poured ridicule on our solemn announcement. 'That emperor of yours,' they said, 'is just an echo fading away in the hills.' 'Once upon a time' is how the tale begins.

FAUST

This rebuff entirely suits the wishes of your faithful supporters. There comes the enemy. Your men are ready for the fray. Order the attack. The moment favours us.

EMPEROR

At this point I withdraw and *to the commander-in-chief* leave it to you.

COMMANDER-IN-CHIEF

Very well. Let our right wing advance. The enemy's left is moving up the slope. We can trust our young forces to check them.

FAUST

Then permit this sturdy lad to join your ranks without delay and in their company show what he's capable of. *He points to his right*

RAUFEBOLD *stepping forward*

Whoever comes near me will have his jaws smashed, upper and lower. He won't get away with less. And if I come at him from behind his head'll be dangling loose from his shoulders in less than a jiffy. Let your fighters pile in with swords and clubs at the same time and we'll drown every man jack of them in his own blood. *off*

COMMANDER-IN-CHIEF

Next let our middle phalanx follow up, circumspectly, but with all its strength. Over there, a little to the right, our forces have already upset their plans.

FAUST *pointing to the middle one*

Allow this one to go with them. He's quick. He'll carry everything with him.

HABEBALD *stepping forward*

Let thirst for booty go hand in hand with heroism and we'll all make straight for the counter-emperor's tent and the wealth we shall find there. He won't be top dog for long. I'll place myself at the head of the phalanx.

EILEBEUTE *canteen-woman, snuggling close to him*

We may not be man and wife, but he's my boy all the same. And now we're running into luck. A woman's ruthless when she robs. She stops at nothing. So on to victory. All's fair in love and war. *They go off*

COMMANDER-IN-CHIEF

As was to be expected, they've thrown the weight of their right wing against our left. We must resist to the utmost the furious drive they're making to gain the narrow pass.

FAUST *pointing to the left*

Then please, sir, don't overlook this man. There's never any harm in adding to your strength.

HALTEFEST *stepping forward*

Don't worry about your left wing. You can trust the old man anywhere. What we have we hold. And in my hands it's lightning-proof. *off*

MEPHISTOPHELES *coming down the hill*

Look behind and see those men pouring out of the rocky chasms and filling the paths, all of them in full armour, with helmets, shields, and swords. A wall of strength at our backs, waiting for the word to strike.

Quietly to those in the know

You mustn't ask where this comes from. But I haven't been wasting my time. I've cleared out the armouries in these parts. There they all were, on horseback or standing, just as if they still were lords of the earth. Once they called themselves knights and kings and kaisers and now they're nothing but empty snail-shells for ghosts and devils to play about in and bring the middle ages back. It doesn't matter just which ones it is. They're serving the purpose. (*aloud*) Just hark at the rage they're in, bumping into one another and rattling their tin armour. And I see flags fluttering on standards, longing for a fresh breeze. Remember this is an ancient tribe, only too eager to get into battle again.

Loud trumpeting from above. Confusion noticeable in the enemy ranks

FAUST

The skyline has gone dark with only here and there an ominous reddish gleam, repeated in the flashing arms and felt everywhere, in the rocks, the forest, the clouds.

MEPHISTOPHELES

Our right wing is holding well. And I can see that nimble giant Raufebold towering above the rest and very busy at his job.

EMPEROR

Where a single arm was raised, I now can see a dozen. It isn't just nature's doing.

FAUST

Did you never hear of mirages, like those on the Sicilian coast? There you see the strangest sights, hovering in full daylight halfway up the sky, all in their own peculiar haze. Cities shifting this way and that, gardens rising and falling, one image relieving another.

EMPEROR

But how disturbing. I see a flashing light playing at the tips of the long spears, flames dancing on the lances in the phalanx. This is too weird for my liking.

FAUST

Forgive me, sir, these are traces of spirits seldom seen now, the Dioscuri, gathering the last of their strength. Sailors swear by them.

EMPEROR

But tell me, to whom do we owe it that nature is assembling these rarities on our behalf?

MEPHISTOPHELES

To whom but that magician who has your welfare at heart. He's deeply concerned about the forces ranged against you. He wants to see you saved, even if it costs him his life.

EMPEROR

They were honouring me with a lively procession through the

city. I felt I was somebody and wanted to show it. And without much reflection I took it into my head to let that old greybeard out into the fresh air again. I spoiled the game of the clerics, they didn't thank me for it. And now after all these years I get the reward for my happy impulse.

FAUST

Generous deeds bring rich returns. But look up. It seems he's sending you a sign. We'll soon see what it means.

EMPEROR

There's an eagle sailing high in the air and a griffin coming at it viciously.

FAUST

Watch out. It seems to me a favourable omen. Griffins are fabulous creatures. Fancy its pitting itself against an eagle.

EMPEROR

They're circling round one another at a distance and now at the same moment they're turning to attack, each bent on destruction.

FAUST

See now, that wretched griffin's got the worst of it, drooping its lion's tail and collapsing into the trees, all tousled and torn.

EMPEROR

A remarkable sign. I accept it and hope things will go accordingly.

MEPHISTOPHELES *turning to the right*

A succession of thrusts by our men has made the enemy pull back and veer towards their right under pressure, and this has confused and exposed their left. Now our phalanx, swinging in that direction, has driven its spearhead into the weak spot. Both sides are going at it madly now, like a sea in storm. It couldn't have worked out better. The victory's ours.

EMPEROR *on the left, to Faust*

But look over this way. It seems dubious to me. Our position is in danger. I can't see any stones flying. The enemy has gained possession of the lower rocks. The upper ones have already been vacated. Now you can see them in large numbers coming closer and closer. They may already have taken the pass. Your wiles have failed. This is what comes of your unholy work. *pause*

MEPHISTOPHELES

Here come my two ravens. I wonder what they have to report. I'm afraid things are going badly with us.

EMPEROR

What are these ugly birds after? Coming straight at us on those huge black wings out of the heat of battle.

MEPHISTOPHELES *to the ravens*

Come and sit close beside me. Your advice can be trusted. With your protection our cause won't be lost.

FAUST *to the emperor*

You must have heard of doves that come from distant lands to nest and breed. It's the same here with a difference. The doves bring messages in peace time, the ravens in war.

MEPHISTOPHELES

Very grave news has come. Look, you can see what difficulties our men are in at the edge of the cliff. The enemy have seized the adjoining heights and if they take the pass, it would go hard with us.

EMPEROR

So you've fooled me after all. I've been uneasy ever since you got me in your clutches.

MEPHISTOPHELES

Don't lose heart. We aren't beaten yet. It's generally a close shave at the last, patience and cunning are called for. I have my reliable messengers. Let me take over.

COMMANDER-IN-CHIEF *arriving*

It's always gone against my grain to see you allied to these two. Jugglery is sure to let you down in the end. I can do nothing in the present situation. They started it. Let them finish. I resign and hand in my baton.

EMPEROR

Keep it till better days that may yet be in store. I shudder at this ugly customer and his trafficking with ravens. (*to Mephistopheles*) I can't give you the baton. You don't seem the right man for it. But take command and try to save us. Do what you can. *He retires into the tent with the commander-in-chief*

MEPHISTOPHELES
Let him keep his clumsy baton. It'd be no use to any of us. It smacked of the crucifix to me.

FAUST
What do we do next?

MEPHISTOPHELES
It's as good as done already. – Now, my coal-black cousins, my eager servants, off you go to the mountain lake, give my best wishes to the undines, and ask them to lend us their water-tricks. They have a women's knack, hard for you and me to grasp, of separating the appearance from the reality so that you'd swear it was the reality.

Pause

FAUST
Our ravens must have flattered those undines no end. Already the water's beginning to trickle. It's flowing strongly now down some of those dry rock-faces. They'll never win.

MEPHISTOPHELES
A rare surprise for them. Their boldest climbers are quite at a loss.

FAUST
I can see streams of water joining, gaining in strength, coming up again out of chasms twice the size they were. One powerful stream has arched high in the air and then spread out over flat rocks, plunging, foaming, this way and that. And stage by stage down into the valley. Any heroic resistance would be wasted here. Those big waves would wash them away. It frightens me to see such a fierce rush of water.

MEPHISTOPHELES
I can't see these deceptions. Only human eyes are fooled by them. But I can enjoy the curious spectacle. There they go, running away in crowds, thinking they're in danger of drowning and ridiculously going through all the swimming motions,

and puffing and blowing, when all the time they're standing on dry ground. Total confusion everywhere.

The ravens have come back

I'll commend you to the master. But if you want to show that you're masters yourselves, make haste to the glowing smithy where the dwarf-folk are striking sparks from metal and stone. Ask them for fire, shining, flashing, exploding, the best they can devise. Sheet lightning far off, or shooting stars, you can see any summer evening. But lightning playing in the thickets, stars sputtering on wet ground, that's another matter. So talk them into it. It shouldn't be hard. Ask them politely first and force them, if necessary.

The ravens leave. The above is enacted

MEPHISTOPHELES

Now our enemies are in dense darkness, can't see a foot ahead, with shifting lights everywhere and sudden dazzling flashes. That's all very well. But now we must have some noise to frighten them.

FAUST

The empty armour that's lain so long indoors in those stuffy halls has come to life again in the open air. They've been rattling and clattering up there for some time. A strange falsetto note.

MEPHISTOPHELES

You're right. There's no holding them. They're fighting away just as in knighthood's golden days. Greaves and armlets renewing the old war of Guelphs and Ghibellines. They're used to it and they'll never be reconciled. There's nothing like party hatred to carry you through to a pandemonium when hell is celebrating. Listen to the noise, sometimes horrible like the god Pan shrieking, sometimes shrill and satanic, and sending a note of terror all down the valley.

Tumultuous noise of war in the orchestra, passing over finally into gay, military music

THE COUNTER-EMPEROR'S TENT
Throne. Rich Setting. Habebald. Eilebeute

EILEBEUTE

So we did get here first!

HABEBALD

There's no raven could keep up with us.

EILEBEUTE

Oh, what a pile of precious things! Where shall I start? Where shall I stop?

HABEBALD

The whole place is so packed I don't know what to choose.

EILEBEUTE

This carpet's just the thing for me after all the hard beds I've slept on.

HABEBALD

And here's a steel-spiked club. I've wanted one of them for a long time.

EILEBEUTE

A red cloak with gold fringes. A dream of a cloak.

HABEBALD *taking the club*

This'll do a quick job. Knock him flat and move on to the next. You've packed a sackful and there's nothing any good in the whole lot. Drop the stuff and take one of these chests. This is the men's pay. Gold. Full of gold to the brim.

EILEBEUTE

It's a cruel weight. I can't lift it. I could never carry it.

HABEBALD

Bend over quick. Quick, I tell you. You're strong. I'll hoist it up.

EILEBEUTE

Oh dear. Oh dear. There it goes. My poor back's broke.

The chest falls and bursts open

HABEBALD

The good gold all spilt on the ground. Quick now and pick it up.

EILEBEUTE *crouching*

I'll grab an apronful. It'll be enough.

HABEBALD

That'll do. Now off you go. (*She stands up*) Oh, your apron has a hole in it. Every step you take the money's falling through.

IMPERIAL GUARDS

What are you doing here? This is no place for you. Ferreting in the emperor's property.

HABEBALD

We gave our services, and we're taking our share of the loot. It's the custom in enemy tents and we're soldiers too.

IMPERIAL GUARDS

This won't do here. You can't be both a soldier and a dirty thief. The emperor must have honest men round him.

HABEBALD

We know what you mean by honest. You mean taxes. We're all on a level. Here, give me that. To show we're buddies. (*to Eilebeute*) Beat it and take what you can with you. They don't like us here. *off*

FIRST GUARD

Say, why didn't you swipe him on the mouth?

SECOND GUARD

I don't know. They were like ghosts. It took the stuffing out of me.

THIRD GUARD

I couldn't see straight. Everything was dancing in front of my eyes.

FOURTH GUARD

It was so hot all day, so close, so frightening, so … I don't know what to call it. You saw one man staying on his feet and the other falling. You fumbled blindly and struck and down the fellow went every time. There was like a veil in front of your eyes and noises in your ears, buzzing and roaring and

hissing. And on and on it went. And now we're here, somehow or other. That's all I can say.

Enter Emperor with four princes. The guards withdraw

EMPEROR
The victory is ours. That much you can't deny. The enemy
forces scattered in flight across the plain. Here stands the
empty throne and here, crowding the place, the traitor's
treasures with these carpets spread over them. And now in
our imperial dignity, with our own bodyguard round us, we
await the envoys of the nations. Good news, glad news, is
coming in from every side, assuring us that the land is quiet
again and happy in its allegiance to us. There may have been
some ghostly forces involved in the fighting, but in the end it
was we who won the battle. There can always be accidents
that work in your favour. A stone falls out of the sky, blood
rains on the enemy, magic noises come rumbling out of
caverns, raising our courage, depressing the enemy's. The
loser loses. Contempt is all he gets. The winner wins, rejoices,
and thanks God. Not he alone. 'Lord, we praise thee,' comes
from a million throats spontaneously. But now, most
devoutly of all, I do what I seldom do. I look within. A
happy young ruler may waste his days. But time teaches him
to value them. And this is why, without delay, I ally myself to
you four, you worthy custodians of our court and country.
To the first
It was you, sir, who shrewdly disposed our troops and struck
boldly at the crucial moment. Carry on now in peace-time and
do what is required. I appoint you High Marshal and invest
you with the sword.
HIGH MARSHAL
Your army, faithful as ever, has been establishing order up
and down the land. But once we have made our frontiers and
your throne secure you must permit me on feast days at your
castle to set the table for the banquet. I shall walk before you
with the shining sword, the eternal token of your supreme
majesty, and stand with it at your side.

EMPEROR *to the second*

You, a man of courage and of gentle manners too, I appoint High Chamberlain. The duties are onerous. You will have complete charge of the household, where I know there is division among the servants and inefficiency. You must make yourself in their eyes the paragon of courtesy to all men.

HIGH CHAMBERLAIN

I shall earn your favour by carrying out your noble wishes which tell me to be helpful to the good people and to go easy on the bad, to be calm and clear-minded, dismissing all cunning and trickery. If you, sir, see me as I am, I cannot wish for more. May I be so bold as to picture that festive scene. When you come to the table, I shall pass you the golden bowl, hold your rings at the happy moment when you dip your fingers and give me a look of approval.

EMPEROR

I find it not easy to turn my thoughts from serious to joyful. But never mind. A lively start helps.

To the third

I choose you for High Steward, to supervise our game preserves, poultry yard, and manor farm. See to it that always month by month the choicest dishes are prepared and well prepared.

HIGH STEWARD

I shall make it my duty and my pleasure not to partake of a dish till it has pleased you. The kitchen staff will co-operate with you in bringing foods from afar and anticipating the seasons, always remembering that your own taste is for simple and healthy dishes, not for the unusual.

EMPEROR *to the fourth*

Since it has to be festivities we deal with today and nothing else, I appoint you, young man, my cupbearer. As High Cupbearer make sure that our cellar is well stocked with wines. For yourself, be moderate. Don't be led astray by the opportunities that come in merry company.

HIGH CUPBEARER

Young men, your majesty, if you give them responsibilities,

quickly rise to the occasion. I too can see myself at that great festival. I shall deck out the imperial buffet with resplendent gold and silver ware. And for yourself I shall select the loveliest of goblets, of shining Venetian glass, comforting even to look at. It improves the wine and never intoxicates. People often rely too heavily on the virtue of this miraculous cup, but your moderation will save you from that.

EMPEROR

What I have bestowed on you you have now heard. It comes with authority in this solemn hour and you can count on it. The emperor's word is supreme and sufficient, but for confirmation we have to put it on paper and I must give you my signature. And now at the right moment comes the right man to draft the formalities.

Enter the chancellor-archbishop

EMPEROR

When an arch locks with the keystone, it can stand for all time. Here you see four of my princes. We have just dealt with problems of the court and the household. And now, turning to the empire as a whole, I rest the full weight and authority on the five of you. I intend you to rank above all others in property and I therefore enlarge your present territories from those of our recent enemies. Not only do I enrich you thus with fair domains. I also give you the right to extend them further by way of succession, purchase, or exchange. Further, I allow you full benefit of all privileges that pertain to your status. Judicially your verdict shall be final, and no appeal is valid. Then, fees, levies, taxes, of every kind, whether excise, transit, or escort, all are yours. Also royalties on mines, salt works, coinage. You see, to give you the fullest evidence of my gratitude I have raised you to positions second only to my own.

ARCHBISHOP

I thank you most deeply on behalf of us all. It strengthens us and strengthens you.

EMPEROR
I now have a further honour to bestow on you. I am still alive, eager to live and serve my empire. But when I reflect on my long ancestry it gives me darker thoughts and curbs my zeal. The day will come when I shall part from my dear ones. It will then be your duty to appoint my successor and solemnize his coronation. May that be a peaceful ending to these stormy times.

LORD CHANCELLOR
Humble in posture, proud in deepest heart, we bow before you, we princes, the first, the highest, on earth. So long as blood flows in our veins, regard us as a single body responsive to your every wish.

EMPEROR
To conclude then, let our deliberations be confirmed in writing and duly signed. Your possessions are yours outright with the sole condition that they are indivisible and, however much extended, must pass on undiminished to the eldest son.

LORD CHANCELLOR
I shall be happy to record this important statute on parchment for the good of the empire and ourselves. The chancery will see to the engrossing and sealing and you, sir, will put your august signature to it.

EMPEROR
And now I can dismiss you, and leave you to reflect severally on this momentous day.

The secular princes withdraw

ARCHBISHOP
Stays behind and speaks with great solemnity
The chancellor has withdrawn, the bishop has stayed behind, warned by an inner voice to speak to you with fatherly affection and with deep concern.

EMPEROR
What can have alarmed you on this happy occasion? Speak freely.

ARCHBISHOP

It pains me grievously at this hour to find you, the emperor whose head is sacred, allied with Satan. True, you seem securely seated on your throne, but it is a mockery to the Lord in heaven and our holy father, the Pope, who, if he hears of it, will quickly inflict the severest punishment on you, shatter your wicked empire with his ban of excommunication. You must consider that he still remembers how on your coronation day you set that cursed sorcerer free, making your first act of pardon an offence to Christianity. But now beat your breast and lose no time in giving a mite out of your impious wealth to the holy cause. Listen to the voice of piety and endow the church with that stretch of hilly country where your tent stood, where evil spirits conspired to protect you and you lent a willing ear to the prince of darkness. The whole extent of mountain and forest, with upland pastures for grazing, clear lakes well stocked with fish, and all the water winding and cascading in countless rivulets down into the valley. Then the valley itself with its meadows and its undulations. In this way you will show your repentance and find yourself in favour again.

EMPEROR

I am so horrified at my offence that I leave it to you to set the boundaries.

ARCHBISHOP

First of all, it must be proclaimed immediately that this desecrated territory is to be devoted to the service of the church. In my mind's eye I can see strong walls rising, the early sunlight lying on the choir, the transept coming next, the nave extending and rising to the delight of all the faithful. Now I see them streaming devoutly through the great porch in answer to the bell that was heard for the first time over hill and dale, booming from the high towers. The penitent come here to start life afresh. At the consecration – may it be soon – your presence will be the chief adornment of the day.

EMPEROR

I trust this great undertaking will show the pious spirit that prompted it. May it glorify God and exculpate me. I am satisfied and already feel my spirits rising.

ARCHBISHOP

In my capacity as chancellor I must go through the formalities.

EMPEROR

Draw up a formal statement, deeding this property to the church, submit it to me and I will sign with pleasure.

ARCHBISHOP *takes his leave and turns back*

Furthermore, you must assign all the revenues from this territory for all time to the cathedral that is to be. Tithes, taxes, payment in kind. Vast sums are needed for maintenance and for administration. You must let us have some of your booty to speed the building on this desolate spot. Besides, you must remember, timber, lime, and slate will have to be brought from a distance. The people will do the hauling, as the pulpit will bid them, and the church will pronounce its blessing on those who give their labour. *off*

EMPEROR

That was a fearful sin I brought upon myself. Those wretched magicians have done me great harm.

ARCHBISHOP *turning back again and bowing obsequiously*

Forgive me, sir, you leased your shoreline to Faust, that disreputable man. But unless you penitently assign all the revenues from there too to the church, it will surely put its ban on him at once.

EMPEROR *annoyed*

But the land isn't there yet, it's still under water.

ARCHBISHOP

For those with justice on their side and patience the time will come. And your word will hold. *off*

EMPEROR *alone*

I might as well write off the whole empire.

ACT V

OPEN COUNTRY

WANDERER

There they are, the dark old linden trees, as strong and sturdy as ever. And to think that I should set eyes on them once again after all my travels. It's the same old place, the cottage where they took me in, when storm and shipwreck landed me on these dunes. A worthy couple they were, so kind and good. I'd like to tell them so and thank them. But they were old then. They may be gone now. It's a question. Shall I knock at the door or give them a hail? Greetings, if you're still there and enjoying the happy life you deserve after what you did for others.

BAUCIS *very old*

Hush, hush, stranger dear. Let my man finish his sleep. Then he'll be able to busy himself for the short time he's up.

WANDERER

Tell me, aren't you Mother Baucis? You must be. So I haven't come too late to thank you for saving my life that time, Philemon and you. I was at the point of death when you wetted my lips. I was young then.

Enter Philemon

And you are Philemon, who stoutly dragged my possessions ashore. I remember your quick bonfire and the silver sound of your bell. It was given to you and Baucis to rescue me in that catastrophe. But now let me step outside and look at the ocean. Let me kneel and say a prayer. I am so moved.

He walks out over the dune

PHILEMON *to Baucis*

Quick now and set the table in the garden. Let him go and look. He'll get the shock of his life. He won't believe his eyes.

Standing beside wanderer

Where you once had that grim struggle with wind and waves is all a garden now, a paradise to behold. I wasn't young any more and I wasn't able to give a hand, but as an ageing man I watched and saw them push the water farther and farther back. The masters knew their job, but the men had to take risks. They dug ditches, built dams, took land from the sea and made it theirs. Look, one green meadow after another, gardens, villages, woods. Come and feast your eyes. The sun hasn't long to go. Far off you can make out the sails of ships heading for home tonight, like birds that know their nests. That's where the harbour is now. The ocean's just a blue strip on the horizon. To right and left of you the land's all thickly populated.

The three at table in the garden

BAUCIS

You haven't a word to say. You're hungry and you don't eat a bite.

PHILEMON

He wants to know about the prodigy. You like talking. You tell him.

BAUCIS

A prodigy it surely was. It bothers me still. There was something wrong, something wicked, about the whole thing.

PHILEMON

Do you mean the emperor was wicked when he gave him the shoreline? Didn't a herald proclaim it, riding past with his trumpet? It was quite close to our dunes that the start was made. They set up huts and tents. And soon there was a palace there with grass and green trees round it.

BAUCIS

The workmen toiled and slaved all day with pick and shovel and got nowhere. At night you could see lights moving, and the next day – there stood a dam. Men's lives were sacrificed, you could hear them groaning in the dark. Torrents of fire flowed down into the water and when the morning came behold a canal. He's a godless man. He covets our cottage and our trees. He's so domineering, he expects us to do what he tells us.

PHILEMON
Didn't he offer us a nice piece of property on the new soil?

BAUCIS
Don't trust that flat land. Stick to your high ground.

PHILEMON
Let us go to the chapel and watch the sun set, ring the bell, kneel and pray, and put our trust in the god of our fathers.

PALACE

Extensive formal garden. A large straight canal. Faust in advanced old age, walking about, meditating

LYNCEUS, THE WATCHMAN *through his megaphone*
The sun is setting. The last of the ships are running in. A freight boat is entering the canal to dock here, its masts erect, its coloured pennants waving merrily. The sailor's joy is centred in you. Fortune greets you at this crowning moment.

The bell rings on the dune

FAUST *starting up*
That cursed bell. It hurts me cruelly like a stab in the dark. Before my eyes my dominion is complete, but from behind vexation teases me, reminding me with taunting noise that my vast estate is not unblemished. I don't possess the linden trees, nor the brown cottage, nor the crumbling chapel. And if I wanted to rest there I should be terrified of ghosts. It's a thorn in the flesh, an offence to the sight. Oh, to be anywhere but here.

WATCHMAN *as above*
How nicely the freighter is coming in on the evening wind. Its pile of cargo in bales and boxes grows bigger and bigger every minute.

A handsome boat, richly laden with the products of remote parts of the world. Mephistopheles. The three giants

CHORUS

Now we've landed. Here we are. Hail to the master. Hail to the boss. *They disembark. The cargo is unshipped*

MEPHISTOPHELES

We've come through well. If the boss approves, it's all we ask. We set out with two ships and we've come back with twenty. What feats we performed, you can see from our cargo. The open sea frees the spirit. Who stops to think there? Quick action's what's wanted. Catching a ship's like catching fish. When you've caught three, you grapple a fourth. The fifth doesn't have a look-in. Might is right. You don't ask how, you ask what. If I know anything about the sea, there's a trinity here, a three-in-one, war, trade, and piracy.

THE THREE GIANTS

Not a word of thanks. Not a word of greeting. He pulls a face at what we've brought. This royal treasure. He thinks it stinks.

MEPHISTOPHELES

You won't get any more from him. You've helped your-selves already.

THE THREE GIANTS

That was just our pocket-money. Equal shares is what we want.

MEPHISTOPHELES

First you must set out the stuff in the halls. When he sees the wealth of it, he won't be stingy. He'll entertain us lavishly. The gay girls will be coming tomorrow. I'll look after them properly.

The cargo is moved away

MEPHISTOPHELES *to Faust*

When I remind you of your great good fortune you take it very gravely, very gloomily. Yet, as you can see, the plan was wise and has succeeded. The sea and the shore are at peace with one another, giving our ships quick and easy access to the open. Standing here in front of your palace, you can say that your arm encloses the whole world. And this is where it all started. Here stood the first log hut. We dug a ditch, where now the oars ply briskly. Your great purpose, the devoted labour of your men, have won the rewards of land and sea. Standing here ...

FAUST

Yes, here, here. It's the cursed here and now that weighs me down. I have to tell you, you man of many parts, that I find it intolerable. I'm ashamed of myself when I say it. Those old people will have to go. I want those lindens for my recreation. This handful of trees, that are not my trees, wrecks everything, wrecks my whole estate. I intended to build platforms there among the branches to let me survey the full extent of my achievement, the supreme achievement of the human mind, setting the nations constructively to work on newly gained land.

This is the worst torture of all, to feel a lack with so little lacking. The sound of the bell, the scent of the lindens, stifles me like being in a tomb. The freedom of my mighty will is brought to nothing here in the sand. How shall I ever lift this off me? The bell tolls on, and I am beside myself with fury.

MEPHISTOPHELES

Of course, of course. There always has to be some one thing to sour your life for you. Don't we all know it? No man of breeding can bear to hear that tinkling sound, that damnable ding-dong that darkens the evening sky and gets into everything that happens from baptism to burial, making life seem no more than an idle dream between one silly note and the next.

FAUST

The stubborn way those people hold out mars all my splendid profit. It hurts me savagely to say it, but I have no choice. I give up trying to be just.

MEPHISTOPHELES

Haven't you been colonizing all this long time? Why make such a fuss now?

FAUST

Very well, go and evict them. You know the little estate I chose for them.

MEPHISTOPHELES

We'll pick them up and set them down. They'll be on their feet again in no time. And they'll forget the rough treatment when they see how lovely the new place is. *He whistles shrilly*

The three giants appear

MEPHISTOPHELES

Come and carry out the master's orders. And tomorrow we'll have a fleet festival.

THE THREE GIANTS

The master received us very coldly. A sweet festival will make amends.

MEPHISTOPHELES *ad spectatores*

What we're doing is an old story. Naboth's vineyard all over again.

DEEP NIGHT

LYNCEUS THE WATCHMAN *singing on the battlements*

Born with these eyes, appointed to watch, pledged to the tower, I like the world. I look at the distant, I look at the near. I see moon and stars, see forest and stag. And enduring beauty in everything. Content with it all, I'm at ease with myself. You happy eyes, when all is said, whatever you saw, it was lovely to see.

Pause

But I wasn't stationed up here for my own enjoyment. See what a horror confronts me in the night. Sparks flying in the dark clump of lindens. A conflagration spreading, fanned by the breeze. The mossy cottage burning inside. No help in sight and the need urgent. Oh, those dear old people, always so careful of fire, and now a victim of the fumes. What a disaster! The whole dark framework blazing red. If only they could escape this inferno. Tongues of flame are mounting in the leaves and twigs, the dry limbs catching and breaking off.

Why must I have to witness this. A pity I'm so long-sighted. The little chapel is collapsing now under the falling branches. The writhing flames have reached the tree-tops and the hollow trunks are glowing down to the roots. *long pause. singing*

What was always so pleasant a sight is one now with the centuries past.

FAUST *on the balcony, facing the dunes*

What plaintive notes are these that reach me from above, reach me too late to be of use. It is my watchman grieving. And I too deplore what I did with such impatience. But no matter. If the lindens are reduced to burnt stems and cinders, we'll soon run up a look-out place, where I can gaze into the infinite. And I can see the old couple housed in their new quarters, contented in their last years and bearing no malice.

MEPHISTOPHELES AND THE THREE GIANTS *speaking from below*

Here we come on the high run. You'll have to excuse us. Things didn't go smoothly. We knocked at the door and thumped at the door and no one came. We shook it and thumped again and the old door gave in. Then we shouted and threatened them and got no answer. They didn't hear; they didn't want to hear. That's the way it is in such cases. But we lost no time and quickly ousted them. The old couple didn't suffer much. They died of shock. And a stranger there who showed fight was soon despatched. In the short encounter sparks were scattered from the hearth and set some straw on fire. Now there's a big blaze, a funeral pyre for the three of them.

FAUST

Were you deaf to what I said? I wanted exchange, not robbery. My curse on this wanton deed. Share it among you.

CHORUS

It's often said: Obey your master. Yet if you stick to him and serve him boldly, you've everything to lose, even your life. *off*

FAUST *on the balcony*

The stars are fading in the sky. The fire has sunk low. But a shivery breeze is fanning it still, bringing a whiff of smoke with it. Haste on my part, over-haste on theirs. But now what shadows are these coming?

MIDNIGHT
Enter four grey women

THE FIRST
My name is Lack.

THE SECOND
My name is Debt.

THE THIRD
My name is Care.

THE FOURTH
And mine is Need.

THREE OF THEM
The door is locked. We can't get in and we don't wish to. A rich man lives here.

LACK
This makes me a shadow.

DEBT
And makes me a nothing.

NEED
From me they turn their pampered faces.

CARE
Sisters, you can't get in and you shouldn't. But Care can slip through the keyhole. *Care disappears*

LACK
Grey sisters away, away from here.

DEBT
I'll come along with you, side by side.

NEED
And I'll be close on your heels.

ALL THREE
The clouds are flying. The stars vanish at a breath. And now, over there, from afar, from afar, I see him coming, our brother coming, our brother Death. *off*

FAUST *in the palace*
I saw four of them come, and only three left. The sense of what they said I couldn't follow. I seemed to hear a word like breath and then another that rhymed with it, a dark word – death. It sounded muted, hollow, like ghost voices. I haven't won my way to freedom yet. If I could only get rid of magic, unlearn my incantations utterly, and stand face to face with nature as a man, just as a man, it would be worthwhile to be a man.

I was that once, before I probed the realm of darkness, damning myself and the world with impious words. The air is now so thronged with spooks and spectres there's no escaping them. The daylight hours may be all sanity and sweetness, but the night involves us in a web of dreams. We come home happy from the fields in springtime. A bird croaks. What does it croak: calamity. Beset, as we are, with superstitions hopelessly, there's always a something ominous that comes, a strange hint, a foreboding. It frightens us. We are alone. The door creaks and nobody comes in. *alarmed*
    Is anyone there?
CARE
The answer must be yes.
FAUST
Who are you? Tell me.
CARE
I'm here. That's enough.
FAUST
Be off with you.
CARE
I'm in the right place.
FAUST *furious at first, then calmer, aside*
Look out now. No more magic spells from me.
CARE
When Care says a thing, whether heard or not, it re-echoes in the heart. In one guise or another I make my cruel power felt. A disquieting companion by land or sea, not wanted, always at hand, cajoled one time and cursed the next. Have you never experienced me?

FAUST

I've just raced through the world, seizing what I fancied by the hair of its head. If it wasn't good enough I let it go. If it eluded me, I didn't bother. I've simply desired and fulfilled my desire and desired again. And so stormed through life, at first in a big way, but now I move more wisely, warily. I've taken the measure of this earth we live on. Into the beyond the view is blocked. Only an idiot would peer in that direction, imagining there were men like him beyond the clouds. Why should he go roving off into eternity? Let him stand where he stands and look about him. The world always has something to offer to a man of worth. When he sees it he should hang on to it and shape his life accordingly. If there are ghosts about, ignore them. And find his pleasure and his pain in moving on and on, knowing all the time that he'll never be satisfied.

CARE

Once I get my grip on a man, the world is no use to him. A dark cloud settles down on him. The sun neither rises nor sets. With outer senses all intact, there are blacknesses within, depriving him of the very riches that are his and letting him starve in the midst of plenty. Happiness, unhappiness – a matter of caprice. Things to do, welcome or unwelcome, he puts them off, leaves them till tomorrow and tomorrow and never quite grows up.

FAUST

Rubbish. No more of that. I won't listen to it. Harping on that note, you might fool the wisest of men. You won't fool me.

CARE

Shall he go? Shall he come? He can't make up his mind. In the middle of the trodden road he totters and he fumbles, seeing more and more awry, getting more and more confused; a burden to himself, a burden to others; panting, choking, not quite suffocating; not yielding, not despairing, just rolling, unable to stop; thwarted, driven; relieved, oppressed; never sound asleep, never wide awake. All this fixes him where he is and prepares him for hell.

FAUST

You wretched ghosts, this is how you've treated the human race times out of number, turning even indifferent days into tangles of torment. Phantoms, I know, are hard to be rid of. The bond with them will never be broken. But your insidious power, O Care, I will not admit it.

CARE

Then taste it now in the parting curse I leave you with. Most men are blind all their lives. Now, Faust, at long last it's your turn.

She breathes on him. Off

FAUST *blinded*

The dark seems darker than before, but my inner light shines clear. No time must be lost in carrying out what I intended. The master's voice is needed here. Up from your beds, you labourers, every one. Let me see with my eyes what I so boldly planned. Seize your tools. At it with spades and shovels. The plot staked out must be finished now, and for strict discipline and speedy work I promise rich rewards. To complete a great project one mind is enough for a thousand hands.

THE GREAT COURTYARD OF THE PALACE
Torches

MEPHISTOPHELES *as custodian, leading*

Come along, come along, you shambling lemurs, you half-begotten contrivances of bone and sinew.

LEMURS *in chorus*

Here we are on hand at once, and as our wits half-tell us, there's a great piece of land going, and we're supposed to get it.

The pointed stakes are waiting there, and the long chain for measuring. You sent for us to come and help. Why us, we can't remember.

MEPHISTOPHELES

This is no job for an artist. Just go by your own proportions.
Let the lankiest of you lie down flat, and the rest of you ease
the turf all round him. Dig out a longish rectangle, like those
men dug for our forebears. Out of the palace into the narrow
room. This is the stupid end it always comes to.

LEMURS *digging with droll gestures*

When I was young and full of zest, I thought it very sweet.
If there was merriment about, it got into my feet.

But now old age has caught me up, and tripped me with his
crutch. I stumbled at the door of the grave. Too bad it
wasn't shut.

FAUST *coming out of the palace, feeling his way by the door-posts*

Oh how I love this clatter of spades. It's my men working for
me, making the shore safe, checking the waves, setting limits
to the sea.

MEPHISTOPHELES *aside*

You with your dams and piers, you're only playing into our
hands. Neptune, the sea-devil, will have a great celebration
over this. You haven't a ghost of a chance. We're in league
with the elements and the end of it all is destruction.

FAUST

Custodian.

MEPHISTOPHELES

Here, sir.

FAUST

Use every means to get more workers. Treat them well, drive
them hard. Pay them, entice them, press them. You must
report daily on the progress of the ditch.

MEPHISTOPHELES *under his breath*

The way I understand it, it's not a ditch, it's a grave.

FAUST

There is a swamp, skirting the base of the hills, a foul and
filthy blot on all our work. If we could drain and cleanse this
pestilence, it would crown everything we have achieved,
opening up living space for many millions. Not safe from
every hazard, but safe enough. Green fields and fruitful too

for man and beast, both quickly domiciled on new-made land, all snug and settled under the mighty dune that many hands have built with fearless toil. Inside it life will be a paradise. Let the floods rage and mount to the dune's brink. No sooner will they nibble at it, threaten it, than all as one man run to stop the gap. Now I am wholly of this philosophy. This is the farthest human wisdom goes: The man who earns his freedom every day, alone deserves it, and no other does. And, in this sense, with dangers at our door, we all, young folk and old, shall live our lives. Oh how I'd love to see that lusty throng and stand on a free soil with a free people. Now I could almost say to the passing moment: Stay, oh stay a while, you are beautiful. The mark of my endeavours will not fade. No, not in ages, not in any time. Dreaming of this incomparable happiness, I now taste and enjoy the supreme moment.

Faust collapses. The lemurs pick him up and lay him on the ground

MEPHISTOPHELES
Indulgence never sated him, no happiness sufficed. One pursuit it was after another, never the same. And now this futile, final moment of all, he wants to cling to it. He stood out mightily against me, but time has conquered him. There the old man lies. His clock has stopped.

CHORUS
Stopped. Run down. Silent as midnight.

MEPHISTOPHELES
It's all over.

CHORUS
It's finished.

MEPHISTOPHELES
Finished. A silly word. Why finished, I'd like to know. Finished and sheer nothingness all one and the same. What use is this interminable creating, this dragging creation into uncreation again? Finished. What does it point to? It might as well never have been at all. And yet it goes its round as if it was something. Give me eternal emptiness every time.

BURIAL

LEMUR *solo*

O who has built so mean a house, with nothing more than a shovel.

LEMURS *chorus*

You sorry guest in a hempen shroud, it's much too good for you, sir.

LEMUR *solo*

And what about the furniture? No chairs, not even a table.

LEMURS *chorus*

We had them on so short a loan. There are too many claimants.

MEPHISTOPHELES

Here lies the corpse and if the soul comes out, I'll quickly show it the blood-signed title-deed. The trouble is there are so many ways now of outwitting me. The old style is out of favour, and they don't like the new. The day was when I could have managed this by myself, but now I need accomplices.

Things are going badly with us devils. Established customs, ancient privileges, you can't trust anything any more. It used to be that the soul came out with the last breath. I'd be on the look-out for it and, quick as a flash, I had it in my clutch. But now it hesitates, loath, it seems, to leave its quarters in that dismal corpse. I know the conflicting elements will bundle it out sooner or later. But meanwhile I have to plague myself day and night with when, how, and where. Death has lost its old vigour. You have to wait and wait to see if it's really there. Many a time have I kept my eye greedily on the rigid limbs. And it was deceptive. The thing began to shift and stir again.

Making strange, mechanical, exorcizing gestures

Come quickly, quickly now, you devils of the ancient cut, some with crumpled horns and some with straight. And bring hell's jaws along with you. I know that hell has many jaws and swallows its victims according to rank. But we aren't going to be so particular in future, even at this stage.

The horrid jaws of hell open, left

See there the tusks. And the raging flames pouring out of the arched gullet. In the murk behind I can see the city of eternal fire. The red surf comes foaming as far as the teeth and the doomed swim up, hoping to escape, only to be gulped down by this monstrous hyena and start all over again. There's lots more to be seen in holes and corners, so many horrors in such narrow space. You do right to strike terror into the hearts of sinners. They don't believe it's true, they think it's a sham.

To the fat devils with short straight horns

Now, you paunchy, short-necked devils with cheeks aflame, fattened on hell's sulphur, keep watch down here for a glint of phosphorus. That's the soul, the winged Psyche. If you pluck its wings off, it's just a nasty worm. I'll stick my stamp on it and then off with it into hell's whirlpool.

Watch the lower regions, you podgy ones. That's your special job. Whether this is where the soul resides, we're not so sure. But it likes the navel. So remember, it may slip out there.

To the scraggy devils with long twisted horns

You ninnies, you lanky dummies, keep combing the air all the time, with your arms extended and your sharp claws spread, so as to catch it if it flutters out. It won't be comfortable where it is now and it'll come shooting up before long.

Gloria, from above, right

THE HEAVENLY HOST

Envoys of heaven, follow us, follow, in easy flight, pardoning sinners, refreshing the dust, with loving-kindness for all creation, as you pass by, passing ever so gently.

MEPHISTOPHELES

Those wretched, harping discords, I can hear them, that boyish-girlish jingle so dear to the sanctimonious, coming down from above in this unwelcome blaze of light. You know that in darkest hell we planned to destroy the human race. Well, the foulest sins we invented are just what their piety thrives on.

They're hypocrites, the young puppies. They've robbed us of many a one that way, fighting us with our own weapons. They're devils too, only in disguise. If you let them beat you, you'll never live it down. So stand by the grave and hold your ground.

CHORUS OF ANGELS *scattering roses*

You dazzling roses, fluttering, hovering, spreading your fragrance, secretly life-giving, winged with your twiglets, ready to blossom, be quick to burst open.

Spring, come out in your greens and purples, bringing paradise to him who is sleeping.

MEPHISTOPHELES *to the devils*

What are you ducking and dodging for? What way is this for hell's denizens to behave? Back to your places, every one of you. They think they can snow you under with their silly flowers. Blow on them and they'll shrivel up. Puff hard, you puffers. – Enough now, enough. Your breath has blanched the whole flight. But steady now. Close your mouths and noses. You've been blowing too hard. You never know when to stop. Have you no sense of proportion? You've not just shrivelled the stuff, you've set fire to it. Now it's coming down on you in flames that sting. Huddle together and hold out. Oh, they've given in, they've lost heart. They sense a seductive heat that is new to them.

CHORUS OF ANGELS

These flowers angelic, these playful flames bring offerings of love and joy, to gladden the heart, like words of truth in the clear sky, the heavenly host's eternal daylight.

MEPHISTOPHELES

Oh damn it. The simpletons, standing on their heads, clumsily somersaulting, plunging backwards into hell. I hope it roasts them. They well deserve it. But I mean to stay where I am.

Beating off the roses in the air

Away, you will-o-the-wisps. For all your brightness, you're

only messy spots of dirt, when I get hold of you. Be off. Stop fluttering round me. You're lodging in my neck like pitch and sulphur.

CHORUS OF ANGELS

What isn't yours, you must shun it. What is disturbing, you must reject. But if we stung you, we must sting harder. Love alone leads lovers to heaven.

MEPHISTOPHELES

My head's on fire, my heart, my liver too. This is a more devilish element. It's much crueller than hell-fire. So this is why unhappy lovers, when rejected, crane their necks in search of the one they wanted.

And it's happening to me. Why do I twist my head towards my sworn enemies, the sight of whom I used to abominate? Some strange spirit has come over me. I like the look of them, these darling boys. I can't abuse them any more, something stops me. And if they can make a fool of me, I'll be a fool for ever. Those cunning youngsters attract me, though I hate them. Tell me, aren't you too descendants of Lucifer? You seem to suit me, you're so lovely, so kissable. It's all so easy, so natural, as if I'd seen you lots of times before. And you're so enticing, you're getting prettier all the time. Come nearer. Let me have a closer look.

CHORUS OF ANGELS

Here we are. Why are you running away? We're coming closer. Stay, if you can stand it.

The angels close round and fill the stage

MEPHISTOPHELES *pushed forward into the forestage*

You call us the damned, but it's you who are the real witch-masters, seducing both sexes at once. What a cursed thing to happen. Is this the element of love? My whole body's on fire, making me hardly notice the agony in my neck. You're floating about in the air, come down lower, work your limbs a little less angelically. I know your solemnity suits you, but I wish you'd smile a lover's smile for once. I'd be delighted. Just a twitch of the mouth, that's all. You, the tall one, are the one I fancy. That clerical look doesn't go with you at all. Why not give me a wicked one? And I'd like to see you not so fully dressed. It would become you better. Those long robes are prudish. Now the rascals are turning round. My, from behind aren't they fetching?

CHORUS OF ANGELS

Turn heavenwards now, you flames of love. And let the sinners be healed by the truth, redeemed from evil, redeemed and happy, blest in the company of all the blest.

MEPHISTOPHELES

Whatever has happened? I'm just like Job, my whole body a mass of sores, making me shudder at sight of myself. And yet I triumph, when I look deeper, and trust again in the stock I'm sprung from. The noble parts of the old devil are unimpaired. That weird attack of sex has come out in a rash. The flames are spent. And now I curse you all, as curse I should.

CHORUS OF ANGELS

Sacred fires, those they encircle will find the good life and share it with others. All together rise and sing praises. The air is pure. The spirit can breathe again.

They rise in the air, carrying off Faust's immortal part

MEPHISTOPHELES *looking round*

But what's this? Where have they gone? Those youngsters have taken me by surprise and are off to heaven with their booty. That's why they came meddling at this graveside. I've lost a rare prize, a unique one, the soul of this great man. It was pledged to me and they've cunningly smuggled it away.

But where can I lodge an appeal? Who will procure me my rightful due? I've been badly let down in my late years, very badly. And it's my fault. I behaved disgracefully. A great effort gone with the wind, all because an erotic impulse of the most absurd variety came over me. It puts me to shame. Fooled at the finish. Me, the tough old devil that ought to have known better.

MOUNTAIN CHASMS, ROCKS, FOREST, WILDERNESS

Anchorites at various levels on the slope, clefts on either side of them

CHORUS AND ECHO

A mountain side begins to show, tree-roots clutching the rock, forest stems rising rank above rank, cascades splashing endlessly, deep caverns for shelter, lions moving about, gentle, noiseless, honouring this sacred place, the abode of heavenly love.

PATER ECSTATICUS *floating up and down*

Joy that burns, love that sears, heart-anguish that scalds, divine rapture that foams. Arrows, come, pierce me. Lances, master me. Clubs, crush me. Lightnings, shatter me. Till all that is worthless is purged away and love's star remains for ever.

PATER PROFUNDUS *lower down*

The abyss at my feet rests on a deeper abyss. A thousand sparkling rivulets unite to form the dread waterfall. The trees soar upwards by their own strength. Each an expression of the almighty love that shapes and cares for all things.

There is a roaring everywhere as if the woods and rocks were in commotion. And yet the torrent sustains its happy flow down to the valley that it waters. The lightning strikes and clears the air of mist and murk.

These again are messengers of love, telling of the creative spirit that surrounds us. Would that it could kindle me, whose mind in cold confusion labours, with senses dulled and unremitting pain. O God, assuage my thoughts. Illuminate my needy heart.

PATER SERAPHICUS *in the middle region*

What morning cloudlet is this, floating through the swaying hair of the pines? I believe I know what it hides. Yes. It is a company of young souls.

CHORUS OF BOY SOULS
Tell us, father, where we're going. Tell us where we are. We know we are happy. Existence sits so lightly on us.

PATER SERAPHICUS
These are boys born at midnight, swept away from their parents with mind and senses barely started. A welcome gain for the angels. You can feel that one who loves you is near, so come closer. You have been spared any knowledge of the rude earth. I invite you to enter me. My eyes are adjusted to the world. Use them as your own and look about you. (*He takes them inside himself*) These are trees. These are rocks. Here is a great rush of water, shortening its steep path downwards.

BOY SOULS *from inside*
Powerful to behold, but gloomy. It fills us with fear. Good father, release us.

PATER SERAPHICUS
Rise to higher regions, growing imperceptibly, as God's nearness and purity gives you strength. It is in the revelation of eternal love, leading to beatitude and ever-present in the ether, that the spirit finds its nourishment.

BOY SOULS *circling around the highest summits*
Join hands in a ring. Sing sacred songs. Be happy, confident now that you will see the god you worship.

ANGELS *hovering in the upper atmosphere, carrying Faust's immortal part*
This noble member of the spirit-world is saved from evil. He who strives and ever strives, him we can redeem. And if love from on high is also his, the angels welcome him.

THE YOUNGER ANGELS
The roses given us by the women penitents helped us to win the fight, rescue this man's soul, and complete the good work. The devils weakened and ran when we pelted them. It was the anguish of love they suffered, not the familiar pains of hell. Even their old chief was stung to the quick. Rejoice, we have succeeded.

THE MATURER ANGELS
To handle a vestige of earth costs us an effort. It might be

asbestos and yet it would be unclean. But when once the spirit welds itself with the elements, it is beyond the angels' power to separate them. Only love eternal can do it.

THE YOUNGER ANGELS

I feel a spirit-life near by, floating like a wisp of cloud round that rocky pinnacle. The cloud is lifting and now I see a lively group of boy souls, freed from the weight of earth, all in a ring, and revelling in the spring-like loveliness of the upper world. Let us put him in their company for a start, to grow along with them towards perfection.

BOY SOULS

We receive him joyfully in his chrysalid state. It will give us weight with the angels. Divest him of these earth-remnants. He is already handsome in his holiness.

DOCTOR MARIANUS *in the highest, purest cell*

Here the view is open, the mind uplifted. Women are passing upwards, our lady in their midst, star-circled. It is the queen of heaven in her splendour.

Enraptured

Supreme mistress of the world, let me see your mystery under the blue canopy of sky. Do not disapprove of the sacred love I bear you in my man's heart.

At your command I am fearless. When you are gracious, the fire quietens. Virgin, mother, purity, our chosen queen, our goddess.

Light clouds play about them. They are penitent women, tenderly breathing the air around her, seeking grace. They in their frailty are allowed to approach you, the immaculate one.

A prey to their weakness, they are hard to save. Who has the inner strength to break the chains of lust? How easily the foot slides on a smooth decline. Who can resist the flattering breath, the seductive word and look?

The mater gloriosa passes by

CHORUS OF PENITENTS

You are ascending to the heights of eternity. Hear our prayer, you the incomparable, you the giver of grace.

MAGNA PECCATRIX

By the love that shed its tears on your son's feet, though the pharisees mocked, by the vessel that poured oil on them and the hair that dried them –

THE SAMARITAN WOMAN

By the well where Abraham once watered his flocks, by the cup that touched and cooled our saviour's lips, by the well-spring that flows from there through all the world in plenty and for ever –

MARY OF EGYPT

By the sacred place where our lord was laid, by the arm that thrust me from the door, by the forty years of penance in the desert that I faithfully kept, by the parting words of blessing that I wrote in the sand –

ALL THREE

We beseech you who permit women that have sinned greatly to come near you and as penitents recover and grow to virtue again eternally, grant your pardon to this poor sinner who fell once and fell in innocence.

UNA POENITENTIUM *formerly Gretchen, joining the others*

You the radiant beyond compare, turn your face to me in my happiness and be kind. My early lover, no longer troubled, has now returned.

BOY SOULS *approaching in a spiral motion*

He has already outgrown us in might of limb. He will reward us well for our care and devotion. We were cut off early, but he is experienced and will instruct us.

WOMAN PENITENT *formerly Gretchen*

In this spirit-company the newcomer hardly knows himself. He barely senses the fresh life beginning. This makes him already like the saints. See how he is shedding the last of his earthly self and, ether-clad, his primal youth and vigour emerges. Allow me to be his teacher. The new light still dazzles him.

MATER GLORIOSA

Come, rise to higher spheres. He will feel your presence there and follow.

DOCTOR MARIANUS *fallen on his face in prayer*
Look up to this saving countenance, all you that are softened
with repentance, thankful now and ready to be transmuted
into blessedness. Put yourselves at her service. Virgin,
mother, queen, goddess, be gracious.

CHORUS MYSTICUS
Transitory things are symbolical only. Here the inadequate
finds its fulfilment. The not expressible is here made manifest. The eternal in woman is the gleam we follow.

SELECTED POEMS

*With translations by Christopher Middleton,
Michael Hamburger and others*

CONTENTS

WILLKOMMEN UND ABSCHIED

Es schlug mein Herz, geschwind zu Pferde!
Es war getan fast eh gedacht.
Der Abend wiegte schon die Erde,
Und an den Bergen hing die Nacht;
Schon stand im Nebelkleid die Eiche,
Ein aufgetürmter Riese, da,
Wo Finsternis aus dem Gesträuche
Mit hundert schwarzen Augen sah.

Der Mond von einem Wolkenhügel
Sah kläglich aus dem Duft hervor,
Die Winde schwangen leise Flügel,
Umsausten schauerlich mein Ohr;
Die Nacht schuf tausend Ungeheuer,
Doch frisch und fröhlich war mein Mut:
In meinen Adern welches Feuer!
In meinem Herzen welche Glut!

Dich sah ich, und die milde Freude
Floß von dem süßen Blick auf mich;
Ganz war mein Herz an deiner Seite
Und jeder Atemzug für dich.
Ein rosenfarbnes Frühlingswetter
Umgab das liebliche Gesicht,
Und Zärtlichkeit für mich – ihr Götter!
Ich hofft es, ich verdient es nicht!

WELCOME AND FAREWELL
(1771; 1789)

My heart beat fast, a horse! away!
Quicker than thought I am astride,
Earth now lulled by end of day,
Night hovering on the mountainside.
A robe of mist around him flung,
The oak a towering giant stood,
A hundred eyes of jet had sprung
From darkness in the bushy wood.

Atop a hill of cloud the moon
Shed piteous glimmers through the mist,
Softly the wind took flight, and soon
With horrible wings around me hissed.
Night made a thousand ghouls respire,
Of what I felt, a thousandth part –
My mind, what a consuming fire!
What a glow was in my heart!

You I saw, your look replied,
Your sweet felicity, my own,
My heart was with you, at your side,
I breathed for you, for you alone.
A blush was there, as if your face
A rosy hue of Spring had caught,
For me – ye gods! – this tenderness!
I hoped, and I deserved it not.

Doch ach, schon mit der Morgensonne
Verengt der Abschied mir das Herz:
In deinen Küssen welche Wonne!
In deinem Auge welcher Schmerz!
Ich ging, du standst und sahst zur Erden,
Und sahst mir nach mit nassem Blick:
Und doch, welch Glück, geliebt zu werden!
Und lieben, Götter, welch ein Glück!

MAILIED

Wie herrlich leuchtet
Mir die Natur!
Wie glänzt die Sonne!
Wie lacht die Flur!

Es dringen Blüten
Aus jedem Zweig
Und tausend Stimmen
Aus dem Gesträuch

Und Freud und Wonne
Aus jeder Brust.
O Erd, o Sonne!
O Glück, o Lust!

O Lieb, o Liebe!
So golden schön,
Wie Morgenwolken
Auf jenen Höhn!

Yet soon the morning sun was there,
My heart, ah, shrank as leave I took:
How rapturous your kisses were,
What anguish then was in your look!
I left, you stood with downcast eyes,
In tears you saw me riding off:
Yet, to be loved, what happiness!
What happiness, ye gods, to love!

MAY SONG (1771)

Marvellous Nature
Shining on me!
Glorious sunlight,
Field shaking with glee!

From all the branches
Flowerlets rush,
A thousand voices
Out of the bush,

And gladness, rapture
From every breast:
O sun, what pleasure!
O earth, how blest!

O love, with a golden
Glow you adorn
The hilltops yonder
Like mist in the morn,

Du segnest herrlich
Das frische Feld,
Im Blütendampfe
Die volle Welt.

O Mädchen, Mädchen,
Wie lieb ich dich!
Wie blickt dein Auge!
Wie liebst du mich!

So liebt die Lerche
Gesang und Luft,
Und Morgenblumen
Den Himmelsduft,

Wie ich dich liebe
Mit warmem Blut,
Die du mir Jugend
Und Freud und Mut

Zu neuen Liedern
Und Tänzen gibst.
Sei ewig glücklich,
Wie du mich liebst!

Splendidly blessing
The meadow trim,
In a haze of blossom,
World full to the brim.

Sweetheart, I love you,
Your glances tell,
Sweet, how you love me,
Love me as well,

So does the lark love
Song and the blue,
And morning flowers
The heavenly dew,

So do I love you,
With hottest blood,
Who give me youth's gladness
And brace my mood

New songs to be making,
New dances to know:
Be happy for ever
In loving me so.

HEIDENRÖSLEIN

Sah ein Knab ein Röslein stehn,
Röslein auf der Heiden,
War so jung und morgenschön,
Lief er schnell, es nah zu sehn,
Sahs mit vielen Freuden.
Röslein, Röslein, Röslein rot,
Röslein auf der Heiden.

Knabe sprach: Ich breche dich,
Röslein auf der Heiden!
Röslein sprach: Ich steche dich,
Daß du ewig denkst an mich,
Und ich wills nicht leiden.
Röslein, Röslein, Röslein rot,
Röslein auf der Heiden.

Und der wilde Knabe brach
's Röslein auf der Heiden;
Röslein wehrte sich und stach,
Half ihm doch kein Weh und Ach,
Mußt es eben leiden.
Röslein, Röslein, Röslein rot,
Röslein auf der Heiden.

MAHOMETS GESANG

Seht den Felsenquell,
Freudehell,
Wie ein Sternenblick;
Über Wolken
Nährten seine Jugend

ROSEBUD IN THE HEATHER
(1771)

Urchin saw a rose – a dear
Rosebud in the heather.
Fresh as dawn and morning-clear;
Ran up quick and stooped to peer,
Took his fill of pleasure,
Rosebud, rosebud, rosebud red,
Rosebud in the heather.

Urchin blurts: 'I'll pick you, though,
Rosebud in the heather!'
Rosebud: 'Then I'll stick you so
That there's no forgetting, no!
I'll not stand it, ever!'
Rosebud, rosebud, rosebud red,
Rosebud in the heather.

But the wild young fellow's torn
Rosebud from the heather.
Rose, she pricks him with her thorn;
Should she plead, or cry forlorn?
Makes no difference whether.
Rosebud, rosebud, rosebud red,
Rosebud in the heather.

A SONG TO MAHOMET
(1772–73)

See the mountain spring
Flash gladdening
Like a glance of stars;
Higher than the clouds
Kindly spirits

Gute Geister
Zwischen Klippen im Gebüsch.

Jünglingfrisch
Tanzt er aus der Wolke
Auf die Marmorfelsen nieder,
Jauchzet wieder
Nach dem Himmel.

Durch die Gipfelgänge
Jagt er bunten Kieseln nach,
Und mit frühem Führertritt
Reißt er seine Bruderquellen
Mit sich fort.

Drunten werden in dem Tal
Unter seinem Fußtritt Blumen,
Und die Wiese
Lebt von seinem Hauch.

Doch ihn hält kein Schattental,
Keine Blumen,
Die ihm seine Knie umschlingen,
Ihm mit Liebes-Augen schmeicheln:
Nach der Ebne dringt sein Lauf
Schlangenwandelnd.

Bäche schmiegen
Sich gesellig an. Nun tritt er
In die Ebne silberprangend,
Und die Ebne prangt mit ihm,
Und die Flüsse von der Ebne
Und die Bäche von den Bergen
Jauchzen ihm und rufen: Bruder!
Bruder, nimm die Brüder mit,
Mit zu deinem alten Vater,
Zu dem ewgen Ozean,

Fuelled his youth
In thickets twixt the crags.

Brisk as a young blade
Out of cloud he dances
Down to marble rocks
And leaps again
Skyward exultant.

Down passages that hang from peaks
He chases pebbles many-coloured,
Early like a leader striding
Snatches up and carries onward
Brother torrents.

Flowers are born beneath his footprint
In the valley down below,
From his breathing
Pastures live.

Yet no valley of the shadows
Can contain him
And no flowers that clasp his knees,
Blandishing with looks of love;
To the lowland bursts his way,
A snake uncoiling.

Freshets nestle
Flocking to his side. He comes
Into the lowland, silver sparkling,
And with him the lowland sparkles,
And the lowland rivers call,
Mountain freshets call exultant:
Brother, take your brothers with you,
With you to your ancient father,
To the everlasting ocean,
Who with open arms awaits us,

Der mit ausgespannten Armen
Unser wartet,
Die sich, ach! vergebens öffnen,
Seine Sehnenden zu fassen;
Denn uns frißt in öder Wüste
Gierger Sand; die Sonne droben
Saugt an unserm Blut; ein Hügel
Hemmet uns zum Teiche! Bruder,
Nimm die Brüder von der Ebne,
Nimm die Brüder von den Bergen
Mit, zu deinem Vater mit!

Kommt ihr alle! —
Und nun schwillt er
Herrlicher; ein ganz Geschlechte
Trägt den Fürsten hoch empor!
Und im rollenden Triumphe
Gibt er Ländern Namen, Städte
Werden unter seinem Fuß.

Unaufhaltsam rauscht er weiter,
Läßt der Türme Flammengipfel,
Marmorhäuser, eine Schöpfung
Seiner Fülle, hinter sich.

Zedernhäuser trägt der Atlas
Auf den Riesenschultern; sausend
Wehen über seinem Haupte
Tausend Flaggen durch die Lüfte,
Zeugen seiner Herrlichkeit.

Und so trägt er seine Brüder,
Seine Schätze, seine Kinder
Dem erwartenden Erzeuger
Freudebrausend an das Herz.

Arms which, ah, open in vain
To clasp us who are craving for him;
Avid sand consumes us
In the desert, sun overhead
Will suck our blood, blocked by a hill
To pools we shrink! Brother, take us,
Take your lowland brothers with you,
Take your brothers of the mountains,
To your father take us all!

Join me then!
And now he swells
More lordly still; one single kin,
They loft the prince and bear him high
Onward as he rolls triumphant,
Naming countries, in his track
Towns and cities come to be.

On he rushes, unrelenting,
Leaves the turrets tipped with flame,
Marble palaces, creation
Of his plenitude, behind him.

Cedar houses he like Atlas
Carries on his giant shoulders;
Flags a thousand rustling flutter
In the air above his head,
Testifying to his glory.

So he bears his brothers, bears
His treasures and his children surging
In a wave of joy tumultuous
To their waiting father's heart.

PROMETHEUS

Bedecke deinen Himmel, Zeus,
Mit Wolkendunst
Und übe, dem Knaben gleich,
Der Disteln köpft,
An Eichen dich und Bergeshöhn;
Mußt mir meine Erde
Doch lassen stehn
Und meine Hütte, die du nicht gebaut,
Und meinen Herd,
Um dessen Glut
Du mich beneidest.

Ich kenne nichts Ärmeres
Unter der Sonn als euch, Götter!
Ihr nähret kümmerlich
Von Opfersteuern
Und Gebetshauch
Eure Majestät
Und darbtet, wären
Nicht Kinder und Bettler
Hoffnungsvolle Toren.

Da ich ein Kind war,
Nicht wußte, wo aus noch ein,
Kehrt ich mein verirrtes Auge
Zur Sonne, als wenn drüber wär
Ein Ohr, zu hören meine Klage,
Ein Herz wie meins,
Sich des Bedrängten zu erbarmen.

Wer half mir
Wider der Titanen Übermut?
Wer rettete vom Tode mich,
Von Sklaverei?
Hast du nicht alles selbst vollendet,

PROMETHEUS (1773)

Cover your heaven, Zeus,
With cloudy vapours
And like a boy
Beheading thistles
Practise on oaks and mountain peaks –
Still you must leave
My earth intact
And my small hovel, which you did not build,
And this my hearth
Whose glowing beat
You envy me.

I know of nothing more wretched
Under the sun than you gods!
Meagrely you nourish
Your majesty
On dues of sacrifice
And breath of prayer
And would suffer want
But for children and beggars,
Poor hopeful fools.

Once too, a child,
Not knowing where to turn,
I raised bewildered eyes
Up to the sun, as if above there were
An ear to hear my complaint,
A heart like mine
To take pity on the oppressed.

Who helped me
Against the Titans' arrogance?
Who rescued me from death,
From slavery?
Did not my holy and glowing heart,

Heilig glühend Herz?
Und glühtest jung und gut,
Betrogen, Rettungsdank
Dem Schlafenden da droben?

Ich dich ehren? Wofür?
Hast du die Schmerzen gelindert
Je des Beladenen?
Hast du die Tränen gestillet
Je des Geängsteten?
Hat nicht mich zum Manne geschmiedet
Die allmächtige Zeit
Und das ewige Schicksal,
Meine Herrn und deine?

Wähntest du etwa,
Ich sollte das Leben hassen,
In Wüsten fliehen,
Weil nicht alle
Blütenträume reiften?

Hier sitz ich, forme Menschen
Nach meinem Bilde,
Ein Geschlecht, das mir gleich sei,
Zu leiden, zu weinen,
Zu genießen und zu freuen sich,
Und dein nicht zu achten,
Wie ich!

Unaided, accomplish all?
And did it not, young and good,
Cheated, glow thankfulness
For its safety to him, to the sleeper above?

I pay homage to you? For what?
Have you ever relieved
The burdened man's anguish?
Have you ever assuaged
The frightened man's tears?
Was it not omnipotent Time
That forged me into manhood,
And eternal Fate,
My masters and yours?

Or did you think perhaps
That I should hate this life,
Flee into deserts
Because not all
The blossoms of dream grew ripe?

Here I sit, forming men
In my image,
A race to resemble me:
To suffer, to weep,
To enjoy, to be glad –
And never to heed you,
Like me!

AUF DEM SEE

Und frische Nahrung, neues Blut
Saug ich aus freier Welt;
Wie ist Natur so hold und gut,
Die mich am Busen hält!
Die Welle wieget unsern Kahn
Im Rudertakt hinauf,
Und Berge, wolkig himmelan,
Begegnen unserm Lauf.

Aug, mein Aug, was sinkst du nieder?
Goldne Träume, kommt ihr wieder?
Weg, du Traum! so gold du bist;
Hier auch Lieb und Leben ist.

Auf der Welle blinken
Tausend schwebende Sterne,
Weiche Nebel trinken
Rings die türmende Ferne;
Morgenwind umflügelt
Die beschattete Bucht,
Und im See bespiegelt
Sich die reifende Frucht.

ON THE LAKE (1775)

And fresh nourishment, new blood
I suck from a world so free;
Nature, how gracious and how good,
Her breast she gives to me.
The ripples buoying up our boat
Keep rhythm to the oars,
And mountains up to heaven float
In cloud to meet our course.

Eyes, my eyes, why abject now?
Golden dreams, are you returning?
Dream, though gold, away with you:
Life is here and loving too.

Over the ripples twinkling
Star on hovering star,
Soft mists drink the circled
Towering world afar;
Dawn wind fans the shaded
Inlet with its wing,
And in the water mirrored
The fruit is ripening.

WANDRERS NACHTLIED

Der du von dem Himmel bist,
Alles Leid und Schmerzen stillest,
Den, der doppelt elend ist,
Doppelt mit Erquickung füllest,
Ach, ich bin des Treibens müde!
Was soll all der Schmerz und Lust?
Süßer Friede,
Komm, ach komm in meine Brust!

EIN GLEICHES

Über allen Gipfeln
Ist Ruh,
In allen Wipfeln
Spürest du
Kaum einen Hauch;
Die Vögelein schweigen im Walde.
Warte nur, balde
Ruhest du auch.

WANDERER'S NIGHT SONG
(1776)

Thou that from the heavens art,
    Every pain and sorrow stillest,
And the doubly wretched heart
    Doubly with refreshment fillest,
I am weary with contending!
    Why this rapture and unrest?
Peace descending
    Come, ah, come into my breast!

ANOTHER NIGHT SONG
(1780)

O'er all the hill-tops
    Is quiet now,
In all the tree-tops
    Hearest thou
Hardly a breath;
    The birds are asleep in the trees:
    Wait, soon like these
        Thou, too, shalt rest.

AN DEN MOND

Füllest wieder Busch und Tal
Still mit Nebelglanz,
Lösest endlich auch einmal
Meine Seele ganz;

Breitest über mein Gefild
Lindernd deinen Blick,
Wie des Freundes Auge mild
Über mein Geschick.

Jeden Nachklang fühlt mein Herz
Froh- und trüber Zeit,
Wandle zwischen Freud und Schmerz
In der Einsamkeit.

Fließe, fließe, lieber Fluß!
Nimmer werd ich froh,
So verrauschte Scherz und Kuß,
Und die Treue so.

Ich besaß es doch einmal,
Was so köstlich ist!
Daß man doch zu seiner Qual
Nimmer es vergißt!

Rausche, Fluß, das Tal entlang,
Ohne Rast und Ruh,
Rausche, flüstre meinem Sang
Melodien zu,

Wenn du in der Winternacht
Wütend überschwillst,
Oder um die Frühlingspracht
Junger Knospen quillst.

TO THE MOON
(1777; this second version published 1789)

Flooding with a brilliant mist
Valley, bush and tree,
You release me. Oh for once
Heart and soul I'm free!

Easy on the region round
Goes your wider gaze,
Like a friend's indulgent eye
Measuring my days.

Every echo from the past,
Glum or gaudy mood,
Haunts me – weighing bliss and pain
In the solitude.

River, flow and flow away;
Pleasure's dead to me:
Gone the laughing kisses, gone
Lips and loyalty.

All in my possession once!
Such a treasure yet
Any man would pitch in pain
Rather than forget.

Water, rush along the pass,
Never lag at ease;
Rush, and rustle to my song
Changing melodies,

How in dark December you
Roll amok in flood;
Curling, in the gala May,
Under branch and bud.

Selig, wer sich vor der Welt
Ohne Haß verschließt,
Einen Freund am Busen hält
Und mit dem genießt,

Was, von Menschen nicht gewußt
Oder nicht bedacht,
Durch das Labyrinth der Brust
Wandelt in der Nacht.

DAS GÖTTLICHE

Edel sei der Mensch,
Hilfreich und gut!
Denn das allein
Unterscheidet ihn
Von allen Wesen,
Die wir kennen.

Heil den unbekannten
Höhern Wesen,
Die wir ahnen!
Ihnen gleiche der Mensch;
Sein Beispiel lehr uns
Jene glauben.

Denn unfühlend
Ist die Natur:
Es leuchtet die Sonne
Über Bös' und Gute,
Und dem Verbrecher
Glänzen wie dem Besten
Der Mond und die Sterne.

Happy man, that rancour-free
Shows the world his door;
One companion by – and both
In a glow before

Something never guessed by men
Or rejected quite:
Which, in mazes of the breast,
Wanders in the night.

THE GODLIKE
(early 1780's)

Noble let man be,
Helpful and good;
For that alone
Distinguishes him
From all beings
That we know.

Hail to the unknown,
Loftier beings
Our minds prefigure!
Let man be like them;
His example teach us
To believe those.

For unfeeling,
Numb, is nature;
The sun shines
Upon bad and good,
And to the criminal
As to the best
The moon and the stars lend light.

Wind und Ströme,
Donner und Hagel
Rauschen ihren Weg
Und ergreifen
Vorüber eilend
Einen um den andern.

Auch so das Glück
Tappt unter die Menge,
Faßt bald des Knaben
Lockige Unschuld,
Bald auch den kahlen
Schuldigen Scheitel.

Nach ewigen, ehrnen,
Großen Gesetzen
Müssen wir alle
Unseres Daseins
Kreise vollenden.

Nur allein der Mensch
Vermag das Unmögliche:
Er unterscheidet,
Wählet und richtet;
Er kann dem Augenblick
Dauer verleihen.

Er allein darf
Den Guten lohnen,
Den Bösen strafen,
Heilen und retten,
Alles Irrende, Schweifende
Nützlich verbinden.

Und wir verehren
Die Unsterblichen,
Als wären sie Menschen,

Wind and rivers,
Thunder and hail
Rush on their way
And as they race
Headlong, take hold
One on the other.

So, too, chance
Gropes through the crowd,
And quickly snatches
The boy's curled innocence,
Quickly also
The guilty baldpate.

Following great, bronzen,
Ageless laws
All of us must
Fulfil the circles
Of our existence.

Yet man alone can
Achieve the impossible:
He distinguishes,
Chooses and judges;
He can give lasting
Life to the moment.

He alone should
Reward the good,
Punish the wicked,
Heal and save,
All erring and wandering
Usefully gather.

And we honour
Them, the immortals,
As though they were men,

Täten im Großen,
Was der Beste im Kleinen
Tut oder möchte.

Der edle Mensch
Sei hilfreich und gut!
Unermüdet schaff er
Das Nützliche, Rechte,
Sei uns ein Vorbild
Jener geahneten Wesen!

ERLKÖNIG

Wer reitet so spät durch Nacht und Wind?
Es ist der Vater mit seinem Kind;
Er hat den Knaben wohl in dem Arm,
Er faßt ihn sicher, er hält ihn warm.

Mein Sohn, was birgst du so bang dein Gesicht? –
Siehst, Vater, du den Erlkönig nicht?
Den Erlenkönig mit Kron und Schweif? –
Mein Sohn, es ist ein Nebelstreif. –

«Du liebes Kind, komm, geh mit mir!
Gar schöne Spiele spiel ich mit dir;
Manch bunte Blumen sind an dem Strand,
Meine Mutter hat manch gülden Gewand.»

Mein Vater, mein Vater, und hörest du nicht,
Was Erlenkönig mir leise verspricht? –
Sei ruhig, bleibe ruhig, mein Kind;
In dürren Blättern säuselt der Wind. –

Achieving in great ways
What the best in little
Achieves or longs to.

Let noble man
Be helpful and good,
Create unwearied
The useful, the just;
Be to us a pattern
Of those prefigured beings.

ERLKÖNIG (c. 1782)

Who rides by night in the wind so wild?
It is the father, with his child.
The boy is safe in his father's arm,
He holds him tight, he keeps him warm.

My son, what is it, why cover your face?
Father, you see him, there in that place,
The elfin king with his cloak and crown?
It is only the mist rising up, my son.

'Dear little child, will you come with me?
Beautiful games I'll play with thee;
Bright are the flowers we'll find on the shore,
My mother has golden robes fullscore.'

Father, O father, and did you not hear
What the elfin king breathed into my ear?
Lie quiet, my child, now never you mind:
Dry leaves it was that click in the wind.

«Willst, feiner Knabe, du mit mir gehn?
Meine Töchter sollen dich warten schön;
Meine Töchter führen den nächtlichen Reihn,
Und wiegen und tanzen und singen dich ein.»

Mein Vater, mein Vater, und siehst du nicht dort
Erlkönigs Töchter am düstern Ort? –
Mein Sohn, mein Sohn, ich seh es genau:
Es scheinen die alten Weiden so grau. –

«Ich liebe dich, mich reizt deine schöne Gestalt;
Und bist du nicht willig, so brauch ich Gewalt.»
Mein Vater, mein Vater, jetzt faßt er mich an!
Erlkönig hat mir ein Leids getan! –

Dem Vater grausets, er reitet geschwind,
Er hält in Armen das ächzende Kind,
Erreicht den Hof mit Mühe und Not;
In seinen Armen das Kind war tot.

'Come along now, you're a fine little lad,
My daughters will serve you, see you are glad;
My daughters dance all night in a ring,
They'll cradle and dance you and lullaby sing.'

Father, now look, in the gloom, do you see
The elfin daughters beckon to me?
My son, my son, I see it and say:
Those old willows, they look so grey.

'I love you, beguiled by your beauty I am,
If you are unwilling I'll force you to come!'
Father, his fingers grip me, O
The elfin king has hurt me so!

Now struck with horror the father rides fast,
His gasping child in his arm to the last,
Home through thick and thin he sped:
Locked in his arm, the child was dead.

MIGNON

Kennst du das Land, wo die Zitronen blühn,
Im dunkeln Laub die Gold-Orangen glühn,
Ein sanfter Wind vom blauen Himmel weht,
Die Myrte still und hoch der Lorbeer steht,
Kennst du es wohl?
     Dahin! Dahin
Möcht ich mit dir, o mein Geliebter, ziehn.

Kennst du das Haus? Auf Säulen ruht sein Dach,
Es glänzt der Saal, es schimmert das Gemach,
Und Marmorbilder stehn und sehn mich an:
Was hat man dir, du armes Kind, getan?
Kennst du es wohl?
     Dahin! Dahin
Möcht ich mit dir, o mein Beschützer, ziehn.

Kennst du den Berg und seinen Wolkensteg?
Das Maultier sucht im Nebel seinen Weg,
In Höhlen wohnt der Drachen alte Brut,
Es stürzt der Fels und über ihn die Flut;
Kennst du ihn wohl?
     Dahin! Dahin
Geht unser Weg! o Vater, laß uns ziehn!

MIGNON
(from *Wilhelm Meisters Lehrjahre*, 1795)

Knowst thou the land of flowering lemon trees?
In leafage dark the golden orange glows,
From azure sky there wafts a gentle breeze,
Calm the myrtle, high the laurel grows,
Knowst thou it still?
                    Aiee, aiee,
There would I go, belovèd mine, with thee.

Knowst thou the house? Its column-bedded roof,
The shining hall, the inner room aglow,
The marble statues gaze but do not move:
What have they done, poor child, to hurt thee so?
Knowst thou it still?
                    Aiee, aiee,
There would I go, protector mine, with thee.

Knowst thou the mountain, stepping up through cloud?
The mule in mist treads out his path; a cave,
And in it dwells the ancient dragon brood;
The crag swoops down and over it the wave;
Knowst thou it still?
                    Aiee, aiee,
There goes the way, father, for thee and me.

(*This translation is dedicated to the memory of Gérard de Nerval*)

RÖMISCHE ELEGIEN

I

Saget, Steine, mir an, O sprecht, ihr hohen Paläste!
    Straßen, redet ein Wort! Genius, regst du dich nicht?
Ja, es ist alles beseelt in deinen heiligen Mauern,
    Ewige Roma; nur mir schweiget noch alles so still.
O wer flüstert mir zu, an welchem Fenster erblick ich
    Einst das holde Geschöpf, das mich versengend erquickt?
Ahn ich die Wege noch nicht, durch die ich immer und immer,
    Zu ihr und von ihr zu gehn, opfre die köstliche Zeit?
Noch betracht ich Kirch und Palast, Ruinen und Säulen,
    Wie ein bedächtiger Mann schicklich die Reise benutzt.
Doch bald ist es vorbei; dann wird ein einziger Tempel,
    Amors Tempel, nur sein, der den Geweihten empfängt.
Eine Welt zwar bist du, o Rom; doch ohne die Liebe
    Wäre die Welt nicht die Welt, wäre denn Rom auch nicht Rom.

Ia

Mehr als ich ahndete schön, das Glück, es ist mir geworden,
    Amor führte mich klug allen Palästen vorbei.
Ihm ist es lange bekannt, auch hab ich es selbst wohl erfahren,
    Was ein goldnes Gemach hinter Tapeten verbirgt.
Nennet blind ihn und Knaben und ungezogen, ich kenne
    Kluger Amor dich wohl, nimmer bestechlicher Gott!
Uns verführten sie nicht, die majestätschen Fassaden,
    Nicht der galante Balkon, weder das ernste Kortil.
Eilig ging es vorbei, und niedre zierliche Pforte

From *Roman Elegies* (1788–90)

ROMAN ELEGIES (c. 1788–90)

I

Deign to speak to me, stones, you high palaces, deign to address me
    Streets, now say but one word! Genius, will you not stir?
True, all is living yet within your sanctified precincts,
    Timeless Rome; only me all still in silence receives.
O, who will whisper to me, at what small window, revealing
    Her, the dear one, whose glance, searing, will quicken my blood?
Can I not guess on what roads, forever coming and going,
    Only for her sake I'll spend all my invaluable time?
Still I'm seeing the sights, the churches, the ruins, the columns,
    As a serious man ought to and does use his days.
That, however, will pass, and soon no more than one temple,
    Amor's temple alone, claim this initiate's zeal.
Rome, you remain a whole world; but without love the whole
      world would
    Always be less than the world, neither would Rome still
    be Rome.

Ia

Fortune beyond my loveliest daydreams fulfilled is my own now,
    Amor, my clever guide, passed all the palaces by.
Long he has known, and I too had occasion to learn by experience,
    What a richly gilt room hides behind hangings and screens.
You may call him a boy and blind and ill-mannered, but, clever
    Amor, I know you well, never corruptible god!
As they did not take in, those façades so imposing and pompous,
    Gallant balcony here, dignified courtyard down there.
Quickly we passed them by, and a humble but delicate doorway

Nahm den Führer zugleich, nahm den Verlangenden auf.
Alles verschafft er mir da, hilft alles und alles erhalten,
  Streuet jeglichen Tag frischere Rosen mir auf.
Hab ich den Himmel nicht hier? – Was gibst du, schöne Borghese,
  Nipotina was gibst deinem Geliebten du mehr?
Tafel, Gesellschaft und Kors' und Spiel und Oper und Bälle,
  Amorn rauben sie nur oft die gelegenste Zeit.
Ekel bleibt mir Gezier und Putz, und hebet am Ende
  Sich ein brokatener Rock nicht wie ein wollener auf?
Oder will sie bequem den Freund im Busen verbergen,
  Wünscht er von alle dem Schmuck nicht schon behend sie
    befreit?
Müssen nicht jene Juwelen und Spitzen, Polster und Fischbein
  Alle zusammen herab, eh er die Liebliche fühlt?
Näher haben wir das! Schon fällt dein wollenes Kleidchen,
  So wie der Freund es gelöst, faltig zum Boden hinab.
Eilig trägt er das Kind, in leichter linnener Hülle,
  Wie es der Amme geziemt, scherzend aufs Lager hinan.
Ohne das seidne Gehäng und ohne gestickte Matratzen,
  Stehet es, zweien bequem, frei in dem weiten Gemach.
Nehme dann Jupiter mehr von seiner Juno, es lasse
  Wohler sich, wenn er es kann, irgend ein Sterblicher sein.
Uns ergötzen die Freuden des echten nacketen Amors
  Und des geschaukelten Betts lieblicher knarrender Ton.

                              V

Froh empfind ich mich nun auf klassischem Boden begeistert;
  Vor- und Mitwelt spricht lauter und reizender mir.
Hier befolg ich den Rat, durchblättre die Werke der Alten
  Mit geschäftiger Hand, täglich mit neuem Genuß.
Aber die Nächte hindurch hält Amor mich anders beschäftigt;
  Werd ich auch halb nur gelehrt, bin ich doch doppelt beglückt.
Und belehr ich mich nicht, indem ich des lieblichen Busens
  Formen spähe, die Hand leite die Hüften hinab?
Dann versteh ich den Marmor erst recht; ich denk und vergleiche,
  Sehe mit fühlendem Aug, fühle mit sehender Hand.

Opened to guided and guide, made them both welcome within.
All he provides for me there, with his help I obtain all I ask for,
  Fresher roses each day strewn on my path by the god.
Isn't it heaven itself? – And what more could the lovely Borghese,
  Nipotina herself offer a lover than that?
Dinners, drives and dances, operas, card games and parties,
  Often merely they steal Amor's most opportune hours.
Airs and finery bore me; when all's said and done, it's the same
      thing
  Whether the skirt you lift is of brocade or of wool.
Or if the wish of a girl is to pillow her lover in comfort,
  Wouldn't he first have her put all those sharp trinkets away?
All those jewels and pads, and the lace that surrounds her, the
      whalebone,
  Don't they all have to go, if he's to feel his beloved?
Us it gives much less trouble! Your plain woollen dress in a jiffy,
  Unfastened by me, slips down, lies in its folds on the floor.
Quickly I carry the child in her flimsy wrapping of linen
  As befits a good nurse, teasingly, into her bed.
Bare of silken drapery, mattresses richly embroidered,
  Spacious for two, it stands free in a spacious room.
Then let Jupiter get more joy from his Juno, a mortal
  Anywhere in this world know more contentment than I.
We enjoy the delights of the genuine naked god, Amor,
  And our rock-a-bye bed's rhythmic, melodious creak.

                              V
Happy now I can feel the classical climate inspire me,
  Past and present at last clearly, more vividly speak.
Here I take their advice, perusing the works of the ancients
  With industrious care, pleasure that grows every day.
But throughout the nights by Amor I'm differently busied,
  If only half improved, doubly delighted instead.
Also, am I not learning when at the shape of her bosom,
  Graceful lines, I can glance, guide a light hand down her hips?
Only thus I appreciate marble; reflecting, comparing,
  See with an eye that can feel, feel with a hand that can see.

Raubt die Liebste denn gleich mir einige Stunden des Tages,
    Gibt sie Stunden der Nacht mir zur Entschädigung hin.
Wird doch nicht immer geküßt, es wird vernünftig gesprochen;
    Überfällt sie der Schlaf, lieg ich und denke mir viel.
Oftmals hab ich auch schon in ihren Armen gedichtet
    Und des Hexameters Maß leise mit fingernder Hand
Ihr auf den Rücken gezählt. Sie atmet in lieblichem Schlummer,
    Und es durchglühet ihr Hauch mir bis ins Tiefste die Brust.
Amor schüret die Lamp indes und denket der Zeiten,
    Da er den nämlichen Dienst seinen Triumvirn getan.

True, the loved one besides may claim a few hours of the daytime,
  But in night hours as well makes full amends for the loss.
For not always we're kissing, often hold sensible converse;
  When she succumbs to sleep, pondering, long I lie still.
Often too in her arms I've lain composing a poem,
  Gently with fingering hand count the hexameter's beat
Out on her back; she breathes, so lovely and calm in her sleeping
  That the glow from her lips deeply transfuses my heart.
Amor meanwhile refuels the lamp and remembers the times when
  Them, his triumvirs of verse, likewise he's served and obliged.

NÄHE DES GELIEBTEN

Ich denke dein, wenn mir der Sonne Schimmer
   Vom Meere strahlt;
Ich denke dein, wenn sich des Mondes Flimmer
   In Quellen malt.

Ich sehe dich, wenn auf dem fernen Wege
   Der Staub sich hebt;
In tiefer Nacht, wenn auf dem schmalen Stege
   Der Wandrer bebt.

Ich höre dich, wenn dort mit dumpfem Rauschen
   Die Welle steigt.
Im stillen Haine geh ich oft zu lauschen,
   Wenn alles schweigt.

Ich bin bei dir, du seist auch noch so ferne,
   Du bist mir nah!
Die Sonne sinkt, bald leuchten mir die Sterne.
   O wärst du da!

NEARNESS OF THE BELOVED (*c.* 1795)

I think of you when from the sea the shimmer
  Of sunlight streams;
I think of you when on the brook the dimmer
  Moon casts her beams.

I see your face when on the distant highway
  Dust whirls and flakes,
In deepest night when on the mountain byway
  The traveller quakes.

I hear your voice when, dully roaring, yonder
  Waves rise and spill;
Listening, in silent woods I often wander
  When all is still.

I walk with you, though miles from you divide me;
  Yet you are near!
The sun goes down, soon stars will shine to guide me.
  Would you were here!

DIE METAMORPHOSE DER PFLANZEN

Dich verwirret, Geliebte, die tausendfältige Mischung
    Dieses Blumengewühls über dem Garten umher;
Viele Namen hörest du an, und immer verdränget
    Mit barbarischem Klang einer den andern im Ohr.
Alle Gestalten sind ähnlich, und keine gleichet der andern;
    Und so deutet das Chor auf in geheimes Gesetz,
Auf ein heiliges Rätsel. O könnt ich dir, liebliche Freundin,
    Überliefern sogleich glücklich das lösende Wort! –
Werdend betrachte sie nun, wie nach und nach sich die Pflanze,
    Stufenweise geführt, bildet zu Blüten und Frucht.
Aus dem Samen entwickelt sie sich, sobald ihn der Erde
    Stille befruchtender Schoß hold in das Leben entläßt
Und dem Reize des Lichts, des heiligen, ewig bewegten,
    Gleich den zärtesten Bau keimender Blätter empfiehlt.
Einfach schlief in dem Samen die Kraft; ein beginnendes Vorbild
    Lag, verschlossen in sich, unter die Hülle gebeugt,
Blatt und Wurzel und Keim, nur halb geformet und farblos;
    Trocken erhält so der Kern ruhiges Leben bewahrt,
Quillet strebend empor, sich milder Feuchte vertrauend,
    Und erhebt sich sogleich aus der umgebenden Nacht.
Aber einfach bleibt die Gestalt der ersten Erscheinung,
    Und so bezeichnet sich auch unter den Pflanzen das Kind.
Gleich darauf ein folgender Trieb, sich erhebend, erneuet,
    Knoten auf Knoten getürmt, immer das erste Gebild.
Zwar nicht immer das gleiche; denn mannigfaltig erzeugt sich,
    Ausgebildet, du siehsts, immer das folgende Blatt,
Ausgedehnter, gekerbter, getrennter in Spitzen und Teile,
    Die verwachsen vorher ruhten im untern Organ.
Und so erreicht es zuerst die höchst bestimmte Vollendung,
    Die bei manchem Geschlecht dich zum Erstaunen bewegt.
Viel gerippt und gezackt, auf mastig strotzender Fläche,
    Scheinet die Fülle des Triebs frei und unendlich zu sein.
Doch hier hält die Natur, mit mächtigen Händen, die Bildung
    An und lenket sie sanft in das Vollkommnere hin.
Mäßiger leitet sie nun den Saft, verengt die Gefäße,

THE METAMORPHOSIS OF PLANTS (1798)

Overwhelming, beloved, you find all this mixture of thousands,
   Riot of flowers let loose over the garden's expanse;
Many names you take in, and always the last to be spoken
   Drives out the one heard before, barbarous both to your ear.
All the shapes are akin and none is quite like the other;
   So to a secret law surely that chorus must point,
To a sacred enigma. Dear friend, how I wish I were able
   All at once to pass on, happy, the word that unlocks!
Growing consider the plant and see how by gradual phases,
   Slowly evolved, it forms, rises to blossom and fruit.
From the seed it develops as soon as the quietly fertile
   Womb of earth sends it out, sweetly released into life,
And to the prompting of light, the holy, for ever in motion,
   Like the burgeoning leaves' tenderest build, hands it on.
Single, dormant the power in the seed was; the germ of an image,
   Closed in itself, lay concealed, prototype curled in the husk,
Leaf and root and bud, although colourless yet, half-amorphous;
   Drily the nucleus so safeguards incipient life,
Then, aspiring, springs up, entrusting itself to mild moisture,
   Speedily raises itself out of encompassing night.
Single, simple, however, remains the first visible structure;
   So that what first appears, even in plants, is the child.
Following, rising at once, with one nodule piled on another,
   Always the second renews only the shape of the first.
Not the same, though, for ever; for manifold – you can observe it –
   Mutably fashioned each leaf after the last one unfolds,
More extended, spikier, split into lances or segments
   Which, intergrown before, lay in the organ below.
Only now it attains the complete intended perfection
   Which, in many a kind, moves you to wonder, admire.
Many-jagged and ribbed, on a lusciously, fully fleshed surface,
   Growth so lavishly fed seems without limit and free.
Forcefully here, however, will Nature step in to contain it,
   Curbing rankness here, gently perfecting the shapes.
Now more slowly the sap she conducts, and constricts the vessels,

Und gleich zeigt die Gestalt zärtere Wirkungen an.
Stille zieht sich der Trieb der strebenden Ränder zurücke,
    Und die Rippe des Stiels bildet sich völliger aus.
Blattlos aber und schnell erhebt sich der zärtere Stengel,
    Und ein Wundergebild zieht den Betrachtenden an.
Rings im Kreise stellet sich nun, gezählet und ohne
    Zahl, das kleinere Blatt neben dem ähnlichen hin.
Um die Achse gedrängt entscheidet der bergende Kelch sich,
    Der zur höchsten Gestalt farbige Kronen entläßt.
Also prangt die Natur in hoher, voller Erscheinung,
    Und sie zeiget, gereiht, Glieder an Glieder gestuft.
Immer staunst du aufs neue, sobald sich am Stengel die Blume
    Über dem schlanken Gerüst wechselnder Blätter bewegt.
Aber die Herrlichkeit wird des neuen Schaffens Verkündung.
    Ja, das farbige Blatt fühlet die göttliche Hand,
Und zusammen zieht es sich schnell; die zärtesten Formen,
    Zwiefach streben sie vor, sich zu vereinen bestimmt.
Traulich stehen sie nun, die holden Paare, beisammen,
    Zahlreich ordnen sie sich um den geweihten Altar.
Hymen schwebet herbei, und herrliche Düfte, gewaltig,
    Strömen süßen Geruch, alles belebend, umher.
Nun vereinzelt schwellen sogleich unzählige Keime,
    Hold in den Mutterschoß schwellender Früchte gehüllt.
Und hier schließt die Natur den Ring der ewigen Kräfte;
    Doch ein neuer sogleich fasset den vorigen an,
Daß die Kette sich fort durch alle Zeiten verlänge,
    Und das Ganze belebt, so wie das Einzelne, sei.
Nun, Geliebte, wende den Blick zum bunten Gewimmel,
    Das verwirrend nicht mehr sich vor dem Geiste bewegt.
Jede Pflanze verkündet dir nun die ewgen Gesetze,
    Jede Blume, sie spricht lauter und lauter mit dir.
Aber entzifferst du hier der Göttin heilige Lettern,
    Überall siehst du sie dann, auch in verändertem Zug.
Kriechend zaudre die Raupe, der Schmetterling eile geschäftig,
    Bildsam ändre der Mensch selbst die bestimmte Gestalt.
O, gedenke denn auch, wie aus dem Keim der Bekanntschaft

And at once the form yields, with diminished effects.
Calmly the outward thrust of the spreading leaf-rims recedes now,
    While, more firmly defined, swells the thin rib of the stalks.
Leafless, though, and swift the more delicate stem rises up now,
    And, a miracle wrought, catches the onlooker's eye.
In a circular cluster, all counted and yet without number,
    Smaller leaves take their place, next to a similar leaf.
Pushed close up to the hub now, the harbouring calyx develops
    Which to the highest of forms rises in colourful crowns.
Thus in fulness of being does Nature now glory, resplendent,
    Limb to limb having joined, all her gradations displayed.
Time after time you wonder as soon as the stalk-crowning blossom
    Sways on its slender support, gamut of mutable leaves.
Yet the splendour becomes an announcement of further creation.
    Yes, to the hand that's divine colourful leaves will respond.
And it quickly furls, contracts; the most delicate structures
    Twofold venture forth, destined to meet and unite.
Wedded now they stand, those delighted couples, together.
    Round the high altar they form multiple, ordered arrays.
Hymen, hovering, nears, and pungent perfumes, exquisite,
    Fill with fragrance and life all the environing air.
One by one now, though numberless, germs are impelled into
        swelling,
    Sweetly wrapped in the womb, likewise swelling, of fruit.
Nature here closes her ring of the energies never-exhausted
    Yet a new one at once links to the circle that's closed,
That the chain may extend into the ages for ever,
    And the whole be infused amply with life, like the part.
Look, beloved, once more on the teeming of so many colours,
    Which no longer may now fill with confusion your mind.
Every plant now declares those eternal designs that have shaped it,
    Ever more clearly to you every flower-head can speak.
Yet if here you decipher the holy runes of the goddess,
    Everywhere you can read, even though scripts are diverse:
Let the grub drag along, the butterfly busily scurry,
    Imaging man by himself alter the pre-imposed shape.
Oh, and consider then how in us from the germ of acquaintance

Nach und nach in uns holde Gewohnheit entsproß,
    Freundschaft sich mit Macht in unserm Innern enthüllte,
        Und wie Amor zuletzt Blüten und Früchte gezeugt.
    Denke, wie mannigfach bald diese, bald jene Gestalten,
        Still entfaltend, Natur unsern Gefühlen geliehn!
    Freue dich auch des heutigen Tags! Die heilige Liebe
        Strebt zu der höchsten Frucht gleicher Gesinnungen auf,
    Gleicher Ansicht der Dinge, damit in harmonischem Anschaun
        Sich verbinde das Paar, finde die höhere Welt.

NATUR UND KUNST

Natur und Kunst sie scheinen sich zu fliehen,
Und haben sich, eh man es denkt, gefunden;
Der Widerwille ist auch mir verschwunden,
Und beide scheinen gleich mich anzuziehen.

Es gilt wohl nur in redliches Bemühen!
Und wenn wir erst in abgemeßnen Stunden
Mit Geist und Fleiß uns an die Kunst gebunden,
Mag frei Natur im Herzen wieder glühen.

So ist's mit aller Bildung auch beschaffen:
Vergebens werden ungebundne Geister
Nach der Vollendung reiner Höhe streben.

Wer Großes will, muß sich zusammenraffen;
In der Beschränkung zeigt sich erst der Meister,
Und das Gesetz nur kann uns Freiheit geben.

Stage by stage there grew, dear to us, habit's long grace,
Friendship from deep within us burst out of its wrapping,
    And how Amor at last blessed it with blossom and fruit.
Think how variously Nature, the quietly forming, unfolding,
    Lent to our feelings now this, now that so different mode!
Also rejoice in this day. Because love, our holiest blessing
    Looks for the consummate fruit, marriage of minds, in the end,
One perception of things, that together, concerted in seeing,
    Both to the higher world, truly conjoined, find their way.

NATURE AND ART
(c. 1800; published 1807)

Nature, it seems, must always clash with Art,
And yet, before we know it, both are one;
I too have learned: Their enmity is none,
Since each compels me, and in equal part.

Hard, honest work counts most! And once we start
To measure out the hours and never shun
Art's daily labour till our task is done,
Freely again may Nature move the heart.

So too all growth and ripening of the mind:
To the pure heights of ultimate consummation
In vain the unbound spirit seeks to flee.

Who seeks great gain leaves easy gain behind.
None proves a master but by limitation
And only law can give us liberty.

NACHTGESANG

O gib, vom weichen Pfühle,
Träumend, ein halb Gehör!
Bei meinem Saitenspiele
Schlafe! was willst du mehr?

Bei meinem Saitenspiele
Segnet der Sterne Heer
Die ewigen Gefühle;
Schlafe! was willst du mehr?

Die ewigen Gefühle
Heben mich, hoch und hehr,
Aus irdischem Gewühle;
Schlafe! was willst du mehr?

Vom irdischen Gewühle
Trennst du mich nur zu sehr,
Bannst mich in diese Kühle;
Schlafe! was willst du mehr!

Bannst mich in diese Kühle,
Gibst nur im Traum Gehör.
Ach, auf dem weichen Pfühle
Schlafe! was willst du mehr?

MÄCHTIGES ÜBERRASCHEN

Ein Strom entrauscht umwölktem Felsensaale,
    Dem Ozean sich eilig zu verbinden;
    Was auch sich spiegeln mag von Grund zu Gründen,
    Er wandelt unaufhaltsam fort zu Tale.

NIGHT SONG (1804)

Pillowed so soft, dream on,
Half listen, I implore,
To this my zithersong,
Sleep, could you wish for more?

To this my zithersong
Is heart's eternal core
Blessed by the starry throng;
Sleep, could you wish for more?

Blessed by the starry throng,
Out of this world I soar
Endless desires among;
Sleep, could you wish for more?

Endless desires among –
Yet you have shut your door,
Cool is the night and long;
Sleep, could you wish for more?

Cool, ah, the night and long,
Only in dreams, on your
Pillow, you hear my song,
Sleep, could you wish for more?

SONNET I: IMMENSE ASTONISHMENT (1807–08)

A river from a cloud-wrapped chamber gone,
Of rock, and roaring to be one with ocean,
Much it reflects from deep to deep, its motion
Never relenting valleyward and on.

Dämonisch aber stürzt mit einem Male –
    Ihr folgen Berg und Wald in Wirbelwinden –
    Sich Oreas, Behagen dort zu finden,
    Und hemmt den Lauf, begrenzt die weite Schale.

Die Welle sprüht, und staunt zurück und weichet,
    Und schwillt bergan, sich immer selbst zu trinken;
    Gehemmt ist nun zum Vater hin das Streben.

Sie schwankt und ruht, zum See zurückgedeichet;
    Gestirne, spiegelnd sich, beschaun das Blinken
    Des Wellenschlags am Fels, ein neues Leben.

WÄR NICHT DAS AUGE SONNENHAFT

Wär nicht das Auge sonnenhaft,
Die Sonne könnt es nie erblicken;
Läg nicht in uns des Gottes eigne Kraft,
Wie könnt uns Göttliches entzücken?

GEFUNDEN

Ich ging im Walde
So für mich hin,
Und nichts zu suchen,
Das war mein Sinn.

Im Schatten sah ich
Ein Blümchen stehn,
Wie Sterne leuchtend,
Wie Äuglein schön.

Ich wollt es brechen,
Da sagt' es fein:
Soll ich zum Welken
Gebrochen sein?

But with abrupt demoniacal force,
By forest, mountain, whirling wind pursued,
Oreas tumbles down into quietude,
And there she brims the bowl, impedes the course.

The wave breaks into spray, astonished, back
Uphill it washes, drinking itself always;
Its urge to join the Father hindered, too,

It rolls and rests, is dammed into a lake;
The constellations, mirrored, fix their gaze:
The flash of wave on rock, a life made new.

SOMETHING LIKE THE SUN
(from *Theory of Colours*, 1810)

Something like the sun the eye must be,
Else it no glint of sun could ever see;
Surely God's own powers with us unite,
Else godly things would not compel delight.

FOUND (1813)

Once in the forest
I strolled content,
To look for nothing
My sole intent.

I saw a flower,
Shaded and shy,
Shining like starlight,
Bright as an eye.

I went to pluck it;
Gently it said:
Must I be broken,
Wilt and be dead?

Ich grubs mit allen
Den Würzlein aus,
Zum Garten trug ichs
Am hübschen Haus.

Und pflanzt es wieder
Am stillen Ort;
Nun zweigt es immer
Und blüht so fort.

DEN ORIGINALEN II

Vom Vater hab ich die Statur,
Des Lebens ernstes Führen,
Vom Mütterchen die Frohnatur
Und Lust zu fabulieren.
Urahnherr war der Schönsten hold,
Das spukt so hin und wieder;
Urahnfrau liebte Schmuck und Gold,
Das zuckt wohl durch die Glieder.
Sind nun die Elemente nicht
Aus dem Komplex zu trennen,
Was ist denn an dem ganzen Wicht
Original zu nennen?

Then whole I dug it
Out of the loam
And to my garden
Carried it home,

There to replant it
Where no wind blows.
More bright than ever
It blooms and grows.

ON ORIGINALITY II (*c.* 1812–14)

My build from Father I inherit,
His neat and serious ways;
Combined with Mother's cheerful spirit,
Her love of telling stories.
Great-grandfather courted the loveliest,
His ghost won't leave me alone;
Great-grandmother liked fine jewels best,
This twitch I've also known.
If, then, no mortal chemist can
Divide the components from the whole,
What is there in the entire man
You could call original?

DIE JAHRE

Die Jahre sind allerliebste Leut:
Sie brachten gestern, sie bringen heut,
Und so verbringen wir Jüngern eben
Das allerliebste Schlaraffen-Leben.
Und dann fällts den Jahren auf einmal ein,
Nicht mehr, wie sonst, bequem zu sein;
Wollen nicht mehr schenken, wollen nicht mehr borgen,
Sie nehmen heute, sie nehmen morgen.

THE YEARS (1814)

The years? A charming lot, I say.
Brought presents yesterday, bring presents today,
And so we younger ones maintain
The charming life that's led in Cockayne.
Then all of a sudden the years change their mind,
Are no longer obliging, no longer kind;
Won't give you presents, won't let you borrow,
Dun you today, and rob you tomorrow.

1109

HEGIRE

Nord und West und Süd zersplittern,
Throne bersten, Reiche zittern,
Flüchte du, im reinen Osten
Patriarchenluft zu kosten,
Unter Lieben, Trinken, Singen
Soll dich Chisers Quell verjüngen.

Dort im Reinen und im Rechten
Will ich menschlichen Geschlechten
In des Ursprungs Tiefe dringen,
Wo sie noch von Gott empfingen
Himmelslehr in Erdesprachen,
Und sich nicht den Kopf zerbrachen.

Wo sie Väter hoch verehrten,
Jeden fremden Dienst verwehrten;
Will mich freun der Jugendschranke:
Glaube weit, eng der Gedanke,
Wie das Wort so wichtig dort war,
Weil es ein gesprochen Wort war.

Will mich unter Hirten mischen,
An Oasen mich erfrischen,
Wenn mit Karawanen wandle,
Schal, Kaffee und Moschus handle;
Jeden Pfad will ich betreten
Von der Wüste zu den Städten.

From *The Parliament of West and East*
(1814–18)

HEGIRA (1814)

North and West and South are breaking,
Thrones are bursting, kingdoms shaking:
Flee, then, to the essential East,
Where on patriarch's air you'll feast!
There to love and drink and sing,
Drawing youth from Khizr's spring.

Pure and righteous there I'll trace
To its source the human race,
Prime of nations, when to each
Heavenly truth in earthly speech
Still by God himself was given,
Human brains not racked and riven.

When they honoured ancestors,
To strange doctrine closed their doors;
Youthful bounds shall be my pride,
My thought narrow, my faith wide.
And I'll find the token word,
Dear because a spoken word.

Mix with goatherds in dry places,
Seek refreshment in oases
When with caravans I fare,
Coffee, shawls, and musk my ware;
Every road and path explore,
Desert, cities and seashore;

Bosen Felsweg auf und nieder
Trösten, Hafis, deine Lieder,
Wenn der Führer mit Entzücken
Von des Maultiers hohem Rücken
Singt, die Sterne zu erwecken
Und die Räuber zu erschrecken.

Will in Bädern und in Schenken,
Heilger Hafis, dein gedenken;
Wenn den Schleier Liebchen lüftet,
Schüttelnd Ambralocken düftet.
Ja des Dichters Liebeflüstern
Mache selbst die Huris lüstern.

Wolltet ihr ihm dies beneiden,
Oder etwa gar verleiden;
Wisset nur, daß Dichterworte
Um des Paradieses Pforte
Immer leise klopfend schweben
Sich erbittend ewges Leben.

SELIGE SEHNSUCHT

Sagt es niemand, nur den Weisen,
Weil die Menge gleich verhöhnet,
Das Lebendge will ich preisen
Das nach Flammentod sich sehnet.

In der Liebesnächte Kühlung,
Die dich zeugte, wo du zeugtest,
Überfällt dich fremde Fühlung
Wenn die stille Kerze leuchtet.

Nicht mehr bleibest du umfangen
In der Finsternis Beschattung,

Dangerous track, through rock and scree:
Hafiz, there you'll comfort me
When the guide, enchanted, tells
On the mule's back, your ghazels,
Sings them for the stars to hear,
Robber bands to quail with fear.

Holy Hafiz, you in all
Baths and taverns I'll recall,
When the loved one lifts her veil,
Ambergris her locks exhale.
More: the poet's love song must
Melt the houris, move their lust.

Now, should you begrudge him this,
Even long to spoil such bliss,
Poets' words, I'd have you know,
Round the gate of Eden flow,
Gently knocking without rest,
Everlasting life their quest.

BLESSED LONGING (1814)

Tell it only to the wise,
For the crowd at once will jeer:
That which is alive I praise,
That which longs for death by fire.

Cooled by passionate love at night,
Procreated, procreating,
You have known the alien feeling
In the calm of candlelight;

Gloom-embraced will lie no more,
By the flickering shades obscured,

Und dich reißet neu Verlangen
Auf zu höherer Begattung.

Keine Ferne macht dich schwierig,
Kommst geflogen und gebannt,
Und zuletzt, des Lichts begierig,
Bist du Schmetterling verbrannt.

Und so lang du das nicht hast,
Dieses: Stirb und werde!
Bist du nur ein trüber Gast
Auf der dunklen Erde.

GINGO BILOBA

Dieses Baums Blatt, der von Osten
Meinem Garten anvertraut,
Gibt geheimen Sinn zu kosten,
Wie's den Wissenden erbaut.

Ist es ein lebendig Wesen,
Das sich in sich selbst getrennt?
Sind es zwei, die sich erlesen,
Daß man sie als eines kennt?

Solche Frage zu erwidern
Fand ich wohl den rechten Sinn:
Fühlst du nicht an meinen Liedern,
Daß ich eins und doppelt bin?

But are seized by new desire,
To a higher union lured.

Then no distance holds you fast;
Winged, enchanted, on you fly,
Light your longing, and at last,
Moth, you meet the flame and die.

Never prompted to that quest:
Die and dare rebirth!
You remain a dreary guest
On our gloomy earth.

GINGO BILOBA (1815)

This tree's leaf that from the East
To my garden's been entrusted
Holds a secret sense, and grist
To a man intent on knowledge.

Is it *one*, this thing alive,
By and in itself divided,
Or two beings who connive
That as *one* the world shall see them?

Fitly now I can reveal
What the pondered question taught me;
In my songs do you not feel
That at once I'm one and double?

IN TAUSEND FORMEN

In tausend Formen magst du dich verstecken,
Doch, Allerliebste, gleich erkenn ich dich;
Du magst mit Zauberschleiern dich bedecken,
Allgegenwärtge, gleich erkenn ich dich.

An der Zypresse reinstem, jungem Streben,
Allschöngewachsne, gleich erkenn ich dich,
In des Kanales reinem Wellenleben,
Allschmeichelhafte, wohl erkenn ich dich.

Wenn steigend sich der Wasserstrahl entfaltet,
Allspielende, wie froh erkenn ich dich;
Wenn Wolke sich gestaltend umgestaltet,
Allmannigfaltge, dort erkenn ich dich.

An des geblümten Schleiers Wiesenteppich,
Allbuntbesternte, schön erkenn ich dich;
Und greift umher ein tausendarmger Eppich,
O Allumklammernde, da kenn ich dich.

Wenn am Gebirg der Morgen sich entzündet,
Gleich, Allerheiternde, begrüß ich dich,
Dann über mir der Himmel rein sich ründet,
Allherzerweiternde, dann atm ich dich.

Was ich mit äußerm Sinn, mit innerm kenne,
Du Allbelehrende, kenn ich durch dich;
Und wenn ich Allahs Namenhundert nenne,
Mit jedem klingt ein Name nach für dich.

A THOUSAND FORMS (1815)

Take on a thousand forms, hide as you will,
O Most-Beloved, at once I know 'tis you;
Conceal yourself in magic veils, and still,
Presence-in-All, at once I know 'tis you.

The cypress thrusting artless up and young,
Beauty-in-Every-Limb, I know 'tis you;
The channelled crystal wave life flows along,
All-Gentling-Tender-One, I know 'tis you.

You in the fountain plume's unfolding tip,
All-Playful-One, what joy to know 'tis you;
Where cloud assumes a shape and changes it,
One-Manifold-in-All, I know 'tis you.

I know, when flowers veil the meadow ground,
O Starry-Twinkle-Hued, in beauty you;
When thousand-armed the ivy gropes around,
Environer-of-All, I know 'tis you.

When on a mountain sparks of dawn appear,
At once, Great Gladdener, I welcome you;
Then with a sky above rotund and clear,
Then, Opener-of-the-Heart, do I breathe you.

What with bodily sense and soul I know,
Teacher-of-All, I know alone through you;
All hundred names on Allah I bestow,
With each will echo then a name for you.

HÖHERES UND HÖCHSTES

Daß wir solche Dinge lehren
Möge man uns nicht bestrafen:
Wie das alles zu erklären,
Dürft ihr euer Tiefstes fragen.

Und so werdet ihr vernehmen:
Daß der Mensch, mit sich zufrieden,
Gern sein Ich gerettet sähe,
So da droben wie hienieden.

Und mein liebes Ich bedürfte
Mancherlei Bequemlichkeiten,
Freuden wie ich hier sie schlürfte
Wünscht ich auch für ewge Zeiten.

So gefallen schöne Gärten,
Blum und Frucht und hübsche Kinder,
Die uns allen hier gefielen,
Auch verjüngtem Geist nicht minder.

Und so möcht ich alle Freunde,
Jung und alt, in eins versammeln,
Gar zu gern in deutscher Sprache
Paradiesesworte stammeln.

Doch man horcht nun Dialekten
Wie sich Mensch und Engel kosen,
Der Grammatik, der versteckten,
Deklinierend Mohn und Rosen.

Mag man ferner auch in Blicken
Sich rhetorisch gern ergehen
Und zu himmlischem Entzücken
Ohne Klang und Ton erhöhen.

SUBLIMER AND SUBLIMEST (1818)

Let our teachings not be thought
A reprehensible offence:
Reasons for them can be sought
In nether grounds of common sense.

So it is you learn that man,
At peace with self in thought and act,
Would keep his being, if he can,
In heaven, as on earth, intact.

As for me, my *ich* has hugged
On earth a need for *tout confort*,
Pleasures such as I have glugged
I'll want hereafter, evermore.

A garden, thus, or fruit, may so
Delight, a flower, a pretty lass
Appeal to us down here below –
To spirits young again, no less.

Friends I'd gather round, likewise,
And be with them, the old, the young,
We'd stammer words of Paradise,
Jubilant, in the German tongue.

Angel and man, when *tête-à-tête*,
Albeit, dialects compose:
A secret grammar, delicate
Declensions of poppy and the rose.

Glad we are when looks of bliss
We interchange as rhetoric;
We rise to heavenly ecstasies,
No sound, no voice in what we speak.

Ton und Klang jedoch entwindet
Sich dem Worte selbstverständlich,
Und entschiedener empfindet
Der Verklärte sich unendlich.

Ist somit dem Fünf der Sinne
Vorgesehn im Paradiese,
Sicher ist es, ich gewinne
Einen Sinn für alle diese.

Und nun dring ich aller Orten
Leichter durch die ewgen Kreise,
Die durchdrungen sind vom Worte
Gottes rein-lebendger Weise.

Ungehemmt mit heißem Triebe
Läßt sich da kein Ende finden,
Bis im Anschaun ewger Liebe
Wir verschweben, wir verschwinden.

Self-evidently sound abates,
Voice its every word repeals;
In Glory, no one hesitates,
Intensely infinite one feels.

If Paradise provide, again,
For Senses Five the wherewithal,
Certain it is I shall obtain
A Single Sense embracing all.

Now lighter through the eternal rings
I pass, no matter where I be —
The Word that penetrates them sings
God's artless living melody.

There unimpeded urges burn
With never an end or latterday,
Till face to face with Love we turn
To floating air and drift away.

URWORTE. ORPHISCH

ΔΑΙΜΩΝ, Dämon

Wie an dem Tag, der dich der Welt verliehen,
Die Sonne stand zum Gruße der Planeten,
Bist alsobald und fort und fort gediehen
Nach dem Gesetz, wonach du angetreten.
So mußt du sein, dir kannst du nicht entfliehen,
So sagten schon Sibyllen, so Propheten;
Und keine Zeit und keine Macht zerstückelt
Geprägte Form, die lebend sich entwickelt.

ΤΥΧΗ, das Zufällige

Die strenge Grenze doch umgeht gefällig
Ein Wandelndes, das mit und um uns wandelt;
Nicht einsam bleibst du, bildest dich gesellig,
Und handelst wohl so, wie ein andrer handelt:
Im Leben ists bald hin-, bald widerfällig,
Es ist ein Tand und wird so durchgetandelt.
Schon hat sich still der Jahre Kreis geründet,
Die Lampe harrt der Flamme, die entzündet.

ΕΡΩΣ, Liebe

Die bleibt nicht aus! – Er stürzt vom Himmel nieder,
Wohin er sich aus alter Öde schwang,
Er schwebt heran auf luftigem Gefieder
Um Stirn und Brust den Frühlingstag entlang,
Scheint jetzt zu fliehn, vom Fliehen kehrt er wieder:

PRIMAL WORDS. ORPHIC (1817–18)

ΔΑΙΜΩΝ, Daemon

As stood the sun to the salute of planets
Upon the day that gave you to the earth,
You grew forthwith, and prospered, in your growing
Heeded the law presiding at your birth.
Sibyls and prophets told it: You must be
None but yourself, from self you cannot flee.
No time there is, no power, can decompose
The minted form that lives and living grows.

ΤΥΧΗ, Chance

Strict the limit, yet a drifting, pleasant,
Moves around it, with us, circling us;
You are not long alone, you learn decorum,
And likely act as any manjack does:
It comes and goes, in life, you lose or win,
It is a trinket, toyed with, wearing thin.
Full circle come the years, the end is sighted,
The lamp awaits the flame, to be ignited.

ΕΡΩΣ, Love

Love is not absent! Down from heaven swooping,
Whither from ancient emptiness he flew,
This way he flutters, borne by airy feathers,
Round heart and head the day of Springtime through,
Apparently escapes, returns anon,

Da wird ein Wohl im Weh, so süß und bang.
Gar manches Herz verschwebt im Allgemeinen,
Doch widmet sich das edelste dem Einen.

ΑΝΑΓΚΗ, Nötigung

Da ists denn wieder, wie die Sterne wollten:
Bedingung und Gesetz; und aller Wille
Ist nur ein Wollen, weil wir eben sollten,
Und vor dem Willen schweigt die Willkür stille;
Das Liebste wird vom Herzen weggescholten,
Dem harten Muß bequemt sich Will und Grille.
So sind wir scheinfrei denn nach manchen Jahren
Nur enger dran, als wir am Anfang waren.

ΕΛΠΙΣ, Hoffnung

Doch solcher Grenze, solcher ehrnen Mauer
Höchst widerwärtge Pforte wird entriegelt,
Sie stehe nur mit alter Felsendauer!
Ein Wesen regt sich leicht und ungezügelt:
Aus Wolkendecke, Nebel, Regenschauer
Erhebt sie uns, mit ihr, durch sie beflügelt,
Ihr kennt sie wohl, sie schwärmt durch alle Zonen –
Ein Flügelschlag – und hinter uns Äonen!

DEMUT

Seh ich die Werke der Meister an,
So seh ich das, was sie getan;
Betracht ich meine Siebensachen,
Seh ich, was ich hätt sollen machen.

So sweet and nervous, pain to pleasure gone.
Some hearts away in general loving float,
The noblest, yet, their all to one devote.

ΑΝΑΓΚΗ, Necessity

Then back it comes, what in the stars was written;
Law and circumstance; each will is tried,
All willing simply forced, by obligation:
In face of it, the free will's tongue is tied.
Man's heart forswears what most was loved by him,
To iron 'Must' comply both will and whim.
It only seems we're free, years hem us in,
Constraining more than at our origin.

ΕΛΠΙΣ, Hope

Yet the repulsive gate can be unbolted
Within such bounds, their adamantine wall,
Though it may stand, that gate, like rock for ever;
One being moves, unchecked, ethereal:
From heavy cloud, from fog, from squall of rain
She lifts us to herself, we're winged again,
You know her well, to nowhere she's confined –
A wingbeat – aeons vanish far behind.

HUMILITY (1815)

The masters' works I look upon,
And I can see what they have done;
When looking upon this or that by me,
What I should have done is what I see.

TRILOGIE DER LEIDENSCHAFT

An Werther

Noch einmal wagst du, vielbeweinter Schatten,
Hervor dich an das Tageslicht,
Begegnest mir auf neu beblümten Matten,
Und meinen Anblick scheust du nicht.
Es ist, als ob du lebtest in der Frühe,
Wo uns der Tau auf Einem Feld erquickt
Und nach des Tages unwillkommner Mühe
Der Scheidesonne letzter Strahl entzückt;
Zum Bleiben ich, zum Scheiden du erkoren,
Gingst du voran – und hast nicht viel verloren.

Des Menschen Leben scheint ein herrlich Los:
Der Tag wie lieblich, so die Nacht wie groß!
Und wir, gepflanzt in Paradieses Wonne,
Genießen kaum der hocherlauchten Sonne,
Da kämpft sogleich verworrene Bestrebung
Bald mit uns selbst und bald mit der Umgebung;
Keins wird vom andern wünschenswert ergänzt,
Von außen düsterts, wenn es innen glänzt,
Ein glänzend Äußres deckt ein trüber Blick,
Da steht es nah – und man verkennt das Glück.

Nun glauben wirs zu kennen! Mit Gewalt
Ergreift uns Liebreiz weiblicher Gestalt:
Der Jüngling, froh wie in der Kindheit Flor,
Im Frühling tritt als Frühling selbst hervor,
Entzückt, erstaunt, wer dies ihm angetan?
Er schaut umher, die Welt gehört ihm an.
Ins Weite zieht ihn unbefangne Hast,
Nichts engt ihn ein, nicht Mauer, nicht Palast;
Wie Vögelschar an Wäldergipfeln streift,
So schwebt auch er, der um die Liebste schweift,
Er sucht vom Äther, den er gern verläßt,
Den treuen Blick, und dieser hält ihn fest.

From TRILOGY OF PASSION (1823–24)

To Werther

So once again, poor much-lamented shadow,
You venture in the light of day?
And here, in blossoms of the fresher meadow,
Confront me and not turn away?
Alive as in the early dawn, when tender
Chill of a misty field bestirred the two,
When both were dazzled by the west in splendour
After the drudging summer days were through.
My doom: endure. And yours: depart forlorn.
Is early death, we wonder, much to mourn?

In theory how magnificent, man's fate!
The day agreeable, the night so great.
Yet we, in such a paradise begun,
Enjoy but briefly the amazing sun,
And then the battle's on: vague causes found
To struggle with ourself, the world around.
Neither completes the other as it should:
The skies are gloomy when our humour's good;
The vista glitters and we're glum enough.
Joy near at hand, but we – at blindman's buff.

At times we think it ours: some darling girl!
Borne on a fragrant whirlwind, off we whirl.
The young man, breezy as in boyhood's prime,
Like spring itself goes strutting in springtime.
Astounded, charmed, 'Who's doing this, all for me?'
Claims like a cocky heir the land and sea.
Goes footloose anywhere, without a thought;
No wall, no palace holds him, even if caught.
As swallows skim the treetops in a blur,
He hovers round, in rings, that certain her,
Scans, from the height he means to leave at last,
Earth for an answering gaze, that holds him fast.

Doch erst zu früh und dann zu spät gewarnt,
Fühlt er den Flug gehemmt, fühlt sich umgarnt.
Das Wiedersehn ist froh, das Scheiden schwer,
Das Wieder-Wiedersehn beglückt noch mehr,
Und Jahre sind im Augenblick ersetzt;
Doch tückisch harrt das Lebewohl zuletzt.

Du lächelst, Freund, gefühlvoll, wie sich ziemt:
Ein gräßlich Scheiden machte dich berühmt;
Wir feierten dein kläglich Mißgeschick,
Du ließest uns zu Wohl und Weh zurück.
Dann zog uns wieder ungewisse Bahn
Der Leidenschaften labyrinthisch an;
Und wir, verschlungen wiederholter Not,
Dem Scheiden endlich – Scheiden ist der Tod!
Wie klingt es rührend, wenn der Dichter singt,
Den Tod zu meiden, den das Scheiden bringt!
Verstrickt in solche Qualen, halbverschuldet,
Geb ihm ein Gott zu sagen, was er duldet.

IM ERNSTEN BEINHAUS

Im ernsten Beinhaus wars, wo ich beschaute,
   Wie Schädel Schädeln angeordnet paßten;
   Die alte Zeit gedacht ich, die ergraute.
Sie stehn in Reih geklemmt, die sonst sich haßten,
   Und derbe Knochen, die sich tödlich schlugen,
   Sie liegen kreuzweis, zahm allhier zu rasten.
Entrenkte Schulterblätter! was sie trugen,
   Fragt niemand mehr, und zierlich tätge Glieder,
   Die Hand, der Fuß, zerstreut aus Lebensfugen.
Ihr Müden also lagt vergebens nieder,
   Nicht Ruh im Grabe ließ man euch, vertrieben
   Seid ihr herauf zum lichten Tage wieder,
Und niemand kann die dürre Schale lieben,

First warned too soon, and then too late, he'll swear
His feet are bound, traps planted everywhere.
Sweet meetings are a joy, departure's pain.
Meeting again – what hopes we entertain!
Moments with her make good the years away.
Yet there's a treacherous parting, come the day.

You smile, my friend, eyes welling. Still the same!
Yours, what a ghastly avenue to fame.
We dressed in mourning when your luck ran out
And you deserted, leaving ours in doubt.
For us, the road resuming God knows where,
Through labyrinths of passion, heavy air,
Still drew us on, bone-tired, with desperate breath
Up to a final parting. Parting's death!
True: it's affecting when the poet sings
To wish away the death that parting brings.
Some god – though man's half guilty, hurt past cure –
Grant him a tongue to murmur: I endure.

LINES WRITTEN UPON THE
CONTEMPLATION OF SCHILLER'S SKULL (1826)

Skull upon skull arranged in fit array
In solemn vault of burial I beheld
And thought of bygone years and times turned grey.

Near neighbours now, in rows they stand tight-held:
Rough bones that clashed in deadly strife before
Lie crosswise here, their rage to quiet quelled.

Unjointed shoulderblades! what once they bore
None now will ask; and limbs once full of grace,
Hands, feet, lie scattered and will move no more.

Welch herrlich edlen Kern sie auch bewahrte.
Doch mir Adepten war die Schrift geschrieben,
Die heilgen Sinn nicht jedem offenbarte,
    Als ich inmitten solcher starren Menge
    Unschätzbar herrlich ein Gebild gewahrte,
Daß in des Raumes Moderkält und Enge
    Ich frei und wärmefühlend mich erquickte,
    Als ob ein Lebensquell dem Tod entspränge.
Wie mich geheimnisvoll die Form entzückte!
    Die gottgedachte Spur, die sich erhalten!
    Ein Blick, der mich an jenes Meer entrückte,
Das flutend strömt gesteigerte Gestalten.
    Geheim Gefäß! Orakelsprüche spendend,
    Wie bin ich wert, dich in der Hand zu halten?
Dich höchsten Schatz aus Moder fromm entwendend
    Und in die freie Luft, zu freiem Sinnen,
    Zum Sonnenlicht andächtig hin mich wendend.
Was kann der Mensch im Leben mehr gewinnen,
    Als daß sich Gott-Natur ihm offenbare?
    Wie sie das Feste läßt zu Geist verrinnen,
    Wie sie das Geisterzeugte fest bewahre.

So all in vain you sought this resting-place,
Poor weary ones! they would not let you lie,
Whom daywards from your shadowy grave they chase,

And none cares now for husks that have gone dry
Though glorious kernels they did once contain.
Yet here was written what my adept's eye,

Though few would guess its sacred sense, read plain:
Amid the rigid throng one shape I saw
Of rare nobility – and at once again

In this cold mouldering chamber's narrow maw
I felt refreshed and warmed, alive and free:
What welling life-spring here outleapt death's law?

O outline traced by God, still clear to see!
O lineaments enchanting to my eyes,
Transporting me to that mysterious sea

Whence transformed forms perpetually rise!
Strange vessel, fountainhead of sapience,
How dares my hand to hold you? Previous prize

Which from decay I snatch with reverence
And into free air, freely there to muse,
Out into sunlight, piously bear hence.

To what more noble end our life we use
Than knowing God-and-Nature, which are one?
Firm matter melts which She as Mind renews,
And She makes firm what fertile Mind has done.

DEM AUFGEHENDEN VOLLMONDE
Dornburg, den 25. August 1828

Willst du mich sogleich verlassen?
Warst im Augenblick so nah!
Dich umfinstern Wolkenmassen,
Und nun bist du gar nicht da.

Doch du fühlst, wie ich betrübt bin,
Blickt dein Rand herauf als Stern!
Zeugest mir, daß ich geliebt bin,
Sei das Liebchen noch so fern.

So hinan denn! hell und heller,
Reiner Bahn, in voller Pracht!
Schlägt mein Herz auch schmerzlich schneller,
Überselig ist die Nacht.

DER BRÄUTIGAM

Um Mitternacht, ich schlief, im Busen wachte
Das liebevolle Herz als wär es Tag;
Der Tag erschien, mir war, als ob es nachte,
Was ist es mir, so viel er bringen mag.

Sie fehlte ja, mein emsig Tun und Streben
Für sie allein ertrug ich's durch die Glut
Der heißen Stunde; welch erquicktes Leben
Am kühlen Abend! lohnend war's und gut.

Die Sonne sank und Hand in Hand verpflichtet
Begrüßten wir den letzten Segensblick,
Und Auge sprach, ins Auge klar gerichtet:
Von Osten, hoffe nur, sie kommt zurück.

TO THE FULL MOON RISING
(1828)

Must you now so soon be leaving?
Moments gone, so close you were.
Sombre clouds around you cleaving,
Now you are not even there.

Yet you feel my feeling darken,
Show a single edge, as star,
Testify that love will hearken:
I am loved, though from afar.

Go your way, in purest splendour,
More and more intensely bright.
Let my heart race and ache, so tender –
Rapturous it is, the night.

THE BRIDEGROOM (1828)

At midnight, I was sleeping, in my breast
My fond heart lay awake, as though it were day;
Day broke: as though by falling night oppressed
I thought: what's day to me, bring what it may?

Since she was lacking; all my toil and strife
For her alone patiently I'd withstood
Throughout the hot noon hours. What quickening life
In the cool evening! Blessed it was, and good.

The sun went down; and hand to dear hand wedded
We took our leave of him, watched the last ray burn,
And the eye said, eye to clear eye threaded:
But hope, and from the East he will return.

Um Mitternacht, der Sterne Glanz geleitet
Im holden Traum zur Schwelle, wo sie ruht.
O sei auch mir dort auszuruhn bereitet,
Wie es auch sei, das Leben, es ist gut.

At midnight! Led by starlight through the gloom,
Dream-wrapt, I go to where she lies at rest.
Oh, may I lie at last in that same room!
Life's good, though worst befall us, life is blessed.

SELECTED LETTERS

*Translated by Dr M. von Herzfeld
and C. Melvil Sym*

To C. G. SCHÖNKOPF*

'Your servant, Herr Schönkopf; how do you do, Madame? Good evening Mademoiselle, and good evening Peter, my boy.'

N.B. You must picture me coming in by the small door. You, Herr Schönkopf, are sitting on the sofa by the warm stove, you, Madame, are in your little nook behind the writing table, Peter has got right under the stove, and if Käthchen is sitting in my place at the window, she must just get up and make room for the visitor. Now I will start talking.

I have been away a long time, haven't I? For five whole weeks and more I have not seen you or spoken to you. That hasn't happened one single time in the last eighteen months, but alas, it will often happen in future. You would like to hear how I have been getting on. Well, I can tell you, fairly well, but only fairly well.

By the way, you have forgiven me now for not coming to say good-bye. I was near the house, I was even outside the door, I saw the lantern burning and went as far as the steps, but hadn't the heart to go up. Knowing it was the last time, how could I have come down again? So I'll do now what I ought to have done then – thank you for all the love and kindness you constantly showed me and that I shall never forget. I don't need to beg you to remember me; there are bound to be thousands of occasions when you will think of someone who for eighteen months made part of your family circle, who must often have given you cause for annoyance, but who always meant well, poor fellow, and whom, I hope,

---

* Father of Käthchen-Annette, Goethe's girlfriend when he was a student in Leipzig.

you will sometimes miss. I know I often miss you. I will say no more, for it is always a sad business with me. I had a safe tolerable journey and found all well here, except my grandfather; he has so far recovered from the stroke which crippled one side, but his speech is still affected. I feel as well as anyone who isn't quite certain whether he has consumption or not. But I am making headway; my cheeks are filling out and I'm not troubled here with worries about either girls or food, so I hope to get better and better every day …

To J. C. KESTNER*

Frankfort,
25th December 1772.
Christmas morning, very early.

It is still dark, dear Kestner. I have got up to write by candle light on this morning; this brings back happy memories of former days. I have had coffee made in honour of the day and I will write till it is light. The watchman has sounded his horn already, it woke me up. 'Praise be to Thee, Jesus Christ.' I love this season and the songs one sings; and the cold that has set in makes me thoroughly cheerful. I had a wonderful day yesterday; I was anxious about to-day, but it has begun well too, so I'm not worrying about the end of it. Last night I promised my two silhouettes that I would write to you. The two dear faces hover like angels round my bed. As soon as I got here, I pinned up Lotte's silhouette. They put my bed in while I was in Darmstadt, and Lotte's picture is now above it – such a joy. Lenchen's is on the other side. Many thanks, Kestner, for this dear picture. It is more like what you wrote to me of her than anything I had imagined. It shows what folly it is for us to guess and dream and prophesy.

*Fiancé, then husband, of Lotte Buff, the original of Lotte in *Werther.* 'Lenchen' was her sister, Helene.

The watchman has turned this way again; the north wind carries his tune across as if he were blowing just outside my window.

Dear Kestner, I spent yesterday in the country with some fine fellows. We were very noisy and very merry, shouting and laughing the whole time. Usually that isn't good for the following day, but is there anything the high gods cannot turn to good if they choose? They gave me a happy evening; I drank no wine, so I looked on nature with a dispassionate eye. A beautiful evening. Night fell as we came back. It always touches a chord in me, you know, when the sun is already low in the sky and darkness has spread from the east to north and south, and now only a disk of fading light glows low in the west. In flat country, Kestner, it is a most magnificent sight. On my rambles when I was younger and felt more warmly, I used to watch for hours and see the sun sink and fade. I stood awhile on the bridge. The dim town to right and left, the calm glowing horizon, the reflection in the river – it made a wonderful impression on me, one that I welcomed with open arms. I ran to the Gerocks', asked for pencil and paper and, happy as I was, sketched the whole picture in a warm soft glow, just as it lingered within me. The Gerocks joined in my pleasure, feeling all I had put into it, and that gave me confidence too. I suggested tossing for it, but they wouldn't; they wanted me to send it to Merck. It's hanging here on my wall at the moment, and I am as pleased with it to-day as I was yesterday. We spent a happy evening together like people to whom fortune has brought some great gift, and I fell asleep thanking the Saints in Heaven for making our Christmas rich with childlike joy. On my way across the Market Square I saw all the candles and toys, and thought of you and the dear boys at home. I can see you coming to them like a messenger from Heaven with your blue Bible in your hand and their joy when you open it. If I could have been with you, I should have wanted to light a feast of wax tapers that would have mirrored the glory of Heaven in their little heads.

The city guards are coming from the Mayor's, rattling their keys. The first grey light of dawn is reaching me over my neighbour's roof, and the bells are ringing Christians together.

Yes, I feel uplifted, in my room up here; it hasn't been so dear to me for many a day. It is bright with the happiest of pictures, bidding me a friendly good-morning. Seven heads copied from Raphael's, inspired by the spirit of God. I have made a copy of one of them, and I am satisfied though not really happy. And there are my dear girls' silhouettes too; Lotte's and Lenchen's as well. Tell Lenchen I am as keen to come and kiss her hand as the Monsieur who wrote those love-letters. He's a mighty poor fish. I would stuff my daughter's coverlet with billets-doux like these, and she will sleep under it as peacefully as a child. My sister laughed and laughed, she has some letters like this from her younger days. That sort of thing must seem as sickening as a rotten egg to any girl with good feeling. I have changed Lotte's comb; this one isn't such a good colour or shape as the first, but I hope it will be more useful. Lotte has a little head, – what a little head!

Daylight is coming fast; if good fortune comes as quickly, there'll soon be a wedding. I must write one more page; I'll pretend not to notice the daylight.

My love to Kielmansegg. Don't let him forget me.

That miserable hound in Giessen,* fussing about us like the old woman in the Gospel about her lost penny, and spying and rummaging about everywhere in our concerns, whose name ought not to defile any letter with your or Lotte's name on it! The wretch is angry because we don't pay attention to him, and he tries to provoke us into thinking of him. He has been so overhasty in writing about my 'Baukunst', obviously it is grist for his mill, and he dashed off a foul review for the *Frankfort Journal*; I've heard about it. He is a real donkey, munching the thistles that grow round my

* Professor Schmidt.

garden, gnawing at the hedge that guards it from creatures like himself, and braying his critical Hee-Haw as if to tell the owner in the arbour: 'I am here too.'

Adieu now, it is daylight. God be with you; I always am. The day has made a festive beginning. I have to waste the good hours, alas, writing reviews; but I'll do it cheerfully, it is for the last number.

Farewell, and don't forget me, an odd creature, sometimes Dives and sometimes Lazarus.

Love to all the dear ones. And let me have news of you all.

To G. A. BÜRGER*

Frankfort,
12th February 1774.

Here is the second edition of my 'Götz'. I have been wanting to write to you for some time, and the few hours I have spent with your friend Destorp have decided me.

I am taking the credit to myself for breaking down the paper wall that separates us. Our voices and our hearts, too, have often met. Is life not short and empty enough? Those whose ways lie side by side ought surely to get in touch with each other.

If you are working at anything, send me it. I will do so too. It gives me confidence. Don't show it to anybody but friends, and I will do the same. And promise never to make a copy.

Destorp and I have been skating together; my heart seemed to thaw in his lovable presence. Farewell.

---

* Best known as the author of the ballad 'Lenore'.

To Countess STOLBERG

Frankfort,
13th February 1775.

Imagine, my dear, a Goethe in a braided coat and from head to foot in finery more or less to match, amidst the empty lustre of sconces and chandeliers, moving among all sorts of people, held at the card-table by a pair of fine eyes, driven from one amusement to the next, from the party to the concert and from there to the ball, and paying his court with all the intensity of frivolity to a charming little blonde.* Imagine this and you'll see the present carnival-Goethe, who only lately was stumblingly telling you some of his dim deep feelings, who doesn't care to write to you and sometimes forgets you because he finds himself quite unbearable in your presence.

But there is another figure, in a grey beaver coat and brown silk scarf and boots. He is sensing the spring in the raw air of February, and soon the wide world he loves will be open to him again. Always living in himself, striving and working, he does his utmost to express youth's innocent feelings in little poems and life's sharper flavours in varied plays. And he tries to trace with chalk on grey paper the outline of his friends and the countryside and his cherished belongings. He doesn't look to right or left, he doesn't ask for any opinion on what he has done, for he has always worked on, reached a new step. Nor does he want to jump to an ideal; he lets his feelings struggle and dally and gradually develop into talents. That is the same man who can't forget you, who on an early morning suddenly feels the urge to write to you, and whose greatest happiness it is to live with the best men and women of his time.

There, my dear, I have told you a great deal about my present state; now do the same and tell me about yours. We

---

*Lili Schönemann, daughter of a Frankfort banker, with whom Goethe was in love.

shall draw closer together like this and think we can see each other – for I warn you I shall often treat you to all sorts of trifles just as they come into my mind.

Another thing that makes me happy is the many excellent people who keep coming here and to me from all over the country; some of course are only mediocre and even tiresome. Some are passing through, others stay longer. We don't realise we exist till we discover ourselves in others.

Whether or not I have been told who or where you are, is of no consequence; when I think of you I feel you akin to me, dear and near. And that is what you will remain to me always, as I too shall certainly remain the same in spite of all my floating and fluttering. Farewell – there Gustchen: a kiss; farewell.

To C. M. WIELAND*

Weimar,
14th April 1776.

A kind of transmigration of souls is the only explanation I can find for the meaning this woman has for me – the power she has over me. Yes surely, once we were man and wife! Now we know one another – darkly, like spirits. I can find no names for us – the past – the future – all –.

To Frau VON STEIN

Torfhaus and Clausthal,
10th and 11th December 1777.

The 10th, before daybreak.

Good-morning, once more, before I leave here again.

* About Frau von Stein.

About seven in the evening.

What shall I say of the Lord with my pen, what kind of song shall I sing to Him? At this moment all prose seems poetry to me, and all poetry prose. No tongue can tell what has happened to me; how then, shall I express it with this sharp tool? Oh, my beloved; God treats me as He treated His saints of old, and I don't know what I have done to deserve it. If I ask as a sign to strengthen my faith that the fleece be dry and the ground wet, it is so, and the other way round too; and above all there is the more than motherly guidance of my wishes. I have reached the goal of my desire, it hangs by many threads and many threads hang from it; you know how symbolic my existence is ... And the humility which the gods delight to honour, and my surrender from moment to moment, and the richest fulfilment of my hopes.

I shall confess to you (tell no-one else) that my reason for coming to the Harz was that I wished to climb the Brocken.* Now, my dear one, I have been at the top of it, quite simply, although for a week everyone has been assuring me it was impossible. But how it happened, and above all why, must wait till I see you again. What wouldn't I give not to need to write now!

I told you I had a wish, for the next full moon. And now, my dear one, I have only to step outside, and there before me lies the Brocken in the glory of the full moon shining above the pines; and I have been at the summit to-day and on the Devil's Altar I offered my heartfelt thanks to my God.

I must fill in the names of the places. At the moment I am at the so-called Torfhaus, where a keeper lives, two hours from the Brocken.

Clausthal, the 11th, evening.

I came back over Altenau from the Torfhaus early this morning, and on the way I told you a great many things. Oh, I'm a talkative fellow when I am alone!

* The highest mountain of the Harz, 3735 ft.

One word, not to forget it. When I arrived at the Torfhaus yesterday, the keeper was sitting in his shirt-sleeves having his morning pint. I began talking about the Brocken, and he assured me how impossible it was to make the ascent, and how often he had been at the top in summer and how fool-hardy it would be to attempt it now. The mountains were hidden in mist, one saw nothing, and 'it's the same at the top', he said, 'you can't see three yards ahead at this season. And if one doesn't know all the tracks', etc. There I sat with a heavy heart, half wondering if I would go back. I felt like the king whom the prophet told to smite upon the ground · and who did not smite often enough. I sat silent and prayed to the gods to turn the heart of this man and the weather, and sat there silent. Then he said to me: 'Now you can see the Brocken.' I went to the window, and there it lay before me, clear as my own face in the mirror. Then my heart leapt and I cried: 'And I am not to get up there! Have you no boy, nobody to –?' And he said: 'I'll go with you.' I cut a sign on the window to witness my tears of joy, and I would feel it wrong to mention it, if I weren't writing to you. I did not believe it until on the highest cliff.

The mist lay below me, and above me it was marvellously clear, and all last night till an early hour, there stood the Brocken in the moonlight; and a dark mass in the dawn as I started off. Adieu. I leave here to-morrow. If you should want to write to me, give the letter to Philipp. I have given my address to him alone. Adieu, dearest. My love to Stein and Waldner, but tell no-one where I am. Adieu.

To CARL AUGUST*

Buttstaedt,
8th March 1779.
At the Townhall.

While the young men are being measured and inspected I will write a few words. Up till now I have always been used to taking everything in this world singly and studying it; so it seems most odd to me now to classify every young man in the country by the physiognomy of army measures! But I must say there's nothing more worth while than pottering about in this sort of thing oneself; looking in from above, one gets a wrong view. Everything happens in such a simple, human way that one has to keep a simple, human outlook to be of any use at all.

I let them tell me all kinds of things and then keep climbing to my old stronghold of poetry for another short spell at my little daughter ['Iphigenia']. But I see at the same time that I am treating this gift of the gods rather too cavalierly, and it is high time I was more economical with my talent if I'm ever to achieve anything more.

I'd like to have come to Weimar the day before yesterday, but rather feared the distraction.

Give your daughter time; after all, the little soul is only a month old. It is from circumstances that we learn, and do what we may, we cannot alter these. Never let the child lack your fatherly care, so that we may bring her up in good health. We shall have plenty of opportunity for thinking and speaking about her by the time she understands what's said to her.

God give Weimar peace within and without; then much may be done for you and your country.

I have noticed all sorts of things to tell you; both funny and serious.

---

*Goethe, as the duchy's defence minister, was on a tour selecting military conscripts, during which he also wrote the first draft of *Iphigenia in Tauris.*

Knebel has just found me writing this; he's been very amusing.

Farewell. He will tell you more. I'm off to Allstädt in the morning.

To Frau CATHARINA ELISABETH GOETHE
Weimar,
Mid-August 1779.

My dear Mother, your answer was just what I wanted; everything is bound to go off easily and be grand. Here are more details about our arrival. We shall arrive about the middle of September and spend a few days very quietly with you. The Duke doesn't want to see his aunts and cousins who will be at the Fair, so we shall leave directly and drift down the Main and Rhine. Once our tour is over, we shall come back and officially take up residence with you, and then I will meet all my friends and acquaintances, while the Duke goes to Darmstadt and visits some other titled people in the neighbourhood. We shall need the following quarters: the Duke will have his bed in the little room, the organ must be removed if it is still there. He will receive in the large room that leads to his own. He sleeps on a clean straw-mattress, with a good linen sheet over it, and has one light blanket.

There's a blot on the paper, so I'll go on here.

The little room with the fireplace will have to be got ready for his attendants and a camp-bed put in.

For Herr von Wedel there will be the back Grey Room with a camp-bed too, etc.

Upstairs in my old room a straw-mattress etc. like the Duke's, for me too.

Please arrange dinner for four in the afternoon; just an ordinary dinner, with no elaborations, just your own, good domestic cooking-masterpieces. It will be good if you can get some fruit for the early morning.

So it amounts to this, that when we come first, we want to take everyone by surprise; a few days should go by before people notice we are there; at Fair-time that's easy enough. Take all the chandeliers out of the Duke's room; he'll think them funny. You can leave the sconces. Otherwise everything as usual, spick and span, and the less apparent fuss, the better. It must seem to you as though we had been living ten years in your house. Upstairs in the attic see there is a place or two for the servants, near ours. Put out your silver things for the Duke's use, basin, candlesticks etc.; no coffee, he never drinks that sort of thing. You will like Wedel; he's better than any of us men you have yet seen.

Strict silence, then. Nobody here knows a thing. Ask me about anything that occurs to you. I'll answer it all, so that everything is well prepared.

Merck mustn't be told yet.

To KRAFFT*

Weimar,
31st January 1781.

You have done right in unburdening your soul to me. I am sure I understand, however little I am able really to reassure you. I have to keep my budget balanced if by the end of the year I am not to be under obligations most unsuitable to my position. So I cannot do any more for you than the 200 thaler. You can count on this; try to manage with it and get what you need by degrees.

I make this express condition; that you do not change your lodgings or place of residence without my knowledge and consent. Every one of us has some obligation; make this the obligation of your love to me, and you will find it an easy one.

---

* Pseudonym of an unidentified bureaucrat who had been disgraced and exiled. Goethe out of charity paid him an allowance of 200 thaler, one sixth of his starting salary as a Weimar minister.

I shouldn't at all like you to borrow from anyone. This unhappy restlessness that is tormenting you at present is the cause of your whole life's misfortunes. You have never been more content with a thousand thaler than you are now with 200, because you always had something more to wish for and you have never made a habit of keeping your wishes within the limits of necessity. I'm not reproaching you with this, I know only too well how it all fits together, and I feel what a torment the contrast between your present and your former position must be to you. But enough of that; just one word more. You'll get your 50 thaler at the end of every quarter; Seidel shall advance you some of the current amount. Economize, then; 'must' is a hard word, but it's the only thing that shows what a man is really made of. It's easy to live just as one wants to ...

To Frau VON STEIN

Eisenach,
17th June 1784.

... My letters will have shown you how lonely I am. I don't dine at Court, I see few people, and take my walks alone, and at every beautiful spot I wish you were there. I can't help loving you more than is good for me; I shall feel all the happier when I see you again.

I am always conscious of my nearness to you, your presence never leaves me. In you I have a measure for every woman, for everyone; in your love a measure for all that is to be. Not in the sense that the rest of the world seems obscure to me, on the contrary, your love makes it clear; I see quite clearly what men are like and what they plan, wish, do and enjoy; I don't grudge them what they have, and comparing is a secret joy to me, possessing as I do such an imperishable treasure.

You in your household must feel as I often do in my affairs; we often don't notice objects simply because we don't choose to look at them, but things acquire an interest as soon as we see clearly the way they are related to each other. For we always like to join in, and the good man takes pleasure in arranging, putting in order and furthering the right and its peaceful rule.

The elephant's skull is coming with me to Weimar.

My rock-studies are going very well ...

Fritz* is happy and good. Without noticing it, he is taken into the world, and so without knowing it, he will become familiar with it. It is still all a game to him; yesterday I got him to read some petitions and give me summaries of them; he laughed like anything and wouldn't believe that people could be in such straits as these petitioners made out.

Adieu, you whom I love a thousand times.

To Frau VON STEIN

Rome,
20th December 1786.

... I am beginning to see the best things a second time, and the first amazement has turned to familiarity and a more accurate perception of the value of what I see.

I simply let everything come to meet me and do not force myself to look for this or that in things. I now look at art in the same way as I looked at nature; I am gaining what I have long striven for, a more complete conception of man's highest achievements, and my mind grows in this direction too and overlooks a wider expanse.

There are certain objects of which one can gain no adequate idea at all till one has seen them, and seen them in the original marble. The Apollo Belvedere towers above everything conceivable; even in the best copies one loses that last touch of warmth of this being, ever alive and young and free as only youth is. The same is true of a Medusa mask, a noble,

---

* Frau von Stein's youngest son, whom Goethe was educating.

beautiful face, where the fearful rigidity of death is most wonderfully expressed. I am trying to get a good copy so as to bring you what I can, but the magic charm of the original marble has not survived and the magic of the translucent stone, its yellowish tinge, almost a flesh-tone, has vanished; plaster never looks anything but chalky and dead in comparison.

What a joy it is though to see a craftsman's workshop where the most beautiful things are gathered together. We bought a huge head of Jupiter; it's in my room now. If only I could put it in your hall.

And yet all this gives me more worry and trouble than pleasure. The re-birth transforming me from within still goes on. I knew I should learn something here, but I did *not* know I should have to go back so far in my studies and unlearn so much. I welcome it all the more. I have surrendered myself entirely and it is not merely my understanding of art but also my moral sense that is undergoing a complete renewal. It would help so much to hear a friendly word from you at this strange, vital period in my life. At present I have to bear it all alone. But I have no wish to extort this from you; follow your own heart and I shall finish my course in silence; Tischbein and Moritz are of the greatest help to me; they do not know how much I owe to them, for here, again, *he* is silent to whom silence is habitual. Farewell. Remember me to the family. I shall go on writing. This year your birthday comes without my being able to enjoy it with you. How happy the next one will be, if you do not wholly shut me out from your heart.

To Frau VON STEIN*

Belvedere,†
1st June 1789.

I am grateful to you for the letter you left me, though it has distressed me in more than one respect. I hesitated to answer it, for in a case like this it is hard to be sincere and not to hurt.

My return from Italy has already proved how much I love you and how well I realize the duty I have towards you and Fritz. I should still be there, if the Duke had had his way. Herder was leaving for Italy, and as I didn't foresee any prospect of being useful to the Hereditary Prince, I have hardly had any other object than yourself and Fritz. I don't wish to reiterate all that I left behind in Italy; you have received my confidence in this matter in an unfriendly enough spirit.

When I arrived you were unfortunately in a strange state of mind, and I must confess I was very much hurt at how you received me and how others did. I saw Herder and the Dowager-Duchess set off, an empty place eagerly offered to me in their coach. I stayed for the sake of those friends for whose sake I had also returned, and yet at that very time I was forced to listen repeatedly to the obstinate assertion that I might as well have stayed away, that I was out of sympathy with others, etc. And all this before there could have been any idea of a connection which appears to offend you so deeply.‡

And what is this connection? Who loses anything by it? Who lays claim to the feelings I bestow on the poor creature? who to the hours I spend with her?

Ask Fritz, ask Frau Herder, ask anyone who knows me well, if I am now less sympathetic, less communicative, less active in the interests of my friends? If, on the contrary, I

---

* Who had gone to Ems to take the waters.
† The ducal summer residence in Weimar.
‡ With Christiane Vulpius, who later became his wife.

do not now for the first time fully belong to them and to society?

And surely it would be a miracle if I were to lose my relationship to you, the best, the closest I ever had.

How vividly I have felt that it still exists on every occasion when I found you disposed to talk about matters of interest.

But I freely admit that I cannot endure the manner in which you have treated me up till now. When I was talkative, you sealed my lips; when I was communicative, you accused me of indifference; when I was active on behalf of my friends, of coldness and neglect. You watched my every look, you criticized my gestures, my manner, and constantly rendered me *mal à mon aise*. How could confidence and frankness thrive when you deliberately repulsed me?

I would add more but for the fear that in your present state of mind it might be calculated to insult rather than appease you.

It is a thousand pities that you have scorned my advice so long in the matter of coffee and have introduced a diet that is exceedingly harmful to your health. As if it were not hard enough morally to overcome such impressions, you are using a physical medium to strengthen the morbid harassing power of your sad fancies. For a while you seemed to acknowledge its harmfulness, and your love for me led you to avoid it for some time, and you felt well in consequence. May the cure and the journey do you good. I do not entirely abandon the hope that you will see me as I am. Farewell. Fritz is happy and comes often. The little Prince is lively and in high spirits.

To CHRISTIANE VULPIUS

*Praucourt,
28th August 1792.*

I arrived at the Duke's camp yesterday and found him well and in good spirits. I'm writing from his tent, with the noise of men felling wood on one side and burning it on the other. We have had almost continuous rain and the men can't get dry day and night; so I'm lucky to be able to spend the night in the Duke's coach. Food is scarce and dear; everybody just tries his best to make life a little more tolerable. On the whole people are cheerful and make jokes of this and that. Yesterday we soon forgot rain and mud over the arrival of two captured flags – sky blue, rose-red and white – some horses, two cannon and a number of rifles ...

I am writing this on French soil not far from Longwy, which the Prussians took a few days ago.

Don't worry about me, I love you dearly and I'm coming back as soon as I can. Kiss our little boy; I think of him often, and of everything about you, even of the kohlrabi we put in the garden and so on. Good-bye, dearest.

To CHRISTIANE VULPIUS

In camp near Verdun,
10th September 1792.

I have written you several little letters and I don't know when they will start arriving one after the other. I didn't number them, but I'm beginning to do it now. Let me tell you again that I am in good health; you know already that I love you tenderly. If only you were here too, now! They have great wide beds here and you wouldn't need to complain like at home sometimes. Oh, my dear one, there's nothing like being together. We'll never forget that once we are together again. Just think! We are so near Champagne and I can't get a decent glass of wine. Things will be better than that with us in the Frauenplan once my dear little one is seeing to the kitchen and cellar.

Be my own dear housewife, and get the house in good order for me. Look after our little boy and go on loving me.

Don't forget to love me. For I often have jealous thoughts and imagine that you might like someone else better, for I find many men handsomer and more likeable than I am. But you must not find that, you must think me the best, for I love you dreadfully, and nothing else pleases me. I often dream about you, all sorts of muddled things but always that we love each other. And that's how I want it to stay.

I've ordered two feather-mattresses and pillows and lots of other good things through my mother. See that our nice house is spick and span; I'll see to everything else. There will be all sorts of things in Paris; in Frankfort there'll be another parcel. I've sent off a small hamper of liqueurs to-day and a little parcel of sweetmeats. It's good to send things for the household. Just go on loving me, be my faithful child, and the rest will settle itself. What use was anything else to me as long as I hadn't your love? Now I have that, I want to keep it. For I am yours. Kiss our little one, remember me to Meyer and love me.

To CHRISTIANE VULPIUS

Marienborn,
3rd July 1793.

You are a very good child to write so often; and you shall have a letter by return. The weather here the last fortnight has been just as bad as it can have been with you. First frost killed the vines, then came cold, rain and gales, and we had a great deal to put up with in our tents. Now it's all the finer and not at all hot. The nights are particularly pleasant. If only there wasn't the sad spectacle of a nightly bombardment; Mainz is gradually being burnt down before our eyes. Churches, towers, whole streets and quarters of the town go up in flames, one after the other. When I tell you about it later, you'll scarcely believe such a thing could happen.

Don't distress yourself about our cucumbers; see to everything nicely, you give me so much pleasure by that. We'll hold together, for we couldn't have anything better. Love me always as I love you. My Mother has sent you an answer, you'll have been happy to get it. She thinks very kindly of you. If there's no thread in the parcel, I must have forgotten to put it in, and it may be at home still with the iron and some other things.

I've written to Councillor Voigt about the small house. I can't send the wine while the weather is so hot. Remember me meanwhile to the building-surveyor and tell him he shall have a keg. Ask him to have a word or two with the gardener so that things get on.

Take very good care of yourself, for the child's sake too; kiss our little boy and love me always.

To SCHILLER

Weimar,
7th July 1796.

Many thanks for your most refreshing letter and for telling me what you feel and think of my novel,* especially the Eighth Book. If it is to your liking, you will not fail to recognize your influence on it; I could not have written it, at least not in this way, but for our relation to each other. I thought many a time of the scenes which are now before you, as we talked about theory and examples, and in my own mind I applied our principles to these scenes. And now, too, your friendly warning saves me from some very obvious errors, and some of your remarks have shown me at once how to put things right and I shall make use of this in the next copy.

Even among the affairs and dealings of ordinary life one rarely finds the sympathetic interest one wants and in a lofty aesthetic matter we can hardly hope for it. For how many can see a work of art as such and how many can comprehend it? Sympathy alone can see all that is in it, and greater

---

* *Wilhelm Meister's Years of Apprenticeship*, which Goethe had just finished writing.

sympathy yet is needed to see what it lacks. I could say still more about our unique relationship.

I had got as far as this after receiving your first letter, when all kinds of outward and inward obstacles prevented my going on. Besides, I feel even if I were completely calm I could not make any observations in return for yours. What you say has now to take shape in my mind, as a whole as well as in detail, if the Eighth Book is really to hold your sympathetic interest. Go on interpreting my own work to me; in my thoughts I have already been working along the lines of your suggestions. Next Wednesday or so I shall give a rough summary of what I mean to do. I should like to have the manuscript back by Saturday, 16th; Cellini is to call on you that day ...*

To SCHILLER

Weimar,
9th July 1796.

On a separate sheet I am indicating the passages which I intend to alter or add, in accordance with your remarks; and I should like to thank you very heartily for to-day's letter. Its suggestions keep my mind on the completion of the whole work. Please do not cease what I may call driving me out of my own limits. The fault which you notice comes from my innermost nature, from a certain 'realistic tic' that makes it seem pleasant to me to withdraw my existence, actions and writings from men's eyes. I shall for instance always enjoy travelling incognito or choose a simpler dress rather than a better one. In conversation with strangers or mere acquaintances I prefer a minor topic or at least a less eloquent expression. I like to appear less serious than I am and place myself

---

* Goethe was translating Benvenuto Cellini's *Autobiography* for Schiller's periodical, *The Horae*.

between what I am and what I appear to be. You know this quite well and some of the reasons too.

After that general confession I am quite ready to go on to this particular one: Had I not been pushed and urged by you, I should have given way to this peculiarity, against my better judgement, in this novel too. And considering the immense trouble I have taken over it, this would have been unpardonable; everything required was so simple to see or so easy to supply ...

There is no doubt that what in the work I mention as *results* is much more limited than the content of the work; I seem to myself to be someone drawing up a long column of large sums and then adding it up wrongly on purpose, yielding to God knows what whim to reduce the total.

I already owe you the heartiest thanks for so much and now comes your timely and candid mention of this perverse manner; I shall certainly follow your sound suggestion as far as I possibly can. I have only to apply your letter to the appropriate passages, and that will be a great help already. It might of course happen that I cannot get myself to say the last vital words – for man's perversity often builds up insurmountable obstacles. In that case I shall ask you to add with a few bold strokes of your brush what the strangest of my natural limitations prevents me from expressing. Do write down your suggestions and during this week encourage me while I help on 'Cellini' and possibly the 'Almanach' too.

To REICHARDT*

Weimar,
5th February 1801.

It is not everyone who gains as much from his travels as I have done from my short absence.

* The composer, with whom Goethe had been out of touch for some time owing to their differing political opinions.

When I returned from the boundary of death's kingdom – so near and so far – many sympathizers were here to greet me. Their presence gave me the flattering assurance of having lived for others also and not for myself alone. Not only friends and acquaintances, strangers and estranged too showed me that they wished me well. My re-entry into life thus brought me the happiness of starting anew, free from any aversion – just as children are born with no knowledge of hatred, their earliest years happy in being a time of liking rather than disliking. Tell yourself with words as affectionate as your own to me what pleasure your letter was therefore bound to give me. Such an old, firmly established relationship as ours, is like kinship, only interrupted by events outside the normal order. It is all the more gratifying, then, when nature and one's own convictions restore it.

I have little to say of what I have suffered. My illness seized me shortly after New Year, not quite without warning. It attacked me in so many strange forms that even the most experienced doctors doubted for a while if I would recover. This condition lasted for nine days and nights of which I remember very little. The most fortunate circumstance was that the moment consciousness returned, I was quite myself again ...

The first higher need I felt after my illness was the need for music; and as far as circumstances would allow they tried to satisfy it. Do send me your latest compositions, and then I'll have a festive evening with some friends.

Please give my grateful regards to my Berlin well-wishers and sympathizers, known and unknown. My greatest wish is to live in future too to be agreeable and useful to the many friends who set such store by my life.

My thanks once again for drawing nearer to me at this time; my best wishes for your continued good health.

To C. G. VOIGT*

Jena,
22nd January 1802.

Koch had Büttner's† rooms opened yesterday, to take charge of some things during repairs, and I went with him. I assure you it would defy the nimblest tongue and the ablest pen to describe the state of the rooms. They seemed a receptacle for books and papers, not a person's home at all. His literary treasures lay about everywhere, in some degree of order, or at random, or jumbled hopelessly together on tables, chairs, trunks, in cupboards, on beds. There were various bits of lumber, notably some old dulcimers and barrel-organs; everything under a coating of dust. There was a ludicrous assortment of old clothes; this was left to Trabitius, to his special delight. The ceiling, walls, floor and . stove in the living-room were all equally black, and several boards were rotting through dampness and under layers of animal filth. There will be a good deal of work for the broom before military smartness can clear up this literary pigsty. It was only when I saw it that I realized how much his Highness has embarrassed his humble servants by his speedy bestowal of these rooms [to the Commandant of Jena]...

Would you believe that while the old man was here, he accumulated from six to eight thousand volumes that we knew practically nothing about. They were not entered in the catalogue but just piled up here. We found a few unopened cases that had come from auctions.

I mean to get everything under way for the great project of a general catalogue for practical purposes. It is a great

* For many years Goethe's closest collaborator in the Weimar administration and with him responsible, among many other things, for the libraries in Weimar and Jena.

† In 1783 Goethe had come to an agreement with Professor Büttner of Göttingen by which the latter arranged for his valuable library to be incorporated after his death in that of Jena University, while he in return was granted a life annuity and the use of rooms in the castle of Jena.

undertaking, I admit, and it all depends on the personality of Dr Ersch. The University as a whole seems willing to help; and the Medical Faculty has already voted an advance of 400 thaler from its library funds ...

I shall make enquiries about Professor Walther.

My best wishes for your recovery and kind regards.

To CHRISTIANE VULPIUS*

Weimar,
12th to 14th July 1803.

We hadn't expected your letter before to-day, so were all the more delighted when it took us by surprise yesterday evening. I'm so pleased that everything you are doing is going well; you deserve that it should, too, for acting so cleverly and tactfully. Don't worry about the expense, I'm glad to meet any for you, and you will come back soon enough to the cares of housekeeping. The purchase-money [for our farm at Oberrossla] will be paid on Saturday, the 16th, and after that there'll be a good deal to think of and see to. For that and other reasons I'm not coming to Lauchstädt; in any case there's no point except to see you.

Instead I advise you to go to Dessau, perhaps taking Mlle Probst with you, just to make things suitable; if others also joined your party that would be quite proper too. But you'll be able to arrange that best yourself. You will need four or five days for the trip, if you want to enjoy seeing everything in comfort, and that would help to pass the month pleasantly. Don't be frightened of the expense. All I want is for you to come back happy and loving me. I'm looking forward to all you'll tell me about it. If I possibly can, I will send August so that you can take him to Dessau with you. He's

* In Lauchstädt where she was acting as deputy for Goethe at the theatre run by the Weimar actors during the summer months.

very good, by the way, and fairly resigned about not making the trip to Lauchstädt ...

Hofrat [Schiller] has come bringing your letter. I am enjoying your enjoyment and am sending this by a messenger dear to us both. I hope he will arrive safely and tell you how much we have thought about you. I've given the coachman a crown piece to pay for August on the way; find out what's left and give the man a good tip. There are six bottles of wine for you too.

Now August is with you don't delay, set off for Dessau and back to Lauchstädt; stay a few days and be back at the end of the month. It will give you much pleasure that way and I'll enjoy what you have to tell me afterwards.

Next time you write send me your latest new shoes you told me about, with their soles danced through, just so as to give me something belonging to you again, to press to my heart. Farewell, love to Mlle Silie and thanks for her charming letter.

Write again as soon as you can.

You see I've got all your letters. There are bound to be people at Lauchstädt who have been in Dessau, so find out how things are done there. Give about a 'caroline' in tips at Wörlitz where there are so many gardeners and guides to pay; that's usually an attendant's business. Be sure to see everything. Farewell and love me.

To Dr NICOLAUS MEYER

Weimar,
20th October 1806.

We are alive!* It was like a miracle; our house was spared, neither looted nor burned down. The Duchess went through the most dreadful hours with us and it is to her that we owe

---

* After the battle of Jena.

snowlines and limits of vegetation. I am sending you a copy of this draft made half in jest and half in earnest. Please add what corrections you like with a pen and with colour, make marginal notes and send it back as soon as you can. For since the end of the war we have started our Wednesday meetings [in my house] again; I bring important objects in nature and art to the notice of her Highness the Duchess, the Princess and a few other ladies. I can think of nothing more interesting or more appropriate than to use your writings and to make them, as you yourself do, a basis for general observations.

But if you could possibly let me have a proof-copy of your own map, that would of course be exactly what I need. And you would do me a great favour if you would send me a sketch (with dates) of your life, education, writings, activities and journey. Some items – I might almost say all of them – are known to me already, but I cannot arrange them chronologically. I have so very little time to search in books and periodicals. When you visit us again, you will find minds and hearts prepared to enjoy at the source what they now have to take at second hand. I shall certainly make the best use of anything you tell me for this laudable purpose.

The problem of colour still occupies me, and the printing of my work is going slowly forward. The didactic part is finished, though mostly rather as a sketch than worked out. Now I am among the thorny polemic paths. It is an unfriendly and also thankless business, showing step by step, word for word, that the world has been in error for the past hundred years. However, I must go through with it, and I am looking forward to the broader historical field in which I hope to stride briskly on, once I have made my way out of the prickly theoretical labyrinth.

Your and Bonplan's works contain several most important cases which I have noted in order to refer to them in the review with which I mean to round off my book; I would I had already the pleasure of knowing the work in your hands and of being able to hope for your opinion of the whole and your observations on the individual parts. But that is likely to take yet another year, which, however, after all is bound to pass like the rest.

It is long since I heard anything from your brother; this too is no doubt my fault, for it is long since I wrote. Do give me news of him.

Our excellent Hackert in Florence has had an attack of apoplexy. He hopes to recover and to serve art again. I could have wished a man like him in your company in those tropical lands.

Do let me know how Hirt is, also Zelter and Bury. I am almost glad now that there are only few people for me to ask about in Berlin.*

His Highness the Duke has given us a good deal of news of you, of your magnetic garden and other investigations. He is well initiated into what you are doing and planning.

My sincerest greetings and wishes.

To HEINRICH VON KLEIST

Weimar,
1st February 1808.

Dear Sir, I am most grateful to you for the copy of 'Phoebus'. I have enjoyed reading the essays in prose very much. I knew some of them already. I have not yet been able to come to terms with your 'Penthesilea'. She belongs to such an unusual race and moves in so strange a region that I must take time to get used to both. And allow me to say – for unless one is honest, it would be better to say nothing at all – that it always disturbs and saddens me to see really talented and gifted young men waiting for a theatre that is still to be. A Jew waiting for the Messiah, a Christian for the New Jerusalem, a Portuguese for Don Sebastian, is not to

---

* Because of the sad situation of Berlin during Napoleon's campaign of 1807.

my mind a more distressing sight. Before any trestle-stage I would say to the true theatrical genius; '*Hic Rhodus, hic salta!*'. On any fair-ground, even on planks put across barrels, I could – *mutatis mutandis* – bring the highest enjoyment to the masses, cultured and uncultured, with Calderon's plays. Forgive my plain speaking, it shows my sincere affection. I realize one might say this kind of thing with friendlier phrases and more attractively. I am content now to have got something off my chest. More soon.

To FRIEDRICH JACOBI*

Weimar,
7th March 1808.

Friends can often differ greatly, so it is most refreshing when we find we can both unreservedly enjoy the same thing. This is indeed the case with your present to me …

The strange pamphlets you sent me at the same time, are less exhilarating. Thinking about Rottmann's book I find I am inclined to rate the Dark Ages higher than you do. I tell myself that in my Father's House are many mansions, and the dim cellar below is as much a part of the palace as the platform on the roof. At the moment I am editing and arranging my collected notes for a history of the theory of colour, so I have to concern myself with the history of art, of science, indeed of the world. And it seems to me that even at times that seem dull and voiceless to us, there was still to be heard from man a chorus that the gods could enjoy. It is always a magnificent sight for me to look into the dark, deep striving of mankind. How fine the individual peoples and races look who guard and carry on a frail but sacred flame of thought! And how splendid are those men in whom this flame flares up once again. I have developed an unbounded respect for Roger Bacon, for instance; but

* Who had sent Goethe a book with lithographs of Dürer's drawings.

his namesake, the Chancellor, seems to me like Hercules, cleansing the stable of dialectics only to let it be soiled again with empiricism...

[Zacharias] Werner has been here almost three months now. We have done all we could to make his tragedy 'Wanda' a success. He has outstanding gifts. His place of birth, his cultural circle and his age explain his adherence to modern Christianity. It was inevitable that German poetry should progress in this direction, and it is the philosophers who are in part responsible if there is anything to blame in it. The ordinary themes which writers of talent usually adopt for their use had all been exhausted and cheapened. Schiller's dramatic characters are noble; to outdo him one had to take what is sacred, which lay to hand in the ideal philosophy.

In the best periods of the Classical Age the sacred had its origin in the beauty of the senses. The Olympian statue of Zeus was needed to perfect the idea of the god. In modern times the sacred rests on moral beauty, opposed, so to speak, to that of the senses. And I don't at all blame you for disliking the mating of what is sacred with beauty or rather pleasure and charm. Even Werner's works show that this leads to a sort of wanton carnival, almost brothel licence, which will even grow worse and worse.

And it is just as logical for the man of talent to seek appreciation for his book and also to be loved and honoured himself, claiming, therefore, to be a kind of teacher and prophet. I can't blame him in the least. Actors, musicians, painters, poets and even scholars seem to bear a strange character, half of the spirit and half of the flesh and appear like fools, indeed almost like knaves, like men with some *levis notae macula* to ordinary people bound to the world of reality from which they sprang. Why should a strange caste, thus handicapped, not produce some astute people who realize that the only way out of this difficulty is to call themselves Brahmins, if not Brahma himself?

Werner's Luther-play (Die Weihe der Kraft) is one of the most fantastic performances ever seen. But can you blame

Iffland for being tempted into acting the role of Luther? He so often plays the rogue and the fool and lowers himself in the eyes of the public that sees nothing but the story; now at last he can appear as the Protestant saint, singing 'A Safe Stronghold' and making an appeal to 'German Strength' in spite of the fact that this went to the devil on the 14th October [1806] because the Germans lacked any sense ...

To ZELTER

Carlsbad,
2nd September 1812.

... I met Beethoven in Teplitz. His talent astounded me, but unfortunately his is a personality of untamed force. He is quite right in finding the world detestable; but that hardly makes it better either for himself or for others. One may excuse and pity him greatly, however, for his hearing is failing; this may do more harm to his sociable than his musical self. He is already laconic by nature and this will make him still more so. A hearty farewell.

To ZELTER*

Weimar,
3rd December 1812.

Your letter, my very dear friend, telling me of your family's great affliction struck and weighed me down with grief, for when it came I was full of earnest thoughts on life. It is only you who have raised me up again. On Death's dark touchstone you have proved yourself to be true, pure gold.

---

* Whose stepson had committed suicide. In this letter Goethe uses for the first time the intimate 'Du' to Zelter. Zelter was the only man to whom he ever gave this sign of friendship after his first years in Weimar.

How magnificent is a character so imbued with mind and spirit, and how fair must be the talent built upon it.

I have nothing to say about the actual deed or misdeed. A man is only to be pitied not blamed if the *taedium vitae* takes hold of him. My 'Werther' can leave no doubt in any mind that every symptom of this strange natural-unnatural illness once swept through me also. I know full well what repeated decision and effort I needed at that time to flee the waves of death and what pains it has cost me to escape and recover from many a later shipwreck ...

... One really cannot wonder nowadays at the misdeeds through which man injures himself and others. There is untold pressure from outside and young people especially yield to their appetites and passions. The sad follies of the age distort and disfigure even what is noble and higher in them; so what should guide to bliss leads to perdition – I could write a new 'Werther' that would make people's hair stand on end, even more than the first. And let me add that most young people who feel there is something in them, demand more from themselves than they should. But it is their gigantic surroundings that urge and force them to this. I know half a dozen who are certain to succumb and for whom there is no help, even if one could make their own possibilities clear to them. People often fail to see that reason and courage are given us to keep us not only from evil but also from too much good.

Let us change the subject and talk of your letters and how they help me. Thank you first of all for your remarks on my autobiography. I have already heard kindly things said of it in a general way, but you are the first and only person to go more deeply into the matter. I am glad that my way of presenting my father made the right impression on you. I must confess I am heartily sick of the German 'head of the family', Lorenz Starke or whatever his name may be, indulging his *philistine* nature freely in a kind of dull humour, blundering in the way of his own good impulses and destroying his happiness and that of those around him. My two next books complete the picture of my father; both father and son would have been spared a good deal, if a grain of understanding of what is really a precious relationship had been given to them. But that was not to be and does not appear to be usual in this world. The best plan for a journey may be upset by a silly chance, and we never go further than when we do not know where we are going.

Do, please, continue your observations ...

To CHRISTIANE VON GOETHE

Wiesbaden,
31st May 1815.

I've more or less settled in here now, in delightful rooms, but expensive; the food's good and cheap, and I've ordered wine from Frankfort, so I'll soon be well off in these important respects. In the morning I drink the delicious Schwalbach water, and then bathe in the healing Wiesbath; it's all very good for me, and I can be busy too. 'Naples' is getting on, so is 'Sicily';* these happy memories entertain me without tiring me in the least. I've spoken of them so often, it's time they were down on paper. The mining director Cramer and the librarian Hundeshagen are friendly, interested and helpful, just as they were last year. Major Luck of Mainz has called on me already; I haven't heard from anyone else and have all the solitude I wanted. I take two walks every day; the country seems lovelier the more you see and appreciate it.

It's the most beautiful weather, though that's bad for the crops and gardens; they have had no lasting rain for ten weeks. We're already enjoying French beans and green peas too. But the very special treat will always be the salmon; for 30 kreuzer you can get a helping in delicious aspic at the Kursaal. This is just the right season; but I must be careful

---

* Sections in Goethe's *Italian Journey.*

not to eat too much of it. There are big cherries too, great baskets of them at the street-corners.

A plant I have specially noticed is the double scarlet lychnis, the loveliest thing you could imagine for a garden; I hope they'll send us plants by the autumn. The roses are in full bloom, the nightingales are singing to one's heart's content so it's not hard to transport oneself to Shiraz. The 'new members* of the Divan' are neatly ranged and a fresh 'address-list' written for the whole 'assembly', which amounts to over a hundred now, not counting the 'attendants' and 'minor servants'.

So you see the days of my journey and my stay here have been happily and usefully spent. More soon . . .

7th June.

Carl is getting on well. We had thunder and showers to-day.

The best is love.

To WILHELM VON HUMBOLDT

*Weimar,
26th June 1816.*

In my sense of loss at the death of my dear little wife it is the greatest comfort to look round and see how much still remains that is good and dear to me.

I have heard nothing from you, my dearest friend, for an eternity, and I long for a kind word and the assurance that you are well. I must, alas, give up my plan of coming to the beautiful Main Valley and of seeing you. The doctors and in some way my own feelings urge me to go to Bohemia, and I cannot yet tell what I shall end by doing. Let me hear from you soon, and send me some important autographs again. Old familiar hobbies like this caress our grief . . .

* The poems of Goethe's 'West-Eastern Divan'.

My best wishes for lasting happiness to you and your family. I have been strangely occupied these days; looking through a mass of old papers. So much begun and abandoned, so many plans, so many intentions not carried out; there is no excuse for it and like a true Oriental one can only hope for God's mercy. Farewell; my very best wishes. Let me soon have good news.

To THOMAS CARLYLE*

Weimar,
15th January 1828.

Should you see Sir Walter Scott, please thank him from me most warmly for his kind, cheerful letter; it shows his noble confidence that men care for each other. It is in this spirit too, that I received his 'Life of Napoleon', which I have read through from beginning to end with great attention during these winter evenings and nights. I was most interested to see how the greatest narrator of the century fares at this unusual task and how he passes in quiet order before our eyes the momentous happenings of which we were perforce the witnesses. His chapters group large, distinct masses of facts, and make these complicated ocurrences perfectly simple to grasp, and every event is told with a clarity and vividness beyond praise. I read the work in the original, so that it produced its own, true effect. Here we have a patriotic Briton speaking, one who cannot, I suppose, look favourably on what the enemy does, who as an honest citizen wants the demands of moral conduct to be met at the same time as those of politics. He threatens his foe in the full tide of success with the direst consequences, and even in that foe's bitterest ruin can hardly bring himself to pity him.

This work means a great deal to me besides, partly by

* Continuation of a letter despatched by the post on 1st January 1828.

reminding me of what I had lived through and partly by showing me a good deal I had overlooked. It made me see some things in a new and unexpected light and think again over what I had taken to be settled points. And in particular it fitted me to judge those who criticize this important work – and there are sure to be some who do – and to appreciate the arguments they put forward. So you see the end of last year could not have brought me any gift I prized more. This work has become a kind of golden net for me, and with it I have been fishing in the waters of Lethe and taking up great draughts of shadowy figures from my past life . . .

Books and journals sent by express-mail are now forming a link between the nations and sensible travellers are doing a good deal to help too. Mr Heavyside who came to see you brings the happiest report of you and your circumstances. And now he is sure to give you a picture of our life here in Weimar. As tutor to the young Hopes he spent some happy years to good purpose in our rather limited but in reality talented and lively circle. I hear the Hope family are pleased too with the education the young men were able to receive here. There is much in Weimar to benefit young men, especially those of your nation. They are kindly and indulgently welcomed at the two Courts, of the reigning House and of the Hereditary Prince. They get a good deal of varied enjoyment there and are encouraged to distinguish themselves by their good manners. Other good society, too, helps to keep them restrained but still cheerful, so that they gradually drop everything rough and awkward. Their intercourse with the beautiful and cultured ladies here provides occupation and food for heart, mind and imagination and holds them back from the dissipation that young people give way to, more because they are bored than because they want to. Weimar is possibly the only place with opportunities for this free service, and we have the pleasure of seeing those who have tried Berlin and Dresden soon coming back to us. Besides, our ladies keep up a lively correspondence between here and Britain, which proves that it is not absolutely necessary to be actually present to keep going any well-established affection, for instance Mr Lawrence has come back from time to time and enjoyed at once taking up the threads of former relations. Mr Parry has rounded off a residence of many years with a suitable marriage.

Please continue your interest in me.

To ZELTER*

Dornburg,
10th July 1828.

I have been so painfully distressed in my mind that I have been forced at least to take care of my health. So I have come to Dornburg to avoid the sad solemnities. It is fit and right that they should be used as a symbol to the general public of their great loss which on this occasion they sincerely feel.

I cannot remember if you know Dornburg. It is a small hillside town, down the Saale valley from Jena. Country seats, large and small, have been built outside it, strung out along the steep limestone ridge. There are charming gardens belonging to the small country houses. I am staying at the last of these to the south, [the Grand Duke's], a dear old place recently freshened up. The views are splendid and cheerful, the flowers in the well-kept gardens are in full bloom, the vines are loaded with grapes, and below my window I see a flourishing vineyard; the late Grand Duke had it planted three years ago on the most barren slope and had the pleasure of enjoying its fresh green last Whitsun. On the other side the rose-arbours are a miracle of blooms, and the hollyhocks and all the rest are blossoming in every shade.

* Grand Duke Carl August had just died.

I see it all with the colours intensified like a rainbow on a dark grey background.

For fifty years I have been spending days of happiness here with him from time to time, and to-day there is no place I could stay in where what he has done shows itself more obvious and delightful. The older part has been preserved and improved, the new acquisition – this house where I am staying used to be private property – is simply and suitably adapted, and charming hill-paths and terraces now join it to the already existing gardens. A numerous suite, if they did not expect too much, found it roomy and adequate. All that a gardener should see to in the way of lay-out and flowers has been done without any pedantry or timidity.

And it will remain as it is now; for the new young owners, too, have a feeling for what is good and appropriate, and for several years have proved it by staying here for varying periods. It is very comforting to feel that when a man dies he hands on to those who follow him some thread to guide them as they go along. And so I too will hold to this symbol he left me, and stay on here.

But you will want to know how your friend spends these long days from sunrise to sunset, in this airy castle from where he can look out over a charming valley with flat meadowland and fields stretching up to the inaccessible steep fringe of the forests. So let me confide to you that a stimulus from abroad has led me to take up my scientific studies again ...

To AUGUST VON GOETHE*

*Weimar,
5th July 1830.*

The safe arrival of your box has made this a day of rejoicing, so let me send you back something cheerful too.

* Goethe's son was on a tour of Italy, during which he died.

Mother and children are delighted to be remembered so charmingly, Alma is running about in her little red frock and the boys, who are still away, will be so pleased with the real Milanese souvenirs when they come back. And as for the collector of coins, he can hardly tell you how overjoyed he is.

Without exaggerating, to begin with the price, I should be embarrassed if a dealer asked twice the amount for them. They are most remarkable examples, dating right on from earliest to later times, and in excellent preservation. Our collection, after a long stationary period, has really entered on a new and happy phase ...

It is a joy to me to see how well you understand these things, what a good judgement and memory you have. When things are at reasonable prices, go on looking at them and considering their value. I am not exaggerating when I say that for me, thinking of what we own so far, this already makes your journey successful.

And go on keeping your diaries as fully as before. Your last letters from Venice have arrived too, and believe me, these pages are doubly and trebly delightful to all who read them, because you are so faithful in recording what you see, and so indefatigable in seeing everything, in going back to it again and taking it in thoroughly. Besides, inner contentment is obviously growing in you, and that after all is what is most important if we are to value and enjoy the present.

I shall keep these coins by themselves and everything else you sent home. It will give point to our conversations in future and make us enjoy refreshing our memories as well as improving our knowledge ...

To WILHELM VON HUMBOLDT*

Weimar,
17th March 1832.

After a long involuntary pause I am beginning like this, and yet simply impromptu. The Ancients said that the animals are taught through their organs; let me add to this, so are men, but they have the advantage of teaching their organs in return.

Every action, and so every talent, needs some inborn faculty which acts naturally, and unconsciously carries with it the necessary aptitude, and which, therefore, continues to act in such a way that though its law is implicit in it, its course in the end may be aimless and purposeless.

The earlier man becomes aware that there exists some craft, some art that can help him towards a controlled heightening of his natural abilities, the happier he is; whatever he may receive from without does not harm his innate individuality. The best genius is that which absorbs everything within itself, knows how to appropriate everything, without this in the least impairing its fundamental dispositions, called its character, but rather enhancing and furthering them throughout as much as possible.

Here begin the manifold relations between the conscious and the unconscious. Take for instance a talented musician, composing an important score; consciousness and unconsciousness will be like warp and weft, a simile I am fond of using.

Through practice, teaching, reflection, success, failure, furtherance and resistance, and again and again reflection, man's organs unconsciously and in a free activity link what he acquires with his innate gifts, so that a unity results which leaves the world amazed.

---

*Whom Goethe had told that he had recently completed his *Faust* and that this had required a more conscious effort than he had made before in writing that poem. Humboldt, in reply, asked for further explanation of this conscious creative process.

These general remarks may serve as a rapid answer to your question, and as an explanation to the note I return herewith.

For more than sixty years the conception of Faust has lain here before my mind with the clearness of youth, though the sequence with less fullness. I have let the idea go quietly along with me through life and have only worked out the scenes that interested me most from time to time. So in the Second Part gaps remained, waiting for this kind of interest before they could be joined to the rest. It was difficult to do through conscious effort and strength of personality something that really should have been the spontaneous work of active nature. But it surely would not be right if this were not possible after my long life of thought and action, and I am not afraid of people being able to pick out the new from the old, the later from the earlier work. We can leave that to future readers.

It would naturally be an infinite joy to me if during my lifetime, too, I could dedicate these serious phantasies to my valued friends everywhere. I have always been grateful for their interest and should like to hear their response. But the present age is so senseless and confused that I know I should only be poorly rewarded for my many years of sincere effort at erecting this strange building. It would be driven like a wreck on the shore and lie there, getting gradually covered by the sands of time. The world is ruled to-day by bewildering wrong counsel, urging bewildered wrong action. My most important task is to go on developing as much as possible whatever is and remains in me, distilling my own particular abilities again and again. You, my friend, are doing the same up there in your castle.

Tell me about your work, too; as you know, Riemer is still busy on the same sort of studies as we are, and our evening conversations often touch on these subjects. Forgive this long delayed letter. In spite of my retirement, there is seldom a time when I am in the mood to remind myself of those mysteries of life.

Ever Yours.

W. H. AUDEN (1907–73) was born in Birmingham and studied at Christ Church, Oxford. After graduation he lived for some time in Berlin. He became the acknowledged leader of the 'thirties poets' after the publication of his *Poems* in 1930. His poetic output was prolific, and he also wrote verse plays in collaboration with Christopher Isherwood. He was elected Professor of Poetry at Oxford in 1956.

LOUISE BOGAN (1897–1970), poet and critic, was born in Maine and spent most of her life in New York. A selection of her life's work can be found in *The Blue Estuaries: Poems 1923–68*.

NICHOLAS BOYLE is Head of the Department of German in Cambridge University and a Fellow of Magdalene College. Volume One (*The Poetry of Desire*) of his biography of Goethe – *Goethe: The Poet and the Age* – was published in 1991; Volume Two (*Revolution and Renunciation*) is to be published in 1999. He has also written a commentary on *Faust. Part One* for Cambridge University Press and a volume of essays on the relation between politics, literature and theology in the modern world: *Who Are We Now? Christian Humanism and the Global Market from Hegel to Heaney*.

DAVID CONSTANTINE is Fellow and Praelector in German at The Queen's College, Oxford. His works include *Early Greek Travellers and the Hellenic Ideal*, and *Hölderlin*; he has also published four collections of poetry and a novel.

BARKER FAIRLEY (1887–1986) was educated at the universities of Leeds and Jena. He taught at the University of Toronto from 1915 to 1957, except for four years in the 1930s when he was Henry Simon Professor of German at Manchester University. He published several books on Goethe, including *Goethe's Faust: Six Essays*, and collections of his letters and poetry.

MICHAEL HAMBURGER's *Collected Poems 1941–94* was published in 1998. His translations from the German include Goethe's *Poems and Epigrams* and *Selected Poems and Fragments* by Friedrich Hölderlin.

M. VON HERZFELD and C. MELVIL SYM translated and edited *Letters from Goethe* for the Edinburgh University Press in 1957.

ELIZABETH MAYER was born in Mecklenburg in 1884 and emigrated to the US in 1936. Her Goethe translations include *Elective Affinities* (in collaboration with Louise Bogan) as well as those of *Italian Journey* and *Werther* included in this selection.

CHRISTOPHER MIDDLETON is a poet and translator. He edited *Volume 1: Selected Poems* of the Suhrkamp/Insel collected Goethe in English in 1983.